Rude in1969
Awakening

Rude Awakening in 1969

Kenneth J Munkens

ISBN 978-0-966-39513-1

For Carol and Paul Blatnicky,

Unexpected inspiration—what a beautiful thing. At the very time when this story was languishing, two remarkable people entered my life, fanned the flames of creativity, and provided just the right amount of encouragement. I will always be grateful for their input, value their friendship, and thank God for sending me two angels.

1: Wednesday - April 10, 1963

Deep green waves churned the North Atlantic Ocean. Unfriendly and dangerous, they twisted and turned and struck at each other with a fury that created an aura of endless conflict. Five, six, eight foot swells rose and fell—driven by a steady northeasterly wind. Everywhere the vast ocean was alive, flexing its massive muscles, and daring those foolish enough to challenge it to come forth and be counted.

The day had been bright and clear, and yet, the ocean remained a swirling storm. In the North Atlantic April comes in like a lion and goes out like one, as well. A bright mid-afternoon sun that had shone upon the restless and chilly waters slipped silently into the west. Two hundred feet below the surface, it was perpetual night—dark, calm, and much colder. In fact, it was colder than the surface ever became. There, beneath the turbulence of the wind and waves a tranquil world existed.

In ghostly shadows a teardrop shaped creature drifted lazily through the water. Its dark gray color made it virtually invisible, in spite of massive size. And yet, in the vastness of the ocean it was but a speck that could easily be missed. Its only outstanding feature bright white lettering SSN-593.

Within the metal confines of the double hull 129 men worked and played and rested. They all wore denim blue shirts and navy blue trousers. Casual dress was the order of the day as they planned to be beneath the turbulent surface for an extended period of time. Three shifts of men worked tirelessly as the craft's many systems were put to the test. It was all part of sea trials that were regulation after a major overhaul.

Seaman Robert Fox sat at a console watching numerous dials, meters, and indicator lights. All was normal. A song kept running through his head—*I Will Follow Him* by Little Peggy March. It had been released two weeks before he and Sharon tied the knot, which was nine days before he had to report back on board. A smile crossed his face as he considered that he would never forget their anniversary given that they had wed on April Fool's Day. He daydreamed as he pictured their wedding night when his blushing bride came out of the bathroom wearing a white negligee singing the words to that song. "I will follow him. Follow him wherever he may go. There isn't an ocean too deep. A mountain so high it will keep—keep me away—away from my love." He pictured her dancing beneath that flimsy material. Her long blond hair swayed with each motion, blue eyes looked only at him, and an inviting smile made him feel more like a man than he had ever felt before in his twenty-two years. The time they had together almost made him not want to return to the boat. Without question, those who felt they shouldn't get married with him scheduled to ship out so soon were wrong. He was glad that Sharon and he had gone ahead and done it. It changed everything. He no longer felt as though he was simply drifting through life. He had responsibility. He had value. He had a reason to live. He had someone to come home to. He had found true happiness.

A light on the console illuminated that caught his eye. It indicated a normal adjustment to the ballast tanks. Immediately, he focused on a number of other dials. The one that he paid most attention to was Rate of Decent. They were doing test-depth dives on this 10 April 63 day and he didn't want to do anything to screw them up. All was normal and they were proceeding according to the designated plan. Again, he smiled. This time remembering how little his friends understood about nuclear submarines. To them you fill the tanks and go down, empty the tanks and surface. He made adjustments to a number of controls as he remembered the blank stares he had gotten when he explained the many methods submarines use to maneuver while submerged. Regulation of the ballast tanks was one element. However, speed, as well as angle of the diving planes also controlled rate of decent and ascent. And then, there were constant adjustments needed to compensate for depth, temperature, and salt content of the water, and . . . at that point he could have said, "and counting the number of mermaids clinging to the hull," and they would have nodded politely while staring across the room at Linda Beal's legs. I guess submarines are only exciting to submariners, he thought.

They were deep beneath the surface where they would remain for at least two days. It was one advantage of nuclear power. Unlike World War II vintage diesel submarines, which could only remain under water for a few hours at a time, nuclear powered craft did not have to surface to recharge batteries. The differences didn't stop there. Because older non-nuclear submarines could only operate under water for a few hours at a time they were built more like surface ships with sharply pointed bows and long slender hulls. In contrast, nuclear powered boats were teardrop or fish shaped with blunt rounded bows and a longer tapered stern. This reduced water resistance when submerged. Because they also had a broader beam, or width, the boat could withstand much greater water pressure allowing it to dive far deeper than its predecessors. This was what they were doing at that moment two hundred miles east of Boston.

A streamlined sail filled with navigational instrumentation and maneuvering apparatus had replaced the familiar conning tower of years past. Even navigation was nothing like it had been just a few years earlier. Complex inertial-navigation systems, based on gravity, the earth's rotation, and submarine speed correlated with detailed underwater maps kept them safe and on course.

The plan for that evening was to submerge to a depth of thirteen hundred feet. At that depth the water pressure would be over twenty times that found at the surface. Seaman Fox continued to check and recheck instruments. They had reached the first holding depth where they would maneuver, check all systems, make readings, and inspect all fittings fore and aft. I will follow him, Sharon's voice whispered in his ear. Not here honey, his mind replied, you'd be banging on the hatch trying to get out. A low creak, not uncommon at those depths, was heard in a distant part of the boat. The craft lazily began to lean ever so slightly as it slowed.

Seaman Fox instinctively looked at the horizontal plane indicator and made a slight adjustment to the trim tanks. The craft stabilized as it continued its silent ballet beneath the surface. While the crew and civilian technicians ran checklists, Robert leaned back and stretched. He glanced at his watch. It was 9:11 p.m. The insignia on the face of the watch once again reached inside of him to touch that indefinable recess in a man that houses his bare emotions. SSN 593 Thresher. How many times a day did he look at that watch and how many times did he feel those same emotions? He loved this boat, all 4,300 tons, and had done so ever since he joined the original crew when she was commissioned two years earlier. Yes, he was proud to serve on the navy's fastest, deepest-diving, and most powerful submarine in the fleet. But, it went much further than that. Everything the Thresher did broke new ground. Everything about her was new and exciting. Even her gentle smooth lines were beautiful to behold. She was gorgeous beyond words, gentle and warm, caring and protective, adventurous and fun, but frighteningly lethal if conditions necessitated that she take action. Yes, he was proud to be a member of the crew of the U.S.S. Thresher. Yes, this was an adventure. Yes, he could love two women at the same time.

A shudder rippled through the craft, imperceptible to some but sickeningly real to others of the crew. Seasoned veterans who know the boat they reside in as well as they know their own bodies and minds took immediate notice. In a submarine an odd creak, out-of-place thump, strange odor, or subtle shudder spoke volumes—sometimes volumes too ominous to think about. Robert Fox was one of those veterans. He sprang forward in his chair and looked feverishly at the many dials and indicators before him on his console. All were normal. He did not alert command of any abnormality. Cross talk was distracting, therefore, only essential information was communicated. Nonetheless, he checked and rechecked the instrumentation before him. What Seaman Fox was unaware of was the failure of a critical circuit in the hull breach indicator system. A fitting somewhere between the inner and outer hull at a pipe, pipe valve, or weld had failed and seawater was flooding into a conduit. Seawater at a pressure far exceeding the most powerful fire hose on earth, entered at a rate that would eventually overwhelm Thresher's pumps. However, without a warning from the failed indicator the problem remained unidentified. A single wire whose insulation had been defective caused it to short, thus keeping the life-saving information from the crew of the Thresher.

As precious time passed, seawater continued its unwelcome entry. Throughout the boat sailors and technicians searched for a cause of the ominous shudder. Nothing was found. Ever so slowly the stern of the craft dropped. It was so slight that it went unnoticed by the crew. It did not go unnoticed by Seaman Fox as he continued to scan his console for any indication of any abnormality. Without panic, he spoke into the microphone on his headset, "We have a two-degree up bubble."

Immediately, adjustments were made to the diving planes and the boat leveled. At that time, Thresher could still maneuver and could still surface. If the wire from the hull breach sensor had not malfunctioned they would have been aware of the problem and been headed for the surface at that very moment. They were not.

Water pressure, eight times greater than that at the surface, forced water through the small breach at an alarming rate. Once again inrushing water caused another drop in the stern. "Three degrees up bubble," Seaman Fox stated into the microphone, a slight indication of nervousness in his voice.

This time the Captain's familiar voice entered his ears through the headphones, "Any indication of hull breach?"

"No, sir."

"Trim tank failure?"

"No, sir."

"Diving plane malfunction?"

"No. sir."

"Indicator calibration checked?"

"Twice, sir. Four degree up bubble, sir."

There was no doubt the stern of the boat was dropping. But without any indication of any malfunction it could be nothing more serious than an anomaly in the distribution of water in the ballast tanks. Or, it could have something to do with that unexplained shudder. Captain John Harvey ordered an increase in the craft's speed and adjustments to the diving planes. Thresher leveled.

Seaman Fox continued to scan his instruments. Something was wrong–very wrong, but he couldn't put his finger on it. He knew the idiosyncrasies of his boat and this wasn't one of them. Everything read normal and no malfunction indicators were lit. Quickly he opened the panel before him. Inside he found the necessary buttons to test each indicator light. He pushed the first and a small red light glowed brightly. Methodically he tested each to confirm that a blown bulb wasn't keeping the truth from him. They all passed the test. When he closed the console his eyes immediately were drawn to a horror only he could understand. "Six degrees up bubble he practically shouted into the microphone." At the increased speed there was no reason Thresher's stern should be dropping. No reason, unless, they were taking on water.

Captain Harvey did not respond. He also knew the implications. Immediately, he decided to abort the test dive. At 9:13 p.m. he radioed the chase sub Skylark that Thresher was experiencing minor difficulties, positive buoyancy, up angle, blowing tanks. He gave the order to surface. Unfortunately, the ice-cold water that assaulted the boat had frozen the valve system through which compressed air passed to blow the ballast tanks. Rising water in the conduit then short-circuited the main engine electrical system. Circuit breakers activated causing the nuclear reactor to SCRAM, or shut down. Alarms echoed throughout the boat. Sailors at their stations, in the mess, or resting in their bunks all jumped. A rush of adrenaline brought each man instantly to peak attention. When submerged any problem is a big problem.

"What the hell's going on?" one seaman asked as he put down his coffee cup and looked to others for an answer.

A different claxon sounded along with the announcement, "General Quarters. This is not a drill. General Quarters."

The main engines cycled down, which caused red battery-powered emergency lights to flood the boat. Crewmembers who a minute earlier had no idea that anything out of the ordinary was happening found themselves in a red wash of light. The effect was dramatic. Fear of the basest kind permeated throughout the craft. Unspoken, it stalked the minds of every crewmember and technician onboard. Being eight hundred feet below the surface, without power, is every submariner's worst nightmare. So frightening is its effect that it is never spoken of aboard ship or on land. It simply is something not to be discussed. Whether superstition or fact, it was believed that to discuss such an event was an invitation for it to enter your craft. No one wanted that responsibility.

"Eight degrees up bubble," Seaman Fox stated calmly even though panic ran through him in cold waves of sweat.

Activity became frantic as each crewmember gave his full attention to their individual task. Without power, they could not surface. Teams searched for the breach they now knew existed but had gone un-indicated. The primary goal was to stabilize the boat. Buy time.

Technicians crawled through work-access tunnels to repair whatever had to be the cause of the reactor shut down. They, unfortunately, had no idea as to the cause. What was clear was the breach was in the stern near the engine room. This was where their effort was centered. Without power, they could not surface.

Thresher's forward speed slowed and the stern began to drop.

"Ten degrees up bubble," Seaman Robert Fox said mechanically. He felt helpless. All he could do was announce their condition, do a play-by-play of their demise. He couldn't pick up a wrench, find the leak, fix it, and single-handedly bring the craft safely home. He couldn't carry a divining rod through the boat, locate the water that was invading them, and assist in their battle to survive. He couldn't help but think of Sharon, his bride, his wife, and his reason to live. The thought of someone to come home to quickly became someone left behind. Sharon sang her little song, I will follow him. Only this time he thought, not here and now, my love–thank God. He couldn't bear the thought of what his passing was going to do to her. He couldn't forgive himself for the self-centered greed that caused him to rush the wedding in order to do it just before he shipped out. He couldn't stand the thought of not seeing Sharon again. He couldn't leave his post, "Eleven degrees up bubble."

In his ears, Sharon kept singing that song, "I will follow him . . ." Suddenly, it was overpowered by another seaman's forcedly calm voice as he announced, "nine hundred fifty feet." They were sinking.

Captain John Harvey responded with a professional calm that only comes with experience and courage and faith as he gave orders to the various teams that fought to find the breach, or recycle the reactor, or stabilize the boat. The calming effect of his voice worked.

There was no panic aboard Thresher. Each man did his job as he had been trained to do. No matter what fears dug at them, they remained at their station. Like some demon in search of prey, fear slithered through the confines of the boat looking for any weakness that would leave some poor soul vulnerable. Those who had it roughest were the ones who did not have an assigned duty. Theirs' was an unrelenting battle to find something other than death to focus upon.

Seaman Fox remembered a chief he once knew who believed there simply was no percentage in panic. The seasoned, weatherworn gob illustrated his point by speaking of a blizzard, "When the snow is so thick you can't see in any direction you have two choices. Stand still and die or start walking in the direction you believe is best." He was a big man who chewed on the small plastic straws that often came in mixed drinks. This always led to odd looks when he would order a beer and ask for a straw. "In a blizzard, if you start walking you may walk right off the edge of a cliff and die," an eyebrow raised as a young seaman listened intently. Then a wry smile foretold better news, "But you could come to a farmhouse and be warm and dry and comfortable with a brandy in your hand." As he told his story for the umpteenth time he explained, "You have a chance, no matter how slim, to survive if you keep going. You have no chance if you stand still. Panic makes you stand still. You see, there is just no percentage in panic."

Every man in the crew had heard some rendition of that story. Every man knew that no matter how small the chance it had to be sought. One last attempt might be the winner. That last desperate act might work. One second before doom, help might arrive or something else unexpected might happen. You just don't know where the point of no return is until you reach it, and if you do, it really doesn't matter.

One seaman's hands shook so violently that he had trouble controlling his movements. Embarrassment overpowered fear. He didn't want his shipmates to see that he couldn't handle the situation with the same courage that they had. The gentle, calm, understanding touch of Captain Harvey's hand on his shoulder immediately vanquished the fear allowing an unexpected and unexplained calm to flow over him. He looked up at the skipper. Two men facing death together shared a knowing revelation. At that moment, there was no difference in age or rank or social standing. One thousand feet beneath the surface, they understood the depth of the human spirit. At a time when survival was paramount in each man's mind there remained enough compassion, strength, and humanity to reach out to make it a little easier for another lost soul.

Torture comes in many forms. One is anticipation. Imagining what will happen often is tenfold worse than what actually does. Fear grows. Imagination runs wild. The mind seeks answers even when none exist. Seaman Fox felt sweat running down his back. "I will follow him," remained in his ears. For some illogical emotional reason he felt that his mistress whom he loved, Thresher, had become jealous of his attentions to another and was taking him far away where she could not follow. He leaned back and sang in his mind, "There isn't an ocean too deep," then whispered, "Shit!"

Thresher twisted in an excruciatingly slow death spiral. A loud bang echoed through the boat as something, somewhere succumbed to the increasing water pressure. Rivets popped. Each condemned man did his job, clung to the life they cherished, did his job, thought of loved ones, did his job, refused to surrender, did his job, made peace with his God, did his futile job, and wept inside where none would see.

Seaman Fox scribbled a letter to his wife. Dearest Sharon; my love, my life. Even though I knew it could happen, I never thought it would happen. Forgive me for putting you in this position, of causing you such pain, of thinking only of myself, of being so blind, of being so thoughtless. Because I love you so much I feared losing you while I was away. My greed is my shame, as you will have to pay the price for me being so self centered. I just couldn't let you go—I can't let you go—I won't let you go. But, I have no power to change what will be. If my last dying words could reach you they would be to forget me and live your life. Don't live half a life because of my unforgivable act of selfishness. Please, Sharon, my Sharon, my . . ."

Thresher settled slowly into its grave fathoms below the raging surface. Slowly, it dropped from the world of man where it was born. Slowly, it descended into darkness. Abruptly, the walls compacted and cataclysmic heat instantly extinguished life's glow. The North Atlantic added one hundred twenty-nine to its count.

At 9:18 p.m. on the evening of April 10, 1963 when the USS Skylark heard a high energy, low frequency sound from beneath the waves of the Atlantic Ocean, Wanda Six Trees gave birth to a six pound eight-ounce baby girl. She was given the name Anna Marie. Her three-year-old brother, Robert, slept through the event.

2: Friday - November 22, 1963

"Leaving early, Mr. Ellis?" Eddie O'Brien asked as he briskly jumped from an old battered dark green metal stool upon which he had been perched.

"Yes Eddie, I'm going to start my vacation a few hours early," the 35-year-old executive replied. Unconsciously, he glanced at the big clock that hung over the automobile elevator servicing three levels of parking garages buried deep in the basement of 811 Sixth Avenue. Time was difficult to tell in the caverns of New York City as the mid-day sun was often obscured. It was 12:45 p.m.

Eddie, a 29-year-old Irish-American who had worked for Margold Garage Management Company for eight years, was thankful that he had not taken his break. He sure didn't want to miss out on the generous two-dollar tip Mr. Ellis rewarded him with every evening. Ten dollars a week, forty dollars a month was a lot of money. In fact, the color television in their living room, making them the first on their block to own one, was purchased with money he had saved from those wonderful tips. In what appeared to be near panic he pushed the intercom button and stated firmly, "Jose, get Mr. Ellis' car—pronto!"

Matthew Ellis felt surprisingly good for a man who had been up most of the night putting together a deal that had come to fruition that very morning. As a result of his hard work, Orztech Corporation would profit greatly in addition to the fact that eventually their product would land on the moon. That was if man ever really did land on the moon. Indeed, there were times when Matt had his doubts. Yes, NASA had successfully orbited men around the Earth. Seven months earlier, in May, Major Leroy Gordon Cooper Jr. did an unbelievable 22 orbits in Faith 7. This, only two years after the United States became serious about the space race. It had taken 34 hours and 20 minutes to complete the final mission of Project Mercury and it had gone flawlessly. However, that was a long way from the moon and it was already late 1963. Now, the Gemini program was underway.

NASA had learned a great deal from the Mercury program, including the fact that half of the electronic components purchased from the open market were unsatisfactory. This led them to pursue private contracts for components that would fit their unique and demanding specifications. High efficiency, low resistance, stranded wire coated with insulation that was impervious to heat and chemical breakdown was just one of thousands of products that were needed—a need filled by Orztech Corporation. The thought of actually making it to the moon before the end of the decade, though, was just too difficult to imagine. And yet, the words of President Kennedy were so confident they could not be ignored, "I believe this nation should commit itself to achieving the goal of landing a man on the moon and returning him safely before the decade is out." The moon! Matt smiled thinking about the possibilities.

Parker Adolphson, president of Orztech, had personally come to Matt's office to thank him for the "above and beyond" effort. Negotiations had been grueling. Long hours and countless conversations led to more long hours and additional conversations. It was the only way. NASA had its own rules, requirements, and demands that had to be met if any deal was to be struck. However, the young vice-president held up under the pressure because he knew the reward was worth the effort. A multi-level, long-term contract had ultimately been written and signed. As a result, Orztech wire products would not only be a part of the space program but would eventually land on the moon.

The NASA deal was actually the second "coup" for the young executive. Three years earlier he had headed negotiations that led to a contract with General Motors' Pontiac Division to provide a flexible drive shaft for the 1961 Tempest. This had brought a well-needed boost in cashflow to Orztech as the corporation diversified into other stranded wire product lines. Much like a speedometer cable the "rope" drive shaft carried rotary motion through a slightly curved tunnel beneath the floor of the innovative Pontiac Tempest. It was much thinner and lighter than a traditional drive shaft and was permanently lubricated. This made possible one of the world's first rear transaxles. The result was the Pontiac Tempest was less nose-heavy giving it exceptional traction. With 100,000 units sold in 1961 and 141,000 in 1962 it had been a boon to Orztech. Unfortunately, that rocket was short-lived as only half as many units were ordered for 1963. However, the new high efficiency, low resistance, Orzcon coated, stranded wire developed by the company and sold to the military, aviation manufacturers, and now NASA more than made up for the decline. And, Matthew Ellis the head of that hugely profitable division was in the catbird seat.

A loud metallic clunk brought Matt back to reality. All who were waiting turned their attention to the massive giver of freedom. Slowly, its maw opened. Eyes of various shapes, color, and age strained to see inside the shadowy bowels of the metal goliath. Light seeped in to reveal a maroon, actually called Marimba Red, 1964 Pontiac Grand Prix. Its unveiling brought about a number of groans and mumbled complaints. Matt, on the other hand, upon seeing his car, felt a rush of excitement.

His baby stood regally and proudly as it waited. Its low, wide-track stance, stacked quad headlights, and distinctive split grille were visions to behold. Eddie launched himself toward the waiting vehicle. A woman tried to stop him by stating, "I've been waiting a long time. . ." The two-bit tipper was ignored.

Matt looked at his pride and joy. It was the first new car he had ever owned whose year designation had not yet arrived. Success is owning a 1964 car in 1963 his mind reminded him. Success is owning a car that cost over four thousand dollars. Eddie started the 421-cubic inch V-8 engine. Its low-pitched growl spoke of power–350 horses of power. Carefully, he eased the car forward to where its owner stood. A few muffled complaints about the obvious preferential treatment were heard. They were ignored by the attendant as he jumped from the car and with a flourish reminiscent of a serf serving a nobleman held the door for the waiting executive. Matt placed a five-dollar bill into the attendant's hand as he slipped gracefully behind the wheel.

"Thank you, Mr. Ellis," the surprised attendant stated with sincere gratitude, "You have a good vacation–we'll miss you." He meant it, as he was saving for a used car.

"Take care Eddie, I'll be back in a week," the T-shaped gearshift lever of the automatic transmission was slipped into drive and Matt drove carefully out of the garage. Behind him unhappy patrons watched his departure in silence.

After a brief battle with midtown traffic, Matt entered the West Side Highway. The near-empty three lane road allowed him to press the accelerator to let his baby run. It responded immediately as the big Pontiac engine purred. He sank slightly into the black leather seat. A glance into the rearview mirror revealed only a few cars that were falling further behind. Once again, he became aware of how much he loved the concave shape of that distinctive rear windshield. Its curve from the roof to the back deck was so aerodynamic, so unique, and so attractive that it alone could have sold him the car.

Exhilaration defeated fatigue. Matt felt fresh, energetic, awake, and alive. It had been a good day–a damn good day.

In Dallas, Texas, 1,548 miles away, John Fitzgerald Kennedy, the thirty-fifth President of the United States, entered the limousine for a short motorcade journey to a planned luncheon. It was a bright and sunny day. His busy schedule had kept him from getting a full night sleep and yet he felt fresh, energetic, awake, and alive. His morning had been filled with negotiation aimed at bringing two disagreeing elements of the Democratic Party in Texas closer together. Although far from an international crisis, it was of paramount concern to the statesman who saw Texas potentially going to the Republicans in 1964 if he didn't solve this annoying problem. To his relief there appeared to be common ground upon which they could fashion a shaky but practical coalition. There were times he was frustrated by ignorance and prejudice. There were times he had to hold his temper at bay. There were times he made a lighthearted remark to defuse potentially volatile confrontations. Over time his resourcefulness, diplomacy, and leadership had paid off. So far, it had been a good day–a damn good day.

The President's spirit soared as he contemplated remarks he was planning to make at the luncheon. The newest and most advanced space center in the nation had been placed in Texas. There were obvious political reasons for this, but what better place to announce it than in Texas. In addition, America was about to test the most powerful rocket ever built–the Saturn. Success of that rocket would give the United States an unquestioned lead in the much-contested space race with the Soviet Union. He looked up as if expecting to see the moon in the afternoon sky. In reality he was looking at the future and the promise that it held. Mankind was on the threshold of something wonderful, that offered infinite possibilities, that made our petty grievances on earth inconsequential, and the first monumental step was the moon.

"The freaking moon!" Matthew Ellis said out loud in the quiet interior of his car. A smile spread across his face until it dominated. He shook his fist in the air to signal victory. As he did his foot pushed down on the accelerator and the sport coupe responded. At seventy miles-per-hour he felt as though he was standing still. This was a far cry from the used 1958 Pontiac Safari Station Wagon his wife, Valerie, drove. Of course, the wagon was older, weighed more, and had 80 fewer horses under the hood. Absently, he reached over and turned on the radio. Immediately, the song *Blue Velvet* filled the car. He pushed the button for FM to see what stereo music he could find. The richness of stereo was so impressive that it made the more popular AM stations sound hollow and flat. Even though he had long listened to 77 WABC's Rock and Roll the newer, better sounding, FM had a lot to offer. As if transforming from a child's tinny musical instrument to the all-encompassing sounds of an orchestra the car filled with music. It was *Scheherazade* by Rimsky-Korsakov, but he didn't know it. All he knew was the car was awash in stereophonic music. Every beautiful tone of the violin solo representing Scheherazade and the Arabian Nights resonated clearly and perfectly.

The NASA contract was a triumphant finale to a glorious year for Matthew Ellis. His direct involvement in getting Orztech into the coated wire arena had proven his instincts to be correct. In three short years that division of the company had become the leader in profitability with the present year the most promising of all. Military contracts had proven to be the key. It still amazed him how much money they represented once you finished jumping through all the hoops and dotting all the i's twice. That, coupled with an arms race that drove the military to order weaponry at an unprecedented rate during peacetime, was the formula for profits. He thought about all of the new Polaris submarines that had been launched that year each containing miles of Orztech wiring. The Nathan Hale, John Adams, and Woodrow Wilson were launched early in the year. Then the largest Polaris submarine of all, the USS Lafayette was launched in April. April, a month of major financial gains, was alas, also a sad month. Matt remembered when the USS Thresher mysteriously disappeared in the Atlantic Ocean during sea trials. All those brave young men lost. It was a crying shame. He wondered if he had met any of the lost men during one of his many trips to the shipyards where the Polaris subs were being built. April was also the month when the USS Jack and USS Daniel Webster were commissioned. He had been at the Daniel Webster commissioning.

Four more boats were launched in June. And, as each submarine slowly slid from its berth into the water it pushed upward the gross income of Orztech Corporation. In one way, there was a degree of luck involved, as Matt had no idea as to how many submarines would ultimately be built when he was negotiating those military contracts.

June was a banner month personally for Mathew Ellis. Parker Adolphson, president of Orztech, invited the young executive to lunch. Over drinks, he thanked Matt for all of his exceptional work, gave him a cash bonus, significant raise in salary, and told him he was a new vice-president of the company. Years of work and dedication had finally paid off. At the age of 35, Matthew Ellis had arrived. He slowed his Pontiac Grand Prix as he made the big wide circle around onto the George Washington Bridge.

President Kennedy's motorcade slowed as they turned left from Houston Street onto Elm Street and entered Dealey Plaza. The President thought for a moment about how much he adored being the leader of this great country. It had been a long arduous, sometimes tumultuous, journey through the perilous arena of politics. He had endured 17 years of dealing with the sharks and snakes and empty suits so prevalent in Washington politics. But now, even with its many challenges and threats he was where he wanted to be most. He was where he was meant to be. Deep inside where a man hides secret desires and dreams he knew this was the culmination of all his life's efforts. It was his destiny to lead because he had the courage to do so. It was essential that he lead because he had the vision to make a real and lasting difference. His "New Frontier" was out there in space, but it was also here on Earth. International conflicts had the potential to intensify and spread until they once again engulfed the entire world. Only this time the stakes would be far greater as mankind had the power to eradicate itself in one mindless act of madness. On a smaller but equally important scale, racial tensions in America were at a boiling point. Let them continue unchecked and the top would eventually blow off setting our nation back decades with generations of promise buried in aimless and fruitless turmoil. This he was committed to avert. When he returned to Washington he was prepared to put into motion programs that he hoped—no he knew—would make America truly a nation of the people and for the people. This was what he wanted to be his legacy.

Matt drove onto the bright cement roadway of the George Washington Bridge. Its brightness hurt his eyes until they adjusted. Once more he accelerated. For some reason, of which he was not sure, he loved that bridge. There was just something about how majestically its two silver towers stood above the water, how its eight lanes of roadway rose and fell in a gentle almost imperceptible arch, and how new it always appeared. He pushed a button and switched the radio back to AM. The song *Walk Right In* filled the car. His mind wandered to their plans for the day. After a short much needed rest in the afternoon, they would go to Piro's for dinner and then he and Valerie and their 12-year-old daughter Stephanie would go to the drive-in movie together. They all had been looking forward to seeing that new "hilarious" comedy *It's A Mad, Mad, Mad, Mad World*. He smiled as he remembered the trailers they had seen where Sid Caesar says, "That's a hard door."

President Kennedy smiled as he waved to the larger-than-anticipated crowd along the motorcade route. He didn't expect it in Texas–a state that was not one of his biggest supporters. At that moment, his attention turned to a 12-year-old girl standing on the curb to his right holding a small American flag. Her eyes were wide and filled with excitement. Her smile was equally wide. Upon seeing the President looking directly at her, she waved her little flag faster in a non-verbal greeting. Their eyes met. There in all its innocence was the future–the future he owed a nation he loved. Suddenly, her expression turned to horror. Her eyes were transfixed upon him and she dropped her flag to the ground. That exact moment of time lasted an eternity in the mind of John Fitzgerald Kennedy as he went from curiosity to confusion to fear. What did she see in him that so upset her? What was it he had done? The small child's rejection struck deeply within him causing excruciating pain. Instantaneously, pain devoured thoughts of hope and promise and a glorious future. His hand instinctively went to his throat where the pain seemed to have concentrated. He had trouble breathing. In desperation he turned to Jacqueline, his wife who sat beside him, but never saw her as his head exploded from an assassin's second bullet.

Matt was nearing home as he traveled north on Route 9W. It was a bright and sunny day offering only promise and a glorious future. The song *I Will Follow Him* rode along with him. Suddenly, it was interrupted by a news bulletin. "President Kennedy has been shot in Dallas. His condition at this time is unclear. However, it is presumed that he is in serious condition. He is presently in emergency room number one at Parkland Memorial Hospital where doctors are working to stabilize the President."

Matt could not believe what he had heard. It was impossible—not on this beautiful day. As he entered the Alpine stretch of Route 9W he reached over to change to a different radio station. Because of a design flaw that would not be corrected until many years and numerous lives later the road dips to the left which caused the big Pontiac Grand Prix to drift across the centerline. It only took an instant. However, that was all that was needed. When Matt looked up he saw only the front of a delivery truck. Time for reaction did not exist.

He blinked.

Before him, stood a beautiful young woman, whom he did not recognize. In fact, he had no idea where he was or how he had gotten there. He attempted to turn his head to look around but no movement followed his mental command. It was then that he realized that his eyes also failed to move around, as they stayed transfixed on the ceiling. Square white tiles stretched out in all directions creating a flat surface. On that surface were odd looking metal tracks that ran on either side of his field of vision. Again, he tried to move. This time, his arm and hand refused to acknowledge his orders. In the distance, he heard odd and yet very familiar sounds that he could not place. In his mind he asked, where am I?

The young woman stood to his left looking away. Her long dark hair hung as straight as anything he could remember curving only where it split to fall on either side of her shoulder. She seemed unaware of him and lost in thought. Beneath her hair, he could just make out an earring. It was silver, long, and narrow and hung straight down mimicking her hair. It appeared to be made of two long metal links with metal beads between them and at the end. It hung motionless, as was its owner, as was its observer.

He blinked. That small involuntary movement brought with it a stabbing pain–a pain that reached up from his eye sockets and buried itself in his brain. He wanted to yell out but couldn't.

Again, he blinked. This time the pain was less intense and the motion slightly more natural. It was much like when one sits in a certain position for a prolonged period of time and then moves. The first movement is the most painful. He wanted to speak, to call out, to ask where he was and how he got there. Unfortunately, that neuro-path seemed foreign and unavailable to him. He couldn't speak because he didn't know how. In his mind, he searched for the right switch, or command, or thought to activate his voice. Nothing.

He blinked, once more. The young woman turned slowly to face him. She was a stranger with a look of someone he knew but didn't know. Her features were clean and fresh and full of the vibrancy of youth. And yet, a shadow hung over her. Within that clean fresh visage was a lifetime of pain. She appeared too serious for one so young, too mature for her unknown years, and too distant. As beautiful as she was with dark brown eyes, high cheekbones, and a long neck that gave the appearance of dignity and poise she lacked the pure beauty and warmth of a smile or for that matter smile lines. There was a sadness that dominated all of those desirable features. Matt stared at her without her knowledge.

Once more he attempted to speak. Nothing. Who are you, he thought. Where am I? And, why are you here? She gazed beyond him seeing him but not acknowledging his consciousness. You must help me, Matt thought, pleaded, and begged. She did not react. Don't you to understand that I am here? Where is here? She ignored him.

The young woman turned to leave unaware of the exchange that had taken place. Matt in desperation didn't want to be left with only those ceiling tiles. From somewhere in his own disconnected mind he found the command that allowed him to yell, "Who are you?" However, what escaped from his throat was a low almost inaudible raspy "who" sound.

The young woman froze. For a moment, she seemed to hang motionless, then turned back to stare at Matt. This time she looked directly into his eyes. They were open! Her eyes were wide open with surprise. She had heard him, but was afraid to admit it, as it would be too much of a disappointment to find out it had been her imagination. Matt tried to repeat the action but could not make his physical prison comply. Finally, after failing again and again, he blinked twice to signal that he was indeed there, awake, with her, and terribly afraid.

"My God, you're awake!" she said in a low voice. They stared questioningly at each other. Then reality sank in and she ran to the big wooden door of the room and began yelling, "Somebody. Come quickly. He's awake!" She returned and whispered, "Daddy, you're back."

Anna Marie Six Trees awoke and stared at the ceiling above her bed. She had been napping. The sounds of plates in the kitchen told her dinner was being prepared. Her brother and mother's voices completed the familiar evening sounds in their small cabin. She didn't know her father as he left one night when she was an infant and never returned. Her nine-year-old brother was the only father figure she had ever known.

3: Thursday - April 17, 1969

On the day Matthew Ellis awoke from his coma, Sirhan Bishara Sirhan was found guilty of murdering Senator Robert F. Kennedy less than a year earlier. The crime took place on the morning on June 6, 1968 in the ballroom of the Ambassador Hotel in Los Angeles, California. Kennedy had just finished celebrating his victory in the Democratic presidential primary in that state and was leaving through a side door. The 24-year-old Jordanian-born assassin fired eight shots from a snub-nosed .22-caliber revolver at Senator Kennedy. Three struck him and he died at the Good Samaritan Hospital 26 hours later. This led to the nomination of Hubert H. Humphrey, the serving Vice-President, as the Democratic candidate for President of the United States, who subsequently lost to Richard M. Nixon on November 5, 1968. The trial of Sirhan Sirhan had lasted three months and he was found guilty of murder in the first degree. Six days later he would be sentenced to die in the gas chamber.

Matthew Ellis was unaware of all of this. His world was a 14 foot by 14 foot hospital room filled with monitoring equipment, nightstand, bed table, two visitor's chairs, and a small window to an outside world that had proceeded along its ceaseless path unaware that one of its own had been left behind. Unrelenting pain commanded his attention. Biting assaults gripped and tore at him every time he moved or attempted to move. Pain had become a constant companion telling him that he was awake, telling him of his fragile condition, but also telling him he was alive. It was welcome. He learned to read the pain, to predict it, to bear its horrific assaults because he knew there was no other avenue of escape from it. Days passed. During that time he faced torture after torture—both physical and emotional. Initially, he was unable to speak which made asking questions impossible. He relied on information provided by well-meaning individuals, however, this left major gaps in the puzzle that had become his life.

Stephanie, his daughter, helped fill in the largest gap by telling him what had happened to him almost six years earlier. On that beautiful sunny November afternoon in 1963 when everything offered so much promise President John F. Kennedy had been assassinated. At approximately the same time Matthew Ellis had a head-on collision with a delivery truck on Route 9W. It occurred so quickly that neither he nor the truck driver ever applied their brakes. They hit each other at over one hundred miles-per-hour. The driver of the truck died instantly. Through a combination of luck and fate, Matt survived. He was trapped in the twisted wreckage of his Pontiac Grand Prix, severely injured, but alive. It had taken the Alpine Fire Department over an hour to cut him free from what very well might have proven to be his metal coffin. And, because he was unconscious, they had no idea as to his identity. Even the police could not determine his identity from the license plates as all government offices had been closed due to the assassination. For this reason, neither Matt's wife nor his daughter had any knowledge of the accident. It was two hours after the accident had occurred when police finally visited the Ellis' home.

Vacation plans were forgotten, movie plans vanished, and dinner was overlooked as Stephanie and her mother waited in a small, uncomfortable, dark, dreary, waiting room in Englewood Hospital. Stephanie remembered how it smelled of alcohol. She hated that aroma. And yet, it became something she had to learn to live with as much of her life over that past six years had involved hospitals and doctor's offices. In that small room they waited. No one would or could give them any information about her father, his condition, or prognosis. Therefore, they could do no more than sit in silence–motionless–and wait.

Stephanie had with her a small red purse she and her mother had purchased that morning for her to carry on their vacation. In a child's mind she wondered if daddy would get well quickly enough to walk through that heavy metal door in time for them to still go on their vacation. She had done all of her homework assignments in advance, read extra chapters, done extra credit work, and even taken two tests in order to get the time off from school. It wasn't fair that she shouldn't get to go now after doing all of that. Still, as each hour of silence passed, hope diminished. Maybe they would leave a day later. Time dragged slowly and agonizingly on. They could go a day later, maybe even two, and still have a vacation. The silence of the room bore down on her. Finally, she lost hope as she realized their vacation was gone. She put her head in her mother's lap and fell asleep.

Dreams visited her from every angle. Good, pleasant, happy visions from the uninhibited joyous mind of a twelve-year-old. Her dreams were quite different from a twelve-year-old child in Texas who could not escape the horror of watching a human being's head explode and hearing the chaotic sounds of a world gone mad. Stephanie saw a forest filled with trees in the early morning as sunbeams were displayed by morning dew. The other child saw bright red streams of blood shooting out of the heads of all the people she knew and loved. Birds sang their merry songs in harmony. People screamed in horror and pain. A stream bubbled and splashed its way to a tranquil sea. Car tires squealed and sirens cried for a fallen hero. One world was enchanted and filled with life–the other a swirling abyss of destruction and death. Stephanie found refuge in a magical world born of a life free of stress and fear and sadness. Only that life was to change in what seemed a blink of an eye.

Abruptly and brutally she was wrenched from her dreams by the loud report of a huge metal door opening with a bang. Lost in the twilight between sleep and consciousness she searched for something familiar. Strange voices spoke in ominous tones as she focused on a small red purse.

"Mrs. Ellis," a monotone impersonal voice said softly, "your husband is alive."

"Oh, Thank God," she recognized the familiar warm caressing tone of her mother's voice. It was strained and gravelly from fatigue, worry, and hours of non-use.

"He's alive, but in critical condition," the voice continued, "the next few hours will tell us a lot. He has internal injuries, both legs are broken, two fractured ribs, a collapsed lung, and numerous other cuts and contusions." After a pause, "Of greatest concern is the fact that he has had severe head trauma. We relieved the pressure but he remains unconscious."

Stephanie listened but didn't understand. She could see the doctor in green scrubs still wearing his mask around his neck. He wore thick-rimmed glasses with dark brown hair that was graying on the sides. To her, he was of monstrous proportion as his size seemed to cover the entire huge green metal door. It was only over time that she had come to know him and to see him clearly as a short, rotund, warm, and caring man. It was over time that she realized the depth with which he cared. It was over time that he became the grounding force in her life. Dr. Gordon Tallman held it all together.

One morning, three weeks after his return, Matt awoke from a restless night sleep. He had that same recurring dream. A dream that was so realistic that its impact remained with him even after he awoke. For a few brief moments he remained motionless. As his eyes adjusted to the light he became aware of the familiar silhouette of his daughter, Stephanie. Once more her presence comforted him. Beside her stood another woman. She was taller than his daughter with long brown hair that hung flowingly down to approximately the middle of her back. She wore a multi-colored and loose fitting blouse. They stood side-by-side looking out the window. Neither talked.

Matt wondered if the other woman was his wife. She had not visited and no one had spoken of her. Even he had not asked the obvious question for reasons known only to him.

Matt ignored the pain as he whispered a familiar greeting, "Are you still my princess?" Those were the words he had said to her every night when he kissed her good night for twelve years.

"Always and always," Stephanie answered automatically as she turned to face her father.

Her smile once again warmed his heart and gave him needed strength to face another day. She walked over to him and kissed his cheek. As she did so, he looked beyond her at her companion who turned to face them. To Matthew Ellis' shock the visitor had a mustache and chin beard. An involuntary gasp of surprise escaped from him in the form of a low, "Uh?"

Stephanie stood up and grasped the visitor's arm as she offered, "Daddy, this is Ritchie. He's a friend of mine."

"Uh."

"Hey, man, I hope you're feeling better, man," the young man said brightly.

"Uh."

"He's an artist," Stephanie stated with shining eyes of adoration, "he's really very good."

"Uh."

"I try to see beyond the eye, man, if you can dig what I mean."

"Uh."

"It's the essence of things that are important not the obvious physical characteristics that anyone can see."

"Uh."

"You see," the young man seemed to get wound up as he stepped closer to Matt to explain his point, "everything that society seems to care about is looks and image and physical things, man. We've lost touch. We're trying to fill a void in our souls with physical possessions. But, all we're doing is covering up our real needs. We're making them harder to find and recognize, therefore, harder to fill. We no longer judge a man by the depth of his character, we judge by the size of his wallet, man. Some schmuck can be a lousy, no good, lying mother, but if he has enough bread he's admired. It's all about money, profits, big business, man. Doomsday hangs over us and all we care about is shit. Give me more shit."

Matt was amazed by the sight before him. He wasn't sure what the young man was saying but he could tell the lad was definitely excited. He was so animated that his long tresses swung one way then another. His eyes glared, but not with hatred. Rather, they were filled with passion. Whatever he was selling he truly believed in it. Around his neck he wore a thin leather chain with an ankh attached. It also swung wildly as the oration continued.

"People are like a bunch of ants, man. Like, they buy what advertisers tell them to buy. They believe what the establishment tells them to believe. That's how we got into this immoral mess in Vietnam."

What mess in Vietnam, Matt wondered.

"The man wants to get his big grubby hands on all that oil over there. So he sets up a puppet government and tries to force it on the people. But, the people, man, don't want us there. So, the establishment tells us we are trying to stop communism because they believe that's the story that will work. We live in a plastic society, man, that's being shaped and molded to fit the needs of big business and the government."

"Daddy," Stephanie interjected, "how are you feeling?"

The young man turned away to once more look out of the window. Matt and his daughter held hands. Conversation was intermittent as speech was still very difficult for him to manage. After a few minutes his visitors turned to leave.

"I love you, daddy," Stephanie said with a wave.

"Peace, man," Ritchie offered as he raised his index and middle fingers.

Matt recognized the victory sign. Once alone, he wondered about that dream.

"Shit!" Wellington Marsh spat as he projected South Carolina red clay from his mouth.

"I'd say that's a pretty good guess," Shortstop responded in a low voice, lest Sergeant Kincaid hear them. His real name was Marvin Press, but early in their training he got saddled with the moniker of Shortstop. How was he to know any better—the teenage son of a black sharecropper from Georgia?

It had happened the very first day, at mess, when one of the other marine recruits asked him to pass the corn bread. Marvin obliged, while casually removing one piece for himself. It was indeed an innocent act very much like what was commonplace back home. Only he wasn't back home and it wasn't innocent. At least to Sergeant Kincaid it was something absolutely intolerable that was one step short of murder.

"Freeze boot!" the huge black Sergeant bellowed from behind. "What in the damn-hell do you think you are doing—recruit?"

A startled Marvin Press looked around not sure who had killed the captain's cat. When he came eye to belt buckle with his verbal assailant he could only mumble through a mouthful of corn bread, "Me? Sir—uh—Sergeant."

"Don't you talk to me with your black mouth exploding with this man's food," a huge arm pointed at the original requester.

After an unpleasant and somewhat painful swallow of half-chewed corn bread Marvin replied, "I don't understand." Burp. "Sergeant?"

"You never shortstop food or anything else that's been requested. Do you read me, boot?"

Marvin could only nod and offer a blank stare.

Sergeant Kincaid wasn't finished. He stood tall and bellowed to all the recruits in his charge, "No one ever shortstops food. Do you read me?" To punctuate his point he slammed his walking stick on the tabletop inches from Marvin's hand. That damn walking stick punctuated many of Sergeant Kincaid's lectures as training progressed on from that day.

There, in the field, flat on their bellies, in mud and grass and animal droppings the last thing Shortstop wanted was one of Sergeant Kincaid's walking stick lessons.

Wellington Marsh came from the opposite end of the country. Instead of being the son of a black sharecropper from Georgia, he was the only son of a black automobile assembly line worker from Detroit, Michigan. He had been drafted shortly after his eighteenth birthday. Slight of build but muscular, Wellington had an air of dignity and confidence. He wasn't an A student, but he was a thinker. He wasn't a fighter, nor was he a coward. He was a philosopher with a sense of humor. Even though getting drafted dashed his hopes of finding a job at a restaurant and learning to be a chef, he didn't lament the loss he simply changed direction. Maybe his army experience would teach him a trade that he would enjoy more. And, he did want to serve his country so he reported for his physical as directed without complaint.

Once through all of the tests and examinations, Wellington and the other draftees were herded into a large room. Young men of various size, build, race, and religious background shuffled uneasily through a narrow door. Wellington saw fear and confusion and dejection and detachment in their eyes. None of them wanted to be there. All of them knew they had no choice. They also knew that they had passed their physicals and were being snatched from their comfortable, safe, happy homes to be pressed into his majesty's service without having any say in the decision. An eerie silence hung over them. Wellington moved along with the slow flow of strangers. The pace and silence was overbearing. Finally, when he could stand no more of it he broke the somber mood with a few well-placed, "moo's." Immediately, it led to other animal sounds like, "Baa," and muffled laughter. Young men began to look around and perhaps for the first time realized they were not alone. They all shared the same anxiety and trepidation. They all shared the same tiny little space. And, possibly they all shared the same fate. Regardless of their apparent differences, at that particular time they were all very much alike.

Once in the room, the young men were told to stand in a number of rows. There was no order or assigned place, simply find a spot and stand still. It was then that a short Marine master sergeant with a chest full of medals entered the room. He stood silently for a moment as he surveyed the day's catch. Then it happened. He went to the first man in the front row and handed each man in the row a piece of paper. As he did so he said, "Army, Army, Marines, Army, Army, Marines." Wellington was one of the lucky one-third who ended up with a green slip of paper and drafted into the Marines that day, which ultimately brought him to this place.

"I'm telling you I'll never get clean again when this is over," Wellington complained.

"That's the plan," Shortstop observed, "they get all this dirt and grime so ground into us that we just naturally blend into the landscape."

From behind, an all-too-familiar voice barked, "The enemy may not see you, but they sure as hell can hear you."

Shortstop tensed.

"What in the damn-hell do you think you are doing? Boot!"

"No excuse, Sergeant!" He had at least learned the appropriate response when caught doing one of the million-and-one things they either shouldn't do, should have done, should have thought of, or should have known.

Wellington Marsh remained motionless. He wanted to hate Sergeant Kincaid but found that he couldn't. The huge black Marine was tough, mean, and intimidating. He was always there, always watching, always waiting ready to strike without hesitation and without pity. To say he struck fear in the young recruits' hearts would denigrate the highly practiced and sophisticated psychological assaults that he delivered.

Sergeant Kincaid reminded Wellington of his father. His old man was tough, mean, and quick with a slap, smack, or verbal barrage. That old man was tough and mean and loud—very loud. But, there was one incontrovertible fact—he cared. He cared so much it almost drove him crazy. He wanted his son to learn how to face life, handle life, and make the best of his life. Meanness was his way of showing love.

Wellington watched as Sergeant Kincaid circled his friend and fellow recruit. The always-present walking stick swung back and forth. It was a wooden junkyard dog waiting for its master's order to attack.

Shortstop knew the blow would come. He just hated having to wait for it. On this particular night it didn't take long. The loud crack of wood against his steel helmet echoed in his ears.

"That's what it sounds like when a bullet hits you in the fucking helmet!" the big sergeant stated emphatically. "But, you wouldn't hear it because your brains would be all over the inside of that helmet."

Shortstop's ears rang and his head ached.

"You dumb, stupid nigger. You got us all killed because you couldn't keep your dumb ass mouth shut."

Shortstop's ears yelled at him as his pulse quickened. He waited for another blow that might come at any moment.

Wellington attempted to come to the aid of his friend as he confessed, "Sergeant. It was my fault. I spoke first."

A huge finger struck out at him, stopping inches from his face, "You shut up!" Sergeant Kincaid added, "I'll deal with you later."

Wellington and Shortstop found out what that meant as they spent the rest of the night digging graves for the entire squad that they had just gotten killed. Twelve holes side by side that, once dug, were filled with rocks, logs, and other debris, then covered over. At the gravesites they said a prayer and asked each fallen comrade by name to forgive them for their stupidity. Finally, exhausted and beat, they had to write a letter to the parents of each slain Marine explaining how their son had died. Finally, they were allowed to clean up and get in the rack. Reveille came thirty minutes later.

Robert Six Trees sat quietly in his room sketching a bird. It was perched on his windowsill. Given the fact that he had never received any formal art training and that he was only nine years old, the quality of his drawing was impressive. As was his habit, he would give the picture to his six-year-old sister, Anna.

4: Sunday - May 18, 1969

"Five, four, three, two, one, ignition."

Matthew Ellis sat in bed in his hospital room as he watched the launch of Apollo 10. A huge Saturn rocket, that dwarfed in size the far smaller rockets he remembered from the one-man Project Mercury series, exploded in flame. Initially, he was alarmed when he thought something had gone terribly wrong. However, the rocket emerged unscathed from an ocean of fire and streaked skyward. In silence, he watched the awesome power that had been unleashed. He couldn't take his eyes off the screen. The huge vehicle bolted skyward at an increasingly fast rate until it became a small white speck. Earlier, he had read in the newspaper that this mission was the final rehearsal before actually landing a man on the moon. Air Force Colonel Thomas P. Stafford and Navy Commanders Eugene A. Cernan and John W. Young were destined to orbit the moon and fly the lunar module to within 9.4 miles of the surface. It was a leap beyond imagination eclipsing the earlier meager attempts to break from the Earth's bonds that Matt recalled. There he sat having been involved in a direct way with the beginning of the space program and now only a spectator at its fruition. To Matthew Ellis it was as though he had begun reading a book and then turned to the end after skipping all the chapters in between. It left him with an empty feeling of having been cheated.

Slowly, over the weeks, movement had returned to his body. Slowly, the medicines and physical therapy brought him closer and closer to physical recovery. However, his mind was still filled with huge gaps where nothing existed. He was mentally trapped on a very small island unable to get to the mainland where all of his history and memories were at hand. The small white speck that was the huge Saturn rocket grew more and more distant on the screen. Finally, it disappeared completely allowing Matt's thoughts to return to the conversation he had with his daughter, Stephanie, the night before.

She arrived at exactly six in the evening as she did every night. They talked and joked and he gave her a progress report on his therapy. Then, he abruptly asked the question with a single word, "Valerie?"

Stephanie froze hearing her mother's name.

Silence hung heavy in the room. Neither spoke. Father and daughter sat in the sterile confines of a hospital room looking at each other—a father looking for answers and a daughter looking for the right words. Matt had asked the question that Stephanie dreaded would come. She knew it was inevitable. She knew he deserved to know. She knew she was the only one who could do it, but she hated having to face it.

Matt failed to tell his daughter that he had not inquired sooner about her mother, his wife, because he couldn't remember her name. Nor, for that matter, could he remember anything about her. For the entire time that he had been awake there existed a void where memories of his wife should have been. As hard as he tried he could not find her. Without telling anyone he labored to mental exhaustion searching and searching but she was nowhere to be found. It was as if she never existed. This left him with a feeling of emptiness, but not remorse for one must have a human connection to mourn. However, he learned quickly that he did not have to have a human connection to feel guilt. Regardless of how hard he searched within his mind, whatever method he used, there remained a frustrating, unnerving, beckoning blank. Nothing seemed to be stored where it should have been. Nothing provided even the slightest of glimpses into a history that must have been lived. Nothing was the hardest thing to face.

Physical pain was something Matt had grown to understand, to interpret, and to deal with. But, as pain became less of a burden, the weight of existence sans memory grew. He had to know. He had to know. He had to know! Yet he had no idea how to find out. And, that recurring dream with its haunting effect continued to plague him.

As often happens, hope presented itself when least expected. Earlier in the day that he made the inquiry of Stephanie, he had been sitting in the dayroom looking out at a beautiful spring afternoon. As had become his habit he read back issues of *Time Magazine* and *Newsweek* in his quest to recapture lost history. Memory for him had become a dynamic thing with images and words and recollections leaping out of dark corners and from behind other thoughts at the most unexpected times. It made him thirst for exposure to as many stimuli as possible with the hope that he would slowly wash away all of the dark mists that masked his life.

The windows in the dayroom had been open allowing a cool refreshing breeze to cleanse the room. Aromas of new growth mingled with the sterile alcohol odor of the hospital. Their sweet perfume brought Matt closer to a world that he missed—the one outside. Somewhere in the distance, he heard the low-pitched buzz of a bumblebee. It beckoned him, fascinated him, and sang to him. Eyes searched for the source of that wonderful sound. It danced somewhere nearby and yet somewhere hidden. Drawn to that dulcet song of life Matt drifted within his mind. It was there that he found Valerie. She wore a wide brimmed sun hat and round oversized dark sunglasses. Behind the brown tinted plastic lenses her brown eyes sparkled. From under the hat her dark hair curled and twisted around her face reaching down until it rested upon her bare shoulders. A yellow sundress covered her pleasingly supple body. With red lips she smiled as she approached. It was at that precise moment that a bee discovered this beautiful flower and began its exploration dance. His wife reacted immediately as she was deathly afraid of bees and wasps and any other buzzing, stinging predator. Quickly she twisted and turned to avoid the creature's infatuated advances. As she did she said in a scolding voice, "Matthew, don't just stand there, help me. Get it away from me." She took off her hat and swung it at the innocent insect. It was then that Matt warned his wife as his mind said in clear revealing welcoming words, "Don't make it mad, Valerie, it will sting you." Her name—finally revealed—reached out to him and caressed him. It gave life and identity to distant shadows. Valerie, once again, existed in his mind and in his heart. Like opening a door, his was led down endless corridors of memories. At light speed they blossomed forth one after another as if fighting to get recognized first. A lifetime of lost images washed over him.

Blood poured from the nose of the larger man, however, Carl Pythacyk wasn't finished. He had a short fuse that ignited red-hot anger, which was hard to extinguish, once aroused. Much like a wildfire, it simply had to burn itself out. Carl ducked as his adversary threw an errant punch in his direction. It was more of a defensive move than an attack. Once more well-aimed calculated strikes weakened his foe further. The man dropped to one knee. With the speed of a striking serpent, hardened knuckles that had struck countless others over the years snapped the man's head back leaving the unnamed, unprepared, unimportant Neanderthal in a helpless heap. Carl exercised compassion by consciously restraining himself from kicking his fallen prey in the ribs. It was his way of minimizing the severity of the infraction that precipitated the event.

The bigger man, now quite unimpressive as he lay on the ground, had bumped into Carl at the bottom of the stairway leading up to the Jerome Avenue elevated subway. Carl had arrived at the bottom of the stairs too late. All he could do was watch the train pull out of the Fordham Road Station. As a result, he was in no mood to be jostled. Then, getting bumped by some six-foot tall oaf walking hand-in-hand with a skinny blond down the stairs as if they owned the place was more than he cared to take. He knew he had already missed the train, but the fact that the two of them blocked his clear passage to the platform above made it abundantly clear that they didn't care. They lived in their own world. Even if the train were there waiting for him, they would have blocked his way. They, in essence, would have kept him from catching the train. They were shit!

When contact was made between the two men words were exchanged.

"You missed it buddy," the bigger man rubbed it in with a sardonic sneer.

"No thanks to you, dickhead," Carl snapped, "Get the hell out of my way."

"Hey, now watch it pal or you might get hurt."

"Up yours!"

"Now listen, punk," the man reached for Carl's shirt.

The first two blows landed before the man knew what had hit him. The next broke his nose.

Carl didn't hear the screams of the young lady who stood in disbelief when the exchange took place. When it was over she crouched next to her fallen boyfriend and spat, "You creep!"

He did, however, hear her subsequent yell for the police. Quickly, he continued up the stairs, entered the lower level below the elevated platform, crossed over, and immediately walked down the stairs on the opposite side of Jerome Avenue. Unnoticed, he disappeared into the darkness.

As Carl walked along Fordham Road in the direction of the Grand Concourse where he could catch a D Train downtown he remembered his very first fight. Why he thought of it at that moment was a mystery. It simply snuck into his mind. The memory was crystal clear.

While in elementary school at PS 86 he lost his lunch money every day to older boys who were bigger than him. They targeted him due to his size. Every morning they were waiting. If he was lucky they simply took his fifteen cents. On those unpleasant days when they were in a cruel mood they would taunt him, call him shrimp, throw his books into the street, push him from one to another, and finally take his money.

One morning Carl carried with him a special book that his father had loaned him. It was from the old country. The book, *The Door,* written in Polish was signed by the author, Kenneth Potenski. Carl was bringing it for show and tell. As luck would have it that was a morning when his antagonists decided to have a little fun at his expense. They took his hat and threw it in a tree, knocked his books out of his hands, and took his money. As usual he did not resist. Fear controlled his actions. Then one of the boys picked up the book written in Polish. He looked at it questioningly.

"Give that back to me," Carl demanded as one of the other boys held him by his jacket sleeve. This was the first time he had offered any resistance, or complained, or spoken for that matter—definitely a mistake.

The young hoodlum looked at Carl as though he was surprised by the affront. He walked over to where the younger boy was being held.

"You want this?" he asked as he hit Carl on the forehead with the book.

"Give it to me," Carl asked in a softer tone, "Please."

"You can't read it. The letters are all mixed up," the tormentor said as he leafed through the book.

"Please," Carl pleaded.

"You want it?" the boy said inches from Carl's face, "then bark like a dog."

This caused the other boys to laugh. Carl looked at each one of them hoping to find some measure of help. None was to be found. With no recourse and desperately hoping to get back the book undamaged, Carl said softly, "Woof."

"What? I can't hear you."

"Woof, woof."

"That's not a bark. Maybe if you got down on all fours you'd feel more like a dog." Laughter filled Carl's ears. The boy who was holding him pushed him toward the sidewalk. Carl resisted. "Maybe, I should start tearing pages out of it."

Carl dropped onto his knees and finally put his hands on the ground.

"Now, bark!"

To hold back the tears Carl closed his eyes and began, "Aarf, Aarf."

"Hey, now that's better," the sneering boy stated grandly. His friends laughed. "You want the book—you can have it." With the flick of his wrist he tossed the book into the street under a passing bus. "Fetch!"

As the massive tires of the bus tore the book into shreds Carl stared in disbelief.

"Oops," the boy said with a broad smile.

Fear became anger, then hate, then uncontrollable action. From the ground where it had been on the dirty pavement a fist traveled with unexpected speed and power to strike his enemy in the left eye. The surprised boy fell backward landing on his rear end. Carl stood up and grabbed the boy who had been holding his jacket sleeve by the collar. Not knowing what else to do he began hitting the boy in the face again and again. Blood from both the boy's mouth and Carl's hand sprayed the air. Something white fell to the ground as did the boy who slumped into a heap offering no resistance.

Two of the other boys ran away. A third grabbed Carl from behind and spun him around. He then punched Carl on the upper part of his right cheek. Carl answered with three quick blows to the upper body and neck of his attacker. While coughing and gasping for air the boy retreated.

Carl's anger, still unquenched, returned to the original target of his assault. The larger boy wanted nothing to do with the unchained fury that came at him. He scrambled to his feet and ran in the direction of PS 86.

As he continued down Fordham Road that memory once again gave Carl an awful sick feeling of shame that refused to abate. By allowing himself to be humiliated in such a manner a permanent scar was left on his psyche. It was a hard and lasting lesson. He had learned the sting of physical pain was far less dreadful than had been believed and, after all, from that you will heal.

The look on his father's face when the old man came to school to pick up his suspended son was etched in his mind. But, far more devastating was the look he endured when he handed his father the destroyed book that had been a prized possession from the old country. The old man didn't say a word. He didn't react in any way at all. He sat at the little kitchen table in their apartment and stared at the small pile of debris. Carl waited for the explosion. He knew he deserved whatever punishment was given. He needed a reaction. He got none. As much as his hands hurt from the fight that he had fought, he found that single moment in time to be far more unbearable. There was nothing that he could say. There was nothing that he could do. He sat waiting. His father, whom he admired, did not move, did not speak, and did not offer any indication of what it would take to once more be an acceptable son. Finally, Josef Pythacyk rose from the table and silently walked out of the kitchen. The soft closing of the apartment door was his final word on the subject. The look on his father's face when he came to school to pick up his suspended son was etched in Carl's mind, however, having so hurt his father and been such a failure as a son would forever be etched in his heart.

He never won his father's respect back. But, years later at the age of nineteen he still lived in a two-bedroom apartment with his parents at 2515 University Avenue in the Bronx, New York. After the book incident they seemed to drift further and further apart with each subsequent year. Carl didn't blame his father for he knew that he didn't give him a great deal of which to be proud.

One major lesson Carl learned that fateful day was that it was far more enjoyable to be on top than on the bottom. Those older boys who once preyed on him quickly found it better to defer to him. Quick and dramatic response became Carl Pythacyk's modus operandi.

When he arrived downtown on Forty Second Street, Carl looked for Miguel. Two nights earlier they had hit a boxcar together and now the greasy little son-of-a-bitch had disappeared. They scored six-dozen Morenz watches that were easily worth a few thousand dollars with any fence in the city. Miguel had claimed he could get the best price so Carl stupidly had trusted him.

"You seen Miguel?" he asked a street barker that he knew who was busy trying to attract young men into a peep show.

"Naw, I ain't seen him for days," the polyester suited, duck-tail coiffed street punk stated. When he spotted a young man walking along the curb he immediately called out, "Hey, live girls. Topless. They're waiting for you inside." He was ignored.

Under his breath he sneered, "Faggot."

"You see him, tell him I'm looking for him."

"Right."

"I mean it. Tell him I want my money."

"What am I your messenger service?"

"Just tell him."

"Sure."

Carl began to leave.

"Hey!"

He stopped.

"I got something for you."

Carl knew what was to follow. Slowly the young man's middle finger shot skyward, he grinned, and disappeared inside the safe haven of the peep show. Carl also smiled. Contrary to appearances that was a sign of respect. Anyone who taunted you and stood his ground was calling you out. To make a gesture and run, on the other hand, was equivalent to a compliment on the street. Carl turned, and continued walking west on Forty Second Street toward Times Square. He knew the many haunts where Miguel hung out. He also knew Miguel was a pimp and had a number of girls who walked over on Eighth Avenue.

Anna Six Trees awoke with a start after having a nightmare. Although the frightening images had faded their effect lingered. In a low pleading voice the six-year-old called, "Bobby, Bobby." Her brother arrived in a few moments and sat on the side of her bed as he had done so many times before. She took his hand and closed her eyes. Sleep returned quickly.

5: Monday - May 19, 1969

"You think I'm a nose?"

"Today, you're a nose. Tomorrow you might be a foot."

"That's grotesque! How can you paint a picture like that and expect me to be happy about it?"

"I don't expect anything. As an artist, I have to reach for new levels of awareness. I have to expand my consciousness. The work I do when straight is different from the work I do on acid, man. You know that," Ritchie explained with a slight tone that betrayed his growing impatience.

"I might as well not have been in the room if—that—is the outcome," Stephanie protested as she pointed at the offending work of art.

"It's what I saw when I tripped, man."

"Do you think my nose looks like that?"

"It did in my expanded consciousness."

"It's terrible, grotesque, horrible."

"It's art."

"So, that's what you see. To you I'm a misshapen monstrous nose."

"Right now, you're an asshole," he spat in anger, only to immediately regret having done so.

Silence followed. Two combatants stood an arm's length apart looking directly at one another. Seething anger sought avenues of expression but was held at bay. Thoughts, both of attack and of reconciliation, entered each mind but remained trapped within. Emotions stirred but were contaminated by words that had been spoken.

Tears welled up in Stephanie's eyes. She turned abruptly and left the cluttered studio. Once outside she let her emotions flow freely. It wasn't Ritchie's art as much as it was her unrelenting need for reassurance, to be accepted, perhaps valued, and—just maybe—loved. For too long her world had been one of disappointment, loss, crisis, and fear. At this time in her life she needed someone to care, to be there, to lean on someone from whom she could draw strength. She thought of the previous night with her father.

Stephanie had told her father what happened to her mother, however, she spared him from all of the details. She spoke in distant, impersonal, medical terms using words such as aneurysm, arteriosclerosis, thrombosis, and numerous other terms that she did not fully understand. All she knew was that her mother literally worked herself to death and that might not have happened if he had only been a little more goddamned careful. And, for the thousandth time she cursed herself for having such a thought.

Back in 1963, that awful night was the end of her childhood, the demise of her family, the first vicious sting of a new reality, and the shaping of Stephanie Elizabeth Ellis. After Dr. Tallman left that horrible little room at Englewood Hospital, Stephanie sat and watched her mother. Before her, she saw the woman she depended on for everything, including life itself, sit motionless unable to determine what was the next thing to be done. Her father had been the one who took care of everything. He had always been there so there was no reason for her mother to learn about any of it.

Stephanie thought, they were getting ready to go on vacation for crying out loud!

That night, that cruel night, was but the beginning of a long journey into a dark and foreboding world of fear, despair, and recurring loss. Her mother, like a deer in headlights, was frozen by fear, confusion, and indecision. She sat unmoving as if that might somehow allow a better alternative to present itself. It obviously did not.

When they finally left the hospital, her mother carried with her a handful of papers that a nice soft-spoken lady in a blue business suit had given her. Stephanie carried a little red purse. The woman had explained very patiently what all of the papers addressed and what needed to be done. Stephanie didn't understand any of it. Terms like "financial responsibility," "insurance coverage," and "deductible" all had no meaning—no meaning at that time.

Life changed so completely for Stephanie that she remained in a state of confusion most of the time. Her father, whom she loved as much as anything in her small world, did not come home. She no longer heard him tell his funny stories at the dinner table. He no longer played dolls with her, took her out for ice cream, did something funny like spill a whole bucket of white paint on the bushes, yell at the television when a ball game was on, or ask her if she was still his princess when she went to bed. She no longer could slip her small hand into his much larger, reassuring, strong, yet gentle hand when they walked together. The warm loving aroma of his cologne faded from their home. Her dreams changed from beautiful sunlit forests to alien landscapes filled with dark shadowy recesses that she dared not enter.

Over time, Stephanie and her mother settled into a routine that allowed them to continue with the remnants of their lives. Things weren't the same. They couldn't be the same. And yet, her mother tried as hard as she could to make it pleasant for Stephanie. Valerie Ellis didn't let her daughter see the worry that she carried inside twenty-four hours a day. She didn't confess her fear that her husband might never recover. Instead, she told Stephanie that her father was simply sleeping while he healed and that when he was stronger he would one day wake up and be with them once again.

In mid-winter, after her father's accident, he remained comatose. To a thirteen-year-old he did indeed appear to be asleep. The illusion was complete with the last of the many bandages removed and all of the cuts and bruises healed. Her father slept peacefully in a hospital bed far from their home, but never far from their hearts. When they would visit, Stephanie would always walk over and touch his arm just to be sure he was real and not imagined. Each time she would stare at his face expecting, wanting, hoping, praying for him to all of a sudden open his eyes and say, hi. He never did.

One particular cold evening, after they returned home from the hospital, Stephanie was quiet and withdrawn. She and her mother ate supper in silence. For some unexplained reason, she missed her father more than ever. In fact, she found that she had less and less of her mother's attention, as well, because of the demands of trying to do everything around the house. Loneliness gripped Stephanie.

They had finished supper and were having chocolate pudding for desert. Stephanie felt weak from the pressure of a life falling apart. She played with the pudding, but did not eat.

Finally, Valerie, having watched her daughter in distress was compelled to ask, "What's wrong, sweetheart?"

Stephanie did not answer as she continued to push milk chocolate pudding around the bowl.

"Please, tell me," her mother pressed, "maybe, I can help."

Still Stephanie didn't answer. It was not that she didn't want to talk to her mother. She simply didn't know what to say.

Valerie waited. She didn't want to push her daughter too hard. Also, she was acutely aware of the fact that it was always Matt who could talk with Stephanie when she was in one of her moods. He knew exactly what to say and how to say it. It was just another example of her many inadequacies as a mother.

Slowly and mechanically Stephanie asked her bowl of pudding, "Do you think daddy will ever wake up?"

The question slashed at Valerie's soul. She wondered the same thing herself—often. She knew there was no answer, but that was no answer to give a 13 year old.

"I know he will," she said softly with all of the conviction that she could muster. "That's why we have to remember as much as we can about what we do so we can share our memories with him when that time comes. You know, he'd be disappointed if we left anything out."

Valerie Ellis had always been the conservative one in the family. She liked to say that she was the voice of reason, but, she knew, it was more that she simply was that way by nature. Throughout her life, she was a hesitator and contemplator. Impulsive acts just weren't something that Valerie ever surrendered to or considered. As a result, it often was Stephanie and daddy against mom. They had a bond forged of fun-loving spontaneity. Without warning, one or the other might fling a marshmallow across the room at the other. Or, Matt might suddenly jump up and declare that he wanted some ice cream and off the two of them would go. Or, they might build an impromptu tent in the living room by dangling a blanket over the card table. One night they began drawing pictures on each other with one of Valerie's lipsticks. Through it all Valerie would sit and watch and smile or warn them that they were going to break something. Only on rare occasions would she participate and that was after lengthy coaxing.

On this cold and desolate night with her daughter so upset and concerned, Valerie did a rare impulsive thing. It seemed like the right thing to do at the time. Unpremeditated, she pulled back on her spoonful of pudding with her thumb and let it snap forward sending a soft brown salvo in the direction of her daughter. Silently, it splat on Stephanie's arm. For a moment, the young girl was surprised. She looked at her mother not sure what to think. What Stephanie saw was an odd smile that was so out of character that her mother had the appearance of a stranger. She looked at the pudding that clung to her arm, then back at her mother who sat silently looking her unflinchingly in the eye. It was a challenge. Had it been her father the war would have been on and her response would have been immediate, however, this was unfamiliar territory. Stephanie didn't know if the assault came from anger and frustration or playfulness.

Chocolate pudding that had endured long minutes of being pushed this way and that in a small white bowl found itself free, flying gracefully across a kitchen table only to land smack on the center of Valerie's chin. It hung there like a brown goatee.

Valerie sat motionless staring at her daughter. Her heart was so warmed by that one silly act that she had difficulty containing herself. How hard life had become for both of them. How desperately she wanted to spare Stephanie from the cruelties of life. How unprepared she was for her new role. How very, very much she loved her little girl. And, how important that simple act that opened a new door for them was to her. She had difficulty holding back tears.

Stephanie sat equally motionless wondering how her mother would react.

Two combatants on a small table of honor remained in mental deadlock. Neither making any move. Then reality penetrated Stephanie's mind as she became fully aware of the vision before her. There sat her conservative, "you might get hurt," "don't do that," mother with a chocolate goatee hanging from her chin. The incongruity was startling. The effect was farcical. Immediately, Stephanie exploded with laughter. A laugh that had long been dormant erupted from the teenager. It was a laugh that had no end. It was a laugh that flowed with abandon. Just short of hysteria, Stephanie laughed at the sight across the table. It was a laugh that warmed and healed and renewed hope. It was a laugh that stopped instantly when a wad of chocolate pudding hit her in the nose.

The Ellis household exploded into all-out warfare. Volley after volley of pudding flew through the air. Valerie took a blast in the ear. Stephanie was laughing so hard that she took a direct hit in the mouth. It was the only pudding that got eaten that night. The refrigerator, stove, sink, cabinets, table, and floor all sustained collateral damage. And then, with no more ammunition, the war ended. Mother and daughter sat on the floor amidst all the damage and laughed until their sides ached. Then silence. A knowing look. A sharing of spirit that can only be felt by those who were involved. A new dawn. Stephanie crawled on hands and knees over to her mother and put her head on her chest and hugged her. Two strangers made peace in a chocolate ruin, forgave numerous unintentional indiscretions, and silently declared allegiance to each other.

The same night that Cassius Marcellus Clay (who two days later would change his name to Muhammad Ali) defeated Sonny Liston to become the new heavyweight world champion, February 25, 1964, Valerie and Stephanie Ellis enjoyed their own victory after a hard-fought battle in their small Alpine, New Jersey kitchen.

"Let me have a double, Harry," a five-dollar bill found its way onto the bar.

Harry Van Ryker, the bartender and owner, filled a glass with two shots of Dewars over ice. He took the offered sawbuck and left the change on the bar. As Harry gazed at the change he considered how bartenders learn a great deal about patrons simply from their actions. For instance, New Yorkers leave their change on the bar while out-of-towners pick up their money. Patrons who come in for a drink and nothing more will look you in the eye, while those with other intentions avoid making eye contact. It was as though they believed that if they didn't look directly at you, you would not pay full attention to them. What it amounted to was an odd but subtle way of hiding. Harry learned quickly that the customer who was in constant motion, shifting this way and that, looking around, and touching his face with his hand was the one to watch. Over the years, he defused many potentially dangerous situations by just being observant and knowing how to read his customers. And now, Jack sat before him with both elbows on the bar. Nothing unusual—nothing unusual to the non-observant. Jack came in two or three times a week, would have a few drinks, and sit sideways on a stool leaning on one elbow. He would quietly watch the room, observing people, letting his reporter's eye seek what it will. When he sits, back to the room, leaning on both elbows that is out of character. Call it experience, bartender's intuition, or whatever you like, it was a sign that something was wrong. The big graying 62-year-old bartender with arms like those of a stevedore leaned forward and asked, "What's the matter Jack? You look all beat up."

"How long has it been, Harry?"

"For what? The last time either one of us had sex?"

The attempt at humor failed as Jack Moore continued in a somber tone, "How long have I been coming in here?"

"Twenty years, but who's counting?"

"That's a lot of damn years," the younger, fifty-year-old man shook his head as he gazed at his visage in the honey colored liquid in his glass. "A lot of years in the blink of an eye."

"Yeah, it is."

"You know, I remember the first time I came in here," he looked deeper into the liquid as if seeing a reflection of times long past. He was thirty-one and had just been hired as an investigative reporter on the *Tribune*. He needed to celebrate. He needed to let New York know he was here. He needed to come down from the high that he was feeling. He needed a drink. As luck would have it the first bar he passed, upon leaving his new place of employment, was More-Or-Less. The name fascinated him. Of course, given his surname of Moore it was sure to catch his eye. Obviously, the owner had a sense of humor and Jack liked that. Humor was a civilized way of releasing emotions and Jack had seen far too much of the other end of the spectrum—violence.

It was late afternoon when he entered the bar, which was deserted. One dark-haired, middle-aged, maybe forty-year-old man was present sweeping the floor.

"You open?"

"To what?"

"Oh, I don't know; running off to Vegas and getting married?"

"And, leave all of this?" a big arm waved across the landscape.

"I see what you mean," Jack took in the room. Its centerpiece was an old, vintage, long, wooden bar with highly polished top. Eight wooden bar stools with swivel backs stood guard. Behind the bar were three antique long handled beer taps, a sink, long table, and rows of clean glasses. Along the wall, behind the bar, on glass shelves were bottles of liquor. A variety of shapes, and sizes, and color formed the typical artwork of an intoxicatorium. Their mix of tone and color were beautiful to behold, as were the promises they offered. Also on the back wall were a number of photographs. One was of two police officers shaking hands, an older man and the man who was in the room with Jack. Another photograph was of a large group of police officers at what must have been their graduation from the academy. Harry, as a young man, stood proudly among his peers with a large grin upon his face. In another frame was a certificate of commendation from the City of New York with the name Harold Van Ryker in gold letters.

Jack turned back to the man with the broom, "Well, it's obvious, I can't beat all of this on a reporter's salary," subconsciously, he wanted to tell someone of his newly acquired position and this wise-cracking bar guy seemed as good a target as any.

"The Trib?"

"Yup."

"Good rag—needs help."

"Well, help has arrived," Jack stated boldly with an arrogance of youth mixed with the seasoning of experience. It was 1949 but the memories of his three years as a combat reporter were still fresh in his mind. He had survived the war in the Pacific theater writing of heroism, valor, sacrifice, and compassion. Then he had covered postwar Japan. Now, he was back in New York City to take on a new and different enemy but was equal to the task. The world lay before him and he was in control of his own destiny. The drink that afternoon tasted of adventure and anticipation. The memory faded and an older more weathered yet still welcoming Harry stood before him.

"So, what is it, Jack?" Harry asked once more in a low and caring tone.

"I think a roach."

"What?"

"That bug over there," Jack pointed to a spot under a shelf behind the bar as he stretched to get a better view, "Yeah, it's a roach alright—a Himalayan Eggsalot—I believe."

The bartender looked where his friend pointed and saw the offending insect. With a snap of his bar towel he smote the creature, "Him-a-layin-dead, now."

"Nice shot."

"You should see me in the shower at the club with a full-size towel."

"No thanks."

Harry poured another two shots of scotch into a fresh glass with ice. He placed it in front of Jack and knocked twice on the bar with his knuckles—a standard signal indicating a drink on the house. "Come-on Jack what's eatin' at you?"

"What makes you think anything is wrong?"

"You just asked how long you've been coming in here. We've known each other a long time—a damn long time. You think I can't read your ugly mug like page six of the Trib? I know when you gotta pee two minutes before you."

"Oh, how do you do that?"

"Your eyes turn yellow," Harry said flatly. He continued in a different tone, "You keep all your troubles bottled up inside and it will eat you up."

"Harry . . . "

"Remember, we've been through thick and thick together."

"Harry . . ."

"You were there for me when I got sick."

"Harry . . ."

"You tended bar for two weeks at night after working all day."

"Harry . . ."

"You think I don't remember that? I almost lost all my regular customers."

"Harry . . ."

"You think I don't want to help you, if I can?"

"Harry . . ."

"What?!"

"There's another one," Jack pointed in the same general area.

Harry turned and looked, "Christ, he's bigger than the other one!"

"You killed his little brother."

The newcomer became a smudge on a rolled-up newspaper.

"That wasn't the Trib, was it?" Jack asked, as though concerned.

"No. *The Times.*"

"Good. Hey, what are you doing reading that lousy paper? And, what's wrong with the *Tribune*?"

"The writers over there stink," Harry deadpanned.

"That's the truth."

The revealing comment did not pass Harry unnoticed. He threw the soiled Times into the trash and leaned on his elbows on the bar opposite Jack, "OK, what's going on?"

This time Jack Moore did not make a wise remark or change the subject. He picked up his near-empty glass and peered at the liquid. Deep in its honey color he saw a sunset—not a beautiful restful end of day glow—but an unwelcome final chapter. There were clouds gathering and darkness waited to engulf him. And, much like with the weather when a storm is gathering there was little that he could do about it. He could shake his fist at the darkness but it would not retreat. It was the natural order of things.

"Jack, don't insult me by not giving me an opportunity to help," the bartender said in a sober and serious voice. He poured another drink.

"You trying to make me drunk?"

"You? I'd go broke."

Both men remained silent. All of the games men play were over. The jousting was complete. It was time to make a decision and the decision was up to Jack. He could open up and seek counsel from a trusted friend or he could keep his problem to himself. They remained silent. There was no need to rush—they had all night. Periodically, Harry would bolt to another part of the bar to refill a glass but then would return.

After one trip away, Harry returned to hear Jack say, "You spend your life trying to amount to something, trying to perfect your craft, and just when you have the most to offer the whole house of cards comes tumbling down."

"You lose your job?" Harry asked with genuine concern.

"Worse, I lost my self-respect." He drained the liquid from his glass and placed it gently on the bar.

Harry looked at his friend not sure what to think about that last remark. What he did know was that Jack Moore was an honest and dedicated writer. He placed a fresh drink in front of his friend and looked closely at him. Jack's hair had started to turn gray, but still was dominated by a deep brown color. Parted on the right side and worn slightly longer than a man of his years ought to let it grow it always looked as though a breeze was lifting it up from his scalp. His eyes were also brown although it was hard to tell, as he seemed to keep them half closed most of the time. Someone once commented that he had bedroom eyes. Not a large man but he had broad shoulders. And, he always wore a brown suit. It was like that was the only color in his world. Brown shoes, brown belt, and a brown hat with a brown hatband completed the monochromatic persona. Jack was certainly not the athletic type but he was strong—very strong. Harry often wondered how he got such strength sitting in front of a typewriter. Through the years, he watched his friend grow and evolve to a point where his exposes and columns were well-respected and well-read. It would be lunacy for the *Tribune* or any paper to fire such a talented writer. But, he didn't say he was fired he said he lost his self-respect. That begged the question, which Harry asked, "Jack, how do you think you lost your self-respect?"

Now that the games were over the conversation flowed more freely. Jack replied, "I've spent a lifetime working to get where I am, today."

"You already said that."

Jack gave Harry a perturbed look. "Yes, well, that's what I'm talking about."

"That's what I'm trying to figure out. What are you talking about?"

"About a month ago Eddie Shank retired."

"I remember."

"He ran a professional shop. He let us do our jobs the way we saw fit, but always insisted that every source be checked and double-checked. He would pick up the phone himself if there ever was any doubt. That old fart wanted accuracy and would go nuts if you based anything on hearsay or opinion." Jack sat silent as if remembering some moment in time. "Eddie and I would debate an issue for an hour but we never lost our tempers or took it personal." Again, he paused, "I liked that old man."

Harry nodded in agreement.

"When Eddie retired we always figured one of us would get his job. That way we could carry on the tradition and turn out a quality paper. But, that's not what happened." Jack looked directly at his friend, "They brought in some snot-nosed kid who doesn't know gaatz about publishing a newspaper. He knows how to talk in freaking clichés though. 'This is where the rubber meets the road.' 'We don't know what we don't know.' 'That's the steak, where's the sizzle?' What kind of bullshit crap is that?" Jack paused and looked around the bar as if to see if anyone from the newspaper was within earshot, then added, "He starts questioning everything. And, I mean everything. Why did you talk to that source? Shouldn't you find out this? How come you didn't follow that line of thinking? Can't we just write that and say it was from reliable sources? He wants to make up whatever will sell more freaking newspapers! He thinks we're writing a damn novel—not reporting the news."

Harry simply nodded, as he listened.

"I spend more time justifying everything that I'm doing than actually doing my job." Jack looked his friend in the eye, "I'm a professional. I've been doing this a lot of damn years. I know more about investigative reporting than that punk will ever know, but here I am sitting in his office answering questions like some junior reporter who just started writing. Sitting in his office wanting to reach over that desk and rip his larynx out and stuff it up his ass."

"Why don't you?"

Jack looked at Harry for a brief moment then answered, "Come' on you're an ex-cop you know they frown on that kind of thing in this town."

"There are many ways to shut him up. I don't have to tell you that."

"This guy's different. He's smart enough to be dangerous and gives the impression he's simply trying to do things right. Unfortunately, all he's doing is getting in the way. He won't let the troops do their job and then complains when the job doesn't get done. And, there's something else—I haven't been able to put my finger on it yet—but I will."

"So how did you lose your self respect?"

Jack leaned back taking his elbows off of the bar for the first time, "I've got this story idea. Not much to it right now, but my instinct is that there is something there beneath the surface. Little bits and pieces that individually mean nothing, but if I can figure out if there is a connection it could be big."

"OK."

"Well, stupidly I ran it by the asshole. His whole demeanor is one of being the authority and he talks to you like you are a child. I felt like some school kid asking the teacher for permission to do extra credit when all I was doing was keeping him informed out of professional courtesy. So, this bastard interrogates me for an hour— wants answers to all the questions that I just told him needed to be answered in order to determine if there really is a story. The worst part is when he starts asking things that make no sense and then acts as though you are incompetent because you have no idea how to answer. Finally, he stands up, walks over to me, puts his hand on my shoulder and says in his effete manner, 'Not this time Jack, there aren't enough legs. Trust me I know these things.'"

"Ouch!" Harry commented, then asked, "Do you have enough to go on with this story?"

"How the hell should I know? That's what I have to find out."

"So, what did you do?"

"I nodded and left his office. Instead of decking him or ripping him a new one, I just left." Jack pushed his empty glass toward Harry, "He wore me down. I just didn't want to fight over it any more. Everything has become a battle. It's like all my years of experience don't mean a thing, except that I'm over the hill and out of touch with the modern world." Before Harry could comment, Jack continued as he spoke to a clenched fist, "He acts like I've been sitting on the sidelines letting the world pass by instead of being a part of it." The slightly inebriated newspaper writer then asked no one in particular, "Who the hell am I—Rip Van Winkle?"

"It stinks, so, what are you going to do?" the bartendologist asked as he led his patient in the right direction.

Jack seemed calmer as he said introspectively, "I don't know, but I'm not ready to quit. Too many years devoted to that rag. Too many good friends there. I'm just not sure how long I will last before I kill the little shit." Jack leaned back on the wooden bar stool and for the first time that evening smiled. "You know, Harry, I've never won a Pulitzer, probably never will, but I've stirred up a lot of pots and smashed a lot of hornet's nests through the years. There's still a lot of fight left in me. Getting older is more of a problem to the people you deal with than to yourself, if you don't let it get to you."

"Tell me about your story idea."

"It's more of a 'what if' than a story right now. And, I could come up empty handed. But, there is something." Jack paused seemingly trying to gather his thoughts through a gentle haze that surrounded his mind. "It deals with NASA and . . ."

From another part of the bar a voice was heard, "Yo! Refill, Harry."

"Hold that thought," Harry directed as he dashed off to fill a glass.

It took only a few moments, but when he returned Jack was gone.

Matthew Ellis sat alone in his hospital room. He tried to read the newspaper. Apollo 10 had been launched a day earlier on a mission that was to be the dress rehearsal for the actual Moon landing scheduled a month later. They were on the doorstep of something wonderful and he felt the excitement of accomplishment. Excitement yes, but also disappointment at having missed out on all of the steps in between. He could now remember the days of negotiation with NASA and the fact that Orztech was also on its way to the Moon. Pride at being a small part of such a noble effort warmed him, but feelings of loss fatigued him. He wanted to read more about the flight but found his mind wanted something else.

Once Valerie reentered his life he found himself returning to her, again and again. Memories were spawned by anything and everything. An odor, color, word, sound—it didn't matter. If there was any connection, no matter how small, the memory played itself out in his mind. In a single day, he went from not remembering her name to reliving endless moments of their life together. And, with every reenactment he found himself missing her more and more. Guilt was replaced by a growing feeling of loss. He mourned for both lost time and a lost love.

A word in the newspaper unfolded another chapter in their lives. The word was ballet. A form of dance where they traipse around on their toes was certainly not something of interest to a kid from New Jersey who grew up building forts in the woods, playing baseball, and spitting for distance. But, it was a passion of Valerie's that slowly became of interest to Matt. This unique and complex art form was somewhat symbolic of their unique and complex relationship.

Matt was brash and young when he first met Valerie in January of 1948. In fact, it was during the great Northeast blizzard that stretched from December 1947 through January 1948. He was nineteen years old and Valerie was seventeen.

The snow started falling at 4:36 p.m. on the evening of December 26th and continued on and off until January 9th leaving a total of fifty-seven inches of white powder in the New York Metropolitan Area. To Matt and his friend Barry it was fifty-seven inches of white gold. Armed with snow shovels they trudged through vacant streets earning a dollar here and a dollar there shoveling people's driveways or businesses' sidewalks. In the beginning, it was easy with only nine inches of snow on the ground. The two boys could whip through a driveway in less than a half hour. But then, the snow would start to fall again. Every day there was more snow and more money to be made. Unfortunately, as the days passed it became increasingly difficult to find places to throw the seemingly heavier and heavier stuff. Along the streets of Bergenfield, New Jersey white mountains began to emerge everywhere—monuments of free enterprise.

On the afternoon of January 6th another layer of snow had fallen leaving the area blanketed in six additional inches. Total accumulated snowfall by that time had reached forty-nine inches. The new arrival might as well have been six feet for there was nowhere else to throw the frozen stuff. Matt and Barry, though fatigued, continued their enterprise as they knew eventually that their moneymaking opportunity would literally melt away.

They had just finished a driveway when Matt spied two girls playing on top of a huge mountain of snow across the street. While Barry collected the money from the homeowner, Matt watched the girls as they climbed their own private Mt. Everest. They were unaware of his presence as he leaned on his well-worn snow shovel and watched. All that snow provided an ideal playground. Giggles and laughter reached his ears as the girls tried to scale the slippery slope. First, one would almost reach the summit only to slip and tumble back to the base then the other would almost make it. Finally, in a close race one of the girls conquered the hill and stood victoriously on top. Then it happened. In an instant, she dropped through the snow and disappeared. The other girl screamed, "Valerie!" and began pawing at the snow. Matt, having witnessed what had happened, sprang across the street and began digging into the side of the snow prison. He was careful not to thrust the shovel in too far or too quickly so as to not injure the trapped girl, but also knew speed was essential because she needed to be saved. The mountain was at least eight feet high and he had difficulty finding a place to throw the snow. No sound came from within. Then, after what seemed a lengthy period of time punctuated by the screams of the other girl, Matt uncovered Valerie's head. She looked directly at him but didn't say a word. He threw down his shovel and began carefully removing snow from around her head and shoulders. What struck him was how she seemed totally calm as she watched him work. She neither smiled nor frowned—simply watched.

"Are you alright?" he finally asked.

"Yes," she replied in a calm and dignified voice that struck him.

"I'll dig you out if you kiss me," he said half joking and half hoping she would say yes.

"I can't stop you, but a stolen kiss is never as good as one freely offered."

In a single sentence she had conquered him and held him as tightly as the snow that held her. He didn't say another word as he worked to free her. He found himself consciously focusing on the rescue unable to look her in the eye, unable to think of another wise remark, unable to remove the sound of her voice from his mind. Finally, Matt was able to pull Valerie out of the white quicksnow.

Valerie brushed snow from her clothing and stood tall before him. She looked directly into his eyes and said with both dignity and sincerity, "Thank you. I don't know what I would have done without your assistance."

"You owe me a kiss," he tried.

"You'll have to settle for some hot chocolate," she answered with a hint of a smile, "Would you like to warm up for awhile?"

Matt, Barry, Valerie, and Gretchen sat in the kitchen of Gretchen's house. Her mother fixed hot chocolate for all of them, thanked Matt again for the rescue, and left the teenagers to themselves. At first the conversation was awkward and mostly between the two boys and the two girls. Matt told Barry about the rescue while Gretchen expressed to Valerie how frightened she had been.

Every once in a while, Matt would glance at Valerie and feel a strange sensation. It was a combination of sexual desire and fear, but fear of what?

Then Gretchen asked, "I don't recognize you, are you from around here?"

Matt explained that they were from the next town further north, Dumont, New Jersey. It was then he learned that Valerie was visiting from New York City and had become stranded when the busses stopped running due to snow. Ah, how Matt was learning to love snow. Both girls were seventeen and seniors in high school. Matt had graduated the year before but hadn't settled on a career path, as yet. Of course, he thought, he could always move to Canada and shovel snow year-round if he wanted.

Barry finished his hot chocolate and announced, "Well, we've got time for some more driveways." He stood up.

"I'm played out," Matt lied. He looked at Valerie for a reaction, but got none. "And, I haven't finished my hot chocolate," he explained as he sloshed the remaining liquid in his cup as demonstration. He knew that he would make that sweet brown fluid last a long time, if he could.

After Barry left there was awkward silence. Matt desperately tried to think of something impressive to say but kept getting tangled up in thoughts he would dare not express. His sips of hot chocolate turned into fake sips. Finally, Gretchen stood up and announced that she was going to change out of her wet clothes. She looked at Valerie giving her an opportunity to also make a graceful exit.

"I haven't finished my hot chocolate, either," Valerie said which sent Gretchen off in silence.

Once they were alone Valerie took a fake sip and asked Matt, "So, what do you do, when you're not rescuing damsels in distress?"

"I . . ." Matt looked into Valerie's eyes and was lost in a world he never knew existed. He couldn't define what it was that he saw or exactly what his feelings were. It was as though he were a little boy meeting his greatest hero in real life. No words came to mind. Only, an overwhelming desire to never leave that spot or that exact moment in time. Without question, he wanted to be everything she desired, to be her knight in shining armor, to have her share the same feelings that he suffered from, but at the same time he felt so inadequate. If not her knight he would be her slave, if it would allow him to remain near her. Those same emotions that caused so many unfamiliar thoughts and yearnings also unleashed the flight or fight response within him and he did the opposite of what he wished by saying, "I'd better go."

"I still owe you a kiss," Valerie said matter-of-factly.

"Yes, you do," Matt heard himself say in a pathetic voice.

"Well, you'll have to earn it."

"How?"

"You'll have to figure that out."

Confusion on top of emotion was more than Matt could bear. He had been summarily defeated and didn't even know he was in the game. She wouldn't offer a kiss unless she liked him, but wrapped it up in a puzzle he had no idea how to solve. For a fleeting moment, he thought of asserting his masculinity and just taking it. But, that would mean looking into those dangerous eyes and risking further defeat. Quickly, he finished the last drop of hot chocolate and stood from the table. "I'd better go and clean up the mess I made in the driveway digging you out."

"You did save my life," Valerie said softly as she also stood.

"I'm glad I did."

"So am I."

Matt turned to leave.

"Would you like to go sleigh riding?" Valerie asked impulsively, which was not in her nature.

Matt stopped and turned back to face Valerie, "I don't have a sled, but I do know where there is an awesome hill that people have been sledding on for the past few weeks."

Matt and Valerie spent the remainder of the afternoon and evening riding a borrowed sled down the McKinley Avenue hill. After each ride, they would trudge back up the hill pulling their sled behind them and talking about their interests, dreams, and lives. Valerie loved ballet and was quite an accomplished dancer, but she secretly knew she wasn't at a level needed to be a professional. At one point, she stopped midway up the hill and said to the cold wind that had begun to blow, "I wish I had the talent to follow that path, but this duckling will never be a swan."

"You are all that is beautiful in my world," Matt heard himself say.

"Thank you," Valerie said maintaining her dignity, "You are my Siegfried and have earned your kiss.

A year later, after Valerie graduated from high school, they were married.

A swan was easy for Robert Six Trees to draw. He especially liked doing the long curved neck that looked like a question mark. He didn't know why his sister, Anna, had asked for a drawing, but was glad to do one for her.

6: Tuesday - May 20, 1969

Jack Moore loved to walk the streets of Manhattan late at night. It was relaxing, and yet, exhilarating at the same time. Life was all around running at hyper-speed and yet somehow under control. Even though it was after midnight, people of every walk of life were hidden in their apartments, walking the streets, or still in the bars and clubs. In his heart, Jack's desire was to meet them all, to hear their individual stories, to know their joys and disappointments, and to share it all with his readers. A vast multitude of humanity stuffed into a concentrated space having an infinite number of tales to tell, feelings to express, and dreams to pursue was more than this reporter could bear.

After he left Harry's bar, More-Or-Less, Jack went home to read through piles of papers that he had gathered pertaining to NASA. Without question, there was a story woven within all those facts and figures. His investigative nose knew it. All that was required was time, patience, and a clear mind. It was the clear mind part that was a problem that night as all the alcohol he had consumed continued its hypnotic dance in his head. He stared blankly at stacks of papers before him. It brought him back twenty-three years to just after World War II in Japan.

The *Newark Star Ledger* had sent him to Japan as a reporter. He was young, energetic, and driven. Yes, he sent back the mandatory daily reports about post-war Japan and an occasional article. But, in his spare time, he searched for anything into which he could sink his investigative teeth. He wanted to know what was going on beneath the surface, what was not being told, what he could uncover that had meat. Whether through luck or perseverance he didn't know for sure, however, he made a contact in the occupying military office of the United States Army. A young sergeant who worked in an analysis and records office filing papers was extra talkative one night at a dinner held by the press corps. As was Jack's nature he began fishing right away. Although the sergeant really had nothing concrete to offer, Jack knew he could be a valuable resource. After that evening, the two men began socializing as they spent many free afternoons exploring the countryside together. It was on one of those trips where they stopped in a small village and wandered from shop to shop. Because of the language barrier they never really knew what was being said to them. They would smile, bow awkwardly, and move on.

When they came to a pottery shop, Sergeant Corey made an offhand comment. He picked up an odd shaped piece of pottery and said, "I wonder if those bombs were shaped like this."

"What bombs?"

"What? Oh, I found this file titled Clay Bombs. I guess the Japanese were running out of raw materials."

The next day Jack visited his friend in an old warehouse building on the outskirts of a rundown airport. There he saw rows and rows of boxed papers and documents that were being labeled and stored for future analysis. In one area, there was a steel fence that ran all the way to the ceiling. Behind that formidable fence were stored materials that had been classified as top secret. Jack wanted to get into that golden treasury of stories in the worst way, but two armed MPs made that possibility simply a reporter's dream. Far from the top-secret cage in a corner of the warehouse, Sergeant Corey worked putting documents in boxes, labeling them, and stacking them in an appropriate section. Most of the documents were innocuous records of general government activities and purchases. Of course, many were written in Japanese, therefore, the sergeant could only go by notes written in English by interpreters on the covers to determine what they were and where they needed to be stored.

The documents that interested Jack most were in a file of interviews that had been conducted with middle level Japanese military officers and scientists. They were found among sixty-seven folders that had been crammed into three torn boxes. Luckily, all were English transcripts of actual interviews. Because they hadn't been labeled as classified, Sergeant Corey let Jack browse through the box. There he found an interview titled "Clay Bombs" and another titled "Fugaku Bombers." Sergeant Corey didn't notice Jack slip those two folders under his jacket before he left.

Cherry Blossoms At Night was a devious and cunningly simple plan that would have had devastating effect on the United States war effort. When Jack read the interview in the Clay Bomb file it made his skin crawl. A Japanese scientist described a strategic plan headed by Major Yoshiro Ishi that involved clay bombs which would be filled with biological agents such as Bubonic Plague or the Laymansrum Virus. If dropped on the west coast of the United States the two-part parachute bombs filled with fleas carrying Bubonic Plague would quickly spread the disease eastward killing thousands before it would even be detected. Scientists had calculated that only a few clay bombs would need to be delivered to start the demonic process. In fact, in Autumn of 1941 they had attacked Chinese troops in Manchuria with Plague and ultimately two-hundred-fifty-thousand died. Further, it was planned that once the original disease was discovered, a second more powerful and different agent would be delivered that would throw the entire nation into chaos. The interviewee went on to detail how Japanese military had tested their biological weapons on captured Chinese and American prisoners. Remarkably, the only obstacle to their planned attack was finding a method of delivery. Unit 731 was given the challenge of finding a way to drop these weapons on the west coast of America. They designed the I-400 submarine aircraft carriers that could carry a limited number of airplanes. Very few planes were needed to execute Cherry Blossoms At Night. Fortunately, these aircraft carriers were never built.

Jack made another frightening discovery in a series of other interviews that he read that night titled "Fugaku Bombers." It was conducted by a different interrogator, with a different Japanese official, at a different location. That man told how Japan had attempted to purchase a number of six-engine, 9,000-mile range bombers from the Boeing Corporation before the war began. Contracts had been signed in March of 1939 and production had been underway but fell behind making delivery of the aircraft in the fall of 1941 impossible. There was speculation in Japan that because of world events delivery would be endlessly delayed. The interviewee believed that the date for a first strike against America had actually been moved twice before the Japanese high command became impatient. Of course, any possibility of getting those aircraft ended on December 7, 1941.

Inadvertently, Jack had gotten his hands on the story of the century. Japan had carefully planned purchasing the very weapons they would use against the United States from the United States and had come damn near succeeding. It didn't take a genius to connect the two plots. If they had taken delivery of the Fugaku Bombers prior to Pearl Harbor the second attack would have been far more devastating than the one that had actually occurred. Jack also believed that had it not been for the quick completion of hostilities, as a result of the use of the atomic bomb, Cherry Blossoms At Night would have eventually been executed.

Jack never got to release his story. All correspondence at that time had to be approved by military censors and Cherry Blossoms At Night caused an explosion of activity that stretched all the way to the White House. Jack was held incommunicado by the military for four days. He was interviewed, threatened, cajoled, warned, and brow beaten. It was explained that if he released the information, whether in written or verbal form, he would be guilty of espionage and could be executed or, at the very least, imprisoned for a very long time. Over and over, he heard different people tell him why it was best that the American people and the world not know about Cherry Blossoms At Night. One Army Major with whom Jack spoke made a great deal of sense. He explained how every country develops plans for various forms of warfare that they never execute or expect to execute. These are hypothetically done to consider all of the possibilities. Even the United States has biological weapons and executable plans for their use. However, we would never actually implement them. It was simply not in anyone's best interest to make public such information, especially when it was based on the opinions of two individuals who were not in positions to know all of the facts. As he listened to the military officer, Jack couldn't help but wonder what other facts were hidden in that top secret caged area guarded by military police. Finally, a telephone call from the state department convinced Jack to drop the story. It was agreed that any charges concerning theft of the files would be dismissed, that the sergeant was in no way involved, and that Jack would never breathe a word about Cherry Blossoms At Night. He was released and over the next two years seemed to get more than his share of scoops from government sources. Jack never saw Sergeant Corey again.

A twenty-three-year-older Jack Moore walked slowly along East Fifty Third Street having given up on the stacks of paper in his apartment. He strolled until he came to a tan-colored brick apartment building. There he paused and looked up. Windows of the many apartments loomed above him. Some glowed with a warm light of life pursuing its dream, while others were dark having been temporarily abandoned by their charge or offering comfort to those who were at that time possessed by dreams.

A light glowed through a shade from an apartment on the sixth floor. Jack stood across the street. As he gazed at that window he took out a cigar and lit it. The bright flame from his lighter seemed harsh and intrusive. Once the brown buck was lit he quickly extinguished the lighter's flame. It took his eyes a few moments to once more adjust to subdued illumination of night. He peered up at that window once more.

He knew she was there. From his vantage point down on the street he could feel her energy. She was alone in her living room, in her underwear, slowly dancing to a sad song—maybe *Don't Worry About Me* sung by Frank Sinatra. It wasn't that her heart was broken, rather that her heart was so full of love and compassion that it needed an outlet to express itself. Her hips led the slow sensuous movement of a clean freshly showered body. She caressed the music as her hands moved slowly along her upper arms. Eyes closed she swayed with the emotion of the music. She turned and felt her hair brush across her bare shoulders, once more enjoying the intoxicating rush of being a woman. As her breathing became deeper her dance continued. Quietly and alone she surrendered to the music.

Jack appreciated that she was a single woman alone in the middle of a churning ocean of humanity who was able to find refuge in an ethereal world of music. She was able to care with every fiber of her being, yet had the strength to decide when and where. So unique and deceivingly powerful was her inner strength that it in itself made her breathtakingly attractive.

Jack didn't want to possess her—simply to know her. But, she was up there alone and he was down on the street. It was not to be. Smoke from his cigar rose slowly into the air until it slightly obscured his view of that one particular window. His imagination had its exercise. He knew it was time to move on.

Five miles is not a long distance. Not if you are riding in a comfortable car, on a bus, or find yourself that far from the epicenter of an earthquake. It is, however, an insurmountable distance if you are trying to run that far while wearing combat boots and carrying both a full field pack and 9.5 pound M1 Garand rifle. To an out-of-shape city boy, five miles was a death sentence.

Wellington Marsh's heart pounded in his chest with such ferocity that it felt as though a caged guerilla was trying to punch its way out of his body. The powerful thuds were so great that he couldn't help but wonder if an eighteen-year-old could have a massive heart attack and die. To the best of his knowledge, they had yet to complete the first mile of a planned five mile run. His leg muscles ached. So did his chest as he tried to pull more and more air into his pollution-filled lungs. Without question, he was ready to quit. The thought of throwing down his weapon, shedding the backpack, and strolling off to a quiet, shady place to rest kept tempting him. Yet, he didn't want to be the first to quit. He would be second, or third, but not the first.

One heavy boot after another slammed the hard red South Carolina clay. In desperation, Wellington looked around for any sign that another recruit was ready to cash it in, or at the very least, pass out. That would count. It really didn't matter, dropping out was dropping out, even if you dropped onto your chin. In his quest, he saw numerous faces that reflected different degrees of torturous pain all around him, but none seemed ready to drop out or drop dead. Even Shortstop seemed determined to continue.

Wellington was certain that his heart was growing larger and larger with each beat. As it grew, it pressed against his lungs denying them room for the air that he desperately needed. Still he continued—not wanting to be the first to quit. Stomp, stomp, stomp. His head began to spin. OK, it would be pass out or die—those were his choices. Stomp, stomp, stomp. Only, he wouldn't make the choice, his body would have that pleasure. Stomp, stomp, stomp. Sweat burned his eyes. Stomp, stomp, stomp. Pulling air into his lungs became ever more difficult. Stomp, stomp, stomp. His head ached. Stomp, stomp, stomp. Numb hands gripped that loathsome weapon he had named Hexcaliber. Stomp, stomp, stomp. His field pack became heavier and heavier. Stomp, stomp, stomp. Then something happened . . .

Wellington crossed an unseen and until that moment unknown to him invisible line. His aching tortured body silently dissolved into a surrealistic state that brought all of his physical actions together into an effortless and coordinated motion. Some call it a "runner's high," but to Wellington Marsh it was a reprieve from imminent death. His breathing became regular, deep, and steady. His boots were weightless. The backpack must have fallen off. His leg muscles no longer ached and his heart fell into a rhythmic, soft, steady pace. Wellington glided effortlessly along the dirt path. This strange new feeling was invigorating, energizing, and completely alien to him. For the first time in his life, Wellington felt absolutely free. It was as though he could run forever and never stop. It felt so good he didn't want to stop. He wanted to run on endlessly. Without realizing it, he began to pass other exhausted, less fortunate recruits with tortured looks upon their faces. His speed continued to increase. The warm breeze felt refreshing on his sweat soaked face. On and on he ran with ease until he was the leader. That's when Sergeant Kincaid ended his bliss.

"Incoming!" the DI yelled and then he blew his whistle.

The platoon scattered in a dozen different directions and dove to the ground. Earlier training had worked as every man reacted instantaneously. Wellington did a hurdle over a small bush and also dropped to the ground. The sudden stop made him feel lightheaded. His breathing remained steady, but deep. Then all was silent.

Wrapped in a blanket of stillness, Wellington became once more aware of his heartbeat. Different from before, it echoed in his ears. Its hypnotic effect drew him back in time to another place when he lay on a rooftop—heart pounding. It was four years prior to that day during the great Staunton Avenue rumble in Detroit.

Outnumbered and outgunned, Wellington and his cohorts had no choice but to break and run. As they did, their retreat took them through familiar alleys, across vacant lots, under elevated highways, and finally up a fire escape to the roof of old man Lund's apartment building. Along the way, they lost their pursuers. Wellington was winded from the chase and climb up a fire escape. His heart pounded in his chest as sweat ran down his face. There he sat with his back against the low wall that edged the roof. The others in his group sat or lay upon the roof—equally exhausted. It had been a rout. From the start, they had been at a disadvantage. Eight against four, but they were not about to back down. Then they were outmaneuvered and outsmarted. It definitely had been a slaughter. Even though it would have been easy to rationalize why they had done so poorly, it wouldn't change the fact that they had been beaten.

Wellington turned and peered over the edge of the low wall. There was no sign of the enemy. They were out there, somewhere, but that wasn't what bothered him. Of far greater concern was the fact that as he and his fellow combatants ran down Alexander Avenue, his father had called to him from their apartment window. In the heat of the chase, he failed to respond. That was never a good idea, because, someone would pay a price for that indiscretion and Wellington knew he would be that someone.

After five minutes, Wellington and his three cohorts were rested. Down on the street there was still no sign of Stewie Nelson or his gang. However, there was no question that they were out there—waiting. The four boys continued to scan the street below. As they did, they failed to notice a large black man who appeared on the roof. He was of impressive stature and stern-faced. To a stranger who might come upon him, he would be frightening. Stealthily, he moved to where the four boys congregated. As he did, a large foreboding shadow slowly crossed over them. Four young faces looked up in unison. Before them a big man stood motionless, a cold unwavering stare punctuated his displeasure. They froze. For a prolonged period, four trapped young men waited for the big man to move or say something. Silence.

"Dad," Wellington finally said, "I can explain."

The big man slightly raised his chin and peered out of the bottom of his eyes in a gesture that asked an unspoken question.

"You see," Wellington continued, "I couldn't stop because we were being chased."

No reaction.

"Stewie and his gang . . ."

A raised eyebrow stopped Wellington in mid-sentence. He began once more, using a different approach, "We ran out of ammunition so we had no choice but to run," he smiled, innocently.

His father looked at each of the boys.

Silence.

"We did pretty well," Backfire said, "being outnumbered and all."

Wellington's father looked at the young man who spoke and thought, I don't ever want to know how he got that nickname.

"It was a massacre," complained another with a soaking wet shirt.

"Yeah," the others agreed.

"Sorry, Dad," Wellington apologized, "I should have stopped when you called."

Finally, Peter Marsh spoke, "Yes, you should have."

"I know."

"Don't ignore me—boy."

"Yes sir."

"I called because I wanted to know if you needed money to buy more balloons."

The four surprised combatants sat in disbelief. There he was a tough, no nonsense father who they all knew. He was feared. He was legend in the neighborhood. And yet, there he was helping his son with a water balloon fight. Finally, Wellington smiled.

"I may not know a lot—but I do know one thing—you can't win a water balloon war without balloons."

"We can't win a water balloon fight when the odds are two to one," one mumbled.

"Sure you can," the older man countered, "Don't try to overpower them—outsmart them."

Silent stares indicated that he hadn't made his point.

Peter Marsh squatted on the roof to look the group of boys in the eye. "Most battles are made up of troops, weapons, and tactics. And, most of the time the tactics are the deciding factor."

"Yeah, we got no tactics," one lad lamented.

"And, no balloons," Backfire added.

Peter Marsh stared him down, "Tactics come from knowing what the other guy is going to do. Then, you can outsmart him."

"Their tactics is easy," the boy with the soaking wet shirt explained, "they come at you from all sides."

"By the time you see them, it's too late, you're surrounded," another added.

"They don't miss," soaking wet shirt offered.

"I can see that."

"They usually all concentrate on one."

"Yeah," the wet warrior confirmed, "and they got runners who bring them more balloons."

"Well, if you know what they are going to do, you darn well know what you need to do," Wellington's father concluded. Blank stares told him that they had no idea what he was talking about. They really didn't know what to do, however, he decided that it was up to them, not him, to see it through. He couldn't resist wanting to help, so he added, "If there is no room for eight—you don't have to face eight." Still, he drew no response, just blank stares. He felt like knocking on their heads and asking if anyone was home. Instead, he continued, "A moving target is harder to hit than one that is standing still."

"I don't know," soaking wet shirt countered, "I got hit in the back of the head—running away."

Wellington's father stood up. He towered over the four boys as he said, "Do the best you can." He slipped five dollars into his son's hand, turned, and walked away.

Newly supplied with ammunition in the form of round balloons of various colors and sizes that would soon be filled with water, the boys were filled with hope. The plan was intricate and required split-second timing, but they were convinced that they could pull it off.

There are two things that you have to remember when preparing a complex plan. The first is to be sure that everyone involved clearly understands their part. Second, which is very important, is to have contingency plans for when something goes astray. This was not the case with the Wellington Plan.

Wellington was to be the hare and Stewie Nelson's gang the hounds. He simply had to locate them and then get them to chase him. The rest was up to his pals. Unfortunately, it all started to unravel when Backfire was unable to climb a fire escape carrying ten water-filled balloons. Ten became nine, then eight, seven, six, and finally when he reached his perch—one. It was obvious that he was not ready.

Young Wellington located the Nelson gang. They sat triumphantly on the steps in front of the apartment building where Stewie lived. They saw him, as he approached. Eight sets of eyes watched him closely. When he was as near as he dared, he threw the single balloon that he carried behind his back. It fell far short of its target. The green balloon exploded on the ground without a single drop of water landing anywhere in the vicinity of Stewie or his bunch. They all laughed at such a meager effort. A small rainbow formed above the puddle. It was erased by eight shadows as they passed. The chase was on.

There were rules in a water balloon fight. No buckets, hoses, or other non-balloon containers of water were ever used. Who established the rules no one knew, however, to break them would result in being labeled a cheat, coward, and scab. In Detroit, a union dominated town, a scab is the lowest form of life. It is what striking union members called those who take their place by crossing the picket line. The offspring of union workers knew the low regard their parents had for scabs. To be branded with such a name was the worst form of insult. Therefore, it was only balloons or risk being called a scab.

The Wellington team member with a soaking wet shirt filled balloon after balloon with water. His fingers were raw from wrapping the open ends around them in order to tie knots. Finally, he had 53 balloons, enough to drench all eight of Stewie Nelson's gang. What he failed to calculate was how heavy fifty balloons were when filled with water. Four shopping bags were needed to carry all of the balloons. Finally, after three failed attempts, he was able to lift all of the bags. Hampered by all of the weight, he slowly staggered in the direction of the rendezvous point where his friend waited and Wellington would soon arrive. Burdened with all the weight he made his way down Malcolm Street. This is where the second breakdown in the plan took place.

Soaking shirt stepped on a slippery substance on the sidewalk causing him to slip and lose his tenuous grip on the four shopping bags. The blood chilling sound of exploding balloons filled the air. Water escaped from its polyethylene prison and ran in every direction. Everywhere the destruction spread with no power on earth to stop it. The young man stared in horror as their hopes literally went down the drain. All was lost with the exception of seven balloons; two green, one blue, three red, and one yellow. As quickly as possible, he retrieved the survivors. He stuck two in his shirt and carried the other five in his arms. Before continuing his desperate journey, he looked back at the offending substance that had caused the accident. There melted the remains of a scoop of vanilla ice cream that most likely fell from a child's cone.

Wellington felt the breeze from a balloon passing his ear as it narrowly missed his head. An explosion of H_2O wet the path before him. He continued his run. For the plan to work Wellington knew that he needed to be exactly 38 feet ahead of his pursuers. He knew, because they had measured. A chalk mark on the curb reminded him of the need for precision. A quick glance behind revealed that they were gaining, but still were farther behind than the plan required. He approached an alley that led between two buildings and faked tripping to slow his progress. After stumbling past the alley, he looked at his opponents. When they reached the chalk mark he darted down the alley. True to the plan he reached a large wooden gate on the right and pushed it open. However, instead of going through he dove into an open doorway opposite the wooden gate. One of his teammates quietly and deftly closed the door. At that precise moment, Stewie Nelson and his cohorts entered the alley. Although they slowed their pace to avoid an ambush, when they saw the wooden gate slowly closing as a group they charged into the adjoining alleyway. At that moment, Wellington and his friend left their hiding place and slipped a metal rod through the metal rings on the gate and post. Stewie and his gang were trapped.

The plan, from Wellington's perspective had been executed like clockwork. Of course, the fact that their water balloon supply hadn't arrived and that Backfire sat on the fire escape with a single balloon did put a crimp in the final phase of the Wellington Plan. Backfire did the only thing that he could—he dropped his single balloon and then beat a hasty retreat. Up he climbed to the roof and disappeared. The water bomb hit Stewie Nelson on the back of the neck. When soaking shirt finally arrived he handed each of his two friends one balloon each. Without saying a word they tossed their balloons over the gate. All three missed. Then Wellington asked, "Where's the rest of the balloons?" Before him stood his friend with two balloons in his shirt looking like a well-endowed girl.

His friend simply replied, "Tactics suck!"

Upon remembering that sight, Wellington began to laugh. Sergeant Kincaid put a quick end to his reverie.

Carl Pythacyk sat quietly at a table in the corner of Stacey's Pub on Fordham Road. It was a small dive of a bar, but they had cold beer on tap and left you alone. It was past closing, 2:00 a.m., however he knew they wouldn't chase him out. Fordham and Kingsbridge Roads in the Bronx were his turf—his home field. He'd busted enough heads and knocked out enough teeth to be well known and left alone. The aroma of stale beer was soothing as were the sounds of empty glasses being washed by Mat, or Nat, or Pat, or whomever. Carl didn't know for sure nor did he care. The old man would pull a beer when needed and then disappear into the woodwork until summoned. He never gave a freebie but kept the peanut bowls full and looked the other way, when necessary.

The corner table was Carl's favorite because it was off by itself in a darkened part of the bar. There he could sit, back to the wall, under an old New York Yankees pennant, in the shadows, and observe the entire bar without himself being observed.

At that hour in the morning the bar was empty, doors locked, and lights lowered. Chairs were upside down on tables and Nat or Mat was busy cleaning.

Carl thought about the events of the evening. He had found Miguel, his partner in crime, who had sold the stolen watches, and then avoided him. Carl had gotten his money—all of it. It could have been easy, but somehow when dealing with the slimy creatures that haunt the underworld of the city it never turns out that way. It seemed that every time Carl looked for Miguel somewhere he was either just a few minutes late, met a group of dullards who claimed they never heard of Miguel Juarez, or encountered a suspicious language barrier.

On that particular night Carl hit pay dirt. He had seen Miguel through the window of El Gato de San Juan. It was one of many places where the elusive hood hung out that Carl regularly checked. He knew sooner or later he would catch the little two-timer at one of the many haunts he was known to frequent. Simple logic told Carl that if he checked these places enough his prey would eventually rear its ugly head.

Upon seeing the little prick, Carl's heart raced. However, he knew better than to storm inside. Any place teeming with Miguel's friends was not one where he wanted to have a confrontation. That was a sure way to get hurt. Instead, he waited. It was a warm spring evening and he didn't have anywhere else that he needed to be. Stealthily, he drifted back into the entranceway of an old dilapidated building across the street that boasted five seedy apartments. The smell of urine was not unexpected. Nor was the cool dampness and mildew odor that mixed with it. Briefly, he turned his back and lit a cigarette. An overpowering cloud of sulfurous gas was a welcomed relief. From his stinking little vantage point Carl peered out into the darkness. Shadows hid most of the landscape, although he could clearly see the front door of El Gato. Its brightness further obscured any view of the surrounding area. Carl knew all-too-well that all of those dark locations represented danger. Deep within each shadow or around any corner or behind any obstacle could be death. A friend or ally of Miguel's could easily be hidden within one of those blinds just waiting for some fool to come along and try something stupid. Periodically, a sound would erupt from an unseen portion of the street. Each time Carl would feel his stomach muscles tighten as he scanned the street for its source. A cat, bum, passing car, even a bag lady pushing a shopping cart made appearances that night. Various people came and went. Most spoke Spanish and laughed as they passed or entered El Gato. At one point, two Hispanic men in their late twenties stopped outside the front door and chatted as they stood guard. At that point, Carl knew he was cooked and that Miguel would once again elude him. He also knew that someday he would cut the little bastard's throat when he finally got his hands on him. After a very long fifteen minutes two young women came strutting down the street wearing their best party dresses. Their hips swayed from side to side as they flirtatiously approached the waiting men. Typical of their age the young men acted like fools while trying to entertain the ladies. Greetings were exchanged and the foursome entered the restaurant. Carl was once more alone. The hunter turned his attention back to that door.

Half a pack of cigarettes later, Miguel walked out through the front door of El Gato de San Juan. Unaware of Carl's presence the young Puerto Rican turned left and headed in the direction of the subway. He was dressed as dapper as usual in a dark gray tight-fitting suit and deep purple shirt with thin lavender tie. His heels clicked as he walked with the casual gait of a man without a care in the world. Silently, Carl moved parallel with his prey on the opposite side of the street. Catlike he moved in silence.

The clicking of Miguel's footsteps echoed loudly in the quiet night. Then in a section where it was relatively dark and secluded Carl bolted across the street and slammed full force into Miguel.

"What the hell—oh, Carlos—I've been looking for you."

"Well, now you found me," Carl said through clenched teeth.

"Si, I see that."

"Where's my money?"

"I've got your money. Those watches they were muy bueno. The old man, he give me six hundred dollars for the whole lot."

Carl pushed his forearm across Miguel's throat and held him against a brick wall, "That means you probably got twelve hundred."

"I wouldn't cheat you compadre."

"You'd cheat your own mother."

"Yes, but I know better than to cheat you."

"That's good because this is your only chance to come clean and tell me what you really got for those watches. Cause, if I find out later that you ripped me off I'll cut your heart out, and you know I'll do it." Carl emphasized his point by putting more pressure on Miguel's throat.

"Argh—I remember now—he gave me six hundred for the men's watches and four hundred for the ladies."

"That's more like it," Carl eased up on the pressure he had been applying. "Now, give me my money."

"Amigo—I don't carry that kind of money around. These streets they're not safe."

"Then let's go and get the money, amigo, because I'm attached to you like your culiones until I get it. So, you better come up with the money before my patience runs out and I decide to leave and take them with me and get blood all over that pretty suit."

"I can get it. I'll have it tomorrow. We . . ."

"Tomorrow, my ass! I get my share tonight or you don't see tomorrow. It's that simple."

Miguel felt the strength in Carl's grip and thought about the .22 caliber revolver he had nestled in his belt in the small of his back. He only needed a moment to reach down, grab the piece, and put a few into his assailant's belly.

"What's it gonna be, amigo?" Carl asked as he attempted to speed things up knowing all too well that at any moment one of Miguel's acquaintances could pass by thus turning the tables on the situation.

"I don't have that much in cash," Miguel pleaded, "I need more time." Time to get my hand on my gun and put some holes in you, he thought.

Carl would not be swayed, "Your time is up—one way or the other." He tightened his grip and put pressure on the other man's throat, as he emphasized, "You've caused me a lot of grief having to hunt you down. That doesn't work for me. No one screws with me and gets away with it!"

With gravelly sounding tones Miguel negotiated as he maneuvered into a better position, "I can put my hands on two hundred tonight and get the rest in acouple of days."

"No good."

"Come'on give me a break!"

"I'll give you a compound fracture if I have to, but I get my money—all of it—

tonight."

Voices were heard from down the street that caused both men to freeze. They were distant and muffled. Miguel was able to shift his weight, which allowed him to move his arm slightly behind his back. His right forearm rubbed against the revolver that waited beneath the cloth of his jacket. The distant voices became fainter. In response, Carl loosened his grip slightly. Contact with the revolver shifted to Miguel's wrist. A little further and he would be able to pay Carl what he deserved. Another shift. It was almost time to show this yallo with whom he was dealing.

"OK, what's it gonna be?" Carl asked as he took his weight off of Miguel.

With fluid quickness Miguel slipped his hand under his jacket and grabbed— nothing. Instead, he looked directly into the barrel of his own revolver.

"You greasy little spic, I ought to empty this into your brain."

"No—wait Carlos, I know where I can get the money—pronto."

"You better, because your life depends on it."

The two men made their way downtown to Times Square where Miguel had a number of ladies who worked for him. He normally kept five girls but Annie had run away. She got tired of life on the street, as well as being beaten by Miguel when she failed to earn enough money. So, like a cockroach she disappeared amongst the garbage of the underground world of the city. He could have found out where she went and dragged her back by the hair, but she wasn't one of his best whores. So, he let her go. Of course, that necessitated that he be especially tough on his remaining four working girls to dissuade them from thinking that they had the same option. He was less concerned about Rita and Rose because they had kids. Kids meant that they needed the money that he let them keep and they feared for the safety of their children should they ever cross him. It was Doris and Claire with whom he was concerned. They had to be shown what would happen if they ever strayed. Therefore, each had been given a demonstration of his authority.

Doris was first. Miguel visited her apartment unannounced early one morning. He used his set of keys to enter and found her asleep on her bed. She had arrived home and fallen onto the bed without taking off her clothes. Before him lay the five-foot three inch, blond, blue eyed hooker. She wore a short tight black skirt and light blue rayon blouse. The skirt had slipped high up on her hips to reveal black satin panties. Silently, Miguel moved to the side of the bed and examined his property. She still had an attractive shape and wasn't too road worn, if you didn't look too close. Although not as pretty as when he first found her, she was still a valuable commodity on the street. Silently, he pulled the thin leather belt from around his waist. Doubled over, it made a resounding crack when the first blow struck her buttocks. Doris screamed as she was ripped from a deep sleep. At first, she had no idea what had happened. A second blow bit into her flesh.

Through blurry vision she saw Miguel and cried out, "What did I . . ."

A third blow slashed across her upper legs tearing her stockings. In fear, she slid off the bed onto the floor. Arms over her head, she cringed in a fetal position. Miguel struck again and again until she simply whimpered on the floor.

"Turn over," he commanded, which she did immediately. "Lift your skirt." He felt a rush of excitement as his abject slave obeyed without hesitation. "Spread your legs!" He placed his foot between her legs and pushed down harshly with his heel. "Don't you ever get any idea about following Annie," he stated with enough venom in his voice to bring terror to her tortured mind.

Doris could only shake her head.

"Don't you ever think that you are free because you're not—you belong to me—until I say otherwise. Is that clear?" He stepped back and waved the belt before her, "This was just a warning. You stray and this will seem like foreplay. It will be so bad you will beg for death. Do you understand?"

Once again Doris shook her head. When Miguel raised the belt she crawled to him and kissed his shoes in the hope that he wouldn't strike again. Miguel smiled.

Claire also received a visit that morning—a visit she would long remember. She made the mistake of talking back and trying to protect herself. Enraged, Miguel knocked out one of her teeth, cracked a rib, and after leaving her half-conscious on the floor took out a pair of scissors and savagely sheared her hair leaving it a horrendous mix of varying lengths. In a few places, he cut it so short that he broke the skin causing little trickles of blood to run down her face. In spite of her injuries he had her on the street that night.

Miguel's girls could each make two hundred dollars on a good night. So, if they didn't hold out on him, he could easily get the five hundred dollars he needed to pay Carl. When the two men arrived none of the girls were to be found. So, in the darkness of West Forty Fourth Street they waited in front of a cheap fleabag hotel. The stench of uncollected garbage completed the seedy scene. Carl kept the revolver in his pocket aimed at Miguel with the index finger of his right hand on the trigger. His left hand had a viselike grip on Miguel's sleeve.

Claire was the first to appear. She walked slowly out of the glass door that led to a dingy lobby with a middle-aged, gray-haired man in a wrinkled and dumpy suit. Immediately, she saw Miguel. Without a word being spoken between the two lovers they parted company. Dumpy suit walked toward Eighth Avenue and Claire walked over to Miguel. It was obvious that she was still in pain, but she had to work so she ignored it the best that she could. She wore a shoulder length auburn wig.

"Brasita, I see you have been busy," he said pleasantly. Then his voice became cold and threatening, "Give me all of your money—pronto!"

Claire didn't protest or ask why. She knew better. She slipped her right hand into her boot and pulled out all of the wrinkled, dirty, stained bills that she had stuffed into it and handed them to Miguel.

As Miguel counted the cash Carl considered the prostitute. She had a face that was once attractive but it now hid behind a swollen jaw, black eye, and misshapen nose. She wore a short red knit dress and black high-heeled boots. Carl wondered why she sported such an unflattering wig, but figured she was a whore so good taste certainly couldn't be expected.

"Cinco, siete, quince . . ."

Claire looked questioningly at Carl. Her eyes were puffy and tired and sad. She did not miss the grip that he had on Miguel's arm. Good, she thought, take everything from the little bastard.

"Ocho, ocho y dos."

An unspoken glance passed between Carl and Claire as they acknowledged that Miguel was the common enemy.

"Eee, ya! Eighty-two dollars is that all you have?" Miguel complained, "What have you been doing all night?"

"It's hard to get anyone to want me looking like this," Claire protested in a pitiful tone.

"Take off your boots!" he ordered.

She obeyed.

"Shake them out."

Another five-dollar bill floated to the pavement. Claire froze for there was no predicting how Miguel would react. One day he would be easygoing and the next lethal.

He picked up the sawbuck and spat, "Get back to work!"

She hurried down Forty Fourth Street barefoot, carrying her boots.

Shortly, thereafter, a man's voice was heard followed by a woman's laugh. From inside the hotel Rose emerged with a young man on her arm who was in his early twenties. He wore dark rimmed glasses and had a crew cut. From all appearances, he was a kid from the suburbs who came to the city for a good time. From all appearances, it was obvious this was the only way he would see a good time. Arm-in-arm, the two turned and headed toward Eighth Avenue. Miguel whistled. The shrill piercing tone was familiar to Rose. She turned, saw Miguel, turned back to her "date," and said, "You go on sweetie, I'll see you again—promise."

The young man, at first appeared as though he was going to protest, then saw Miguel and Carl, turned on his heel, and quickly walked away.

Rose sauntered over to the two waiting men. "Hey, hon, you're early," she said to Miguel, "who's your friend?"

"Carita, I need your money, all of it," Miguel said in an unexpectedly soft and friendly tone.

"Sure baby," she reached into a hidden pocket that she had sewn into the inside of her tight-fitting skirt. From it she removed one hundred forty dollars in bills of various denomination and handed them to Miguel. As he counted the money, Rose glanced seductively at Carl. "Are you a special friend of Miguel?" she asked in a teasing manner, "cause, I know how to treat special friends of Miguel."

"Don't worry about him," Miguel said as he finished counting. "Give me another fifty and you can have tomorrow night off," he tested.

"That would be nice sweetie, but I have to work because you just took all of my money," she lied as she straightened his lavender tie.

Miguel liked Rose. She never complained and produced a steady income. It seemed as though she liked life on the streets and the sex that came with it. Whereas, she never gave him a hard time he never laid a hand on her. Of all his girls, she was the one he treated the best. He pulled a twenty-dollar bill from the handful of money that he held and slipped it into the right cup of her bra. She smiled for two reasons. First, it kept Miguel under control and second because he didn't pick the left cup where he would have found the money she had skimmed off the top. "Thanks, baby. You're sweet." She ran her hand up his arm and leaned on his shoulder.

Miguel smiled and put his hand on the back of her neck. When they were forehead to forehead he said softly, "Go, make me some real money."

"Why don't I make you feel good instead?" she purred.

"Ahh, that cannot be, brasita," he nodded toward Carl, "I have business to handle."

"Well, you handle your business," she glanced at Carl with a look he was unable to interpret, "take this if it helps." Rose removed the twenty-dollar bill from her bra and seductively slipped it into Miguel's hand.

"Caramia," he put his free arm around her shoulder and said softly into her ear,

"You will always be my favorite. Someday. Someday."

Rose's face lit up and she turned to go back to work. A soft pat on the rear sent her prancing down the street dreaming of "someday."

There was a long lull during which time Rose returned with another john. They turned into the lobby of the seedy hotel. As they entered Rose looked over toward Miguel and winked.

Moments later Rita emerged alone.

"Yo, Rita," Miguel yelled angrily, "What the hell are you doing, taking a coffee break?" He snapped his fingers, "Get the hell over here."

She obeyed but didn't say a word.

"What are you doing? You know you have to make it while they're out there. I should smack the shit out of you for cheating me."

"I'm sorry. I was sick," she responded weakly, "I'm throwing up all the time. I think I'm pregnant."

"Ah, Madre de dios," he spat, "how could you let that happen?"

"I don't know."

"Well, you better know because I can't have you laid up like last time." Miguel looked around as he tried to calm down, "Give me your money, now!"

The mousy dark-haired girl, not yet twenty-one, produced a handful of neatly folded bills from somewhere. Miguel grabbed them greedily and counted quickly.

"Is this all of it?"

"Yes."

"I'll strip you naked right here on the street to find out. Now, give me the rest."

An additional few bills that were neatly folded were offered by the frightened girl. Combined she had given Miguel one hundred twenty-three dollars.

He slipped the money into his pocket and ordered, "Get back to work. Get sick on your own time. And, we're going to take care of that little problem, muy pronto." She turned and rushed off as Miguel attempted to kick her in the rear but missed.

The last hooker in Miguel's stable came walking down the street with a well-dressed middle-aged businessman.

Miguel motioned for her to join him. She hesitated then said something softly to the businessman and watched him enter the hotel. She then walked over to Miguel.

"Give me your money, I need it."

"Sure Miguel," Doris reached into the lining of the short bolero jacket that she wore over a very revealing blouse. From it she retrieved one hundred forty dollars.

Miguel snatched the money and said coldly, "Go take care of your friend."

With all the money he needed to pay Carl, Miguel wanted to fling it into his ex-partner's face. That's what he wanted to do; instead he handed the money to his captor and simply said, "OK, we're even." It was the appropriate thing to do for Miguel was well aware of the Pythacyk temper and the busted-up bodies it left in its wake when aroused. He decided the right time would come and when it did it would be final.

Carl stuffed the money into his pocket. He didn't count it, he simply pushed the muzzle of the revolver up under Miguel's chin and stated flatly, "I know it's all there because if I'm short one dollar I'll come back and I won't collect payment in money. Comprende, amigo?"

"It's all there, you can trust me."

"Right," Carl stepped back and held the revolver at arm's length pointed directly at Miguel's nose. After taking a few more steps backward he aimed the muzzle skyward and flipped the cylinder out. Six .22 caliber long rifle cartridges fell into his hand. Idiot, Carl thought, he didn't leave an empty cylinder under the hammer. The little greaser was lucky he didn't blow himself a new asshole. With the twist of his wrist he flipped the empty cylinder back into place. "Next time, don't make me come looking for you. Because, next time I might not be in such a good mood." Carl tossed the empty revolver to Miguel, turned slowly and stepped into the street.

Then began the macho dance. Carl walked casually away from where Miguel stood. As he did he tossed the cartridges under a parked car. Every move was easy and calm so as not to show nervousness. After all, a coward would run—a man would show no fear. Carl only hoped that Miguel didn't have any spare ammunition or if he did that he would not be able to load the revolver quickly enough.

Behind him Miguel fumbled in his pocket for the extra shells that he carried.

Carl stopped to wait for two taxicabs to pass. He didn't look back as that would betray fear.

Miguel cursed himself for wearing tight pants. Slowly, he was able to retrieve three cartridges and rushed to slip them into the cylinder.

With the street clear Carl crossed to the other side. He continued with an "up yours" easy gait. His heart pounded as he put distance between himself and Miguel. It was then in the darkness of West Forty Fourth Street with city sounds echoing all around that he heard the unmistakable click of a revolver's cylinder slipping into place. Although he had reached the other side of the street, Carl knew he was still dangerously close.

Miguel quickly turned the cylinder to where one of the bullets lined up with the hammer. It would be a relatively easy shot inasmuch as he knew Carl would not run. What he wanted to do was put one in Carl's lower back and cripple the bastard.

Time, distance, angle, obstacles; Carl tried to calculate all of the possibilities and what movements would look casual while making him less of a target.

Miguel stepped into the street and raised his arm to take aim when a pair of headlights caused him to hesitate. Quickly he hid the firearm by his side. A large newspaper delivery truck rumbled slowly past. It headed in the direction of Ninth Avenue. For a brief moment, it obscured the view and then passed. Immediately, Miguel raised his arm and aimed. Carl was gone. The sidewalk on the other side of the street was empty. Miguel crouched down to peer under the parked cars for a sign of his prey. There was none. With five quick lengthy strides, he reached the other side of the street and glanced first left, then right. He found no sign of Carl.

"Damn it!" he cursed as he slipped the revolver into his belt in the small of his back.

In the cover of darkness Carl leapt from the rear bumper of the newspaper delivery truck and disappeared down Ninth Avenue.

Matt awoke in his dark hospital room. At first, he was disoriented and unsure of where he was. Such was the effect of that dream. Every time he had it he lived it. He lived it so completely that it crossed over into his consciousness. Waking up did not remove it from his memory as often happens with run-of-the-mill trips into the world of dreams.

When his eyes adjusted to the dark he looked at a small clock radio on the nightstand. The small hand of the clock was pointed at the two while the large hand pointed at the seven. Two thirty-five in the morning, he had been asleep three hours. The haunting image of the dream lingered, beckoning him, teasing him, seducing him. He wanted so much to go back to sleep to rejoin phantom images that came to him only in the night, but he knew it wouldn't happen. As hard as he tried he was never able to revisit fading images in his mind. Awareness of that fact gave Matt reason to wish to stay awake. Desperately, he fought to hold onto those precious images, to see beyond memory, to possess those feelings just a little longer. He searched the distant vision that moments earlier was sharp and distinct as it flooded all around him. It dissolved away, yet emotional memory lingered.

In the darkness, he searched. In the darkness, he continued to experience intense feelings. In the darkness, he reached out for answers. Finally, the darkness won and he drifted back into the world of the id—only he traveled beyond the dream.

In a dream Robert Six Trees saw his sister Anna far across a field. He tried to run to her, but no matter how fast he ran she remained the same distance away. She stood motionless looking directly at him. He continued in his quest to reach her but failed to make any progress. Finally, when she turned as if to leave he called out her name. His own voice woke him up.

7: Wednesday - May 21, 1969

"The trouble with grass is sometimes you get a good buzz and sometimes—nothing." Ritchie took another deep drag on the roach he held in an alligator clip. Blue white smoke snaked its way into his lungs. Hold—caress the drug—seek its wisdom—surrender to its effect—exhale. The desired relief eluded him. "That's some bad shit, man," he complained, "What is it—monkey grass?"

"No man, it's good stuff, direct from Turkey via Canada," Toby took the offered burning weed and sucked in its smoky mixture of marijuana, twigs, and animal droppings. Without exhaling he said, "This is pure D, top of the line, Mary Jane, man."

The two young men sat in a sparsely furnished second story loft over a Pontiac Dealership in the middle of town. It was where Ritchie lived and did most of his artwork. The rest of the time he worked down by the railroad tracks painting cars at Finley's Auto Body Shop. He worked flexible hours and generally when he felt like it. Big Bob Finley didn't mind because Ritchie did a great job, which helped to build the quality reputation of his shop. He knew, he could put customers off a few days when Ritchie wasn't in the mood.

Ritchie got up from the faded hardwood floor and walked over to a row of windows that wrapped around the curved outside wall. He wiped his sleeve across the dusty glass. Below him was the intersection of Washington and Madison Avenues, which is the center of Dumont, New Jersey. Diagonally across the street stood the regal white-pillared bank building. Across Washington Avenue stood the aged and historic North Reformed Church with its tall steeple reaching hopefully into the sky. Its big clock always present, always chiming on the hour and half hour as it counted down the remaining minutes of a man's life. On the corner across Madison Avenue was a row of stores. Ritchie's dilated eyes caught a glimpse of Reinhardt's bakery. Oh, how he loved their German chocolate cake, although he rarely was able to afford one. Hunger grew inside of him until it reached a crescendo. Too bad that bakery was closed for the day. Absently, he watched the traffic signal as it switched from green to red to green to red. Finally, he said with a voice that could be considered reflective, pensive, or sad, "It's out there, man, I know it."

"What's out there?" Toby asked as he sat up on the torn and dirty couch, hid the roach behind his back, and craned his neck to get a better view. "Not the fuzz, man?"

"No ace, the truth, that's out there. What it's all about. Why we are here, man."

"That's easy—to smoke grass and get laid, man."

Ritchie smiled, turned, and looked at his friend. They had grown up together, gone to school together, and dropped out together. Each supported the other without even knowing it. In school, they had the same interests, failed the same courses, and didn't fit in with the same popular crowd. Only, none of that bothered them. Together, they found a world into which they fit. It might have been on the fringe, but they didn't know it. They drifted through life finding pleasure and excitement wherever it was to be discovered. When none was present—they created their own.

Toby was of Lithuanian decent, which probably meant very little except for the fact that he had a different perspective on "how things were done." At times, he could be inflexible while clinging to the most preposterous points-of-view. Other times, he was patient and forgiving to a fault. Ritchie often believed that Toby's well-developed tolerance was the reason they were such good friends. Toby simply overlooked all of his many faults or was totally unaware of them.

Even though they were best of friends they literally came from different sides of the tracks. Toby lived in a small Cape Cod house on a side street that boasted 50 by 100 foot lots. His father was a civil service worker who delivered the mail. On the other side of town where great old Victorian houses stood regally on tree lined streets with grass-covered medians, families of corporate executives and business owners lived a life of privilege. Ritchie grew up in one of those houses. Two young men from opposite sides of town with nothing in common found a bond that only they understood. It worked for them and outlived the shallow friendships of many others who graduated from Haworth High School.

"Yeah, that's the secret of life—get high and get laid," Ritchie commented with his back to his friend as he had resumed watching the traffic light to see if he could catch it making a mistake. "But, which is better; get high then laid or laid and then high?"

Toby thought for a brief moment then replied with a straight face, "Man, it doesn't matter."

Ritchie began to laugh. The weed had taken effect. At that point, a car wreck would have been funny. Uninhibited laughter filled the room, reached over to Toby, and drew him in. The young men spiraled into almost uncontrollable laughter.

When they finally settled down, Ritchie stated, matter-of-factly, "Man, she's getting those picket fence eyes."

"Huh, Steph?"

"Yeah, she's starting to make demands." Ritchie thought about the argument that he and Stephanie had a few days earlier. It wasn't so much that she didn't like his painting of her. It was more that she wanted him to see her as special and beautiful and important. "She wants me to go establishment, man, settle down, raise a family, pay taxes, nine-to-five, fit in, sell-out, man."

"Wear a collar, get your wings clipped, become PW'd man."

"That's not my bag."

"It's hers."

"It's an empty bag, man."

"It's a dangerous bag. It sneaks up on you and before you know it, you change, man."

"Not me—I'm not Joe Corporation—you know that."

"Yeah," Toby sat silently for a moment, then added, "Heard from your old man, lately?"

"Naw," Ritchie offered, "I think he's given up. No way am I ever going to fit into his mold."

"You will," Toby smiled as he needled his friend.

"No way, man," Ritchie, countered. He began to pace back and forth. It was difficult to understand why he felt the way he did, but he just couldn't join the masses, the lemmings, marching in time step to their doom. There just had to be more to life than that. "Why man?"

"Why what?"

"Why is everyone trying to make me fit into their world? Why do I have to be what they want, instead of what I want? Everyone seems to have an opinion of what

I'm supposed to be."

"It's the way of the world, man."

"Not my world!"

"You're right it's not your world—it's their world—and because of that they control your world."

"Not if I don't let them."

"Yeah, try that and see what jail cell you end up in."

"You're bumming me out, man."

"Just layin the truth on you, you know that."

"Yeah."

"So, how is Warbucks—anyway?"

"Stinkin rich and outa touch, as usual."

"And, you haven't seen him?"

"Not lately—been too busy," Ritchie shrugged.

"Yeah, busy getting PW'd."

"Better than GW'd"

"GW'd? What's that?"

"Goin without."

Toby sat silently, staring at his friend. It was as though the comment was taking time finding a brain cell onto which to latch. Then he suddenly laughed.

Ritchie continued, "I dig her. I just don't dig her trip, man. It's not for me. I've seen what Mr. Straightarrow is all about and it ain't me." Ritchie thought about his father. He was the perfect example of a successful businessman. Most of all he pictured the big heavy gold wristwatch that his father always wore. He couldn't remember a time when the old man didn't wear it. It was a permanent part of him—his trademark. When Ritchie was young that wristwatch was a thing of fascination. His father would sit in the den and watch a Yankee baseball game on television and unconsciously twist that watch around his wrist.

When Ritchie was young he admired his father. His father was a kind and benevolent man who took good care of his family. They lived in a comfortable and spacious house, rode in a new car every other year, and took exciting vacations. On spring evenings, his father would come home and after dinner get out the gloves. Then Ritchie would become Whitey Ford as he pitched to his father in the driveway. Everything was idyllic. Everything was pleasant. Everything was perfect. Then Ritchie grew up and broke his father's heart.

Ritchie really didn't remember when he realized that his father was not the kind and wonderful person that a gullible son had once believed. Maybe it happened when he overheard a conversation the old man had on the telephone one eye-opening Thursday evening. He and his father were on their way out to the driveway to play catch when the telephone rang. His father took the call and Ritchie waited by the front door. Although he could only hear one side of the conversation, he got a pretty good idea of what it was about.

"You tell that Jew that next time he should read the contract. Nowhere does it state that we pay in thirty days, or sixty days. I don't care if he did pay an upcharge to get that paper shipped on time. We never agreed to it, so he eats the cost. And, the fact that he needs the cashflow isn't our problem." There was a pause as his father listened. Then he added, "I know we have the money, but we stick to the ninety-day schedule. If he goes under we don't pay anything and come out ahead—that's all."

Over time, Ritchie became more and more aware that his father had two distinct personalities. The kind man that he grew up with and admired contrasted with the one that was calculating, cold, and as unfeeling as a virus that snuffs out the life of an infant without any remorse. As Ritchie grew so did his discomfort. Inevitably, he distanced himself from the man that he had looked up to for such a large portion of his life. His father, who had steadfastly remained the same man, who was once loved by his son, found himself at a loss. The publisher of numerous vertical magazines, those that deal with a specific subject, never understood what he had done that was so wrong as to lose the love of the boy he cherished. In his mind, he did everything that he could to provide a good home and the best of everything for his family.

As if the gap was not bad enough, when Ritchie began to let his hair grow longer and longer the arguments began. "You look like a girl—get a haircut for crying out loud!"

"I'm just being me!"

"What are you—queer?"

"I like the way I look!"

"You look ridiculous. You look like one of those potheads who walk aimlessly down the street."

"Maybe, they're not aimless. Maybe, they simply haven't found any acceptable target."

"What the hell does that mean?"

"Maybe, they just see things differently, that's all. Why judge them—they're not judging you."

Ritchie found himself torn between a parent that he loved and disillusionment with a capitalistic society that seemed to reward the greedy, the heartless, the liars, the cheats, the thieves, and a father who caught his son's pitches in the seventh game of the World Series. It seemed to him that the very people with the means to help others were the ones who most often turned their backs on the needs of society. These good family men failed to hear the cries of the average Joes trying to raise their own families. What Ritchie couldn't understand was how they could be so unaware of their cruelty. They were insensitive, uncaring, self-centered despots who only cared about profits without any feelings of shame. Instead, they felt pride and pleasure and fulfillment without hearing the bones cracking beneath their feet. When a man needs water, do you not give it to him without condemning him for failing to have the resources to own a well? Is the real value of a man based on the size of his fortune or the depth of his compassion?

Red became green, as Ritchie wrestled with his emotions. He thought of the father who was always there and had given him everything—the father he now rejected. Unexpectedly, his mind jumped to Stephanie and the father who lay in a hospital bed in a coma for six years. She not only didn't have the joys of a father's smile but also was denied the security of a father's strength. Instead, she had the endless fear of him one day breathing his last without ever regaining consciousness. Green became red. Ever since her mother died, she had no one, just the endless beeping of a medical monitor that could fall silent at any moment. It made Ritchie feel ashamed for making her cry. Red became green. He saw her eyes, her tears, her desperate need to be comforted and knew he had failed her. His mind leapt to his father, standing in the driveway, baseball glove in hand, waiting. All he wanted was to see a smile on the face of his son that he loved more than life itself, but Ritchie wasn't there. Green became red.

Matt found himself living the experience as he read an article in *Newsweek* magazine. There were two reasons why the space program had become his focal point for filling in missed years. It was one of the last things he had been involved with before his accident and that big NASA contract had been the crowning glory in his career. As a result, he found himself reading everything that he could get his hands on that pertained to NASA and the quest to reach the Moon 239,000 miles away. How they got from the Mercury program to Gemini and now Apollo was a fascination that he pursued in earnest. On this evening, he read an account in *Newsweek* about the tragedy of Apollo 1.

What had started out as a routine test on a Friday afternoon had ended in a silent shroud of disbelief. The unimaginable not only happened, but it struck at the very time when optimistic anticipation was at its highest point. Apollo was the final step in a long series of steps designed to ultimately place a human footprint on the surface of the moon. It was the culmination of millions of hours of work by thousands of dedicated scientists, technicians, and support staff. NASA had faced each obstacle and found a solution. A whole new science was being learned day by day and America was up to the task. Confidence had been high and a belief spread among all involved that it really could be done before the end of the decade as President John F. Kennedy had ordained. Everyone knew there was danger—there always would be danger—but they grew to believe that danger resided above the clouds, not in the relative safety of controlled tests and rehearsals.

On January 27, 1967, ten weeks after the final Gemini flight, three astronauts entered the command module of Apollo I. Lieutenant Colonel Virgil "Gus" Grissom was the oldest at forty-one years of age. He was one of the original seven astronauts originally recruited when the space program began. During the early days, he was the second American astronaut to go into space. On July 21, 1961, he flew a sub-orbital mission in Liberty Bell 7. This flight was controversial as the hatch of the capsule blew off as it bobbed in the Atlantic after splash down and it sunk. Grissom was rescued after almost drowning but the question remained as to whether or not he had panicked and blown the hatch. Four years later, March 23, 1965, he commanded Gemini III with astronaut John Young. It was the first manned Gemini flight.

At thirty-six years of age, Lieutenant Colonel Edward White was next oldest. He also was an experienced astronaut who had gone into space during the Gemini program. From June 3rd through 7th in 1965 he orbited in Gemini IV. In fact, Ed White had the honor of being the first American to walk in space during this mission.

The rookie on the team was Lieutenant Commander Roger Chaffee who was the youngest at age thirty-one. Three men with different backgrounds, levels of experience, and of varying ages had been brought together to train as the first crew of the new Apollo program.

At one in the afternoon on that bright and clear day the three space-suited men entered the Apollo I capsule high atop a Saturn rocket 218 feet above launch pad 34 at Cape Kennedy. With helmet faceplates closed and suits fully pressurized they sat in a row in the command module. Once sealed, pure oxygen was pumped in to a pressure of fifteen pounds per square inch. Oxygen was used because it is lighter than air, thus reducing the overall payload of the capsule. All power was disconnected in what is called a "plugs out" test. They were rehearsing the planned countdown for a launch sequence that would be executed in reality a few weeks later.

During the test, Gus Grissom complained that his oxygen had a sour smell. Then a live microphone breaking into transmissions caused communications problems. There seemed to be a rash of small annoying difficulties that hindered progress. Testing dragged on for hours. At 5:40 p.m. Grissom complained once more about continued communications problems, as he grew frustrated. By 6:30 p.m. everything seemed to be back to normal. At that point, the three men had been in the capsule for five and a half hours.

At 6:31 p.m. startled technicians heard the frightening words, "Fire! I smell fire." Whose voice it was wasn't clear. Immediately, the radio delivered more ominous and fateful words, "Fire in the cockpit!" Then silence.

Inside Apollo 1 three brave men who were trained to face death followed procedures. For, at times like those that is the only route. Normally, it took ninety seconds to evacuate the capsule. At least, that was what had been the case during earlier tests. This time, however, the pressurized capsule kept Ed White, who was seated in the middle, from opening the hatch. Due to a design flaw, the hatch opened inward, which meant he had to overcome tons of pressure but couldn't. An instant before the other two astronauts, Ed White realized it was hopeless. A calm unlike any he had ever experienced before washed over him followed by a burning flash as the pure oxygen ignited.

It took NASA technicians five minutes to open the capsule. What they found were the lifeless bodies of the space program's first casualties in a charred spacecraft. No one spoke a word, as no words were adequate to express what they felt. They did their jobs and fought feelings of loss and guilt.

It was the worst of all starts for the new program. Apollo, the Greek god of light, in a single blinding flash reminded all involved in the space program of the day-to-day dangers involved when pushing the limits of man's knowledge. As a result of that disaster, design changes were made to Apollo command modules and the 100% oxygen was replaced with a mixture of nitrogen and oxygen.

The cause of the accident had not been determined, as yet. However, it was believed to have been caused by faulty wiring, a bad connection, or static electric buildup. Matt stared at the sentence gripped by the words "faulty wiring." It couldn't be! He couldn't accept the possibility. Faulty wiring pierced his mind like an intrusive flashing red neon sign. Could it be? No, it must have been a bad connection or static charge. Faulty wiring felt like being accused of cheating on your wife. It just couldn't be the case. He recalled how hard he had worked to get that NASA contract. The space agency established incredible standards that had to be met. Matt met them all; gauge, tensile strength, stranded minimums, alloy composition, conductivity, variances, insulation tolerances, even delivery date. NASA got exactly what it needed. There were so many requirements that it was virtually impossible for there to be faulty wiring. It just couldn't happen.

Matt couldn't help feeling as though he had just lost three friends. Even though the event had occurred over two years past, it had just happened in his catching-up world. He sat in silence.

A quote by Gus Grissom ended the article, "If we die, we want people to accept it. We are in a risky business and we hope that if anything happens to us it will not delay the program. The conquest of space is worth the risk of life."

Without thinking, Matt looked skyward as if trying to see the three astronauts,

Eugene Cernan, John Young, and Tom Stafford, aboard Apollo 10 who had entered orbit around the moon at 3:45 p.m. that day. "Safe journey and God's speed," he whispered.

Matt's rehabilitation had come a long way. He could slowly walk on his own for short distances. Every day he worked as hard as he could with the goal of leaving the hospital before the planned Moon landing in July. He grew weary so he stopped reading. The magazine dropped to the floor as his grip failed once more. His muscles still did not have the stamina needed for any prolonged activity. Fatigue brought with it images—new glimpses of a past that had been misplaced.

Valerie sat in a rocking chair holding a baby in her arms. Slowly, she rocked back and forth, all the while looking at her little miracle. She was lost in the glorious reverie of motherhood. Stephanie Elizabeth Ellis represented everything that was good and pure and beautiful in the world. If there was any way for Valerie to give that innocent, yet magnificent, infant a better chance at life—she would.

Matt entered the room covered in sawdust and other assorted substances that he had accumulated while working on the nursery. "How's my little princess doing?" he asked.

"Mother and daughter are fine," Valerie answered in her slightly formal and dignified manner.

"Can I hold her?"

"Not covered in all that dirt and grime." She wrinkled her nose and drew the baby closer as if trying to protect it. This was her time—mother and child. There is never a closer more fulfilling moment than those first few months when a human being of infinite potential and promise is completely dependent on another for survival. Valerie held her gift and treasure close and prayed for only good things to come her child's way. It was a prayer not unlike that of every parent. Unfortunately, it was one that could not be realized. And yet, it is a universal desire.

Valerie held Stephanie up in front of her and looked at her perfect features. Their eyes met. Innocence gazed into a loving parent's eyes. A proud new mother said, "This baby needs changing—yuck!"

Now, there's one thing about babies and parents. In the beginning the yuck factor is very high, then slowly it loses its impact and becomes commonplace, as well as a way of life. Spit-up, diapers, and snot lose their offensive potency and become quite innocuous to those who deal with it all the time. Parents become desensitized, which often causes consternation among their single friends. However, it doesn't matter to a proud parent.

As Stephanie grew and began eating solid food the adventure changed. Matt recalled one infamous night when they were in a hurry to go to a friend's house. They decided to quickly change the baby before leaving. Valerie placed Stephanie on their bed and removed the old diaper. That's when it happened. Their beautiful, perfect, enchanting princess shot a projectile past Valerie. It hit a dresser and fell to the floor.

"Wow!" Valerie exclaimed.

"What did you do?" Matt asked.

As usual, Valerie answered in a somewhat formal and dignified voice, "It wasn't me. I didn't know she was loaded."

As Matt recalled that moment he began to laugh. It was something that had to be seen to be fully appreciated. The event itself was hilarious. But, the surprised look on Valerie's face contrasted with the contented look on the face of their princess was an image he was glad to have recalled. It was a time he wished he could relive. It was a time to which he wished he could return.

Valerie smiled lovingly in his memory. She looked at him as no other person ever had. Her spirit caressed his tired and struggling mind. From a past long gone, she reached out and soothed him as she had done so often. He wanted to hold her once more, or at least one last time. His Odette was his life. She gave meaning to his life. And, now she was gone. It was difficult for him to let go. He held back tears that welled up in his eyes.

Matt knew a Valerie that others missed. She was warm-hearted, caring, and gentle, even though, she hid her depth of feelings behind subdued expressions and dignified words. Some might have thought that she put on airs. Instead, she was the most real, unpretentious, pure individual he had ever known. He wished that others could have been able to see how delicate and beautiful she really was. Her sensitive and caring nature was genuine beyond belief. Her dignity was not one of self-importance but more a need to be kind and loving to the world and all who resided in it, for she felt insignificant among all of the talented and successful people that surrounded her.

Memories of their first apartment unfolded in Matt's mind. It was small and cramped in a four-story walk-up building in Bergenfield, New Jersey. It was a coincidence that they moved into the town where they had met. When they moved in they had an old armchair, one bookshelf, and Valerie's old bedroom set. Money was tight, but they both had jobs, so they were full of hope. Valerie was a teacher at a local dance studio. Matt loaded trucks and did maintenance work at a factory in Hackensack. Early each morning he would board the old number 72 bus and ride to within a few blocks of work. Unfortunately, it didn't run at night so he had to take two buses to get home. This made his arrival time somewhat unpredictable.

Every night, Valerie would be waiting with dinner ready and her secret smile just for him. She loved her knight in sweaty armor. He protected her and nurtured her dreams. His strength gave her confidence. The future lay before them filled with promise. Together, they would build a life filled with all the wonderful things that they discussed in their small cramped apartment. They both wanted a house in the woods, one, maybe two, children, and the opportunity to travel. Sir Matthew was not afraid to work hard to give Lady Valerie a castle and dreams. However, it wasn't until he landed a job with Orztech Corporation that their dreams began to become reality.

Jack sat on his favorite bar stool, leaning on one elbow, watching the early evening crowd.

"Things looking better, these days?" Harry asked in a friendly tone.

The newspaper reporter turned to face his friend. As always, Harry had a welcoming and pleasant expression on his face. He always seemed to be easy-going and amiable. In fact, Harry was the epitome of the nice guy. So much so, that Jack had trouble picturing him as the tough New York City cop that he had once been. He just didn't fit the stereotype. Of course, Jack didn't meet Harry until after he had been forced to retire due to wounds received in the line of duty.

As the story went, Harry had followed a robbery suspect into a tenement on the lower east side. The armed thief ran up three flights of stairs and pushed his way into an apartment behind an old woman who was bringing in laundry that she had hung on the roof to dry. Harry was not far behind. He arrived in the hallway just as the apartment door closed. Inside he could hear the woman screaming. A well-trained officer, he knew better than to blindly rush into the apartment. The screams from inside, though unsettling, provided clues as to what was happening on the other side of the door. The sound moved toward the back of the apartment. Silently, Harry tried the door and found that it was unlocked. With great care, he turned the old tarnished brass knob and pushed the door inward. A small foyer stood empty before him. Farther inside a woman's voice cried out telling him where they had gone. The patrolman entered and moved as quickly as he dared in the direction of that voice. Slowly he crept down the hall that led to the bedroom. It was from there that he believed the cries had come. Every movement was made as silently as possible. This was no easy task with all of the equipment that a patrolman wore. Finally, he reached the doorway to the bedroom and paused. Inside the room the confrontation had ceased and silence prevailed. Shadows told him the room was occupied, but he couldn't tell who was where.

Training is a wonderful thing. It prepares you for situations that you would not encounter on an average day. It also keeps you from reacting emotionally when logic is needed. For this reason, Harry was able to fight the instinct to rush in and attempt to save the old woman. Instead, he ducked low and in a squatting position peered through the doorway. Shadows confirmed that two people were in the room, but he still couldn't tell exactly where they were. He spotted a mirror on a dresser and decided to move to a position where he could scan the room. Cautiously, he crept forward. Suddenly, it happened.

Out of nowhere, Harry was assaulted. Pain struck from above. Loud and unfamiliar sounds of mad aggression ripped at his ears. Confusion butchered training. In an instant, the hunter had become the hunted. He found himself completely vulnerable to unseen attacks. He dove to the floor in a desperate act of self-preservation. A shot echoed in his ears as he once more came under vicious attack. He rolled to his right and looked in the direction from where the shot had come. A Flash of lightening struck his hip. Thunder exploded all around. Painful blows struck his head, again and again. Fear-driven action caused Harry to swing his left arm above his head to grab at the source of the assault. Another flash of lightning struck his right wrist knocking his revolver from his hand. However, before the thunder was heard he flung the object that he held in his left hand at the source of the lightening.

The thief, who stood in front of an open window, was caught completely off guard. A green mass struck him full in the face. He took two fateful steps backward and tumbled out of the window. He couldn't fly, however, the green mass could. The assailant fell to his death, while the parrot flew to a fire escape across the street.

Harry had been shot twice as well as been viciously pecked by a frightened and angry South American Mandril Parrot. Yet, he saved the old woman and killed the felon without firing a shot. This fact, of course, led to a great deal of ribbing. "When you give a guy the bird you really give him the bird." "I'll bet the feathers flew during that shootout." "Next time, use a bullet—it's cheaper." The last remark referred to the fact that the old lady sued the city for five thousand dollars because her bird escaped.

Jack smiled thinking about that story.

"OK, what has you in such good humor?" Harry asked his friend as he delivered a scotch on the rocks.

"There's an old Japanese proverb—I'm not sure if I have it right—but I believe it is 'a-ki-ra-miru.'" He looked at the blank stare that dominated Harry's face. "I don't know the exact translation, but basically it means, 'If something is such that I can't change it—make the best of it.'"

"Uh-huh."

"So," Jack said slowly as if that would help, "I'm making the best of a bad situation."

"What was that? A key in your rear? Doesn't sound like a situation you can make any best out of—if you ask me."

Jack stared at his friend considering his lame attempt at humor. "I guess it depends on what kind of key we are talking about," he finally offered.

Harry returned the stare as he considered his friend's remark. Finally, a grin morphed across his face, "Yeah, and how many years in prison you get." He turned to go pull a beer, stopped, turned back and added, "But, then we're back to that rear thing again—aren't we?" His attention returned to the demanding patron and stated as he approached, "Hold on, I'm coming—it ain't medicine."

Jack laughed.

When Harry returned, the subject became more serious, "So, how are things going in the world of yellow journalism?"

"Same old crap. Probably worse, but I'm kind of numb to the whole thing. I avoid the kid. Or, kid the void, whichever works best."

"So, you haven't quit yet?"

"You know me—I'm resilient—I bounce back."

"You bounce checks, I know that."

"Bullshit! I don't even pay you with checks, you lyin' bastard."

"Now, that's the Jack Moore I know and love. Welcome back." Harry turned and wandered off to tend to business.

Jack assumed his standard position; one elbow on the bar, sitting sideways so that he could watch the room. The bar had become quite crowded with individuals or couples at all of the tables. Those who couldn't find a place to sit stood in little circles of conversation. The crowd was a fine mix. Young professionals, old newspaper hacks, single middle-aged businessmen in search of a lost past, a couple of construction workers, and cops. This was a bar that had long been a favorite watering hole for off-duty police. It was probably a combination of the fact that an ex-cop owned it and that it was close to the twelfth precinct house. Jack liked the mix because it always kept him entertained.

People fascinated him. They were unpredictable. You never could figure them out. That, of course, was one of the advantages of being a reporter. You didn't have to try to figure out why they did what they did or try to predict events, only report them as accurately as possible. He watched a young couple who sat near the door. It was obvious that they were on a date and each was trying to impress the other. How tough that must be, he thought, as he tried to remember the last date that he had been on.

"Come on, Jack," Harry blurted when he returned, "You just screwed your best friend's wife and you're not talking about it." He planted both elbows on the bar and asked, "What did you do?"

"I don't know what you're talking about."

"Don't play that stupid game with me."

"What makes you think I did anything?"

"Because you've been like a constipated yak around here and all of a sudden it's the morning after the honeymoon."

"You're nuts."

"You've got that blushing bride glow. Now, tell me what happened."

"What did you do buy a book on how to master the metaphor?"

"You're busting at the seams. You can't wait to tell me. So, come on."

"OK, now this . . ."

A patron called Harry a number of derogatory names and pleaded for a refill. "Hold that thought," Harry ordered as he rushed off.

When he returned, Jack continued, "Now, this is just something that I heard. I don't know that it's true—mind you."

"Cut the malarkey, this is freakin' Harry Van Ryker you're talkin' to."

"Let me see . . . I told you about the new managing editor."

"The young jerk."

"Right. Well, he is the most arrogant, obnoxious, irritating son-of-a-bitch that you'd ever want to meet," Jack took a sip of his scotch. Harry ran off to serve a customer. After a few minutes they were together, once more. "This young arrogant jerk got a telephone call from a headhunter. The guy knew all about him and told him that he was perfect for a position as publisher of a national magazine."

"Wow!"

"Wow, is right. The headhunter told him it was a sure thing–if he wanted it. But he couldn't tell him what magazine it was because they were keeping the search hush, hush. The salary was in the stratosphere, perks up the yahzoo, and a free hand to run it the way he thought it should be run. All he had to do was meet with the COO of the division and the deal would be done. He was assured that all parties involved were well aware of his qualifications and background and were excited about the possibility of his joining them."

"So, you're getting rid of him," Harry concluded with a congratulatory smile.

"Not exactly."

"Why not?"

"The headhunter, it seems, explained to our boy that the COO wanted to meet him, but was traveling. He asked if it was possible to meet at a hotel in Detroit."

"So, he went off to Detroit?"

"Yup. Using his own credit card, he books a round trip flight to Detroit. Only, when he got to the hotel there was a message waiting for him that said this big executive got delayed in Pittsburgh. He would be flying to Dallas with a stopover in St. Louis and asked the soon-to-be-publisher to join him for dinner at a restaurant near the airport. So, off he goes to St. Louis."

"So, they met in St. Louis?"

"Not exactly, the big guy missed the plane and was still stuck in Pittsburgh."

"I see a pattern developing here."

"The headhunter delivered the message by telephone to the restaurant. He explained that the COO was so embarrassed that he would make every effort to meet our little buddy wherever he wanted. He went on to explain that the executive would wait in Pittsburgh or get a later flight to St Louis or could get on a flight ready to leave for Nashville."

"I smell a rat."

Jack smiled, "Well, there weren't any flights from St. Louis to Pittsburgh. And, the Pittsburgh to St. Louis flight wouldn't have arrived for three and a half hours. The good news was that there were regular hedgehopper flights from St. Louis to Nashville so the two of them could get together in about an hour and a half, if they met there."

"This was getting to be a very expensive evening."

"Yeah," another smile, "it seemed like it was going to be impossible for these two to get together."

Harry got hit with a peanut from a frustrated regular who had been staring at an empty glass for what seemed an eternity. "Hold that thought. Don't lose your place." He hurried off. Upon return, he asked, "What happened in Nashville?"

"Nothing."

"Nothing?"

"Nothing."

"You can't say nothing and not explain what you mean," Harry complained, "What happened?"

"Nothing."

"What kind of nothing?"

"The guy didn't show."

"So, what did he do?"

"Instead, a young businessman shows up and picks Andy out of the crowd and walks right up to him. He introduces himself and tells the tired young lad that Mr. Kirchenbaum got called back to the meeting he had been at because the publisher of the magazine had gotten wind of the fact that he was being replaced and quit. He went on to explain that the position was his if he would join the team in Pittsburgh that night."

"He bought all that?"

"Ego is an incredible thing. You believe because it feels good to believe. By questioning, you question your own stature or value. Normal people would ask a lot of questions, but he didn't. He booked a flight to Pittsburgh." A grin blossomed on Jack's face, "After all, he had a name and address and big new job."

"You son-of-a-bitch."

Jack took a sip of his scotch.

"What was the address—really?"

"A hospital for the criminally insane."

"He's gonna kill you."

"I don't know what you are talking about. Besides, how can he say anything to anyone when he was out interviewing for another job?"

"That's a key in the rear, alright."

"A-ki-ra-miru."

Harry looked at Jack and considered how ingenious the scam had been. The guy can't make a big deal out of it, yet would love to get his hands on the perpetrator. Jack ran him ragged, cost him money, and dashed his dream all in one night. It was ruthless and cold-blooded. It was sadistic. It was mean-spirited and underhanded. It was the funniest damn thing he had heard in a long time. Revenge is sweet. He tapped his knuckles on the bar twice to signify that the next drink was on the house.

Robert and Anna sang along with the song "Hey Jude" by the Beatles, on the radio as they rode in their 1964 Ford Fairlaine driven by their mother. It was one of the few things she kept after the divorce.

8: Friday - May 23, 1969

Awake. The miracle Stephanie had prayed for as a child and lost faith in as a young adult arrived with a single blink of an eye. It seemed an understatement for such a momentous event. But, that was how it happened—her father simply strolled back into her life without any fanfare or cheers or heroes' welcome. For the past month, she tried to become reacquainted with a long-lost father. Only, the frail man who lay in a hospital bed was but a shadow of the past—a past that abruptly shifted from pleasure to pain on a dark November night as a nation mourned.

Her father's memory was, at best, faulty, as well as frozen in time. Six long years of events, news, and life had passed unnoticed. As a result, he remained in a past when life seemed to be less frantic and the world was not so turned upside down and chaotic. Matt shared a few memories with Stephanie about her as a little girl—his princess. However, he was consumed by a desire to catch up with a world that had left him behind.

They were two strangers connected by their hearts but separated by time. Divergent lives pulled worlds apart only to be abruptly thrown back together when least prepared. And, given the circumstances, it was inevitable that parent became child and child became parent.

It broke Stephanie's heart each time a new memory would emerge and her father would reminisce as though it was yesterday, because to him, it was yesterday. Matt's yesterdays had long shadows that obscured Stephanie's recollections, yet he spoke of them with incredible clarity. Time played tricks on their mingling of past and present as it created a mismatched tapestry of life.

During this evening visit, her father spoke of a yesterday as he explained, "Your mother loved ballet." A smile of resignation crossed his face. "She dragged me to so many that I actually began to like them. Of course, I showed my pedestrian taste because my favorite ballet is *Swan Lake.*" He looked at the wedding ring on his finger as he concluded, "I guess I became a sort of balletomane."

Stephanie could not remember her mother ever going to the ballet after that cruel night.

"Your mother would call me at the office and ask me to pick up tickets when a new ballet opened," he continued, "Sometimes, I'd surprise her with tickets unexpectedly." He paused as his mind reminded him, once more, that it had been only a few days since he learned of the loss of his Valerie and the pain returned until it overwhelmed him. Even though years had passed, Matt was still in the first stage of mourning. "I loved the glow of excitement that would cross her face. She never disappointed me. It was like I had just given her a diamond ring." He paused once more as he pictured the small engagement ring that he had given Valerie with its miniscule diamond which was almost too minute to be seen by the naked eye.

Stephanie could not remember ever seeing a glow of excitement on her mother's face.

"One time she wanted tickets to *Eugene Onegin.* I splurged and bought front row center balcony seats. I think it was the Stuttgart Ballet," he smiled at having been able to remember. "We did the whole thing; the ballet, a late dinner at O'Neal's Balloon, and a handsome cab ride in Central Park." He gazed through Stephanie into a past to which she knew he wished he could return. "I loved to make her smile," he continued solemnly, "it meant the world to me."

Stephanie cherished those rare times as well when she saw her mother smile.

"On that particular night, Valerie told me . . ." Matt paused, "she said . . ." His gaze turned inward, "She . . . said . . . I was . . .the . . . best thing . . . that ever happened to her." He fell silent holding his lost love in his arms far away from a cold sterile hospital room. Tears refused to be held abated as they escaped to slowly begin their mournful journey down his cheeks. He had never been the best thing that ever happened to anyone. But, to be thought of in that manner by someone as precious and kind and wonderful as Valerie was something he could never feel he deserved.

Stephanie looked at her father and felt alone—so awfully alone.

Wellington Marsh lay on his rack with his hands behind his head. The lights in the barracks were out, but he didn't feel like sleeping. His head was awash with the events of the evening—more accurately, some of the events of the evening. He was totally unprepared for what had occurred and it left an impression on the young Marine from Detroit.

Five hours earlier Sergeant Kincaid stood in the doorway of those same barracks large and imposing and stern-faced. The room was empty, with the exception of one lone recruit. All the others had long since gone to town with their treasured overnight passes. Methodically, the drill instructor scanned the room searching for any oversight or infraction that a sloppy inexperienced boot might have inadvertently left for him to discover. Nothing immediately presented itself. This irritated the Sergeant whose job it was to find infractions. Then he spotted it, a blatant boldfaced breaking of regulations.

"Marsh!" the big man bellowed.

Wellington jumped from his bunk and stood at attention, "Sir. Yes sir."

The menacing D.I. walked slowly down the corridor between the rows of bunks. As he did, out of habit, he examined each man's meager domain looking for any transgression that he could use against a poor soul at a later time. Finally, he stood tall and imposing before Wellington Marsh.

For some odd and unexplained reason in the quiet of that big room Wellington felt extremely vulnerable. He knew it was ridiculous to have such feelings but he did. After all, there had always been other recruits around to act as witnesses. At this given moment there were no witnesses around. Whatever happened, regardless of what, it would be Sergeant Kincaid's word that would be believed.

Nose to nose with Wellington the drill instructor barked, "Were you lying on that rack, boot?"

"Yes, Sergeant."

"Do you know it is against regulations?"

"Yes, Sergeant."

"So, you purposely broke regulations?"

"Yes, Sergeant."

"Do you have an excuse for this blatant disobedience?"

"No excuse, Sergeant."

"So, you feel you can disregard regulations any time you wish?"

"No, Sergeant."

"Do you think you know more than the corps?"

"No, Sergeant."

"Did you do it to irritate me?"

"No, Sergeant."

Then why did you do it?"

"No excuse, Sergeant."

Sweat began to run down Wellington's face. He knew the standard answers he was supposed to give but that was getting them nowhere. Finally, he just said without thinking, "I wasn't thinking, Sergeant. Or, I was thinking, Sergeant. I was thinking that I'm afraid of Vietnam. It seems like I'm trying to learn so much so quickly that I won't know anything when I get there."

Sergeant Kincaid stood silently looking at the young recruit. Without saying anything he fully understood what the poor lad was going through. In fact, he shared the recruit's concern. Recently, training had been cut from twelve weeks to eight because of the demand for men. He thought, some things just take time and when you rush you only create more problems than you solve. Sergeant Kincaid knew he had to do all that he could to train these men. He also knew he couldn't work miracles, but he had to try.

Reality knocked the wind out of Sergeant Kincaid. Every day he saw the numbers. He heard the reports. He knew the odds. In fact, he knew the name of every recruit that he had trained who had been killed or wounded in combat. Wellington Emanuel Marsh, age eighteen, from Detroit, Michigan—would that name some day be on the list? And, was there anything that he could do that he wasn't already doing to improve the odds that it wouldn't be?

"Why aren't you in town?" he asked in an unexpectedly calm manner.

"No excuse, Sergeant," a surprised Wellington answered before thinking, "Uh—well—I missed the bus, Sergeant."

"Be ready in ten minutes," Sergeant Kincaid barked as he turned smartly and strut off.

On the ride to town, Sergeant Kincaid was a completely different person. He was soft-spoken, compassionate, and exhibited something that Wellington had been convinced the non-com failed to have any capacity for—a sense of humor. It revealed itself when a red convertible driven by a young Marine approached them from behind, tailgated for a few seconds, then swung onto the right shoulder, passed them, and cut back in front with little room to spare.

The tough, intimidating, show-no-mercy Sergeant Kincaid that Wellington knew would have barked some great expletive and run the offending automobile off the road. The new and improved Kincaid simply smiled and said good-naturedly, "I hope they don't put him in armor."

"Do you know who he is?" Wellington asked.

"It would be easy enough to find out, but what would be the purpose? I'd wager tomorrow morning his own body is gonna punish him far more than I could. Besides, I ain't no traffic cop!"

Silence followed for the next three curves. Sergeant Kincaid shifted from fourth gear to third, back to fourth, third, and again fourth. The whole time he watched the road ahead like a hawk. It was clear that this man took the art of driving very seriously.

In the dark quiet confines of a 1959 Ford Fairlane 500 a question was asked,

"So, what are your plans for the evening?" However, before Wellington could utter a sound, the older man added in a friendly, non-threatening tone, "You don't have to tell me—I'm just curious."

"Shortstop said he was going over to the Halftrack, so I thought I might go and see if he's there."

"Yes—Marvin." Sergeant Kincaid said using Shortstop's given name, "he'll make a good Marine—someday."

Wellington was immediately impressed by the fact that the drill sergeant knew Marvin Press' real name—even more so that he used his familiar name.

Sergeant Kincaid continued, "We had a Shortstop when I came up. I'll bet every class has a Shortstop. It's funny how some guys get tagged with a nickname and some are immune. There really isn't any way to predict it. It just happens and when it does it sticks like glue."

"Did you have a nickname?" Wellington asked absentmindedly as he forgot to whom he spoke.

"I sure did," the sergeant answered, "but, if I told you it—I'd have to kill you."

"That bad, huh?"

Silence filled the car along with the reflection of occasional headlights. Wellington decided not to press the point. After all, Sergeant Kincaid might not have been joking.

The D.I. broke the silence, "You have to remember we were young men, just like yourself. It was peacetime, but we all still remembered World War II and training was still a serious thing." He shifted the car into fourth, "You know, every class has its clown. Every group needs its clown." There was a brief moment of silence. "Ours was Benjamin Cerbowitz. He was a Jewish kid from Philadelphia. Always spoke of that city like it was some kind of Shangri La. No doubt about it that boy loved Philadelphia."

Wellington heard the warmth in the Sergeant's words.

"Bennie was a cut-up right from the start. He could find something funny in everything."

In the darkness of the car one could hear the big man smile.

"One morning we were on the rifle range learning to shoot M-1s. We were all pretty poor shots in the beginning. Maggie's drawers waved a whole lot of times that first day."

"Tell me about it," Wellington remembered his first day on the range.

"Yeah. Now Ben, he is the worst shot of all. He wore these thick rimmed Marine issued glasses and couldn't see through the sights all that well." Sergeant Kincaid let out a slight laugh as he continued, "I'll never forget when he took his first shot. We were shooting at big targets that were twenty yards away. Well, he was supposed to shoot at target number eleven, but he hits ten, which was my target. Sergeant Monroe—he goes nuts—starts screaming at Ben, calls him every name in the book, makes up a few new ones, and ends by asking what the hell did he think he was doing."

"Bennie stays as calm as can be, looks at the target, then at me, then at Sergeant Monroe and finally says, 'Annie Oakley here was doing so poorly that I wanted to help him out,' and he smiles. It was the only time Sergeant Monroe didn't have an answer. He just stood there. Ben lays there proud as he could be and I just wanted to run and hide. Finally, Sergeant Monroe turns to me and says, 'OK Annie you owe this man a bullet and I don't care where you put it," and he walks off."

"I got pinned with that damned nickname for the rest of boot camp. It's just a good thing that it didn't follow me after that or I'd have hunted down Congressman Cerbowitz and wrung his wisecracking neck." A slight pause was followed by an afterthought, "That is after I burned down Philadelphia."

Wellington thought about the fact that the big sergeant that he and the other men feared so much being called Annie and started to laugh. Immediately, Sergeant Kincaid hit the brakes and stopped the car on the side of the road. Old Sergeant Kincaid jumped inside the car and threatened with unmistakable seriousness, "You tell anyone, you slip in any way, you talk in your damn sleep, and your life won't be worth living! Do you read me?"

"Your secret is safe with me, Sergeant," Wellington reassured the drill instructor. His tone was friendly and easy as he had come to be comfortable with the monster he once feared. "I'd hate to have some retaliatory hard to live with name hung on me."

"Good. Then we understand each other."

The ride to town continued.

Unexpectedly, Sergeant Kincaid asked warmly, "Have you written your mother, lately?"

"Not this week."

"Write your mom," the older man suggested, "as hard as it is for you here, it's twice as hard for her. She doesn't know what is going on and that's the worst feeling of all. She probably thinks there is some big black bastard with a walking stick making your life a living hell."

Wellington smiled in the dark. Yes, this man was very much like his father and just as unpredictable. Memory of his childhood swept across him. It brought Wellington back to when he was thirteen-years-old.

He remembered a stolen bicycle and his father's huge hand coming down like a building collapsing upon him. The left side of his face was numb from the blow but he didn't cry. He also didn't talk back because he knew better. All he could do was stand there. He knew he was wrong and he knew his old man was not going to let his son start down that path—not without a fight.

"I'm not about to raise no common thief," Wellington's father bellowed as he removed his belt.

Wellington knew he was going to get a whipping. His cheek ached from the open hand blow he had received but he knew far worse was to follow. However, that wasn't exactly what happened. Not out of fear, but due to unrelenting shame Wellington said to his father, "I'm sorry, dad, you can beat me—I deserve it." Tears washed his face. "I know I was wrong. I'm sorry. Please, don't hate me."

In the silence of their living room lit by an old table lamp with a green shade a belt dropped to the floor and a father hugged his son. Peter Marsh said with all of the love and concern that a parent can have for their child, "Boy, you can't make it in this world if you're gonna go against the law. They always catch up with you. And, once you get locked up and in the clutches of them no-accounts your life won't be worth a nickel." Wellington's father held him at arm's length with his strong autoworker's hands on his son's shoulders, "I can't walk behind you watching every step you take. You have to be a man if you want to be treated like a man. No one can make you go right and no one can make you go wrong. It's up to you."

It was the last time his father hit him, but it was the most memorable. Why that memory chose that exact moment to surface Wellington didn't know, but his father's words remained with him, "No one can make you go right and no one can make you go wrong. It's up to you."

"It's up to you," Wellington heard Sergeant Kincaid say, "you can bum a ride back to the base but this bus leaves at midnight. So, don't be late, Cinderella."

The D.I.'s mischievous tone made Wellington laugh, "I read you, sergeant."

It was at ten minutes past midnight when Wellington came trotting down the street later that evening. He headed to where Sergeant Kincaid had parked the car fully expecting to find an empty space where a black and red 1959 Ford Fairlane 500 was once parked. Instead, he found Sergeant Kincaid standing in front of a statue of a Revolutionary War general. The military leader was mounted on a horse that stood high on its two rear legs. Sergeant Kincaid seemed lost in thought.

Wellington, somewhat out of breath, approached the big man from behind not sure whether the D.I. was aware of his presence or not. However, when he drew near Sergeant Kincaid said without turning around, "Do you know the significance of a statue of a soldier on a horse with both front hooves off the ground?" His question was asked in an almost solemn manner.

"No Sergeant," Wellington gasped trying to control his breathing.

Sergeant Kincaid turned to face the young recruit, "It means he was killed in battle." His dark brown eyes stared directed into Wellington's as if waiting for a reaction.

Wellington stood silently as he looked at Sergeant Kincaid, then the statue, then back to Sergeant Kincaid.

The older man continued his explanation, "If one hoof is raised it means he was wounded in battle and died at a later date due to his injuries. If all four hooves are on the ground he didn't die in battle or as a result of a wound."

"I never knew that," Wellington admitted, "are there any other symbols in military statues?"

"Yeah, if the guy's head is up the horse's ass that's where his sergeant shoved it for being late," Kincaid answered in a deadpan manner, "get in the car."

On the ride back to base Sergeant Kincaid spoke in a remarkably friendly tone as he told a story of a man who could neither read nor write. He was uneducated but by no means was he ignorant. This man knew the forest and the land and animals and plants and everything in nature. If it was alive he seemed to have a sense about it. People turned to him whenever they had an injured pet, sick cow, or some kind of crop problem. Although he never had money, his family never went hungry and they were welcomed guests in many homes. He was a man who was respected by people for miles around. This man's son was the father of a Marine Drill Instructor.

Sergeant Kincaid spoke of his grandfather in admiring terms. The old man died fifteen years earlier in 1954 at the age of one hundred. Nathan Kincaid was twenty-seven at the time. However, what he remembered most was a conversation that he had with his grandfather ten years before the old man died. It was 1944 and World War II was still raging in both Europe and the Pacific. His grandfather was ninety years old at the time. The old man had just finished supper and was sitting on the porch rocking in his favorite chair. He seemed more quiet and reflective than usual. Nathan arrived home from working at the mill and though tired and dirty stopped to visit with his grandfather, as he was apt to do.

The old man rocked slowly as he gazed out over the fields lush with cotton across the dirt road on which they lived. Through tired eyes he looked at distant trees swaying in the breeze and clouds on the horizon and said, "It's going to rain tonight."

Nathan knew better than to question his grandfather's instinct for he was rarely wrong when it came to nature. The then seventeen-year-old lad had a long piece of straw in his mouth as he looked out at the fading sky. The breeze felt good and the rain would be welcome, even if the old tin roof on the house would surely leak as it always did. A fly landed on his cheek and he brushed it away. Then his grandfather talking to no one in particular began reminiscing. Absently, the old man told a story that would live in Nathan's heart for the rest of his life—a story he would share with a young recruit twenty-five years later.

His grandfather spoke of a time long gone. It was a time Nathan Kincaid could never fully appreciate. As he told his tale his voice revealed a strange mix of nostalgia and sadness, "It was an evening like this when I was told by my mother that the war was over and that we were free. I didn't know what she meant at the time. I was eleven years old, I believe. It seemed that a whole lot of men fought a great war in which many of them died and even more got scarred and broken and lost parts of themselves. Men from the south fought men from the north and somehow we ended up free."

"We lived on a plantation in Darlington County in this state of South Carolina. I was born on the plantation. I was a part of the plantation. My world was the plantation. Mastah Tyler fed us and gave us a place to sleep and taught us how to do things on the plantation and told us what we needed to do. Most of the time he was kind and soft speaking, but he was not to be disobeyed. He went off one time when the war was still going on and I never saw him again."

"Those were stormy times when the war was over. People everywhere was lost. White people and us darkies all kind of found ourselves displaced. We were told that we were free. Free to leave the plantation, free to go wherever we wanted, free to do what we wanted. Freedom was a beautiful word but it didn't count for nothing in the general store."

"This freedom was a heavy burden. Before the 'man's anticipation proclamation' we only had to make sure that Mastah Tyler's orders was followed. We had a roof over our head and food in our belly. This freedom took all of that away. We didn't have no roof or no food and we didn't know where to get them. There was hundreds of us wandering around the countryside looking for something, but we didn't know what it was. Some turned to stealin' and some begged for handouts. My mother, she did laundry and cleaning and other jobs at some of the houses, but those people seemed to be as poor as we was."

"Those were also mean times. There was enough hate goin' round to fill the biggest barn. White folks hated other white folks who came from the north. They also hated us only I wasn't sure why. Many darkies who had been through hard times hated white folks. They also hated other darkies who had found work or stayed on the plantations where they was born. It was one big festering human wound."

"We kept heading north because that's where people told us the work was. One day we came to a farm in Lancaster County. Two men was squatting down over a calf. The animal looked dead or a bunch ill. I had helped take care of some stocks when I was on the plantation. The calf was very young and near dying. I don't know why, but I walked over to the calf and started moving it around, talking to it, and rubbing it. The men, they didn't say nothing and I didn't say nothing to them. They just let me work on the animal. In no time, it was standing and looking at me like I was its mama," the old man rocked back with a toothy smile dominating his wrinkled, weathered, tired face. "That's when one of the men shouted, 'By Jove, you are a vetnarian.' I didn't know what that meant so I just grinned. The calf trotted off full of vinegar."

"We stayed on that farm and worked. They gave us food and let us sleep in an old shed. My mother did jobs around the house and I took care of the animals and worked the fields some. That's when we first accumulated some of our treasures. They give us some old pots and pans, a kerosene lamp, a wooden table and chairs, and some old clothes."

"They had a boy about my age. Together we worked that farm for all it was worth. We grew turnips and corn and greens and tobacco. In time, we became friends. His name was Edwin. He showed me how to fish. He taught me to count and to read some. Most of all he taught me about people. I never knew someone who could see the good in people like him. With all the hate that was going around he didn't seem to have any he wanted to use. Even when someone was being downright mean he felt sorry for them, because he felt something must be wrong for them to act that way. That boy just made you feels good being around him."

"Edwin, he had this hat—a western hat like the soldiers wore with a wide brim and leather band. It was something to see. I really admired that hat. Well, one day he hands it to me and tells me to try it on. At first I didn't want to. I thought I'd get it dirty or ruin it. He told me not to worry, so I put it on my head. It was the most wonderful thing. It made me feel like a fully-grown man—free man. Edwin, he looks at me and simply says, 'Yes,' and turns and walks away. I yelled at him that he forgot his hat. He didn't look back, he just said, 'I don't have no hat.' Now, you may think me odd, but I loved that hat—wore it for years—wore it until it didn't exist no more. That hat Edwin gave me lifted me out of the dirt. That hat was mine and it became my identity. It outlived Edwin. He died the next winter of the fever."

"Over the years, more and more people began asking for my help with their animals and crops. They started calling me doc, although I didn't have no schooling. I birthed calves, fixed broken bones, fought off blight with mixtures of sugar and lye and alcohol, made fertilizers for the fields, and even helped the ladies in their flower gardens. After my momma passed away people just seemed to all want to bring me food. I had some good eatin' in those days."

"Twenty years after we was freed I met your grandma. She was working at the Haskell farm. I was there helping Mister Haskell start a chicken egg business. She was a young girl and brought me some lemonade. Her name was Lilly. She was short and round and shapely in all the right places. When she walked she just sorta bounced from place to place like a young calf frolicking in a field. Her hair was short which made her smile stand out all the more. But, most of all, I remember her hands. They were so clean and pretty compared with my working-in-the-dirt rough ones. I was afraid to touch her for fear that I might hurt her. From the very first moment that we met we both knew. I think she liked my hat. A year later we was married. That's when all the good eatin' stopped. I want to tell you that girl she could burn water. Some nights I had to chew til my jaw hurt just to get it down. Only, truth be known, I'd have eaten a tree stump to be with her."

"One morning Mister Harper comes bangin' on the door of our little one room shack that they had let us live in. He's all puffed up and angrylike. He looks at me and says that we can't live there no more, that we gotta leave right then and there. Lilly grabbed hold of my arm as we stood in silence while a group of the local men loaded all of our belongings onto a wagon. I didn't know what to say or do. I must have done something bad wrong but couldn't figure out what. When everything was loaded, I put on the hat his son, Edwin, had given me. Then Lilly and I followed the wagon as it carried our things to who-knows-where. About a half-mile down the road they turned onto a small path that went into the woods. I was scared but I didn't let Lilly know. It was not uncommon for darkies to suddenly disappear and never be heard from again. What struck me was that they didn't say nothin and they didn't look at us. Lilly hugged my arm as she bounced alongside."

"We followed a stream in the woods. After a while, I could hear voices up ahead. It was then that we came to a clearing. There, other folks I knew and a lot of the ladies stood in front of the prettiest three-room house with a shiny tin roof and a porch. In front of it they was roasting a pig and cooking other good things my stomach had forgotten about. Mr. Harper turns to us and says in as angry a voice as he could, 'Doc, you no longer can live on my land. I just won't have it. So, I guess you will have to live on your own land,' and he grins. It was an Edwin grin if I ever saw one."

"This house and ten acres was what Lilly and I got that day. Of course, we've added rooms and plumbing since then, but that's how we came to be here. I went from slave to landowner in one lifetime—not bad at all. You see, in life you gotta plant the seeds that you are given and do all you can to make them grow. Some seeds will grow and some won't, but you can't spend your time cryin' over the ones that don't grow cause it will make you neglect them all."

Sergeant Kincaid finished the story about his grandfather, "I learned from that old man that freedom is something you can't hold in your hand but you can hold in your heart. But, freedom doesn't mean a thing if you don't put it to good use. I also learned that there are good people and there are bad people in this world. There are those who do good things everyday, there are those that take advantage of people everyday, and there are those no-accounts who have this wonderful thing called freedom but can only complain. An old slave/landowner, now there is someone who really understood what freedom is all about."

"Is that what we are fighting for in Vietnam—freedom?" Wellington asked in a somber questioning tone.

"That's what we are being told. I guess that's what we must believe," Sergeant Kincaid stated with a tone of acquiescence.

Wellington sat in the darkness of the car watching shadows float past. He was deep in thought. Sergeant Kincaid, the grandson of a slave, tough as nails drill instructor, was far more than he appeared to be. There was a depth to this man. Wellington found that he really liked the grandson of a slave/landowner. Was it by chance or design that they spent this time together? And, if by design—why? It must have been so difficult in those early days after the Civil War. Suddenly, Detroit seemed like heaven.

"Did your grandfather ever express anger about being a slave?" Wellington heard himself ask as a passing car's headlights illuminated Sergeant Kincaid's face. As usual, the big man was intently staring at the road ahead.

"I asked him that same question myself, one day," was the reply, "he told me that people do bad things. Often, they regret it later or learn better. Rome had slaves, the Egyptians had slaves, African tribes had slaves, American Indians had slaves, probably every people at some time in its history had slaves. I'll always remember what he said next, 'What they did is less important than what they do.' Do you have any idea what he meant by that?"

Wellington felt like he was back in high school and had just been called upon while he was daydreaming. "Did he mean that the fact that there was slavery is less important than the fact that it was abolished?"

"Exactly. We shouldn't condemn America for having had slavery, we should applaud her for being the kind of nation that would recognize that it was wrong and abolishing it. Let's face it our forefathers did a lot of things that weren't that honorable throughout our history. The Indians had their land stolen and were killed off. Japanese Americans were put in camps during World War II. Blacks have been denied opportunities. Big businesses have cheated, lied, and stolen. A whole lot like a child growing up, America has made a lot of mistakes. The good news is that she learns from her mistakes. We should be proud of the fact that it changed for the better and hopefully will continue to change for the better. My grandfather told me we have to leave the dark days and the bad things in the past."

Silence once again left Wellington to his thoughts.

"Have you seen combat?" Wellington asked in a somber tone. He was scared even though he hadn't even finished basic training. The only thing he could do was seek answers, try to imagine what it would be like, and prepare himself the best he could.

"Korea, 50-51."

"What was it like?"

"I'm not gonna lie to you. Combat is rough—don't let anyone tell you otherwise. You're scared all the time, only you learn to live with the fear. It keeps you alert and can save your life. But, if you let fear get the best of you, you don't come home." Sergeant Kincaid thought about the first night he spent in the field in a mountain pass somewhere north of Seoul. It was cold, quiet, dark, and terrifying. He continued, "Me and three other guys had a middle of the night watch. For two hours, I sat alone in a damp, smelly, dirty, little hole staring into the darkness. It was a cruel and scary darkness—not like the darkness in your warm and friendly bedroom—it was a darkness filled with bad and evil things. As hard as I tried, I couldn't see anything but shadows. In those shadows may have been nothing or there could have been death inches from me. It got so that everything appeared to be reaching for me, coming closer and closer. I wanted to run, but to where, in which direction? K Rations I had eaten earlier pushed their way up into my throat. The shadows watched as I quietly as possible wretched into the damp, smelly, hole in which I hid. I didn't know exactly what I was looking for but I kept looking."

"When it happened, I'm not sure, but I heard something off to my right. It was a soft rustle-like sound like an animal would make. I heard it but saw nothing. It was chilly, but I began to sweat. There was something out there but I couldn't tell what. I desperately tried to see better, to force my eyes to see into those hellish shadows, but I couldn't. My heart beat faster and faster. I wanted to yell out and start shooting, but at what? A breeze cooled my face. I sniffed the air and that's when I picked up a faint odor. It wasn't that of an animal but of a man—many men. Like magic the shadows took on a form of men moving toward our bivouac. I yelled and started shooting. Immediately, the sky lit up and before me were hundreds of North Koreans coming at us from every direction. Machine gun fire came from the camp and explosions from grenades and mortar blew men and pieces of men in every direction. The Koreans blew horns and whistles as they came at us. I fired my weapon again and again at whatever moved." One of the very few times during the ride Sergeant Kincaid turned to look at Wellington. His face was serious, but not panic stricken or remorseful. Slowly an odd grin crossed his face as he added, "I don't know that I hit anything, but I sure made a lot of noise."

Wellington looked into the older man's eyes. He expected to see the terrible effects of war. In the changing dull light within the car he found none. There was no pained look or residual fear. The sergeant appeared as normal and composed as any average man.

"Almost as quickly as it started, it was over," the D.I. continued. "The attacking forces seemed to dissolve back into the darkness beyond the flares. Absolute silence followed. There I squatted in my stinkin' little hole looking out where a moment earlier a hundred bad guys had been. Nothing moved and there were no sounds. I could see small heaps on the ground where bodies lay. Some of them might have been alive but there was no way to tell. If they were they lay dying in the dying light from the flares. Slowly, darkness completely covered the area. I was in my first action and I didn't freeze or run away. What struck me most was how calm I was. I was still scared but I was calm—in control."

"You were very brave."

"Brave—nothing. I was scared shitless. I just didn't have time to think about it. All I could do was my job." Sergeant Kincaid shifted the old Ford Fairlane 500 and then concluded, "Maybe that's the secret. Stay focused on what you have to do and do your job. When nothing is happening you have all the time in the world to worry about all the scary possibilities. When you're busy doing what you were trained to do there's no time to worry."

"I don't know. I'm scared and I haven't even left the states."

Sergeant Kincaid pulled over to the side of the road. He took the car out of gear and stomped down on the parking brake. In the shadowy darkness of the car he turned to face Wellington and said with a tone that was hauntingly familiar, "Son, I'm a good judge of character. I see all kinds. Some I know right from the beginning don't have what it takes, some are unknowns, and then there are those that have that certain something. They are the ones that I want with me when I'm in a stinkin' hole in a dangerous darkness. You are in that group. Don't you worry. When the time comes, you'll do your job." It was at that moment that Sergeant Kincaid shared a secret with Wellington.

Wellington laughed a deep and soothing laugh that washed over him and refreshed him.

The remainder of the trip took but a few minutes. They rode down Route 802, the only road that leads to the only gate into Parris Island. When they passed through the front gate a remarkable thing happened. Old Sergeant Kincaid returned with the same sudden impact as a screen door that is unexpectedly let free in a strong breeze to spring into one's face. "Tomorrow morning get your regulations-breaking ass up and report to Sergeant Markenston for five days KP for lying on your rack."

Four strangers entered More-Or-Less. Their arrival immediately caught Jack Moore's attention. To begin, he knew all of the regulars who frequented the bar owned by his friend and that they were not. He also had a trained reporter's eye which raised his power of observation dramatically. Observe, deduce, clarify, and confirm. Finally, he was the curious type who was fascinated by people. It was his belief that every individual, no matter how apparently insignificant, had a story—a magnificent story far more interesting and remarkable than any novelist could ever conjure. For it was his opinion that the complexity of human life simply could not be distilled into words. Ravenous curiosity drove him as he sought to know all about the endless line of characters that crossed his path as he lived his own unfolding story.

Three men and an Asian woman had sauntered into the bar and selected a table. They exhibited an air of confidence, or more accurately, of being in control. The men were large, each more than six feet tall, and appeared to be in excellent shape. One of them stood out because he was older than the other members of the group. Jack guessed that he was in his late forties. The other two were in their thirties and could have been body builders. At least, that was Jack's opinion from physical appearances although they were covered by outdated sports coats. By contrast, the female stood out as contemporary and fashionable. A turquoise silk blouse with matching tie open at the collar seemed a perfect complement to her skin color. Her black skirt, much like any businesswoman would wear, somehow seemed softer as it hung loosely from her hips. She walked with the same air of confidence as her companions, but with a definite feminine, soft, enticing motion. However, there was something else—hidden beneath the surface—something lurking inside born of the story of her life. It was something waiting to get out to flourish in freedom, or something better left in its lair. Jack wondered. Long, shiny, straight, jet black hair hung seductively past her shoulders. Her high cheek bones, oval face, and small nose indicated to Jack that she was of Japanese decent. Obviously, the time he had spent in Japan after the war allowed him to become familiar with the subtle differences among Japanese, Chinese, Korean, and other Asians from the Vietnam Peninsula and elsewhere. In fact, he could tell them apart almost as well as they could, although Eurasians and Amerasians were the most confusing. Dominant genes messed up the features so that it was almost impossible to tell. He tried to guess how old she was, but knew it would be an exercise in futility as Asian women just don't age like other women.

The four customers pulled out chairs to sit as they scanned the room. Uninhibitedly, they looked around, not shy about making eye contact with other patrons. Indeed, all four at one point in their examination of the establishment made eye-to-eye contact with Jack. It might have been brief or passing in nature, however none let their gaze drop or looked away. Jack was familiar with that look. It was one he had seen before. In fact, he had seen it many times. He quickly surmised one undeniable fact—they were cops. Cops are observers. They use it as a tool, a means of defense, or just plain out of habit. Each looked for any overt sign of anything that was out-of-place or worthy of investigation. Jack figured, in this case, he was probably the most suspicious character they came across.

When the female police officer's eyes met his, Jack instinctively looked away. It was a sign of weakness. Why he did it he wasn't really sure—he just did. As a cover-up, he looked at his drink and rationalized that it wouldn't pay to piss off a cop. Hesitantly, he looked up once more only to come eye-to-eye across the room with the same rare beauty to whom he was indisputably attracted. She continued to look in his direction with no change in expression. Damn Japanese, he thought, you never know what's going on in their mind. Once more he looked away. I'm the damn girl he mentally chastised himself for being a coward. For some inexplicable reason he felt naked, vulnerable, and defenseless under that relentless stare. Finally, he turned to face the bar so that he could order another drink. Only, to his surprise, he came eye-to-eye with Harry. A second set of piercing eyes questioned him.

"See something you like?"

"What the hell are you talking about?"

"Come-on, Jack," Harry teased, "You look like a dog in heat behind a fence."

"I wouldn't be pointing any paws, if I were you," Jack attempted to cover up.

"Why don't you buy her a drink?"

"Why don't you go away?"

"I can't—I work here."

"Then do your job and give me a refill," Jack pushed his empty glass at Harry.

Harry shrugged, took the glass, and walked away leaving Jack to his voyeurism. To his relief, the Japanese policewoman had turned her attention to her three cohorts. Jack was no longer an object of interest. She looked so out-of-place among those gargantuan, no-neck, enforcers of the law. And yet, she also looked quite at home dealing with them. He couldn't hear their conversation, therefore, had to write his own story based on body language. They were detectives—as their lack of uniforms clearly indicated. Maybe they were working on a case together or had just solved one of the great mysteries that had baffled the city for years. If that were so, he should talk with them, get the scoop, and write a story.

There they sat four stories that were probably spellbinding. However, there was one story at that table that Jack was most interested in hearing. Suddenly, the older cop in a grey jacket seated to the right of the lady pounded his fist on the table and cursed. There was a moment of tense silence. Then his three companions began to laugh. Cop humor was self-effacing, macho, and more of an expression of respect and affection than any outsider ever realized. Lotus Blossom briefly turned her head to look in Jack's direction. Her smile was a picture of beauty and charm. Jack checked to see if his refill had arrived.

After a short period of time, the cop with a mustache, wearing a brown tweed jacket, got up and walked over to the bar. Two stools down from where Jack sat, he could hear the big man's order.

"Draw three and a Shirley temple."

Aw, a clue, Jack thought, it seemed the lady didn't drink. However, when Moustache returned to the table he placed the innocuous, non-alcoholic beverage in front of Grey Jacket.

"What the hell is this?" could be heard throughout the bar, followed by more laugher.

Jack watched as Grey Jacket rose and stomped over to the bar and bellowed, "Hey, birdman—give me a boiler maker."

Harry walked over and stood in front of the detective. The two locked eyes. Jack watched wondering what pearl of wisdom his friend might use as a retort. Finally, Harry didn't disappoint when he said, "Your father told me he had a daughter. He just didn't tell me how ugly she was."

"My father had a partner once, a clumsy son-of-a-bitch, let a parrot take his revolver and shoot him in the ass."

"Don't let him fool you—that was one tough mother bird," Harry smiled as he offered his hand. "How is Roy doing?"

"He's still riding that freakin' motorcycle," Grey Jacket said warmly, "Sixty-six years old and he acts like a kid."

"That's the way to be."

"I guess so. He sure didn't have any trouble retiring from the job."

Jack heard the remorse in the detective's voice. It was obvious that retirement was looming in this man's near future and he wasn't ready to get off the ride. That's when Harry once again demonstrated a depth of understanding and range of wisdom that made him a very special person.

"The job is not your life. It takes over your life, but you gotta take it back. Buy a Harley, buy a typewriter—it doesn't matter—just redirect all of that energy." He added with a smile, "Just don't buy a bar."

"I don't know," Grey Jacket lamented, "sometimes facing the clock is harder than facing a gun."

"Ignore the clock—it never did anything for you."

Grey Jacket nodded resignedly as Harry put a shot and beer in front of him.

"What's the celebration?" Harry asked the question that had been on Jack's mind.

Jack stared at Grey Jacket waiting for the answer.

"Conroy was promoted to first grade," the thirsty detective said as he downed the shot in a single gulp. "Not that he deserves it," he exclaimed over his shoulder for all to hear.

The third man in the party, Suspenders, raised his glass in recognition.

Jack watched as Grey Jacket returned to the table. Bits and pieces of information had given him a sense of what was taking place. As a mental game, he decided to attempt to determine who was whose partner.

It was impossible to tell by how they were seated or by their conversation. No, the solution lay in more subtle clues. Maybe a look or nod or other gesture would give them away. All that was needed was a keen eye, patience, knowledge of human behavior, and another damned drink.

"Hey, birdman!"

Harry glared at Jack and flung his bar towel at the reporter so quickly that there was no time to duck. With a loud wet splat, it found its mark. After striking Jack on the side of the face it dropped to the bar. In addition to a biting sting, it left a wet patch on his face. Jack made a mental note; don't ever call Harry "birdman."

"Sir, could I please have another drink?"

As the night progressed, Jack gathered clues. At one point, Suspenders and Lotus Blossom ganged up on Mustache. In another instance, Grey Jacket made a motion like he was going to hit Lotus Blossom with the back of his hand. Still at another time, both Suspenders and Mustache said the same thing at the same time ending in a flourish as they pointed at each other. It went on and on until Jack had all of the information he needed to conclude without hesitation that he had no earthly idea who partnered whom.

Slowly, More-Or-Less began to empty as the hour grew late. Jack had lost interest in his game. It also had become somewhat uncomfortable remaining in the same position for such a prolonged period of time. In defeat, he turned toward the bar and leaned on both elbows. He decided to nurse his last drink and then go home. In the gold liquid he saw memories of another time in Japan. It was a strange world, at first, but slowly became his second home. The green hills and deep blue ocean had a richness of color that he had never seen before or experienced since leaving Japan. The whole landside was lush and filled with life that seemed to be compressed together to utilize the limited amount of space. Even the grass in a meadow grew so thick that it was difficult to see or even reach down and touch the dirt. The large island of Japan, part of the Ryu Kyu island chain, was formed from volcanic eruptions, therefore was filled with minerals and nutrients. The soil was so rich that it supported anything that had the courage to grew.

Jack was fully aware that he would always be attracted to Japan; the landscape, culture, and dark haired, dark-eyed beauties that were common there. However, when he was in that country he had little to do with women. It was too close to the war and fraternizing was frowned upon by both sides. Twenty years later, things were different, but, only slightly different. Most Japanese families remained very clan oriented and race conscious. They frowned on their daughters having anything to do with Gai Jin, or outsiders. Tradition and culture were hard obstacles to overcome. They reach all the way inside where an individual's belief systems reside and values are formed.

Harry poured himself a cup of coffee and joined his friend. The two men looked at each other but neither spoke. It was a form of mental sparing. Jack had pissed Harry off and Harry had lashed out at his unsuspecting friend. They were both wrong. The bartender glanced over Jack's shoulder at the four police detectives who appeared to be finishing their final drinks before heading home.

"This is your last chance," he warned as he motioned toward the table where Lotus Blossom sat.

"Last chance for what?"

"To show some backbone—be a man—meet the lady."

"I wouldn't know where to begin," Jack admitted.

"After your birdman comment," Harry stated, "I shouldn't even let you back in the bar."

"I'm really sorry. I wasn't trying to hit a nerve."

"Wait here," Harry said as he walked from behind the bar over to the table where the detectives sat. Jack watched, but couldn't hear what was being said. All four police officers began to laugh, which made Jack uncomfortable and self-conscious. He faced the bar and stared into his glass that held what could best be described as a memory of Scotch. Behind him there was more laughter. The birdman was getting even.

The sound of chairs squeaking along the hardwood floor caught Jack's attention. Muffled voices made their departure and the bar grew still and quiet. At last, Jack thought.

"I want to thank you for the offer, but I'll have to take a rain check," a voice far more sweet, innocent, and pleasant than expected surprised Jack from behind. He turned to face Lotus Blossom. "It was nice of you," a sly and seductive smile, "and very intriguing." She offered her hand which Jack shook.

"Uh."

"I guess, you need my name and number."

"Uh, yes."

"It's Ryoya Akimoto. You can reach me here," she presented a business card on which the crest of the New York City Police Department was emblazoned. Under it was the name Detective Ryoya Akimoto. She smiled and turned as she said, "Very intriguing, indeed."

Jack sat in stunned silence as he watched her walk away. What had just happened? And, more importantly, what was so intriguing? He watched as she returned to the table where moustache waited. Together, they left the bar. Through the window, Jack watched dark shadows disappear into the night.

"So, how'd you do?" Harry's familiar voice bit Jack's ear.

"What did you say to her?"

"What does it matter?"

"Don't answer a question with a question."

"Why not?"

"Because it's not an answer."

"Do you think you deserve an answer?"

OK, you're going to keep it up until you drive me nuts—aren't you?"

"Is that what you think?"

Jack pushed the remaining money he had left on the bar toward Harry. He stood and turned in the direction of the door.

Harry couldn't help himself. He had to take one more shot. The target was just too easy. "Should I keep the change?"

Jack stormed out.

Wanda Six Trees gave Robert and Anna their ice cream sandwiches. It was their Friday night treat when they could afford it. Robert teased Anna by acting as though he was going to bite her sandwich. She smiled and pushed him away.

9: Saturday - May 24, 1969

At precisely 5:25 a.m. Command Module Pilot John W. Young initiated the transearth injection sequence that started the spacecraft toward home. No longer burdened with the lunar module, the lighter vehicle slingshot easily from lunar orbit and sped toward Earth. It had been, literally, a picture-perfect dress rehearsal for the upcoming Apollo 11 flight and planned moon landing.

The day before, astronauts Thomas Stafford and Eugene Cernan had climbed into the lunar module, completed a two-hour checkout procedure, undocked, and separated from the command module. For six hours they tested various systems and executed maneuvers that brought the tiny, spiderlike craft within eight miles of the lunar surface. A distance that made it extremely difficult to keep from breaking all the rules and touching down, however, professionalism and military discipline won out. Or, could it have been the fact that the lunar lander was short-fueled in the takeoff module which meant if they had landed they could not take off and get back to the command module?

While in close proximity of the surface they took numerous photographs with modified Hasselblad 500 EL cameras, using both 80-millimeter and 250-millimeter Zeiss panacolor lenses. Because of its higher degree of resolution many of the landmarks and landing site shots were taken in black and white. Their primary interest was the Apollo 11 Landing Site 2 in Mare Tranquillitatis. Dozens of stereoscopic photographs were taken with each subsequent picture overlapping the previous one by about 60%. This allowed scientists back on Earth to view the surface in sixteen mile segments.

The Apollo 10 mission also allowed for a test of the new tracking and control network on Earth. Communications with the spacecraft was far superior to previous missions and various alternative protocols were tested. In addition, the lunar module's radar and ascent engines were put through their paces and checked out AOK. All too soon for them, the two astronauts completed the planned mission tasks. A simulated ascent from the lunar surface was performed and rendezvous with the command service module executed. It had indeed been a superb adventure and everything worked as designed.

With all mission objectives completed the day before three brave explorers were headed home.

Her gait had a regal air as she sauntered across the deep green grass in the park that surrounded Cooper's Pond. Noble and proud, her every movement was a reflection of confidence and dignity. Whether or not anyone noticed her presence, she could care less, for she was lost in her own world—a world she found exquisitely fascinating. To her, life was rich and promising and full of possibilities.

Each fluid motion step gave the impression that she was gliding effortlessly across a soft green sea. With shoulders back and head held high her poise was indeed something to behold. Her demeanor was such that it caused anyone who was near to take notice. Only, she was unaware of the effect that she had on them. Or, was she?

A cool spring breeze rustled her short hair refreshing her. She always loved the way it felt. Off to her right children laughed and played. She paused. Children were always entertaining. Silent and motionless she watched. To some, her uninhibited stare was often quite disarming, but children never seemed to notice. She continued to watch.

The sound of children's laughter filled her ears. Unnamed games played with unwritten rules brought perpetual motion to the playground. It was as though this island of fun was separate from the rest of a chaotic world. It was a refuge of innocence. It was a celebration of life.

"Fetch," a distant voice was heard to say.

The children's play continued to entertain her. A small boy fell, began to cry, was rescued by his mother, and rejoined his playmates. She looked at the mother and saw the natural bond that existed between mother and child. It bewildered her.

"Fetch," once more a voice echoed from behind her.

Her attention was drawn to the scream of a little girl that pierced the air. It was followed with disharmonic giggles and children running in every direction. A symphony of human voices accompanied an energetic human ballet.

"Fetch!"

Finally, her pointed black ears stood straight and tall as she turned in the direction of the voice. It was a voice she treasured—a voice she obeyed—even if she did demonstrate a little streak of independence every now and then.

"Fetch!"

After one last glance at the children, she turned and pranced toward the owner of that voice. When she reached Ritchie her tightly curved tail spun, rather than wagged. Head slightly down she glanced at him through the tops of her brown eyes in a coquettish manner. Ritchie attempted to show his displeasure with having to call four times, but a grin betrayed him as he was completely taken in by her act.

"You better come when I call you," he scolded in a friendly non-threatening voice that lacked anger.

Her stare continued—undaunted.

Ritchie began to laugh as he attached a leash to her collar. By his judgment, she was the perfect dog—beautiful, obedient most times, affectionate, and quiet. The basenji breed is known as the African barkless dog. They are not completely silent, however, rather than bark they have a distinctive yodel. Generally, the breed is brown and white in color, but a few oddballs, such as Fetch, exist. She was completely black with just a wisp of white on her chest appearing much like a tie. The basenji is an ancient dog depicted in early Egyptian art. A pointed snout, short hair, pointed ears, lean body, and long legs made it clear that this was an athletic creature capable of speed and agility. Together the two walked out of the park.

Ritchie looked at her distinctive gait and remembered when he had found her. She was huddled on the side of the road under a guard rail on Route 80. It was late in the afternoon and daylight had already begun to fade. A chilly rain drizzled down on the road and the pitiful little creature that had nowhere to go. Ritchie was tired from a long drive to Pennsylvania to pick up an old couch and chair that his cousin had given him.

He was driving his dark blue 1966 Ford Econoline van. It was a unique vehicle in those days. Squared off and flat-nosed the driver literally sat on top of the front wheels and next to the engine compartment that was between the two front seats. As a result, there was nothing in front of the driver except the windshield, dashboard, front panel and bumper. The steering wheel stood almost straight up and down like that of a bus. Ritchie's version had windows all around but only a driver and single passenger seat. Two swing-out doors were on the passenger side of the van. A small six cylinder engine cranked out a paltry 170 horsepower that, coupled with a three speed manual transmission, made "Hilda" a slow and cumbersome vehicle to drive.

The four-hour trip to his cousin's house and almost four hours on the return trip wore on Ritchie. He was tired and wanted to get home. It was just plain luck that he had glanced at the side of the road looking for a mile marker when he spotted the poor soaked creature. At first, he thought it was a fox or skunk. However, something told him otherwise. Quickly, he pulled off the road about a hundred feet beyond. He smiled as he remembered calling himself a "dumbass" for backing up on the shoulder of the highway.

When he arrived at the spot where he saw the lost animal, he stopped, took the van out of gear, pushed down on the emergency brake pedal, climbed into the back, and opened one of the two side doors that swung outward. To his surprise, the small black dog jumped in, just as if she had been waiting for her ride. Further, she jumped up onto his newly acquired, until then without muddy paw prints, slightly used, couch and curled up to go to sleep.

"Come in," Ritchie said after-the-fact, "make yourself at home."

Fatigue made Ritchie somewhat giddy. As a result, he continued the drive homeward carrying on a one-sided conversation with his new passenger.

"Been waiting long?"

"I tried to get here sooner, but you know how those government, freedom-denying tight asses are about speed limits. If I got pulled over, they would want a sales receipt for this stuff."

"Where you coming from?"

"Car break down?"

"You look tired—been on the road long?"

He glanced over his shoulder to see a sleeping dog.

"Guess you don't feel like talking."

"Where are you headed?"

"I'm going to Dumont. Is that anywhere near where you're going?"

"If you don't tell me—I won't know where to drop you."

"Look, you can't stay with me."

"I'm just not prepared for a guest."

"You wouldn't like it anyway."

"I'm an artist—there's paint everywhere—and I'm a real slob. It just wouldn't work."

A cold wet nose touched his right forearm. It was so unexpected that it caused Ritchie to abruptly change lanes. Once he regained control of the van, he looked down into two deep brown eyes that instantly captured him. Quickly, he turned his attention back to the road, then those eyes, the road, eyes, road.

"OK, but only for a little while until I can find you a good home."

As if she understood, the wet black canine jumped into the passenger seat and once again settled down to sleep.

Two years had passed and that little dog didn't come to visit—she took over. At first, it was subtle. When she wanted to go for a walk she would sit and stare at him until she got her way. That same steady undaunted stare insured that she always got a portion of whatever Ritchie was consuming. And, no matter how bad a day he had, she could make him smile.

Her unique name was also a thing of her own doing. After a week of not knowing what to call her, Ritchie decided they should visit a local park where he could think. Together, they strolled along a gravel path to a lush green softball field. Ritchie stopped and looked at his new friend, "You've gotta have a name."

Two brown eyes stared back at him. Her pointed ears, that had the capacity to lay flat on her head or stand straight up, rose to peak listening position.

Ritchie smiled. Then he picked up a stick and threw it. His expectation was, a dog being a dog, she would go and get it. However, Basenjis are not retrievers—they are sight hounds. So, true to her breed, she stared at where the stick landed. Her point was true and accurate, but she took not a step in the direction of the stick.

"Fetch," he commanded. But, instead of running off, she walked over to where he stood and sat.

Ritchie walked a few paces from where she sat and threw another stick. She took two paces in the direction of the throw and pointed at the escaping arborage.

When Ritchie yelled, "Fetch," she pranced back to him.

No matter what he did or what he threw, every time he said, "Fetch," she returned to him. It became clear that she thought her name was Fetch, and who was he to argue with those brown eyes? So, Fetch it was and had been ever since.

She was not a vicious dog, but she was an alpha. Also, she was a one-person dog. If another dog came near she was ready to defend her turf. Another human was safe as long as they didn't get between her and Ritchie. If they did, she would push her way between and express her displeasure with a low no-nonsense growl. However, she never bared her teeth.

Ritchie grew accustomed to having Fetch around. She was always by his side. At night, she slept in his bed. She would jump up turn three times clockwise and settle down in the center of the bed. In the beginning, Ritchie pushed and shoved her to the side, but she always returned to her spot. The battle of wills raged for a week. Finally, Ritchie learned to sleep on his meager portion of the bed while Fetch lay on her side with her long legs straight out taking up most of the bed.

So, Ritchie became the guest of Fetch and all was right with her world.

Stephanie sat cross-legged on the couch in her small apartment. It was in a two-story brick building nestled among single family homes on Roosevelt Avenue in Dumont, New Jersey. She was within walking distance of Ritchie's loft, but had not spoken with him since their argument two days earlier concerning his nose painting. It wasn't that she was still angry or upset; it simply had been a very busy time. Her father was making excellent progress and was expected to be allowed to leave the hospital shortly. Stephanie knew he would have to live with her but didn't know how they could share her small single bedroom apartment. She thought how nice it would have been if they still lived in their comfortable house in Alpine. It had plenty of room, a quiet back yard, and a basement for storing things. Oh, how she missed having a basement.

Stephanie remembered how much she loved her room in that wonderful house. It was upstairs in a loft overlooking the den on one side and the front yard on the other. There were wooden shutters that allowed her to close the den side when she wanted privacy. Many times, she opened the shutters just enough to see what was going on below when she was supposed to be in bed. Her room was spacious and bright. Lavender walls accented with white crown molding, ruffled white curtains, and a white bedspread created a distinctively feminine feel. In one corner of the room was a three-story wooden dollhouse complete with furniture, rugs, pictures, and people. It was the home of the Bass family. She named them after her daddy's favorite beer—Bass Ale. It had been a family joke that every time they ate dinner out he would innocently ask the server if they had Bass Ale. The inevitable answer was that they would have to check. In her room, Stephanie felt safe and comfortable. Everything was familiar and the outside world never penetrated her space. It was where she found refuge when the telephone calls started.

Eight months after her father's accident the telephone rang and Stephanie heard her mother say, "I'm doing the best that I can. The bills are simply adding up faster than I can earn the money to pay them." Her mother got phone call after phone call every night of the week. No matter how she tried to explain the situation it was clear that the caller didn't care. Moreover, each caller wanted their money without regard to whoever else was owed money. On more than one occasion her mother hung up the telephone and abruptly left the room. A few minutes later, she would return, but it was obvious even to a thirteen-year-old that she had been crying.

On one particular Tuesday evening the telephone rang again and again. Stephanie's mother spent the whole evening trying to explain over and over why she couldn't do any more than she was doing. Stephanie had needed help with her homework but ended up working on it alone in her loft bedroom.

It began that night. She made an inventory of her most treasured things; a small bracelet her father had given her, Mingo the bear, a letter from her grandmother written just before she died, five photographs of her parents, numerous favorite items of clothing, three select books, various toys, and a child's red purse. An inventory was essential, lest she forget something if they had to leave their home suddenly. As time went on she added and added to the list. It grew as she grew with her unable to remove any item. Deep inside where superstitions hide that influence one's actions she believed removing one item would create a domino effect of catastrophic proportions. She just could not take that risk. Because she had lost so much in life she was determined not to be the cause of any more loss. What if she removed that old blouse that no longer fit? Could the result be the loss of something of greater importance? She needed the list. The list was the binding force that held everything together. Without it, things would disappear and be lost forever. She protected it, cared for it, added to it, and checked it regularly. Over time, she had essentially lost her father and feared the loss of her mother, so people began to be included on the list.

Keeping the world in order became Stephanie's mission in life. The list was her way to take control of an out-of-control world. One day when she arrived home from school she was horrified to find that her mother had cleaned out her closet and removed her old no-longer-worn clothes. Cold waves of panic engulfed her. She screamed at her unsuspecting mother who had given the old items to charity. It was two days before she could eat, or sleep, or with shaking hands remove the lost items from her list. Her present list filled three notebooks. Ritchie was included, as well as everything in her apartment. Meticulously, she maintained an inventory of her life.

Miguel sat quietly at his table in the coffee shop on the second floor of the Port Authority Bus Terminal. The aroma of frying bacon mixed with that of coffee filled the air around him. For ten minutes he had watched a steady stream of customers arrive, buy coffee, a donut, or a few brave souls breakfast. His coffee had grown cold but it was of no concern. He had also been observing a young girl who sat in a booth at the other end of the little coffee shop. She was maybe fifteen years old with that clean just washed white skin, blond hair hanging below her shoulders, and innocent look of a child.

She exhibited all of the telltale signs of being a runaway—disheveled appearance, small bag to carry her meager belongings, and lack of concern about time. In a bus terminal, there was one universal concern—time. Everyone was arriving, waiting for a bus, or meeting someone. For this reason, they all are keenly aware of the time. Runaways, on the other hand, have nowhere to go and no need to be there by a certain time. To them time does not exist. Most often, they are in turmoil trying to decide whether or not to go through with their plan to escape parents that don't understand them or return home. Finally, she was sipping a Coke. Miguel wondered why they always order a Coke and sit with it for hours. It was like waving a sign—runaway, come and get me.

Once he was sure that no parent or boyfriend would show, Miguel decided to make his move. Experience taught him that he couldn't wait too long lest he lose this fine catch to a competitor. After taking one last glance around, Miguel rose from his table, went to the counter, purchased a Coke, and walked over to the booth that held his prey.

"Brasita," he smiled, "It looks like you could use this."

The surprised girl looked up.

"I thought you could use a fresh drink."

Innocent eyes stared at the smooth slick pimp.

"Please."

"What?"

"I was sitting over there and noticed you have been waiting a long time. So have I," he smiled.

Instinctively, she said, "I don't think I should take that."

"Why?" Miguel said with a sincere tone of being hurt that could have won a Tony Award.

"I don't know you."

"My name is Miguel and I have been waiting for my sister. But, it looks like I'm being stood up. Ah, carumba," he shook his head.

The child smiled. Miguel returned her smile and glanced once more around the coffee shop.

"I saw you waiting for someone and thought you could use a fresh drink," Miguel offered. Then with perfect timing he added, "I didn't mean to offend a beautiful young lady, like you." His smile was so pure and so inviting it painted a picture of gallantry and warmth.

"I still don't think that I should," she looked down.

"If you don't feel right about it—don't take it. My feelings won't be hurt. It's only a Coca Cola," again the smile, "You know what is best and are smart enough to make your own decisions."

Abruptly, the young girl looked up at Miguel. He had struck a nerve. It had been quite easy. He knew most runaways felt unappreciated and treated like children who were incapable of making a decision. How many times he had seen it before? Once more he smiled. They had reached a crossroad. If she continued to refuse, he would have to take another approach. If she took the soda—she was his.

As the silence continued, Miguel reached out and put the glass on the table in front of the young girl. There was a long pause and then slowly she reached out and took the offered drink.

"I guess it won't hurt."

As if invited, Miguel sat down opposite his prey, "So, who are you waiting for?"

"Oh, I'm not waiting," she stated sadly, "I was just resting."

"Ah, there must be better places than this to rest," his hand waved to point around the coffee shop. "Did you just get off of work?"

A broad smile crossed her face, "No, I don't work—I wish I did."

"I guess I ask too many questions," he tested, "forgive me."

"It's OK," she said sadly, "I'm not sure where I'm going. Only, I'm not going home—that's for sure."

"You have runaway?" he said sounding surprised, "Carumba, little one, you should go home."

"No!" she pushed the glass in his direction, "Keep your Coke. You don't know what it was like."

"Forgive me," the Coke was moved back toward the young girl, "I won't tell you to go home—promise. You can make up your own mind. But, you can't live here in the bus terminal."

"I haven't worked that out, yet."

With precision, Miguel sat back and remained silent. She was near the snare, but too quick a move would cause her to rabbit. There had to be a sense of spontaneity. No pressure could be applied. It was time to build trust, remove doubt, and then snap the trap shut.

"I'm not sure," he said as if thinking out loud, "but I have a friend. She might put you up for a few days—if I ask her."

The girl, whose life hung in a balance, looked up. She tried to read the expression on his face. Was this a man to be trusted or feared? He hadn't done anything that would make her think he was a threat. In fact, he told her she should go home. Now, he offered to ask a female friend to let her stay with her. That seemed like a kind gesture. Was she just lucky to find a good and generous person in her hour of need? He wasn't telling her to do anything, like her parents always did. The decision was hers. She asked, "Why would she do that?"

"Because we are friends. I've helped her and she has helped me. This is a tough city; you have to rely on friends to survive," he sat back in the booth as the bait drew her in, "If you want, I'll call her. If not, I'll go away. It's entirely up to you." Again, Miguel gave the child a sense of being grown up and fully capable of making a decision.

"Who is she?"

"Her name is Doris. You'd like her. She has a kid."

A mother sounded safe, indeed. "Are you sure that she wouldn't mind?"

"She is a good friend," as if an afterthought, "Maybe she can help you find a job."

A young girl's life went from hopeless to full of hope with a single sentence.

"You know, if you stay away a few days your parents will treat you differently when you go home."

"I'm not going home!"

Miguel knew that all he needed was a few days to take ownership of her life and there would be no going home after that. Ah, his mind smiled, he had netted a good one that promised many years of income.

"What kind of work do you think I could do?"

"A pretty girl like you?" Miguel smiled once again as he began his pitch, "Ah, brasita, you could be a secretary or receptionist and get by." He paused knowing she didn't have any of the necessary skills. "Or, you could be a waitress—but that's hard work." Upon seeing the reaction he wanted, Miguel dangled the carrot that she could not resist, "Of course, a pretty girl like you could be a model." She smiled hesitantly and looked away revealing her shy side. Step two, "Ah, come'on you know how pretty you are."

"Not really."

"You are one in a million. Young ladies with your looks make big money modeling." He paused to let the effect of his words sink in. "Of course, you have to know the right people to get a chance."

"How do you get to know the right people?"

Miguel leaned forward, "It's not that hard."

Olivia Samantha Everett sipped a Coke and looked at her benefactor. He had filled her head with hope and promise and dreams. Dreams; the power that helped carry a man to the moon, bring meaning to so many lives, get the tired and weary to take one more step, now stood ready to drag an innocent young girl to the gates of hell.

Jack began to dial the number Detective Ryoya Akimoto had given him the night before. To his surprise, his hand shook. At one point, his finger slipped from a dial hole causing it to register the wrong digit. "Damn it!" he cursed as he hung up the receiver. He couldn't understand why he felt so nervous. In the quiet calm of his East Sixty Third Street apartment he had sat motionless for thirty minutes trying to decide whether or not to call. During his mental debate, he counted the books on the shelf opposite the torn easy chair in which he regularly fell asleep. One book in particular reached out to his troubled mind. *The Godfather,* by Mario Puzo sat on a shelf lonely, waiting, wanting to be held and opened and read. It was a new novel about the mafia which Jack planned to read. It had just been published and gotten good reviews in the *Times.* Unfortunately, his attention was consumed with the space program. There was a story there hidden among the millions of dollars and thousands of people involved in this historic endeavor. Jack knew it and was drawn to it.

He turned his attention back to the telephone. Why he was so nervous he really couldn't fully understand. It was reminiscent of when he was a young man in high school. At that time, he was deathly afraid of talking with Andrea Holtz. She was his first love. Yet, she didn't know it because he was too frightened to tell her. Every morning he would tell his mirror image that this was the day that he would talk to the girl of his dreams. And, every night he would look into the eyes of a coward.

It wasn't until that wonderful fire drill that he finally was able to make contact. At 10:30 in the morning while they were both in the same English class the alarm bells began their chime of three rings—silence—three rings—silence.

OK, everybody," Miss Levy stated, "You all know what to do. Line up on that side of the room."

Jack was a little slower than usual getting up from his desk. As a result, he lost his place in line. Fate, however, was on his side as he ended up directly behind Andrea. Immediately, he noticed that she had that clean, freshly washed, aroma mixed with some kind of girl smell. Whatever it was—he loved it! There he stood inches from the girl he dreamt about. Inches away, but it might as well have been miles because he couldn't think of a thing to say to her.

Once they were in an orderly line Miss Levy directed, "OK, this way. Jordan, close the door when you leave."

The group began the school-line shuffle down a long hall toward the stairs. Jack couldn't help but wonder if there was a real fire how they wouldn't all perish as a result of the slow-motion evacuation. Onward they trudged. Jack became transfixed on Andrea's long brunette hair as it swayed back and forth. Like silk it flowed so gently in soft waves. It was a haunting vision of beauty—so lovely, so feminine, so pure. He wanted to reach out and touch her hair, stroke it, and feel its softness, but dared not.

Suddenly, without warning, he sneezed. It was an ambush sneeze—one you don't feel coming. There is a fact about sneezing that most people do not realize. It is impossible to sneeze and keep your eyes open. This was the case with Jack. When he opened his eyes before him stood Andrea the vision of loveliness that he worshipped with a huge wad of spittle hanging in her exquisite hair. Jack was shocked by the sight before him. It was the worst of catastrophes. He had defiled the very thing that he adored. Panic set in as he wondered what he should do. There it hung an abomination on a thing of beauty.

While he froze in confusion as to what to do, Andrea turned around and said, "Bless you."

His reply was, "I don't deserve it," which he sincerely meant.

Andrea laughed.

The sweet sound of her laugh caused him to melt. She was the perfect human being. Without question the perfect human being—with spit in her hair.

Impulsively he said, "You have something in your hair," as he quickly ran his hand lightly along the back of her hair.

"It's not a bug?" she panicked and shook her head.

"No, I got it. Some kind of dust bunny," he lied.

"Thank you."

After that day talking with Andrea was much easier. When she saw him in the hall, she would smile and say hi. If he saw her coming he would reply, but if he was caught off guard his response was often a blank stare. They remained friends, but Jack never found a way to tell Andrea how he felt about her.

Jack went back to dialing the telephone number that his new Andrea had given to him. After five digits, he hung up the receiver. A man whose job involved the careful crafting of words didn't know what to say. For a brief moment he sat and stared at the telephone. Then he got up and walked into the bathroom, stood at the sink, and stared at the coward in the mirror.

A Coke was not a great gift but it was the only one left. Robert opened the bottle poured equal amounts into two glasses. Splitter's rules applied. The one who pours has last choice of glass. This insures that every effort is made to pour as equally as possible. Anna watched every drop flow into the glasses, examined them carefully, and took the one on the right. Children's solutions to complex issues often are pure, simple, and fair.

10: Monday - May 26, 1969

At 11:52 a.m. Stephanie sat with her father in the business office of the hospital. He was being released and an endless number of papers had to be signed to convert him from being a ward of the state back to that of a private citizen. As Matt slowly and methodically affixed his name on various lines he was struck by the fact that his signature looked completely foreign to him. The strokes were awkward and sloppy, much like an elementary school student's writing might look as they learned how to do cursive. The lady with a brass nametag that read Elizabeth Jones, Business Management Supervisor, seemed to have a canned statement for each document. She presented the facts in a monotone, starkly unemotional, and disconnected voice. It was easy to allow her words to drift into the background until they dissolved into a dull hum. Paper after paper appeared, was signed, and then disappeared into a neat manila file. Matt's mind wandered back to the closing on their house in Alpine. The memory simply returned from its hiding place in his mind. He and Valerie had worked so hard to save the down payment. Then looking for the right house became a study in ying and yang. When he liked a house, she was unimpressed. When she was attracted to one, he was underwhelmed. This went on weekend after weekend. Finally, when they visited the ranch house in Alpine they were simultaneously captivated and agreed immediately. It was a magic time and those memories that were so welcome still seemed so distant as he signed an endless assortment of unread documents.

At 11:52 a.m. Wellington squeezed the trigger of his M-1 rifle one final time. The weapon recoiled back into his shoulder as it ejected the spent shell. He had learned on day one to hold it tight against his shoulder in order to avoid getting smacked in the face with the butt. He smiled as he remembered how many recruits sported a black eye after the first day on the range. After a few moments, a black dot on a long stick was raised to indicate on the target where the bullet had struck. Just to the right of bull's-eye which meant that he qualified. In a short amount of time he had developed quite good target shooting skills and was awarded a Sharpshooter rating. Basic qualifying earns a Marksman Badge, next higher is Sharpshooter, and the highest Expert. Wellington was pleased with his performance and rating.

Sergeant Kincaid stood behind Wellington as he took his final shot. "Boy, you have a good eye, I'll give you that."

Wellington looked up and smiled at the shadowy figure silhouetted by the bright light blue sky.

"Now, if you can just start acting like a Marine, you might just graduate." The big man turned and sauntered off to harass another recruit.

At 11:52 a.m. a young girl awoke in hell. She had spent two days being starved, raped, beaten, and chained to a radiator. In a mere 48 hours, she had lived a lifetime and at numerous times prayed for death. However, death would not come, but the devil would in the form of Miguel, again and again. No longer was he the charming young man from the coffee shop who promised her a job and money and happiness. Now, he was her tormenter and as he put it, over and over, her owner. She would learn to obey his every order without question. Fear and self-deprecation would destroy the remnants of Olivia Samantha Everett and leave an empty, obedient, pitiful, unloving shell. In the beginning she would perform under close supervision. Then she would go on the streets but would be closely supervised by his other ladies. Indeed, they each knew the penalty for letting her escape or under-perform. Miguel was satisfied because over time, this runaway would become a valuable replacement for Annie who had herself run away.

At 11:52 a.m. Carl sat in the detective's office of the 37th precinct. A Detective Hahn was questioning him about his whereabouts two nights before. It seemed there had been a break-in at a local liquor store. Carl had been seen in the area and was a known thief. It didn't take long for Detective Hahn to grow impatient with the snide remarks and dumb routine. In the end, he told Carl that it was going to be a pleasure putting him behind bars some day and that he would make it his personal goal. As he left the building Carl spat on the sidewalk.

At 11:52 a.m. Ritchie put the finishing touches on a 1968 Buick Riviera that had been repaired at Finley's Body Shop. His long hair was pulled back into a ponytail and pushed up under his cap. The effect made him look almost clean cut. With an artist's eye and technician's skill he waved the paint sprayer across the repaired surface of the car. To a casual observer, he made it look simple. However, simple it was not. Many young men who tried their hand at auto painting found the outcome had streaks, uneven coating, runoffs, swirls, and more. A Richard Carlton Anderson paintjob never had any imperfections.

At 11:52 a.m. Jack picked up the telephone in his office and dialed the number that had haunted him throughout the weekend. As the first ring chimed in his ear he reread the business card she had given to him—Ryoya Akimoto, Detective. The distinctive emblem of the New York City Police Department gave him pause. Second ring. Sweat began to run down his forehead as he wondered if any words would form when he tried to speak. Third ring. She wasn't there. What a relief.

He took the receiver from his ear just as a click erupted and a pleasant female voice said, "Detective Akimoto."

"Uh."

"Yes, who is this?"

"Uh," Jack knew his first words would define him forever. Unfortunately, if he said "gopher guts" which had popped unexpectedly into his head it would end the relationship before it began.

"At least give me your name so I know with whom I am speaking."

"Uh, Jack."

"Jack, that's good." She coaxed, "Jack Who?"

"Moore."

"You don't have to tell me any more, Jack. Just tell me your last name."

"No, my name is Jack Moore," Jack finally found his power of speech. After all he did know his own name. "We met the other night at More-Or-Less."

"Oh, yes, I remember," she said with noticeable friendliness, "You sent the bartender over with that intriguing proposal."

What damn proposal Jack thought. I'm gonna kill Harry! "Yes, I'm glad you remember."

"Why, of course, how could I forget something like that?"

"I really don't know," Jack said as he wondered what he had gotten thrust into by his soon-to-be-no-longer-a-friend, "I hope I didn't call at an inopportune time."

"This time is fine."

"I realize a police detective has odd hours, and I'd like to take you to dinner, but I'm not sure when you could go," he paused, "That is, if you even want to go, which is OK if you don't. I know . . ."

"I'm free tomorrow if that's not too soon," Ryoya said pleasantly.

"No," Jack replied somewhat surprised, "That would be fine. I'll see you tomorrow."

"Jack."

"Yes."

"Don't you want to discuss when and where and at what time?"

"Oh, Of course," he felt like he was back in high school. In fact, he felt as though he was about to sneeze. "What kind of food do you like?"

"I'll let you decide," was the response that didn't help at all. "Why don't you surprise me?"

"OK, what time would you like to go?"

"I'm off tomorrow so any time will do. What suits you?"

"How about six?"

"Six it is."

"Great I'll see you there." Jack hung the telephone up. Then he sat staring at the instrument of doom. In his mind, he heard the fire alarm bell three rings, silence, three rings, silence. There it hung a mental spit wad. No way to hide it or avoid the embarrassment. Slowly he redialed the number.

"Detective Akimoto."

"OK, there is no way to not seem like a bumbling idiot," he began.

"644 West 23rd Street, Apartment 6D," Ryoya said pleasantly, "You'll have to press my apartment number and I'll buzz you in."

"Thank you," Jack said sincerely, "I'm looking forward to it."

"So am I. Remember your offer. Bye"

Harry is a dead man, Jack thought.

At 11:52 a.m. Harry Van Ryker, the owner of More-Or-Less, washed the last few glasses from the night before. The smell of stale beer filled the air. He wondered why he liked that aroma so much. Somehow, it made him feel at home. Because it was Monday he had come in early to receive a scheduled delivery from his supplier. A siren outside caught his attention. He listened as it disappeared into the distance and for an uncountable time, his heart wanted to be back on the job.

At 11:52 a.m. Apollo 10 splashed down at about 15°S latitude, 165°W longitude. This placed it approximately 200 miles east of American Samoa in the Pacific Ocean. After eight days in space and traveling 240,000 miles from Earth the landing was pinpoint accurate less than 4 miles from the target area. John W. Young, Thomas Stafford, and Eugene Cernan were picked up by helicopter and transported to the USS Princeton. Their spacecraft was retrieved an hour and a half later. Given the success of this mission the stage was set for a moon landing two months later.

At 11:52 a.m. Robert Six Trees tried to remember the names of the first thirteen colonies of the United States. He had studied for the test but somehow never was very good at memorizing facts. The bane of a creative mind is its desire to wander.

11: Tuesday - May 27, 1969

When Matt Ellis awoke in his daughter's apartment he was glad to be out of a confining sterile hospital room. Even though everything was strange he felt at home in Stephanie's bedroom. His only regret was that she was forced to sleep on the couch. He hoped, over time, once on his own to be out of her way. A survey of the room gave him an impression of how she had been living. It was neat and sparsely furnished with a small white dresser in the corner. Except for the pale blue walls everything was white. On a little table next to the bed was a white teardrop shaped lamp and a small digital clock radio with numbers on little plastic cards that flipped down with the change of minutes and hours. Matt hadn't seen such a clock radio before. One could get hypnotized watching the number cards drop. Sheer white curtains hung over a single window. He watched them move from a breeze entering the room through the open window. The motion was also mesmerizing. From the other room he heard a song. He didn't recognize *Both Sides Now* sung by Joni Mitchell, but the words talked directly to him.

> Bows and flows of angel hair
> And ice cream castles in the air
> And feather canyons everywhere
> I've looked at clouds that way
> But now they only block the sun
> They rain and they snow on everyone
> So many things I would have done
> But clouds got in my way

Dark clouds had engulfed him for six years that blocked his sun and stood in the way of all the things he would have done. A storm of indescribable proportion had destroyed his life, taken his love, washed away precious memories, laid waste to all he had tried to build and then moved on leaving a path of destruction. He was a castaway among the living.

> I've looked at clouds from both sides now
> From up and down, and still somehow
> It's cloud illusions I recall
> I really don't know clouds at all

Without intending, he had brought this destructive storm into the lives of those he loved. They had suffered their own anguish and despair, as a result. A heavy sense of responsibility flowed over him and he felt a tremendous sense of guilt. For it was by his hand that the accident occurred, through his negligence that his family was put through unimaginable hardship, and he alone caused dear sweet Valerie to perish. He lay in the bed looking at the ceiling, tears escaped his eyes as he wondered how he could repair all the damage he caused or live with the irreparable loss of his life's partner.

> Moons and Junes and Ferris wheels
> The dizzy dancing way that you feel
> As every fairy tale comes real
> I've looked at love that way

The dancing curtain and words of the song brought forth a vision of Valerie in a white dress walking down the aisle at St. James Episcopal Church on Jerome Avenue in the Bronx. The old stone structure smelled of mildew and was dark and mysterious inside, but it had a powerful feeling of holiness. Matt almost felt as though he was an interloper to be in such a hallowed place. There he stood in a rented tuxedo, hands sweating and knees shaking watching the most beautiful lady he ever saw gliding gracefully toward him. It just seemed so impossible that she would say yes when he had asked—but there they were.

> But now it's just another show
> And you leave 'em laughing when you go
> And if you care, don't let them know
> Don't give yourself away

It was a small wedding mainly attended by her friends and family. Matt's parents and his best friend Toby Catrell were there, but no one else. After all, it was a long trip into the city and many who knew him didn't own a car. In Matt's mind though it really didn't matter the only person he wanted to be there was walking gracefully toward him.

> I've looked at love from both sides now
> From give and take, and still somehow
> It's love's illusions I recall
> I really don't know love
> Really don't know love at all

Mrs. Matthew Ellis taught Matt how to love. When she plunged into his life through a mountain of snow she awakened emotions within him that he was unaware existed. His world had consisted of earning money and blowing it on a pool game, car parts, or some other useless thing. A cold shallow world without meaning filled his days. Valerie brought kindness and dignity and awareness of the many beautiful things presented every day to brighten one's life. In the beginning, he saw the world through her eyes. The warmth he experienced came from her. In the end, he eventually developed the ability to recognize the light on his own and embrace its beauty. Yet, the beauty he embraced with the greatest passion was his snow queen whose love he cherished and now ached to have once more.

> Tears and fears and feeling proud
> To say "I love you" right out loud
> Dreams and schemes and circus crowds
> I've looked at life that way

Together, they built their world that was just for them. It was pure and honest. One life on its own is destined to circle in small pools of stagnation. The commonplace becomes the only place. Routine defines actions and actions become predictable. Time moves on while one stands still. Then the explosive introduction of another ignites emotional responses, disturbs the routine, and unveils all of the glory and hope and opportunity that is life. The catalyst removes self-constructed barriers to possibility. A transformation occurs. Tomorrows beckon, promising dreams and adventures worth pursuing.

> Oh but now old friends they're acting strange
> And they shake their heads
> And they tell me that I've changed
> Well something's lost but something's gained
> In living every day

In the end, time moved on while one poor soul stood still. And, in that stillness, loneliness emerged leaving Matt longing for a time long past. So distant were the images that they could only be perceived as fleeting wisps of illusion.

> I've looked at life from both sides now
> From win and lose and still somehow
> It's life's illusions I recall
> I really don't know life at all
> It's life's illusions I recall
> I really don't know life
> I really don't know life at all

Matt slowly sat up in bed. The pain of atrophied muscles remained evident though not as intense as prior to physical therapy. He reached out to the gently swaying curtains as if asking his new bride to dance.

Jack arrived at the corner of Third Avenue and West 23rd Street at 5:30 p.m. He was a half hour early. Shoes shined, brown suit, white shirt, and racy maroon tie confirmed that he had done all within his power to put his best foot forward. He thought about the lady with whom he was about to have dinner. She was indeed beautiful. It was true that Asian women had something that he found extremely attractive. Was it their long dark hair, their eyes, shape of their face, physique, mannerisms, poise, or chemistry? Yes, he thought. Other than her appearance and the limited knowledge that he had of Ryoya Akimoto she was a complete unknown. Yet, he was drawn to her. He needed to know more, to enter her world, to see if there was a connection, a future, a dream realized. She had risen in the ranks of the police department to detective so he knew she had to be exceptional. He was certain there weren't very many female detectives; much assume female officers in the department. A Bob Dylan song from 1963 came to mind; *The Times They are a-Changin.*

The evening sun lay low on the horizon illuminating the sky above creating fanciful shadows at street level. Rows of brownstones lined both sides of West 23rd Street. Small trees planted next to the curb the length of the block gave it a park-like appearance. The building that housed his dreams was at the other end of the block.

With so much time to spare, Jack decided to take a leisurely walk around the block. It was a welcome interlude as he never tired of watching people on the street or through the windows of stores, offices, or apartments. It was life—life in the big city. As he strolled he observed countless individuals pursuing countless dreams, numerous dramas unfolding, heard laughter and tears, observed day to day chores, children playing, impatient drivers, and enjoyed the mingled aroma of a thousand dinners being prepared a thousand different ways. All around, there were mysteries to be solved and the totally unpredictable nature of human beings for him to discover, write about, touch, and experience.

On his journey, he wondered what lay ahead. Would the evening be a wonderful surprise or a disastrous disappointment? Ryoya Akimoto was indeed a beautiful woman. He became attracted to her from the first moment he saw her. In his mind, he stared once more into her dark exotic eyes. What he should have been doing was looking at the dark and hazardous sidewalk for when he planted his next step his foot slid across the pavement causing him to twist and turn in order to recover his balance. A familiar stench told him what had happened.

"Damn dog owners," he cursed aloud, "Why don't they curb their dogs?"

Jack stormed over to the curb and attempted to scrape the offending substance from his shoe. When only limited success was achieved, he continued his walk dragging his shoe periodically in an attempt to finish the cleanup job. A quick glance at his watch told him he still had plenty of time. However, instead of looking at his watch he should have been looking where he was going because a raised concrete slab of sidewalk that had been pushed skyward by the roots of a tree caught him by surprise and he tripped. With little identifiable grace, he felt to one knee tearing his trouser leg.

"Son of a bitch," he spat, "this can't be happening."

It was a small tear, but to Jack it was a gaping hole. In his mind, he might as well have been standing there with no pants on at all. Frustration welled up inside yet no avenue of release was available. He heard laughter across the street and angrily turned his attention in the direction of its source. There he saw a young couple clowning around laughing at each other totally unaware of Jack Moore or his dilemma.

A few minutes later he reached Second Avenue and breathed a sigh of relief as he escaped the street from hell that he vowed to someday burn to the ground. He turned left to go uptown one block.

Street cleaners in New York City spray water at a low angle across the pavement to wash debris to the curb. Unknown to Jack a street cleaner had come through a few minutes earlier. While it was no longer a threat to him at that point, the puddles of water left in its wake turned out to be one more disaster. A yellow cab speeding close to the curb sent a tsunami of dirty water that drenched the newspaper writer's right leg from the knee down. Jack stood there in silence. No curse escaped from his lips. No shaking of a fist. No throwing of a rock at the escaping vehicle. He had reached that inevitable moment in time we all understand. Beyond anger and frustration there is a point where one becomes either homicidal or just has to laugh.

Jack looked up as if expecting to see God watching the comedy below from above the rooftops. He raised his arms and said, "If you're holding back a meteor, let it go now." Then he laughed.

Ryoya opened her door and Jack immediately was awestruck. She stood before him wearing an exquisite blue silk dress open at the neck with three quarter length sleeves and bias cut skirt. Her hair hung long and straight held back by a barrette on either side. A thin gold necklace with a jade stone hung around her neck. The picture was completed by makeup that brought out her exotic features and haunting eyes.

Jack quickly said, "Before you say anything, if first impressions count, this bum has come to take you out to dinner." He pointed at his worse-for-wear pants. Her broad smile was one of understanding, not cruel humor. It brightened his—until then—dismal evening and caused him to smile, as well.

"What happened?" she asked with sincere concern, "Are you alright?"

On the cab ride to Le Cav du Henri Quatro Jack told his tale. Ryoya offered a mix of sympathy and unsympathetic laughter. She was amazed that he would circle the block just to be sure to arrive on time rather than be early. All in all, Jack's adventures with the Twenty Second Street curse broke the ice and gave two strangers a feeling of openness that might have taken hours to establish or might not have happened at all. Maybe the Lord does work in mysterious ways.

At one point during the ride Ryoya wrinkled her nose and said, "What is that smell?" knowing full well what it was, thus demonstrating her ability to tease.

Impulsively, Jack opened the cab window, removed his shoe, and acted like he was going to toss it out into traffic.

Ryoya laughed. It was an innocent, almost childlike, genuine laugh that was so endearing that it was worth any effort to hear it once again.

When they arrived at the restaurant Jack escorted his date into the establishment, asked about their reservations, and led Ryoya to their table. He excused himself, went to the men's room and made sure he would no longer be offensive in any way.

As they examined their menus Ryoya inquired, "Do you read French?"

"Absolutely," Jack opened his menu, "not." He closed the menu and added, "When all else fails—ask the waiter."

"Do you think he reads French?" she asked with a mischievous smile.

It is a universal fact that waiters in French restaurants are rude, arrogant, and snobs. Some believe it is an essential part of the ambiance. However, on this particular evening of unexpected events the waiter dressed in a fine tuxedo with slicked back hair gave every impression that he was from western France.

"Howdy, how are you folks doing this evening?" he said with a drawl that would make any Texan proud.

After a short pause needed to regain his train of thought, Jack confessed, "Neither of us reads French."

"Well now, that makes three of us."

Jack and Ryoya looked at each other and laughed.

"Now, don't you worry," the waiter pointed at his head, "I've got the whole kit and caboodle stored in here in English." He took the menus and began to describe different appetizers that they might consider. "This restaurant is famous for its escargot which is snails baked in their shells with parsley butter. So, if ya'll are feeling adventurous you might want to start with that."

Convinced by their new guide and friend they accepted the challenge. The waiter disappeared. As they waited for their appetizer there was the inevitable period of uncomfortable silence. Jack searched his mind for something intelligent to say, or at least something that wouldn't be embarrassing or inane. Ryoya considered the man who sat opposite her. He was dressed well. Given his adventure prior to their date he definitely had a sense of humor. There was warmth in his voice and his words were educated and intelligent. He was impulsive, yet a little inhibited. A tell revealed his nervousness. He was constantly adjusting the knot of his tie.

"I'd like to go to Disney World when they open it," Jack stated out of the blue.

"Disneyland, in California?"

"No, Disney World. They broke ground today in Florida somewhere around Orlando. It's going to be a theme park, like Disneyland, but also is going to have a futuristic city, international exhibits, a monorail, and super modern hotel. Walt Disney died three years ago from cancer, but there is an interesting story about how he approached the idea of building a park on the east coast."

Their waiter returned with the escargot. "Now, if you've never had these little gomers you dig them out like this. Enjoy."

"He really is a nice man," Ryoya concluded.

"What I want to know is," he looked directly into her eyes, "what the hell is he doing in a French restaurant." They both laughed.

When Jack tried the escargot he chewed and chewed and chewed, then swallowed, upon which he commented, "It's like trying to eat a rubber band."

Ryoya smiled and nodded as she continued chewing.

"Disneyland was a great success," Jack returned to the subject, "but three quarters of the population live east of the Mississippi River. Now, Walt Disney may have been a creative genius but he was also a sharp businessman. As the story goes he started scouting sites for an east coast park back in 1963. I don't know if it is true but I read that he first flew over the site near Orlando, Florida November 22, 1963—the same day President Kennedy was assassinated."

Ryoya listened attentively as she watched Jack. He was nervous which is to be expected on a first date, yet he also had an ease about him. An energy, born in enthusiasm, gave him a spark that was endearing. There didn't seem to be any pretense about him. No false impressions, simply the real thing. What struck her most was that he was friendly without being fawning.

"When they built Disneyland in California all sorts of sleazy dives and tourist traps sprang up around the park. Walt Disney felt that it cheapened the family experience but couldn't do anything about it. Because the price of land skyrocketed in the area around Disneyland, Walt Disney was secretive about his plans in Florida. They created fake corporations and began buying land. Walt Disney showed his sense of humor with some of the names of these corporations. There was Ayefour Corporation because it was near Interstate 4, Retlaw Corporation which is Walter spelled backwards, and Reedy Creek Ranch Corporation. In the end, they bought land that is double the size of Manhattan Island."

"OK, How did you like the escargot?" their waiter's voice drawled as he approached.

"Very good," Ryoya said pleasantly.

"Now, for the main course what are you in the mood for; beef, fish, poultry, or vegetables?"

Jack looked at Ryoya who stated, "I think I'd like something with vegetables."

"You would enjoy the Ratatouille which is a vegetable stew with olive oil, aubergine—which is eggplant—courgette—which is zucchini—bell pepper, tomato, onion, and garlic. It's very good."

"That sounds fine."

"And you sir?"

"I'd like something with beef."

"For you I'd recommend the Boeuf Bourguignon, which is beef stewed in red wine."

"That sounds like a winner."

"Now as far as wine, I'd love to sell you a bottle of Chateauneuf-du-Pape which is a wine made near the village of Chateauneuf-du-Pape in the Rhone Valley in southeastern France but the price is about the same as a new Chevy. Personally, I think a Jin Da Li Cabernet Sauvignon from Australia is very good and far more reasonably priced. It also goes well with vegetables and beef."

"We'll trust your judgment," Jack answered.

After the waiter left Jack finished his story about Disney World. "They finally announced the project in Florida in November of '65. Roy Disney, Walt's brother, took over the project when Walt died. The price of property in Orlando quickly became inflated, but it was too late. In 1966, the Reedy Creek Improvement District was incorporated with all of the rights and powers of any other town or city in Florida. Only the sole owner is the Walt Disney Company."

Sixteen blocks away Carl walked into a seedy little bar that hid among pawn shops, discount stores, and an Army/Navy store. Inside he found a dark shadowy room that stunk of stale beer. Two men he didn't know sat at a table against a wall. One had the look of a longshoreman past his prime. He wore a blue denim shirt with the sleeves rolled up high on his muscular arms. A tattoo on his forearm depicted a knight with a sword raised above his head. The other man was younger with short brown hair, a mustache, and a faraway look. It was the kind of distant stare that comes from use of cocaine or is the warning sign of a disturbed individual capable of anything.

Edna sat at the end of the old beat up bar. She turned and looked at the new arrival, recognized Carl, smiled a sad and defeated smile, and returned to her drink. When life on the street becomes too difficult one option—the one she chose—is to dissolve into a dirty, non-descript, low-end bar and do whatever is needed for free drinks while waiting to die. Twenty-four years on the street marked her face like the annual rings of a tree. Wrinkled and discolored, deep sunken eyes, and thin colorless lips made the forty-year-old hooker appear to be sixty years old. Life had begun full of promise for Edna, but a poor decision here, bad luck there, and absence of any value system or ambition took its toll.

Carl had utilized Edna on more than one occasion, but he never showed her any kindness or treated her as any more than a source of quick oral sexual service or street information. He had no use for her on that particular night so he sat far away from Edna, the beast of the bar. Before the old, ex-school teacher, child molester, bartender could say a word, he placed a dollar on the bar and spat, "Draw one!"

As they sipped the wine that their waiter had chosen for them, Jack inquired, "What caused you to join the police department?"

"It was quite by accident," Ryoya answered, "I had a job in midtown in an office checking orders and issuing invoices for a company that imported watch parts. It wasn't anything thrilling but gave me a salary. One night I had to work late because a large order had been processed and they wanted the invoices out immediately. I stayed and finished my work finally leaving the office at 7:30 in the evening. It was July so I was somewhat happy that I didn't have to ride in a stuffy, overcrowded, smelly subway during rush hour. I lived in the Bronx at that time so I took the D Train up to Yankee

Stadium where I needed to change to the Jerome Avenue Line. There's a passageway leading from the D train upstairs to the elevated Jerome Avenue Line."

"I know it well," Jack injected not explaining that he was familiar with all of the subway lines in the city. In his line of work getting somewhere quickly was often the difference between a good story and a lead gone cold. Jack knew more ways to travel underground than, most likely, any transit official in the city.

Ryoya continued, "Because of the hour there wasn't anyone else around. I probably was careless but a man surprised me in a secluded part of the passageway. He stepped out in front of me holding a knife. 'Give me your purse, lady,' was all he said as he grabbed the strap. I didn't fight and let him have my purse. When it happened, to my surprise, I was completely calm. I considered every move. What to do to keep it from getting more dangerous and which way I would move if he slashed at me with that knife. I memorized his face, including a small scar on his left cheek. He was 5 foot 10 inches tall with longish brown hair that was not combed. He wore a grey tee shirt with the letters TTL on it. His blue jeans were dirty and he wore an old pair of Keds. I also noticed that there appeared to be blue paint on his left forearm. Once he had my purse he turned and ran off."

"When I gave my report to the police they were very nice. They told me that unfortunately they rarely catch muggers unless they see them in the act. A Sergeant Hawk told me that my description was amazing considering the situation. He said jokingly, 'You should be a cop.' They offered to give me a ride home but I declined and borrowed ten dollars from the Sergeant."

Ryoya leaned slightly forward as she stated, "I was driven to do more than just give a report and forget about it. I wanted to catch that thief. Without thinking, I found myself going in the direction the mugger had gone. I don't know—maybe I was tracking him. As I did I looked everywhere that he might have thrown my purse. It just seemed logical that no man would want to be seen running along carrying a woman's purse. Believe it or not, I found it behind a garbage can. Everything but my wallet was still in it. Even my keys were there. This told me that he was looking for quick cash. He definitely wasn't a professional thief or else he would have been on his way to my apartment with keys in hand."

"I exited the subway and found myself on a busy street corner not knowing what to do or where to go. There I stood in front of a bank—I don't remember which. Across the street was a small grocery store. On my right across the street were other stores but I don't recall what they were. Diagonally, across the street was a small park. In the fading daylight, I could see benches and a lot of bushes and a fountain in the middle."

"Adrenalin is an interesting thing—it energizes and drives you to action—however it doesn't offer a clue as to what action to take. So, I stood looking at that park. Then it hit me. I knew he wasn't a common thief getting rent money or he would have taken my watch, bracelet, and ring in addition to using my keys. Therefore—and this was a big assumption—he was looking for a quick score so he could buy some wine or drugs. If he was looking for drugs he'd be headed to his supplier and I'd be out of luck. Wine he could get in that little grocery store. It had been twenty minutes, so if he bought wine he probably went somewhere to drink it. The park seemed like a logical place to look. It wasn't a big park, but there were plenty of secluded areas and bush-obscured hideaways. I walked slowly along a path looking in every direction. Nothing. Dusk was making it increasingly difficult to see and also increasingly dangerous."

"How do you like the wine? It's real nice, isn't it? I'll have your meals in a moment." The waiter asked and was gone before they could answer.

"I'd like to add to that man's tip," Ryoya offered with a warm smile as she took Jack's hand.

As he held her hand Jack expressed his thoughts, "I spend countless hours looking for stories about people with whom we share our city and our lives. In some ways, I've become numb to the evil that people are capable of doing. It doesn't seem to be that hard to find. Then, once in a while, I unexpectedly discover a truly good remarkable individual who reflects the best of humanity and it makes me feel sad."

"Sad? Why?"

"Sad because they seem so rare, so wonderful, and so precious that I want to keep them as a part of my world, but I know that can't be," he paused and looked down at the table, "In truth, I'm not worthy of being a part of their world. I would pollute it."

"What an awful thing to say," Ryoya remarked.

Jack looked up, "Oh, I didn't mean that the way it sounded. I just feel that in many ways I've seen the seedy side of life and my influence might inadvertently cause a truly kind and innocent person to lose faith in people."

"Then you think the same about a police detective, I assume?"

Jack quickly changed the subject, "You were telling me about how you joined the department."

Ryoya recognized the diversion but let it pass, "Yes. I was just about to give up when I spotted a leg under a bush. Slowly, I crept up on the lying figure. When I got closer I recognized my assailant. He lay before me next to an empty wine bottle. He must have downed the whole thing in three gulps. He was asleep or passed out. At first I stood there trying to decide my next move. In my quest to find the culprit I hadn't given much thought as to what I would do if I was successful. He didn't move but I could hear him breathing. I noticed a little pile of things next to his left hand; a cork screw, ring with numerous keys, some change, a few dollars, a couple of business cards, a knife, a billfold, and my wallet. Carefully and quietly, I picked up the knife, the billfold, and my wallet. After I slipped away I went to a phone booth and called the number Sergeant Hawk had given me. He wasn't there so I left a message that they radioed to him. When he pulled up I was standing across the street from the park. It was funny what he said. He climbed out of the patrol car and said, 'Detective Akimoto I hear you caught your man.' We went into the park and I pointed out the perpetrator, he was roused from his sleep, handcuffed, and taken away."

"A week later, Sergeant Hawk called and asked me to stop by the precinct. I thought it had to do with the mugging, but when I arrived he introduced me to his captain and told the story of how I tracked down and nabbed a mugger. It was an interesting meeting. The captain asked why I did what I did. I told him I wasn't sure, only I wasn't going to let some cheap thug take my property and just walk away. He asked if I was scared. The truth was that I wasn't. I didn't fight a man with a knife, however was ready to do something if he tried to stab me. He then wanted to know how I tracked the man down. I told him my tale and he began laughing. He looked at Sergeant Hawk, as did I, because I didn't know what was funny. Finally, he said to Sergeant Hawk, 'You're right, she is a pistol, good head on her shoulders, and guts.' The two men then spent the next hour convincing me to enter the police academy. And, here I am, today, Detective Akimoto."

Jack picked up his wine glass and toasted, "Here's to Detective Akimoto a beautiful and remarkable woman."

Carl sipped his beer and waited. It wasn't long before two young punks entered the bar and made a beeline to where he sat. They both sat on stools to his right. Whether they realized it or not he had positioned himself on the last stool to ensure that they couldn't sit on either side of him. He had learned an important lesson a long time ago through a bad experience in a bar in New Jersey when he thought he was meeting two possible cohorts for a robbery. He ended up on the floor bleeding from the bottle that the creep who sat on one side hit him with while he was looking at the other. One day he figured the score would be settled. There was little chance that one of these wannabees would pull anything on this particular night. They looked up to Carl and made every effort to gain his trust.

Moe, whose given name was Morris, said in a whisper, "There's a guy on the docks who said he could point out to us high value cargo for a piece of the action."

"Oh, how big a piece?" Carl inquired.

"He said he'd leave it up to us," Moe offered, "However, he did say if he wasn't satisfied he wouldn't give us any more info."

"You think this is a good deal?"

"It could be, if his information is good."

Carl looked at the other young man who sat behind Moe, "What do you think?"

Sylvester, whose voice was higher than he liked, tried to sound as tough as he could as he offered his opinion, "If we get good leads and make a big score it could be a good thing. Maybe it's worth the risk."

Carl slapped Moe across the face practically knocking him off the stool. "You asshole! Who owns the docks?"

The stunned punk didn't answer.

"I'll tell you who owns the docks—Carmine Spacini. The quickest way to find yourself in the mud under the docks is to mess with him."

Moe wiped his cheek, "Jeeze Carl I didn't . . . "

"Right, you didn't think." After a pause he asked, "You know Miguel Juarez?"

Moe answered, "I know him—bad ass dude."

"Keep your ears open. I don't trust him. He may be planning something and I want to know about it before anything happens."

"Count on me."

Carl pulled out a pack of Winstons and offered one to Moe. When Sylvester reached for a cigarette Carl lifted the pack to his own mouth and pulled out one with his lips. He put the pack away.

"What have you done for me lately?" he inquired of the surprised punk. A flame offered by Moe lit Carl's cigarette. These actions established the pecking order where Sylvester found himself the odd man out.

The waiter from heaven, not a region in France, returned to the table where Jack and Ryoya were finishing their meals.

"Did ya'll leave a wee bit of space for desert, coffee, or digestif, uh, after-dinner drink?"

Ryoya was the first to speak, "You've been so nice and hospitable all evening, please tell me your name."

"Now miss, I think your gentleman might object to me becoming too familiar with his lady," a warm friendly, ya gotta like this guy, grin flowed across his face.

"I object!" Jack feigned sounding much like a lawyer in a courtroom.

"You see."

"Over-ruled," Ryoya declared.

For a brief moment three relative strangers gazed at each other and felt that indescribable pleasure one experiences with honest human interaction. There existed a fleeting bond among them couched in trust and contentment.

The unnamed waiter broke the silence, "OK, for desert we have a wide variety of decadent choices. Would you like . . ."

"No answers until you reveal your name," Ryoya interrupted with a petulant smile.

"Ah, now, don't be that way," he said soothingly, "My job is to make your experience pleasant, fulfilling, and memorable. When you leave, you should savor the flavors you tasted, feel sated and relaxed, perhaps experience the delight of a well-fed burp, and want to return to Le Cav du Henri Quatro." He waved his arm to encompass the splendor of the dining room. "The waiter is inconsequential. He is but a fixture in the dining room designed to make your visit pleasant."

"Remember, we are in a French restaurant," Jack interjected with deadpan accuracy.

After a pause and knowing glance, the waiter continued, "I'm simply here to make sure you get what you need."

"I need your name," Ryoya pressed on.

"You need desert. In fact, the word dessert comes from the Old French 'desservir' which means 'to clear the table.' One of our most enjoyed desserts is 'Gateau au Noix' or nut tart."

"Who are you calling a nut tart?" Jack exclaimed.

"Oh, now you know I wouldn't do a thing like that. It's made with walnuts, is very rich and tasty. It's a traditional recipe of the people who live in the Aquitaine region in the southwest corner of France."

"Why won't you tell me your name?" Ryoya inquired.

"For you, my lady, I recommend Pompe aux Pommes du Perigord. It is actually apples and almonds in a flaky pastry." He quickly turned toward Jack and added, "No sir, you are neither flaky nor pasty."

"OK, you win," Ryoya relented, "I'll try the pomp poms."

"Clafouti is a famous traditional dessert also from the Southwest of France made with wild cherries. It's a cross between a pancake and custard. More like a runny pancake with cherries. Go with the tart." When both diners stared accusingly at him he quickly stated, "I have to help another table," and he rushed off.

After the laughter subsided, Ryoya announced, "I'll be right back," and she left the table.

Olivia Samantha Everett lay on a mattress on the floor in the corner of a dirty, smelly nondescript room that was empty. The single window across the room was covered with cardboard. Outside she heard dogs barking which brought her home.

That terrible place with clean sheets, good food, television, security, and strict parents from whom she tried to escape had become her dream and prayer. A chain around her ankle attached to a massive eyebolt screwed into the floor kept her from moving more than four feet in any direction. Within reach was a bottle of water and a dented, rusty metal pail she used as a toilet. Her clothing consisted of a stained pair of jeans and filthy T-shirt. She wore no underwear. Her blond hair was disheveled and stuck to her head from sweat and filth. Body odor from days without soap and water offended her senses. The horror of the past four days drained her of tears and left her contemplating suicide. Yet something deep inside kept her from seriously considering such an escape.

A sound in the hall made her start. Was it the devil once again coming to torture her? She lay still as she listened. It was inevitable that he would return. Fear added more sweat to her rancid body. With no place to run she was forced to wait for the next visit.

Juan had broken her on day three and she now complied with all of his orders. In fact, she found that on those rare occasions when he said something in a kind tone that strangely she was grateful. Hate on a scale she had never known before in her life boiled within but was kept at bay by fear and conditioning. He would come to continue her training until she was ready to be put out on the streets to earn him money.

A runaway lost in the soulless world of exploitation and slavery pulled once on the chain but was too weak to make a serious effort. Pain of the most intimate kind gnawed at her and hunger made her lightheaded. She closed her eyes to return to the nightmares that mirrored her conscious world.

When Ryoya returned to the table Jack stood and greeted her. She smiled and sat just as their waiter returned with their desserts. After he placed them in front of each guest, Ryoya looked him in the eye and said, "Thank you, Colt."

The surprised waiter froze. Then as a warm and endearing smile blossomed upon his face he stated, "Someone in this establishment has loose lips."

"Don't blame them." She implored, "I can be very persuasive."

"Well, now you've gone and removed all of the mystery from the evening."

"Don't be angry, I have an insatiable curiosity."

"Oh, no, I'm not angry. I don't know why knowing my name was so important, but now that you do it isn't anything to be angry about. Please, enjoy your deserts." He turned and walked toward another table.

"Now see, you upset the man," Jack chided in jest.

Ryoya stated, "His name is Colt MacIntyre and he's been working here for three months."

"Is that all?" Jack tasted the walnut tart that he had ordered, "Given all his knowledge of French food one would conclude that he has been doing this for a long time. This is very good."

"He isn't what he seems to be," Ryoya stated with conviction. "The manner in which he carries himself reflects a sophisticated upbringing. And, his demonstrated ability to learn quickly shows intelligence. Obviously, he'all didn't grow up in New York." She smiled as she took a forkful of the Pompe aux Pommes du Perigord. "Mmmm, Colt was right. This is delicious. An air of confidence and dignity betrays his 'I'm just a country boy act.' And, his grooming is impeccable."

"Not like the guy who showed up at your door earlier this evening," Jack said trying not to show a hint of jealousy.

He failed as the police detective picked up immediately on the slightly hurt tone of his voice. "Don't get me wrong. I wasn't comparing you or making a judgment. I just can't leave a puzzle unsolved." She leaned forward and continued, "I'm having a lovely evening and enjoy your company very much." Her innocent glance and slight tilt of her head melted Jack's heart. Ryoya explained, "There are some side effects to being a police detective. You're always looking for the incongruous, questionable, or potentially dangerous. We develop an ability to notice things that others overlook. Anything, no matter how insignificant, that we can't readily explain we are compelled to analyze and then seek answers."

"You sound like a newspaper reporter."

"Yes," she smiled, "In many ways we are alike."

"So, how is dessert?" Colt asked as he approached, "Is it everything that I suggested it would be?"

"You steered us in the right direction, my friend" Jack offered.

"Delicious; a perfect ending to an outstanding meal and exceptional service." Ryoya smiled.

"Why thanks, it was my honor to serve y'all and my pleasure to have succeeded in making your visit to Le Cav du Henri Quatro satisfying."

On a whim, Jack commented, "My name is Jack Moore. I have a column in the *Tribune*. I'd like to interview you for a story."

"Why, I'm truly complimented but I must decline."

"Let me assure you, I'm not an ambush reporter. My intent is to show New Yorkers the people with whom we share our city. There are good, bad, pitiful, odd, admirable, funny, unique, and a thousand other types of individuals in our town. I believe the more we know about them the better we understand each other and this wonderful place we call New York."

"There really isn't any story here," the waiter seemed to be trying to put a quick end to the issue, "I'm just a waiter trying to make a living."

"A friendly and polite waiter in a French restaurant. That doesn't strike you as news?" Jack inquired.

Colt picked up some empty plates from the table. He smiled and nodded as he turned to leave. Jack decided not to press the point. They had enjoyed a wonderful evening, delicious meal, and good conversation. What could be better? He decided that Colt deserved the respect of privacy, if that was what he wanted, at least for now.

Wanda Six Trees sat on the steps of their cabin with her nine-year-old son Robert. He was confused because in the school history book the tribe in Northern Minnesota was called Chippewa, yet they were on that reservation and were Ojibwe. His mother explained that they were the same. It was a matter of language and pronunciation. Chippewa was the American spelling. Put an "O" in front and pronounce it with a different accent and it is Ojibwe.

12: Saturday - May 31, 1969

Fillmore East was a small performance space that seated 2,700. Located on Second Avenue near East 6th Street it began as a Yiddish theater in 1926, eventually became a movie theater, then fell into disrepair, and finally was reopened by promoter Bill Graham as a rock concert performance space on March 8, 1968. From the street, Fillmore East appeared to be quite small, however, it was spacious inside. This unique venue quickly became known as the Church of Rock and Roll. Several nights a week concerts were performed at 8:00 p.m. and 11:00 p.m. by many well known bands. On this evening, the British blues oriented band Led Zeppelin was scheduled to perform.

In the loft apartment over a Pontiac dealership Ritchie and Stephanie prepared to attend the 8:00 p.m. concert at Fillmore East. He combed his long, below the shoulder, brown hair as he waited for Stephanie to get out of the bathroom. Based on history he knew it would be a long wait. Fetch his dog, a black Basenji, lay in her chair. She knew he was going out and didn't like it. Her displeasure would be demonstrated while Ritchie was away.

Stephanie hated the bathroom in Ritchie's apartment. It was odiferous, cramped, and uncomfortable. Those were its strong points. There was a much bigger problem. Ritchie had turned this innocuous little room into a true work of art. Painted on all four walls was a mural of the outdoors. The ceiling resembled an afternoon sky with indirect lighting adding to the illusion. The sink had been transformed into a birdbath, complete with two birds perched on one side of the rim. On the right wall was depicted a park with gently rolling greens, trees, a few distant boulders, path, and park bench. Upon that bench sat an old couple. Both were looking in the direction of where a visitor to this unique room would be seated. The man, in fact, was pointing to that spot, therefore, directly at Stephanie.

As disconcerting as the old couple viewing your every move could be, it was minor compared with the wall behind the toilet. On it was a road in the distance on which was a bus filled with people all looking out the window at whatever poor soul had become the center of attention. There were times when male guests who attempted to relieve themselves experienced some difficulty doing so while standing and facing that bus full of onlookers. Finally, on the left wall was the final insult. On it appeared a line of people apparently waiting for their turn. By the looks on their faces they were non-too-patient as they stared woefully at the occupant of the throne. Lighting was also a marvel. Ritchie had placed diffusers in such a manner that it was nearly impossible to tell where the light source was located. A faux grass floor completed the image.

All in all, this was not a room where one felt at ease or for that matter alone. So, there Stephanie sat in the middle of a busy park not because she wanted to, but more so because she had no alternative. Without question, whoever visited "the park" was left with both an enduring image, and an enhanced awareness of their own individual modesty.

Stephanie used "the park" only on rare and unavoidable occasions when she was desperate. She often tried to find a way to turn the lights off, preferring darkness. However, she never figured out how. What Ritchie failed to explain was that it was a simple automobile door switch. When the door was closed the lights came on, when open they turned off. So, a visitor had a choice sit in the middle of a busy park in the afternoon sunshine or with the door to the bathroom left open.

She pulled up her pantyhose and marveled at how much easier and comfortable they were than stockings and a girdle or garter belt. Pantyhose had been introduced a few years earlier and caught on quickly with over 600 million pair manufactured in 1969, up from 200 million pair the previous year.

As Stephanie touched up her makeup she remembered a conversation that she had with her father earlier that day. He seemed lost in thought as he sat at their little kitchen table playing with some coins.

"What are you doing?" she had asked.

"These coins—they're counterfeit," her father explained. He held up a quarter and added, "It's made of something, but not silver. Look at it." The offending coin was dropped on the table making a dull thud sound rather than the melodic ping common with silver coins.

In 1964, a rapid rise in the cost of silver caused many to horde dimes, quarters, and the new Kennedy half dollar. The result was a growing shortage of these coins. In addition, minting operations were depleting the treasury's stock of silver. H.R. 8746 The Coinage Act of 1965, signed by President Lyndon Johnson, created copper-nickel clad dimes and quarters and reduced the silver content of half dollars from 90% silver to 40%. Quarters and dimes went from a mix of 90% silver/10% copper to 92% copper/8% nickel. Between 1965 and 1967 these new quarters were struck without a mint mark.

Stephanie told her father of the change that had taken place with coins. She finished saying, "They may not sound the same but a quarter will still get you on the subway—at least for now—they're planning to raise the fare to 35 cents."

"I used to hop the subway and ride up to the Polo Grounds to watch the Giants for 15 cents," Matt had answered, then added, "Now that new team, the Mets, play there."

"Actually, the Mets play in Shea Stadium on Long Island," Stephanie corrected.

Stephanie touched up her lipstick and thought of that conversation and how much the world changed during the six years her father "slept." He was an alien discovering new things every day. In many ways, their roles had reversed. He was the child and she the guardian. Abruptly her mind reached back to a memory of her mother. It was a spring evening three years after the accident. The windows of their apartment were open to let a cool breeze flow through. Her mother sat at their kitchen table with a stack of bills. Slowly she sorted them into piles of current, past due, and gone to collections. Stephanie was then fifteen years old and in high school. As she did her homework she looked over at her mother. Still dignified and proper her mother had aged. Her face had a shadow of sadness, lines from worry, and pallor of someone who had not spent adequate time in the sun.

The telephone rang causing Valerie to jump. Her mother answered it. Stephanie watched as her mother listened for a long time. The look on her face made it clear that this was neither a welcome nor pleasant phone call. Finally, her mother said, "I can't make arrangements to pay. There simply isn't any money." She paused and listened once more. "Our insurance . . ." she waited. "I know what my responsibility is . . ." Stephanie became annoyed as she watched her mother suffer. "There is nothing I can do." A tear ran down her mother's cheek which she quickly wiped away. "I told you

I know what my responsibility is. It is to my child! You will just have to wait." Her breathing became shallow and faster. "This is not going . . ." "I'm doing all . . ." "We can only . . ." "Don't threaten me!" She hung up.

Like clockwork calls came every evening at dinner time. On each occasion her mother would begin calmly, attempt to explain, and finally hang up with her hands shaking from anger. They finally took the telephone off the hook at dinner time only to be serenaded by a shrill off-the-hook indicator sound. Valerie then began unplugging the telephone at dinner time but worried she would forget to plug it back in and miss a call from the hospital if there was a change in Matt's condition.

The venomous callers changed their tactics. Calls began arriving early in the morning, late at night, and on weekends. It got to a point where her mother would answer and as soon as she knew it was a collections agent she would hang up and unplug the phone. This, of course, only caused them to call at different times and to use tricks like offering to set up a credit account where she would only pay the interest.

Stephanie didn't realize it at the time but not only was her mother unable to pay mounting doctor and hospital bills but was also falling behind on other bills, as well. It was later that she learned that after his vacation time, sick time, and long term disability ran out her father had been terminated from Orztech Corporation. They offered paperwork whereby Valerie could pay for Matt's health insurance. She did for as long as possible but eventually let it lapse.

"Steph, we gotta go," Ritchie's voice echoed in The Park.

That warm Saturday night Led Zeppelin shook the foundation of the Fillmore East. An enthusiastic audience set the stage for an exciting evening. The band took the stage and glided into a towering rendition of *Train Kept A Rollin'*. Jimmy Page on guitar and Robert Plant, singer, jousted on stage as they stepped onto each other's phrases in a manner that made for an over-the-top performance. Then came *I Can't Quit You Baby, Dazed and Confused, Black Summer, White Summer, Black Mountainside,* and more. After two hours, the audience was so energized and aroused the applause was, in fact, a demand for more. Led Zeppelin responded with a dynamic version of *Communications Breakdown*.

Stephanie and Ritchie left the Fillmore hand in hand and headed to the Port Authority Bus Terminal where his van was parked.

Ten o'clock on Saturday night is always a busy time for New York City detectives. Assaults, robberies, domestic violence, drug overdoses, rapes, break-ins, solicitation, and murder all rise in occurrence at that hour. Ryoya Akimoto and her partner, Michael Donovan, were on their way to the scene of an assault. It occurred on 59th Street along the edge of Central Park. They left the house, their precinct headquarters at 306 West 54th Street, and headed uptown. Donovan drove as usual. As the senior officer, it was his prerogative which he exercised because as he put it, "Asian women are damn dangerous behind the wheel."

"It appears two thugs came out of the park and jumped this guy," Ryoya read the report they had been given when they left. "He fought back but got beaten up pretty good. Lost his wallet. Ambulance is on the way."

"If they take him before we get there we'll check out the scene and then visit him in the hospital," Donovan stated and then asked, "Any description of the skells?"

"No."

They turned onto 59th Street and saw red flashing lights up ahead. Both detectives became silent. It was indicative of a switching from relaxed to investigative mindset that was common, yet never realized by police officers.

The victim was still at the scene resting on an ambulance gurney. Ryoya reached him first and stated, "Sir, my name is Detective Akimoto may I ask you a few questions?"

He nodded and said, "I already gave all of my information to the police officer."

"I'll get that information from him so as to not keep you any longer than necessary. I just need a few answers to start the investigation. Can you tell us anything about your assailants?"

"One was Puerto Rican, the other was smaller and had a high voice."

"Do you remember what they were wearing?"

"No," he paused, "Wait, the Puerto Rican had on a black tee shirt. That's all I remember."

"Where were you coming from when you were attacked?"

"I had stopped in a small pub on 58th Street for a few drinks before returning to my hotel. I don't remember the name but it was lit mainly with red colored lights on the tables. There was a pool table on one side and a bar on the other."

"When you left the bar did you notice anyone else leaving the bar?"

"No, not really. Those two creeps came out of nowhere."

The paramedic indicated that they needed to leave. Ryoya joined her partner who was examining the crime scene. Together they looked for any clue that would help them identify the perpetrators. They both also knew that a run-of-the-mill mugging rarely got solved without witnesses or a lucky police officer happening on the scene at the moment of the assault. The only lead they had was a bar on 58th Street.

Michael Donovan and Ryoya Akimoto left their car on 59th Street and walked one block down Avenue of the Americas to 58th Street. As they walked they looked for anything unusual. Mike asked casually, "So, this newspaper reporter, what do think?"

"Give it a rest, Mike, you've been asking me all week."

"Hey, I'm your partner, I want to know what's going on."

"He was very nice. We had a pleasant evening. He called and asked me out tonight but I'm on duty."

"Yeah. Yeah. But did he get your blood boiling?"

"None of your business."

"Yeah it is, I got to look out for you. If your head's in the clouds it might not be on the job. That could get me killed."

"No, keeping on asking about my date could get you killed. This looks like the place." They stopped in front of a bar named Red's Rendezvous.

Detectives Akimoto and Donovan entered the proverbial hole-in-the-wall. Inside they confirmed that it was the place the victim had visited. There were small tables on which sat small lamps with red lampshades. A bar with six barstools was located on the right. Only one stool was occupied by a scruffy looking male, about 40 years old, wearing a denim shirt and dungarees. He turned to face the door to see who had entered. For a brief moment, he observed the two new guests then went back to his beer. Three young men were shooting pool on the table covered with red cloth. They appeared to be blue collar workers out on a Saturday night. Two couples shared a table in a corner. There didn't appear to be any other patrons. Detective Michael Donovan walked up to the bar and asked the bartender if he remembered serving a middle-aged man, sandy hair, wearing a dark blue suit. The bartender gazed at the detective as if he were hard of hearing. Then he shook his head in the negative. Donovan asked if any customers had left the bar in the past half hour. This time the pain-in-the-glass booze tender shrugged. With little help from the proprietor Donovan turned to the patron on the bar stool and asked if he had seen a middle-aged man, sandy hair, wearing a dark blue suit.

"I mind my own business," was the response.

"How long have you been here?" Detective Donovan inquired.

The unhelpful patron picked up a half empty glass and replied, "I just got here."

Across the room, Detective Ryoya Akimoto questioned the two couples in the corner. From them she learned that a middle-aged man, with sandy hair, wearing a dark blue suit had been there. He sat at a small table alone and drank a mixed drink. They didn't pay much attention to him. He may have been there 45 minutes to an hour. One young woman noticed when he left because he bumped the table and caught the small lamp that was about to fall over. She said the three pool players had been there the entire time that the two couples were there. They also remembered two men sitting next to the one still at the bar but they didn't know when they left.

Detective Donovan questioned the men playing pool. The tallest of the three told him people came and went but that unless they were of the female persuasion they didn't pay much attention.

"Yeah, and there haven't been any of those for hours," a heavyset player who just missed a shot that Detective Donovan knew he could make complained.

The third player added, "This joint is dead. With the little red lights and fancy tables, we thought it would be crawling with chicks."

"What'd this guy that you're lookin for do?" heavyset inquired.

"Got himself beat up."

"There was no fight here," the tall pool player stated.

"If there was we would've been a part of it," the third player smiled and bragged as he turned his cue around to show how he would use it as a club.

"You couldn't beat a drum," the heavier man quipped.

"I can beat you at pool!"

"Yeah, like you been doin all night?"

"I was just warming up. Now, let's put some money on the table," after his remark he glanced at Mike Donovan with a guilty, I shouldn't-have-said-that, look and shrugged.

Detectives Akimoto and Donovan left Red's Rendezvous. They informed the bartender that he would be cited for obstruction and probably would lose his liquor license. At that point, he became very cooperative but didn't know the names of the two men who left the bar directly after a middle-aged man, with sandy hair, and wearing a dark blue suit. One was Hispanic the other a young punk with a high voice. He didn't know anything else.

As they walked back to their car Michael Dovovan suddenly stopped and turned to face Ryoya Akimoto, "Ra, you know I'm just bustin your chops about this newspaper guy. Your happiness is important to me. If he treats you right and you like him I'm all for it. We're partners so we look out for one another." He looked deep into her eyes and added, "I'm just glad someone as ugly as you could get a date."

Ryoya punched Donovan in the stomach.

Olivia Samantha Everett sat on a bed in a seedy hotel room on West 44th Street. She had been given a good meal and been allowed to take a shower. Her hair was now clean and brushed and she wore clean underwear, a tank top, mini skirt, and four-inch high heels. On this night, Rita was her keeper. She would bring the johns, collect the money, and make sure Olivia provided the services. It had been made clear to Rita that she would not see the sunrise if the little flower escaped. Rita explained to Olivia what was expected and what consequences awaited if they didn't do exactly as they were told. The older hooker felt sorry for her young charge because she knew the life that lay ahead. Yet, while she felt sympathy she also was keenly aware that her own life and that of her child depended on her. For this reason, there would be no failure to follow Miguel's instructions to the letter.

Olivia was so emotionally defeated and scarred at this point she couldn't think clearly. Miguel had done his job well. His new young whore had no self-respect or self-identity. She no longer was a human being. Instead she was a mindless entity that learned that her compliance brought kind words, food, and some semblance of peace. Disobedience brought pain, degradation, and fear of the most primal nature. There was no question of what Miguel was capable of doing when angered. She endured numerous horrific punishments. Even more frightening was his threat to kill her parents if she ever tried to leave. On her knees, she swore complete allegiance and obedience to Miguel Juarez. A free Coca Cola one short week ago had a life-alteringly dear price.

Robert Six Trees stood in the woods overlooking a lake. In his hand were three red feathers. They were a treasured gift from one of the tribal elders.

13: Saturday - June 7, 1969

United States Marine Corps Values have been handed down from generation to generation. To join the brotherhood of Marines it is essential to understand and draw upon this legacy of the Corps. It defines a Marine and gives them a sense of something bigger than each individual. Three simple values are a bond that has linked millions of warriors past and present.

> **Honor:** Honor guides Marines to exemplify the ultimate in ethical and moral behavior; to never lie, cheat or steal; to abide by an uncompromising code of integrity; respect human dignity; and respect others. The quality of maturity, dedication, trust and dependability commit Marines to act responsibly; to be accountable for their actions; to fulfill their obligations; and to hold others accountable for their actions.

> **Courage:** Courage is the mental, moral and physical strength ingrained in Marines. It carries them through the challenges of combat and helps them overcome fear. It is the inner strength that enables a Marine to do what is right; to adhere to a higher standard of personal conduct; and to make tough decisions under stress and pressure.

> **Commitment:** Commitment is the spirit of determination and dedication found in US Marines. It leads to the highest order of discipline for individuals and units. It is the ingredient that enables 24-hour a day dedication to Corps and country. It inspires the unrelenting determination to achieve a standard of excellence in every endeavor.

Most civilians are unaware that Marine recruits are required to memorize a great deal of information. In addition to United States Marine Corps Values, Wellington Marsh knew the Code of Conduct, 11 General Orders for a Sentry, the first part of the Marine Hymn, and Marine Rifle Creed. On this Saturday evening, he was on guard duty. As he walked along a fence he kept going over the General Orders of a Sentry lest he foul up and get quarterdecked.

> 1. Take charge of this post and all government property in view.
> 2. Walk my post in a military manner, keeping always on the alert and observing everything that takes place within sight or hearing.
> 3. Report all violations of orders I am instructed to enforce.
> 4. To repeat all calls [from posts] more distant from the guardhouse than my own.
> 5. Quit my post only when properly relieved.

6. To receive, obey, and pass on to the sentry who relieves me, all orders from the Commanding Officer, Officer of the Day, Officers, and Non-Commissioned Officers of the guard only.

7. Talk to no one except in the line of duty.

8. Give the alarm in case of fire or disorder.

9. To call the Corporal of the Guard in any case not covered by instructions.

10. Salute all officers and all colors and standards not cased.

11. Be especially watchful at night and during the time for challenging, to challenge all persons on or near my post, and to allow no one to pass without proper authority.

Half a world away another Marine, Private First Class Dan Bullock, was on guard duty at An Hoa Combat Base in Quang Nam Province. The last thing he thought about were the 11 General Orders for a Sentry. This was his first experience as a sentry at a combat base. He was scared and unprepared for the role he was playing. With no other option, he walked his post at the northern end of the base's airstrip and strained his eyes to see any movement or indication of an enemy he knew was out there. At that moment, he felt very small.

Dan Bullock arrived in Vietnam a month earlier on May 8, 1969 and was assigned as a rifleman in 2nd Squad, 2nd Platoon, Fox Company, 2nd Battalion, 5th Marines, 1st Marine Division. He spent the first few weeks working in a support capacity. During this time, he watched seasoned Marines leave on missions and return tired and spent or in body bags.

Earlier that day he had been assigned to cleaning duties but after light-hearted sparring with fellow Marine Steve Piscitelli, who accidently broke his thumb, Pfc Dan Bullock was reassigned to front-line duty in the injured man's place. He joined other Marines who were choppered out to An Hoa Combat Base and ultimately ended up staring into a dreadful darkness.

The wilderness was alive with sounds emanating from every imaginable animal, bird, and insect. Mosquitoes fed freely on every exposed portion of his body. There was a humid breeze that was heavy with so much water it made it hard to inhale deeply. The breeze also carried foul odors. Sweat burned his eyes and he found he was incredibly thirsty. He wanted to run, but to where?

All Dan Bullock's senses failed him. Relentless sounds from the jungle made it impossible to hear any movement. Endless black shrouded any visual signs of an enemy. He couldn't smell or taste an approaching threat and he didn't, by God, want to feel it.

Wellington Marsh was relieved from his post at 0200 hours (2:00 a.m.). He followed proper procedures to be relieved and climbed into a jeep to be returned to the barracks. When he finally lay on his rack he found it hard to get to sleep. In the quiet darkness his thoughts traveled to Vietnam. What would it be like? What would he face? What was happening at that moment in that far away war ravaged country? His mind was filled with haunting, yet unrealistic, images of soldiers fighting.

At 0200 hours, the darkness Dan Bullock watched intently went ominously silent. Immediately, rockets and mortars rattled the base. Sentries cried out and the base came to life. For a brief thirty second interval the only defense of An Hoa Combat Base were the sentries. Each man desperately searched for an indication of where the attack was coming from and from where an assault might be initiated. Dan heard gun fire he recognized as coming from M-16s. He didn't see any target to shoot at but held his position. Suddenly, flood lights from the base washed the area and probed the surrounding terrain. The young Marine was then joined by twenty half-dressed fully armed Marines. Tangle wire with cans attached alerted them to the left. Out of the jungle spilled a regular North Vietnamese Army unit carrying wooden ladders that they flung onto the wire to allow those who followed to cross. A fire fight began.

Dan Bullock and his fellow Marines opened fire. A rocket hit one of the floodlights leaving Dan's group of defenders without a clear view of the attackers. Small arms fire came at them from in front and from the right side. Over the loud report of various M-16s and AK47s he heard the cry of a Marine who had been hit. Then another. Flares were fired into the air and the battleground was once more illuminated. Dan was shocked at how close the North Vietnamese were and the large number that kept running toward them. He pressed the release on his M-16 to drop an empty magazine and slid another in locking it in place. He fired again and again. The small group of defenders were joined by more Marines some of whom fired M60 7.62mm caliber machine guns. This effectively stopped the main attack. Skirmishes erupted in different sections of the base and the Marines were directed by now fully involved officers to provide support.

Wellington knew they would begin field training in the upcoming week. As part of that training they would face a ten-mile march with full field packs. Even though he knew it would be tough and test his improved physically conditioned body it was still a better alternative to what lay ahead after boot camp. He remained awake for another hour.

After an hour, the attack on An Hoa Combat Base in Quang Nam Province was over. Thirty-one Marines had been wounded with nineteen needing to be evacuated. Marine Pfc. Dan Bullock had been killed instantly from small arms fire. Four other Marines died that night LCpl Larry J. Eglinsdoerfer, Pfc Donald W. Bunn, Pfc Jason D. Hunnicutt, and Pfc Steven H. Montgomery.

Dan Bullock was born December 21, 1953 in Goldsboro, North Carolina. His mother died when he was eleven years old. Subsequently, he and his younger sister, Gloria, moved to Brooklyn, NY to live with their father who had remarried. Dan was never happy in Brooklyn and dreamed of becoming a Marine or police officer. He made that dream come true when he altered the date on his birth certificate to fraudulently show that he had been born December 21, 1949. On September 18, 1968 Dan Bullock enlisted in the United States Marines. At Parris Island as a member of Platoon 3039 he trained under Drill Instructor Sergeant Nathan Kincaid and coincidentally slept in the very rack that Wellington Marsh occupied. Dan Bullock graduated from boot camp December 10, 1968 and ultimately ended up being the youngest American serviceman killed during the Vietnam War. He was fifteen years old.

Years later former Marine Franklin McArthur, Jr., started the Pfc Dan Bullock Foundation to raise funds for a monument to be erected outside the Brooklyn Marine Corps recruiting station where the young man enlisted. The Marine whose place Dan took on that fateful day, Steve Piscitelli, who was a sculptor, volunteered to design the statue. Another former Marine who worked for Sally Jessy Raphael told her of the young man and the fact that he was forgotten by his nation and buried without fanfare or even a headstone. The talk-show host donated a headstone for Dan Bullock's grave. Members of the New York Rolling Thunder motorcycle club left Brooklyn for North

Carolina and were joined at the Virginia/North Carolina border by the North Carolina Rolling Thunder motorcycle club as they caravanned to Goldsboro, NC. The North Carolina National Guard provided an Honor Guard and a headstone would finally be placed at Dan Bullock's grave site in the Elmwood Cemetery, Goldsboro, North Carolina. Once a Marine, always a Marine. Semper Fi.

Matt tossed and turned as he once more experienced the dream that haunted him. When he awoke, the images remained fresh in his mind. A woman, who was definitely not his wife Valerie, remained in his mind's eye. She had long dark hair, deep green eyes, high cheek bones, olive skin reflecting Greek or Italian heritage. Her smile was pleasant but had harshness to it as though it was hiding a treacherous secret. Matt whispered in the darkness, "Lida."

On Sand Island 0600 hours brought renewed activity. It is the larger of the two islands that make up Midway in the Pacific Ocean. The other smaller island is called Eastern Island. For the past week Navy, Air Force, and Marine personnel prepared for President Nixon's meeting with South Vietnam President Nguyen Van Thieu on Sunday.

Inside an empty hanger Chief Aviation Boatswain's Mate Danny Cooper watched along with Secret Service and other security teams as Navy personnel began washing two white Lincoln Continental limousines and twenty or more other cars that had been flown in for the Presidential motorcade. It struck Chief Cooper as funny how before him were three times the total number of cars on the island. We don't even have a traffic light, he thought. The whole damn place is less than 4 square miles. The motorcade will travel barely a half mile from the runway to Captain Yesensky's quarters where the meeting would take place.

They had spent the whole week painting buildings, washing windows, and trimming shrubs along the route but only on the side that would face the motorcade.

Outside there were five recently delivered howitzers for a 21-gun salute.

With all the secret service, communications technicians, cooks and service staff, Navy intelligence, reporters, military brass, additional air-traffic control personnel, and a Marine band flown in from Hawaii the island was overrun with people and vehicles. Others who would be in attendance were Secretary of State William Rogers, Secretary of Defense Melvin Laird, the U.S. Representative at the Paris Peace talks Ambassador Henry Cabot Lodge, Ambassador to the Republic of Vietnam Ellsworth Bunker, and the Commander in Chief Pacific Admiral John S. McCain, Jr., whose son John McCain was a prisoner of war in Vietnam.

Chief Cooper leaned over to one of the Secret Service Agents and asked, "Is it always like this?"

Agent Rufus Youngblood, who was famous for having thrown himself on top of Vice President Lyndon Johnson in Dallas when President Kennedy was shot November, 1963, replied in a non-emotional, almost monotone voice, "This is a dream because we can control almost everything here on the island. The greatest concern is transportation to and from the island. Other locations don't give us such a luxury."

"You think I could get ten minutes with the President?" Chief Cooper joked.

"No." was the unemotional response.

Saturday afternoon in New York City was bright and clear and warm. Jack Moore, newspaperman, and Ryoya Akimoto, police detective, sat side by side along the first base line on the upper deck at Yankee Stadium. The flagging Yankees (25-28) were host to the just as inept Chicago White Sox (21-24). It was destined to be a battle of the basement teams. However, in the eyes of a diehard Yankee fan like Jack Moore every game was a new beginning and start of a record setting winning streak. The season was still young and things could turnaround at any time. While he didn't get to go to many games each year when an opportunity arose he would happily escape into the confines of the house that Ruth built.

Jack turned to Ryoya and said, "Do you have to wear that thing?" His eyes burned into the blue baseball cap she wore that had the orange New York Mets emblem on it.

"Yes," she replied, "I'm loyal."

"The Mets?"

"The Mets," she replied and began to sing the Mets theme song, "Meet the Mets. Meet the Mets. Step right up and greet the Mets! Bring your kiddies, bring your wife. Guaranteed to have the time of your life . . ."

"Stop! This is Yankee Stadium!"

"And I'm a Mets fan." Ryoya looked at Jack and presented a mischievous smile.

"You're too much," he smiled.

"Maybe. Maybe not."

"The Yankees are New York's team. The Mets haven't finished in better than next to last place since they invaded New York six years ago."

"At least the Mets have a winning record (26-23) this year. How are the Yankees doing?"

Jack looked at Ryoya with feigned displeasure but reality was the exact opposite. He was overjoyed that she had agreed to go to the game with him. Their work schedules had made it difficult to get together. They had lunch together once and late-night drinks on another occasion. This Saturday afternoon promised to give them a chance to spend more quality time together. Jack enjoyed being around Ryoya. She was a study in contradictions. She could be a no-nonsense detective on the job yet a softer gentler woman when she wished. Her piercing stare could make the toughest criminal confess while those same eyes had a childlike innocence to them. With verbal banter she could give it as well as take it. She was also both generous as well as demanding.

"I want a hotdog," Ryoya pouted.

"OK."

"And a big beer."

"Anything else?"

"Surprise me."

When Jack returned, he had four hotdogs with everything on them, french fries, two beers and Ryoya's surprise. He handed her a brand-new navy blue baseball cap with the famous white Yankee "NY" on it.

"What am I supposed to do with this?" she asked.

"Wear it."

"I don't know. I'd feel like such a traitor."

"You might be a traitor, but it will help us get out of here alive."

Ryoya could have stated that she had her off-duty gun and would protect him but was quite familiar with the fragile male ego. Besides there was a part of her, steeped in Japanese culture, that welcomed being taken care of by her strong protective beau. After a moment of thought she raised her chin and offered, "I'll make a deal with you," she bounced the Yankee cap on her fingertips, "I'll wear the Yankee cap if you agree to go to a Mets game with me and wear a Mets cap." A slight rising of her eyebrows punctuated the challenge.

"You know tomorrow is Mickey Mantle Day," Jack changed the subject. "Just try getting tickets for that game—a double header." He handed her a hotdog as he continued, "They're going to retire his number, seven, and Joe DiMaggio is going to give him a plaque that will be hung on the centerfield wall near the Babe Ruth, Lou Gehrig and Miller Huggins monuments." He pointed at centerfield and smiled.

"You're changing the subject. Do we have a deal or not?" Ryoya spun the Yankee cap on her finger.

Reluctantly, Jack agreed, "We have a deal. Now, take off that cap and get in the spirit of the game."

By the third inning the Yankees were ahead 4 to 0. Ryoya had supported the team with enthusiasm. She enjoyed baseball so it was easy to root for the Yankees and enjoy the game. A warm breeze blew her hair into her eyes. Her obstructed view revealed another time and place. For an unexplained reason, that warm breeze brought her back to Gila River, Arizona in July, 1942. She was twelve years old. Gila River was a relocation center run by the War Relocation Authority (WRA) where she and her family lived from July 28, 1942 to October 11, 1945.

Immediately after Pearl Harbor was bombed by Japan on December 7, 1941 public opinion was hatred of Japan while there was little animosity toward Japanese Americans. There were the expected isolated incidents aimed at Japanese but they were not widespread. However, as news spread of a Japanese national accompanied by two Hawaiian-born Japanese violently freeing a Japanese naval airman who had been captured on the island of Niihau in Hawaii, public opinion and military trust of Japanese in America deteriorated rapidly. Relentless media pressure followed the incident with countless editorials questioning Japanese loyalty.

A *Los Angeles Times* editorial reflected the hate promoted by the media that had a definitive effect on public opinion. "A viper is nonetheless a viper wherever the egg is hatched. So, a Japanese American born of Japanese parents, nurtured upon Japanese traditions, living in a transplanted Japanese atmosphere, notwithstanding his nominal brand of accidental citizenship almost inevitably and with the rarest exceptions grows up to be a Japanese and not an American. Thus, while it might cause injustice to a few to treat them all as potential enemies, I cannot escape the conclusion that such treatment should be accorded to each and all of them while we are at war with their race."

Columnist Henry McLemore also lashed out at unsuspecting and innocent Americans. "I am for the immediate removal of every Japanese on the West Coast to a point deep in the interior. I don't mean a nice part of the interior either. Herd 'em up, pack 'em off and give 'em the inside room in the badlands. Personally, I hate the Japanese. And that goes for all of them."

Public opinion and military pressure caused President Franklin D. Roosevelt to issue Executive Order 9066 on February 19, 1942 and the internment of Japanese Americans began. The order allowed the military to create exclusion zones from which "any or all persons may be excluded." As a result, the entire west coast of the United States to about 100 miles inland was off-limits to all people of Japanese ancestry. In fact, it also included Koreans and Taiwanese as both Korea and Taiwan had been conquered and were Japanese colonies.

December, 1941 Ryoya Akimoto, her father Takashi and mother Mitsuki lived in Yuba City, California. Takashi Akimoto was Chief Engineer at the Yuba City power plant. By virtue of his position it made him a primary suspect for potential sabotage. After the attack on Pearl Harbor and subsequent freeing of a Japanese prisoner in Hawaii, Takashi Akimoto was no longer allowed to work unsupervised at the power plant.

Thirteen years earlier, 1928, Takashi Akimoto and his wife had immigrated to the United States at the ages of 24 and 22 respectively. A year later, before the stock market crash, their daughter Ryoya was born. In the beginning life in America was difficult. Takashi did laborer work even though he had a degree in electrical engineering. After five years, he was hired by Pacific Gas and Electric Company to work on high tension wires that travelled twenty-two miles from the Folsom hydroelectric power plant on the American River to Sacramento, California. Eventually, his hard work, knowledge, talent, and perseverance earned him the position of Chief Engineer at the Yuba City power plant forty-two miles north of Sacramento.

The Akimoto family lived in a small cabin walking distance from the hydroelectric power plant. When Ryoya started school, she walked hand-in-hand with her mother two miles each way every day. Her father gave her a bicycle when she turned eight which she then rode to school. Life in America had improved greatly and the future looked as bright as the street lights lit with electricity that Takashi Akimoto helped provide. With the bombing of Pearl Harbor a dark shadow extinguished the light. The few Asian students in school became outcasts and singled out for ridicule and contempt. Ryoya's mother was subjected to rudeness and foul comments. She understood the reasons for such treatment and would bow and apologize trying to assuage their anger.

Lieutenant General John L. DeWitt was head of the Western Command. He was authorized by Executive Order 9066 to unilaterally decide what geographic areas were restricted and to whom. His feelings were well known as he was quoted in newspapers numerous times and told Congress, "A Jap's a Jap. I don't want any of them here. They are a dangerous element. There is no way to determine their loyalty. It makes no difference whether he is an American citizen, he is still a Japanese. American citizenship does not necessarily determine loyalty. But we must worry about the Japanese all the time until he is wiped off the map."

March 11, 1942: Executive Order 9095 created the Office of the Alien Property Custodian and gave it authority over all alien property interests. Japanese assets were frozen creating immediate financial difficulty for the Akimoto family.

May 3, 1942: General DeWitt issued Civilian Exclusion Order No. 34, ordering all people of Japanese ancestry, whether citizens or non-citizens, who were still living in "Military Area No. 1" to report to assembly centers, where they would live until being moved to permanent "Relocation Centers." The Akimoto family was given forty-eight hours to settle their affairs and pack two suitcases each. They could take no more of their personal belongings. The Office of the Alien Property Custodian would safeguard what remained. This, of course, was a goal that was never met. A truck arrived that already contained four other families. Takashi, Mitsuki, and Ryoya Akimoto climbed aboard the big Army truck to be taken to an assembly center run by the Wartime

Civilian Control Agency (WCCA). In this case, it was a migrant workers' camp in Sacramento. As the behemoth vehicle pulled away Ryoya looked back at their small cabin and the blue bicycle her father had given her leaning against the wall.

After two months in a crowded, dirty, poorly facilitated camp Takashi, Mitsuki, and Ryoya Akimoto were transported to the Relocation Center on the Gila River Indian Reservation thirty miles southeast of Phoenix, Arizona. The trip was grueling and difficult for the very young and very old. Some died enroute or shortly after arriving at Gila River. One casualty was Iva Toguri the mother of the American woman of Japanese descent who was later condemned as Tokyo Rose.

Gila River Relocation Center was actually made up of two camps, Canal and Butte. The Akimoto family was assigned to Butte Camp. They lived in a harsh desert environment with oppressive heat, water shortages, rattlesnakes, and scorpions. Barracks made of wood with fireproof shingles designed to block out the desert heat had been hastily built, each to house four single families in separate apartments. In truth, Gila River was nicer than many of the other camps spread around the Midwest but they had no way of knowing that fact. It was the only camp surrounded by fences without barbed wire and the administrators tried to make life in the camps as close to normal as possible. The relocated Japanese built a theater and playgrounds, planted trees and vegetable gardens, established a medical clinic, and built a 6,000-seat baseball field.

The baseball field was designed by Kenichi Zenimura. He and his family were on the same truck with the Akimoto family when they were transferred from the Sacramento assembly center to Gila River. At the time, Ryoya's father was thirty-eight years old and Kenichi Zenimura was forty-two. Takashi Akimoto immediately recognized the famous Japanese baseball player and manager known as "The Dean of The Diamond." On the long arduous trip the two men talked in English and Japanese for hours. Ryoya was fascinated by how animated her father became after months of looking deflated and half-dead. At one point, she heard Kenichi Zenimura say in Japanese, "Shikata ga nai." Later she asked her father what that meant. A re-energized Takashi Akimoto explained to his daughter that it meant "it cannot be helped." The baseball player who had lost so much because of the internment understood the events that led to their situation were not of their doing but that they were paying the price as a result of fear.

Kenichi Zenimura was born January 25, 1900 in Hiroshima, Japan. His family moved to Honolulu, Hawaii a few years later. He was introduced to the game of baseball at Mills High School. In 1920 he moved to Fresno, California and worked as a mechanic as well as in a restaurant. Here he founded the Fresno Nisei baseball team and eventually created a ten team Nisei league. Nisei were second generation Japanese born in the United States. He was dubbed the Dean of The Diamond because he excelled at all nine positions although he most often played shortstop. He was short of stature at five-foot-tall and to look at him he seemed rather frail at 105 pounds. Nothing was further from the truth. His muscles were exceptionally strong while not showing bulges. They also were remarkably quick in response to his highly developed reflexes.

A love of baseball drove Kenichi Zenimura throughout his life. He played in numerous leagues, managed teams, and opened international doors. In 1927, he helped arrange a playing tour to Japan for the All-Star Philadelphia Royal Giants of the Negro-league. In 1934, Zenimura made it possible for Babe Ruth to tour Japan. He was indeed an international ambassador for baseball.

When the Akimoto and Zenimura families reached the Gila River Relocation Center Kenichi and Takashi began planning a baseball field. Construction of the 6,000-seat stadium brought the community together and gave them a purpose. Eventually, a 32 team league was created. Her father and Kenichi Zenimura played on the same team. Ryoya remembered the many games at which she worked and how it helped during those dark days. Kenichi Zenimura died November 13, 1968. Ryoya and her parents flew to California for the funeral. This special man made a real and lasting difference at a time when people had lost faith and lost direction in their lives.

Those memories, though harsh, rekindled a feeling of family and community. These wonderful people who came to America, were productive, didn't ask for anything, endured mistreatment, were strong, continued their interrupted journey in life without complaint, and offered forgiveness making them a source of immense pride in being Japanese American. One might hate America for what had been done to 120,000 Japanese but they didn't. For that would condemn a nation, founded on the promise of freedom, for a single emotional overreaction that could be understood.

A tear ran down Ryoya's cheek. Quickly she wiped it away before Jack could see. She looked at him and saw a caring, intelligent, poorly dressed, funny, honest man who filled a void in her life. How ironic that the game of baseball that was a young girl's salvation was now a grown woman's possible escape from loneliness.

Shikata ga nai.

So, there it was. The track was clear and led into densely treed woodland. It was a bear—most likely a black bear. Robert Six Trees looked in the direction of travel and found another paw print made by the huge creature. On his back the young native-American boy wore a backpack. In it he carried his sketch pad and a wide array of pencils. He moved cautiously as he didn't want to scare it off before he could capture it on paper.

14: Thursday – June 12, 1969

On this day, Niagara Falls went dry. More accurately, the American Falls portion of Niagara Falls ceased to flow. It was the work of the Army Corps of Engineers. For the following five months, no water would travel the path to this portion of Niagara Falls.

Originally, the falls had been a single entity until approximately 800 years ago when Goat Island caused the river to split into two channels. For 12,000 years, the Niagara River carried 60,000 gallons of water over the falls every second. After the split occurred the main channel carried 90% of the water to the Horseshoe Falls and the remaining 10% went to the American Falls. Rock slides in 1931 and in 1954 piled up tons of scree at the base of the American Falls. Erosion added to the debris.

In 1965, a reporter for the *Niagara Falls Gazette* wrote an article predicting the imminent death of the American Falls. He warned that another rockslide could destroy the falls forever. His impassioned story got the attention of the United States Congress which quickly authorized an International Joint Commission to study the issue. Four years later a decision was made to remove some of the rock at the base of the falls and to take measures to prevent further rockslides. To achieve this goal they had to essentially turn off the American Falls.

Jack Moore arrived mid-morning to cover the event for the *New York Tribune*. He rode the train to Buffalo, New York, rented a car, and drove to Niagara Falls. Earlier in the week water flow had been reduced by opening the gates of the International Water Control Dam upriver as well as diverting more water to the hydroelectric generating stations. These actions reduced the river flow from 60,000 gallons a second to a much tamer 15,000 gallons per second. Workmen then labored for three days on a cofferdam and pushed the final three boulders into place at 10:40 a.m. It took 1,264 truckloads of fill consisting of 27,800 tons of rock and earth to stop the flow of water. And, stop it they did. By midafternoon only a trickle of water meandered its way down to the crest and over the falls to a pile of rubble below. Jack stood on the bank along with countless other reporters and a swelling crowd of tourists. It was indeed a surreal sight looking out over the riverbed that had been at the bottom of eight feet of rushing water.

Jack had a photographer with him who began taking pictures of the many lost items, including a 10-ton pontoon float which had become grounded in the rapids 600 feet above the falls in 1959. A more gruesome discovery was made at the base of the falls as two bodies were recovered. One was a young man who committed suicide the day before. The other was a badly decomposed body of a woman who's only identifying mark was a ring with the inscription, "forget me not."

That sentiment made Jack wonder who gave her that ring and what kind of relationship they had. The romantic in him which drove him to wander New York City streets late at night and fabricate stories about women he never met behind those shades or curtains caused his imagination to work overtime. A love that could never be, or the untimely passing of a lover, or breakup story after story entered his mind. He finally decided that he would never know the story behind that ring. He also thought of Ryoya and knew he wouldn't be gazing up at any windows late at night anymore.

Matthew Ellis walked along Veterans Plaza in the direction of Madison Avenue and the center of Dumont, New Jersey. He walked slowly with the aid of a cane but was making steady progress. His balance had improved and weakened muscles, though complaining, were gaining strength. It was a pleasant spring day and the afternoon sun felt good on his face and arms. Even though his world was a combination of mental confusion and physical pain Matt was determined to become strong enough to gain employment and independence. He knew his intrusion into Stephanie's life was a very heavy burden for one so young to bear.

A train whistle in the distance caught Matt's attention. Instinctively, he quickened his pace. Trains are a fascination to all males. Maybe it's their brute power, or size, or noise. Whatever the reason they are fun to watch. When Matt arrived at the railroad crossing the signal had not yet begun to ring. He paused. In less than a minute the bell began to clang and the gates lowered into place to block traffic. Matt looked to his left up the track and saw a single headlight in the distance. The rhythmic ringing of the crossing bell gently pulled him into another lost memory.

It was Christmastime and the ringing of the Salvation Army Santa's hand bells filled the air. Matt and Valerie had eaten dinner at a small restaurant in Greenwich Village and taken a taxi to Rockefeller Center to ice skate under the big Christmas tree. He had worked at Orztech for a year and their financial situation was improving. This Saturday night the skating rink was crowded but not to a degree that it was difficult to skate. Because Matt had played some pond hockey he could skate. Valerie—not so much. After he tied the laces on her figure skates, which they had purchased earlier in the week, he led his wife to the ice. However, when she stepped out onto the ice her skates immediately went out from under her and she dropped onto her rear with a thud.

"I guess I needed more rosin," Valerie said softly referring to the practice of ballet dancers stepping in rosin to give their pointe shoes more grip.

"What you needed was a husband who did a better job of holding onto you," Matt apologized.

She looked up at her strong, caring, wonderful partner and feigned criticism, "You did miss your mark."

"Did you hurt—your self?" Matt inquired as he helped Valerie up.

"My 'self' is not only sore but also wet," she attempted humor.

Matt guided Valerie as she picked up the art of skating quickly. She had strong legs and excellent balance. More importantly was the fact that as a dancer she had strong ankles so unlike many new skaters she was not skating on the sides of the skates. The biggest problem she encountered was the serrated teeth on the front of the blades that had an uncanny way of digging into the ice at the most inopportune times. More than once Valerie found herself diving forward toward the ice. Eventually, she developed a unique technique to keep from falling. When the teeth on the blade caught the ice, she would go on pointe, do a kind of pirouette, and step in the direction she was falling. It might not have looked very graceful, but it worked. Matt watched his young bride and marveled at how she was always willing to try things, most times wasn't very good, yet never got frustrated or angry.

After skating, they walked down Fifth Avenue with their skates draped over their shoulders and looked at all of the incredible window displays at Bloomingdales, Saks Fifth Avenue, Abercrombie & Finch, Lord & Taylor, and various other stores. There were depictions of English villages, fantasy toy stores, family Christmas scenes, and one window that mesmerized Valerie. It had a stage scene with two mechanical ballet dancers that moved and spun. Matt watched as Valerie looked at the display with the fascination of a young child. She wore white mittens and a white snowball looking hat that completed the image of innocence he knew to be reality.

"I'm sorry," Matt said with sincerity.

Valerie looked up at her husband and asked, "For what are you sorry?"

"For taking away your dream of being a dancer."

For an excruciatingly long moment she looked at him. Then she took his gloved hand in her mittened hand and held it to her cheek. "You didn't take away my dream—you are my dream." She glanced at the mechanical dancers in the window then back to Matt, "Dancers are partners for a short period of time going through well-rehearsed, choreographed steps portraying a story that is already written. We are writing our story at this very moment and will continue into the future. We are partners forever. For us the music will never end. For me there is no role I would prefer to dance than that of the wife of Matthew Ellis." She leaned her head back and Matt responded by kissing her gently, then more forcefully, and finally with a passion they both shared.

Matt and Valerie walked arm-in-arm down Fifth Avenue. A Salvation Army Santa rang his bell on a corner providing the traditional sound of Christmas in the city. Valerie stopped, slipped off her mitten, and opened her small purse. From it she retrieved a handful of change and dropped it in the red bucket that hung from a familiar tripod. This was repeated with other Santas as they walked down the avenue.

"I hope we still have food money," Matt joked.

"We do. That was the money I saved for your Christmas present," Valerie answered with a smile.

"So, no Cadillac?" Matt responded.

"No Cadillac."

"No expensive watch?"

"No watch."

"New underwear?"

"Maybe." She spun from his grip and giggled as she went to another Santa to drop more coins in a bucket.

Their magic night ended at home. Matt massaged Valerie's sore bottom and they sipped wine in candlelight. Little was said as they enjoyed simply being together. To the best of their knowledge Stephanie was conceived that night as they danced their pas de deux of love.

Matt became aware of the railroad crossing gate rising. The ringing of the signal ceased. He realized that he didn't recall seeing the train pass. What he did see was a past, a past too wonderful to forget, too personal to share, and too painful to have lost.

Carl Pythacyk sat at his personal table in Stacey's Pub on Fordham Road in the Bronx. He drank a beer as he considered what Sylvester Attoro had told him. The young hood with a high voice who Carl had snubbed when he and Moe and Sylvester met in a bar downtown had gotten his attention. This time he treated Sylvester with respect.

Sylvester revealed that Miguel Juarez had made contact in South Carolina with a straw buyer for guns. A straw buyer is a person with a clean record who can legally purchase firearms and does so for less reputable individuals. Miguel had invested $2,500 to purchase five Smith & Wesson 9mm pistols, two Remington 870 pump action 12 gauge shotguns, hundreds of rounds of ammunition, and a chrome plated Ruger 357 Magnum revolver. The Ruger was Miguel's choice for personal use. He mentioned a piece-of-shit Polack who would be an early target. Sylvester seemed to get some thinly veiled pleasure when furnishing that last bit of information. He also was pleased by the fact that he had impressed the older hoodlum. Carl listened attentively as Sylvester described, in detail, the planned operation.

Miguel and his cohorts had planned the endeavor down to the minutest detail. While getting the firearms purchased was somewhat complex a greater challenge was transporting them to New York. Public transportation was out of the question. Therefore, it had to be a car. They selected a 1963 Ford Falcon because it was an older, common, low-priced vehicle that wouldn't stand out. In preparation, they sent out a team that searched for Ford Falcons in each state along the route and stole the license plates. As part of the plan when the courier entered each state he would find a remote location and switch plates. In addition, he would change the decal in the window to an in-state college. These two steps would greatly decrease local police interest. They also knew any Hispanic driving the north-south corridor would arouse too much attention. Therefore, Miguel chose a young white male who could pass for a college student. Due to illegal transportation of cigarettes from the Carolinas, marijuana from Mexico, undocumented workers, and even moonshine being so common on the main corridors of vehicle transportation these routes were carefully watched by law enforcement. To avoid these high-risk highways, they laid out a more remote route that followed Route 77 in the Carolinas to Route 81 in Virginia and West Virginia to Route 80 in Pennsylvania and New Jersey. The driver would cross the Hudson River on the George Washington Bridge and end his journey in the south Bronx where he would park the car in an alley between two tenement buildings at 163rd Street and College Street. Finally, he would go to a public telephone booth and call Miguel to report his arrival.

Transportation of firearms across state lines is a federal offense with stiff penalties. Miguel wanted the guns. What he didn't want was to make a costly mistake that would bring with it heavy prison time.

After Sylvester finished describing the plan with obvious admiration of its designers he gave one final detail. It turned out that he was to be the courier. The excitement and pride that he felt was easy to see.

"How come Miguel has so much trust in you?" Carl had inquired.

"I don't know." was the response, "we did a few things together and, I guess, I fit his needs."

"You could end up in federal prison or dead."

"Naw, I'm gonna be careful." After a pause Sylvester added, "Hey! Do you want me to pick up a gun for you?"

"No, I don't need a gun to do what I do."

"I'm thinking of getting one if I can pull together the cash."

"When is all of this going to happen?"

"I leave next week and drive down to Anderson, South Carolina. Miguel will give me a phone number to call when I get there. If all goes well I'll be parking the car in the alley next Friday." As an afterthought, Sylvester suddenly asked, "You aren't pissed that I'm doing this for Miguel, are you?"

"Hell no. I asked you to keep tabs on him. It looks like your keeping pretty good tabs. I appreciate it." Carl pulled two twenties and a ten out of his pocket and offered them to Sylvester. "Here put this toward your gun purchase."

"Geeze, Carl, thanks."

The meeting had ended and Carl wished the young punk luck. Now, he sat and considered what he knew and pondered what he could do with this valuable information. Obviously, as much as he hated Miguel he wouldn't inform the police. He wasn't a rat. It was also out of the question to ask Sylvester to double-cross Miguel and bring the guns to him. Someone put a quarter in the jukebox and the song *I Heard It Through The Grapevine* by Gladys Knight & the Pips began to play. The appropriate nature of the song caused Carl to laugh out loud. At that same moment, he had a solution to the gun running plan and laughed even louder.

Anna Marie Six Trees played butterfly hide and seek with other little girls of the village. One girl covered her eyes and sang, "Butterfly, butterfly, show me where to go." All the others quietly hid. The singer would then track the others by the marks they left. It was a game of skill while also celebrating the butterfly. Ojibwe children were taught to never hurt a butterfly. In fact, it was considered good luck if you stayed so quiet that a butterfly landed on you.

15: Friday - June 20, 1969

Stephanie Ellis sat alone in Doctor Tallman's waiting room. It was late in the day and she didn't have an appointment. As she waited, she read an article in the May 26, 1969 issue of *Newsweek* about an up and coming singer named Janis Joplin. It was titled "Rebirth of The Blues." She was a creative, unfortunately drug addicted, singer with a style that was all her own.

Janis Lyn Joplin was born January 19, 1943 in Port Arthur, Texas. She was a loner in high school who craved attention. Originally, she was a painter but found more of what she needed in music. One of her very few friends, who was also in the less popular group, had record albums by African-American blues artists Bessie Smith, Ma Rainey and Lead Belly whom Joplin admitted influenced her to become a singer. After high school, she attended the University of Texas at Austin, though she didn't graduate. The campus newspaper *The Daily Texan* ran a profile of her in the issue dated July 27, 1962, headlined "She Dares to Be Different." The article described the young iconoclastic singer in the first sentence, "She goes barefooted when she feels like it, wears Levi's to class because they're more comfortable, and carries her Autoharp with her everywhere she goes so that in case she gets the urge to break into song it will be handy. Her name is Janis Joplin."

As Stephanie read the article she found herself identifying with Joplin, not as a singer but as a lost soul who desperately needs attention and validation. She admired the blues singer for having the courage to be different. What freedom that must be to have the ability to impulsively stop what you are doing, plop down, and break into song without regard for what others think. It also made her wonder if what attracted her to Ritchie was his comfort with being a nonconformist. Stephanie considered how twisted and tangled her own life seemed in comparison as she was consumed with simply trying to survive. She neither had the option of acting out nor would know how to do so. Ah, the acorn, she thought, really didn't fall far from the tree as she realized that she was very much like her mother.

As Stephanie read further the article in *Newsweek* told of how Joplin moved to Haight-Ashbury and in 1964 recorded a number of blues standards with Jorma Kaukonen, who later was a guitarist with Jefferson Airplane, and Margareta Kaukonen who accompanied them on a typewriter. They recorded seven songs; *Typewriter Talk, Trouble in Mind, Kansas City Blues, Hesitation Blues, Nobody Knows You When You're Down and Out, Daddy, Daddy, Daddy,* and *Long Black Train Blues.* It was during this time that Janis Joplin became a heavy user of speed, user of heroin, experimenter with psychoactive drugs, and heavy drinker of Southern Comfort.

Once again, Stephanie thought of Ritchie. His use of marijuana and LSD bothered her. Initially, she attributed it to a creative mind seeking freedom, but lately it appeared to be simple indulgence. She never joined him in these activities which disappointed him. Drug addicts and alcoholics never seem satisfied with drowning in their destructive passion alone. They always attempt to bring others down with them. Come on in the water's fine.

Joplin joined the psychedelic rock band Big Brother and the Holding Company on June 4, 1966. Their first album together included the singles *Down on Me, Bye Bye Baby, Call On Me,* and *Coo Coo,* on all of which Joplin sang lead vocals. April 7, 1966 Joplin performed with Jimi Hendrix, Buddy Guy, Joni Mitchell, Richie Havens, Paul Butterfield, and Elvin Bishop at the "Wake for Martin Luther King, Jr." concert in New York. Joplin left Big Brother and The Holding Company to form her own group the Kozmic Blues Band. By early 1969 she was a heavy daily user of heroin.

Dr. Tallman entered the waiting room still wearing his white lab coat. "Stephanie, it's been a while. Sorry to keep you waiting. How's your dad doing?"

A familiar feeling of calmness embraced Stephanie as she put down the magazine, rose, and walked over to meet Dr. Tallman. When she reached him she hugged him and buried her head in his chest. For a short time they stayed motionless. Then Dr. Tallman held her by her shoulders and moved her to arm's length so that they could look into each other's eyes. "And, how are you doing?" he asked with a warmth she needed at that very moment.

Stephanie looked at Dr. Tallman and remembered the first time she ever saw him. It was he who came through that big green metal door at the hospital on the night of her father's accident. He still wore the familiar thick-rimmed glasses and his heavy weight remained a distinguishing factor. His dark brown hair was now more grey than brown. Funny she hadn't noticed it changing over the past six years.

"I guess I'm doing as well as can be expected," Stephanie stated in an unconvincing voice.

"Now, we both know better than that," he replied, "what's bothering you?"

"I'm not sure," she admitted while looking down at the floor.

"OK, let's start there. What aren't you sure of?"

"Everything."

"That's a lot," he said humorously.

Stephanie let out a small chuckle and smiled, "You know what I mean."

"Yes, I do. You're happy that your father is improving but feel responsible for him and his well-being. You want to do more than work in a clothing store but aren't sure what you want to do. Your boyfriend, what's his name?"

"Ritchie."

"Right, he isn't showing you the attention that you desire. Money is a problem. You miss your mother. And, you just don't know why you're not happy. Does that sum it up?"

"Now, I feel worse," she said half kidding.

"Stephanie, you have every right to be anxious and concerned and a little depressed. You've been through a lot. Don't try to make everything right all at once. And stop blaming yourself. You are a wonderful, caring, intelligent, sensitive, and strong young woman. These tough times will pass and you will find . . . no . . . happiness will find you."

"Sometimes that's hard to believe."

"When things seem hopeless you have to go on faith. Someday when you're a mother holding your daughter and your life is filled with promise and all the good things that come your way you'll forget these tough times." Dr. Tallman put his arm around Stephanie and led her back to the chair where she had been sitting. He sat next to her.

"Why did my mother have to die?"

"From what I was told she had a congenital heart defect that was never diagnosed. The stress and long hours may have exasperated her condition but she could have had congestive heart failure at any time. That's the medical explanation. From a spiritual perspective, we are all born and given the miracle of life, but with no guarantees. Why does a child die within the first year of life? Why do others live to be one hundred? By the very nature of not knowing how much time we have we need to value every minute and use it wisely. Your mother was a very special person. Her warmness and grace are so very rare in today's world. She died way too young. But even with limited time she did a wonderful job raising you. We are all lucky to have known her."

"I was reading about this singer," Stephanie picked up the copy of *Newsweek,* "she appears to be so confident and strong, able to be whatever she wants to be, but does all kinds of drugs."

"You and I have talked about the dangers of illegal drugs," Dr. Tallman said in a stern and serious voice, "they never are a solution. In fact, they are the cause of far more serious problems."

"I know. You've given me the lecture more than once. Don't worry. I don't ever want to use drugs."

"Then I overreacted—I'm sorry," Dr. Tallman brushed a hair out of Stephanie's eyes.

"It's Ritchie—my boyfriend. I know that I never will be able to get him to stop using drugs. It seems all creative people are compelled to destroy themselves. I really care about him, but we don't have a future if it includes drugs."

"Stephanie, you are a wise young lady. I'm very proud of you."

Stephanie remembered the first time Dr. Gordon Tallman said he was proud of her. About six months after her father's accident Dr. Tallman visited their house in Alpine, New Jersey. He and her mother had a lengthy conversation. From a child's perspective, she understood that he wasn't going to bill for his services after the insurance stop paying. She also heard him say that he would contact the other doctors involved. The hospital unfortunately was another story as they would want full payment. Eventually, he walked over to where Stephanie was sitting and asked, "How are you doing, young lady?"

"When can my daddy come home?" was her response.

"Your dad was hurt very badly," he explained, "all we can do is wait until he heals enough to leave the hospital."

"I miss him and want him home."

"I know you do. We just have to be patient and wait for him to get strong enough to wake up. How are you doing in school?"

"Last report card I got all A's except for one B."

"Very good. I'm very proud of you."

After that visit, Dr. Tallman helped Stephanie's mother find a job. In addition, he sent babysitting jobs to Stephanie. He would come to the house from time to time with boxes full of food. Even after they sold the house and moved into an apartment Dr. Tallman continued to visit. He never stayed long but always had time to ask how she was doing, to listen to her stories, or answer her questions. More than once he helped her with her homework. He never asked for anything and simply did what he could to help the struggling family. In many ways, he became a stand-in father to Stephanie. She remembered his motivational talks as well as his stern lectures. Another characteristic about Dr. Tallman that others missed was his dry sense of humor. He really tried but more often than not his audience didn't know when he was kidding. This led to awkward situations where people didn't know how to react. Stephanie was fortunate because she connected with him and had an uncanny ability to understand his humor. Over six years, there were much needed smiles and caring words that helped Stephanie live as normal a life as possible.

"My mother was a ballet dancer, but never fulfilled her dream." Stephanie continued, then added sadly, "I don't even know what my dream is."

"Some people have to live a long time and have many experiences before they finally recognize what would make them happy," Dr. Tallman explained. "You haven't had your magic experience, yet."

"My magic experience?"

"Someday, maybe tomorrow, you will meet someone, see something, read about something, or experience something that will have a special kind of effect on you. The thing is, it isn't the same for everyone and there is no way to predict it. However, if you remain open-minded and allow yourself to be honest with yourself it will happen."

"I'm not sure that I understand."

Dr. Tallman stood and paced the room, "Let me explain it this way. Almost every school student at one point wants to be a teacher. The reason is that they are impressed by their teachers who most often are the only role models with whom they have had extensive interaction. Some students continue on that path and become teachers. Others meet different people, have unique experiences, or discover their interests in other ways. For some it happens early in their lives. While with others, it takes longer. Your magic experience is out there. And, when it happens, you'll know it. It will light a fire in you and create a passion for something that will be a driving force in your life."

"I hope so, because right now I feel like a leaf in the wind."

"Then drift, sweetheart, let life take you and show you all of its promise," Dr. Tallman walked over to Stephanie, she stood, and they embraced. "You know that you can talk with me anytime you want. I love you and want you to be happy. But, now, your father is back, so I have to remain in the background. He needs you and, more than you realize, you need him."

"How do I thank you for all you did for us?"

"Make your life count."

Less than two years later, on October 4, 1970, Janis Joplin was found dead in her hotel room by producer Paul A. Rothchild. She had been scheduled to do the vocals on the song *Buried Alive In The Blues* but didn't show. The official cause of death was an overdose of heroin combined with alcohol. Some believe it was accidental because several other customers of her supplier also overdosed that week from a more potent mix than usual.

Carl stood on the corner of Thirty-Fifth Street and Broadway as he had been instructed. He wore a blue shirt, black pants, and dress shoes which wasn't his normal attire. Yet, it seemed appropriate. This was not a blue jean, black tee shirt, and sneakers event. The normally unflappable hood was nervous. He paced slowly as he watched the evening traffic that had dwindled down to a few passing cars. A glance at his watch indicated that it was seven-thirty. He had been there for twenty minutes after arriving early to be sure that he was there at the designated time. A taxi pulled up in front of him. Immediately, he looked inside. Two young women paid the driver and exited the cab which drove off. Carl returned to his pacing. He wanted a cigarette but didn't want to be smoking. A breeze carried the aroma of pizza from the open-front pizza shop on the corner across Thirty Fifth Street. Carl waited.

At seven-forty-five a midnight blue 1969 Lincoln Continental pulled over to the curb a short distance from the corner. The driver flashed the high beams to get Carl's attention. The young tough, who at that moment didn't feel very tough, walked casually over to the car. The driver's power window went down and a large dark haired man in a charcoal suit with a black shirt open at the collar said, "Get in." The rear suicide door opened. A suicide door is one that is hinged at the rear rather than the middle pillar. They are called suicide doors because if it was hit by traffic it would slam shut on someone entering or exiting the vehicle. A conventional door would break off.

Carl climbed into the vehicle and found himself sitting next to another large man with dark hair greying on the sides. This individual wore a dark green sport coat, black pants, and a black shirt open at the collar. Carl thought, he should have worn a black shirt. In the passenger seat in the front sat a third man. Carl's anxiety increased threefold. He closed the door and the car sped off.

Olivia walked along the east side of Eight Avenue. It being a Friday night she had been told that she would earn at least three hundred dollars or else she would be whipped. It was not an empty threat. Five stinging lashes gave her a taste of what punishment awaited and that she would receive one lash for every dollar short of three hundred. Her approach to johns was awkward but her young age and attractiveness made up for inexperience. She tried to get ten dollars for oral sex and thirty for intercourse. Unfortunately, a majority of patrons either bargained with her or simply didn't have that much money. As a result, after an hour, she had only sixty dollars. Fear drove her to work harder. Fear pushed her shame and degradation aside. Fear made her numb to pain and discomfort. Fear stole her personality and soul. "Hey, baby want a date?" a voice she didn't recognize flowed from her bright red lips.

As the Lincoln Continental traveled down Broadway Carl sat in silence not sure what to say or do. The vehicle turned right and headed toward the Hudson River. The three other occupants of the car remained silent. Sweat ran down Carl's back and his mouth was dry. In the darkness, he felt very small and at that moment very vulnerable. Whenever he moved the leather seats would burp filling the silent void with an explosion that pointed directly at Carl. They reached the docks and turned into an alley and stopped. All three men exited the car. The large man in the green sport coat who had been sitting next to Carl motioned for him to get out on the passenger side. He simply said, "Come'on."

They entered the rear door of a restaurant. The sounds of dishes and pots and pans and silverware filled the air. Green sport coat led the way followed by Carl with the two other confederates bringing up the rear. Voices joined the other restaurant sounds as Italian cooks shouted directions, orders, or curses at each other. The aroma of real Italian cuisine dwarfed the pitiful smell of pizza Carl had enjoyed at Thirty Fifth and Broadway. They passed through the kitchen. It was steamy hot and all of the activities made it feel chaotic. They came to a door and stopped. Green sport coat knocked twice and waited. After a moment, the door opened and they were ushered into a private dining room.

At the far end of the room was a long table much like a dais that sat at least eight. Spread around the room were five smaller tables. Each had a red and white checkered tablecloth, empty straw covered Chianti bottle with a lit candle, tableware, and multiple bottles of wine. The large table was empty. At one of the smaller tables sat a man dressed in a blue suit with a black shirt and light blue tie. By all standards, he was impeccably dressed and perfectly coiffed. He motioned for Carl to join him. Carl's companions silently drifted away. The nervous young man walked over to the table and stood in front of his host.

"Sit down," the man said pleasantly.

Carl obeyed.

"Have something to eat. I recommend the lasagna al forno. Or, how about some spaghetti?"

"That will be fine," Carl answered in a low voice that was near a whisper.

"Gino; spaghetti per il mio amico." The mobster with whom Carl sat ate a forkful of lasagna. He picked up a bottle of red wine and poured a half glassful in a glass in front of Carl. "Have some wine."

Carl picked up the glass and tried not to show his hand shaking.

"So, Carl, what made you decide to make contact with Don Spacini?"

"I, uh," Carl took another sip of wine, "I thought you . . . uh, he . . . would be interested in what was going on."

"We were."

"When I found out about the guns I didn't want them in the hands of . . . " Carl hesitated as he wanted to use ethnic slurs but thought better of it, ". . . of low-level punks like Miguel Juarez and his gang."

The spaghetti arrived.

"Mangiare," the unnamed mobster said, "Well, you did right. That spic won't get those guns."

"Good," Carl said sincerely. He tasted the spaghetti and couldn't believe how delicious it was. The flavors seemed strong yet pleasantly blended together. It was the best spaghetti he had ever tasted.

"How's the spaghetti?"

"It's great! I never tasted anything like it," Carl stated enthusiastically.

"Good," his host said, "You come here any time, ask for Gino, and tell them you're a guest of Ray Esposito. They'll take good care of you."

"Thanks," Carl said surprised. He felt more at ease as he asked, "So, you have the guns?"

"What guns?"

"Uh, well, I thought . . ." Carl sipped more wine and fell silent.

Ray Esposito ate some more lasagna, wiped his mouth with his napkin, and asked, "How did you know how to contact us?"

"I didn't know, really. All I do know is Mr. Spacini owns the docks. That's why I stay away from there." Carl drank more wine and Ray refilled his glass, "I called the union hall and said I had a message for Mr. Spacini. They wanted to know what the message was but I said I needed to talk with him or someone who works for him. I left a telephone number for a phone booth at a bar where I hang out. When I got a call back I gave the information about the guns."

"You did the right thing."

"Is the driver of the car OK?"

"What do you care?"

"He is sorta a . . . an acquaintance."

"He fell down walking to the phone booth, but he'll be fine." Ray explained, then added, "His story is more believable that way. Besides, he needs a little toughening up." Ray reached into his pocket and pulled out a money clip. He peeled five one-hundred dollar bills from the roll and placed them on the table in front of Carl.

Carl didn't know what to do.

"Ci prendiamo cura dei nostri amici," Ray said then offered a translation, "We take care of our friends." He stood up and walked around the table and put his hand on Carl's shoulder, "From now on you contact me." A piece of paper with a phone number was placed on the table, "Memorize that and destroy it. Call me next week. I might have something for you." Ray turned to leave and said as he walked away, "Enjoy your meal, Carl."

Carl sat alone in the large private dining room. A wave of excitement passed through him. Adrenaline made him want to jump up and move, but he remained still. He looked at the money on the table. He wanted to grab it and stuff it in his pocket. Yet, he had that unexplainable feeling that he was being watched. Irrational thoughts dominated his mind. The wrong move could be fatal—the right move profitable. Yet, this was a new world for Carl. One he was fascinated with but also feared. The wine had reached his brain and he wanted more. Alcohol has a unique effect. It makes one thirsty, therefore they drink more adding to their thirst. This is why so many who decide to limit what they drink often fail. The wine glass was now empty. Carl almost jumped when Gino refilled his glass. How long had he been there? Were there others? What should be his next move? Carl decided to finish the incredibly tasty meal. When he did he picked up the money and stood. The wine tried to spin him in place but he fought it. For a moment, he remained still hoping to become steady on his feet. As he scanned the table his mind wanted to believe that he was in—a part of the crew. He peeled a hundred-dollar bill from the folded money and left it on the table as a tip. Yup, he was a big-time spender, but he could afford it. Carefully, he staggered through the kitchen and out into the alley. The midnight blue Lincoln Continental was gone.

During the next to last week of basic training field exercises are emphasized, numerous long marches take place, recruit's skills are tested, and the dreaded Confidence Course is run one final time. Recruits have to pass physical, skills, and written tests. On this day as the week came to an end those recruits who passed were given the revered Eagle, Globe, and Anchor emblem and they became Marines. This brings with it very noticeable changes in protocol. No longer do you refer to yourself in the third person, "This recruit doesn't understand Drill Instructor Sergeant Kincaid." Also, the title Drill Instructor is dropped and only rank and name are required. Another standard, which has become a habit that is hard to drop, is starting a sentence with "Sir" when speaking to drill instructors. In fact, the whole atmosphere changes dramatically as the new Marines are welcomed into a select and proud group of warriors.

Wellington Marsh was now a Marine. It was hard for him to believe that he had survived. Even more amazing was that he was promoted to Private First Class which meant he would wear one stripe and receive a higher pay grade. A basic training promotion results from extraordinary performance, testing scores, and Drill Instructor recommendation. Wellington had done well in all three areas.

As he sewed the stripes onto his uniform Wellington Marsh felt a sense of pride, as well as belonging to something bigger than himself. He was a part of the greatest fighting force in history, therefore, in a small way he was a part of history. He experienced a unique sense of accomplishment.

The last week of training is called "Marine Week." It consists of classes, learning about the heroes of the Corps, Battalion Commander's inspection, more core value classes, graduation practice, family day, and graduation. Private First Class Wellington Marsh hoped that his parents would be able to be there.

Vietnam was half a world away and not on his mind this particular day. Fear did not haunt him. He felt good, and strong, and alive—at least for one day.

Nine-year-old Robert Six Trees approached the cave. He would stay as long as was needed without food or water until Manitou sends him a spirit in a vision. This coming-of-age ritual, when completed, would make him a full member of the tribe. He was not afraid because he was about to become something bigger than himself.

16: Tuesday – June 24, 1969

Lida Petropoulos reentered Mathew Ellis' life in the form of a memory. She sat at a wooden table in a dark restaurant whose name Matt could not recall. He did remember that the inside of the restaurant had high brick walls with windows above giving the impression that you were sitting outside. Lida had arrived wearing a designer sweater dress with solid cowl-neck top, short sleeves, elastic black waistband and a zebra-printed skirt. Upon seeing him she smiled, waved, and pranced lightly over to him in knee length black boots. She threw her arms around him and they kissed.

As the memory unfolded Matt observed his shame. This young woman and he were more than friends or business associates. He didn't want to know more. If he could, he would push that memory back into the dark recesses of his mind, hide it in his id, and never acknowledge its existence again. Yet, that was impossible. Memories flow at their own pace at the time and place of their choosing. And, this particular memory had been fighting to be recognized for some time. Matt remembered that dinner. However, so many facts and events that preceded it or followed still hid in his slowly awakening mind.

Lida was young and energetic and exotic and seductive. Her long dark hair hung down across her shoulders and caressed her full breasts. Mawsitsit green eyes gazed unfaltering at Matt. His pulse quickened when she smiled. Even as a shadow in his memory he was attracted to her.

He remembered her talking about her apartment and getting a new color television. This put her in the 3.1% of American households that owned a color television in 1963. It wasn't until 1966 when the three national broadcasting networks ran their primetime schedules in color that sales began to soar.

As the memory unfolded he remembered other bits and pieces of their conversation.

"I still have your favorite wine at my apartment."

"Not tonight, I have to get home."

"Oh, but I'll be lonely without you."

"I know, but I do have a wife and child," reality bit into his being causing guilt to flow from within.

"You can have them later," she pouted, "I want you now."

They walked hand-in-hand along a New York City street. Was that the same night? Memories overlapped and time became irrelevant. Matt did recall that Lida was always playful. As a result, one never knew what to expect next. She might break away and run into a store or park, she might start a conversation with a stranger, or push him into pedestrians walking in the opposite direction. One time, she ran her long fingernails down his chest leaving dark red marks and mischievously said, "Try explaining that."

They stopped in front of a jewelry store window and Lida stood looking at a matching gold and diamond necklace and earrings set. It was obvious from the intricate design and size of the diamonds that this was not a reasonably priced collection. Another hint was the lack of a price. If you have to ask, you can't afford it.

"You can get me that," Lida stated with authority as she pointed to the extravagant bauble.

Matt's memory skipped to another time and place. However, there was a link. Lida wore a floor length deep blue evening gown with a high neckline, sleek bodice with low-key vertical pleats, and sheer see-through full length sleeves. Draped regally around her neck was the gold and diamond necklace from the store window enhanced by matching earrings.

"Thank you for coming," Lida said welcomingly.

"It is our pleasure, thank you for inviting us," Matt heard Valerie respond. His wife's voice startled him as he now remembered that the two women had met—but where? What party or event was it? Did Valerie know about Lida? Had the two women had a conversation? Why had he even agreed to attend? When did it take place? Where did Lida get that necklace?

Frustration joined guilt as Matt tried to remember how Lida and he met, how long they had known each other, and how far the relationship had gone. Unfortunately, the fog of lost years remained in place. Lida was there in these memories but they began to fade. He had a name, face, and small glimpses of a past long gone but the mystery remained.

Eastern Airlines flight 172 had departed Charlotte, North Carolina at 11:20 a.m. Its destination was Newark Airport. Thirty-seven minutes into an hour and ten minute flight the captain called air traffic control, "Pan-pan, pan-pan, pan-pan, Washington Center, Eastern flight 172 heavy declaring an emergency. We have smoke in the cockpit. Over."

"Eastern 172 this is Washington Center, is the aircraft stable? Over."

"Affirmative, Washington Center. Request clearance for uninterrupted approach to nearest airport. Over."

"Eastern 172 switch to private frequency 128 Megahertz. Over."

The captain switched the airplane's radio to the designated frequency and spoke, "Washington Center we are over North Carolina/Virginia border, heading zero, three, seven at three, two, zero feet (32,000). Airspeed five, nine, zero. Aircraft is Boeing 727 with 126 onboard. Over."

"Eastern 172 we are clearing your route to RIC (Richmond Airport). Change course to zero, four, four. Over."

Smoke in the cockpit grew more dense and smelled of burning insulation. The three crew members in the cockpit of the Boeing 727 donned oxygen masks and an announcement was made to the crew and passengers.

"This is Captain Tully, we have a mechanical issue and will be landing at Richmond Airport. There is no cause for alarm. Please remain in your seats and keep your seatbelts on. Cabin crew, please review emergency landing procedures. I will advise when we are coming in for a landing. Thank you." His practiced calm voice was meant to comfort passengers and cabin crew. Unfortunately, it did little to help his anxiety. It is difficult enough to face death but dragging 125 other souls along raises the stress level 125-fold. Smoke means fire and fire onboard an aircraft means inevitably that there is only limited time to find the cause and extinguish the fire or get the hell on the ground. In this case, they had no way to determine where the fire was located.

"Eastern 172 please descend to two, zero, zero feet (20,000) and continue on present course, Over."

"Descending to two, zero, zero feet. Over."

"Captain," the co-pilot interjected, "Heading indicator and altimeters are out."

"Mayday, Mayday. Washington Center, we have failure of heading indicator and altimeters. We are flying blind. Over."

"Eastern 172, continue on present course and altitude. We will clear for VFR (Visual Flight Rules) landing at RIC. Handoff to RIC TRACON in three minutes. Over."

This is going to get hairy," Captain Tully stated to no one in particular. Visually landing a 727 without an altimeter was not something for which pilots trained. A missed judgment or optical aberration and he could plant the aircraft into the ground short of the runway or touch down too far down the runway to stop. In addition, he had no way of determining speed of descent. Eyesight can be deceiving. What appears to be a slow descent might be far faster than realized too late. It was going to be very difficult to not bounce the aircraft down the runway. And, this was going to be a one-shot endeavor. An aborted landing and going around was out of the question as it presented far too many risks that could lead to a catastrophic outcome. Other gauges and indicators became inoperable.

"Let's make sure we know what we have," Captain Tully stated.

"The attitude indicator is operable, airspeed indicator, oil pressure, uh, oh, flaps and slats out." After two minutes the two pilots had made an inventory of what they had to work with and it wasn't much.

"Eastern 172 this is RIC Control. We are aware of your emergency and will provide all assistance necessary. Over."

"RIC Control, we have instrumentation problems that are deteriorating rapidly. We do have the magnetic compass and will have to manage with it. Your assistance with glide path and altitude would be appreciated. Over."

"Eastern 172 there are some low clouds at one three zero feet (13,000). Visual approach above that level will be diminished. Begin a slow turn to zero one three degrees and start a slow descent. When you enter the clouds you will know that you are above one three zero feet. Continue descent until you have surface visual. At present, you are being tracked by secondary radar which relies on transponder information. Therefore, we have zero data on your altitude or speed. When you are close enough for primary radar we will provide altitude data. Over."

"RIC Control heading approximately zero one three degrees. Still above cloud cover. Over." Captain Tully turned to the co-pilot, "Jim, we need flaps or else we will come in too hot for this runway. When we adjust them there won't be any degree indicator confirmation. I need you to go back into the cabin and visually confirm. You'll probably get a lot of nervous questions from passengers. Reassure them but don't give any details. Tell them the engines are all operating correctly and the structure of the aircraft is fine. Then get back here as quickly as possible. I need your eyesight, experience, instincts, and freakin good luck here with me."

"Just don't rub my head," the co-pilot nervously quipped.

The aircraft now flew inside the cloud cover. Without instruments, it was an ominous feeling. Until they emerge below the clouds they had no idea how high they were and whether or not they actually were descending. Done incorrectly they could miss the airport in a cloud cocoon. On a positive note the smoke in the cockpit was not becoming heavier. It raised hope that the fire was small and concentrated or, if luck was with them, could burn itself out.

"Easter 172, you are approximately thirty miles from RIC. You are cleared for unobstructed approach on runway zero, two. True bearing zero, one, three. Magnetic variation zero, nine, west. Glide slope angle three degrees. Elevation one, five, nine. There is a nine zero foot tower three, three, zero, zero feet from the runway four, five, zero feet left of the centerline. Three four to one slope to clear. The runway is six, six, zero, seven feet in length and one, five, zero feet wide. Wind is minimal at east, southeast three miles per hour. The runway is dry. Please advise when you have surface visual. Over."

Captain Tully spoke to the co-pilot, "The good news . . . this aircraft can land on a runway under five thousand feet. That gives us over a thousand feet extra . . . if we misjudge touch down." After a pause, as he gazed out the windshield, "I just wish we would break out of these clouds." He picked up the internal microphone, "This is Captain Tully. We are approaching Richmond Airport, the aircraft is flying well, and we anticipate an uneventful landing. As a precaution please follow the instructions of the cabin crew and follow crash landing procedures. When the aircraft stops moving deplane through the emergency exits over the wings or the built-in airstair that opens from the rear of the fuselage. By all indications this will be a normal landing."

"I like your definition of a normal landing," the co-pilot deadpanned.

"I thought it was better than saying we're not sure we can even reach the airport."

"If we don't get out of these clouds we won't even find the airport."

"You're right,"

Captain Tully considered the aircraft he was flying. The Boeing 727 began flying in 1963. Eastern was the first airline to fly the 727 on February 1, 1964. He was among the first Eastern pilots to captain a 727. The Boeing 727 is a mid-size, narrow-body, three-engine aircraft that carries 149 to 189 passengers. It has three Pratt & Whitney JT8D engines below a tall T-tail, one on each side of the fuselage and a third center engine that goes through the tail. Because no engines are mounted on the wings leading-edge slats and trailing edge flaps can run the full length. This produces maximum wing lift which makes the 727 remarkably stable at very slow speeds compared with other jets. This would be a welcome advantage as they try to put the aircraft down as slowly as possible. He made a note to remember to raise the flaps as soon as they touch down to reduce lift and get full effect from the brakes. It would be tough but they could do it. He loved this aircraft and trusted it. By God, he would bring his wounded bird home.

Captain Tully stated with conviction, "Let's get down to where we can see something." He pulled back on the two outboard engine throttles to reduce airspeed. It was hard to tell if the pitch of the aircraft changed. Airspeed of the 727 dropped to 320 miles-per-hour. They didn't dare drop airspeed too dramatically without an operating altimeter.

"Eastern 172, you are approximately twenty miles from RIC. You should be below the cloud cover at this point. Over."

"RIC Control we are still in cloud cover. Reducing airspeed. Will advise when we have surface visual. Over."

"Eastern 172, RIC has standard VASI on left side of runway. Over."

Basic visual approach slope indicators (VASI) consist of a set of lights on one side of the paved surface 23 feet from the start of the runway. The lights are designed with lenses that appear either white or red depending on the angle from which they are observed. When on the glide slope the left set of lights appear as white while the right set appear as red. If both sets appear white the aircraft is too high. Both sets red—too low. Captain Tully concluded a combination of these lights, ground radar altitude readings, and an operating airspeed indicator would make the landing reasonably routine.

"Tull," the co-pilot used a familiar nickname, "I think we have visual at eleven o'clock." He pointed in the direction where the clouds were disappearing. In just a few moments the fog literally cleared and below was the state of Virginia.

"RIC Control, we have surface visibility. Over."

"Eastern 172, maintain altitude. Turn to zero, two, two to line up with runway. You are approximately, ten miles from the airport. Primary radar indicates altitude of one, two, seven feet. Over."

Captain Tully said to the co-pilot, "OK, this is it. Give me 30 percent slats and flaps, go back and confirm, and get back here, pronto."

The co-pilot set the flaps, unbuckled his seatbelt, removed his oxygen mask, and departed the cockpit. Captain Tully pulled back slightly on the stick to keep the nose level, then moved the throttles for all three engines back to half power. He wanted to come in slow but knew there was a fine line between descending speed of 170 miles per hour and stall speed which was 107 miles per hour with 30 percent flaps. Was it his imagination or was the smoke once more getting thicker in the cockpit? As he completed his turn he watched the magnetic compass swing between 15 and 30 degrees. Precision was not possible and it would take a few seconds for the device to stabilize. Unfortunately, in their present situation seconds were precious.

"Eastern 172, you are zero, zero, two degrees off the centerline. Adjust right. Outer marker at six, point, six miles. You are below minimums of one, four, zero feet due to cloud cover. Maintain altitude. Over."

"RIC Control, adjusting approach." The aircraft shuddered and smoke began billowing out of the instrument panel. "RIC Control smoke has increased in intensity. Have fire emergency vehicles at the end of the runway. Over." Silence followed. Captain Tully changed frequencies on the radio but no signal was found. The radios joined other instruments that had ceased to operate. "Damn!" the now sweating veteran pilot spat.

When the co-pilot returned, he exclaimed, "Shit; it's getting worse! Flaps are down. Did we lose anything else?"

"The radios."

"That tears it. We are really on our own. What's the procedure?" He slipped the oxygen mask over his face.

"We're going in. We are on the glide path. As soon as we have a clear view of the runway and I can focus on the VASI lights we're going in. You have to be the visual heading indicator and keep me on the centerline. There's no airspeed indicator and most of the engine gauges are out. Oh, is the attitude indicator on your side operational?"

"No."

"Then we both have to do the left window, right window exercise to make sure the wings remain level. It will be tricky but we're up to it."

"Let's do it."

"Lower the landing gear before the switches no longer operate."

The co-pilot moved the levers to put the landing gear down. Both men strained to listen for the gear locking in place. As expected, there were no indicator lights to confirm that the landing gear was, in fact, down and locked. The captain pulled further back on the throttles and the aircraft slowed as well as descended.

"We don't know if the gear is down and locked," the co-pilot warned.

"I'm going to put her down as gently as possible. If there are wheels it will be smoother than if there aren't."

"There it is!" the co-pilot exclaimed as he waved his arm to clear some smoke and pointed slightly to the left. The runway, their salvation, lay ahead. "Slight left rudder," he instructed.

"Keep me on the centerline, Jim."

As the visual approach slope indicator lights became visible both sets were white. They were too high. Captain Tully thought that's far better than too low at this distance. He eased back on the throttles to increase the rate of descent. His ears strained to hear a difference in the engines but because they are located at the rear of the plane he couldn't. With the landing gear down, if it was down, they had greater drag which increased the potential for a stall if the airspeed dropped too low. The nose of the jet dropped. No chimes or whistles or stick shaker gave any warning. As they had been rendered inoperable none would have anyway.

The runway crept closer and closer.

"Rudder right slightly," the co-pilot instructed.

The two sets of white lights became one set red and one set white. They were on the 3-degree glide path. Closer and closer. Suddenly, the lights all appeared red. They were too low. If Captain Tully pulled back on the stick at such low speed they would stall and drop into the countryside short of the runway. Quickly he moved the center engine throttle forward to provide more power. Again, they couldn't hear the engine rpms increase. Both pilots stared with the intensity of someone going over a cliff and hoping for something to grab onto. They were seconds away from judgment day.

Captain Tully grabbed the intercom, hoped it was functioning and yelled, "Brace, Brace, Brace."

"You're dead on," the co-pilot whispered as they passed the end of the runway and the VASI lights.

Captain Tully raised the nose slightly and pulled slowly back on the center throttle. The Boeing 727 seemed to be hanging just above the runway as it consumed its length. The center throttle was drawn back to 10 percent yet the jet refused to give up its flight. Over five hundred feet of the runway had passed under them. When he pulled back on the outboard engine throttles the wheels touched the runway so gently it was almost unperceivable. Nose high they rolled down the remaining runway.

"Raise the flaps!" Captain Tully commanded.

The co-pilot moved the lever to the "no flaps" position.

The end of the runway was in sight as they applied the brakes. Eastern Flight 172 came to a stop with room to spare. They shut down the engines.

Both pilots looked at each other for a long moment, extended their hands, and shook with an unspoken emotion two people who share a crisis and come through together experience. They were there for each other and didn't waiver. On this day two new pilots entered a brotherhood no one ever sought but once in were among a select few who faced the demon whose name translates as 'the Cannibal at the North End of the World, Hokhoku and lived to tell about it. Thankfully, it was a small club. Or, maybe not thankfully, because there was a far larger club of those who perished at the hands of Hokhoku.

"This is the captain; please leave the aircraft in an orderly fashion. Follow the instructions of the crew. Thank you."

When service crews entered the Boeing 727 they removed dash panels, extinguished the fire, and concluded that it had been caused by faulty wiring.

A storm formed in the west. Clouds rolled over clouds rising higher and higher into the sky creating a wall of green-grey hues. An ever-growing creature lashed out at the countryside. Coils of lightning struck at distant objects sinking in its fangs again and again. Robert Six Trees watched through his window imagining that it was one of the seven great miigis (radiant/iridescent) beings striking down their enemies. His creative mind guided his hand as he drew the spirit in the sky.

17: Friday - June 27, 1969

Wellington Marsh put on his Service C uniform that consisted of green trousers with khaki web belt, khaki short-sleeve button-up shirt, no tie, hard-framed round Barracks Cover, and black shoes. On his sleeves were the single stripes of a Private First Class. His Sharpshooter insignia hung proudly on the left breast pocket of his shirt. He thought of the previous day which was family day and how much having his parents there meant to him. The day began with a motivational run where they yelled Marine Corps cadences as they circled the base past their families ending at the parade deck. They were then dismissed for on-base liberty until evening.

Peter Marsh was amazed how ten weeks had dramatically changed their son. The young man looked stronger and more muscular, stood taller with his shoulders back and head held high, but he also looked more serious. That easy-going, wise cracking teen was no more. Peter had a father's pride in a son that had accomplished a difficult task, but he also had a father's fear of what lay ahead. Wellington and his mother, Judith, and he had spent a wonderful afternoon touring the base. It was an impressive place. They visited all of the non-restricted training facilities where more recent recruits were being put through their paces, the Parris Island Historic District, and the barracks for Platoon 2099, Kilo Company, 2nd Recruit Training Battalion, Wellington's home for the past ten weeks.

Recruits had to report back to their barracks at 6:45 p.m. On this night before graduation they were challenged to do skits depicting training and lampooning the drill instructors. Sergeant Kincaid's walking stick was highlighted in various routines. One of the more memorable bits had a recruit in front of a blanket held by two other recruits. He held up a toothpick and stated, "Sergeant Kincaid's walking stick from his perspective. The blanket was walked in a circle revealing another recruit holding a pipe. He stated, "Sergeant Kincaid's walking stick from our perspective. The two recruits holding the blanket again walked in a circle revealing the first recruit who held a twig. "Sergeant Kincaid's perspective." Once more the blanket turned and a recruit held a baseball bat. "Our perspective." Another turn and the recruit held a feather. "Sergeant Kincaid." Finally, the last turn and a recruit held a live snake. "Sergeant Kincaid."

When Private First Class Wellington Marsh came out wearing a white cowboy hat and announced, "The Ballad of Annie Oakley" Sergeant Kincaid sat up straight in his seat. The two exchanged quick knowing glances. The tough drill instructor knew that a nickname he had escaped many years past was about to be made public and pinned on him forever. He was not pleased but could do nothing but watch. As he did Kincaid wondered why he ever recommended the little bastard for promotion. Wellington Marsh read his poem.

> Annie Oakley could really shoot,
> Most of us couldn't and didn't give a hoot.
>
> Sergeant Kincaid took us to the range,
> To a bunch of recruits it was very strange.

I'm just a city kid so what did I know,
I'd pull the trigger and watch the shot go.

Sergeant Kincaid was gentle and kind,
Tapping my head with his stick from behind.

But then after one kindly blow,
Everything around me began to glow.

And there she was in my mind's eye,
Sweet little Annie saying ignore this guy.

It's easy to make that bullet go true,
Picture the nose of you know who.

That is how I learned to shoot,
So now I'm a Marksman—not just a boot.

A very relieved Sergeant Kincaid stood and remarked, "Private Marsh, I'm glad Annie helped because I couldn't do a thing with you." He paused and then for the first time in ten weeks smiled and said, "Get some rest Marines, tomorrow's your day."

Graduation began at 7:45 a.m. in front of Barrow Hall with the Morning Colors Ceremony (flag raising) with musical accompaniment by the Parris Island Marine Band. Later at 9:00 a.m. all of the graduating Marines formed up on the Peatross Parade Deck. It was here as each platoon waited to march past the reviewing stands and officially graduate that Wellington remembered a fateful Friday night when Sergeant Kincaid shared something with him. No, it wasn't his horrible nickname. However, it was fun making him sweat the night before. It was something he was about to see, or more accurately hear—if true. All of the platoons were ready and the Sergeant Major raised his sword to begin the ceremony. His command, "Pass in review." And at that single moment Wellington knew what Sergeant Kincaid had told him was true. Sergeant Major Whitney Coleman had actually said, "Piss in your shoe." No one noticed. He said, "Piss in your shoe" and the Marine band struck up with *National Emblem* loud and proud. The platoons stepped off and the ceremony began. Wellington Marsh held in laughter, found he had trouble getting in step, and glanced at Sergeant Kincaid who froze him with his stare.

After graduation, all new Marines are authorized ten days leave. After this much-needed rest Wellington was to report to Camp Lejeune, North Carolina for Marine Combat Training (MCT). For fourteen days, he would learn to operate in a combat environment. His MOS, Military Occupation Specialty was designated 0311 Rifleman. This required additional training. After that he would be assigned to his first permanent duty station—Vietnam.

Once again, Carl stood on the corner of Broadway and Thirty Fifth Street. This time he wore his best suit. Truth be known, it was his only suit. He wore a dark grey, three button suit with out-of-style large notched lapels, center vent, and three button cuffs. The fit was tight as he had grown since he last wore it. He felt uncomfortable and a little self-conscious. A white shirt and blue striped tie completed his outfit. He had shined his black dress shoes to as high a gloss as possible. In his mind, he saw Ray Esposito in his sartorial splendor and knew there was no way he was in that league.

A familiar aroma from the street-front pizza shop on the corner reached him. It smelled good but was no match with the real Italian meal he had enjoyed a week earlier. He definitely wanted to return to that restaurant. Problem was that he had gone in the back door, sat in a private room, and his meal was ordered without a menu. For these reasons, he didn't know the name of the restaurant. At least he knew he could find the back door.

Ray Esposito hadn't given him any idea as to what the job was that he had been enlisted to do. It didn't matter. He was in. Unlike a week ago he was neither anxious nor fearful. This time he was filled with anticipation.

A police car slowed as it approached the corner. Carl cursed under his breath, "Just what I need to be rousted by a couple of cops with nothing better to do." The driver of the patrol car stared at Carl as he turned the corner. After sizing him up the police officer completed the turn and accelerated down Thirty Fifth Street. Carl was once more alone. He thought about the past week. Sylvester was home resting. He had a broken arm, lacerations, and concussion. In time, he would heal. Miguel certainly wouldn't think he had been double-crossed by someone in that condition. Ray had played it right. Carl hadn't heard much about Miguel's activities but now he was small potatoes of little concern.

After ten minutes the midnight blue 1969 Lincoln Continental arrived and pulled to the curb about ten yards from where Carl stood. Carl walked casually over to the big car, the driver's window went down, and a familiar face said, "Get in."

Ray Esposito sat in the front passenger seat. As usual he was impeccably dressed. Carl once more felt self-conscious about his dated and dumpy suit. Ray neither said anything nor acknowledged the fact that Carl sat alone in the back seat. The car pulled away and headed downtown. Carl also didn't say anything assuming that proper protocol was that they would be the first to talk. In silence, they continued their ride toward Greenwich Village.

"Carl," Ray finally asked, "What do you know about poker?"

"Enough to get into trouble," he answered honestly.

"There's a game downtown. I need you to help out."

"Whatever I can do, but I'm not . . ."

"I don't want you in the game. These sharks would eat you alive. It's one of our games. I need you to serve drinks, run errands, do whatever is needed to keep them happy and at the table. Keep your eyes and ears open and mouth shut. A player wants a sandwich or drink—you get it. A pissed-off player throws his cards across the room— you pick them up. Capisce?"

"Sure, but . . ."

"Carl, these games are important," Ray said in a friendly sharing voice, "A lot of big money changes hands and we get our vigorish. We give whales a safe place to have some fun and they pay for the security. The longer they play the more they bank and the more we make. Understand?"

"Ray . . . I don't know . . . if I will do a good job," Carl explained, "What if I piss off one of the players?"

"Then I shoot you," Ray replied. He turned and in the darkness of the automobile Carl could see he was smiling. "Get what they need when they need it.

Don't ask them anything. If they want something they'll tell you. For the whole night you don't have to say a single word. The losers will curse you and the winners will tip you. Just stay alert. Don't daydream or fall asleep. Constantly scan the room for a sign that a player needs something. This is your opportunity kid. I know you'll do a great job. Ho fiducia in voi. I have faith in you."

Greenwich Village was a tapestry of diversity. Writers and artists lived in small apartments over strange, outlandish, unique, quaint little shops. Dancers and performers called historic old buildings home. Beatniks, anarchists, and a growing population of hippies with their long hair, bell bottoms, beads, and peace symbols roamed the streets. Restaurants, offering every kind of cuisine, wedged themselves into any open space among the dissimilar structures and architecture. Up and coming professionals in the financial district resided in upgraded apartments in reclaimed sections of the Village. Performance spaces, pubs, and evangelical churches nestled with open arms among the inhabitants who seemed to be in perpetual motion. Street kids slept in the parks. And, a large homosexual population called Greenwich Village home. Any visitor to New York City, that had a chance, made at least one visit to The Village. A Friday or Saturday night was the best time to get the full effect.

This Friday night was warm and clear. By eight o'clock the sidewalks in Greenwich Village had already become crowded. People shuffled along window shopping, people watching, gazing at street side art galleries, or looking for a place to eat or drink. Among the many pedestrians, Andrew Newell walked south on Seventh Avenue. He was nervous and kept having second thoughts. More than once the five-foot-nine-inch eighteen-year-old stopped and stood like a deer in the headlights unable to move. Then after a mental wrestling match he continued his journey. He had taken the bus to the City from Teaneck, New Jersey where he lived with his parents while attending Fairleigh Dickinson University. They had no idea he was in Greenwich Village. To Andrew the crowds were exciting but also unnerving. He would much rather have been walking alone. When he reached Christopher Street he paused. Across the street was Christopher Park. He watched the many characters that wandered into the park and those leaving. There were young couples, tough looking individuals, hippies, and homosexuals. Once more he hesitated and considered returning home. Two young punks jostled Andrew from behind as they passed. He attempted to stand farther back out of the way of the flow of pedestrian traffic. Still he wrestled with himself and couldn't choose his next action.

A midnight blue 1969 Lincoln Continental traveled west on Christopher Street and stopped at the light at Seventh Avenue. The occupants didn't notice Andrew Newell standing against a building on the corner. He, in turn, was unaware of the automobile or its passengers. Inside the Lincoln, Ray Esposito pointed at an innocuous building that was two stories tall with three windows on the second floor. There was a brick arched doorway and large glass window on the first floor. The sign on the building read Stonewall Inn.

"That's a homosexual bar," Ray stated, "In 1966 the Genovese family invested $3,500 to turn a restaurant into that fag bar."

"Why would they want a fag bar?" Carl asked.

"Because, it's a good investment. The sodomites need somewhere to go, pay for over-priced watered-down drinks, fill the place every night, and they don't make trouble," he explained. He didn't reveal the other source of income. Many successful persons who frequented a homosexual bar desperately wanted anonymity. When they were identified, they became easy prey for blackmail. And, they were the last to go to the police. Many thousands of dollars in cash and negotiable bonds changed hands to protect reputations.

The light changed and they rode one block farther, made a left turn onto Bleecker Street, went to the next intersection and pulled over on the right at the corner of Grove Street and Bleecker Street. On that corner was a three-story red brick building with shops on the ground floor and an ornate door leading to the upper floors.

"OK Carl, this is the place," Ray stated. "The game begins at nine, so we have time to get ready for our guests,"

Two blocks away from the planned poker game Andrew Newell stood like a statue against a building on the corner of Seventh Avenue and Christopher Street. He could feel his heart pounding in his chest. This was something he had to do, but wasn't sure he would be able to do it. His palms sweat and his legs felt weak. For six years, he carried a burden that tortured his mind. Again and again, he tried to eliminate it from his life. Yet it remained. This night he was going to do something about it—if he had the courage. Slowly he took a step. Then another. He turned left onto Christopher Street. His hands shook. He moved east in a dreamlike state along the street until he was in front of the Stonewall Inn. In the window, he saw a reflection of himself. A young man with acceptably long blond hair wearing a light blue dress shirt, open at the collar, and black chinos. In the reflection, he also saw the faces of his parents and knew how angry they would be if they knew. Some passersby bumped him shaking him from his introspective thoughts. He stepped forward and tried the door but found it locked. When the door opened and a large bouncer stood before him he jumped.

"I don't recognize you. You been here before?" the large man asked.

"No . . . I . . . this is . . . my first time . . . maybe . . . I should leave . . . ," a nervous young man with a voice that cracked said.

"Relax kid," a friendlier voiced bouncer said welcomingly, "Come in." He waved Andrew to a stand with a book and pen on it. "Ya gotta sign in. We're a private club." He smiled, "At least as far as the cops know."

Andrew entered and looked at the book. He didn't want his parents or friends or relatives to know he was here.

"Sign any name. It doesn't matter."

Andrew Newell picked up the pen and signed Michael Cobb. He smiled as he thought about the school mate who was always picking on him now listed among the patrons of a homosexual bar.

"That'll be three dollars," the bouncer stated.

Andrew paid the entrance fee and was given tickets for two drinks.

Inside there was a main bar next to a dance floor. The walls were painted black with colored lighting adding to a subdued dark atmosphere. He could see couples dancing, heard laughter, and smelled an odd mixture of colognes. Some of the patrons seemed as normal as anyone you might meet on the street. Others were more obviously effeminate. And, in the back he saw a number of women who he assumed were transvestites.

"Hi," a voice came from his right.

Andrew turned and came face to face with a young professional man in his twenties wearing a well-tailored blue suit. He stood confidently holding a drink and looked Andrew in the eye. Andrew was immediately attracted to him. Yet, years of hiding from the truth caused him to be aloof, "Hi."

"Are you here alone?"

"Yes."

"Why don't you join me over here?" he waved toward an open part of the main bar. Andrew followed.

"What's your name?"

"Uh, Michael."

The young professional stared directly into Andrew's eyes and asked, "What's your real name?"

"Uh . . . it's . . . Andrew."

"That's better. Relax. You're among friends. My name is Jerry. Yes, that's my real name."

The card room where Carl would be working was professionally decorated with wood paneling, ficus trees, bookshelves, a couch and coffee table at one end, and a poker table in the middle of the room that was a work of art. A thick octagonal wood top sat on an ornate, wood carved, pedestal. Plush green felt covered most of the tabletop. In front of each player's position was an indented wooden tray with places for chips, cards, an ashtray, and a cork lined drink holder. The edge of the table was covered with cushioned leather for comfort. The chairs were matching soft leather with arm rests and nylon casters for quiet movement. Hung on the walls were various paintings depicting hunting and other outdoors activities. Polished oak wood floors completed a very masculine look and feel.

"Back here down the hall is the bar and kitchen," Ray pointed out. "The bartender and the chef will fill all orders." He stopped and looked at Carl's suit, "That's your best suit?"

"I haven't worn it in a while."

"You do good tonight, you use some of that tip money to buy a good suit. Go to Antonio's Custom Suits on Thirty Fifth Street. Tell him I sent you." He ran his hand down Carl's thread-worn lapel, "You don't work any of my games in shit like this. Capisce?"

"Capisce."

Ray laughed and slapped Carl on the cheek, "I'll make a gumba out of you yet."

By any standards, the Stonewall Inn was a dive. There was no running water behind the bar so used glasses were simply rinsed out in a water filled pan. Bathrooms were disgraceful, smelly, and always overflowing. There weren't any fire exits. The biggest draw was the two dance floors. At the time this was the only gay bar that offered dance floors. Andrew sat on a wooden bar stool that rocked back and forth on uneven legs. He held a bottle of beer in his hand that his new-found friend had suggested was the most hygienic drink to order.

"You're new to the bar scene so I better give you some pointers," Jerry offered. "Be very careful who you hook up with because there are a lot of different types in gay bars. If you're not careful you could go home with a sadist." He chuckled, "Unless that's what you want."

"I . . . right now . . . well . . . maybe I shouldn't have come."

"Look, I'm not trying to scare you. You're gay—right?"

"Uh . . . I'm . . . it's all . . . I guess."

"If you were still guessing you wouldn't be here," Jerry put his hand on Andrew's hand. "You're young and pretty and there are a lot of masters/tops who will grab you up before the night is over." He squeezed Andrew's hand, "You have to know what you want."

Andrew didn't move his hand and rather enjoyed the physical contact with another man. He didn't answer because, in truth, he didn't know what he wanted or needed.

"In every relationship one is dominant and the other submissive. It might be subtle or dramatic," Jerry explained. "In time, you'll know which you are more comfortable with. Right now, why don't you just enjoy the experience? Do you dance?" Again, Andrew didn't answer but allowed himself to be led to the dance floor.

At nine o'clock the players arrived. Ray Esposito greeted each man in a formal, yet familiar, manner. Each man's choice of drink had already been placed at their favorite seating position. In front of the five cigar smokers places was a cigar and cigar cutter.

"Tonight, my cigar selection is from Cuba, where else?" Ray announced, "The brand is Fonseca. It is milder than other cigars but the flavors are magnifico. Cigarette smokers we have your brand."

The players indicated the number of chips they wanted and the correct number were placed on the table. Carl stood by the door to the hallway and observed the entire operation. He was amazed at how smoothly everything was run. It was impressive. He didn't recognize any of the players but they all obviously were very well-heeled. They also were serious about poker as was evidenced by how quickly they sat and began the game. Antes were placed, cigars and cigarettes lit, cards dealt, and each gambler began his private routine. Ray handed Carl a piece of paper on which was a diagram of the table with the drink preferred by the player at each position. Also indicated was a signal they might use to get a drink or something else. Carl started to feel nervous.

In the early 1960s Mayor Robert F. Wagner, Jr. decided to rid the city of gay bars before the planned 1964 World's Fair. To accomplish this, the city revoked the liquor licenses of gay bars and undercover police arrested any patron that even remotely tried to leave with them. The bars survived by paying off police, getting tip offs about raids, and hiding liquor in walls or parked cars down the street to replace what was confiscated. Luckily, raids generally occurred early in the evening allowing bars to reopen after the police left. By ten o'clock the patrons at the Stonewall Inn had relaxed because no raid had taken place even though there had been raids at other gay bars earlier in the week.

"Where are you from, Andrew?" Jerry asked as the two men sat once again at the large bar.

"New Jersey."

"How did you hear about the Stonewall?

"I have friends who have been here. Now that I'm eighteen and can legally drink in New York, I decided to find out what it is like."

"Well, if you're going to swim with the sharks you better know the rules."

Andrew looked at Jerry and was so thankful that he met up with someone who was friendly and kind. He liked Jerry and wanted to go home with him, but didn't have the courage to ask. Even though he was a homosexual and had intimate encounters in New Jersey they were spontaneous and anonymous. He was totally unfamiliar with the New York City gay scene.

Jerry continued, "To begin, there is an unspoken language to keep you from making a terrible mistake when meeting partners. Keys and handkerchiefs are the main signals. Worn on the left means master, on the right—slave. The color of the flag tells you what they are into. Navy blue on left means pitcher—right catcher. Light blue on left wants a blowjob—right gives them. Grey means bondage, red fisting, yellow means golden showers, fuchsia spanking. The one you have to be careful about is black. Worn on the left means they are into applying heavy S and M. You get the idea."

"How do you know . . . what . . . you want?"

"You don't know til you try it," Jerry laughed.

Carl watched the game and understood what Ray meant when he said these guys would eat him alive. They were all business. Their betting and movements were practiced to eliminate any "tell" that would give away the quality of their hand. When they won a pot they simply retrieved the chips, left an ante, and continued playing. There were no emotions. As the game, continued Carl checked and rechecked the paper that Ray had given him to make sure he didn't miss a sign from a player. A heavyset player, wearing an expensive grey suit, smoking a cigar tapped a chip on his empty drink glass. Immediately, Carl walked over picked up the empty glass and went down the hall to the bar. He checked his cheat sheet and ordered Chivas Regal straight up. Quickly he returned to the table and placed the drink in the cork lined holder. As he did he said, "There ya go."

The player looked up from his cards and spat, "What the hell did you say?"

Carl was caught off guard and confused. He opened his mouth to respond but before a word could pass his lips a strong hand grabbed the back of his jacket and dragged him out into the hall.

"What part of say nothing didn't you understand?" Ray asked angrily.

Carl remained in shock and didn't know what to say. He decided not saying anything was the best approach. It turned out that he was right.

Ray continued, "These guys have so many requirements, superstitions, habits, and hang-ups that it doesn't take anything to throw them off their game. If Martin Eliot starts losing, it will be your fault. You broke his lucky streak or train of thought or concentration. Don't inject yourself into his game or any player's game. Get back in there and keep your eyes and ears open and mouth shut."

Carl returned to the game room. For the next few hours he got drinks, cigars, snacks, even a wet towel but never said a word.

At exactly 1:20 a.m. two policemen, four plainclothes police officers, Detective Charles Smythe, and Deputy Inspector Seymour Pine entered the Stonewall Inn. They announced, "Police! We're taking the place!"

Two undercover policemen and two undercover policewomen had infiltrated the bar earlier in the evening to gather evidence. When they were satisfied that they had enough to close the place down they called the Sixth Precinct on a pay telephone.

The music was turned off and main lighting turned on causing most of the crowd of over 200 to temporarily have trouble seeing which added to the confusion. Everyone was ordered to line up and have their identification ready. Managers and staff were taken into custody.

Andrew Newell was slightly inebriated and completely confused. He turned to his friend and asked, "Jerry, what's going on?"

Jerry stood and stated, "I'm officer Campbell and you're under arrest for solicitation. Turn around and put your hands behind your back."

"What's happening?" Andrew pleaded.

"Turn around and put your hands behind your back!"

Andrew complied as he shakily turned around and put his hands behind him. Cold metal handcuffs circled his wrists and he was led to the lobby. His head spun more from emotion than alcohol. What would his parents think? They didn't know about his sexual orientation and now to find out this way. He had trouble standing. Tears ran down his cheeks. If he could he would cut his wrists then and there and end the nightmare that was his life. Officer Jerry Campbell guided Andrew by the arm through the front doors out of the Stonewall Inn.

Two blocks away within sight of the Stonewall Inn the card players were unaware of the police raid. Big money was changing hands and a number of players had to go to the bank for more chips. This, of course, meant the house received more vig. The heavyset player, wearing an expensive grey suit who had confronted Carl earlier was on a winning streak. Twice he had drawn three cards and filled a full house. He called Carl over.

"What was it you said to me kid?" he asked in a friendly voice.

Carl was reluctant to answer and looked toward Ray Esposito, who nodded. He then answered, "I said, there ya go."

"Right," the big man replied, "From now on when you're at the game you make sure you say 'there ya go' before we begin." He slipped three chips in Carl's jacket's breast pocket.

The game resumed and Carl watched for signals and fulfilled orders.

Patrons of the Stonewall Inn who were lined up waited. Those men who were dressed as women were asked to go into the bathroom with policewomen to have their gender verified. On this night, for whatever reasons, they refused to cooperate. This was followed by the other patrons refusing to show their identification. At this point the police decided to take them all to the Sixth Precinct which required additional patrol wagons. They also had to transport confiscated liquor, twenty-eight cases of beer and nineteen bottles of liquor.

Outside, Officer Jerry Campbell led Andrew Newell along the street close to the building. They got to the corner at Seventh Avenue and turned uptown. Once out of sight of the activity at the bar he stopped, turned Andrew around and said, "Look, you seem like a good kid. Stay in New Jersey. This scene isn't for you. You'll only get hurt." He removed the handcuffs from Andrew's wrists and added, "Take off and don't look back."

In disbelief Andrew looked at his wrists and then Officer Campbell. Through tears he said in a soft, almost whisper, "Thank you."

"I don't know what makes a homosexual a homosexual. Maybe you are just born that way. Go home. Tell your parents. I think they will surprise you. At least you won't have to keep living in fear of them finding out. They probably will give you the support and love you need. Take care of yourself, Andrew." Jerry Campbell turned and returned to the Stonewall Inn.

Andrew Newell walked slowly up Seventh Avenue. It seemed so long ago that he hesitantly walked in the opposite direction. Until the police raid he had really enjoyed himself. He cared about Jerry. He felt safe with him. He would miss him. He knew he could have loved him.

Ray Esposito and the players became aware of sirens outside. The poker game ceased and eight nervous men prepared to leave. At that point, one of the guards at the door downstairs came in and told the group that there had been a raid on the Stonewall Inn. Given this reassurance the game resumed.

Police vans were slow to arrive and the crowd that stood in line inside the Stonewall Inn became impatient. Police decided to let those who cooperated and showed identification to leave. Steve, who called himself Maria Ritter later admitted, "My biggest fear was that I would get arrested. My second biggest fear was that my picture would be in a newspaper or on a television report in my mother's dress!" Approximately 100 patrons were allowed to leave. Yet, instead of disappearing into the night as was the custom, they congregated outside the bar. Quickly they were joined by others from Christopher Park and the surrounding area. The crowd swelled to more than 200 outside the Stonewall Inn.

When the first police wagon arrived and those who were being arrested were escorted out of the bar the crowd outside became silent. It was an ominous sign of something about to happen. Someone yelled, "Gay Power" and others began singing, *We Shall Overcome*. One police officer shoved a transvestite toward the van and she turned and hit him on the head with her purse. The crowd booed and started throwing pennies at the police. Then a beer bottle flew out of the crowd and hit the van. Things were at a breaking point needing no more than the slightest provocation—which promptly occurred.

A woman, who could have been mistaken for a man based on how she was dressed, in handcuffs was escorted to the police van. After being placed inside, she jumped back out and wrestled with police who put her back into the van several times. At one point a patrolman struck her on the head with his baton. She yelled to the crowd, "Why don't you guys do something?" as she was roughly thrown into the van a final time. That spark set off the events that followed.

The game was finished and all the players settled up with the bank. Some were pleased and others looked forward to getting even next time. None were overly concerned with cash gains or losses as they could all easily afford the cost of an evening's entertainment and challenge. It was the competitive spirit and drive to best other powerful men that was the attraction.

At this point the atmosphere changed as eight combatants finished their drinks and chatted with each other while waiting for their rides to arrive. Sirens continued to sound outside which raised the anxiety level slightly.

"Either there were a boatload of faggots in that bar or they're putting up a fight." One player observed.

"I don't think a fight, so much as a flair," another player added which resulted in laughter.

The doorman announced the arrival of two limousines and two players departed.

Carl stood by the door and said nothing as the men passed. One, who had been a loser brushed right by while the other slipped a bill into Carl's breast pocket.

"Next time, Ray, a little quieter location," a player quipped, "This is hard on my concentration. I played like shit, tonight."

"Maybe we can get the back room at the Stonewall," Ray Esposito answered.

After a pause and some muffled laughter, the player replied, "Here will do."

More cars arrived and additional players left.

When the heavyset player, wearing an expensive grey suit who had confronted Carl earlier left he said, "Remember kid, next time I want to hear 'there ya go' before the game begins." He slipped three more chips into Carl's pocket and left. He was the big winner of the night.

When the room was empty Ray walked over to Carl and said, "You did good, Carl. Better cash in those chips before we leave."

It was then that Carl removed the contents of his pocket. He had six $100 chips and five $100 bills. He couldn't believe that he made so much money for a single night's work. Being on the inside was looking better and better.

Ray walked over to Carl and said, "Clean the place up. I want it immaculate. When you're done tell Tommy, the bartender. He'll lock up." Once again Ray fingered Carl's lapel, "And, for chrisakes get a new suit." He turned and left.

After witnessing the woman being thrown into a police van the crowd became unruly. They rushed the van and two police cars. Rocks and bottles were thrown and tires on the police cars were slashed. Immediately, the police cars and van left the scene. More people from surrounding areas joined the crowd which grew to over 500 persons. Someone yelled that the police raided the place because they hadn't been paid off. Someone else added, "Then, let's pay them off." Coins were thrown at the police followed by beer cans, bottles and bricks from a nearby construction site. Inspector Pine and ten police officers found refuge in the Stonewall Inn. Officer Jerry Campbell held a handkerchief to a cut on the side of his head.

Emboldened by the police retreat the crowd began throwing bricks, bottles, and garbage cans. They lit garbage cans on fire and tossed burning debris at the building. The windows were broken and the crowd used a parking meter as a battering ram on the doors. When the doors flew open the police drew their weapons.

Before any shots were fired, the Tactical Police Force (TPF) of the New York City Police Department arrived along with the fire department. Given the larger number of police they began arresting the perpetrators and dispersing the crowd. Some realized that it was over and left the scene but an indignant and angry group of transvestites formed a chorus kick line to mock the police. They sang an impromptu song to the tune of the *Howdy Doody Show.*

> We are the Stonewall girls,
> We wear our hair in curls,
> We don't wear underwear,
> We show our pubic hair.

Unimpressed the tactical police formed a line and marched toward the kick line swinging their night sticks. The transvestites were subdued and arrested. By 4:00 a.m. relative calm had returned to Christopher Street.

Carl walked one block west on Grove Street, turned left onto Seventh Avenue, and walked one block north to Christopher Street. He planned to catch the Number 1 train to Times Square, the Shuttle to Grand Central, and the Number 4 to the Bronx. As he approached Christopher Street he smelled smoke and saw fire engines and numerous police cars. Debris covered the streets and sidewalks and small groups of young men milled around. Immediately, he thought about the eleven hundred dollars that he carried. If anyone came too close to him they were going to be on the receiving end of a quick takedown. When he reached the entrance to the subway he could see the damaged front of the Stonewall Inn. Two young street punks came in his direction. Years of experience told him he was being sized up. They wouldn't do anything in the open with all of the police around but down in the subway it would be a different story. Carl turned on his heel and started up Seventh Avenue. When he saw a taxi with its light on he quickly flagged it and made his escape.

Anna Six Trees listened as her mother told her about wild rice which the Ojibwa people call manoomin, meaning "harvesting berry" or "good berry." She explained how the plant was not really rice but an aquatic grass or water oat. This highly nutritious grain that was a staple in their culture was considered sacred and knowing how to cultivate and harvest it an essential part of their education.

18: Saturday – June 28, 1969

Ritchie Anderson pulled his long hair back into a ponytail to keep it out of his eyes. It was a warm summer morning. He and Fetch were riding in Hilda his 1966 Ford Econoline van. As it didn't have air conditioning all the windows were open. This was fine with Fetch who enjoyed hanging her head out of the window and letting the wind blow across her face. They were headed to New York City. Over the past five years Ritchie had become fervently interested in the World Trade Center ever since he saw the original artist's concept drawings in 1964. At that time, he devised a plan to document the transition of lower Manhattan in photographs, sketches, and paintings. To do so he had to keep track of and record progress of the project from planning to completion.

The idea of building a World Trade Center in New York City actually was first proposed in 1943. Nothing happened and the idea languished. Throughout the 1950s most of the growth in Manhattan had been in the midtown area. That was until one individual, David Rockefeller, who was chairman of a committee to determine where Chase Manhattan Bank would build their new headquarters got involved. He believed in the future of the financial district in lower Manhattan. Given his influence the 60 story One Chase Manhattan Plaza bank headquarters was built in 1960 on Liberty Street in lower Manhattan. Directly across the street from the Federal Reserve Bank of New York, it became the largest bank building with the largest bank vault in the world. Initially, the plan was to build a World Trade Center on the east side of lower Manhattan. However, the Port Authority required agreement from the governors of both New York and New Jersey. New Jersey Governor Robert B. Meyner objected to the location and plans were shelved. Finally, in 1961 everything came together. Newly elected New Jersey governor Richard J. Hughes and Port Authority director Austin J. Tobin agreed that the World Trade Center should be on the west side of lower Manhattan where New Jersey's Hudson and Manhattan Railroad (H&M) terminal was located. In addition, the Port Authority agreed to take over the flagging railroad which was renamed the Port Authority Trans Hudson (PATH). It was a logical solution as commuters from New Jersey could take the train directly into the World Trade Center.

On September 20, 1962, the Port Authority selected Minoru Yamasaki as lead architect and Emery Roth & Sons as associate architects. Yamasaki considered over one hundred designs before settling on the twin towers. His original plan called for the towers to be 80 stories tall, but to meet the Port Authority's requirement for 10 million square feet of office space, the buildings had to be increased to 110 stories. This required a unique style and type of construction.

Tishman Realty & Construction Company was the general contractor on the World Trade Center project. The revolutionary design of the buildings required the use of many new technique. Outside walls consisted of 59 columns per side closely aligned which only allowed for narrow 18 inch windows. Some believe this was a reflection of Yamasaki's fear of heights. The center core of the towers were rectangular in shape 87 feet by 135 feet containing 47 steel columns which ran from the bedrock to the top of each tower. Inside the core were elevator shafts, restrooms, stairwells, and utility shafts. Large open space floors were made possible through the use of prefabricated floor trusses that were attached to the outer frame and inner core. Viscoelastic dampers were used on the connections to the perimeter columns to reduce the amount of sway felt by building occupants.

With tall buildings, a great deal of floor space is lost to facilitate elevators. To reduce this impact the World Trade Center towers' engineers devised a new system with "sky lobbies" at the 44th and 78th floors. High-capacity elevators would lift people to these two levels where they would transfer to local elevators. This configuration allowed the local elevators to share the same shafts at different heights thus reducing the footprint of elevators. The final design for the World Trade Center was unveiled to the public on January 18, 1964. On that day, Richard Carlton Anderson was hooked.

The fact that the tallest buildings in the world would be right in his backyard struck a chord with Ritchie. He wanted to start at the beginning and follow the undertaking through completion with photographs, sketches, and paintings. When he first became engaged and learned where the buildings would be located he traveled to downtown Manhattan to record what was originally there. Thirteen square blocks of low rise buildings and the well-known radio row commercial district bounded by Vesey Street, Liberty Street, Church Street, and West Street were demolished to begin construction. Before that occurred Ritchie photographed all of the buildings and streets. He spent time sitting on stoops sketching the neighborhood. In a sense, he was ravenous to capture as much of the doomed structures, thoroughfares, and way of life as he could before the wrecking ball of progress erased it from the city forever. For five years Ritchie periodically drove into Manhattan to visually document the birth of the World Trade Center. Generally, he would venture there on Saturdays or Sundays when traffic was lighter and parking places could be found.

This was the first time that Ritchie had brought Fetch on his World Trade Center sojourn. His plan to mainly do photography led him to believe Fetch wouldn't be a problem. Funny thing about beliefs—they are not always true. It seemed every time Ritchie discovered a picture worth taking Fetch discovered something worth chasing. He succeeded in taking an entire roll of motion-blurred shots of the building site.

The north tower was already twenty-one floors tall while the south tower had just begun to sprout above ground. Like some colossal garden the grand visions of man were beginning to grow, take shape, and reach bravely to the sky to fulfill their promise. To an untrained eye the building site was chaos. Different pieces of heavy equipment strewn about like toys spread across a child's bedroom floor. Building materials stacked here and there. Garbage and refuse piled in various out-of-the-way places. Evidence of the involvement of human beings could be found everywhere. These, of course, were impossible to ignore by an artist. A discarded workman's glove in the dirt covering part of a footprint made by a steel toed work boot, a lone paper cup on a steel beam two floors above the ground, cigarette butts forming what appeared to be a map of the United States, and a twisted piece of metal which might have been a harbinger of the future of this great manmade endeavor.

Included in Ritchie's portfolio was Battery Park City. This 92-acre area off the southwestern tip of Manhattan was created using over three million cubic yards of rock and soil excavated during the construction of the World Trade Center and other projects throughout the city. It was to be the home of the World Financial Center along with numerous housing, commercial, and retail buildings.

Ritchie and Fetch walked around the building sites. While Ritchie took pictures, Fetch explored new and exciting venues, chased squirrels, cats, and a number of other unidentified creatures. It was destined to be the last time Fetch would be allowed to accompany Ritchie to the World Trade Center.

Jack Moore entered More-Or-Less late in the afternoon. Harry Van Ryker, the bartender, didn't see him. He was chatting with another regular customer. The bar was relatively quiet for a late Saturday afternoon, however, Jack found his favorite barstool empty and occupied it. When Harry finally did see him he walked over, placed a shot glass in front of his friend, and filled it with Dewars.

"Hey lover, how you been?" The bartender quipped.

Jack picked up the glass and sipped the liquor, "Down boy. You're a little ahead of yourself. Detective Akimoto and I are just getting to know one another."

"What's it been? A month?"

"Four weeks and four days, but who's counting."

"All I know is you haven't been here as often, so you must be spending your time somewhere . . . with someone."

"Jealous?"

"Jealous? Me? Remember, I'm the one that got you in this predicament."

"And, what predicament is that?"

"Running headlong into captivity. Giving up your free will. Having your individualism surgically removed. Watching your confidence erode. Need I go on?"

"You make it sound so wonderful," Jack concluded.

"How the hell would I know," Harry said in an uncharacteristically melancholy voice, "I let my opportunity slip away."

Before Jack could reply Harry bolted to the other end of the bar to refill a patron's glass. Jack watched his old friend and for the first time in all the years they'd known each other wondered if Harry was lonely. He always assumed that Harry had lady friends when not working the bar but, then again, they never broached the subject. It was then that Jack realized that they were only part-time friends. Yes, they did things together away from the bar but it was on rare occasions. Neither man had really allowed the other into his life.

Harry returned and said lightheartedly, "Hey, I'm glad things are going well. Name your first born after me."

"Who'd you let slip away?" Jack pressed.

"Drop it. OK?"

"No, we're friends. I want to know the real Harry Van Ryker." Jack explained in a serious tone, "It's a dimension of you I haven't seen. I'm interested."

"What if I don't want to talk about it?"

"Then I'll drop it. But, if it is something that you would share with an old friend, I'd appreciate it."

"It was a long time ago and not very interesting," Harry offered.

"That's OK, I've got nothing to do until tonight."

"Your lady working?"

"Yeah."

Harry ran off to take care of a number of customers. Jack looked around the room. He recognized some regulars, nodded to those who waved, and decided that there weren't any unusual characters worth watching.

When Harry returned he immediately said, "Wait a minute! I must be losing my power of observation. Is that Jack Moore in a blue, freakin, suit? I knew something was different, but this is inconceivable. There's not a touch of brown on you." Harry grabbed Jack's lapels and yelled, "Where is Jack Moore and what have you done with him?"

Jack laughed.

Harry began without coaxing, "When I was on the job I was seeing this young lady. She was a school teacher. Taught problem students in a school in Washington Heights. It wasn't an easy job. From what I heard it would test the patience of a saint. Yet, she always seemed to see the good side of things. Those kids would pull every kind of stunt, act up, not do the work, exhibit every kind of social maladjustment, fight, be disrespectful and, no-matter-what, she would try to focus on their good attributes and nurture them."

"Sounds like quite a lady," Jack observed.

"When we were together we tuned out the world. What was so funny was that we would talk. I mean about nothing and everything. Neither one of us had to think of something to say; we always had something to say—to each other. Hours would pass and we wouldn't notice." Harry poured himself a ginger ale, "Jack, don't ever tell anyone this, but I even enjoyed shopping with her."

Jack held up his hand, "Scout's honor."

"As I said I was on the job, foot patrol. There were times the streets were quiet and other times when the streets tested your resolve. After those rough tours, I wasn't always the happy-go-lucky guy that you know."

"Uh, huh."

"Even those times when I might have been a little gruff, she smiled, deflected my barbs, and brought me back to the world of human beings. In many ways, I was her worst student." Harry stopped talking. He poured another Dewars for Jack and then uncharacteristically poured one for himself. Jack didn't comment letting his friend gather his thoughts or come to terms with his emotions. Harry left to refill a patron's glass. When he returned he still had a dispirited countenance. Jack remained silent.

"We were together for almost a year. It was a good year. It was my best year." Harry sipped the scotch in his glass as he considered the accuracy of that statement. He looked down at the bar, "I had a tour one night when I caught three punks breaking into a car. I chased them into a dead-end alley and found myself face to face with them. One had a wood stick, another a garbage can lid, and the third a knife. Without a doubt, I was scared. I pulled my service revolver and threatened to shoot all three of them if they didn't face the wall. Fortunately, they complied. Later that evening when she and I were together my adrenalin was still pumping and I was nervous. It was an arrest—that's all. But, I couldn't let go of it. Was it because I now had someone I cared about? Had I lost my nerve? My whole body was electric. I paced. She tried so hard to make me feel better. However, this time she couldn't talk me down. Somehow, having someone you leave behind made a difference. Out of the blue I realized that it could affect my judgment. Then she asked if I liked being a cop. I took it the wrong way, you know, when people ask that question with a sneer. I snapped and told her if a cop wasn't good enough for her she could go to hell. She just looked at me with a shocked look on her face. She wasn't judging me as a cop, she wanted to know if I truly was happy being a cop. My head was screwed up. I had to leave. As I went for the door she reached out and grabbed my arm. I swung my arm back to get her to let go and hit her in the face." Harry looked up with a stricken look and stated, "I hit the woman I loved!"

Jack didn't speak but nodded to indicate that he had heard. He could have said it was an accident and not to be so hard on himself but how would that help. It was a long time ago and if he did convince Harry that he was mistaken it would only cause additional pain as he would realize that he unnecessarily gave up the woman he loved.

Harry continued, "There's no way I could be forgiven for that or trusted again. More importantly, I couldn't trust myself. What if it happened again? She deserved better. I left and didn't call or return calls. The only honorable thing I could do was to never put her at risk again. And, as time passed it became impossible to retrace steps or return to those terrific times. I let it slip away, but I had to." Harry finished the scotch. "You asked."

"What was her name?"

"Carol."

Thousands of people gathered in front of the Stonewall Inn after the previous night's riots. They began harassing pedestrians and people in cars. Garbage cans were set on fire and chaos spread to surrounding neighborhoods. Over a hundred police officers were on hand but had trouble controlling the unruly crowd. By 2:00 a.m. the Tactical Police Force was called in once more.

Allen Ginsberg, a poet and longtime Greenwich Village resident who lived on Christopher Street visited the Stonewall Inn for the first time. While walking home, he declared to Lucian Truscott, "You know, the guys there were so beautiful—they've lost that wounded look that fags all had 10 years ago."

However, not every homosexual was in favor of the antics and rioting. Older members of the gay community, who worked so hard to show that they were no different than heterosexuals, found the violence and effeminate behavior embarrassing. A gentleman, Randy Wicker, who had marched in front of the White House in 1965 said, "Screaming queens forming chorus lines and kicking went against everything that I wanted people to think about homosexuals ... that we were a bunch of drag queens in the Village acting disorderly and tacky and cheap." Many felt the closing of the sleazy Stonewall Inn was a good thing.

Regardless of one's opinion, emotions ran wild and were contagious. And, like the race riots two years earlier in cities across America a single event often leads to greater events which change society in ways that cannot be predicted. The fairy was out of the bottle and would never be recaptured.

Robert Six Trees had his vision. He saw Chibiabos who was murdered by water spirits which was followed by events that led to the destruction of the earth by flood. According to Ojibwe legend Chibiabos became ruler of the underworld as a kind being who takes good care of the land of the dead.

19: Thursday - July 3, 1969

Miguel was still angry about losing his guns. The whole plan was too well-thought-out for the theft to have been a coincidence. It was either an inside job or someone had a big mouth. Only a limited number of trusted associates and that little dipshit driver were the ones who knew where the car was to be parked and when. After highly contentious questioning he was convinced that none of his people had anything to do with the loss. This was why he was where he was at that moment.

Two young men were tied to chairs in the basement of an abandoned tenement building in Harlem. They had each been abducted by members of Miguel's gang. Sylvester Attoro was grabbed as he sat on the stoop of the apartment building he lived in with his parents. Moe Black, Sylvester's friend, had just left a candy store where he lifted a *Playboy Magazine*. Now they were tied to two mismatched old beat-up wooden chairs back-to-back against a pole. Rope was tied around their necks holding their heads upright against the pole. Both had been beat up displaying numerous bruises and abrasions.

"Now, I want to know who you told about my gun run," Miguel stated menacingly as he patted his left hand with a cut-off broomstick that resembled a police baton.

Moe mumbled through swollen lips, "I don't know anything about any guns."

"So, your friend—who tells you everything—whose dick you suck—didn't tell you where he was going, man?" Miguel asked inches from Moe's face.

"No!"

"You lie to me, man, and I'll cut off your balls and make you eat them. You understand me, man?"

Sweat ran down Moe's face and he was near tears, "He didn't tell me nothing. I swear!"

"We'll see," Miguel moved in front of Sylvester, "What did you tell your faggot friend?"

Sylvester was in severe pain as his broken left arm hung at his side after the cast had been smashed. His eyes showed intense fear as he was near panic wanting to flee. That, of course, was impossible as he was held in place against the pole. In a gravelly voice he said, "I didn't tell him anything. Honest."

"You didn't brag about making the gun run?"

"No."

"You didn't tell him where you were going?"

"No."

"You didn't tell him where you got the car?"

"No."

"Is he your lover? You trying to protect your lover?"

"I didn't tell him anything." Sylvester stated as he shook his head as far as the rope would allow.

Miguel hit the broken arm with his club. A high-pitched scream filled the basement followed by a gurgling sound as Sylvester pulled against the rope around his neck. "Who did you talk to?"

Tears ran down Sylvester's face and his breathing became short and quick as he hyperventilated. The room began to spin and he felt lightheaded. He couldn't form words as he slurred, "No . . ."

Miguel returned to Moe. The young hood had a stricken look on his face.

"Your friend, he says, you know nothing," Miguel said in a friendly voice. "Whether or not that is true you are here and you know what is taking place here."

Moe didn't respond. He stared at the menacing interrogator with wide open eyes.

"If I let you go, how do I know you won't talk?"

In a desperate attempt to save himself Moe said as convincingly as possible, "I won't say nothing, ever. You can trust me. Honest. He's just someone I know. He never said nothing. Please, believe me."

Miguel leaned close to Moe. The smell of his breath was intense. "Two guys are going to take you back downtown. You were never here. If you ever speak of it, worse than what happens to that piece of shit will happen to you. Comprende?"

"Yes," Moe whispered.

Five thousand nine hundred thirty miles away a Russian N1 rocket stood on a launch pad at The Baikonur Cosmodrome. Many historic flights had lifted off from the world's first and largest operational launch facility. Sputnik 1, the first man-made satellite, launched October 4, 1957; Luna 1, the first spacecraft to fly close to the Moon, launched January 2, 1959; Yuri Gagarin flew the first manned orbital flight April 12, 1961; Valentina Tereshkova, the first woman in space, lifted off in 1963.

On this day, vehicle serial number 5L – Zond L1S-2 was ready to launch. Atop the N1 was a new lunar package known as the L3. It was comprised of an adapted Soyuz spacecraft and the new LK lunar lander. There were also three cosmonauts onboard as Russia made a desperate attempt to beat the United States by putting a man on the moon two weeks before Apollo 11. Whether or not they could safely return to Earth was not an issue.

The Russian N1 rocket was their answer to the American Saturn V. It was shorter but wider that the Saturn with the first stage made up of thirty smaller rockets. The Russian rocket used only kerosene fuel in all three of its stages while the Saturn V used higher energy liquid hydrogen as fuel. The Saturn V also had a superior reliability record having never lost a payload, while three previous N1 launch attempts all resulted in failure.

With the countdown complete the huge N1 rocket lifted off the launch pad. The night sky became bright as enormous flames pushed the rocket skyward. Then seven seconds after liftoff a loose bolt was ingested by an oxygen pump. As a result, the automatic engine control shut off 29 of the 30 rockets causing the N1 to fall back onto the launch pad. What followed was one of the largest artificial non-nuclear explosions in human history.

The Russian story for the press was that the rocket was headed for Moon orbit to photograph possible manned landing sites. Three brave souls were never acknowledged as, according to the Russian space bureau, they never existed.

Another strike on Sylvester's broken arm brought screams of agony from the terrorized hood. He coughed as his throat was compressed from pulling against the rope around his neck. Tears ran down his face and he sobbed uncontrollably.

"Tell me who you talked to before I start to twist that arm until the bone snaps completely," Miguel warned.

"Please . . ."

"Tell me now and I might let you live."

"I . . . told . . . Carl . . . Carl Pythacyk . . ." Sylvester weeped.

"I knew that Polack asshole had something to do with it. Does he have the guns?" Miguel queried.

"I . . . don't know . . . who . . . took them. I . . . was hit . . . from behind."

Miguel stood back from the bound captive, "I knew Carl was the one. He will pay. I'm going to make him beg for his life."

Moe Black was dropped off on Sixty Third Street. Nothing was said to him. They simply pushed him out of the car. He was beaten and bruised, had rope burns on his neck, and was still shaking. As he staggered to a low brick wall and sat down he didn't hear the pain-driven shrieks of his friend as his tongue was cut out.

When Carl told a salesman at Antonio's Custom Suits on Thirty Fifth Street that Ray Esposito had sent him he wasn't prepared for the reaction. The man became nervous and stammered, "Antonio, he'sa not here now. If he know'sa you were coming he'sa be here ready."

"That's no problem," Carl replied, "I simply need a new suit."

"Antonio, he insist that he take care of all of Mister Esposito's friends."

Reality hit Carl as he looked at the frightened salesman. He'd seen that kind of fear before when he intimidated some young punks. Once more he felt the power of being "in" with Ray Esposito. A growing feeling of respect and loyalty to Ray flowed over him. He was aware of a dichotomy of roles. When with Ray he was the bottom of the totem pole, the hired help, a servant. Yet, with outsiders his association with Ray made him bigger than life, someone to be respected, someone to be feared. He knew that he would have to keep his sometimes-quick temper in check. This was the big leagues. This was for real. A slip could be fatal. On the other hand, the potential payoff could be more than he ever dreamed. For that reason, if ordered to he would shine Tony's shoes without complaint because in time that would change. He would prove himself and move up the ladder with greater rewards on every rung.

"When will Antonio be here?" Carl asked.

"He'sa come back soon."

"How soon."

"Maybe, half an hour, or maybe less."

"I'll wait."

A press conference was held in Hartfield, Sussex, England. The head investigator stepped up to the podium and announced that Brian Jones, former lead guitar player of the Rolling Stones, had been found dead. He went on to describe that around midnight Jones was discovered motionless at the bottom of his swimming pool at Cotchford Farm. His girlfriend, Anna Wohlin, was at home at the time. He was pronounced dead at the scene. A preliminary coroner's report indicated that it was most likely "death by misadventure" as there were no signs of foul play.

Lewis Brian Hopkins Jones was born February 28, 1942. Louisa, his mother was a piano teacher. Lewis, his father, was an aeronautical engineer who also played piano and organ, as well as led the choir at a local church. Brian had an IQ of 135, did well in school in spite of making very little effort, but had trouble conforming. A childhood friend remarked, "He was a rebel without a cause, but when examinations came he was brilliant."

When Brian Jones heard Cannonball Adderley's music for the first time he became interested in jazz. On his seventeenth birthday his parents gave him an acoustic guitar.

Jones moved to London where he became friends with Alexis Korner, Paul Jones, and future Cream bassist Jack Bruce. They and others made up a small London rhythm and blues scene. While in London, Brian Jones and Paul Jones started a blues group called the Roosters. When they both eventually left in January 1963, Eric Clapton took over Brian Jones' position as guitarist.

In May of 1962 Brian Jones ran an advertisement in Jazz News seeking musicians for a new R&B group at the Bricklayer's Arms pub. Pianist Ian Stewart was the first to respond. Later Mick Jagger joined the band and recruited his childhood friend Keith Richards. As the story goes, Brian Jones came up with the name Rolling Stones while on the phone when a club owner asked what the band was called. He looked at The Best of Muddy Waters album lying on the floor and used the title on track five, side one—Rollin' Stone. The Rolling Stones first played on July 12, 1962 in the Marquee Club in London. The band was comprised of Brian Jones, Mick Jagger, Keith Richards, Ian Stewart, Dick Taylor, and Tony Chapman.

One of the distinct sounds of the Rolling Stones was what Keith Richards called "guitar weaving" whereby both guitarists, he and Brian Jones, play rhythm and lead without boundaries. It often makes two guitars sound like four or five.

Brian Jones founded the group and was its leader. However, over time Mick Jagger and Keith Richards overshadowed him when they began writing original songs together. His role diminished more due to a growing alcohol and drug problem. He frequently used LSD, pills, and cannabis.

Keith Richards and Brian Jones didn't get along. This affected their relationship and performance together. Then in March of 1967 Jones' girlfriend of two years, Anita Pallenberg, left him for Keith Richards. It happened in Morocco where the three were visiting and Jones had been hospitalized.

On May 10, 1967 Brian Jones was arrested for drug possession. He was arrested a second time on May 21, 1968. Due to his substance abuse and mood swings it became difficult for him to participate in the band. Attendance at rehearsals and recording sessions became erratic and he had trouble playing music. Finally, he was asked to leave the Rolling Stones in June 1969. Less than a month later he was dead.

At the time of his death Brian Jones was twenty-seven years old. In the music world this made him a member of the 27 Club—musicians who die at the age of twenty-seven. Prior to his death a number of other musicians died at that age. Among them;

Louis Chauvin–ragtime musician–neurosyphilitic sclerosis–3/26/1908
Robert Johnson–blues musician–unknown–8/16/38
Nat Jaffe–blues musician–high blood pressure–8/5/45

Jesse Belvin–R&B singer and songwriter–car wreck–2/6/60
Rudy Lewis–vocalist of The Drifters–drug overdose–5/20/64
Malcolm Hale–member Spanky and Our Gang–carbon monoxide–10/31/68

These deaths might be a coincidence if not for the fact that more than 25 musicians died at the age of 27 after Brian Jones' death. Among the more famous:
Alan Wilson–lead singer of Canned Heat–suicide–9/3/70
Jimi Hendrix–Jimi Hendrix Experience–drug overdose–9/18/70
Janis Joplin–singer/songwriter–drug overdose–10/4/70
Jim Morrison–member the Doors–drug overdose–7/3/71
Linda Jones–R&B singer–diabetic coma–3/14/72
Ron McKernan–member Grateful Dead–alcoholism–3/8/73
Wallace Yohn–Organ player of Chase–plane crash–8/12/74
Dave Alexander–member The Stooges–pulmonary edema–2/10/75
Peter Ham–member Badfinger–suicide–4/24/75
Gary Thain–member Uriah Heep–drug overdose–12/8/75
Jacob Miller–member Inner Circle–car wreck–3/23/80
Freaky Tah–member Lost Boyz–gunshot–3/28/99
Amy Winehouse–alcohol–7/23/2011

One last coincidence; Jim Morrison of the Doors died exactly two years after Brian Jones. The legend continues, whether true or not—one fact is undeniable—rock and blues musicians average lifespan is 36.9 years compared with the average lifespan of 75.8 years. Indeed, the price of fame often is paid in years.

Antonio returned in approximately ten minutes. When he walked in the door the salesman ran over to him and spoke rapidly in Italian. The shop owner looked over at Carl, put down the package he was carrying, and rushed to where he sat.

"Marone, I didn't know you were coming today, Mr. Carl."

Carl stood, "No problem."

"I will personally help you, eh. You're here for a suit, yes?"

"Yes. I . . . "

"Let me show you our best custom Italian suits." Antonio led Carl to a rack near the back of the store. He moved a few suits one way then another. Examined other suits and picked a rich dark green with black pinstripe three-piece suit. "This, Gino Valentino wool/silk blend suit perfect for year-round use." He held it up, "You see modern business cut, two button, side vents, and vest make you look molto sofisticato."

"I don't know," Carl looked for a price tag but found none.

"I take care of you," He slipped the jacket off the hanger and held it up for Carl to try it on. "Trust Antonio."

Carl slipped into the jacket. It felt cool and soft. The fit was perfect and he liked the color. Antonio guided him to a three-angle mirror. What he saw amazed him. Instead of a young punk in a black tee shirt he saw a grown man who could be a successful businessman, lawyer, or banker. "It looks great. How much?"

"The fit, she is not right," Antonio pulled the front of the jacket out, put his fingers between the inside of the jacket and Carl's stomach. He moved to the back and marked the shoulders with soap. Carl was amazed as the small Italian man moved around him tugging and marking with soap here and there. Then he stood in front of Carl and slipped his hand under his left arm and asked, "Do you need room?"

"Room?"

"Romm per una pistola?"

"I don't understand."

"A pistola. Capisce. Uh, gun."

"Oh, no, no pistola."

"OK, try on the trousers."

"Wait. How much does this suit cost?"

"This suit, she is nine hundred dollars."

"Whoa, I can't afford that."

"Siete cliente speciale. Uh, you are special customer. Two hundred dollars. Now, you try on trousers, Mr. Carl."

Carl didn't answer. He simply followed instructions. Once more he was amazed at the power of the Ray Esposito name. He was becoming addicted to the lifestyle and knew he would do whatever was necessary to remain in it. He thought of Sylvester Attoro and decided he owed the little twerp a dinner.

Wanda Six Trees crafted a dreamcatcher out of feathers, beads and leather. The Ojibwe believe that if one is hung above the head of a sleeper, it will capture and destroy bad dreams preventing them from reaching the dreamer. She planned to place it over Anna's head because she had experienced nightmares a number of nights.

20: Tuesday – July 8, 1969

Private First Class Wellington Marsh reported to Camp Lejeune as ordered. His first impression was amazement at the size of the facility. There were hundreds of buildings and thousands of military and civilian personnel wandering this way and that. Military vehicles were in constant motion and training activity could be heard in all directions. The base was alive with activity.

As he waited in a large room with other Marines who were to report that day he read the materials that had been given him. Camp Lejeune covers 246-square-miles, has 11 miles of beach, 48 tactical landing zones, 80 live fire ranges, obstacle courses, living facilities, museum, and much more.

From behind, Wellington heard a familiar voice and an unwelcome familiar name, "Annie Oakley," his fellow recruit, Marvin "Shortstop" Press, said when he saw Wellington. The young Marine from Georgia had no idea what he had just done.

Wellington quickly turned to face his friend and said in a low voice, "Cut that out you want to . . ."

"Hey Annie, your slip's showing," an unidentified Marine remarked.

"Marvin, if that gets hung on me, you're a dead man," Wellington snapped.

"How was your leave?" Marvin continued undaunted, "Man, I had some good eatin. Some good sleepin, too."

In spite of the nickname issue Wellington was glad to see Marvin.

Wellington thought about his ten days leave. The car ride home took two of those days with his father insisting on doing a majority of driving. One thing he noticed immediately was how his father treated him. Some of the tough edge was missing. His old man talked with him more man to man than father to son. But, there was also something undefinable that Wellington didn't fully understand or pick up on at first. There was a feeling like when you say goodbye to someone and you want them to know how much you care or that you will miss them. It can't be adequately put in words. It's a combination of tone, expression, and actions—a kind of mental hug.

Once home Wellington found his room ready for him and he was ready to enjoy its comforts. Little had changed. Yet, he had changed. Basic training made him more aware of his surroundings and his responsibility to keep them neat and clean. He also decided to follow a regimen of exercise and roadwork to maintain the physical conditioning that had been so painfully developed. Toward that end, each morning he rose early, worked out, and ran two miles.

When some of his childhood friends invited him to a party he put on his civilian clothes and attended. It was good to be with them and a lot of reminiscing took place. Some remarks were made about his short haircut or developed muscles or Vietnam, but mostly it was just good old times.

At one point, Teresa sat next to Wellington and began to flirt. She asked him why he wasn't drinking. Wellington explained that he was underage and also didn't feel like drinking. She mainly did small talk about school, the neighborhood, Danny the pig she used to date but he was too immature, her father not understanding her, and more. Slowly, she got around to Wellington, "Do you like being in the Army?"

"Marines."

"Do you like being in the Marines?"

Wellington answered honestly, "I don't really know. The training was very hard. I did meet some great guys, the food was pretty good, not much comfort or privacy, and my D.I. was a mean mother."

"What did he do?"

"For one thing, he used his walking stick to make sure you remembered what he told you. From out of nowhere he'd appear and wham. I don't think a single recruit escaped without a few welts. He also could find the smallest infraction to have a reason to quarterdeck you."

"What does that mean—quarterdeck?"

"Oh, it's punishment. Mainly push-ups, bends & thrusts, leg lifts, running in place, that sort of thing. And he always had that junk yard dog to keep you going."

"He had a dog?"

"No, I mean his walking stick. We called it a junk yard dog because its bite was something you remembered. There's more. Every few days you'd get put on the firewatch list. That meant getting up in the middle of the night, when you're dead tired to do some meaningless thing for an hour."

"You must have hated it," Teresa cooed as she ran her hand along his arm. "They did make you muscular."

"I hated it, but there were times it wasn't so bad or I felt like I was a part of something," Wellington said, then continued as if contemplating his own words, "Sergeant Kincaid, though, he was mean and scary and unpredictable, but he was a man with a history and a way of thinking about things. Slave to landowner."

"What?"

"He told me about his grandfather who went from slave to landowner in one lifetime. There was no reason for him to do that. And, I don't know why me. Maybe, it was just luck. I hated him and I liked him, most of all I will always respect him."

"Why didn't you wear your uniform?" Teresa inquired teasingly.

"When on leave you don't have to wear your uniform except when traveling to or from the base."

"Hey," one of Wellington's male friends interrupted, "we're gonna go down the school yard and chase the young punks off the court. Then we might stir things up at the Seven Eleven. Come'on."

"Not for me," Wellington said with authority. It was at that moment that he realized kid's games and acting out no longer were of interest to him. Further, he became acutely aware that his father had taught him to follow the right path a long time ago. Now, Sergeant Kincaid gave him the strength to do so.

Teresa chimed in, "He's staying here with me." She hugged his arm and waved the other youth away. "When do you have to go back?"

"In about eight days. I have to check on transportation." Wellington looked at Teresa. She was small in stature with short brown hair. Her skin was what could be called cappuccino. She had a gap between her two front teeth and definitely had curves in the right places. Her voice was soft and overall she would be considered cute. The aroma of her perfume was sweet and flowery. Wellington found that he liked the feel of her hand on his arm or her leaning against him. "What do you do, Teresa?"

"I just graduated high school," she replied. "I'm looking for a job, but I'm not having very good luck."

"What kind of job are you looking for?"

"Anything," she answered, "when you're right out of school you really don't have much choice."

"Yeah, I know that feeling. Don't give up you'll find something."

Teresa paused and sat silently, then commented with a smile, "I found you."

They spent the rest of the evening together and the next day. Teresa made Wellington feel alive and gave him more to think about than Vietnam. However, the shadow of that faraway war hung over them. Because of it Wellington decided that this was not a time to have a girlfriend. He knew after MOS school his next destination would be San Diego and then the Republic of Vietnam. Fear would creep into his dreams, be brought on by a word, or take shape as a result of a news story. Regardless of the cause one fact remained Wellington Emanuel Marsh was going to war not with the bravado of someone who believed in a cause and signed up voluntarily. He had been conscripted into service much like eighteenth century British sailors who made the mistake of being in the wrong place at the wrong time when press gangs were afoot. Wellington Marsh was going to war to risk his life for a cause he neither understood nor cared about. The pleasure he found with Teresa therefore would have to be fleeting. Good times would fill the gap between coming home and leaving, but his immediate future had already been decided and it was something he had to face alone.

When it came time for Wellington to leave, his parents drove him to the bus station. Teresa rode along. She commented as to how handsome he was in his uniform. The good byes were difficult and Teresa slipped a note into his hand. On the bus ride, he read it.

"We've only known each other a few days. They were wonderful days. Next time you are home I hope you want to see me. I'll be waiting."

As Wellington sat in the staging room at Camp Lejeune he thought about Teresa and how he couldn't start any relationships with his future so questionable. However, he saved Teresa's note.

They rode the Number 7 line out to Flushing, Queens. Ryoya had the day off and Jack took a "mental health day" which meant if he didn't take the day off he would go crazy. Game time was 2:09 in the afternoon. With plenty of time to spare they arrived at Shea Stadium. It was Ryoya Akimoto's expedition so she procured the tickets and planned the event. Their seats were on the first-tier loge level section 9 which were located to the right side behind home plate. This placed them in front of the Diamond Club and press box seating. Jack looked up at the press box and recognized a sports writer for the *Tribune*.

It was a beautiful day for attending a baseball game. A clear blue sky hung above them accompanied by a temperature of 78 degrees, low humidity, and a slight breeze. Jack wore a brown knit short sleeved shirt, tan pants, and brown topsider shoes. Ryoya looked captivating in a blue sundress and sandals.

They began the day with breakfast at the elegant Marriot Hotel at Grand Central Station then passed the time visiting various stores along Madison Avenue. Jack couldn't help but remember Harry Van Ryker's confession about enjoying shopping with his lost love. The newspaper reporter admitted to himself that he also experienced such a pleasure. It was then Jack decided he had something that needed to be done.

OK, he was at a Mets game, something he never envisioned ever happening.

He would be a good sport and root for the . . . uh . . . amazing Mets. The Mets were in second place 5.5 games behind the Chicago Cubs who they played that day. It promised to be a good game. The Yankees? They languished in fifth place 17.5 games out of first. It was clearly not their year. These facts were not lost to Ryoya and were part of some stimulating debate over breakfast. In truth, Jack enjoyed their verbal sparring. Lotus Blossom was smart, quick witted, even tempered, and had a sense of humor. She also was the most beautiful woman in the city of New York.

They found their seats and settled down for a good afternoon of escaping from day-to-day demands. Jack had purchased a program as he was not very familiar with the Mets lineup. He liked baseball. Therefore, he would better enjoy the game by being more familiar with the team he was there to support.

Abruptly, Ryoya stood and announced, "I'm off to get hotdogs and beer."

"I'll go," Jack offered.

"No, you stay here," she insisted, "today is my treat."

In her absence, Jack read the program. Jerry Koosman, a 27 year old left hander, was on the mound for the Mets. He was 6 and 5 for the season—not very impressive. Fergie Jenkins was to pitch for the Cubs. His 11 and 6 record was more respectable. The Cubs were hot and expected to go all the way in the National League. Jack decided he should plan on consoling Ryoya after the Mets lost.

Ryoya returned with the refreshments and something else. She presented Jack with a pink New York Mets cap. "A deal is a deal," she stated with a mischievous smile. Jack looked at the hat and thought, "Console her? . . . I'm gonna rub it in!" A man of his word, Jack took the loathsome headgear and put it on. Ryoya laughed and Jack bravely smiled. He also quickly glanced up at the press box to see if he would hear about his humiliation later. Fortunately, all the writers were busy studying notes.

Ryoya looked at Jack and her competitive nature screamed victory in her ear. What she saw in reality was a man she cared about, respected, and found easy to turn to for support. He was her knight in shining armor—not a pink baseball cap. Because her world was one of endless competition with men just to survive, weakness had no place. Like in an aikido match she knew it was a matter of using one's opponent's strength against them. Ryoya Akimoto had a well-known reputation at N.Y.P.D. of being a force to be reckoned with. She didn't earn respect she demanded it. It was clear that she had successfully developed that side of her personality. What remained abandoned was the other essential part of her being. Like a little girl hiding from some unseen threat her vulnerable side wanted so much to be found and rescued and loved. Yet, it was overpowered by tough Rita. She looked at Jack wearing the offensive cap and knew he deserved better. Indeed, she wanted him to have better. Detective Ryoya Akimoto reached up and took the pink cap off Jack's head and replaced it with her blue cap. She then placed the pink cap on her head. With a smile, she leaned over and rested her head on his shoulder.

National Association of Broadcasters President Vincent T. Wasilewski announced a four-year phase-out plan of cigarette advertising on television. The move came after Congress passed an extension of the Cigarette Labeling Act of 1965 and was considering stronger government action. The plan was immediately criticized by anti-smoking groups as taking too long, being too complicated, and allowing broadcasters to continue to make significant amounts of money from a product that threatens children.

Senator Frank E. Moss (D-Utah) said, "Today I sense that the cigarette industry is turning away from stubborn conflict and preparing to accept the heavy burden of its public responsibility." He added, "we must also make certain that other forms of promotion; magazines, billboard, couponing, points-of-sale are adequately circumscribed and restrained."

National television networks derived approximately 10% of revenues from cigarette advertising while 5% of local spot television sales were to this industry. It was argued that replacement of these significant amounts of money required time.

Tobacco-industry spokesman Joseph F. Cullman lll issued a statement, "I have been authorized by each cigarette manufacturer for whom I speak to inform this committee that each company is prepared to agree to discontinue all advertising of cigarettes on television and radio in September 1970, when the major existing contractual arrangements will expire, provided that 'Congress enacts legislation which provides that an agreement to this effect shall not be deemed illegal under the antitrust laws."

Further debate would take place but the road to elimination of broadcast cigarette advertising had been paved only the distance to the final destination was in question.

After three innings, the score was 0 – 0. It was turning into a pitcher's duel and Jack found himself getting into the game. Although not the Yankees, the Mets were fun to watch. An added incentive was seeing how Ryoya was also involved and enjoying herself. They definitely had one thing in common—baseball. They also had one thing in conflict—Yankees or Mets.

"I love baseball," Jack disclosed. "Wanted to play. However, I throw like a girl and hit like a duck. The only position I was good at was sitting."

"Is that why you chose to be a reporter, because you were so good at sitting?" Ryoya asked while still watching the game.

"What?"

"You never told me how you got to be a reporter."

"There really isn't much of a story." Jack offered.

"However, there is a story."

"There was a girl."

"How come that doesn't surprise me?"

"Hush."

Ryoya's first reaction to Jack's rebuff was to verbally take him down a peg. Let him know she will not tolerate being spoken to in that manner. However, this was not the squad room and Jack was not an antagonist. Her second reaction, though somewhat unfamiliar, was to hush and wait.

"The girl I speak of was in my high school English class," Jack continued. "We had to write a short story over a weekend. I wrote a humorous story about how two inept boys tried to steal a car. The teacher picked a few of us to read our stories in front of the class. As luck would have it, I was one of them. I read my tome and this one girl laughed and laughed at my story. After class, she told me I should be a writer which is when I showed her my paper. On the top in red ink was a large D and the comment, 'This is godawful trash.' She was surprised by the grade and remark. What struck me most was what she said, 'Mr. Granson is a stickler for proper grammar, sentence structure, and punctuation. These things can be learned. He has no understanding of the essence of a story, the characters, or the emotional context. Your story was creative, funny, and interesting. You painted a picture with words and left a lasting impression. I liked it.' From then on I was hooked. A silly funny story that reached one person in a class of twenty-four gave me a taste of what words could achieve. Don't get me wrong. I don't want to change the world or promote a particular point-of-view. If I can get my audience to think, or feel, or experience, or learn, or chuckle, or react—that's success."

In the bottom of the fifth inning with one out Ed Kranepool hit a homerun to center field. The Mets led the game one nothing. However, the lead was short lived as the first batter up in the top of the sixth inning, Ernie Banks, hit a homerun to tie the game. It went from a pitcher's duel to a battle of the first basemen as both homeruns were hit by players in that position. The Cubs scored one run in the seventh inning and Jim Hickman hit a homerun in the eighth inning. When the Mets came to bat in the bottom of the ninth they were behind three to one.

Some fans headed for the exits but Jack and Ryoya stayed. They were both true baseball fans who enjoyed the game. They preferred to win but didn't abandon a team when it was losing.

The first batter for the Mets was Ken Boswell as a pinch hitter for Jerry Koosman. Number 12 hit deep into centerfield for a leadoff double.

"Now it's a game!" Ryoya exclaimed. "Good job Kenny!"

Jack continued to enjoy watching Ryoya. He wondered, how many men are fortunate enough to date a woman who likes sports? That might be an interesting column. Hey does your wife or girlfriend like sports? No. Leaves the room. Calls you a what? Stop laughing, it's a serious question.

The Mets top of the order was coming to bat with nobody out and a man on second. Tommie Agee hit a pop foul that was caught for the first out.

"Put in a pinch hitter for Pfeil. He's been off all day," Ryoya yelled.

Ryoya was leaning forward in her seat. The afternoon sun illuminated the pink hat she wore. Jack loved that hat—on her. Here she was a tough New York City police detective and all he could see was a captivating woman. She was enjoying the game with childlike innocence and he was enjoying the game like a smitten suitor.

Ryoya got her wish as Donn Clendenon pinch hit for Bobby Pfeil. Mets manager Gil Hodges must have heard her. The crowd grew quiet as Fergie Jenkins wound up to pitch. They remained silent until with the count two balls and two strikes Clendenon ripped one to leftfield for a double moving Ken Boswell to third. Shea Stadium exploded with cheers.

"Wheeeeew Yoo!" Ryoya yelled while standing up. "We're gonna win this one."

Jack hoped they would win it for Ryoya. If he could he would go down and pinch hit a homerun for his lady. But, wait, I hit like a duck. Better leave it to the professionals.

Cleon Jones stepped into the batter's box and on the third pitch hit a double into leftfield. Ken Boswell and Donn Clendenon scored and the game was tied.

Jack jumped to his feet and cheered along with Ryoya. She smiled seeing a dyed-in-the-wool Yankee fan cheering for her lowly Mets.

Art Shamsky came to bat with the winning run on second base. With one out and the threat of Shamsky's hot bat the Cubs intentionally walked him. This set up a potential double play to end the inning. At this point, Chicago was playing for a tie and extra innings. Wayne Garrett almost gave the Cubs what they wanted when he hit a slow grounder to the right side of second base. Glenn Beckert, the Cubs second baseman had to run in to field the ball. His only play was to throw Garrett out at first. This allowed Jones to stop at third and Shamsky at second.

Two out in the bottom of the ninth with the score tied, Ed Kranepool came to bat. The crowd began to chant, "Kranepool, Kranepool, Kranepool." Jack and Ryoya joined them. Fergie Jenkins had pitched a brilliant game until the ninth inning. Luck or fatigue? The Mets batters had only four hits through eight innings. Jenkins got ahead of Kranepool one ball and two strikes. "Kranepool, Kranepool, Kranepool." Ed Kranepool, the six foot three-inch-tall Bronx native who signed as an amateur free agent in 1962 at the age of seventeen, was one of the original Mets. The left-hand batter swung at the next pitch and hit a foul ball back into the seats behind home plate. The ball bounced off of the rail in front of the press box and rose straight into the air and back down into Jack's waiting left hand.

"Maybe you throw like a girl and hit like a duck, but you can catch," Ryoya concluded.

"In all the years I've attended baseball games, I've never caught a ball."

"Don't tell anyone, you looked pretty good just then."

"You brought me luck."

"I brought you to your senses." She tugged the Mets cap that he wore.

The next pitch Ed Kranepool hit into left centerfield between Billy Williams and Don Young. Cleon Jones scored the winning run. The entire stadium thundered on a cloudless day. Impulsively, Jack grabbed Ryoya and pulled her to him and kissed her. She reciprocated and their relationship moved gently toward their destiny.

On this same day in Baltimore the New York Yankees lost a double header to the Orioles 10 to 3 and 4 to 1. Their record dropped to 40 wins and 47 losses. The Mets record was 46 wins and 34 losses. It was going to be a day when crow was on the dinner menu.

Robert Six Trees checked his traps but found none had served their purpose. He had hoped for a rabbit, but decided he preferred fish on this day. It was a pleasant day so he decided to bring Anna along and teach her the finer points to catching the big ones.

21: Wednesday - July 16, 1969

JoAnn Morgan, instrumentation controller, Apollo Launch Control, arrived at Kennedy Space Center before 3:00 a.m. The sight of the Saturn V three stage rocket with the Apollo 11 spacecraft on top at Launch Complex 39-A gave her pause to consider the threshold of history that was about to be crossed. The combined vehicle stood 363 feet tall, 53 feet taller than the Statue of Liberty. Giant xenon lights bathed the launch complex as the final liquid propellant was loaded. Venting of liquid oxygen sent wisps of gases into the darkness. As gaseous streams reached for the heavens they dissolved into the atmosphere. For a brief moment, JoAnn stood before the surreal sight watching the many technicians attending to their jobs. She knew that no single individual was unimportant. Each had to do his or her function perfectly for this great endeavor to reach the goal set by President Kennedy nine years earlier.

"I believe this nation should commit itself to achieving the goal of landing a man on the moon and returning him safely before the decade is out."

JoAnn Morgan was one of tens of thousands of people who were a part of man's quest to conquer the next frontier. Every day she woke up thinking about NASA and the Moon and went to bed dreaming about this day. Now, she stood awestruck by the enchanting sight of the powerful steed that was to carry three brave riders to their destination and mankind to its destiny.

The Apollo 11 space vehicle consisted of a Saturn V rocket, the Command Module, Service Module, and Lunar Module. Saturn V was the most powerful rocket ever built. Fully fueled it weighted 6.5 million pounds. Most of its mass at launch was propellant. It generated 7.6 million pounds of thrust at launch which meant that the rocket lifted relatively slowly. For this reason observers often were fearful that something was wrong and that it wouldn't clear the tower. It took a very long twelve seconds to clear the tower. However, as the Kerosene fuel burned at an incredible rate the vehicle became lighter causing it to lift faster.

The Command Module housed the crew and re-entry equipment. The top of this cone-shaped module had a hatch and docking assembly for connecting to the lunar module. Also at this end were three main parachutes, two drogue parachutes, and mortar pilot chutes for landing in water. A Heat Shield was located at the bottom of the Command Module. In the center was the crew quarters with three couches. A large hatch was located above the center couch. There was a total of five windows; one in the large hatch, one next to each of the outside seats, and two forward looking. The crew compartment held the controls, displays, navigation equipment and other systems used by the astronauts.

The Service Module carried consumables and the main propulsion system. It was cylindrical in shape and was attached to the back of the Command Module. At the bottom of the Service Module was a gimbal mounted hypergolic liquid propellant engine with a cone shaped nozzle. Around the upper part of the module were four sets of four reaction control thrusters each 90 degrees apart. These were used to make course adjustments. Hydrogen oxygen fuel cells to generate electricity, cryogenic oxygen and hydrogen tanks, and fuel tanks were also carried in the Service Module.

At 3:00 a.m. in a dark alley on West Forty Fourth Street Detectives Ryoya Akimoto and Michael Donovan were investigating an assault. A young dark-haired hooker had been beat up and robbed. She drifted in and out of consciousness as paramedics placed her on a gurney. Blood dripped from her nose and a large gash on her forehead. Pitifully, she looked up at Ryoya and whispered, "My baby."

"Can you tell us who did this?" Ryoya pressed on while the girl was coherent.

In a faint voice she replied, "Two, black, young . . ." her voice faded and fell silent.

"What's your name, hon?" Ryoya asked.

The injured girl seemed to not understand the question. The paramedics rolled the gurney toward a waiting ambulance. Ryoya signaled her partner that she would ride in the ambulance with the victim. Detective Donovan remained at the scene to gather clues and evidence. As is the case most of the time, there weren't any witnesses. At least, any that would come forward.

In the ambulance, Ryoya remained out of the way of the paramedics as they attended to the victim. An oxygen mask had been placed over her nose and mouth. Ryoya examined the young girl from a distance and made notes. From the number of welts and bruises on the left side of her face it appeared that she was beaten by a right-handed assailant. She wore a red rayon blouse that had been torn open in the front. A black mini-skirt also had been ripped. No panties and no shoes. Ryoya made a note to have a rape kit employed by the hospital. Even hookers have rights. Blood on the underside of her white bra appeared to be from the attackers, not the victim, because of the location. Her hands also had blood on them, some near the finger tips. Samples from under her nails would be needed.

For a moment, the victim seemed to become aware of her surroundings. She tried to sit up but the attending paramedic held her down. Through the oxygen mask she said, "Trojan."

Ryoya made a note and tried to ask what she meant but the young girl once more fell into unconsciousness.

Apollo 11 Commander Neil A. Armstrong, the 39 year old retired Navy pilot who flew the 4,000 miles-per-hour X-15, as well as over two hundred other aircraft stepped onto the elevator at launch complex 39A. Along with him was Michael Collins, the 38 year old Command Module pilot, who was a West Point graduate who ultimately served in the United States Air Force. Interestingly, Michael Collins designed the Apollo 11 mission patch. Jim Lovell, the backup commander, was the one who suggested the use of an eagle which was a symbol of the United States. Michael Collins agreed and traced a photo from a *National Geographic* magazine. To that he added the earth above the lunar surface in the background. An olive branch was added as a symbol of peace. The third member of the crew, Lunar Modular Pilot Edwin E. "Buzz" Aldrin Jr., was also a West Point graduate—a year earlier than Collins. He finished third in his class in 1951. During the Korean war, Buzz Aldrin flew 66 combat missions shooting down two Mikoyan-Gurevich MiG-15 aircraft. In fact, the June 8,

1953, issue of *Life* magazine featured gun camera photos taken by Aldrin of a Russian pilot ejecting from his damaged aircraft.

Because he would be the last to board the spacecraft, Buzz Aldrin was let off the elevator one landing below the level for the capsule. As he stood on the swing arm looking out he watched the ocean waves far below. The sun was gradually rising in the east. It was a peaceful moment. He experienced the same unspoken anxiety that all astronauts carried with them just prior to a launch. It wasn't so much fear as it was a sense of reality and awareness of the risks attached to what they were about to do. Much like the combat missions that he flew, you know something bad could happen but you focus on the present. Anticipation of what could happen was a waste of energy. Buzz Aldrin saw the beauty of the planet he was about to leave and was thrilled to have an opportunity to see it through the eyes of God.

Ryoya was given a ride back to the crime scene in a marked patrol car. The investigation team was doing their job. She spotted Michael Donovan and caught up with him.

"It's now a homicide investigation," she told her partner.

Detective Donovan nodded. There wasn't anything else to be said. To protect their sanity and to do an effective job a detective had to remain impersonal. Panties found in the dirt next to a cardboard box were evidence—not the intimate apparel of a young girl who desperately fought for her life alone, afraid, and in pain. A pair of shoes collected from the gutter might offer some clues—not be what carried someone's daughter to her death at far too young an age. The investigation would continue, it would follow proper protocol, and ultimately lead to a conviction—if they were lucky. Both detectives were keenly aware of the statistics. Slightly more than 60% of homicides were solved. And, when the crime is random where the victim does not know the perpetrator the success rate drops precipitously. This case fell into that category and with no witnesses it would be in the cold case file within a week.

"She was pregnant," Ryoya informed Michael who was shining a flashlight into the dark recess of a doorway.

"Don't do it, Rita," Michael warned.

"I'm not."

"You are." Detective Donovan countered. "I can hear it in your voice. You are making it personal. This is your Davie Hanshaw." He referred to a case of a young boy who disappeared years before that haunted him because it never was solved. It tested him as an investigator, as a cop, and as a man. Anger, frustration, self-doubt, and poor judgment almost ruined his career as he pursued that case. His captain finally took him in the back and literally slapped some sense into him. "Take a step back, Ryoya," he used her correct name for emphasis.

"Hookers are human beings," she replied, "not garbage left in an alley."

"We do our job and if we get lucky there will be a conviction. Focus on the job, not the crime, or the victim."

Ryoya gathered her wits and asked in an official voice, "What have we got?"

"Not much." Michael Donovan suggested, "Let's go back to the house and allow the crime scene folks to finish their work."

On the drive back to the precinct Ryoya discussed the clues they did have, "She said 'two, black, young' at the scene. In the ambulance, she said only one word,

'Trojan.' That really is a lot to go on."

"OK, we have two young blacks. Could be male or female. The rape kit could answer that question. Trojan? A name? Condoms? Picture or symbol? Or, a different word that only sounded like Trojan." Michael Donovan surmised.

The world watched Launch Complex 39-A at the Kennedy Space Center, Florida. Matthew Ellis was among them. He sat in front of the small black and white television in Stephanie's apartment. The countdown was going along smoothly. Matt watched knowing three brave souls were on the trip of a lifetime and Orztech wire, that he helped provide, was part of the vehicle that was to take them to the Lunar surface.

The last thirty seconds of the countdown were the most nerve racking for all involved. It was during this short period of time that automatic systems were engaged and functions initiated that were difficult to abort. At 8.9 seconds before liftoff the ignition sequence started. First, the center engine ignited then opposing outboard pairs of rockets fired at 300-millisecond intervals to reduce the structural impact on the rocket. When the onboard computers confirmed thrust the hold-down arms were released. At this point the Saturn V still had to fight for half a second to escape from tapered metal pins pulled through dies. The slowing effect allowed for the rocket to lift smoothly from the launch pad at exactly 9:32 a.m. Neil A. Armstrong, Michael Collins, and Buzz Aldrin knew this was one of the most dangerous moments of the mission. If the rocket failed to liftoff after release there was little chance of surviving a two-kiloton explosion that would result. For this reason, there was a thirty second shutdown delay built into the system but it didn't improve the odds very much if there was a malfunction.

As the Saturn V slowly rose from the launch complex Matt realized that he was holding his breath. It took twelve seconds for the vehicle to clear the tower and begin its flight into space. The propellant in the first stage of the Saturn V made up about three-quarters of the vehicle's entire launch mass. As it consumed over 13 tons of fuel per second the vehicle grew lighter which caused it to rise ever faster. Greater thrust and thinner air added to the acceleration of Apollo 11. Overall, the first stage burned for 2 minutes and 41 seconds, lifting the rocket to an altitude of 42 miles and a speed of 6,164 miles per hour while burning 4,700,000 pounds of fuel.

At T+135 seconds the main engine shut down. Four smaller engines then burned until all fuel was depleted. At this point eight small solid fuel separation motors pushed the depleted first stage away from the vehicle and the second stage ignited. The second and third stages were powered by hydrogen fuel which was lighter than kerosene and more efficient at higher altitudes. With the Saturn V it was the first-time hydrogen fuel was used successfully in a rocket. Stage two burned for 6 minutes and propelled the spacecraft to 109 miles above the Earth at a speed of 15,647 miles-per-hour. Finally, after separation of the second stage, the third stage burned for 2.5 minutes increasing velocity to 17,432 mph and placing Apollo 11 in orbit at an altitude of 118.8 miles above the Earth.

"Here's something," Ryoya announced from her desk, "George Washington High School, in Washington Heights, athletic teams are called Trojans."

"Got possibilities," Detective Donovan conceded.

"We need to find out what apparel students might wear that would have the word Trojan on it. What was the temperature last night?"

"It was chilly. A sweatshirt or light jacket."

"Let's take a run up there and have a talk with the principal. It's on 549 Audubon Avenue," Detective Akimoto stated.

The third stage of the Saturn V remained attached to the spacecraft as it orbited the Earth. Three astronauts and mission controllers checked all systems and determined everything was AOK. Apollo 11 was given a go for TransLunar Injection (TLI). This required that the third stage engine that had been shut down reignite successfully. At T+2 hours and 44 minutes the S-IVB stage fired again and burned for six minutes which increased Apollo 11's speed to 25,053 miles-per-hour—escape velocity.

Forty minutes after TLI the combined Apollo Command and Service Modules separated from the third stage, turned 180 degrees and docked with the Lunar Module that was stored below the CSM during launch. In a process known as transposition, docking and extraction the completed Lunar spacecraft turned back 180 degrees and reattached to the third stage of the Saturn V. It was now ready for its journey. Apollo 11 separated from the third stage 50 minutes later. To avoid a collision between Apollo 11 and the third stage of the Saturn V an auxiliary propulsion system was fired to move the third stage away. This caused the rocket to head toward the Moon on an angle that would slingshot it into solar orbit. Finally, Apollo 11 was off on its three-day journey to the Moon.

Detectives Akimoto and Donavan spoke with the principal of George Washington High School. They didn't reveal the fact that it was a homicide investigation. Rather, they indicated that there was a possibility that one or more students from the school might have been witnesses to a crime. While he was cooperative he really didn't provide any useful information about school-related clothing or paraphernalia. It being July, only summer school was in session. The two detectives left knowing that a potential lead had led nowhere.

Television coverage of the launch of Apollo 11 had ended. Matthew Ellis sat at the small kitchen table in the apartment and thought about what was happening. A great adventure was taking place and he was, in a small way, connected to it. He decided that it was time to visit Orztech Corporation to catch up on all that had taken place since his departure. Before the accident, he had been successful in negotiating contracts with NASA, the Navy, aircraft manufacturers, and others that he had trouble recalling. He expected that the folks at Orztech were celebrating this monumental event.

A Soviet unmanned spacecraft streaked toward the Moon ahead of Apollo 11. It had been launched three days before Apollo 11. The Lunik 15 was on a mission to land on the Moon, measure the lunar gravitational field, photograph the lunar surface, determine the chemical composition of lunar rocks, and gather samples of soil for return to Earth. It was the Soviet Union's attempt to demonstrate their capability in light of the expected triumph of America in the much-publicized space race. When the launch of Lunik 15 was confirmed a concerned Houston Control had Astronaut Frank Borman call one of the leaders of the Soviet space program, Dr. Mstislav Keldysh. Remarkably, the Soviets released the flight plan for Lunik 15 to allay fears that it might pose a collision threat to Apollo 11.

Late in the evening Detectives Akimoto and Donovan returned to work. They had each gone home for a few hours of sleep and to freshen up. Immediately, they drove over to Eighth Avenue where the prostitutes generally strolled. They brought pictures of the deceased with them. After talking with three girls who claimed no knowledge of the victim they stopped a prostitute named Claire. Her face showed signs of having been beaten in the past and she wore a shoulder length auburn wig.

"That's Rita," she said sadly.

The name struck both detectives as they were aware that Rita was the nickname by which Ryoya was often called.

"Did you see her last night?" Ryoya asked.

"Yeah, early in the evening. She wasn't feeling well. I don't remember seeing her after that. I wondered where she was. Who did it?"

"That's what we are trying to find out," Detective Donovan stated.

"I know this is difficult, but did you see any young men who acted suspicious last night?" Ryoya added.

"They all act suspicious," she replied half kidding then catching herself added in a serious tone, "We all try to avoid those who seem odd or dangerous. I can't think of anyone who stood out."

"Does the word Trojan mean anything to you?" Detective Donovan asked and immediately realized what the obvious answer would be from a hooker.

Claire smiled and answered, "It's a brand of condom."

Ryoya added, "Besides condoms does the word Trojan mean anything else to you?"

"No. There was the story about a Trojan Horse, but I don't know much about that."

"Did you see two young black boys around here last night?"

"Is that who did it? Two black boys?"

"We don't know. We simply want to talk with them," Ryoya explained.

"I mean, this area is a huge melting pot. Look around. No one would stand out," Claire explained.

"Do you know Rita's last name or where she lived?"

"Umm, it's Rita Craig. She lives, uh lived, on West Ninety Third Street. I don't know the number. She has a kid. I think someone in the building watches the kid. She was pregnant, you know."

"Did she have any enemies or persons who might want to hurt her?" Michael Donovan asked.

"No. None I can think of. She was a sweet person." Claire looked around and saw Miguel standing across the street. "Look, I have to go. I'm sorry about Rita, but I really don't know anything."

Both detectives picked up on her abrupt change in demeanor and knew most likely what was the cause. Ryoya shook Claire's hand placing her business card in it and said, "If you think of anything that might help, give me a call. We appreciate your help."

As they walked away Michael asked, "Did you pick him out?"

"Not in this crowd," Ryoya replied and then added, "But, if we keep our eye on her, he'll reveal himself."

Half a block away they stopped another street walker. While questioning her they kept Claire under surveillance. It didn't take long. Miguel walked up to Claire, grabbed her arm, and walked her around the corner. Two N.Y.P.D. detectives followed. Miguel had the prostitute up against the wall and was talking fast. What he was saying was inaudible from the detectives' vantage point. They waited. When he slapped her, grabbed Ryoya's business card, tore it up, and threw it on the sidewalk they intervened. Michael Donovan reached Miguel first and slammed the pimp against the wall none too gently, "You're under arrest."

The surprised punk blurted out, "What the hell! What did I do?"

"You have the right to remain silent," Detective Donovan started. Based on a 1966 Supreme Court decision in Miranda v. Arizona, police must inform individuals who are under arrest as to their right to remain silent, have an attorney present, or have an attorney provided. The court found that the Fifth and Sixth Amendment rights of Ernesto Arturo Miranda had been violated during his arrest and trial for armed robbery, kidnapping, and rape of a mentally handicapped young woman. The opinion stated:

> ... The person in custody must, prior to interrogation, be clearly informed that he/she has the right to remain silent, and that anything the person says will be used against that person in court; the person must be clearly informed that he/she has the right to consult with an attorney and to have that attorney present during questioning, and that, if he/she is indigent, an attorney will be provided at no cost to represent him/her.

Ernesto Arturo Miranda was subsequently retried and convicted.

"Anything you say, can and will be used against you in a court of law," Michael Donovan continued. "You have a right to have an attorney present during questioning."

"I don't need no stinkin attorney."

"If you cannot afford an attorney one will be provided at no cost to you."

Claire watched Miguel getting manhandled and enjoyed every second of it. However, she didn't dare show her pleasure.

"What am I under arrest for?"

"Do you understand these rights?"

"Si, muy comprende. Now, what are you arresting me for?"

"Right now, assault. We saw you strike this woman," Donovan stated.

"Ah, you were mistaken. I didn't touch her." He told Claire, "Tell them."

"He didn't touch me," the frightened woman conceded.

"See, it's all a misunderstanding," Miguel offered with a smile.

Ryoya pushed the torn-up business card with her shoe, "Then we have you for littering."

Detective Donovan put handcuffs on the litterer. He turned Miguel to lead him away. Behind their backs Ryoya slipped another business card into Claire's hand and said loud enough to be heard, "You can go, Miss."

Robert and Anna Six Trees looked up at the stars trying to see Apollo 11. Instead, they saw a shooting star streak across the sky. Robert told Anna it was Chakapesh a dwarf with immense strength who can shoot his arrow farther than the largest men. He lives on the Moon and will protect the astronauts from evil spirits.

22: Thursday – July 17, 1969

Detectives Akimoto and Donovan read through the preliminary coroner's report on the victim tentatively identified as Rita Craig. Death caused by an intraparenchymal bleed within the medulla oblongata due to traumatic brain injury. A cerebral hemorrhage in this area is almost always fatal as it can damage cranial nerve X and the vagus nerve which controls heartbeat and breathing. Injury caused by multiple strikes by a blunt instrument. Bruises, vaginal tears, and semen indicated rape. The victim was in the first trimester of pregnancy—the fetus did not survive. The cornea of her right eye had been torn by a hard object, possibly a large ring. Skin and blood found under her fingernails suggested that the victim fought her attackers. Blood and skin fragments on her teeth and in her mouth implied that she bit one of her killers. Various other cuts, abrasions, and bruises were the result of a prolonged beating.

Among her effects were her clothes, house keys, condoms, and twelve dollars. Also, tangled in her clothing was a black with orange and white trim wrist sweatband.

Ryoya opened a folder on her desk. "We need to go back to that school. The colors for the George Washington High School Trojans is, you got it, black, orange and white."

"We'll hit it after we go to her apartment on West Ninety Third Street," Detective Donovan replied.

The Soviet spacecraft, Lunik 15, entered lunar orbit. Its four-day journey was flawless. Technicians began a series of systems checks and preparation for touch down on the lunar surface. Further out in space, traveling at over 25,000 miles-per-hour, Apollo 11 executed a 3-second mid-course correction burn of the main engine. It then began a coast to its planned lunar orbit. All three astronauts were in good spirits while very busy checking and rechecking systems for the planned Moon landing.

Matthew Ellis took a bus into Manhattan on his quest to fill in the many blanks and gaps in his life. The ride, while familiar, was noticeably different. The bus was far more modern than busses he occasionally rode. Square windows had been replaced by larger forward angled rectangular windows. Cushioned seats were more comfortable and covered with cloth. The ride itself felt smoother. The interior of the bus was also quieter and it had air-conditioning. When he arrived at the Port Authority Bus Terminal on Eighth Avenue Matt found a telephone booth and looked up Orztech Corporation in the white pages. He knew it was downtown on Sixth Avenue, known as Avenue of the Americas, but couldn't remember the exact address. To his surprise there wasn't a listing for Orztech Corporation.

Miguel wasn't pleased about losing one of his income producers. Rita had been a steady earner and dependable. It pissed him off that she would be so careless.

When he heard of the murder he quickly moved Olivia out of Rita's apartment and decided to keep his new young hooker off the streets until the police stopped nosing around. By that time, Olivia did what she was told without question. However, she was young and stupid. She might say something that the police could use against him. That was not going to happen. He left her with Rose, one of his stable who had a four-year-old child, with instructions to take a few days off and watch over his property.

Still using a cane Matt walked down Sixth Avenue. He believed that if he saw the building where Orztech Corporation was headquartered that he would recognize it. At least, that was his hope. As he passed various buildings and storefronts along the way a sense of déjà vu surrounded him. He knew these places. From time to time he stopped and looked around. Memories emerged from dark corners of his mind. He'd made this walk numerous times. It hadn't changed very much. On the corner of Thirty Fourth Street and Sixth Avenue was a coffee shop—a familiar place he had visited often. Impulsively, he entered. The welcoming aroma of coffee, sounds of plates and cups, and cacophonous voices brought Matt back six years. He walked over to his favorite table where he could look out onto the street. It was 1963—he had returned. So much was going on. He was extremely busy. Contracts, negotiations, logistics, profit margins, projections, receivables, presentations, and more all could wait while he sat in his oasis for a half hour and enjoyed a not-so-healthy breakfast.

It was here that he first met Lida. Yes. They had an appointment. Here. On a rainy morning in 1960. She was late. He had grown impatient and was about to leave when she arrived. She wore a navy-blue business suit with a white blouse. Long dark hair caressed her shoulders. As she approached, an enchanting smile lit up her face.

"Did you ever try to get a cab when it rains in this town?" she said pleasantly. It was less of an apology for being late as it was a presupposed acceptable explanation. She had an air of confidence which allowed for her somewhat inappropriate familiarity at a business meeting. Her actions weren't overtly flirtatious but her sexuality seemed to be ever present. Lida was the epitome of feminine charm. Whether she came by it naturally or carefully developed the talent Matt didn't know, but how wasn't an issue. Yet, it was there adding heat to any encounter. Matt was attracted to Lida from the start. It was she who had suggested that they meet away from the office. A breakfast meeting in a coffee shop seemed harmless.

As a result of successful negotiations and robust contracts Matt was busy sourcing raw materials and perhaps finished products. Automotive, airline, and military orders for specific wire products created demands that were beyond Orztech's present manufacturing capabilities. Management was considering expanding their operation but unfortunately that wouldn't satisfy the significant immediate needs. Matt assured all of them that he would make sure contracts were fulfilled. This is what brought Lida and Matt together in a small coffee shop on May 1, 1960, the same day that a Soviet missile shot down an American U-2 spy plane piloted by Francis Gary Powers over Sverdlovsk.

Lida Petropoulos was from the Peloponnese peninsula in the southernmost part of mainland Greece. She represented a consortium of international manufacturers under the business name LPAmerica LLC. Lida contacted Matt upon learning about a sizeable military contract won by Orztech Corporation. The timing was perfect as he was facing a challenge to deliver significant amounts of product to three different industries. Hence, the meeting at this coffee shop.

"Who exactly do you represent?" Matt inquired.

"Numerous manufacturing facilities around the world," Lida acknowledged, "I am certain that I can deliver whatever amount and type of wire product you require. In addition, I'll deliver ahead of any other manufacturers."

"You sound pretty confident."

"I know what I'm doing."

"If I provide you with a detailed list, how quickly can you provide a bid?"

"Never."

"Never?"

"I don't bid," Lida stated. "We either work together or we don't." She leaned forward causing her long dark hair to cover a portion of her face. In a sultry voice she promised, "You will not be disappointed." As she gazed directly into Matt's eyes she softly ran her finger across her lips and allowed her mouth to open slightly.

Matt was caught off guard and didn't know whether he was reading something that wasn't there or was indeed being seduced. Regardless of which, a stirring confirmed sexual attraction.

"When forced to bid, companies cut corners or make promises that they can't keep," Lida looked at Matt as if implying that he was trying to fulfill product promises that he had made knowing full well Orztech Corporation didn't have the capability of delivering.

"I need . . ."

"You need a partner that will deliver product, at a price you can afford, and one whom you can trust," Lida placed her hand on top of Matt's hand. He didn't move, however looked directly at her. With just a hint of a smile and a subtle head movement that caused a wave to run down her silky hair like a gentle waterfall she stated, "You can trust me."

"That's easy to say."

Abruptly, Lida sat upright. Her chin up, she had a regal countenance. She paused long enough to make a dramatic non-verbal point. Then she said, "You, my friend, are on the spot. Fail to deliver on time at the agreed upon prices and you'll never get another contract from the government or other industries." She brushed her hair away from her face. Matt noticed her perfectly manicured nails with maroon polish. "I imagine you have a penalty clause for failure to deliver on time." Lida glanced at her nails as if to indicate that she was aware of his observation. "Any other manufacturer you contact is going to take you to the cleaners. Your margins will be sliced to the bone, but you'll pay. And, even then, you will worry as to whether or not they will deliver on time. If they don't—you lose." She took an imported cigarette out of her purse, held it between her fingers, and waited. Matt fumbled for his lighter, found it, and brought the flame to her cigarette. "I'm going to provide all the product required to fulfill your contracts at a price you can live with." Lida inhaled deeply and waited as if thinking whether or not to make the next statement. As she exhaled smoke drifted over toward Matt. For some reason, he felt even more aroused and found himself wanting this woman.

"You're right. I'm in a bind," Matt agreed. "I did such a great job selling I failed to consider production limitations."

"You're a good salesman. That's something to be proud of," Lida consoled Matt. "It's not as bad as you might think. Together we can make this a highly profitable proposition for Orztech Coporation, LPAmerica, and Matthew Ellis." She looked directly at Matt and offered him her cigarette. He accepted it, noticed the red lipstick on the filter, and put it to his lips. As he drew in smoke he had a sensation of kissing the beauty sitting across the table. The two sat in silence for a moment. At that point in the negotiations Lida knew the first to speak—lost.

"I want to believe you," Matt admitted.

Lida took his hand in hers and said softly, "Then believe."

George Washington High School was relatively empty. A few classrooms were occupied by those poor souls who had failed during the school year. Detectives Akimoto and Donovan sat in the principal's office, once more.

After finding nothing at Rita's apartment, on their way to the school the two detectives had discussed the case. They could only assume that it was a student from George Washington High School because of the victim's description of two young black men and the black wristband with orange and white trim found with the body. Ryoya surmised that the injury to the cornea could have indeed been caused by a ring—a class ring. A logical conclusion could be that one or both of the perpetrators were recent graduates who had played on one of the sports teams at the school. They both knew it was a stretch but it was the only clues they had. Fingerprints, blood type, hair samples, clothing all would be corroborating factors once they identified a suspect, but first they had to find a suspect.

"Mr. Hobarth, how many students were in the graduating class?" Michael Donovan asked.

"We had 347 graduates this year," principal Hobarth replied.

"Could we get a list of the graduating class and their addresses?"

"And, we'll need a copy of the yearbook," Ryoya added.

The Moody Blues latest album, *On The Threshold of a Dream,* was released April, 1969. Words from the first track, *In The Beginning,* filled the room.

I think, I think I am, I think.

Of course you are my bright little star.
I've miles
And miles
Of files
Pretty files of your forefather's fruit
And now to suit our
Great computer
You're magnetic ink.

I'm more than that, I know I am, at least, I think I must be.

There you go, man, keep as cool as you can.
Face piles
And piles

Of trials
With smiles
It riles them to believe
That you perceive
The web they weave
And keep on thinking free.

A lone mind folding upon itself, swam among the words and music unable to differentiate the two, tangled in images that tore at perceived flesh, wanting to run without legs, dripping blood from unseen wounds, falling into a web of flashing lights; green, amber, red, green, amber, red. Then they came. Grotesque hands reached out from the darkness. From all directions, including above and below, leaving no path of escape. All within inches. Sensations of being touched on every naked exposed part of the body. Desperate attempts at defense with an elongated arm weighed down with a huge gold watch.

Lysergic acid diethylamide-25, known as LSD, was discovered by the Swiss chemist Albert Hofmann in 1938. He was studying the medicinal uses of a fungus found on wheat. On April 16, 1943 while doing a laboratory experiment a tiny amount of lysergic acid diethylamide-25 dropped onto his finger. "I had to leave work for home because I was suddenly hit by a sudden feeling of unease and mild dizziness," he wrote in a memo. He also told of "wonderful visions. It lasted for a couple of hours and then it disappeared." Three days later a heavier dose resulted in a frightening experience. "Everything I saw was distorted as in a warped mirror," he said. On his bicycle ride home he described, "I had the impression I was rooted to the spot. But my assistant told me we were actually going very fast." Hofmann later wrote, "The substance which I wanted to experiment with took over me. I was filled with an overwhelming fear that I would go crazy. I was transported to a different world, a different time."

Timothy Francis Leary was an American psychologist and writer who advocated psychedelic drugs. At Harvard University, he experimented with LSD and psilocybe mexicana mushrooms. The research focused on treating alcoholism and reforming criminals. May, 1963, Harvard terminated Timothy F. Leary. He continued experimenting and promoting the use of entheogenic substances as a means of expanding one's consciousness and reaching higher levels of mental power. He was credited with the phrase, "turn on, tune in, drop out" which was inspired by Marshall McLuhan. LSD usage spread across America and was finally made illegal on October 6, 1966. It was considered so dangerous that mere possession was criminalized and all research with the drug ceased.

Ritchie was on a bad trip. One he was destined to ride to the end. His senses misled him. The odor from his paints made it difficult to breathe. Yet, whenever he tried to move them they bolted away from his outstretched hand. The Moody Blues played in his mind discordant notes that echoed deeper and deeper throughout caverns within. Then one tone caused burning pain as each time it vibrated a bare raw nerve. Ritchie screamed. The floor became liquid and he fell drowning in wood. Slowly, on hands and knees he made his way into the small bathroom in his loft apartment. There he found himself in a park. He stared at the bus full of passengers all looking at him. They seemed to be laughing. Then the bus turned and began driving at him. He tried to run. Movement was impossible. The bus blew its horn and its big engine roared. He couldn't escape. The vehicle came closer. He could see the driver. It was President

Nixon with a sardonic smile as he bore down on Ritchie. Curled up on the floor he waited to die. Colors spun around him, amber, red, green, and he lost all concept of time. Then, after two hours, a cold, black, wet nose was a bridge to reality.

Detective Ryoya Akimoto made a list of the names and addresses of black male athletes who graduated that past June. A total of 77 names were included. In an attempt to narrow the list, they had the names checked for prior arrest records. Fourteen were found to have been arrested in the past. They decided to start with those and then expand to the others if nothing was found. This is the part of being a detective that requires patience and stamina. The two detectives would question graduate after graduate with the hope that they would identify a suspect. If that approach failed they would question black athletes who were juniors becoming seniors. However, with so little to go on they both knew all their efforts could come up empty.

"Once we start interviewing, the word will get out," Detective Michael Donovan observed.

"I agree, we need to use a diversionary approach."

"We know she fought for her life. Most likely scratched one or both attackers."

"Also, may have bitten one."

Michael Donovan offered, "There's a good chance the injuries will be visible."

"OK, we're investigating vandalism that took place at the school Tuesday night. It seems the perpetrators did a lot of damage and scrawled 'class of 69' on one of the walls." Ryoya folded the list and put it in her purse.

"So, we're talking to all of the graduates to see if they know anything about it."

"OK, let's go see all the smiling faces."

Anna Six Trees went outside to play. Her face had charcoal patted on it as a sign that she was sorry for disobeying her mother. Ojibwa did not believe in hitting their children.

23: Friday - July 18, 1969

The coffee tasted good. It always did in the early morning after a late night. Ryoya drank her coffee with milk and sugar while Michael was more macho preferring his black. Both Detectives drank from Styrofoam cups as they drove up to Washington Heights. The previous day they had contacted and talked with two dozen black male athlete graduates from George Washington High School. As luck would have it, they hadn't spoken with any youth who seemed nervous, suspicious, or had scratches or other visible injuries. The cover story of investigating vandalism at the school seemed to be accepted without question.

"We should get through the rest of the list today with the exception of those we can't locate," Ryoya concluded.

"It's the ones in the wind that interest me most," Michael Donovan said while driving their unmarked police vehicle uptown. "If they know that they killed the girl they could be hiding out in New Jersey by now."

"Well, their friends and families are here and we can garner information from them as to their whereabouts."

"I just want one kid to answer the door wearing one black, orange, and white wristband with long scratches across his face." Michael stated.

"How about a tattoo on his forehead saying Trojans?"

"That would work."

Ryoya asked, "Have you ever had a case that went that easily?"

"Actually, I have," Detective Donovan admitted. "There was a mugging in the Bronx. I was stationed in the 44th Precinct at the time. It seems this Asian chick got robbed in the subway at Yankee Stadium. I was a beat cop. Well, Wonder Woman wouldn't let the mugging go. So, she tracks the perpetrator down. Found him drunk and asleep in a park with her wallet. Can't get any easier than that."

"Very funny," Ryoya commented.

"If we don't turn something up today this case could go south very quickly," Detective Donovan admitted.

"Let's start with these four who all live in the same building," Ryoya recommended.

Carl had been nervous due to the fact that he hadn't been able to reach Ray Esposito. However, that changed a day earlier when he spoke with the organized crime capo. There was a card game this evening and Ray wanted Carl to work the room. Some of the same heavyweights would be there, including the heavyset player in an expensive grey suit that got lucky after Carl said, "There ya go."

"You're his good luck charm," Ray Esposito said over the telephone. "He wants to make sure that you are there."

"I'm glad," the young inexperienced hood replied.

"Don't be. If he loses you'll be to blame. This guy blows hot and cold. If he's losing stay an arm's length away. He'll smash your head into the table. And, I don't want to have to refinish it." Ray chuckled and then asked, "Did you get a new suit?"

"Picked it up yesterday from Antonio's."

"Good. You looked like shit, last time. Cheapened my game. Did you get a shirt and tie?"

"Antonio threw them in—insisted that I take them."

"Good." Ray said, "Shine your shoes. Be at the same corner at the same time." The telephone clicked ending the call.

Matt sat at the small kitchen table in Stephanie's apartment and thought about the previous day. After leaving the coffee shop, where he reminisced about Lida, he had continued downtown on Sixth Avenue. When he crossed Twenty Eighth Street he immediately recognized the building where Orztech Corporation had its offices. There was an arch over the doors leading to an ornate lobby. Large brass numbers above the arch gave the address 811 Sixth Avenue. Inside he found the business directory on a wall to the right. He scanned it five times but could not find Orztech Corporation. Yet, everything was familiar. This was the correct building, but no Orztech.

Outside, he walked around the corner and recognized the parking garage entrance. Out of curiosity he entered. The attendant, Eddie O'Brien, looked at the new arrival for a few seconds. Then recognition set in and he jumped from the green stool upon which he was sitting.

"Mr. Ellis. It's really you," he offered his hand and grasped Matt's firmly and expressively, "How are you doing?"

"I'm doing much better, thank you," Matt didn't use Eddie's name because he didn't remember it. He did however remember the face and voice.

"Did you park here earlier?"

"No. I was in the neighborhood and decided to stop by." Impulsively, Matt asked, "What happened to Orztech Corporation?"

"Beats me. One day three or four trucks arrive, load up all the office equipment, and poof—they're gone." Eddie walked over to the little counter where he kept all the records. "I think it was two years ago—May, 67."

"Did they move to another location?"

"I don't know. But, there was something odd about it. Usually, when a company moves in or out, building management sends out a memo. This way we can answer questions, when asked. With Orztech—nothing." Eddie looked up at Matt and asked, "How are you feeling? It was a terrible accident. Made the TV news and everything."

"Every day a little better," Matt replied. "Now, I'm trying to put the pieces together from a lost six years."

"I wish I could help," Eddie scratched his head as if thinking. "When they moved out it seemed like a wake. No joking or excitement. The movers said nothing. They loaded their trucks and drove off. As I said—poof."

"Did you see the president of the company . . . what was his name?"

"Parker Adolphson? Yeah, I saw him that day. He came, got his car, but never said a word. He looked tired." Eddie thought for a moment then added, "He used to smile and call me by name. Gave me a bottle of Scotch one Christmas. It didn't make it to New Year's." Eddie smiled, then with a serious look added, "Mr. Adolphson wasn't happy when he left here for the last time."

After leaving the garage, Matt wandered around the area rekindling memories with familiar sights. A small bookstore he frequented was still there. There were numerous new releases in the window. *The Peter Principle* by University of Southern California professor Laurence J. Peter which examined middle management at corporations. It was credited with the theory that ". . .every employee tends to rise to his level of incompetence." *Master and Commander* by English novelist Patrick O'Brian. It depicted the adventures of Jack Aubrey and his surgeon friend Stephen Maturin in the Royal Navy during the Napoleonic wars. *The Godfather* by New York novelist Mario Puzo who wrote a compelling story about the Mafia. Matt was tempted to buy all three books but settled for *The Godfather.*

Most of the surrounding neighborhood appeared the same as far as Matt could remember. Stores and restaurants dotted the streets with apartments above many. Old office buildings remained filled with businesses and sidewalks still had a constant flow of pedestrians. On the streets automobiles jousted with delivery trucks and Checker Cabs. Matt considered how Checker Cabs hadn't changed in years. Their boxy 1950s style made them easy to spot and also provided a kind of a charm. They were designed to have expansive back seats and large trunks. It was in 1958 when the laws changed that they added quad headlights. He remembered reading how Checker Cabs came to dominate New York City. Mayor Jimmy Walker in the early 1930s settled a taxi fare war by creating the New York Taxi Cab Commission, which ruled that all cabs in New York had to be purpose-built, not consumer cars. This gave Checker the advantage that they kept all those years.

Matt's mind drifted back to a taxi ride he, Valerie, and Stephanie had taken. It was 1958. Stephanie was seven years old. One Saturday morning they decided to take their daughter to the Bronx Zoo. They took the bus to the George Washington Bridge bus terminal and hailed a cab. Once inside the Checker cab they gave the driver their destination and off they zoomed.

"Ah, the Bronx-a zoo. It is-a nice-a day for the zoo," the middle-aged Italian driver said pleasantly. He pushed down the flag on the meter, pulled away from the curb, and then asked over his shoulder, "Has-a the little girl been to-a the zoo before?"

"This is her first time," Valerie answered running her hand through Stephanie's hair.

"She will-a enjoy it," the driver concluded. He maneuvered the taxi onto the Cross Bronx Expressway. "Some-a day, I'm-a gonna take my-a little girl to the zoo."

"You should," Valerie agreed.

"We live so-a close-a. But I . . . I-a work at the bakery during the week and drive-a the taxi on weekends."

"How old is your daughter?" Valerie asked as she continued a conversation with the friendly cabbie.

"She-a eight yearsa old," he answered and added, "beautiful, just like-a her mother. May she rest-a in peace."

Silence filled the cab for a minute.

"Make-a sure she sees all the beautiful birds in the aviary," the cabbie recommended.

"So, you have been to the zoo?" Valerie asked.

"A long time ago. Before-a Maria was-a born. Stephania, my wife, and I, we go to the zoo. She loved the aviary. After she sick and I work so much we . . ." the cabbies voice trailed off.

Matt had listened to the conversation. He remembered looking at Valerie and Stephanie and thinking how lucky he had been and how difficult it must be for a single parent to raise a child. A parent's love gives them the strength to carry on in spite of overwhelming demands and emotional strain. In his recollection, Matt saw Valerie conversing with a total stranger, yet caring about a cab driver's story. What happened next surprised him.

"You live in the Bronx?" Valerie asked the driver.

"One hundred-a eighty third street."

"I grew up in the Bronx—Riverdale."

"Ah, Riverdale, such-a beautiful place. I love to take-a fares-a to Riverdale."

Matt's conservative, never impulsive wife then said, "We could take Maria with us to the zoo."

"Excusa please?" the equally surprised driver exclaimed and then added, "No, that would be-a too much. You take-a your little girl. She doesn't need no interference from someone else's-a child."

Valerie and Stephanie spoke with each other after which Valerie stated, "My daughter would love to have a friend go along to the zoo. Would you like us to take Maria?"

The taxi driver didn't say anything as he exited the Cross Bronx Expressway onto Jerome Avenue. Once on a surface street he pulled the taxi to the curb and stopped. He turned to face the Ellis family and said, "Mrs. Lady, that's-a very nice of you but you don't-a know me or Maria and-a we couldn't ask-a such a big-a favor."

"It would be our pleasure. Can Maria go with us?"

"No, but thank you," his voice cracked slightly revealing deep emotion.

"She would be no problem and we'd love to have her. Wouldn't she like to go?"

There was a long pause and silence filled the Checker cab once more. Finally, the driver said in a slightly raised voice, "She can't-a go." He turned back toward the front of the cab and put the car in gear.

"I'm sorry," Valerie said, "We didn't mean to intrude."

The cab remained at the curb, "Mrs. Lady, I don't-a want to insult you. With the doctore bills and . . . other bills . . . Maria canna go."

It was then that Valerie understood. She looked at the license card on the back of the driver's seat and immediately said, "Mr. Vittori, I didn't make it clear that Maria would be our guest. We will pay for her."

"No, that's-a too much to ask."

"But, you are not asking—we are. We'd love to have Maria join us. Please, say yes."

Matt remembered that day. The two girls got along famously, laughing and running and pointing. They ate hot dogs and bought souvenirs. When they brought Maria home Angelo Vittori made an authentic Italian meal for all of them. It was a perfect day at the zoo.

Ramona Jefferson answered the door. Before her stood a man and a woman who held out police detective shields as they introduced themselves. Although confused she heard them ask if her son, Tyrone, was at home. After a short pause, she nodded wondering if he was in trouble.

"Tyrone, there are police here who want to talk with you," Ramona called in the direction of the bedroom.

When they heard a commotion in the back room Michael Donovan and

Ryoya Akimoto pushed by the surprised woman and headed toward the bedroom. They entered the room just in time to see a leg disappear up the fire escape.

"The roof!" Michael shouted as he pursued the young man.

Ryoya ran out of the apartment and began climbing the stairs. They were on the eighth floor of a twelve-story building. Two steps at a time Detective Akimoto devoured the stairs. When she reached the roof door she paused and listened. Footsteps approached the door. Detective Akimoto took a step to the side of the door and waited. Almost immediately, the door was pulled open and a young black male bounded through the doorway. He never saw Ryoya until he looked up from the floor where he had fallen after being tripped. An aikido wristlock incapacitated the youth.

Tyrone Jefferson had a bandage on his left hand and obvious scratch marks on his neck. Detective Michael Donovan arrived, saw the wounds, looked at Ryoya and said, "Bingo!"

The detectives read Tyrone Jefferson his Maranda rights and took him downtown to the Midtown North precinct headquarters at 306 West 54th Street. Once there, photographs were taken of his injuries and he was placed in an interview room. Ryoya conducted the interview.

"Tyrone, why did you run?"

"I was scared," he replied. "Police comin' to your door ain't ever a good thing."

"We just wanted to ask you a few questions," Ryoya began, waited, and then asked. "How did you hurt your hand?"

"You wanted to ask me how I hurt my hand?"

"It looks like a bite mark. Did someone bite you?"

"Yeah, my girlfriend."

"Did you have a fight?"

"Yeah. She gets really mad and then gets rough."

"Did she scratch your neck?"

Impulsively, Tyrone's hand went up to his neck and felt the scratches—then he answered, "Yeah."

"What's your girlfriend's name?"

"What's my girlfriend's name?" He repeated the question, hesitated, and then answered, "Shirley . . . uh . . . Shirley Madden."

Ryoya knew he was lying. When he repeated the question he was buying time to think. The practiced detective neither said a word nor did she show any facial expression. She looked directly into the youth's eyes. He was blinking quickly—another tell. Unconsciously, he hid the bite mark on his left hand with his right hand. His head was tilted slightly toward the left, as well, as if trying to minimize the exposure of scratches on his neck. The silence made him more nervous.

"Her name's Shirley," he repeated then looked away.

Ryoya stood and picked up the folder that was in front of her, "I can't help you, Tyrone," she turned to leave, "if you're going to lie to me."

"I ain't lying," he insisted.

Abruptly Detective Akimoto turned and tossed the folder on the table. "Your partner will implicate you to get a deal. You, on the other hand, will play dumb and lie and ultimately end up in jail."

"What did he say?" Tyrone asked taking the bait.

"He had nothing to do with it. You were the one who raped that girl and beat her up." Ryoya left out the fact that the victim had died.

"He's lying!" Sweat appeared on the young man's forehead.

"He convinced me," Ryoya said softly as if thinking. "Of course, it wouldn't be fair to just take his word for it." Ryoya sat down opposite the suspect, "Why don't you tell me your side of the story."

"I didn't rape no one. And, I didn't hit her," Tyrone started. "She was a hooker. We were just going to take her money so we could go downtown and get high. Dewayne, it was his idea. He picked her up and I waited around the corner. When they came down the street the two of us grabbed her and dragged her into the alley. She went nuts. Started screaming and fighting. I put my hand over her mouth and she bit me." The young mugger held up his hand. "I let go and she spun around and scratched my neck. Dewayne grabbed her and hit her with a heavy wrapped pipe he carries. Then he pulled her farther back into the alley and beat her up and raped her. I wanted to leave but Dewayne has a bad temper and he'da come after me. So, I waited." After a pause he suggested, "Ask the hooker. She'll tell you it wasn't me."

Detective Akimoto had observed the young man's gestures and remembered the description of the victim's injuries. She asked Tyrone, "Are you left handed?"

Surprised, he looked at his left hand and acknowledged, "Yes."

From all indications, the victim had been struck by a right-handed assailant. This added credibility to Tyrone's description of events. She now needed to get him to name and implicate his partner. He appeared to be cooperating, therefore, she decided to use an old technique. She placed a yellow writing tablet and pencil in front of Tyrone. He looked up.

"I believe you, Tyrone," Detective Akimoto said in a friendly voice, "but, I need your help." She stood and instructed, "I need you to write down what you just told me. Put down everything that happened and who did what. Make sure you include your full name and Dewayne's full name so there aren't any questions later." She walked to the door, stopped, and turned back toward the suspect. "Make sure you also include what each of you were wearing." After a pause, she asked, "Do you have a class ring?"

"No."

She didn't want him to know that they didn't have Dewayne, so she added, "Make sure you put down any jewelry, hats, sweat bands, or other items either of you were wearing." Pause. "Do a good job and be honest, Tyrone. I want to help you." Detective Ryoya Akimoto left the room.

The bright afternoon sun danced on the water of Nantucket Sound. Sails of various colors and size could be seen in the distance. Along the eastern shore of the island were over four miles of pristine beach. The name Chappaquiddick came from a Wampanoag Indian word "cheppiaquidne" meaning "separated island." Indeed, it was a small island separated by a narrow channel from the larger Martha's Vineyard Island in Massachusetts.

Senator Edward Kennedy stood on Pogue Beach looking out at the water. He was participating in the annual Edgartown Yacht Club Regatta with his nephew, Joe Kennedy. For over thirty years the Kennedy family had been participants and Ted kept up the tradition.

The 37-year-old U.S. Senator had finished the competition for the day and was thinking about the cook-out he and co-host Paul F. Markham, former United States Attorney for Massachusetts were having at the Lawrence Cottage on

Chappaquiddick Island. In attendance were Joseph Gargan, Ted Kennedy's cousin; Charles Tretter, an attorney; Raymond La Rosa; and John Crimmins, Kennedy's part-time driver. All were married men with the exception of one. No wives accompanied them. Instead, six young women, known as the "boiler room girls," who had worked on the late Robert Kennedy's 1968 presidential campaign had been invited. Kennedy fully expected to get lucky that night.

Luck was with Carl as the heavyset card player in an expensive grey suit was winning. When Carl brought the player his first drink he made sure to say, "There ya go." This, of course, raised some mumbles from the other players. Poker players are worse than baseball players when it comes to superstitions.

"Hey pal, when you gonna bring some luck my way?" asked an older player who chewed on that night's featured cigar. It was a new cigar that had just been introduced in Cuba by Zino Davidoff. The Davidoff No.1 was a hand-made long Panatela that measured about seven and a half inches long. It followed the tobacco blend of Cohiba with a slightly lighter wrapper to make the cigar smoother and more refined. Cuban Cohiba is filled with tobacco that comes from the Vuelta Abajo region of Cuba which has undergone an extra fermentation process. It was established in 1966 as a private brand exclusively for Fidel Castro and high-level officials in the Communist Party of Cuba and Cuban government. After Ray Esposito gave his description of the featured cigar he was asked how he got his hands on them. He simply smiled.

Robert Six Trees sat on the bank of a lake. He watched a deer on the other side of the water. Silently, he observed how it carefully approached the water, took a drink, looked around, another drink, looked around, and finally darted back into the woods. When he got home he sketched the beautiful creature from memory.

24 : Saturday - July 19, 1969

After an afternoon and evening of heavy drinking most of the partiers at Lawrence Cottage on Chappaquiddick Island were in various stages of intoxication. Senator Edward Kennedy, a long-time imbiber, held his liquor well. As the cookout progressed Kennedy targeted a 29-year-old blond secretary who had worked in Washington D.C. for Senators Robert F. Kennedy and George Smanthers. Her name was Mary Jo Kopechne. He spoke with the young lady throughout the evening and turned on the charm. She had been an ardent admirer of Robert Kennedy and was taken in by the Kennedy mystique. Shortly after midnight Senator Kennedy convinced her to take a ride with him out to the beach on the eastern shore of the island where he had been earlier that day. Kennedy got the keys to his mother's 1967 Oldsmobile Delmont 88 from John Crimmins, who sometimes drove for the Kennedys. Edward Kennedy and his object of interest that night got into the car. Mary Jo left her purse and hotel keys at the party.

Ted Kennedy had a history of wild driving. He had been cited for reckless driving four times while attending law school at the University of Virginia. Once he drove 90 miles per hour through a residential neighborhood with his headlights off.

On this night a combination of alcohol and testosterone prodded him to demonstrate his driving prowess to his young rider. Impaired judgment and speed caused him to miss the sharp right turn onto Dike Road which led to the beach. Instead, the big Oldsmobile left the pavement and entered a dirt road that lay straight ahead and led to a cemetery. Kennedy braked hard and brought the car to a stop.

At that same moment Christopher "Huck" Look, a deputy sheriff working at the Edgartown regatta dance, approached the intersection of Chappaquiddick Road and Dike Road. He had left the dance at 12:30 a.m., taken the yacht club's launch to Chappaquiddick Island, gotten in his parked car, and was driving home on Chappaquiddick Road. The road curves sharply to the right at the point where it intersects with Dike Road. When the deputy sheriff saw headlights approaching from the right he slowed. From experience he knew drivers often misjudge the curve and cut it close crossing the white line. He witnessed a dark car occupied by a man and woman go straight, leave the pavement, enter the private Cemetery Road, and stop. The Deputy stopped, got out of his car, and approached the vehicle to see if he could help. When he was approximately thirty feet away the car started backing toward him.

As Ted Kennedy backed the Oldsmobile onto the road his lights illuminated the badge and uniform of Deputy Sheriff Christopher Look. He was shocked to see a law enforcement officer approaching and knew the consequences of being found driving drunk with a young female in the car. In a near panic he decided to run. The deputy called out but Kennedy pushed down on the accelerator and drove off on Dike Road leaving a cloud of dust in his wake. Deputy Sheriff Look noted that the car's Massachusetts license plate began with an "L" and contained two "7s."

At nearly forty miles-per-hour Kennedy drove down the rutted, rough road. As he did so he kept looking in the rearview mirror to see if the police were following. He knew getting caught would be a disaster. Thirty seconds later the real disaster occurred. It was too late when he saw the bridge. Alcohol slowed his reaction time and clouded his judgment. He braked the car and turned the steering wheel. The big Oldsmobile skid 17 feet along the road and 25 feet onto the bridge where it hit the rub rail. At twenty miles-per-hour the car left the bridge, flew 25 feet over Poucha Pond, flipped over, and hit the water on the passenger side. On impact Mary Jo Kopechne was thrown into the back seat, the driver's door sprung open, and the car sank into the cold dark water.

Carl looked at his watch. It was 12:47 a.m. The card game had become quite interesting with some rather large bets being made. Ray Esposito was pleased as more chips were purchased and the house took its cut. He also saw that his young pupil had gotten the hang of working the room while staying invisible. The kid had potential. He had done some checking and learned of Carl Pythacyk's prowess with his fists. There would be other jobs he could have the kid do.

Ted Kennedy swam to the surface and looked around. In the darkness, it was difficult to identify the shoreline. A light on a cottage to the left helped him find his way. He swam to the bank and climbed out of the water. Meanwhile, in the sunken Oldsmobile Mary Jo was dazed and disoriented. It was completely black and she was under water. Instinctively, she let her body float until she could tell which way was up. She then attempted to swim but when she broke the surface she made contact with the carpet in the back floorboard of the overturned car. Air filled her lungs and she yelled, "Help!" In the enclosed space her yell sounded flat and muffled. Unable to see anything in darkness, she felt around the air pocket trying desperately to find a way out. Fear and cold caused her hands to shake and her breathing was rapid. Slowly she walked her hands across the carpeted floor above her to the driver's side rear door. Her heart beat rapidly. When she found the handle she tried to open the door. It didn't budge. "Help me!" she whispered. She found the door window with her feet and tried to kick it out but the water hindered any quick motion. Rapid currents caused the automobile to rock causing her to feel nauseous. To keep her head above the water she held onto the lower portion of the seat. With tears running down her cheeks she prayed that help would come soon.

Ted Kennedy looked out over the water. There was no sign of the car. In his alcohol fogged mind he tried to think of how to get out of this career threatening situation. The girl was probably dead. Nothing he could do. Now, he had to save himself. For 15 minutes, he sat on the bank and mumbled, "This can't be happening. What do I do?"

At 1:00 a.m. the card players took a break. Some ate sandwiches that were provided, others used the facilities, and a few wandered up to the roof for some fresh air. As usual, Ray was charming, funny, and accommodating. These were big fish that were well-known. It was a coup for Ray Esposito to have assembled this group. He made money on the game, as well as gained allies with great influence in New York City. Across the room, he heard Judge Markinson laughing. A rivalry had developed between the judge and another player. This was good as testosterone-fed betting increased the pots. However, there was a risk that it could get out of hand and disrupt the game. Ray decided to get the two together on his boat for a day of fishing.

In complete blackness Mary Jo Kopechne didn't know how deep the car had sunk. She thought of swimming down toward the roof of the vehicle and then the front seat to see if there was a way out. Fear that she wouldn't be able to find her way back to the air pocket kept her from making the attempt. Each time she heard a noise from the car settling or water pushing against it she hoped it was help arriving. "Here, I'm in here. Help!" she screamed. She tried knocking to get a rescuer's attention but the rug on the floor and padded door didn't allow for any sound. Cold and darkness gnawed at her soul.

Senator Kennedy decided the best action was to get back to the party and enlist the aid of the two lawyers, Joe Gargan and Paul Markham, who were in attendance. They would be able to make this go away. He staggered to his feet and began walking west on Dike Road. As he did he passed a number of cottages that were clearly visible but knew he couldn't knock on their door in the middle of the night and admit what he had done. One of the houses he passed belonged to Fire Captain Foster Silva. For thirty minutes, he walked the 1.2 miles from the bridge to Lawrence Cottage where the party was still ongoing.

When Ted Kennedy arrived at Lawrence Cottage he saw Ray LaRosa, one of the guests. LaRosa was a former fireman and had not been drinking at the party. However, instead of asking for help Kennedy asked LaRosa to send out Joe Gargan and Paul Markham, the two lawyers. He then climbed into the back seat of a white Plymouth Valiant that was parked outside of the cottage.

"There's been a terrible accident. The car's gone off the bridge down by the beach, and Mary Jo is in it," Kennedy told Gargan and Markham when they arrived.

The two shocked men jumped in the car and headed to the accident scene. Joe Gargan drove across Dike Bridge and parked the car on the beach with the headlights aimed at the water. There was no sign of the Oldsmobile.

Both men removed their clothes and dove into the water. They fought a strong current to get to the sunken vehicle. Paul Markham had injured his leg in the regatta and was highly intoxicated. As a result, he had trouble swimming. Joe Gargan found the car and felt for a door handle. When he found one he pulled on it but the door wouldn't open. The car was nose down on its roof. Gargan moved around the car and found an opening. He entered the car through a broken window but couldn't see anything. He felt around but found nothing. As his breath ran out he pushed free of the vehicle cutting his arms and chest. Frantically, he fought his way to the surface. When Joe Gargan reached the surface and inhaled deeply he saw Senator Kennedy on the bridge illuminated by the headlights of the Valiant. He was lying on his back with his hands clasped behind his head looking up at the sky. Kennedy rocked back and forth and kept repeating, "Oh my God. What am I going to do? What am I going to do?"

Sounds inside the car had alerted Mary Jo and she tried to call out. Her voice was weak and overpowered by the sound of the current. Did she imagine it or was rescue on its way? Weakly, she tried kicking any part of the car that might make a sound. Then there was silence. Mary Jo Kopechne was exhausted and trembled from the cold. The air smelled of sea water and seemed heavy making it difficult to breath.

Both men, Gargan and Markham, made additional attempts to open the car's doors but failed. With each attempt, Mary Jo tried to signal that she was inside but was unable to make contact. Finally, the men gave up and climbed onto the bridge.

"I just can't believe this happened," Senator Kennedy said.

"Well, what the hell happened?" Joe Gargan asked.

"I was driving down the road and before I knew it, I was on the bridge," Kennedy said. "The car went over the side. I thought for sure I was going to drown. And the next thing I know, I'd come to the top of the water." He paused then whined, "I don't believe this could happen to me. I don't understand it. I don't know how it could happen."

"Well, it has happened," Paul Markham stated.

"What am I going to do?" Kennedy said. "What can I do?"

"There's nothing you can do," Markham said.

The three men got into the Valiant and drove toward the ferry landing. As they rode they discussed the accident and made sure that their stories matched. Joe Gargan insisted that they needed to report the accident immediately.

Senator Kennedy surprised the two men when he suggested, "Why couldn't Mary Jo have been driving the car? Why couldn't she have let me off and driven to the ferry herself and made a wrong turn?"

Joe Gargan told Kennedy that they didn't know Mary Jo very well and had no idea if she even had a license. He added, "You told me you were driving!" Finally, he explained to Ted Kennedy that they had been at the scene of the accident and that someone might have seen them and recognized him. He knew making a false report to police could cost him his law license. Gargan insisted that Kennedy report the accident.

"OK," Kennedy replied, "Take me to Edgartown."

The card game broke up at 2:00 a.m. A great deal of money had changed hands but all the players seemed satisfied with the competition. Ray Esposito was pleased. Carl also was happy as he net nine hundred dollars from tips. He started picking up glasses and ashtrays without being told by Ray.

"I have another job for you," Ray said as he approached Carl. Carl looked up but didn't say anything.

"Wednesday morning 10:00 a.m. be back here." With that Ray left.

When the three men reached the ferry landing Joe Gargan once more recommended that the accident be reported. There was a pay phone where they parked. "All right, all right, Joey! I'm tired of listening to you. I'll take care of it. You go back. Don't upset the girls. Don't get them involved," Kennedy said not hiding his anger. He then left the car and jumped into the water and swam in the direction of Edgartown. The ferry had stopped running at midnight.

Joe Gargan and Paul Markham were shocked by Kennedy's action. After standing and watching him swim away they returned to the party at Lawrence Cottage but didn't tell anyone about Mary Jo Kopechne.

A vehicle silently drifted in darkness surrounded by an uninhabitable airless environment. Within its shell life so fragile found temporary refuge. Refuge from which there was no escape. Life, small and insignificant by comparison to what lay beyond the man-made metal conveyance, was sustained and protected from the outside. Mortality on the edge. In a void time is nonexistent. Yet, it passes and with each moment an ultimate destination grows closer. Apollo 11 was on a direct course toward the Moon.

Two hundred thousand miles away trapped in the sunken Oldsmobile a young woman clung to life in silent frigid darkness. Terror had dissolved into acceptance and then an inexplicable wave of calm came over her. The effects of carbon dioxide fogged her mind and sleep brought images of home and safety. Ever so slowly her fragile life drifted over the edge. On a warm summer night, clear skies revealed a tapestry of stars and the Moon. The world gazed upward at an unseen spacecraft destined to make history and prayed for their safety. In a dark cold pond, no one noticed the passing of Mary Jo Kopechne.

Senator Edward Kennedy snuck back to his room at the Shiretown Inn in Edgartown. He dressed in a jacket and slacks, left the room, and stood at the bottom of the stairs until a clerk named Russell Peachey came by. The clerk asked if he could help and Kennedy said he had been disturbed by noises coming from a party. Kennedy also commented that he had lost his watch and inquired what time it was. Peachey looked through the office window at a clock and told Kennedy it was 2:25 a.m. The Senator returned to his room. He made numerous calls to family and legal advisors and ultimately decided that his only hope was to lie.

After reviewing Tyrone Jefferson's written statement from the night before the police arrested DeWayne Martin at 6:00 a.m. at his home without incident. He sat in an interview room at the Midtown North precinct headquarters. Detective Michael Donovan entered the room and sat opposite the suspect. Neither spoke.

"Why was I arrested?" a defiant DeWayne Martin finally asked and then added, "I had nothin to do with no vandalism at G.W.High." It was clear that word had spread based on their cover story.

"Oh, then where were you on Tuesday night?" Donovan asked taking the lead from the suspect.

"I was downtown. Nowhere near the school." DeWayne spat.

"Where downtown?"

"The Village."

"Where in the Village?"

"Just roamin around. No place in particular."

"Can you prove you were there?"

"Yeah." The young man hesitated, then stated, "I was with a friend."

Detective Donovan looked at the class ring on Dewayne's left ring finger. On the side of the ring was the word Trojans. He asked, "Who were you with?"

"I was with Tyrone. All night. We were nowhere near the school." The young hood figured the mugging of a hooker wouldn't even get reported. And, what he told the police was the truth. After they took a hundred fifty dollars off Rita Craig they took the subway downtown to Greenwich Village.

"What time were you in the Village?"

"I don't know—it was dark. And, I ain't got no watch."

"So, you and Tyrone were in Greenwich Village Tuesday night?"

"Right." DeWayne sat up tall and stated, "Now, can I go."

"You're right DeWayne, you and Tyrone had nothing to do with vandalism at George Washington High School." DeWayne nodded and started to rise. "Sit down!" Michael Donovan ordered. DeWayne complied, shrugged, and smiled at the detective. "Were you on West Forty Fourth Street on Tuesday night?"

The smile dissolved from DeWayne's face. He looked around the room as if looking to see if someone else might be present. The mugging had been reported after all. But, who's gonna believe a hooker? And, it's her word against his and Tyrone's word. If they both deny it they are each other's alibi. Then he remembered Tyrone's injuries. Nah, that could've happened anywhere. He looked at the detective across the table, elevated his chin, and stated with complete sincerity, "We got on the subway at One Hundred and Sixty Eighth Street and rode all the way down to the Village."

Detective Donovan made a note on the pad in front of him, looked up, and informed the arrogant murder suspect, "We have a team searching your mother's apartment as we speak." DeWayne looked shocked but didn't move. "If they find the pipe that you used as a weapon you will be charged."

"They ain't gonna find nothing," DeWayne bluffed but he knew they would find it under his bed.

"Do you want to tell me what happened on Forty Fourth Street?" Detective Donovan asked. This question was followed by a long period of silence. Dewayne knew he was caught. He also knew his only defense was to lie.

At 7:00 a.m. Senator Edward Kennedy, dressed in yachting clothes, entered the lobby of the Colonial Inn which was located next to the Shiretown Inn where he was staying. With a smile he asked the desk clerk, Mrs. Frances Stewart, to save a copy of both the Boston Globe and the New York Times for him. In addition, he asked to borrow a dime for the public telephone.

Outside on the porch where the telephone was located Ted Kennedy called Helga Wagner. She was a former German airline stewardess with whom he had an affair. He contacted her because he knew that she had the telephone number for where Stephen Smith and his wife were staying in Spain. Stephen Smith was Ted's brother-in-law and the Kennedy family business manager. With the number in hand he returned to the Shiretown Inn. On the way, he met Ross Richards and Stan Moore who were friends and joined them on the porch outside Richard's room. They had casual conversation and no mention was made of the accident on Chappaquiddick Island.

Joe Gargan, Paul Markham, Charles Tretter, Rosemary Keough, and Susan Tannenbaum left Lawrence Cottage in time to catch the first ferry back to Edgartown at 7:30 a.m. When Gargan arrived at the Shiretown Inn and saw Kennedy chatting with his friends. It was clear that the accident hadn't been reported. He was enraged.

"I'd like to see you right now! Get in there!" Gargan yelled as he pointed toward Kennedy's room.

Inside Kennedy's room the Senator explained that he had not been seen when he arrived during the night, changed clothes, established his presence by asking an employee for the time, and hadn't told anyone about the accident. He expressed disappointment that Gargan hadn't reported the accident and explained that Mary Jo had driven the car alone. Kennedy had expected Gargan to protect him.

While the two men argued, events took place on Chappaquiddick Island. Two fisherman crossing Dike Bridge saw a reflection in the water. When they looked closer they discovered that it was a submerged automobile. Immediately, they went to the nearest cottage and told what had been seen. At 8:00 a.m. Mrs. Malm called the police.

In Edgartown, after being informed of the sighting of a submerged vehicle, Police Chief Dominick Arena had the dispatcher call the fire department's scuba diver and then headed for the ferry. John Farrar, captain of the search and rescue division of Edgartown's volunteer fire department, went to the fire station retrieved his gear and also headed to Dike Bridge on Chappaquiddick Island.

A half hour after receiving the call Chief Arena arrived at Dike Bridge. Due to the outgoing tide the rear wheels of the Oldsmobile poked slightly above the water. Arena swam out to the car. The license plate read L78 207. Under water he couldn't see into the car and had difficulty fighting the current. Finally, he climbed onto the automobile and sat on the undercarriage to wait for the scuba diver.

"She said she'd give both of us a blowjob for ten bucks," DeWayne Martin explained. "Then she pulled a knife on us and tried to rob us." DeWayne looked directly at Detective Donovan and continued, "Tyrone, he got a temper, so he hit her with a pipe and dragged her into the back of the alley. I stayed out front. She fought him—even bit him—then he raped her. I didn't do nothin."

"We didn't find a knife at the scene," Michael Donovan stated.

"Tyrone, he picked it up."

"What happened to the pipe that was used?"

"Tyrone give it to me and told me to hide it," DeWayne explained. "It's under my bed. I was gonna give it back to him."

"Did you hit her?"

"Nah, I barely touched her. Tyrone grabbed her, hit her, and raped her."

"What would she tell us?" Detective Donovan tried an old ploy.

DeWayne hesitated, considered the question, and then offered an explanation, "It was dark. She don't know one of us from the other. Besides she bit and scratched Tyrone. If she says I did anything—she's lying."

So, when did she pull the knife on you?" Detective Donovan asked knowing that a lie is hard to remember so by asking the same question different ways the suspect gets confused.

"When we was in the alley. She points the knife at me and says to give her my money. Tyrone grabbed her and dragged her into the back of the alley."

"Did she drop the knife?"

"Uh, yeah."

"And, you picked it up?"

DeWayne didn't answer. Detective Donovan sat back in the metal folding chair. He stared at the suspect making eye contact. The young thug looked away. He tried to devise a way for explaining how the nonexistent knife ended up with Tyrone. Finally, he offered, "I left it there. I was scared. When Tyrone came out from the alley he picked it up."

"Is that when he gave you the pipe?"

"No. He gave it to me later."

Michael Donovan leaned forward and asked, "Why did he give you the pipe?"

"He wanted me to hide it."

"Couldn't he hide it?"

"I don't know. He hands me the pipe and says hide this for me."

"When did he give it to you?"

"On the way home. He just hands it to me and says hide it."

"What kind of knife was it?"

"It was like a big kitchen knife."

"So, Tyrone carried a big kitchen knife and a pipe around all night?"

"Yeah."

"This thing is worse now than it was before. We've got to do something. We're reporting the accident right now!" Joe Gargan stated emphatically.

"I'm going to say that Mary Jo was driving," Kennedy insisted. In his mind, it was his way out.

"There's no way you can say that!" Gargan said. "You can be placed at the scene. Jesus! We've got to report this thing. Let's go."

On Chappaquiddick Island John Farrar, the scuba diver, and Fire Chief Antone Silva arrived at Dike Bridge. Over the car radio they were informed that license plate # L78 207 had been issued to Edward M. Kennedy, Room 2400, JFK Building, Government Center, Boston, Massachusetts. John Farrar feared that the Senator was dead in the sunken Oldsmobile. He entered the water holding a safety line. Underwater, he found the automobile. Based on its location he concluded that it must have been going pretty fast to have landed so far out in the channel. It balanced on the front part of the roof with the engine side down and rear tilted upward. The driver's side window was open or broken out. Through it he saw the front seat was empty. When he looked in the rear window he saw a woman's feet wearing sandals. He entered the car through the open window and found Mary Jo Kopechne's body. Her head was tilted upward, face pressed into the footwell, and hands gripped the front edge of the back seat. The scuba diver removed the body from the car through the open window. Due to rigor mortis it was a difficult task. Once out, he tied the safety line around the body and brought it to the surface. The recovery took ten minutes.

"When Tyrone dragged her back into the alley did she scream?" Detective Donovan asked.

"Tyrone had his hand over her mouth"

"So, Tyrone grabbed her from behind and dragged her back into the alley?"

"Yeah, and raped her."

"When did he hit her with the pipe?"

"Back in the alley."

"Is that when she dropped the knife?"

"Yeah."

"OK, when Tyrone came out of the alley what did he say?"

"He said, 'the bitch bit me'"

"Did she say anything?"

"Nah, she was in the back lying in a pile of garbage. I didn't hear nothin."

Michael Donovan paused. There were enough inconsistencies in DeWayne Martin's answers to show he was lying. However, the detective wanted more.

Chief Dominick Arena ordered Officer Robert Bruguiere to call the medical examiner and have a tow truck brought to the scene. He then instructed John Farrar, the scuba diver, to search downstream for other bodies. As Officer Robert Bruguiere was leaving Arena called out, "And see if you can find out where Ted Kennedy is and get him down here."

Joe Gargan, Paul Markham, and Ted Kennedy had taken the ferry to Chappaquiddick Island where there was a secluded public telephone in the ferry house that could be used. Senator Kennedy made a number of calls. While Kennedy was on the telephone Paul Markham observed a tow truck with flashing lights arrive by ferry.

At this point, Joe Gargan exclaimed, "You've got to do what I've been saying all along. Get your ass over there and report it as fast as you can."

Police officer Antone Bettencourt arrived at the ferry landing from the accident scene and asked ferry pilot Dick Hewitt, "Do you know about the accident? It's Ted Kennedy's car and there's a dead girl in it."

The young man looked toward the ferry house and answered, "Well, he's standing right over there with two men."

Officer Bettencourt was surprised. After looking at the three men in amazement he walked over to the group and asked Kennedy, "Senator, do you know there's a girl found dead in your car? Do you need a ride down to the bridge?"

"No," Kennedy replied, "I'm going on over to town."

"When we get the pipe, which we will, whose fingerprints will be on it?"

"What?" DeWayne asked surprised.

"Whose fingerprints, DeWayne? Let me say it another way. Will we find Tyrone's fingerprints anywhere on the pipe?"

"He wiped it clean, then gave it to me."

"Come'on, DeWayne, he never touched the pipe, did he?"

"What are you saying? Tyrone hit the bitch with the pipe, then dragged her back in the alley, and raped her."

"How do you know he raped her?"

"Huh? He told me," DeWayne Martin became agitated as his story unraveled.

"There wasn't any knife, was there, DeWayne?"

"She had a knife!"

"Then where is it?"

"Tyrone picked it up!"

"No, he didn't. He never mentioned a knife in his statement."

DeWayne sat in silence. He had to find a way to put the blame on Tyrone. If he could convince them that Tyrone hit the hooker he would be nothing more than an accomplice. "Tyrone said there was a knife. That's why he hit her. I said there was a knife to cover for him. Maybe there wasn't a knife, but he beat her up and raped her."

Joe Gargan suggested that Paul Markham and Senator Kennedy go to the police station in Edgartown. He had an ulterior motive for this suggestion. If Ted Kennedy stuck to his story about Mary Jo driving, Gargan wanted to be as far away from the lie as possible. In this case, it would be at Lawrence Cottage. On his way, driving the white Valiant, Joe Gargan met Ray LaRosa, John Crimmins, Nance Lyons, Mary Ellen Lyons, and Esther Newberg walking on Chappaquiddick Road heading for the ferry landing. He stopped and told them, "The Senator has been in an automobile accident and we can't find Mary Jo." Because he didn't know what Senator Kennedy would ultimately say he didn't offer any other information about the accident.

The group returned to Lawrence Cottage and hastily cleaned up any signs of a party. They went so far as to empty the outside garbage containers leaving no evidence at all.

While the cleanup was taking place, the tow truck arrived at Dike Bridge. The driver was told it was Ted Kennedy's car at which time he commented, "Gee, I just saw him at the ferry landing on the Chappaquiddick side."

Chief Dominick Arena called the station and told the dispatcher to send someone to the ferry landing to get Kennedy. He was told that the Senator was at the station and wanted to talk with him.

Over the telephone Arena said, "I'm afraid, Senator, I have some bad news. There's been another tragedy. Your car was in an accident over here. And the young lady is dead."

"I know," Kennedy replied.

"Can you tell me, was there anybody else in the car?"

"Yes."

"Are they in the water?"

"No," Senator Kennedy said, "Can I talk to you? Could I see you?"

The police chief asked, "Do you want to come over here? Or do you want me to go over there?"

"I prefer you to come over here."

"We found a black wristband with orange and white trim out by the street."

"That's mine. See, I told you I was out front," DeWayne Martin smiled.

"That's funny Tyrone told us it was his."

"He's lying. He wasn't on the wrestling team."

"So, you're sure that the wristband is yours?"

"I said so, didn't I?"

"OK, DeWayne, I need you to write down everything that you told me. Don't leave out any detail. Then we'll go from there," Michael Donovan pushed a yellow writing tablet and pencil in front of the suspect. He looked at his watch. It was 10:00 a.m.

When police Chief Dominick Arena arrived at the police station he found Senator Edward Kennedy in his office using the telephone. Paul Markham was also in the room.

"I'm sorry about the accident," Arena stated.

Kennedy replied, "Yes, I know. I was the driver." After a short period of silence Kennedy asked, "What would you like me to do? We must do what is right or we will both be criticized for it."

The police chief considered it a routine automobile accident so he replied, "The first thing we have to do is to have a statement from you about what happened."

Once Lawrence Cottage was spotless the group returned to the Katama Shores Inn where they joined Charles Tretter, Rosemary Keough, and Susan Tannenbaum. Joe Gargan then told the group, "I think what you should do is get off the island as soon as possible. Nobody knows at the moment that any of you are here, so go home and just keep quiet. Don't talk to anybody until we see what develops. That's the best advice I can give you right now." He knew there were too many witnesses who saw Kennedy drinking heavily.

While Ted Kennedy and Paul Markham worked on the accident report, Chief Arena returned to Dike Bridge. He told John Farrar, the scuba diver, to call off the search that they found the driver and there weren't any others in the car. The car was dragged from the pond and Deputy Christopher Look, who had arrived and watched from the bridge, saw the license plate and confirmed, "That was the car I saw last night."

"Do you know who was driving that car?" Chief Arena asked.

"It appeared to be a man and a woman."

"Well, it was Senator Ted Kennedy," the Chief stated.

Deputy Look was stunned. He finally said, ""Holy Jesus!" then added in jest as he backed up, "I didn't see a thing."

After the Oldsmobile was back on land, John Farrar observed that there was probably a large air bubble in the car and that the young woman could have been rescued if they had been called early enough. He went on to explain that he had equipment to supply air to a trapped individual or to maintain an air pocket. She probably was alive for over an hour.

Detectives Ryoya Akimoto and Michael Donovan discussed the statements of the two youths. They also looked at the physical evidence. Searches of the apartments where each boy lived turned up a number of items. From Tyrone Jefferson mother's apartment the search team found some marijuana in his room but nothing else. DeWayne Martin's room turned up far more. They found the pipe, a black wristband with orange and white trim that had blood on it, a tee-shirt with blood stains, and eighty dollars. The detectives also had the coroner's report and supplemental analysis of each boy's blood, hair, skin, etc. It was time to talk with the district attorney, present the evidence, and make an arrest.

"If Rita Craig hadn't lived long enough to give us a lead we might not have solved this one as quickly," Ryoya said.

"I'm glad that we did because you weren't going to be able to let this one go," her partner commented. He then asked, "What was it about this case that struck a nerve?"

"I knew her for ten minutes. Yet, in spite of hustling, she seemed like an innocent human being who could have had a wonderful life if things were different. I don't know why. Maybe it's the 'stray dog syndrome' where you feel they deserve better. Those two boys, if they got away with it, were going to go on with their lives, possibly live a long time and enjoy lots of pleasures. Would they even care that a young woman would not have that opportunity? Or, was she just another stray to be forgotten?"

"We can't save them all."

"No, we can't save them all," Ryoya sipped her cold coffee, "Shikata ga nai."

Paul Markham finished Senator Kennedy's statement and gave it to Chief Arena. As the law enforcement officer read the statement he was shocked to learn that the accident had occurred more than ten hours earlier.

> On July 18, 1969, at approximately 11:15 PM in Chappaquiddick, Martha's Vineyard, Massachusetts, I was driving my car on Main Street on my way to get the ferry back to Edgartown. I was unfamiliar with the road and turned right onto Dike Road, instead of bearing hard left on Main Street. After proceeding for approximately one-half mile on Dike Road I descended a hill and came upon a narrow bridge. The car went off the side of the bridge. There was one passenger with me, one Miss Mary Jo Kopechne, a former secretary of my brother Senator Robert Kennedy. The car turned over and sank into the water and landed with the roof resting on the bottom. I attempted to open the door and the window of the car but have no recollection of how I got out of the car. I came to the surface and then repeatedly dove down to the car in an attempt to see if the passenger was still in the car. I was unsuccessful in the attempt. I was exhausted and in a state of shock. I recall walking back to where my friends were eating. There was a car parked in front of the cottage and I climbed into the back seat. I then asked for someone to bring me back to Edgartown. I remember walking around for a period of time and then going back to my hotel room. When I fully realized what had happened this morning, I immediately contacted the police.

The police chief had Kennedy's statement typed out and gave it to the Senator. Kennedy requested that it not be made official until he spoke with Burke Marshall a family lawyer. Arena then asked for Kennedy's driver's license but was told that the Senator had lost his wallet. After refusing to answer any more questions the Senator was allowed to leave. He and Paul Markham boarded a charter flight back to Hyannis.

For a long three days the astronauts had to make constant adjustments, done things with the fuel cells, gotten rid of water in the system, and kept the spacecraft rotating so that the sun wouldn't make one side too hot. Because it was like the slow turn of a pig on a spit they called it barbecue mode. Throughout the mission there was also careful outgassing and venting. Every action had to be calculated and compensated for because it could change the trajectory of the craft. The ultimate goal was not to hit the moon, but to miss it at the correct angle and altitude to go into orbit.

Edwin E. "Buzz" Aldrin Jr., lunar module pilot, noticed out the window that the Moon covered the sun. This huge black object, backlit by the sun, was unlike any eclipse pictures that he had ever seen on Earth. In fact, the Earth was out of sight. Apollo 11 had passed behind the Moon at 1:21 pm Eastern Daylight Time. At this time Michael Collins, command module pilot, executed a maneuver that flipped the spacecraft over allowing for a six-minute burn of the main engines putting Apollo 11 in an elliptical orbit. Out of contact with Earth the three astronauts drifted 60 miles above the lunar surface.

Jack Moore was in his apartment typing a story when the telephone rang. He picked up the receiver and heard a familiar voice.

"Jack, are you busy?" Ryoya asked.

"Hey, how is the case going?" he responded cheerily.

"They've charged two perpetrators with murder. It's in the hands of the legal system, now." There was a pause, then she continued, "I need a shoulder."

"I've got two—pick one."

"Either will do. However, your left one is a bit boney."

Jack laughed. Even fatigued and possibly emotionally drained Ryoya Akimoto could be witty. He missed her. He understood once she was elbow deep in an important case there was no time for socializing. Regardless, he still missed her. It was a good thing they were talking over the telephone, he thought, because she couldn't see the dumb smile on his face.

"Want to get a cup of coffee?" Ryoya asked.

"If you're tired I'll bring coffee to your apartment," he offered.

"That would be great."

"Have you eaten?"

"Here and there. Not really."

"I'll take care of it. See you in half an hour."

Mission Control sat in complete silence while Apollo 11 was behind the Moon. This was necessary, as well as a point where they could do nothing but wait. If all went well the spacecraft would emerge from the dark side of the Moon in orbit. Seconds ticked by. No contact. Intense silence continued. No contact. An errant cough was heard somewhere in the large room. No contact. Steve Bales, guidance officer, White Team, Mission Control, looked around the room. Everyone was between the age of 25 and 28 with the exception of Gene Kranz the flight director who was 35 years old. NASA attracted young, intelligent, bold, and driven individuals. He smiled as he considered all these young unproven professionals doing the impossible. Fact was, experienced persons were unavailable as they had never done this before. No contact. Chuck Deiterich, retrofire officer, Black Team, Mission Control sat and watched the many monitors. Five hours before the spacecraft went behind the Moon they had gone over a number of maneuvers where the spacecraft could return to Earth if lunar orbit wasn't achieved. He hoped they would not be needed. No contact.

"Mission Control, we have achieved orbit."

A cheer filled the room.

Shortly after Apollo 11 entered orbit, Frank Borman at Mission Control received a message from the Soviet Union, "Congratulations on reaching lunar orbit. We have Lunik 16 also in orbit around the moon." They provided the orbital parameters of their craft. "If it presents any problem, please advise and we will move it."

After two orbits around the Moon Apollo 11 executed a 17 second burn, also on the dark side, to fall into a circular orbit. Everything was AOK.

Jack arrived at Ryoya's apartment laden with an assortment of fine Italian delicacies. He carried an open top cardboard box.

"That's a heck of a cup of coffee," Ryoya remarked.

"Coffee?" Jack said, "Damn, I forgot the coffee."

Ryoya laughed. It felt good to have something to laugh at after a long three days of dealing with a murder. She looked at Jack who was busy unloading his box of goodies. He really was fun to be around. In her exhausted state-of-mind she wanted to run to him and be held in his arms—to feel protected and loved. For so long she hid her feelings and controlled her actions. She almost didn't know how to let go, but deep inside she so wanted to experience the simple joys of being a woman.

"We have antipasto, chicken parmigiana, fettuccini alfredo, lasagna with meat sauce, breads, and a fine bottle of Cabernet Sauvignon."

Ryoya walked up behind Jack and gently put her arms around him. He paused, turned around, and they embraced. Nothing was said. Nothing needed to be said. Two people found comfort simply being together and holding each other. Ryoya looked upward and they kissed. There were no pretenses as they both knew they wanted— needed each other. Together, they moved into the bedroom. In the heat of passion their food grew cold.

Robert Six Trees sat on a rock and looked at the beaded bracelet that his younger sister, Anna, had made for him. She did a fine job at such a young age. He tied it onto his wrist.

25: Sunday - July 20, 1969

Matthew Ellis and his daughter Stephanie sat at the small table in her apartment. She had prepared a Sunday morning breakfast of bacon and eggs. As he ate Matt read the Sunday *Bergen Record.* The headline that morning was "Apollo 11 in Moon Orbit, Landing Planned Today." He looked out the window at the cloudy skies and said, "They have a good day for it."

"What was that?" Stephanie asked looking up.

"They have good weather for the Moon landing."

She hesitated, thought about the comment, then concluded, "But, they're on the Moon."

"It was a joke, you know, ha, ha," Matt sipped his coffee.

"Oh."

"This is an historic day," her father continued, "In nine short years, man has made strides that were unheard of and considered impossible. To go from barely being able to get a rocket to liftoff without blowing up to landing on the Moon—it's incredible." He grew silent for a moment than added in a low voice, "I'm just sorry I missed most of it."

"You're here to see it happen, now," Stephanie said. A secondary thought intruded into her mind, "which is more than mom is." She immediately fought the anger that still seethed inside. The complaint, "If you had only been more careful" once more whispered in her ear.

Steve Bales, Guidance Officer, White Team, arrived early at Mission Control. Excitement of what was about to happen magnified the fear of what could happen. Out in space 238,000 miles away the Lunar Module was dormant, waiting to be awakened and powered up. It involved a lengthy process with many steps and tests. In the back of his mind he was keenly aware that this was the phase in all of their simulations where lay the greatest risk. In training, he recalled they had never had a 100% successful initialization of all elements. He considered the entire sequence of events that would lead to a lunar landing and, all-too-well, knew this time there was no reset button or do-overs. If the LEM functioned flawlessly two human beings would make history, if not, two human beings would be history.

After a week and a half Wellington Marsh had grown accustomed to the routine of MOS training at Camp Lejeune. In the early stages of this training it was mostly classroom instruction of common skills. The young Marine knew he couldn't possibly remember everything that was being thrown at him so he tried to gain a basic understanding of formations, combat marksmanship, support functions, use of different weapons, patrol tactics, communications, navigation, and emergency medical treatment. Mixed with the classroom work was conditioning through marches, calisthenics, and an obstacle course. Then there were barracks inspections, although these were not the strict, guaranteed to find a speck of dirt, exercises used in basic training. If you kept your rack made, uniform clean, and personal items stowed you got by. All-in-all it was long tough weekdays followed by weekends off. On weekends when most Marines would head to town and get wasted, Wellington found he better enjoyed some quiet time reading or listening to music. This Sunday morning, he sat on a small beach on base writing a letter to his mother. A song by rhythm and blues singer Otis Redding was playing on his portable radio. The song, *The Dock of the Bay*, had a melancholy sound that found its way into Wellington's words to his mother.

> Sittin' in the mornin' sun
> I'll be sittin' when the evenin' come
> Watching the ships roll in
> And then I watch 'em roll away again, yeah

Mom,
I know I have to do what I am doing. There is no choice. Yet, I find that I'm being trained to do something that I really don't want to do.

> I'm sittin' on the dock of the bay
> Watching the tide roll away
> Ooo, I'm just sittin' on the dock of the bay
> Wastin' time

Some of the guys are gung ho ready to be combat Marines. They welcome the training and get excited by it. I wonder if with me it's a waste of time.

> I left my home in Georgia
> Headed for the 'Frisco bay
> 'Cause I've had nothing to live for
> And look like nothin's gonna come my way

I wish I were home learning a trade or how to be a chef or just working at the Ford plant.

> So I'm just gonna sit on the dock of the bay
> Watching the tide roll away
> Ooo, I'm sittin' on the dock of the bay
> Wastin' time

Here I sit putting in the time and obeying orders but still feeling like an outsider who doesn't fit in.

> Look like nothing's gonna change
> Everything still remains the same
> I can't do what ten people tell me to do
> So I guess I'll remain the same, yes

They can make me a Marine and teach me how to kill, but they can't be sure that I will because I can't be sure that I can.

> Sittin' here resting my bones
> And this loneliness won't leave me alone
> It's two thousand miles I roamed
> Just to make this dock my home

You know I'll do my best. But, I wish I was home where I'm not all alone just drifting with the tide that is going to carry me to, who knows where.

> Now, I'm just gonna sit at the dock of the bay
> Watching the tide roll away
> Oooo-wee, sittin' on the dock of the bay
> Wastin' time

I guess I've always been an oddball. It's just that I feel like my life isn't my own anymore. They're going to tell me where to go, what to do, who to kill, and to die if necessary. It seems like such a waste.

Otis Redding was born September 9, 1941 in Dawson, Georgia. Not far from where Wellington's friend Marvin Press, known as Shortstop, was born. The singer/ songwriter left school at the age of fifteen to help support his family. He toured the south with different bands performing at talent shows for prize money. Redding was discovered by Stax Records which released his first single, *These Arms of Mine,* in 1962 and his first album, *Pain In My Heart,* in 1964. He grew in popularity and after appearing at the 1967 Monterey Pop Festival wrote and recorded *The Dock of the Bay* with Steve Cropper. *The Dock of The Bay* was recorded in December, 1967.

On December 9, 1967, after completing concerts at Leo's Casino, Otis, pilot Richard Fraser, and members of the Bar-Kays; Matthew Kelly, Jimmy King, Phalon Jones, Ronnie Caldwell, Carl Cunningham, and Ben Cauley climbed aboard Redding's Beechcraft H18 for a flight to Madison, Wisconsin. They were scheduled to play the next day at the Factory Nightclub near the University of Wisconsin. As they approached Truax Field in Madison a short in the wiring that controlled the aircraft's twin engines caused the plane to rapidly lose altitude and it crashed into Lake Monona four miles short of the runway. Ben Cauley was the only survivor who hung onto a seat cushion to remain afloat. Police recovered Otis Redding's body that was strapped to a seat in the rear of the aircraft.

The Dock of The Bay became the first posthumous number-one record on both the Billboard Hot 100 and R&B charts.

Gene Kranz, flight director, White Team, Mission Control went around the room and asked for each station's status. Everyone was anxious. They all knew that any malfunction or miscalculation could result in an aborted landing, or worse, the loss of the two astronauts aboard the LEM. As Kranz polled the room a nervous Steve Bales Guidance Officer, White Team, suddenly bellowed, "Go!" The outburst helped break the tension in the room as many snickered. Those who were questioned afterward answered with a calmer more professional, "I'm go. Or, OK to go."

Ritchie worked on a painting depicting the World Trade Center building site. He used a photograph that he had taken looking up as the girders and metal skin grew skyward as a guide. Metallic tones against a blue sky reflected the perpetual battle between man and nature. As he added touches to his work he couldn't help but think that on this very day man will conquer one more challenge—the ultimate reach skyward. On a whim, he added an afternoon moon to the painting. Now, the structure reached for the moon as if offering a stairway for the astronauts.

While contemplating man's ability to build, Ritchie lamented the human ability to devise ways to kill. As magnificent as his towers may be, man tarnishes them with blood. He builds great machines designed to eliminate other men and cities and dreams. Ritchie stopped painting. Anger grew within as he stared at the artwork. Two towers would someday stand tall and erect proclaiming conquest of the skies over Manhattan. Would they be a beginning of better understanding of people around the world? Could glass and steel be a symbol of peace? Or, would insignificant human lives continue to be snuffed out on battlefields, in jungles, on city streets, and elsewhere by governments hell-bent on enslaving more and more innocent victims?

Ritchie felt powerless to stop the insanity that he saw everywhere. His was not a voice that would be heard. He had no power to intercede. Pointless killing would continue. Villagers that lay dead in the mud in Vietnam had no quarrel with anyone. Which side killed them was irrelevant. They were dead. Life, the greatest gift of all, was brutally taken from them by those who did not see or respect the beauty of the human spirit. Evil power-hungry despots were simply driven to dominate and destroy. An insatiable need for power left in its wake the bodies of the powerless. Ritchie looked once more at his painting. Two towers just beginning to grow like great redwoods seeking the sun. He wondered, "Are they the hope for the future?"

Early in the afternoon, Eastern Daylight Time, Neil Armstrong and Edwin "Buzz" Aldrin entered the Lunar Module. They went over checklist after checklist. All stations at Mission Control also made their final checks. The Lunar Module was powered-up without any abnormalities. Therefore, at 2:11 EDT, when Apollo 11 was at the low point in lunar orbit, there was nothing left to do but separate the LEM from the Command Module. The two craft drifted apart. Mike Collins, the lone member of the team who remained in the Command Module, then did a visual inspection of the Lunar Module and gave the AOK. Given the "go" Neil Armstrong maneuvered the capsule to go backwards, engine first, and face down. A 30 second burn was initiated at 3:08 EDT to put the Lunar Module in a low orbit.

On Earth, at that very moment when the Lunar Module entered orbit, Mission Control computers lost data. It was quickly picked up from backup systems but due to the interruption in data transmission the guidance officer indicated that there were questions about the trajectory. He also noted that based on flight guidelines they were halfway to the abort limit and hadn't even begun the descent.

Approximately 2 minutes into the powered descent Neil Armstrong told Buzz Aldrin, "I think we're gonna be a little long."

Aldrin wondered how Armstrong came to that conclusion, but from experience knew that Neil had an uncanny way of accurately figuring things out. In this case, Armstrong had been timing the craft's angular rate over the craters on the surface to calculate their altitude. He estimated, at the point of engine ignition, that they would be a few miles further down range than planned. On the dark side of the Moon, Apollo 11 had done some venting which was not known on Earth or input into the computers, therefore timing of the engine start was 4 or 5 seconds late. Neil Armstrong was correct.

After the arrest of Tyrone Jefferson and DeWayne Martin, Miguel felt safe putting Olivia back on the streets. He made sure that she understood that she had to make up for the lost income from Rita. To punctuate his point, he had thrown her on the floor, ripped off her tee shirt, and with his knife made a three inch cut in her left side under her arm. He assured her if she didn't do exactly what he said or failed to produce enough income her face would be next. Even with little remaining self-esteem or hope Olivia shuddered from the thought of being disfigured. Late on a cloudy Sunday afternoon she walked Eighth Avenue and offered herself to passing men. It didn't take long as being young and pretty she was in great demand. Olivia Samantha Everett lived in fear and self-loathing. She despised what she had become. Yet, a kind word from a John was something she cherished.

Tension was building. In the Command Module Michael Collins watched the Lunar Module drift away. The Lunar Module, named Eagle, descent engine was fired and the craft slowed down dropping into an orbit 50,000 feet above the surface. Collins knew what happened in the next hour was out of his control and that he was simply an observer. He knew Neil Armstrong was an excellent pilot. Yet, he also knew the entire flight to touchdown had not been completed in a single session in the simulator. Word came from Mission Control, "You are go for PDI (powered descent insertion)." At that point man, machine, and computer had to work in perfect synchronization for there to be success. Michael Collins had faith in the men, respect for the machine, but concern about these relatively new devices called computers. The thought of a long journey home alone entered his mind but was quickly dismissed.

At Mission Control, everyone followed procedures and did their job. Joe Gavin, director, Lunar Module Program, Grumman Aerospace Corporation was accustomed to flight testing aircraft before they were delivered to customers. In the case of the Lunar Module that was impossible. This was the ultimate flight test. If the vehicle worked as planned all would be well, if not, it could be the end of the program not to mention the lives of two brave individuals.

Gene Kranz flight director, White Team, Mission Control previously had called the team together and said, "I want you to figure out every possible alarm code that can happen in flight so that we're prepared." It turned out that his action had primed them for what actually did happen.

Early in the descent they got a 1202 alarm. Red lights came on and a loud klaxon sounded. Aldrin and Armstrong looked at each other. They knew the problem was defined in the guidance and navigation dictionary but didn't have time to search. Neil Armstrong asked Mission Control, "What's the reading on the 1202 alarm?" Before he received an answer, they got a 1201 alarm. Charlie Duke, astronaut, capsule communicator, White Team, Mission Control reached for the guidance and navigation checklist. Almost immediately, Jack Garman literally yelled, "It's okay! It's okay, as long as it doesn't keep going on!" And, Steve Bales, who knew what the alarms indicated, said, "We're go on those alarms, flight." What led to the alarms was a wiring dysfunction in the rendezvous radar that wasn't needed during the descent to the moon.

In addition, unknown to the astronauts in the Lunar Module the computer on the ground was processing so much data that five times the software was flushed and reconstructed in terms of what was being executed. This load-shedding allowed it to provide necessary guidance system support while ignoring other data. Without quite knowing how, they had built a fault-tolerant computer.

During the final phase of the landing the Lunar Module was coming down into an area littered with rocks and boulders. In response, Armstrong took manual control of the attitude of the spacecraft in order to fly along the surface in a direction that would bring them to a more hospitable landing site. Computers controlled the throttle that maintained the descent rate. The Lunar Module, in fact, was the first craft ever to have an adjustable throttle descent engine. This was necessitated by the fact that at the beginning of the descent it had to generate 10,000 pounds of thrust and then be slowly adjusted down to 2,000 pounds thrust as they approached the lunar surface. Due to consumption of a great deal of fuel the vehicle became lighter requiring less thrust. NASA had successfully developed a rocket that was capable of smoothly making the required transition.

In the simulator, the Lunar Module took a relatively straight path down to the surface. This was not the case on this Sunday evening. Armstrong was propelling the vehicle 20 feet per second in a forward direction which was eating up fuel. He was looking for a boulder-free landing site. All involved knew if the Lunar Module hit a boulder or rolled over on contact with uneven ground the Moon would be their final resting place.

A red alarm light suddenly lit indicating "low level" in the propellant tank. This surprised everyone at Mission Control as it had never occurred in all of the simulations that had been run. Low fuel was never considered a factor, however now it was. There was about 120 seconds of propellant remaining at the hover throttle setting. Mission Control became eerily quiet as all they could do was watch. Bob Carlton, Lunar Module control officer, White Team, Mission Control had a stopwatch. He started the watch and considered the altitude of the craft. Reality gave him a sinking feeling that they weren't going to make it. There was just too far to go on too little fuel. He called out, "30 seconds." What he was unaware of was that the Lunar Module had passed over a deep crater. As a result, the landing radar gave a false reading on altitude. The Lunar Module finally touched down softly in Mare Tranquilitatis or the Sea of Tranquility. When the engine shut down they were 18 seconds from having to abort the landing.

"Tranquility Base here. The Eagle has landed," Neil Armstrong transmitted from the surface of the Moon.

Charlie Duke, astronaut, capsule communicator, White Team, Mission Control had been using the call sign Eagle for so long when he responded, in his excitement he said, "Twank—I mean, Tranquility. Roger, Tranquility, we copy you down."

The time was 4:17 p.m. EDT.

At Mission Control there were spontaneous cheers, whistles, and applause. On the cold barren surface of the Moon two men accustomed to under-reaction looked at each other and smiled. Then they went about the business at hand.

Jack Moore and Ryoya Akimoto entered More-Or-Less carrying four pizzas. They sat at a table near the color television set that stood upon a shelf mounted on the wall. Harry Van Ryker, the owner/bartender, walked over and greeted them. He looked at the pizzas and said, "I serve food here, you know."

"You serve crumby sandwiches and bar pies that you heat in a toaster oven," Jack replied.

"I make money with those crumby sandwiches and bar pies," Harry stated, then added, "They were good enough for you before you got domesticated." He smiled and nodded in the direction of Ryoya.

Ryoya took Jack's hand and said to Harry, "We just thought we would have a party as we watched the first man step onto the Moon." With her other hand, she took Harry's hand and said, "We couldn't think of anyone we would rather share this historic moment with. After all, you are the one who got us together."

"Yeah, I'm sorry about that."

"You are?" a surprised Ryoya asked.

"Yeah, I'm not sure saddling you with a clown like this was such a good thing."

Jack ignored the dig and asked, "What will you have Pepperoni, Italian Sausage, extra cheese, or a garbage can?" He looked around the bar which was relatively empty because it was closing time on a Sunday night. There were two couples at other tables and three off-duty police officers at the bar. He announced to the patrons, "Anyone want pizza? Join the Moon walk celebration. Help yourself. Drinks are on the house."

Harry turned abruptly to look at his soon to no longer be a friend, smiled, then said, "OK, you win, drinks are on the house."

Once all systems were checked and double-checked Mission Control gave the Lunar Module crew the "stay" call. They were going to remain on the surface of the Moon. Unnecessary Lunar Module systems were shut down. The original plan had been for the astronauts to get eight hours sleep and then step out onto the surface in the morning. Everyone involved and the media knew that wasn't going to be the case. There was no way anyone was going to keep those guys inside the lander. All three broadcast networks announced that the astronauts would step onto the Moon that evening. They had been told it would be sometime between ten and eleven.

Inside his spacesuit, Neil Armstrong carried a piece of fabric from the 1903 Wright brothers' plane, Flyer 1. He reached the lower rung of the ladder and extended his left foot and tested the surface. Then at 10:56 p.m. Eastern Daylight Time he stepped onto the lunar surface. As he did he said for the world to hear, "That's one small step for a man, one giant leap for mankind." Unfortunately, due to static what the world heard was, "That's one small step for man, one giant leap for mankind." Bruce McCandless, astronaut (CAPCOM), Green Team, Mission Control felt that Neil nailed it. He remembered a conversation that he had with Neil Armstrong before the mission. He had asked the astronaut what he was going to say at such an historic moment. Armstrong replied. "I'm a test pilot; I'll probably just say how dusty it is or something like that. Don't worry."

Once on the surface, Armstrong immediately bent down and scooped up a sample of the lunar surface in case they had to make a quick departure. There had been concern that the dust could be pyrophoric and when exposed to escaping oxygen as the module door was opened could explode. This, of course, didn't happen. Armstrong loped across the lunar surface and commented, "The surface is fine and powdery, it adheres in fine layers, like powdered charcoal, to the soles and sides of my foot."

Matthew Ellis had tears in his eyes as he watched the grainy, ghostly images on the small portable television in Stephanie's apartment. Man was on the Moon. And, in a small, almost insignificant, way he had been a part of this great endeavor. Orztech wire was in the lunar lander and aboard the Command Module. Deep inside, Matt had a feeling of pride. He was also sad, though, that Valerie wasn't there to share the moment.

Unexpectedly, Lida Petropoulos entered his mind. He remembered a conversation that he had with Lida concerning the various orders for wire that she was going to fulfill. Specifications on some, especially for NASA, were strict and delivery dates inflexible. Matt asked Lida for reassurance that all orders would be correct and delivered on time.

"Orztech, and you will be completely satisfied," was her response as she ran her hand up his thigh. With a mischievous smile she added, "Especially you."

As it turned out LPAmerica LLC, Lida's company, delivered all wire orders on time. Wire was delivered for the military, airline industry, automotive industry, and even a rush order for a railroad.

Two months after payment for the first LPAmerica LLC's orders had cleared, Lida invited Matt to go to the play *Cats* that was playing on Broadway. During the intermission, as they sipped champagne, Lida handed Matt an envelope. In it he found five one hundred dollar bills. He looked up at her with a quizzical expression. To whit she stated, "Every good salesman gets a commission."

"I received a commission from Orztech," he innocently replied.

"But, you didn't get one from LPAmerica."

"I'm not supposed to . . ."

"Why not?"

"Because it's a kickback."

"I didn't offer it before the sale," Lida explained, "Let's just say I got a better deal and it's a refund."

"Then give it to Orztech."

Lida shook her head and sighed and replied, "Get serious. I saved them enough money. I saved their asses."

"You saved my ass."

Lida ran her hand along his, glanced around behind his back, and cooed, "yeah."

"But . . ."

"This is my special reward for you. The first of many to come."

"But . . ."

"Give it to charity," she said, then with a noticeable amount of venom hissed, "Or, give you wife a present." She turned on her heel and walked back into the theater. With a wave of her hand she said over her shoulder, "It's yours. Do with it what you wish."

Matt followed Lida back to their seats. Before the night was over he apologized.

Nineteen minutes after Neil Armstrong had stepped onto the lunar surface Buzz Aldrin left the Lunar Module and placed his boot upon the Moon. He said just two words, "Magnificent Desolation." The two astronauts then deployed the Early Apollo Scientific Experiment Package (EASEP). A seismometer was set up to measure any moon quakes or other movements. Also, a lunar retro reflector was set up and aimed at Earth for scientists to bounce a laser signal off to more accurately measure the distance to the Moon.

President Nixon wanted to speak to the astronauts but Mission Control kept delaying him to allow the astronauts to collect rock samples and take numerous photographs of the surface, Lunar Module, and each other. Actually, because Neil Armstrong had the camera most of the photos were of Buzz Aldrin. Finally, at 11:49 p.m. Eastern Daylight Time, President Nixon spoke with Neil A. Armstrong and Colonel Edwin E. (Buzz) Aldrin, Jr who stood in front of the American Flag on the Moon.

"Hello Neil and Buzz, I am talking to you by telephone from the Oval Room at the White House, and this certainly has to be the most historic telephone call ever made from the White House," President Nixon stated. "I just can't tell you how proud we all are of what you have done. For every American this has to be the proudest day of our lives, and for people all over the world I am sure that they, too, join with Americans in recognizing what an immense feat this is."

"Because of what you have done the heavens have become a part of man's world, and as you talk to us from the Sea of Tranquility, it inspires us to redouble our efforts to bring peace and tranquility to earth."

"For one priceless moment in the whole history of man all the people on this earth are truly one--one in their pride in what you have done and one in our prayers that you will return safely to earth."

Neil Armstrong replied, "Thank you, Mr. President. It is a great honor and privilege for us to be here representing not only the United States, but men of peaceable nations, men with an interest and a curiosity, and men with a vision for the future. It is an honor for us to be able to participate here today."

"Thank you very much, and I look forward, all of us look forward, to seeing you on the Hornet on Thursday," the President replied.

"Thank you. We look forward to that very much, sir."

The entire Moon walk lasted two hours and twenty minutes in duration. Neil Armstrong collected a wide variety of rocks and scooped up lunar regolith before closing the collection box. With the scientific equipment deployed the two astronauts entered the Lunar Module and closed the hatch.

Neil Armstrong left behind a size 9½ B footprint that the world would come to see as symbolic of man's achievement.

Robert Six Trees lay in bed full of wonderment. Men were on the Moon. In the darkness, he asked Gichi-Ojiig, an animal spirit represented by the Big Dipper constellation, to watch over the brave warriors.

26: Monday - July 21, 1969

After completing fifty-two orbits of the Moon at various altitudes and all systems were checked by Russian controllers on Earth, Lunik 15's main retrorocket was fired at 11:47 a.m. EDT. The craft began its descent for a planned soft landing on the Moon. The objective of the mission was to retrieve soil from the lunar surface and return it to Earth. Per plan it would arrive on the same day as the returning Apollo 11 crew. Once again it was Russia's attempt to detract from the American man-on-the-moon success.

A few minutes into the descent Russian controllers lost contact with Lunik 15. The craft crashed into Mare Crisium at 11:50 a.m. EDT. The crash site was approximately 740 miles north of Apollo 11's Lunar Module where astronauts Armstrong and Aldrin were stowing gear in preparation for their takeoff. They were unaware of the crash.

Ryoya Akimoto sat at her desk on the fourth floor of Midtown North precinct headquarters at 306 West 54th Street. She turned a pencil around and around in the air as she pondered something that she had observed in Rita Craig's apartment on West Ninety Third Street. They hadn't found any evidence that could be used in the case against Tyrone Jefferson or DeWayne Martin. Nothing was expected. It was a case of following proper procedures to investigate every possible source of information no matter how remote. If they had found any connection between the suspects and the victim in Rita's apartment, a letter or photograph, it might change the charge to first degree murder. While in the apartment Ryoya noticed something that would easily escape her partner, Mike Donovan. She noticed that there were pairs of two different size shoes in the closet. This most likely indicated that there was another woman living with Rita Craig. Here again, if there was any connection between this "other" woman and either Tyrone Jefferson or DeWayne Martin then Rita Craig's death was more than a mugging/rape gone wrong. Yet, from all indications it was simply that. Ryoya tried to decide whether or not it was worth department time to follow up on this small detail.

H. David Reed, flight dynamics officer, Green Team, Mission Control had come in early to compute the proper launch time so that the Lunar Module could rendezvous with the Command Module. He knew if the calculations were off the two craft might miss each other by too great a distance and due to fuel limitations might find it impossible to dock with each other. It all depended on knowing the exact locations of the Command Module and the landing site. The problem was that they had five different locations for the landing site. There was the site where the Lunar Module thought it landed, then where the backup guidance system thought it landed, where radars on Earth tracked them, where they were supposed to land, and finally geologists claimed they were at a different location. Mike Collins in the Command Module orbiting overhead used a telescope to try to locate the Lunar Module but failed in his effort.

Reed took off his headset and whispered to Gene Kranz, flight director, "We have a problem: We do not know where the hell they are."

After a serious discussion, they decided to have Buzz Aldrin do a rendezvous radar check one rev early. Because they knew relatively accurately the location of the Command Module the vectors would allow them to translate back down to the surface and determine the location of the Lunar Module. As it turned out it was 5 miles from any of the other believed locations. Mission Control calculated the proper launch time and uploaded it to the crew.

The original concept was for a combined vehicle to land on the Moon and then for the Command Module to take off from there. It was scrapped because it relied on a larger vehicle that had to carry sufficient fuel. The craft would have been so tall that the astronauts would have had a long climb down to the surface. The two craft configuration, even with its inherent risks, was subsequently adopted.

After a 21 hour and 36-minute visit, Neil Armstrong and Buzz Aldrin prepared for takeoff. There remained one last challenge. The head of the engine-arm circuit breaker, the one that's got to be in to get electricity to turn on the ascent engine, was broken. Aldrin figured that he had hit it with his backpack when he reentered the craft. While there was a way to manually start the engine, this was not a preferred approach. Buzz Aldrin solved the problem by using a pen to push in the remaining part of the circuit breaker. Thus, began the least understood and most dangerous part of the mission. Explosive bolts connecting the two stages had to fire releasing the ascent craft, the main engine had to ignite on time, the craft had to liftoff on the correct trajectory, and the computer calculations about burn time and rendezvous coordinates had to be correct. All in all, nothing to worry about.

At 1:54 p.m. Eastern Daylight Time the ascent stage lifted off. Unlike on Earth where the atmosphere and greater gravity holds a vehicle down the departure from the Moon was quick. Neither astronaut felt the force of the ascent but saw the surface drop rapidly away. Due to uneven fuel in the tanks the craft veered off the planned trajectory. Over approximately the next four hours the Lunar Module executed four burns to correct its course and speed. Two of these were when it was behind the Moon. Finally, at 5:34 p.m. Eastern Daylight Time the Lunar Module docked with the Command Module. The astronauts, gear and lunar samples were transferred to the Command Module and the LEM was jettisoned into Lunar orbit at 8:35 p.m. Eastern Daylight Time. This created one last challenge. When they released the Lunar Module it drifted up and away which meant when they came around the Moon once again the LEM would be in the same spot the Command Module had to pass through. As a result, they were forced to do a retrograde burn to slow down the speed of their orbit. This avoided a collision but also created the need for new calculations for a trans-Earth injection.

"I must say that you are persistent," Colt MacIntyre commented as he grabbed a piece of chicken with chopsticks.

"I told you, I'm a newspaperman who wants to tell our readers and neighbors about the many different folks with whom we share our city," Jack Moore responded. He added, "Nothing more than that. I believe the average New Yorker has a curiosity about the guy or gal sitting next to him on the subway. Or, wonders who the people are that walk down Fifth Avenue looking in store windows. Or, why there's a polite waiter at a French restaurant. There was a movie in 1948 and a television series that ran from 1958 to 1963 titled *The Naked City.* At the end the announcer stated, 'There are 8 million stories in the naked city. This has been one of them.' You're one of the eight million stories."

"Shucks, not a very interesting one, I assure you."

"Maybe not, but I think there is more to you than meets the eye."

"I'm a simple cowboy from Victoria, Texas."

"You're neither a cowboy nor simple," Jack countered. "Come'on, tell me who Colt MacIntyre really is." He paused, then added, "Tell you what. I won't print anything unless you agree to it." Jack picked up a piece of green bell pepper with chopsticks but they snapped together shooting it across the table at Colt.

"OK," Colt said as he ducked, "you don't have to get violent."

"You seem too smart and, might I say sophisticated, to be simply a waiter at a French Restaurant."

"Le Cav du Henri Quatra," Colt pointed out with pride. "Being a waiter is a mighty tough job. Fine people do it every day pulling in fewer pieces than they deserve. They have to put up with rudeness, unreasonable demands, and complaints about things over which they have no control. Sometimes it's all sixes and sevens. I've met some good, honest, smart, hardworking people with sore feet, tired muscles, lots of cares, and hearts as big as Texas."

Jack responded, "Maybe I'll talk with some of those persons. However, today, I want to talk with you. After all, it's costing me a dinner. And, I let you pick the place."

"That surely was kind of you. Hope you like Szechuan food."

"As long as there's plenty of water," Jack added, "What is sixes and sevens?"

"Sixes and sevens—confused, messed up—you know."

"Uh-huh. OK. Tell me about yourself."

"There's not much to tell," Colt shook his head.

"Then start at the beginning. Tell me about Victorville."

"Victoria, Texas," Colt smiled, "Shoot you're not much of a newspaperman. Can't even get the name of my hometown straight."

Jack had purposely said the wrong name to essentially break the ice. The fact that Colt corrected him gave him confidence that the young man would be mostly honest during the interview. Also, the "cowboy's" good humor was a sign that a human connection had been made and Colt might just trust Jack enough to provide additional honest answers. He wasn't ready for where the interview eventually led.

"Tell me about growing up in Texas and how you ended up in New York City," Jack requested.

"Victorville," Colt began with a sarcastic smile, "is a small town about 120 miles southeast of San Antonio and 90 miles northeast of Corpus Christi. It's cattle country that runs along the Guadalupe River. There are oil wells, as well. The big draw, I believe, is the Victoria Children's Zoo."

"Did you grow up in Victoria?"

"Sure did. Or, at least outside of Victoria on my daddy's ranch."

"So, you are a cowboy?"

"That's what I've been telling you. I wasn't stretching the blanket."

"OK, you grew up on a ranch."

"Right."

"Was it a big ranch?" Jack inquired.

"Well it's not the King Ranch, but it will do."

"How many acres?"

"I don't rightly know. Between twenty and twenty-five thousand, I suppose."

"That's huge!"

"The King ranch is eight hundred seventy-five thousand acres."

Jack whistled. He sat for a minute and tried to put the size of the MacIntyre ranch in perspective. Jack knew that Central Park in Manhattan is 843 acres and that is really big. Quick, not too accurate, calculations in his head told him the MacIntyre ranch was approximately the size of 30 Central Parks. The King ranch would equal 1,000 Central Parks. New York may be the big apple but in Texas apples don't appear to be very impressive. As he continued to envision the ranch he remembered that Central Park is about 6% of the island of Manhattan. That meant that the MacIntyre Ranch was the size of almost two Manhattans.

"You're pulling a kite," Colt said as he watched Jack.

"What?"

"Making a face."

"Oh, I just was trying to put the size of your daddy's ranch in perspective. It's bigger that the entire island of Manhattan."

"Yeah, I guess it is."

"What do you raise on all that land?"

"Cattle, horses, hay, oil, and gas."

"Oil? You mean your daddy is also an oil baron?"

"He's no baron. Although, he is the biggest toad in the puddle around Victoria."

"So, how come a rich guy like you is waiting tables at a French Restaurant?"

"Le Cav du Henri Quatra . . . "

"Yeah, I know," Jack sighed.

"I'm not rich—my daddy is," Colt explained.

"OK. But, he didn't throw you out, did he?"

"No, quite the contrary," Colt explained as he grabbed vegetables with his chopsticks. "When I graduated from the University of Texas my daddy wanted me to learn the business so I could take over for him someday. For four years I worked the ranch, labored in the oil fields, and even beat the devil around the stump at the refinery."

"Huh?"

"I avoided taking on responsibility. Well, just before I turned twenty-five my daddy and me had a heart to heart on the veranda along with a shot and a beer or two or ten."

"Boilermakers."

"Right. Now, my daddy is not one who is easily honey-fuggled, even when he's been in the sun."

"Wait. What?" Jack asked.

"You can't pull the wool over his eyes, even when he's drunk."

"Are we from the same country?"

"I'm from the country—you're from the city." Colt sipped some green tea and smiled.

"And, you're giving the city-boy the business."

"Are you throwin' off on my manner of speech?" Colt feigned surprise.

"You know, I still have more green peppers here and a one-eyed cowboy might have a little trouble roping them doggies," Jack threatened.

Colt MacIntyre laughed in a genuine good-spirited manner. "OK, pilgrim, I think you're splashing but you're no moss back."

"I'm not even going to ask," Jack smiled, "But, I know a bartender that you have to meet. He deserves you."

"I said, you're talking but not making a lot of sense even though you catch on quickly."

"Let's get back to the veranda and your heart to heart with your daddy."

Colt leaned back in his chair and looked toward the ceiling as if returning to the event. "When I was growing up my daddy made sure I walked the chalk, uh followed the straight and narrow. Believe me I got hided a bunch of times. But there on the veranda he treated me like a man. I was no longer between hay and grass, neither man nor boy. He told me he was proud of me. I'm not sure he ever said that before. Don't get me wrong we got along all right, but he had a lot of sand. When he'd walk into a room wearing his grey John B., that's a cowboy hat named after hat maker John B. Stetson, people would stop what they were doing and wait. He wielded power and made tough decisions, but I never saw him be mean. I saw him shoot a horse with a broken leg, or kill a prairie tenor, uh coyote, put a wrangler in his place, and sing in church off key. Clinton MacIntyre carries around a lot of responsibility, I'm sure many heartaches, maybe regrets, if he has fears he doesn't show it, but shows people respect. I'm not even a patch in the cloth from which he's made. For that man to be proud of me just seemed out-of-place. I hadn't done anything worthy of it."

"Is that why you left?"

"I told him that I wasn't sure that I was the one to someday take over. He didn't say a word. He let me pop my corn, uh have my say. I told him I didn't think I had enough life's experiences to run a big complex company. I needed to see the elephant before I would even know if I was up to the task."

"What elephant?"

"The world, different places, life. Ain't you had no learning?" Colt grinned and tossed a fortune cookie at Jack.

Jack caught the cookie and said, "So, instead of the elephant you came to the apple."

"Not exactly."

"Of course." Jack broke open the fortune cookie and read the paper strip. It read; "Listen carefully." He laughed and handed it to Colt.

Colt read the advice, nodded, and stated, "I was wondering why you're having so much trouble understanding."

"Yeah, that's it."

"Well, my daddy doesn't say anything." Colt leaned forward and put his elbows on the table, "You know how hard it is to talk to someone who doesn't respond? He was playin me to see where I was headed. So, I finally told him that I wanted to get out on my own with no backup to see how I fair. If I can't make a living on my own then I'm not his huckleberry."

"Huckleberry?"

"Man for the job. Someone he could count on." Colt shook his head and smiled, "I thought he'd be as hot as a whorehouse on nickel night. But he knew I wasn't barking at a knot."

"Uh, huh."

"Wasting time."

"Right."

"We made an agreement that I would go out and take on the world and return on my thirtieth birthday. That was five years ago. I'm going to be thirty years old on October 16 of this year."

"So, you're going home."

"I am."

"Did your elephant hunt work?" Jack asked sincerely.

Colt got a look of exasperation as he replied, "I saw the elephant. I saw different walks of life. And, I saw what it takes to make a living. Whether or not this makes me better prepared to run a business, only time will tell."

"What did you do for five years?"

"I worked in retail, as a bank teller, truck driver, newspaper reporter, teacher, gas station attendant, advertising media buyer, union official, car salesman, and now a waiter."

"You were a newspaper reporter?"

"Yes, a member of the fourth estate. And, I got the names of cities correct."

"What newspaper?"

"*Richmond Times Dispatch.*"

"I can see the headline, 'Rustlers Skedaddle with Loot'," Jack offered.

"How'd you know?"

"Mayor And Gamblers in Cahoots."

"Hobble your lip if you want to hear the rest of my story," Colt warned.

"Consider it hobbled."

"Much obliged. Over five years I've seen the good and the bad . . ."

"And the ugly," Jack interrupted. "Clint Eastwood, Lee Van Cleef, and Eli Wallach, 1966 Spaghetti Western directed by Sergio Leone." Jack shrugged and produced an innocent grin, "OK, the hobble came loose."

Colt continued, "This is a big country and there are a lot of good people out there. I think business owners get a raw deal by always being portrayed as greedy and heartless. When I worked at Taylor Distributing in Florida one of the employees was having marital problems. As a result, he was constantly skipping a cog, uh making mistakes. So, Keith Taylor, the owner, told him to go home and work out their problems. He said they would send his checks home until he was ready to return. After a few weeks, the employee separated from his wife and Keith let him use a company truck to move out. The guy came back to work and not only was a model employee but also very loyal. You don't read about things like that in the newspaper," Colt gazed accusingly at Jack.

"You would if you read my column."

"I do read your column," Colt admitted, "That's one reason I finally gave in and agreed to meet with you."

"I'm complimented. And, I do appreciate you telling me your story," Jack said. He then asked, "Do you think the five-year odyssey was worth it?"

"Absolutely, in addition to all of the wonderful people I met, scoundrels I had to deal with, and jobs I worked at, I grew up, developed values, and gained confidence. When I return to Victoria I'm going to begin a concerted effort to learn every phase of my daddy's business. Someday, I might even jump the broom."

"Say, what?"

"Get married." Colt leaned back once more and said, "There is one thing I want to do right away when I get back to Texas." He looked directly at Jack Moore, "I met a couple when I worked as an advertising media buyer who told me they had a Holt baby. I had no idea what that was—coulda been a disease for all I knew. It seems that they adopted this little Korean baby through an organization named Holt International Children's Services. She was the cutest little nub. The couple, Marlene and Hank, were so proud and so happy with their daughter. If you ever wanted to see the essence of love that was it." Colt leaned forward once more and continued, "You want a story about people, Bertha and Harry Holt are two you would be inspired by. It seems in 1954, shortly after the Korean War, they saw a documentary film about 'G.I.Babies' in orphanages in Korea. They had a farm and Harry had a successful lumber business in Oregon. Even though they had six children and were both over fifty years old they decided to adopt some Korean Orphans. In order to do it they literally had to have an act of congress because it was an international adoption. After the Holt Bill was passed Harry brought back eight orphans in 1955. Harry died a few years ago and Bertha has run their international adoption agency ever since. If I can, I want to bring such a service to Texas."

"Do you know anything about adoptions?"

"Nothing."

"That's sort of a problem."

"I didn't know anything about any of the jobs I've held and I did OK. However, I don't plan to run the organization, just create the non-profit, help fund it, and guide it. We can hire the right people to run it."

"There are government agencies, I'm sure."

Colt scratched his chin. Then in a storytelling voice said, "You're walking down the street and come upon a hungry man. Being the good natured caring individual that you are, you buy him a five-dollar sandwich. He gets to eat and you feel good. If the government were involved there would be a bureaucracy running the thing. They would create rules and forms and lists of approved sandwiches. Numerous people would be hired, offices opened, accounting, and when all is said and done each sandwich would cost $500. Leave it to individuals and $500 would feed one hundred hungry persons, not just one."

"You sound like an anarchist," Jack kidded.

"If I learned anything during my five year experiment it is that it always comes down to the individual. Everywhere that I worked there were those who worked hard and those who did just enough to get by. Yet, it was always those who did just enough to get by that complained the loudest. When I was a union official we protected the weakest at the expense of the hardest working. Now, that may sound reasonable, but eventually the hardest working folks left. With nothing but ten-cent men the factory couldn't be profitable. It eventually closed. So, everybody lost. Funny thing, though, they blamed the factory owners, not the union or themselves."

"So, you're anti-government and anti-union . . ."

"I'm not anti-anything. I am for freedom. Give people the opportunity and they will do great things. Tie them down and you kill their spirit."

"What do you think of the Moon landing?" Jack asked.

"I'll bet all them boys are walking in tall cotton." Colt displayed a large grin.

"Did you follow the landing?"

"Shoot, yeah," Colt replied, "In all my born days I never thought I'd see something as miraculous as that. I have to give Rusty a call."

"Who's Rusty?"

"Rusty? He's a good ole boy I met at UT. Some kind of science major. He works at NASA. We stay in touch once in a while. Got an excuse to call him now."

Jack thought about the investigative report he had been trying to do concerning NASA. It was all based on little tidbits here and there. Nothing solid. He never seemed to be able to find a contact on the inside. This could be that entry. "You think you could introduce me to Rusty?" Jack asked, adding, "I would like to do a story on NASA."

"I tell you what, I'll give him your name."

Robert and Anna Six Trees listened to their mother as she explained how they had to protect the wild rice paddies to insure a good harvest in September. She explained how the stalks had begun to appear above the water. They should watch for light green kernels which will gradually turn dark brown or black. When that happens, they are ready for harvest.

27: Wednesday - July 23, 1969

Carl Pythacyk arrived at the three-story red brick building on the corner of Grove and Bleecker Streets in Greenwich Village half an hour early. He tried the handle on the ornate door that leads to the upper floors where the card games were played. It was locked. All he could do was wait. This time he wasn't nervous. Rather, he was filled with anticipation. Carl knew that Ray now trusted him which meant that he was getting inside. Whatever Ray needed done, short of murder, Carl was prepared to do.

As he waited, Carl glanced over toward the Stonewall Inn on Christopher Street where the gay riots had taken place a month earlier. All was quiet. Of course, it was 10:00 o'clock in the morning and the bar wasn't open. In the park across the street he noticed a number of questionable characters wandering around. They most likely would be patrons of the Stonewall later in the evening.

Twenty minutes later a familiar midnight blue 1969 Lincoln Continental pulled to the curb. This time the driver didn't roll down the window or tell Carl to get in. Instead, Ray Esposito and two other associates got out of the car and headed for the ornate door. Carl followed. Upstairs in the kitchen used to service the card games the three men sat at a small table. Carl stood and waited to be asked to sit.

"You know how to make coffee?" Ray asked.

"I've seen it done," Carl replied.

"Forget about it," Ray motioned for one of his cohorts to make coffee. "The kid would probably poison us. Come, here. Sit down."

Carl sat at the table. In his mind, he felt that it was symbolic—that he was sitting at the table with an underworld captain.

"You like the card games?" Ray asked.

"Yeah! I like them a lot."

"Good. You do a good job. I appreciate that," Ray said as he lit a cigar. "You got lucky, kid. That tip on that merchandise was a good one. Then the fact that one of my crew got a vacation upstate gave you a chance to taste the honey." Ray leaned forward and looked Carl right in the eye, "Now it's time to shovel some shit."

Carl didn't say anything.

Ray grabbed Carl's left hand and asked, "You good with these?"

Carl wasn't sure what Ray was asking but he wanted to continue having good luck so he replied, "Yeah."

"OK, I got a job that needs to be done. You do it right—there's more honey. Wrong—well, shit flows downhill."

Carl didn't respond.

"You know much about Queens?"

"The place or homos?"

Ray laughed. He took a long draw on his cigar and responded, "The place."

"Not really. I never go there."

"Not even to go to a Mets game?"

"I'm a Yankee fan."

Ray jumped up from the table so quickly it almost caused Carl to fall out of his chair. "Who the hell are you to not like the Mets?" Ray bellowed. "Sona-fa-bitch, if I had known that—you wouldn't be sitting here."

The sudden outburst threw Carl off so much that he didn't know what to say or do. He just sat there with a surprised look on his face.

Ray stepped around the table and came toward Carl. He walked past the confused young man and went over to the counter to pour a cup of fresh coffee. All three men began to laugh. Ray said to the other two hoods, "Check to see if his pants are wet." This brought more laughter.

Carl was relieved to find it was a joke. He also was slightly angry but knew better than to show it.

"The only thing I know about the Mets is don't bet on them," Ray finally said as he returned to the table.

Carl nodded.

"OK kid, here's what I need you to do. There's a guy who's into me for three large. He's late on his payments. He drives a beer truck in Queens. You got a pencil and paper?"

Carl shook his head in the negative.

Ray jumped up again and yelled, "Who the hell are you to come here unprepared?" The other two men in the room laughed, once more. This time Carl smiled. Ray also smiled as he was getting a kick out of acting up for his crew. He instructed one of the men, "Give him something to write on."

With a paper napkin and pencil Carl waited.

"The guy's name is Casey Holmes. He drives for Emmitt Distributing. They have big red trucks. You can't miss them. He drives around Queens making deliveries to liquor stores and bars. I don't have no picture of him, but all the drivers have their first names on their shirts. So, how many freakin Caseys can there be? You have two days to find this guy and put a beatin on him. Now don't break any bones unless you have to. The guy's got to work to be able to pay. But, I want him to feel it and to fear a return visit from you. Don't use my name but tell him to pay his gambling debts."

One of the other two men offered, "After work, before he goes home, he often stops in at a bar named Gil's Tavern at Seventy Ninth Street and Thirty Seventh Avenue in the Jackson Heights neighborhood."

"You got that?"

"Yeah, but I don't know if I can find him in two days."

"There's a card game Friday night. You be here at eight and tell me the job's been done. If it's not—you better leave town."

Carl didn't know if Ray was once more joking or not. He knew better than to try to find out. "I'll take care of it, Mr. Esposito," Carl said as he rose to leave.

"Where you goin?" Tony asked.

"I thought . . ." Carl sat back down, "that I'd get to work finding this guy."

"I'm not finished," Ray warned Carl. "You leave when I tell you to leave. Capice?"

Carl nodded.

"You know how to drive?"

"Yeah," Carl lied.

"You got a license?"

"No."

"Then what the hell are you doing driving—that's illegal." All three men broke into laughter, once more. Carl didn't respond.

"Get yourself a license. If you need to borrow a car, call Murray Hill 9-6712. Ask for Angela, she'll set you up. You gonna write that down, or what?"

Carl quickly made notes on his napkin.

"Another thing," Ray continued, "learn how to make coffee!"

Carl smiled.

Ray struck, "You think it's funny that someone else had to do your job?"

"Uh, no," Carl stammered, "I thought . . ."

The three men laughed and Ray waved his arm as he said, "Go'on, get the hell out of here. Go find Casey Holmes. What the hell are you sitting around for?"

"Right, I'm on it," Carl practically ran for the door. He heard laughter behind him. Part of him was pissed off. However, a larger part of him felt the fact that they joked around was a good sign. A really good sign. He decided to look up the address of Emmitt Distributing and head for Queens. "Go, Mets," he said in a whisper and smiled.

Matthew Ellis had gone to Grand Central Station late in the morning to purchase a ticket on the New York Central to Pelham Station. To his surprise, New York Central and Pennsylvania Railroads had merged the year before to become Penn Central. In addition, the Pelham Station which was built in 1893 by the New York, New Haven, and Hartford Railroad was transferred to Penn Central in 1969. Once the confusion subsided, Matt purchased his ticket and proceeded to a lower platform to wait for his train. As he did he was amazed by the sights that he witnessed. There were soldiers everywhere, some on leave, or on their way home, or on their way to war. Scruffy young men with long hair, beards, tie-dyed tee shirts, cutoff jeans, and sandals also roamed through the terminal. One hippie spit on a soldier who was then held back by his buddy. Young girls with mini-skirts, peasant blouses, long straight hair that looked ironed, and large costume jewelry carried flowers. Business men sporting the latest wide ties rushed to and fro. Fashionable women wore fitted jersey dresses that clung here and there and moved as they did. Hemlines seemed so high that Matt wondered how the young ladies remained respectable. The terminal teamed with life from many different walks of life.

Matt was working on a hunch based on a dim memory. Parker Adolphson, president of Orztech Corporation, lived in the Village of Pelham in upstate New York. At least he lived there seven years prior. Matt was unable to find a telephone number but had an old Christmas card with a return address of 691 Young Avenue.

The 15.1 mile trip took approximately half an hour. As the train grew closer to its destination, Matt found himself getting more and more nervous. What was he going to say and what did he want to know? He was still trying to put the many pieces of his past together that remained in dark recesses of his mind. Then, he wanted to know what took place while he slept for six years. Where was Orztech Corporation? Did the NASA contract get filled? Did he know where Lida Petropoulos was? Were there any positions available at Orztech? He smiled at that last thought knowing it was an impossibility. After departing the train Matt found a taxi at the Pelham Station and rode the short distance to 691 Young Avenue. Before him stood a large two story house surrounded by trees on a very large plot of land. The driveway curved upward toward a courtyard positioned between two peaked two-story elements of the house. In the courtyard were well managed flowers and bushes and a park bench. Matt walked up to the double front door with beveled glass panels and rang the bell.

A short man with grey hair wearing a blue golf shirt and white pants opened the door. Upon seeing Matt, he said, "I'll be damned. The grim reaper." He neither smiled nor offered his hand. He asked in a not-too-friendly voice, "What are you doing here?"

"Mr. Adolphson," Matt began, "I had to find you to fill in many gaps in my memory and to find out what happened to Orztech."

"What do you mean, what happened to Orztech?"

"I went by where the offices were and they aren't there anymore."

"Of course they're not there anymore!"

"I'm sorry, I don't understand," Matt admitted.

"Why don't you ask your little girlfriend what happened?"

"Lida Petropoulos?"

"Who else would I be talking about?"

"I don't know where she is," Matt explained, "It's been six years."

"Well, I can't help you." Parker Adolphson started to close the door.

"Please, Mr. Adolphson," Matt pleaded, "I only remember little bits and pieces of my past. I need your help."

"Sorry."

"Just help me fill in some of the blanks." Matt pleaded, "I don't know why you are so angry."

"You really don't know—do you?" Parker said with a slightly softer voice.

Matt shook his head, "I don't know. I only know that Orztech wire went to the Moon."

"And, those three brave men will be damn lucky to get back to Earth alive if they depend on that wire."

Matt was shocked by Parker Adolphson's comment.

"What's wrong with the wire?"

"Oh, you are beautiful. You and your girlfriend substitute inferior wire made in China, or Korea, or Mexico, or India, or wherever she got that poison rope manufactured, make sure the first few rolls that would be tested meet specifications, charge full price, and pocket the difference. How much did you and that bitch take for yourselves? You must have a Swiss bank account hiding your blood money."

"Blood money?"

"Yeah, blood money. Every time I hear of a disaster in the military, aviation, or NASA my heart stops. And when it's faulty wiring I get sick to my stomach. Worst of all—I'm complicit. How many millions of feet of wire did we sell before we caught on to your scheme? That's right; we discovered what was going on a year after your, uh, accident. At that point, we got out of the wire business. We hung on for about three years and then had to close the shutters."

"I'm sorry . . ." Matt began.

"Sorry won't feed the bulldog. The damage is done and the time bombs keep on ticking."

"Can't something be done?" Matt asked knowing full well there was no solution.

"What would we do tell the military to rewire a hundred nuclear submarines, have Boeing rewire every 747, inform NASA that their multi-million-dollar spacecraft could fail, try to find out the thousands of other uses our wire has been put to that could present a risk? We're lucky that we aren't in jail!"

Matt looked down at the ground. He shook his head and stated, "I remember Lida Petropoulos. She assured me that the wire we subcontracted would meet all specs."

"You really expect me to believe that?"

"I don't know what to expect you to believe because I don't know what the truth is. I only get to see small glimpses of my past."

"Let me give you some facts. She couldn't have substituted inferior wire without inside help—that was you. After your accident, it took us a year to catch on—that was my fault. There are millions of feet of wire out there that could fail at any time. It could be something as simple as brake lights that don't come on. Or, it could be a connection to a propulsion system that shorts out and leaves better men than you or me stranded on the Moon. There's no way to track it all down and no way to replace what has been installed. So, I wait. Every time there is a disaster, I wait. And, when I hear it was due to a faulty wire I take one more step downward toward hell."

"Mr. Adolphson . . ."

"Don't bother. There's nothing more to say. You and that tart have planted the seeds of tragedy and, like me, you have to live with it. Now, get out of my sight." Parker Adolphson slowly closed the door.

Matt stood motionless, stunned by what he had just heard. Was it true? Could he have done something like that? Was he responsible for lives lost and those to be lost? How could he find the truth? And, if it turns out to be true, how could he live with himself?

At approximately 8:00 p.m. Chuck Deiterich, retrofire officer, Black Team, Mission Control told the astronauts, "Hey, we've got bad weather where you're going." At that point in the flight it was impossible to slow the approach to allow the Earth to rotate enough for them to splash down downrange. Therefore, they had to use a different somewhat more risky solution.

Robert Six Trees laughed as he watched his sister, Anna, chasing a chicken around the yard. Those plump birds are fast on their feet and can instantly change direction. Little Anna was no match for it, but it was fun to watch.

28: Thursday - July 24, 1969

Valerie never doubted her knight in shining armor. He was her strength. Stephanie knew this by of the way her mother spoke of her father. Whenever her mother told stories about their early married life her face would light up and voice reflect love and adoration. Her mother never faulted him for their predicament. Unlike her daughter, who couldn't escape gnawing feelings that he should have been more damn careful.

Before they lost the house, on one warm spring evening sitting out in the backyard, Stephanie remembered her mother telling how they came to live in Alpine, New Jersey, an expensive upscale town along the Hudson River. When the three of them lived in an apartment in Bergenfield, New Jersey, her parents often talked about buying a house. Again and again, the dream ended with them needing to save up a down payment. Yet, somehow, whenever they thought they might have a few extra dollars to put aside an unexpected expense would arrive with outstretched hand. Then one Friday night her father came home early from work and took Stephanie and her mother out to dinner at The Wagon Wheel. Stephanie always got a hamburger and fries with a vanilla milkshake. Her mother loved the Lemon Trout Almondine. Her father ordered a steak. Because Stephanie was nine-years-old at the time and rarely listened to her parent's adult talk she didn't remember the conversation from that particular night. At the age of fifteen, however, when her mother told the story Stephanie was far more interested.

Valerie explained, "Your father seemed to have something on his mind all through dinner. I could tell. He fidgeted and seemed preoccupied. Twice I had to repeat what I had said because he wasn't listening. I was afraid something was wrong at work. Yet, he didn't seem distressed. Finally, over coffee, he just blurt out, 'Let's buy a house.' I was so surprised that I didn't say anything. He continued by saying, 'We can start looking tomorrow.' When the shock wore off, I told him that we still hadn't saved enough for a down payment. Once again, I was surprised when he told me that we had more than enough money. My only response was, 'How?' It seems your father had received some bonuses and invested them in some risky, but potentially fast growing stock, of which he knew I wouldn't approve. As he put it, he guessed correctly and, as a result, we had a sizeable down payment. It was that money that made it possible for us to even consider a house in this upscale community. Your father worked hard, had courage, and had a business sense that gave us the lifestyle that we enjoyed."

Stephanie thought about that conversation and how smart and resourceful her father must have been. It was quite a contrast from his present weakened state after his long sleep. On a positive note, he was making progress and seemed to be getting stronger, although, on the previous evening he seemed to be withdrawn. Something was on his mind. After a few failed attempts at conversation, Stephanie decided to leave her father alone.

In the morning, Stephanie's father still remained lost in his thoughts. She didn't push him and essentially remained out-of-the-way. By noon he was glued to the small portable television watching coverage of the Apollo 11 return to Earth.

The velocity of Apollo 11 returning to Earth was 36,000 feet per second. This is significantly faster than an in-Earth orbit which is 25,000 feet per second. Because of this higher rate of speed the spacecraft cannot come directly into the atmosphere because it would exceed the capability of the heat shield. A combination of this fact and the need to splash down farther downrange to avoid bad weather in the landing zone made it necessary to change the trajectory to skip off the atmosphere and re-enter at a slower speed. Even with this maneuver the impact on the heat shield pushed its limits. Parts of the shield burned off creating a huge ionization cloud around the craft. This cloud prevented all communications. When the craft entered the atmosphere and rapidly decelerated the three astronauts were pushed into the back of their couches. This continued until there was a jolt followed by a swaying motion which told them the parachutes had deployed.

Clancy Hatleberg, a diver with underwater demolition team 11, United States Navy rode in helicopter 66 off the aircraft carrier USS Hornet. The seas were rough and he could see that they were skirting a storm. Dark clouds filled the sky to the east. Over the clouds the sun could be seen rising. As he watched the storm he suddenly saw what appeared to be a meteor streak across the sky until three parachutes opened above the glowing craft. Apollo 11 splashed down in the Pacific Ocean four hundred miles South Southwest of Wake Island at 12:50 p.m. Eastern Daylight Time. The USS Hornet was fifteen miles from the point of landing.

Helicopter 66 hovered over Apollo 11 and Clancy Hatleberg jumped into a raft that had been lowered. He washed down the Command Module with liquid from decontamination bottles. Neil A. Armstrong, Edwin E. "Buzz" Aldrin Jr., and Michael Collins then left the spacecraft, were washed down, and slipped into biological isolation garments. The three astronauts finally stepped off the helicopter onto the deck of the USS Hornet at 1:53 p.m. EDT. Apollo 11 arrived on the aircraft carrier at 3:50 p.m.

It took nine years, 400,000 people, and over 10 million different parts to put two brave men on the moon. Left behind was a plaque on the Landing Module descent stage with the inscription: "Here Men From Planet Earth First Set Foot Upon the Moon. July 1969 A.D. We Came in Peace For All Mankind."

Detectives Ryoya Akimoto and Michael Donovan rang the bell at the apartment that was formerly occupied by Rita Craig, the murder victim. There was no answer. Once more, they enlisted the aid of the building superintendent to let them into the apartment.

"It looks like nobody has been here since we were last week," Detective Donovan observed.

"Whoever shared the apartment with her must be afraid to return, traveling, in the hospital, unable to return, or dead," Ryoya concluded.

As they did an extensive search of the premises Michael Donovan called from the kitchen to the bedroom where Ryoya was searching, "So, how are things going with Horace Greeley?"

"Fine."

"Come'on I need more than fine," Michael responded. "Are you getting serious? Is he married? Have you done the dirty? Is he any good? Did you run his name through I.D.?"

Ryoya appeared in the doorway. "You're a jerk—you know that—don't you?"

"We both know that. It's what makes me so lovable. Now, give. What's going on with you and Jeff?"

"Jack."

"Yeah, him too. Look if you don't give me something to work with I'm going to have to make things up and spread rumors around the house."

"Spread whatever you want. If they come from you nobody will believe them."

"Look, I'm your partner. I care about you. I don't want to see you get hurt. This guy is different. He's gotten under your skin. Not to mention your skirt," Michael smiled and ducked as Ryoya made a half effort to punch him.

"I appreciate you caring but let it drop."

"Oh, this is serious," Michael said in a concerned tone.

"Yeah."

"So, you like this guy?"

"I do."

"And, he likes you?"

"He does."

"Well, that's good, then. You should be happy." Yet, Michael Donovan could see that Ryoya wasn't bubbling with the joy that should come from having a fulfilling romantic relationship. He walked over to his partner and asked in a serious voice, "What's wrong?"

"Drop it—OK."

"If it was anybody but you, I would." Michael put his hands on Ryoya's shoulders, "But you, Ryoya Akimoto, are my partner, my friend, my little sister."

"Look at me."

"OK."

"What do you see?"

"I see a beautiful woman, who is one hell of a good detective," Michael offered.

"I am nisei, second generation Japanese. I am an American, but Japanese traditions remain strong in our family. My father will be 68 years old this year. He would love nothing more than for me to get married. A traditional Japanese marriage to a traditional Japanese man."

"Oh, now I get it. How stupid of me. Your old man would never accept Jack."

"I will never put him in the position to have to make that decision. I am an American woman but I have been raised to respect my parents and my Japanese heritage."

"So, they don't know about Jack."

"No."

"Well, what are you going to do?"

"At some point, I'm going to have to break it off with him."

"Ryoya, this is America. You shouldn't have to give up love because of some ancient tradition."

"My father worked hard to support our family. He went to the internment camps without complaint. He brought us to New York and made a new life for us. All he expects in return is for me to honor our heritage and traditions. The fact that I am a New York City police detective was difficult enough for him. That's not a traditional role for a woman, much assured a Japanese woman. He never said anything but I see it in his eyes. Tradition is fading and his identity along with it. I just can't do it to him."

"Have you said anything to Jack?"

"No."

"So, this poor slob is going along dancing on a cloud not knowing that a storm is coming?"

"I know it's a bad situation but I'm not ready to give him up. Maybe it's selfish. It is selfish. I just want to make it last as long as it can, before . . ." her voice trailed off.

Michael Donovan looked at his partner who was obviously fighting an emotional battle with herself. She was not the tough, take no prisoners, in your face detective that all of the officers in the Midtown North precinct knew. She was in pain. Being a man he wanted to fix the situation. Only, it was not something that could be fixed. It was a beautiful thing that sadly couldn't exist torn between two cultures. Jack and Ryoya surely would both be scarred by the eventual outcome. So, at present, one of the players wrestles with a difficult decision while the other drifts toward a painful experience totally unaware that it is coming. "Crap," Michael said in a low voice.

"What was that?"

"All this crap. There's nothing to indicate that more than one woman ever lived here."

Ryoya went into the bedroom and returned carrying two pairs of high heels. She held out one pair and said, "Size nine," then the other pair, "Size seven. Two people lived here. Only I don't think there is anything that might lead us to believe there is any connection to the case."

"I agree. We can . . ." Michael Donovan stopped. He spotted a book on a shelf that was upside down. It could be a simple mistake or a way of remembering it or a signal. He took it off the shelf and examined it. Ryoya joined him. When he opened the book a piece of white paper floated to the floor. Ryoya retrieved it. It was a letter written with an unsteady hand. She read it out loud.

> Mom, Dad,
> I know you will never see this letter or me again. By now you've probably stopped looking for me. I made such a mess of things. And now, I can never come home. You could never love what I've become. Maybe I will die and save everyone the horror of knowing. I never knew there were people in the world who were so cruel. There is no escape for me. My tears have run out along with my hope. He controls everything and I dare not disobey, or run, or fail to make enough money. Everything in my life before seems like such a dream. Now, life is a nightmare. Please, forgive me and forget me.

The letter wasn't signed. Ryoya handed it to Michael and said, "Sounds like a runaway."

"Based on Rita Craig's profession, I'd say she is under the thumb of the same pimp we arrested for littering."

"We need to turn this over to vice."

"You know what will happen," Michael Donovan said.

"Yeah. They'll question every young girl on the avenue and they'll all deny being a hooker or writing the letter," Ryoya concluded.

"We can't save them all."

"Someday, I want to travel to the edge of the nation and see the oceans," Robert Six Trees told his sister Anna. "They cover most of the Earth. Great waves smash upon the shore. And you can't see the other side. I just want to see these vast givers of life. Maybe a spirit will make itself known to me."

29: Friday - July 25, 1969

"Is this Jack Moore?" an unrecognizable voice asked.

Jack replied into the telephone receiver in his office that he had just answered, "It is. Who is this?"

"My name is Russell Samuels," the voice said, "Colt MacIntyre asked me to call you. He said you were writing a story about NASA. I work at NASA. Can I be of help?"

"I hope you can," Jack replied as he grabbed a yellow pad and a pen. "Colt didn't waste any time, did he?"

"That's the kind of guy he is. If he says he's going to do something—you can take it to the bank. He's quite a character."

"How do you mean?"

"Colt MacIntyre is one of the smartest people I have ever met. He graduated with honors, with a double major. He's a crack shot with a long gun and a handgun. Seems to be able to learn anything rapidly, does complex math in his head, really cares about people, and is an honorable and honest man."

"With a strange vocabulary," Jack added.

"Ha, did he pull that country jargon on you?"

"He popped my corn, I was splashing, and half the time I had no idea what he was talking about?"

"I've been there. Don't feel bad. He's a bangtail, but keep in mind, he's definitely not all hat with no cows."

Jack laughed. He then explained his interest in NASA, "I've been following the space program along with one hundred million other Americans. Congratulations on the successful moon landing."

"Thank you. We are all very excited and the parties are still going on down here."

"Being a news reporter I am inquisitive and pick up on subtleties that others miss. Sometimes it's the way something is said while other times it is what is said or what isn't said. Anyway, when something stands out in my curious mind I have to follow it to see where it leads."

"Uh, huh."

"I'll get to the point. In various stories and interviews over the past few years there seems to be an air of frustration by different NASA personnel about materials and parts that they purchased or had manufactured that didn't perform as expected or required. It may be nothing. However, it could be a story if NASA had to overcome gravity, the unknown, design obstacles, and the failure of American industry to deliver needed materials."

"Mr. Moore," Russell said more formally, "we started with nothing but a concept. From there we had to design, test, redesign, test, and make further adjustments. Initially, we tried to use parts and equipment that were readily available to save time and money. Unfortunately, due to the unique nature of what we were creating, available parts just didn't work or exist. That might be the frustration that you picked up on."

"That was my first impression. But, later in the program it seems that there were numerous occasions where parts that were designed by NASA and manufactured by private companies fell short in terms of quality or consistency. There were stories about bolts that weren't tooled correctly, or parts that didn't fit when delivered, or parts that failed when tested."

"That's common in the realm of design. As hard as we might try for a smooth transition from drawing board to installation, in the end it often requires numerous changes and adjustments in order to get the prototype right. I wouldn't . . . condemn . . . American industry . . . for needing . . . more than one attempt to . . . get it right."

"So, you believe it was simply a process that had to take place to get it right rather than any failure on the part of any companies to provide what was needed?"

"When there were shortcomings we would issue Problem/Failure Reports, or PFRs, for every incidence of hardware or software failure. From there an analysis was done and corrective steps taken. When things don't go as planned, of course there is frustration. There were thousands of cases of something not working as expected due to design flaws, unexpected results, parts that didn't work, mistakes, and more. You have to understand there were no guidelines or blueprints. We were the ultimate inventors on a tight timetable. Under these conditions there are going to be false starts and missteps."

"From what you are telling me there was nothing out of the ordinary with the relationship between NASA and its suppliers. NASA was satisfied with the products they ordered and received from various companies."

There was a prolonged period of silence. Then Russell answered, "I am not in a position to draw a conclusion on whether or not everything NASA received functioned as ordered. I'm an engineer that works in the area of propulsion. We did an enormous amount of experimentation. Did everything work as expected? Absolutely not. Was it because some supplier provided something that didn't work? Sometimes. But, remember they were creating things from scratch just as we were. Of course, there would be failures. In the end, the process worked, as demonstrated in the past week. I think you are seeing things in the shadows that aren't there."

"You're probably right," Jack admitted. "Being a reporter I'm acutely sensitive to any aberrations that I see and compelled to find out if they reflect something worth investigating. More often than not, there is nothing there."

"We've just had an historic success with an unbelievably low number of issues. This is something that couldn't have been imagined nine years ago when we failed to get a rocket to launch without blowing up. Thousands of scientists, mechanics, engineers, computer whizzes, and other dedicated people worked countless hours with one goal— the Moon. We, by God, did it! That's your story."

"I think you're right," Jack concluded.

It had been an interesting week. Early on they spent time at the firing range learning about all of the weapons they would have at their disposal. Each Marine fired an M-1, M-16, 1911 sidearm, and finally the M60 machine gun. Wellington did well with the two shoulder-fired weapons and didn't embarrass himself with the pistol. It was the M60 machine gun that proved to be a problem. The instructions were to fire the machine gun in short bursts of five to ten rounds from a prone position. After two sequences, they were to secure the weapon and move on. The first burst of ten rounds that Wellington fired went without incident. However, when he fired the second time and released the trigger after ten rounds the machine gun kept firing on its own. Before Wellington could do anything a rather large sergeant landed on his back, held the machine gun on target, and broke the ammo belt to stop the runaway weapon.

Wellington groaned, "Thanks," as the big man rolled off of him.

The next day they were introduced to booby traps. They were marched into an area that had a facsimile Vietnamese village. Orders were to secure the village and establish a landing zone. Right from the beginning the exercise turned out to be a journey into terror. When the first team entered the abandoned village, one Marine tripped a booby trap that caused a branch that had been pulled back to swing around and hit him in the stomach with rubber spikes. Had the spikes been real he would have been severely and painfully wounded. Another Marine stepped in some grass that covered a pit with large rubber spikes aimed upward. These "punji sticks" would have impaled his feet and lower abdomen. These two incidents made everyone more observant and cautious. Unfortunately, innocent kids were no match for devious minds. As each trainee was designated as killed or injured they would be tagged and then continue in the exercise as observers. Wellington Marsh learned quickly. After seeing two comrades go down he started examining everything. After a few minutes, he found a wire stretched across a path and signaled for the team to stop. The wire was attached on both sides to a grenade, with the pin removed, that had been inserted into a tin can that was tied to a tree. If the wire was stepped on or otherwise yanked the grenades would pull out of the cans and explode. Right after disarming the path trap another marine stepped into a Venus Fly Trap. This booby trap was made out of a metal frame that formed a cube. Attached to the four top bars were downward and inward facing rubber spikes with fish hook style points. The cube was then buried in the ground and covered with sticks and leaves. The victim is injured when stepping in but more severely injured trying to pull his leg out. There were cases in Vietnam where they had to dig out the entire metal cube and send the injured soldier back to have it surgically removed.

Some of the trainees began to panic and froze in place afraid to move. Others used sticks to probe the ground before stepping onto any unknown surface. This allowed them to find additional booby traps without falling prey to them. There was a spike board on a swivel that would have spun upward if a soldier had inadvertently stepped on the other end of the board that hung over an open pit. Shortstop reached the hut first. Carefully, he pushed the door open. When he did a two-part booby trap that consisted of two lengths of bamboo tied end to end with a piece of rope with rubber spikes swung down from above the door opening. The upper bamboo spike weapon struck Shortstop in the chest while the lower bamboo spike segment swung up between his legs hitting him in the groin. He yelled out from a combination of surprise and pain. Wellington ran over to his friend.

Shortstop sat on the ground and gasped, "This place scares me."

"Me too," Wellington agreed.

"I don't want to go there—to the war."

"Me either."

"What can we do?"

"We better learn all that we can. Because we're going. And that's that."

Wellington entered the hut. He stopped and looked around for any sign of a booby trap. There were multiple traps in that hut. This much he knew. What or where he had no idea. His eyes searched frantically. On one side of the hut there were two grass mattresses. In the corner was an AK47 propped against the wall. Wellington knew that rifle had to be booby trapped. As hard as he looked he couldn't see any wire or other sign of a booby trap. On the opposite wall, there was a table with a radio transmitter, maps, and a book. In the middle of the hut was a table with clay plates and cups. Then he spotted it. A wire ran from one of the legs of the table across the floor to where the radio transmitter was located. Wellington moved slowly following the wire with his eyes. It went around a nail and up behind the radio. Fascinated, he crouched down to look under the table. That move was fortuitous as from that vantage point closer to the ground he saw a slight indentation in the ground directly in front of the radio. With the butt of his rifle he pushed down on the dirt floor and a trap door dropped down revealing rubber punji sticks waiting for an overzealous victim. Wellington returned his attention to the wire. Up behind the radio was mounted a claymore mine aimed directly at the center of the hut. He carefully cut the trip wire. Once more Wellington surveyed the room. He thought that he saw movement under one of the grass mattresses and opened fire. A mattress rose up and a trainer gave Wellington a thumbs up. Two other soldiers entered the hut. Wellington pointed at the table and trap door. They froze. Wellington reached the radio and examined the maps before carefully picking them up. Finally, he picked up the book, examined it, and opened it. A snake popped out of the hollowed-out book launched by the effect of opening the book which stretched paper that had been attached to both covers. The serpent hit Wellington in the neck. An observer entered the hut and tagged Wellington.

After the frightening and high body count exercise Sergeant Custer proceeded to show the trainees all of the technique used to set up booby traps. "Listen closely, learn, become sensitized to your environment, it could save your life." In addition to describing all of the booby traps, he held up the AK-47 that had been leaning in the corner of the hut and said, "The second shell in this weapon had the powder taken out and C4 explosive added. If any of you fired this weapon the second time you pulled the trigger would be the last thing you did on Earth. He finished by walking over to Wellington carrying the rubber snake, "This, my friend, is a common Krait, or Bungarus Caeruleus. It is one of the most venomous snakes in Vietnam. They have highly potent neurotoxic venom. If you are bitten you will experience severe abdominal cramps accompanied by progressive muscular paralysis. The first signs might be ptosis or the drooping of your eyelids. Then you will have trouble breathing and finally die. You've got four maybe eight hours. So, if you're out in the bush you might die before you can be evacuated. And, gentlemen," he held the snake above his head, "anti-venom, which is in short supply doesn't always work. On a happier note, most of the reptiles in Vietnam are nocturnal which means they are active at night. Shake out your boots and anything else that you might have removed before you put them back on. You might have a friend who is not so friendly."

Later in the day Wellington was ordered to see the Company Commander, Captain Strong. He reported as ordered.

When he entered the office, Captain Strong threw a rubber snake at Wellington. The young Marine leapt aside. "What is that?" asked the commanding officer.

"That's a Krait, sir"

"What do you know about it?"

"It's one of the most venomous snakes in Vietnam. Causes droopy eyes, paralysis, and death," Wellington paused, then added, "and it likes to read."

Captain Strong laughed. "Damn right it likes to read. You found that out."

"Yes, sir."

"Sergeant Custer tells me you were flawless in the booby trap exercise until you met our little friend there."

"That's because others found booby traps first, sir."

"Yes, by tripping them and dying."

"Yes, sir."

"How did you do so well?"

"Sir?"

"You hadn't been taught what to look for. That was part of the training. We can tell trainees all day long that it's dangerous out there. Only half will hear us. However, throw them into the experience unprepared, let them get a taste of it first, and they will be far more attentive. But you, Private Marsh, you had a sense of what to look for. Can you explain that?"

"Not really sir," Wellington said. His mind returned to the great Staunton Avenue rumble balloon war in Detroit. He looked at Captain Strong and said, "My father once told me, 'Tactics come from knowing what the other guy is going to do. Then, you can outsmart him.' I just tried to think of what the enemy might be thinking. They knew what we would do and booby trapped the village based on our tactics. So, I figured if I know our tactics then I know what they would be using as a guide for booby trapping. Shortstop, uh Private Marvin Press, shouldn't have pushed open that door and stood there. He should have stood to the side and pushed it knowing something would be rigged. And the radio transmitter with the maps was a perfect type of bait. A Marine would rush over to it, step on the trap door and get stabbed. I bet they study our every move and then create traps based on our tactics."

"Your father is a wise man."

"He is, sir."

"Son, you are a born leader. You think fast and you think straight. If I were a Marine Private on patrol I'd want you leading the way."

"Thank you, sir."

"I'm putting you in for promotion to Lance Corporal. Given the needs of war we can dispense with the eight-month time in rank requirement. For now, you will be acting corporal in your platoon. Keep up the good work. That's all."

"Yes sir," Wellington saluted, executed an about face, and left the office. Once outside he had mixed feelings. Yes, he was proud to have been recognized as doing well and getting promoted. Yes, there were things about the Marines that he liked. Yes, his father would be proud. No, he didn't want to go to Vietnam. Yes, that is exactly where he was going.

> When the moon is in the Seventh House
> And Jupiter aligns with Mars
> Then peace will guide the planets
> And love will steer the stars
> This is the dawning of the age of Aquarius
> Age of Aquarius
> Aquarius!
> Aquarius!

The two song medley, *Aquarius/Let the Sunshine In,* written by James Rado, Gerome Ragni, and Galt MacDermot of the 5th Dimension for the 1967 musical *Hair* played on the radio of a car parked across the street. Carl listened to it as he stood in front of the ornate door on the corner of Grove and Bleecker Streets in Greenwich Village. He ran his fingers over his left cheek and swollen eye. It was a reminder of his encounter with a truck driver named Casey Holmes.

> Harmony and understanding
> Sympathy and trust abounding
> No more falsehoods or derisions
> Golden living dreams of visions
> Mystic crystal revelation
> And the mind's true liberation
> Aquarius!
> Aquarius!

After striking out on Wednesday, the next day Carl hung out at the wide driveway where the Emmitt Distributing trucks entered and left the warehouse. He identified Casey Holmes by the name on his shirt when he arrived at work in the morning. At the end of the day he waited for the drivers to return. His target drove through the open warehouse door at 6:10 pm. Carl waited. When Casey Holmes left the building, Carl followed. He didn't want to confront the welsher near Emmitt Distributing where his co-workers could come to his aid. As he walked behind, he considered his prey. The man was about five foot seven inches tall with broad "truck driver's" shoulders. He had a bit of a saunter of one who was sure of himself. A beer belly indicated that he liked the suds.

> When the moon is in the Seventh House
> And Jupiter aligns with Mars
> Then peace will guide the planets
> And love will steer the stars
> This is the dawning of the age of Aquarius
> Age of Aquarius
> Aquarius!
> Aquarius!
> Aquarius!
> Aquarius!

Three blocks away from the warehouse, Carl saw an area with a secluded parking lot. He quickened his pace and caught up to his target. He called, "Casey." To his surprise the man suddenly pivoted on his left foot and hit Carl in the cheek and eye with his right hand. Before Carl could react, his opponent hit him in the stomach with his left followed by a right to the head. Carl stepped back.

Casey Holmes motioned with both hands as he challenged Carl, "Come'on punk. Get some more."

Carl stepped in but his opponent sidestepped and hit him in the chest followed by another blow to the left side of his face. It became clear that Casey Holmes was no pushover. However, one thing was proven, Carl could take a punch. He feigned being hurt and bent over. A confident boxer moved in to finish the fight. That was his mistake. Carl dove forward and grabbed the man's shirt. While hanging on he spun around and dragged his adversary with him throwing him to the ground. Before the fighter could regain his footing, Carl kicked him in the head. The stunned man saw the fist that broke his nose but didn't see the one that knocked him flat onto the pavement on his back. A kick to the kidney further incapacitated him. Carl grabbed Casey Holmes by the hair and pulled him to his feet. Another blow to the kidneys kept the fighter from resuming his attack. Carl slammed the man's head onto the hood of a parked car and held him down while bending his arm behind his back. He then said into the man's ear, "Pay your debts. You don't want me to come back because then I might be pissed. And, when I'm pissed I do bad things. You get it."

"I get it," Casey Holmes groaned.

"Pay your debts," Carl repeated as he kicked the man as hard as he could where the sun don't shine. He wanted the truck driver to remember him every time he sat down.

> Let the sunshine, let the sunshine in, the sunshine in
> Let the sunshine, let the sunshine in, the sunshine in
> Let the sunshine, let the sunshine in, the sunshine in

The two-song medley, *Aquarius/Let the Sunshine In,* became one of the most popular songs of 1969 worldwide. In the United States, it reached the number one position on the Billboard Hot 100 and the Billboard Adult Contemporary Chart. Around the world, it topped sales charts and ultimately was ranked as the #1 single for 1969.

The midnight blue 1969 Lincoln Continental pulled to the curb. Ray Esposito and two cohorts got out of the car and approached Carl. When they got to him Ray asked with a smile, "Did you get the license of the truck that hit you?"

Carl answered with a slight tone of annoyance, "That guy was a boxer and expected trouble."

"Was Casey a boxer?" Ray innocently asked his two associates.

"I think he did do some fighting in the welterweight division," one said.

The other man followed up with, "Yeah, he was pretty good. Called himself, Casey The Bat."

"That would have been nice to know," Carl complained.

Ray peeled two one hundred dollar bills off a money roll and handed them to Carl, "Here, buy yourself some Band Aids."

"Thanks."

"Casey made a payment this morning. My guy tells me he wasn't moving any too gingerly and walked a little funny," Ray examined Carl's eye, "You did good." He then lightly slapped Carl on the cheek.

At the card game that night Carl took a lot of ribbing.

"Hey, 'here ya go,' your girlfriend get mad at you?"

"You forget to duck at a ball game?"

"Next time don't try to clip one of Ray's cigars."

The card game was unusually friendly that night. Even the losers were talkative and joked. There was a discussion about the moon landing and the bravery of the astronauts. Ted Kennedy was also a subject of interest.

"You think he was drunk?"

"No question about it."

"They'll never get him on anything."

"Smart move, leave the scene until you sober up."

"His chances to be president sunk with that car."

"What do you want to bet?"

That night Ray introduced another luxury cigar for those who smoked. The Aguila rolled on Tenerife, the largest and most populated island of the seven Canary Islands. The cigars were blended with long filler Cuban tobaccos and a Havana wrapper. They were mild but exquisitely flavorful. After the players who wanted to taste the Aguila were given this fine cigar Ray slipped one into Carl's breast pocket of his suit jacket. "For later," he stated.

Gary Allen Hinman was born in Colorado on Christmas Eve in 1934. While he graduated with a degree in chemistry from UCLA he was also an accomplished musician. His curly brown hair, short cropped beard, and mustache supported his image of being a creative musician but hid the fact that he was quite an intellectual, as well. He worked at a music store teaching bagpipes, piano, trombone, and the drums. Always easy-going and friendly he opened his home at 962 Old Topanga Canyon Road, Santa Monica, California—in the hills above Los Angeles—to those who needed a place to stay. In 1968 Gary became interested in Nichiren Shoshu Buddhism and planned a pilgrimage to Japan the summer of 1969.

May of 1968 Gary had come home from visiting Dennis Wilson, a member of the Beach Boys, with a group of hippies. They needed a place to crash. There were two men, five women, and a newborn. The group left the next day. Over the next year, they returned periodically to borrow things and get food. One of the members of that group was a wannabe musician named Chuck Summers. Over time Gary and his ex-wife, who was living with him, became increasingly uncomfortable with this group of individuals. She was especially terrified of them.

When word got out that Gary Hinman had inherited $20,000, Chuck Summers sent Robert Kenneth "Bobby" Beausoleil age 21, Susan Denise Atkins age 21, and Mary Theresa Brunner age 25 to visit Gary and invite him to join their family. This, of course, would include turning over the inherited money and his two cars. The group lived at the Spahn Ranch and used Chuck Summers' given surname the Manson Family.

Shortly before midnight, Bruce Davis drove the three family members to Gary Hinman's house and dropped them off. They decided that the two girls would go to the house first and if they found Gary alone would signal in the window. Inside the house, Gary and his ex-wife were getting ready for bed. When they heard noises outside Gary became concerned and told his ex-wife, "Get up the hill and hide in the shed. There might be trouble."

Gary's ex-wife picked up the telephone and began to dial the police when there was a banging at the front door. Quickly, Hinman took the telephone from her and pushed her out the back door and locked it. Wearing only a thin nightgown and robe, she made her way into the hills behind the house and hid in a storage shed.

Susan Atkins and Mary Brunner entered the house and finding Gary alone signaled Bobby Beausoleil. The three intruders then demanded that Gary give them the money that he inherited. When he refused Bobby Beausoleil pulled out a gun and told the frightened Hinman that they weren't kidding. A short fight ensued and the gun went off. No one was hit by the bullet. Bobby Beausoleil then beat Gary Hinman with the gun. Gary's ex-wife hearing loud voices, a shot, Gary cry out in pain, and the stereo turned up to full volume crept out of the shed fled to the road and eventually hitchhiked to Malibu. She stayed with friends but never called the police.

Lauma White Feather, a classmate of Robert Six Trees, had become an object of interest to the young man. He had spoken with her often at school. Yet, after watching her as a jingle dress dancer everything changed. The jingle dress, also called a prayer dress, has small metal pieces sewn to ribbons that create a sound much like rain.

30: Saturday - July 26, 1969

He awoke early in the morning from a dream. It had begun as shadows and voices and echoes. Movements and sounds surrounded him creating a surrealistic world with Matt as an observer. Slowly, clarity came and the faces and words became clear. Matt heard his own voice. He was at the NASA meeting where he presented the Orztech proposal for high efficiency, low resistance, stranded wire coated with insulation that was impervious to heat and chemical breakdown. Scientists and other staffers sat around a conference room table. At one end of the table Matt held a flip chart which showed the many tests that had been performed to confirm that the wire developed by Orztech met or exceeded all of the specifications required by NASA.

The dream transitioned to a small office where Matthew Ellis and Lida Petropoulos sat at a small meeting table with papers strewn upon it.

"What is the problem?" Lida asked impatiently.

"I'm concerned." Matt replied.

"Why? You win the bid, Orztech makes money, the order gets fulfilled, and we get rich." Lida sat back and stated emphatically, "You can't win that NASA contract without a cost advantage. I'm your ace in the hole." She smiled and patted his leg as she added, "And, in many ways you're my ace in the hole."

Matt understood the double entente and was embarrassed. He commented, "There are so many risks . . ."

"Risks exist in every business. Do you doubt I will deliver the product on time?"

"No, you've delivered every order as promised."

"Have there been any complaints?"

"No, yes, one."

"I see. You're still hung up on that one auto manufacturer that got a bad spool of wire." Lida took out a cigarette and held it to be lit. "We replaced it and everyone is happy."

"It shouldn't have happened."

"You know I raised holy hell and got a refund for part of that order. The factory has been more vigilant than ever to make sure no more bad spools are sent." She leaned forward and added, "Even Orztech factories screw up from time to time."

"I know. That's not really the problem."

"What is it? You don't like your rewards?" Lida ran her hand up his leg, "Either of them."

"I don't feel right."

"Shit, Matt, I thought we were past all that!" She stood and walked over to a window. "Don't you like the money? Because, if you don't, I'll be happy to take it off your hands."

"I just don't understand how you get wire manufactured at such a low cost."

"Here we go again." Lida walked back over toward Matt swinging her shapely hips in an inviting manner. She leaned over Matt letting him have a view of her cleavage. "It's simple economics. I outsource overseas. There's a factory that can provide all the wire we need at a fraction of the cost of manufacturing it here in the United States."

"Child labor."

"Sure it's child labor and stinking lousy working conditions. But we didn't create them. We simply are taking advantage of a cost savings."

"I don't like the thought of it."

"Matt, you have to be a realist." She stroked his hair, "Look at it this way, some nine-year-old in Sri Lanka works ten hours a day, seven days a week, and gets paid seven dollars. Those seven dollars will feed his family. Which do you honestly believe? Would that child rather work hard and eat or not work and starve?"

"We're taking advantage . . ."

"We pay the manufacturer what they want. They establish salaries and working conditions. Over time things will change, but right now this is the way it is. Remember, there were sweatshops in the United States until unions came along." Lida sat down next to Matt put her hand on the back of his hand. "We are helping the process along. As manufacturers make more profits they will improve conditions and salaries."

"I'm not so sure."

"Well, you can be sure of this. I will deliver on time at the price we established. NASA will get to the Moon and you and I will hold hands all the way to the bank."

"The money still bothers me."

"You like that fancy house, nice clothes, and new car, don't you?"

"Somehow, I feel like I'm cheating."

"You are, but in a different sense," Lida ran her hand down between his legs. "It feels good, doesn't it? Well, having money feels good, as well. You are not cheating anyone. You're just ahead of the curve. Mark my words, big corporations are going to outsource overseas more and more as they find labor costs in America are putting their profits at risk. There's going to be plenty of work for those nine-year-olds and ten-year-olds. And, eventually they will organize. That's when the gravy train leaves the rails"

Olivia Samantha Everett sipped her coffee as she listened to Claire, the hooker with whom Miguel had her room when Rita was murdered. "You see this," Claire showed the young girl bruises and abrasions on her arms. "Miguel wanted to know where you were and I couldn't tell him. He threw me against a wall and punched me in the stomach." She walked over to the sink and filled a glass with water. "He's a son-of-a-bitch and capable of anything." Claire wasn't wearing her shoulder length auburn wig so Olivia could see the wretched condition of her hair from when Miguel cut it off. "Honey, all we have is each other. He won't stop with beating me. He'll get to you. So, like it or not, we have to watch out for each other." Claire sat at the small kitchen table, "You have to let me know where you are or are going so I can either tell Miguel or cover for you."

"I'm sorry," Olivia said sincerely not wanting to lose the only friend she had left in the world.

"If you run away, Miguel will kill me." Claire warned, then looked directly at the young girl and added, "And, he will find you and savagely beat you or kill you."

"I know."

"We have to be smart. It's a matter of survival."

"It was really hot, I was thirsty," Olivia apologized. Her mind jumped back less than a month when she had a good life, comfortable home, and a loving family. How she regretted leaving. But, those days were gone. She could never go back, so she had to learn how to survive on the streets and under the watchful eye of Miguel.

"Just let me know, that's all I ask," Claire said softly.

"I will. I promise."

"Do you want some waffles?" Claire asked as she stood.

Olivia smiled, "That would be nice. Can I help?"

"No. But, you can do the dishes."

"OK."

The two roommates ate breakfast and continued to talk about nothing. Neither asked any personal questions. For both it was too soon. However, in their cold, impersonal, soiled world a small degree of companionship was welcome.

Bobby Beausoleil took the .22 caliber Hi Standard Longhorn revolver from Susan Atkins who had been guarding Gary Hinman. He asked Hinman once again for the money and pink slips for his two cars. The musician continued to refuse and asked them to leave.

Charles Manson, a.k.a. Chuck Summers and seventeen other documented names, arrived with Bruce Davis, a petty thief who lived at the Spahn Ranch with the family. Manson was a cold, calculating, heartless predator who was unpredictable. That made him highly dangerous. When he walked in he was carrying a sword. Bobby Beausoleil told him that Gary Hinman was not cooperating which caused Charlie to abruptly raise the sword and strike. He slashed Gary Hinman's left ear almost off and left a gash in his face.

Charlie Manson was an illegitimate child born November 12, 1934 in Cincinnati, Ohio. His mother, Kathleen Maddox, ran away from home at sixteen and was both promiscuous and often in trouble with the law. Manson's father, Colonel Scott from Ashland, Kentucky had nothing to do with either of them. At one point Kathleen Maddox briefly married a William Manson from whom Charlie took his last name.

There was a story, though not substantiated, about how one afternoon Charles Manson's mother sat in a café with him in her lap when a waitress joked that she would buy him from her. His mother replied, "A pitcher of beer and he's yours." After she finished the beer she left without him. Several days later his uncle located him and brought him home.

When his mother and her brother were sent to prison for armed robbery Charlie was sent to live with his very religious aunt in McMechen, West Virginia. Charlie kept to himself and became a petty thief. At nine-years-old he was sent to reform school. In 1947, at the age of twelve, he was caught stealing and sent to Gibault School for Boys in Terre Haute, Indiana. Less than a year later he escaped and tried to return to his mother. She didn't want anything to do with him. Subsequently, he lived on the streets and survived by stealing. When he again got caught he was sent to Father Flanagan's Boys Town. This didn't go well either as he and another boy committed multiple armed robberies while there. At thirteen-years-old Charles Manson was sent to the Indiana School for Boys for three years. In 1951, Charlie and two other boys escaped but eventually got caught in Utah. He was sent to the National Training School for Boys in Washington, D.C. While there it was determined that he had an IQ of 109 (average), he was illiterate, and in need of psychiatric help. Charlie was small in stature which added to his feelings of inadequacy. At one point while being considered for parole he held a razor blade to another boy's throat and sodomized him. As a result, authorities concluded that he was "homosexual, dangerous, and safe only under supervision." He was transferred to the Federal Reformatory at Petersburg, Virginia. In 1952 Charlie was transferred to a more secure institution in Chillicothe, Ohio. There he learned to read and basic math. He was paroled in May, 1954 at the age of nineteen.

Charlie Manson married a waitress in 1955. During that time he worked at menial jobs and supplemented his income by stealing cars. In fact, he took his pregnant wife to Los Angeles, California in one of the stolen cars. After he was caught and sent to prison at Terminal Island in San Pedro, California his wife divorced him. He was paroled in 1958 but was arrested in 1959 on two federal charges; stealing a check from a mailbox, in addition to attempting to cash a U.S. Treasury check for $37.50. He got lucky when a young woman pretended she was pregnant and pleaded with the judge. The gullible judge believed her and sentenced Charlie to ten years, immediately placing Manson on probation. A few months later, he was once more arrested for stealing cars and using stolen credit cards. The charges were dropped for lack of evidence.

Late in 1959 he conned a young woman out of $700, got her pregnant, and raped her roommate. Even though he fled to Texas he was caught and sent to prison to serve his ten-year sentence. The judge said, "If there ever was a man who demonstrated himself completely unfit for probation, he is it." Charles Manson was sent to the U.S. Penitentiary at McNeil Island, Washington.

In prison, Charlie became friends with an aging gangster, Alvin Karpis. The sole survivor of the Ma Barker gang taught Charlie how to play the steel guitar. Manson's dream was to get a job as a guitar player, drummer, or singer with a band. He spent most of his free time writing songs and became obsessed with the Beatles.

At the age of thirty-two, after spending more than half his life in prison, he was released. He didn't want to leave stating, "Oh, no, I can't go outside there. I can't adjust to that world not after all my life being spent locked up and where my mind was free. I'm content to stay in the penitentiary, just to take my walks around the yard in the sunshine and to play my guitar."

Manson fit well in the hippie scene in San Francisco. He wasn't impressed by the hippie culture, but lived off it. He learned about drugs and to use them to influence people. Slowly, he gathered a group of followers, mainly emotionally troubled young women with little self-esteem. He manipulated them bending their personalities to fit his world view. LSD and amphetamines were among the tools that he used.

In spring of 1968 the Manson family left San Francisco in an old school bus. Charlie met George Spahn that year and convinced the old man to let him and his followers live on the abandoned Spahn Ranch. One of Charlie's girls, Squeaky Fromme, made sure that the elderly man's sexual needs were fully satisfied. During this time, the Manson Family survived by stealing and scavenging. Much of their food was taken from what the supermarkets discarded each day. They eventually met Gary Hinman and were frequent visitors to his home.

The visit on Friday, July 25, 1969 was highly unwelcome. With Gary Hinman bleeding and moaning in the background Charlie told his minions to keep the pressure on and get that money. He and Bruce Davis left in one of Gary Hinman's cars.

Robert Six Trees welcomed the rain. It had been a long dry spell. Smaller streams dried up and even larger lakes and streams were below normal. He loved the smell of the forest when it was fresh and wet and let drops of water run down his face.

31: Sunday - July 27, 1969

Carl Pythacyk walked along Thirty Fifth Street. He looked quite debonair in his custom tailored Gino Valentino suit. Given his new look and new business associates the young hood carried himself differently. Without realizing it he had mentally been studying and adopting the movements and mannerisms of Ray Esposito and his colleagues. There was a slight swagger to his step and he had an air of confidence. His shoulders were back and head held high. He knew, at present, he was just the hired help but had a sense of belonging. In time, he also knew he would gain their respect and become a trusted member of Ray's crew. No longer a street punk—Carl was connected.

Carl had just left a meeting with two of Ray Esposito's henchmen at a coffee shop. He only knew their nicknames, Fat Tony and East River Vito. Following instructions given him by telephone the night before, he arrived at the coffee shop at ten in the morning and waited. After approximately twenty minutes he saw a tan Cadillac pull up outside and park in a no parking zone. Two men, who Carl recognized, got out, entered the coffee shop, and sat on either side of him at a table.

Fat Tony started the conversation, "Ray has another collection job for you."

"OK," Carl replied.

"This time he wants you to break something. An arm or leg or thumb. This guy's in deep and he has to know we are serious."

East River Vito added, "Before you leave you take his wedding ring. Then you tell him if he doesn't pay up immediately, arrangements will be made for his wife to work off the debt."

"He has until Friday," Fat Tony said, "When he doesn't pay, his wife will start work on Saturday."

Carl had a pretty good idea what kind of work they were referring to but didn't say anything.

"You have something to write on?" Fat Tony asked.

Carl pulled a notepad and pen out of his jacket pocket.

East River Vito laughed and said, "The kid learns fast."

"The guy's name is Barney Halverson. He lives on the upper east side. Swanky place, 236 East Sixty Third Street," Fat Tony explained. "There's a doorman."

Carl nodded.

Fat Tony continued, "The time to get him is early in the morning, around 6:00 a.m. He jogs in Central Park. You'll know him because he wears fancy jogging gear and a red baseball cap with the StL for the St. Louis Cardinals on it."

"They won the World Series two years ago," East River chimed in.

"I know. I lost a bundle on that series," Fat Tony complained.

"I won a bundle," East River replied.

Fat Tony glared at East River then returned his attention to Carl, "The guy works on Wall Street. He has access to the money so we'll see how much he loves his wife."

"She's a looker," East River Vito commented. "I'd like to see her get her nose out of the air and between some guy's legs."

Fat Tony laughed which drew a laugh from Carl, as well.

"I'd get to him tomorrow, if you can," Fat Tony advised. "He will need time to gather the money together."

"I'm on it," Carl stated.

"You know, Ray likes you, kid," Fat Tony said. "You can go far."

"I'll do my best for Mr. Esposito," Carl said sincerely.

East River Vito replied, "There's one thing you better do."

Carl turned toward him and asked, "What's that?"

"Learn to make coffee," Vito replied through a laugh.

"Take off kid," Fat Tony said, then added, "Nice threads."

"Thanks, I ordered another suit from Antonio's," Carl said.

"That's good. It pays to look good," Fat Tony said.

Carl left the coffee shop. Fat Tony and East River Vito stayed and ordered coffee.

As Carl walked down Thirty Fifth Street he planned his next day's activities. It would mean getting up really early to be on Sixty Third Street before six. He decided to carry a short metal rod, just in case. It also could be used to break something. Carl was so lost in thought that he didn't see Miguel until he stepped out of the recessed entrance of a closed store.

"Hey, ladron, fancy meeting you here," Miguel said as two other hoods stepped out of the doorway behind Miguel. The three punks blocked Carl's way.

Immediately, Carl looked over his shoulder just in time to see two more of Miguel's compatriots cross the street to stand behind him. He had nowhere to go.

For two days Gary Hinman lay on the floor in his house in pain, bleeding and reciting Buddhist prayers. Bobby Beausoleil once more demanded that Hinman give them the inherited money and sign over ownership of his two cars. His patience had run out and he was none too gentle with the injured captive. Susan Atkins and Mary Brunner cheered him on saying, "Hit him. Hit him."

Once more Gary Hinman stated that there was no money. He begged them to leave which brought on more punishment. The injured musician drifted in and out of consciousness.

Carl stood motionless as he considered his options. Five to one weren't very good odds. He could turn and attack the two thugs behind him and hope to escape. Unfortunately, there was too little distance between the three in front and two behind for that strategy to work. If he broke and ran across the street they could still block him, but it would spread them out. No matter what he considered it ended with him at best taking a beating. It wasn't looking good.

"This has been a long time coming pobre tipo," Miguel said.

Carl didn't answer.

"I see you have been doing well for yourself," Miguel motioned toward Carl's suit. Buen Traje, uh, nice threads. Too bad they're going to get all bloody."

"It won't be my blood," Carl warned as he bluffed.

"Ah, muy valiente," Miguel said to his cohorts.

Anger grew in Carl. He decided he might go down, but it wouldn't be without a fight or him having something to say. "I should have cut your throat for what you did to Sylvester," he spat.

"Si, the cobarde who told you about the guns."

"What guns?" Carl feigned ignorance.

"You know damn well what guns. My guns! Where are they?" In a friendlier voice Miguel said, "I might let you live if you give me my guns."

"I don't know what you're talking about."

Miguel changed the subject, "I bet you are wondering how I found you."

Carl once more remained silent.

"One of my people saw you in the coffee shop sitting alone. He called me. I have a bounty on your head." Miguel pulled a switchblade knife out of his pocket, pushed the button, and it snapped open. "Enough small talk. I'm going to cut off your cojones and make you eat them. Then maybe I'll put you out on the street with my girls." Miguel took a step forward but abruptly stopped.

Carl heard the screech of tires and the sound of someone being knocked to the ground. He glanced over his shoulder to see Fat Tony and East River Vito standing over two hoods lying on the pavement. He then heard the familiar sound of the slides of two pump-action shotguns being shifted to load a cartridge in the chamber.

Miguel backed away slowly, "No problem here. We are leaving."

Fat Tony said to Carl, "Get in the car," as he motioned with his shotgun.

Carl and his two new best friends climbed into the Cadillac. As they sped away East River Vito said, "Can't you stay out of trouble?"

"That was a close one. I don't know what I would have done if you hadn't come along. Thanks," Carl replied.

"No problem, Kid," Fat Tony said. Then he asked, "You got trouble with that punk?"

"Yeah, he cheated me and I got even. Now, he's out for revenge."

"That suit you ordered," East River suggested, "Get it made a little loose across the back so you can carry a piece."

Carl looked at East River Vito who made a shooting motion with his fingers.

"This sucks!" Ritchie spat as he looked at the letter from the Selective Service System that had arrived the day before. He had been reclassified as 1-A—registrant available for military service. While this was not a notice to report it was, indeed, a forewarning that such a letter would arrive in the near future.

Fetch, the black basenji, jumped up on the couch and settled down next to Ritchie. She could tell that something was amiss and pushed her nose up under his arm. Unconsciously, Ritchie scratched the back of her neck. He knew it was inevitable that a letter was going to arrive. It would tell him where and when to report and his freedom would be gone. "I won't fight the man's war," Ritchie stated. Fetch replied with a low yodel. "It's immoral, man." Fetch pawed his arm. "I should have known it would happen as soon as I turned twenty." Fetch pushed up against Ritchie. "That's the prime age of draftees."

He pondered his options—jail or Canada. There was no need to toss a coin. Ritchie decided he better buy a map or two and chat with some people who have a little more experience with crossing the northern border. Bobby Evans escaped to the great white way a year earlier. After digging through a desk drawer to find the number, Ritchie picked up the telephone and called a friend with whom he went to high school.

Paul was still in college, therefore enjoyed a 1-S, student deferment.

When the phone was answered Ritchie said, "What the hell's a Hoya?" He referred to the term that was adopted for all Georgetown University athletic teams. A long time ago the teams had been called "The Stonewalls." That was until a student used the Greek and Latin terms "Hoya Saxa" which meant "What Rocks." By 1894 the chant became well established and the name Hoya stuck. Since then students of Georgetown University have for decades had to answer the question, "What the hell's a Hoya" ad infinitum.

"Hey man, how's it hanging?" Paul replied.

"Draggin on the ground, man." Ritchie said, then got serious, "What do you know about Canada?"

"I know there's no war there, if that's what you mean, man," Paul answered.

"Yeah, I got a letter from big brother."

"No shit? You drafted?"

"Not yet, just got my 1-A. But you know the greetings from the government can't be far behind."

"Like imminent."

"How do I get to Canada?"

"You go north until the cops wear red."

"Come'on man, you know guys who did it. Give me a clue. What's the best way?"

There was silence for a few seconds. Then Paul said, "You can't cross at a regular crossing. The marshals are hip to dudes trying to just walk over. If they stop you and ask for your draft card and see that you're 1-A—you're toast."

"OK, kemosabe, how then do I fly the coop?"

"Funny you should use what Tonto calls the Lone Ranger because the best route out is through an Indian reservation," Paul stated.

"Really? Where?"

"You'll have to do a little research but I know a couple of guys who went up through Minnesota, past Duluth, and through an Indian reservation. There are old lumber roads and paths there that go all the way to Canada. Once you're in Canada they can't touch you."

"Great."

"But, you know man, you can't come back—ever."

"Yeah," Ritchie answered reflectively, "But, if I'm lying dead in a rice paddy in Vietnam, I ain't coming back—ever."

"Point taken."

"What are you going to do when you graduate next year," Ritchie asked his friend.

"Man, I'm staying in school and going all the way to a freakin' PhD if I have to."

"Does that count?"

"In education, man. Teachers are considered essential, man. I'll teach my ass off, so I don't get it blown off."

"Good plan."

"Hey," Paul asked, "You taking that fox you've been porking with you?"

"She doesn't know about it, yet."

"Well, if she doesn't make the trip, give me her number, man. I'll show her what being with a man is supposed to be like."

"Yeah, who you gonna introduce her to for that?"

"I'm gonna introduce her to Mister Johnson."

"More like Missing Something."

"When you plan to tell her?"

"I don't know. I'll have to find the right time, man."

"You think she'll go with you?"

"Probably not. She's taking care of her old man who was in a coma for years."

"Oh yeah, that's right." Paul recalled. "She's not going, man."

"I know."

In the evening Gary Hinman could fight no more. He agreed to sign over ownership of his VW bus, which Charlie Manson had taken two days earlier, and his Fiat 1100 station wagon. His hope was that they would accept this gesture and leave. Bobby Beausoleil asked about the money one last time. Hinman could do no more than shake his head because there wasn't any money. Bobby Beausoleil looked at the two girls in the room and pointed at Hinman. "I guess there's no money," he concluded as he spun around and stabbed Gary Hinman in the chest two times with a Mexican-made bowie knife.

Gary Hinman lay on the floor bleeding with his prayer beads in hand, chanting "Nam Myo Ho Renge Kyo Nam Myo Ho Renge Kyo," a Buddhist chant. Bobby Beausoleil, Susan Atkins, and Mary Brunner took turns holding a pillow over the face of the mortally wounded man until he died.

Beausoleil then used Gary Hinman's blood to write "Political Piggy" on a wall and drew a paw print under it. Charlie Manson had told them to do it in order to make the police think the murder had been done by the Black Panthers.

Charlie Manson preached that the black man would rise up and start killing whites and burning down the cities. He believed that the black race would win but wouldn't be able to govern. From the Book of Revelations he spoke of a "bottomless pit" that would be found in a cave in Death Valley. There the family would hide and wait for the violence to end at which time they would emerge and take over. His drug addled followers were convinced that he, Charles Willis Manson, was Jesus Christ and would rule the world.

While Charlie was predicting a race war the Beatles released their white album which included the song *Helter Skelter*. Manson felt the lyrics fit his racial Armageddon, therefore, Helter Skelter became its name.

Charlie forecast that black men would start killing whites in various despicable ways starting in the summer of 1969. As the summer wore on it appeared that the prophet was wrong. He couldn't allow this. "The only thing blackie knows is what whitey has told him," he told one of his followers. He then concluded, "I'm going to have to show him how to do it."

On a trail Robert Six Trees came upon a stranger. He raised his hand and said, "Aaniin." This was short for "Aaniin gidoodem?" which meant "What is your 'doodem'?" A doodem was their clan named primarily for animal and bird totems.

The young man replied, "Moozwaanowe or Little Moose-tail."

Robert replied, "Baswenaazhi or Echo-maker," which meant Crane.

32: Tuesday - July 29, 1969

Carl stood in the shadows on the corner of Park Avenue and East Sixty Third Street. He sipped coffee from a Styrofoam cup. On Monday he had waited across the street from 236 East Sixty Third Street where his prey lived. Barney Halverson came out a few minutes after 6:00 a.m., stretched, did deep breathing exercises, and then jogged two and a half blocks over to Park Avenue. Carl followed at a discreet distance. Halverson turned right and jogged four blocks north to Sixty Seventh Street. That was where Carl's plan fell apart. Barney Halverson met up with another jogger and they proceeded over to the Sixty Seventh Street entrance to Central Park. After that, no opportunity to confront Barney Halverson alone ever presented itself.

On this morning, Carl needed to determine whether having a jogging partner was a regular thing or one time occurrence the day before. Unfortunately, it turned out to be the same as Monday. Carl didn't bother following the two joggers into the park. He was pissed off and thought Ray's guys keep leaving out important details. On a brighter note he did shadow Halverson the day before and found a few places where he would have an opportunity to fulfill his assignment. Unfortunately, as with the truck driver, Casey Holmes, Carl assumed that his target was aware of the fact that he had unpaid gambling debts and might get a visit from one of Ray Esposito's associates. Barney Halverson would be on his guard ready for an assault and he wasn't any lightweight. He had at least three inches on Carl and probably twenty pounds, as well. How good a fighter the man was would have to be determined. The thought of losing a fight and having to admit it to Ray Esposito made Carl shiver. He decided that there was no way that he was going to lose. Toward that end, Carl knew anything he did would have to be quick and decisive.

Time passed. A few people were on Park Avenue but East Sixty Third Street remained empty. The sun was up and Carl could feel both the humidity and heat rising with every minute. He glanced at his watch. If Barney Halverson did the same as the prior day he would come down Park Avenue any moment. Carl glanced around the corner but there was no sign of his target. In the area where he waited there were numerous buildings that housed medical offices. At that early hour they were all closed. Also, because there were no apartment buildings on East Sixty Third Street between Park Avenue and Lexington Avenue the block was deserted. He glanced around the corner once more. Half a block away Barney Halverson was jogging in his direction alone. Quickly, Carl moved down the street to where a building was set further back from the street. It was a perfect place to remain unseen.

In a few minutes Carl heard the footsteps of a jogger. He turned and placed his weight on his rear foot ready to spring into action. When Barney Halverson appeared in the middle of the sidewalk jogging in the direction of his apartment building, Carl sprung. Before the jogger could react Carl grabbed his shirt and used his momentum to swing him into the recess of the building. Instinctively, Halverson raised his hands to brace himself as he slammed into the wall. Immediately, he cried out in pain, "Ooow, I broke my finger." The frightened man turned to face Carl and pleaded, "Please don't hurt me." He raised his arms over his face in a defensive posture.

Carl realized his prey was a coward and wasn't going to put up a fight. He placed his arm across the man's throat and pushed hard enough to make it difficult for him to breathe. "You have gambling debts. Pay them."

"Aargh, pleaadth."

"You have until Friday."

"I cathn't."

"You have no choice," Carl struck the man in the stomach. He slumped downward and Carl let him slide to the ground.

"I broke my finger," Barney cried as he showed a misshapen middle finger on his right hand.

Carl laughed realizing that part of his assignment had been done for him.

"Give me your wedding ring," he ordered.

The fallen man stared in disbelief.

"Give it to me now or you won't have any fingers that work."

Barney said, "Please don't hurt me," as he pulled and pulled on his wedding band. "I need more time."

"You have til Friday, or your wife will work the debt off."

"What?" The ring came off and he handed it to Carl, "What do you mean?"

"Use your imagination," Carl spat. "Pay by Friday or your wife goes to work." Carl added as he improvised, "And, don't go to the police or try to hide her or get her out of town. You have a lot of bones."

"Please!"

Carl turned and walked away saying over his shoulder, "Friday."

In a quiet corner in the Dixon Homestead Library, Matthew Ellis sat reading a back issue of *Time Magazine*. It was dated Friday, August 4, 1967. He read an article about a fire on the USS Forrestal. It occurred on Saturday, July 29, 1967, exactly two years earlier.

The aircraft carrier USS Forrestal (CVA-59) left Norfolk in early June, 1967. It was operating in the Gulf of Tonkin off the coast of Vietnam. Sailors were preparing for a second strike for that day. Seven F-4B Phantom II fighters were on the port side of the deck. The F-4B Phantom II was a large fighter capable of carrying 18,000 pounds of ordinance, including air-to-air missiles, air-to-ground missiles and bombs. Across from these aircraft were twelve smaller A-4 Skyhawk attack aircraft. The Skyhawk had a delta wing so compact that it did not need to be folded for carrier stowage.

At about 10:50 a.m. an Mk-32 Zuni rocket on the underwing rocket pod of F-4B Phantom II number 110 accidentally fired due to an electrical power surge. Many factors could have caused the surge. High winds could have blown free the safety pin that is normally kept in place until just before takeoff, or the decision to plug in the "pigtail" system which connects the jets electrical system to the missile pod early to increase the number of takeoffs, or defective wiring in the pigtail which allowed a surge when the pilot switched from external to internal power. Whatever the cause the Zuni rocket flew across the flight deck and struck a wing-mounted external fuel tank on A-4E Skyhawk, Number 405, piloted by Lieutenant Commander Fred D. White. The warhead safety mechanism prevented it from detonating, however, the impact knocked the fuel tank off of the wing spilling JP-5 fuel which ignited. In seconds other external fuel tanks overheated and ruptured. The additional fuel fed the fire on the flight deck.

The Zuni rocket also dislodged two 1000-lb AN-M65 bombs, which fell to the deck and lay in the pool of burning fuel between Lieutenant Commander Fred D. White's and Lieutenant Commander John McCain's aircraft. Upon noticing the flames, John McCain climbed onto the nose of his jet and dropped to the flight deck. Damage Control Team #8 moved in to fight the fire. Chief Gerald Farrier led the way without protective gear. He began spraying the bombs with a PKP fire extinguisher in an effort to keep down the fuel fire long enough to allow the pilots to escape.

If they had been using more modern Mark 83 bombs which featured relatively stable Composition H6 explosive filler and thicker heat-resistant cases there would have been a 10 minute window in which to extinguish the fire and prevent the bombs from detonating. Unfortunately, due to shortages, they had been supplied surplus World War II 1000-lb. AN-M65A1 "fat boy" bombs. These thin skinned, highly volatile, bombs had been stored in open-air Quonset huts for almost thirty years exposed to the heat and humidity of the Philippine jungle. After approximately one minute, despite the efforts of Chief Farrier, one bomb suddenly split open and began to glow cherry red. He shouted for the team to withdraw but the bomb detonated. It was only one minute and thirty-six seconds after the fire started. Chief Gerald Farrier and all but three of Damage Control Team #8 along with pilot Lieutenant Commander Fred D. White were killed instantly. Two other A-4 Skyhawk aircraft were heavily damaged and began to burn. Additional bombs detonated. A crater had been blown in the armored flight deck. Two other pilots were unable to escape the conflagration, Lieutenant Dennis M. Barton and Lieutenant Commander Gerry L. Stark.

In all nine bombs exploded on the flight deck which left gaping holes. This allowed flaming jet fuel to drain into the interior of the ship, including the living quarters, directly underneath the flight deck, and the aircraft hangar. The crew got the fire under control one hour and twenty-five minutes after the rocket had accidentally fired. Due to hot spots and flare ups it was not declared over until 4:00 a.m. the next day. One hundred thirty four crewmen were dead and one hundred sixty one injured. Twenty one aircraft had been destroyed or jettisoned into the sea. Initial investigations focused on a malfunctioning electrical connection.

When Matt finished reading the news story he understood what Parker Adolphson, president of Orztech Corporation, meant when he said, "Every time there is a disaster, I wait. And, when I hear it was due to a faulty wire I take one more step downward toward hell."

Matthew Ellis sat alone in a musty reading room in an old building converted to a local library. He tried desperately to reach into his mind. Was he the monster Parker Adolphson described? Why couldn't he find the answer? Where was the key to open hidden memories? As much as he feared finding the truth—he had to know. Without knowing, he had no real identity. He was an apparition, a non-being. Was he responsible for the deaths of all those men on that ship? Or, was there no connection, at all? If he finds the truth, can he live with it? Finally, he got down on his knees and prayed, "Lord, open the shades and shed light on my past. Let me see what I have or haven't done. Punish me, if need be, but don't leave me alone in bewilderment living without living. Guide me to the truth—the blessed truth that will free me or condemn me." At that moment he knew the answer, Lida.

Jack Moore sat at his desk and read the morning newspaper. The Baltimore

Orioles had won again. They were in first place with a record of 60 wins and 31 losses. His Yankees, on the other hand, were coming off of another loss. Their record was 48 wins and 54 losses which put them in fifth place, 23 games behind The Baltimore Orioles—a team that he hated. He hated the Baltimore Orioles but also knew that the Yankees were actually the first Baltimore Orioles back in 1901. The team was purchased by two bartenders for $18,000 and moved to New York. From 1903 to 1912 they were called the New York Highlanders. Then in 1913 they became the illustrious New York Yankees. This year he thought they were more inept than illustrious. Interestingly, the Baltimore Orioles began as the Milwaukee Brewers in 1901, became the St. Louis Browns in 1902, and the Baltimore orioles in 1954. To Jack it was obvious that the Orioles were heading to the World Series and would probably make short work of a National League team.

The telephone rang and Jack answered it.

"Jack Moore?" a strange voice asked.

"Speaking. Who is this?"

"Let's just say that it is the friend of a friend."

"OK, F.O.F. what can I do for you?"

"It is more of what I can do for you."

"OK, what can you do for me?"

"Let me begin by saying that this is very difficult for me. I'm not one that likes to make waves or tell secrets."

Jack grabbed a yellow pad and pencil, "I know it's difficult, but it obviously is something important enough for you to want me to know. Take your time."

"I work at NASA."

Jack's mind became active. Was this another friend of Colt MacIntyre or a friend of Russell Samuels, the engineer who worked in propulsion, with whom he spoke the previous Friday? He decided to be cautious as the caller already sounded nervous. It wouldn't take much to cause him to rabbit. So, he simply replied, "Yes."

"I believe you are doing a story on inferior products supplied for the space program by outside sources."

"I haven't decided whether or not there is a story."

"There is."

Jack sat upright, "I'd be very interested in hearing what you know or what you have been told."

"Most suppliers provided good quality products with an occasional bad one in the mix. That's to be expected. Overall, they did very well and we were highly satisfied. There were, however, three cases where it could be said . . . that . . . um . . . that their products . . . were . . . misrepresented. One was a computer hardware company that claimed their product could do far more than it turned out it could actually do. We replaced them early in the program. The second was a tool manufacturer. They were expensive and claimed to be able to provide any type of specialized tool we required. They couldn't. And, what they did provide was nowhere near the caliber that they originally presented. These two companies were an irritant and caused some development delays, but we identified them early without any real damage being done. The third company is a different story." There was a pause.

Jack waited in silence. He knew from years of experience that being too pushy can cause an informant to have second thoughts. He would wait for a few moments but not too long. If FOF didn't continue, he would have to attempt to gently pull the information out of him.

The caller continued, "You would think something as simple as this product would not be a problem."

Jack waited.

"Unfortunately, it turns out that it has and will continue to have a dramatic and deadly impact on the space program."

Jack wrote down the quote underlining the word "deadly." He wanted so much to ask questions—dozens of them. Instead, he let the caller continue at his own pace.

"Three brave men died on January 27, 1967."

Jack literally held the telephone receiver in front of him and stared at the earpiece as if trying to make sure that he heard what he heard. Quickly, he returned it to his ear.

"We determined that the fire that killed Command Pilot Gus Grissom, Senior Pilot Edward White, and Pilot Roger Chaffee in Apollo 1 was caused by faulty wiring. More accurately—a faulty wire."

"Wow," Jack let slip out.

There was silence.

Jack broke the silence, "Can you tell me what was wrong with the wire?"

Silence.

"Listen, I can't do an investigation or write a story if I don't have more facts."

Silence.

"Don't you want the truth to be told about the deaths of those brave men?"

"I want the truth to be known about them but the threat remains."

"What threat?"

"NASA purchased a significant amount of high efficiency, low resistance, stranded wire coated with insulation that is impervious to heat and chemical breakdown. The original order was tested and found to meet all specifications. That wire was used in every area of development and construction. It wasn't until the Apollo I fire that we suspected anything. The wire that caused that fire was a cheap alloy that had a tendency to heat up and the insulation was inferior to wire that you could buy off the shelf in any electronics store. Yet, it was stamped with the high grade markings of the wire that we ordered. It couldn't be a mistake. It was a deliberate attempt to substitute cheap inferior merchandise for what was ordered."

"What is the name of the manufacturer?"

"Orztech Corporation. Their headquarters was in New York City."

"Was?"

"Our investigation led us to the wire. We examined new spools that were in inventory and they seemed fine. Yet, the wire that was in the Command Module was the culprit. The insulation had broken down. We ran further tests. After a number of tests we were shocked to find low-grade wire turned up. It was found on the spool approximately after 50 feet of wire had been rolled off. Tests on other spools found the same thing. With the exception of the first fifty feet all spools contained a cheap, inferior substitute. We tried to contact the manufacturer but found they were no longer in business."

"That's outright fraud. Possibly manslaughter. Did you contact the legal authorities?"

"I don't know what steps were taken other than replacing the wire that was in inventory."

"What about the wire that was already used? Did you have to replace it?"

"That's the problem. This wire is pervasive in the system. We would have to rebuild practically everything to replace it. That is impossible."

"So, you're telling me . . ."

"Right. There are potential disasters throughout the space program."

"So, the decision was made to do nothing?"

"The decision was to no longer use the tainted wire and when up fits or changes were made to replace whatever wire was accessible."

"That's all?"

"If we were to replace all of the wire, in addition to the cost, it would shut the space program down for two years."

"But, that means proceeding knowing the risks are elevated," Jack exclaimed.

"There are always risks. The risks were greater before we made the discovery. Now, as we develop new systems and do upgrades the risk coefficient from substandard wire will decline."

"And, NASA finds that acceptable?"

"NASA accepts reality and the necessity to continue the program." Friend of a friend added, "I'm not justifying or defending the decision. I called to give you information that you might find useful. It is now less about NASA. There might be other companies out there who are unknowingly still using defective wire after being defrauded by this Orztech bunch. Maybe, if you shine a light on the subject other potential disasters can be averted. Maybe, the legal system will get involved and bring the perpetrators to justice. Maybe you will be instrumental in righting a wrong."

"I will pursue this," Jack confirmed.

"I know you will."

"Is there anything else that I should know?"

"If I think of anything, I'll call. But, don't wait for it."

The connection ended.

Wanda Six Trees and her daughter Anna worked in the garden. It was time for the first harvest of maize and squash. Even though only six years old, Anna followed behind her mother dragging her basket and carefully placing squash into it.

33: Thursday – July 31, 1969

Stephanie Ellis noticed a change in her father. She wasn't sure what to make of it. He seemed distracted and preoccupied. Physically, he was getting stronger and he often took long walks or went out for hours at a time. In her mind it was a good thing that he was getting out but his odd mood was a concern. She chose not to confront him. After all, he was an adult and was still trying to find a way of fitting into a world that had passed him by. For whatever reason that thought made her think of her mother, Valerie.

It was two years earlier, in the fall. Stephanie was a junior in high school and had just started a new school year. She was sixteen-years-old. They had moved into an apartment in Bergenfield, NJ during the summer so everything was different. With no friends and everything new and strange, Stephanie had become quiet and withdrawn.

On a Friday afternoon when she arrived home from school she found a note on her pillow. It said, "Don't get undressed. We are going rabbit hunting. Mom." Stephanie smiled. She wasn't sure what it meant but looked forward to spending some mother/daughter time together. While many sixteen-year-olds might not feel that way, Stephanie was a latchkey kid therefore she valued time with her mother. In the afternoons when she was alone she often felt lonely. During those times, she fell prey to her record keeping obsession. Notebook after notebook was filled with her lists. Anything that she valued was listed. Then she began to list things she saw and words whose definition she didn't know. On some occasions she would focus on her homework in order to not get into listing. A side effect was improved grades.

On the night of the rabbit hunt her mother arrived home at five thirty. She was obviously tired but put on a happy face and enthusiastic front. "Happy Weekend," she exclaimed.

Stephanie replied, "Happy Weekend!"

"Are you ready to go rabbit hunting?" Valerie asked her daughter.

"Do I need a gun or bow and arrow?"

"Nope, all you need is to come with me."

Mother and daughter left their apartment and walked the few blocks to Washington Avenue which runs through the center of Bergenfield's retail district. "Now, you have to keep your eyes open or you might miss the rabbit," Valerie warned.

Stephanie was confused but played along. It was rare for her mother to joke and kid. "I've never seen any rabbits on Washington Avenue," Stephanie observed.

"You just didn't look in the right place."

"Where is the right place?"

"Right over here," Valerie said as she directed her daughter into a record shop. They walked over to where the new album releases were and Valerie picked up *Surrealistic Pillow* by Jefferson Airplane. She pointed at the second song, *White Rabbit*, and said there's the rabbit. The album contained nine songs 1. *Somebody to Love*, 2. *White Rabbit*, 3. *She Has Funny Cars*, 4. *Today*, 5. *My Best Friend*, 6. *Comin' Back to Me*, 7. *D.C.B.A. -25*, 8. *How Do You Feel*, 9. *Embryonic Journey*.

Stephanie stood looking at the album not sure what to say. Then reality set in and she said in a slightly higher tone of voice, "You mean I can have it?"

"If you want it."

"I do," Stephanie held the record to her chest and said, "I love Grace Slick." After a pause she added, "You said you didn't want me listening to this kind of music."

"I changed my mind," Valerie said. She then asked, "Are you hungry. Do you want to get a pizza?"

"I can't. I'm on a diet," Stephanie answered sadly.

"Since when?"

"Since never—let's go," Stephanie smiled and took her mother's hand. After they purchased the record album they walked up Washington Avenue, turned down a side street, and entered a small Italian restaurant that they went to on rare occasions.

Over pizza they talked about school, work, the weather, her father, braces that they couldn't afford, and more. Finally, Stephanie asked her mother, "Why did you decide to let me buy this record?"

She remembered her mother sitting back and straightening her napkin looking very poised and dignified. Valerie answered, "When I was sixteen-years-old we listened to music on the radio. I remember Eddie Howard singing *For Sentimental Reasons*, Frank Sinatra *Day By Day* and *They Say It's Wonderful,* and Sarah Vaughn singing *If You Could See Me Now.* Because . . . I . . . was . . . a dancer . . . I also listened to classical music. When we kids got together we often would listen to jazz. People like Dizzie Gillespie, John Coltrane, Charlie Parker and bebop with Lester Young, Joe Oliver, Fletcher Henderson, Andie Kirk and Count Basie. We listened to Billie Holiday sing *Me Myself and I, Foolin' Myself,* and *Mean to Me.*"

Stephanie ate a piece of pizza and listened to her mother reminisce.

Valerie continued, "I know these names don't mean anything to you. To us they were swell." She smiled having used an outdated word. Her mother continued, "Of course, we didn't have Dick Clark and *American Bandstand.* We didn't even have television."

"Wow."

"And, our parents were as concerned about us listening to the devil's music as we are today. But, when I thought about it I decided that you are a smart young lady. You are responsible and we have already had our sex and drugs talks. In other words, I trust you."

"Thank you."

"Because I trust you I know simply listening to music isn't going to drive you to drugs or promiscuous behavior. The world is getting pretty wild and young people are acting out in so many ways. All I can do is give you the best advice that I can and hope for the best. For that reason I decided not to censor your music."

"I appreciate that and won't let you down," Stephanie replied.

"In many ways, I feel that I have let you down," her mother lamented.

"No, you haven't."

"If I had been smarter, maybe I could have gotten a better job and we would still be living in Alpine."

"That doesn't matter."

"I always wanted the best for you—my little girl. From the time you were a baby, I feared that I wasn't doing things correctly. The last thing I want, is for you to have to overcome my poor parenting. My mother always knew what to say or do and made everything work. Sadly I've come to realize that I'm not my mother."

"You're a great mother," Stephanie said holding up the record album.

Valerie smiled and then went on to say, "Right after Pearl Harbor my father joined the Army. I remember him and my mother talking at the kitchen table. I was eleven. He was old enough to miss the draft but felt it was his duty. They spoke so softly I couldn't hear what they were saying. Every now and then my mother would nod. What struck me most was the fact that they were holding hands."

"When he left for the Army he kissed me and told me to obey my mother. Then he and my mother embraced and held each other for a long time. Finally, he walked out and I saw that my mother was crying. I don't remember ever seeing her cry before."

"While my father was in the Army my mother ran our store. It was a small grocery store on a corner in Riverdale. Times were tough. The Office of Price Administration (OPA) froze prices on practically all goods, starting with sugar and coffee. Rationing was enforced on sugar, coffee, meat, butter, fats, cheese, oil, gasoline, and hundreds of other products. Coupon books were issued and ration coins for different products. It was quite a problem keeping up, but my mother did. We had a car but were given an A Sticker which meant we could get only four gallons of gasoline a week. B Sticker cars were considered essential therefore they could get eight gallons a week. Truckers, members of Congress, and other V.I.P.s could get as much gasoline as they wanted. Mom worked long hours but kept that little store operating."

"After school I would go to the store or dance class. When I went to the store I helped as much as I could or did my homework. Through it all my mother stayed strong and positive. All alone she kept our family going. She did a far better job back then than I am doing now."

"I think you are doing a great job."

"Thank you sweetheart. I am trying. However, I'm no Harriet Louise Matheson."

"I'm sorry that I didn't know grandmother."

"She died in 1950, the same year your father and I were married. She was only thirty-eight-years-old. It was an undetected heart abnormality." Valerie sat in silence for a moment as if trying to picture her mother once more. She then said, "At least she was able to see me get married." After an additional pause Valerie added, "I'm just so sorry that she didn't get to see you and come to know how wonderful you are."

Stephanie remembered that day as clearly as if it was the day before. She and her mother enjoyed the rest of the day and even listened to the Jefferson Airplane album together. It struck Stephanie that her mother's mother died of a heart abnormality at the age of thirty-eight—the same as her mother. A thought entered her mind that could not be ignored. It was more of a question that one would rather not ask. Could she have the same genes that caused an undetectable heart ailment that would dramatically shorten her life? Was she destined to live thirty-eight years and no more? She went over to a shelf and retrieved the record album *Surrealistic Pillow* and placed it on her record player. The first song, *Somebody to Love,* filled the room. Grace Slick's pure voice sang directly to Stephanie.

When the truth is found to be lies
And all the joy within you dies
Don't you want somebody to love?
Don't you need somebody to love?
Wouldn't you love somebody to love?
You better find somebody to love. (love, love, love)

When the morning flowers, baby are dead, yes.
And your mind, (your mind) is so full of dread.
Don't you want somebody to love?
Don't you need somebody to love?
Wouldn't you love somebody to love?
You better find somebody to love.

Your eyes, I say your eyes may look like his,
Yeah, but in your head, baby, I'm afraid you don't know where it is.
Don't you want somebody to love?
Don't you need somebody to love?
Wouldn't you love somebody to love?
You better find somebody to love.

Tears are running, yeah running down your vest.
And your friends, baby, they treat you like a guest.
Don't you want somebody to love?
Don't you need somebody to love?
Wouldn't you love somebody to love?
You better find somebody to love.

Stephanie sat in silence holding a photo of her mother. She stood in front of a church. Her shoulder-length brown hair and brown eyes complemented the green dress she wore. Even in a photograph she had an air of sophistication. Or, was it the trained posture of a dancer? Stephanie thought how beautiful her mother was and how warm, caring, and gentle she could be. Yet, she endured a lack of self-confidence. It had been a year since her mother died but the pain remained. The next song, *White Rabbit*, began.

One pill makes you larger
And one pill makes you small
And the ones that mother gives you
Don't do anything at all
Go ask Alice
When she's ten feet tall

And if you go chasing rabbits
And you know you're going to fall
Tell 'em a hookah smoking caterpillar
Has given you the call
To call Alice
When she was just small

When the men on the chessboard
Get up and tell you where to go
And you've just had some kind of mushroom
And your mind is moving low
Go ask Alice
I think she'll know

When logic and proportion
Have fallen slowly dead
And the White Knight is talking backwards
And the Red Queen's off with her head
Remember what the dormouse said
Feed your head, feed your head

As the song ended Stephanie carefully placed her mother's picture on a table. She looked at it for a long time then whispered, "You were better than Harriet Louise Matheson." She sobbed as she felt so small and so alone.

"Kiss me, Rita." Detective Michael Donovan bellowed loudly in the squad room.

"Kiss yourself," Detective Ryoya Akimoto replied without looking up. This drew laughter from the other detectives present.

"Is that any way to talk to your partner?"

"Ahh, did I hurt your feelings?" Ryoya purred as she continued to review the papers on her desk.

Michael Donovan put on a sad face and replied, "Yes, you did."

"Good."

Detective Donovan sat on the edge of Ryoya's desk. He reached into his jacket pocket and pulled out two tickets. "Then I guess you don't want these. Two tickets to tomorrow's Mets game," he announced.

Ryoya Akimoto finally looked up from her paperwork. "Where did you get those—off your bookie?"

"No, someone owed me a favor and dropped them on me."

"Well, why don't you go to the game?"

"And root for the Mets? You got to be kidding me."

"They're doing better than the Yankees."

"I don't care. I'm a Dodger fan."

"Oh that's right. Still can't believe they left Brooklyn?"

"They'll be back."

"Don't count on it."

"I figured you and Jerry could go to the game."

"Jack."

"That's right. Well, anyway, they're yours if you want them."

"What's the catch?"

"No catch. I know you're a Mets fan and they're playing the first-place Atlanta Braves. Should be a good game. They'll get their asses kicked, but still should be a good game," Michael Donovan explained. After a pause, he added, "We are off tomorrow."

"And, in return you want?"

"Nothing."

"I don't believe you."

Donovan lowered his voice, "Rita, Jack's a good guy. Regardless of where this relationship is ultimately going the two of you like baseball and enjoy going together. Why not have a good time tomorrow and stop worrying about the future." He didn't tell Ryoya that he purchased the tickets.

Ryoya took the tickets offered by her partner and simply said, "OK, you talked me into it."

Donovan smiled and said, "What about my kiss?"

Detective Akimoto stood turned to go to the filing room and patted her rear end while saying, "Kiss this."

Michael Donovan laughed.

Mike Irwin called the Malibu Sheriff's station. He told the deputy that he, John Nicks, and Glenn Giardinelli had gone to 964 Old Topanga Canyon Road to check on a friend, Gary Hinman. They hadn't heard or seen him in a week which was unusual since he was very dependable as a music teacher. It was unlike him to not show up for work and not call. Upon arrival at Hinman's house they noticed that his cars were missing. When they went on the porch they detected a strong odor at which time they went to a neighbor's house and made the call to the police.

At 8:05 p.m. Deputies Paul Z. Piet, badge 761 and Donald Lang, badge 1336 arrived at the scene. They walked around the house and observed numerous flies at a southeast window that was partially open. Deputy Piet found a ladder and climbed it to look in the window. Inside he saw a body on the floor leaning against a wall. The two deputies entered the residence through an unlocked window in the kitchen.

The police report stated: "Victim had a blanket covering his body and a pillow partially covering the left side of his face. Victim was observed to be in a decomposed condition, face blackened with maggots on and around the head area. We observed splotches of blood on the blanket in the area of victim's chest."

Deputy Paul Piet contacted Sergeant Wheteley of the homicide division and was advised to secure the scene. Sergeant Wheteley arrived at 9:45 p.m. and Deputy Coroner Greene arrived at 11:30 p.m. and removed the body.

Because the victim's vehicles were missing a "want" was put out for them. Sadly, three days earlier Los Angeles Deputies Olmstead and Grap had visited the Spahn Ranch on another matter and had seen the Fiat station wagon that belonged to Gary Hinman. When they ran a check on the plates and determined he was the owner they didn't think anything of it because Deputy Grap knew he was a friend of the people at the ranch. Unfortunately, both deputies were busy on other assignments and didn't learn of Gary Hinman's murder until much later.

When Robert Six Trees awoke he knew what he had to do. It was the fourth time that he had dreamed of a fox. According to their culture any animal that visits a dreamer four or more times becomes the individual's spirit guide. Robert would create a fox totem which would bring him luck, protection, and guidance.

34: Friday - August 1, 1969

"There's a trail going this way right to the LZ," Two Tone said as he looked at the map with Wellington Marsh.

"That would be easy, but I don't like it," Wellington replied. They were at the end of a night field exercise and only had to make it to the landing zone (LZ) to complete the assignment.

"Easy is good."

"Not in the Marines. Easy is a setup. They want us to walk into an ambush to teach us a lesson."

"Well, do you have a better idea, squad leader?" he emphasized the title squad leader.

"I think we should go east to this stream. Then follow it northwest until we get to this clearing. If we stay just inside the tree line we can come into this area here from behind where I think they'll be waiting to smoke our tails."

"That will take twice as long."

"Maybe even more, but it is better than walking into an ambush."

"If there is an ambush," Two Tone lamented.

"This whole night has been filled with the unexpected. Now that its sunup it doesn't mean the tricks will stop."

"You're the squad leader."

In the Marine Corps, a squad is typically composed of three fire teams of four Marines and a squad leader, who is typically a Sergeant or Corporal. Wellington told the twelve Marines that he led of his plan. There were a few tired grunts and groans by those who just wanted to get back to the barracks and into the rack. Other than that—no protests. So, fire team Whiskey, Echo, Lima headed east. Tom Drewsberry was on point. At first, it was slow going as they were moving directly into the rising sun making visibility limited. As they progressed Wellington checked the map again and again. He became concerned because they should have reached the stream by his reckoning, yet hadn't. Fatigue and inexperience opened the door to self-doubt. Did he get them lost in the North Carolina wilderness? Did the planners of this exercise anticipate his decision to not use the obvious path? Is there any way to not go to Vietnam?

Just before Wellington was going to order his team to go back to the path the point man raised his arm to stop the team. He returned to Wellington and said, "I see it. The stream. It's right up ahead. It doesn't look too deep."

"Good. We'll head upstream."

For the next hour the team of exhausted Marines moved silently up stream. The sun heated the countryside making it more and more uncomfortable. August humidity caused them all to sweat profusely. They were hot, tired, hungry and filthy but none complained. Then they broke out of the trees into a clearing. Wellington called a stop and five minute break. He studied his map.

Shortstop came over and asked, "Are we almost where we are supposed to be?"

Wellington smiled, looked up, and replied, "We are where I decided we would be. I'm just trying to figure out what our next step should be."

"Get back to the barracks for a shower, food, and sleep."

"I'd like that too. But, I want us to get there without failing the test."

"What test?"

"They want to train us to be Marines."

"We are Marines."

"Well, they want to train us to be live Marines."

"Yeah, til we gets to Vietnam."

"We have a better chance of staying alive over there if we learn all we can here," Wellington explained.

Jackson Smith, a large black Marine from Louisiana came over to where Wellington was sitting. His large frame made it look as though he was about to explode out of his fatigues. Big hands wrapped around the M-14 that he carried. He stopped in front of Welling and said, "Boy, where you from?"

"Detroit."

"A city boy. Well, city boy you is sitting in poison ivy."

Wellington jumped up and turned to look at the offending plant.

"Get yo ass over to that stream and sit it in the water. Don't touch your pants or y'all be itching for a week."

Wellington did as Jackson told him.

"What the hell?" one of the Marines asked.

Jackson told him, "City boy done sat in poison ivy."

The fire team laughed which embarrassed Wellington. But, then comments like, "Better you than me. What's that stuff look like? I feel like I'm itchy all over," made Wellington realize that most of the team didn't know poison ivy from a head of lettuce.

"Jackson," Wellington called out, "Show the team what poison ivy looks like so we can avoid it."

With the rest period over and Wellington's pants soaking wet they continued on, skirting the forest on their left. Twenty minutes later the point guard came back and said he saw movement in the trees ahead. Fire team Whiskey, Echo, Lima entered the woods and slowly made their way in the direction of the observed movement. In a few minutes they were on a ridge looking down into a low area that ran along the path that they had declined to follow. In the low area were approximately twelve Marines with M-14s and two machine guns waiting to ambush them when they came down the path. Wellington wasn't sure what his next move should be. He tried to remember the orders given them twelve hours earlier when they were dropped off in the wilderness. They were ordered to find their way to a designated LZ by noon the next day. It would mean moving at night if they were going to make it by noon. They were to avoid contact with the enemy as this was a reconnaissance mission. With their orders in mind, Wellington had the team work their way around the ambush and onto the path out of their sight. He warned all team members to be on the lookout for any kind of booby trap. So close to their destination he didn't want to have any mishaps.

At ten-forty-seven in the morning team Whiskey, Echo, Lima entered the LZ. A mobile kitchen had been set up with hot coffee and food. Wellington reported to a surprised Staff Sergeant who asked, "Where'd you come from? I didn't hear gunfire."

"We snuck around the ambush," Wellington explained.

"Well, I'll be damned," the sergeant replied.

"Takaramono. It means treasure," Jack Moore told Ryoya. "I chose it because you are my treasure."

Ryoya sat in silence holding the gold necklace with small Japanese figures. She fought back tears. It had been a long, long time since she felt so touched by something someone did for her. As it turned out that someone was her father. He was a strong man who took care of his family without complaint or any show of weakness. This strength often made him seem insensitive, rigid, or self-righteous. What emotions he felt always remained unseen. Four years earlier, Ryoya had a glimpse of the depth of his feelings when she got her gold shield designating her as a New York City Police Detective. She and her father sat in the small back yard of her parent's house in Brooklyn. The yard was immaculate with gardens surrounding a small pagoda style gazebo. She had just told him of her promotion and handed him her gold shield. Takashi Akimoto held the shield in his hands. He had made it clear that he didn't support his daughter becoming a police officer. It didn't fit his vision of Ryoya learning the tea ceremony, marrying a successful Japanese man, and having children. Over the years, though, he slowly accepted her choice of career but never said much about it. On this night, holding her gold shield, he looked at his daughter and said, "Watashi o yurushite (forgive me)." Ryoya started to speak to tell him no apology was necessary but he held his hand up silencing her. He continued, "Watashi wa anata o hokori ni omotte (I am proud of you)." He then fell silent. Ryoya waited. When he tried to speak once more his voice cracked and he turned away. For a prolonged period father and daughter remained in the gazebo in silence. Finally, he rose bowed and took Ryoya's hands in his and pulled her toward him. He kissed her cheek and said, "Anata wa watashi no taiyō no hikaridesu (You are my sunshine)." He turned and entered the house. Her gold shield sat on the table reflecting the light from a lantern that hung above. As important as her gold shield was to her, her father's praise was the jewel of that evening.

Over breakfast Jack had given Ryoya the "treasure" necklace. He told her it was for no particular reason. When he saw the gold necklace in a small shop it was among a number of necklaces with different Japanese characters and meanings. They all made him think of Ryoya, however, when the girl told him the meaning of this piece of jewelry he was sold. It was perfect because it clearly defined what he thought of her. Ryoya was his treasure—a treasure that through some wonderful quirk of fate had come his way. He also knew that he owed Harry Van Ryker a steak dinner.

When he gave the gift to Ryoya he didn't expect any more reaction than a simple thank you. The fact that she sat opposite him in silence holding the necklace lost in thought caught Jack off guard. He decided the best approach was to wait. So, he ate his breakfast.

Their waitress arrived with a coffee pot to provide refills. She spotted the necklace and proclaimed, "Oh, hon that's beautiful."

"Thank you," Ryoya said, adding, "it means treasure."

The waitress looked at Jack and smiled as she said, "That's sweet. Why do the good ones always get away?" She hurried off to another table.

Ryoya took Jack's hand and started to speak but quickly stood and said, "Excuse me." She left and headed for the restroom.

Jack sat sipping his coffee wondering if he did a good thing or a bad thing. Sometimes women confused him. When he does something for which he should apologize they act as though it was their fault and try to make him feel better. Now, when he does something nice he feels like he should apologize. Go figure, women are a mystery with a logic that is all their own and it's a no men allowed club.

When Ryoya returned to the table she was wearing the necklace. Jack rose and after Ryoya sat he followed. Neither spoke for a few minutes. Ryoya looked at Jack and saw a wonderful man, a man she enjoyed being with, a man she respected, a man who cared about her, a man who made her laugh, and a man she was destined to hurt. Ultimately, it would have to come down to a choice between Jack and her father. She knew which she would choose. Her Japanese culture was too deeply instilled in her. Respect and honor outweighed personal desires.

That afternoon the New York Mets hosted the Western Division first-place Atlanta Braves. The Mets were in second place in the Eastern Division behind the Chicago Cubs by a significant six and a half games. This was the first year that each league had been split into East and West Divisions. They also added four expansion teams; Kansas City Royals, Montreal Expos, San Diego Padres, and Seattle Pilots.

The seats that Detective Donovan had given them were perfect. Located on the first base side of the field just past first base in section 25 of the Loge Level they provided a perfect view. Both Ryoya and Jack wore Mets caps. Jack had given in and decided to root for the Mets but made it clear if they ever played the Yankees his loyalty was with the Bronx Bombers.

The game didn't start out well for Ryoya's Mets. Don Cardwell was the starting pitcher for the Mets. Filipe Alou led off with a single to right field. Tony Gonzalez was hit by a pitch. Then Hank Aaron drew a walk. It was loaded bases with nobody out. Jack couldn't help himself and he said, "I hear there's a good movie at the Rialto." Ryoya stared at him but didn't reply. A run scored when Orlando Cepeda was also walked.

Ryoya looked at Jack who knew better than to say anything and said, "Shut up!"

Clete Boyer hit a pop up foul ball which was caught for the first out of the inning. Unfortunately, Felix Milan hit a single to left field allowing two more runs to be scored. Jack more seriously said, "It's not his day. They have to take the pitcher out, his control is not there." No sooner had he said that when Gil Hodges, the Mets manager, came walking out of the dugout. He waved for Cal Koonce to replace the pitcher. After an intentional walk to set up a double play the next two batters grounded out and hit a pop fly for the final outs of the inning. After half an inning the Mets trailed by three runs.

Ryoya turned to Jack and said, "Don't be so pessimistic. We have nine innings."

"Anything can happen."

"Exactly."

"Right." Jack looked up toward the cloudless sky and said, "Maybe it will rain."

Things got better when the Mets came to bat. Bud Harrelson hit a single to right field. This was followed by singles by Bobby Pfeil and Tommie Agee loading the bases with no one out.

"It's about to rain," Ryoya commented.

Wayne Garrett hit a fly ball to shallow left field holding all the runners. One out. Ed Kranepool came to bat and was struck out. Two out.

"Looks more like a drizzle," Jack stated.

Ryoya shoved him causing him to splash beer on his paints. "See, it's raining," she observed.

Then it happened, Ron Swoboda was walked which drove in a run. Rod

Casper followed with a single to right field driving in two runs and tying the score. Ryoya jumped up and yelled, "Way to go Rod."

When Jerry Grote came to bat Jack got into the spirit of rooting for the Mets. "Come'on Jerry bring em home," he yelled. This must have shaken up the pitcher because his next pitch was wild and got past the catcher. The passed ball allowed Ron Swoboda to score. Eventually, Jerry Grote walked. Cal Koonce, the relief pitcher, struck out ending the inning. After one inning the Mets led the Atlanta Braves four to three.

"Quite a pitcher's duel, wouldn't you say," Jack said sarcastically.

"They shouldn't have started Cardwell. He's 3 and 9 this season and hasn't had anything on his fast ball. Back in 64 he hurt his arm and I don't think he ever got it all back—controlwise. He hit at least ten batters last year," Ryoya stated.

"And one today."

"He's 34, at that age you have to be a control pitcher. Last year he won 7 and lost 13," Ryoya pointed out.

"So, you think they should trade him or send him down to the minors?"

"No, I think he has to change his choice of pitches and pitch a controlled game. He needs to throw a splitter that looks good until it drops into the dirt. Power hitters generally miss or top the ball hitting a bouncer into the infield. If he uses a forkball he can throw slower than with a fastball or splitter. Then mix in off-speed pitches and sliders and save the fastball for a setup pitch."

Jack was impressed by her knowledge of baseball. He thought for a second and then asked, "Do you mind if I use your recommendation in my column?"

"I don't want to be quoted."

"I won't quote you, I just want to point out what he should consider doing."

"That's fine, just don't quote me."

Jack looked at Ryoya and knew she was something very special. Upon seeing the necklace he thought, you are a treasure. The game continued with no scoring until Mets player Jerry Grote hit a lead-off homerun in the bottom of the fourth inning extending their lead to five to three. Jack and Ryoya enjoyed a great afternoon with the Mets going on to win the game 5 to 4.

"What did you break?" Ray Esposito asked Carl knowing full well the answer.

Carl held up his middle finger aimed at East River Vito who warned, "Hey, watch it, kid. I may take that personally." They all laughed.

"Why that finger?" Ray asked.

"It really wasn't my choice," Carl admitted. "When I slammed him into the wall he broke it so I figured, OK, that takes care of that."

"He hasn't come across with the scratch, yet," Ray stated. "He has until midnight. After that we have to make some decisions. If he doesn't make a payment I will have another job for you."

"Whatever you say."

"I heard you had some trouble with some spic."

"Yeah. These two bailed me out. I'm not sure what would have happened if they hadn't come along."

"We take care of our own," Fat Tony said. Carl didn't react but the fact that he was described as "one of their own" made a distinct impression on him. He knew he was where he belonged. It was where he wanted to be. Whatever the outcome he had an identity and a place in a crew. In his mind he was home.

"I put the word out to lay off of you," Ray said. "That doesn't mean to let your guard down. These street punks don't always take good advice."

"You should get yourself a piece," East River advised.

Ray added, "Tony, take the kid to the range tomorrow. Teach him how to shoot. I don't want him armed and then have him shoot himself in the nuts." The three men laughed. He turned to Carl and ordered, "Get ready for tonight's game, kid."

Robert Six Trees carved on a piece of wood. His sister, Anna came over and asked, "What is that?"

"It's going to be a fox," he answered.

"It doesn't look like a fox," she said.

"Not yet, but it will."

She sat down next to him and watched as he continued to work.

35: Wednesday – August 6, 1969

At approximately 10:50 a.m., California Highway Patrolman Joe Humphrey was traveling northbound on Highway 101 south of the Cuesta Hotel when he spotted a car on the shoulder of the road. He stopped to investigate. As he approached the vehicle a young man in a sleeping bag in the rear of the station wagon sat up.

Robert Kenneth Beausoleil explained that his car had broken down during the night. He produced the owner's certificate and registration card but couldn't show any personal identification. He gave his name as Jason Lee Danials. Beausoleil further told the officer that he had purchased the 1965 Fiat 1100 station wagon from three black men in Los Angeles for $200 cash. When Patrolman Joe Humphrey did a check of the license plate, OYX 833, the car came back as stolen and wanted by the Los Angeles Sheriff's Office. He was told that the car was to be impounded and held for prints. Given that information Beausoleil was placed under arrest for a 10851 of the California Vehicle Code, driving or taking a vehicle not his or her own without the consent of the owner.

At the San Luis Obispo County Jail Beausoleil gave his real name. In his wallet the investigating officer found the owner's certificate, registration card, and a Union Oil credit card belonging to Sheryl A. McAdams. When the detective saw APB BC-10 Date 8-3-69 from the Los Angeles Sheriff's Office which stated that the owner of the car was deceased he placed Beausoleil under arrest for 187 of the Penal Code—murder.

Jack Moore sat in his office at the *New York Tribune* and reviewed his notes. On Monday he had researched public records on Orztech Corporation and found that the company had been headquartered at 811 Sixth Avenue, New York but closed for business May 21, 1967. The president of the corporation had been a Parker Adolphson whose last known address was 691 Young Avenue, Pelham, New York. He found an annual report for Orztech Corporation and saw that the company manufactured numerous products, including wire, and was profitable at the time it closed its doors.

On Tuesday Jack had ventured out to Pelham and found Parker Adolphson at home. The retired president of Orztech Corporation didn't wish to talk with the press. He tried to close the door numerous times but Jack kept pushing for answers. Finally, Jack said, "Fine, if you won't tell me the truth, I'll print what I know. Parker Adolphson, president of Orztech Corporation knowingly sold inferior wire products to NASA thus putting America's astronauts in jeopardy."

At that point the older man opened the door and simply said, "OK, what do you want to know?"

From their conversation Jack had learned that, in fact, inferior wire had been sold to NASA. It was done without the knowledge of anyone at Orztech Corporation except for the perpetrator of the fraud, a Matthew Ellis, the then vice-president of Orztech in charge of the wire division. Due to demands that exceeded their capacity he had outsourced the manufacture of high efficiency, low resistance, stranded wire coated with insulation that was impervious to heat and chemical breakdown. He made all arrangements and approved the product. Adolphson gave the name of the company that manufacturing was outsourced to as LPAmerica and the contact as Lida Petropoulos. He didn't know how to contact them. Invoices had been processed through the Orztech billing department and most of those files had been destroyed. Jack also learned that Matthew Ellis had been in an automobile accident in 1963 and was in a coma for six years. Earlier in the current year Ellis woke from the coma and was recuperating. His last known address was in Alpine, New Jersey. Parker Adolphson did not share the fact that the same suspect wire had been sold to the military, aviation and automotive industries, as well as other businesses. He did state that after they made the discovery of the inferior wire that they had contacted NASA immediately. This jack knew wasn't true. He asked who they contacted at NASA and Adolphson couldn't recall. Finally, Jack asked why they went out of business while still profitable. Adolphson simple told him that the board-of-directors, himself included, decided that it was time. Jack thought, "Time to distance themselves from major lawsuits and possible criminal prosecution." Inside the house a telephone rang giving Parker Adolphson the opportunity to end the conversation and shut the door.

Tuesday afternoon brought more research as Jack tried to locate Matthew Ellis. He and his wife did indeed own a house in Alpine, New Jersey but it had been sold. There was no forwarding address. Hospitals rarely gave out patient information and Englewood Hospital that had cared for Matthew Ellis was no exception. Even when Jack turned on the charm, if that was what it could be called, he received little assistance. One nurse, however, did provide a clue when she said, "We were all surprised when the patient suddenly woke up. Even Doctor Tallman was amazed." Jack followed that lead right to the office of Dr. Gordon Tallman.

"I'm writing an article on NASA and have been told that Matthew Ellis and Orztech Corporation supplied wire that was used on the moon landing vehicles," Jack explained over the telephone. "Unfortunately, I don't know how to contact him."

"We aren't allowed to give out personal information about patients," a female voice responded.

"All I ask is a telephone number or address."

"I wish I could help but there are strict rules."

"May I speak to Dr. Tallman?"

"He's with a patient."

"If I leave you my name and telephone number would you give him a message and ask him to call me?"

"He's very busy."

"Well, give it a try," Jack added, "What is your name?"

"Why?"

"Well, I might put you in my story as being warm and helpful in my search to find Matthew Ellis."

"It's Ginger Harbough," a far more enthusiastic voice answered, "The *New York Tribune* you say?"

"Yes, Jack Moore with the *Tribune*."

"I'll give Doctor Tallman your message."

"Thank you, Ginger."

Jack didn't expect much to come from that conversation. He was wrong. Later in the day Dr. Gordon Tallman called. After a short conversation he told Jack that Matthew Ellis was living with his daughter, Stephanie, in an apartment in Dumont,

New Jersey. The doctor explained that he was not at liberty to discuss Matthew Ellis' medical status but felt there was no issue with providing contact information.

On Wednesday, Jack called the Ellis household and a young woman answered. After determining that she was Stephanie Ellis, Matthew's daughter, Jack explained the reason for his call. "Your father worked for Orztech Corporation that supplied wire to NASA. I'm doing a story on all of the companies that are a part of the historical moon landing. I'd very much like to interview him."

"He's not at home at the moment," Stephanie explained.

"Do you know when he will be back?"

"He's very unpredictable. Sometimes he goes out for an hour and other times he disappears for a whole day."

"I heard that he is recovering from being in a coma for six years. How is he doing?"

"Remarkably well. He no longer is using a cane and is building up his weakened muscles with exercises. The biggest problem he has is lost memory." She paused then added, "Oh, and he keeps being surprised by all the changes in the world."

"Changes?"

"I guess we don't think about it, but when you miss six years, things are really different when you wake up. He was amazed that I had an AM/FM radio."

Jack thought about that comment. It was true. We experience change slowly so we take it in stride like it is nothing unusual. However, if you are disconnected for a period of time the changes are startling. Much like when you reconnect with a childhood friend after twenty years. He commented, "That's understandable because FM was first offered in cars as an option in 1963. And, in 1964 the Federal Communications Commission (FCC) ordered radio stations to stop simulcasting their AM programs on their FM frequencies. This caused stations to have to program their FM broadcasts. Your father was in a coma when all of this was happening."

"FM is so much better."

"That's because it is frequency modulation, or FM, which creates a superior sound free of static that you experience with amplitude modulation, or AM."

"What?"

"With AM the strength of the signal varies while with FM the frequency of how often the current changes direction varies with the signal strength remaining constant."

"I don't understand."

"Well, all it means is the FM signal is better than the AM signal."

"FM stations also play more music and some stations play whole albums. That is so cool."

"Yeah, I like that, too."

Stephanie lamented, "My father missed the entire Beatles' invasion."

The meteoric rise of a British band made history and changed the music industry forever. Teenagers John Lennon and Paul McCartney had a chance meeting at a church event in the late 1950s. The two hit it off and decided to form a band. McCartney recruited his younger schoolmate George Harrison to play guitar and Lennon talked art college friend, Stu Sutcliffe, to play bass. The group broke into the Liverpool club scene and, after hiring drummer Pete Best, also played clubs in Hamburg, West Germany.

In 1960 they went by the name Beatals in honor of Buddy Holly and the Crickets. May of the same year they changed it to the Silver Beetles. Once more, while on tour in Scotland in early July, they changed it to the Silver Beatles and finally in

August settled on The Beatles. For the next two years they played in clubs in England and Germany gaining a loyal following. Stu Sutcliffe, who never really learned how to play bass, remained in Hamburg, where he later died of a brain hemorrhage related to a head injury. McCartney began playing bass.

Brian Epstein, a record-store owner and music columnist, became their manager in January, 1962. At that time the Beatles dressed in jeans, smoked, swore, and ate onstage during performances. He told them if they wanted to be taken seriously they would have to dress and behave more professionally. They listened. Epstein traded their leather look for tailored suits and long, thin ties and helped polish their overall presentation. A musical instrument retailer and designer, Ivor Arbiter, sketched a logo that had a capital B and T in the name. It stuck and was adopted by the group. The Beatles had a new image, a repertoire of music, and growing number of voracious fans. EMI decided to sign the Beatles in 1962 and a studio session was arranged. It was decided that their original drummer, Pete Best, was not right for the group and he was replaced with Ringo Starr in mid-August of 1962.

By 1963 the four members of the group, John Lennon, Paul McCartney, George Harrison, and Ringo Starr agreed that they would all contribute to the vocals. Lennon and McCartney also formed a songwriting partnership.

February 11, 1963 the Beatles recorded ten songs at the Abbey Road Studio during a single session for their debut album, *Please, Please Me.* The album reached number one in the United Kingdom. In August, the band's fourth single, *She Loves You,* generated the fastest sales of any record in the United Kingdom selling three-quarters of a million copies in under four weeks. Success brought increased media exposure. In November, they released their second album, *With The Beatles.* The band's public relations officer wrote the sleeve notes for the album. He used the phrase "fabulous foursome" which the media made "The Fab Four." After two albums and three United Kingdom tours they were well-established and often greeted by screaming and riotous fans. The press called this enthusiasm—Beatlemania. And yet, they were unknown in the United States.

Art Roberts, music director of Chicago radio station WLS, played *Please Please Me* in late February 1963. This was the first time a Beatles record was heard on American radio. In August 1963, Philadelphia-based Swan Records released *She Loves You,* which failed to receive airplay. An airing of the same song on Dick Clark's *American Bandstand* was greeted with laughter from American teenagers when they saw the group's hairstyles.

A five-minute news story shot in England about the phenomenon of Beatlemania aired on CBS Morning News on November 22, 1963. It had been scheduled to air on the evening news, as well, but with the assassination of President John F. Kennedy all programming was cancelled. Matthew Ellis never heard of the Beatles when an automobile accident on this very day sent him into a six year hibernation.

The news story eventually aired on the CBS evening news December 10, 1963. After seeing the program about the Beatles a Silver Spring, Maryland teenage girl named Marsha Albert wrote a radio disc jockey at radio station WWDC, Washington, DC requesting that he play Beatles records. The radio personality, Carroll James, played *I Want to Hold Your Hand* on December 17 and the audience response was overwhelming. Capitol Records took advantage of the increasing interest in the Beatles and released the single three weeks ahead of schedule on December 26, 1963. New York radio stations began playing *I Want to Hold Your Hand* on its release day and the response was just as enthusiastic as was experienced in Washington, D.C. Support spread to other markets and the first Beatles record released in America sold one million copies in ten days.

The Beatles came to America on February 7, 1964. When they landed at Kennedy Airport they were met by a crowd of three thousand screaming fans and countless reporters. At 8 o'clock on February 9, 1964 the Beatles appeared on the *Ed Sullivan Show*. 73 million people watched.

Ed Sullivan made the introduction, "Now yesterday and today our theater's been jammed with newspapermen and hundreds of photographers from all over the nation, and these veterans agreed with me that this city never has witnessed the excitement stirred by these youngsters from Liverpool who call themselves The Beatles. Now tonight, you're gonna twice be entertained by them. Right now, and again in the second half of our show. Ladies and gentlemen, The Beatles! Let's bring them on."

They opened with *All My Loving*. Then Paul McCartney sang *Till There Was You*. And, they wrapped up the first set with *She Loves You*. Throughout the performance teenage girls in the audience screamed. Other performers on the show that night were eclipsed by the Beatles. The Fab Four ended the night with *I Saw Her Standing There* and *I Want to Hold Your Hand*.

A week later, the February 24th issue of *Newsweek* magazine's cover featured a picture of The Beatles with the title, "Bugs About Beatles." The review of the *Ed Sullivan Show* went as follows, "Visually, they are a nightmare: tight, dandified, Edwardian/ Beatnik suits and great pudding bowls of hair. Musically, they are a near-disaster: guitars and drums slamming out a merciless beat that does away with secondary rhythms, harmony, and melody. Their lyrics (punctuated by nutty shouts of "yeah, yeah, yeah!") are a catastrophe, a preposterous farrago of Valentine-card romantic sentiments." At the end of the article the writer wrote, "The big question in the music business at the moment is: will the Beatles last? The odds are that, in the words of another era, they're too hot not to cool down, and a cooled-down Beatle is hard to picture. It is also hard to imagine any other field in which they could apply their talents, and so the odds are that they will fade away, as most adults confidently predict."

By the time the Fab Four headed back to England in late February 1964, over 60 percent of all records sold in America were Beatles records.

Because of the increasingly complex music that the Beatles incorporated in their songs that was hard to reproduce live and the interference of all the screaming fans they stopped doing concerts in 1966.

Brian Epstein died in 1967. His organizational skills and business acumen had been invaluable to the group. While they artistically continued to evolve, their lack of business experience led to disagreements and poor decisions. The creation of Apple Records was a costly mismanaged endeavor. John Lennon and Paul McCartney stopped collaborating on songs with each working on their own. George Harrison wasn't happy with the amount of representation that his works were getting. Adding to the tension, John Lennon refusal to go anywhere without Yoko Ono, his future wife.

The group got together in the summer of 1969 to record the album *Abbey Road* which turned out to be the last time they worked together. Just as with the space program Matthew Ellis missed most of these historic events.

"What else surprised your father?" Jack asked.

"Money is made different. Coins, I mean. They make a dull thud when dropped instead of a musical sound." Before Jack could comment Stephanie continued, "And football, he was surprised that the two leagues now have a championship game. He was really surprised that the American Football League New York Jets beat the National Football League Baltimore Colts 16 to 7 this year."

"It was called the Super Bowl," Jack added. "Joe Namath predicted the win and he delivered."

"I wonder if that name Super Bowl will stick."

"I doubt it. Sounds like something some newspaper reporter created," Jack concluded with a laugh. As a dialogue had started Jack wanted to continue it with well-placed questions about Matthew Ellis. He asked, "Was your father as impressed as we all were with the moon landing?"

"He was glued to our little TV. He reads everything he can about the space program," Stephanie answered. She added, "More than once he stated that Orztech was on the moon. He was very proud."

"Did he ever show any concern for the safety of the astronauts?"

"No. He had confidence that the scientists and designers knew what they were doing."

"Boy, I bit my nails until they were safely on the aircraft carrier."

"I don't know how they do it. I would be a basket case."

"Me too. Did your father ever mention a person named Lida Petropoulos?"

"No," Stephanie answered. She then asked, "Who is she?"

"I'm not sure. I think she helped with the manufacture of the wire."

"Oh, I don't know anything about that." There was a noise and Stephanie announced, "My father just came in. Let me tell him you want to speak with him."

After a pause and some inaudible discussion a man's voice came on the telephone, "Hello."

"Is this Matthew Ellis?"

"Yes, who is this?"

"Jack Moore with the *New York Tribune*." Jack added, "I enjoyed talking with your daughter."

"You want to know about NASA?"

"I have some questions that you might be able to help me with."

"You probably know more about NASA than me," Matt stated. He added, "I was injured in an automobile accident and in a coma for six years."

"I heard. I'm sorry that you had to go through all of that. The questions that I have pertain to Orztech Corporation and specifically wire supplied to NASA."

"I really don't know that I can help. My memory was affected by the accident and long coma. I only remember bits and pieces of my past."

Jack had the impression that the man was telling the truth and not trying to be evasive. He didn't try to quickly end the conversation as most guilty persons generally do. Jack decided to proceed as though he were dealing with a cooperating witness. He said, "I understand. Let's do our best and maybe that will be enough."

"I don't know if I'll be of any help."

"You were a vice-president at Orztech Corporation. Is that correct?"

"I believe so."

"You believe so?"

"I know that I worked there. I dealt with wire and NASA, but details, including my actual role and title, are not clear."

"Did you supervise the manufacture of wire sold to NASA?"

"No."

"No?"

"I remember meeting NASA and that a contract for high efficiency, low resistance, stranded wire coated with insulation that was impervious to heat and chemical breakdown was finalized the day of my accident."

Jack made notes as he considered what he had been told. He continued the interview, "Did you make arrangements to outsource manufacture of the wire?"

"I have vague memories of making arrangements, but I can't give you any details or tell you whether or not it was for NASA wire."

"Does the name Lida Petropoulos mean anything to you?"

"Yes."

"What can you tell me about her?"

"I've had fleeting images of meeting with her about manufacturing wire for Orztech. She would get it done overseas. After that, I'm not too clear."

"Do you know how I could reach her?"

"No."

"Have you contacted her after . . . uh . . . waking up from the coma?"

"I don't have any idea how to contact her."

"Do you know Parker Adolphson?"

"Of course, he was the president of Orztech."

"So that you are clear on?"

"Yes." After a pause, Matt added, "I went to his home . . . uh . . . two weeks ago . . . yes . . . it was exactly two weeks ago."

"Did you talk with him?"

"Yes."

"Why did you go to see him?"

"I was hoping he could help fill in the gaps in my memory. Also, to tell me what happened to Orztech."

"What did he tell you?"

"He was very angry with me and accused me of substituting inferior wire for what was ordered."

"Did you?"

"I don't know. I don't think that I would or did. Only, my memory is so limited that I can't say anything for sure. When I went there I was seeking answers. I left with more questions."

"Are you seeking answers to those questions?"

There was a long pause. Jack waited patiently not wanting to pressure a very cooperative interviewee. Finally, Matt answered, "I have been trying to fill in all the blank spaces in my memory. After speaking with Mr. Adolphson I don't know where to turn. The obvious next step is to find Lida Petropoulos, but I have no idea how to find her or where to begin looking."

"For the record," Jack said, "I have confirmation that NASA received inferior wire from Orztech Corporation. From how the spools were delivered it was deliberate fraud." There was no response from Matthew Ellis. Jack continued, "Either Parker Adolphson, Lida Petropoulos, you, or all of you perpetrated this fraud." There was still no answer. Jack asked, "Who do you believe was responsible?"

"I don't know."

"I've spoken with Adolphson and now you. It seems to me the next step is to find Lida Petropoulos."

"I wish I could help."

"Maybe you can."

At approximately 8:15 p.m., detectives went to the impound lot, Jim's Garage, 31 Higuera, San Luis Obispo, California. They took pictures and searched Gary Hinman's 1965 Fiat 1100 station wagon. Hidden in the tire well beneath the matting was a 5-inch hunting knife with a 1 ½-inch width blade in a leather scabbard.

Wanda Six Trees was concerned about the maturing wild rice. High summertime temperatures and very high humidity create ideal conditions for Helminthosporium disease. This and other blight conditions can wipe out a weak overcrowded stand in a matter of days.

36: Friday - August 8, 1969

"Now, that's a paint job," Big Bob Finley, owner of Finley's Auto Body, said.

Ritchie had just finished painting a 1966 Corvette Stingray. The right side of the car had dragged along a guard rail damaging the entire side. After repairs had been made to the fiberglass Ritchie told the owner the only way the Corvette would look factory fresh was to paint the entire care. Big Bob liked hearing that because he could charge more. After the owner agreed Ritchie went to work.

He began by sanding the entire car with 120 grit sand paper. Then wiped the car with wax and grease remover and applied three coats of urethane primer. After all coats had dried he lightly sanded the surface with 1200 grit sandpaper to remove the top layer of primer. Again, he wiped the car down with wax and grease remover using a lint-free cloth. The color of the Corvette was Nassau Blue. Ritchie sprayed four coats of paint onto the primed fiberglass. Finally, he applied three coats of clear varnish. The finished product was a vehicle that looked better than when it came from the factory.

Big Bob knew an artist when he saw one. His shop enjoyed a reputation as offering the best paint work in the New York Metropolitan area. A reputation that allowed for higher prices and one that drew customers from miles away. He grabbed his Polaroid Camera and took pictures of the finished Corvette. He then spoke to his paint star, "Ritchie, you have some talent." He peeled back the negative to reveal the photograph he just took and looked up, "Look how beautiful that is."

Ritchie nodded, but didn't say anything.

"OK, what's bothering you? Is it money?" Big Bob asked.

"No."

"Well, it's something. How can I help?"

"You know any congressmen or senators?"

"I know a hooker who knows some politicians," Big Bob laughed.

Ritchie smiled, "I doubt she'd be much help with the draft board."

"You drafted?" a shocked Big Bob asked. In his mind he pictured all the problems he would have with customers because of inferior paint jobs done by pimple-faced kids who couldn't make a light bulb shine.

"Not yet. I got reclassified 1-A."

"That's tough. Any idea when you might get the notice?"

"No. But it's coming. The war is still raging regardless of what Nixon says."

"Listen, maybe you'll flunk the physical."

"Not a chance. If you're breathing you're in."

"I'll buy you a dress."

"Naw, that's been tried."

"How 'bout I drop a car on your foot. You can't march with a broken foot."

"That would only delay the inevitable and they'd probably draft me anyway and make me stay in a hospital or on base until I heal. I'm screwed, man."

"We gotta do something. I need you here."

"Well, I don't know what. It's the army, jail, or Canada."

"Does your father know? He's got connections."

"I haven't talked with him in weeks. He'd probably tell me it would be good for me. At least I'd get a haircut."

"Listen, he's your father. He doesn't want you going to war."

"No. But, he'll tell me to join the navy or air force to stay out of the fighting."

"That is a point. Problem is, those services have more volunteers than they need. They actually turn people down."

Ritchie thought for a minute, then admitted, "I'm no good for the military. I hate authority."

"Tell me about it," Big Bob joked.

"It's a free country—isn't it? So, why do they have the right to make me a military slave against my will?"

"It's the law. What can you do?"

"I can load up and head to Canada before they draft me. If I don't get the freakin letter then I'm not draft dodging."

"I don't think it works that way."

"I work that way."

Two thousand eight hundred miles away in Los Angeles, California Sharon Tate had lunch with two friends, actresses Joanna Pettet and Barbara Lewis. Sharon was pregnant and approximately two weeks away from giving birth. She was filled with anticipation and looking forward to being a mother. The three actresses chatted about the movie industry and their upcoming roles. At one point Sharon admitted that she was disappointed that her husband, director Roland Polanski, was delayed returning from London.

Sharon Tate was an Army brat many of whom share a common characteristic of being shy. Most likely this occurs due to constantly moving around. Without the opportunity to make long-term friendships and learning how to communicate, one's lack of confidence causes interpersonal relationships to be difficult to build. Another contradiction is that shy people often do well in the entertainment industry as actors. Somehow it's easier to portray someone else than to be yourself.

After early appearances on the television programs *Beverly Hillbillies* and *Petticoat Junction* Sharon Tate landed minor roles in the movies *The Americanization of Emily* and *The Sandpiper*. Her first feature role was in *Eye of the Devil* with David Niven and Deborah Kerr. She then landed the lead role in Roman Polanski's wild film *The Fearless Vampire Killers*. Director and actress on that film fell in love and with its completion they were married.

In mid-February, 1969 Mr. and Mrs. Roman Polanski rented a house at 10050 Cielo Drive, Los Angeles, California from Rudi Altobelli who represented stars like Katherine Hepburn and Henry Fonda. He had purchased the house from Terry Melcher, Doris Day's son.

A month after the Polanski's moved in Charlie Manson showed up at the house looking for Terry Melcher. One of their house guests answered the door. From inside Sharon Tate asked, "What does the creepy looking guy want?" Manson overheard this and was angry when he was sent away.

Charlie Manson had met Terry Melcher through his contact with Dennis Wilson, vocalist and drummer of the Beach Boys. Manson hoped to interest Melcher into financing a film that included his music. At the time Melcher owned the house at 10050 Cielo Drive. On a number of occasions Charlie had been to that house. Terry Melcher also had visited the Spahn Ranch and listened to Charlie sing his own compositions and play the guitar. After a second visit, Melcher decided he wasn't interested. Manson, who had unrealistically built up the possibility in his mind, was disappointed. It quickly turned to anger.

In the evening, Sharon Tate went to her favorite restaurant, El Coyote, with Jay Sebring, Abigail Folger, and Voytek Frykowski. Jay Sebring was an internationally known hair stylist who had been an item with Sharon Tate before she met Roman Polanski. They remained friends. Abigail Folger, the twenty-five year old heiress to the Folger coffee fortune, was an investor in Jay Sebring's men's toiletries and hair styling business. Voytek Frykowski, a longtime friend of Roman Polanski, was Abigail's boyfriend who had been introduced by Sharon Tate.

After dinner they returned to 10050 Cielo Drive. It was 10:30 p.m. They settled down for a pleasant evening together. Jay Sebring was excited about his planned franchising of men's hair styling shops and introduction of his line of hair products. As a top men's hairstylist he served an elite clientele that included Frank Sinatra, Steve McQueen, Peter Lawford, George Peppard, and Paul Newman. Abigail Folger was a little withdrawn because she had made the decision to break it off with Voytek Frykowski due to his shiftless ways and lack of ambition. She didn't know how or when she would tell him.

The house at 10050 Cielo Drive was secluded with the nearest neighbors over a hundred yards away. Approximately a hundred feet from the house was a locked gate and there was a guesthouse on the property occupied by a caretaker.

At approximately 11:45 p.m. Steven Earl Parent, an 18-year-old recent high school graduate, arrived at the estate. He had come to visit William Garretson the caretaker who lived in the guesthouse. They both shared an interest in electronics and Parent hoped to sell a Sony AM-FM Digimatic clock radio to his friend. Garretson wasn't interested. After half an hour Steven Parent left. Parent got into his father's 1966 white AMC Rambler and drove down to the entrance of the estate and stopped to push the button that operated the electronic gate. When he rolled down his window Charles "Tex" Watson stepped up to the car and shouted, "Halt!" He held a .22 caliber Hi Standard Longhorn revolver in one hand and a buck knife in the other. A frightened Steven Parent begged, "Please don't hurt me. I won't say anything." He raised his arm to protect himself and Watson swung the knife slashing the palm of his hand. Watson then shot Parent four times, hitting him in the face, chest, and abdomen.

Neighbors thought that they had heard shots from the direction of 10050 Cielo Drive, but when nothing else was heard they went to bed.

Charles "Tex" Watson, Susan Atkins, Patricia Krenwinkel, and Linda Kasabian, all members of the Manson Family, entered the estate. Watson told Linda Kasabian to stay by the gate and watch out. The other three proceeded up to the house. Watson removed a screen and entered through a window and let Atkins and Krenwinkel in through the front door.

Detective Ryoya Akimoto received the call. After a minute she told her partner, Detective Michael Donovan, "We have a road rage incident on the West Side Highway with injuries."

They drove out to Twelfth Avenue turned right and headed toward the Westside

Highway that runs along the Hudson River. Ahead in the distance they saw red flashing lights. In fact, the night was filled with what appeared to be hundreds of red fireflies.

"This doesn't look good," Michael Donovan observed.

The wreck was located at the entrance of the West Side Highway where Twelfth Avenue ends and a ramp leads up to an elevated highway. Traffic was being routed around the wreck onto Fifty-Seventh Street and then north on West End Avenue. A fire truck blocked the ramp up to the West Side Highway. Two other fire engines were parked at the scene. An ambulance waited on the side of the road for victims that might need transport to a hospital. Four marked police cruisers, lights flashing, were parked around the scene. Michael Donovan parked the car and he and Ryoya approached the accident on foot.

They were approached by a uniformed patrolman who had been first on the scene. He recognized the detectives and said, "This is a bad one."

"Victims?" Ryoya asked.

"Two. Male and female. Probably, late twenties. Both trapped in the vehicle. Fire is using the jaws of life to cut them out. Injuries look serious. Oh, and the female is pregnant."

"Witnesses?"

"An old couple. They were behind the vic's vehicle. Patrolman Bronson is taking their statements."

"What do you know, so far?"

"Original statement from the witnesses indicated that a light colored, perhaps tan, car driven by a woman forced the victims into the piling. She was behind the witnesses going north on Twelfth. They said she passed them and then started to pass the victims. When they got to the ramp she swung over, hit the front of their car, and forced it into the piling. It looked like she did it on purpose. Then she drove off on the West Side Highway."

"Did anyone get the license plate number?"

"No, but they think it was a Jersey plate."

"Anything about the car?"

"Very little. It was tan or yellow. The wife said it was bigger than the vic's car. The perp had no trouble forcing them into the piling. Sick bitch."

"Who's working the accident investigation?" Michael Donovan asked.

"I'm not sure. I was the first one on the job that got here. The car was a mangled mess. Two people inside. I couldn't tell if they were gone or not. When fire arrived I got out of the way."

"How do you know the female is pregnant?" Ryoya asked.

"Fire rescue told me. Said they were both alive but trapped. Woman kept mumbling, 'My Baby.' They're working to get her out first. The male may not make it. They're going to take the female to St. Luke's, Tenth Avenue and Fifty Ninth Street."

Detectives Akimoto and Donovan walked toward the accident rescue scene.

Inside the house at 10050 Cielo Drive the three invaders found a man on the couch and a woman reading in a chair. The startled occupants protested but were held at gunpoint. Susan Atkins and Patricia Krenwinkel went into the bedroom and found Sharon Tate sitting on the bed talking to Jay Sebring. They tied nooses around their necks to keep the two of them from moving.

Back in the living room Tex Watson brutally beat Voytek Frykowski in the face and on the head with a the butt of the revolver. The injured man tried to run but one of the girls stabbed him in the leg. Frykowski was stabbed several more times and shot. In blind desperation he broke loose and ran out the front door screaming, "Help, help, somebody please help me." The murderers finished the job on the lawn.

A man supervising a campout less than a mile away heard the screams. He got in his car and drove around but didn't find anything unusual.

Abigail Folger, wearing a full length nightgown, also tried to escape when they were busy attacking Frykowski. She didn't get far as they fell upon her and killed her with twenty-eight stab wounds. Her body was left on the front lawn near Voytek Frykowski.

A neighbor's dogs began barking frantically and he went outside to investigate. When he found nothing, he went back to bed.

Sharon Tate and Jay Sebring had been led into the living room, the rope thrown over a ceiling rafter, and nooses placed back around their necks. They could do nothing. Without warning Sebring was shot and stabbed seven times. Sharon Tate watched in horror as he died. She then pleaded for her life saying, "Please don't kill me. Please don't kill me. I don't want to die. I want to live. I want to have my baby. I want to have my baby."

Susan Watkins looked Sharon straight in the eye and said, "Look, bitch, I don't care about you. I don't care if you're going to have a baby. You had better be ready. You're going to die and I don't feel anything about it." A few minutes later they stabbed Sharon Tate sixteen times penetrating her heart, lungs, and liver causing massive internal hemorrhaging. Her unborn son, Paul Richard Polanski, died with her.

The pregnant victim was finally removed from the wreckage of the car and placed in an ambulance. She was on her way to St. Luke's while the driver of the car was being extricated. Detectives Akimoto and Donovan would have loved to have been able to speak with the victims but knew that would have to wait until they were cleared at the hospital. The fire chief in charge of the operation, a big ruddy faced Irish gentleman, approached the detectives. He said, "It looks like she has a chance. The status of the fetus is unknown."

"What about the driver?" Donovan asked.

"Touch and go. The quicker we get him to a hospital the better his chances. He's broken up pretty severely. My boys will get him out as fast as they can. After that—it's in the hands of God." The big man looked around and sighed, "It's a bloody shame."

From a distance Michael Donovan examined the wreck. It looked like what used to be a Ford Falcon. Year he didn't know. It was a coupe. Dark Blue. Then he saw it. It had New Jersey license plates. Might be nothing or might indicate that this was more than road rage. Maybe the perp knew the victims. He heard a fireman yell, "Oxygen!"

They were losing the driver. As other firemen cut, bent, and twisted metal away from the trapped man others did all they could to keep him alive. It was a race against time.

Charles "Tex" Watson, Susan Atkins, Patricia Krenwinkel, and Linda Kasabian went to work creating a crime scene that would shock the world. 10050 Cielo Drive had been selected because it was secluded and Charlie knew and disliked the owner. Who was living there was of no consequence. Their devil's work complete the four butchers drove to a place where they changed their clothes and washed their hands.

A private security guard for an upscale community thought he had heard gunshots. He called his employer who relayed the information to the Los Angeles Police Department. The officer who received the call said, "I hope we don't have a murder; we just had a woman-screaming call in that area."

A patrolman called out to the detectives. He was carrying something. When they arrived he handed them what appeared to be a taillight lens. It was pyramid shaped with four stacked red lenses of decreasing size. "Maybe it came from the other car," he concluded.

"Bag it," Detective Donovan said.

Headlights from an arriving vehicle caught their attention. They turned to see the coroner's station wagon drive slowly toward the accident scene.

"Looks like it's a murder investigation, now," Detective Donovan said.

Robert Six Trees finished carving his fox totem. He strung a piece of leather cord through a hole and made a necklace. Once around his neck it would remain there to guide and protect him.

37: Saturday – August 9, 1969

At the entrance of the West Side Highway, NYPD forensic officers gathered evidence. Statements had been taken from the only two witnesses and they were allowed to leave the scene of the accident. Given their account of events, it could more accurately be defined as a crime scene. The police had to operate under that assumption. Detectives Ryoya Akimoto and Michael Donovan proceeded to St. Luke's Hospital at Tenth Avenue and Fifty Ninth Street. When the detectives arrived at the hospital they were informed that the female victim was in surgery—condition unknown. They were told that they would have to wait until the doctor in attendance was available.

From the information in the victim's handbag they determined that her name was Frances Herde. She was twenty-six years old and a resident of New Milford, New Jersey. Her business card identified her as a bank teller at North Church Community Bank in New Milford. There were two credit cards and a membership card for the Little Community Theater.

"It could be simple road rage," Michael Donovan commented.

"That would make it manslaughter, at the very least," Ryoya replied.

"We're going to New Jersey, you know that."

"Yes, I know. I'll bring my Skin So Soft."

"Your what?"

"It repels mosquitoes."

"Oh. Yeah. Maybe I'll use a little of that Skinny Stuff," Michael Donovan replied. Then being the great detective that he was, he noticed something for the first time and asked, "Hey, nice necklace. What does it mean?"

"It means treasure."

"You mean like buried treasure? Jim give you that?"

"Jack. Yes, at the baseball game. I've been wearing it for a week." Ryoya shook her head, "You're so observant."

"Hey, wait a minute, I noticed that you had on a green dress on Monday."

"Red."

"And that you wore that blue suit of yours on Tuesday."

"Brown."

"Well, you didn't notice that I'm wearing new socks."

"Jeeze, I'm sorry Mike. With the number of times you put your foot in your mouth I should definitely have realized that you had on new socks."

"That's better." Michael Donovan stood, stretched, and exclaimed, "Listen, I'm hungry. You hungry? It will probably be a long wait. Unfortunately, there's not much open at this time of night."

"Morning."

"Right. I'm gonna run out and find an all-night deli or diner. You want something?"

"There's a place on Sixty Second, an all-night grocery. They also will make take-out sandwiches. Get me a turkey on rye with lettuce, tomato, and mayo. And, coffee."

"OK, treasure."

"Off limits, Mike."

Detective Donovan knew his partner well enough to recognize the serious nature of her comment. He knew it was definitely an area to be left alone. He also knew it revealed an unmistakable depth of emotion. Given their earlier discussion about the status of her relationship with Jack, yeah he knew his name, it was best to avoid a direct confrontation. A part of him wanted to tell Ryoya to hang tradition and be happy. However, a rumbling storm cloud told him there was trouble ahead. Or, was that his stomach? He simply replied, "OK, Rita, I'll be back."

Ryoya Akimoto sat alone in the waiting room. Unconsciously, she touched the Japanese symbol that hung around her neck. In her life there had been other men but somehow they always remained more distant. Or, did she keep them at arm's length? The conflict between Japanese and American cultures was constantly being fought on so many levels within her. American culture won with her occupation. It was not planned, however circumstances led to where she was at that moment. She liked being a cop. In the beginning, though, it was a difficult thing for her parents to accept. Also, the few Japanese men that she saw socially wanted a traditional Japanese wife. Submissive, obedient, well-versed in the tea ceremony, ready to raise children and prepared to stay at home. That was not going to happen. Ryoya was aware that her parents saw their culture dissolving into the American fabric and she once more felt guilt that should not be hers to bear. Her parents left Japan for a better life. That better life brought with it changes. She shouldn't be required to carry the banner for a country she didn't know or had never visited. Yet, family is a powerful force. Family traditions are to be protected and cherished. There is a limit as to how far one can stray without destroying the very thing that is one's identity, values, and strength.

Winifred Chapman, housekeeper for Sharon Tate, arrived at the front gate of 10050 Cielo Drive at around 8:30 a.m. She noticed a wire hanging from a nearby telephone pole draped over the gate and running along the ground on the property. What it was for or how it got there she didn't know. Hesitantly, she pressed the button to open the gate and half expected it to not work. The gate swung open. She picked up a newspaper from the driveway, walked to the garage, and switched off the overhead lights. As was her habit she went to the service porch and retrieved the key that was hidden on a rafter above the door. She remained concerned about the fallen wire and decided to check the telephone in the living room to make sure it was working. Upon entering, she proceeded through the kitchen and dining room to the entry hall. Once there, she was surprised to find the front door wide open. She peered outside and saw a blood-soaked body lying on the front lawn. In a state of shock Winifred Chapman quickly looked around and saw pools of blood on the porch and in the entry hall. There was also a blood soaked yellow towel. The frightened housekeeper ran back through the house retracing her steps and leaving the residence. As she started down the driveway she noticed for the first time Steven Earl Parent's white AMC Rambler with his body inside. In near panic, Mrs. Chapman ran to a neighboring house and frantically rang the bell but there was no answer. At the next house she told the owner what she had found and he called the police.

A radio call, "Code 2, possible homicide, 10050 Cielo Drive" was transmitted at 9:14 a.m. to West Los Angeles Police Units 8L5 and 8L62. The first on the scene was Officer Jerry DeRosa in Unit 8L5. Near the gate he examined the 1966 white AMC

Rambler with the body of a young man slumped inside drenched in blood. The victim was wearing a red, white and blue plaid shirt, blue denim jeans, white socks, and black shoes. Officer William Whisenhunt arrived and joined Officer DeRosa. Guns drawn, they searched the other cars in the parking area. A third police office, Robert Burbridge, arrived. On the lawn the police officers found two bodies. One was a white male, approximately thirty-five years old wearing a purple shirt, multi-colored pants and brown high-top shoes. Multiple wounds and trauma to his face and head were observed. The other victim was a young female with long brown hair, wearing a white, full-length nightgown. There were numerous stab wounds on her body and deep lacerations on the left side of her face. Both victims had defensive wounds on their hands.

The three officers approached the house cautiously not knowing if the perpetrators were still on the premises. Officer Whisenhunt found an open window on the side of the house. He and Officer Robert Burbridge entered through that window. Meanwhile, Officer Jerry DeRosa approached the front door. On the door he saw the word "PIG" in what appeared to be blood. He entered the residence.

When the officers entered the living room they were shocked by what they found. A young, obviously pregnant, blond female was lying on the floor covered in blood. A three-strand white nylon rope noose was around her neck that went up over a rafter and ended with a noose around the neck of a male also covered in blood. The female was in a fetal position wearing a nightgown consisting of bra and pants. She had been stabbed multiple times. Four feet away the male victim lay on his side. He was wearing a blue shirt, white pants with black vertical stripes and black boots. There was a light-colored, blood-drenched towel over his face. Numerous stab wounds were noted. The three officers searched the rest of the house. It was eerily silent, yet they heard music from somewhere outside. When they investigated they saw the guest house and heard dogs barking. A man's voice said, "Be quiet." The three police officers entered the house through the front door and found William Garretson, the caretaker, in the living room on the floor. He was placed under arrest.

A nurse arrived and told Ryoya that the victim was in recovery and the prognosis was good. She also said that the attending physician, Doctor Phillip Hartz, would be available shortly. Detective Michael Donovan arrived with their food. As they ate they discussed what they knew.

"A larger vehicle, either tan or yellow, passed the witnesses' vehicle and attempted to pass the victim's vehicle or purposely forced it into the stanchion," Detective Donovan said through a mouthful of food.

"There was no other suspicious activity witnessed prior to the event," Detective Akimoto added.

"The driver was female with long hair, but in the dark little could be told about her features or clothing."

"No gestures or threatening actions took place before, during, or after the accident or attack."

"The abrupt sideways movement of the vehicle made it appear to be intentional rather than an accident."

"The driver made no attempt to stop and left the scene via the West Side Highway."

"Possibly New Jersey license plates on the perp's car but no letters or numbers observed."

"We have one dead, the driver, and one in unknown condition."

"Two in unknown condition—mother and child."

"Right."

Ryoya sipped her coffee. She looked at her notepad and added, "The victim's car also had Jersey tags."

"The perp might have known the victims."

"According to the witnesses there wasn't any other traffic on the road at the time. They were about to enter the West Side Highway so there would have been multiple lanes. No problem passing another vehicle. It makes no sense to cause an accident passing a slower car one hundred feet before it would be clear sailing." Ryoya sat back and concluded, "This was either road rage or premeditated. It was not an accident."

"The difference between manslaughter and murder—intent."

"How fast were they going?"

"According to Mr. Trumane, the witness, he was doing approximately forty-five."

A doctor arrived in the waiting room. "Detectives? I'm Doctor Hartz."

"How is the woman?" Michael Donovan asked.

"She is stable. Compound fracture of the left tibia, possible concussion, separated ribs, ruptured spleen, facial lacerations, and multiple contusions. We had to do a caesarian to save the fetus. It wasn't too great a risk as the mother was near term. The infant appears healthy but we have to keep it under observation. All in all, the prognosis looks good for mother and child."

"When can we speak to her, doctor?" Detective Akimoto asked.

"Not for a few hours. She's in recovery but still under the effects of anesthesia. Then she will be sedated and given a morphine drip." He looked at his watch and said, "I'd say she will be coherent by noon."

Olivia Samantha Everett woke with a start. What had caused her to wake she didn't know at first. Then she heard it once more. A familiar voice with a Spanish accent was yelling in the bedroom. There was a thud and she heard Claire groan. More yelling, a slap or punch, sobbing, something crashed to the floor and shattered, then silence. Olivia remained motionless on the couch, afraid to move. When Miguel walked through the room headed for the door Olivia feigned sleep. Her heart raced as she feared that she would be the next recipient of a beating. For what, they often never knew. He neither spoke nor looked in her direction as he stormed out of the apartment.

Immediately, Olivia jumped from the couch and headed to the single bedroom of the apartment to check on her friend. Inside she found Claire lying on the floor with a blanket over her head. A lamp lay on the floor in multiple pieces. She gently pulled the blanket back to reveal Claire's face. Without her wig the older woman's hair was a mass of different lengths, twisted, and disheveled. Claire looked up at Olivia with a lost, broken, pitiful countenance. She didn't say a word. Her left eye was swollen and lip was bleeding. The electric cord from the broken lamp was wrapped around her neck. She remained silent and motionless. Olivia carefully removed the cord revealing deep red marks around Claire's neck. With neither speaking, Olivia went into the bathroom and wet a towel, returned and softly dabbed the wounds, then helped Claire onto the bed. It was obvious that moving was painful as Claire had also been struck elsewhere on her body.

Finally, Olivia spoke, "Why?"

Claire looked at her friend unable to speak. She shook her head ever so slightly. The look in her eyes was no different from those often shown of abused animals in cages by non-profits to raise money. Indeed, she was just as helpless, as lost, and without hope. Only there were no good Samaritans who would rescue her.

For an hour Olivia tended to Claire's injuries. She made tea and brought a cup to her friend. The first sip caused pain and Claire winced.

"That bastard," Olivia spat.

Finally, Claire was able to speak. She told Olivia that Miguel was angry because she didn't make enough money for the past three nights. He accused her of pocketing money and wanted her to give it to him. She had none to offer. He beat her and strangled her until she blacked out. That's when he stormed out of the apartment.

"How does he expect me to earn more when he keeps beating me up?" Claire complained. "Look at me. I'm the last one they choose on the street. I get the bargain hunters, the weird ones, the cheats. Maybe, I'll get lucky and one will kill me."

Olivia wanted to console her friend but couldn't find the words. There was no question that they were living in hell. How do you tell someone like Claire that things will be alright? They won't be alright. Maybe death was the only escape.

Claire stumbled into the bathroom and threw up. She gagged and cried at the same time. Olivia followed her in and dabbed her face with a damp towel. Claire reached out and took Olivia's hand and held it. Together they sat on the bathroom floor comforting each other.

After thinking for a while Olivia said, "I'll give you some of my money each night."

"You can't do that Miguel will beat you for not making enough."

"He won't know. I'll work harder and still give him what he's been getting."

"He'll know. He always does."

"Not this time. We'll make sure."

"Honey, I can't let you do it."

"It's how we are going to survive," Olivia said as she dabbed blood from Claire's lip. "We need each other." She brushed a strand of hair out of the older woman's face and added, "We will protect each other." Olivia stood and walked to the doorway. She turned to face Claire and said, "It's that simple."

"It's from a 1966 Mercury Monterey," stated Officer Patrick Kelly, an automotive expert with the NYPD. He held a plastic bag in which was the broken taillight lens from the crime scene. "From paint scrapings we determined that the color was light beige. Actually the color name is Sandstone." He looked at a piece of paper and stated, "There were 65,688 Mercury Montereys produced in 1966 with an average price tag of $2,900. Good news; only 3,941 were Sandstone. We ran New Jersey registrations and found 158. We're compiling a list of owner's names and addresses." He looked up and smiled.

"Thanks for getting on that so quickly," Detective Michael Donovan said to his colleague.

"No problem. You'll have the list this afternoon."

Off the coast of Africa thunderstorm activity concentrated in a small area. It grew into a tropical disturbance with a distinct circular motion and began to track westward along the 15th parallel north.

At noon Detectives Akimoto and Donovan arrived at St. Luke's Hospital. They received clearance from Doctor Hartz to speak with Frances Herde, the surviving victim of the incident at the West Side Highway. He explained that she was still slightly disoriented and had not been told of the death of the driver of the car.

The detectives had examined the dead victim's effects and determined that his name was Walter Marshall. He lived at 237 Cooper Avenue, Oradell, New Jersey. His business card indicated that he was a sales rep for a contact lens manufacturer. They had no idea what the relationship was between the two victims. A telephone call to his residence resulted in a woman answering who identified herself as Mrs. Marshall. Ryoya had the difficult task of informing the unsuspecting woman of her husband's death. Mrs. Marshall explained that she had been distraught when her husband failed to return home after a business event in the city. She told Ryoya that she had called the local police to report him missing. They had not gotten back to her.

"Do you know what event he attended?" Ryoya had asked.

"No, he doesn't . . . uh . . . didn't tell me," she said with a quivering voice. "He rarely gave me specific information about the events he attended because he said it would mean nothing to me."

"Did he attend a lot of events in New York?"

"Not a lot. About once a month he had to stay late. It was his job."

"Did he have any enemies or persons who might want to harm him?"

"No. Why do you ask? Do you think it wasn't an accident?"

"We don't know. The other vehicle left the scene of the accident. For that reason we have to approach it from all angles—including an intentional act."

"My God, you think someone killed Walter?"

"It's too soon to conclude anything," Ryoya explained. She then asked, "Did he receive any threats or have any problems with people at work?"

"No. Everyone liked Walter."

An appointment was made to meet Mrs. Marshall at her home later in the afternoon. They didn't reveal that there was another passenger in the car.

When Detectives Akimoto and Donovan entered the hospital room they saw a young woman with her left leg in a cast and elevated by a sling. An intravenous drip was attached to her right arm. She appeared to be asleep. A nurse in the room spoke to her and told her that two detectives wanted to ask her some questions.

"Walter?" the young woman asked in a strained voice.

"You don't have to worry about him," the nurse replied as she patted the patient's arm.

"My baby?"

"Your baby is fine. He's in the maternity ward being well taken care of. Why don't you answer these detective's questions."

Frances Herde looked over at Detectives Akimoto and Donovan and nodded.

"I know you are in pain and somewhat disoriented but we need to ask you a few questions if we are to find the person who caused the accident," Ryoya began.

The young woman didn't respond. She stared blankly at Detective Akimoto. Ryoya continued, "Did you see the car that caused the accident?"

"No."

"Did Walter Marshall say anything about a car trying to pass?"

"No."

"Did he say anything when your car was hit?"

"I don't remember. You'll have to ask him. How is he? Is he hurt?"

Ryoya ignored the young woman's question and continued, "Where were you coming from?"

"We had dinner at a restaurant downtown. Why is that important?"

"We're trying to determine if anything happened that might have caused the other driver to be angry."

"You think it was intentional?"

"We don't know but the other driver left the scene of the accident. Because of that fact we have to investigate all possibilities. At any time during the evening did you or Mr. Marshall have any disagreement or argument with any other individual or individuals?"

"No."

"Where were you going?"

"We were heading home."

Although Ryoya already knew the truth she asked, "Do you and Mr. Marshall live together?"

"No."

"So, he was taking you home."

"Yes."

"What is your relationship with Walter Marshall?"

Frances Herde's answer surprised both detectives. She said, "He's the father of my baby."

Ryoya paused briefly. Then, she changed the direction of the interview. "How long have you and Mr. Marshall been seeing each other?"

"Two years. We met each other at a fundraiser for a theater group. Then one thing led to another. You can ask him. How is he?"

"Right now we need to get as much information from you as we can," Ryoya used a common technique of ignoring any question that dealt with a subject that they were unprepared to address. "Do you know of any person who might have wanted to harm you or Walter Marshall?"

The injured young woman thought for a moment. She shook her head slightly and winced from pain. Finally, she answered, "No one."

"What about his wife? Does she know about you and Walter?"

Even in her weakened and drugged condition the look of surprise on her face was obvious. She turned away from the detective. There was a long pause before she said in a low voice, "No, she doesn't know about us."

"Are you married?"

"Not anymore."

"Did your . . . relationship with Walter break up your marriage?"

"Not really. It was already bad. We're divorced."

"What is your ex-husband's name?"

"Jason Lassiter."

"Where does he live?"

"I'm not sure. Somewhere in Hackensack. Why do you want to know about him?"

"We are just covering all bases. When was the last time that you had contact with your ex-husband?"

"I don't remember. It was over a year ago. We met in a lawyer's office when the divorce was made final."

"Was he upset by the divorce?"

"Yes, but he got over it."

"Does he know about you and Walter Marshall?

"I don't think so. No."

After half an hour the nurse informed the detectives that they had to let the patient rest. They thanked Frances Herde and wished her a speedy recovery. It had been a long night, but there was still more to be done.

"Well, we certainly have motives for a premeditated attack," Donovan surmised.

"We've got to find the car, that's the key," Detective Akimoto offered.

Homicide Division personnel arrived at 10050 Cielo Drive at about 1:30 p.m. Lieutenant R. J. Helder, Supervisor of Investigations, Homicide Division, assigned the case to Sergeants M. J. McGann and J. Buckles.

Detectives found a pair of reading glasses on the floor in the hall, as well as a broken wooden gun grip. The gun grip was originally seen in the hall but had been kicked into the living room by one of the investigators.

At 2:00 p.m. Deputy Coroner Finken examined the five bodies and took liver temperature readings to determine time-of-death.

Ritchie stood at the site of the World Trade Center. The twin buildings rose before him. He took photographs of the progress but his heart was heavy. Once he receives his greetings from the government he knew he would be whisked away to Vietnam and never would finish his World Trade Center project. Or, he would be freezing his ass off in Canada, but that also meant that he would not finish.

His eye caught a pigeon gliding gracefully on the updrafts common between New York City's skyscrapers. It fascinated him, yet he wasn't sure why. Every so often it would flap its wings to gain altitude. Then it would once again swim in the sky. There was an exquisite beauty about the movements. He then realized that he was observing ultimate freedom. The bird landed on a girder of the World Trade Center six stories above the street.

Ritchie photographed the grey and white pigeon on the massive structure and wondered if he would ever get to see the completed buildings. He felt cheated. Here, right in his own backyard, was the soon to be tallest buildings in the world. It was a monument to man's achievement and progress. It would stand for decades as a symbol of international cooperation and hope. Through trade, not war, the world would eventually come together and know real and lasting peace. What a glorious future these two magnificent structures would offer. Sadly, he would not be there to see it. The pigeon took flight. As Ritchie watched it soar he knew one thing for sure. Flight was the answer.

At their downtown headquarters Los Angeles police detectives questioned William Garretson, the caretaker at 10050 Cielo Drive. He claimed that he had slept through the entire incident. What he left out was the fact that he did hear what he believed were firecrackers when Steven Earl Parent, his 18-year-old friend, was shot to death. Also, that he heard screams and when he peeked out the window of the cottage saw Abigail Folger running across the lawn being chased by another woman—Patricia Krenwinkel. He heard Folger scream, "I'm already dead."

Upon further questioning and having been shown photographs of the crime scene he wrongly identified the body of Abigail Folger as "the maid" and the body of Voytek Frykowski as "the younger Polanski."

Jack Moore entered More-Or-Less. He sauntered over to his favorite barstool and sat. When Harry Van Ryker, the bartender and owner, saw his old friend he walked over and said, "Well, I'll be damned. I thought you were dead or in jail."

"Neither, my friend—just busy. Let me have a Jameson neat."

"What! Since when did you embrace the Irish? You've always been a scotch man."

"I've developed a more discerning taste."

"Then, I would have thought you would order sake."

"Why the hell would I want with a fish?"

"A fish? Who said anything about a fish?"

"Sake in Japanese means salmon. The term for rice wine in Japanese is nihonshu. You can use the term sake but it depends on how you pronounce it as to whether or not you get a drink or a fish."

"That's very interesting," Harry stated sarcastically.

"There's more. Sake isn't really wine. Wine is produced by fermenting sugar that is naturally present in grapes. Sake is produced by brewing like beer."

"Knowing all of that is really going to help my business."

"Beer contains like 3%-9% alcohol, wine 9%-16%, and nihonshu 18%-20%. That stuff will kick you in the head real quickly."

"I'd like to kick you in the head."

Jack ignored his friend and continued, "In Japan, nihonshu is served warmed in a small bottle called a tokkuri. It is then sipped from a small porcelain cup called a sakazuki."

"Well, I don't have any sock-it-to-me's around so you'll have to stick with the Irish." Harry poured Jack's Irish whiskey and placed it in front of his friend. He commented, "I take it from your enhanced knowledge of all things Japanese that you and the lady detective are still seeing each other."

"We have been, but right now she's on a case and I'm developing a story."

"So, you had nothing better to do and decided to come here."

"Why, are your feelings hurt? Are you jealous?"

"Hey, the place has been quieter, more friendly, a better class of clientele. You not being here has improved business."

"Glad to help." Jack sipped his Jameson and concluded, "It's not in a sakazuki but it will do."

Harry left to serve a customer at the other end of the bar who had been tapping his glass feverishly. "Keep your shirt on," he shouted as he came to the rescue of the desperate imbiber.

Jack thought about the past week and how much information he had gathered on the NASA story. He had an appointment to meet Matthew Ellis in person on Monday. The man intrigued him. He could be a monster who caused the deaths of three brave astronauts and put an untold number of people in danger. Or, an innocent dupe. That would have to be determined. At present, he was being very cooperative and almost apologetic about not remembering what took place. It was either a great act or a real sad situation. At least Jack knew there was a story and he was determined to dig up all the skeletons.

Harry returned. "Did you hear the news today?" he asked. "Those murders in California? So damn senseless. I hope they find the mad dogs that did that before they do it again."

"What's your retired-cop opinion of who would do something like that?"

"Every mass killing is different. Though, generally stabbing is an act of passion. Up close and personal. It might mean that the perps knew the victims and had a score to settle. It could be that it was actually the premeditated murder of one individual and the others got in the way. Wrong place at the wrong time. Or, and this is the most frightening scenario and most difficult to solve, it was meant to leave a message. The victims might have been randomly selected and the crime executed in as grisly a manner as possible to generate a lot of media coverage. That would be the work of a sick mind."

"Those poor souls. That must have been a terrifying ordeal. No one should ever have to die that way."

At that moment, Jack noticed a new arrival at the pub. It was the guest that he had invited. Colt MacIntyre, the waiter from Le Cav du Henri Quatra, saw his friend and waved as he approached the bar. Harry Van Ryker had wandered off to serve a customer.

"Welcome to Le Cav du Harry Van Ryker," Jack said.

"It's quite charming," Colt replied.

"Listen, before Harry comes back, he's a friend of mine and deserves some of your country jargon, if you know what I mean."

"Shoot yeah. You want me to be your cat's paw and throw around some corral dust. Get the old guy all balled up with windies."

"Right. I think."

Colt smiled and said, "Like lickin' butter off a knife."

"Good. Here he comes."

"Wipe your chin."

"huh?"

"Be quiet."

Harry arrived and looked at Colt MacIntyre and asked, "What'll you have?"

Colt replied in a clear and unmistakable English accent, "You have a smashing establishment here, Gov'nor. Antwacky with quite a hum. Money for old rope, I'd say what. I'm keen as mustard to try one of your American libations. What do you say to Bourbon and Adam's Ale? Yes, bring that, and Bob's your uncle."

"We don't have Adam's Ale, whatever the hell that is," Harry replied.

"Pardon me, I appear to have dropped a clanger. Adam's Ale is called water in the colonies, old chap."

"Yeah, right," Harry wandered off shaking his head.

"What the hell are you doing?" Jack asked in a low voice. "Who are you?"

"Keep your hair on and don't girn, I'm doing what his nibs requested, am I not?"

"His nibs expected rodeo Bob, not your uncle Bob whatever that means."

"Don't get collywobbles—enjoy the show."

"What?"

"A nervous stomach."

Harry returned with the bourbon and water. "Here ya go Chauncey."

"I see you're not backward at coming forward. I like that in a bloke."

Harry turned to Jack and asked, "This a friend of yours?"

"Something like that."

"Well, tell him in America we speak American not some limey, snooty, gobbly gook."

Before Jack could respond, Colt said, "Don't bloody blank me, you blighter."

"I'll bloody your nose, you putz."

"Just because you have a bag on doesn't mean I have to listen to your tommy-rot." Colt turned to Jack, frowned, and said, "This bugger's barking mad. He's throwing a benny."

"I'll throw you out of my place," Harry replied. "How about that?"

Other customers in the bar watched the escalating confrontation with interest. Among them were a number of off-duty police officers.

"You're daft as a brush. And, as welcome as a fart in a spacesuit."

"That's it!" Harry threw down the bar towel.

"Wait!" Jack stood up and moved between the two men, even though there was a bar separating them. "Both of you calm down. I wanted you to meet each other not beat each other."

"Are you talking to me or chewing a brick?" Harry asked.

"Huh?"

"Bang on, Gov'nor. I believe this bamstick is interfering in our do."

"Quite. He is a cheeky monkey," Harry replied.

"Well he's no oil painting done up like a dog's dinner. And a bit toffee-nosed for sure, I'd say," Colt added.

"Not ones cup of tea."

"Bloody right."

Jack caught on that he was the butt of a well-planned joke. He backed up raised his hands into the air and said, "OK, kill each other."

"What ho? My friend Harry is as right as rain."

"And, my friend Colt is a bit of all right."

"And, I was a bit of a patsy," Jack stated as a number of customers applauded.

"You just had a blonde moment," Colt said soothingly.

"Let the dog see the rabbit," Harry said. He then added, "Get out of the way. There are two attractive ladies opening the door."

"Ah, yes," Colt said with his English accent, "Dead heat in a Zeppelin race."

"What?" Jack asked.

"Large breasted."

"OK, let's leave the British Isles and return to good old America," Jack said to both friends.

Colt looked at Jack for a moment then turned to Harry and said, "Colt

MacIntyre, glad to make your acquaintance," he offered his hand.

Jack wiped his brow and said, "Let me have a Scotch."

Robert Six Trees sat and listened to the elders of the tribe as they spoke. This was his first council meeting. He would endeavor to learn their laws and system of kinship which was quite complex. This was the first step to being recognized as a full grown member of the tribe.

38: Sunday - August 10, 1969

In the middle of the night early Sunday morning Pasqualino Antonio "Leno" LaBianca, his wife Rosemary, and her daughter Susan Struthers drove back from Lake Isabella where they had spent Saturday boating. They had joined Struthers' fifteen-year-old son, Frank Struthers, Jr., who was vacationing at the lake with a friend, Jim Saffie, and his mother, Mabiha Saffie.

It was past midnight when they completed the one hundred fifty mile drive towing their speed boat. After dropping Susan off at her apartment at 4616 Greenwood Place the couple then stopped at a gas station on the corner of Hillhurst and Franklin to buy fuel at approximately 1:00 a.m. Rosemary purchased a newspaper and saw on the front page a story about the murders of Sharon Tate, Jay Sebring, Abigail Folger, Voytek Frykowski, and Steven Earl Parent. She expressed her horror and concern to John T. Fokianos, the clerk, about such a heinous crime being committed in the Los Angeles area. They continued home to 3301 Waverly Drive in the Los Feliz area of Los Angeles.

Leno LaBianca's father was the founder of State Wholesale Grocery Company. His son entered the family business right out of college. Those who knew Leno described him as quiet, conservative, and well-liked. Unfortunately, he had a gambling habit that caused him to misappropriate over two-hundred thousand dollars of company funds. It was not uncommon for him to bet five hundred dollars at the track on a given day. Also, he owned nine thoroughbred race horses, including Kildare Lady, one of the better-known horses. His wife Rosemary was an attractive 38-year-old Mexican who had been an orphan and adopted at the age of twelve. She was an accomplished businesswoman who ran the Boutique Carriage and also made investments in securities and commodities. Rosemary was a self-made millionaire after starting out as a waitress and carhop.

Charlie Manson was not pleased with how the murders at Cielo Drive had been carried out the night before. He particularly didn't like the fact that the victims had been told they were going to be murdered which resulted in panic. For this reason, he decided to take charge of the next executions. He wanted their prey to be misled so that they would be compliant and easily restrained.

Seven Manson Family members rode through the Los Angeles suburbs in the night looking for the right house to invade. They stopped at a number of houses but rejected them for various reasons. Inside, occupants slept peacefully having no knowledge of how close they had come to breathing their last. Finally Charlie Manson remembered a house where he had attended a party. The house next door was very secluded separated from the rest of the neighborhood. They proceeded to 3301 Waverly Drive in Los Feliz.

When they arrived, Charlie Manson and Tex Watson entered the home through an unlocked side door and caught the LaBiancas by surprise. They assured the couple that their only motive was robbery and that they would not be harmed if they cooperated. Once the victims were tied up, Charlie left the house and sent Patricia Krenwinkel and Leslie Van Houten in with instructions to listen to Tex Watson. Charlie Manson, Linda Kasabian, Susan Atkins, and Steve Grogan then drove away.

Krenwinkel and Van Houten took Rosemary LaBianca, who was wearing a nightgown and peignoir, into the bedroom. Van Houten put a pillow case over Rosemary's head and tied a heavy lamp cord around her neck. She then held the frightened woman down on the bed. In the living room Leno LaBianca, wearing pajamas, also had a pillow case over his head and a lamp cord tied around his neck. His hands were tied behind his back with leather thongs using a double square knot. Both victims believing that it was a robbery didn't resist.

Tex Watson then pulled out a bayonet and stabbed Leno LaBianca. The stricken man screamed and tried to break his bonds. He was stabbed again and again. When Rosemary heard her husband scream she also screamed and tried to fight back. Patricia Krenwinkel stabbed Rosemary LaBianca but the knife struck her collarbone and bent. Rosemary rose from the bed and fought for her life. Other attempts to stab her with kitchen steak knives proved less than effective. The two girls called Tex Watson for help. He entered the bedroom and killed Rosemary LaBianca with the bayonet. In all, Leno had been stabbed twenty-six times and Rosemary forty-one times.

Officer Patrick Kelly sat in the break room sipping a cup of coffee. Detectives Akimoto and Donovan joined him. They had with them the list of 158 owners of a Sandstone color 1966 Mercury Monterey registered in New Jersey.

"Well, you don't need that anymore," Officer Kelly stated as he pointed at the list. "We found the car."

"Where?" Detective Michael Donovan asked.

"Port Authority Bus Terminal parking deck—third level. It was stolen. The ignition was punched. We're going over it now."

"Preliminary info on the owner?" Donovan asked.

Officer Kelly handed the detective a piece of paper. "Owner is a woman living in Fort Lee, New Jersey. Her name is Brenda Carrington. She didn't report it stolen because she only uses it occasionally and was unaware that it was gone. It was parked on the street. Her address is there." He pointed at the paper. "We made initial contact. Didn't tell her that the car was involved in an accident. Simply told her that we found her car."

"Looks like we are going to Jersey," Ryoya said the Michael Donovan.

A heavy thunderstorm moved westward through the Lesser Antilles into the southernmost portion of the Caribbean Sea. Gale force wind warnings were issued as ominous black clouds dominated the sky.

Detectives Akimoto and Donovan met with Brenda Carrington, owner of the 1966 Mercury Monterey that was involved in the accident killing Walter Marshall. After twenty minutes of questioning they were both convinced that she had nothing to do with the crime.

With the interview complete they left Brenda Carrington and drove to Hackensack, New Jersey to locate Jason Lassiter, Frances Herde's ex-husband. His last known address was 745 Colton Street. In a combination industrial and residential area they located a small Cape Cod house that badly needed a paint job, roof, new windows, and extreme yard clean-up. The front door was open. Inside they could hear a baseball game on television. It was WOR-TV carrying the Mets at Atlanta. Through the door they observed a man, approximately thirty years old, with long hair below his shoulders sitting on a couch with a can of beer in his hand. He wore dirty jeans and white tee shirt.

Even though he was staring at the television he seemed to be looking far off in a daze. Detective Donovan knocked on the door. The man didn't respond. Donovan knocked louder. Still no response. Finally Detective Donovan yelled into the house through the screen door, "Hey!" This time the man turned slowly to gaze with a faraway look at the door.

"You have a minute? We'd like to ask you a few questions," Detective Donovan stated through the door.

The man raised his beer can but didn't reply.

"Can we come in?" Detective Donovan asked.

The man took a drink of beer.

Michael Donovan turned to Ryoya Akimoto and said, "I'll take that as a yes."

"Clearly an invitation," she replied.

The two NYPD detectives entered the house. The man on the couch watched them without making a sound. It was obvious that he was high on more than alcohol. The detectives stopped in front of the juiced Jerseyan.

"Are you Jason Lassiter?" Michael Donovan asked.

The man ran his hand through his long hair and seemed to be trying to understand the question. When he brought his hand down he bumped the hand that held the beer can which caused some liquid to splash out onto his jeans. Vacantly, he stared at the wet spot. Then he poured some more beer on his leg to compare the stains.

"Hey!" Detective Donovan yelled, "Are you Jason Lassiter?"

The man looked up. It was as though he saw his two visitors for the first time. "You want a beer?" he slurred.

Detective Donovan answered slowly, "Are you Jason Lassiter?"

"I don't know—are you?"

Detective Akimoto pulled her partner aside and said, "Obviously, we are not going to get any answers from him in his condition. Why don't you ask if we can look around?"

Detective Donovan said, "Jason, can we look around your house?"

The inebriated man looked around the room, "It's around here somewhere."

"We'll find it. You watch your game."

They left the man staring at the television and began searching the house. There was garbage everywhere, clothes strewn here and there, the kitchen qualified as a bio hazard, and Ryoya wouldn't go into the bathroom. The bedroom was equally disheveled and cluttered. What stood out immediately was a photograph of Frances Herde on the dresser. That portion of the dresser was clear of any clutter and appeared to be free of dust. "That reads volumes," Ryoya said.

"Our boy hasn't extinguished the torch."

"It speaks of motive."

"Maybe Walter Marshall was the target and Ms. Herde was collateral damage."

"It's going to be hard to prove without physical evidence."

"We do have two witnesses."

"Who say a woman was driving."

"Or, a man with long hair."

The two detectives continued their search of the room. Ryoya picked up a newspaper and a cockroach scurried for cover. It didn't make it. She tossed the stained newspaper aside.

"Hey, what about this?" Detective Donovan called as he held up an I.D. tag.

"What does it say?"

"Tishman Realty, Horizon House, Fort Lee, NJ. Jason Lassiter, NJ Carpenters Local 487. He works in Fort Lee," Donovan said.

"Means. It would be easy for him to snatch a car, drive into the city, kill Marshall, and dump the car in the Port Authority terminal."

"Now, all we need is opportunity."

"Did he know where they were? Did he follow them? Was this a planned assault?" Ryoya said, "I'd love to interview him when he knows what his name is."

"That won't be today. Hello!" Detective Donovan held up a notebook. Inside he found handwritten notes on the whereabouts of Jason Lassiter's ex-wife, "Opportunity."

At four o'clock in the afternoon with his attorney present and upon his attorney's advice, William Garretson, the caretaker at 10050 Cielo Drive and only survivor of the carnage two days earlier, submitted to a lengthy polygraph examination conducted by Lieutenant Burdick, S.I.D. Polygraph Section. He was sober and alert. However, his responses were vague and evasive. In the opinion of the investigating officers it was highly unlikely that the young man could not have heard the gunshots, screams, and other noises that came from a residence in such close proximity. In the end William Garretson passed the polygraph test. As a result there was no doubt on the part of the Los Angeles Police Department that he was not involved in the grisly Sharon Tate murders.

Mabiha Saffie dropped Frank Struthers, Jr. off at home at 8:30 in the evening. The first thing that he noticed was the family's 1968 Thunderbird with boat trailer still attached parked in front of the house on the street. He knew it was his step-father's practice to put the boat away in the morning which had not been done. He then noticed that all of the window shades had been drawn which he had never seen his parents do before. A feeling of concern washed over him. He walked up the driveway and saw his mother's 1955 Thunderbird parked by the garage with water skis from the boat lying on the fender. When he got to the back door that led to the kitchen, he noticed a light on inside. The door was locked. He knocked but there was no answer. By this time it was dusk and Frank Jr. was becoming alarmed. On one side of the house he found louvered windows opened and he yelled inside for his parents. When he still got no response fear engulfed him. He left 3301 Waverly Drive and walked several blocks to the Char Burger diner located on Hyperion Boulevard. From a telephone booth he called the Great Scot Restaurant where his sister, Susan Struthers worked. Unfortunately, she was not on the schedule that night. The manager of the restaurant telephoned her at home and relayed Frank Jr's message about being concerned about their parents. She called the telephone booth number and the two siblings spoke.

After their conversation, Susan telephoned her fiancé, Joseph Dorgan, and the three of them went to 3301 Waverly Drive. They arrived at the residence at

10:25 p.m. Immediately, Susan noticed from outside the house that there were lights on in the kitchen and the master bedroom closet. Because they knew that Rosemary had a habit of leaving her keys in the ignition of her '55 Thunderbird they checked her car. They found keys to the house. Frank Jr. opened the rear door and he and Joseph Dorgan entered the kitchen. When they reached the living room they found Leno LaBianca lying on the floor dead. Quickly, they returned to the kitchen and stopped Susan from going into the living room. At that time they noticed the words "HELTER SKELTER" scrawled on the refrigerator door. Joseph Dorgan thought of calling the police using the kitchen wall phone but decided it was best not to disturb the crime scene. The three left the house.

Frank, Susan, and Joseph ran to 3308 Waverly Drive and banged on the door. They yelled that someone had been cut and to call the police. The resident became alarmed and called police to complain about the three intruders. A call "See the man, 415 juvenile" was sent to car 6A39.

In near panic Frank, Susan, and Joseph went to 3306 Waverly Drive, the home of Doctor Merry J. Brigham and asked to use her telephone. They were so upset that they rambled about somebody being stabbed. Finally, Dr. Brigham made the call to the Los Angeles Police Department for them. Officers W. C. Rodriguez and J. C. Toney in car 6A39 responded and proceeded to 3301 Waverly Drive. They were met in front of the house by the three young people. Officer Rodriguez tried the front door and found that it was unlocked. When he opened the door he immediately observed the body of Leno LaBianca. He didn't enter the residence. Instead, Officer Rodriguez called for a backup unit, a supervisor, and an ambulance. Officer Toney went to the rear door to secure the crime scene.

Sergeant E. Cline and an ambulance arrived on the scene. They entered 3301 Waverly Drive. Leno LaBianca was pronounced DOA at 10:40 p.m. Sergeant Cline found Rosemary LaBianca in the master bedroom and she was pronounced dead at 10:43 p.m.

Robert Six Trees gave his sister Anna a birch bark hoop. Children played with such objects by rolling them around. He laughed as he watched her first feeble attempts.

39: Monday – August 11, 1969

"Lida Petropoulos lives here," Matt pointed at his forehead. "I dream about her and have glimpses of memories but I don't know what is real and what isn't."

Jack Moore sat across the table from Matt Ellis. They were in a small restaurant named Lido located in an old house in New Milford, New Jersey. It was past two in the afternoon so they had avoided the lunchtime crowd. "Maybe, together we can separate fact from fiction," he offered.

"I never gave much thought to what it was like to be crazy," Matt said into his sandwich, "But, now I know. When you can't tell what is real—you're crazy." He shook his head, "What do I believe? Am I guilty or innocent? Does Lida Petropoulos even exist? Why can't I find the answers in my own head?"

Jack was a seasoned interviewer. He quite often could tell when an individual was telling the truth, stretching the truth, omitting the truth, or outright lying. His opinion of Matthew Ellis was that he was being honest about his confusion and trying to provide whatever answers he could. This was a new situation for Jack—a cooperative subject who didn't know how to cooperate. He knew this was going to be a process that could take time. All he could do was try to be a catalyst to finding answers. He said to Matt, "Let's start with Lida Petropoulos. We know that she does exist. Parker Adolphson confirmed that she billed Orztech for wire products. She operated under the business name LPAmerica. That much has been confirmed."

Matt nodded.

Jack looked at his notes. "I couldn't find any record of LPAmerica in Dunn and Bradstreet, Thomas Register, the Chamber of Commerce, Better Business Bureau, and other business listings. Without the Orztech records we don't know where the invoices originated from or where the checks were sent or deposited. Adolphson was not the most accommodating contact. From a legal standpoint the IRS requires that records be kept for seven years. Therefore, we'll continue to search for them." Jack looked up, "Where do you recall meeting Ms. Petropoulos?"

"I have one memory of meeting her in a coffee shop in New York City. I believe it was our first meeting. She had contacted me after it was announced that Orztech had won a government contract. This was before the NASA negotiations. It was a military contract. She arranged to have the wire manufactured outside the United States at significant savings."

"Was the product up to the standards that you required?"

"I don't know."

"You have no memory of examining the product that was delivered?"

"None."

"But, you used her services again for the NASA order?"

"Somewhere in my mind I have a recollection of a conversation with Lida about the NASA bid. I didn't feel right about outsourcing overseas—child labor and all that. But, it was the only way we would be competitive—pricewise. It was our only chance."

"And, she delivered the product as ordered on time?"

"I don't know."

"You don't know?"

"We won the bid on November 22, 1963. The day President Kennedy was shot. That was when I had my accident."

"And, you came out of a coma this year."

"Correct."

"So, other than Lida Petropoulos' participation in the bidding process you don't know if she had anything to do with manufacture and delivery of the wire." Jack made some notes.

"I don't."

"Is it possible that after your accident Orztech found a different source for the wire?"

"Anything is possible."

"Did anyone, other than yourself, at Orztech meet with or have any contact with Lida Petropoulos?"

"I don't know."

Jack knew he had to tread lightly with the next questions. "How well did you know Lida Petropoulos?"

"I told you. She contacted me after learning about the government contract and we met at a coffee shop."

"You had other meetings."

"I think so, but only remember one in an office. But, I don't remember whose office."

"Did you meet her socially?"

"No," Matt's voice changed tone slightly.

It was an easy "tell" for Jack to pick up. He continued, "Think carefully, did you have any contact with Lida Petropoulos outside of the work environment?"

"I didn't."

Jack sat quietly and didn't ask another question. The two men each nibbled at their lunch. Jack wrote a few more notes on his note pad.

Finally, Matt said, "A necklace."

"What was that?"

"There was a necklace. She wore a diamond necklace at a party. Valerie and I attended a party and Lida was there wearing a diamond necklace that she and I had seen in a jewelry store window."

"So, your wife knew Lida Petropoulos?"

A rapid and decisive, "No," revealed that there was in fact more to the relationship between Matthew Ellis and Lida Petropoulos.

Jack said in a consoling manner, "Mr. Ellis, we both want to uncover the truth. Sometimes that truth hurts or is embarrassing or seems threatening but it always comes out in the end." Jack paused and looked at his subject. Matthew Ellis was hiding something, however it was important to get him to reveal the truth rather than make an unsupported accusation. "Why do you remember the necklace?"

"I don't know. It just came to me." Before Jack could respond Matt continued, "Wait, I think she said to me, 'You can buy me that,' when she saw it in the window. It was very expensive and she was kidding. That's why I was surprised to see her wearing it at the party." Matt seemed to be reliving the events as he stared at the wall behind Jack. He and Lida were holding hands. That was not indicative of a business relationship. His hand unconsciously went to the spot on his chest where she had playfully scratched him. "Try explaining that," she had said. Another memory erupted in his mind. He was in his office when he opened his attaché case and found a pair of Lida's panties. They were lace, yet almost transparent. A floral pattern in violet/fuchsia gave them the look of fine art. The label was from Aubade a well-known and expensive French lingerie emporium. A note was attached. It read, "Don't let these get into the wrong hands. Hand wash and return." Immediately, he recalled the night that he returned those panties to Lida. She had prepared dinner—kotopoylo yemisto, roasted stuffed chicken, with briami, baked summer vegetables. Matt brought the desert—halva. Lida wore a dark blue cotton French terry dress with a Henley neckline and elbow sleeves. Over dinner she playfully confessed, "I'm not wearing any panties."

"Oh," was Matt's brilliant response.

"I seem to have misplaced my favorite pair," she purred over the top of her wine glass.

"I believe I can remedy that situation," Matt replied as he handed her a flat box. Inside, hidden by tissue paper, were the fresh, clean, carefully folded panties that he had found in his attaché case.

"Did your wife do this?" she sarcastically inquired with a mischievous smile.

Matt didn't answer. Instead, he produced another box, placed it on the table, and slid it over to Lida. Inside was the necklace and earrings she had admired in the jewelry store window. When the memory unfolded he said in a whisper, "My God."

"Something come to mind?" Jack asked.

"Yes. Uh, no."

Army Corporal Nick Richardson lay bleeding in the dirt. A North Vietnamese People's Army of Vietnam (PAVN) soldier's bullet had pierced his lung and caused significant internal bleeding. It was at the beginning of a new offensive by the Viet Cong that involved over one hundred fifty cities, towns, and bases, including An Loc where Corporal Richardson clung to life. Gary "Doc" Pope was the 68W10 (68 Whiskey 10), line medic, in attendance.

A 30 caliber AK-47 round had entered Richardson's chest in the front and exited out his back. It was a classic "sucking chest wound." Pope observed bright red foamy blood escaping from the wound. Corporal Richardson was conscious but couldn't talk. Helpless, he lay in the dirt watching Doc do his job. He heard a voice say, "I called for MedEvac."

Pope used the paper from a large battle dressing package to cover the exit wound and taped it in place. He ignored Richardson's cries as he rolled him onto his back to give his attention to the entrance wound. With each breath blood sprayed from the wound. The smell of death engulfed Gary Pope. Doc knew he had to seal both wounds if Corporal Nick Richardson was to live long enough to be evacuated to a hospital.

Whiskeys are assigned by platoon. However, in this war they cared for larger groups of soldiers and were spread pretty thin. In spite of that fact, most medics knew their team members quite well. They remembered soldiers' previous injuries, allergies, and personalities. In many cases, they knew about their personal lives back in the world, as well. Corporal Richardson was not married, but was engaged. Doc had seen a picture of a sweet little Alabama girl with innocent eyes who waited for her soldier to come home. If he had anything to with it, Doc was going to get Nick home. The sealing of the entry wound was posing a problem as the dressing wasn't working and

Corporal Richardson was going into shock.

Fifty clicks away Lieutenant Dan Dryfus of the 57th Medical Detachment climbed into the pilot seat of the only Bell Hu-1, Huey, MedEvac helicopter not in use at that time. The coordinated attacks with resulting casualties put a strain on their resources. He was on standby and having heard the call located An Loc on the map and began startup procedures on the helicopter. After initial turbine windup he engaged the twin rotors. They slowly began a counterclockwise spin increasing in speed with each revolution. Lieutenant Dryfus focused on the RPM dial waiting for the needle to enter the green zone. Just before it reached minimum rpms an alarm sounded and the engine shut down. Before the pilot could say a word Sergeant Byrd, the crew chief, was on the skid looking in the pilot's window.

Doc twisted the gauze dressing to make it firmer and applied it to the wound. He taped it fast and wrapped a belt around the fallen soldier's chest to put pressure on the wound. With the quick yet accurate moves of a pianist he inserted an IV into Corporal Richardson's arm and held the pouch above him. The frightened soldier stared at him. Doc attempted to comfort him, "You're going to make it. Just hang in there. We'll get you evac'ed right away." The medic looked skyward hoping to see a MedEvac helicopter approaching.

Sergeant Byrd examined the instrumentation and tried a number of switches to, as quickly as possible, determine the cause of the shutdown. With no response he climbed over to the cowl that covered the engine and opened it. There weren't any obvious pools of oil which was a good thing. He quickly examined the fuel line and main electrical connections.

Army Corporal Nick Richardson began to lose consciousness.

"Stay with me!" Doc ordered. He took the soldier's hand and said, "Squeeze my hand." He felt only slight pressure on his hand.

Lieutenant Dryfus, following Sergeant Byrd's instructions, began the startup sequence, once more. The two large blades atop the Huey began chasing each other around and around picking up speed. Sergeant Byrd watched the inner workings of the turbine engine. As the blades began to reach full speed, they caused a vibration, there was a pop, an alarm, and the engine shut down. "Son-of-a-bitch!" he exclaimed. "There's a damn wire shorting out." He reached into his pocket a retrieved a roll of black electrical tape. He wrapped the offending wire making a mental note to replace it when the helicopter returned. Lieutenant Dryfus began the startup sequence a third time. When the blades reached full power they continued without any further problems. Sergeant Byrd shut the engine cowling, jumped from the helicopter, and yelled "God's speed. Bring em home!" Lieutenant Dryfus lifted off and headed toward An Loc.

Corporal Richardson's breathing became shallow and raspy. Doc checked the IV and the dressing. He couldn't do any more in the field. "Where's the damn chopper?" he asked no one in particular. With gunfire and mortars and air strikes and yelling and other sounds of battle in the background the only sound that Gary "Doc" Pope heard was the death rattle of a brave young man named Nick.

A MedEvac helicopter flew in low over the trees and landed.

The name of the restaurant where Carl first met Ray Esposito was Santino's. This time Carl entered through the front door with Susan Friedlander on his arm. She was a girl from the neighborhood that on an impulse he asked to dinner. They were more friends than boyfriend/girlfriend. He wanted to go back to Santino's and felt it would be more fun with a companion. Dressed in one of his expensive designer suits they took a taxi from the Bronx down to West Twenty Third Street. Susan was impressed by the "new" Carl Pythacyk. Little did she know that in many ways he mimicked the debonair style of Ray Esposito, a captain in the Carmine Spacini crime family. He also reflected greater maturity as evidenced by better control of his explosive temper.

Upon entry, Carl announced that he had reservations. The maitre d' nodded and immediately brought them to a choice table in the corner. They had just been seated when Gino arrived at their table. "Mr. Carl," he said in a friendly and respectful tone, "how nice to see you and your lady. We will take good care of you."

"Thank you, Gino," Carl responded.

"Allow me to suggest as an appetizer Crostino, sliced and grilled ciabatta bread with a variety of toppings that include cheeses, meats, and vegetables. And, a bottle of Taurasi Riserva, a red wine from the Aglianico grape grown in the Province of Avellino in the Campania Region. It will enhance the flavor of the herbs used on the Crostino."

"Sounds good to me Gino," Carl said with authority.

Gino nodded and ran off.

Susan Friedlander looked at her friend from the Bronx and considered the dramatic change that he exhibited. He was poised and confident. His manner was that of a powerful man in charge. She liked it. Although, she knew well his reputation and violent past it didn't matter because he was always nice to her.

Gino returned with the appetizer and wine. He poured a few ounces in a glass and handed it to Carl. This was unfamiliar to the young hoodlum but he remembered that it was ladies first. He handed the glass to Susan. Gino leaned down and whispered in Carl's ear, "Mr. Carl, you taste it first to decide if it is acceptable."

Carl took the glass back from Susan and downed the wine. Its warm full-body flavor was a combination of sweet and tangy with a slight tannin aftertaste. Carl stated, "That's fine."

Gino filled the glasses, placed the bottle on the table, and stated, "For your salad I will personally prepare a Mediterranean delicacy of house greens, Kalamata olives, Feta, red onions, roasted red peppers, pepperoncini, marinated artichokes and tomatoes with our special Santino's dressing. You will enjoy." He disappeared.

Carl looked at Susan and admitted, "I have a lot to learn." He nodded in the direction of the wine glass.

"You've already learned a lot," she replied with an admiring smile.

They nibbled on the Crostino in silence. Carl was stunned by the flavors he experienced. Italian food, to Carl, was spaghetti and meatballs and pizza. The tastes he enjoyed at Santino's were nothing like the bland faux Italian food with which he was familiar. The flavors were also dramatically more satisfying than Polish food he was raised on. He smiled as he thought he really was becoming a gumba.

For the main course Carl ordered Carne Campania, veal sautéed with roma tomatoes and basil in white wine with garlic topped with Parmesan cheese. Susan, with the help of Gino, selected Pollo Amatriciana, Julienne strips of chicken sautéed with bacon, onions, and roma tomatoes in garlic and oil. It was served tossed with cheese tortellini. Over their dinners and second bottle of wine, for no particular reason, Carl told Susan a story, "When I was a kid I went to school at PS86. One day I brought a book written in Polish named *The Door* to show and tell. Some older kids took the book and threw it under a bus. It got run over and destroyed. Until then," he paused not wanting to say the words that he ultimately did, "I was a coward. There were four of them. I beat up two and the other two ran away. From that day on I learned it was far nicer being on top. I hit first and take no shit from anyone."

Susan Friedlander watched her host attentively but didn't say anything.

Carl continued, "My father never forgave me for letting that book get destroyed. He and I don't know each other. We barely speak. On my birthday my mother gives me a small present and bakes a cake. My father always has some reason to not be at home on those days."

Susan was compelled to speak and said, "Carl, I'm sorry." She put down her fork, reached over, and took his hand. He was surprised and instinctively pulled away. Then, he took her hand and held it.

After drinking some wine Carl went on, "I'm doing OK now. Things are really looking up. I went to a Polish grocer and asked if he had any contacts in Poland. With the war and all Poland is not the same. He wrote some letters and found me a copy of *The Door*. It's not signed by the author but is an original. Cost me three-hundred bucks. I got it yesterday."

"That's so nice. Did your father like it?"

"I left it on his dresser before picking you up."

"Do you think it will bring you and father back together?"

"Doesn't matter—the debt is paid."

"Doesn't matter," Sergeant Hicks said as he answered the trainee's question. "If you get too low on the net and trapped between the landing craft and the side of the ship your legs will be crushed."

All of the trainees looked at the side of the ship where cargo nets had been hung over the side. They were all dressed in full battle gear including helmets, Kopeck lifejackets, and packs. It was time to learn amphibious assault, the hallmark of a Marine. Each man carried a 9.5 pound M-1 rifle. The Corps didn't want to risk valuable M-16's on an exercise.

In the water below, waiting for their passengers were flat-bottomed landing craft that were WWII vintage. Waves that appeared to be as large as tsunamis caused the craft to rise and fall aside the ship. A whistle blew and they knew it was time. Acting Corporal Wellington Marsh led his squad over the rail of the ship. The bulky lifejacket and M-1 rifle slung over his back threw off his center of balance causing movement to be awkward. He began climbing down the cargo net and concluded that all the physical training and obstacle course cargo net climbing had prepared him for that specific moment. Slowly he made his way down. He looked in the direction of the landing craft and his stomach tightened as the height of the ship he was leaving became apparent. When he looked up all he saw were a million boots coming in his direction. The climb seemed endless. It tested his strength. The pitching of the ship gave the impression that it was trying to shake them loose. It was a frightening experience. Yet, it was one of those instances where the only solution is to continue. He approached the bottom of the net and looked at the landing craft. In the dark it was difficult to judge distance. A wave raised the craft toward Wellington. Instinctively, he knew this was the best opportunity. He placed one foot on the side of the landing craft and it immediately slipped on the wet metal causing him to tumble into the boat. He made it without crushing his legs. Another trainee fell on top of Wellington landing on his legs. They quickly untangled themselves and, as instructed, moved to the front of the landing craft near the huge metal ramp that would be lowered when they hit the beach. Then they heard someone yell, a splash, followed by two more splashes as rescue swimmers came to a fallen Marine's aid.

Once the landing craft was loaded it pulled away from the ship. Because of its flat bottom the ride was quite bouncy throwing Marines into the air and off balance. The abrupt motions caused some Trainees to get seasick. Unfortunately, when that many men in full battle gear are squeezed together in a tight space vomit splashes everywhere and on everyone creating the worst-smelling, uncomfortable conditions imaginable. Chain-reaction vomit followed. Then there was the heat. It was a humid night compounded by the heavy gear and closed-in space which raised their body temperatures. One Marine passed out but no one knew because there wasn't any open space where he could fall. There was silence aboard the craft. No one felt like talking, no jokes came to mind, and orders were to remain silent.

The landing craft started to circle as it waited for other craft to be boarded and to join the flotilla. Wellington was pressed against the ramp at the front of the boat. The coolness of the metal was welcome. As they bounced along he considered that this position was certainly not a preferred spot as when that ramp dropped he would be among the first to be shot. Or, if he stumbled onto the beach dozens of other Marines desperately wanting to get somewhere safe would trample him to death. He smiled as he tried to decide which he preferred a bullet or a boot. Strange what your mind does when you are stuck in limbo in a hostile environment.

Wellington was a senior in high school. It was Thursday April 4, 1968, late in the school year, and they were all looking forward to, or perhaps hoping for, graduation. On this night, his only concern was History. Somehow he never mastered the art of memorizing names and dates. Only on this evening, he was about to experience history.

In Memphis, Tennessee Dr. Martin Luther King, Jr. addressed a gathering at the Mason Temple (World Headquarters of the Church of God in Christ). He had traveled there in support of black sanitation workers who were on strike because Memphis paid black workers far less than whites. It was here that he gave his "I've Been to the Mountaintop" address that lasted over an hour and ended with the words:

> "Well, I don't know what will happen now. We've got some difficult days ahead. But it doesn't matter with me now. Because I've been to the mountaintop. And I don't mind. Like anybody, I would like to live a long life. Longevity has its place. But I'm not concerned about that now. I just want to do God's will. And He's allowed me to go up to the mountain. And I've looked over. And I've seen the promised land. I may not get there with you. But I want you to know tonight, that we, as a people, will get to the promised land! And so I'm happy, tonight. I'm not worried about anything. I'm not fearing any man. My eyes have seen the glory of the coming of the Lord!"

After his speech they returned to the Lorraine Motel in Memphis, room 306. Reverend Ralph David Abernathy was King's roommate in the motel room that day.

After saying to musician Ben Branch, who was to perform at an event later that evening, "Ben, make sure you play 'Take My Hand, Precious Lord' in the meeting tonight. Play it real pretty," King went out onto the balcony. At 6:01 p.m. a single .30-06 bullet fired from a Remington Model 760 struck Martin Luther King Jr. in the right cheek. It broke his jaw, traveled down his spinal cord, severed the jugular vein, and lodged in his shoulder. The impact ripped off his necktie. He was rushed to St. Joseph's Hospital but never regained consciousness and was pronounced dead at 7:05 p.m. As the media reported the assassination of Martin Luther King, Jr. anger grew in black communities across America. Riots erupted in Baltimore, Boston, Chicago, Detroit, Kansas City, Newark, Washington, D.C., and numerous other cities.

Wellington Marsh received a telephone call from Gerald Young. His friend was screaming that they killed Doctor King. The eighteen-year-old said it was time to go to war and burn the city down. White America had to answer for its crimes. Wellington didn't admit that he never heard of Doctor King. Yet, as he heard what happened he felt anger grow within him. After ten minutes listening to Gerald Young he was filled with anger, as well. He remembered the riots a year prior that destroyed parts of Detroit. Now, it was time to finish the job. Wellington and Gerald agreed to meet at a corner gas station and go downtown together to join the protests.

Peter Marsh, Wellington's father, stood at the front door. He had a look on his face that gave Wellington pause.

"Where are you going?" Wellington's father asked in a stern voice.

"Downtown. To protest!"

"No, you are not."

"They killed Dr. King!"

"You are not joining the mobs that burned Detroit last year and are going to do the same tonight."

"But, we have to fight back!"

"Destruction and violence are not the answer."

"But, dad . . . "

"Wellington, I didn't raise you to be a criminal. And, I didn't walk through hell to have you throw it away." Peter Marsh took his son's arm and led him into their small living room. They sat and the elder Marsh continued, "When I was your age I quit high school to get a job because we needed the money. I started as a janitor at the Phillips Street assembly plant. There was a lot of 'yes sir' and 'no sir-in' in those days. Sometimes I was treated like garbage but I swallowed deep and did my job. You think I didn't want to hit someone or break something? No man should have to put up with being treated the way I was treated. But I had a goal and I wasn't going to let them keep me from it. I learned it takes a lot more courage to take it and not fight than to fight. So, today, I'm a foreman and they yes sir to me. We live in a nice house, have a new car, and eat well. And, my son wants to set fires and become a looter. I put up with humiliation so you wouldn't have to. There's a lot wrong in the world and we still have a long way to go. But, son you have no reason to complain. You fight when there is a real reason to fight." Wellington thought about his father's words as he leaned against the landing craft ramp. A reason to fight. He was being trained to fight but wasn't sure of the reason. And, his father wouldn't be there to keep him from going. He also remembered Gerald Young who as a result of an injury sustained during the riots was sentenced to a wheelchair for the rest of his life.

The flat bottom landing craft finally straightened its course and along with the others headed for the beach. The craft was tossed into the air slamming back down as it rode over waves. When the landing occurred it was with a sharp jolt. A whistle sounded and the big landing ramp fell onto sand. Marines poured out onto the beach under the sounds of gunfire and explosions. In a realistic war environment they spread out and dug in grabbing a foothold on an unnamed beach to fight an anonymous enemy.

Wellington rolled onto his back to unhook his lifejacket. His gaze went skyward. In the black heavens he saw a streak of light travel across the sky.

Robert Six Trees sat on top of a hill with his sister Anna. In the dark they watched a large meteor burn across the sky. It was followed by other meteors, as many as 60 per hour, from the annual Perseids meteor shower associated with the comet Swift–Tuttle. He never heard of Perseids but knew early each August the spirits danced in the sky.

40: Wednesday - August 13, 1969

In a psychedelic office at 47 West 57th Street in Manhattan four young men discussed their upcoming event that was three days away. At the time, they had an unexpected problem. Almost 60,000 people had already arrived at the venue and were setting up camp.

Artie Kornfeld and Michael Lang had long wanted to produce an outdoor music festival in upstate New York. Michael was an experienced promoter who had organized the Miami Pop Festival where an estimated one hundred thousand people had attended the two-day event in 1968.

The challenge that they initially faced was funding such an event. In early 1969 John Roberts and Joel Rosenman ran an ad in the *New York Times* and *Wall Street Journal* under the name of Challenge International, Ltd. It read, "Young men with unlimited capital looking for interesting, legitimate investment opportunities, and business propositions." Kornfeld and Lang saw the ad and the four young men got together and formed Woodstock Ventures.

Originally, the music festival was planned to take place in Woodstock, New York on property owned by Alexander Tapooz. Unfortunately, local residents fought the plan and another venue was sought. They found a property in Saugerties, New York but the owner's attorney quashed that deal. Kornfeld and Lang then discovered a 300-acre plot of land in the Mills Industrial Park in Wallkill, New York. They leased the land for $10,000 in the spring of 1969. Almost immediately, those opposed to the concert went to work. The town board passed a law that required a permit for any gathering over 5,000 people. On July 15, 1969 the Wallkill Zoning Board of Appeals voted down the project based on there not being a sufficient number of portable toilets allocated.

Finally, a realtor introduced a frustrated Michael Lang to Max Yasgur. He owned a 600-acre dairy farm in the town of Bethel, New York. The land was perfect as it formed a natural amphitheater sloping down to a pond. However, local opposition once more arose with signs appearing in yards that read, "Buy No Milk. Stop Max's Hippy Music Festival." The protests failed and the festival was allowed to proceed. So, the Woodstock Music & Art Fair, billed as "An Aquarian Exposition: 3 Days of Peace & Music," was actually scheduled to take place in the town of Bethel, New York—43 miles southwest of the town of Woodstock.

Due to all of the changes in location the four producers were unable to properly prepare for an expected 50,000 people. And now, three days before the concert, there were already 60,000 people at the site. They quickly realized that they had a tiger by the tail. Only they had no idea how big a tiger it was going to grow to be.

"So, how goes the case?" Jack asked when Detective Ryoya Akimoto answered the phone.

"I have five open cases. Which one are you referring to?" Ryoya said in a monotone voice.

"The one keeping us apart."

"I have a job to do, Jack. It takes time."

Jack realized his subtle attempt at humor had fallen flat so he took another approach, "The Mets have a double header Saturday against the Padres."

"What makes you think I'm going to have time on Saturday?"

"That's why I called—to find out," Jack replied.

"Well, there's no way I can know now, is there?"

"OK, forget the Mets. I'd like to but they're doing better than the Yankees."

"Most of the league is doing better than the Yankees," Ryoya quipped.

"Most of the league is doing better than I am."

"What does that mean?"

"It means, I don't know what to say that isn't going to be taken wrong."

"Maybe you're better off saying nothing."

"That sounds about right. Have a nice day, detective." Jack hung up the telephone. He didn't know what had just happened. To begin, Ryoya wasn't prone to being moody. She could be a tough detective but with him she was always pleasant and fun. Something was bothering her and he hoped it wasn't something that he did.

Ryoya sat at her desk reviewing all of the reports from the various departments pertaining to the murder of Walter Marshall. She knew it couldn't be officially classified as a murder given the evidence but in her mind it was. They had just come back from the hospital. Francis Herde, the injured girlfriend and mother of Walter Marshall's baby, had learned of her married boyfriend's death. It wasn't a pleasant interview but one that had to be done.

Herde once again confirmed that her ex-husband, Jason Lassiter, didn't know of her affair with Walter Marshall. The detectives didn't tell her that in an interview that they had conducted the day before her ex-husband indicated that he knew she was sleeping with a married man and his identity. Further, he admitted to informing Walter Marshall's wife of the affair. The two of them in an act of retaliation had an affair of their own. According to Lassiter it only happened one time.

Between tears Francis Herde once again gave all the details of the accident that she could remember. She also answered their questions about any out-of-the-ordinary things that might have happened in the past six months. Did she receive any telephone calls where the caller hung up before speaking? At any time did she get the feeling that she was being followed or observed? Had she had any arguments with anyone, no matter the reason, over the same time period? Was there any unexplained damage to her car or other property? Did her employer receive any complaints about her? Did they have any other near accidents individually or when they were together? They also inquired as to whether or not Mr. Marshall had told her of any strange occurrences that he might have experienced. She was visibly shaken by the news of her boyfriend's death and couldn't offer any insights that might help Detectives Akimoto and Donovan solve the case.

Ryoya subconsciously toyed with the gold Japanese symbol for treasure that hung from her neck. Why she treated Jack the way she did she wasn't sure. Maybe it was the case on which she worked. Maybe, just bad timing. Maybe, there was more to it. Maybe, it was time to face the inevitable and make the break. That would, in the long run, be the kindest thing to do.

Michael Donovan arrived at Ryoya's desk eating a candy bar.

"Nice lunch," Ryoya said, "Did you bring enough for everyone?"

Michael broke off a piece and offered it to Ryoya.

"No thanks."

"I took it off the side that I hadn't bitten into."

"Doesn't matter."

"Connoisseur?"

"Better than being a common sewer."

"OK, I think the wife did it," Detective Donovan stated.

"Why?"

"She's the only one who lied to us. Lassiter freely admitted to boinking Marshall's wife. He also stated emphatically that he still loved Herde and was a stalker. Someone who plans a murder doesn't leave such a perfect trail to their own door."

"When we interviewed the wife on Saturday afternoon," Ryoya added, "she acted upset."

"Put on a good show."

"And, she kept referring to it as an accident. She asked, 'Why would someone cause an accident and leave?' Later she said, 'I always worried about him having an accident while driving home alone late at night.' Like she kept trying to steer us into concluding it was, in fact, an accident."

"I'll wager there's a life insurance policy somewhere with a double indemnity clause for accidental death."

"There's one big hitch in this theory."

"What's that?"

"We have nothing to connect her to the car."

"Let's go back over those forensic reports on the car."

"Man, I can't believe Cream broke up," Ritchie said as he lay on the couch with his head in Stephanie's lap in his apartment listening to *Strange Brew.*

> Strange brew, kill what's inside of you
>
> She's a witch of trouble in electric blue
> In her own mad mind she's in love with you, with you
> Now what you gonna do?
> Strange brew, kill what's inside of you
>
> She's some kind of demon messing in the glue
> If you don't watch out it'll stick to you, to you
> What kind of fool are you?
> Strange brew, kill what's inside of you
>
> On a boat in the middle of a raging sea
> She would make a scene for it all to be ignored
> And wouldn't you be bored?
> Strange brew, kill what's inside of you
>
> Strange brew, strange brew
> Strange brew, strange brew
> Strange brew, kill what's inside of you

By 1966, Eric Clapton had earned a reputation as the premier blues guitarist in Britain. At the same time Peter Edward "Ginger" Baker was recognized as one of the most influential drummers in both the jazz and rock 'n' roll worlds. Both musicians ached to do more and felt stifled by their present band affiliations. One day, after watching Clapton play, Ginger Baker approached Eric about forming a new band. Clapton agreed with one condition that the band include Jack Bruce as bassist/vocalist. This was quite a surprise to Baker who had worked with Jack Bruce in another band. The two musicians were notorious for their arguments, on-stage fights, and sabotage of each other's instruments. In spite of their volatile history, Ginger Baker agreed and a new band was formed.

The band was originally called Sweet 'n' Sour Rock 'n' Roll. After it was suggested that the three musicians were the cream of the crop in blues and jazz they settled on the name Cream. Their official debut was at the Sixth Annual Windsor Jazz & Blues Festival on July 31, 1966. In the following two years they produced four albums that sold over 15 million copies. Yet, three powerful music personalities found it hard to continue to work together and Cream disbanded May, 1968.

"Damn, they were good," Ritchie said as he listened to the music. He rose to change the record and inadvertently kicked a newspaper on the floor. When he looked down he couldn't believe his eyes. An ad read, "Woodstock Music & Art Fair. An Aquarian Exposition in Wallkill, N.Y. 3 Days of Peace And Music."

"Holy shit! Look at this," Ritchie exclaimed as he picked up the paper. "It's this weekend. Where the hell is Wallkill? Look at all the bands that are going to be there. Joan Baez, Arlo Guthrie, Tim Hardin, Ritchie Havens, Incredible String Band, Ravi Shankar, Sweetwater, Keef Hartley, Canned Heat, Creedence Clearwater, Grateful Dead, Janis Joplin . . ."

"Janice Joplin?" Stephanie asked as she interrupted.

"Yeah, she's singing on Saturday, man. Look at this Jefferson Airplane, Mountain, Santana, The Who, The Band, Jeff Beck Group, Blood, Sweat and Tears, Joe Cocker, Crosby, Stills and Nash, Jimi Hendrix, Iron Butterfly, The Moody freakin Blues, and Johnny Rivers. Practically every known group will be right there in the same place for an entire weekend." Ritchie turned to Stephanie and said, "We gotta go, Steph! It's like music city!" He started looking around the room for something, "Where the hell is Wallkill?"

"How can we go?" Stephanie asked.

"We'll crash in the van. Fill a cooler with food and drinks. I got that air mattress we can inflate. You, me, and Fetch. It'll be a blast, man. That's so far out, all those bands in one place grooving."

"I'd like to see Janis Joplin and Johnny Rivers."

"That's my girl. We're gonna make the scene, babe. You, me, Fetch and endless vibes. Like, I'm getting a rush just thinking about it."

"OK, let's do it," Stephanie said hoping that somehow in all that music she could find a way to convince Ritchie to change his getting-high ways.

An editorial meeting was called at the *Tribune.* Jack Moore and his colleagues sat in chairs, leaned against walls, and looked out the window of the conference room. The Editor-In-Chief entered the room and immediately announced, "I need a volunteer."

Mumbles and groans echoed in the room.

"There is a big music festival in upstate New York that seems to be taking on unexpected proportions. It starts on Friday and there are already thousands of teenagers and hippie-types camping out on this farm that is the performance venue. We need someone to cover it. With that many kids in one place there is going to be sex, drugs, and violence."

"Makes it sound like fun," an unidentified voice remarked.

"We've rented a room in a house in the town and have access to their telephone. All you have to do is report what happens, how the police respond, and how many casualties. Think of it as a weekend vacation in the Poconos."

"I'll go," Jack Moore stated.

"What the hell? You never volunteer," another voice spoke out.

"I can use a little time away from the city," Jack said.

"OK, it's yours," the Editor-In-Chief replied. "Marcia has all the information and contacts." He left the room.

As the other staff members began to leave Jack asked, "Anybody want two tickets to the Mets Saturday?"

His question was answered with laughter.

Anna Six Trees watched her brother leave to hunt with some of the men of the tribe. To her he was the father that she never knew.

41: Thursday – August 14, 1969

A tropical depression passed over the southern coast of Jamaica. It moved slowly to the northwest. As it did a deepening low-pressure center pulled up moist air and thermal energy from the ocean surface. The rising warm air collided with higher pressure in the upper atmosphere pushing it outward. Wind currents began to spin counter-clockwise forming clouds into a circle. Shortly after dawn winds reached 60 mile-per-hour and Tropical Storm Camille was born.

Jack Moore picked up a rental car from the Hertz downtown garage. Carefully, he pulled out onto Tenth Avenue and headed north. The car that he drove was a 1969 Chrysler New Yorker. At over eighteen feet in length he felt like it was as long as a city block. The big 440 cubic inch V-8 engine thrust the 4,387 pound vehicle forward with ease. As he drove Jack found that it was easy to accelerate faster and faster without noticing it in the luxurious comfortable interior. He concluded, "It's like driving your living room."

His journey took him across the George Washington Bridge, onto Route 4 West, then Route 17 North, and ultimately the New York State Thruway. He was on his way to cover a hippie music festival. When on a two-hour drive the mind often goes in a different direction than the car. This is what happened to Jack. He thought about the last conversation that he had with Ryoya. It had caught him off guard. As far as he could tell he had done nothing wrong. That was until he looked down and saw the speedometer at ninety five miles-per-hour. He removed his foot from the accelerator and let the car slow to the speed limit of sixty-five. The big Chrysler wasn't happy. Neither was Ryoya. He shook his head as he tried to understand the female of the species. Things had been going so well. It would be understandable if he had stood her up, insulted her, or been caught kissing another woman. All he had done was buy tickets to a double header—a double header for the freakin' Mets! He smiled. They were fun to watch because they were so unpredictable. He missed Ryoya. The car was traveling at eighty five. Once more Jack slowed his speed. He felt homesick, but why? A once loner who traveled to foreign lands and covered wars was becoming a nester. What the heck? Ninety miles-an-hour wasn't good. Slow down Bessie! Maybe she wants space. Maybe she found someone else. Maybe he was a bad lover. No, whatever they had wasn't bad he knew that much. He pictured Ryoya with her Mets cap on, long hair caressing her shoulders, wearing the treasure necklace he had given her. Part of him wanted to turn around and head back to Manhattan. The newspaper pro kept heading toward Bethel. For an unknown reason Jack remembered that he never told Ryoya how he chose to become a newspaper reporter.

It all began when he was fifteen-years-old growing up in Great Neck, Long Island, 20 miles east of Manhattan. As was the case with most young industrious males, Jack delivered newspapers to earn a buck. It was Saturday, May 5, 1934. He had gone to a matinee movie, *Treasure Island* with Wallace Beery and Jackie Cooper. The show also included the first Three Stooges short *Woman Haters*. Afterward, Jack picked up his newspapers and started his route on his bicycle. It was a warm spring day which Jack enjoyed. Great Neck was not that well developed, as a result houses were somewhat distant from each other. This gave Jack a great deal of exercise each day.

Halfway through his deliveries Jack began to smell smoke. He looked around to find the source but didn't see anything. At the next corner he looked down Pond Terrace Road and saw smoke rising from a two story clapboard house at the end of the road, approximately 50 yards away. He quickly peddled down the road to see the fire. When he arrived he found the house smoking from three of the upstairs windows. After dropping his bicycle to the ground, he ran to the front door and pounded on it. An old woman answered. She was shocked to hear that her house was on fire. Jack told her that she needed to leave the premises which she did. They moved away from the structure which now had visible flames erupting from the roof. Suddenly, the woman grabbed Jack's arm and screamed that her dog, Winkie, was in the house. She pleaded with him to save her dog. Without thinking, Jack ran into the house. Inside he could smell smoke and feel heat. He called for the dog but to no avail. Frantically, he searched each room on the first floor. Finally, he entered the master bedroom and saw a small Boston Terrier huddled in a corner. He called the dog but it ran away from him. It stopped in another corner of the room and growled at him. Jack became aware that the smoke was growing thicker and feared the house would collapse on both him and the dog. To keep the frightened canine in the room he pushed the bedroom door closed. Once more he approached the dog speaking to it in a calm soothing voice with intermittent cough. The dog scampered off to another part of the room. Above Jack heard something heavy fall. He assumed it was part of the roof and knew his time was running out. The fifteen-year-old approached Winkie again and almost got a hold of the dog when it scurried to another corner. It was then that he decided to try something else. He slipped off his belt and fed the length of it through the buckle to create a loop. Slowly he moved in toward the frightened animal and just as it darted away got the loop around its neck. He pulled the dog on his makeshift leash out of the house and handed the lead to the old lady who was waiting outside. She grabbed her dog and thanked Jack for saving its life. At that very moment part of the upper wall fell down as did Jack's pants.

"Oh, my!" the woman exclaimed and Winkie barked.

By the time the volunteer fire department arrived Jack had his belt on and pants securely in place. Shortly after, a reporter from the local paper arrived. The woman was too upset to speak with him. When he questioned Jack the young man explained that the woman, whose name was Elizabeth Pennington, was unaware that her house was on fire. He told of his arrival and efforts to save the dog but left out the part about falling trousers. Further, he explained that Mrs. Pennington had lived at 1309 Pond Terrace Road for twenty years. Her husband worked for the Long Island Railroad as an engineer. It appeared that the fire had started in the upstairs rear of the house where they had some electrical repairs done recently. The reporter was impressed and said that Jack had a keen sense of detail. He asked how Jack had found out so much so quickly.

Jack replied, "I was trying to keep her mind off the fire and her loss by having a conversation."

"You'd make a good reporter," the man replied and invited Jack to visit the newspaper office.

For the next few years Jack spent time at the newspaper office running errands, doing odd jobs, cleaning up, and learning the trade. From time to time he was given opportunities to cover simple events or to do research. In every case he did an outstanding job. He was hooked and never looked back.

The red lights and siren behind him caused Jack to look back. He then looked down and saw the speedometer at eighty miles-per-hour. The Chrysler was slowed and pulled to the side of the road.

A New York State Trooper approached the car and asked, "You in a hurry?"

"I'm not, but this stinkin' car seems to be."

"I clocked you at eighty."

"You should have been behind me twenty miles back I was doing ninety-five."

The trooper laughed, "Are you confessing?"

"It's a rental. Damn thing refuses to go the speed limit. If you don't watch the speedometer like a hawk it creeps up."

"Now, that's a new excuse."

"Not an excuse. I deserve a ticket."

"Where are you headed?" the Trooper inquired.

"Bethel, to cover a rock concert. I'm a reporter for the *New York Herald*."

"I see. You know there's a traffic jam headed to Bethel. Kids from all over driving every kind of vehicle you can imagine going that way."

"Can't believe I gave up double-header tickets to the Mets to go to this thing."

"You a Mets fan? They're having some year, eh?" the Trooper smiled.

Without thinking Jack said, "You want to go? Call the *Tribune,* give them my name, and tell them the tickets are in my top desk drawer."

"You trying to bribe me?"

"Hell no! Give me the ticket and go to the game. It's a shame for the tickets to go to waste."

"What day?"

"Saturday. I was going to take my lady friend but she's working a case."

"What kind of case?"

"I think it's a murder, but I'm not sure."

"She's a cop?"

"NYPD Detective."

"You don't deserve a ticket. You deserve an award."

"Tell me about it."

"That's funny," the Trooper remarked.

"What is?"

"You're a reporter dating a cop."

"Yes?"

"I'm a cop married to a reporter—local paper. Only she's a damn Yankee fan."

Jack laughed, "How's that working out?"

"OK, for twelve years. This year is especially good given the Yankee's crashed and burned and the Met's continue to climb."

"A lot of bragging rights, I'm sure."

"You got it. Saturday, huh? That'll work."

Jack handed the Trooper his business card. "Call that number. Ask for Martin Hewitt. He works with me and will leave the tickets at the front desk. I'll call him from the next gas station. This bucket not only wants to fly it drinks like a sailor."

"You deserve a ticket, you know that," the Trooper said. He then stood straight up and stated in an official voice, "Tell you what. Get that taillight fixed and I'll let you off with a warning."

"I'll do that," Jack smiled. "Enjoy the game and think of me having my hearing permanently destroyed."

"Watch the speed. There are a lot of us on the Thruway because of the concert." The Trooper returned to his cruiser and drove off.

As he continued to drive toward Bethel, NY Jack unconsciously checked his belt to make sure it was buckled. It was a habit he had picked up a long time ago.

"We scored a break," Detective Michael Donovan said as he entered the squad room. He held up a sheet of paper and added, "Fingerprints from a Jason Lassiter, ex-husband of Frances Herde, found in the suspect vehicle."

"Where?"

"Under the dashboard. Clear prints. Let's go pick up the bastard."

"Wait," Ryoya cautioned, "We've got him in the car and the car was used in an assault, but we don't have him driving. It's thin. Plus, he's not in our jurisdiction— remember?"

Michael Donovan sat opposite Ryoya Akimoto. "We need a confession or a witness that saw him driving the car."

"Well, it won't be the Trumanes, our only witnesses."

"We need to do another interview," Detective Donovan admitted.

"Right. Another trip to Jersey."

Tropical storm Camille gained strength as it moved across the Caribbean. A small tight storm, its gale force winds spread out for 100 miles causing thunderstorms to develop over Cuba. As Camille approached the island it attained Hurricane Status with winds of 110 miles-per-hour.

Robert Six Trees felt the warm breeze off of the lake. He had been fishing for an hour and only had two catches. He decided to try a little longer before taking home their evening's dinner.

42: Friday - August 15, 1969

Ritchie and Stephanie loaded his dark blue 1966 Ford Econoline van with everything that they would need for the weekend. They decided to get an early start due to all of the news stories about traffic jams and thousands of attendees to the concert. It was 4:00 a.m. Fetch wasn't happy being sequestered in the back of the van even though Ritchie had made a comfortable bed for her.

"It's gonna be a long drive," Ritchie offered.

"Wake me when we get there," was Stephanie's response. She wore cutoff denim shorts, a Tee shirt with Pepe LePew on it, and sandals.

"Babe, this is like going to be the greatest happening of all time. It will go down in history!"

"You don't even have tickets."

"We'll get them at the gate."

"My father thinks I'm nuts."

"You are, but that's what I love about you." Fetch growled in the back of the van.

Jack Moore woke up in a bed in the guestroom of Bertha and Teddy Schumacher. It was seven in the morning. At first, when he awoke, he found himself confused by his surroundings. Some of it the residual effect of the bottle of scotch that he had brought with him. It took a moment for him to remember that he was a paying guest in a home that was approximately two and a half miles from the site of the Woodstock music concert. The day before had been uneventful except for a very long drive. In the end, it had taken Jack over four hours to make the two-hour trip to Bethel, NY.

The opening performance by Sweetwater was scheduled for 3:00 p.m. This gave Jack plenty of time to get to the performance venue. The house, second on the right on West Shore Drive, would be his home for the next three days. From the kitchen window he could see the main—actually only—road leading to the concert, West Shore Road. West Shore Drive, West Shore Road—very creative he thought. I wonder where West Shore Lane, Place, Street, Circle, and Avenue are located. Not far from here, I'm certain. While eating a sumptuous country breakfast prepared by Bertha Schumacher, Jack looked out at the road leading to the concert. It was filled with traffic that was moving intermittently. There were cars, vans, mini-buses, and pickup trucks filled with young people. Jack knew, before the day was over, it would evolve into the West Shore parking lot. One fact was clear; the big Chrysler New Yorker wasn't going to move from its spot in the driveway. Jack asked Bertha how they were going to get around given the traffic situation. With a big smile she told him that they had stored up enough supplies to not have to go anywhere. She went on to explain that if they did have to go somewhere there were dirt trails through surrounding farms that were familiar to the locals.

Jack decided to do a little scouting in the morning before calling in his report. He was glad that he had planned ahead and brought casual pants, short sleeved knit shirts, and sneakers. After breakfast he walked the short distance from the house to

West Shore Road. Instead of turning left and going in the direction of the concert he went to the right to see how far the traffic jam extended. As he walked, a steady flow of young people passed him going in the opposite direction. They were the hip, enlightened, idealistic, beat, music-loving generation on a pilgrimage to Valhalla. Teenagers and young adults passed wearing individualized outfits of self-expression. There was no common look. Cutoff jeans, tee-shirts, leather vests, ankle-length peasant dresses, short tie-dyed mini-dresses, headbands, bell bottoms, sandals, long jeans, brocade shirts, beads, sunglasses, music oriented tee-shirts, floppy hats, hoop earrings, ponchos, peace symbols, moccasins, bras, long straight hair, beards, platform shoes, flowers, sun dresses, leather bracelets, boots, mini-skirts, and bandanas. They carried guitars, beaded bags, suitcases, lawn chairs, duffle bags, coolers, paper bags, tents, blankets, backpacks, and so many different items it was impossible to tell what was being transported. To Jack they looked like refugees leaving a war zone carrying all of their worldly possessions on their backs. Yet, they didn't have the sad, frightened, lost look of refugees. The entire scene, as far as Jack could see, was high-spirited, happy, care-free, bright, and innocent faces filled with anticipation. Some sang, some played musical instruments, some laughed, some talked, and some smoked marijuana.

As he walked against the flow, many of God's children said things to him, including, "You're going the wrong way, man. The happening is that way. Peace daddy. Join us, man, dig the return to nature. Hey, you're not a narc, are you? Come with us to music city, man. Get hip to the beat, join us. Right on, brother, I dig your threads. Come 'on man, straight arrows are welcome. Don't split, man, it hasn't even started." Jack found all of the invitations and light-hearted banter refreshing. He couldn't help but smile. When a teenage girl with long, straight, brown hair flashed him a peace sign he couldn't help but return it. "Right on, man!" someone shouted. The teenage girl ran over to Jack, took a string of beads off of her neck, and placed them around his neck. She then kissed him on the cheek to the applause of the passing crowd. "Dig it, big daddy, this is where it's at," a young man in his early twenties said, "Join the odyssey of awareness, man." Jack turned and began walking with the crowd.

"What do you expect to find here?" Jack asked his new friend.

"The truth, man."

"What truth?"

"Why we're here, man. The cosmic meaning of it all? Ya gotta get away from the manmade world to find yourself."

"I do."

"Get hip, man. Don't you feel trapped? Forced to live the way society tells you to live? Is this the real you or the commercial you? Living your antlike life is keeping you from contacting the spiritual you that is dying to be set free. Mother Nature and music—the ultimate key to a higher plane."

At that moment two teens who were carrying a cooler stumbled and dropped the blue and white box. One dropped to his knees with a grunt. Two other hippies told them they would help and picked up the cooler. The four continued along with thousands who moved inexorably on toward Yasgur Farm.

Jack was amazed by what he saw. If there was a definition of innocence and human cooperation this was it. It challenged Jack's preconceived opinion of the younger generation.

Detective Ryoya Akimoto hung up the telephone. She looked over at her partner and said, "The District Attorney is processing the paperwork for extradition. It's out of our hands now, partner."

"What a freakin' turn of events," Detective Michael Donovan stated. He added, "It's like a soap opera. The ex-husband tells the wife being cheated on about her husband boinking his ex-wife. Then he and the ex-wife join each other in the sack to get even. But, that's not enough. The wife convinces the ex-husband to steal a car for her so that she can follow the couple and confront them. But, that's not what happens. She sees them kissing when they come out of the restaurant and she loses it. She follows them and with the intention of killing the girlfriend forces them into the stanchion. Problem is she ends up killing her husband."

"And, the ex-husband is an accessory, before and after the fact."

"That was quite a bit of interviewing that you did yesterday," Michael Donovan said with a nod of approval.

"Once we had the fingerprints we had Lassiter. When he knew he faced murder charges he had to come clean. Breaking Mrs. Marshall was our only hope."

Detective Donovan remembered, "She denied everything. Finally, turned on Lassiter telling us that he told her that he did it. It would have worked too, if you didn't pull that rabbit out of your hat."

"It wasn't a rabbit—it was a bold-faced lie," Ryoya admitted.

"Security cameras in the Port Authority Terminal parking deck showing her behind the wheel," Michael Donovan laughed.

"I got worried when she still didn't crack."

"You didn't sound worried. When you said, 'You wear glasses when you drive,' my jaw dropped. How did you know?"

"I didn't. I took a calculated risk. More than half the drivers who are her age wear glasses." Ryoya smiled, "The way you drive, I think glasses are in your future."

"I drive better than you, ya kamikaze bumper car jockey."

"Right," Ryoya said sarcastically.

"When she started to cry I knew we were home free," Michael Donovan said.

"Even that was an act."

"It was?"

"She knew we had her and was building a case for an act of passion. It wasn't. It was premeditated murder all the way. That lady was cold. One thing I don't know for sure."

"What's that?"

"I don't know if she really did intend to kill just the girlfriend or if she wanted to kill them both."

"At this point it doesn't matter."

"I just don't like not knowing."

"It's been a long week. Why don't you clock out early?"

"I might do that."

"Plans for the weekend?"

"There is a double-header at Shea but it doesn't look like I'll be going."

"Jack not interested?"

"He had tickets but we haven't spoken in a few days," she paused, "It's probably for the better."

The Woodstock Music & Art Fair was scheduled to begin at 3:00 p.m. Unfortunately, its first act, Sweetwater, was stuck in a fifteen-mile-long traffic jam. Ritchie, Stephanie, and Fetch were also stuck in that same slow-moving mass of vehicles. They had been on the road for eleven hours and were far nearer the concert venue than was the overdue band. As they inched closer they started seeing areas where cars had pulled off the road to park or had run out of gas. The line of traffic stretched before them as far as they could see.

"Eventually, everything is going to come to a stop," Ritchie said. "I wonder how close we are."

"From what I can tell by this map the water on our left is White Lake and we are just a few miles away," Stephanie stated.

"We need to start looking for a place to park."

"It looks like a thousand others had the same idea."

"Not to worry, there has to be a few square feet somewhere."

They continued to inch along for a half hour until everything came to a complete stop. After about ten minutes the passengers of the vehicle in front of them got out of their car, opened the trunk, and started to gather their supplies.

Ritchie took the van out of gear and pressed on the emergency brake, "We're here."

"We're still on the road."

"The road is closed."

"What if they tow it away?"

"How?"

"I . . . well . . . I guess we're here."

They gathered their gear, hooked on Fetch's leash, locked the van, and joined the exodus of young people that was moving slowly toward the promised land.

"Hey, cool dog, man," someone in the crowd declared.

Fetch must have understood because she raised her head and proudly strode along fascinated by all of the strange people she observed. They reached the site late afternoon. Before them was an ocean of humanity. Every inch of the 37 acre alfalfa field was occupied. Buried under human bodies were cars and other vehicles that had been parked along the edge of the field. Ritchie was mesmerized by the vast mixture of colors that moved and undulated like a great kaleidoscope. Thousands and thousands of young Americans waited patiently for the concert to begin. There was no shoving or arguing or complaining. Some strummed guitars, others ate and drank, some found pleasure with each other, and some were far off in drug induced worlds. Ritchie and Stephanie found a small open space so far away from the stage that it appeared tiny. They sat down on the blade of grass they called their own.

Michael Lang, one of the concert promoters, asked Richie Havens to open the concert in place of Sweetwater that was still among the missing. He agreed. At 5:07 p.m. Richie Havens opened Woodstock and performed for almost two hours. Because other bands were still tied up in non-moving traffic the promoters had asked him to keep singing. When he ran out of songs he improvised a song based on the spiritual *Motherless Child* in which he sang about freedom so powerfully it became one of the most memorable performances of the concert.

At 7:10 p.m. Sri Swami Satchidananda gave the opening invocation for the Woodstock Music Festival when he addressed the crowd of nearly 500,000.

"My Beloved Brothers and Sisters: I am overwhelmed with joy to see the entire youth of America gathered here in the name of the fine art of music. In fact, through the music, we can work wonders. Music is a celestial sound and it is the sound that controls the whole universe, not atomic vibrations. Sound energy, sound power, is much, much greater than any other power in this world. And, one thing I would very much wish you all to remember is that with sound, we can make—and at the same time, break. Even in the war-field, to make the tender heart an animal, sound is used. Without that war band, that terrific sound, man will not become animal to kill his own brethren. So, that proves that you can break with sound, and if we care, we can make also."

Sweetwater had finally arrived and coincidentally began with the song *Motherless Child.*

Carl was busy setting things up for the Friday Night poker game when Ray Esposito entered the room. He walked up behind Carl, put his hand on his shoulder, and said, "Kid, I need you to do something for me, tomorrow."

"Whatever you say," Carl responded.

"You like to travel?"

"Haven't done much."

"Well, I need you to go to D.C. Take the train. When you get there call this number," Ray handed Carl a slip of paper. "When they answer the phone you tell them that Ray sent you. Don't use my last name. Set up a meet, but make sure it's a public place. A restaurant, museum, or public street." Ray looked around as if making sure that they remained alone. "You don't need to know what's in a package I'm gonna give you." Ray pointed directly at Carl, "Don't open it. It's better that you don't know anything."

"OK."

"You don't give your contact the package until they give you 100 grand. That's the hard part—making the exchange."

"You want I should count the money before giving them the package."

"Exactly. You can count to a hundred, can't you?" Ray smiled.

"With my shoes on," Carl replied.

"Once you're sure you have the hundred G's get your ass back here." Ray walked over to the counter and poured a cup of coffee from the pot that Carl had started. "You know why I picked you, Carl?"

Carl didn't answer.

"I know that I can trust you to follow orders. And, you're a thinker. Some of my other guys would blow the whole deal." Ray sipped some coffee, "You know where the problems will be?"

Carl poured himself a cup of coffee, "The way I see it there's something in the package that my contact wants—real bad. That means they could try to get it from me from the moment that you give it to me. So, just getting to D.C. with the package will be a challenge. Then in D.C. the same goes. Making the exchange will be when I face the greatest risk. Once I have the money and they have the package there will be a good chance that they will want to take the money back. So, until I put it in your hands I'm a target."

"You got a good head on your shoulders, kid." Ray stated. "You need to know that the person you will be dealing with is a public figure and they aren't happy about the whole thing. You understand?"

"Yeah."

"They may send someone with the money, but I don't think so. They want this to be hush, hush."

"Any chance cops will be involved?"

"Not likely. That kind of publicity they definitely don't want."

"When do I get the package?"

"Tomorrow morning. I'll give you more on that later tonight," Ray put down his cup. "Good coffee," he left the room.

Jack stood amidst the thousands of young people. He took photographs with his Nikon Photomic camera with a through the lens center-weighted metering system. As far away from the stage as he was the sound still seemed uncomfortably loud. Sound engineer Bill Hanley designed the system. He built 70 foot speaker columns that had 16 loudspeaker arrays on the hills.

After other singers who Jack didn't recognize finished their sets Ravi Shankar took to the stage. Due to his friendship with Beatles guitarist George Harrison, Shankar was a well-known sitar player. He began at 10:00 p.m. The rain began at 10:30 p.m. which caused him to cut his performance short. He was followed by Melanie and then Arlo Guthrie at 11:55 p.m. When Guthrie came on stage he announced, "The New York State Thruway's closed, man!"

Jack decided that he had witnessed enough and was wet enough to call it a night. He worked his way through the crowd and began his two mile hike back to the Schumacher house.

Robert Six Trees lay in bed listening to the thunder. He thought how welcome the rain was and that the next day would be full of promise.

43: Saturday – August 16, 1969

Joan Baez, who was six months pregnant, walked onto the stage at 12:55 a.m. She was the last performer of the first day of the Woodstock concert. Rain continued to fall as a drizzle. In the audience, young people huddled under tents, umbrellas, blankets, ponchos, and anything else they could find to fend off the incessant drops. Baez walked up to the microphone and proceeded to dedicate *Joe Hill,* her first song, to David Harris, her husband in prison for evading the draft. In 1967 Harris had formed an organization called The Resistance which worked to convince young men to return their draft cards and refuse to cooperate with the Selective Service. During the Vietnam War approximately half of those who received draft notices actually showed up for their physical. This made it impossible to prosecute them all. Instead, the government went after the leaders of the anti-draft movement. David Harris was arrested in July, 1969 and convicted of a federal felony—draft evasion. He was sentenced to 15 months in prison. Baez finished her set with the song *We Shall Overcome.* At 2:00 a.m. she left the stage as the rain began to fall more heavily. Thunderstorms proceeded to drop five inches of rain throughout the night on many totally unprepared children of God.

Ritchie, Stephanie, and a soggy doggy trudged back to the van. They left before Joan Baez took to the stage. Over two miles in the rain wasn't the most fun that they had that day but they made the best of it. Upon reaching the van they climbed inside and tried to dry off. A wet Basenji is not the most pleasant odor in a confined space.

"At least we're out of the rain," Ritchie said. "That's more than a lot can say."

"Can you believe how many people are here?" Stephanie asked.

"It's a revolution, babe! Power to the people!"

"I've never seen so many people in one place."

"They're, like, beautiful. Free spirits—diggin' the music."

"I can hear the music in the distance."

"Yeah. They might go all night."

"I hope we don't miss Janis Joplin."

"We won't," Ritchie said. He then turned serious, "Hey Steph, I gotta tell you something."

Stephanie, somewhat surprised and concerned, looked directly at Ritchie, "What?"

"Well, I sorta got reclassified 1A."

"You've been drafted?" she exclaimed.

"No, but the letter can't be far behind," Ritchie said. He added, "Once they make you 1A you're as good as drafted."

"What are you going to do?"

"Like, I'm heading to Canada. What else?"

"Canada?"

"I know your dad lives with you and all, but why don't you come with me?"

"I can't. You know that."

"Maybe there's some way you can get your father some help."

"I can't leave him, now. I won't," Stephanie stated. Inside she thought this was an opportune time to end the relationship that she was becoming more and more uncomfortable with due to Ritchie's drug use. She asked, "When do you plan to go?"

"In a week," Ritchie answered. "I've got to make a few more arrangements. Then I pack up and go."

"You won't be able to come back, you know that?"

"I'd rather be alive in the great white north than dead in North Vietnam."

"How will you cross the border?"

"I'm studying that. I've been told there is a way to cross into Canada through an Indian reservation in Minnesota. From all the maps I've seen the Rain River creates the border. I haven't found the secret crossing point yet. But, I will."

"How does Canada feel about all these Americans coming into their country?"

"They love us," Ritchie joked. Then he said, "Seriously, I read that the Canadian Parliament granted amnesty to American war resisters who entered Canada illegally and even offered them an opportunity to apply for immigrant status. In fact, this past May it was announced that immigration officials would not ask about military status of anyone who showed up at the border seeking permanent residence in Canada."

"So, you're really going?"

"I have to," Ritchie shrugged.

Fetch shook, spraying water onto the two humans in the van.

Ray Esposito walked into an Italian bakery on Mott Street in Little Italy, south of the East Village. His driver waited in the 1969 Lincoln Continental. As usual Ray was impressive in his sartorial splendor. His two-button Italian Ramp Brown Linen suit was perfectly tailored by Antonio. While rare for him to enter any establishment alone it was necessary on this day. He walked past the counter and the few customers waiting for their turn into the back of the bakery. Three bakers were busy at work kneading dough, checking ovens, and preparing pastries. They recognized Ray Esposito immediately but made no sign of noticing. It was better that they kept busy and minded their own business. Ray continued past them out the back door into the alley. There stood Carl Pythacyk wearing one of his custom suits by Antonio. Carl had arrived an hour before Ray, as instructed, and waited.

"Did you try the Pasticciotti?" Ray asked.

"I tried everything," Carl replied with a smile.

"I love the smell of a bakery early in the morning. It brings me back." Ray looked around the alley. It was small, surrounded by old brick buildings with no windows. At the far end there was a brick wall where the alley split at a T going right and left. He knew both branches led to the back door of other businesses that were no longer open. One of his men stood guard at the front door of each abandoned store. "You remember everything that I told you, right?"

"I went over it again and again in my mind all night."

"Good. You can never be too prepared."

Carl nodded.

"Kid, we're talking about a big fish, here. One that is capable of anything. Don't underestimate the danger. If he has the opportunity to put out your lights and take the package and keep the cash he will in a heartbeat."

"I'm not going to let that happen."

"Good," Ray smiled, "I kinda like your coffee."

"There's no accounting for taste," Carl observed.

Ray laughed and smacked Carl on the back. "I got a lot of muscle. You know, brawn but no brains. I push a button and they take care of it." He pointed at Carl, "You got a brain. I can use it lots of ways. So, don't get yourself smacked." Ray reached up under the back of his jacket and pulled out an envelope that was tucked in his belt. It was a 9" x 12" manila envelope. "Remember, don't open it. The less you know the better." He handed the envelope to Carl who immediately slipped it into an attaché case with lettering on the outside, Plymouth Chess Sets.

Carl looked up and said, "I sell chess sets."

"Where'd you get that?"

"Couple years ago we hit a warehouse. Got a bunch of new games and electronic stuff. I saw this and took it. It's a sample case with a couple chess set designs. Thought, I might learn someday."

"Good idea, but it will make you easy to identify."

"This," Carl lifted the case, "will get me back to the Bronx. There I pick up my wife and we head to the train station."

"Your wife?"

"A girl I know. She and I are going to Baltimore to visit her mother."

"Baltimore?"

"If they're watching the ticket counter they will be taking a second look at anyone buying round trip tickets to Washington, D.C.—not Baltimore."

Ray nodded.

Carl continued, "I leave the girl in Baltimore and take a bus to Washington. Then I scope it out to find a safe place for the exchange. Once that's done I board a train for New York. Before it leaves I sneak off and get my ass to the bus terminal and go back to Baltimore. From there, Mr. and Mrs. Pythacyk take the train from Baltimore to New York, only we get off in Newark. From there a bus ride brings us home."

"That's quite a plan," Ray admitted. "Can the girl be trusted?"

"She's a friend and doesn't ask any questions. She not only has no idea what I'm doing but doesn't know where I'm going when I leave her. She will stay in Baltimore and wait for me to return."

"There are parts of the plan where you are vulnerable. After the exchange, you have to get to the train station. That may be harder than you think. Once on the train you may be watched or approached before you can sneak off the train. Even if you do get off the train there could be backup watching the platform."

"No plan is perfect. Going down they don't know who they are looking for. Coming back—they will know. I'm still working on that."

Matt sat at the small kitchen table in Stephanie's apartment. He sipped coffee as he read the New York Daily News. The headline shouted, "TRAFFIC UPTIGHT AT HIPPIEFEST—Go-Go Is a No-No." He thought about his sweet innocent daughter, Stephanie, spending the weekend with a long-haired, hippie, freak at a rock concert that might get out-of-control and violent at any moment. The newspapers, radio, and television news all stressed the fact that the concert was poorly planned, lacking proper facilities, had little security, and was attracting thousands more than expected. He didn't want her to go, but couldn't tell her not to. His long illness and slow recovery had changed the dynamic of their relationship. He was her father but was unable to reclaim that role in a traditional sense. Stephanie was old enough to make her own decisions and he had to accept that fact. Yet, it didn't mean that he wouldn't worry about his little princess.

Since his meeting with Jack, the newspaper reporter, Matt continued to try to remember his pre-accident life. Unfortunately, it is nearly impossible to force memories to reappear. Lida Petropoulos was somewhere out there in the world. She could fill in the gaps and answer unanswered questions about Orztech and the wire products that were manufactured. Once found, she could exonerate or condemn one Matthew Ellis.

A number entered his mind—5594. What it meant he didn't know. It was familiar but why he didn't have a clue. It was too few numbers to be a telephone number. Four digits? The idea of four digits immediately ignited another unexpected memory. The number 6174 entered Matt's mind. But why? Suddenly, he once again entered a world of memories.

Valerie was sitting in the den of their plush Alpine, New Jersey house. It was winter and snow covered the ground outside. A fire danced in the fireplace providing a warm glow and flow of air. She was on the couch with her legs pulled up beneath her. Her full attention was to a magazine and yellow writing pad. When Matt entered the room carrying two cups of hot coffee he observed his wife writing numbers on the pad, doing calculations, repeating the process, then saying, "It works!"

"What works?" Matt asked as he sat next to Valerie.

"There's an article here that explains how the number 6174 is always the result when four digit numbers are rearranged and subtracted. It's called Kaprekar's Operation. It was invented by an Indian mathematician named D. R. Kaprekar in 1949"

"Oh, how does it work?"

Valerie sat up straight, sipped some coffee, and explained, "You start with any four digit number. But all four digits can't be the same number."

"Why?"

"I don't know—yes I do. If all four numbers were the same when you do the subtraction it would equal zero."

"Nice trick," Matt said sarcastically.

"Hush! Whatever number you pick, say 4733 you rearrange the digits to form the largest number possible and the smallest number possible. In this case it would be 7433 and 3347." Valerie wrote the numbers on her yellow pad. She continued, "Then you subtract the smaller number from the larger one." She did the math and said, "There, it equals 4086."

"That's not your magic number."

"No silly, you do it again. Let's see 4086 would become 8640 and 0468. Subtract again and the result is 8172."

"That's still not, what was the number, 6174."

Valerie looked at her husband, tilted her head, and then returned to her calculating, "8172 would become 8721 and 1278. Subtract and the result is 7443."

"It's not working," Matt said.

"It can take up to seven subtractions," Valerie explained. "OK, 7443 becomes, hey, 7443 and 3447. Subtract and we have 3996."

"I'm getting bored,"

"You have the attention span of a gnat. 3996 becomes 9963 and 3699. Subtract and you get 6264." Matt made a snoring sound at which point Valerie slapped his arm,

"Pay attention. This could save your life."

"How so?"

"Do I have to tell you? Just listen. 6264 becomes 6642 and 2466. Subtract and you get 4176."

"You know, if you do it enough any number will eventually appear."

Valerie ignored Matt, "4176 becomes 7641 and 1467. The result 6174." She held up the yellow pad showing the calculations. Also, on the page were five other examples of how the number ultimately reached was always 6174. "How about that?"

"It works every time?"

"Every husband doubting time. Fascinating. The article shows algebra formula and gives an explanation but I really don't understand it."

Matt took the pad from Valerie, placed it on the table, and put his arm around her. She leaned against his shoulder. "I wonder how much it's going to snow," Valerie said.

"Not as much as when we met, I hope," Matt replied. He then added, "Because I'm not digging through a mountain of snow to save you."

Valerie sat up and looked hurt, "You wouldn't save me?"

"I don't know. What would I get for saving you?"

"If I recall the price was a kiss."

"Well, that's a lot of work for a measly kiss."

"My kisses are not measly," Valerie pouted.

"Let's see," Matt pulled his wife toward him and kissed her. "Well, if it's not too big a mountain. Maybe I'd save you."

"Thanks," Valerie returned to leaning on Matt's shoulder. She then told a story. "When I was in high school I took ballet lessons at a school in Manhattan. It was associated with one of the ballet companies so was very competitive. I worked hard and seemed to get noticed now and then. There was a girl my age who was very good. Much better than me, she had natural talent. She kept to herself which made some of the other girls feel she was a snob. In reality, it was the opposite. Her clothes and hair revealed that she came from a poor family. I think she stayed and worked at the studio as part payment for lessons."

Matt wondered why Valerie was telling the story but continued to listen. "One day we were getting ready to audition for roles in *Swan Lake*. I had a new pair of pointe shoes that my parents had given me for my birthday. As I was preparing them I heard the girl say, 'Oh,' that's all, just, 'Oh.' When I looked over I saw that the ribbon on one of her shoes had pulled off. At first I didn't think much about it because it's quite common. You just have to sew it back on. We all kept needle and thread in our dance bags. After a few minutes I looked over once more and she was just sitting there. I asked her if she needed some thread but she didn't answer. Then I went over to her to give her some thread." Valerie sat up and motioned with her hands, "She held her pointe shoe in her hand and I could see that it was well worn. It was worn out. The material was so riddled with holes there was no way to sew a ribbon onto the shoe. I don't know how she even danced in them or how she danced so well. She looked at me but didn't say anything. In fact, her face was expressionless. It was like she had come to a point, no pun intended, where there were no more solutions and she was resigned to the fact that her dancing had come to an end. I was still holding my new pointe shoes and noticed her shoe size was the same as mine. In my bag was an old pair of pointe shoes. Now I knew that if she didn't audition, I had a real chance at the lead dual role of Odette/Odile, the white and black swans. For a moment I was tempted to not help. As I said, the school was very competitive. The ugly side of ballet. I stood, dropped the new shoes to the floor, and walked back to my bag. As I put on my old shoes she walked over to me and handed me my new ones. 'I can't,' she simply said. I refused to take them and replied, 'You have to.' She put them down next to me. At first, I didn't know what to do. I tried to help so my conscience was clear. Then it struck me. I finished putting on my old pointe shoes, stood, pointed at the shoes on the floor and said, 'If you want to dance there's your chance. If you're too proud to accept a little help then maybe you weren't meant to be a dancer.' I went into the studio and left her alone."

Valerie sipped some coffee and stared into the dark liquid. She spoke softly as she said, "A part of me wanted to see her enter the studio while another part of me hoped that she wouldn't. I wanted that role so much. The work and practice and pain that I endured to have that chance did not escape me. Then, she came into the room wearing my new shoes and began to warm up. It's hard to explain how two emotions can clash within you. I was glad that she chose to dance while I was also disappointed because I knew that I couldn't outperform her. After the auditions, back in the dressing room, she came over and handed me my shoes, smiled, and said, 'I danced my best for you.' I didn't know what to say. She wanted to please me. What a strange thing to say. Why should she care what I think? I remember her smile. Even though fleeting it was so different from what we were accustomed to seeing. As I prepared to leave it struck me that she had nothing else to give. It was her way of saying thank you. All she had was her dance and she gave it to me. I couldn't help but feel honored by her gesture. A gift from the heart is a rare and wonderful thing. I walked over to where she sat and dropped the pointe shoes onto the floor before her. We looked at each other for a moment and I left. I never told my parents about giving away the shoes. Not sure they ever noticed. Marguerite got the role and went on to be a prima ballerina with the Boston Ballet." Valerie smiled.

Matt said, "The same Marguerite we get a Christmas card from every year?"

"The same one."

Matt remembered that story and the look on Valerie's face. She was truly proud of her friend. There was no envy or regret reflected in her eyes. Instead there was innocence and purity. How he was the one who was fortunate enough to win her heart he never could understand.

Detective Ryoya Akimoto walked along Third Avenue carrying a bag of fresh bakery items and a large container of coffee. Under her arm was a copy of the *Tribune* that she had picked up on a whim. She missed Jack but as each day passed she wondered if it was the right time to end the unacceptable and doomed relationship. It would indeed be kinder than putting off the inevitable.

Once home, she settled down at her dining room table to eat some of her goodies. A Saturday off duty was a welcome change of pace. When she unfolded the newspaper an article caught her eye.

AN UNEXPECTED WELCOME
by: Jack Moore

Bethel, NY: I came to this small village in upstate New York to cover a music festival billed as "An Aquarian Exposition: 3 Days of Peace & Music." The term Aquarian refers to the Age of Aquarius loosely based on the belief that the world will soon enter the astrological age of love, light, and humanity. More accurately, it probably came from the 1967 musical *Hair* and the song by The 5th Dimension. Whatever the motivation a rural farm in New York did enter a different and unique age.

After a long arduous drive among countless odd looking vehicles filled with odd looking individuals I arrived at the musical promised land. If you have ever been in Times Square on New Year's Eve you have a slight idea of what an ocean of humanity looks like. Add to that image an array of colors, movement, and music coming from all directions and the picture is complete. Well, maybe not. Look more closely and something wonderful will strike you. Smiling faces, nods of acknowledgment, peace signs, pats on the back, hugs, sharing, dancing, and laughter. The Age of Aquarius.

Young people everywhere were setting up tents and laying down blankets in preparation for a concert to end all concerts. Remarkably, there weren't any shoving matches or territorial disputes. Quite the opposite, there were invitations to join them. I stood out like a sore thumb but wasn't treated as such. Wherever I went I was welcomed. I felt more at home than I do at a family dinner.

If there be fault to point out it has to be with the promoters of the festival. Facilities are sorely lacking. There are not enough food services available. The event started two hours late and the sound system is of poor quality. Even the venue, while shaped like an amphitheater, is too small to accommodate the massive audience. Mother Nature didn't help bringing rain later in the evening. Yet, thousands of young people made their own fun. If they represent the future there is hope that better days lie ahead.

I have one major concern—the use of drugs. Marijuana, LSD, amphetamines, and an array of drugs I've never heard of were openly in use by far too many. Police presence is non-existent and wouldn't be effective if it was with such a large crowd. So, these young people who seek peace, love, and more might just be clouding that possibility with blown-out minds. I wish I could tell them that there is a real difference between peace and rest-in-peace.

Ryoya could envision Jack in a massive crowd of hippies somehow fitting in. He was a likeable guy with a hard to describe charm. Only he could write an article from a positive perspective while all the other media condemned everything about the festival. She smiled. In a funny way she was proud of her man, even if he was her man only for the moment.

At 6:00 a.m. Pacific Time more than 100 Los Angeles County Sheriff's Deputies descended on the Spahn Movie Ranch at 1200 Santa Susana Pass Road in Chatsworth, California. They were looking for stolen cars and illegal guns. Their early arrival caught most of the Manson Family asleep.

Charlie Manson was located hiding underneath the floor of the building called "Longhorn Saloon." He was face down in the dirt between foundation timbers. After being told to come out two times he finally crawled out to waiting deputies. As he stood a black credit card holder fell out of his right shirt pocket. In the holder were four stolen credit cards.

Gulf Oil credit card #118-692-588-7 issued to Irvin H. Weiland
Atlantic Richfield credit card #R-18-221-424 issued to T.H. Weiland MD
Enco Oil credit card #185-112-654-4 issued to T.H. Weiland MD
Phillips 66 credit card #1-89-109-3899 issued to Ayman Weiland MD

Deputies didn't notice the leather thong around Manson's neck that was very similar to the thongs used to tie up the LaBiancas.

In all a total of 26 suspects were arrested on the 200-acre ranch. Among those arrested was Johnny Swartz who owned the car used during the Tate-LaBianca murders. Unfortunately, due to a technicality with the warrant, all suspects were subsequently released. Sadly, the police made no connection between the members of the Manson family and the Tate-LaBianca murders.

Mr. and Mrs. Pythacyk boarded the train at Penn Station. It was scheduled to stop in Philadelphia, Baltimore, and Washington, DC. As agreed they talked about their upcoming visit with her mother in Baltimore. They actually had fun making up stories about non-existing events and relatives. Anyone nearby would be convinced that they were a young couple making a family visit. To complete the image they carried old worn suitcases.

After buying one way tickets to Baltimore, Carl carefully screened the ticket counter area and the train platform to identify any individual who might be paying too much attention to them. As part of the ruse Carl wore a black tee-shirt and jeans. Susan Friedlander, his pretend wife, wore shorts and a cotton top. She had been surprised by Carl's call but quickly agreed to be an accomplice. The dinner they had together at Santino's on the previous Monday night made quite an impression on her. She knew Carl was involved with organized crime, but he was always nice to her. His confidence and newfound sophistication was exciting. With him she felt safe. It was an easy decision to spend a day together and when told to ask no questions she readily agreed. Pretending to be a married couple to Susan was a hoot.

A hurricane watch was issued for the Gulf Coast extending from Biloxi, Mississippi eastward to St. Marks, Florida. Wave heights in the Gulf were as high as seventy feet. Camille was a Category 2 storm moving in a northwesterly direction over warm Gulf of Mexico waters. In her wake she left five dead in Cuba.

Jack made his way back to the music festival after a large country breakfast with Bertha and Teddy Schumacher. The sky was overcast and the road wet. Overnight rain added one more challenge for the thousands of attendees who sought music and nature. It was a long two-mile trek on West Shore Road so Jack paced himself. He passed cultivated fields, a few old homes, a horse ranch, and forests. The rain made all the green colors appear far more vibrant. Up ahead, Jack heard laughter. It came from around a bend on the left. On that side of the road was Forsythia Cove, a pond with a small waterfall.

The sight Jack saw when he rounded the bend in the road was something for which he was unprepared. In the water young men and women were skinny-dipping. Dozens of them were swimming, washing off mud, sitting on the bank, and walking around naked without embarrassment or concern. His first thought was of young savages. Then his mind pictured the Garden of Eden. Innocence, pure and unfettered by social mores, was free to exist as one with nature in Bethel, which ironically means House of God.

A female voice behind Jack said, "Don't stare. It's impolite."

Jack started and turned. Before him was a young woman. She was approximately twenty five years old, long straight auburn hair with a headband made of flowers, wearing rimless glasses, through which peered dark green eyes. No makeup was apparent yet the tones of her skin highlighted sharp sculptured features. Her lips were slightly parted and a tilt of her head gave the impression of one looking upon a thing of wonder. She wore a tee-shirt on which was painted a skunk holding the green ecology flag. Over her shoulder hung a tan cloth bag on which was painted a pastoral scene. Yellow shorts and sandals completed the picture. "You definitely didn't come for the music," she concluded.

"How do you know?" Jack responded.

"Just a hunch," she tilted her head in the other direction and looked out of the corner of her eye as she asked, "Narc, reporter, or father looking for his daughter?"

"Does it matter?"

"To me? No."

"Reporter, *New York Tribune.*"

"I see." She took Jack's hand and said, "Walk with me."

Jack complied both due to attraction and curiosity. They continued down West Shore Road in the direction of the concert. It was before noon therefore no performers were scheduled to play. In silence, they walked along with the returning crowd. Jack couldn't help but think of the song by the Cowsills, *The Flower Girl.* He didn't remember that the title actually was *The Rain, the Park & Other Things.* However, the lyrics whispered in his mind.

> I saw her sitting in the rain
> Raindrops falling on her
> She didn't seem to care
> She sat there and smiled at me
>
> And I knew (I knew, I knew, I knew, I knew)
> She could make me happy (happy, happy)
> Flowers in her hair, flowers everywhere

I love the flower girl
Oh, I don't know just why
She simply caught my eye
I love the flower girl she seemed so sweet and kind
She crept into my mind

I knew I had to say hello (hello, hello)
She smiled up at me
She took my hand and we walked through the park alone

But I knew (I knew, I knew, I knew, I knew)
She had made me happy (happy, happy)
Flowers in her hair, flowers everywhere

I love the flower girl
Oh, I don't know just why
She simply caught my eye
I love the flower girl she seemed so sweet and kind
She crept into my mind

Suddenly the sun broke through (see the sun)
I turned around she was gone (where did she go)
And all I had left was one little flower from her hair

But I knew (I knew, I knew, I knew, I knew)
She had made me happy (happy, happy)
Flowers in her hair, flowers everywhere

I love the flower girl
Was she reality or just a dream to me?
I love the flower girl
Our love shall lead the way
To find a sunny day
I love the flower girl
Was she reality or just a dream to me?

Strange as it was he was walking hand-in-hand with a flower girl. She had appeared from nowhere and found him. Why? He looked over at his unnamed companion. As if she sensed his gaze she turned her head to look into his eyes. Finally, Jack said, "Are you here for the music?"

"Not the music you think."

"Oh. What music then?"

"The rhythm of life." She led Jack over to a rail fence and looked into the pasture on the other side. "Have you ever listened to *Bolero* by Maurice Ravel?"

"I've heard it. Interesting piece."

"He originally wrote it for his patron, Blanche Lapin, as a ballet. Most people hear each instrument as it solos and feel the energy building until the final climax. They don't hear all of the instruments as they play or the unique drumbeat throughout playing in a constant 3/4 time with a prominent triplet on the second beat of every bar." She turned back toward Jack and said, "There are tones and sounds behind the music. There are sounds to life behind the obvious. What do you hear?"

"What? Oh, I hear voices and distant music."

"Do you hear the cow?"

"No," Jack listened more carefully but didn't hear a cow.

"What about the hammering?"

Once more Jack listened. In the cacophony of sounds that came from the crowd at the concert he couldn't hear anything clearly. Then, as if a microphone had been turned up, he heard it. There was indeed a hammer being used somewhere in the distance. He smiled, "Yes, I hear a hammer."

The flower girl smiled. She took Jack's hand and they continued in the direction of the concert. A young male hippie passed them going in the other direction. He raised his right hand showing the familiar V-peace sign and said, "Peace, man."

"Did you hear that?" Jack's companion asked.

"Yes. He said peace," Jack replied.

"No. He stepped on an acorn cracking it as he passed."

"He did?"

"Yes."

Jack stopped and turned toward the young woman. He looked at her and asked, "What is your point? That you have supernatural hearing?"

She smiled and said, "I don't have super hearing. My point is that you don't need drugs to reach a higher plane or expanded awareness."

"I don't use drugs," Jack remarked.

"Do you drink alcohol?"

"I do."

"Why?"

"I like it."

"No one likes poison."

"One man's poison is another man's refreshment," Jack said. Then he asked, "Do you drink alcohol?"

"Of course."

"Then why are you giving me a hard time?"

She laughed, turned, and continued walking toward the concert. Jack fell in step with her and they walked in silence. The young woman fascinated him. He couldn't put his finger on it but there was a story. Obviously, she was a conservationist, a tree hugger, but there's nothing wrong with that. He thought how polluted the Hudson River had become. You wouldn't dare swim in it. If persons like the flower girl raised awareness . . . awareness—that's her point! Impulsively, he took her hand and turned her toward him, "What do you hear?"

She looked up into his eyes and replied, "Your heartbeat." She leaned forward and wrapped her arms around him placing her right ear on his chest.

Once more Jack was caught off guard. He indeed had stepped through the looking glass. A middle-aged, straight-arrow, conservative newspaper reporter was among a plethora of strange creatures that he had failed to see until then. Where were they hiding when not at a concert? With a young attractive woman hugging him he wasn't sure if he felt like a father or lover.

The Pythacyks arrived in Baltimore. They exited the train at Penn Station on North Charles Street. A man in a dark blue suit, white shirt, and maroon tie also exited the train at that station. Carl and Susan didn't notice. They hailed a cab and jumped in. Carl asked the driver where the bus station was where he could catch a bus to Washington, D.C.

"That'd be the Greyhound station on Haines Street," the driver stated. Before starting to drive he turned and said, "Didn't you just get off the train?"

"Yeah," Carl answered as he considered the driver. He was Caucasian, most likely German or Belgium, had a bald head covered with a Baltimore Orioles baseball cap worn in a manner where the brim pointed straight up, and had a half-burned unlit cigar in his mouth.

"The one that goes to DC?"

"Yeah, now drive."

The taxi left the stand and began driving north on Charles Street. As he drove, the driver said over his shoulder, "It's none of my business, but you coulda just stayed on the train. The bus, when it runs, takes forever."

"I like buses," Carl said.

The taxi made three right turns and entered a highway headed south. The driver looked into the rearview mirror and commented, "Well, whoever is following us might also like buses."

Carl glanced out the back window and saw another Baltimore taxi behind them. "How do you know?"

"Could just be a co-ink-a-dink but that cab left the station right behind us." He slowed his taxi to the speed limit. The taxi behind did the same. "Yeah, he's got his nose glued to my butt. Want me to lose him?"

"No," Carl said, "If they're following us they know where we are going." He leaned forward and asked the driver, "How much to take us to Washington?"

"Jeeze, that'd be at least fifty bucks."

"If you take us to Washington and then lose that cab once we're there I'll give you a hundred bucks."

"Let me see the money," the cabbie said.

Carl waved a hundred dollar bill and two fifties in front of the driver's face. He then handed the driver one fifty and said, "Fifty now, the rest when we lose our tail in DC."

At 12:15 p.m. a little known band named Quill that was formed by two brothers, Jon and Dan Cole, from Boston took to the stage. Just before they walked onto the soaking wet platform the sun broke through clouds. They played a four song set that lasted forty minutes. Earlier in the week they had been hired to play concerts at prisons, mental hospitals, and halfway houses by festival organizers as a goodwill gesture to the community. Country Joe McDonald followed and played for half an hour.

The first Mets game featured Tom Seaver on the mound who was 16 – 7 for the season. The team he faced, San Diego Padres, was in last place so expectations were high. Attending the game was New York State Trooper Nelson Arvin and his wife, the

New York Yankee fan. It turned out to be a pitcher's duel that remained scoreless until the fifth inning. Batting for the Mets, Jerry Grote grounded out. He was followed by Bud Harrelson who singled to centerfield. The pitcher, Tom Seaver, bunted moving Harrelson to second. Tommie Agee then singled to right field allowing Harrelson to score the first run of the ballgame. The Mets added a second run in the seventh inning when Bobby Pfiel drove in Jerry Grote with a single to right field. Tom Seaver pitched eight innings of shutout ball and won his seventeenth game of the season 2 - 0. Ryoya listened to the game on the radio as she cleaned her apartment. She thought about Jack upstate covering a concert that the media had labeled a disaster.

Jack and the flower girl could barely hear the music from as far from the stage as they were. The massive crowd before them had the appearance of a huge mass of bees swarming on the hillside. Mud covered filthy bees, but bees none-the-less. Flower girl led Jack away from the concert toward a wooded area. There was a gravel path and she started in that direction. When Jack attempted to follow she turned and held up her hand, "There are some things a person prefers to do alone." Immediately, Jack understood and stopped.

When she returned Jack asked, "Did you wash your hands?"

Flower girl reached into her bag and retrieved a bar of soap, "A lady is always prepared. There's a stream on the other side of those trees."

"Good to know."

The two odd concert-fellows headed toward the concession tents that were located on a hill behind the audience. Promoters had hired a catering firm named Food For Love to provide hamburgers and hotdogs. Unfortunately, the small operation was overwhelmed by the unanticipated large crowd. They quickly ran out of food and went out of business.

Another group known as the Hog Farm had been hired to help with preparations by clearing trails and building fire pits. The Hog Farm was founded by Hugh Nanton Romney, a comedian and political activist in California. After being arrested numerous times during demonstrations he decided to take on a clown persona. In his words, "He would be less likely to be arrested if he dressed as a clown."

In the early 60's when he needed a place to live he was told that a hog farm owned by Claude Doty needed caretakers. Romney took the position and the mountain-top hog farm soon became a haunt for artists, actors, musicians, and hippies. Hugh Romney and his partner, Bonnie Beecher, both had jobs in Los Angeles. He taught improvisation at Columbia Pictures and she was a television actress. By 1966, the Hog Farm had become an entertainment troupe doing light shows for musical artists, such as; Jimi Hendrix, Cream, and the Grateful Dead.

Members of the Hog Farm had also been recruited to act as security for the Woodstock festival. Concert promoters simply overlooked telling them. The Hog Farm people didn't have the brawn or experience of a normal security force, however, nothing at Woodstock was shaping up to be normal. They found out about their new responsibility when Romney was asked by a reporter how they planned to keep the peace. He replied, "Cream pies and seltzer bottles." They called themselves the "Please Force." When they found someone doing something they shouldn't they would say, "Please, don't do that. Please, do this instead."

When the food ran out the Hog Farm's Lisa Law, who was seven months pregnant, convinced the promoters to give her $3,000. She borrowed a truck and drove to Chinatown in New York City. There she bought cooking pots, cleavers, stainless steel bowls, 50-gallon plastic garbage cans, 160,000 paper plates and other items. She then purchased 1,500 pounds of rolled oats, 225 pounds of currants along with dried apricots and almonds. These were all the ingredients needed to make granola. On her way back she purchased bulgur, a kind of dried cracked wheat, which cooks faster than rice, corn, onions, cabbage, squash, and carrots. In the large plastic garbage cans she mixed up bulgur and granola sweetened with honey to feed thousands. Local farmers and residents also pitched in when they heard of the food shortage. They made peanut butter and jelly sandwiches and other meals for the hungry crowd. Finally, the National Guard dropped food from helicopters.

Jack and the Flower Girl volunteered and helped distribute food. As they did John Sebastian walked on stage following Santana. He was not on the bill and was simply attending the concert. Due to late arrivals of other performers he was asked to perform. He was high when he took the microphone wearing a tie-dyed suit and said, "You know, like, the press can only, uh, can only say bad things unless there ain't no fuck-ups, and it's looking like there ain't gonna be no fuck-ups. This is gonna work." He went on to play *I Had A Dream, Rainbows All Over Your Blues, Darling Be Home Soon* and *Younger Generation,* which he dedicated to a newborn baby at the festival.

Carl and Susan arrived in Washington D.C. The taxi driver asked if he wanted to lose the other cab at that time and Carl said yes. With precision only a skilled driver or maniac could muster the bald driver wearing a Baltimore Orioles baseball cap cut in and out of traffic, made abrupt turns, and a few well-timed illegal moves to leave the other car far behind. Once far out-of-sight of their shadow he drove into an alley and stopped. With the unlit cigar still hanging out of his mouth he turned and said, "Never had a chance." Carl smiled and handed the driver fifty dollars. It was then that he had a flash of brilliance that completed his plan.

"There's another hundred in it if you can help me do one more thing."

"As long as it's legal—I'm in."

Game two of the Mets/Padres double hitter started at 2:30 p.m. Threatening clouds hung in the sky. Jim McAndrew was on the mound for the Mets. In the second inning ex-New York Met, Larry Stahl of the Padres, hit a homerun to give his team the lead. It held until Cleon Jones hit a homerun in the fourth inning to tie the game. In the bottom of the seventh Ron Swoboda hit a ground ball that should have been an out. However, a bad throw caused the first baseman to miss the ball and Swoboda was able to make it to third base. Bud Harrelson was intentionally walked. With runners at first and third Jerry Grote singled to right field. That was all the Mets needed. They won the game 2 – 1. At Shea Stadium 19,940 fans enjoyed watching the Mets sweep the double header. Rain began to fall as they left to head home.

Hurricane Camille stalled over the Gulf of Mexico 310 miles due south of Pensacola. Winds were at 150 miles-per-hour. Forecasters tried to project the path of the storm but had to admit that they weren't sure if it would track east, west, or north.

Carl left the Baltimore taxicab in the alley. Susan remained with the driver who they determined was named Sid. When he found a public telephone he dialed the number that had been given to him by Ray Esposito. A man answered with a single word, "Yes."

"I have a package for you," Carl replied.

"Yes."

"Do you have something for me?"

"Yes."

Carl was getting impatient with the one-word answers but continued, "Here is how it's going to go down. Neither of us trusts each other. So we will make the exchange in public. Now, I don't know what is in my package, but I'm sure you will want to inspect it."

"Correct."

"I studied a map of DC."

"OK."

"Do you know where Mount Vernon Square Park is?"

"Yes."

"How soon can you get there?"

"Ten minutes."

"OK. Be at the front gate on K Street. It's in the middle of the block."

"OK."

"A Baltimore Taxi will pull up. You get in."

"How do I know I can trust you?"

Finally, more than one or two words, the young hood thought. Carl explained, "Listen, I don't know you and you don't know me. Let's keep it that way. If my employer wanted to hurt you he already would have. My instructions are to make the exchange and return what you give me to him—the money that I will count. Let's make this painless." Carl added in a tone that made his point very clear, "Understand, I know how to make it as painful as necessary. But, that wouldn't be good for either of us."

"I understand."

"One final point. Any attempt to take the package from me without payment will end any chance for an exchange. And, my employer is one person you don't want to piss off."

"Understood."

"Ten minutes at the gate of Mount Vernon Square Park."

A Baltimore taxicab slowed to a stop in front of the gate of Mount Vernon Square Park ten minutes after Carl spoke with his contact. After a few seconds a man stepped out of the shadows and walked toward the cab. He wore a white golf shirt, tan pants, and brown docksiders. In addition, he wore a white baseball cap with an unidentifiable logo and dark glasses. Under his arm was a leather portfolio. As he approached the cab he looked around. Carl knew this was a critical time as the man could try something stupid or he could have accomplices who swarm the taxi. The man reached the taxi and entered the back seat.

"Did you bring the payment?" Carl asked.

"The Package?"

Carl had the package on his left side away from the new passenger. He patted it. It was then that he said to the taxi driver, "Sid, take us out onto a highway and keep the cab moving at least forty miles-per-hour. Don't stop." Carl turned to the man he didn't recognize and stated, "I don't want anyone jumping in or you jumping out. We'll make the exchange when we are on the highway."

"You are careful," the man said without emotion.

The tone and statement rang an alarm in Carl's mind. The man was too calm and the statement was meant to put Carl at ease—or off guard. Carl said to the driver, "Sid, anything happens to me use the gun."

The driver picked up on the ploy and replied, "Got it."

The man's tone changed and he said, "There's no need for that."

"Why don't you put the weapon on the floor?" Carl suggested.

"I don't have any weapon."

"Don't make me search you."

"You're not going to search me," the man said as he raised his right arm to aim a 9mm semi-automatic pistol at Carl.

There was something surreal about the whole Woodstock experience. It was a combination of Marti Gras, Jones Beach, Vatican on Christmas Eve, and Grand Central Station all mixed together and put to music. In spite of all the problems with lack of food, poor facilities, rain, mud, crowding, and bad acoustics the massive gathering of counter-culture rebels were uncommonly calm, generous, and in good spirits. Albeit, some were stoned, or asleep, or engaged in lovemaking. Jack wondered what it was that made this enormous group of grubby homo sapiens so different and so rare. There was every reason to look down on them as losers, dropouts, or useless individuals but he couldn't. Beneath the mud and filth there were pure honest welcoming creatures who were searching. Their search had brought them here by the thousands and it would shape their lives in ways they never could imagine. At his side stood the Flower Girl. Whatever she was, she was genuine. For an unknown reason she had attached herself to him. Yet, she asked nothing of him. Together they experienced Woodstock in their own private manner.

At sunset, Canned Heat walked onto the stage. An established blues band, they were one of the featured groups at the festival. The band was founded in 1966 by two record collectors, Alan "Blind Owl" Wilson and Bob "The Bear" Hite. They were joined by Henry "The Sunflower" Vestine, Larry "The Mole" Taylor, and Adolfo "Fito" de la Parra. Vestine had played with Mothers of Invention and Taylor with Jerry Lee Lewis. Adolfo de la Parra, the drummer, had played with well-known Latin American bands, Los Sinners and Los Hooligans. They began to play blues oriented songs with psychedelic features which brought the crowd that could hear them to their feet. Canned Heat played seven songs ending their set with their best known song, *On the Road Again*.

> Well I'm so tired of cryin' but I'm out on the road again
> I'm on the road again.
> Well I'm so tired of cryin' but I'm out on the road again
> I'm on the road again.
> I ain't got no woman just to call my special friend

You know the first time I traveled out in the rain and snow
in the rain and snow.
You know the first time I traveled out in the rain and snow
in the rain and snow.
I didn't have no fairo, not even no place to go.

And my dear mother left me when I was quite young
when I was quite young.
And my dear mother left me when I was quite young
when I was quite young.
She said "Lord have mercy on my wicked son."

Take a hint from me mama please don't you cry no more
don't you cry no more.
Take a hint from me mama please don't you cry no more
don't you cry no more.
Cause it's soon one morning down the road I'm gone.

But I ain't going down that long and lonesome road - all by myself.
But I ain't going down that long and lonesome road - all by myself.
I can't carry you baby, gonna carry somebody else.

Wellington Marsh sat on his footlocker shining his boots. On his small portable radio he listened to a blues station that played Canned Heat, *On The Road Again*. Most of the other Marines had headed out to town. He preferred to stay on base and catch up on some chores. For some reason he thought about Teresa, the girl who waited back in Detroit. He hadn't written to her because he didn't know what to say. The last thing that he wanted to do was lead her on, then leave for Vietnam, and be killed. A cold wave flowed through his body. Starting a relationship wouldn't be fair, yet he looked forward to seeing her once more.

The last week of training was coming up after which he would get two weeks leave. He would then have to report to his next duty station which there was no doubt would be southeast Asia. He heard Alan Wilson of Canned Heat sing, "Take a hint from me mama please don't you cry no more." Wellington wondered how many mothers cried for a lost son because of this damned war.

Acting Corporal Marsh had learned a great deal during his training at Camp Lejeune. If not for the war the Marines were not a bad place to be or to make a career. He smiled as he realized the ridiculousness of his thinking. The Marines prepare for war, fight wars, and die in war. Wellington's mind drifted back to Sergeant Kincaid, his basic training D.I. The young Marine smiled as he recalled the story of Sergeant Kincaid's grandfather going from slave to landowner. That story proved one thing for sure—you cannot accurately predict the future. Most likely he will go to Vietnam. After that whether or not he sees action or not is an unknown. Whether he lives or dies is an unknown. He simply has to see it through to find out. Alan Wilson sang in the background, "But I ain't going down that long and lonesome road—all by myself." Wellington looked around the large room at all of the empty bunks.

"I was going to drop you off where we picked you up," Carl said. He then added, "However, given the circumstances a walk will do you some good." Carl told the driver, "Take the next exit, Sid."

"Got it."

Events had happened quickly. When the 9mm pistol had been aimed at Carl, Sid hit the brakes of the taxi hard throwing the threatening man to the floor. Carl reacted quickly by kicking his assailant in the face and grabbing both the gun and the portfolio. A punch made sure the man stayed down.

"Did you see that dog?" Sid said with a smile.

"I hit mine," Carl stated. He then turned his attention to his nemesis. With his foot on the man's hand holding him in an awkward position Carl said, "It seems you lost both your gun and the payoff. And, the package you wanted goes back to my employer."

"Please," a subdued and pitiful individual moaned, "I wasn't going to shoot you. I just wanted to make sure you didn't take the money and not give me the package."

"We've got a tail," Sid interrupted.

"Lose it."

"Can do." The taxi cut across three lanes of traffic at the last moment and exited the highway. Unable to follow the suspect car had to continue on. Quickly, Sid turned right went up one road turned onto another, then another and disappeared into the maze of streets. "It won't be easy to hide an out-of-state cab," he said.

Carl appreciated the efforts of his new friend and realized he could become a target for reprisal from this powerful, yet at the moment cowering, man. In an effort to protect the driver he said, "We have to get rid of it anyway before the driver we took it from reports it stolen." A quick glance at the back of the driver's seat showed no identification photo or name. "Let's finish this business and get back to our car."

Sid caught on and replied, "I'll be glad to get out of this piece of crap. It handles like a bus."

While Sid continued to weave through local streets Carl opened the portfolio and found four stacks of bills. In all there were 200 five-hundred dollar bills. They looked real. With the money counted Carl had to make a decision. Ray hadn't given him any instructions about what to do if the man tried anything. Most likely, he had duplicates of whatever was in the package. The slightly pissed-off hood was tempted to open the package and see what all the trouble was about. Yet, he was smart enough to heed Ray's warning that it was safer not knowing. "Pull over," he commanded. When the taxi stopped Carl took his foot off the man's hand and let him get back into the seat. He then said, "This is yours," as he handed the man the sealed package. "You don't get to check it and I'm keeping the gun. Now, get out." The man was about to protest, thought better of it, and climbed out of the cab. They left him standing on the side of a road.

"You did good, my friend," Carl said to the driver as he patted him on the back. "Now, let's get back to where we left the missus."

Ryoya Akimoto entered More-Or-Less. Harry Van Ryker, the owner/bartender, recognized her immediately. He walked over to where she sat at a table near the window, "You slumming?"

"I don't consider your fine establishment slumming," Ryoya replied with a smile.

"Thank you." Harry added, "I do the best that I can." He thought for a moment than asked, "You know Jack is up at that Woodstock music festival?"

"Yes, I read his article this morning."

"Only Jack Moore could go up to a music festival that was poorly organized, drenched in rain, and filled with all kinds of wild characters and find the bright side," Harry commented.

"It's a gift."

"Could be a curse."

"Either way—it's Jack."

"Yes, I guess it is," Harry replied. He then asked, "How are you two getting along?"

Ryoya hesitated which was not missed by Harry. Then she replied, "Jack's quite a character." More hesitation as she chose her words carefully, "I care about him and wouldn't want to do anything to hurt him."

"He's a big boy. Anyway, why would you hurt him?"

Ryoya ignored his question, "You know Jack is the first man that I can remember, upon learning that I am a cop, who didn't ask if I carry a gun or if I ever shot anyone."

"Yeah, that age-old cop question," Harry agreed. "When I was on the job it seemed like that was the first question a lady would ask when we went out."

"But, not Jack."

"Jack is an observer—not an inquirer," Harry concluded. He looked around the bar and nodded at a few frantically waving hands, "I'll be right back."

To Harry's surprise, Ryoya stood and said, "I'll help you."

For the next hour Ryoya drew beers, mixed a few drinks with which she was familiar, and served tables. She wore a spare apron that Harry had in the back. As the bar is frequented by off-duty police officers there was a certain level of banter and cop humor. Ryoya gave better than she received. One officer put his arm around her waist and invited her to join them.

"It's a good thing that you're right handed," Ryoya said, "because I'm going to render your left arm inoperable."

The off-duty police officer quickly withdrew his left arm and smiled, "No offense meant."

"None taken."

During a slow period Harry said to Ryoya, who was washing glasses, "Jack thinks the world of you."

"It's what the world thinks," she answered without thinking.

"Who gives a shit what the world thinks," Harry replied. "Someone say something to you?"

"No," she said sadly.

"If you and Jack are happy nothing else matters," Harry stated. He added, "As cops, we see how screwed up the world is and how rare it is to find a truly good person."

"I remember when you introduced us. That was quite a joke making him think that you told me he had made some intriguing offer that interested me." Ryoya smiled a warm and endearing smile.

"It must have driven him crazy for quite a while."

"How can you tell?" Ryoya joked.

Harry walked over to Ryoya and put his hands on her shoulders and said, "Both of you are good people who deserve each other. In this crazy mixed up world every once in a while the gods smile and make something beautiful happen. I would hate to see Jack, or you, be hurt."

"Shikata ga nai," Ryoya whispered. She remembered its meaning as "It can't be helped."

After getting lost here and there Sid and Carl found their way back to the coffee shop where they left Susan Friedlander. Carl went in and brought her back to the waiting taxi. He peeled two hundred dollars off his money roll and gave them to Sid. He then asked, "What would you charge to drive us to New York?"

"Hell, you already gave me enough. You pay gas and tolls and I'll take you," Sid said through his cigar.

"Tell you what. Get us there without a tail and I'll give you another five hundred."

"Naw. That's too much."

"You and that dog were a great help. I appreciate it. I'd give you more but it's all I have left."

"Make it two hundred and I'll do it."

The Grateful Dead started their gig at about 10:30 p.m. The blues, jazz, folk, country, rock band had a style all their own and ardent followers. Jack and The Flower Girl were deep into the crowd at that time. It was like swimming in neck deep water. In the dark Jack found that he had to be careful not to step on a sleeping, passed out, or otherwise engaged individual or couple. As the Dead sang *Mama Tried* Jack told the Flower Girl that he had to leave. In the golden glow of stage lights she looked up at him and said her Volkswagen Beetle sleeps two. Her innocence and authentic beauty was indeed tempting. They had spent the day together. In all they helped prepare and serve food, took drug ravished kids to the medical tents, listened to amateur musicians who played in the crowd, did tai chi with a group in a pasture, gotten rained on, chatted with local farmers who had brought food, milked a cow, got chased by a bee, and forgot a world away from the magic of the festival. Jack kissed her on the forehead and told her he had to write a story and get it in to the paper. She smiled, hugged him, and said, "Be kind. They earned it."

Robert Six Trees sat in the large meeting house and listened to Adam Fortunate Eagle, a hereditary member of the Ojibwa Nation, as he spoke of his experiences and desire to promote better understanding and lives of all Native American people.

44: Sunday – August 17, 1969

Just after midnight Creedence Clearwater Revival went on stage as rain once more dampened the festival. Members of the band grumbled about the late start due to the long set played by The Grateful Dead leaving them with a non-responsive audience. John Fogerty, lead singer and guitarist, looked out into the darkness and saw bodies everywhere. He was angry because in his mind they were playing for the dead. Then way in the back on the far edge of the pasture he saw a lone figure flicking his Bic and heard a voice yell out, "Don't worry about it, John. We're with you." Fogerty played the set for that young man.

Creedence Clearwater Revival played their distinct style of Rhythm & Blues and Country Rock. Included in their set was *Born on The Bayou, Green River, Bad Moon Rising, Proud Mary, I Put a Spell on You, Night Time is The Right Time,* and *Suzy Q.* Unfortunately, because of the late start most of their audience were asleep or rendered unconscious by drugs.

Two miles away in a dark blue 1966 Ford Econoline van Stephanie sat on an inflated air mattress looking at Ritchie who was a thousand miles away in a drug induced catatonic state. His long hair was damp and tousled draping partially over his face. When she brushed the hair from his face, Fetch, the basenji that lay against him, watched her with a protective glare. Stephanie thought as she considered the canine's jealous gaze, "Don't worry he's all yours." In her heart, Stephanie knew that Ritchie had many fine qualities and exceptional artistic talent. So, how come she had come to a point where his running off to Canada was a welcome solution to a growing problem? From the beginning she knew he did drugs and overlooked the fact. In many ways she saw it as him being a little boy who was rebelling and acting out. Subconsciously, she might have hoped that he would grow up and leave the destructive drug world behind. Or, maybe she thought that the love of a good woman would motivate him to clean up his act. In yet another rationalization she envisioned him being arrested and forced to mend his ways. None of this happened.

Raindrops on the metal roof of the van created a pleasant and reassuring feeling of shelter from the ever present elements that dampened the concert. Yet, Stephanie was determined to leave her refuge and endure the weather in order to return to the concert to see Janis Joplin. While there weren't any schedules of when artists would perform, she had heard that Joplin had arrived at the scene. She, therefore, made the decision that if she had to remain at the venue all night, she would.

In a corner of the van Stephanie found a red umbrella. Armed with that polyester shield and wearing a blue tee-shirt, black shorts, and sneakers she left the dry protective cocoon of the Ford. It didn't take long for every inch of her to become wet with the exception of her head and shoulders. In soaking wet sneakers she squished along heading in the direction of the concert. It was dark yet Stephanie was able to follow the road. Every once in a while she found a deep puddle. As she walked she thought about her life. Her mother, Valerie, was first to come to mind. How she missed mom. Stephanie knew, if her mother were alive, she wouldn't be at Woodstock. In fact, she wouldn't be with a pot-smoking, LSD dropping hippie and would probably still be a virgin. But, her mother wasn't alive and once more the thought, "if he had only been more careful," emerged from a dark corner of her mind. In the end, Stephanie realized that she hadn't really done very much of which her mother would have been proud.

In the eerie darkness, shadows drifted by traveling in different directions. No voices could be heard as these unrecognizable apparitions shuffled along like so many ghosts searching for their souls. Stephanie had the strange feeling that this must be what it is like after a battle with combatants lost and disoriented aimlessly moving along with no destination. All they could do was keep on moving. However, Stephanie had a destination and it lay ahead around a bend. She wanted to see and hear Janis Joplin. Another puddle, hiding in the dark, soaked her up to her ankle. As she shook her foot a female voice nearby said, "It got me too." In the shadows was the shape of a young woman.

"They're hard to avoid in the dark," Stephanie said.

"A branch killed my umbrella and nearly knocked me down," the voice in the shadows added.

"You can share my umbrella," Stephanie offered.

"Thanks, but I'm all wet so an umbrella isn't necessary," the shadow came forward to reveal a young Asian girl with long black hair. "It's sorta like shutting the gate after the horse already ran away. Isn't it?"

"I guess so," Stephanie replied.

"My name is Barbara," the girl said. "It's an old Korean name. It means the kimchi is hot," she laughed.

"What's kimchi?"

"Pickled and fermented cabbage."

"That's what Barbara means?"

"No, I made that up," Barbara said. "My Korean name is Min Kyung-Soon. My adopted American name is Barbara Fortune. Quite a difference, huh? I have no idea what Min means, but Kyung-Soon means 'gentle and honorable'—that's me."

"I'm just plain old Stephanie Elizabeth Ellis. No meaning, but it spells 'see.'"

"I see," both girls laughed.

"I'm going back to hear Janis Joplin if she sings," Stephanie explained.

"I'm looking for my sister," Barbara answered. "She and I snuck out to come over here and see all the people. We got separated and now I'm searching in the dark."

"What does your sister look like?"

"She looks like me. Except she's blond, blue eyes, taller than me, light skin, and skinny."

"Your sister's not Korean?"

"No, I'm the only one in the family with that honor."

"That's right, you're adopted."

"No," Barbara leaned forward and whispered, "we had this Korean gardener." Then laughed.

Stephanie also laughed. "You're still welcome to share my umbrella."

"Put that thing down the rain stopped."

"Oh." The two girls began walking together in silence toward the concert. After considering how to broach the subject without offending her companion, Stephanie asked hesitantly, "What's it like, being adopted?"

Barbara Fortune stopped which caused Stephanie to do so also. She turned to face Stephanie with a serious look, "For me it was a life saver. In Korea, without a father you don't exist. Can't go to school, have no rights, you are nothing. I was in an orphanage because my birth-mother was unmarried and couldn't take care of me. We were hungry all the time. Hand-me-down clothes that were worn by countless other children were barely able to keep us warm. Bunched together we would sleep three in a bed. It wasn't a happy place." Her face brightened and she smiled, "Then this lady came by and took me by the hand. I was five. She spoke kindly and seemed nice. Before I knew it I was in a car, then on a train, then an airplane. Everything was so different and so frightening. I went from lady to lady. It was very confusing. I have to admit I remember wanting to be back at the orphanage. It was the only world that I knew. Finally, I arrived at Kennedy Airport and was led to my mother. She had a teddy bear, knelt down, and handed it to me. I was so confused and frightened that I dropped the bear on the carpet. Then she gently pulled me close and hugged me. She looked strange and smelled odd. And when she spoke to me I didn't understand a word. I remember crying." Barbara turned and took a step then turned back. With a smile she finished, "I was a handful at first, but my family loved me. We all had a lot of adjusting to do. They didn't understand why at dinner I would scoop all the crumbs off the table to save. In Korea that might be your next meal. Or, why that teddy bear eventually had to go everywhere with me. At the orphanage if you put a toy down you most likely would never get to play with it again. And, I was stubborn and aggressive. My parents called it OA—orphanage attitude. They were right. In the orphanage you had to grab what you wanted and fight to keep it. Over time things got better and better and better. No more OA, just a teenager who snuck out and is going to catch hell when I get home."

"What will they do?"

"My mother will lecture us and my father will yell while threatening to take off his belt and beat us."

"Does he beat you?" Stephanie asked, surprised.

"No, he threatens, but even his yelling is put on," Barbara started walking toward the concert. "Our parents love us and are great. But, my sister, who is two years older than me, says we have to get in trouble from time to time or they wouldn't have anything to do." Barbara laughed.

"So, getting adopted was a good thing," Stephanie concluded.

"Like I said, for me, a very good thing, it was a life saver and a life changer," Barbara answered, then added, "I only wish I could help other children escape from hell and come to heaven, like me."

The two girls proceeded on to the concert venue. They arrived just in time to hear Creedence Clearwater Revival do their last song, *Suzy Q.* Silence fell over the soggy, crowded, Yasgur farm pasture.

"I hope I didn't miss her," Stephanie said with a concerned voice.

"Who? Oh, yeah. Janis Joplin. She hasn't sung as long as I've been here."

In a porta potty Janis Joplin and her friend Peggy Caserta shared a needle as they shot up heroin. Joplin had arrived by helicopter ten hours earlier and was awe-struck by the enormous crowd. As time passed she became more and more nervous which led to continued consumption of her favorite drink, Southern Comfort. So, by the time she was scheduled to perform she was wasted on alcohol and drugs. Twenty minutes after Creedence Clearwater Revival finished Janis Joplin and Kozmic Blues Band walked onto the stage. In spite of her condition, Joplin exploded into song with *Raise Your Hand.* The audience so enthralled by her presence never noticed her slurring her words or her voice cracking. As the performance continued she staggered rather than danced but her adoring fans continued to be mesmerized. At the end, they cheered and pleaded for an encore, which she delivered in the form of *Ball And Chain.*

Stephanie and Barbara had pushed their way toward the stage when Janis Joplin appeared. Together they watched the incredible performance of the blues legend. However, her condition did not escape them.

"She's drunk," Barbara concluded.

"She's stoned on drugs," Stephanie corrected remembering the *Newsweek* article that she had read.

"What a waste to have so much talent and to throw it away."

An abrupt odd feeling flowed over Stephanie as she turned from the stage and surveyed the audience. Almost everywhere she looked there were half-conscious and unconscious young people massed together into a writhing, pulsing, oozing, life-sucking pustule. Half a million souls were on a path to self-destruction. She turned to look at Barbara and saw a clean, fresh, alive young woman with a life filled with promise. A child who traveled half way around the world to a place called America where food was abundant, opportunities limitless, lifestyles unimaginable, and luxuries everywhere had to face a new and ominous threat. Over indulgence and self-centered arrogance hell-bent on dragging down that which others around the world would cherish and risk their lives to have. The contrast was striking. When Barbara looked at her and smiled Stephanie began to cry.

Barbara was caught off-guard and asked with concern, "What's the matter?"

"I have to get away from here," Stephanie responded as she turned and tried to rush through the throng of bodies. Barbara followed.

When they finally emerged from the crowd Barbara asked, "What's wrong?"

Tears still flowed as Stephanie stopped. She faced Barbara and said, "You have to go home. Stay away from these people. Drugs are dangerous and evil. They promise to make you feel good or expand your consciousness but all they do is destroy your life."

"I don't do drugs."

"Understand, druggies don't like to travel alone. They do everything that they can to convince you to join them. Their arguments can be compelling and difficult to fight. I know. I've almost surrendered a few times, but have stayed clean."

"There you are," a voice yelled behind Stephanie. She turned to see a tall blond girl rushing toward them.

"Evie, I've been looking for you," Barbara said.

"We have to get home," Evie, Barbara's sister, stated, "before we get into even more trouble."

"Oh, I wouldn't worry about that," Barbara said, "We are at the top of the trouble meter already."

Evie smiled, "Yeah, I guess we are." She noticed Stephanie and said, "Hi, I'm Evelyn, Bab's sister."

"I'm Stephanie. We've been looking for you."

"I was so worried."

"Stephanie was lecturing me on not taking drugs," Barbara offered.

"You don't have to worry about that. We're two farm girls," she put her arm around her little sister. It was obvious that the two loved each other. Together they walked off into the darkness. It was then that Stephanie remembered what Dr. Tallman had said and realized that this was her magic experience.

Carl tossed in bed. It was the middle of the night and he had yet to fall asleep. The day's activities kept running through his head. Sid, the Baltimore taxi driver, turned out to be the best thing that happened to Carl during his encounter with Senator William Reed. After the exchange, they picked up Susan Friedlander, Carl's faux wife, at the coffee shop in Washington, D.C. The drive to New York City was uneventful and quite pleasant.

It began with a heated discussion about the Baltimore Orioles dominating the American League East. After beating the Seattle Pilots that day 4 to 1, Baltimore was securely in first place with a record of 84 wins and 35 losses. Detroit was in second place a distant 16.5 games behind. The Yankees languished in fourth place, 23.5 games out of first with a record of 61 wins and 59 losses. The heated discussion was more of an opportunity for Sid Grolier to brag—and brag he did. Carl had very little he could say, but he liked Sid and had to laugh at the cabbie's good natured taunts.

"Remember Sid, I still have a gun," Carl said with no tone of malice.

Unfazed, Sid replied, "Damn, there are a lot of dogs on the roads these days."

Carl laughed while Susan remained confused. Throughout their journey there was no sign that they were being followed. At one point Sid exited the highway and filled the taxi with gasoline. Carl sat in the back with his hand on the gun that he had taken from the Senator guarding a portfolio filled with cash. Both he and Sid kept watching for any sign of a threat.

It was early evening when they reached Manhattan. Carl had Sid pull over next to a telephone booth. While holding the portfolio close Carl dialed the number that Ray Esposito had given him. It was not the number that he usually used to reach his boss. After four rings it was answered, "Mario's," an unfamiliar voice stated.

Caught off-guard Carl hesitated, then asked, "Ray Esposito there?"

"Who wants to know?"

"Carl Pythacyk."

"Hold on."

Restaurant sounds filled the receiver, then a clunk, and finally Ray's voice, "You have good news for me?"

"I do."

"Where are you?"

"Ninth and Forty-Fifth."

Ray gave Carl instructions to go to the location where they held the card games and to wait for him. Carl had Sid drive him to the location, paid him, and asked him to drop Susan home in the Bronx. He thanked Sid and told him things wouldn't have gone as well as they did without him. In addition, Carl got Sid's telephone number so that, as Sid put it, they could go to the World Series together and root for Baltimore.

For twenty minutes Carl waited outside the three-story red brick building on the corner of Grove and Bleecker Streets in Greenwich Village. He stood by the ornate door leading to the upper floors. The fact that he held one-hundred-thousand dollars under his arm significantly raised his stress level. It had been a long day and Carl was a little jumpy. He realized that he hadn't eaten any more than a few candy bars all day. A meal at Santino's sounded molto bene at that moment. His use of Italian caused him to smile. At that moment a black 1970 Cadillac Fleetwood Series 75 Limousine pulled to the curb. The rear door opened and Ray Esposito's voice said, "Get in."

Carl complied. Inside the huge car sat Ray Esposito and another man. Carl slid into one of the jump seats facing the two occupants. In the dark it was difficult to see the features of either man. There was a glass partition between the back seat and the driver. It was open. The other man in the back seat told the driver to go to "the club." Without saying a word the driver closed the partition and drove the car away from the curb.

"You have something for me?" Ray Esposito asked.

Carl found the situation uncomfortable, therefore he spoke in a more formal tone, "I do. And, I'm glad to get rid of it." He handed Ray the portfolio that contained the money.

"Do I need to count it?"

"No sir, it's all there."

"Did the contact give you any trouble?"

"He tried," Carl reached into his pocket then thought twice about such a move and asked, "I took a gun away from him. Can I give it to you?"

"Where is it?"

"In my right pocket."

"I'll get it." With that, Ray leaned forward and retrieved the 9mm pistol, dropped the magazine, and cleared the chamber. He examined the gun and said to no one in particular, "The son-of-a-bitch had to make waves." Ray then asked, "How did it go down?"

Carl gave Ray Esposito and the stranger that sat next to him a detailed description of events in Washington, D.C.

"You improvised," Ray stated, "that was good."

Silence hung in the big limousine. Carl knew better than to speak. If Ray or the other man wanted to know any more they would ask. Finally, Ray asked, "So, did you look in the package?"

"No."

"You telling me the truth?"

"You told me not to look. I figure it was none of my business."

"Molto bene."

A slight laugh escaped from Carl before he could stop himself.

"What the hell's funny?" Ray spat.

"I'm sorry. When I was waiting at the building I was hungry and thought how good a dinner at Santino's would be. Only in my head I thought molto bene."

The stranger on Ray's left laughed. The two men then conversed in Italian. Carl sat silently. Finally, Ray turned to Carl and introduced the stranger, "Carl, this is Don Carmine Spacini."

Carl's first instinct was to stand but that was impossible in the car. For a fleeting moment he considered offering his hand to shake but quickly decided that was also wrong. As a last resort he bowed while sitting and said, "Don Spacini, this is an honor."

"Ray tells me you have brains," Carmine Spacini said as he sat in the shadows. "From what you just told us about D.C., I agree."

Carl didn't answer for fear of saying the wrong thing.

Carmine continued, "You listen to Signore Esposito, learn from him and you will go far." After a pause, he cautioned, "You listen, you learn, but you also remember. Sometimes those with brains think too much. Then they start to think that they could do it better, that they should sit on top. That is a dangerous thing."

Carl couldn't see the man's facial expression in the shadows but knew he was as serious as a switchblade knife in a confined space. He also knew there was nothing to say. Only his actions would prove his loyalty.

"Respect," Carmine continued, "that is what makes our thing work. Without respect there is no trust, no control, no future. You know what I mean?"

"I do. I respect Signore Esposito," Carl caught himself and quickly added, "and you Don Spacini."

"Good. Then we understand each other," Carmine stated.

Ray Esposito then spoke, "Carl, I told Don Spacini about you. He remembered that you alerted us about the gun shipment. Since then you have proven yourself. The D.C. exchange was important and as you found out dangerous. You did good. From now on you work for me with Don Spacini's blessing. You'll get more chances to earn and have an expanded role as a soldier in my crew."

"Thank you, Senore Esposito. Thank you Don Spacini."

Carmine Spacini leaned forward and lightly slapped Carl across the face. "You may not be Italian but you act molto bene," he laughed and sat back.

As Carl considered what had transpired he found that regardless of how tired he was sleep was elusive. He was in! All because of that little spic Miguel Juarez.

At around 5:00 a.m. Roger Daltry, Pete Townshend, Keith Moon, and John Entwhistle walked onto the stage. They comprised the band known as The Who. The band proceeded to play their new rock opera, *Tommy.*

The double album Tommy had been released by Decca/MCA Records on May 17, 1969 in the United States and May 23, 1969 in the United Kingdom. It sold 200,000 copies in the United States in the first two weeks.

The Who had been known for their hard rock style with Pete Townshend smashing his guitar and Keith Moon destroying his drums. As they grew older the bad boy image lost its appeal. Townshend wanted the band to go from standard three-minute singles to more ambitious projects. The Who co-manager, Kit Lambert, coined the term "rock opera." At about the same time a friend of Pete Townshend, Mike McInnerney, introduced him to the works of Indian spiritual leader Meher Baba. Townshend found Baba's philosophy about compassion, love and introspection captivating and began developing a rock opera in an attempt to put his teachings into music. Interestingly, Mike McInnerney did the cover art for the album.

The rock opera *Tommy* was not an easy story to follow. After the album was released a synopsis was published to help listeners.

Overture: British Army Captain Walker goes missing during an expedition and is believed dead.

It's a Boy: The Captain's widow gives birth to their son, Tommy.

1921: Years later, Captain Walker returns and discovers that his wife has a new lover. The Captain murders the man. Tommy's mother brainwashes him into believing he didn't see or hear anything, making him deaf, dumb and blind to the outside world.

Amazing Journey/Sparks: Tommy relies on his sense of touch and imagination, developing a unique inner psyche.

The Hawker: A quack claims his wife can cure Tommy.

Christmas: Tommy's parents become increasingly frustrated that he will never find religion in the midst of his isolation.

Cousin Kevin: Tommy's parents neglect him which allows his sadistic cousin to torture him.

Do You Think It's Alright? & Fiddle About: Tommy is molested by his Uncle Ernie.

The Acid Queen: The Hawker's wife gives Tommy LSD.

Underture: Tommy's hallucinogenic experience is expressed musically.

Pinball Wizard: Tommy discovers he can feel vibrations sufficiently well to become an expert pinball player.

There's a Doctor: Tommy's parents take him to a respected doctor who determines that his disabilities are psychosomatic rather than physical.

Go to the Mirror!: The Doctor tells Tommy to stare at his reflection in a mirror.

Smash The Mirror: After extensive time staring at a mirror, his mother smashes it out of frustration.

Sensation: The broken mirror recovers Tommy's senses.

I'm Free: Tommy starts a religious movement.

Welcome & Tommy's Holiday Camp: Tommy starts a retreat for followers.

We're Not Gonna Take It: Tommy's teachings are rejected and the followers leave the retreat.

See Me, Feel Me: Tommy retreats inward once more.

Originally, they considered names, such as; *Deaf, Dumb and Blind Boy, Amazing Journey, Journey into Space, The Brain Opera,* and *Omnibus* but eventually settled on *Tommy* because it was a common nickname for British soldiers during World War I.

When The Who performed *Tommy* at Woodstock just after *Pinball Wizard,* as Pete Townshend was adjusting his amplifier, Abbie Hoffman, an anti-war protester, went on stage and grabbed the microphone. He yelled, "I think this is a pile of shit while John Sinclair rots in prison." He referred to another political activist who was sentenced to ten years in prison in 1969 after giving two joints to an undercover narcotics officer. Townshend, hearing the announcement, looked over his left shoulder and became enraged. He charged Hoffman and hit him in the back with his guitar knocking him off the stage.

Pete Townshend screamed, "Fuck off . . . fuck off my stage!" He then said, "I can dig it." He paused, then warned, "The next fucking person that walks across this stage is gonna get fucking killed."

The Who played *See Me, Feel Me,* the finale of the performance as the sun rose at 6:05 a.m.

At 6:00 a.m. Eastern Daylight Time it was projected that Hurricane Camille would make landfall at Mobile, Alabama. Winds had increased to 160 miles-per-hour. This was equivalent to a Category 5 hurricane on the Saffir-Simpson Scale. The measurement system was actually developed in 1969 by an engineer, Herbert Saffir and Dr. Bob Simpson, director of the National Hurricane Center. Saffir devised a five level scale based on wind speed. Simpson added the effects of a storm surge and flooding. The Saffir-Simpson Scale was introduced to the general public in 1973.

Olivia Samantha Everett and Claire Payton sat at the kitchen table sipping coffee. A combination of Olivia slipping Claire money and Claire increasing her production as her injuries healed kept Miguel at bay. There had been no other visits or incidents with the pimp. On the table was the *Daily News* with the headline: Hippies Mired In a Sea of Mud. Neither woman read the newspaper.

"I'm going to church today. Do you want to come?" Claire asked.

"I don't think I belong in church," was Olivia's sad response.

"Honey, if anyone belongs in church—it's you." Claire placed her hand on Olivia's hand and explained, "You are a victim. And, even as a victim, you reached out to help me. What greater charity is there than to help another when you yourself need help?" After taking a sip of coffee, Claire concluded, "God, would be proud to have you in His house."

"I probably wouldn't be charitable in church. I'd pray for Miguel to get arrested."

Claire smiled, "I'd pray for him to get a dread disease."

"Or, to get run over by a bus."

Claire laughed, "Or, to get bitten by a rat and get rabies."

"To get beat up in Central Park."

"And, gang raped," Claire added, which caused both woman to laugh.

"I'd pay to see that."

"I'd like to make him walk the streets and service men."

"The punishment would fit the crime." Olivia sat in silence for a moment. It seemed so long ago that she made the fateful decision to leave home. How petty and foolish she had been. A child's temper tantrum led her to a world of degradation and pain. Much like cutting off one's arm your life is changed forever and there is no going back. Only, she didn't cut off an arm, she tossed away her soul. Had it been so long since she was in a church? It had been Easter. Yes, she wore a white dress and gloves. White, that would never be her color ever again. Easter? Isn't that when Jesus rose from the dead? Yes, but how do you rise from the dirt in the gutter? Or, do you accept your fate and embrace the sin? Is that the secret to survival? Olivia looked across the table at Claire. The older woman no longer thought of escaping. She lived each day going through the motions not expecting more or trying for anything better. Submission was easier than fighting. Claire stopped being Claire a long time ago. But, was there any vestige of the innocent girl that she had once been? It seemed hopeless. The devil is a cruel master leaving broken beings in his wake. He takes everything—including your life, your soul, your dreams, and your identity. Who was Claire? Where did she come from? Did she have a good childhood, loving parents? Were her dreams bright and full of promise? Obviously, she didn't choose this life. Olivia saw her future across the table. "I'll go to church with you."

It had been a busy night for the Midtown North precinct. A number of robberies, numerous domestic violence arrests, destruction of property, auto theft, attempted rape, DUI's, B & E, assaults, and a rat attack. Ryoya looked at the activity sheets and couldn't help but smile as she commented, "Rat attack?"

"It's getting mean out there," Detective Michael Donovan commented.

"Was the rat taken into custody?"

"No, it got away."

"You mean it's still at large?"

"From what I heard it was very large," Michael said. He then changed the subject, "Rita, did you read Jack's column?"

"Not yet."

"I think you should," he tossed a copy of the *Tribune* onto Ryoya's desk.

She saw the teaser, *The Naked Truth About Woodstock,* page 3. After sipping some coffee, Ryoya turned to page three and read Jack Moore's column.

THE NAKED TRUTH ABOUT WOODSTOCK
by: Jack Moore

When you stand in the shower naked there is no hiding those extra pounds, that mole, hair where it's not supposed to be, or any other flaw that makes your body imperfect. Like it or not you have to face the naked truth. However, there is a good side to coming face to face with such truth. It allows you to change what can be changed and to accept that which you have no control over.

Today, Woodstock lay naked before me, both figuratively and literally. It began when I came across young people of both sexes totally naked frolicking in a waterfall. I must admit I was uncomfortable and felt that I had crossed some moral boundary. Yet, they didn't care. They didn't even notice me. In their innocence they washed the mud from their bodies while filth was gathering in my mind. Call it a generation gap or changing mores. We each viewed the situation differently. Naked Truth 1: as Bob Dylan says "the times they are a changing."

I then met a young woman I dubbed "The Flower Girl." To say she was on a different plane would be an understatement. Her view of life was so foreign to me that it was as though we were from unrelated species. She had an awareness of life that I never knew existed. The Flower Girl heard and saw things that I simply overlooked in my busy, only aware of the obvious, life. Without the use of any kind of drugs she had expanded her mind and enhanced her awareness. Next time you are someplace where there are multiple sounds listen for the hidden sounds that nestle among the obvious. Naked Truth 2: We are missing a lot in life.

The Flower Girl and I spent a part of the day preparing and serving meals to the hungry thousands of attendees at Woodstock. A group called the Hog Ranch made it possible. Though hungry, tired, covered in mud, and crowded into a tight space young people waited patiently in line for their turn. Many offered to bring food to others or volunteered to help prepare meals. Even with all of the elements present that could lead to a riot none occurred. Quite the opposite there was an atmosphere of sharing. Don't get me wrong I also heard of stealing and assaults did happen. However, if this concert is a microcosm of America's youth it was revealing. Naked Truth 3: Good caring people vastly outnumber the bad apples.

The music at Woodstock is ear-shatteringly loud. Speakers spit out distorted sounds and emphasize the base to such a degree that my ears actually felt pain. I had to remain at a distance or cover my ears during some performances. Naked Truth 4: A good number of the population will be deaf or hearing-impaired by the time they are forty years old.

Without question Woodstock was poorly planned. The fact that significantly more people showed up than expected does not excuse the glaring lack of facilities or security. This could have been a disaster of enormous proportions. From what I have read and heard from other news outlets it is being portrayed that way. Naked Truth 5: If you go looking for dirt you inevitably will miss the flowers that grow there.

Finally, there are the ever present drugs. In their attempt to get back to nature in a search for meaning and higher consciousness these misguided souls have turned to chemicals. They could learn so much from The Flower Girl. A clear head is capable of perceiving far more than one muddled with drugs. My fear is that manipulating the body's chemistry will become the trend in psychology, medicine, sports, education, and more. Naked Truth 6: We are about to embark on a path toward a drug-dependent society from which no good will come.

In closing I have this to say. Rain, rain go away. I only have to stay one more day.

Ryoya Akimoto smiled at the last line of the story. She could see Jack trudging around in the mud and trying to make the best of it. When she put the newspaper down Michael Donovan commented, "Flower Girl?"

"Jack meets people. It's what he does."

"Flower Girl?"

"If you are baiting me, don't bother," Ryoya stated flatly. She neither showed nor would admit to jealousy. If she allowed herself to let her emotions come to the surface she would have to face the fact that she missed Jack. He was unique and charming and sensitive and funny. But, he was a Yankee fan and that was a deal breaker. Detective Ryoya stood from her desk and said as she headed for the door, "Let's go catch a rat."

As the sun rose Grace Slick led Jefferson Airplane onto the stage at Woodstock. The lead singer walked up to the microphone and stated, "You have seen the heavy groups, now you will see morning maniac music, believe me. Yeah, it's a new dawn."

Stephanie had been in attendance all night. Barbara, the adopted Korean, and her sister Evie had gone home. They would catch hell, but it would quickly turn to heaven once again. After The Who finished their set there was silence. Welcome silence in the dark was all Stephanie needed to think about her epiphany. Two sisters living on a farm in upstate New York, one biological the other adopted, demonstrated how dramatically different an individual's life can be due to the efforts of persons they didn't even know. How she would like to be a part of something that gave children a brighter future. Her attention turned to the endless mass of shadows around her that were sleeping or drug-addled. Many were here to protest, but few offered solutions. Around the world there were children who would gladly trade places with them. Ritchie, the kid with wealthy parents, planned to run away rather than take responsibility and find a solution. He didn't have to fight in a war. He could join the Navy, Coast Guard, or National Guard. The answer was not dropping out, but getting involved. Stephanie knew what she wanted to do. Unfortunately, she had no idea about how to do it.

When Jefferson Airplane started their performance, Stephanie remembered the wonderful night she and her mother went "rabbit hunting." Grace Slick began singing *White Rabbit* as Stephanie walked on the road headed back to the blue van.

Sullivan County declared a state of emergency and New York Governor Nelson Rockefeller called John Roberts, one of the festival producers, to inform him that he was going to order 10,000 New York State National Guard troops to the festival. Roberts was able to convince the governor to not make such a move as it would have a destabilizing effect that could lead to disaster.

The New York Mets played a second double-header of the weekend against the San Diego Padres at Shea Stadium. In game one all they needed was a three-run homerun by catcher Duffy Dyer in the fifth inning to beat the Padres 3 to 2.

In game two the Padres had 11 hits compared to the Mets 5 hits. Unfortunately for the Padres, they were spread out while the Mets were concentrated where they did the most good. After six scoreless innings, in the bottom of the seventh Ed Kranepool led off with a single to right field. Al Weis was put in as a pinch runner. Clay Kirby, pitcher for the Padres, then walked Jerry Grote. With runners on first and second and nobody out Bud Harrelson tripled to centerfield. Weis and Grote scored. The next batter, pinch hitter J.C. Martin, hit a fly ball to centerfield which scored Harrelson. At the end of the inning the Mets had a 3 nothing lead. San Diego would score two runs in the eighth inning on two hits and an error but it wasn't enough as the Mets won 3 to 2 sweeping the double-header.

Thirteen hundred miles away from Shea Stadium a C-130 weather aircraft tracked Hurricane Camille. The storm was located 250 miles south of Mobile, Alabama with wind gusts estimated to be over two-hundred miles-per-hour.

Hurricane Camille began moving west at fifteen miles-per-hour. With it a surge of water sixteen feet higher than the Mississippi River slammed against water flowing out of the river delta. Huge whirlpools were seen and the river began to flow backward. As far north as Carrollton, Louisiana, 120 miles from the delta, the Mississippi River was running northward. Hurricane warnings were issued from the entire Mississippi coastline to New Orleans, Louisiana.

Chip Monck, who had designed the stage lighting and was the announcer at Woodstock Music Festival, walked up to the microphone and issued a statement, "The warning that I've received, you may take it with however many grains of salt you wish, that the brown acid that they're circulating around us is not specifically too good. It's suggested that you do stay away from that. But it's your own trip, so be my guest. But please be advised that there is a warning on that."

At two in the afternoon Joe Cocker and The Grease Band took to the stage. The highlight of his performance was his shrieking, seemingly unhinged, version of *With a Little Help from My Friends*. It was a great hit and the last song in the set after which a huge thunderstorm blanketed the festival bringing the heaviest rains of the weekend.

Jack Moore was wandering among the crowd when thunder rumbled in the distance. Much like reacting to an air raid siren young people began preparing for the coming storm. Some opened umbrellas, others unfolded plastic tarpaulins, still others pulled wet blankets from beneath them, and a few left to find shelter. Due to the previous night's rain many sat in mud or wet grass.

The rain came. At first, large drops fell from the sky in small numbers. While they were few each contained what seemed like a gallon of water. Then like a crescendo a bright flash, immediately followed by a deafening explosion of thunder, brought a deluge from the sky.

Jack was caught in the open vulnerable to the elements. He resigned himself to the fact that he was going to get very wet. He heard a voice but didn't realize it was directed toward him. Slightly louder it yelled, "Hey, dad, there's room in here. Come'on, man."

When Jack found the source of the voice he saw a young man with long messy hair, not wearing a shirt, holding up a side of a tent-like canvas structure. The man repeated, "Come'on, man." In an instant Jack was under the canvas roof. On the ground was another sheet of canvas. The flap on the side that faced the stage was raised on an angle that kept the rain from coming in while also providing air circulation and light. Above he heard rain drumming on the canvas at an increasingly faster pace.

Inside the makeshift lean-to Jack found four persons. His host, who invited him out of the rain, appeared to be twenty-years-old. No shirt, cut-off jeans, sneakers with holes in them, and a necklace with a peace symbol hanging on it made up the attire of the young man with long tousled brown hair. At the far end away from Jack was a girl who at most was nineteen. She had unnaturally straight black hair that hung past her shoulders, a flower painted on her right cheek, long beaded earrings, and a vest that covered bare breasts. Because she was sitting and partially hidden behind the others he didn't see what she wore below the objects of his attention. Next to Cleavage sat another young man. He had an afro-style haircut that made him appear like a large dandelion. On his face he sported a chin beard and mustache. His tie-dyed tee-shirt was quite colorful but in conflict with his native American beaded pants. Something unfriendly or morose was reflected by his expression. Finally the other girl in Jack's refuge was a tiny blond wearing a blue peasant dress. Her hair was short and pixie-like. What struck Jack immediately was her eye makeup. Bright blue eye shadow formed wings, while dark mascara and eyebrow pencil created large doe-eyes. Her whole appearance gave new meaning to the terms cute and innocent.

"You can crash here, man," his host stated.

"Thanks. I was about to get my evening shower early."

"All this rain is a bummer, man."

"Go with the flow," Pixie said as she looked up with those big inviting eyes. "It's nature doing her thing. We just happen to be in her way."

"I think nature's a music critic," Cleavage said with the hint of a smile.

"Why'd you bring in the square, man?" Dandelion asked in a none-too-friendly tone.

"It's raining, man. You don't leave a stray dog out in the rain."

"Woof," Jack commented with a smile. He added, "If it's a problem, I'll take my chances."

"All are welcome, no matter how square," Pixie said as she patted an open space near her. Jack sat.

"He's gonna impede my relaxation, man," Dandelion complained.

"You're not the fuzz, are you?" Host asked.

"No. Newspaper reporter."

"Aw, hell man. That's worse. He's part of the plastic establishment. Delivering the man's lies. Brainwashing the masses."

"What's your bag man? You here to dig the music, or condemn the people?" Host asked.

"I'm here to witness the festival and tell readers what happened here. Nothing more."

Dandelion pounced, "Headline; hippies fuck up a farm and exhibit anti-social behavior."

"That's good. Can I use it?" Jack asked with a smile. Dandelion frowned, gave Jack the bird, and picked up a bag of marijuana.

"What do you think is happening here?" Cleavage asked.

"Something very interesting—perhaps transformational. It's nothing like I expected. Aside from the rain, mud, lack of facilities, bad planning, and loud music the festival is very revealing."

"How so?" Host asked as he showed interest in what the old man had to say.

"Your friend is correct. Many reporters came here to write derogatory stories about young people getting out of hand, doing drugs, and causing problems. They want to condemn your lifestyle, music, and attitudes."

"What about you?" Cleavage pressed.

"Me? I want to learn, to be an observer not a judge."

Dandelion finished rolling a joint. He handed it to Cleavage, who exclaimed, "You made a dovetail!" She referred to a European style of joint rolled to look like a bird. Her attention returned to Jack, "So, what have you observed?" Dandelion held up a lit Bic lighter for Cleavage to utilize.

Jack ignored the fact that they were smoking marijuana. He stated, "When I arrived I was greeted with friendliness and warmness. I watched young people help each other and help strangers. Everything was good natured in spite of the traffic jams and over-crowding."

"The power of love," Pixie commented.

Cleavage handed the burning joint to Dandelion. Jack continued, "Yesterday, a young woman taught me that there is so much to life that I am missing. Without drugs," he emphasized the word drugs, "she showed me how to hear things that I normally missed and to see beyond the obvious."

Once more the Dandelion, with a chip on his shoulder, attacked, "You have a problem with us blowing grass—there's the door, man."

In a calm voice Jack answered, "As I said I'm not here to judge. I'm simply relating my experience." He became conscious of the distinct aroma of marijuana.

Pixie leaned forward close to Jack and asked, "How did she increase your cosmic awareness?"

Jack picked up the scent of Patchouli. It overpowered the smell of the marijuana. He didn't know the name of the scent but became fully aware of its flowery and earthy aroma. "You have to slowly remove the surface sounds, like the rain hitting the canvass." Large doe-eyes stared at him with anticipation of learning a new mind-expanding technique. "Then other dominant sounds, like the talking and laughing occurring outside because they mask lesser tones." There was silence in the tent as all listened to Jack. "When your mind filters out what is reaching your ears you begin to pick up unexpected sounds. Like that cow that is mooing, or something metal tapping against some other metal object in the distance, or a bell like one on a cat's collar."

"I hear the cow, man," Host stated with excitement.

"Far out," Dandelion said as he handed his friend the smoking joint.

Pixie turned to Host and exclaimed, "Shotgun me!" At which point Host put the lit end of the joint in his mouth and the other end in Pixie's mouth. By blowing through the marijuana cigarette he forced the smoke into Pixie's mouth. She inhaled and held the intoxicant for as long as she could than exhaled. Jack was fascinated by all of the activities that took place before him. He never knew the art of smoking marijuana was so complex. What he didn't realize was that second-hand smoke was filling his lungs with tetrahydrocannabinol, the active ingredient in marijuana that makes one high. After taking a toke Host offered the joint to Jack who shook his head.

"Not a head, huh? That's cool. Last week I got burned on some fake Acapulco Gold. It was a rose bush, man," Host admitted.

Pixie interrupted, "What else did you do?"

"We worked with the folks at the Hog Farm making food."

"That was killer, man," Host said, "I had some of that funky food."

"So, what are you going to write about this scene?" Cleavage asked as she took another drag on the joint.

"I haven't decided," Jack answered. "I might write about you. There was no reason to offer an old, establishment, straight arrow like me shelter—yet you did."

"Well, leave me out. I don't want anything to do with big money, big government, big machine murderers," Dandelion snapped.

"Chill, Jerry," Host said.

"You chill! Your brother isn't lying dead in a jungle halfway around the world."

Jack immediately understood the young man's abrasive attitude. He knew that there was nothing he could say that would ease the pain the young man was feeling so he simply said, "I'm sorry."

"Everyone's sorry. But, my brother's not sorry—he's dead. He joined the Marines and went to fight the man's war and what for? Nothing!"

Jack said in a soft tone, "During World War II I covered the Pacific Theater. I saw a lot of dead. Every single one was a price too high, but one that had to be paid. Millions of families received the news that their loved one was not coming home. War steals lives and destroys families. Mankind would be so much better off if there was never another war."

"Right on!"

"I can dig it."

"Make love—not war."

"Unfortunately, we are an aggressive species. It seems there is always an individual, group, or nation that seeks more power through conquest. After World War II in postwar Japan I discovered things that our government never told us. Frightening things. Things that I can't tell you. Sometimes we don't know all of the facts which would affect our opinion about a war. But, I will say I'm glad we fought the Japanese and I thank God that we won. Yet, it doesn't change the fact that there are always families that pay an awful price."

Cleavage lamented, "Why can't we just love each other and live in peace?"

"From what I've seen here at Woodstock you've made a good start. Maybe we can learn from you," Jack stated, "Based on the experience that I've had I feel like growing my hair and buying some beads." At that comment Host, Pixie, and Cleavage began to laugh. For some reason Jack also began to laugh. It was an uninhibited laugh that he couldn't remember experiencing before. His laugh was out-of-control. Yet, he didn't care, it felt good. He felt good.

Cleavage shuffled through her things and produced a string of beads. She climbed over Dandelion and leaned toward Jack. As she placed the beads over his head he couldn't help but get more of a view than he felt was appropriate. "These are love beads. I made them myself. They mean we are friends and love each other. You're no longer a square—you're a yo yo." With that comment all the young people laughed. Even Dandelion couldn't keep from joining in.

Jack found himself still giddy and asked with a grin, "What's a yo yo?"

Pixie answered, "A weekend hippie."

"Thank you, I think," Jack said with his head feeling strange. Not dizzy but also not grounded. Then out of nowhere he became aware of extreme hunger which he commented upon. "You know, I'm really hungry."

In unison his new friends said, "The munchies!"

"The what?"

"Munchies," Host remarked. "You're high, man."

"But, I didn't. . ."

"A contact high, man. Secondhand smoke."

"There goes your cherry, man," Dandelion said with a smile.

It was the first time that Jack saw the young man smile. He was driven to comment, "Hey, you have teeth." More laughter followed.

Pixie moved closer to Jack, looked up at him with her big doe-eyes and said, "Why are there wars?" Upon hearing the question Dandelion looked directly at Jack waiting for his answer.

"There are wars where people defend themselves from aggression, or stop atrocities, or in some way protect people's individual rights. They have to be fought or else all mankind would become victims of power-hungry entities that use violence." Jack looked directly at Dandelion, Jerry, and admitted, "Vietnam? I just don't know. We are told it is to stop the spread of communism. Those against the war say we are trying to get their oil. Just like with World War II there might be things that the government is not telling us that justify fighting. Or, just like with Korea, it is destined to never have an outcome. I don't see a good end to this war. It is not clear who the enemy is, the regime we support is corrupt, the people simply want to live their lives, we don't have a workable strategy, and young men are dying."

Host held up the peace symbol on his necklace and said, "Peace, man. Just stop making war."

Jack, upon seeing the symbol, changed subjects, "That peace symbol," Jack pointed at Host's necklace, "It actually was created by a British philosopher and political activist. His name is Bertrand Russell, the Earl of Russell. He was protesting for nuclear disarmament back in the late fifties. The symbol is actually a combination of semaphore flag signals for the letter N," Jack held his arms at the five o'clock and seven o'clock positions, "and the letter D," he held one hand straight up with the other straight down.

"N,D?" Cleavage asked.

"Nuclear Disarmament," Jack answered.

"Wow, that is so cool, man," Host said as he examined the symbol.

"Russell is quite a character. He won the Nobel Prize in Literature, was a pacifist, a mathematician, and political activist." Jack felt something on his arm. In his relaxed state he looked down. Pixie was drawing a peace sign on his arm using an eyebrow pencil. He found the whole process fascinating. It seemed as though he was watching artwork being applied to someone else's arm.

"Dad, you're alright," Host stated.

"Thanks. Try telling my lady friend, I don't seem to be doing well lately," slipped out of Jack's intoxicated mind through his mouth.

"That's a drag, man," Host said, then asked, "Is she here at Woodstock?"

"No, she's back in the city. She's an NYPD detective."

"Holy shit!" Exclaimed Dandelion, "Hide the stash."

Jack laughed, once more.

"What's her hang-up? You seem like a cool dude," Host stated.

"I am a cool dude. At least, I think I am. Things were going great then all-of-a-sudden they weren't."

"She's buying rice or you're twirling a lasso," Cleavage concluded.

"What?"

"Either she's getting serious and it scares her or you're showing signs of greater interest than she is ready for. It's a typical timing conflict. A real relationship killer."

"I like her and don't want to lose her."

"Then go after her, man," Dandelion screamed.

Cleavage slapped him on the arm. She looked at Jack and said, "That is the worst thing you can do. Any pressure at this time will flip her out and you'll see her heels running away. If she's serious and scared, that's her hang-up, you only need to be there. Give it time. Tick, tock, it's in the hands on the clock."

"I'll give it time," Jack said. He then asked, "Where are all of you from?"

"Connecticut, Danbury," Host replied.

"I'm from an egg," Pixie revealed to Jack's surprise.

"She goes by the handle Night Bird," Cleavage explained.

Dandelion broke into a song to the tune of *White Bird*, "Night Bird with the big blue eyes just wants to fly. She's got to fly or she will die."

"I'm on a quest," Pixie said innocently.

"A quest for what?" Jack asked with sincere interest.

"The meaning of life."

"Aw, baby, philosophers have sought better understanding of that for time immemorial. There isn't a singular clear-cut answer. The only thing we know is that we are here. What we do while here is up to us," Jack stated. He then asked, "Do you want some advice from an old straight arrow?"

"Yo yo," Cleavage corrected. Everyone laughed.

Pixie leaned forward, put her elbow on Jack's knee and rested her head in her hand, "Lay it on me."

Jack gave his philosophy, "Don't waste your time trying to understand the meaning of life. It's an unanswerable question. Instead spend your time living your life. Experience life but avoid harmful things. They'll steal life from you. Learn to like yourself and believe in yourself. Let the world spin around you. Your life is unique and will continue to be as long as you live. Remember what The Flower Girl taught me, open up to the world around you and you will make discovery after discovery."

"That's heavy," Pixie, Night Bird, said. "It's, like, a head trip. I'm freaking out." She sat back and looked at the roof of the tent and continued, "Like, I don't have to travel the world seeking answers because they're all around." She raised her arms and announced, "But, I still have to fly. Give me a hit!" When Dandelion handed her the exceedingly short joint she said, "Too bad we don't have a lemon."

"A lemon?" Jack asked.

Host explained, "You put a hole through a lemon, insert a joint in one side, and inhale from the other. It cools the smoke and gives it a flavor."

"That's where the band that sang *Green Tambourine,* the Lemon Pipers, got their name," Dandelion added.

The rain stopped. Jack gave his four friends his business card and told them to call him when they are in the city. With a crooked smile on his face he left the head shop. By 6:30 p.m. when Country Joe and The Fish took to the stage Jack Moore was driving his rented 1969 Chrysler New Yorker on the New York State Thruway headed back to Manhattan.

Wanda Six Trees sewed a fancy pattern on a shirt that she was making for her son. His birthday was still more than a month away but she knew it would take every bit of that time to finish the job in time.

45: Monday – August 18, 1969

Johnny Winter, a blues artist from Texas, began his performance at Woodstock just after midnight on the morning of August 18, 1969. His long straight shoulder length blond hair flowed as he strummed his Gibson guitar and sang *Mama, Talk To Your Daughter*. Contagious energy and a driving blues beat roused the interest of the tired and much smaller audience. Many attendees had headed home throughout Sunday. A downpour in the afternoon was the final blow to long-suffering music aficionados. Ironically, as Winter began his second song, *Leland Mississippi Blues*, Hurricane Camille made landfall in Bay St. Louis, Mississippi.

The ferocious storm had wind speeds of 201 miles-per-hour and generated a storm surge of 28 feet above sea level. This was the highest storm surge in U.S. history. A last-minute change in direction spared New Orleans from a direct hit by Camille. Mississippi was not as lucky. With energy exceeding that of an atomic bomb the massive hurricane blanketed the state. It began off the coast when a combination of wind, rain, and storm surge cut Ship Island in half. Located on the island was Fort Massachusetts, a small defensive structure built after the War of 1812, and a lighthouse. They remained on West Ship Island across from East Ship Island separated by a body of water subsequently named Camille's Cut.

In Pass Christian, Mississippi, on the corner of Henderson Avenue and U.S. 90, twenty three people took refuge in the three story Richelieu Manor Apartments on the Gulf Coast. When the storm made landfall the storm surge literally reached the third floor and swept the entire building away. One lone survivor was swept along with all of the debris. In a matter of minutes everything from the coastline to over a mile inland was completely destroyed.

Johnny Winter went on to sing B. B. King's *You Done Lost Your Good Thing Now*, Bo Diddley's *I Can't Stand It*, and Chuck Berry's *Johnny B. Goode*. He finished his set at 1:05 a.m.

Matthew Ellis woke with a start. Thunder had rattled the windows of Stephanie's apartment. As he became aware of his surroundings flashes of lightning assaulted the room followed by additional claps of thunder. He had been wrenched from a vivid dream. It was a dream that had been opening doors in his memory long hidden from his conscious mind. Lida Petropoulos was ever present as dreams seemed to be the only avenue of contact with his former partner in crime.

They were sitting at an outdoor café in a foreign country. He couldn't tell what country but based on the people he observed it was in the Far East. Lida sat across from him wearing a light blue flowered sundress and sunglasses. She seemed more animated than usual. After taking a sip of an exotic, yet unidentified, drink she continued with what she had been saying, "My tech assures me that the product will perform as well as the specified wire." She leaned forward and said in a hushed voice, "It will, however, have a significant impact on cost."

"Orztech already agreed on the price," Matt replied.

Lida Petropoulos sighed and leaned even closer to Matt and explained, "Not Orztech's cost, silly—our cost."

"Our cost?" Then a light went off in his slow-to-catch-on brain, "Oh, I see." He leaned back in his chair and thought for a moment. Finally, he asked, "How much of a difference?"

Lida explained. "It is spec'd to be tinned wire to prevent corrosion. Tin is the most expensive element used to manufacture the wire. We reduce the tin in the tinning process and add more zinc which costs a fraction of the price. The anti-corrosion property remains the same," after a pause, "or very close to it. Because it's stranded wire a small number of aluminum strands will be substituted for copper strands further reducing cost. Finally, the insulation thickness will be microscopically reduced as the wire is coated. Of course, the first one hundred feet will remain exactly to spec." She smiled and concluded, "The wire will perform exactly as desired. And, as we all know, they always over-estimate needs and over spec products."

The dream changed abruptly as they are apt to do. Lida and Matt were in New York. Matt couldn't identify where they were as all he could see was Lida's face. Her makeup was perfect, as usual. Green piercing eyes smiled at him with just the right hint of mischief. Long dark flowing hair aroused him. Her voice echoed in his mind from a time long past, "As of today you have $768,000 in your account." With a slight tilt of her head she cooed in a little-girl voice, "What are you going to buy me?"

"What do you want?"

"Hmmm, something silky and soft and easy to remove," she laughed.

"I'll see what I can do."

"Now, don't forget your pseudonym and account number. It's the only way to access your money in the private Hong Kong account. They have your signature on file but will not make any transaction without that name and number. It's very confidential."

"I won't forget," Matt assured her. In his mind, he repeated the number "4 . . . 4 . . ." A loud clap of thunder slammed the lid on the dream leaving the remaining six digits buried in a fog that may never lift.

Matt lay in bed trying hopelessly to remember the number. Lightning flashed like a neon sign outside a cheap hotel. His pseudonym and account number remained hidden deep in a dream.

Blood, Sweat & Tears played at Woodstock between 1:30 a.m. and 2:30 a.m. They were followed by Crosby, Stills, Nash & Young at 3:00 a.m. When they took the stage Stephen Stills remarked, "This is the second time we've ever played in front of people, man. We're scared shitless."

The group was formed in 1968 after the breakup of The Hollies, The Byrds, and Buffalo Springfield. Originally, it was comprised of David Crosby, Stephen Stills and Graham Nash. Stephen Stills played the instrumentals. Neil Young joined them after their first album was released in May, 1969.

The band was so new that it was actually introduced as Buffalo Springfield. They would go on later to record the song *Woodstock* written by Graham Nash's girlfriend, Joni Mitchell, who did not attend the music festival. It did, however, sum up the feeling that many had about that unforgettable weekend.

Well I came upon a child of God
He was walkin' along the road and I asked him
"Tell me where are you going?"

This he told me, said, "I'm going on down to Yasgur's farm
Gonna join in a rock and roll band
I got to get back to the land and set my soul free"

We are stardust, we are golden
We are billion year old carbon
And we got to get ourselves back to the garden

Well then can I walk beside you
I have come to lose the smog
And I feel myself a cog in somethin' turnin'

And maybe it's the time of year
Yes and maybe it's the time of man
And I don't know who I am, but life is for learnin'

We are stardust, we are golden
We are billion year old carbon
And we got to get ourselves back to the garden

By the time we got to Woodstock
We were half a million strong
And everywhere was a song and a celebration

And I dreamed I saw the farmers
Just play his ridin' shotgun in the sky
Turning into butterflies above our nation

We are stardust, we are golden
We are caught in the devil's bargain
And we got to get ourselves back to the garden

As the sun rose Jimi Hendrix appeared on stage. He had been scheduled to play at midnight but preferred sunrise closing the festival. By that time the crowd had dwindled to approximately 30,000. At 8:00 a.m. Chip Monck walked up to the microphone and introduced the group as the Jimi Hendrix Experience. Hendrix wearing a blue-beaded white leather jacket with fringe, a red head scarf, and blue jeans stepped up to the microphone and stated, "We decided to change the whole thing around and call it Gypsy Sun and Rainbows. For short, it's nothin' but a Band of Gypsies."

By 1969 Jimi Hendrix was the world's highest-paid rock musician. He was also a main draw at the festival and even though he accepted a lower-than-usual fee he was the highest paid performer. In eight short years Jimi Hendrix had gone from rags to riches.

James Marshall "Jimi" Hendrix was born in Seattle Washington. He began playing the guitar at age fifteen. The first tune Hendrix learned to play was the theme from the television series *Peter Gunn*. He was a self-taught musician with enormous talent. In 1961 when he was eighteen years old he was arrested twice for riding in stolen cars. A judge gave him a choice of joining the Army or spending time in jail. He enlisted on May 31, 1961. After basic training Hendrix was assigned to the 101st Airborne Division and stationed at Fort Campbell, Kentucky. He never really adjusted to Army life and was frequently disciplined for neglecting his duties, napping while on duty, and failing to report for bed check.

He had his red Silvertone Danelectro guitar sent from home. On it he had hand-painted his girlfriend's name Betty Jean. Hendrix and fellow soldier Billy Cox began performing in base clubs.

Even though he earned the prestigious Screaming Eagles paratrooper patch on January 11, 1962 his lack of commitment continued to cause him problems. Finally, on May 24 of that year, Hendrix's platoon sergeant, James C. Spears filed a report in which he wrote, "He has no interest whatsoever in the Army. It is my opinion that Private Hendrix will never come up to the standards required of a soldier. I feel that the military service will benefit if he is discharged as soon as possible." Jimi Hendrix was granted an honorable discharge due to unsuitability on June 29, 1962.

At Woodstock, Hendrix, who was part Cherokee Indian, wore a fringed tribal jacket and moccasins. He played a cream-colored, left-handed Fender Stratocaster. Prior to his set he had been ill which was why his performance was weak in the beginning. Three-quarters of the way through his act he introduced the, "new American anthem until we get another one," and proceeded to play a psychedelic version of the *Star-Spangled Banner*. He used amplifier feedback, distortion, and sustain to create a work of which Pop critic Al Aronowitz of *The New York Post* wrote, "It was the most electrifying moment of Woodstock, and it was probably the single greatest moment of the sixties." Hendrix followed with *Purple Haze*, a four minute Woodstock jam, *Villanova Junction*, and his acclaimed version of *Hey Joe* after which he unplugged his Stratocaster and simply said, "Thank you." Thus was the official end of the Woodstock Music Festival.

By the time Hendrix went on stage he had been awake for more than three days. When he left the stage he collapsed from exhaustion.

The organizers had invited Roy Rogers to sing *Happy Trails* as the finale but he declined.

After delivering a crushing blow on coastal communities Hurricane Camille weakened quickly upon making landfall. Two-hundred miles inland at Jackson, Mississippi wind speed dropped to 67 miles-per-hour and Camille was downgraded to a tropical storm.

The New York Herald lay on her desk in pristine condition. Detective Michael Donovan had placed it there. Detective Ryoya Akimoto sat reading a number of DD5's from overnight arrests. She knew quite well why her partner had placed the newspaper there and wasn't going to take the bait. When it was convenient she would get to it.

Michael Donovan changed his tactics and announced, "I have a confession for you to review."

Ryoya looked up, "Oh, a confession to what?"

"Use of a controlled substance," he handed her his copy of the *Tribune* folded to Jack Moore's column titled, A Confession.

A CONFESSION
By: Jack Moore

I smoked marijuana. Yes, I freely admit it. However, before you condemn or arrest me it happened completely by accident but gave me first-hand experience with the weed due to second-hand smoke. Late in the afternoon the rains came once more testing the resolve of thousands of young people at a music festival who simply wanted to get back to nature. Unfortunately, nature wasn't having any of it and tried to wash the unwashed away. After days of bad weather, mud, lack of food, over-crowding, bad acoustics, and more you would think tempers would flare, violence would erupt, and the Woodstock Music Festival would degenerate into a disaster. I witnessed quite the opposite. Acts of kindness, cooperation, good-natured acceptance, playfulness, and generosity were ever present. To quote my newfound friends, "they dug the scene, mellowed out, and went with the flow."

When the rains came I was caught out in the open destined to receive a good soaking. That was until I was invited to join four young persons in their canvas shelter. They had no earthly reason to invite the old guy into their abode except as a gesture of kindness and act of caring about your fellow man. Inside I found that I had entered another world—their world. If you've read Robert A. Heinlein's *Stranger In A Strange Land* you understand my inability to "grok" the situation. I was out-of-place yet felt unexpectedly comfortable.

They were a newspaperman's dream—pure and honest. Their attitude and lifestyle is authentic. Nothing about them was an act for my benefit. With the rain trying to beat its way into our shelter the five of us shared our thoughts, dreams, frustrations, and feelings. Hard as it might be to admit; I learned about relationships from a young lady who was, let's say, impressive. Tick, tock. She gave me handmade love beads that I will forever value. These four young people neither spewed hate nor condemned anyone. I've experienced more venom around the office watercooler.

One young lady in a blue dress with big, warm, inviting eyes is on a quest seeking the meaning of life. Philosophers tell us it is a futile effort. Yet, when the others complained about the rain her comment was, "It's nature doing her thing. We just happen to be in her way." In her innocence she is closer to the answer than most of us will ever be. The mud of Woodstock could not touch her. I hope the filth of the world fails to thwart her quest. Fly Night Bird lead the way.

Marijuana is illegal. Therefore, I do not condone its use. From firsthand experience, though, I understand its attraction. The buzz is relaxing and enjoyable. There appears to be no hangover. I haven't seen any of the aggressiveness that often happens when someone is drunk on alcohol. It does reduce one's inhibitions and definitely affects appetite. They called it the munchies. I think marijuana is not as dangerous as it is depicted to be. Of course, it is smoking which we know can be a health hazard as stated on every pack due to the Cigarette Labeling and Advertising Act of 1965. And, those who call it a gateway drug that leads to more and more addictive drugs could be right. Woodstock certainly supports that argument. If there was one factor that I found disturbing it was the widespread use of other drugs, primarily LSD. I have to wonder if they aren't happy with the "system" or the evil power structure how is destroying their brains or becoming addicted to a substance going to make things better?

Woodstock is destined to become a defining moment for the counter-culture in America. It's easy to point out things that are unfair or unreasonable. It's not as easy to make a difference. And, I know one thing for sure; you don't change things that you believe are wrong by running away. That's the coward's way out.

Ryoya put down the newspaper. She smiled thinking of Jack high on grass and hanging out with four hippies. Only he could get himself into such a predicament. There was one thing for sure. Being around Jack Moore was never dull. She did miss him. Slowly she opened a compact and lifted it up to gaze into its little mirror. Staring back at her was a coward bound by thousands of years of tradition.

Downtown in the offices of the *New York Tribune* Jack Moore sat at his desk. Upon arrival he was greeted by comments, such as, "Hey man, can I have a hit," "Far out man, the colors!" "You have some stash to share?" One of the more playful women in the office said, "Call me Night Owl. I stay up late if you want to come by and get mellow." Jack, of course, expected a response from his colleagues and took it with good humor until he was called into the editor's office.

The young punk that Jack had no use for stated, "You slipped one by me, didn't you?"

"Slipped what by you?"

"This column. You submitted it so late that it got printed without my OK."

"I submitted it the same time that I did the previous two nights. Besides, there are no facts to be checked. I was there and simply gave my account of what I observed." He added for effect, "Without, I might add, the negative spin that all of the other media seemed so intent on doing."

"So, everyone else is wrong but Jack Moore." In a fake high voice the editor imitated a woman reiterating an old joke, "Look everyone is out-of-step but my son."

"The truth, sadly, can be presented many ways. A man carrying a large box doesn't see a child and accidentally pushes him into the street. Headline A: Man

Accidentally Pushes Child Into Street. Headline B: Man Shoves Child Into Street. Both are true. The impression each generates is distinctly different."

"And, 'Man Shoves Child Into Street' will get read by more readers. It sells newspapers which pays your salary. When are you going to get it? This paper doesn't exist for your personal ranting and self-righteous pontification."

Jack was tired and not in the mood for this confrontation. Fortunately, he was professional and mature enough not to take the bait. He simply replied, "Is that all?"

"No, it's not!" The young editor picked up a copy of the morning's *Tribune*, "You give the impression that you support the legalization of marijuana and by association that the *Tribune* supports the use of illegal drugs."

"What are you talking about? Read the column. You can read, can't you? I state, 'Marijuana is illegal. Therefore, I do not condone its use.' That's about as clear as it can get."

"You will write a retraction and scathing—yes, I said scathing—condemnation of marijuana," the editor said with more than just a subtle threat evident.

Jack sat in silence for a minute. This confrontation was a long time coming. And, now it was here. He tried to sublimate his anger and control his emotions. A vision of Cleavage came to mind. He saw her placing the necklace around his neck and saying, "These are love beads. I made them myself. They mean we are friends and love each other. You're no longer a square—you're a yo yo." Jack slipped his hand into his jacket pocket and felt the beads. He thought of another comment that she made, "Why can't we just love each other and live in peace?" Because it's easier to hate than to love, Jack answered in his mind. Finally, Jack said, "Headline; Hippies fuck up a farm and exhibit anti-social behavior."

"What?" a surprised newspaper editor asked.

"That's what you want."

"It's a start." He sat back and ordered, "I want your retraction and condemnation of marijuana on my desk by noon."

"Not gonna happen."

"Why not?"

"I have a dentist appointment," Jack lied.

"By end of day, then."

"Listen, you want me to do an article on marijuana, I'll do it. But, I'll tell the truth and present the facts. I'll talk with law enforcement, the medical profession, and users. Then I will write a factual examination of the drug. No retraction, because there's nothing to retract."

"You do it or I'll write one for you."

"You print anything with my name on it that I didn't write and I'll go to every media outlet in this town."

"Get the hell out of my office!"

Jack returned to his desk. He was surprisingly calm. Maybe it was a little residual mellow from the day before. Or, maybe he was more affected by his weekend than he realized. Whatever it was he wasn't going to let the little twerp ruin his day. He also wasn't going to be blindsided. Since he lied about a dentist appointment he decided he would gather some important papers and other valuable files and shepherd them home. In this way, if he got the boot it wouldn't hurt as much. He leafed through an untidy mass of files around his desk on the floor, the file cabinet, and the desk. All his files dealing with the NASA story that he had labeled as The Changing DMV had remained undisturbed as he expected. After placing the chosen files in his briefcase he checked his desk drawer for any contact information that he might have missed. Inside the drawer he found a white envelope with his name on it. Was he already fired? That little shit didn't have the courage to tell him to his face. He opened the envelope. Inside he found a note that read, "I couldn't take the tickets without paying for them. Let's hope the Mets win both games. Watch your speed and drive safely, Trooper Sal Milano." The envelope contained a ten dollar bill that more than covered the cost of two Mets tickets.

The Rolling Stones did not attend Woodstock. Their lead singer, Mick Jagger, was in New South Wales playing the lead role in an upcoming movie *Ned Kelly.* Shooting had begun on July 12, 1969.

Ned Kelly was a famous 19th century Australian Outback criminal who wore an iron mask. Because of police persecution Kelly was forced into crime to feed his family. Called a bushranger he robbed several banks, was eventually captured, and hanged.

The production was plagued with numerous problems. Descendants of Ned Kelly complained about the film being shot in New South Wales, rather than in Victoria where most of the events actually took place. Marianne Faithfull, Jagger's girlfriend, went to Australia to play the lead female role, Ned's sister Maggie. Unfortunately their relationship was not going well and she took an overdose of sleeping pills shortly after arriving in Sydney. After being hospitalized in a coma, she recovered and went home. An unknown Australian actress, Diane Craig, replaced her.

On this day of filming Mick Jagger was shot in the hand when a pistol misfired.

Anna and Robert Six Trees followed a bee to find the hive. Robert carried a makeshift torch to smoke the hive long enough to gather some honey with the minimum number of stings.

46: Tuesday – August 19, 1969

Jack was in no hurry to get to the office. He hadn't returned the day before and decided that whatever the risk he wasn't going to take any more bullshit from his boss and nemesis. As a professional he knew he had done nothing wrong and steadfastly resolved that his integrity was not for sale. The weekend at Woodstock still clung to him. There was something about the idealism, perhaps naiveté, or beautiful innocence that stirred hope that a better world was possible. All those young people enduring trial after trial and remaining upbeat and positive was something that had to be seen to be believed. In a funny kind of way he missed the Flower Girl and his four compatriots in the tent. Once more he played with the love beads in his jacket pocket. They made him think of Ryoya. Was he doing the right thing giving her room? How long was he supposed to wait? He didn't want her to think that he was angry. However, he didn't want to cause her to feel pressured either. Tick, tock, it was in the hands of the clock.

When Jack entered his office he found a note on his desk from the editor. It simply said, "See me." He tossed it aside. As he looked at the other messages on his desk he became aware of the aroma of Patchouli. It was familiar however at first he wasn't sure where he had experienced it before. At the very moment that he connected the aroma to a person, Night Bird appeared in his doorway. The tiny blond wore a yellow peasant dress that reached the floor. She carried a cloth bag with flowers painted on the side. A headband held her blond hair back away from her face, although it wasn't long enough to require one. In the brighter light of his office he was drawn to her blue eyes. They were more indigo than blue—the color that lies between blue and violet in a rainbow. Deep enchanting eyes drew him in and captured his gaze. Jack blinked realizing that he had been staring straight into Night Bird's eyes.

"I heard the cow," she said as she smiled with the innocence of a young child.

"Night Bird, what are you doing here?"

"You visited our digs. It's only fair that I visit yours." She walked over to Jack's desk and sat on it pulling her legs up in front of her with her chin resting on her knees. The long skirt of her dress covered her legs completely. "It's depressing. You are too free a spirit to be in this cage."

"An accurate description."

"I heard your anguish and had to come to rescue you."

"How do you propose rescuing me?"

"I'm continuing my quest to find the meaning of life," Night Bird reached out toward Jack as she added, "Come with me."

"I appreciate the invitation, but my life is here. Besides I'm way too old for you."

"Age is a mark on a calendar. It means nothing in the metaphysical spiritual world. We are all the same age in the now. Two beings interacting, sharing, existing. Would you count the number of eyelashes you have, or the number of steps you take in a day, or how many words you speak? They are pointless numbers just as the number of years you have been wandering aimlessly around means nothing."

"That's a nice way to look at it." Jack concluded. The young woman who sat upon his desk continued to look directly at him. For some unexplainable reason it gave

Jack the impression that she saw right through his professional facade into the rebel that was kept at bay. He changed the subject, "Where is your quest taking you?"

Night Bird leaned forward as if telling a secret, "There's a commune in Western Pennsylvania that's led by a transcendental enlightened guru."

"How are you going to get there?"

She held up her thumb, "Thumb, man, the magic digit, the transporter."

"A pretty young girl like you? That can be dangerous."

"This bird has a stinger," Night Bird reached into her bag and held up a long thin knitting needle that had a sharpened point.

"A formidable weapon," Jack admitted. "However, I still worry about you being out on the road alone. It's just not safe." He paused then impulsively offered, "Why don't I rent a car and drive you there?"

Night Bird smiled and her doe eyes grew large as she said, "Then you will join me on our quest."

"No—not our quest—your quest. I'll drive you to your destination and then leave. Nothing more than that."

"You have the soul of a free spirit and need to fly, but you can't break the chains that keep you grounded. You're selling out and it's stealing your life. Come with me and find Jack Moore."

"I'm sorry Night Bird but this Jack Moore is trying to make things work here. My quest is to find happiness here in New York City."

"Let's make love," Night Bird requested catching Jack quite off guard.

"Excuse me?"

"You're in my mind, now I want you in my body," she said without inhibition or embarrassment.

"I . . . uh . . . don't think . . . that's a good idea."

"It's a great idea. We can share our essence and always be a part of each other."

Jack was about to respond when his telephone rang. He picked up the receiver and heard Ryoya's voice, "You're under arrest for use of a controlled substance. You have a right to remain silent. Although, I doubt you have the capability. Anything you say will be used against you in every way possible."

"Guilty as charged under extenuating circumstances."

"I read your columns. There seem to have been some very incriminating circumstances."

"I said extenuating."

Night Bird slid off of Jack's desk into his lap. The surprised reported exclaimed, "Hey!"

"I'm sorry, I'm interrupting," Ryoya said.

"No. Well, at the moment I'm busy but . . ."

"We do need to talk. Are you available for dinner, tonight?"

"I am. That would be good."

Night Bird rolled her hips and leaned against Jack's chest. She then ran her right hand up his leg which caused him to stand abruptly. Night Bird slid to the floor with a thud.

"Say, six o'clock at Maria's?" Jack asked.

"Six is fine," Ryoya answered. "I'll see you then."

As Jack hung up the telephone Night Bird said, "We have til six to get into it."

"We're not getting into anything." Jack helped the girl up. "You have to understand that I care about you as a friend—nothing more. There will be no getting into or sharing essence or anything else. My offer to drive you to Pennsylvania stands but it is only a ride."

"OK, I understand. It's a downer but you have your thing and I have mine. I still think you're groovy, a closet freak, and my yo-yo."

"That's on the weekend. This is Tuesday, so I'm a straight arrow."

"Mmmmmm, that sounds promising," she teased.

"Stop. It's not going to happen."

"Too bad. I really could turn you on. Well, I better split and get on the road."

"What about the ride?"

"Part of the quest is the journey. Don't miss the cows in this big noisy city. I hope your bird sees the soul I do. Peace." Night Bird flashed the peace sign and left Jack sitting in his office.

Hurricane Camille was a tropical depression when it reached the northern border of Mississippi. It dropped 3 to 5 inches of rain in Tennessee and Kentucky in the afternoon. Forecasters predicted the storm would continue to dissipate over land.

Jack Moore waited outside Maria's Napolitano Restaurant. He wore a dark blue knit shirt and khakis. This represented quite a change from the old, conservative, pre-Woodstock, always in brown Jack Moore. For a lot of reasons he was nervous. Ryoya gave the impression that something was wrong. His weekend among the counter-culture had made an impact on how he looked at things. The fact that he didn't see the editor, as requested, meant there would be repercussions the next day. And, his manner of dress was out of character.

He heard a woman's footsteps and turned to see Ryoya approaching. She wore a tan business suit with a white blouse. Obviously, she had come directly from work. Lifted by a breeze, her long black hair danced gaily behind her. Jack had the impulse to run to her and hold her in his arms. Everything about her stirred emotions within him, however, he kept his composure and simply waved.

Over dinner the relationship between Ryoya and Jack remained strained and distant. Jack attempted to lighten things up by describing the many costumes he saw at Woodstock. Ryoya nodded and nibbled at her food. She was lost in thought and conflicted. It was clear where the relationship was going or, more accurately, not going. Yet, she liked Jack and enjoyed being with him. The problem was that the longer they remained together the more painful a breakup would be. Without question, it would be kinder to end it now. The tough NYPD detective could do it without a second thought. Unfortunately, Jack had succeeded in reaching the softer female that hid inside her longing for a gentle touch, kind words, and warm smile. Difficult as it was to admit she enjoyed being taken care of and finding comfort in another's strength. If Jack were Japanese she could easily surrender to his charms and be complete. The problem was Jack was not Japanese and never would be. That was the undeniable truth and reason for her next actions. Ryoya put down her fork, looked at Jack and said, "Jack, you are a wonderful man . . ."

"But?"

"I enjoy your company . . ."

"But?"

You make me laugh . . ."

"But?"

Any woman would be happy to be with you . . ."

"But?"

"You're a pain in the butt!" Ryoya exclaimed. "Shut up and let me finish a sentence."

"If I do, I'm afraid I won't like what I hear."

"I don't want to hurt you."

"Then don't. Eat your dinner, drink some wine, and enjoy the stimulating conversation," Jack said trying desperately to change the course of the conversation.

"Jack," Ryoya unconsciously reached up and fondled the Japanese symbol for treasure that hung on her necklace.

Jack noted her action and immediately everything became clear. It embarrassed him how a seasoned reporter could miss such obvious signs. Too much, too fast. Tick tock—thank you Cleavage. What he had to do was turn back the hands of time. That would not be easy, but he had to try. "Ryoya, I enjoy your company . . ."

"But?"

Jack smiled, "Let's get one thing straight. I care deeply about you . . ."

"But?" this time Ryoya smiled.

"I'm not trying to tie you down—unless that's what you like." Ryoya laughed and Jack's heart soared. He continued, "We are two adults who for the most part get along. You're a Mets fan, but I forgive you."

"Thanks. Hell of a weekend. Sorry, I didn't say yes."

"Maybe, I tried to show my affection in ways that made you feel uncomfortable. That was not my intent. Yes, I am attracted to you. You are a vision that stirs me there's no denying that fact. You're quick and insightful. I'm never bored when with you unless you're rambling on and on about the Amazing Mets."

"But, you already forgave me. Remember?"

"Right. What I'm trying to say is that we are two adults who enjoy each other's company and add something to each other's life. I'm not going to press you for any more than that."

"Jack, I don't want to hurt you but it can't ever be any more than that."

"Then, let's enjoy each other and if you grow tired of me or, impossible as it seems, find someone better we will part ways without regret."

"I just don't want to mislead you."

"Listen, put your mind at ease. I'm a big boy. I know the risk. You don't have to worry about me getting too serious." Jack leaned back in his chair and said with a broad smile, "I'll propose to you on the day the Mets win the World Series—and we know that's never going to happen."

Camille's remains still had a lethal punch. The storm had sufficient strength and low pressure to absorb additional moisture as it moved east. Filled with replenished moisture the dark menace swept over West Virginia and Virginia. It stalled on the eastern side of the Blue Ridge Mountains dropping a world record 27 inches of rain in a three-hour period. The hardest hit area was Nelson County, Virginia where almost every road and bridge was washed out. Telephone and electric service was completely lost. Flash floods and mudslides wiped out entire communities. The rain fell so hard that those caught outside or forced from their homes had to cup their hands over their mouth and nose in order to breath. Mud, debris, dead bodies, dead livestock, and more flowed down the James River. In the end, over 1% of the population of Nelson County was missing or dead. With no way in, emergency services were unavailable.

So much rain fell in such a short period of time in Nelson County meteorologists at the National Weather service theorized that it was probably the maximum amount of rainfall that was physically possible. Entire hillsides broke loose and changed the topography of the area forever.

The James River crested in Richmond at 28.6 feet swamping downtown areas. After five hours, more than 37 inches of rain had fallen in Virginia.

Robert Six Trees rubbed tree sap on the twenty bee stings he received. The smoke would have worked if it hadn't been for that strong breeze that came along at the worst time. He was glad that his sister was far enough away to be spared.

47: Friday – August 22, 1969

Wellington Marsh was ordered to report to the Company Commander, Captain Strong. He knew he hadn't done anything wrong, therefore, wasn't concerned. In the uniform of the day, Service C which consisted of green trousers, web belt, khaki short-sleeve button-up shirt, and black shoes, he stopped in front of the officer's desk, saluted, and stated, "Private Marsh reporting to the Company Commander, as ordered, sir."

Captain Strong returned the salute and in a friendly voice corrected Wellington when he said, "At ease, acting Corporal Marsh." He picked up a sheet of paper and stated, "You've had an impressive record at the MOS school. No quarterdecks, write-ups, or deficiencies, a number of leadership commendations, and excellent test scores."

Wellington was proud of his accomplishments, but deep inside the demon resided that whispered in his ear it will all ultimately lead to one place. His mind recalled images of Marines in Vietnamese jungles that he had seen in newspapers, magazines, and on television. None of them looked happy. In fact, they all had that determined, tired, intense look of someone under extreme stress simply trying to survive. The reality of war was brought home for everyone to experience for the first time with the Vietnam War. Until then, war was an abstract. Something that happened over there with no burning images that were hard to forget. A bleeding Marine on a stretcher reached out for a cigarette but in Wellington's mind he was reaching out to an acting Corporal as if asking, "Why?"

"Your promotion to Lance Corporal has come through," Captain Strong's voice pulled Wellington back to the moment at hand. He handed Wellington a sheet of paper confirming the promotion.

"Thank you, sir."

"You earned this rank, son. Based on what you have demonstrated I expect that you will do well in the Marines," Captain Strong said. "You might want to make it a career. Just stay away from those snakes that like to read," he added with a smile.

A spontaneous smile crossed Wellington's face. He quickly caught himself and returned to a serious countenance. The Marine Corps wasn't a bad life if it wasn't for the fact that you could be sent into a war zone at any time and die.

"Have a seat Corporal," Captain Strong motioned to an open chair. He then walked around his desk and leaned on it. "You're going to Vietnam—you know that."

"Yes, sir."

"Vietnam is a tough grind. A lot of good Marines have served there. Some with distinction and far too many have lost their lives. There's no question that guerilla warfare is the toughest to fight. To be successful you have to not only use overwhelming force but also use your head. Corporal, you use your head."

Wellington didn't answer. All he could think about was how he was going to use his head to survive a tour in the jungles of Vietnam.

Captain Strong continued, "There is a strategy that we have initiated in Vietnam called the Combined Action Program, or CAP. We began using this approach in 1965 and found it to be a most effective counterinsurgency tool. It's different from the search and destroy strategy designed to wear down an enemy. In truth, nobody wins a war of attrition. CAP, on the other hand, partners our forces with local home guard militia to help protect villages and keep them from being sanctuaries for Viet Cong guerillas. In effect we are helping local villages protect their homes. This changes the dynamic of the relationship with the locals."

Lieutenant Colonel William W. Taylor started the CAP program in August, 1965. He was assigned a Tactical Area of Responsibility (TAOR) in the Phu Bai area that encompassed six villages and an airfield within ten square miles. He knew his forces were spread too wide to be effective. When his Executive Officer, Major Zimmerman, suggested that they use local militia Taylor devised the CAP approach and sent it to Colonel E. B. Wheeler, Commanding Officer of the 4th Marine Regiment. It was forwarded to III Marine Amphibious Force (IIIMAF) and Fleet Marine Forces Pacific (FMFPAC) for review. Major General Lew Walt, Lieutenant General Victor Krulak, and General Nguyen Van Chuan, the local Army of the Republic of Vietnam (ARVN) Commanding Officer all agreed to the proposal.

Captain Strong explained, "The way it works is a thirteen-member rifle squad with a Navy Corpsman is assigned to a geographic area. They operate in conjunction with older youth and elderly men from the villages who have not been drafted into the Army of the Republic of Vietnam (ARVN) to create a defensive force. The home guard has knowledge of the people and terrain. Highly trained Marines give them greater fire power, tactical capability, American medical services, artillery, air-support, and leadership. It gives them a distinct edge. We've had relatively good success with this approach."

"Originally, the Marine squads stayed in assigned villages but this left them vulnerable to attack. Today, the CAP squad is mobile. It moves among a number of villages in a random order so that the VC never knows where they will be at any given time. We have 102 CAP operations ongoing in Vietnam and are expanding that number."

"All Marines involved are carefully selected volunteers. CAP squads operate independently and are supported by the nearest American battalion, either Marine Corps or Army. Most often CAP squads are commanded by a sergeant, but there are units led by a Corporal. You've demonstrated the leadership ability and clear-headed thinking that we need to lead a CAP squad. I'd like to recommend you for the position. However, it remains a voluntary duty."

"But, I don't know anything about Vietnam, sir," Wellington said when Captain Strong paused and appeared to be waiting for a comment.

"If you volunteer you will be given ten days of training near Da Nang. You'll learn some Vietnamese phrases, customs, geographic data, first-hand insights from CAP commanders, threat assessments, and be introduced to your local militia counterpart. You and your squad will become partners with the defenders of the villages under your care."

"I just don't know," Wellington admitted. "When do I have to decide?"

"Right now, here," Captain Strong answered. "Now, I'm not going to tell you it's a walk in the park. But, it's better duty than trudging through the jungle doing recon or S&D. With the support of the villagers you have a much better handle on where the unfriendlies are so there's less chance of walking into an ambush. There are always the sympathizers that you have to watch out for. However, if you win over the villagers and they see you as a good thing then they will make your job easier. It all comes down to the leadership ability of the squad leader. The Marine Corps has confidence in you

Corporal Marsh. The question is; do you have confidence in yourself?"

Wellington's head spun. He was going to Vietnam. That was a given. The CAP program did sound better than being out in the jungle. Yet, Captain Strong was correct, the unanswered question was did he have what it takes to make it work? It stacked responsibility upon responsibility with other Marine's lives in his hands. His fear of dying in Vietnam just grew exponentially. What would his father do? He knew. That tough old man would take the lead and make it work. Without question he'd rather have control of his destiny than to be dependent on someone else's decisions. Confidence must be a nice thing. Suddenly, Wellington remembered the village exercise and how many trainees were designated as killed because of mistakes that they made. In other instances during training he kept them out of trouble which in a real-life situation would have saved lives. Maybe, just maybe, he could help save lives in Vietnam if he accepted the CAP squad leader position. In his heart he knew he would do everything in his power to protect his team and the villagers. Yes, at least he would know what his objective was which was better than wandering aimlessly in a jungle. He prayed that he would be smart enough as he said softly, "I'll do it, sir."

"Good," Captain Strong said as he stood and returned to his chair behind the desk. "You will receive your orders before you leave the post tonight. They will show your next duty station as Da Nang, Vietnam. You will report back here no later than 21 September to be issued equipment and arrange transport to your duty station."

Wellington stood, saluted and said, "Aye, aye, sir,"

"Hey I appreciate you giving me a heads-up, but I'm not in the small time anymore," Carl told Moe Black, the friend of Sylvester Attoro who had his tongue cut out by Miguel Juarez.

"This isn't small time," Moe insisted.

"Not interested," Carl said as he looked around the diner on Kingsbridge Road. Even though this was his home turf, he liked to be careful. It was after the breakfast rush and still too early for lunch so the place was essentially empty. Two old ladies sat in a booth at the other end of the restaurant and unless they had super hearing or high power hearing aids they couldn't hear the conversation.

"Your bigshot friends would be interested."

"Then take it to them."

"I don't have your connections," Moe stated. He then changed his tone to one of pleading, "Listen, just meet the guy and tell me if he's legit. You know how to tell the scammers from the real thing. I don't have your talent. If it's for real it could be my big break," he looked down at his hands and mumbled, "Besides, you owe us after what happened to Sylvester."

Carl grabbed Moe by the shirt and pulled him out of the booth to a standing position, "What the hell are you talking about? I owe you nothing! Sylvester must have spilled the beans to more than me because I didn't rip him off. I don't know what the hell happened to those guns." Deep inside, Carl knew he was indirectly responsible for Sylvester's injuries. He also suspected that the young hood told Miguel everything before he was shut up forever. Still, he didn't owe these punks anything. Of course, the compliment about him being the real deal didn't go unnoticed. Ego being what it is, Carl relented, "OK, I'll meet the guy and tell you what I think. But, I'm not getting involved no matter how sweet the deal."

"That's all I ask. Just meet him and hear what he has to say," Moe said with excitement. "You tell me whether or not to get involved. You're the expert. If you tell me to walk—I walk."

"Set up the meet."

"What's a good time for you?"

"I'm not working a card game, so tonight will do."

"I'll set it up."

"The Mets are playing the Dodgers tonight, tomorrow, and Sunday at Shea," Jack said into the telephone receiver.

"Tell me something that I don't know," was Ryoya Akimoto's response.

"Well, you don't know that it is sold out tonight but I know a guy who can get me two tickets," Jack explained. "That is, if you are interested."

"What no dinner?"

"Hot dog and a beer. What kind of fan are you?"

"Good point."

"Of course, the Mets are six games behind the Cubs in the Eastern Division which means the fair-weather fans aren't compelled to attend."

"Fair weather fans!? That's a hot one. Didn't you just tell me the game is sold out? Let's see, the Yankees are what, uh, yes, here it is, 25 games out of first place. In fact, they are in fifth place."

"It's not their year."

"And, when was the last time you went to a Yankee game?"

"You know because you were with me."

"That's right. I still have my Yankee cap." After a pause, Ryoya asked, "If I agree to go will you wear your Mets cap?"

"Absolutely, when you go to a game you support the team. So, are we on?"

"As long as you don't bring any illegal drugs."

Stephanie sat on the couch in Ritchie's apartment. It was without emotion that she listened as he told her of his plan. He was leaving early the next morning heading west to Warren, Pennsylvania. There he will spend a few days at a hippie commune.

"You remember Nick?" he asked.

"How could I forget?" was Stephanie's response.

"While I'm there I'll get better directions. The trip will probably take me through Ohio, Indiana, Illinois, Wisconsin, Minnesota, and then up to Canada. I have to sneak across the border on an Indian Reservation. It's easy to get across. Unfortunately, it's also easy to get hopelessly lost." Ritchie threw the last of his art supplies into a cardboard box. He picked up his collection of photos of the construction of the World Trade Center and shook his head. That was one project he wouldn't get to complete. How he wanted to see the finished product and travel to the top of that awesome building. After a few seconds he dropped the photographs into the box. He looked at Stephanie and asked, one more time, "You sure you don't want to join me?"

"I can't with my father and all. Besides I don't want to give up my citizenship and run off to Canada."

"You don't have to. You can come back anytime. Think of it as a vacation."

Stephanie knew that she had made the decision while at Woodstock and her direction had become clear. Rather than telling Ritchie that it was over for more reasons than his running away to Canada she chose to use her father as an excuse. "I simply cannot leave my father here alone at this time."

"Well, maybe you can come up later."

"We'll see."

Matthew Ellis sat outside in front of the three story brick building where he shared an apartment with his daughter, Stephanie. The cement retaining wall was perfect for sitting in the sun on a clear day. He read a back copy of *Newsweek*. An article of interest pertained to the first flight of the Boeing 747 which took place on February 9, 1969. Test pilots Jack Waddell and Brien Wygle were at the controls and Jess Wallick at the flight engineer's station. All involved with the project were elated because the enormous aircraft handled extremely well, better than anticipated. As Matt looked at photos of the 747 he was awestruck by how far aviation had come in a mere six years.

Slowly, images of aircraft began to form in his mind. However, they weren't commercial aircraft. He put down the magazine and let his mind uncover distant memories. Before the NASA contract in 1963, Matt had been fortunate to land a number of military contracts for mil spec wire products. Most were for use in the construction of an aggressive number of nuclear submarines. An image of the USS Thresher floated into his mind. Yes, he remembered. It disappeared in April of 1963. That tragic loss hit close to home as Matt knew by that time Orztech had supplied wire to the military for three years. They supplied the wire that was used in numerous Polaris class nuclear submarines. In fact, it was that military connection that led to the sale of wire to Boeing.

In the early 1960s, when Orztech Corporation was providing miles of wire for the Navy, Matt learned of another potentially lucrative military project. For years the United States Air Force relied on propeller-driven aircraft to move personnel and equipment. However, military leaders realized that a switch to jet aircraft was essential for a modern Air Force. Toward that end, the Air Force issued Specific Operational Requirement 182 with guidelines for a new aircraft that could be used for various purposes. The jet would have to be capable of flying missions of at least 3,500 nautical miles with a 60,000 pound payload. It had to be able to make low-altitude supply drops, as well as support combat paratroops. Finally, the jet had to allow for loading and unloading large military equipment. Three companies responded to SOR 182, Boeing, Lockheed, and General Dynamics.

Matthew Ellis was unable to find an appropriate contact at Lockheed or General Dynamics but did get an audience at Boeing. His experience with mil spec wire for the Navy was the key to that lucrative door. In the end, the Lockheed C-141 Starlifter was selected by the Military Air Transport Service (MATS). The Boeing design had been a wide body aircraft powered by four wing mounted engines. To allow for doors to open on the front of the jet for loading and unloading oversize military equipment the designers moved the cockpit above the fuselage in a pod that ran from just behind the nose to just behind the wing. While Orztech didn't profit from the bid process it gained entry into the aviation industry.

At the same time as the military project was being developed Boeing designed and built the 727, a mid-size narrow-body three-engine jet aircraft that could carry 149 to 189 passengers. It first flew in February 1963 and entered service with Eastern Air Lines in February 1964. The high quality and outstanding pricing of Orztech wire led to its extensive use in the 727 and succeeding aircraft. For over a decade more 727s were built per year than any other jet airliner.

The Boeing 737 followed shortly thereafter. This short to medium range, twinjet, narrow body aircraft was developed to serve more airports economically. Design began in 1964 with the first flight in April, 1967. Lufthansa put the Boeing 737 into service in February, 1968.

Finally, the "Jumbo Jet" Boeing 747 was developed. Interestingly, it used the same basic design that had been used for the failed Air Force Military Air Transport Service bid. The hump-like upper deck designed to allow large cargo doors on the front was converted into a first-class lounge and extra seating. Designers kept the basic configuration because Boeing management expected supersonic aircraft to become standard in the passenger segment of the industry. With the upper deck hump the 747 could easily be redesigned for carrying cargo. Development of the high-bypass turbofan engine that delivered double the power of earlier turbojets while consuming a third less fuel was the technology that made the 747 possible.

Matt's mind cleared as he remembered fulfilling orders for miles of wire to be used in the 727 and other aircraft in development. It was then that he knew Orztech wire was used in the Boeing 747. Immediately, he also questioned whether the wire was authentic mil spec wire or the inferior replacement provided by Lida Petropoulos through her company LPAmerica LLC. "I'm going to provide all the product required to fulfill your contracts at a price you can live with," Lida stated once more in his mind as he remembered her making that promise in a coffee shop May 1, 1960.

Jack Moore and Ryoya Akimoto arrived at Shae Stadium shortly before game time. The sun was still high in the sky and the humidity drew sweat out of every pore. Their seats were in Section 21 of the Mezzanine Level. This put them on the first base side half way between first base and the outfield foul pole a significant distance from the field. Upon seating, Ryoya stated, "When the Mets play in the World Series I want to sit down there." She pointed at the box seats along the first base line behind the Met's dugout.

"By the time the Mets play in the World Series we'll be seated in a new stadium," Jack snorted. Ryoya pulled the brim of his Mets cap down over his eyes. Jack straightened the cap and added, "There's practically nobody here."

"What are you talking about?" Ryoya responded, "The game is sold out. There are over fifty-thousand fans here."

"Well, last weekend I was with five hundred thousand in about the same size area. Look at all that open space."

"Woodstock flashback?"

"Yeah, kinda makes New York City seem less crowded."

The game started with an odd play. Mets pitcher, Jerry Koosman, was ahead on the count when Maury Wills unexpectedly bunted up the first base line. He was safe at first. Manny Mota bunted moving Wills to second and Willie Davis grounded out moving him to third. With two out and Wills on third Koosman struck out Wes Parker, looking.

"Koos is off," Ryoya stated.

"How the hell do you know so early in the game?" a heavyset middle-aged fan that needed a shave sitting in front of them grumbled.

"He's a control pitcher. Even from here I can tell he's struggling. A few of those pitches got away from him. If he doesn't settle down they'll start getting hits off of him."

"You're nuts lady!"

Ryoya answered, "Koosman pitched in the Army at Fort Bliss, Texas. He had a reputation of putting the ball right where he wanted. He led the International League in strikeouts in 1967 with a combination of control pitches that kept batters off balance. His strength is control."

Bottom of the first inning saw Bud Harrelson hit a single but he was stranded on the bases. In the top of the second inning Ryoya's prediction came true as the Dodgers hit two singles but failed to score. On the other hand, the Mets scored two runs in the second inning when Ron Swoboda hit a homerun with Wayne Garrett on base.

When the Mets batted in the third inning Tommie Agee, Cleon Jones, and Art Shamsky all singled and with a passed ball two more runs were scored. After three innings the Mets led four nothing.

The fan who sat in front of Jack and Ryoya turned to face them and said, "Any other useless observations?"

When the Dodgers came to bat in the fourth inning Wes Parker led off with a single. Then, with two out, Ted Sizemore and Jeff Torborg both singled driving in Parker for the Dodger's first score. They got two more hits in the fifth but didn't score. By this time they had accumulated eight hits.

"We're lucky the hits have been spread out," Ryoya commented.

"I'm lucky to have Ms. Baseball expert behind me," fat fan mumbled.

A foul ball was hit that drifted over the section where Jack and Ryoya sat. It was clearly too far to their left to be caught. Jack jumped up and yelled, "I got it!" The abrupt motion caused what was left of the beer in his cup to splash out. Golden cold liquid arced forward making a perfect twenty point landing atop the head of the offending fan.

In the top of the seventh inning pinch hitter Bill Russell singled to centerfield. Mets pitcher Jerry Koosman then balked allowing Russell to go to second base. A single by Maury Wills drove the base runner to third base. With runners on first and third and no one out Mets manager Gil Hodges walked out to the mound.

"Give him a break—take him out," Ryoya yelled.

Hodges must have heard her because he signaled to bring in relief pitcher Tug McGraw. Nothing was said by the cooled-down fan. McGraw struck out the next batter but then allowed two singles which drove in two runs. He got out of the inning as the result of a double play. The Mets lead was cut to one at 4 to 3.

In the bottom of the eighth inning Cleon Jones drove in Tommy Agee with a single and the Mets went on to win the game 5 to 3.

As he walked west on 44th Street Carl couldn't help but smile as he remembered the night that he got the best of Miguel. The seedy hotel the pimp's girl's used was on the right. Carl looked into the dingy lobby when he passed but didn't see any familiar faces. The address he sought was further up the block, 346 West Forty-Fourth Street,

Apartment 3C. The guy's name was Oscar—no last name. Moe was going to meet him there at eleven. Carl's ego swelled as he thought, "OK, I'll help the little punk out. But, I don't get involved. From now on, I only do what Ray Esposito and Don Spacini tell me to do."

The street was quiet with little traffic at that hour of the night. Carl looked ahead and saw only an empty sidewalk. He liked it that way. No one to size up and make an instant decision as to friend or foe.

Halfway down the block he came to an alley between two buildings. As he passed, a figure stepped out of the shadows.

Jack and Ryoya arrived at her apartment door. When he went to kiss her goodnight she said in a soft, inviting, and distinctly feminine voice, "Would you like to come in for a drink?"

"I don't know. Do you think I might spill it?"

"Only if there is a foul ball within fifty yards," Ryoya smiled. "You didn't have to defend me, but I appreciate your gallant effort."

"He was being a jerk."

Nothing else was said as the door was opened and Ryoya smiled.

Fatigue set in as Wellington Marsh waited for the Southern Railroad Southerner train that would take him to Philadelphia where he would make a connection to Detroit. MOS training had been long, arduous, and very challenging. Yet, he knew reality was that it was only a small sample of what he would face in Vietnam. The cool night air was a welcome relief from the hot, humid, oppressive days he had endured during training.

Once more he glanced at his sleeve at the single stripe over crossed rifles designating him as a Lance Corporal. A sense of pride flowed through his mind as he admitted to himself in the quiet of the night that he had earned the rank. Unfortunately, it quickly reminded him that he would now be responsible for thirteen Marines, a Naval Corpsman, and an untold number of villagers. A cold wave of sweat passed over him.

In the distance he heard a train whistle. He hoped it was his train and that he would soon be on the first leg of a welcome trip home. Wellington pictured his mother and father. He knew that his old man would be proud of his rank. Unexpectedly, another face entered his mind—Teresa Champion.

Miguel Juarez stood before Carl Pythacyk. In the Puerto Rican's hand Carl recognized the twenty-two caliber revolver he had taken away from the punk not that long ago. For a prolonged period nothing was said. Then Miguel spat, "Well, Puerco, I told you I always get even."

Carl didn't answer. He wasn't going to give the little shit the satisfaction. As he considered the situation he couldn't help but wonder if Moe had set him up. It didn't take long for him to conclude that this was more than a coincidence.

"Into the alley, pronto!" Miguel ordered.

Carl realized that once in that secluded place his chances of coming out in one piece were slim. He hesitated.

"I'll blow your nuts off, right here," Miguel threatened as he aimed the revolver at Carl's groin. Once more he motioned in the direction of the alley.

Without a better alternative Carl complied. Slowly, with a forced hint of arrogance he walked into the dark abyss that would seal his fate one way or another.

Ryoya walked seductively into the living room carrying two glasses. One had Scotch on the rocks. The other contained Cabernet Sauvignon. Jack watched as she approached. The same feelings that he had at More-Or-Less when he first saw Ryoya returned. Ryoya Akimoto was a beautiful, exotic, mysterious woman with piercing eyes that made one self-conscious. He wondered what did she see in him? What had she discovered that worked in his favor or against him?

His treasure handed him the glass that contained Scotch on the rocks and sat next to him. A light floral scent with top notes of lilac and apricot reached Jack adding to the attraction that he was experiencing and increasing the desires he felt. A simple aroma vastly enhanced her seductive charms. Jack slipped his arm around Ryoya and she surrendered to his touch. In silence they enjoyed each other's presence.

Jack enjoyed just sitting quietly with Ryoya. He surveyed the room in an attempt to gain greater insight into the extraordinary person he considered his treasure. What immediately struck him was that everything was neat and orderly and clean. Right away he knew if she saw his living room she would run screaming into the night. On the other hand she might just pull her weapon and shoot the damn place. The décor in Ryoya's apartment was an interesting mixture of western modern and traditional Japanese. All in all, he liked it.

The couch upon which they sat was simple with clean lines. Brightly colored fabric depicting cherry blossoms made the piece unique and personal and Japanese. Jack had seen a lot of cherry blossoms when he was in Japan after World War II. Called Sakura, the cherry blossom is the flower of a number of trees. While there, Jack learned of Hanami a centuries-old practice of picnicking under a blooming sakura tree. The custom began in the imperial court, spread to the samurai, and eventually the common people. Most public buildings and schools in Japan have cherry blossom trees around them.

In Japan, cherry blossoms symbolize the ephemeral nature of life. The concept of "mono no aware" dates back to the 18th-century scholar Motoori Norinaga. Cherry blossoms bloom en masse, are extremely beautiful, and die quickly. Mono no aware is a philosophy of enjoying the beauty of a thing because it is transient and will not last. Jack looked at Ryoya and appreciated every second of the time he was spending with her.

During World War II, the image of cherry blossoms was used to motivate the Japanese people and to stoke nationalism. Japanese pilots painted them on the sides of their planes or took branches of the trees with them on their missions. One of the first kamikaze units was called Yamazakura or wild cherry blossom.

Jack continued to study Ryoya's apartment. A comfortable-looking easy chair and accompanying pole light with table sat in one corner. It looked like an ideal place to sit and read. A bookshelf stood tall against a wall. A combination black & white television, record player, and radio console in dark wood was placed directly across the room from the couch. In front of the couch was a low square black liquored coffee table with four glass inserts on the top. Upon the table were a number of magazines and an ash tray. The magazines covered an interesting choice of subjects. As would be expected there was the latest issue of *Time Magazine*. Also present, was *Psychology Today*, *Natural History*, *Redbook*, and a totally unexpected *Motor Trend*.

"*Motor Trend?*" Jack asked no one in particular.

Ryoya jumped up and said, "Have you seen the new Datsun sports car? It's called the 240Z." She picked up the Motor Trend magazine and leafed through the pages until she found an article. As she handed the magazine to Jack she added, "It looks something like a Jaguar—only better. A 2.4-liter single-overhead-cam inline six produces 151 horsepower giving it a top speed of 125 miles-per-hour. For $3,526 you get all independent suspension, MacPherson struts, rack-and-pinion steering, front-disc brakes, and a Corvette-style dashboard." She smiled and in a little-girl voice said, "I want one."

"I can tell," Jack replied. He looked at the article and concluded, "It says here that it is being introduced in 1970."

"They're in showrooms, now."

"Are you going to buy one?"

"On my salary? No, I'll just go by the showroom and gaze in the window." Ryoya returned to her position leaning against Jack's chest. Jack let his cheek touch her hair and slowly turned his head toward her. Ryoya responded and looked up to accept his tender kiss. They embraced.

Carl's eyes adjusted to the darkness. One thing he immediately concluded was that he and Miguel were alone. That was a good thing as he didn't have to contend with more than one adversary. On the other hand, it meant that Miguel already had planned the next steps that were to take place. This left no room for negotiations. Carl decided that if he survived this night Moe would beg for a quick death.

"Over there," Miguel motioned toward a railing that ran around the opening to a flight of cement stairs leading down to a basement door.

Carl moved toward the stairs. Fear that he had not felt for many years erupted in the pit of his stomach. Bile creeped up to his throat. A mental slap kept him from pleading for his life. From what he could determine the alley left no opportunity for escape or cover. Brick walls on both sides were both windowless and doorless. At the inner far end was a ten foot wrought iron fence. The only way out was the way they came in and that was not an option.

When Carl reached the railing Miguel ordered, "Stop there! Turn around!" Carl obeyed. What he saw was Miguel holding the twenty-two caliber revolver in his right hand aimed at Carl and a length of rope in his left hand. With a venomous smile Miguel outlined his plan. "I thought a long time about what I was going to do to you. It would be easy to simply shoot you and be done with it. But you embarrassed me in front of my puta—my girls. This has to be avenged. So, I'm going to tie you to that railing. Then I'm going to have one of my girls bring the others to watch me pork you up the ass. You're gonna cry like a baby, Puerco!" Miguel took a step closer to Carl making sure to remain too far away to be vulnerable to attack. He tossed the length of rope to Carl. It had a loop with a slipknot on one end. "Slip that around your right wrist." he ordered.

Carl still had no choice but to comply. His heart beat faster now that he knew the horrendous plan formulated by Miguel. Thoughts of Sylvester Attoro confirmed that the little prick was capable of anything.

When the loop of rope was around Carl's wrist, Miguel instructed, "Pull it tight." Carl obeyed. "Tighter!" Once more, Carl complied. "Now, turn around, put your wrist on top of the railing, and tie the rope to it."

Carl knew this was a critical point as once he was secured to that railing there was little he could do.

"Hurry up, Puerco, tie your paw to the railing."

No option came to mind so Carl reluctantly tied his right wrist to the railing.

"Bueno. Now, hold your left hand out behind your back."

Carl hoped desperately that Miguel would make a mistake and come close enough for him to grab the shirt of the son-of-a-bitch. He knew the gun would still be a threat, but if he could grab Miguel and pull him down with enough force to smash his head against the railing he might have a fighting chance. Unfortunately, the opportunity failed to materialize as Miguel stayed a safe distance away as he tossed a widened slipknot loop around Carl's left wrist. With a savage tug on the rope the knot slid tight around Carl's wrist causing his to gasp.

"That's it. Learn to like pain. You're going to learn to lick my hand after I beat you." He pulled once more to make sure the knot was tight and announced, "Oh, you should know that I'm also going to have one of my girls photograph you losing your virginity. That way I'm sure you will behave and do whatever I tell you." Miguel draped the rope over the railing and proceeded to tie Carl spread eagle on the wrought iron pillory.

Wellington sat in a window seat and watched the dark scenery pass by. It would be morning before the train reached Philadelphia. He looked at his watch. It was midnight. In just a few minutes he was asleep.

Robert Six Trees sat with his mother and discussed a planned trip north. He was excited about visiting the place where his mother grew up.

48: Saturday – August 23, 1969

Sweat dripped off of Carl's chin. He knew one thing for sure; if his left hand got tied to the rail he was finished. Fortunately, he knew something else. The railing had rusted which caused the horizontal crosspiece to separate from the vertical upright post where his right hand had been tied. When he tied the rope around the railing he discovered this weakness. Knowledge of the fact that Miguel would not check the rope until after Carl's left hand had been secured allowed the captive to leave enough slack for the rope to move freely. While it offered a glimmer of hope, Carl knew that timing would be everything. If he moved too soon he would be shot, too late and his left hand would be secured to the railing vastly limiting what he could do.

Miguel had draped the rope that was attached to Carl's left wrist over the rail. Quickly he grabbed the end and pulled on it to draw his adversary's wrist toward the railing. The pimp/rapist was careful to remain out of reach by approaching the rail from the left. He said nothing as he concentrated on the final step to rendering his victim helpless.

Carl slowly slid his right hand toward the gap between the railing and post. He knew that he needed a diversion to slow Miguel's progress. In a voice that reflected more fear than he wished, Carl said, "Listen, Miguel, you know that I'm in with the Spacini family. Let me go and I'll get you in. We can work together again. What do you say?"

Miguel took the bait and looked up at Carl, "I let you go and I'm a dead man. No, compadre, I'd rather have you on your knees sucking . . ." He never saw the fist that struck him when Carl's freed right hand swung full force through the darkness. The blow knocked Miguel backwards to the ground. Contact with the cement was so violent that it knocked the revolver out of Miguel's hand. In an instant Carl was free. He saw the gun and kicked it away from his foe. Although groggy, Miguel produced a five-inch switchblade knife. As Carl approached, the Puerto Rican swung the blade back and forth in a defensive motion. Carl Pythacyk was seeing red. Fear had morphed into anger—red hot unstoppable emotion hell-bent on destruction. No punk with a puny knife was going to thwart his assault or escape his punishment.

Miguel had a different idea and plenty of fight left in him.

Ryoya slid scrambled eggs onto Jack's plate. He nodded as he sipped his coffee. She joined him at the small table. After a few minutes of silent eating, Jack looked at Ryoya and said, "There's something I've been wondering." She looked up not knowing what to expect from the person she had come to realize often does the unexpected. Jack hesitated, then began in a halting manner, "There's something, I'd like to ask you." Immediately, Ryoya thought that contrary to what he had said earlier Jack might be getting ready to pop the question—a question that she knew would end their relationship. She looked at Jack and knew that she would miss him but it was the way it had to be, shikata ga nai. Jack asked, "What did Harry tell you I offered the night we met at More-Or-Less?"

Relief caused Ryoya to laugh, almost uncontrollably. It was definitely not the question that she expected. Once more the king of the unexpected had struck.

Jack wasn't sure why Ryoya reacted the way she did, so he added, "Seriously, it's haunted me. What was the damn intriguing proposal that Harry told you I made?"

Ryoya again laughed. She took Jack's hand and said, "He told me that you would let me be me without any judging or attempt to change me. It was refreshing and intriguing." Ryoya sipped some tea. With a smile she added, "He also told me to keep you guessing to drive you crazy." She put down her cup and concluded, "I see it worked."

"I'm going to kill him. You know that."

"Is that a confession? You know, I can arrest you for intent?"

The telephone rang. Ryoya answered. Jack heard her side of the conversation. "Are you kidding me? Yes, I recognize the location. I also recognize the name of the vic. They need to fence-off that alley. Yes. OK, pick me up in fifteen minutes. Who? None of your damn business!" Detective Akimoto hung up the telephone, turned toward Jack, and said, "I'm sorry, Jack. I just caught a case." She nodded in the direction of the telephone, "You heard. You can stay. Just lock the door when you leave." She grabbed a piece of toast from her plate and rushed into the bedroom.

"Yeah, I'll stay and rifle through your things and look for loose change in the sofa."

Ryoya walked out with a toothbrush in her mouth and mumbled, "I know I can trust you." She returned to the bedroom.

"Ouch!" Jack said with a smile. He knew that he would respect her privacy and not go snooping. The fact that Ryoya knew and trusted him locked that fact in stone, no concrete, no steel. "What kind of case is it?" he asked.

From the bedroom he heard, "Murder."

"I'm sorry, it's Saturday, there are no buses to Detroit until Monday," the ticket clerk told Wellington Marsh.

"Damn," the young Marine replied as an aside. "It's hard to believe that there's no way to get to Detroit on a weekend." He asked, "What's the best route to hitch to Detroit?"

The clerk was surprised at first, then after a moment's thought said, "There are a couple of ways to get there. You could take 176 West to Pittsburgh, then 80 to Toledo. From there I'm not really sure but you're a lot closer. The other way is to go North on 476 past Allentown and pick up 80 there. It's a long way to hitchhike."

"I know, but at least I'm moving in the right direction. Thanks," Wellington turned to leave.

"Wait, Corporal!" The clerk called out. "I get off in an hour. I live in Allentown. I'll take you that far to get you started."

"Thanks."

"You can wait over there," the clerk pointed toward a coffee shop in the terminal. "I'll come and get you when I get off." After a pause he added, "Hell, I'll drive you all the way to Route 80. It's only an hour more. The damn lawn can wait. I was a Marine once, semper fi."

Miguel Juarez' body was found in an alley on West 44th Street. His throat had been cut. When the call went out a WINS-News Radio reporter picked up the story. As a result, the Puerto Rican's murder hit the airwaves just after dawn. Luckily, the police were able to suppress the method used to end the young man's life. In this way they could eliminate the inevitable false confessions that are often offered, as well as use that information omission to potentially confirm the actual perpetrator of the crime.

In his parent's apartment at 2515 University Avenue Carl packed as much as he could into a single suitcase. He only packed one of his custom Italian suits as the other had blood on it. From his dresser he gathered all of the cash that he had on hand. Finally, he packed the twenty-two caliber revolver that he brought home in the middle of the night.

Without saying anything to his parents, Carl left the apartment. When he exited the building into a courtyard he half expected to be met by a cordon of police. Instead, he was met by a number of kids who lived in the building. They waved and yelled, "Hi, Carl." What was generally a common innocuous occurrence, on this day seemed like he was being pointed out to the authorities. He quickly moved on and headed toward Jerome Avenue. The Number 4 to Yankee Stadium, D train to 145th Street, and A Train to 175th Street brought Carl to the George Washington Bridge bus terminal. At this point he knew time was working against him and the police might already have circulated his picture. He also knew there were always transit cops in the passageway from the subway to the bus terminal. For this reason he exited the subway onto the street and walked a block to the bus terminal on a side street. Without incident he arrived at the upstairs platform and took the first bus across the bridge.

Carl did not have a destination. The only thing he had was a desire to get as far away from New York City as possible—as quickly as possible. Once in New Jersey he began to hitchhike on Route 4. Before long, a truck driver picked him up and they ended up traveling west on Route 80. Unfortunately, the driver had to exit in Parsippany, NJ so Carl was once more on foot waving his thumb. At that time he wasn't far enough from New York to feel comfortable.

Ritchie loaded Hilda, his dark blue 1966 Ford Econoline van, with as many of his possessions as possible. There was only room for his clothes, art supplies, books, records, and Fetch. She took her place in the passenger seat. Little did she know that they were embarking on a long journey from which they could not return.

The draft-dodger had to negotiate with his landlord to get out of his lease. The lord-of-the-manor wanted two month's rent and to keep the security deposit. Ritchie decided the security deposit was sufficient and decided to sneak out of town under the cover of sunlight. He told the landlord that he would be leaving the following week.

Big Bob Finley, owner of Finley's Auto Body, was sad to see his accomplished artist leave but understood the reasons. It was clear that, no matter what, he was going to lose his painter either to the army or the great white north. He handed Ritchie a box. Inside Ritchie found a hockey puck and a hundred dollars. Bob offered his hand, "You take care, ya hear?"

Mid-morning two fugitives from Uncle Sam left Dumont, NJ. They drove south on Washington Avenue until it became Teaneck Road and crossed Route 4. Ritchie turned right onto Route 4 and headed west. As it was Saturday morning there was little traffic. When they merged onto Route 80 west Fetch perked up. It was as though she recognized the highway where she had been abandoned, wet and alone. She turned and looked at Ritchie wondering if history was going to repeat itself. A low yodel escaped from the throat of a concerned basenji. Ritchie looked over and said, "Calm down, we have a long way to go."

Claire Payton woke Olivia Samantha Everett by saying, "Miguel is dead!"

"What?" a foggy Olivia replied. "Who is?"

"I just heard that Miguel was murdered last night," Claire said with a smile that she couldn't contain. She then got serious as she said, "Listen, you have to leave, go home, get out of this hell before one of Miguel's cohorts takes over."

"I can't go home," Olivia uttered sadly, "you know that."

"Yes, you can," Claire asserted. She sat on the edge of the couch. "You are the victim here. You have nothing to be ashamed of. All you did was survive the best way you knew how. Your parents will welcome you home with open arms and tears of joy."

"How can I ever go back after all that I've done?"

"Honey, nothing will erase the nightmare that you've lived through. It happened and is a part of you. But, it doesn't have to destroy you. There is a good, sweet, caring, incredibly strong person inside you. You're young. You can put this behind you and have a long and happy life. What is most important is that you take the opportunity now, while you can. Don't let Miguel, or his kind, win. Their evil cannot triumph. Miguel can only win if you let him."

Olivia began to cry, "He has won. There is nothing left inside me. Olivia Samantha Everett is dead along with her innocence and dreams. He took them away. I'm lost. The awful, filthy stain cannot be washed away. It goes too deep. I will forever be an Eighth Avenue whore."

Claire's heart sank as she felt the same unwashable definition of self. She felt so inadequate as she searched for the correct words to save a poor child from a life of misery. She looked at the young girl. Fifteen years old with long blond hair and blue eyes, the picture of innocence, not yet scared by ravishes of life on the street. Deep inside where Claire hid her emotions she felt like the surrogate mother of Olivia Samantha Everett. She had to save her. Nothing else mattered. She would give her own life to give Olivia back her life. Claire decided to try a different approach. "Olivia, am I an Eighth Avenue whore?"

Olivia looked up through tear-soaked eyes and replied, "Yes . . .no . . .you are a good warm loving person . . .you are . . .my friend."

"But, no matter what I do from now on I will always be an Eighth Avenue whore."

"No."

"I can get a job, become a nurse, help people but will always be an Eighth Avenue whore."

"No!"

"I could never get married, have a home, a dog, a yard because I am an Eighth Avenue whore."

"Stop it!" Olivia screamed, "You are a kind and good woman. You aren't a whore. Look at you—you were beaten and forced to do what you do." She reached out and said with the deepest most sincere emotion, "You are my friend and I love you."

The last comment was unexpected. It caught Claire completely off guard. She found herself welling up with tears. Spontaneously, she also reached out and pulled Olivia close and hugged her. How could this child be so misguided as to love an Eighth Avenue whore? More than ever she was committed to saving her only true friend.

After a few moments embrace, Claire held Olivia at arm's length and asked, "Do you believe that I can be saved and live a good life?"

"I do—you deserve it."

"Then you have to believe that you can also."

"I . . .I just . . .don't know."

"You have to know and you have to believe. If our friendship counts for anything you have to accept what I am saying. If you go home and make a life for yourself, I'll stay off Eighth Avenue. You will be saving us both."

"What if I can't?"

"Then you will confirm that I'm an Eighth Avenue whore not worth anything. It's up to you."

Suddenly, Olivia broke down completely. Emotions hidden inside, held at bay, beaten into hiding, forcefully numbed escaped as a fifteen-year-old child wailed, "I'm so ashamed!"

Claire held Olivia in her arms, once more, and comforted her. Softly, she said, "Of what? Being a captive, tortured, and enslaved?" She stroked Olivia's hair and soothed her, "You cry. If anyone in this world has a right, it's you." Patiently, Claire waited for Olivia to cry it out. She couldn't remember when she did the same thing so many years before. When Olivia settled down Claire told her, "I have some money squirrelled away. I'm going to give you some to get you home. But, you have to leave today, this morning. Miguel's gang of goons won't take long fighting among themselves for control. When they get organized it will be too late."

"But . . ."

"You have to decide. Would you rather face loving parents who will welcome you home or one of Miguel's underlings who wants to try you out before putting you back on the street?"

"What about you?"

"I have an aunt in Virginia who would take me in. See, we both will get away from Eighth Avenue. Now, you pack up quickly and get out of here. Where is your home?"

"Bridgeport, Connecticut."

"I'm going to give you enough money to take a taxi home. We can't be too careful. They might already be watching the bus and train stations. A hundred dollars should be enough."

"When will you leave?"

"I have a little more than you to pack, but I'll be out this afternoon."

In less than an hour Claire hugged Olivia and put her in a taxi. She smiled and waved as the yellow automobile disappeared down the street. For a period of time she stood motionless. All she could do was pray that everything would work out for her emotionally adopted daughter. Claire Payton did all that she could, more than Olivia realized or would ever realize, to save a cherished friend. She did everything, including lie. There was no aunt and the hundred dollars was almost all she had. None of that mattered because Claire knew the destiny of an Eighth Avenue whore had already been determined.

Detectives Ryoya Akimoto and Michael Donovan arrived at the crime scene on West 44th Street. The victim, Miguel Juarez, was slumped against a wall. His body was covered with a sheet. Crime scene investigators were gathering evidence while uniformed officers guarded the entrance to the alley. The two detectives stopped by the first officer on the scene.

He described what he found from his notes. "I received the call at seven twenty six a.m. The super from the building on the right, 340 West 44th, saw the victim in the alley and thought it was a drunk or bum. He went in to chase him away. When he got within three feet he saw the blood and backed out of the alley and called the police. I arrived about ten minutes after the call. I checked the vic for life and found no vital signs. After calling in on my car radio I secured the scene."

The two detectives entered the alley and uncovered Miguel's body. "Look familiar?" Ryoya asked.

"Sure does," Michael Donovan answered. "The pimp we ran in for manhandling the toot. Juan something."

"Miguel Juarez," Ryoya corrected.

"That's what I said." Detective Donovan observed, "Looks like he was in quite a fight. One he lost."

"The apparent cause of death is having his throat cut, but we better wait for the coroner's report."

When the lead crime scene investigator approached, Ryoya asked, "Did you find a weapon?"

The young woman with short dark hair wearing a blue pullover shirt with POLICE on the breast pocket and blue jeans answered, "Sure did. A five-inch switchblade lying right next to the body."

"Maybe it was suicide," Michael Donovan joked.

The investigator smiled and continued, "We also found two lengths of rope with slip knots. There's blood on both walls and two of the vic's teeth were found over there. We also found an expensive silk tie with the label; Antonio's, Thirty Fifth Street, New York, NY. And finally, a variety of other bits and pieces of clothing and debris."

"Something went on in this alley, that's for sure," Ryoya stated. She turned to Michael and said, "We better canvass the area for witnesses and later we will talk with his girls."

As the sun rose in the sky the temperature and humidity rose along with it. Carl sweat as he walked along the highway while holding his left hand out with his thumb pointing in the direction he travelled. Dozens of cars and trucks ignored the lone pilgrim with a suitcase.

Carl thought about Miguel's demise. The prick deserved to die. With what he had planned for Carl death seemed too quick and easy. Unfortunately, now Carl was on the run. Obviously, he had no idea where he was running to but west seemed as good a direction as any.

A blue van pulled onto the shoulder of the road and blew its horn. Carl trotted to the passenger side door. The window was open. "Thanks, I was getting tired," Carl said.

"Where are you headed?" Ritchie asked.

"West."

"Well, I'm going that way, hop in."

Carl looked at the black dog in the passenger seat that was staring at him. For a brief moment there was a staring contest that Fetch won. Finally, Carl asked, "What about the dog?"

"Fetch—in the back," Ritchie ordered.

Reluctantly and with a parting snarl Fetch relinquished the passenger seat. The canine jumped into the back of the van and lay down on a blanket that Ritchie had spread for her before she yelled, "Shotgun!"

"I'm headed to Warren, Pennsylvania."

"What's in Warren, Pennsylvania?"

"A commune where a friend of mine lives," Ritchie explained. "It's not my final destination, just a stopping off point. I'm really headed to Canada."

"Canada, huh?"

"Yeah, but I have to sneak across the border."

This was good news to Carl. "Why do you have to sneak across the border?"

"I'm evading the draft," Ritchie said nonchalantly.

Oh, you a coward?"

"I don't know. What I do know is I don't want to serve in the Man's army."

"Yeah, I get that," Carl agreed. He then said, "Canada? I've never been to Canada. Mind if I go along?"

"You're welcome to go with me but it could get hairy crossing the border."

"I'll take my chances."

They came to the Delaware Water Gap and crossed into Pennsylvania. For an odd reason, Carl felt slightly relieved now that he had a state between him and New York. He also felt very lucky to have been picked up by a guy who planned to sneak into Canada. What could be more perfect?

"I figure it's another four hours or so to Warren," Ritchie offered.

About a half an hour later, outside of White Haven, the travelers came upon another lost soul. A Marine Corporal was walking along Route 80 carrying an overnight bag. Ritchie pulled onto the shoulder of the road and stopped under a sign that read "NO STOPPING." Wellington Marsh ran up to the van on the passenger side where Carl had the window open.

Ritchie yelled to Wellington, "Where you headed?"

"Detroit."

"That's cool, man. Get in back."

Wellington opened the side door and climbed in. When he did he realized that there wasn't any back seat. There were boxes and bags and papers spread throughout the back of the vehicle, but no seat. There was also something else and it was alive. His eyes adjusted to the dull light and he found himself face to face with a dog. "Does he bite?" the Marine asked.

"She hasn't bitten me," Ritchie answered.

Wellington wasn't sure what to do. He was hesitant not wanting to upset the animal. Fetch grew weary of the whole encounter and walked over to her blanket and settled in for a nap. "There's no back seat," Wellington stated.

"Use the folding lawn chair," Ritchie replied.

Wellington found the chair, opened it, positioned it behind the two front seats, and sat down.

Ritchie accelerated and drove back onto the highway. It was at that moment that Wellington learned a valuable lesson about riding in an unsecured seat. As if shot in the chest, he flew backwards falling on a canvas bag filled with clothes. He also found himself face to snout with a growling black dog. Her look was one of displeasure, discomfort, distrust, and to Wellington possibly distemper. Slowly, he backed away.

"Detroit, is that anywhere near Canada?" Ritchie asked.

"Yeah. As a matter-of-fact Canada is south of Detroit."

"Get out of here," Carl spat, "Everyone knows Canada is north of the United States.

"There's a part of Canada that juts west below Detroit. Most people don't know that. You go due south on Randolph Street through the Detroit Windsor Tunnel and you're in downtown Windsor Canada."

"No shit?" the hood on the run said.

"Cause of death; loss of blood due to having his throat cut," Detective Donovan read the preliminary coroner's report out loud. "Like we didn't already know that." He continued to read the three page typed document. "He got beat up before he ran out of blood—that's for sure," Donovan commented. "Broken jaw, four teeth knocked out, broken ribs, contusions on the back of his head, concussion, broken fingers on his right hand, bruises, scrapes, and cuts. This guy got hit by a truck! I think he bounced into the alley from the street."

"Is that how you're going to report it," Ryoyo smiled.

"Yeah, hit by truck bounced into alley—accidental death. Case closed."

"How do you explain the cut throat?"

"Hit a car antenna as he flew through the air."

"That makes sense," Ryoya agreed sarcastically. "OK, you write it up. I'm going home." She was handed a piece of paper by a lab assistant. She read the paper and said, "Fingerprints on the switchblade belong to the vic and a known petty thief named Carl Pythacyk."

"It was a Chevy antenna. I'm telling you. I know by the angle of the cut," Detective Donovan continued.

"Last known address; 2515 University Avenue in the Bronx." Ryoya stood, picked up her purse, and headed for the door.

Michael Donovan followed, "What about the crime scene?"

"Dozens of prints everywhere. Clear set of prints belonging to Mr. Pythacyk on a railing."

"Hey man, how long you been a soldier?" Ritchie asked over his shoulder as he drove.

"Marine," Wellington corrected.

"OK, how long you been a Marine?"

"A couple of months, since April."

"Join up or drafted?"

"Drafted."

"You know you're going to go to Vietnam?"

"Yes."

"So, why do you want to go to Vietnam?" Ritchie asked innocently.

"I don't want to go—it's where they are going to send me," Wellington explained.

"You know, if you go, you'll kill men, women, and children."

"I hope not to kill anybody."

"It's what you'll do because it's what you'll be ordered to do."

"If I have to kill anyone, it will be another soldier."

"Don't count on it, man."

Wellington didn't respond. He thought about the fact that he was going to participate in the Combined Action Program, or CAP, and would be defending villagers from the Viet Cong. That was very different from attacking villages and not knowing if they were friend or foe. A chill ran through him as he wondered if he could kill anyone when the time came.

"You ought to come with us, man. I'm dodging the draft."

Carl added, "We're headed for Canada."

"Carl isn't home," Mrs. Pythacyk, Carl's mother, told Detectives Akimoto and Donovan.

"Do you mind if we come in and check his room?" Michael Donovan asked.

"What has he done, my Carl?"

"At the moment he hasn't done anything," Detective Donovan lied. "He may have witnessed a crime."

"When was the last time you saw your son?" Ryoya asked.

"Yesterday afternoon. My Carl, he went out before dinner and came home after I went to bed."

"So, you don't know for sure that he came home at all?" Ryoya asked.

"He comes and goes. I thought he came home. Yes, I heard him," Mrs. Pythacyk stated. "But, he left again before I got up. Why are you looking for Carl?"

"May we look in his room?" Ryoya repeated Detective Donovan's request.

"Please, it is here on the left," Carl's mother led the two detectives to her son's room. "Is my Carl in trouble?"

"Not at this time," Ryoya said knowing that he was indeed a suspect in a murder.

The room was small and cluttered. A single bed lined one wall. It appeared slept in and had clothes strewn upon it. Opposite the bed was a five drawer dresser. On the top was a book, *Beginning Italian*. Next to it was a wooden jewelry box that was empty. A glass ashtray with an expensive cigar butt was on the rear next to a picture of Carl and his mother and father. Carl was likely eight-years-old. A wooden bookshelf was against the wall at the foot of the bed. Various books, magazines, and records were on the shelves. In the corner a wooden chair had an expensive Italian suit draped over it. Ryoya picked up and examined the suit. Immediately, she noticed blood stains on the right sleeve and front of the jacket. Inside was a label—Antonio's, Thirty Fifth Street, New York, NY. "Look at this," Ryoya said, "blood and the same label that was on the tie found at the crime scene.

"Carl, you have some splaining to do," Michael Donovan said with a very poor Ricki Ricardo Spanish accent.

"We need to get an evidence team in here and have Carl Pythacyk picked up."

Detective Donovan examined the empty jewelry box and concluded, "He's already in the wind." He then picked up the book, *Beginning Italian*, and added, "We better check with the airlines."

Ryoya Akimoto walked to the bedroom door and called to Mrs. Pythacyk. When the old woman arrived the detective requested a recent photograph of Carl Pythacyk. The woman stared blankly at the detectives. Finally, Ryoya asked, "You do have a recent photograph—don't you?"

The old woman stood motionless. A stricken look upon her face told a story of a long unhappy history. After taking in a labored slow breath she nodded toward the dresser and said, "We don't have any photographs of my Carl since he was a boy."

Three unique travelers and a black dog rode west on Route 80. After Clearfield they turned north on Pennsylvania 153, took Exit 111 onto Route 219 north, and entered Warren, Pennsylvania. From there they went east on Fifth Avenue out of town until they found a gravel road that wound into the woods. At the end of the road they came to a wooden gate. Next to it was an empty barrel. On the fence was a plaque which read, "Deposit your anger in the barrel and open your heart as you open this gate."

The gravel road continued up a hill and around a bend in a wooded mountainside. When they rounded to the left the landscape opened up to reveal an old 1800s vintage farm house. It was two stories tall covered in white clapboard with a stone foundation. A screened porch wrapped around the structure which gave it an inviting look. On one side there were clotheslines covered with laundry drying in the warm August sun. Many items fluttered in a breeze. A chicken ran across in front of the van as they approached.

On the right and a short distance farther an aging barn stood majestically against time and weather. Red barn planking on the walls appeared fresh and new despite their considerable age. The brown tin roof also looked to be in good repair. A young woman walked out of the barn. She wore cut-off jeans, a tie-dyed tee shirt, and cowboy boots. Upon seeing the van she smiled and trotted over to the driver's side. "Welcome to Lark's Run," she said with enthusiasm, "It's about time you came to visit us." She leaned into the vehicle and kissed Ritchie.

"Pine Tree, it's good to see you," Ritchie remarked.

"Penelope," she corrected him with a smile, "Rickety." They both laughed.

"I'm on the run."

"Avoiding the draft. Nick told me. You know that you're 1A in my book." Penelope looked over Ritchie's shoulder at the two passengers in the van.

"This is Carl and the Marine is . . . What was your name?"

"Wellington, ma'am."

"And, that's Fetch in the back," Ritchie pointed to the black Basenji that stared at the new intruder.

"Come in, we are about to start preparing dinner. I guess we are ten for dinner. There is a couple passing through—I believe it is Dennis and Tania. We have a new member, Night Bird, and of course Audra and Larry. Nick and me and you three." A low yodel from the back of the van caused her to correct herself, "You four. We are eleven for dinner."

Dinner began with Nick saying grace. "From the earth we receive nourishment. To the earth we give our care, protection, and love. Life is given for life, therefore, let us honor all creatures for their part in the great circle of nature. Through our actions may we be worthy."

Ten individuals sat in two long wooden church pews on either side of a large wooden table. On the table was a bounty—chicken, sausage, vegetables, bread, butter, honey, and relishes. Everything a product of the commune farm that welcomed all, fed all, and celebrated life.

Nick was a tall, slender man with long brown hair tied back into a ponytail. His dark brown eyes stared directly at whomever he spoke with but were not intimidating. Instead, they were welcoming and friendly and attentive. One got the impression that he truly cared about what they were saying. He had a small scare on his left cheek. Facial features were strong and somewhat weathered. Although he was a city-boy who grew up in Cincinnati he had the appearance of an outdoorsman. Without saying a word or making a gesture it was clear that he was the leader of this community. This fact was confirmed by the actions of the others. When he spoke they listened. If a question arose they turned to see his response. Yet, if he did wield power he did not overtly demonstrate the fact. His smile was subtle while also genuine. He waited while the others took food from the table. It was his habit to make sure all had food before he took any.

Ritchie spoke first, "Nick, I'm headed to Canada."

Nick responded, "The path of least resistance."

"The path to avoiding the draft."

"You're welcome to stay here, you know that?"

"I know, but I don't want to bring trouble to Lark's Run."

"No trouble."

"What if you just don't show up?" Penelope asked as she passed Ritchie a bowl of mixed vegetables.

"I'd end up in jail," Ritchie answered, "and that's another place I don't want to be."

Dennis, one of the hippie couple who were passing through seeking shelter for the night, stated, "I burned my draft card and we keep moving so they don't know where to look for me."

His partner, Tania, added, "We're gypsies experiencing the world first-hand, free and unencumbered."

"There are thousands of draft-dodgers," Dennis continued, "The military machine can't catch us all." When he took a bowl that Wellington had passed to him he realized what he said and added, "No offense meant."

"None taken," Wellington responded. "Maybe, if I was a little braver, I'd be headed for Canada."

"You're welcome to join us," Ritchie offered.

A small, blue-eyed, blond girl, known as Night Bird, spoke up, "I was at Woodstock."

"How cool was that?" exclaimed Dennis.

"Man, I was too," Ritchie said. "If it wasn't for the damn rain it would've been a gas."

Night Bird continued, "At Woodstock I met a newspaper reporter. He was older and so out-of-place, but he was really cool. He said we fight wars because there are always those who try to use force to control others. He said man is aggressive by nature."

"Man is aggressive by nature," Nick said, "however, a better word might be driven. Man is driven to achieve. If we weren't compelled to explore, experiment, build, hunt, and dream we would still be living in caves."

"So, there will always be wars?" Night Bird asked with a tone of disappointment. Nick looked at the young woman and replied, "Sadly, yes. And, crime. And, betrayal." He gave her a moment to feel dejected, then added, "And, inventions, medical advancements, art, music, great structures, space exploration, new products, advancements in every area improving our lifestyle, and longer life expectancy." Nick smiled and Night Bird returned his smile.

"What about illegal wars—like Vietnam?" Ritchie asked.

"All wars are illegal in some form or another," Nick answered. "It was illegal for Germany to attack Poland or Japan to bomb Pearl Harbor precipitating World War II. The Civil War had two sides, both of which believed they were in the right. Often, it depends on what side you are on as to which side is considered wrong."

"What about Vietnam?" Wellington asked seeking some reason for going to a far off place to die or a far north place to escape.

"Did you ever get into an argument with someone and start seeing their side? You intellectually get their point but are emotionally invested in the debate. It becomes impossible, or at the very least very difficult, to surrender your position. Vietnam is like that. The peninsula has been colonized for centuries. In the late 1800s the French colonized what was called Indochina which encompassed Vietnam, Cambodia, Laos, and other areas. All developed nations were gobbling up parts of the world in a race to create an empire. During World War II the Japanese occupied Vietnam. The United States supported a dissident named Ho Chi Minh in the fight against the Japanese. In fact, Roosevelt didn't want the French to have control over the region after the war and in 1945 President Ho Chi Minh declared independence for the Democratic Republic of Vietnam. France tried to reassert itself into Vietnam. Bitter fighting ensued until 1954, when the Viet Minh won a decisive victory against French forces at Dien Bien Phu. At that point there was a conference held in Geneva where North and South Vietnam were established and plans were made for a national election to reunify the peninsula. The United States and the South Vietnamese government refused to sign the agreement fearing that a fair election in the communist portion could not be held. At that point we became involved. That involvement grew and grew until we find ourselves mired in a conflict that we don't know how to get out of. We won't win because we don't colonize. Legal or not, with Vietnam you have to ask yourself is the goal noble enough to die for?" Nick picked up a carrot and examined it, "For my money, I'd rather grow things."

Carl remained quiet feeling out-of-place with the group of nonconformists and draft dodgers. Inside a part of him sneered at the oddballs while another part envied them.

Wellington lamented, "I don't have a choice. They pointed at me and said you go there."

Nick continued, "In every relationship one is dominant and the other submissive. It might be subtle and to small degrees but is still there all the same." He looked at the three travelers and said, "With the three of you Ritchie is the dominant one. That's because he has the keys to the van." They all laughed.

Penelope added, "Without those keys you're a doormat." More laughter.

"Here without question, Penelope rules the roost," Nick admitted.

"Right," Penelope responded sarcastically showing disbelief. "Nick is the rooster here at Lark's Run and I wouldn't have it any other way."

"Dominance is dynamic changing all the time. When I walk into the kitchen I can literally feel my power drain from my body. I do what I'm told or I don't eat. And, brother, I like to eat." He turned to Wellington and said, "You feel like you have no choice, but you have many choices. If you go to Vietnam it is because you chose to go."

Wellington pondered what Nick had said. Indeed, he could choose to escape to Canada, or refuse to go and end up in prison, or jump off a high ledge and break his leg, or become a conscientious objector, or go gay. Yes, he had choices but they weren't the ones he preferred.

Suddenly, Nick changed the subject when he asked, "Would anyone like a glass of ale?"

All at the table answered in the positive. Nick retrieved a glass pitcher from a cupboard and disappeared from the room. When he was gone, Penelope whispered, "He is real proud of his Lark's Run Ale, so make sure you all tell him how bad it is." She displayed a mischievous smile.

The proud brew-master returned with his golden ale. Carefully, he filled each glass.

Ritchie tasted the liquid and found that it was quite good. He looked at his friend and with a straight face stated, "A little on the sour side—wouldn't you say?"

"You think so?" a surprised Nick said as he examined his glass.

Then Dennis said, "Not my cup of tea. Sorry." He put his glass down on the table.

Nick looked around the table hoping to find someone who enjoyed the ale.

"I don't normally drink ale, so I can't tell if the after taste is normal or not," Tania said as she pushed her glass away.

Audra simply looked down into her lap. Night Bird offered a "nice try" smile and shrugged.

The tall host of the feast said apologetically, "I'm sorry, I thought it was quite good. My taste must be different from others."

Carl downed his glass and proclaimed, "Damn good ale. Don't let these liars throw you."

"Ah, an honest man," Nick stated as he saluted Carl with his glass and filled the glass of his new found friend. All at the table laughed and compliments poured forth along with the pouring of more ale.

Detective Michael Donovan asked, as he wandered around the alley where Miguel Juarez' body had been found, "Tell me again what we are looking for."

"A Chevy antenna," Detective Ryoya Akimoto quipped.

"Ah, so you buy my 'hit by a truck' scenario?"

"Let's say there's something about this that doesn't add up."

"Two guys fight—one wins. The winner is pissed off so he finishes the job by cutting the other guy's throat."

"What about those two lengths of rope? And, if you're going to commit a murder why leave the murder weapon? Also, why were they here? Did they know each other? Were there more than two involved in the conflict? The victim had 22 caliber cartridges in his pocket—where's the gun? Is that spider walking up your arm poisonous? There are just too many unanswered questions."

Michael Donovan looked, shook his arm, and asked, "Don't you think the crime scene folks found everything that could be found?"

"Probably, but I just have to have a look for myself. So, humor me."

"OK, but we've got the body, fingerprints on the murder weapon, blood on the suspect's clothes, and he's in the wind. It looks pretty straightforward to me."

Ryoya wandered around the alley looking at the ground, the walls, and down the flight of stairs that was surrounded by a railing. When she grabbed the railing it came loose. Upon closer examination she found where rust had been rubbed off and a strand from a rope tangled on the rough surface. As she looked at it she told her partner, "A lot more went on in this alley than we suspect."

Carl Pythacyk sat mesmerized. It was the quietest and calmest he had been in as long as he could remember. Before him sat a vision that reached inside his armor, beneath his muscular chest, past his hardened heart to the very essence of his emotional being.

Laurel Fitzpatrick sat on the floor in front of an old stone fireplace singing softly. She sang a Celtic ballad, Ē Horō. The words that she sang were foreign to him— not English—but what? Her smooth soft white hands danced upon the strings of an Ovation guitar as she sang. Behind her the motion of the flames kept time with her voice. The brightness of the fire kept him from seeing her eyes but her other features stirred him. Long dark red hair hung straight to her waist framing a perfect face with high cheek bones, small nose, and long neck. Soft melodic words filled the room making it the only place he ever wanted to be. What he didn't understand was how he could be struck so quickly or so thoroughly. Love at first sight, a myth of novels and movies, wasn't reality. And, even if such a thing were possible it couldn't happen to a useless, no account, son-of-a-bitch who never did anything of any value and was certainly destined to never amount to anything.

He moved closer as she began another song, An Fhideag Airgid, soft and slow and filled with emotion. Melodic tones of such beauty pulled Carl into an unfamiliar world of unfamiliar words but warm and inviting, all the same. Carl was alone in that room with the only creature on the face of the earth he ever cared about.

Laurel Fitzpatrick had arrived after dinner. She was a member of the commune who had been away visiting a sick friend. All present sat in the large great room listening to unfamiliar words and soft melodies that took them to quiet places in their heart.

Robert Six Trees finished memorizing an Ojibwa prayer.

Oh Great Spirit, whose voice I hear in the winds. And whose breath gives life to everyone, hear me. I come to you as one of your many children; I am weak; I am small; I need your wisdom and your strength. Let me walk in beauty, and make my eyes ever behold the red and purple sunsets. Make my hands respect the things you have made, and make my ears sharp so I may hear your voice. Make me wise, so that I may understand what you have taught my people and the lessons you have hidden in each leaf and each rock. I ask for wisdom and strength, not to be superior to my brothers, but to be able to fight my greatest enemy, myself. Make me ever ready to come before you with clean hands and a straight eye, so as life fades away as a fading sunset, my spirit may come to you without shame.

49: Sunday – August 24, 1969

Detectives Akimoto and Donovan compared notes from the night before. They had located and interviewed three prostitutes who walked Eighth Avenue and were known to be associated with Miguel Juarez.

"Let's start with Rose Fallon," Detective Akimoto said. "She was the most forthcoming and cooperative."

"Yeah, she liked the little prick—go figure."

"There's no telling what love will do," Ryoyo leafed through her notepad and added, "She gave us the names of two other girls and described a young girl with blond hair and blue eyes, but didn't know her name. Also, that she hadn't seen the young one since Miguel was killed."

"She also saw the vic walking down Forty Fourth in the direction of the alley," Michael Donovan added. "After that he didn't show to collect her money as was his practice."

"And, she identified the photo we showed of Pythacyk as the person who strong-armed Juarez for money a few weeks ago. So, they have history." Ryoya Akimoto looked at her watch. It had been a late night and being back in the office at eight in the morning wasn't ideal but necessary to move the investigation forward. She moved onto the next interview. "Doris Eskendorian didn't see the vic Friday night but also ID'ed Pythacyk as having had a run-in with Juarez a few weeks ago. She saw a gun at the time. Didn't mention a young girl."

Detective Michael Donovan started, "The last one, Claire something. . ."

"Payton."

"Yeah, that's it. Did she seem a little twitchy to you?" he asked.

"She was definitely being evasive," Ryoya stated, "I think she knows more than she admitted. A second interview is in order."

"Agreed."

As the sun rose over the Allegheny Mountains in Warren, Pennsylvania Bad Temper Barney crowed to welcome the dawn. Wellington, Carl, Ritchie, Dennis, and Tania stirred in their beds. Outside the farm was alive with activities. Nick, Penelope, Audra, Larry, Laurel, and Night Bird had already been at work for a few hours. With a farm, the day begins before dawn and often lasts past sundown. The work is hard but to those who value a return to nature and simpler life it is remarkably rewarding. End-of-day fatigue is rather pleasant as it is sans stress and anxiety. Hospitality was their main form of entertainment as they were always eager to share their bounty while neither charging a dime nor expecting their guests to work.

At Lark's Run the residents had a loose definition of responsibilities with each doing whatever task was at hand at the time. Night Bird was a good fit. She worked hard, never complained, and seemed hungry to learn more, experience more, and discover more. When she first arrived the young hippie asked if they had any marijuana. Nick took her out into the woods up to a rock overhang that looked down onto a waterfall and running spring. He pointed out at the view and simply said, "There—get high." She became a regular visitor to that spot.

In the kitchen on a coal fired stove a sausage, potato, onion, and greens mixture simmered in a pot to stay warm for the guests. Fresh milk, eggs, bacon, and orange juice were available along with homemade biscuits. The five travelers, two heading east and three west, gathered at the table and ate breakfast.

"We plan to leave this morning," Dennis stated as he buttered a biscuit.

"What's your next stop, man?" Ritchie inquired.

"Not sure, but we're heading toward Maine and the coast."

"That's cool, man."

"When are you leaving?"

"Either late today, early tomorrow, before the first snow, not really sure," Ritchie replied. "I need to get some better directions from Nick. It looks like we will go west and run along Lake Erie to Cleveland and then Toledo." He leaned back and looked at Wellington and added, "We might make a detour to Detroit to drop off our warrior friend."

"I appreciate it," Wellington said.

"Ultimately, I've been told we can make it into Canada from an Indian reservation in Minnesota."

"Good luck, my friend," Dennis said. He flashed a peace sign.

Matthew Ellis and his daughter Stephanie sat quietly at the little table in her apartment. They had finished breakfast and each was reading a different section of the Sunday *Newark Star Ledger*. After a few minutes Matt sat back and asked, "Do you remember the little church in Alpine that we used to go to?"

Stephanie looked up and answered, "The little stone church? Yes, I remember."

"For some reason it just came to mind," her father said reflectively. "It was on Old Dock Road and the minister was named Rex."

"Mom loved that church."

"She also loved Rex. He was quite a minister. You never knew what to expect on Sunday. That was part of the draw. With other churches it's the same old thing Sunday after Sunday. But with Rex . . . well you didn't want to miss his act." Matt rubbed his chin as he focused on new memories that unfolded in his mind. "After the service we would go across the street to a small community house and have coffee and donuts."

Stephanie didn't respond as she allowed her father to relive the experience.

"I remember the time mom and Rex got into a debate on why God was a man." Matt smiled, "That was something to see. It all began when Valerie commented that she believed God was neither male nor female. Rex countered with references from the Bible. Your mother then asked him, 'Who wrote the Bible? Men, correct?' Rex smiled and added that it was written that God created man in his image. Your mother answered, 'Yes, and I'm a rib, I know.' She then went on to say that God is spiritual and gender is a physical trait. I remember Rex nodding and saying 'God is a spirit, John 4:24.' Then mom pounced by saying, 'sex is for procreation. Does God have a honey on the side?' I never saw someone laugh as hard as Rex did that day." Matt smiled as he recalled the exchange. He then missed Valerie so very much that he couldn't continue.

Stephanie upon seeing her father's pain said, "Let's go to that church. There's still enough time for us to get there."

"Rex won't be there anymore."

"But, mom's spirit might be."

Carl wandered around Lark's Run in the mid-morning warmth. Everything seemed to be well-kept and neat. Chickens roamed freely, rows of various vegetables grew in fields, cows leisurely ate grass in fenced meadows, a pond fed by a mountain stream promised many fish, goats played in their pens, and birds sang in the trees. To Carl it was peaceful and calming. It made him almost forget the trouble back in New York that he was fleeing. He hoped to find Laurel Fitzpatrick as he roamed around the farm. She remained sharply in his mind after capturing his heart the night before with her songs. He deeply desired her, but knew it was impossible given his situation. Yet, he still wished to see her, talk with her, and just be near her even if for only a brief period of time.

"There's a lot more to see up this path," a voice tapped Carl on the shoulder from behind. He immediately recognized who it was and turned to face Nick.

"It's quite a farm," Carl said.

"A home, a refuge, a stopping-off point, a cathedral, an experiment, it's all of those and more."

"It must be nice," Carl noted sincerely.

"It's hard work, but honest work. There's no fame and fortune only peace and quiet." Nick walked over and picked up a fallen branch and moved it from the path. "Contrary to appearances, I am not the lord of the manor. If anything I am only a guide. We all share responsibility and do whatever is needed to keep Lark's Run operating." Nick turned in the direction of the path that led into the woods and said matter-of-factly, "You were looking for Laurel."

"Well, I, uh . . ."

"Come with me," Nick led the way up the path that he had cleared. "Every day is an adventure here."

Carl followed. After a slight rise the path turned to the left and opened into a small clearing. Before Carl was Laurel wearing shorts and a tee-shirt and sandals. Her back was to them. When he got a better look Carl saw that she was leaning over a row of wooden boxes. She was singing softly and moving gracefully. Nick grabbed Carl's shoulder and said softly, "Don't interfere." Carl stopped. Nick pointed in the direction of Laurel and said in a low voice, "bee hives." Carl turned and looked realizing that she was removing honey from the hives without any protective gear. It was then that he saw the bees dancing around Laurel, landing on her, taking off, circling, and flying into the woods. Carl looked back at Nick and without saying a word asked how she was not being stung. "She sings to them and somehow it calms the entire hive. Maybe it's the vibration. She has smoke if she needs it, but she never does."

Carl's fear of bees was fierce therefore the sight before him was terrifying. In no way did he want to go a step closer to that buzzing chaos. Laurel's song reached his ears. The dulcet tones had a calming effect. Carl was drawn to her having to hold himself back. She was an angel of the highest order. If only he wasn't the devil on the run.

Laurel turned and saw Nick and Carl. She smiled and continued to sing as she slowly moved away from the bee hives. Some yellow fuzzy insects rode upon her for a short distance and then took off to replace the nectar that they had paid for the song.

Detective Ryoya Akimoto sat in an interview room in the Midtown North precinct. Across the table sat Claire Payton the prostitute who they had spoken with the night before.

"You know more than you are telling," Ryoya stately factually without it sounding accusatory.

Claire didn't answer. She stared directly at the detective not revealing any emotion. Only one thing betrayed her—she briefly parted her lips than closed them tightly. Ryoya picked up the subtle movement. It was a sign that the woman wanted to talk but wasn't ready. Experience taught Ryoya any attempt to push the interviewee would only result in her becoming even more defensive and closed.

Ryoya adjusted her approach, "Who is the young girl that we have been unable to locate?"

Once more, Claire refused to answer.

"We simply wish to talk with her."

A hardened stare.

"She lived with you. Is that correct?"

A nod.

"Do you know where she is?"

Finally, Claire spoke, "She's safe—leave her alone!"

A breakthrough and a tell. Ryoya sat back and didn't speak. The woman knew where the child was and was being protective. It was clear that she cared about her roommate or ex-roommate. This time Claire looked nervous. Her eyes searched the room as if looking for a means of escape. More than a physical attempt it was a mental desire. Another delicate subject to be handled carefully had presented itself. Ryoya once more had to pivot. "Would you like something to drink?"

"Coffee?"

"How do you take it?"

"Black."

"Good. It's never easy getting cream or sugar around here." Ryoya smiled and left the room. She let Claire sit alone with her thoughts for a short period of time then returned with coffee. "Do you think it would be better that we not involve the child in the investigation?"

For the first time Claire showed emotion. She smiled and said in a motherly sort of way, "It would be far better for her and she knows nothing about what happened—I can assure you of that."

Ryoya continued in a friendly tone, "Is she a working girl?"

"Not by choice and not anymore."

"And she lives with you?"

"No longer." Claire sipped her coffee, put the Styrofoam cup down, leaned forward, and said, "Listen, she went home. When we found out that Miguel was dead it was her chance to escape. Let her be. Let her have her life back."

"You care about her?"

"Enough to never reveal her name or location."

"That may be all right as long as we are convinced that she had nothing to do with the murder."

"I know her whereabouts the entire night right up until we got home. She was not involved."

"I believe you," Ryoya commented, "As long as we get all we need from you we can leave the girl alone."

"Thank you."

To protect the child Ryoya knew that Claire would be more cooperative. "Let's go over this one more time," Ryoya went back to business. "You saw Miguel Juarez on the night that he was murdered."

"Yes."

"When and where did you see him?"

"I saw him on Eighth Avenue earlier in the evening. Then again on Forty Fourth Street when he stopped and talked with me in front of the New Haven Hotel."

"What did he say?"

"He said that he had a thing to do down the street and that he would see me later."

"Did he give you any idea what kind of thing he planned to do?"

"No, but he smiled. It was an evil smile."

Ryoya changed the subject, "What happened to your hair?"

Instinctively, Claire's right hand went to her wig. She attempted to cover up her reaction and said nonchalantly, "Bad haircut."

"Did Miguel give you that bad haircut?"

Claire stared into her coffee cup and said in a low almost imperceptible voice, "Yes."

"Why did he do that to you?"

"With Miguel there isn't always a reason. One day he showed up, went crazy, and this is the result."

"After Miguel told you that he had a thing to do did you see him anymore that night?"

Claire hesitated and looked to her right as she said, "No."

Ryoya knew that the woman was lying. After giving an agreed upon signal by brushing her hair out of her face, Detective Michael Donovan entered the interview room. He placed a file folder on the table as he sat down. "How's it going?"

"Claire is being helpful—if not completely honest," Ryoya commented.

Claire looked at detective Akimoto and wondered what lie she picked up on. There had been a few lies as well as omissions. She picked up her coffee cup and took a sip. The warm liquid felt good but the caffeine did nothing for her nerves.

Detective Donovan continued the interview, "Did Miguel own a gun?"

"Yes, one of those with a wheel that holds the bullets."

"Do you know if he had it with him on the night that he was killed?"

"I don't remember seeing it."

"Do you recognize this man?" Detective Donovan showed Claire a photograph of Carl Pythacyk.

"He, uh, maybe, a few weeks ago he and Miguel were together in front of the New Haven Hotel. Miguel needed money to pay this man."

"Were they friends?"

"Hell no! That guy had a death grip on Miguel. Miguel was scared."

"Did the man say anything?"

"Miguel did all the talking."

"What happened next?"

"I gave him, Miguel, what money I had and left."

"Did you see this man on the night Miguel was killed?"

"Did I see him? No."

Both detectives knew that she was lying because Claire repeated the question before answering. Michael Donovan continued, "When did you learn that Miguel Juarez had been killed?"

"Yesterday morning. I heard it on the radio."

"Didn't you wonder why he didn't make his collection the night before?"

"He sometimes misses making the pick-up. But, he always shows up the next day to collect. Or, at least, he did."

"Do you know anyone who might have wanted to hurt Miguel?"

"The list would be a mile long."

"Would you be on that list?"

"Yes," Claire said without hesitation.

"Did Miguel carry a knife?"

"I don't know."

Michael Donovan slid the photo of Carl Pythacyk closer to Claire and asked, "And, you're sure you didn't see this man on Friday night?"

"I'm sure."

"Where can we find the young girl you are protecting?" Ryoya asked which surprised Claire.

"You said we could leave her out of this," Claire protested.

"If you cooperated," Ryoya replied, "You've been lying to us."

"I haven't," Claire insisted, but her nervous actions of moving her coffee cup and looking around betrayed her.

"You saw this man on Friday night," Ryoya stated emphatically. "Why are you lying?"

"I'm not!"

"You also saw Miguel again later that night. When did you see him?"

"I didn't see him!"

"What is the girl's name?" Michael Donovan asked impatiently.

"I won't tell you. She's safe—leave her alone!" Claire shouted.

"We can place you under arrest for withholding evidence and interfering with an investigation," Detective Donovan warned.

Claire rested her cheek on her left palm and stared at the table. In a defeated resigned voice she said, "This Eighth Avenue whore just doesn't care."

Wellington Marsh wandered in the woods above Lark's Run. Everything was green and lush and filled with life. Trees protected him from the heat of the afternoon sun and a cool breeze found its way to him. Because it was eerily quiet he could hear each step that he took. In that place at that time the young Marine found himself at peace. The beauty of nature made him feel alive and he cherished the very act of being.

His eye caught movement to his right. When he peered in that direction he saw in the distance a deer. It was full grown nibbling on a bush. Wellington froze not wanting to scare it off. For a long period of time Wellington observed the deer. It chewed on leaves and berries without a care in the world. For its world was this beautiful peaceful hillside. Wellington envied the deer. It didn't have to listen to small arms fire or mortar shells echoing in the distance. Or, dodge bombs dropped from above. It heard no screams of wounded and dying. All it had to hearken to was the melodic sounds of nature. Suddenly, the deer looked up, sniffed the air, saw Wellington, and disappeared into the trees.

An image entered Wellington's mind. It was of a three room cabin with a shiny tin roof and a porch. The one Sergeant Nathan Kincaid described when he spoke of his grandfather who went from slave to landowner in one lifetime. The old man had said, "You see, in life you gotta plant the seeds that you are given and do all you can to make them grow. Some seeds will grow and some won't, but you can't spend your time cryin over the ones that don't grow cause it will make you neglect them all." For months his entire life had been focused on only one thing—Marine training. Wellington wondered, what seeds were he neglecting. It was then that he realized that he really liked Sergeant Kincaid, the mean old bastard.

A voice brought Wellington out of his reverie, "Over there would be a good place."

Wellington turned and met Nick eye-to-eye, "What?"

"That's a good place for a cabin. High enough to be away from the threat of floods, close to water, and with the removal of a minimum number of trees a great view."

"You read my mind."

"It's not that hard. All of us experience those thoughts when we get out here alone close to nature."

"It is peaceful."

"A refuge from a world gone mad."

"A world that I have to return to," Wellington lamented.

"You always have choices."

"Yeah, great choices, go to Vietnam, or go to jail, or go to Canada."

"Those and more."

"Like what?"

"You could be a conscientious objector, stay at Lark's Run and drop out of the world, enroll in college, confess to being a homosexual, renounce your citizenship, join the communist party, commit a felony and hope for probation, smash your foot with a rock, or commit suicide. Lots of choices."

"I get it.

"No, you don't get it." Nick explained. "Yogi Berra once said, 'When you come to the fork in a road—take it.'" Wellington laughed. Nick continued, "In life we constantly face challenges and have to make decisions—some that are tough. What Yogi meant was make a decision. Indecision is a killer."

Jack looked over his notes on the NASA wire scandal. Lida Petropoulos remained the key missing ingredient in unravelling the Orztech wire conundrum. She and jogging addition memories out of Matthew Ellis were his only leads. He decided that another meeting with the hapless long-term sleeper was in order. With that decision made he turned on the black and white 19" television set in his living room to watch the end of the Yankee game on WPIX.

It hadn't been a good weekend for the fifth place Yankees who were 24½ games out of first in the American League Eastern Division. They lost two games in a row to the Minnesota Twins who were in first place in the American League Western Division.

On Friday they were shutout 6 to 0 and on Saturday after three innings were behind 8 to 0 and ultimately lost 8 to 3. The games were being played in Metropolitan Stadium in Minnesota. When Jack began viewing it was in the fifth inning of a scoreless tie. A pitching duel had ensued between Yankees Al Downing (4-4) and Twins Tom Hall (6-4). In fact both pitchers were working on no-hitters, at that point. Then in the top of the sixth inning the Yankees got two hits, both singles, but failed to score. That ended Tom Hall's no-hitter. In the bottom of the sixth the Twins got a single ending Downing's no-hitter. The duel continued. Both teams went three up and three down in the seventh. In the eighth inning both teams had a single but failed to score. The ninth inning began with a nothing/nothing tie. The Yankees got a single but their at bat ended with a double play. In the bottom of the ninth Tony Oliva, the right fielder, hit a high fly ball and reached third base on an error. Jack yelled at the television. With nobody out the Yankees then intentionally walked Bob Allison and Leo Cardenas to load the bases. "What the hell are you doing?" Jack yelled. He knew they were trying to pitch to the bottom of the order but it was a huge risk. It was a risk that ended the game when the Twins catcher, George Mitterwald singled to left driving in the winning run. Jack cursed and turned off the television.

Lark's Run settled down for the evening after dinner. Dennis and Tania had left in the morning to continue their journey to Maine. Nick and Ritchie sat in the great room looking at roadmaps and discussing possible routes to the Indian reservation in Minnesota by way of Detroit, Michigan.

Wellington Marsh sat on the front porch enjoying the cool evening air. The sun had dropped behind the mountain while the sky remained a bright blue. Everything at Lark's Run seemed so peaceful it was hard for the young Marine to believe such a place actually existed. How nice it must be to wake up in the morning in this enchanted garden day after day. Penelope walked out onto the porch. She saw Wellington, walked over, and sat on a rail, "This is the best time of day."

"I think every time is the best time of day, here," Wellington said.

"It is our little piece of heaven."

"When did you come here?" Wellington asked.

"Nick and I bought this farm in 1962 after he got out of the Army."

"He was a soldier?"

"Special Forces, Green Beret," Penelope stood and walked away from Wellington a few steps, turned to face him, and continued, "Before Vietnam became a full-fledged American war, Nick was sent with other advisers to help train the South Vietnamese Army. He was a Master Sergeant specializing in hand-to-hand combat. At one point, he was part of an eight-man American Military Assistance Advisory Group (MAAG) team at a base in Bien Hoa, 20 miles north of Saigon. They were training the South Vietnamese 7th Infantry Division. It was early 1959 and in his letters he told me things were going well. Then, on July 8 of that year when six of the team were in the mess watching a movie Viet Cong terrorists attacked. Major Dale R. Buis and Sergeant Chester M. Ovnand and two Vietnamese soldiers were killed. Nick was not in the mess at the time. He was able to retrieve his weapon and helped fight off the attack. There is a scar on his cheek where a bullet grazed him. Major Buis and Sergeant Ovnand were the first Americans killed in Vietnam. They had been a close knit team and Nick took it hard. He remained in Vietnam until he got out in 62."

"No wonder he knows so much about Vietnam," Wellington concluded. As an afterthought he asked, "How come he isn't bothered by Ritchie running to Canada to avoid the draft?"

"Nick was a soldier by choice. He originally joined to defend the freedom that we enjoy in America. It isn't in him to sit in judgment of others. I don't think that he likes the fact that there are so many young men fighting in Vietnam who have been forced into service."

Carl wandered around the farm impressed by everything that he saw. Fields were filled with growing and ripening vegetables. Cows were huddled in the pasture ready to settle down for the night. Goats were in their pens, chickens their coops, and pigs wherever they spend the night. From a distant place to his left he heard the musical tones of a flute. Soft and soothing, they drew him in that direction. He followed his ears. In a short distance he came to a garden—not a vegetable garden—a garden filled with flowers, shrubs, and other plants that he had never seen before. It was carefully landscaped and beautiful to behold.

In the center of the garden was a gazebo constructed of polished hardwood. Its design was unconventional with circular rails attached to posts that were angled outward giving the impression of a bowl. The roof was made of cedar shakes. Inside the structure was a circular wooden bench that allowed occupants to sit and face in any direction.

The flute music that attracted Carl emanated from the center of the gazebo. Carl moved closer and recognized Laurel the young woman who sang the night before and captured his heart. She sat upon the circular bench with her back toward him. Initially, he didn't want to disturb her so he stood quietly a short distance from the structure and listened to the music.

Suddenly, she stopped playing and turned to face Carl. How she knew that he was there he couldn't figure out. She neither spoke nor showed any sign of recognition. The two looked at each other in silence. Laurel wore a full length white lace dress and a small silver tiara.

Finally, Carl was compelled to speak and he said the first thing that came to mind, "Why the crown? Are you a princess?"

Laurel smiled and replied, "I find a tiara empowering."

"I like your music," he added.

"I am the voice of the wind."

Carl, of course, had no idea what she meant but he did enjoy the sound of her voice. "I enjoyed your singing, last night."

"Thank you."

"Of course, I couldn't understand the words."

"It is Gaelic or Irish."

"It was beautiful as are you," Carl became embarrassed as that statement slipped out.

"It's the tiara," Laurel replied.

Carl allowed that comment to semi-save him. He nodded agreement and changed the subject, "Why don't the bees sting you?"

"They're Irish," she replied with a smile.

Carl laughed softly then asked, "Seriously, how come they leave you alone?"

"It must be the vibration from my song. Their wings vibrate which is why they buzz. Maybe my vibration is soothing," she surmised. After a pause she added, "They probably think I'm a huge bee."

"What would you do if one stung you?"

"Change the song I'm singing."

"Doesn't it scare you?"

"No. We've gotten used to each other. Sometimes when I'm working in a field a bee might fly by or circle me. When it does I start to sing and it might land on me or hover for a while and then fly off."

"You must like honey."

"Honey is the only substance with everything needed to sustain life," Laurel explained. She thought for a moment and then replied, "Yes, I like honey."

"I hate to admit it, but I'm afraid of bees."

"Stay away from the hives. Fear sometimes gives off a pheromone that could get them agitated."

"Don't worry." Carl took a step closer and made a request, "Would you play some more?"

Without replying, Laurel brought the wood flute to her lips and began to play. Inside the gazebo the sound was more pronounced as it filled Carl's ears and stirred his emotions. He leaned against one of the polished wood posts. At that moment, in that place, New York City did not exist and Carl's past dissolved into a hazy mist.

Over the Rocky Mountains the pilot of a charter Boeing 737, a medium-range twinjet narrow-body airliner, struggled to keep the aircraft on course. Something in the electrical system had shorted out which caused the starboard engine to shut down. A fully loaded 737 can remain aloft on one engine, however there are challenges. In this case, the jet had fifty-nine passengers and six crew on board.

When the engine stopped the aircraft immediately began to turn to the right due to unequal thrust. To compensate for the yaw the pilot had to keep one foot on the left rudder pedal, adjust the trim, set the ailerons in opposing positions, and increase the power in the operating engine. He was grateful for one thing; the engine had cycled down rather than stop abruptly which would, by design, cause it to rip from the wing and drop off. If that had occurred a whole new set of challenges would have had to be faced.

The pilot declared an emergency. Based on their location Colorado Springs was the closest airport but Denver had a larger airport. After a conversation with air traffic control the decision was made to proceed to Denver. The navigator developed a flight plan and calculated the time required to reach Denver Airport. When he was finished he gave the pilot a new heading and simply said, "Twenty-two minutes." He looked at his watch and noted that it was five minutes before midnight.

Robert Six Trees awoke from a dream. He was on the bank of a river. On the opposite side was a fox, his spirit guide. It stared at him and then picked up something with its teeth. In its mouth, held like a mother fox would hold its baby, was Anna.

50: Monday – August 25, 1969

Air traffic controllers, emergency crew, airport personnel, and members of the media watched as lights in the sky grew larger and larger. It was a charter Boeing 737 limping toward Denver airport on one engine. To add to the air crew's problems crosswinds gusted across the runway. With its rudder full over and ailerons in opposing positions the jet had limited ability to make adjustments. A combination of engine thrust and changes of control surfaces allowed the aircraft to make right turns. For this reason it approached from a left off-center glide path. The pilot modified the approach right as needed as they neared the runway. Unfortunately, as airspeed decreased the ability to maneuver declined with it. Closer and closer the lights came. When the jet passed the outer marker lights on the glide path it was in line with the runway. Five seconds before it reached the runway threshold a cross wind pushed the aircraft off-center. With no way to realign with the runway the pilot was forced to go around. From the ground observers heard the high pitched roar of the one engine as the aircraft clawed for altitude. Once aloft it would circle to the right and make a second attempt for a safe landing.

Carl rose at five in the morning along with the other members of Lark's Run. He knew the three travelers would be leaving that day and wanted to see Laurel once more. She was on her way to milk the cows when he caught up with her. She wore a brown peasant dress and sandals. Her hair was held in place by a scarf.

"What no tiara?" he joked.

Laurel looked at Carl and brought a finger up to her lips, "Shhh, the cows get jealous." Her smile warmed him in the chilly pre-dawn air. She then asked, "Have you ever milked a cow?"

"I've never seen a cow," he admitted.

Laurel laughed. "We have two milking cows, Hazel and Taffy. Hazel is seven years old and has a calf. We keep the calf in the stable overnight so that Hazel will produce more milk. Taffy is five." They entered the barn and Laurel placed a harness on Hazel and led her out. As she did the cow mooed loudly. "She is a very calm cow but wants her calf so she is complaining." They got to a fence and Laurel tied the lead to keep the cow from running off.

Carl walked behind the cow and Laurel warned, "She doesn't normally kick but you don't want to take a chance." Carl moved quickly out of danger. He was amazed at the size of the cow. Hazel mooed once more.

Laurel had two clean pails with her. She explained, "Hazel is a Jersey so she gives very creamy milk. She can give up to four gallons of milk. We won't take that much as she has to have enough for the calf." Laurel used a washcloth to clean the teats and udder. "She has three teats. We will empty two and leave the third for the calf." Hazel mooed impatiently. Laurel reached under and grabbed two teats and pulled shooting two short streams of milk onto the ground. "I squirt the first milk on the ground to remove any bacteria."

Carl was fascinated but also a little queasy as he watched Laurel alternate pulls on the large teats spraying white liquid into a pail. As the pail filled he could see that the milk foamed.

Laurel continued to milk Hazel as she explained, "The creamier milk is in the top of the udder." One pail was full and the other was quickly placed under the udder. Laurel continued her lesson on cow milking, "You press on the top of the udder to get the last milk out. We have to make sure to empty the udder every day to keep Hazel from getting sick." When Laurel finished she stood and went into the stable and returned with Hazel's calf. It immediately went to the udder and began nursing. She then turned to Carl and said what he dreaded to hear, "Would you like to try?"

Jack woke at six in the morning. He put on the coffee and turned on the Today Show on television. Immediately, he saw that they were covering a plane crash in Denver Colorado. He sat and watched as the announcer summarized the incident.

"A charter flight on route from Salt Lake City to Dallas, Texas declared an emergency and was diverted to Denver, Colorado. With only one engine operational, on a second attempt to land a cross wind caused the aircraft to dip one wing which contacted the ground and it cartwheeled across the runway breaking into several pieces. A fuel-fed fire engulfed the fuselage and all sixty-five aboard perished. No information is available on who was aboard the aircraft or who chartered it."

Not much was visible on the television screen as it was still dark in Denver. Jack stared at ghostly images that passed in front of flames and spotlights and wondered what Parker Adolphson, retired president of Orztech Corporation, and Matthew Ellis would be thinking when they became aware of the tragedy. Then he heard the fateful words of the announcer.

"We've been told that due to an electrical problem the aircraft's right engine shut down which was the reason for the unsuccessful emergency landing."

A cold chill raced through Jack. He then knew what they would feel.

When Carl returned to the farmhouse he found Ritchie and Wellington eating breakfast. Ritchie looked up over a biscuit and asked, "Where have you been?"

"Milking a cow."

"You're kidding me. That's so cool, man."

"Yeah, it's quite a trip."

Wellington picked up a pitcher and asked, "Want some milk?"

"I don't think so," Carl said as he sat and made his breakfast selections.

"You really dig that chick," Ritchie concluded.

"Another time, another place, under different circumstances, who knows?" Carl said somewhat sadly.

"Nick would welcome you. They can always use a good cow milker," Ritchie teased as he smiled.

"Keep it up and you'll be looking for a good dentist."

Wellington calmed the situation by saying, "Nick would welcome all of us. He told me that he created Lark's Run as a refuge from the world. Even though he fought in Vietnam he doesn't hold it against anyone who is opposed to the war. So, you are welcome to stay and work and become a part of the commune."

"It sounds really good," Ritchie said, "but I wouldn't want to bring any trouble to Nick." He leaned back and stated, "The Canada Express leaves at noon."

"I'll be there," Carl said reluctantly.

"We'll drop you in Detroit," Ritchie said to Wellington.

Wellington Marsh sat in silence. He thought about other statements made by Nick. One in particular stayed with him. Wellington desperately wanted to know what was waiting for him on the other side of the world. He had asked Nick. Nick described the rank and daunting jungle conditions that caused illness, rot, sores that wouldn't heal, the effects of poisonous plants, and the wide range of creatures that assault or threaten a man every minute of the day. He spoke of fear and stress and sleepless nights. However, it was when he told Wellington when you kill a man it changes you for life that it left an indelible impression on the young Marine. He didn't want to kill anyone. He didn't know if he could kill anyone. He didn't know if what was happening there was worth a person's life. He wanted to get back in bed and pull the covers up over his head. Finally, Wellington looked at Ritchie and said, "You don't have to go to Detroit. I'm going with you to Canada."

Detective Michael Donovan entered the office carrying two cups of coffee. It was mid-morning and both detectives had already consumed more coffee than they cared to admit. The crime scene reports were in and their prime suspect, Carl Pythacyk, was still in the wind. Donovan handed one cup to Ryoya, "Thought you could use this."

"Thanks, but I'm so wound now I'm surprised my face isn't puckered."

"What makes you think it isn't?"

"I can still talk. So, do you have any additional thoughts?"

"I think we need to find the young hooker to see if she can add anything."

"Remember that letter that we found in Rita Craig's apartment when we were investigating her murder?"

"Vaguely."

"It was written to her parents. It was in desperation. She was obviously a runaway who had been enslaved by a pimp. I think it was Miguel Juarez. That letter was heartbreaking. She wrote, 'You could never love what I've become,' and, 'My tears have run out along with my hope.'"

"Your point being?" Detective Donovan asked.

"My point is if Claire Payton rescued that child and convinced her to go home we could do irreparable harm by involving her."

"What if she knows something?"

"I don't think she does. This Claire Payton is hiding something, but I believe her when she says the young girl doesn't know anything." Ryoya picked up a supplemental report of what the evidence team found in Carl Pythacyk's bedroom. "It says here Mr. Pythacyk didn't have anything incriminating in his room aside from the blood stained suit and a shirt. The blood type matches the victim."

"And, he is probably sunning in Florence, Italy by now."

"It would be nice to interview him, however, without that we only have the ladies."

Detective Michael Donovan stated, "A canvas of the neighborhood turned up nothing. Therefore, without any other evidence our only conclusion has to be Carl

Pythacyk murdered Miguel Juarez. We've got witnesses who put him in the vicinity, his fingerprints at the scene and on the murder weapon, the victim's blood type on his clothes, history between the two, and he is on the run. Case closed."

Jack Moore called Stephanie Ellis' apartment late in the afternoon. He wanted to make an appointment to meet with Matt Ellis in the next few days. Stephanie answered. She explained that her father had been reading the afternoon *Bergen Record* and abruptly stood and left the apartment.

"He seemed to be upset when he just walked out," she explained, "He didn't say anything."

"So, I guess you don't know where he went or when he will be back."

"I don't. He might go out for a few minutes or half a day. He never tells me."

"You say he was reading the newspaper?"

"Yes. Terrible about that plane crash—isn't it."

"It is. Was your father reading about the crash?"

"I really don't know." Stephanie then surprised Jack when she said, "I read your columns on Woodstock. They were very good and a good description of what went on over that weekend."

"Thank you. It was quite an experience."

"I know I was there."

"You were? I didn't see you," they both laughed.

"I met a girl who was adopted from Korea," Stephanie went on. "She seemed so happy and well adjusted. Her sister and she were so cute together. It made me think of all the other children out there who deserve a better life. That is what I've decided I want to get involved with."

"A Holt baby," Jack said softly.

"A what?" Stephanie asked somewhat confused.

"A Holt baby. I was recently told a story about a couple, somebody Holt, in Oregon that started an adoption agency in Korea. A friend of mine wants to do the same thing in Texas. I should introduce you two to each other."

"Are you serious? That would be wonderful!"

"I'll make a note to try to contact him," Jack stated. "In the meantime I still want to talk with your father. Would you ask him to call me? He has my card."

"As soon as he gets home, I'll tell him."

After hanging up, Jack thought about Stephanie. She seemed to be a sweet and caring individual. If what her father was suspected of doing turned out to be true it would break her heart. Jack didn't like the fact that he would most likely be the one to deliver the blow.

Robert Six Trees looked at his sister, Anna, who was picking flowers. He wondered why his spirit guide, the fox, was watching over her.

51: Tuesday – August 26, 1969

Matthew Ellis literally spent the last evening wandering aimlessly. After reading about the plane crash due to apparent electrical problems his mind raced searching for answers where there were none. He walked and walked driven by nervous energy. As he did he tried to find a way to unlock lost memories, but failed. At one point he seriously considered banging his head into a wall to jog loose missing recollections. Exhausted and dejected he returned to the apartment late at night. Stephanie was asleep on the couch when he entered. He moved quietly to the bedroom trying not to disturb her. It was an unnecessary effort as she was not actually asleep. She turned on the light and was relieved that her father was safely home.

"I'm sorry. Did I wake you?" Matt said softly.

"No, I was awake waiting for you. Where did you go?"

"I just walked."

"You shouldn't stay out so late after dark. Something could happen to you."

"I'm fine. Nothing is going to happen."

Stephanie changed the subject, "That reporter, Jack Moore, called. He asked for you to call him."

"What does he want?"

"He didn't say." She added, "You know he wrote those great stories about Woodstock. I think he's a nice guy, trying to help."

After a night of restless sleep, Matt sat by the telephone and tried to decide whether or not to call the reporter. He had nothing new to add. Yet, Matt wondered if the reporter had any news. Could he have located Lida Petropoulos? If he had, that would be a major breakthrough. It could fill in a lot of blanks in his memory and shed light on the wire scandal. Slowly, Matt dialed the telephone.

"Jack Moore."

"Mr. Moore, this is Matthew Ellis."

"Matt, thank you for calling," Jack said in a welcoming tone. "I'd like to get together with you to compare notes and see if we can recover any additional memories."

"Have you found Lida Petropoulos?"

"No. As a matter-of-fact I haven't found any trace of her or her company— LPAmerica. Not even tax records. It appears to be one of two things," Jack paused for effect, "LPAmerica was either a strawman or a concoction made up by you and/or Parker Adolphson to cover yourselves."

"She wasn't made up and neither was her company!" Matt protested.

"Matt, I'm just giving you the possibilities given the few facts that we have," Jack explained. "I don't know what the truth is."

"The truth is that there is a woman out there—someplace—that can shed light on this whole subject."

"Frankly, I don't know where else to look," Jack said, "except in your mind."

"If only it was that easy," Matt lamented. "I've tried everything that I know to dig up past history but to no avail."

"Can we meet and try some more?"

"It may be for naught."

"Well, it's worth a try."

"I'm willing to try anything. Having blank spaces in your mind and your life is disturbing and frustrating. It's like an itch you can't locate."

"How about this afternoon?"

"Tell me again why we didn't leave yesterday at noon," Wellington Marsh asked Ritchie as they walked along a path in the woods.

"I wanted to give Carl a little more time with his honey, no pun intended," Ritchie replied with a broad smile.

"Seriously?"

"No, man, I just wanted another day or two here," he stopped and turned to look at Wellington, "You know we can't come back."

Wellington looked out over the valley on their right and said introspectively, "I know. There are lots of things that we can't come back to."

"Man, here we are, two strangers, from different parts of the good old USA, who are both in the crosshairs of the man because of a military conflict on the other side of the world—a conflict that we don't even support. It's fucked-up, man!"

"Home of the free," Wellington muttered as he picked up a rock and examined it.

"Free to report as ordered. Free to be cashiered into the Army. Free to go to a faraway land. Free to kill people we don't even know."

Wellington threw the rock into the valley, "I wanted to be a chef. Cook good food, nourish people. Now, I'm trained to extinguish people."

"I'm an artist. I'd rather draw people than draw-down on them."

"You know the truth?" Wellington Marsh said, "I'm not sure that when the time came that I could take a life. Given that fact and all my other options, Canada seems the most logical answer."

"Maybe you can be a chef in Canada," Ritchie said, then added, "Do you have a good recipe for moose?"

Wellington laughed, "Moose under puck served with French wine."

"Ha, you'll do fine in Canada."

"Yeah, but it's gonna kill my father. He's going to be disappointed in me."

"At least you'll be alive for him to be disappointed in."

"It still hurts."

"My father gave up on me a long time ago," Ritchie said. After a few moments thought he said, "Or, I gave up on him."

Wellington walked over and sat on a fallen tree trunk. He looked out over the landscape and pictured his father. He said to no one in particular, "My old man is tough as nails. He worked in an automobile factory before it was common to see a black face. He started at the bottom, worked his ass off, and became a foreman. And, he raised me to be responsible and face things straight on. Me running away won't go down easy for my father."

"The opposite is true for mine. He would expect me to run away. So, I'm just living up to his expectations," Ritchie quipped. After a pause he continued, "My father is publisher of a whole bunch of vertical magazines."

"Vertical magazines?"

"They are magazines that appeal to a small audience like birdwatching or woodcarving. Horizontal magazines appeal to a wide audience," Ritchie explained. "He wanted me to get interested in the business and join him."

"Why didn't you?"

"I don't have the killer instinct he does."

"How so?"

"Let me give you an example. He found out that the writers were thinking about joining a union to get better pay and benefits. So, for six months he secretly had freelancers write articles that he kept in a file. When his in-house writers joined a union and the negotiators threatened to stage a strike my father told them anyone who didn't report to work without a valid excuse was fired. A strike was called and my father retrieved the stories he had stockpiled out of the file and the magazines went to press on time without interruption. When the union convinced the printers to not cross the picket line for the next edition my father had the magazines printed out-of-state at another provider he was holding in reserve. After four months the strike collapsed and the writers begged for their jobs back. My father hired about sixty percent back at reduced salaries. The printer also was allowed back at a lower cost. I remember my father saying, 'We need a strike from time to time—it's good for the bottom line.'"

Carl came up the path and asked, "What are you guys doing?"

"Talking about our fathers," Wellington answered.

"Well, leave me out. Mine disowned me years ago," Carl stated without any emotion.

"What'd you do?" Ritchie asked.

"When I was in grade school I destroyed a book of his."

"He disowned you for that?" Wellington said surprised.

"It was from the old country—I wasn't," he shrugged.

"I'm sorry to hear that," Ritchie said sincerely.

"I got over it a long time ago," Carl lied, "besides I paid that debt."

"Why are you going to Canada?" Ritchie asked Carl unexpectedly.

"None of your damn business."

"Yeah, I guess it isn't," Ritchie agreed. He changed the subject, "What are you going to do when we get to Canada?"

Carl responded, "I haven't thought that far ahead."

"I guess I'll look for a job," Wellington said, then asked, "You?"

"First thing I'm going to do is find the Maryjane supply." Ritchie walked over to a tree and patted it with his hand, "Maybe I'll be a lumberjack."

Carl and Wellington both laughed. Then Carl joked, "You probably can't even lift an axe."

"What's in Canada?" Wellington asked. "I mean where we plan to enter."

Ritchie turned and faced his two friends and answered, "Northeast of where we will enter are two small towns, Port Arthur and Fort William. They are on the shore of Thunder Bay on Lake Superior."

"What's there?" Carl asked.

"Well, from what I've been told it is a real artsy community with a lot of festivals and events. I guess it's like a resort." Ritchie walked back over to his friends, "There's this rock formation made out of high cliffs called The Sleeping Giant because that's what it looks like. I don't know if I got the name right but the Indians call it Nanabijou. Legend has it that it is a giant that was turned to stone for revealing the location of a silver mine."

"Maybe we can find the silver mine," Carl quipped.

"If it's a resort then there might be jobs available," Wellington said sticking to the subject.

"You could open a restaurant," Ritchie offered

Carl turned to Wellington and asked, "You cook?"

"Not really, but I wanted to learn. I can do the basics—that's about it."

"He's got a moose recipe that's out of this world," Ritchie said.

"Moose?"

"Why don't we wrap this up, give it to the district attorney, and leave it with suspect at large," Detective Michael Donovan stated as he threw a folder on his desk.

"You're probably right. Everything points toward Mr. Pythacyk. When he is located and arrested we'll have a chance to interview him."

"Unless Italy won't extradite him," Donovan remarked, "You know with the mafia and all, he could be a hero."

"This definitely was not a mob hit—too sloppy."

The telephone rang and Ryoya picked it up, "Detective Akimoto."

"Happy August 26," Jack Moore replied.

"And, to you. Why happy August 26th?"

"You're a detective and you don't know."

"Sadly no," Ryoya smiled knowing Jack had some obscure fact to drop on her.

"Allow me to enlighten you," Jack said, "On this day in 1883 Mount Krakatoa exploded blasting ash 50 miles into the air and creating tidal waves over 100 feet high. But that, my dear, was not as big a tidal wave as in 1920 when the 19th Amendment to the Constitution was ratified granting women the right to vote. You lucky doll."

"Long past due, if you ask me," Ryoya deadpanned.

Jack continued, "On this day in 1939 the first baseball game was broadcast on television. It was a double header between the Cincinnati Reds and Brooklyn Dodgers at Ebbets Field."

"Who won?"

"Uh, I don't know."

"Typical reporter—incomplete information."

"Ouch!" Jack remained undaunted, "In 1957 two events took place; introduction of the Edsel and the USSR successfully tested an intercontinental ballistic missile."

"You're not very busy—are you?"

"Actually, I am, but I wanted to make sure you started your week with information that might come in handy."

"I see. If only I knew who won the game between the Reds and the Dodgers. You always do that Jack, leave me wanting for more." Ryoya hung up the telephone and smiled.

"Nice," Ryoya's partner commented, "Now, he'll spend all day trying to figure out what that meant exactly."

"He's just going to have to figure out if he's an Edsel or an intercontinental ballistic missile."

"What the hell are you talking about?"

"You have no idea what happened on this day in history, do you?"

"You're right."

"Peasant!" Ryoya picked up the Miguel Juarez file and opened it. She then said out loud, "Those two had history." She read the file and added, "He said that he had a thing to do down the street and that he would see me later." Ryoya looked up, "That's what Claire Payton said about Juarez. In addition, she said he had an evil smile. I'm also convinced that she saw Pythacyk that night."

"So, why would she protect him?"

"I don't know that she is, but the pieces still don't fit together."

"If she saw Pythacyk and Juarez ends up dead, she's smart enough to put two and two together. But, why deny it?" Michael Donovan asked.

"Unless there is also history between Claire Payton and Carl Pythacyk."

"Another interview?"

"Unless we can locate Carl Pythacyk and ask him."

Jack arrived in Dumont, New Jersey in mid-afternoon. He and Matthew Ellis had agreed to meet at the Ellis' apartment. It was a strange situation, to say the least. Jack believed that Matthew Ellis was telling the truth within the realm of what he could recall. The man never denied that there was a distinct possibility that he was directly involved in the scandal. However, he really didn't know.

"I want to know the truth," Matt stated sincerely, "You must believe that. But, I fear the truth. If it turns out that this Lida Petropoulos and I perpetrated this fraud and it cost peoples' lives I'm not sure that I can live with myself."

Jack observed the soft-spoken tortured soul in front of him. Was this the same man who had an automobile accident six years ago? He didn't seem the type that would commit such a crime. Or, had six years in a coma changed his personality? It did one thing for sure—it erased important portions of his memory. And, if it did turn out that before him sat a monster what should be done? The reporter in him pushed Jack to seek the truth even if it was truth that Matthew Ellis feared. Jack had his own fears. How much of that suspect wire was out there performing critical tasks that could fail at any time. Finally, Jack said, "I've talked with a number of doctors about memory loss. Most believe, if it was caused by trauma, that it may never be recovered. A few suggested hypnosis. One doctor in particular intrigued me. He said often memory is hidden in the mind until some trigger brings it to the surface. For example, you might try to remember the telephone number in the home where you grew up. As hard as you try it just won't come to you. Then, weeks, months, or years later you see or hear the number 59 and out of nowhere you remember your childhood home telephone number as Cyprus 8-5912. His theory is that memories have a wide range of links attached to them. When something, whether it's an aroma, word, sound, taste, sight, or something else activates a link it brings that memory and millions of others connected to that stimulus closer to the surface where it is easier to recall. Sometimes a stimulus brings forth only a single memory."

"Right now, my memories about Lida Petropoulos seem to reside in my sleep. I have no idea what triggers them."

"What was the last dream that you had about her?"

Matt thought and remembered it pertained to a secret Hong Kong bank account. That was something he wasn't going to share. Instead, he lied, "I dreamed about meeting her in New York, but I can't identify where."

"What happened? What did you talk about?"

"She was flirtatious. That's all there was."

"Did she wear a certain perfume? Or, any unique jewelry?"

"I don't really know."

"What about her voice? Was there anything distinctive about her voice?"

"It changed."

"How did it change?"

"There were times when she was sweet and soft-spoken, almost like a little girl. Then there were times when she was abrupt and harsh or very businesslike. And, then there was . . ." Matt paused.

"There was what?" Jack pressed.

"One time," Matt seemed to be searching through his mind. He spoke slowly, "Her father. She once mentioned her father. Yes, and when she did there was sadness in her voice." Matt became silent.

Jack waited before speaking allowing Matt to gather his thoughts. Eventually he asked, "What did she say about her father?"

"I don't remember. I just remember the crestfallen sound of her voice. There was something terrible that happened, but what I don't know. I'm not even sure that she told me. Yet, that was the time when she seemed the most vulnerable. Aside from that she always seemed in control."

"Where were you when this happened?"

"We were alone in a hotel room," Matt suddenly stood up from the couch as a new memory flashed before him. He and Lida were in Central Park. They had met there to discuss the final NASA proposal. It was going to be a close bid worth millions with Orztech the underdog. To be competitive they had to do something dramatic. It was a warm summer day perfect for sitting in the grass in the meadows. Matt remembered that he was pessimistic about the outcome. Even though they had passed the product evaluation phase the last step was the greatest hurdle. Three finalists had been asked to present final proposals with costs and timing. On both counts Orztech could not easily compete. Matt recalled his surprise when Lida told him to reduce the cost twenty percent and move delivery date up three months.

"How can we do that?" Matt had asked Lida.

"I'll take it out of your share," Lida joked.

"Seriously, we can't make promises that we can't fulfill."

"I'll twist some arms," Lida said confidently, "break a few legs, if necessary."

Matt knew that those adjustments gave Orztech an edge—a profitable and prestigious edge. As he thought about her suggestion he remembered that he found a four-leaf clover and picked it. He gave it to Lida when he agreed to her proposal and said, "Here, for luck."

"We don't need luck," she responded as she took the clover.

She held the four-leaf clover between her fingers and studied the small green leaves. After a few moments, she looked up and said, "Thank-you, it's not every day someone gives one luck. I'll keep it with me and wish my luck to be shared with you on your journey." Laurel slipped the four-leaf clover that Carl had given her into her apron pocket.

Carl knew luck was something he needed in the worst way. If he got stopped at the border he would surely be sent back to New York to stand trial for murder. A part of him felt angry. Of all the dumb luck, to meet an angel like Laurel at a time when it was impossible for them to have any type of meaningful relationship. Once again, fate was toying with him and he heard the distinct sound of a lever flushing a toilet.

"You know you can stay at Lark's Run," Laurel said softly as she picked up baskets filled with vegetables that she had just picked.

Carl immediately took the baskets and carried them for her.

"What were you thinking?" Jack's question brought Matt back to reality.

"Lida and I discussed the NASA bid while in Central Park," Matt shook his head. He looked at Jack Moore and stated, "I let her control the manufacture of the wire. That shouldn't have happened. It was an Orztech product. I was responsible. Whether it was desperation or laziness or fear, I don't know. However, I abdicated my power."

"To an apparition."

"No!" Matt protested, "She is a real, flesh and blood, human being who is somewhere on this planet."

"Well, until we confirm that, the only real, flesh and blood persons connected to this scandal are you and Parker Adolphson." Jack made a note to revisit the retired president of Orztech Corporation, Mr. Parker Adolphson.

Carl spent the day following Laurel around helping her with her chores. She didn't seem to mind as they chatted about everything and nothing. Of course, Carl didn't reveal much about his past or his present situation. Laurel also remained a mystery. She was neither evasive nor forthcoming about her past. The few times that Carl asked a question about her childhood her answers were simple and direct but vague. He did determine that she came from a wealthy family, had a wonderful childhood, was not running away from anything, and seemed to possess a spiritual sense that only she could understand.

Another fact was clear to Carl; Laurel was completely suited to life at Lark's Run and content with her lifestyle. She went about her chores with effortless abandon. Sometimes she would hum or sing a soft song. Completely at ease with her surroundings, Carl watched in amazement and wondered how that must feel. Everywhere she went she had a calming effect. This included Carl.

Ritchie had announced that they would leave in the morning. As a result, Carl wanted to have as much time as possible with Laurel. To do so he helped prepare dinner and do the dishes afterward.

Later, after dark, Carl and Laurel walked out to the garden where he had watched her play the flute. A bright, almost full, moon lit the way. Laurel caught a lightning bug on her arm and showed it to Carl. "It's a male."

"How can you tell?" Carl asked in disbelief.

"The male flies around while the female waits in a tree or shrub. If she likes him she signals with a flash."

"Sounds like human beings. Does the male pick up the check too?"

Laurel laughed and replied, "He does if he knows what's good for him." She walked into the gazebo and sat on the circular bench in the middle, "Or, he helps with the dishes."

This time Carl laughed, "In truth, I just wanted to be with you."

"I know."

"We are leaving tomorrow," Carl looked down at the ground that was covered with crushed gravel. There was a great deal he wanted to say to Laurel, but didn't know how. He thought of inviting her to go to Canada, but knew it would be the wrong thing to do. His angel was here in heaven. Lark's Run was where she was happy. In no way would he wish to deprive her of such satisfaction. A part of him wanted to stay although he knew that couldn't be. Finally, he was compelled to make a statement before leaving Laurel forever. "I've never known anyone like you. You are beautiful, but the word beautiful isn't enough. I would have to invent a new word to describe what I see when I look at you. I mean, wow! But, there's more, so much more. Everything that you do, your voice, music, taming bees, milking cows, it all adds up to make you the most remarkable lady that I have ever known. You are the best thing that has ever happened to me if even for just a few days. I'm going to remember you and miss you for the rest of my life." Carl paused.

Laurel looked at him with deep green eyes. She didn't speak wanting to allow Carl to fully express himself.

"Laurel, I have to leave Lark's Run. If I could stay, I would. But, that doesn't mean you'd want anything to do with a mutt like me. And, I wouldn't blame you. Someone as good and pure and innocent as you should have a knight in shining armor and that's something that I'll never be." Carl paced around the gazebo searching for words or searching for courage.

Laurel waited.

Finally, Carl stopped, turned, and walked over to Laurel. He sat next to her and said, "Right here, right now, no matter what tomorrow brings, I want you to know that you are the first and only woman that I have ever told I think I love you. You don't have to say anything. After tomorrow I'll be gone and you won't have to deal with me. But, for whatever silly reason, I just want you to know how I feel—that's all."

In the darkened shadows of the gazebo two people sat in silence. Crickets conversed in the woods and an occasional owl made its presence known. A breeze delivered an enchanting scent from surrounding flowers in the garden. In the distance a dog barked. Carl recognized it as Fetch. At that point, Carl began to stand to leave. As he did Laurel put her hand on his arm and brought him back beside her. In the shadows he looked at her. She raised her chin, pursed her lips, and welcomed Carl's kiss. They embraced and tomorrow was held at bay as two lovers found words were no longer necessary.

Anna Six Trees was excited as she handled the Kodak Instamatic camera her mother said they could take with them when they went to visit where she grew up.

52: Wednesday – August 27, 1969

Detectives Ryoya Akimoto and Michael Donovan stood outside Claire Payton's apartment door. It was nine in the morning. With Carl Pythacyk's whereabouts still unknown an additional interview of the Eighth Avenue hooker was deemed necessary. Detective Donovan knocked on the door. There was no response. He knocked once more with greater force. After a few minutes with still no response he pounded on the door with his fist and announced, "Police, open up."

They heard movement inside the apartment. After a moment locks on the door were flipped and the door opened with the security chain still in place. Claire Payton looked out and recognized the detectives. She shut the door, unhooked the chain, and opened the door. "Detectives? What can I do for you?"

Immediately, both detectives became aware of the fact that Claire Payton had a black eye, swollen lip, and abrasions on her face, neck, and arms.

"We would like to ask you a few more questions," Ryoya Akimoto said, "Can we come in?"

"Uh, well, I guess," Claire said with a weak and hoarse voice. She walked with an obvious limp to the couch in the living area of her apartment. The act of sitting was executed with considerable pain.

"What happened?" Ryoya asked with concern as she examined Claire's eye.

"One of Miguel's lieutenants has taken over. He wanted to know where the young girl who lived with me was. I wouldn't tell him."

"If you give us his name, we'll arrest the son-of-a-bitch for assault," Michael Donovan stated.

Claire shook her head, "That wouldn't do any good. He'd be out in a few hours and I'd be even worse off."

"You know, he will continue to try to force you to reveal the girl's location?" Ryoya said.

"I'll never give it up, not to him or you or anyone."

"We need to get you to a hospital."

"No, I'll be alright."

Ryoya moved a strand of tangled hair out of Claire's face and reassured her, "We don't need to speak to the girl and won't ask you where she is as long as you are sure that she had nothing to do with the murder of Miguel Juarez."

Claire looked directly at Ryoya and stated without hesitation, "She had no idea that he was dead until I told her Saturday morning."

"Then, we will leave it at that," Detective Akimoto said. She then surprised Claire with the next question, "Why didn't you tell us that you saw Carl Pythacyk on West Forty Fourth Street on the night of the murder?"

"What?" Claire looked around the room, hesitated, and then responded, "I didn't see him. Why do you think that I did?"

"Because he was there and Miguel was going to meet him."

"If he was I had no idea that was his plan."

"Do you know Carl Pythacyk?"

"No."

"But, you recognized his picture when we showed it to you."

"I recognized the man who strong-armed Miguel a few weeks ago. That's all."

"So, after Miguel Juarez left you in front of the New Haven hotel and walked west on Forty Fourth Street you neither saw him nor Carl Pythacyk at any other time that night, correct?"

"Yes."

"Claire Payton you are under arrest for withholding evidence," Ryoya stated authoritatively. "Please, get dressed and come with us."

A surprised look on her face, Claire stood slowly and went into the bedroom.

Michael Donovan looked at his partner and turned palms up in a silent question of why.

Ryoya whispered, "At least we can get her to a hospital while she's in custody."

Detective Donovan nodded and smiled.

Matthew Ellis leafed through papers he had found in a box in the closet. His hope was that he would find one physical piece of evidence that Lida Petropoulos actually existed. With the records from Orztech Corporation gone this was one last desperate hope. He was convinced that it was impossible to have an ongoing affair with a specter in dreams. That coupled with many recollections while awake could not be manufactured out of thin air. He found medical bills, legal documents, and personal letters. One letter stood out. It was a letter from an unfamiliar person to Valerie.

> Dear Mrs. Ellis,
> I'm writing to thank you. You didn't know at the time that I was desperate. I tried to keep that old car running way past its limit. When money is an issue you have to make do. No one else would stop to help, but you did.
>
> The fact that you went out of your way to take me to my destination was far more than I expected. When you asked if I had a ride home I had no idea that you would offer to wait and then take me. I've never experienced such kindness.
>
> As I told you I was going to a job interview. Because of you, I got the job. I didn't know at the time but was called the next day. I'm a single mother and this job will make a big difference in our lives.
>
> I guess you get to know someone when you spend time with them in a car. With your husband in the hospital and all that you have to face I really can't imagine why you gave me so much of your time. I guess there really are good people in the world and I was lucky enough to find one.
>
> I will always remember you.
> Thank you,
> June Udell

Matt put down the letter and thought it was typical of Valerie. She selflessly helped others without giving it a second thought. Because of her somewhat formal demeanor people sometimes felt she was aloof while the opposite was true. Valerie Ellis quietly reached out and made a difference in other's lives without any recognition or reward. A vision of Lida Petropoulos floated into his mind. She was the polar opposite of Valerie. Lida was outgoing while Valerie was reserved. Lida could be tough which was different from how Valerie was strong. Valerie was generous and giving while Lida was driven by money and quite self-centered. He could trust Valerie completely unfortunately she was unaware that the same could not be said for her husband. Shame and regret descended upon him and he wondered what kind of man would make such terrible choices.

Carl didn't want to leave Lark's Run. He wrestled with the decision but knew there wasn't any alternative. Up at five, he rose early to help Laurel with her chores. Those few hours seemed to pass at lightning speed—far too quickly for a fellow lost in a world he never knew existed. Love was a new experience for Carl. It brought to the surface strange new feelings, painted wondrous pictures of what could be, ignited intense desires, and presented reflections of a life squandered. The light of reality burned in his heart. What he wanted he couldn't have. For what he had done he would be punished one way or another. The ultimate pain of letting Laurel go was a price that had been ordained by fate.

"You gave me luck," Laurel said as she held the four leaf clover between her fingers. "I give you hope," she said as she handed him her tiara. "Someday, when you place it on my head you will find your peace."

Carl held the sparkling adornment in his hand and pictured Laurel on that night in the gazebo playing her flute while wearing the tiara. She had said, "I find a tiara empowering." If only there was a power on earth that could change destiny. He looked at Laurel and said without embarrassment, "If I live to be a hundred, these few days will remain the highpoint of my life. I love you, Laurel Fitzpatrick." He kissed Laurel and slowly walked over to the waiting Ford Econoline van.

"You can stay, you know," Ritchie said.

"Shut up and drive," was Carl's response.

Detectives Akimoto and Donovan arrived at Antonio's Custom Suits on Thirty Fifth Street. Inside they found Antonio working on a suit. He was not happy with their visit and noticeably nervous. After looking at a picture of Carl Pythacyk he stammered, "I'a make'a suits for him—that's all."

"When did you make suits for him?" Michael Donovan asked.

"I see," Antonio walked over to an old wooden desk and opened a box that contained copies of invoices. After a few minutes he said, "I deliver two suits on July, uh seventeen'a."

"May I see the invoice?" Ryoya asked.

Antonio hesitated, then reluctantly handed the paper to Ryoya. She examined the invoice. After a moment she said, "It shows two $900 suits delivered at $200 each and a notation R. Esposito. That wouldn't be Ray Esposito, would it?"

"I don't know what you ask."

"Why the big discount and the note R. Esposito?"

"It was'a a mistake." Antonio thought quickly and added, "It should have said Gino Valentino. They were'a Gino Valentino suits on sale—that'sa all." He looked at both detectives hoping for a nod or other sign that they accepted his explanation.

"It says here that you included two shirts with matching ties at no charge," Ryoya responded.

"Uh, that's'a part of the sale," the sweating tailor explained. "It was'a a big'a special."

"I see."

Ryoya left Antonio's Custom Suits and walked toward their car. As they did Michael Donovan said, "Mother, our boy has been up to no good."

"I think a visit to the organized crime unit is in order," Ryoya replied.

In less than twenty minutes they arrived at the downtown central command of the NYPD Organized Crime Unit. The two detectives sat in the ninth floor window office of Captain Emanuel Lewiston. The greying, slightly overweight, middle-aged police Captain was friendly and unassuming. He leaned way back in his chair behind a large maple desk and examined a photo, as well as listened to the findings of Detectives Akimoto and Donovan. When they finished he smiled and said, "On 16 August we tracked Ray Esposito to an Italian bakery on Mott Street. The reason we were on him was an anonymous tip that he was planning something. Uncharacteristically, he went in alone. Our best guess is that he was meeting someone to make arrangements. For that reason we photographed everyone who came out of the bakery after Esposito. You're in luck, I recognize that punk as one of the individuals who came out." Captain Lewiston picked up his telephone and requested a surveillance folder from that date. In a few moments a young policewoman delivered the folder. From the folder the senior law enforcement officer retrieved a photograph of Carl Pythacyk leaving the bakery. "We didn't know his name and had no reason to think he was anything more than a customer." He patted the photo and said, "It's safe to say, we now think differently and have a name. What is your interest in him?"

"He's a suspect in a murder," Michael Donovan stated.

"Oh? Do you think Ray Esposito put him up to it?"

"No, this was a cheap pimp with whom Pythacyk had history."

"Well, it's still no coincidence that he and Esposito were in the bakery together."

"Do you have any idea what Ray Esposito was planning?" Ryoya asked.

"No." Captain Lewiston stood and offered his hand, "Hell, what do we know stuck here in the basement."

Ryoya smiled, looked around, and replied, "Nice basement."

Ritchie, Carl, and Wellington left Warren, PA and rode in silence—each man lost in his own thoughts. Wellington wrestled with his decision to desert. There he said it to himself. All those who placed their trust in him would soon know the truth. He was a coward running away. But, his mind interrupted, was it fear of dying or refusal to kill that led to his decision? Either way it was hard to swallow. At that time, rocking precariously in a lawn chair behind the driver's seat, Wellington didn't much like himself. More accurately, he didn't really know himself.

Carl thought about Miguel Juarez and hate burned in his mind. That little shit! If Miguel hadn't tried to cheat Carl or kill him or torture him he would be alive and Carl wouldn't be on the run. But then, if Carl wasn't on the run he wouldn't have met Laurel. What irony, to discover love as a result of an act of hate. Damn! If he hadn't killed Miguel he could surrender, do a few years, and return to Laurel. Carl felt weary. He was tired of life throwing him curves.

Ritchie looked forward to getting to Canada. It was an adventure. He had to let fate take him where it would. After all, art is where you find it. Maryjane is also where you find it. Looking back was not a habit Ritchie wanted to develop. He also believed that over time he would convince Stephanie to join him in Canada.

"We'll get to South Bend mid-evening," Ritchie offered. "We have to go to Notre Dame University and find Sorin Hall. It's a four story building with a large attic. I got the name of a guy who will sneak us in for the night.

Fetch slept in the back of the van.

Wanda Six Trees told Robert and Anna that they would leave Friday for a long weekend visit to where she grew up.

53: Thursday – August 28, 1969

"Can you see?" Carl asked.

"I can see the windshield," was Ritchie's reply.

"That's comforting," Wellington said from his perch on a lawn chair behind the driver's seat.

Rain had come quickly and in such intensity that I-90 literally disappeared. For all intents and purposes they were driving into a waterfall. Ritchie reached up over the sun visor and retrieved a pair of sunglasses. When he put them on Carl exclaimed, "What the hell are you doing? There's no sun out there!"

"I read in one of my father's magazines that sun glasses help you see in heavy rain," Ritchie said. He continued driving and concluded, "Damn, they do."

"They do?" Wellington remarked from behind Ritchie.

"How much can you see?" Carl asked.

"Oh, about two car lengths, but that's better than seeing nothing."

"Hope this doesn't keep up all day," Wellington commented.

"Me too," Ritchie said as he kept his eyes squarely on the small portion of road that he could see. "We should reach Chicago in about two hours. After that it will take the rest of the day to get to Duluth, Minnesota. And, tomorrow we cross into Canada—ay," Ritchie faked a Canadian accent.

"Or, we get stopped at the border," Carl warned.

"You know, this rain reminds me of Woodstock, man," Ritchie offered, "Rained all freaking weekend. Mud everywhere. You just remained soaking wet all the time. Yet, we were all in good spirits. It was really strange."

"You're really strange," Carl quipped.

"Thank you. I work at it. It's a badge of honor."

A tractor trailer passed the van in the left lane throwing back a tsunami.

Detectives Akimoto and Donovan entered the hospital prison ward. Claire Payton appeared to be asleep as they approached her bed. Upon their arrival she opened her eyes.

"How are you feeling, today?" Ryoya Akimoto asked.

"They say I have a broken rib."

"Tell us who did it and we'll put him away," Detective Donovan said with a hint of anger.

Claire didn't respond, simply looked at him with a sad expression that reflected someone who was resigned to their situation knowing there was no solution or escape.

Ryoya adjusted Claire's pillow. She then stated, matter-of-factly, "We found a connection between Carl Pythacyk and Ray Esposito a capo in the Don Carmine Spacini family." Claire lay on the bed showing no reaction. Ryoya asked, "Do you know if Miguel ever had any dealings with Ray Esposito or Don Spacini?" Claire slowly shook her head in the negative. "Would there be any reason why either of these two men would want Miguel dead?" Claire shrugged. "Listen, we know that Carl Pythacyk murdered Miguel Juarez. What we are looking for is motive. Is there anything that you can do to help." Claire again slowly shook her head.

Matthew Ellis sat in his room. The afternoon sun filtered in through the window and lit a square on the floor. He was lost in thought. What if there wasn't any problem with the wire? Maybe, it was all a hoax. Could he be racked with guilt for something of which he was innocent? He didn't have a single strand of the questionable conductor, so how did he know that it actually exists? Lida Petropoulos was a phantom. She could neither confirm nor deny the accusations. Maybe, the wire was something conjured up by an overzealous newspaper reporter. Perhaps, his dreams and memories were an elaborate fantasy created by an idle mind asleep for six years.

He heard the ticking of his watch that lay on the dresser. It seemed louder than usual. What if the whole story was real? Did he consciously decide to commit fraud? Was he part of or the architect of an evil conspiracy? Tick, tick, tick. If he did commit this heinous crime how many feet of tainted wire were out there? How many have been killed or injured? How many wait for their turn to fall victim to Matthew Ellis' evil plot? Only time would tell.

Ritchie, Carl, and Wellington all sported sunglasses as they continued north on I-90 in the rain. Wellington and Carl had picked up a pair at the Quick Fill when they stopped. It was late afternoon and the rain had not subsided throughout the day. Carl's mind wandered to Lark's Run. By then the rain had most likely reached the farm and Laurel would have welcomed it in some strange ethereal way. She was probably dancing barefoot in a field singing one of her Celtic songs that no one understood. He smiled. Then a wave of sadness engulfed him. It was a feeling with which he was unfamiliar. Deep, gnawing despair made him want to jump from the van and head back to Lark's Run. Yet, the cold slap of reality told him that was impossible. Therein was the pain. The only thing that made life worthwhile was not only something he couldn't have but it was drifting farther and farther away. Out of reach—forever. Her voice, her smile, her beauty, her strange endearing view of life were memories Carl would cherish until they faded into a distant past in a far off land. He wiped a tear from his eye making sure that his two companions didn't notice.

Colt MacIntyre entered the Top of The Sixes on the thirty-ninth floor of 666 Fifth Avenue. He looked around and spotted his dining companions. At a table along an outside wall overlooking the city sat Jack Moore and Ryoya Akimoto. Colt wore a tan suit, white shirt, and a brown plaid tie. Most noticeable was that he wore black Lucchese Heritage Anson western boots and carried a tan Stetson Palacio cowboy hat with a cattleman crease.

"I like your boots," Ryoya said when Colt arrived at their table.

In a fine Texas accent he replied, "Why thank-you, ma'am. My daddy gave them to me."

"You're looking rather Texas, tonight," Jack commented.

Colt turned toward Jack and smiled, "The clock is ticking. I return to Victoria shortly after October 16."

"When you turn 30 years old."

"Yup, that's when I have to post the pony."

"Here we go," Jack commented as soon as he heard the cowboy jargon. "Go ahead, pop your corn just don't kick up any corral dust."

"Now, you've got it, cousin. You ain't no moss back."

"Wait," Ryoya interjected, "if this is going to go on all night you better provide translations or I'm going to dine with that nice elderly couple over there."

Colt looked real sullen and said, "I'm sorry, ma'am. When you post the pony you pay your debt. Pop your corn means to speak your mind and corral dust is a tall tale." He pointed at Jack and said, "Jack here is not behind the times or an old fogy so he's not a moss back. This Monkey Ward Cowboy, uh tenderfoot, is just try'in to make me feel at home." With a distinct New York accent, he added, "Don' worry bout it. We'll speak New Yawk so you's undastand.

Ryoya smiled and said, "I appreciate it."

"How's the restaurant business?" Jack asked.

"Funny thing about that," Colt said as he sat down, "it seems the French don't have much of a sense of humor."

Both Michael Donovan and Ryoya Akimoto gazed at Colt with increased interest.

"It seems Chef Andre was having trouble keeping up and orders were taking longer and longer. I made sure to speak with all my tables to inform them that their meal would be coming soon. Then as the time dragged on I decided to bring each table more bread. Well, the manager goes crazy. He starts yelling in the kitchen, 'le pain est de l'argent' which one of the chefs told me means 'bread is money.' I picked up a piece of bread from the basket on the table, examined it, and asked, 'How do you get it in your wallet?'" Ryoya and Jack smiled. Colt continued, "Well, during my break I went across the street to the Gristedes market and bought four loaves of Wonder Bread. You know the one with the colorful polka dots on the package? I slipped them onto the bread rack. They looked so pretty there among the loaves of French bread." He leaned back in his chair and continued, "Well, the manager walks in and darned if he didn't spot the bread imposters. He screams like a little girl and yells, 'Qu'est-ce que c'est Merveille pain.' I believe it means 'what is this Wonder bread.'" Colt looked at his two companions and asked, "Do you know 'fichez le camp' means 'get out?'"

Jack replied, "I believe it means get out and stay out."

"Well, I figured that it was best I skedaddle, especially when that ten-cent man picked up a cleaver," Colt smiled.

"So, you're unemployed," Ryoya noted, "What are you going to do for money?"

Colt held up what he was holding and said, "I have bread."

All three laughed.

"How are you fixed for money?" Jack asked seriously.

"I live in a sublet on Thirty Fifth Street. Me and twenty-thousand roaches. I'm paid up until I have to leave at the end of October. I haven't been living the high life so money isn't an issue."

"What do you plan to do for the next two months?" Ryoya asked.

"I haven't decided. Stay around New York for sure. Maybe, I'll just wander the streets and soak up the local culture."

"Are you still interested in adoption?" Jack asked unexpectedly.

"Shoot, yeah, why do you ask?"

"Recently, I met a young lady who is also interested in the subject. She, like you, has no experience in that area but there's something about her that makes me feel you two should meet."

"I'm not in a position to offer her anything."

"When you talked about that Holt baby there was an energy or enthusiasm that reflected a real desire and dedication on your part. I was convinced that you would indeed pursue an adoption service in Texas. You felt that strongly about the need and sincerely cared."

"I'd say your analysis is correct," Colt admitted.

"This young lady exhibited the same level of desire after meeting an adopted Korean teen at Woodstock. You and she both have that fire in the belly. I believe you two should meet—not for a job interview—to share your feelings about adoption. You might be good for each other."

"Well, it appears that I have some free time, so go ahead and set it up." Colt turned his attention to Ryoya and asked, "How do you put up with this fellow?"

"Someone has to keep the moss off his back. Besides, he's not boring," she answered.

Rain finally began to subside as the three escapees passed Duluth, Minnesota on I-35 North. The highway ended and they began driving north on State Road 61, a two lane thoroughfare that ran along Lake Superior to Canada. It was dark by the time they arrived in Beaver Bay, Minnesota. They stopped at the Lemon Wolf Café.

"Let's grab a bite and figure out where we're going to spend the night," Ritchie said.

Three tired travelers entered the small wooden structure and sat at one of the four tables in the establishment. A young couple sat at another table chatting quietly and a middle-aged man wearing a golf shirt and shorts sat at the counter. No other patrons were in the café.

After the waitress took their order Carl asked Ritchie, "What do you have in mind?"

"Churches are generally good for a single night. Sometimes there are community houses, bus terminals, campgrounds, and the always accommodating jails."

"No jails," Carl replied holding up his hands, "I'm allergic."

"It seems pretty sparsely populated around here," Wellington offered, "We might have to settle for whatever is available. Maybe, even pay for a room."

Four large Ojibwa lumberjacks entered the café. They stood in the center of the room and surveyed the layout and customers. Wellington had his back to the room but turned when he observed a change in the expressions on Carl's and Ritchie's faces. Immediately, he realized that the four men were looking in their direction. The café seemed eerily quiet. Wellington's mind drifted back to his high school gym, after school had been dismissed. He and a few friends were shooting baskets when a group of older boys entered. A silent standoff ensued. All present knew something was about to happen. It could be good or it could be bad—most likely bad. The new arrivals could challenge them to a game, leave without incident, or initiate a confrontation. In that case it was bad.

One of the lumberjacks led the others over to the table where Ritchie, Carl, and Wellington sat. He stated with authority, "You're sitting at our table."

"There's a table right over there," Carl answered immediately as he pointed toward another table.

"You don't understand—this is our table."

"We can move," Ritchie said as he gathered his things.

"No!" Carl spat, "I'm comfortable here. Tonto can sit someplace else."

The man showed visible anger at the affront and reached for Carl. He fell to the floor after being hit in the solar plexus and the jaw. Carl was on his feet facing the other three men. Wellington was by his side. Ritchie protested, "Wait, wait, this isn't necessary, man. It's just a table."

"It's not the table; it's our dignity and self-respect that's on the line. I don't take shit from anyone, especially when I didn't do anything to deserve it," Carl said.

The three Ojibwa men rushed Carl and Wellington. Carl struck one and was hit by the other who followed. Wellington sidestepped his attacker and shoved him headfirst into a wall. The original combatant regained his feet swung at Carl who ducked and then hit his opponent on the side of the head. Carl was grabbed from behind by one of the other attackers. Wellington came to Carl's defense when he jumped on the back of the man who held his friend. The two of them fell to the floor. The man who had been knocked down twice once more gained his footing and pulled a knife out of his pocket. He approached Carl.

"Ishkwaataa!" a voice said loudly. Then in English, "Stop!"

All participants stopped and looked in the direction of the command. There at the door stood an old man—an Ojibwa elder. Even though age had left its mark he stood tall and proud with an air of confidence. The four men who had fought with Carl and Wellington moved away. One of the men whispered, "Chief Michael."

"You bring shame to Ojibwa people." He pointed at the door, "Maajaa!"

Without saying a word the four men left the Lemon Wolf Café.

Carl rubbed his hand. He looked at Wellington who stood next to him and said, "Thanks."

The old man studied the three visitors with deep piercing eyes and a stern face. It was obvious that this man was a force to respect and obey. He slowly turned his attention to Carl and said, "Tonto was Potawatomi—not Ojibwa." Something changed in his expression. What exactly wasn't clear, but he seemed less threatening. The old man added, "In Spanish, Tonto means fool."

"I really didn't mean anything by my remark," Carl replied sheepishly.

"In anger, meaningless words are sent as arrows to conquer an enemy only to strengthen their resolve," Chief Michael remarked.

"They were the ones who came over to us and told us to move," Ritchie explained.

"In school we are taught of how the white man told the Indian to move and to move and to move. Perhaps they were seeing how it is the other way around."

"Perhaps," Ritchie agreed a little embarrassed.

The old Indian chief smiled and said, "Or, they were just oshki maazhi-bimaadizi, young men living a bad life—punks."

Carl laughed, "I guess I'm oshki ma-whatever-dizi."

Chief Michael faced Carl and stared directly into his eyes, "You conquer fear. You are zoongide'e—brave." He spoke to the three travelers, "Be strong enough to stand alone, be yourself enough to stand apart, be wise enough to stand together when the time comes." A glance at Ritchie chastised the young hippie.

In response, Ritchie nervously invited Chief Michael to join them. The old man walked around the table and sat facing the room. He waved his arm inviting the others to sit. After they sat the chief observed each man. The four sat in silence.

When the food came, Ritchie told the waitress to give Chief Michael what he wanted and to put it on his bill. She smiled and left.

"She didn't take your order," Ritchie said surprised.

"She knows what I wish to have." The chief raised his hand over the table and said, "May you be strengthened by yesterday's rain, walk straight in tomorrow's wind, and cherish each moment of the sun today. This is an Ojibwa Prayer."

"Thank you, but I think we cherished the sun yesterday and got soaked by the rain today," Wellington said with a smile.

Chief Michael turned his attention to the young Marine, "You run from yourself which is a race that can never be won."

"It seems I've spent my life running," was Wellington's response.

"When you stop, the fog will be lifted." He then addressed Ritchie, "Canada is in your head, but not in your heart. Animinizhimo—you run away scared. It will not bring you peace. Fear drives you away from never toward a destination."

Finally, he spoke to Carl, "You do not run—my brave. Yet, you seek your destiny in the wrong direction. Nandawaabandan—search for it. It is difficult, but worth the effort."

The waitress returned with a tray upon which was baked lake trout and wild leek, mint leaf tea, and traditional fried bread. As the elder ate Ritchie posed the question, "Are there any churches or community houses where we could spend the night around here?"

The chief waved his arm and stated, "You will stay in my lodge. In the morning you can continue your journey." He put down his fork and leaned forward as he added, "If you plan to cross the border in the dense forest be very careful. There are dangers you cannot see. It is easy to get lost. Many spirits wander the crossings where they fell." The old man warned, "Beware the Bagwajiwinini, the little people of the forest. They will mislead you and keep you lost until all is lost."

"Will we see Bagwajiwinini?" Anna Six Trees asked as they prepared for their trip. Her brother Robert laughed. He held up his fox totem that hung by a leather strand around his neck and said, "Waagosh will protect you."

54: Friday – August 29, 1969

Fetch, Ritchie's black Basenji, stretched her legs straight back poking Ritchie in the back. The three travelers shared a bedroom in Chief Michael's log home. It was a good size room with two bunkbeds.

The previous night they sat on the spacious porch enjoying the evening air and conversing with Chief Michael, his wife, and adult daughter. Life on the reservation was completely foreign to all three young men. Carl and Wellington, having grown up in big cities, were amazed at how challenging living in the wilderness could be. Chief Michael walked five miles to get to the Lemon Wolf Café and would have walked an equal distance back if they hadn't given him a ride. It was a regular Thursday ritual for the Ojibwa elder.

Ritchie was fascinated by his three host's acute awareness of the beauty of nature. The twisted gnarled roots of a tree, shape of a stone, sunlight touching a single leaf, changing colors in a pool of water, or a footprint made by a wolf all were pleasing to the eye of the Ojibwa. Chief Michael explained, "The Great-Circle-of-Life is the Circle of Unity with all things in the universe, including the Great Spirit, our Creator, about which all life revolves. We are all equal in the Circle, no one is in front of you and no one is behind you, no one is above you, no one is below you. We are all related."

At one point in the evening Chief Michael told a story about a tree. "Up north in Grand Portage there is a tree called Manidoo-giizhikens, which means Little Cedar Spirit Tree. The white man calls it the Witch Tree. It grew out of granite rock on the shore of Hat Point on Lake Superior. Before our time the tree was struck by lightning leaving only the trunk. But its spirit was mighty and a new root sprout arose entwining the original trunk with new growth. The roots also grew down into the water where fish swim among them and its branches became strong offering safe haven to the eagle. This tree has survived more than three hundred winters on the edge of Lake Superior. It is believed by the Ojibwa people that the spirits of this eternal tree are strong and will protect travelers. Ojibwa people leave tobacco, ribbons, and other gifts to appease Mishipizheu, the Underwater Lynx." Chief Michael lit his pipe and as smoke floated off the porch into the woods he said, "You should visit this tree and leave a gift to request that the spirits protect you on your planned journey."

"Our journey is almost over," Ritchie said.

"Yes, you are near your destination, but your chosen route is filled with danger," Chief Michael nodded and instructed, "Visit Manidoo-giizhikens and leave a gift."

"Where is the tree?" Ritchie asked.

"Grand Portage is about one hundred miles north on Highway 61 at the Canadian border. Before you get to the border, in Grand Portage, go right on Store Road. When you can only go right or left go left on Mile Road. When you again have to go right or left go right on Bay Road. Follow this road to its end. From there walk the path through a grove of light-green lichen and down a steep trail to the shoreline. Before you, will be centuries of life. This tree witnessed history before America was born."

The three travelers looked at each other. Finally, Ritchie said, "We'll visit the witch tree and leave a gift."

"Good."

Chief Michael's daughter handed Ritchie a small beaded bag strung on a thin leather thong. "Please leave our gift for Manidoo-giizhikens."

Ritchie nodded and took the bag.

"Because I believe your words are iron and that you will visit Manidoo-giizhikens the spirits will guide you through me."

Ritchie wasn't sure what the chief meant. He waited.

Chief Michael continued, "You wish to enter Canada by a less-traveled path."

All three young men were surprised as none of them had expressed that desire.

"After you leave Manidoo-giizhikens return to Route 61 North. On the left you will find a small street named Joe's Road," he smiled, "We are not creative with our naming of roads. Take this road into the forest. It will wind as a snake around its prey. You will go deeper and deeper into the wilderness. In the middle of the day the sun will be as dusk. The road will narrow. Be very careful those hills are treacherous and with yesterday's rain water will flow searching for streams and rivers. Do not cross rushing water—wait. Patience is the use of time as a tool. After a steep rise you will find a dirt road. It will be on your right and easy to miss. This old path is little used but will lead you to where the Pigeon River is wide and shallow and lazy. There you will be able to cross the border undetected."

After a small breakfast Ritchie, Carl, and Wellington thanked Chief Michael, his wife, and daughter for their hospitality and kindness. Ritchie assured them that they would visit the Witch Tree before leaving America forever.

When they drove off Chief Michael's daughter said, "Three distinctly different young men brought to this place for three different reasons with a common goal."

Chief Michael peered down the road as the blue van disappeared into the distance. He commented, "I fear they will not reach their destination."

TWA Flight 840 from Rome was scheduled to stop over in Athens, Greece and then continue on to Tel Aviv, Israel. The Boeing 707 aircraft cruised at 35,000 feet in an afternoon sun. Inside the cabin all seemed normal. Ninety-five passengers and twelve crew members left Leonardo Da Vinci International Airport in Rome in the morning. It promised to be a pleasant flight. Unfortunately, it would never reach Tel Aviv.

Shortly after takeoff a stewardess rushed down the aisle from the rear of the aircraft all the way to the flight deck. Shortly after, with a stricken look, returned to the back. It was obvious that something was terribly wrong. Passengers began looking out the windows to see if they could determine what the problem was. The flight continued with everything seemingly normal.

"Attention, attention. This plane has been taken over by the Popular Front for the Liberation of Palestine. Put your hands on your heads, don't move, there are Israeli assassins aboard, we're going to a friendly country," an unfamiliar female voice came over the loud speaker in half French and half English. It was that of twenty-five-year-old Leila Khaled. Her PFLP accomplice was Salim Issawi. They had boarded the plane in Rome and sat in the first class section. Khaled boarded Flight 840 wearing a wide-brimmed hat and carrying a book, My Friend Che, about her hero Che Guevara. She and Issawi, armed with grenades, stormed the cockpit and took control of the flight.

They believed that Yitzhak Rabin, the Israeli Ambassador to the United States, was to be aboard the flight. He wasn't.

After circling in a holding pattern over Lode Airport in Tel Aviv, the hijackers hurled insults at the Israeli air traffic controllers and ordered the plane to head north. At that point they had an Israeli fighter jet escort. The jet headed for Damascus, Syria.

Ritchie, Carl, and Wellington stood silently on the edge of Lake Superior gazing at the Witch Tree. Indeed, its gnarled, stunted, twisted branches, and leafy crown created an image of a woman standing on the shore. Each of the young men was lost in his own thoughts. Chief Michael had successfully instilled the spiritual nature of the sacred ground upon which they stood. How insignificant a man feels among thousands of years of history. How inadequate he feels among unseen spirits who are aware of far more than he can comprehend. How vulnerable one is to the unknown forces that determine his destiny. How strange it was to be beckoned by the Witch to do her bidding. Ritchie placed the beaded bag given him by Chief Michael's daughter among the branches. He then placed an artist's paintbrush at the base of the tree. Wellington held his gift for a long period of time before he placed the globe and anchor Marine insignia next to Ritchie's paintbrush. Carl was last. In the tree he saw a lost love. A row of leaves gave the impression of a tiara. Wind off the lake sang a Celtic song. Sadness engulfed him. The Witch reached out to him. He knew there would be no peace for him, no place to hide, no joy to compare with what he left in the Pennsylvania mountains. He took a four leaf clover out of his pocket, kissed it, and placed it as high among the branches as he could reach. Carl turned and slowly walked away.

"Attention, attention, this is PFLP flight number one, Israeli assassins, we're going to a friendly country, and we'll hear your just demands when we get on the ground." Stewardesses began collecting passenger's shoes, watches, pens, rings, and anything else that might become a projectile upon impact. It was standard practice to place all loose items in large plastic bags and stow them in the lavatories when a crash landing was anticipated.

Remarkably, they found Joe's Road. It began as a paved two-lane thoroughfare that wound around a rising mountain. Chief Michael was correct—the forest became more and more dense as they proceeded. Ritchie had to drive slowly to avoid going off the road, hitting a protruding boulder, or ruining a tire in a massive pothole.

"I wonder how many people enter this forest and are never heard from again each year," Carl mused.

"I don't know, but I don't want to be the next on the list," Wellington said from his lawn chair behind the driver's seat.

"Considering how bad this road is I really am concerned about the condition of the dirt road we're supposed to take," Ritchie commented.

Carl added, "That old Indian is sitting on his porch laughing his ass off about sending the three white," he looked over his shoulder, "uh, two white guys and one bluecoat soldier to their doom."

"Naw, he spoke the truth," Ritchie countered, "We have to trust him."

From seemingly nowhere a woman ran in front of the van. She was obviously panic stricken and distraught. Ritchie had to make an abrupt stop which threw Wellington against the back of his seat. The woman threw herself on the flat hood of the van and wailed in a shrill tone that brought chills to all three men. As they left the van she shrieked, "My children!"

Carl reached her first and put his hands on her shoulders and turned her toward him, "Where are your children?"

"Please, help me!" she pleaded, her face distorted with fear and agony.

"Where are they," Carl repeated impatiently.

"In the water!" she screamed. Wanda Six Trees turned and ran up the road in the direction that the three had been driving. Ritchie, Carl, and Wellington followed. When they rounded a bend before them was rushing water that had washed out the road. She pointed down a slope where the flashflood water was flowing into a river below. Half way down the slope was a red 1964 Ford Fairlaine sedan. The automobile was hung up on a log in rushing waist deep water. Inside they could see a young boy sitting in the front passenger seat.

Water is a thousand times denser than air. For this reason a two-and-a-half mile-per-hour flow is equivalent to an F1 tornado. At eight miles-per-hour it has the destructive power of an F5 tornado.

Carl tried to wade into the water but was quickly knocked down and only saved himself by grabbing a tree branch. As he hung helplessly clinging to the branch Ritchie and Wellington were able to grab his shirt and pull him out of the water.

"We have to get to that kid," Carl said breathlessly.

"The rush of the water is too strong," Wellington said.

"We can make a chain and get out to the car," Carl suggested.

"It looks too far," Ritchie said.

"We'll have to start above it and edge over toward the car as the water pulls us downstream," Wellington suggested.

"Well, we gotta try," Carl stated as he removed his belt and wrapped it around a small tree. He slipped the belt through the buckle and then wrapped the end around his wrist. With a tug he made sure the anchor was solid. After moving down the edge of the running water he offered his free hand and said, "Come'on who's next?"

Wellington Marsh slipped off his belt and looped it around his left wrist through the buckle. He offered the other end to Carl who wrapped it once around his wrist and held it tight.

Ritchie was last and would be the lead rescuer. With his belt securely around his wrist he handed the end to Wellington. He yelled to be heard over the water, "I'll start here next to Carl." With that he entered the water. He didn't expect the force to be as great as it was and almost fell when the water tried to pull his legs out from under him. Wellington felt the yank and was almost pulled into the water. He was able to keep his footing and waded slowly into the flow. Ritchie felt like a huge weight was pulling him farther out. Carl was still on the edge of the water straining to hold the two others. He held on. Wellington's belt cut into his wrist. He moved into the rush of water. The additional force of water upon his body combined with the weight of the other two stretched his arms. Tears involuntarily dripped from his eyes. He hung on with all of the strength he could muster. The pain gnawed at his mind.

In the middle of the chain Wellington fought to keep his footing. The water was just below his waist but moved with such force that he had to lean against it. Pain in both his wrists and arms became unbearable. Then he heard Sergeant Kincaid yell at him, "Damn you Marsh—you gonna give up!" His father joined in the chastisement, "You can do anything—if you have the courage. Do you have the courage, boy?"

At the end of the chain Ritchie had trouble keeping his feet as the water rushed past him. At an awkward angle he leaned into the current to stay upright. He focused on his target, a red Ford which was bobbing in the water still lodged against a log. Inside he saw the face of a child. With unblinking eyes the little boy watched as Ritchie edged closer and closer. The young artist saw that the water was approximately ten inches below the open window of the car. That was higher than when he first observed the stricken automobile. He realized that he and the water were in a life and death race.

"Attention, attention, we're blowing up the aircraft 60 seconds after we get on the ground," the evil voice warned. Fearful passengers were brought to near panic. Some cried, others prayed, and still others sat in silence. The Boeing 707 landed hard on a stone runway in what looked like a desert. Emergency doors were flung open and escape chutes deployed. Passengers rushed to escape the aircraft before it was blown up. In bare feet they ran into a field of prickly briars. The long spines stabbed them causing some to fall to the ground. Crying screaming passengers scrambled to get away from the runway. A woman had broken her leg and a man his ankle when jumping from the wing of the aircraft. They were helped to safety. A short distance from the airplane passengers hid behind a row of sandbags that lined a shallow trench. Suddenly, a loud bang was heard as the front third of the jet went up in smoke.

Ritchie came to within two feet of the incapacitated car when he found that he couldn't go any farther. He yelled, "Give me some slack," but couldn't be heard over the sound of the hungry water. A large branch that flowed down the wash like a huge spear struck Ritchie in the back causing him to cry out in pain. He dipped below the surface of the water and came up coughing. He thought of letting go of his tether and slamming into the car. The only problem was he saw no way to get to dry land on either side of the vehicle. A smaller branch floated past and he grabbed it. In desperation Ritchie pulled the branch above the water and toward his wrist where his belt was looped, the other end held by Wellington. He yelled, "Hang on kid," as he removed the loop from his wrist and wrapped it around the branch.

"Hurry up," Wellington yelled, "It's getting worse." Ritchie couldn't hear him.

The outgrowths from the branch allowed the belt to hold tight and also gave Ritchie a handhold. He reached the car. For a moment the enormous pull on his arms was replaced by a battering as he was pushed into the side of the car by pounding water. He reached into the vehicle and said, "Come'on kid, it's time to go."

"Take my sister," Robert Six Trees yelled to be heard over the sound of the water.

"I'll come back for her—come on!"

"No!" Robert pulled six-year-old Anna Marie from the back seat. The panic stricken little girl stared wide-eyed at Ritchie but didn't say a word. Ritchie considered taking both children but in his heart knew he didn't have the strength. "I'll come back for her," Ritchie repeated.

"No! Take her!" Then in a surprisingly calm voice Robert said, "Please, take her. I'll be alright. She's too little and too scared." With that he took the fox totem from around his neck and placed it around Anna's neck.

Ritchie grabbed the frightened girl and said, "I'll be back." With the girl in his right arm held above the rushing water Ritchie moved away from the car. He yelled, "Pull me in." Carl and Wellington couldn't hear what Ritchie said but saw him move away from the vehicle. They tried to pull him back but were no match with thousands of cubic feet of water.

Wellington yelled, "Swing for the shore."

"Hurry!" Carl gasped.

Ritchie moved sideways and like a great pendulum the human chain swung toward the bank. The rushing water tried to pull him under but he stayed upright. At one point Ritchie stepped into a hole and twisted his ankle. Then the branch that he had used to reach the car broke. Carl and Wellington watched Ritchie disappear down the slope carried by muddy water filled with debris.

Syrian soldiers raced across the field. They rounded up the passengers of TWA Flight 840 and loaded them onto buses. The two hijackers were arrested but would be freed a day later. All were transported to Damascus Airport. An officer said with malice and authority, "You will all be interrogated."

Once out of the water Carl and Wellington called out to Ritchie but got no answer. Wanda Six Trees stood silently on the edge of the water looking downstream. Wellington and Carl moved down the slope yelling Ritchie's name. Only rushing water could be heard. It echoed in the small valley that seemed devoid of any other sounds. The two men traveled fifty, then one-hundred yards. The banging of a storage shed torn from its foundation and tumbling in the water caught their attention. With one last metallic clunk it bounced the final fifty yards into the rushing river below.

"Ritchie," Carl yelled.

They continued to look for any sign of two lost souls.

"Ritchie," Wellington yelled.

Carl tripped over a branch and fell with a hard thud onto the muddy ground. "Son-of-a-bitch," he cursed. Then yelled, "Ritchie."

"Here!" a weak voice could barely be heard over the roar of the rushing water.

"Where?" Carl shouted with excitement.

Before Ritchie could answer, Wellington exclaimed, "There!" He pointed to a hollow on the edge of the wash. In a tangle of branches and debris Ritchie lay against a log still holding Anna Marie Six Trees in his arms. His two friends rushed to his aid.

"Help me get up," the exhausted and battered rescuer said weakly.

Quickly, the two fellow travelers climbed down and pulled Ritchie and Anna out of the debris and mud. Wellington took Anna from Ritchie. With a gasp, Ritchie said, "We've got to save that little boy."

As the three men climbed back up the slope each knew that their strength had been greatly depleted. A repeat of what they had just done seemed impossible. Carl asked, "Is there anything in the van that we could use to gain a better hold on whoever goes out to the car?"

"I just don't know," Ritchie replied.

Back on the road Wellington handed Anna to Wanda Six Trees. She hugged her daughter and ran her hand through the little girl's wet and muddy hair. She then stopped and looked at the three young men and pleadingly asked, "My boy?"

Ritchie looked out over the flashflood. The water was higher than before. It had risen to a point where it was over the side of the car door. The little boy had rolled up the window to keep the water out. "We don't have time to go to the van. We have to go now." He picked up a branch that would give him the extra distance needed to reach the car. "Let's go!"

Carl wrapped his belt around the tree and the around his bruised and bleeding wrist. Wellington followed suit. With the chain recreated Ritchie entered the water. It was more treacherous and deeper than before but he ventured out into the swirling water. When he looked up he saw the helpless child in the car who appeared to be looking only at him. The vicious stream with a mindless desire to devour all that got in its path tore at Ritchie's clothes and skin.

Wellington followed Ritchie into the water. Immediately the current pulled him roughly downhill. He fell and went under the water. With the human chain at full length the water swung them back against the bank. Without saying a word they regained their footing and ran a short distance further upstream to try to get farther out before the current swung them back toward the bank. Wellington picked up a branch and used it to prop himself against the massive sideways pull of the water created by the fulcrum that Carl created at the tree. Ritchie fought to get in line with the auto.

Then over the roar of the water they heard the sickening sound of metal creaking. In unison they looked at the car. It heaved and rocked. Then there was a sickening crack as an underwater branch that had been holding the car in place broke. Immediately, the steel cocoon moved with the flow of the water. At a torturously slow rate it began to float down the slope toward the river below. Inside, a small boy looked at the three men. He neither yelled, nor cried, nor showed any outward sign of fear. He simply looked at the three would-be rescuers with a haunting stare that said nothing and everything. Ritchie prayed that the automobile would hit something or get snagged on something. The red Ford Fairlane turned in the current and slid down the slope to disappear below the churning water in the river.

Wellington and Ritchie slammed against the bank and Carl released himself from the tree. As Ritchie and Wellington climbed out of the wash Carl ran down the slope searching desperately for a sign, any sign, of the lost automobile or its occupant. In the swirling murky water he saw all kinds of debris that had washed down from upstream but no evidence of the car. Faster and faster he ran catching his clothing on brambles and branches, tearing his skin, stumbling, on and on. It had to be out there and he had to find it. He couldn't stop. He couldn't give up as long as there was any hope. Carl didn't hear his friends calling from behind. All his strength, all his effort, and all his consciousness was focused on one objective. Nothing else mattered. In his mind he saw the river running faster than he could follow. Unaware of the cold, or cuts, or bruises that he sustained he pressed on. If he was to achieve one thing of value in his entire sad existence it was going to be the resurrection of this lost soul. On and on he pushed downstream until he came to a point where the river split and his path was blocked. Out of breath and out of hope he scanned the demonic waters. The cruel river refused to give up its bounty. It continued on its destructive course without acknowledging the poor devastated soul that stood on its bank so helpless and overwhelmed.

In a slow steady display of defeat Carl dropped to his knees and settled back into a sitting position. The worst beating that he had ever experienced would have been a welcome relief from the massive pain he felt at that moment. Sitting in the mud, somewhere in Minnesota, Carl Pythacyk lost hope.

Wellington and Ritchie caught up with Carl. Three men from three disparate worlds shared a common emotion. None spoke. They remained on the bank of an unnamed river looking at the unleashed fury of nature and ultimately saw themselves.

Finally, Wellington spoke, "I'm going back."

"Back where?" Ritchie asked.

"To Detroit, the Marines, Vietnam," he shrugged. "I can't run away from myself, anymore."

"I'm going back, as well," Carl said in a low voice. "Even if I only get to spend one day with Laurel it will be worth it. I'm going back to Lark's Run." He stood and faced his friends. "We have to take that mother and child to Chief Michael and tell him what happened."

Ritchie looked at Carl and then Wellington. They had come so far and now at the last minute his friends change their minds. He understood why. In fact, he was having doubts himself. Chief Michael was accurate when he said Canada was not in his heart. The eyes of a child haunted him. A young Ojibwa brave knew the risk of sending his sister first and faced it with dignity and courage. Ritchie felt shame. There was no way he could hide in Canada with those eyes staring at him in his mind. Ritchie became aware of a searing pain in his back.

After making their way back to the road and breaking the news to Wanda Six Trees five travelers rode in silence over one hundred miles to Chief Michael's lodge. He comforted the mother and daughter and listened to the new plans of the three battered and beaten young men. He nodded and said, "You will all stay here tonight."

Anna Marie Six Trees cried softly in her bed as she held her brother's fox totem in her hand.

55: Saturday – August 30, 1969

Three young men rode south on Highway 61 in silence. Each was lost in his own thoughts and feelings about the previous day. A child perished and there was nothing they could have done to prevent it. Yet, each man was saddled with his own individual guilt and speculation about what he might have done differently.

Chief Michael was correct when he said Robert Six Trees chose his fate when he sent his sister to safety first. The rising water and delicate balance of the automobile upon an unseen anchor could not have been missed. The Ojibwa elder commented, "The spirits were strong in him. When he gave his totem to his sister he knew Waagosh, the fox, could only protect one of them. Her life will now be manidoowaadizi, spiritual in nature. His jichaag, spirit within, now travels four days to the afterlife in the sky." Chief Michael offered tobacco to the spirits in tribute to a young warrior. He turned his attention back to the tired and beaten young men, "Canada was never in your future. You came a long way to save a child and to learn to accept your own destinies. Do not ignore the wisdom of the spirits."

As the silence weighed heavy on Ritchie he turned on the radio. Immediately, Jim Morrison and The Doors filled the van with the song, *Touch Me*.

Yeah

Come on, come on, come on, come on
Now, touch me, babe
Can't you see that I am not afraid?
What was that promise that you made?
Why won't you tell me what she said?
What was that promise that you made?

Now I'm gonna love you
Till the heavens stop the rain
I'm gonna love you
Till the stars fall from the sky
For you and I

During the instrumental portion of the song Carl thought about Laurel. How he looked forward to placing the tiara back on her head. How he just wanted to be with her. However, he didn't look forward to confessing about his past or admitting that he was a murderer. She would surely reject him and he would find himself heading back to New York City to face justice. A vision of Robert Six Trees flashed in his mind. Courage, he thought.

Ritchie knew that his return would surprise Stephanie. He also figured that she would be glad to have him back and that they could return to what they had even if for only a short period of time. Inevitably, the draft board would separate them once more.

Wellington Marsh thought about the letters he received from Teresa Champion.

She wrote the sweetest things and, as it turned out, had a sense of humor. She related a story of how she was on a midtown bus going to the movies when an old man got on a saw that there were no seats left. He walked over to her and said that she was young and he was old and she should give him her seat. She refused. She wrote in the letter, "So, he grabbed my leg and started pulling it—like I'm pulling yours." Wellington smiled as he remembered laughing at her joke.

Jim Morrison began singing once more. He was the iconic lead singer of the relatively new band The Doors. Born December 8, 1943 in Melbourne, Florida, his father was a naval officer, therefore, the family moved quite regularly. James Douglas Morrison was the oldest of three children. Young Jim was a voracious reader interested in philosophy, poetry and Native American Mythology. His high school English teacher indicated that he read more than any other student, but the books he selected were so obscure that she suspected that he was making them up. They dealt with sixteenth and seventeenth century demonology. In the end, she found that they were real.

Morrison attended St Petersburgh Community College in Florida and in 1962 transferred to Florida State University in Tallahassee. While attending FSU, Morrison was arrested September 29, 1963 following a home football game. He had arrived at the game very drunk. By the end of the game he was drunk and disorderly. On his way out of the stadium he came upon the belongings of a police officer that had been set aside and impulsively took an umbrella and the officer's helmet. He was immediately arrested for petty larceny, disturbing the peace, resisting arrest, and public drunkenness. All charges were subsequently dropped.

In 1964 Jim Morrison transferred to UCLA in California where he majored in film. At the time his father Captain George Stephen Morrison was aboard his flagship USS Bon Homme Richard directing activities off the North Vietnamese coast. On August 2, 1964 the destroyer USS Maddox under his command was on an electronic intelligence gathering mission in the Gulf of Tonkin. At 3:05 in the afternoon Captain Herrick of the Maddox radioed that it was under attack from three North Vietnamese Navy P-4 torpedo boats. The Maddox evaded two torpedoes and opened fire with its five-inch guns claiming to have made a direct hit on one attacking boat. Four F-8 Crusader jets were launched from the aircraft carrier USS Ticonderoga. They sunk one and heavily damaged another torpedo boat. North Vietnamese general, Phùng The Tài, claimed that Maddox had attacked fishing boats forcing the North Vietnamese Navy to "fight back."

After the skirmish, President Lyndon Johnson ordered Maddox and another destroyer USS Turner Joy to stage daylight runs into North Vietnamese waters, testing the 12 nautical miles limit and North Vietnamese resolve. A second unconfirmed attack occurred on August 4, 1964. Within thirty minutes, President Johnson had decided on retaliatory attacks stating, "The determination of all Americans to carry out our full commitment to the people and to the government of South Vietnam will be redoubled by this outrage." One hour and forty minutes after his speech, U.S. aircraft reached North Vietnamese targets bombing four torpedo boat bases and an oil-storage facility in Vinh. Accounts of what exactly happened varied with some claiming it was simply staged to provide an excuse to bomb the north. What was fact or fiction is not clear, however it was these events that escalated U.S. involvement in the Vietnam War.

In the summer of 1965, after graduating with a degree from the UCLA film school, Jim Morrison lived on a building rooftop in Venice Beach, California. One day Jim Morrison and fellow alumnus Ray Manzarek had a chance meeting on Venice

Beach. Manzarek had always been impressed by Morrison's poetry believing it sounded much like music lyrics. The two agreed to form a band. Drummer John Densmore joined the band and introduced them to guitarist Robby Krieger. The Doors name came from the title of Aldous Huxley's book *The Doors of Perception* in which he supports the use of psychedelic drugs.

November, 1966 the Doors produced a film to support their first single record release *Break On Through To The Other Side*. However, it was *Light My Fire* that brought them national attention and remained number one on the Billboard Hot 100 chart in July/August of 1967.

Admiral Morrison was not supportive of Jim's career choice. After an acquaintance played a Doors' debut record for Morrison's family his father wrote him a letter telling him "give up any idea of singing or any connection with a music group because of what I consider to be a complete lack of talent in this direction." Jim Morrison had little contact with his family after that.

In September of 1967 the Doors appeared on the Ed Sullivan Show. Sullivan requested that they sing two songs; *People Are Strange* and *Light My Fire*. However, Sullivan's censors insisted that the lyrics in *Light My Fire* be changed from "Girl we couldn't get much higher" to "Girl we couldn't get much better." They wanted to avoid any perceived reference to drugs. After agreeing to the request in the dressing room, Morrison sang the lyrics as they were written. Ed Sullivan was so angry that he refused to shake the hands of any member of the band. He had a producer tell them that they would never appear on the Ed Sullivan show again. Jim Morrison replied with a smile, "Hey man, we just did the Sullivan Show."

On December 9, 1967 Jim Morrison became the first rock star to be arrested on stage during a performance. Before the concert, backstage at the New Haven Arena Morrison was making out with a female fan. A police officer providing security for the band didn't recognize the lead singer. He told the couple to vacate the area. Morrison replied, "Eat it." The officer threatened them with a can of Mace and warned, "Last chance." The singer replied, "Last chance to eat it." He got sprayed in the face with Mace. When the Doors' manager identified Jim Morrison the police officer apologized and the concert began after a long delay. Still angry, Morrison recounted what had happened backstage during the song *Back Door Man*. He shouted, "The whole fucking world hates me," and taunted the cop in question calling him "a little blue man in a little blue hat." When he said, "I'm just like you guys, man—he did it to me, they'll do it to you," the police walked onto the stage and placed him under arrest. He was charged with inciting a riot, indecency, and public profanity. The charges were later dropped. Thirteen additional arrests were made when the angry audience took to the streets.

By 1968, Morrison, who had long been a heavy drinker, came to recording sessions drunk. Frequently, he was late for performances forcing the band to play instrumentals or for Ray Manzarek to pick up singing duties. Morrison grew a beard and mustache and gained weight. Then March 1, 1969 during a concert at the Dinner Key Auditorium in Miami Jim Morrison was accused of exposing himself. Four days later the Dade County sheriff's office issued a warrant for his arrest. He was charged with felony lewd and lascivious behavior and five misdemeanors; two counts of indecent exposure, two of public profanity, and one of public drunkenness. A jury found him guilty of misdemeanor indecent exposure and profanity on September 20, 1970. All of the problems and arrests essentially ended the Doors concert tours.

Jim Morrison had a girlfriend named Pamela Courson. He knew her from before he gained fame. She encouraged him to continue with his poetry. It was an open relationship making her more a companion than lover. As a result, they had frequent loud arguments and separations. Morrison regularly had sex with fans and flings with musicians and other professionals in the music industry. Among the more notable were Grace Slick of Jefferson Airplane and Janis Joplin. Well, with Janis Joplin—not so much.

Record producer Paul Rothchild worked with both Joplin and the Doors. In his opinion he considered Jim and Janis the king and queen of rock 'n' roll. He got them together at a party in Hidden Hills, California. Janis Joplin and Jim Morrison were notorious imbibers. On this day they both arrived sober. Janis enjoyed sex and when she saw Jim she said, "I want that!" The two singers got along well—at first. Unfortunately, Morrison quickly got inebriated and became rude and obnoxious. Joplin, on the other hand, held her liquor well and became irritated by Jim Morrison's antics. Ultimately, she decided to leave the party. Before she could drive off Jim staggered over to the car and mumbled something. She told him in no uncertain terms that she was not interested. Because he was a violent drunk Jim reached into the car and grabbed Janis Joplin's hair. Janis clocked him on the head with a bottle of Southern Comfort. They never saw each other again although Jim Morrison remained interested.

In the end, Jim Morrison joined the 27 Club July 3, 1971. Janis Joplin preceded him into the infamous group of musicians who died at the age of 27 nine months earlier on October 4, 1970. Morrison was found in a Paris apartment that he shared with Pamela Courson in the bathtub. The official cause of death was listed as "heart failure" but it is widely believed that he suffered a hemorrhage from an overdose of heroin.

"I love the Doors," Ritchie said breaking out of his melancholia.

Neither Wellington nor Carl answered so Ritchie added, "We should get to Detroit in twelve or thirteen hours. Wellington, do you know someplace where Carl and I can get some sack time before we go on?"

"My parents will put you up," after a pause he said, "Just don't tell them that I was running away."

"Your secret's safe," Ritchie reassured his friend.

Carl still didn't speak.

"What's it like," Ritchie asked Wellington, "basic training?"

"I don't know about other military branches, but in the Marines it's tough. If you don't take it personally and do what you're told you get through. Keep two things in mind. First they want you to get through it and second you can do far more than you think. When you think you can't do another pushup you can probably rip off another ten. When you have to run until you feel like your lungs are going to explode push past it—you'll be surprised. They want you to learn that you can do more than you think and to not give up. It could save your life someday."

"I don't know man, I'm kinda a coward, you know?"

Carl spoke, "The hell you are! After you got washed down into a pile of shit and held onto that girl then went right back out into that water. You got guts. You're a goddamned long hair hippie freak but you're alright in my book."

"Thanks, Carl, that means a lot to me," Ritchie answered.

"Do you think Chief Michael was right?" Wellington asked from his perch on the lawn chair behind the driver's seat, "Some unknown forces brought us here to save that little girl?"

"Then why didn't they let us save the boy?" Carl asked.

"Maybe we were meant to be there and could save one. Who got saved was in the hands of the boy," Ritchie speculated.

Wellington said, "If that lady didn't stop us it would have been us in that wash."

"True," Ritchie agreed, "I would never have seen the washed out road when I came around that bend."

"Just don't tell me that a little boy had to die to save us," Carl spat, "I don't want that hung on me."

"Why we arrived at the exact time that car was there in the middle of a wilderness just seems like more than a coincidence," Wellington concluded.

"If that didn't happen," Ritchie asked, "would you have gone to Canada?"

"I'd have gone, but I don't know if I would have stayed," Wellington admitted.

Carl said, "I'd have gone and probably stayed. Going back is the stupidest thing I can do. But, I have to go back as far as Lark's Run. I just have to take the chance."

"Yeah, she's worth it," Ritchie said.

"She's worth risking my life."

"What are you running from?" Ritchie asked.

"None of your damn business."

"Stephanie Ellis, this is Jack Moore," he said into the telephone receiver.

"Mister Moore do you want to speak with my father?"

"Actually, this time I want to talk with you."

"Really? What about?"

Jack explained, "You made a comment about being interested in pursuing a career in adoption services."

"I did."

"Now, I don't want to get your hopes up. This might be nothing. I know a young man who also expressed an interest in that area. However, he doesn't have any experience either. He is really bright and I'm confident that if he decides to pursue this direction he will be successful. I'll get to the point. I think the two of you should meet if for no other reason than to offer each other moral support."

"I don't know," Stephanie said, "I am interested but I haven't done anything in that field. I have nothing to offer."

"You can tell him about the girl you met at Woodstock." Jack paused and thought for a moment. He then said, "Maybe, I'm over thinking this, but I see two people who have a similar interest and believe that somehow they might be the spark to make something happen."

"I've never even gone to college."

"This young man has and earned numerous degrees. He is also very smart." Suddenly, Jack had a thought about what he was doing and stated emphatically, "I'm not matchmaking. Colt is going to be thirty this year. He's going back to Texas to help run his daddy's business, but first wants to start a non-profit adoption service. As he said, he's not going to run it, just make sure it gets started."

"Texas?"

"Yes, Victoria, Texas."

"Well, I always wanted to meet a cowboy."

Jack laughed, "You won't be disappointed."

U.S. Route 94 East became U.S. Route 90 East around Tomah, Wisconsin. It was just after noon and they had been on the road for approximately five hours.

Carl had a map they got at an ESSO station. He detailed their route, "We stay on 90 through Chicago and somewhere around Gary, Indiana we get on 94. Then straight through Kalamazoo, Battle Creek, and Ann Arbor on to beautiful Detroit. We dump the soldier," he looked over his shoulder and smiled, "and find a place to sleep. Then it's like five or six hours back to Larks Run."

"I told you, you can spend the night at my house," Wellington said. "Just no talk about Canada."

"What's it worth to ya?" Carl asked mischievously.

Before Wellington could answer, Ritchie said, "Shit! We've got company."

A siren and red lights on a blue and white Wisconsin State Patrol Plymouth Fury following the van told Wellington and Carl what Ritchie already knew. He pulled the van onto the shoulder of the highway. Carl considered jumping out and running but decided to see how things progressed.

The state trooper wearing a dark blue uniform and Smokey-the-bear hat approached the van. Carl asked Ritchie, "Were you speeding?"

"No."

When the law officer got to the driver's window he said, "License and registration."

Ritchie handed the requested documents to the patrolman and asked, "Why did you stop me?"

"I'll ask the questions—hippie," was the response which told all three occupants of the van the reason for the stop. As the officer examined Ritchie's license he asked, "Where are you headed?"

"East," was Ritchie's response.

"You being a wiseass?"

"No."

"I'll try again. Where are you headed?"

"Detroit."

"Where are you coming from?"

"Duluth."

"Did you pick up drugs in Duluth?"

"What?"

"Are there drugs in this vehicle? Take the hair out of your ears!"

"No, there aren't."

"Why don't you show where you have the drugs hidden so I don't have to have you unload the van on the highway?"

"There aren't any drugs."

"Your license is from New Jersey. What were you doing in Duluth?"

"That's really none of your business."

"I can make it my business, princess."

Fetch growled in the back of the van. The state trooper was briefly distracted. He peered at the boxes and bags in the back of the van. He then made eye contact with Wellington followed by a glance at Carl. Carl stared directly back at the lawman.

"You have identification?" the state trooper asked Carl.

Carl knew by that time his name was in the hands of all law enforcement nationwide as a fugitive from justice in New York City." His mind pictured Laurel. How close he had come to returning to her.

Matthew Ellis sat in the New York City Public Library at Fifth Avenue and Forty Second Street. He was in the reference section searching for any information on Lida Petropoulos or LPAmerica. It just didn't make sense that there would be no records of her or her business. He looked through volume after volume of every business and personal record he could think of. Frustration gnawed at him but an overwhelming desire to know drove him. Hours had passed and nothing.

"OK, all of you, out of the car," the state trooper ordered.

Slowly, the three travelers climbed out of the Ford Econoline van. They stood on the passenger side of the van while the police officer looked accusingly inside. Fetch growled. "This dog bites me and I'll shoot his ass."

"Let me take her out," Ritchie offered.

The patrolman turned and faced the group, "So, where are the drugs, hippie?"

Before Ritchie could protest, Wellington spoke up as he offered his military identification card, "Officer, I'm Lance Corporal Wellington Marsh United States Marines. These two are my friends who were kind enough to pick me up in Duluth and are taking me home to Detroit to visit my parents before I'm deployed to Vietnam." The state trooper took Wellington's ID and examined it. Wellington added, "In fact, both of these guys are scheduled to report for basic training in the next two weeks."

The officer abruptly looked up, then at Carl, then Ritchie and said, "Oh, Alice is going to get sheared?"

"High and tight," Wellington smiled.

The patrolman laughed.

"They may be sick, lame, and lazy but after day one they'll be squared away," Wellington added. He pointed at Carl and said, "This one volunteered," then at Ritchie, "this one volun-told."

"I can believe that." In a friendlier voice he asked Wellington, "When do you deploy?"

"I report back 21 September and transport immediately."

"My brother's there. Stay alert and keep your head down." He spoke to the group, "OK, you can go. Watch your speed and drive carefully."

When they got back in the van and the patrol car left Carl asked, "What the fuck was that?"

"A little hippie harassment," Ritchie replied. He addressed Wellington over his shoulder, "Nice touch saying we were entering the military."

"It was all I could think of at the time."

Carl stated, "Well it worked." He thought of how close he had just come to being arrested and returned to New York. A shiver passed through his body.

Matt sat at a wooden table in the library. His hands shook as he looked at the page in the reference book—LPAmerica, there it was in black and white—reality!

56: Sunday – August 31, 1969

Wellington Marsh lived in a small brick ranch house in the Cambridge Village neighborhood in Southfield, Michigan. The family had moved there the year before Wellington graduated from high school. Just after dark the previous night the Ford Econoline van had pulled into the driveway. Peter and Judith Marsh, Wellington's parents, were surprised, yet overjoyed that their son was home. He had neglected to tell them the exact time when training would be complete, therefore no explanation for the time lag was necessary. Wellington's parents enjoyed meeting his two friends and all five had an enjoyable evening of conversation. Nothing was said about Canada or the tragedy in the woods. Ritchie slept in the guest room and Carl slept on the couch. Carl always hated that rock, paper, scissors game.

After thanking Wellington's parents the three young men moved outside. As they stood next to the van, Ritchie said, "Take care of yourself, ya hear?"

"I'll do my best."

"You have my address—write me."

"I'll try."

Carl spoke, "Sergeant, thanks for pulling our bacon out of the fire with that cop."

Wellington nodded, "Lance Corporal."

"Thanks for backing me in that fight."

Wellington nodded, once more.

"And, thanks for helping save that little girl."

Wellington looked down and shook his head demonstrating continued disappointment that they couldn't do more.

"I don't have many people I trust or call friends, but I consider you one of my best friends," he offered his hand.

Wellington shook hands with Carl.

Carl said with all sincerity, "Don't do anything stupid. Get back home safe."

The ride back to Lark's Run began in silence. When emotions are involved men retreat into the safety of their id. Carl's focus was on Laurel. How he wanted to hold her and never let go. How he wanted to express his love without sounding wimpy. How he longed for life in the quiet refuge of Lark's Run. How the hell was he going to confess his crimes? Ritchie kept his eyes on the road. For some odd reason his thoughts were about his father. At least his old man wouldn't be disappointed in him again for running away. He'd report for his physical, get drafted, go through basic training, and die in Vietnam. At least his father wouldn't be disappointed. The World Trade Center buildings slipped into his mind. Maybe he could do a little more work on his art project before being dragged away kicking and screaming.

"Hey, Alice, why don't you push your hair up under your hat so we don't get pulled over again?" Carl suddenly said.

"Fuck you, I'm going to wear my hair the way I want, proudly man. Screw'em."

"Yeah, I get it. You're right. Screw'em."

By mid-afternoon the dark blue 1966 Ford Econoline van made its way up the winding gravel road that led into the woods. At the wooden gate they once more noted the empty barrel and sign that read; "Deposit your anger in the barrel and open your heart as you open this gate." They drove up the gravel road and around a bend in a wooded mountainside until they arrived at the old 1800s vintage farm house.

"Last stop—Lark's Run, everybody exit the vehicle," Ritchie announced sounding like a train conductor.

Carl laughed and Fetch barked.

No one met them, as all were out doing their assorted chores. Carl looked around and inhaled deeply enjoying the many fragrances. He was home—if only until they threw him out after hearing the truth about him. "I do love this place," he said to no one in particular.

"So, you're staying here?" Ritchie semi-asked, stating the obvious.

"Time will tell," was Carl's somewhat somber response.

They began walking toward the farm house when they heard a male voice stating with authority, "You can't park there! I'll have the damn thing towed away."

Ritchie turned recognizing Nick's voice and smiled.

"What happened," Nick asked, "you couldn't find Canada?"

"It's a long story, but Canada is no longer an option," Ritchie said.

"You can tell us at dinner." Nick looked at Carl and said, "She's with the bees."

"Of course, had to be the bees," Carl complained. He looked in the direction of the hives trying to decide his next move. A decision made he reached into his bag and retrieved the tiara. Without saying a word he walked slowly in the direction of his fear.

Nick commented in a low voice, "I could have offered him some smoke."

"No need. He gave a gift to the Witch Tree."

"You do have some stories to tell, I see." Nick looked around and asked, "Where'd you leave the Marine?"

"He's at home in Detroit."

Carl came to the edge of the clearing and stopped. Twenty yards away was what he desired most. Twenty yards away was the one thing in the world that was pure and good. Twenty yards away was his last chance for happiness. Twenty yards away was buzzing death.

Ever so soft, Carl heard Laurel's song. It soothed him, it intoxicated him, it called to him. Carl left the shelter of the woods and walked slowly toward the bee hives and his heart's desire. A bee buzzed around his ear, but he could only hear Laurel's song. Step by step he approached her. His focus was on her gently swaying red hair and soft ethereal mesmerizing movement. As he drew near from behind he was concerned that startling her would initiate a bee stampede. A stampede that would most definitely engulf him. He was about to speak when Laurel, without changing the beat or tone, sang, "A brave knight bearing gifts, I presume." She slowly turned and faced him. She continued singing, "It's better that we move to a quieter place." Together, they left the hives and walked into the woods.

Rocky Marciano retired as the undefeated Heavyweight Champion of the World on April 27, 1956 at the age of 32. He finished his career 49-0. After retiring he was an actor, television host, sports commentator, and businessman. He was a partner in a San Francisco based franchise business named Papa Luigi Spaghetti Dens.

On this evening Rocky Marciano boarded a privately-owned 1967 single engine

Cessna 172 at Midway Airport in Chicago for a short flight to Des Moines, Iowa. He intended to go to Des Moines for a few hours and then return to Chicago to catch a commercial flight to Fort Lauderdale. It was important for him to return home in time for his birthday party the next day planned by his 16-year-old daughter Mary Ann.

Rocky was going to Des Moines as a favor to Frankie Farrell and his father to make an appearance at ringside at the fight of a young fighter they had an interest in. Marciano didn't know that a surprise birthday party was waiting at the Charcoal Room steakhouse in Des Moines.

The 334 mile flight was expected to take approximately two and a half hours. Frankie Farrell, 28, was in the back of the four seat aircraft. He was the oldest son of Marciano's childhood friend Lew Farrell, also a former boxer. The pilot Glenn Belz, 37, president of a Des Moines construction company was relatively inexperienced with only 231 total flying hours time of which 35 hours were at night. They took off at 6:00 p.m.

At dinner Carl and Ritchie told their tale of meeting Chief Michael, visiting the Witch Tree, and saving the young girl. Silence hung over the table as they told of their failed efforts to save the young boy. Carl finally said in an uncharacteristically soft voice, "His name was Robert Six Trees."

After dinner Carl asked to speak privately with Nick. They walked out onto the porch and Carl told Nick of his interest in joining the group at Lark's Run but had to first tell something about himself. He stated that he didn't want to bring any trouble to the farm.

Nick held up his hand and asked, "Do you plan to do anything illegal or harmful to Lark's Run if you join us?"

"Absolutely not."

"Then whatever you are running away from is of no interest to me."

"But, it's important."

"Carl the man who risked his life to save a child and who so cared about the one lost is welcome here."

"But . . ."

"A man who worked as hard as you did when you were here is a value."

"I . . ."

"Any man who likes my beer shows good taste."

"Nick . . ."

"Laurel has taken a liking to you and she is a good judge of character."

"She is my next conversation—one that I fear most."

"You don't have to lay bare your soul."

"I do. She has to know who I am, what I was, what I am guilty of. And, in the end, if she wishes me to leave, I will," Carl looked down thinking of that possibility.

Nick walked over and put his hand on Carl's shoulder, "Carl, you've got a lot to learn about Lark's Run and people. I can't speak for Laurel, but as far as I'm concerned you are welcome here. You have to do what you feel is best. I'll send Laurel out." Nick disappeared into the farmhouse.

An hour and a half into the flight Glenn Belz started having engine trouble. An intermittent spark caused the engine to sputter and almost cease running. To add to their problems a storm system was building in the distance. They could see flashes of lightning and a cloud cover already obscured the ground. At 8:50 p.m. the pilot contacted Des Moines Radar Approach Control to request radar assistance. He told his passengers that he intended to land at Newton Airport which was 35 miles east of Des Moines to avoid the storm and refuel. A faulty wire again caused the engine to sputter and the aircraft lost altitude. This caused them to break out of the clouds and see the ground. With renewed confidence Belz headed toward the airport.

Approximately, one and a half miles from the airport, Coleen Schwartz in her farm home heard an airplane flying low. She looked out of her window and saw the Cessna that seemed to be trying to climb, the engine increased speed, sputtered, stopped, sputtered, and quit. The plane came down in a corn field hitting a lone oak tree, skidding for about 235 feet, and coming to rest near a drainage ditch. Upon impact the wings were torn from the aircraft and the motor from the fuselage. Glenn Belz and Frankie Farrell were thrown clear of the plane, while Rocky Marciano remained belted in his seat. All three died instantly.

Eventually, the National Transportation Safety Board report would say, "The pilot attempted operation exceeding his experience and ability level, continued visual flight rules under adverse weather conditions, and experienced spatial disorientation in the last moments of the flight." The shorting wire would go undetected.

Laurel walked barefoot out onto the porch. She wore a white smocked waist peasant dress with capped sleeves. Waist-length dark red hair hung straight down her back. Her expression was one of curiosity.

Carl's first instinct was to run up to her and hug her and hold her close but he knew better than that. He was about to lay bare his crimes and sordid past to this pure, innocent, unblemished creature. His expectation was that she would listen, stare at him with contempt, and go back into the house not wanting to be near him ever again. The words he was about to speak would be the provocation. He knew by comparison he was untreated sewage to her clean mountain spring and when the truth was known she would view him quite differently. A part of him wanted to heed what Nick said and not bare his soul. Yet, something inside him made that impossible. If anyone in this crazy twisted world deserved honesty it was Laurel. Carl thought, if this were New York City in a bar I would tell her whatever it took to get her. Only, here in this place with this person New York City didn't exist. She was unlike anyone he had ever known. If he knew what love was this was probably it.

Tentatively, he began, "Laurel, I asked Nick if I could stay at Lark's Run." She smiled. "Wait! He said I could, but I will only stay if, after you hear what I have to say, you wish me to."

Laurel walked over to one of the wooden chairs and sat. Dark green eyes looked up at Carl.

Carl walked over but remained standing. "I'm not a very nice person," he began.

Laurel tilted her head slightly without saying a word. She waited for an explanation.

"Back in New York I was a thug, a criminal, a bad seed."

Laurel sat motionless.

"I stole, and beat people up, and got involved with organized crime."

Laurel waited.

"I'm on the run—a wanted man. I killed someone."

Lauren raised her eyebrows, but remained silent.

"When I met you I discovered that the world is not simply a jungle with survival of the fittest. For the first time I saw beauty in the world, in life, and in a human being. It made me aware of the ugliness that was my life. I can't deny what I was. But, I can say it is not what I wish to continue to be. I wish I were a good man who could declare his love for you and offer you something of value—something you deserve." Carl realized that he just told Laurel that he loved her. He became embarrassed and lost his train of thought. He turned and walked to the edge of the porch. Without looking back he said, "I won't stay at Lark's Run if my presence here bothers you, or if you fear me, or if you no longer see any good in me. I'll return to New York to face the music. But, not to return to the life I led before meeting you."

Laurel spoke in a soft voice, "Why did you kill?"

"I didn't intend to do it. He was going to do terrible things to me. I had to fight back to stop him," Carl replied still looking out into the night.

"Was he also a criminal?"

"He was a very bad man."

"Do you plan to kill again?"

This time Carl turned and looked into Laurel's eyes, "Nothing can change what I did. And, in truth, if I was in the same position of having to defend myself, I would fight back. It is not my wish to kill. That night it was the farthest thing from my mind. But, with a gun pointed at me and my life at risk I had no alternative." Carl paused. He looked around and then with a tear in his eye looked back at Laurel and confessed, "The child we couldn't save up north haunts me. If saving him had cost my life it would have been a bargain. Maybe, my redemption."

Laurel rose and walked into the farmhouse.

Carl stood alone on the porch. His emotions were raw as he had an overwhelming sense of loss. He decided to return to New York with Ritchie. His mind concluded that Miguel had won, after all. Without knowing it, he had inflicted in Carl the worst of all pain. In defeat, Carl walked over and sat on the wooden steps leading from the porch.

An owl hooted in the woods.

Laurel walked out of the house carrying brown sandals. She sat next to Carl and put them on. As she rose she said, "Come with me," and led him down the path away from the house. Carl followed as they walked down the gravel road toward the entrance of Lark's Run. His addled brain wondered if she was showing him the road and telling him to leave. They got to the gate and Laurel opened it. Much like an automaton Carl followed. He was prepared to go where she led him. What was it Chief Michael had said? "You seek your destiny in the wrong direction." Canada was the wrong direction. Is New York the right direction?

Laurel stopped outside the gate. Her features were enchanting in the moonlight. A slight breeze caused her hair to dance seductively. The light caught her eyes causing them to sparkle. Her body, though covered by a full-length dress, was caressed by the soft material. An aroma of flowers surrounded him. Carl never wanted her more. The pain of losing her intensified. He wanted to scream but stood in silence. Laurel spoke, "Who is standing at the gate, the man I have known or the criminal from New York?"

"The criminal from New York is no more," Carl said softly.

She patted the empty barrel and pointed at the sign on the fence that read, "Deposit your anger in the barrel and open your heart as you open this gate." Laurel then asked, "Is there anger in your heart?"

"I can't be angry anymore."

"Can you be happy on the other side of this gate?"

"I've never known such peace as I found in Lark's Run."

"And, happiness?"

"Yes, happiness—happiness I never knew existed. And love."

"You love me?"

After a long pause, Carl attempted an answer, "Laurel, just saying your name brings out feelings foreign to me. When I see you I want to run to you and hold you. Everything about you excites me. I want to be with you and a part of your life and for you to be a part of my life. When we headed to Canada all I thought about was you. Now, if you tell me to leave—I will. If you allow me to stay I will prove to you that I love you and that you can always trust and depend on me."

Laurel walked to the side of the road and picked up a round stone. With a marker she wrote upon the stone, "criminal Carl." She handed it to Carl and said, "Throw it as far away from Lark's Run as you can.

Carl examined the rock and walked down the path. When he came to a ravine he threw the stone as far as his strength would allow.

Laurel stood at his side and smiled. In a different and more inviting tone she said, "I believe you have something of mine."

In the moonlight, Carl reached into his pocket and took out the tiara. He kissed it and gently placed it on her head.

57: Monday – September 1, 1969

At five in the morning the residents of Lark's Run sat around the large wooden table eating breakfast. This time Ritchie joined them, rather than remaining in bed. The day promised to be sunny and warm. It would be a pleasant drive back to New York. Everyone at the table appeared to be in good spirits as bacon and eggs and biscuits were passed and coffee poured.

Nick picked up his coffee cup and said, "I would like to welcome our newest member, Carl Pith-something, to Lark's Run. He will take over tending the bee hives."

Carl choked on a piece of bacon.

Nick looked over at the stricken young man, smiled, and concluded, "Well, maybe it's too soon. I'm sure there are other tasks that would be better suited to your talents. We have some serious need for fence mending." He turned his attention to Ritchie and said, "And, a safe trip Rich back to the big city. Sorry we don't have a witch tree but you can give a gift to one of the witches at the table. Maybe that will protect you from tight-ass traffic cops." A piece of biscuit hit Nick on the side of his head.

"Thanks," Ritchie replied. He handed Fetch a piece of bacon and added, "I have a favor to ask." With everyone's attention, Ritchie said, "Where I'm headed will not be conducive to keeping a dog and my parents surely wouldn't take her in while I'm away so I would appreciate it if Fetch could stay at Lark's Run." Fetch looked up at Ritchie upon hearing her name.

"Of course," Nick said, "Does she like beer?"

Ritchie patted Fetch on the head and looked into her big brown innocent eyes and realized how attached he had become to the little lost critter. His mind reflected another set of innocent eyes as a child drifted away out of reach. Emotions tugged at him. At least this time, he thought, he was leaving those eyes in a better and safer place. He looked at the black basenji watching his every move and said, "You'll be happy here. Plenty of food, squirrels to chase, people who care, warm beds." Fetch put her head on his leg still looking up. "You can't go where I'm going." He then spoke to Nick, "I'd keep her on her leash when I leave until she gets comfortable here."

Laurel answered, "We'll make her feel at home."

"It will be nice having her around," Carl added.

After breakfast the members of Lark's Run prepared for their day's work. Nick, Ritchie, and Carl stood outside his blue van. Nick and Ritchie hugged and Nick said, "Use your head and stay safe."

Carl shook Ritchie's hand and said, "It was good traveling with you. What we shared will always make us brothers. I'll look forward to when you come back to Lark's Run." He brushed Ritchie's long hair with the back of his hand and added, "Of course, I probably won't recognize you."

Ritchie replied with a smile, "By then, it will have grown back."

"Yeah, well, on you it looks good." Carl started to turn then thought of something and returned his attention to Ritchie and asked, "By the way, when that cop stopped us and asked where you had the drugs. Where was your stash?"

"You see those curtains?" Ritchie pointed at the van window. "Guess what they're made of."

"Oh that's sneaky. Hidden in plain sight," Carl gave Ritchie a thumbs up, turned, and left.

Through a window in the farm house Fetch watched the blue van disappear down the road.

Detective Ryoya Akimoto spoke on the telephone with Sergeant Madden who was the Investigative Supervisor of their squad. "We feel pretty good about one Carl Pythacyk but without interviewing him I'm not ready to close the case." She listened, then replied, "I realize Lieutenant Parissi is on your back but with the suspect in the wind . . ." She listened, once more having been interrupted. "We're following the few small leads we have as to possible locations where he might be." Another interruption. "I think he's no longer in the state." More diatribe. "This guy was a loner. We don't have a long list of acquaintances to point us in the right direction." She held the phone away from her ear and looked at her partner, Detective Michael Donovan, and mouthed the words, "pain in the ass." Into the telephone she said, "If you could assign a few patrol officers." A response. "I didn't think so." More blather. "By end of week? Close the case?" Blah, blah, blah. "How are the wife and kids, Sarge? Hell-o?" Ryoya put the receiver in its cradle.

"Does he know that today is a holiday?" Michael Donovan asked.

"Does he care?"

"So, he wants us to close the case by Friday without a suspect in custody."

"Those are the orders from on high."

"If I shoot him will you swear it was an accidental discharge?"

"I'll swear it was a suicide."

"What's our next step?"

"Let's hit the parents, again. See if there are any distant relatives out-of-state who Carl might have decided to visit."

Half a world away evening fell over Libya. The son of an impoverished Bedouin goat herder, Muammar Muhammad Abu Minyar al-Gaddafi, led a bloodless coup d'etat and replaced King Idris as the leader of the nation. Idris had gone to Turkey for medical treatment allowing a group of Libyan Army officers under the leadership of Gaddafi to initiate "Operation Jerusalem." Gaddafi's "Free Officers" occupied airports, police stations, military barracks, anti-aircraft batteries, radio stations, and government offices in Tripoli and Benghazi. They arrested crown prince Sayyid Hasan ar-Rida al-Mahdi as-Sanussi, and forced him to relinquish his claim to the throne. The monarchy was abolished and Muammar Gaddafi became the Revolutionary Chairman of the Libyan Arab Republic. He proclaimed that the revolution meant "freedom, socialism, and unity."

Muammar Gaddafi was born in a tent in the deserts of western Libya. His parents were nomadic Bedouins and illiterate, therefore, there were no birth records. It is believed that he was born in 1942 or 1943. When he was eight or nine-years-old, in 1951, the United Nations created the United Kingdom of Libya under the leadership of the pro-western monarch, King Idris.

Unlike his parents, Gaddafi attended school and even spent a short period of time studying history at the University of Libya in Benghazi, before dropping out to join the military. He hated the presence of the British military even though they trained Libya's armed forces under Idris. Gaddafi was rude to British officers and sighted for insubordination numerous times. They even accused him of being involved in the assassination of the military academy's commander in 1963. By 1964, Gaddafi founded the Central Committee of the Free Officers Movement as a clandestine revolutionary group. He traveled around Libya enlisting sympathizers and gathering intelligence but the government never considered him a threat.

Gaddafi admired President Gamal Abdel Nasser of the Arab Republic of Egypt who supported Arab nationalism, rejection of Western colonialism, and a transition from capitalism to socialism. Nasser's book, *Philosophy of the Revolution,* influenced Gaddafi by outlining how to initiate a coup and was the inspiration for revolution. Colonel, as he called himself, Gaddafi learned his lesson well.

After Matthew Ellis found the listing of LPAmerica in a reference book in the library he was confident that he would eventually discover more facts. Even though a part of him feared the truth he knew for his sanity he had to find it.

Stephanie, his daughter, entered the apartment hauling an obviously heavy suitcase. She placed it just inside the door with a huff.

"What's that?" Matt asked.

"Last week when Ritchie left I had to take this and a couple boxes of papers out of his apartment. I stored them there because there isn't much room in this apartment. They've been in the trunk of my car."

Matt showed increased interest, "What kind of papers?"

"I don't know." Stephanie admitted. "Each time we moved we filled boxes with assorted documents and other papers and took them with us. After mom died, I continued the practice."

"I'd like to look through those papers." Matt asked, "You say there are more boxes in your trunk?"

Ritchie drove east on Route 80 in New Jersey. He slowed when he passed the location where he saved a lost basenji. Fetch stared at him through the windshield and he missed her a lot more than he thought he would. How easy it had been to become attached to that uninhibited, unpredictable, beautiful, crazy canine. Here was another reason why getting cashiered into the military pissed him off. He and Fetch were a team, a family, and the man was tearing—had torn—them apart. A sharp pain in the middle of Ritchie's back caused him to grimace and call out.

It was mid-afternoon when Ritchie pulled into the driveway of the large Victorian house he once called home. Suddenly, he had an odd feeling of being a stranger—a visitor. The last time he visited the atmosphere had been cool and uncomfortable. He and his parents found little to talk about and he left after only a short period of time.

How he was going to break the news about being drafted and needing a place to live until then he didn't know. From inside the van he examined the house and yard. Well-kept and immaculate were the terms that came to mind. His parents lived an orderly life which was probably why they were ill-equipped to deal with an iconoclastic and rebellious son. In turn, he was unprepared for their harsh criticism and severe judgement. It ended with an uncomfortable truce. Ritchie was certain that his father would welcome the news about his impending military service. "It will make a man out of you," the old man would declare. The old bastard would rather see him dead in a rice paddy than walking around town with long hair. His mother would simply repeat what she said in the past, "What will people think?" Anger clouded his thinking and he considered going to his friend Toby's house and requesting temporary shelter. Fortunately, Chief Michael's words spoke to Ritchie, ". . . you run away scared. It will not bring you peace. Fear drives you away from never toward a destination." Ritchie shut off the van and got out.

His mother answered the door. When she saw Ritchie her face lit up and she called out his name. After hugging they walked through the house into the kitchen. "Are you hungry?" his mother asked.

"I could eat."

"I'll make you a sandwich."

"That will be fine."

In silence, his mother made a sandwich and Ritchie sat trying to figure out where to begin. When she placed the plate in front of her son she said, "What's the matter, Richard? You look worried."

"I'm more tired than anything else, but I do need to ask you and dad something."

"What is it?"

"I'd rather talk with both of you together. When will he be home?"

"You know your father, there's no predicting when he will get home." She paused and thought for a moment and then offered, "Today is a holiday. He just ran out to the store." In a different tone she asked, "How's your little girlfriend?"

"I'm not really sure," Ritchie responded, "I haven't seen her in a while."

After twenty minutes the front door opened and Nathan Anderson entered the house. "I see a familiar vehicle in the driveway," he announced cheerfully. "To what do we owe this pleasant surprise?" He walked through the house into the kitchen.

"Richard has something that he wishes to speak to us about," his mother announced.

"Oh," Nathan Anderson sat at the table, "What's on your mind?"

Ritchie said, "I have a lot to say so if you let me get through it that would probably be best and avoid a lot of questions." His parents looked at each other but remained silent. "I just got back from a trip," Ritchie told his parents that he had been reclassified as 1A by the Selective Service and the tale of his journey to the Canadian border and back. When he described the rescue and tragedy on the washout his mother exclaimed, "Oh, my." Ritchie finished by telling his parents that he had his mail forwarded to their house because he had no idea where he would end up living. At that point his father rose and left the room. Ritchie and his mother sat in silence. In a minute his father returned carrying a tan envelope. The return address read: Selective Service, Official Business, If not delivered in 5 days return to, and a stamp in a box read: Local Board No. 36, 744 Broad Street, Newark, NJ 07102.

"This came last week," his father said. "I know what it is. When I tried to call and your telephone was disconnected I had an idea where you were headed."

"Well, I'm glad I didn't disappoint you," Ritchie remarked.

His father ignored the sarcasm and asked, "What do you plan to do?"

"First, open the letter, then follow the instructions."

Nathan Anderson nodded and handed his son the letter.

It was an Order To Report For Armed Forces Physical Examination. It read, you are hereby directed to present yourself for Armed Forces Physical Examination by reporting at: Assembly Room, 10th Floor, 744 Broad Street, Newark, NJ 07102 on September 15, 1969 at 7 A.M. He carefully read the paragraphs below the instructions with all the requirements, legalese, and threats. Slowly he put the notice down on the table. Ritchie considered getting back in his van and heading north but a child's eyes haunted him. In his heart, he knew there was no more running left in him.

In a dreamlike state he heard his father say in a low voice to his mother, "It will make a man out of him."

Jack Moore took a bite of his roast beef on a soft roll followed by a sip of a draft beer. "I don't know where McCann's gets its meat but nothing beats it."

"This was a good idea," Ryoya admitted.

"You have to eat."

The police detective nibbled at her sandwich. A visit to Carl Pythacyk's parents proved worthless. They hadn't heard from him and the few relatives and friends where he might seek refuge were all in New York City and hadn't seen or heard from the young man. In addition, the nationwide fugitive alert turned up nothing. Carl Pythacyk had disappeared.

"You're lost in thought," Jack observed.

"I have this case—pretty open and shut—but the suspect is at large and I'm running out of ideas of where to look."

"It's a big country."

"I hate loose ends. I'll have to close the case with suspect outstanding," Ryoya picked up a pickle, looked at it, placed it back on the plate. Thinking out loud she said, "He had a connection with Don Spacini but I think it was ancillary. The murder was definitely not a mob hit—too sloppy. Besides, he had history with the victim."

"What's the suspect's name?"

"Why?"

"I have contacts in low places. I'll be happy to make a few inquiries."

"You don't have to do that. It's my job."

"It's not any trouble."

Ryoya thought for a moment than decided it couldn't hurt so she said, "His name is Carl Pythacyk and the victim was Miguel Juarez, a pimp."

Jack wrote down the names and said, "I'll check into it." He then changed the subject, "How'd you like to go to a movie some night this week?"

"That sounds like fun. Do you have any movie in mind?"

"There's a western, *Butch Cassidy and the Sundance Kid* with Paul Newman and Robert Redford just been released. You pick the night. I'm flexible."

"OK, but I'll have to let you know." It was Ryoya's turn to change the subject, "Are you going to get Colt and that girl together?"

"I'm working on it. My only concern is Colt could put a scare into her—damage her for life."

Ryoya laughed which Jack welcomed. "Maybe, he'll be on his good behavior. Tell him to act like a waiter in a French restaurant."

"He might do that—literally."

"He is unpredictable. I must admit, I will miss him when he returns to Texas."

"Something tells me that we will stay in touch," Jack reassured her.

After a short span of silence with each eating their sandwich, Jack asked, "Have you seen those new potato chips that come in a can? I think they're called Jingles or something like that."

"Pringles. They are made from potatoes but I don't think they can be called potato chips. I have some at home. You're welcome to try them," Ryoya's smile said all that Jack needed to hear.

58: Tuesday – September 2, 1969

Twenty-three miles east of New York City, Rockville Centre was considered a bedroom community for commuters riding the Long Island Railroad. The quiet village had a total area of 3.4 square miles and population under 20,000. Yet, on this morning Rockville Centre made history.

All newspapers with significant circulation in Nassau County, New York carried an ad for Chemical Bank with the headline, "On Sept. 2, our bank will open at 9:00 and never close again!" It referred to the introduction of the first Automatic Teller Machine (ATM) in America at its Rockville Centre branch.

The nondescript metal machine was installed in a wall at the bank. It was invented by Don Wetzel, an executive at Docutel, a Dallas company that manufactured automated baggage-handling equipment. He got the idea while standing on line at, of course, a bank. Rather than ATM the machine was called the Docuteller and could only dispense cash. To withdraw cash customers had to insert a magnetically coded card. Because the machine couldn't confirm that enough funds were available to be withdrawn a $150 daily limit was established.

Without really knowing the future impact of this innovation a sleepy village on Long Island woke up to a new era.

Matthew Ellis woke up in the chair that he had been sitting in while going through a mountain of papers. He had started with the suitcase that his daughter had dragged into the apartment. In it he found personal papers for the family including; birth certificates, bank accounts, Stephanie's medical records and school report cards, mortgage statements, diplomas, and his and Valerie's marriage license. He held that document and read it over and over subconsciously wanting to return to that exact moment in time. They were both happy and filled with anticipation as the future lay ahead. Together, they would build a family and live the American dream. It was a glorious time when everything was possible, the world offered so much promise, and most desirable of all his hands were clean.

They didn't have a lot of money when they married so decided to honeymoon for two days at a small hotel on the Jersey shore. It was off-season so rates were low and crowds non-existent. The new Mr. and Mrs. Ellis boarded the New Jersey Southern Railroad in Jersey City. As he recalled the events, Matt clearly saw Valerie in his mind. She wore a dark blue sleeveless casual dress flared below the knee with a lace scoop collar. For two hours they watched New Jersey scenery drift by the window. Two newlyweds spoke of their hopes and dreams and plans for the future. It was 1949, World War II was behind them and America seemed to be coming alive once more. Businesses were being opened, developments promised affordable housing, automobile sales were brisk, help wanted signs popped up like spring wildflowers, postage stamps cost 3 cents, the average annual salary was $3,600, and this new thing called television was spreading across the nation at a rapid pace.

Their train arrived at the Asbury Park Station in the late afternoon. It was a short walk from the station to their small two-story hotel on Ocean Avenue overlooking the ocean.

"Oh, this is so beautiful," Valerie exclaimed.

"It's still not too cold why don't we take a walk on the beach," Matt suggested.

An afternoon breeze brought a slight chill to the air. Matt put his arm around Valerie to warm her. She looked up at her husband and said, "We met in a snowstorm, a breeze doesn't have a chance."

It was a magical time for young lovers. They ate seafood in a small restaurant on the south end of the boardwalk, went to the Grand Arcade between the Paramount Theater and the Convention Hall, rode through the Tunnel of Love, and finally took a quiet walk on the beach in the dark. Waves broke offshore spilling water onto the beach. Valerie played cat and mouse with the water. A crescent moon and lack of city lights made the night sky appear huge filled with glimmering stars. Together they gazed at the tapestry of light. Toward the north was the Big Dipper made up of seven stars—four create a rectangular bowl and three comprise the handle. The brightest star appeared to be the one forming the handle closest to the bowl. Unknown to Matt that star was named Alioth.

"See that star?" Matt asked as he pointed skyward. "The bright one in the Big Dipper."

"That star?"

"Yes." Matt turned and looked at his wife and said, "I'm naming that star Valerie and as long as it is in the heavens I will love you and be faithful."

Two lovers alone on a deserted beach kissed.

Matt still held the marriage license in his hands after spending the night asleep in a chair. The memories he relived the night before remained with him. In the most heartfelt way he missed Valerie. He thought about all the events that followed that night and felt so terribly ashamed.

"One of these days, Jack, you're going to go too far."

"It's the truth."

"The truth can get you in trouble."

"Not from those who respect truth."

"There are those who will take that truth and shove it down your throat in a dark alley and make you choke on it."

"Those aren't honorable men."

"They are business men," a fist pounded the table causing all of the bottles and glasses to bounce and clank against each other. "Jack, you're bad for business."

"That's a matter of perspective. I'm bad for some business."

"You're bad for my business," Don Carmine Spacini glared intensely at the newspaper reporter.

The two men sat across the table from each other in a silent duel of wills. To an observer it would appear that it was only a matter of time before Carmine would make the move to eliminate an itch he couldn't scratch. How difficult would it be to create an accident and "have nothing to do with it?" The standoff continued.

"So, how's Anne doing?" Jack asked.

Carmine sat back. He poured a glass of wine and replied in a friendly and calm voice, "Good—she's doing good."

"I'm glad, she's a sweet kid."

"A sweet kid with an attitude."

"Ah, come'on, look where she comes from."

"Shit," Carmine took a sip of wine, puffed on his cigar, and through a cloud of smoke stated, "She wants to become a goddamn District Attorney when she finishes law school!"

Jack poured a glass of wine for himself. He stared at the deep red liquid in the glass, swirled it around, inhaled the aroma, and took a sip. Over the lip of the glass he glanced at the mob boss. Carmine made no move only stared at Jack. Jack laughed and said, "Then my work is done."

"You poisoned her mind!" Carmine declared.

"I cleansed it."

"You turned her on her family."

"I gave her a chance to have a family."

"You . . ." Carmine paused, looked Jack in the eye, and admitted, "You're one helluva god father."

"I'll take that as a compliment. She is a wonderful and impressive kid. You gave me an honor I can never repay."

"What is truth?" Carmine began.

"Truth is the foundation of trust," Jack followed the lead.

"Truth is all we have."

"Truth is to be shared between friends."

"Truth is a gift."

"Truth is responsibility."

"Truth is yours, my friend, you have my word," Carmine stated.

"Your word is truth as mine is to you—you have my word," Jack replied as he had done countless times before.

The two men stood and embraced each other for the untold thousandth time since they were young boys growing up together in Great Neck, Long Island. Their lives followed distinctly different paths but they remained friends. It was a relationship that wasn't public but was clearly defined. In fact, when they were young men Carmine established the rules in no uncertain terms. They had gotten together on the roof of the apartment building where Jack lived. It was a friendly meeting with a few shared beers, some laughs, and small talk. Out of nowhere a gun appeared in Carmine's hand. The muzzle was pushed into Jack's throat as he was backed against a wall. "Understand this; you come after me with all you got. Leave no stone unturned. Turn a blind eye to nothing. Come after me. Because, if you don't . . ." in a softer almost mournful voice Carmine stated emphatically, "If you don't then I know I'm right and you are wrong and there is no goddamned good in the world. You will be a lie and better off dead. If I give you an opening it's my problem. If you bring me down with your fancy words it's my fault. But if you sellout that's your fault and there's no hope left. And, on that day my friend I will rid the world of lies."

Carmine had power and prestige. He could make captains of industry and political leaders do his bidding. With just a glance he could ignite fear. Yet, he admired Jack and knew he was in all respects a better man.

Numerous times Jack shined the light of truth on the Spacini family. Often, other reporters wondered why Jack Moore was still walking the streets of New York City. What they didn't know was that behind closed doors alone Don Carmine Spacini would read the scathing accusations, smile, and raise his glass as he said, "Saluto!"

Jack got to the reason for his visit to Don Spacini's place of business. "I want to know about a kid who is associated with your organization. His name is Carl Pythacyk."

"Are you asking as a shit-nosed reporter or a friend?"

Jack picked up a bottle of wine and poured an amount into Carmine's glass. It was a symbolic gesture of friendship.

Carmine sipped from the glass and said flatly, "I know of him. Is there something that I should be aware of?"

"Are you asking that as a friend or a cheap crook?" Jack inquired.

Carmine smiled and poured wine into Jack's glass. "He's a bright young man. What's your interest in him?"

"He's wanted for murder only no one seems to know where he is."

"Murder? Who is he accused of killing?"

"A Miguel Juarez."

"That pimp?" Carmine waved his hand, "That punk was a hot head. You know, macho madness. These spics blow into town full of fight and full of shit and think they can take over. They got no respect."

"Do you know where Carl Pythacyk is?"

"If I did I wouldn't tell you, but I can tell you this, Carl Pythacyk wouldn't waste his time on that pimp."

"You know this—how?"

"The kid was earning respect, showing smarts, gaining favor he wouldn't throw that away on a useless murder." In a serious tone Carmine said, "He learned enough to not make a move without permission."

"All the evidence points directly at him."

"Are there any witnesses?"

"No."

"Then it's circumstantial. You know that. He didn't kill that prick. Look someplace else."

"Then why did he run?"

"Who says he ran? Maybe he's on vacation."

Jack sat in silence and considered Carmine Spacini's opinion. Then he asked the question that had to be asked, "Was it a hit?"

Carmine pushed his glass away and called his bodyguards, "Lonnie, Cootch."

Jack and Carmine stood simultaneously. The two large intimidating men who had escorted Jack into the room entered and stood on either side of him. Carmine pulled a one-hundred dollar bill from his pocket, folded it lengthwise, stuffed it into Jack's breast pocket, and stated authoritatively, "There's nothing cheap about me." He turned to his guards and ordered, "Throw this bum out!"

As Jack walked down the street he remembered a conversation that took place a lifetime ago between friends.

"You can't save me. I know what I am—what I've become. I have no illusions about the past or the future."

Jack knew his friend was right. He wanted to say that it's never too late to change, but that would be a lie.

Carmine continued, "You can't save me, but you can save my daughter. Give her what a man in my position can't."

"I don't know," Jack began.

"Today, in her eyes I am perfect. She loves me unconditionally. But, the time will come when she hears things and becomes confused. She will come to a crossroads and I want her to choose the right path—even if it means turning her back on me."

"I can't do that—turn a daughter against her father."

"You have to."

"Why me?"

"Because you are the only human being on the face of the earth that I truly trust."

"Don't put that burden on me."

"I have to. I don't have any other choice."

"I can refuse."

"You won't."

"How do you know?"

"Because you are my friend, know the difference between right and wrong, and know that I am right."

Carl Pythacyk stood at the gate of Lark's Run looking out at the outside world. The adage about the grass always being greener on the other side of the fence came to mind. Before him were the picturesque mountains of western Pennsylvania and the world lay beyond. Indeed, there was plenty of green for comparison. However, in his case the greener pastures were on his side of the fence. Lark's Run had everything he could want and more.

Carl loved Laurel. That was a fact he couldn't escape. Everything about her drew him to her. Her hair, features, voice, view of life, the way she moved, fresh clean scent, even her touch all aroused feelings he didn't know he could experience. It created a pleasant ache. Mentally, he chastised himself, "Buddy, you've got it bad. You used to mock guys who fell prey to the feminine mystique." Only on this occasion he wasn't embarrassed—he was proud. Through some miracle he had unlocked the door to deeper emotions. As a result, he grew as a human being. Or, more accurately, he discovered what it was like to be a human being.

On the other side of that fence 342 miles east was New York City. It was the jungle in which he prowled. It was cold and sterile and unfeeling. In that world he was a predator unaware of anything more important than coming out on top. Now, it all seemed pointless. Ray Esposito, Don Carmine Spacini, and the whole being "in" thing was no longer important.

Carl thought of his parents. His debt to his father had been paid. While his mother might miss him she was better off not having him around. She would miss him just as much if he were in prison. No question Lark's Run was preferable.

Carl turned and began to walk back toward the farmhouse. As he did he made a decision. He would do all that he could to earn Laurel's love but if she ever wished that he leave her alone he would do so without complaint. He cared deeply enough to not wish to upset or hurt her.

A noise caused him to look up the path. Laurel wearing her white peasant dress was walking in his direction. He picked up his pace.

"I was looking for you," Laurel said as she drew near.

"I was down at the gate," Carl replied.

"You're not having second thoughts, are you?"

"Absolutely not."

"I'm glad," Laurel took Carl's hand and they walked back toward the farmhouse together, "I would miss you."

Jack dialed the telephone number of the Midtown North precinct. After talking with the operator he was connected to Detective Akimoto's desk.

"Detective Akimoto."

"Ryoya, Jack."

"Jack, how are you?"

"I'm fine. Listen, I have some information you might be able to use. My source doesn't believe that Carl Pythacyk killed Miguel Juarez."

"Based on what? Can he provide an alibi?"

"No, but he has knowledge about the guy and stated emphatically that it couldn't have happened."

"What kind of knowledge?"

"I can't say."

"Come on Jack, help me out here. You tell me the suspect who left clues all over the crime scene didn't do it but you have no proof what-so-ever."

"I know, it's real thin. However, my source is in a position to know things. I'm not trying to screw up your case. All I can tell you is there are missing pieces to this particular puzzle."

"Jack, I appreciate you making inquiries but this case will be closed on Friday and I have no valid reason to keep it open."

"I understand, sorry I couldn't get anything more concrete for you as to the kid's whereabouts."

"You tried—that's enough," Ryoya said, "Movies tomorrow night?"

"Works for me. I'll let you know the show times."

"You bring the Pringles."

59: Wednesday – September 3, 1969

Detective Ryoya Akimoto sat at her desk in the squad room of the Midtown North Precinct and thought about her conversation with Jack the night before. Could they have missed something? Was there any evidence that could raise even the slightest degree of reasonable doubt? She did the only thing any good detective would do. Remove all evidence that points toward Carl Pythacyk and then approach the case as if none of it exists.

A dead body identified as Miguel Juarez was found in an alley on West 44th Street with his throat cut. Multiple bruises and lacerations on the body indicated a struggle. Swelling on the back of the head and accompanying concussion could have been inflicted by a blunt object or as a result of falling against a brick wall or on cement. The victim might have been unconscious at the time of the murder. A knife that subsequently was found to be the murder weapon was found near the body. Wound across the throat ran from his left to right which meant that the assailant was most likely right handed. Pieces of rope were found near a railing along the top of a flight of cement stairs leading down to a basement storage room. The door was locked. No witnesses. Victim bled out and died. Coroner put the time of death at between 11:00 p.m. and midnight. No car antenna was found at the scene. Ryoya smiled at that thought. Last person to see the victim alive was one Claire Payton a prostitute. Miguel Juarez was her pimp. She had seen the victim in front of the New Haven Hotel on West 44th Street shortly before eleven. She had recently been beaten and had her hair cut by the victim. Ryoya sat back. "That would be motive," she said softly. "And, we have opportunity."

"What's that?" Detective Michael Donovan asked from his desk.

"I'm thinking about the Juarez case."

"Oh, how so?"

"Now, go with me on this," Ryoya requested. She then explained, "Jack had a contact that emphatically stated that Carl Pythacyk couldn't have done it."

"Did they provide an alibi?"

"No."

"Were they a witness?"

"No."

"Did Pythacyk tell them that he didn't do it?"

"No."

"Who was Jack's contact?"

"I don't know."

"Well, then I guess Carl Pythacyk didn't do it."

"Don't be an ass." Ryoya explained, "I've been reexamining the facts leaving out all that incriminate Carl Pythacyk. This way if we overlooked something it might become clearer."

"So, what have you got?"

"Nothing."

"That's promising."

"Nothing concrete."

"That sounds solid."

"Cut that out," Ryoya warned. "If all the evidence didn't point to Carl 'The Missing' what would we have?"

"My antenna theory."

"No. The missing blond blue-eyed young girl being protected by Claire Payton."

"Why?"

"She was held hostage by Juarez, forced into prostitution, hated him, and was desperate. Remember her unsent note to her parents?" Detective Akimoto said.

"She did run away. We only have a lying prostitute's word that the kid went home. However, we still can't discount all the evidence that implicates Pythacyk."

"Consider this; the murder weapon was left at the crime scene. That is not the M.O. of a seasoned criminal. It's the sloppiness that's more common with an emotional act. And, where is the gun? That is if he had a gun. He did have cartridges."

"Then who beat him up?" Michael Donovan asked.

"Carl beat him up and left him unconscious. Blondie comes along and in a rash impulsive act finishes Mr. Juarez off. Then she hightails it out of town."

"You know," Detective Donovan admitted, "That is reasonable doubt."

Ryoya stood and slipped her detective special 38 caliber service revolver into her holster, "We need to visit Claire Payton, once more, and get that kid's name and whereabouts."

North Vietnamese officials announced on this day the death of Ho Chí Minh the previous day at 9:47 in the morning Vietnam time from heart failure at his home in Hanoi at the age of 79. They withheld news of the death of the president for a day because he died on the anniversary of the founding of the Democratic Republic of Vietnam (North Vietnam).

Born Nguyen Sinh Cung in 1890, he was the son of a Confucian scholar and teacher who became an imperial magistrate in a small remote Vietnamese district. His father was later demoted following an incident where a man died a few days after receiving 102 cane strokes as punishment for breaking a law. He later resigned purportedly in protest against French domination of his country.

As is a common practice in Confucian tradition when Cung reached the age of 10, his father gave him a new name: Nguyen Tat Thành ("Nguyen the Accomplished"). At the age of 21 the young man signed on as a kitchen helper on the French steamer Amirale de Latouche-Tréville using the alias "Văn Ba."

Nguyen Tat Thành traveled the world and even claimed to have lived and worked in New York City for a period of time. While living in France between 1919 and 1923 he was influenced by Marcel Cachin, a member of the Socialist Party of France. He also joined a group of Vietnamese nationalists in Paris that published newspaper articles advocating Vietnamese independence.

In 1923 he journeyed to Moscow using a passport with the name Chen Vang, a Chinese merchant. He studied at the Communist University of the Toilers of the East and in 1924 moved to Canton, China using the name Ly Thuy. There he gave lectures on socialism to young Vietnamese living in Canton at the Whampoa Military Academy. Thus, he planted the seeds of communism in Vietnam.

He married a Chinese woman named Zeng Xueming telling his friends, "I will get married despite your disapproval because I need a woman to teach me the language and keep house."

Around 1940, he began regularly using the name Ho Chí Minh. It was a combination of the common Vietnamese surname Ho with Chí meaning "spirit" and Minh meaning "bright." He returned to Vietnam that year to lead the Viet Minh independence movement. The guerrilla force initiated military actions against the French and, during World War II, the occupying Japanese. During the war his forces were supported by the United States Office of Strategic Services. After the war in August of 1945 the Viet Minh organized a revolution, convinced Emperor Bao Đai to abdicate his throne, proclaimed independence of the Democratic Republic of Vietnam, and made Ho Chi Minh provisional chairman of the new government. To their surprise the new government was not recognized by any nation.

Ho Chi Minh's socialist government ruled through brutal intimidation, by purging all rivals, imprisonment, and execution. In fact, the Viet Minh collaborated with French colonial forces to massacre supporters of the Vietnamese nationalist movements. Then, once the communists secured complete control, they declared war against the French Union on December 19, 1946 commencing the Indochina War.

Four years later, February, 1950, Ho Chi Minh met with Joseph Stalin and Mao Zedong in Moscow. At that meeting it was agreed that China would be responsible for providing training and material support of the Viet Minh. Given this support the Viet Minh were able to continue the war. It is estimated that the Viet Minh assassinated between 100,000 and 150,000 civilians during the war.

The Battle of Dien Bien Phu between the Viet Minh and French Expeditionary forces began on March 13, 1954. While this battle was being fought a conference was held in Geneva, Switzerland with a goal of solving the issues on the Korean peninsula and the Indochina War. The Soviet Union, United States, France, United Kingdom, and People's Republic of China were participants throughout the conference while other countries were represented during discussions of interest to them. There were no resolutions pertaining to Korea, but a number of documents known as the Geneva Accords were produced that addressed Indochina. Vietnam was divided into two zones 1) Northern Zone governed by the Viet Minh, and 2) Southern Zone governed by the State of Vietnam and headed by emperor Bao Đai who had been forced to abdicate power nine years earlier. While the conference was going on the French were defeated at Dien Bien Phu.

A final declaration was issued at the conference by the British chairman that called for a general election by July 1956 to create a unified Vietnam. Neither the State of Vietnam (South Vietnam) nor the United States agreed to this provision, because they didn't trust the communists to hold an honest election. The United States offered what became known as the "American Plan" which recommended that unification elections be supervised by the United Nations. The Soviet Union and North Vietnamese delegations rejected the proposal.

Following the Geneva conference a 300 day grace period was established that allowed people to travel freely between north and south. More than one million North Vietnamese fled to the south while a far smaller number traveled north. It is estimated that an addition two million would have left the north if they hadn't been stopped by the Viet Minh.

North Vietnam proved to have a brutal government that operated with significant political oppression. Through what they called "Rent Reduction" and "Land Reform" programs it is estimated that over 100,000 were executed. Many faced a firing squad while others were buried up to the neck and then plowed over. Those who were not executed were sent to hard labor camps where most died.

In 1959, North Vietnam invaded Laos aided by the Pathet Lao, the communist revolutionaries controlled by the Viet Minh, and built supply routes known as the Ho Chi Minh Trail. This move dramatically increased the capabilities of the insurgency in South Vietnam.

By the mid-1960s fighting increased as did foreign involvement. China sent as many as 320,000 volunteers to North Vietnam allowing an equal number of PAVN troops to head south. The United States sent combat troops to protect the airbases around Chu Lai and Da Nang. Eventually more and more American troops arrived and took on the fighting. Widespread aerial and artillery bombardment across North Vietnam by the U.S. Air Force and Navy began with Operation Rolling Thunder in July 1967. Ho Chi Minh and his staff concluded that the United States military had brought the war to a stalemate. Rather than sending more troops to the south the Viet Minh had to use a majority of their resources to maintain the Ho Chi Minh trail.

On January 31, 1968 the Viet Cong made a daring move called the Tet Offensive with hopes of achieving a decisive victory that would end the grinding conflict that frustrated military leaders on both sides. Hanoi selected the lunar new year Tet holiday because it was traditionally a time of truce. Also, numerous Vietnamese traveled south to spend the festival with their relatives which provided cover for the movement of South Vietnamese National Liberation Forces (NLF) who supported the communist forces.

The initial phase of the assault began when NLF forces simultaneously attacked a number of mostly populated areas and places with heavy U.S. troop presence. They also struck the major cities of Hue and Saigon which produced a significant psychological impact by demonstrating that the NLF troops were not as weak as the Johnson Administration had claimed.

A second phase began on May 4 with simultaneous assaults on smaller cities and towns throughout the south. The final phase began in August and lasted six weeks. In the end, U.S. and South Vietnamese forces fought back and retook lost territory at great military and civilian losses. Ho Chi Minh had shocked the world. However, the greatest victory he enjoyed was a turning of public opinion against the war in America as they witnessed the horror of combat in their living rooms. President Johnson ordered a halt to the bombing of North Vietnam above the 20th parallel and the Ho Chi Minh trail, placed a limit on U.S. troops in South Vietnam, and negotiators began to discuss how to end the war.

By 1969 negotiations dragged on and Ho Chi Minh's health began to deteriorate from multiple health problems, including diabetes which prevented him from participating in further active politics. After his death, People's Army of Vietnam soldiers often sang a famous song written by Huy Thuc *Bác van cùng chúng cháu hành quân* which meant "You are still marching with us, Uncle Ho."

Detectives Michael Donovan and Ryoya Akimoto arrived at the apartment of Claire Payton. She had been released from the hospital earlier in the day. They knocked but there wasn't any answer.

"You think she's not home?" Michael Donovan asked his partner.

"I think she's afraid to open the door," Ryoya replied. "Did you notice the two nice young men down on the street?"

"I did. Most likely members of Miguel Juarez crew. Real upstanding citizens if you ask me."

"Claire's no fool. She saw them when she came home. If she doesn't get out on the street at the appropriate time they'll come up here and make sure she does."

Michael Donovan banged on the apartment door with his fist and announced, "Police. Open the door."

The sounds of multiple locks could be heard inside then the door opened slowly with the security chain still attached. From inside Claire Payton peered out. When she saw the detectives she shut the door, unhooked the chain, and opened the door all the way. She didn't mutter a word.

Ryoya said, "We have a few more questions. Do you mind if we come in?"

Claire stepped aside to allow entry but remained silent.

"How are you feeling?" Ryoya asked.

In a hoarse voice the hooker answered, "As well as can be expected under the circumstances."

They sat at her small kitchen table. "We have some new evidence that clears Carl Pythacyk of the murder of Miguel Juarez," Ryoya lied. She got the look of a surprise response that she had expected. Detective Akimoto continued, "After Miguel went west on 44th Street did you see anyone follow him or any suspicious persons in the area?"

"I didn't see anything."

"Did you see the young blond girl who you say went home head in the same direction as Miguel at any time?"

"What? Uh, no. She was on the Avenue or in the hotel the entire night."

"We need to interview her."

"Leave her alone. She's just a child."

"She is a suspect in a murder," Detective Michael Donovan interjected with perfect timing.

"No. She had nothing to do with it."

"How do you know?" Michael Donovan pressed, "Were you with her the entire night?"

"Yes. Well, I saw her off and on."

"And, during one of those times when you didn't see her she had time to go up the block, commit the crime, and return."

"She didn't do it!" Claire Payton yelled.

"She fled. That's a sign of guilt," Detective Donovan stated as he stood and paced around the small room.

"Where is she?" Ryoya took her turn.

"I won't tell you."

"Then you'll go to jail for hindering an investigation," Ryoya warned.

"Then I'll go to jail."

"We will find her, I assure you of that," Ryoya stated. "We will arrest her and bring her back here to stand trial."

"Leave her alone."

"We can't do that."

"She had nothing to do with it."

"How do you know?"

"Because, I did it!" Claire Payton looked down at the table. In her hand she held a small silver cross. She spoke into her coffee cup, "Miguel told me to come to the alley at 11:30 and to bring a camera that he had given me. He didn't offer any explanation. Just before 11:30 I walked up the street toward the alley. With Miguel, you do what you're told when you're told to do it. As I drew near I heard two men fighting. Slowly, I approached the alley. In the shadows I saw the struggle but couldn't tell who was involved. Then one man was knocked down. As he got up he pulled out a knife. I heard the switchblade snap into place. The other man kicked the knife out of his hand and struck him hard. The one who had the knife fell backward and struck his head on the concrete. After that he didn't move. The other man picked up something and walked quickly out of the alley. He didn't see me because I hid against a brick column. It was that guy Carl something. He turned right and disappeared up the street. I went into the alley and found Miguel unconscious on the ground. When a car passed on the street its headlights reflected off the blade of the knife lying on the ground about four feet away. The glimmer of light seemed so bright. I retrieved the knife and went back to see about Miguel. He started to stir but was groggy. In the darkness he must have mistaken me for his opponent because he cursed at me and grabbed my arm." Claire paused as if reliving the incident. She looked up and made eye contact with Detective Akimoto, "I slashed the knife across his neck. Blood spurt out with so much force it startled me. I jumped back, Miguel gurgled, grabbed his neck, and then it sounded like the air just leaked out of him. I knew he was dead. I tried to wipe the blood off my hand and the knife with my scarf but in the dark couldn't see if I was successful. In a daze, I dropped the knife and left the alley. I didn't return to the hotel or Eight Avenue. Instead, I went to Ninth Avenue, turned uptown, and walked home. When I got home I just sat not knowing what to do." Claire turned to Detective Donovan and said softly, "The child had nothing to do with it. Let her forget about what she went through." She looked down and added, "and forget about me."

"You'll have to come with us," Ryoya said gently.

Matthew Ellis' eyes were tired from examining countless documents found in the suitcase that Stephanie, his daughter, had dragged into the apartment. Everything he read painted a picture of a lone woman doing all that she could to carry the burden of raising a daughter, facing a mountain of medical bills, dueling with collection agencies, and handling a demanding job—all without complaint. He couldn't ignore the guilt that he felt for not being there. In addition, that dream about a Hong Kong bank account with over $750,000 gnawed at him. His family could have used that money while he slept. But, even now, he had no idea how to access the account. All he had were the first two of eight numbers and no memory of the pseudonym used for the account. Unless he could miraculously return to that dream and retrieve the information the money would languish unclaimed. Blood money, tarnished and evil, waits for its malevolent master to put it to use.

Slowly, Matthew Ellis was rebuilding his past. Unfortunately, it was a past of which he wasn't proud. How could he have let things spiral so out-of-control? How could he have done the things that it was becoming clear he had? How could he have let a life filled with promise slip away?

"You were right."

"Hey, that's a first. Say it again."

"Don't push your luck."

"OK, how was I right?"

"Carl Pythacyk didn't kill Miguel Juarez." Ryoya Akimoto admitted.

Jack leaned back in his chair. In his right hand he held the telephone receiver. He asked the obvious question, "Who did it?"

"One of his girls from Eighth Avenue."

"Is this on the record?"

"I'd prefer that you not share this until she is charged," Ryoya said, "There are extenuating circumstances that I have to discuss with the District Attorney."

"You know me. If something is confidential it stays that way. Are you sure she did it?"

"Thank you and yes."

"So, Carl P is off the hook?"

"Yes. Somewhere out there is an innocent man hiding from the law believing that he is wanted for murder."

60: Friday – September 5, 1969

Two days after her arrest Claire Payton was in the Manhattan Criminal Court at 100 Centre Street. A court appointed lawyer who specialized in homicide cases was with her. She was there for her arraignment. In her case, it was more of a formality than legal procedure.

When Claire had been taken into custody Detectives Akimoto and Donovan did not inform her of her Miranda Rights, therefore anything that she had said during their interview could not be used against her. On the ride back to the Midtown North Precinct on West 54th Street Ryoya explained the situation to their detainee.

"Claire at present you are being detained for questioning. We have not placed you under arrest nor read you your Miranda Rights. What this means is that everything that you have told us thus far is inadmissible as evidence."

"But, I confessed. You know that I murdered Miguel."

"Get the hell out of the way—shit for brains," Michael Donovan cursed and blew the horn at a driver who had double-parked blocking the lane.

Ryoya clarified her point, "We know that you killed Juarez. The circumstances under which the event took place will determine what crime was committed, if any. It could be anything from first-degree murder, to manslaughter, to self-defense."

"I didn't go there to kill him."

"What you need to think about is after we put you under arrest and read your rights everything you say or write will be used in court. How you word things will make a big difference."

"I can only tell what happened."

They arrived at the Midtown North Precinct. Ryoya said to Detective Donovan, "Go around the block—make it two."

"How bout we take a drive to Jersey?" Michael Donovan said sarcastically as he drove west on 54th Street.

Ryoya returned her attention to Claire, "Claire, Miguel Juarez was a monster. What he did to you and the others is reprehensible. And, yes, you killed him. But as you said you didn't go there to kill him. That pretty much eliminates First Degree Murder."

"Does it really matter? I'm going to jail," Claire said with a tone of certainty. "At least that will get me off the street. And, Olivia, uh, shit, the girl got her life back."

"It does matter," Ryoya stated. "Once we arrest you, we have to show probable cause. Your statement, though inadmissible, tells us that you did kill Miguel Juarez. Our arrest report coupled with your written statement will paint a picture of the events that led up to his death." Detective Akimoto paused and looked at her partner.

"Don't look at me." Michael Donovan said, "You're the one offering a 'get-out-of-jail-free' card." He blew the horn at a taxicab.

"We have to agree or the card goes back in the deck," Ryoya replied.

Detective Donovan pulled over to the curb, put the car in park, and turned toward Ryoya. He stated flatly, "If you want to coach the suspect into claiming that Juarez, in a dazed condition, grabbed her and attempted to assault her causing her to fear for her life and wildly swing the knife in self-defense, don't ask me to do it."

"You just did," Ryoya said with a straight face.

Michael Donovan turned toward Claire Payton in the back seat and asked, "Did you hear what I just said?"

Before she could answer Ryoya ordered, "Say no."

Claire complied, "No."

"There," Detective Donovan said smugly, "I suggest you keep your trap shut and let the District Attorney make the decision on charges." He began to drive and added, "We're cops, all we do is arrest 'em."

At the precinct, Claire wrote her statement and the detectives their arrest report. She was taken through the arrest procedure and placed in a holding cell.

The next morning Assistant District Attorney for Manhattan, Reeves Vermillion, reviewed the documents and interviewed Claire Payton. When he finished he said, "According to NY Penal Code Section 125.15 a person may be found guilty of the crime of Manslaughter in the Second Degree when he or she recklessly causes the death of another person." He looked across the table at Claire and her attorney. "If you plead guilty we are prepared to ask the judge for leniency. It's a class C felony which carries a minimum sentence of 1 to 3 years. We'll recommend the minimum with a suspended sentence."

Maxwell Hall, her attorney, replied, "Come'on Reeves you know as well as I do that it was self-defense."

"The use of self-defense requires that the action match the level of the threat in question. She used a knife on a half-conscious man. I could make a case for second degree murder."

"We both know that wouldn't fly."

"He beat her up in the past—that's motive. He's lying helpless on the ground—opportunity. A knife is available—means. We have her statement which proves without a shadow of a doubt that she did it."

After the lawyers finished their argument there was nothing left but the arraignment the next day.

Claire Payton sat in the gallery with her lawyer. She wore a blue skirt and white blouse that Ryoya had given her. The auburn wig remained upon her head. Detectives Akimoto and Donovan also sat in the gallery in case they were needed as witnesses. District Court Judge Horace Dalrymple sat on the bench. He was an older man in his sixties, near retirement. He wore dark rim glasses, had thinning hair, and an expressionless face. After two preceding arraignments Claire's case was called and the judge was handed a file.

The bailiff announced, "The people of the city of New York vs. Claire Payton."

Led by her lawyer Claire walked up to the defense table. Assistant District Attorney for Manhattan Reeves Vermillion sat at the opposite table. Judge Dalrymple read the charges, "Claire Louise Payton, you are charged with Manslaughter in the Second Degree. I see that you have council. How do you plead?"

Maxwell Hall, her attorney, replied, "Your honor, per a plea agreement with the state of New York the defendant pleads nolo contendre." A plea of "no contest" meant that she did not contest the charges but at the same time did not admit to guilt.

Judge Dalrymple asked her attorney, "Is there a factual basis for the plea?"

"If it pleases the court," Assistant District Attorney for Manhattan Reeves Vermillion spoke up, "based on the facts in evidence the defendant agreed to nolo contendre in exchange for a minimum sentence and, if you agree, a suspended sentence."

"I do not agree," Judge Dalrymple said in a deep monotone voice.

In a small military courtroom in Fort Benning, Georgia Lieutenant William Calley stood in silence as he listened to the charges preferred against him with four specifications alleging premeditated murder in violation of Article 118 of Uniform Code of Military Justice:

> Specification 1: In that First Lieutenant William L. Calley, Jr. ...did, at My Lai 4, Quang Ngai Province, Republic of South Viet-Nam, on or about 16 March 1968, with premeditation, murder an unknown number, not less than thirty, Oriental human beings, males and females of various ages, whose names are unknown, occupants of the village of My Lai 4, by means of shooting them with a rifle.

> Specification 2: In that First Lieutenant William L. Calley, Jr...did, at My Lai 4, Quang Ngai Province, Republic of South Viet-Nam, on or about 16 March 1968, with premeditation, murder an unknown number, not less than seventy, Oriental human beings, males and females of various ages, whose names are unknown, occupants of the village of My Lai 4, by means of shooting them with a rifle.

> Specification 3: In that First Lieutenant William L. Calley, Jr...did, at My Lai 4, Quang Ngai Province, Republic of South Viet-Nam, on or about 16 March 1968, with premeditation, murder one Oriental male human being, whose name and age is unknown, by shooting him with a rifle.

> Specification 4: In that First Lieutenant William L. Calley, Jr...did, at My Lai 4, Quang Ngai Province, Republic of South Viet-Nam, on or about 16 March 1968, with premeditation, murder one Oriental human being, an occupant of the village of My Lai 4, approximately two years old, by shooting him with a rifle.

The criminal charges referred to an incident that took place March 16, 1968. Lieutenant Calley was a platoon leader in Charlie Company, 1st Battalion, 20th Infantry. They had been conducting a search and destroy mission as part of the yearlong Operation Wheeler/Wallowa. My Lai 4, was actually part of a cluster of hamlets that made up Son My village in Son Tinh District in Quang Ngai Province in the coastal lowlands. It was believed that Viet Cong forces were being sheltered in this area.

For weeks prior to the incident Calley's troops had been losing men to snipers, mines, and booby traps left by an enemy they could neither see nor find. They were tired, jumpy, frustrated, and angry. Orders had been given to destroy the villages. Add to that a statement by four-star General William Westmoreland that he wanted a body count and all the elements for a breakdown of discipline were present.

When their helicopters landed in the village there was no enemy fire or signs of an enemy. No enemy combatants were present but the soldiers knew they were among enemy sympathizers. Suddenly, one of the infantrymen bayonetted a civilian. It came as a complete surprise. What happened next was a slaughter. They began shooting people as they ran from their huts, forcing survivors into a ditch, and executing them. Madness overwhelmed military procedure. One soldier later said, "Yes, they were children, women and old men. However, women and children can kill you just as easily as a grown-up. These people were not sympathetic to us. They were just as much an enemy as the ones doing the fighting."

At one point, Warrant Officer Hugh Thompson, an aero-scout helicopter pilot, observed what was happening and landed his helicopter between the Americans and the fleeing Vietnamese. As quickly as it started the action stopped.

On March 16, 1968, the same day, in the official press briefing humorously known as the "Five O'Clock Follies" a mimeographed release included this statement: "In an action today, Americal Division forces killed 128 enemy near Quang Ngai City. Helicopter gunships and artillery missions supported the ground elements throughout the day." General William Westmoreland, the Military Assistance Command, Vietnam commander, congratulated the unit on an outstanding job.

An initial investigation of the operation was undertaken by the 11th Light Infantry Brigade's commanding officer, Colonel Henderson, under orders from the Americal Division's executive officer, Brigadier General George H. Young. Henderson's report in late April claimed some 20 civilians were inadvertently killed during the operation.

Specialist 5 Ronald L. Ridenhour, a former door gunner from the Aviation Section, Headquarters Company of the 11th Infantry Brigade, learned about the events at My Lai secondhand from talking to members of Charlie Company over a period of months after the incident. He was so disturbed by the stories that three months after being discharged from the Army, in March 1969, he wrote a letter to thirty members of Congress asking them to do an investigation. All ignored him with the exception of Congressman Mo Udall and Senators Barry Goldwater and Edward Brooke. In the letter he included the name of Michael Bernhardt, an eyewitness who agreed to testify. Mo Udall urged the House Armed Services Committee to request that Pentagon officials conduct an investigation. As a result of the investigation charges were preferred against Lieutenant William Calley

The public information office at Fort Benning issued a press release regarding charges against Lieutenant Calley without providing any details.

When the judge refused to accept the plea agreement a cold chill ran through Claire Payton. The man before her held her life in his hands and he just threw out the deal that would have meant no jail time. She wasn't sure what would happen next. In desperation she looked at her lawyer. He simply nodded and patted her arm. She then looked back in the gallery at Ryoya Akimoto and Michael Donovan. They sat motionless. Her attention returned to Judge Dalrymple.

"I cannot accept a plea of nolo contendre." The judge stated. "Manslaughter in the Second Degree includes reckless cause of death. From what is written here that is not the case. This is either Second Degree Murder or Self-Defense. In my opinion the facts can only bring me to one conclusion. This is a case of self-defense and shouldn't even have been brought before this court. All charges are dismissed. You are free to go." The sound of his gavel echoed throughout the courtroom. Claire stood in a daze.

If it could be called relaxation that was what Wellington Marsh attempted to do. Unfortunately, too many images kept sneaking into his mind for him to drift into the comfort of a blank mind. In sixteen days he would report back to Camp Lejeune and be whisked off to Vietnam. Then he would be placed in a strange village with people that spoke a strange language who he wasn't sure he could trust. As the CAP Squad leader he would be responsible for fourteen American and an untold number of Vietnamese lives. And yet, he couldn't save one young Indian boy in a rushing stream. Carl and Ritchie came to mind. What was Carl guilty of doing that had him running to Canada? He seemed like a decent sort. At least he was the kind of guy Wellington would welcome by his side in a strange village with people who spoke a strange language. Maybe Carl could hide out at Lark's Run—maybe not. Wellington was concerned about Ritchie. A peacenik, long haired, hippie, artist would be eaten alive in basic training. He'd seen it happen when a Drill Instructor took a personal interest in a recruit. It wasn't pleasant to watch. It wasn't something he wished for his friend.

A voice brought Wellington back to reality. It was Teresa Champion the girl he had decided not to get involved with as he was going to war. She had other ideas.

"If you keep getting lost in your thoughts I'm going to think you don't like me," she said as she carried two bottles of Coca Cola out to the patio where Wellington sat.

"I explained to you," Wellington replied, "It has nothing to do with liking or not liking you. I'm going to a dangerous place and may not return. Or, I may return seriously injured. I don't want to put anyone in a position to have to face that. It's not fair."

"Maybe, I think otherwise," Theresa countered. "We have now and the next day and the next day. And when you are away you will have someone who will write to you and wait for you."

"No. I don't want any commitments. If I come back I may be changed, or I may see you differently. There is just too much that could go wrong."

Theresa didn't reply. She sat next to Wellington on the chaise lounge, leaned over, and kissed him. At that moment Wellington knew that tomorrow could wait.

61: Tuesday – September 9, 1969

"He's dead and you can't change that," Laurel said consolingly.

"I have to admit there is a part of me that is glad about that," Carl admitted.

"I understand."

"I mean, it's not like I purposely did it."

"You were the innocent party."

"Damn right. He attacked me."

"Well, that's not exactly correct. You attacked him."

"Not intentionally."

"I know," Laurel soothed, "Let me see it."

Carl held up his arm. There on the underside of his bicep was a bee sting. The stinger was still pumping venom.

"Stand still," Laurel ordered. She dragged her fingernail across the sting site pulling out the stinger.

"Owww!" Carl complained.

"It had to come out," Laurel said. "The longer it stays in the more venom that is injected."

"All I did was put my arm around you," Carl lamented.

"Yes, right on top of a bee."

"What the hell was he doing there?"

"Resting."

"That's great. You're being funny and I'm dying."

In a serious tone Laurel asked, "You aren't allergic, are you?"

"I've never been stung before."

Laurel took Carl's hand and led him back to the farmhouse. Once there she went into the bathroom and came out with a tube of toothpaste.

"I don't think brushing my teeth will do much good," Carl concluded.

"No, silly, toothpaste is alkaline in nature while bee venom is acidic. It neutralizes the venom. Also, there is glycerin in toothpaste that will dry up any residual venom on your skin." Laurel spread a dab of toothpaste on the wound and said, "Smile."

Carl didn't.

"You don't have any swelling other than where you were stung. Do you feel like you have any difficulty breathing or dizziness?"

"No."

"Let me know if you get hives or a rash anywhere."

"I will. Thank you."

Laurel leaned forward, kissed Carl, and said, "After the pain subsides I'll put some honey on the wound."

"Honey?"

"Honey is a natural antibacterial agent. Those little critters may sting you but they also provide the cure," Laurel smiled.

Detective Ryoya Akimoto was enjoying an overdue day off. Jack Moore was writing his column for the *Tribune*. They were together at Shea Stadium early in the afternoon. The Mets (82-57) were playing the first-place Cubs (84-58).

Tom Seaver (21-7), the Mets ace pitcher, was on the mound. It had been a rough August for the Cubs as they squandered a nine game lead in the standings. The Mets, on the other hand, had a fantastic August and were only a half-game behind the Cubs. They had won 21 of 31 games played that month. This included two six-game winning streaks.

"So, you've had a few hours since lunch to decide. What is your column going to be about?"

"About a thousand words," Jack remarked.

"Sounds more like zero words, if you ask me."

"Ha, ha, something will come to me."

The Chicago Cubs led off. A fly to right field and a strikeout eliminated the first two batters. Then Billy Williams came to bat. As he did Ron Santo, the Cubs slugger, Third Baseman, and cleanup batter walked into the on-deck circle and began to loosen up. At that very moment to the surprise and amusement of the more than fifty-one thousand fans a black cat sauntered onto the field. It walked down the third base side of the field and circled Santo. The crowd of mostly Mets fans cheered and laughed. As if aware of its new found celebrity the cat looked around at the stands. Finally, after basking in the limelight for a few seconds, it disappeared under the stands. Ron Santo later said, "I knew right away we were in trouble. I wanted to run and hide."

"I believe I just got my story," Jack observed.

"Are you superstitious?" Ryoya asked.

"Not as superstitious as baseball players."

Billy Williams hit a pop fly to the shortstop to end the inning. In the bottom of the first inning the Mets scored two runs when Tommie Agee and Cleon Jones, who both had been walked, were driven home by a Ken Boswell double to right field.

"I love that cat," Ryoya remarked.

By the end of the third inning the Cubs had been hitless and the Mets scored two more runs on a Donn Clendenon homerun. Finally, in the top of the fourth inning the Cubs scored one run on three hits. The Mets answered with a run in the bottom of the fourth making the score 5 to 1. The Cubs went hitless for the next three innings and the Mets added two more runs. In the end the Mets won the game seven to one and moved into first place in the National League Eastern Division.

That evening Jack went home and wrote his column that would be in the next day's newspaper.

THE LEGEND OF CASEY THE BLACK CAT
by Jack Moore

Throughout history black cats have been feared, maligned, and murdered. Most likely it all started in 1232 when Pope Gregory IX issued the Vox Rama a papal bull that condemned all devil worship. In this document he officially mentioned that black cats are the incarnation of the devil ordaining that they should be burned. Pity the poor kitty in the Thirteenth Century. All the killing of that century decreased the cat population which in turn allowed the rat population to flourish. The resulting Bubonic Plague of the Fourteenth Century killed an estimated 200 million people. That is, as they say, the unexpected consequence. By the Sixteenth Century black cats were no longer thought of as the devil but as witches' companions called "familiars" or demonic animals given to them by the devil.

An old English folktale told a story of a man and his son traveling home late at night when a black cat crossed their path. The son threw a stone at the cat and hit it in the left leg. The cat let out a wail and fled under a house where an old woman, long believed to be a witch, lived. Next morning the father and son saw the old woman at the marketplace. She was limping on her left leg. From that day on the people were sure that the woman was a witch that prowled the town late at night in the shape of a black cat.

The Pilgrims came to the New World in the early 17th century. They brought their "black cats are witches" beliefs with them and during the Salem witch trials, many pet black cats were burned at the stake with their "witch" owners. While this was going on King Charles I of England had a black cat he absolutely loved and protected. When the cat died he lamented that his luck had run out. The next day he was arrested for treason and publicly executed.

During the 18th century pirates also had superstitions about black cats. They believed if one was walking toward you that brought bad luck, walking away good luck. They also believed that if a black cat boarded your ship and then left, the ship would sink on its next voyage. Likewise sailors kept black cats aboard their ships for good luck. Even their wives kept black cats at home to protect their men at sea.

So, our friend the ebony feline has gone from being the devil to a symbol of luck, both good and bad. In England, a black cat given as a wedding present is thought to bring good luck to the bride. Scottish people believe a strange black cat on your porch is supposed to bring prosperity. In Germany, the direction a black cat takes when crossing your path determines if it represents good luck or bad. If the mouser crosses from right to left it means bad luck, while from left to right there are good things ahead. In Japan a woman with a black cat in her home is supposed to attract many suitors. Finally, in Russia a black cat is always considered a good sign.

Now, with all of this as a backdrop let's take a look at Casey The Black Cat. I named him Casey in honor of the Mets first manager Casey Stengel. Known as The Old Professor, Stengel was involuntarily retired in 1960 from the Yankees, because he was believed to be too old to manage. At the time he remarked that he had been fired for turning 70, and that he would "never make that mistake again." A year later Stengel came out of retirement to manage the expansion team he dubbed the Amazin' Mets.

I don't have to tell Mets fans that they lost a lot, I mean a record setting number of games, their first season. Even Casey Stengel admitted that they found ways to lose games that even he had never seen before. It was as though they were cursed. But, remember this, they were never losers. The Mets had spirit and a lovable charm that made them stand out. They were the ultimate underdogs that you just had to root for.

Now this year, 1969, the Mets are finding ways to win that sometimes seem magical. This is the same team that finished 9th in 1968 with a record of 73-89. To be fair a lot of credit goes to their second year manager Gil Hodges. His platoon lineup of eleven players and on field decisions have been a major factor. But, there have been times when a ball took an odd bounce finding its way into a waiting mitt. Or, a long fly ball seemed to curve just enough to miss the foul pole and give a Mets hitter a homerun. There are forces at work here, my friends, that baseball observers are hard pressed to explain.

Does it strike any of you as a coincidence that Casey The Black Cat showed up at the very game where, if won, the indomitable Cubs would be vanquished and the under-rated Mets would step into first place for the first time in club history? No, it wasn't coincidence; it was the magic of Casey The Black Cat. The bringer of luck and harbinger of misfortune appeared on the Cub's side of the field and circled their most imposing player. And, as a result, shut down one of the league's most powerful offenses. In two games at Shea Stadium the Cubs only generated three runs while the Mets scored ten.

I believe that Casey has been with us all season bringing the Mets that degree of luck that proves the difference between a win and a loss, or gets that third strike called on a close pitch, or causes a shortstop to move one step over just before a ball is hit that would have been out of his reach, or any of a thousand other elements that change the outcome of a game.

So, as an outside observer, I offer this advice. Next time you go to a Mets game beckon him to appear once more. Yell, "Casey, Casey." Show proper respect and acknowledge the supernatural forces at work. Or, go ahead, be a doubter and put this incredible season at risk.

Matthew Ellis held a piece of paper tightly in his hand. It represented verification that Lida Petropoulos did, in reality—not dreams—exist. He had found the letter the night before. She had written to him on LPAmerica stationery. It was incontrovertible proof that Lida Petropoulos was flesh and blood. Once again, he read the contents of the letter that had been addressed to Matthew Ellis.

RE: Wire Production

This confirms our agreement for LPAmerica to provide Orztech Corporation with a variety of stranded wire products manufactured at our facilities to exact specifications as defined in each individual work order.

All products and packaging will display the Orztech Corporate logo and identification information as provided by the customer.

Delivery will be to the designated Orztech Corporation warehouse on or before the agreed upon due date. A twenty (20) percent penalty will be incurred for failure to meet this date.

Payment terms are net thirty after credit is established. A two (2) percent charge will be added if payment has not been received sixty (60) days after invoice date.

This agreement will remain in effect until cancelled in writing by either party.

Lida Petropoulos
President
LPAmerica

Of even greater interest than the contents of the letter was the address; 347 Madison Avenue, Suite 333, New York, NY.

Earlier that day, Matt had gone to Manhattan and visited the offices of LPAmerica. When he arrived he found 347 Madison Avenue was a narrow twelve-story building tucked between two larger buildings one block south of the Roosevelt Hotel. There was a single revolving door between two swinging doors.

Matt entered the building with a sense of excitement seasoned with a pinch of fear. Could this be the day that he comes face to face with the specter that visited him so often in dreams and in random memories? Would he learn directly from Lida Petropoulos the truth? Could he face the truth?

The lobby was small with one bank of four elevators on the right side. Matt examined the business directory on the wall. An advertising agency, Dancer-Fitzgerald-Sample occupied the fifth through twelfth floors. To his disappointment LPAmerica was not listed. From the letterhead he knew it was Suite 333 so Matt entered an elevator and ascended to seek the truth.

On the third floor Matt found a number of small business offices. He followed the corridor, turned right, and before him was a single wooden door with the number 333 emblazoned on it in gold. When he tried the knob the door opened. To his surprise the inner office was dark. No lights were on nor any sound heard. With his hand he explored the wall, found a switch, and turned on the lights. The office was empty. No people, furniture, filing cabinets, telephone equipment, or anything else—just a big open room with blue carpet.

Further in, there were three offices with closed doors. Matt went to the nearest door and opened it. Inside was an empty office. The second door opened to the same. In the third office he saw a small pile of trash in a corner. Empty cardboard boxes, a broken lamp, Styrofoam cups, newspapers, empty manila folders, a piece of cloth, dead potted tree, and numerous other items that had been left behind. His hopes dashed, Matt knew he wouldn't get any answers from this abandoned center of operations. In his mind he saw people working at desks, answering telephones, typing, and scurrying about. The room he stood in, which was the largest office, was most likely Lida's. She sat at a large desk wearing a white silk blouse and dark blue skirt. Her makeup and hair were impeccable, as always.

Something shiny caught Matt's eye. He moved an empty box to reveal a spool of Orztech wire. Dark gray wire wound around a metal spool like a venomous snake. He almost feared touching it. After a moment, Matt picked up the roll of wire, looked at it, and wondered if he had it tested what would be the results. He decided to take it with him.

Upon closer examination, he realized the piece of cloth in the debris pile was actually a scarf. A dark blue and Kelly green paisley pattern made it rather fashionable. Impulsively, he brought it to his nose and sniffed. While very faint he recognized Lida Petropoulos' perfume. The aroma acted as an intoxicant. In a trancelike state Matt found himself sitting in that very office in a comfortable padded chair. The office reflected a definite European style of practical, yet comfortable furnishings.

Before him was Lida Petropoulos sitting on the arm of a couch holding a manila folder. She wore a blue dress with a wide black leather belt. Matt was keenly aware that the hem was slightly above the knee. Around her neck was the scarf that he held in his hand. She smiled and said, "Then we understand each other."

Matt heard himself say, "Your less expensive substitutes seemed to work well with the military, automotive, and aviation industries, but this is NASA. Are you sure that they won't catch on?"

"Honey, it's wire. They aren't going to waste a lot of time testing every inch."

"What if something goes wrong?"

"Nothing is going to go wrong."

"I'm sure what we are doing is illegal."

"What bankers do is immoral. No one cares. In the wild, wolves look out for themselves. They don't create laws that favor one wolf over another. The strong, or in our case innovative, survive. In the end you and I will prosper and all of Orztech's customers will get what they need." Lida moved over to where Matt sat and added, "Stop worrying. It will give you wrinkles." He felt her run her hand through his hair.

"I do like the rewards," Matt heard himself say.

"And, there's plenty more if we play our cards right."

"I'll peddle the steak, you provide the hamburger," Matt said. They laughed.

Matt left 347 Madison Avenue carrying a spool of Orztech wire, a scarf, and the burden of knowing that he was a willing co-conspirator in a fraud that threatened countless lives. He had come face to face with what he had perpetrated. He also recognized another reality—there was no practical way to eliminate the danger.

62: Thursday – September 11, 1969

It was a rare clear, cool, low-humidity morning in New York City. Ritchie drove south on the West Side Highway toward the World Trade Center building site. He couldn't help but feel that something was missing traveling alone without his basenji pal. Part of him missed her while another was happy that she was in an ideal place for a lunatic dog. As it was late morning rush hour had subsided and traffic was moderate to light. Ahead he could see the North Tower that had progressed to a point where it was visible from a distance. He tried to envision what the completed project would look like with twin towers holding up the sky.

In five days he would report for his physical, pass, and get cashiered into his majesty's army. This thought caused him to reflect on his new friend, Wellington Marsh, a bright young Marine who was scheduled to make that journey into hell and possibly never come home. His mind did an unexpected calculation trying to determine the odds of both of them going to Vietnam and returning safely. They weren't good.

The North Tower of World Trade Center loomed large in the distance. In just a few weeks since his last visit it had progressed to a point where its incredible size was now apparent. Ritchie knew this would be his last photo shoot of the project. He had doubts that he would ever see the completed buildings. After parking on a side street he walked in the direction of the World Trade Center construction site. While still two blocks away he stopped and considered the vista before him. Wide open sky dominated the lower Manhattan skyline. Ritchie took numerous photographs of a view future New Yorkers would never see once the massive buildings changed the focal point of the Island of Manhattan. He had no idea what the future would hold thirty-two years ahead on this very date on a beautiful clear morning like this one.

Jack Moore sat in his office and thought about the telephone conversation he had just completed with Matthew Ellis. The "Sleeper" informed him that it was his belief that Lida Petropoulos did not exist, had never had anything to do with Orztech, and that the idea that there was anything wrong with wire provided NASA was absolutely wrong. Further, he stated that the manufacture and delivery of the wire was executed while he was in a coma. The conversation was ended with Matthew Ellis declaring that he was finished with this subject and would now focus on getting back to his life.

Many years as a reporter helped Jack develop a talent for reading between the lines. The sudden turnaround and denial of any involvement with a Lida Petropoulos indicated that Matthew Ellis had found new evidence of a connection between the mysterious lady and Orztech. The man's denial that there was any possibility that the wire was defective didn't ring true. And, his coma defense confirmed that something was irregular as he was distancing himself from the subject. Finally, he made it clear that he would not cooperate any longer in the investigation. At that point Jack knew this was a story worth pursuing.

A reporter walked into Jack's office and tossed the first American issue of *Penthouse Magazine* on his desk. It was the September 1969 issue and featured Evelyn

Treacher on the cover. Jack had no idea who she was but, after examining the issue, knew a great deal more about her. She was a twenty one year old, London-born, ex-stewardess who flew the London-Nassau-Miami run until she fell in love with the Caribbean climate. She gave up her British citizenship but softened the blow by stating, "I always enjoy going back despite the weather. I've got loads of friends in London and it's really a marvelous city in its own special way. What I love about the Bahamas goes a little bit deeper. It's something you could never find in London or any other big city and I don't mean the sun. This is a very peaceful place; it's wild, primitive and yet strictly non-competitive. The people are warm and somehow they don't seem to expect anything from you. They live their lives and you live yours." Jack contemplated the brunette's blue eyes—right! Yes, the Bahamas were looking pretty good. With his memory of Woodstock as a reference, Jack fully understood Ms. Treacher's perspective, "The things I left behind are like those little ships that men build in bottles—perfect little replicas glued to their painted sea—little ships with nowhere to go."

Penthouse Magazine was founded in 1965 in the United Kingdom by Robert Charles Joseph Edward Sabatini "Bob" Guccione. He was the son of an accountant who worked for Nathan Anderson, Ritchie's father, the publisher of numerous magazines. Guccione grew up in Bergenfield, New Jersey and at one time considered entering the priesthood. While still in his teens he got married but it didn't last. He then traveled to Europe to be a painter. While there, he met and married an English woman named Muriel and they moved to London. There he managed a chain of laundromats until he was hired as a cartoonist for *The London American* a weekly newspaper. At the age of thirty five he launched his own magazine.

Penthouse was a men's magazine that combined urban lifestyle articles, investigative reporting, and stories about government corruption caressed by softcore pornographic pictorials. Due to limited funds, Guccione did most of the photography in the early issues. His knowledge of painting influenced the photographic creative approach of using a diffused, soft focus look that became a trademark of the magazine's pictorials. The magazine's centerfold models were known as Penthouse Pets who ordinarily wore a distinctive necklace with the Penthouse logo—a stylized key incorporating both the Mars and Venus symbols in its design.

Besides the obvious, something on the cover of *Penthouse* struck Jack. It was a teaser that announced an exclusive interview with Clay Shaw—the only person prosecuted in connection with the assassination of President John F. Kennedy. Now, that was an interview he would have loved to have done. Clay Shaw was a New Orleans businessman who was arrested March 1, 1967 and charged with being involved in a conspiracy with the Central Intelligence Agency (CIA) and right-wing activists to assassinate John F. Kennedy. The trial began in late January 1969 and lasted 35 days.

New Orleans District Attorney Jim Garrison believed Shaw used the alias "Clay Bertrand" and had attended a party in September 1963 at the apartment of anti-Castro activist and airline pilot David Ferrie. His main witness Perry Russo, an insurance salesman, testified that after other guests left he heard Lee Harvey Oswald, David Ferrie, and Clay Shaw openly discuss killing Kennedy. The conversation included plans for a triangulation of crossfire and alibis for the participants.

The case quickly fell apart as many inconsistencies were revealed and a memo from Assistant D.A. Andrew Sciambra, who interviewed Russo, indicated that Russo met Shaw on two different occasions, neither of which occurred at a party. Another witness, Charles Spiesel, said under cross-examination that he regularly fingerprinted his children, because he feared they had been replaced with cloned lookalikes by the US Government. On March 1, 1969 Shaw was acquitted less than one hour after the case went to the jury.

Jack read the *Penthouse* interview. In it Clay Shaw claimed that he never met Perry Russo, the primary witness against him, until the day before his arrest. He explained that a friend had visited his house and they were having a drink when the doorbell rang. It was Russo. Only Shaw didn't know it because the visitor had given him a business card with a false name. There was another person with him from the District Attorney's office.

In spite of all the allegations Shaw concluded, "I think that it was just Lee Oswald, a poor psychotic loser, who got a lucky shot at the President. People find it difficult to believe that the great golden prince should be killed by this psychotic little man, crouching behind paste-board boxes, with a cheap mail-order rifle. But the fact that it is inappropriate doesn't mean that it didn't happen. Life is full of inappropriate things, and I believe that I am a well-qualified person to make that statement. I speak from first-hand experience."

In the end the whole ordeal was extremely costly. In addition to legal fees, Shaw had to hire private investigators to check on some of the peculiar witnesses that popped up in the case. He stated, "Before Garrison accused me, I was rather comfortably fixed. Now I'm broke."

Members of the New York Mets team settled into their seats on the chartered Boeing 737. To say their spirits were high would be an understatement. They were on a seven game winning streak having beaten the Montreal Expos that afternoon 4 to 0. In addition, they had sole possession of first place in the National League Eastern Division. And, someone had smuggled a black cat aboard. At one point before the plane left the gate a chant of, "Casey, Casey, Casey," began. Jack Moore's column the previous day had been passed around the locker room and baseball players being baseball players fell into the superstition trap.

It was to be a short flight to Pittsburgh to play a doubleheader against the Pirates the next day. At eight-fifteen the aircraft pushed away from the gate at LaGuardia Airport for a one and a half hour flight to Greater Pittsburgh Airport. Skies were clear over both airports and no weather systems were present that would impact the flight. Takeoff was normal and the Amazin' Mets were headed to Pittsburgh. Because Greater Pittsburgh Airport was located northwest of the city the flight plan had them flying north of Allentown and Altoona.

The Mets player who brought the black cat aboard confessed that it wasn't Casey but an imposter that he named Gil in honor of the team's manager Gil Hodges. A chant of "Gil, Gil, Gil," filled the plane. The manager was not amused.

Just west of Altoona, at 41,000 feet, the #2 fuel tank low pressure light illuminated. Thirty seconds later, the center tank fuel low pressure light illuminated. On a 737 each wing forms a fuel tank. Near the bottom of each wing are two pumps which feed fuel into pipes that lead to the plane's engines. Electricity for each pump comes through a 110-volt wire, enclosed in a conduit, which runs from the front of the wing down to the pump. Upon seeing the warning lights, the captain turned to look at the circuit breakers and noted that the center tank right pump circuit breaker was out and the right tank forward circuit breaker was out. The right tank aft pump was still in. Fuel was still being fed to the twin engines, however, to avoid fuel contamination, he opened the crossfeed manifold. The co-pilot radioed air traffic control and declared an emergency. Given their location and the fact that the aircraft was still functioning it was decided that they would continue to Greater Pittsburgh Airport. The flight was given priority.

Back in the cabin one of the trainers seated mid-cabin noticed an electrical odor. He looked around to see if any of the other passengers might have noticed. On every baseball team there are fearful flyers. They love the sport enough to endure the near-panic experienced when in the air. Keenly aware of this fact the trainer opted to not cause any alarm. He kept his own fear of flying to himself.

In the cockpit they prepared for a straight in landing on runway 28 at Greater Pittsburgh Airport. The glide path kept them mainly over rural areas. As they descended the crew checked the Quick Reference Handbook (QRH) which included the precaution to not reset the circuit breakers. A spark at the wrong time in the wrong place could cause the aircraft to explode. The left center fuel pump continued functioning and by all indications would provide enough fuel for landing. A normal landing was executed to the captain and crew's relief. As they taxied to the terminal an electrical smell floated into the cockpit.

The Mets, plus Gil the cat, exited the plane unaware that their season might have ended prematurely.

Later that night the maintenance crew repowered the circuits. Immediately, a master caution light illuminated and numerous circuit breakers snapped open. Technicians isolated an electrical short in the forward cargo compartment. Damaged wiring bundles at station 420 above the forward cargo compartment ceiling on the right side of the airplane were found. Numerous wires appeared to have been severely damaged by electrical arcing. A total of 110 conductors were involved in the electrical arcing. It was concluded that a breakdown in the insulation of a single wire most likely led to the electrical arcing but given the damage they would not be able to identify the specific wire. Years later, the FAA would ground Boeing 737s from this era to inspect for this exact problem.

63: Monday – September 15, 1969

The Military Selective Service Act of 1967 expanded the age of conscription to those aged 18 to 35. Student deferments were still granted, but ended upon either completion of a four-year degree or 24th birthday, whichever came first.

Richard Carlton Anderson was ripe for the picking. He was young, healthy, a non-college student, not married, and had all of his teeth. During World War II men without enough teeth to eat K-rations were rejected. Ritchie wore a blue cotton shirt, tan pants, and loafers. He figured it was better to dress conservatively rather than piss off the wrong people. Stories were rampant about some belligerent anti-draft malcontent being a pain-in-the-ass summarily passed and loaded onto a bus headed for basic training.

Ritchie's father dropped him off at the draft board office in Hackensack ten minutes before 5:00 a.m. A drab green school bus was parked at the curb with its motor running. Beside it stood an Army sergeant holding a clipboard. Ritchie provided his name and was instructed to board the vehicle. He climbed onto the bus and looked into the dark interior. There were shadows spread throughout the bus. Unidentified young men seated here and there waiting to take the ride that would define their future. No conversation was heard. Each individual was left with their own thoughts and fears about what lay ahead. Ritchie found a set of empty seats and plopped down among the shadows. He thought of Wellington Marsh, Lance Corporal in the Marines, and wondered what he was doing at that moment. A smile crossed Ritchie's face as he concluded; the son-of-a-bitch was probably sleeping in his bed at his parent's house without a care in the world.

In a small brick ranch house in Southfield, Michigan a lone figure sat at a kitchen table in the dark. Wellington Marsh couldn't sleep. Too many images danced in his head. The flashflood was the most disturbing as he saw that car floating away carrying its passenger into oblivion. A child whose life lay ahead of him would not get the opportunity to live it. Wellington twisted and untwisted a paper napkin. What could they have done differently?

At five minutes after five the Army sergeant with the clipboard boarded the bus. His voice shattered the silence, "Listen-up! You are going to the Newark Military Entrance Processing Station (MEPS). Keep the shit out of your ears and follow orders. You'll be evaluated to determine if you are qualified to serve in the armed forces of the United States of America. It's going to be a long fucking day. So, don't screw around and make it any longer than necessary. Keep in mind this is a military facility. Follow orders, show respect, and listen up. Profanity, off-color language, and anti-American comments will not be tolerated. Hats, watches, jewelry, and other valuables are not permitted. They will be taken from you upon entry and returned when you leave. Good luck and have a nice day." He smiled and left the bus.

Ritchie looked out at the night obscured streets as the bus made its way to the New Jersey Turnpike. What fascinated him were the houses they passed. Most were dark but a few sported a light in one room or another. Those houses left Ritchie with a warm feeling as he imagined someone going about their business feeling comfortable and safe in their home. He did not share that feeling.

The illuminating overhead light caught Wellington by surprise. He turned to face the doorway and his father came into focus.

"Having trouble sleeping?" the older man asked.

"Yeah, just too much on my mind, I guess."

Peter Marsh walked over and sat opposite his son at the table. He immediately noticed the strangled napkin. His initial reaction was to make inquiries in order to determine what was bothering his son. Instead, he decided that it was up to Wellington to share his concerns if he wished. If not, he would respect the young man's privacy.

"Before we came here," Wellington began, "we came across a washed out road. There was a car with two children inside floating down a water run. Carl, Ritchie, and I made a chain and we were able to save a little Indian girl." He looked at his father who was paying close attention. "We tried to get back to the car for her older brother but it broke loose and floated away before we could get there." Wellington noticed his father slightly raise his chin in response. "I keep seeing those dark eyes staring at us while drifting away." The paper napkin endured more twisting. "He knew he was going to die but didn't scream or yell or show any sign of panic. We could only watch." Father and son looked into each other's eyes. One seeking answers the other wishing to help. "What kind of courage does it take to face death so calmly?"

The bus arrived at the Newark Military Entrance Processing Station and another sergeant came onboard. "Listen up! When you disembark this vehicle you will enter the building and make an immediate right into the staging area. Form four lines in front of the four admission tables. There you will check in and receive your personnel jacket. Put your name and Selective Service Number on it. Keep that jacket with you throughout the process. You will also place your name and Selective Service Number on a property envelope. Deposit all valuables in this envelope and give it to the designated staff member. From there follow instructions." His voice increased in volume as he added, "Now, Move it! Move it! Move it!"

Wellington's father leaned back in his chair and said softly, "Years ago, when you were just a boy, I was sent with a driver to pick up a machine part that was needed at the plant. We rode in a large panel truck. It was snowing and the roads were treacherous. I'm not sure how much experience the driver had in that kind of weather with that size vehicle. On our way back we were on a winding road along Lake St. Clair. It was on a pretty steep downgrade when we went into a skid. The driver couldn't get out of it and we headed for a low guard rail and a long drop to rocks by the lake. There wasn't time to jump even though it felt like slow motion. It was clear that we were going to be killed. At that moment a strange feeling of calm came over me. I don't know how to describe it. It was a peaceful sensation. I was prepared to die and didn't fear it." Peter Marsh sat up straight and concluded, "The truck hit the guard rail and somehow spun around without going over. We spun to the bottom of the hill." Wellington's father rubbed his chin and stated, "I hope you never have to come that close to death to experience the feeling."

The first room Ritchie and his fellow captives entered was a classroom style. In it were more than fifty small desks and on each was a packet of papers. The twenty victims in his group shuffled in. An Army specialist stood next to the door. He gave his prepared short speech, "Take any seat. There are three forms on the desk in front of you. A medical history, a background questionnaire, and a multiple choice test to measure intelligence. It's not a difficult test to pass so any of you guys who had student deferments that fail will be immediately drafted. Don't get cute. Put your name on the top of each document as you fill it out. Last name first, first name, middle initial. You have half an hour. Start now."

Wellington considered his father's story. He had never heard it. "I find that I'm like a traffic light. One day I feel strong and believe I can face what lies ahead. Then the next moment the light changes and I have no confidence at all."

"When the time comes and you need to make a decision to act that light will be bright green," Peter Marsh stated with conviction. "You've already proven that fact by doing so well during training." He stood and walked over to the stove, "Do you want some coffee?" Wellington nodded. As his father made coffee he added, "I've watched you grow up and you are smart—real smart—and you have more courage than you realize."

After finishing the intelligence test they were marched down a hall and lined up in the corridor. One by one each young man entered a room and a few minutes later returned. When Ritchie entered he was ordered to sit on a stool. A set of earphones was placed on his head and he was told to raise his hand when he heard a tone. With that test completed an eyechart was projected onto a wall and he was told to read the smallest line that he could. He obviously passed both tests.

As the coffee percolator erupted on the stove Peter Marsh returned to the table and sat. Both men sat in silence not knowing what to say. Finally, Wellington's father spoke, "When you face something difficult or frightening the best way to handle it is to look beyond it. Make plans, create a vision of the future. If you look past the bad part it becomes smaller in your mind." He stood and went to the stove. "One time when I got laid off and we didn't have any savings I didn't know what we were going to do. I'd break out in cold sweats. Your mother talked me into drawing up plans for a house we would build someday. I told her she was crazy. Well, I got so involved with doing that plan that our money troubles stopped haunting me. We picked up odd jobs and made it through the hard times." He placed a cup of coffee in front of Wellington, "I still have those plans."

The next stop for the gang of twenty was a long tiled room. Each man was given a beaker and told to piss in it. Some did right away while others stood there desperately hoping that a stream would start. Ritchie was able to squeeze out an acceptable amount and handed the beaker to a young corpsman. As he moved down the line he looked back at two members of the group who stood there hopelessly unable to urinate. There was something sad, pitiful, and unbelievably funny about that sight. They looked like Maple trees with buckets attached to collect the sap. Only the sap wasn't running on that morning. Ritchie swallowed a laugh but couldn't hide his smile. Blood was taken at the other end of the room and once more they found themselves in a corridor waiting.

Wellington saw his reflection in the coffee. He almost didn't recognize the visage that stared back at him. An older, more mature face with certain—oh, my God—features that resembled his father floated in the liquid.

A burly sergeant entered the corridor. He gave the order, "Strip down to your shorts," as he walked past the line of men. When he got to Ritchie he looked at his long hair with disdain. The two then had a staring duel. Finally, the big sergeant looked down at Ritchie's shirt and said, "Nice shirt. Does it come in men's sizes?" He moved on. While carrying their clothes the group was ushered into yet another room. Once inside they were lined up ten on each side facing each other. An Army Captain wearing medical corps insignia entered the room and ordered, "Drop your shorts and skin them back." Ritchie assumed that second part was for those fellows who were not circumcised. The doctor was followed by a corpsman who carried a box of gloves and a trash bag. Each candidate was examined and then tested for hernia. When he finished the Captain shouted "About face. Bend over and grab your ankles." The final indignity was a rectal exam. Someone passed wind.

"I remember the time when we went to that park and rented a rowboat. You and I were in the boat and mom was really nervous about getting in."

Peter Marsh finished the story, "Yeah, when she put one foot in the boat it moved away from the dock and she dropped like a sack of potatoes into the water."

Wellington laughed, "I can still she her with one foot on the dock and the other in the boat slowly doing a split."

"She was mad as hell at me for the rest of the day."

"It was a funny sight," Wellington smiled wide.

"It was."

Judith Marsh, Wellington's mother, entered the room, "What are you laughing about?"

The final stop for Ritchie was a quick medical exam and interview by a doctor. While waiting outside the examination room Ritchie looked at his personnel jacket and saw that he had passed all the previous tests. He was in—in trouble. The door opened and he walked slowly into the room and handed his personnel jacket to the doctor.

"You appear to be in pretty good shape," the middle-aged man in a lab coat stated, "any pain or ailments?"

"Not really."

The doctor went through his routine without saying anything else. When he listened to Ritchie's lungs with a stethoscope he tapped his back which caused the young man to jump in pain. "Did that hurt?"

"Yes."

The doctor ran his hand down Ritchie's spine pushing slightly on each vertebra. When he pushed one in the middle of his back Ritchie jumped and let out a low groan. "Have you been in an accident?"

Ritchie told the story of how they rescued a little girl. He remembered being hit in the back by a log or some other debris in the rushing water. The doctor listened intently, nodding from time to time. When Ritchie told how they were unable to save the girl's brother the doctor shook his head in sympathy. He picked up Ritchie's folder and as he made a note stated, "You have a cracked or dislocated disk. I'm giving you a medical deferment for six months. You should get that looked at by your doctor. X-rays will provide a more accurate diagnosis." He handed Ritchie the folder and added, "Son, sometimes as hard as you try there are some that you can't save. You have to let it go so that you can focus on those you can still help."

Ritchie knew the man was not referring specifically to the lost boy. Impulsively, he reached out and offered his hand. The doctor took it and they shook hands.

The Mets had won ten games in a row until they finally lost a game to the Pittsburgh Pirates on Sunday afternoon. From there they traveled to St. Louis. On this day they won 4 to 3 as a result of two homeruns hit by right fielder Ron Swoboda.

Jack Moore sat at the bar at More-Or-Less. He was waiting for Ryoya Akimoto. They had decided to meet for drinks after getting off from work. Harry Van Ryker, the bartender and owner, walked up behind Jack who was sitting in his observation pose scanning the room. "I heard you visited your old pal recently," Harry commented.

Jack turned to face his friend, "I spoke with Carmine Spacini—if that's who you are referring to. He's no friend. He's a criminal."

"Come' on Jack, use that line on the public," Harry replied. "You're seeing a cop. Word gets out about you being a chum with the godfather will hurt you and her."

"I simply went to get some answers," Jack countered. "As a matter-of-fact I got ushered out of the place unceremoniously for something I said."

"Yeah, nice act," Harry winked and Jack smiled. "Just be forewarned." Harry looked around and asked, "Where's your lady?"

Jack looked at his watch, "She's late. Probably got stopped on her way out. Hope she didn't catch a case. I might not see her for weeks."

"She's aces. How did a gazoonie like you ever get past a first date?"

"Charm, wit, good looks . . ."

Detective Ryoya Akimoto entered More-Or-Less. She didn't have to look around to find Jack. He was a creature of habit. As she made her way to where Jack sat he once again noted how seductively beautiful she was. Her long black hair hung below her shoulders draping a combination dress and vest ensemble. The dress had a dropped waist black skirt with self-belt and a bamboo beige top with wide lapels that hung over a black vest. A hemline above the knee revealed shapely legs that neither Jack nor countless other men in the bar could miss. Jack said, "Did I ever thank you?"

Harry replied, "You don't deserve it, ya bum. Besides you'll blow it, if I know you."

Jack stood when Ryoya arrived and the two hugged. Over his shoulder he heard Harry say, "Evening detective, what can I get you besides a better companion?"

"It's been a long day, Harry. Let me have a Margarita."

"Anything for you, sweetie."

"Anything?"

"Uh, oh," Jack said.

Ryoya gave Jack an accusing glance then turned her attention back to Harry, "I'll let you know what you just agreed to, later."

"I didn't agree to anything," Harry protested.

"You said anything," Jack reminded Harry. "I'm a witness."

Harry shook his head and wandered off to make Ryoya's drink. The couple walked over to an empty table and sat. Jack noticed that Ryoya was wearing the necklace he had given her with the Japanese figures which meant "treasure."

Jack broke the silence, "Colt and Stephanie hit it off. Not romantically, but philosophically. He is more intent on creating an international adoption agency than ever. My understanding is that he has agreed to help Stephanie go back to school and get an appropriate degree in order to be involved."

"He's quite a character. I like him."

Jack feigned a sad look and complained, "What about me? What am I chopped suey?"

"It's chopped liver and I rather think of you as an enlightened baseball fan. Before long I'll get you to sing the Mets theme song."

"Yeah, that'll happen. The day they win the World Series I'll sing it in the middle of Grand Central Station."

"That's two promises you've made. I better start writing them down," Ryoya smiled. She looked across the table at Jack and wished they were in her apartment where she could lose herself in his arms and leave the tough New York City Police Detective on a shelf. He was her oasis, her refuge, her opportunity to be a woman or on occasion a little girl. His other promise to marry her if the Mets won the World Series, although tempting, was destined to never happen. Some barriers were impenetrable and beyond the ability of individuals to defeat. Shikata ga nai.

Harry arrived with Ryoya's Margarita and another scotch-on-the-rocks for Jack. He gave Ryoya an inquiring look to which she replied, "Later."

Once alone again, Jack asked, "So, what have you in mind for our favorite barkeeper?"

Ryoya sipped her drink. That simple action aroused Jack. He wished they were alone at her place where he could find out what color underwear she was wearing.

"I have been given four tickets to Saturday afternoon's Mets game against the Pittsburgh Pirates," Ryoya broke the spell.

"Oh, and are you taking Colt?"

"Keep it up and I will. You can go to a Yankee game if you prefer. What are they in fifth place, like thirty games out?"

"Twenty-nine and a half."

"Right. Well there's always hope. With luck they could finish in fourth place."

"So, you have tickets to Saturday's game?" Jack changed the subject.

"Yes, would you like to join me?"

"Of course, I'll bring my hat." Ryoya smiled and nodded and Jack was back to wondering about her underwear.

Ryoya looked in the direction of Harry who was serving drinks to another table. "I was wondering if we could get Harry to join us."

"An afternoon game? We might. It'd be good for him to get out." Jack looked at Ryoya and saw something he recognized and didn't like. No longer was he interested in her underwear. It was definitely there and you didn't have to be a New York City detective to see it. Jack leaned forward and in an accusing voice asked, "Alright, who is going to use the fourth ticket?"

Ryoya sipped her drink.

"What's her name?" Jack pressed.

"What makes you think that I've decided who should get that ticket? It could be Colt for all you know."

"What's her name?" Jack repeated.

"You would be a poor detective because you jump to unfounded conclusions."

"What's her name?"

"If that's all you are going to say all night I might as well leave. I wonder what Colt is doing."

"What's her name?"

"Amanda."

"Why?"

"Because that's what her parents named her."

Jack laughed. He then forced a serious look and asked, "Why are you doing this?"

"Because I have four tickets."

"Harry will never go for it."

"I didn't plan on telling him. He doesn't have to know."

"For a detective, you sure didn't read Harry Van Ryker correctly. We'll be banned from the bar."

Ryoya stared at Jack for a prolonged period of time. He wasn't sure if she was angry or sad or considering what he said. Abruptly, she stood and walked over to the bar. She and Harry had a conversation that Jack couldn't hear. He observed Harry stand up straight, shake his head, and look around. The conversation continued. Finally, Ryoya turned and walked back to the table.

"Did he tell us to get the hell out of his bar?"

"No."

"Well, what did he say?"

"It was a private conversation."

By that time Harry arrived at the table. He addressed his comment to Ryoya, "Tell your Amanda not to expect much, but that I'm looking forward to meeting her."

64: Friday – September 19, 1969

Matthew Ellis wanted to run and hide to escape his past. Yet, he knew you can't un-ring a bell. And when that bell brings forth malevolence, pain, and suffering beyond imagination there is no escape from responsibility. He wondered, who was this man that callously put countless lives at risk for personal gain. What kind of mind could justify his actions or, for-that-matter, live with them? He began thinking of himself, pre-accident and coma, as Nightmare Matt because of all he wrought upon the world. Worst of all there was no way to stop the monster he and Lida Petropoulos created and unleashed. Even if they could identify where every inch of Orztech wire had been installed it was physically impossible to replace it.

Matt thought of Valerie, his wife, and Stephanie, his daughter. Two innocent souls who had no idea what an evil creature he was. His mind drifted. He and Valerie were sitting on a bench in a garden. Trees formed a dark green canopy above them and hedges sheltered them from an outside world. All the colors seemed sharper than normal as is the effect after a rain. Valerie had on a white sleeveless dress with cobalt blue roses. A tea length waist, pleated skirt, and white pumps completed an innocent and captivating image. As usual she sat very prim and proper. She was indeed a rare and beautiful flower that stood out in a world filled with weeds. A few birds were heard up in the trees otherwise it was quiet—overwhelmingly quiet. Matt looked into Valerie's deep brown eyes. She waited. He remembered a snowy evening so long ago when he breathlessly had stated, "You are all that is beautiful in my world." How true that comment had come to be. A tortured mind brought them here to a quiet garden. It was time for a snake to confess his sins. The innocence of Valerie magnified the guilt Matt felt. He didn't know where to begin.

A rustling sound caused Matt to turn. Through the bushes walked Lida Petropoulos. Confident and without hesitation she approached the couple on the bench. In contrast to Valerie, Lida wore a black silk chiffon cocktail dress with a fitted bodice, sheer straps, and black satin detailing. The gathered waist and full skirt emphasized her seductive movement as she drew near. Immediately, Matt recognized the matching gold and diamond necklace and earrings set he had given her. Nervously, he looked toward Valerie. She sat quietly and neither smiled nor frowned—simply watched. Lida stopped before them and said, "Aren't you going to introduce me?"

"I don't think this is a good idea," Matt responded.

"It's been a long time coming."

"No good can come from it."

"Ahh, but you are wrong—as usual." Lida stood before Valerie and introduced herself, "Mrs. Ellis, I'm the other woman. Your husband and I have been having an affair for quite some time."

Valerie didn't respond.

Lida glided over to Matt and ran her hand through his hair, "He can be quite a naughty boy. A lot more naughty than you have any idea."

Matt whispered, "Please don't."

"He bought me this," she held out the necklace. "I see you don't have a necklace.

Face it, sweetheart, you don't have a man either."

Valerie sat unmoved.

"It was easy bringing him under my spell. More easy than I anticipated." To Matt's surprise Lida raised the skirt of her dress to reveal lace panties with a floral pattern in violet/fuchsia. "He hand washed these panties for me." Embarrassed and ashamed Matt looked at his wife. She sat showing no emotion quietly watching Lida. "With a little corrective encouragement he makes quite a lover but you don't appear the type to draw that out of him." Matt felt anger well up inside but was unable to speak.

Lida continued, "Your husband and I were also business partners. We made quite a killing," she giggled and added, "killing in more ways than one, unfortunately. A little miscalculation in the manufacturing process." After moving to a few inches from Valerie's face Lida asked, "Do you know Mattie has over three quarters of a million dollars in a Hong Kong account?" She then stood back up, "Of course you don't. You scratched by raising a daughter on pennies unaware of the wealth I brought to your husband." Once more next to Matt, Lida said, "Take a good look at your knight in shining armor. Remove the façade and you have a filthy little rat scurrying in a sewer."

Valerie didn't move.

"You wholesome, pure, dignified, blind little bitch. Life isn't a ballet. You're not Odette, the white swan in Swan Lake. You are a misled, unappreciated, housewife whose entire life is a lie. There's no dignity in being a fool." Lida turned to Matt, gave him an icy stare, and said, "There, I did your dirty work, made your confession, and bared your soul. Do you feel redeemed?" She turned and left.

Matt's mind continued to paint its vision of what might have been had his accident not occurred. He looked at Valerie filled with remorse and shame but could not speak. Valerie slowly turned to face Matt. He watched a lone tear makes its way down her cheek.

After winning three games in a row, the New York Mets lost both games in a double header played against the Pittsburgh Pirates on this day. The first loss was 8 to 2 and the second 8 to 0. It was not a pleasant day for Met pitchers who gave up sixteen runs. Or, for that matter, for the offense who could only squeeze out two runs in 18 innings.

Dr. Tallman walked into the waiting room and smiled upon seeing Stephanie Ellis. "You're looking good. Happier than I've seen you in a while."

"I am," Stephanie stated emphatically with a smile.

He nodded.

"I think I've had my magic experience."

"You have?" he replied with enthusiasm.

"When I was at Woodstock I met an adopted Korean girl. She and her sister seemed so happy. For some reason I couldn't get the two of them out of my mind. It was such a beautiful story offering a child who didn't have much of a future a new and better life. That is something that I want to be a part of even though I don't have the training or education. I shared my feelings with a newspaper reporter who has been talking with my father and he introduced me to a man who has the same desire to get involved with adoption. He's from Texas and his family has a big ranch and money.

We're discussing me going back to school and he researching what is involved to start an adoption agency."

Dr. Tallman smiled, "Your magic experience."

"Yes, just as you predicted I found something that excites me. I just wanted you to know."

"Have you shared this with your father?"

"Not yet. He seems so preoccupied with something but won't tell me what."

"Regardless, you should talk with him—he's your dad and I know he will be interested."

"I will."

"Have you looked into schools?"

"I've just started. It's too late for the fall semester so the best I can hope for is the spring. I can take some courses at the community college but right now can't afford the tuition."

"Stephanie, get the information for the community college and bring it here. I'll cover the cost of tuition."

"No, I couldn't, I didn't come here, you don't, that wouldn't . . ." her voice trailed off.

Dr. Tallman took her hand, "I don't have any children. My practice takes all my time. In a way, if I help you and it, in turn, leads to you helping other children I'll have an extended family living better lives. Seems like a good investment to me. Besides, I believe in you—always have."

"You've already done so much."

"Nonsense, I didn't do that much. So, allow me to share in a small way your passion and dream."

"I don't know how to thank you."

"You just did." Dr. Tallman stood and walked around the waiting room. As if thinking out loud he commented, "I know the president of Farleigh Dickenson. I'll give him a call next week."

Wellington Marsh sat on the right side of the Greyhound bus so that he could watch countryside pass rather than stare at the oncoming lanes of a highway. He was on his way to Philadelphia where he would catch the Southern Railroad Southerner to Jacksonville, North Carolina. From there it would be a short ride on the regularly scheduled bus to Camp Lejeune. He looked at his orders that designated his next duty station as Da Nang, Republic of Vietnam.

The week seemed to fly by. First, he received a telephone call from Ritchie. Now, there is one lucky hippie, Wellington thought as he smiled. He was glad his new found friend had been spared the draft. The journey he and Carl and Ritchie made to almost escape to Canada came to mind but seemed so long ago. A part of the Marine Lance Corporal wondered if he hadn't made a mistake not crossing the border.

Teresa Champion spent as much time as possible with Wellington. More than once he explained that due to the fact that he was going into a dangerous war zone he didn't want any serious relationships. She would nod and then go right back to snuggling or clinging or stroking. Her intent was clear and the night before he had to leave Wellington succumbed to her alluring charms. He conquered and was conquered in one impulsive act. Teresa insisted that she was on the new birth control pills but that was a lie. When he told her goodbye he was more than aware that her efforts had worked.

When Wellington's mind drifted to Carl he wondered what that young man was running from but was glad that he found refuge at Lark's Run. Carl Pa-whatever was a man you could count on. He was solid as a rock and had tremendous courage. A bit rough around the edges, but Laurel would polish that gem. Wellington considered Carl a true and honest friend. He hoped the CAP squad he was about to take charge of would be filled with men like Carl. For some unknown reason his mind created a picture of thirteen men in fatigues all with long hair like Ritchie aimlessly milling around. "My God," he thought and he shook his head to remove the image.

The final thought the young Marine had was of Sergeant Kincaid. That tough, no nonsense, D.I. had to turn children into men and men into Marines in record time. In truth he was being asked the impossible. No wonder he had such a bad temper. Wellington smiled as he admitted to himself that he liked the bastard.

Unhappy with the progress of the police investigation of Sharon Tate's murder her father Colonel Paul Tate, a retired Army intelligence officer launched his own investigation. He let his hair grow long and grew a beard. Night after night he visited hippie joints looking for any clue to who murdered his daughter and her unborn child.

It seemed everybody had a theory as to who had done the crime. The most unique theory put forth suggested the murders never took place and were staged. It was based on the fact that Sharon Tate's father, Colonel Paul Tate, was one of the top brass at The Presidio base in San Francisco. With public support of the Vietnam War weakening a significant number of Army 'dissidents' against the war had established themselves at The Presidio and were gaining political strength. Major Peter Folger, father of Abigail Folger, who was purportedly killed along with Sharon Tate, worked in the same military intelligence operations as Colonel Tate and lived in San Francisco. In addition, the Folger family owned one of the largest coffee operations in the United States and had extensive interests in the low-cost production of coffee in Vietnam. Another officer, Colonel Michael Aquino, a military intelligence officer specializing in psychological warfare, was stationed at The Presidio and worked with Anton Szandor LaVey author, musician, circus/carnival performer, and occultist. In 1969 Aquino joined LaVey's Church of Satan that was headquartered two blocks south of the base. This connection was important because one of the persons who would later be accused of the murders, Susan Atkins, was a regular actress in occult-themed soft porn plays produced by LaVey's Church of Satan. Those who put forth this theory believed the faked murders were intended to sway public opinion against the anti-draft counterculture. Coincidence or conspiracy no arrests had yet been made.

65: Saturday – September 20, 1969

Nathan Anderson was sitting in his den reading when his son Ritchie entered the room. In silence the two looked at each other. The days of getting the baseball gloves and going out to play catch had long faded into a distant past. Semi-strangers waited for the other to speak. Ritchie walked over to a couch in the room and flopped down. His father waited. The ticking of a clock on the mantle over a fireplace dominated the room. Nathan Anderson looked at his long-haired, hippie son and wondered why the young man had chosen to drop out when he had so much going for him. He had talent, a quick mind, sense of humor, and stubborn streak much like his mother. Rather than a generation-gap there was a culture-gap between them. Hard as he tried he couldn't understand the anti-establishment mindset. Before him was his son from whom he felt detached. A degree of guilt presented itself but was tempered with the knowledge that he had done everything he could to raise the boy right and offer him the best possible start in life. Somehow it didn't work. The world had spun off in a peculiar direction and dragged Ritchie with it.

"How's your back?" Nathan Anderson asked his son.

"The doctor says it's a slightly slipped disc. It might find its way back into place or require manipulation. He wants to look at it again in two weeks."

Nathan nodded.

Ritchie moved nervously where he sat. He paused, looked at his father, and stated, "You know the World Trade Center they're building. I've been taking pictures of it from the beginning before they even knocked down the buildings that were originally there. My goal is to document this world-changing project. It's a first step in man's drive for world peace. Now that I don't have to worry about the draft for six months I can continue." Ritchie looked out the den window. It was a clear day and the morning sun cast long shadows on the yard. They moved with the breeze. One shadow resembled Manidoo-giizhikens, Little Cedar Spirit Tree, that the white man calls the Witch Tree. A fertile imagination caused Ritchie to wonder if the tree's spirit had followed him home.

Nathan Anderson waited.

Ritchie returned his attention to his father, "I have an idea I want to run by you."

"OK."

"You publish a lot of magazines," Ritchie waved his arm in the direction of a number of framed magazine covers that hung on a wall. "They are all nice, basic, and dull."

"And, put food on the table."

"I'm not saying they're bad. I'm saying they could be better." Ritchie leaned forward and stated with obvious enthusiasm, "They all look alike—a photo and a logo. I'd like to work for you and give each title a style of its own and updated fresh design. Make it stand out on the newsstand and you'll increase circulation," he paused then added, "and increase advertising sales."

Increased revenue was definitely of interest to the elder Anderson. Of greater interest, if that were possible, was the opportunity to bring his son into the business.

He'd seen Ritchie's artwork and found it to be highly imaginative and creative. It would have to be reined in to fit the needs of magazine publishing as commercial art is quite different from creative art. Nathan looked at the framed magazine covers on the wall. They could definitely use a facelift. He then turned his attention to his son. Could he depend on him to meet critical deadlines, take direction, accept criticism, dress appropriately, and get a damn haircut? What about his suspected drug use? That would not be tolerated. Unconsciously, he toyed with his gold watchband. It would be easy to hire the young man—not so easy to fire him. His businessman side cautioned against it. The father side ignored the advice and wanted to leap at the chance. Finally, he spoke, "I don't doubt that your talent would improve our magazine products. But, I'm running a business. I can't introduce a discordant note into the operation. You would have to adjust to working within a corporate environment. No artistic tantrums."

"Dad, I painted cars without complaint."

"Proper dress is a jacket and tie."

"I'll look in the back of my closet."

"And, absolutely no drugs of any kind."

"Does that include aspirin?"

Ritchie's father gave him an icy stare, "No being a wiseass either."

"I'll try."

"And, get a haircut."

Ritchie stood and walked toward the door as he said, "Well it was nice while it lasted."

His father watched him walk to the door and asked, "Having long hair is that important to you?"

Ritchie turned, "It's who I am—a statement. One man may grow a beard another shave his head. It's all about self-image—being comfortable in your skin. Force a change and you're a stranger to yourself. If you worked for a company and they required that you have long hair like mine you'd never survive. You'd be so uncomfortable it would affect your work and attitude." Ritchie walked back toward his father, "I want to do this. It would be a creative challenge. I can live within the rules, wear a suit, let some poltroon criticize my work, but not as Mr. Someone-else."

"I see."

"How about this? When at work, I'll wear a ponytail."

Nathan Anderson sat and thought about his son's offer. Ritchie was making a gesture, a compromise, although slight. He wondered what would be the reaction of the staff. Would other male employees feel that it was acceptable to grow long hair? Would the office start looking like a commune? Would they have to spray for lice? He smiled. A good business decision weighs the ROI, considers risk, and looks long term. Ultimately, the decision made, he said, "We can try that. One requirement; the ponytail has to be tied with a ribbon and a large bow." Nathan laughed seeing the look on Ritchie's face.

Jack Moore met Harry Van Ryker at More-Or-Less. From there they took a taxi to Ryoya's apartment where they were to meet the ladies. Jack was dressed casually with a black golf shirt and brown pants. Harry was slightly more formal with black slacks a light blue shirt and gray sport jacket.

"You're looking dapper," Jack commented as they rode in the cab.

"I'm meeting a lady. Far better to put my best foot forward."

"Just don't put your foot in your mouth."

"I'm not you."

Jack nodded with a half-smile indicating that he didn't have a response.

"Do you know this Amanda?" Harry asked.

"Never met her. Never heard of her until last night," Jack confessed.

"I like Ryoya and think I can trust her, but you know when it comes to blind dates it's totally unpredictable."

"It's a day at the ballpark. Nobody's asking you to marry her," Jack reminded his friend.

"That's good because I'm too set in my ways to change my life now."

The two gentlemen arrived at Ryoya Akimoto's apartment promptly at 1:00 p.m. which gave them plenty of time as the game was scheduled to start at 2:08 p.m. When the door opened Ryoya stood before them wearing red shorts and a grey Mets tee shirt.

"Right on time," Ryoya smiled, "an endearing trait of Mr. Moore." She led them into the living room where a slim woman in her mid-fifties with auburn brown hair pulled back into a ponytail sat. She wore tan slacks, a turquoise blouse, and blue Mets baseball cap.

Upon seeing Amanda, Harry said, "Amy? How are you?"

"Hi, Harry."

Ryoya looked at each of them and asked, "You know each other?"

"Tom and Harry knew each other, on the job, but that was a long time ago," Amanda explained.

"How long has it been since he passed?" Harry asked.

"Two years."

"He was a good man."

"He was a good husband."

A period of awkward silence hung in the room. Jack broke the spell when he reached into a bag he was carrying and retrieved a stuffed black cat. He handed it to Ryoya, "If Casey doesn't show up here's a stand-in. I named him after the first New York Mets player to ever hit a home run."

"I know that I shouldn't ask," Ryoya stated, "But, who hit the first-ever Met home run?"

Jack began his oratory, "April 11, 1962, it was a cool overcast day when the brand new expansion team took to the field. The first game of the first season of the New York Mets was played at Bush Stadium against the St. Louis Cardinals. Trailing 5 to 2, the lead-off Met batter in the fourth inning hit a home run to centerfield. After playing 16 years with the Dodgers in Brooklyn and Los Angeles, Gil Hodges was one of the original New York Mets. The 38 year-old first baseman with ailing knees hit the Mets first home run. Unfortunately, they went on to lose the game 11 to 4—a portend of things to come."

"You've been reading again," Ryoya concluded.

Amanda decided to address the discomfort obviously being felt by Harry. "Harry, when Ryoya invited me to go to the ball game and told me you would be going I welcomed the opportunity. I was blessed to have the time that I had with Tom. After two years, it's time that I start to live once more and I couldn't think of a better person to start with." Her countenance changed and she added, "If you'd rather not, I understand."

Harry replied, "You wore a light green dress and white hat at the Captain's party one year. I thought you were ravishing and couldn't take my eyes off you. You didn't notice but I avoided you all night so that I wouldn't make a fool of myself. You still have that effect on me."

Ryoya looked at Jack who glanced upward in disbelief.

They rode the 7 Line to Mets-Willets Point arriving with time to spare. Their seats were on the mezzanine level along the first base line. Harry and Amanda had disappeared to get beer and hotdogs leaving Ryoya and Jack alone.

"I guess you did OK," Jack nodded in the direction of the concession stands.

"I think they're cute."

"Cute is not a term that I would ever attach to Harry Van Ryker."

"Well, I would." Ryoya played with the stuffed black cat. Jack watched and thought how innocent and sweet she could be in spite of being a tough New York City detective. Of course, he also knew she could be a loud obnoxious Mets fan.

It was Bob Moose (12-3) pitching for the Pirates versus Gary Gentry (11-12) for the Mets.

Harry and Amanda returned with food and beer. They were laughing and acting well below their ages. When Jack and Ryoya looked in their direction, Harry said, "Can you believe that Amy went to the Broadway show *Hair*? I asked her if she took off her clothes."

Amanda answered, "I told him that I didn't because I was in the balcony." They sat down and Amanda continued, "It was quite an experience. What story there was wasn't very clear. It was about a tribe, as they called themselves, of hippies living in New York City. The leader is named Claude. He passes his draft board physical but is torn as to what to do next. One of the Negro hippies says the draft is white people sending black people to make war on the yellow people to defend the land they stole from the red people. They try to convince Claude to burn his draft card. He fakes it and burns his library card. The whole production was somewhat bizarre but interesting. They explain the significance of long hair by saying kids should be free, no guilt and do whatever they want, just so long as you don't hurt anyone."

Jack added, "I remember a theater writer who called long hair the hippie's flag and that they consider themselves patriots for trying to save America."

"I don't know that I would go that far but there was an innocence about their views and attitudes." Amanda looked at Jack and asked, "You were at Woodstock. What is your opinion of the hippie movement?"

"Innocence is a good word. What I found were thousands of young people wanting to 'drop out' of a world they didn't create nor that they believe in. Naïve is another accurate word. They are opposed to the evil system but drive up there in cars with coolers and tents and expect someone to provide basic services. It's like a ten-year-old wanting to run away from home with no idea where to go or how they would survive. I find their openness and welcoming of strangers the most appealing element. Also, they were authentic. None of it appeared to be an act. However, the use of drugs was so rampant it will sink the movement into hallucination and death."

Harry handed Ryoya a hotdog as he commented, "I told Amy that I would take her to see *1776*. It's a Broadway play about the writing and signing of the Declaration of Independence. That's more my speed."

"I don't know," Amanda said with a captivating smile, "there's probably no nudity."

Matty Alou had a leadoff single for the Pirates to start the game. After that both teams failed to have a hit for three innings. Then, in the top of the fourth, Pirates Dave Cash walked and Willie Stargell singled. Roberto Clemente came to bat. During Clemente's at-bat Cash stole third and Stargell stole second. Then a wild pitch allowed Cash to score. Clemente ultimately walked and the next batter, first baseman Al Oliver, was hit by a pitch. This loaded the bases with no one out.

Jack looked at Ryoya. Ryoya looked at Jack. Then she blew, "Hey, Gentry, which side are you playing on? Get your head in the game."

Jack waved the stuffed black cat at Ryoya.

Manny Sanquillen, the Pirates catcher, came to bat. The third pitch to him was a wild pitch and Stargell scored from third.

At that point Harry Van Ryker got into the spirit of the game. He yelled, "Ah, come 'on, they don't need your help. Make em earn their runs."

Sanquillen grounded out to 3rd base allowing Clemente to score. The next two batters hit fly balls for the final two outs.

"Three runs on one hit is not a winning formula," Ryoya observed.

The Mets went down in order in the bottom of the fourth. In the fifth inning both teams had a walk but no hits. After five innings the Mets had yet to have a hit. Harry tapped Ryoya on the arm and asked, "I'm new to this game. Aren't the Mets supposed to hit the ball and get on base or something like that?"

Ryoya glared at the sixty-two year old bartender but couldn't help but smile seeing his lovable face.

The Pirates had two hits in the sixth inning but didn't score. The Mets went down in order. Both teams went down in order in the seventh inning. In the eighth inning Tug McGraw was the relief pitcher for the Mets. Again, both teams went down in order.

At the beginning of the Ninth inning Jack tried to start a chant of Casey, Casey but found he was a solo act. "I guess they didn't read my column," he stated, "that's depressing."

Ryoya comforted him, "Don't feel bad. It's loud, they just didn't hear you." She smiled at Amanda.

In the top of the ninth the Pirates had two singles and scored on a wild pitch. The leadoff batter for the Mets was walked. Ryoya jumped to her feet and yelled, "Bring em home. Rally, rally, rally!" She also was a solo act.

"Don't feel bad," Jack offered, "they didn't hear you."

Unfortunately, the next three batters fouled out, ground out, and ground out to end the game. The Mets were on the losing side of a 4 – 0 no-hitter. Even worse it was their third loss in a row as they were trying to win the National League East title.

Jack handed the black cat to Ryoya. She took it and said, "Your cat is defective. Like you—defective," she paused, "but cute." She kissed Jack. "I need a drink." Ryoya turned to Harry and asked, "Whose minding the store?"

66: Sunday – September 21, 1969

Lance Corporal Wellington Marsh arrived at Camp Lejeune early in the morning. He immediately, reported to the adjutant's office who directed him to report to Company Commander, Captain Strong.

"Corporal Marsh here are your orders," Captain Strong said as he handed folded papers to the Marine. "You will depart from New River Air Station at 1115 hours. Sergeant Oldenburg will get you there. Your equipment voucher is included with your orders. Stop by supply and get squared away. Any questions?"

"No sir."

Captain Strong rose from his desk and walked around to where Lance Corporal Wellington Marsh stood. "Son, I'm confident that you have what it takes to make the CAP program a success. You exercise good judgement. Don't second-guess your decisions. What we taught you are the basics. In the field you'll learn far more. Learn quickly and take care of your men. Make us proud, Marine."

"Aye, aye, sir."

"Semper fi."

"Ooh Rah."

"Get the hell out of here."

Wellington couldn't hold back a smile. He saluted, turned smartly on his heel, and left Captain Strong's office. At base supply he was issued the uniforms and equipment on his voucher. Weapons, ammunition, field uniforms, and military equipment would be issued in Vietnam. Sergeant Oldenburg drove him the few miles to New River Air Station. When he dropped the young Marine off in front of an administration building he said, "This is Airforce Military Airlift Command (MAC). They will have all of your travel arrangements." He turned in his seat to face Wellington, "Those yahoos in the five-sided squirrel cage believe in the CAP program. You'll make it work if you stand tall and stay frosty. Just don't become a Lance Colonel—listen to your men, especially those who have been there. They'll get you home for Christmas. Semper fi."

"Ooh Rah," Wellington departed the vehicle and headed toward the building.

Inside the building he found five other Marines of various ranks. The highest rank was a First Lieutenant. Wellington handed his orders to the on-duty clerk. After checking his records, the clerk said, "OK, Corporal you will be taking the U-21 to Raleigh where you'll board a chartered 727 to Travis Air Force Base and then a charter flight to Cam Ranh Bay airbase in Vietnam. Your flight leaves in an hour."

"What is a U-21?" Wellington asked.

"That's a U-21," the clerk pointed out a window to a Beechcraft King Air Multirole Transport. It was a twin engine turbo-prop airplane that seats eleven. There was a fuel truck next to it.

Nick walked up behind Carl Pythacyk, "Do you know how to drive a tractor?"

Carl turned, "No, but I'm willing to learn."

"Good. There's a field that we want to start to utilize. I can't do it and, don't say anything to the ladies lest we have an uprising, I don't want any of them put at risk."

"I understand."

"In some ways, I'm old school. Hold the door for a lady, ladies first, show respect, and there are some tasks that require strength. This is one of them."

"So, if I tell them you didn't want a woman to do this job?"

"The memorial service will be tomorrow." Both men laughed. Nick liked Carl. He didn't want to know what Carl was hiding from. From his experience with the young man he was dependable, honest, hard-working, non-complaining, and smitten with Laurel Fitzpatrick. Many years in the military gave Nick a perspective on judging character and Nick would welcome Carl along heading into a hot LZ. "Meet me by the tool shed in an hour."

Wellington found a place to sit. He no sooner sat down when another Marine entered the room. It was Marvin Press, known as Shortstop, with whom Wellington had trained. Both men saw each other at the same time. "Shortstop, you heading west, too?"

"More than that, I'm going with you."

"What are you talking about?"

"The CAP program—I volunteered. I asked Captain Strong and he said he'd arrange it that I get assigned to your squad."

"Are you sure you want to do that?"

"Too late now."

The First Lieutenant overheard the conversation and asked, "What's CAP?"

"Combined Action Program, sir," Wellington answered. "We partner with local home guard militia to help protect villages and keep them from being sanctuaries for Viet Cong guerillas."

"Sounds dangerous. How do you know the militia aren't VC or sympathizers?"

"I guess you find out over time."

"If you live long enough."

"Yes, sir."

"Who is leading this squad?"

"I am, sir."

"You! A Lance Corporal! How much time have you spent in Nam?"

"Never been there, sir." Wellington was getting annoyed and didn't wish to continue the conversation. What wasn't needed at that time was negativism. He was nervous enough and had a head filled with images of a disaster. Twelve Marines and a Navy Corpsman would depend on him to make the right decisions. Thirteen lives would be in his hands. Fourteen if he counted his own. Funny how the thirteen seemed more important.

"You've never been in-country and you're going to lead a squad in the bush? That's suicide."

"Yes, sir."

"Have you ever driven a car with a standard transmission?" Nick asked.

"I've never driven a car," Carl replied as he remembered Ray Esposito telling him to get a license.

"OK, well, that makes it a little more complicated." Nick showed Carl all of the pedals and levers that controlled the 1952 International Harvester McCormick Farmall general-purpose red tractor. He spent the next half hour demonstrating the clutch, brake, transmission, gas, and more. "The important thing to remember is that this is a direct drive vehicle. When in doubt press the clutch. If it gets bogged down the front will come right up over you if you let it."

"Sounds dangerous."

"More farmers are killed in tractor accidents than any other cause."

"I'm the guy who liked your ale. Why are you trying to kill me?"

Nick smiled, "Also, these tractors are very unstable. They will roll over quickly if you aren't careful. Don't drive crosswise on a steep incline. If you do feel it leaning too much turn downslope."

They spent the next half hour with Carl driving the tractor around in front of the tool shed. After some rough first attempts, Carl began to get the hang of it and gained confidence. Nick told him to drive around the farm on the paths to practice.

After a short flight from New River Air Station to Raleigh-Durham Airport Wellington Marsh and the other Marines walked across the tarmac and boarded a chartered Boeing 727 using the airstair that opened from the rear of the underbelly of the fuselage. This was a unique feature of this aircraft. Inside there were rows of three seats on either side of a center aisle. Wellington was surprised to see that the aircraft was more than half full with military personnel from all branches. He and Shortstop slipped into seats on row twenty over the wing. They could just barely see upfront to first class where a number of men in suits were seated. Obviously, these were government officials. Wellington's group was the last to arrive as the airstair was closed and the jet prepared for takeoff.

When they began to taxi Shortstop said in a low voice to Wellington, "What was the idea of the LT telling us we are going to get killed?"

"Probably just warning us to stay alert," Wellington responded.

"Well, it gave me the heebie-jeebies."

"We all just have to watch out for each other. Maybe, because we are new they will give us a less threatening group of villages to protect," Wellington said hopefully. "You know, let us get our feet wet before we are thrown into the middle of things."

"Yeah, that's what I want, less threatening."

The chartered plane moved into line and approached the runway.

"You ever fly before?" Shortstop asked.

"No."

"Me neither," Shortstop admitted, "I'm starting to not feel so good right now. There are too many people on this thing. It's too heavy. It'll never get off the ground."

"I don't think it's going to be running down a highway all the way to California," Wellington said. "Relax, planes are flying all over the world right now."

"Yeah, and they drop like refrigerators too often if you ask me."

"When we're in a jungle in Vietnam, you're going to look back on flying as a walk in the park."

The jet turned onto the runway and stopped.

"Why'd we stop? Did something break?" Shortstop said.

Before Wellington could answer the three engines of the aircraft roared into takeoff mode and the jet rushed forward generating lift. On the Boeing 727, due to having all three engines in the rear, leading edge slats and trailing-edge flaps could extend the entire length of the wing. These allowed it to takeoff on short runways, as well as remain stable at slower speeds. Charter flight ML349 became airborne at 1240 hours.

"Oh, my God!" Shortstop commented.

An Air Mexicana Boeing 727 taxied from the gate at O'Hare Airport in Chicago at 12:50 p.m. in the afternoon. A bright midday sun and clear blue sky promised a pleasant flight. Flight MX801 was bound for Benito Juárez International Airport in Mexico City. There were 111 passengers and 7 crew onboard the jet. Total flight time would be approximately four and a half hours.

One of the flight attendants, Graciela Guadarrama, did the safety presentation that she had done countless times before. This was the last leg of a three day schedule that had taken her to Puerto Vallarta, Corpus Christi, Dallas, Los Angeles, and Chicago. She was tired and couldn't wait to get home. Her husband, Carlos Guadarrama, was a pilot for Air Mexicana and would be arriving home later that day. They planned on a two day mini-vacation.

Flight MX801 reached cruising altitude of 30,000 feet approximately twenty-five minutes after takeoff at which time the cabin crew began serving lunch and drinks.

Charter flight ML349 reached cruising altitude and proceeded due west at 575 miles-per-hour. The non-stop trip would take five hours and seventeen minutes. After his initial panic Marvin Press fell into a catatonic state mumbling from time to time. Over Mississippi the flight hit turbulence. Marvin didn't say anything but his eyes grew large and he had a death grip on the armrests. Wellington was fascinated by the whole experience. He was glad that he had taken the window seat. Below countryside, roads, and towns silently slid beneath them. Every once in a while a wispy cloud would pass. For the next few hours at least he would not have to think about Vietnam, war, or death. He would simply soar with eagles over a beautiful world below.

Air Mexicana Flight MX801 followed the flightpath toward Mexico City. The flight had been smooth and uneventful. By all indications they would arrive approximately ten minutes early. At that moment they were over Texas still enjoying clear skies.

Over Texas, charter flight ML349 encountered a problem. Unknown to the passengers, the flight crew scrambled to find the cause of an electrical failure. The first indication was an engine one fire warning lamp and audio signal. They quickly shut down the engine which also shut down the number one generator. An overload condition on number two generator, caused by a sudden shift of operating load led to its failure and loss of all electrical power. Without lights or instruments the flight crew had no way of determining altitude, attitude, climb/descent, or direction of the aircraft. The pilots would have declared an emergency but without radios didn't have that opportunity. In fact, trying to visually fly an airliner without instruments was nearly impossible even though the flight-control system wasn't affected by the loss of electrical power, since it relied on hydraulic and mechanical lines. However, much like trying to judge how fast one is driving a car without a speedometer it is damn near impossible to judge airspeed, angle of decent, direction, trim, and more only by visual observation. Not to mention the fact that the landing gear couldn't be lowered.

The pilot thought of the many instances where 727s were flown into the ground or water. August 16, 1965, United Airlines Flight 389 had a controlled flight into the waters of Lake Michigan while on approach to Chicago. November 8, 1965, American Airlines Flight 383 flew into a low hill during approach to Cincinnati airport. November 11, 1965, United Airlines Flight 227 crashed about 340 feet short of the runway after an excessively steep final approach in Salt Lake City. February 4, 1966, All Nippon Airways Flight 60 flew into the waters of Tokyo Bay about 6.5 miles from Haneda airport. February 16, 1968, Civil Air Transport Flight 010 impacted trees short of the runway in Linkuo, Taiwan. January 5, 1969, Ariana Afghan Airlines Flight 701 hit trees and a house about 1.5 miles short of the runway near Gatwick Airport, England. January 18, 1969, United Airlines Flight 266 reported an engine one fire warning then crashed at high speed into Santa Monica Bay. June 4, 1969, Mexicana Flight 704 hit high ground during approach in Monterey, Mexico. He knew of all these incidents because it seemed like more than a coincidence that so many Boeing 727s were having similar accidents. It was simply a case of making sure you know the aircraft you are flying.

It was then that the pilot noticed that the aircraft was nosing down. And, it appeared to be doing so at an increasing angle. He pulled back on the yoke as he called over his shoulder to the flight engineer. "Switch to the backup electrical system before we crash this goddamned thing!" When the engineer found the switch and flipped it instruments came back to life. Number three generator carried the load but for how long they couldn't be sure.

With radios operating they declared an emergency and were diverted to Dallas-Ft. Worth Airport. With the autopilot once more engaged the jet remained stable. The pilot followed air traffic control instructions for course adjustments and landing approach. While he was focused on getting the aircraft safely on the ground his mind also analyzed what had occurred. The plane definitely nosed down when they lost electrical power. Why? In but a few seconds the reason became obvious. The horizontal stabilizer was operated by a main electric trim motor, an autopilot trim motor, or by manual control cable. When the power went out air pressure on the elevator caused it to move. He realized, if an aircraft was on approach and descending the loss of electrical power might cause the elevator to abruptly shift in a direction that would dramatically increase the pitch downward. Without electrical power to the instruments the flight crew wouldn't realize what was happening until it was too late. If that were indeed the case the question became why had so many 727s lost all electrical power.

Nick heard a tractor motor and turned to see Carl approaching. The young man had a large grin on his face. It was obvious he was having fun. From his vantage point Nick concluded that Carl had definitely gotten the hang of the thing. Now, all he had to do was teach him how to use the plowing attachment and point him in the right direction.

Dallas-Ft. Worth Airport came into view. Charter flight ML349 approached on two engines. Engine One remained shut down due to fire indication. They were cleared for an uninterrupted approach on Runway 31R. It was a 9,000 foot runway with Fire Station Number Three located near the end.

The pilot brought the aircraft onto the glide path. As he did, he kept his eyes on the instrument panel and prayed that it wouldn't disappear. They were on back-up electrical power which meant if that was lost there weren't any other options. He made the decision to lower the landing gear earlier than normal with that potential hazard in mind. It was at that time when he made the announcement, "This is the captain; we have experienced a mechanical problem and will be landing at Dallas-Ft. Worth Airport. There is no reason for concern. The landing will be routine. However, as a precaution I request that you follow the cabin crew's instructions for an emergency landing."

"Emergency landing!" Marvin Press yelled. "What emergency landing?"

"It's just a precaution," Wellington said trying to calm his friend.

One of the stewardesses stood in the aisle and explained that when told they should place their feet and knees together with their feet flat on the floor and tucked behind the knees to prevent shins and legs from being broken against the base of the seat in front. Next they should place their head in their lap and grip the seat in front of them. This was called a brace position.

"We're gonna crash!" Marvin said.

"We are not going to crash," Wellington insisted.

The passenger section of the aircraft became very quiet.

In the cockpit the captain strained to see the visual approach slope indicator (VASI) lights next to the runway. This airport had standard three bar lights. When they came into view all three sets of lights were white indicating that they were too high on the glide path. He expected that and ordered that the landing gear be lowered. Electric motors whined as the gear came down.

"What's that?" Marvin asked in panic. When the gear locked into place with a thump he said, "It broke—what broke?"

With the landing gear down the increased drag slowed the aircraft which caused it to lose altitude placing it precisely on the proper glide path. They came in over the end of the runway and the pilot announced, "Brace, brace, brace." Charter flight ML349 touched down softly and rolled to the end of the runway.

Air Mexicana Flight MX801 was cleared for landing on runway 23L at Juarez International Airport, Mexico City. They were using the Instrument Landing System (ILS) on approach. Using radio signals the jet lined up with the glide path and passed the outer marker at 4.74 miles from the end of the runway. The middle marker, located .6 miles from the end of the runway, was where the pilot would switch to visual landing rules (VLR). He ordered that the landing gear be lowered. As the wheels locked into place the instrument panel went dark. They were .9 miles from the runway. The pilot knew he had to abort the landing, however, before he could do anything the jet nosed down and hit the ground short of the runway. After bouncing on the landing gear undercarriage it went airborne until the wheels and forward part of the aircraft hit a railroad embankment. The 727 broke into pieces. No information pertaining to the crash could ever be retrieved because the Flight Data Recorder had been incorrectly installed two days prior to the accident. Also, the Cockpit Voice Recorder had been previously removed and no replacement had ever been installed.

Twenty two of the one hundred eleven passengers were killed and five of the seven crew including the flight crew so no details about lost electrical power would be shared. Flight attendant, Graciela Guadarrama, was one of the two crew survivors. She escaped essentially uninjured. Two years after the crash she retired. Almost seventeen years after the incident, on April 2, 1986, she and her sons Rodolfo 10, and Juan 8, were aboard a Mexicana Boeing 727 that had taken off from Mexico City heading to Puerto Vallarta, Mazatlan, and Los Angeles. Her husband, the aircraft's pilot Carlos Guadarrama, had arranged for the family to go on a delayed Easter vacation to Disneyland. Less than 30 minutes after taking off the jetliner unexpectedly nosed down and slammed into the Sierra Madre mountainside about 80 miles northwest of the capital. All 158 passengers and 8 crew members perished.

Two hours after Charter flight ML349 landed in Dallas-Fort Worth a replacement aircraft arrived to take the military personnel to Travis Air Force Base. The original pilot remained with the stricken 727. Examination of the aircraft revealed a bundle of wires whose melted insulation and subsequent heat was probably enough to set off the engine fire sensors that prompted the engine one shutdown. The wire bundle was part of new wiring that had been used when generator upgrades were installed.

67: Monday – September 22, 1969

The earth shook. It took the form of a rolling vibration that continued for thirty to forty seconds. Reaching outward from the epicenter, the motion traveled for hundreds of miles. For villagers along the Taklamakan desert of Xinjiang Autonomous Region the tremor was no surprise. Yang Liang instinctively stopped what he was doing and looked in the direction of Lop Nor. Neither a flash nor cloud of dust was visible. With no other physical sign he wondered if his senses had misled him. They had not. On this day the Chinese government detonated a 19.2 kiloton nuclear device in an underground tunnel at Lop Nor. This was their ninth nuclear test, designated CHIC-9, by the newly emerging nuclear power.

China, under the guise of developing peaceful nuclear energy, initiated its nuclear weapons program in 1953. The communist nation had earlier signed a secret agreement with another communist nation in 1951 whereby in exchange for technical assistance China would export uranium ore to the USSR. The Soviet Union sent advisers to assist with construction of uranium-enrichment plants in Baotou and Lanzhou, a plutonium facility in Jiuquan, and nuclear test site at Lop Nor. In October 1957 the USSR agreed to provide a prototype bomb, missiles, and related technology.

Unfortunately, relations cooled between the two nations in 1958. Mao was unhappy with Soviet leader Nikita Khruschev's decision to discuss arms control with the United States and Britain. By June 1959 the two nations ended their agreement to cooperate and the Chinese nuclear program was temporarily halted when all Soviet technicians left in July 1960.

At the same time the President of the United States made a commitment to land a man on the moon, China made a commitment to join the world's nuclear powers on its own. The Soviet head-start allowed for accelerated progress in the development of a weapon.

The first Chinese nuclear test, designated Project 596, was conducted on October 16, 1964 at the test facility at Lop Nor. A fission device with a yield of 25 kilotons was detonated in a tower. Uranium 235 was used as the nuclear fuel. This fact was a clear indication that Beijing sought to create high-yield nuclear weapons as quickly as possible. China launched its first nuclear missile October 25, 1966 and detonated its first hydrogen bomb June 17, 1967.

At the test site Chinese soldiers served in a unit called "Nuclear 8023." Immediately after each nuclear detonation, 30,000 soldiers were sent to ground zero in tanks, trucks, and on foot for maneuvers. They then lived at the site for approximately six months. The only protection offered was their military uniforms. Little was known or said about radiation. Both in the short term and long term as numerous soldiers suffered a wide range of health problems but received little or no treatment. China was determined to be a nuclear power no matter the cost.

When the call came Detective Ryoya Akimoto felt her stomach muscles tighten as she listened to the voice of the duty sergeant. A woman's body had been found in an alley on West 44th Street. There was little other information available. She and Detective Michael Donovan were assigned the case and headed to the location. As they drove to the crime scene Ryoya attempted to prepare herself for what she feared. "I don't have a good feeling about this," she admitted to her partner.

"I thought they were going to fence that alley off."

"Obviously, they didn't."

Michael Donovan inquired, "You think it's the hooker that killed Miguel?"

"Her name is Claire Payton."

"Yeah, her."

"I hope that it isn't, but the location, timing, circumstances all point in that direction," Ryoya said sadly.

"If she didn't go into hiding or agree to work for Miguel's crew it could easily be her."

They arrived at the scene and parked on the sidewalk along with two patrol cars and the coroner's station wagon. Yellow crime scene tape once again cordoned off the alley. There were remnants of tape from two previous homicides.

In the alley Ryoya saw a body. It was a female in a sitting position leaning against a metal railing that surrounded cement stairs leading down to a basement. Her arms were tied to the top of the rail creating an image of a crucifixion. From all indications she had been severely beaten before her throat was cut. It was Claire Payton.

Michael Donovan came up behind Ryoya and looked at the victim, "Damn!"

"She would have been better off in jail," Ryoya stated in an angry tone.

"This is payback."

"The evil of Miguel Juarez lives on."

Detective Donovan knelt next to the body and stared at the gaping wound. The expression on the victim's face struck him. Where one might expect to see terror or pain there was an odd look of peace. He thought, at least life can't hurt her anymore.

"I want these bastards!" Ryoya said.

"We'll get them," he replied.

Ryoya Akimoto squatted down. She looked into the open eyes of Claire Payton, the woman who saved a young girl from a life in hell, and saw a lost soul.

A long sleepless night concluded with touchdown at Cam Ranh Bay Airbase in the province of Khanh Hoa, Vietnam. Wellington Marsh, along with twenty-three other military personnel, had boarded the C-130E Hercules Transport by climbing up the ramp at the rear of the aircraft. Inside they found two jeeps and stacks of munitions and supplies destined for the war zone. The passengers shuffled along until they found a row of fold down seats along the outside walls of the big plane. Seats were only slightly cushioned and the backs consisted of a wide crisscross weave of red canvass straps. Lap belts were available for takeoffs and landings. Wellington found a seat and Shortstop plopped down next to him. The young Lance Corporal looked around the cavernous interior of the aircraft. He guessed the cargo compartment was at least ten feet wide and over forty feet long. The ceiling seemed far above while being about nine feet high. Above he saw pipes, tubes, wires, and some padding. A row of lights hung on each side just below where the body started to curve to form the ceiling. There were recesses along each wall where tools, lash-down chains, chain tensioners, and other equipment was stowed. Small portholes dotted the forward portion of the cabin. One would have to stand to peer out. A distinct odor of jet fuel mixed with packing materials and an aroma from the lashed down jeeps made Lance Corporal Marsh feel like there wasn't enough air in the compartment. Opposite him was an emergency exit that curiously had a warning in red "propeller." He thought, that would be no fun to have to evacuate and run into a spinning prop. After the huge ramp rumbled and creaked until it was closed and the aircraft began to move it became clear to Wellington that the next time he saw the sky it would be on the other side of the world.

Once they were airborne they were allowed to move around the compartment even though there was little space to do so. At one point, Wellington found himself in front of a Marine Gunnery Sergeant. By the ribbons on his chest it was clear that he had combat experience. Wellington asked, "Any advice for a first-timer?"

"Don't get killed."

"That is my intent."

"You misunderstand. You can be killed but don't get killed. You get killed if you do something stupid."

Wellington stared at the older man not knowing what to say.

The Gunnery Sergeant continued, "Say you come up on a hooch, what do you do?"

"Carefully look inside."

"You just got killed."

"OK."

The man leaned forward, "You look around first. A lot of times the VC wait in the brush or on a hill for some green kid like you to stumble in."

"Good advice."

"You gotta think like them to beat em."

"If I live long enough."

"You will if you approach every situation like it's an ambush. Maybe one time in fifty it will be, but get sloppy that one time and you get sent home in a bag."

"Thanks, I'll do that."

"You know where you'll be stationed?"

"I'm not sure but I volunteered for the CAP program."

"No shit?" The sergeant looked at Wellington with a crooked neck, "You have a death wish?"

"Is it that dangerous?"

"A single squad out in the middle of nowhere, among locals you aren't sure you can trust, with unfriendlies everywhere—you tell me."

"Well, when you put it that way."

"Just listen to your sergeant. Stay close to him and follow his lead."

"That might be a problem."

"Why?"

"We don't have a sergeant."

"Who's the squad leader?"

"That would be me."

"You! That's suicide!"

"That's encouraging," Wellington said and then asked, "Anything I can do to be better prepared? There's more than my life at risk."

"Desert, punch an officer and go to the stockade, shoot yourself in the goddamn foot, just don't go."

"As nice as all that sounds I'm pretty much committed," Wellington smiled a sad smile. "I'm not gung-ho or anything like that but I'm here and soon will be somewhere out there. All I know is that I'll do my job." Wellington turned to leave.

"OK, kid, it's a long flight. Shut your mouth and open your ears." The Gunnery Sergeant led Wellington over to one of the lashed down jeeps, "Get in." They sat in the jeep and the seasoned combat veteran began his lesson. "When you go into a village, everyone is the enemy until they prove otherwise. They might all be VC sympathizers. Or, an American patrol might have gone through and shot up the place leaving a shit-bag full of hate in its wake. That ten-year-old girl carrying vegetables might have a hand grenade mixed in her salad. Trust no one, not even your interpreter."

An airman arrived at the jeep and ordered, "Get out of there. You can't sit there."

"You've got one second to get the fuck away from me before you go Tango Uniform," the gunny said with such authority that the airman immediately dissolved into the darkness.

"Tango Uniform?"

"Tits Up—dead." The sergeant looked around, "Where was I? Oh, yeah, the only way you can know if you can trust any locals is to test them. Tell each of them that you are sending a number of men to investigate a different location. After they're gone send your men to observe the different locations and intercept any possible ambush at one of the locations. If VC show up you have a traitor—the location will tell you who it is."

"What if they're VC?"

"Tango Uniform." The sergeant looked directly at Wellington with a no-nonsense gaze, "This is war. You're not going to some afternoon social with Jody. You want to come home alive you eliminate those who are trying to see that you don't." The older Marine sat back and inquired, "You ever kill anything? Go hunting? Splat a rat? Snake? Fuckin Cockroach?"

"Not really."

"Then listen-up. The first time affects everyone differently. Those who dwell on it get zipped in. In war people die and people kill. It's that simple. When you make that first kill be glad it wasn't you and move on. If you feel guilty—you're a putz. Sounds cold, but if they neutralize you they won't give it another thought. Stay frosty and stay alive."

Wellington Marsh wondered how he would react to killing another human being.

Gunny read his mind, "You're not killing another human being you're killing a combatant who would kill you. Don't get into a fucking moral head battle. You can have all the guilt you want when you're back in the world. Go to church—light a candle—light a hundred candles, just be glad you're still around to do it."

Wellington nodded.

"Don't yes-ass me! I'm trying to keep you alive. Deal with your moral hang-ups now. Accept your role as a squad leader responsible for your men and yourself." Strong fingers poked Wellington in the head, "What goes on up here will be the difference between life and death. You make your first kill, say 'Ah, shit,' and move on. It's over."

"I'll try."

"Yeah, that convinced the hell out of me. Don't Bravo Foxtrot your team."

"What's that mean?"

"Blue Falcon, buddy fuck, let them down." The Gunny shifted in his seat and looked directly at Wellington, "You were volun-told to accept this assignment for a reason. My guess is that you got a brain and think good on your feet."

"Or, I was stupid."

"I don't think so. Nam is not a conventional war. It's a guerilla war. No soldiers in uniform lining up opposite you on a field. Truth is, it can't be won. Like Korea they're hoping for a stalemate." He looked around and then added, "What you are going to try to do may be more important than all the military victories put together."

"Great. Just pile a little more pressure on me."

"Hey, you volunteered."

"I did, but it's a lot like going on a blind date after being told she is beautiful, intelligent, and sexy only to discover she's psychotic."

Gunny laughed, "Yeah, don't turn your back on her."

For the rest of the night the seasoned Marine tutored Lance Corporal Wellington Marsh. No punches were pulled or sunshine blown up any skirt. The older man found that he liked the young Marine. He would have been glad to have him assigned to his platoon. That not being the case he tried to instill as much knowledge as possible to help keep the fresh meat alive. Unfortunately, he was keenly aware of the mortality rate of green second and first lieutenants who had significantly more training than the kid sitting in that jeep. In the end he was willing to give up a night's sleep if it would improve the odds—even if only a little.

The self-propelled cargo were the first to leave the C-130E. Twenty-three men walked slowly down the rear ramp. It was raining. When Wellington cleared the ramp he looked around. Where they stood was flat and paved but everywhere else he observed was sandy. In one direction he could see a large body of water and a beach. Opposite that were a number of buildings constructed of concrete blocks, wood, sheet metal, and canvas. Beyond the buildings, in the distance, he saw a mountain range.

The largest building in the immediate area had a sign reading; 14th AERIAL PORT SQ PASSENGER TERMINAL. Below that sign was a smaller sign which read; PASSENGERS MOVED DURING 1969 – 953,719 and TONS CARGO MOVED DURING 1969 – 153,787. A third sign was below that one. It read; AIR MILES FROM CAM RANH BAY and listed various cities in the United States, such as; Chicago, Ill. 9372, Miami, Fla 10590, New York, NY 10062. He noticed an important omission and commented out loud, "Where's Detroit?"

An airman walking the other way said, "Boy, did you get on the wrong plane buddy."

Half a world away a much more peaceful battle was being waged. First place San Francisco Giants were on the diamond versus the San Diego Padres who occupied sixth place. On a sunny afternoon where other ballparks would be packed there were only 4,779 fans at San Diego Stadium. There was a price to be paid for a losing season. It was the top of the seventh inning with the score tied 2 - 2. Ron Hunt had hit a lead-off single. Willlie Mays was then put in as a pinch hitter for George Foster. The thirty-eight-year-old veteran who had been plagued with injuries that season was still a considerable threat. He proved it on this afternoon when he hit a towering homerun more than 370 feet over the left field fence. The "Say Hey Kid" came through once more with his 600th homerun. He became only the second man in Major League history to reach that mark joining Babe Ruth who retired with a total of 714 homeruns.

Willie Howard Mays Jr. was born in Westfield, Alabama May 6, 1931. His father was a baseball player in the Negro League. By the age of five he was playing catch with his father and at ten he sat on the bench during his father's games. Willie played multiple sports at Fairfield Industrial High School, among which being basketball and football. His professional baseball career began in 1947, while he was still in high school. During that summer, he played for the Chattanooga Choo-Choos in the Negro League.

A number of Major League teams scouted Mays and were interested in signing him. However, it was the New York Giants who signed him and sent him to their Class-B team in Trenton, New Jersey. In 1951 Mays moved up to the AAA Minneapolis Millers. He batted .477 and was a standout in the field. On May 24, 1951 Willie was at a movie in Sioux City, Iowa when a message flashed on the screen which read, "WILLIE MAYS CALL YOUR HOTEL." He had been called up to the New York Giants.

His Major League career did not start well. He had no hits after his first twelve at-bats. Willie Mays first hit in the Major Leagues was, in fact, a towering homerun over the left field roof of the Polo Grounds off of pitcher Warren Spahn. Well into the future after Mays had proven to be a formidable opponent Spahn joked, "I'll never forgive myself. We might have gotten rid of Willie forever if I'd only struck him out." Willie Mays batted .274 and won the 1951 Rookie of the Year Award.

Willie Mays was drafted into the Army the following year and missed the next two seasons. In 1954 he returned to the Giants and won the National League Most Valuable Player Award. He was an all-star year after year consistently playing outstanding ball. One of his most memorable performances came on Sunday April 30, 1961 against the Milwaukee Braves in County Stadium, Milwaukee, Wisconsin. He went four for five hitting four homeruns leading the giants to a 14 to 4 win. The game proved to be a slugfest with Jose Pagan hitting two homeruns for the Giants and Hank Aaron hitting two homeruns for the Braves.

While playing for the Giants, Willie Mays became friends with fellow player Bobby Bonds. When Bobby's son, Barry, was born he asked Willie to be his godfather. In the end, Barry Bonds would become the all-time homerun leader with 762, followed by Hank Aaron (755), Babe Ruth (714), Alex Rodriguez (695), and Willie Mays (660).

Age and injuries reduced Willie Mays time on the field. May 1972, the 41-year-old, Mays was traded to the New York Mets for pitcher Charlie Williams and $50,000. The trade was less of a slap-in-the-face as it was a way of looking out for the beloved San Francisco Giant. Due to money issues, Giant owner Horace Stoneham could not guarantee Mays an income after retirement. The Mets offered Willie a coaching position upon his retirement. Mets owner Joan Whitney Payson, who had been a minority shareholder of the Giants when the team was in New York, long desired to bring Willie Mays back to his baseball roots and was instrumental in making the trade.

On a rainy Sunday afternoon at Shea Stadium on May 14, 1972 Willie Mays made his debut as a Met. His fifth inning homerun led the Mets to a victory over the Giants. Then on August 16, 1973, in a game against the Cincinnati Reds Mays hit a fourth inning home run over the right-center field fence. It was the last homerun of his major league career. Willie Howard Mays Jr. retired after the 1973 season saying, "Growing old is just a helpless hurt."

68: Wednesday – September 24, 1969

Na Na Na Na Na Na Na Na
Hey Hey Hey Goodbye

He'll never love you
The way that I love you
Cuz if he did, no no
He wouldn't make you cry
He must be fooling baby
For you my love
My love

So will you kiss him
I wanna see you kiss him
I'm gonna see you kiss him, Goodbye

Na Na Na Na,
Hey Hey Hey Goodbye

Na Na Na Na Na Na Na Na
Hey Hey Hey Goodbye

Mathew Ellis woke to the rock song *Na, Na, Hey, Hey Kiss Him Goodbye* by Steam. It was an unusual song with the chorus in the background singing Na, na, na, na, na, na and upbeat music that gave the impression of a celebration.

He's never near you
To comfort and cheer you
When all those sad tears are
Falling baby from your eyes

He must be fooling baby
Fooling my love
It's alright love

I wanna see you kiss him
I'm gonna see you kiss him, goodbye

Na Na Na Na
Hey Hey Hey Goodbye

Na Na Na Na Na Na Na Na
Hey Hey Hey Goodbye

A musical interlude with a distant chorus slowly coming closer and closer brought a dimension to the performance Matt had never experienced before.

> Na na na na, hey hey-ey, goodbye
> Na na na na, na na na na, hey hey-ey, goodbye
>
> I really love you girl
> I really need you
> I need to have you near me everyday
>
> You know that's true girl
> I really need you girl
> I can't let you be with him
> When it's not right
>
> Na Na Na Na Na Na Na Na
> Hey Hey Hey Goodbye

Na Na Hey Hey Kiss Him Goodbye was written and recorded by Paul Leka, Gary DeCarlo and Dale Frashuer. It was recorded in one session at Mercury Records studios in New York City in the fall of 1969. The band, Steam, was a fictitious entity. In fact, the group seen on the album cover was a road band that had nothing to do with the recording. They lip-synched the song. Originally, it was recorded as a B-side filler. That changed when a DJ in Georgia played *Na Na Hey Hey Kiss Him Goodbye* on the radio. The station was flooded with calls for a replay. Then other stations began to play it and it continued to be well-received. As a result, Mercury Records ordered 100,000 copies which put it on the Billboard popular hit chart. *Na Na Hey Hey Kiss Him Goodbye* reached number one in the United States for two weeks in December 1969.

Matt enjoyed the music but the lyrics hit a nerve. He hadn't been fair to Valerie. She never complained and had been the kind of loving, supportive, loyal wife most men dream of marrying. Unfortunately, he didn't know what he had. He was too busy looking in the mirror at the successful executive with dirty hands.

After breakfast Matt found himself aimlessly wandering the streets of Dumont, New Jersey. Leaves on trees had changed color and many had fallen to the ground. A slight breeze brought with it a reminder that fall had arrived. After half an hour Matt found himself on top on McKinley Avenue looking down the hill. This was where he and Valerie had sledded the night they met. It had been a magic time. They were both young and innocent and filled with dreams. A world of possibilities lay before them. The white snow made everything appear clean and pure. And, in Matt's mind, Valerie was all that was beautiful in his life. As it turned out she was too beautiful for the dark soul within him. He tried to return to that wonderful evening but spinning dead leaves blocked the way.

"Shikata ga nai," Ryoya Akimoto said in a soft voice as she stared into her beer.

"What does that mean?" Jack asked.

"It has many meanings. I guess the most understandable is that it refers to something that cannot be helped." Ryoya looked up and explained, "If you walk out into the rain you get wet—shikata ga nai. As the years pass you grow older—shikata ga nai." Her voice took on a tone of sadness, "You become a New York City detective and you see the worst humanity has to offer—shikata ga nai."

Jack reached across the table and took Ryoya's hand, "Obviously, this latest murder really bothers you. I'm sorry."

Ryoya looked into Jack's brown eyes. What she saw was the best that humanity had to offer—a strong, unassuming, intelligent, caring, funny individual who would make any woman happy. A mix of gratitude for him being there and sadness knowing that it was destined to be only temporary flowed over her.

Colt McIntyre arrived at the table and sat down. His contagious smile and Texas drawl, "Howdy!" broke the spell.

Ryoya smiled and returned the greeting, "Howdy."

"Well, that filly, Stephanie, started her classes and is all fired up. Only one thing—she could be my huckleberry if she's not barkin' at a knot."

"I see," Ryoya said with interest.

"You do?" Jack asked in amazement.

Ryoya turned to Jack and explained, "Colt thinks she could be right for the job, but is concerned she isn't serious enough."

"Exactly," Colt confirmed. "You see, her daddy is still on the mend and she feels like she can't leave the Garden State until he's in the pink. She's his cats-paw."

"I need a drink," Jack decided.

"It shouldn't be a problem as she is in school right now," Ryoya observed.

"Well, we talked about her making tracks to Texas after this semester. She could go to the University of Texas, you know, 'hook em horns' and all that. We then could start to put the pieces together for our itty-bitty adoption service. Then, when she gets certified, we're off and running lickety-split." Colt paused, put his elbows on the table, looked at Ryoya, and asked, "So, why are we here?"

"We're here to watch a baseball game," she replied.

"The Mets can clinch first-place in the National League East Division if they win," Jack said with feigned distaste.

"Tarnation. I didn't think that dog would hunt. You think they'll win the whole kit and caboodle?"

"She does," Jack nodded toward Ryoya who smiled.

"Little lady, that calls for some Mormon Tea."

Ryoya explained, "This is their last home game. If they beat the St. Louis Cardinals that would be five wins in a row and clinch the title. So far, in September they are 19 and 7."

"Well, I don't want to be a wagon jumper but I guess I better give these boys my support."

"I thought you would so I brought you a present," Ryoya stated as she reached behind her to retrieve a large paper bag which she handed to Colt.

"And, it's not even my birthday, yet." He opened the bag and pulled out a black cowboy hat with the distinctive blue and orange Mets "NY" embroidered on it. "It's beautiful," he stated, then added, "It will get me shot in Texas, but it's beautiful."

Jack told nobody in particular, "The first team the Mets ever faced was the St. Louis Cardinals. The Mets lost 11 – 4. It seems apropos that they win their first title by beating that same team." When no one showed interest Jack pressed on, "The Mets played their first home game at the Polo Grounds on April 13, 1962. They lost to the

Pittsburgh Pirates 4 – 3. They played their first game at Shea Stadium on April 17, 1964 and lost to, you guessed it, the Pittsburgh Pirates 4 – 3."

Ryoya looked at Jack. She appreciated the fact that he showed interest in her team. What she didn't expect was a history lesson that came flowing her way.

Jack continued, "After the Brooklyn Dodgers and New York Giants left New York for California in 1957 the Mayor of New York, Robert Wagner, began searching for ways to bring a National League baseball team to New York. He turned to William Alfred Shea of the law firm Shea & Gould. Bill had a reputation of getting things done. First, he tried to convince an existing team to move, but the Cincinnati Reds, Philadelphia Phillies, and Pittsburgh Pirates all refused his overtures. He then tried to get the league to add a new team but was turned down." Jack took a sip of his drink. This time he had an interested audience. "Now, Bill was a man who did not give up. His next move was to form a third baseball league, the Continental League. It was formally announced in 1959 with the first games scheduled to be played in 1961. It was a brilliant move because Major League Baseball didn't want additional competition so they agreed to expand the American League by two teams, the Washington Senators and Los Angeles Angels in 1961 and two National League teams, the New York Mets and Houston Colt .45s in 1962. In recognition of his tenacity, creativity, and success, the City of New York named the stadium after William Alfred Shea."

"You've been reading, again," Ryoya stated with a smile.

"There's more."

"Of course there is."

"Relax and be enlightened. Shea was the first major league stadium in America to have two moveable stands. The left and right field-level stands move inward to run parallel with a football field layout. Shea also was the first stadium to utilize a light ring around the roofline to illuminate the field. The only light towers are in the outfield. And, when Bill Shea christened the new stadium he used two symbolic bottles of water. One filled with water from the Gowanus Canal which was near Ebbets Field the former home of the Brooklyn Dodgers and the other filled from the Harlem River near the Polo Grounds home of the ungrateful New York Giants."

Harry Van Ryker, the owner and bartender, turned on the television that hung over the bar and put on Channel 9, WOR-TV. A commercial for Rheingold Extra Dry Lager Beer was being broadcast. The well-known jingle filled the bar.

> My beer is Rheingold the dry beer;
> think of Rheingold whenever you buy beer.
> It's not bitter not sweet;
> extra dry flavored treat.
> Won't you try extra dry Rheingold beer?

"Makes me want a Rheingold beer," Colt MacIntyre said while staring at the television set wearing his new cowboy hat.

Jack added to his history lesson, "The Rheingold Beer Jingle was based on the melody of an old European waltz tune, *Estudiantina Valse, Opus 191, No. 4*, known as *The Students' Waltz*. While it sounds like the kind of music heard in a German Beer Hall the tune was composed by a pair of obscure French composers. The tune itself was written by Paul Lacome (1838 - 1920), but it is often attributed to Emile Waldteufel (1837 - 1915) who arranged it in a Strauss-like arrangement for two pianos."

"That's it, I'm taking your library card away from you," Ryoya stated.

Amanda joined the group. She announced, "Harry told me you would be here tonight to root for the Mets."

Ryoya made the introductions, "Amanda Shay this is Colt MacIntyre. You know Jack."

"Shea?" Jack said, "Not any relation to the stadium?"

"No, wrong spelling. Mine is S-H-A-Y."

It was fan appreciation day at Shea with souvenir keychains presented to all attendees. Gary Gentry with a record of 12 – 12 was on the mound for the Mets. He retired the Cardinals in order in the top of the first inning. Bud Harrelson led off for the Mets and singled to right field. Then Tommie Agee was walked. After Cleon Jones struck out, Donn Clendenon hit a homerun putting the Mets ahead 3 nothing. The fans in More-Or-Less cheered along with the fifty-four thousand in the packed stadium. Ron Swoboda was then walked and third baseman Ed Charles followed with a homerun. Steve Carlton, the Cardinals pitcher, was replaced after a third of an inning with Dave Giusti. Then after Jerry Grote doubled to centerfield a fly out and strike out ended the inning. The Mets led 5 – 0.

"Come'on where is it?" Jack asked Ryoya.

"I don't know what you are talking about," Ryoya insisted.

"Yes, you do."

"Stop being obnoxious."

"Stop being evasive."

Colt looked at Amanda and asked, "Do you know what this is about?"

"I have an idea," she replied.

Jack stared at Ryoya with an accusing expression. At first, she ignored him. He began drumming on the table. She watched the television. Then he began scratching the table and meowing. Ryoya couldn't hold back a laugh, "OK, you win." She reached into the same bag that had held Colt's hat and brought out the stuffed black cat. "Happy?"

"I knew it! You couldn't take the risk, like not stepping on the first base line."

"Fine. Now, can we watch the game?"

Clendenon hit a second homerun in the fifth inning to give the Mets a 6 – 0 lead which ended up being the final score.

Mets announcer, Lindsey Nelson, proclaimed, "At 9:07 on September 24th the Mets have won the championship of the Eastern Division of the National League."

After arriving at Cam Ranh Bay, Wellington Marsh was given a DA Form 3078 for issue of basic combat tropical clothing. When the clerk handed Wellington his boots he stated, "Man, these are the latest in jungle boots. They got the nylon canvass tops and removable ventilating insoles. They also got a stainless steel plate inside the sole to protect you from Victor Charlie Toothpicks."

"From what?" Wellington asked.

"Punji stake traps, man."

In addition to boots, Wellington received shirts, trousers, OD underwear, tee shirts, socks, jungle jacket, towels, and handkerchiefs. After leaving that station he entered the supply depot where he was issued basic field gear; an ERDL camo pattern boonie tropical hat, two one quart canteens made of olive drab polyethylene plastic, individual load carrying web equipment belt, mess kit, rubber coated fabric poncho with hood, lightweight tropical rucksack, machete, a coil of rope, map case, compass, binoculars and case, wrist watch, and first aid kit.

A final piece of equipment was a water-repellent mildew-resistant cotton duck dyed olive green half of a tent panel with triangular flaps. Two of these could be buttoned together to form a complete tent. Each Marine carried a half tent, one tent pole, and tent pegs. When the clerk gave it to Wellington he said, "You're gonna learn to love this little item. Don't lose it."

Wellington's final stop was the weapons depot. The Army sergeant in charge examined Wellington's DA Form, looked at him, returned to the form, then back to Wellington and finally said, "It says here you are to be issued an XM177 and M1911A1. Those weapons are assigned to platoon leaders."

"That's correct."

"You, a lance corpuscle, a platoon leader?"

"That's what they tell me."

"What kind of platoon—motor pool guard?"

Wellington got irritated by the condescending attitude of the sergeant—an Army sergeant at that. He looked the older man in the eye and said with authority, "A Marine combat platoon operating independently in enemy territory on special assignment. We're going where it's raining shit not hanging out in an air-conditioned hut giving Marines a hard time."

The sergeant felt anger well up inside, however it was overpowered by the slap of reality that Lance Corporal Wellington Marsh was going into combat. A slight pang of embarrassment kept him silent. He issued the XM177, which was a CAR-15 carbine with an 11.5 inch barrel, and the M1911A1 45 caliber automatic pistol. After recording the serial numbers he simply said, "Sign here."

Once squared away sixteen Marines were loaded onto a Boeing CH-47 Chinook tandem-rotor helicopter and flown from Cam Ranh to Da Nang. The trip took an hour and forty minutes. Eleven of the sixteen marines accompanied Wellington to the Combined Action Program (CAP) training facility. After two days they had a better understanding of the geography of Vietnam, political climate, basic customs, culture, and a few Vietnamese phrases. Wellington found it interesting that the term Viet Cong came from the Vietnamese phrase "Viet gian cong san" which translated to "Communist traitor to Vietnam." He also was amazed to learn that the pejorative term "gook" originated during the Korean War when American soldiers heard the Korean term "guk" which means country. In addition, they misunderstood the Koreans who said "miguk" meaning "American" and thought they were saying "me gook." Wellington laughed as he stated, "We're the gooks."

69: Monday – September 29, 1969

Once again the earth shook. Yang Liang felt the shudder and instinctively looked toward Lop Nor. This time a powerful three mega-ton thermonuclear device had been dropped from an aircraft. Even at a great distance, a huge ominous cloud of brown dust became visible on the horizon. Like some awakening monster it grew and grew. There appeared to be no end to its expansion. Yang didn't realize that the cloud was both moving skyward and in the direction of his village in Xinjiang Province. Boiling hot gasses pushed tons of dirt, sand, and debris into the atmosphere where winds carried it over the dried lakebed of Lop Lake and the desert.

In a few hours the sky over Yang Liang's village became dark with a menacing brown cloud. School children asked their teacher what was happening and they were told there was a storm on Saturn. Saturn's Chinese name translates to "soil planet." Night fell in mid-day as the sun was completely obscured. A deathly silence blanketed the area. Yang Liang felt something touch his cheek. He wiped it with his hand and found it was dirt—a fine powder of brown dust. For the next three days earth would fall from the sky as it rained radioactive dust on unsuspecting participants in the nuclear arms race.

Captain Rembrandt Robinson of the Joint Chiefs of Staff read the memorandum from Roger Morris and Anthony Lake. He recognized the names as aides to Henry Kissinger who was the National Security Advisor. The memo stated that the President should be prepared to accept two operational concepts: Duck Hook "must be brutal and sustainable" and "self-contained."

Richard Nixon was elected President partially due to his promise to end the war in Vietnam. Therefore, this objective became a priority when he entered office. To help reach that goal Henry Kissinger created a National Security Council planning committee referred to as the "September Group." They were charged with finding solutions to the Vietnam enigma. In the end, they recommended developing a plan for greater strategic bombing combined with widespread diplomacy. For the combat element the Joint Chiefs of Staff in Washington, DC worked with armed forces leaders in Saigon to create a strategy the White House called "Duck Hook" that was code named "Pruning Knife" by the military.

Duck Hook called for a wide range of actions to be taken if North Vietnam failed to yield to Washington's terms at the Paris peace negotiations. There would be a price to be paid for further delays. The military response would be dramatic and decisive. It called for bombing of military and economic targets in Hanoi, mining Haiphong Harbor and other ports, breaching the Levee System in the Red River Delta, destruction of the Northeast Rail Line, bombing bridges at the Chinese border, as well as air and ground attacks on other targets throughout Vietnam. The use of tactical nuclear weapons was very seriously considered.

Numerous diplomatic and military scenarios were created in an attempt to answer numerous important questions. What would be Hanoi's response? Would they continue to receive outside economic aid? How would it impact Hanoi's internal politics? What would be the Chinese and Soviet reactions? How long would sustained military action be required? What would be the reaction of the American media and public?

Captain Robinson understood the implications of the sentence in the memo that stated, "The President would need to decide in advance the fateful question of how far we will go. He cannot, for example, confront the issue of using tactical nuclear weapons in the midst of the exercise. He must be prepared to play out whatever string necessary in this case." From a military perspective laying waste to an enemy to render them unable to continue was a valid strategy. However, the worldwide implications were enormous. Captain Rembrandt Robinson was glad that he wasn't the one who would make this momentous decision.

Detective Ryoya Akimoto kicked the waste basket sending it across the room. One of the other detectives in the room ducked and yelled, "Incoming!"

Ryoya glared at the man but didn't remark. She left the room and walked down the hall in the Midtown North Precinct at 306 West 54th Street. It had been a frustrating week since the body of Claire Payton had been found. The ladies of Eighth Avenue weren't talking, no witnesses turned up, associates of Miguel Juarez knew nothing, and forensics had come up blank. Time was running out and they had no lead, not even a whisper of a lead, to follow. In her heart she knew she was taking this case personally. Claire Payton deserved better. When the judge dismissed charges Ryoya thought it had given the woman a chance at a better life. What it did in reality was give her a death sentence. How had a seasoned detective been so naïve as to overlook the potential for vicious retaliation? She was complicit in this particular murder—there was no denying that fact. Ryoya couldn't shake the guilt that she felt. She also feared the anger. If the perpetrators were in a room in that building at that moment she would have to fight the desire to go in and empty her Smith & Wesson 38 caliber detective special into them. Ryoya found the door and entered the ladies room. She looked in the mirror and saw a stranger.

Wellington Marsh looked in the mirror and saw a Marine. What caused the changed attitude and mindset he didn't know. Maybe, it was due to the fact that he was in a foreign country no longer with the safety net of knowing he could go home. Perhaps the last week of a steady diet of tactics and military jargon had their affect. Or possibly, for some unexplained reason, he simply found himself. Whatever the cause, he was a Marine preparing for a mission and he had to give that his full attention. Lives were at stake and he was an essential element in their protection.

Wellington had spent the last week seated among nine sergeants and three second lieutenants. When he first arrived the group peered at him as though he had inadvertently walked into the wrong room. Questioned by one second lieutenant he produced his orders which confirmed his reason for being there. While not overtly ostracized, he quickly became aware of the camaraderie among the sergeants and the connection shared among the second lieutenants. By virtue of rank he was the odd duck out.

On this day a number of Vietnamese interpreters joined the group. They were polite and friendly but stayed among themselves. Once again, Wellington was reminded of the child's game where they sing, "the cheese stands alone." Training covered the relationship between the village Popular Forces militia members (Nghia Quan) and each CAP squad. As a result of aggressive recruiting by the South Vietnamese Army in most cases village militia consisted of those too young, too old, or physically unfit for service. Their weapons were mostly old French-era firearms, machetes, hand tools, and other farm implements. They were neither trained in tactics nor taught discipline. From experience, Marine instructors explained that in most cases villagers relied heavily on the CAP squad to provide security. Out of fear of reprisal, lack of training, or doubts that the Americans would stay around very long, locals were reluctant to take an active role. Instructors did, however, offer numerous warnings about communist sympathizers who would betray the squad in a heartbeat. This brought protests from some Vietnamese interpreters and agreement from others.

The picture Wellington was developing was bleak. He envisioned an undermanned police force in the worst possible ghetto trying to weed out organized crime where the people actively protect them. What on earth had he gotten himself into?

During a break, one of the Vietnamese interpreters walked over to Wellington and said, "I choose you."

"Me? Why?"

"These others, they all already think they know everything. They not listen, not hear, not need me."

"What have you chosen me for?"

"The Combined Action Platoon for my village," he smiled, "Together we fight Viet gian cong san."

"What is the name of your village?"

"Quy Hoa. It actually three villages, together Quy Hoa."

"What does Quy Hoa mean?"

The short, very slender, late thirties interpreter with a weathered face looked surprised. No one had ever asked him that before. No one cared. His village was coordinates on a map—coordinates he didn't want used for an artillery barrage. Dark Asian eyes peered at the brown American Marine and he knew he had chosen well. He answered, "Quy Hoa means Precious Flower." A glow of pride surrounded him.

"Precious Flower. It sounds like a nice place," Wellington said. "If I am assigned to Quy Hoa you will have to tell me more." The young Marine Lance Corporal offered his hand, "I'm Wellington Marsh."

"Nghiem Duc Hung," the interpreter answered. He went on to explain, "Nghiem is my family name—well respected. Hung my given name. In Vietnam we referred to by given name. You call me Hung."

In 1946 an exhibition best of three baseball series was played between the Yankees and the Giants. It was called the Mayor's Trophy Series and was used to raise money for New York City's Amateur Baseball Federation, which included sandlot baseball programs. The Yankees won the first game 3 – 0 on July 1 at the Polo Grounds. They won the second game 3 -2, thus winning the series, on August 5 at Yankee Stadium.

Due to scheduling and logistical difficulties the series was transformed into a single game in 1948. On the evening of August 16 the game was played at the Polo

Grounds. Sadly, during the game the festive atmosphere was dashed with the announcement that at 8:01 p.m. George Herman (Babe) Ruth, The Sultan of Swat, died of cancer at Memorial Hospital. He was fifty-three years old. The crowd and players rose to their feet in tribute. The Yankees won 4 – 2 in eleven innings.

The Brooklyn Dodgers entered the inter-league competition when they played in the 1951 Mayor's Trophy Game. On June 25th at Yankee Stadium the Yankees defeated the Dodgers 4 – 3 in ten innings. In subsequent years the Yankees won two of the next three games against the Dodgers. It was in 1955 that the Giants returned to Yankee Stadium but lost 4 – 1.

May 23, 1957 the final Mayor's Trophy game was played at Ebbets field. The Yankees beat the Dodgers 10 -7. Afterward, both the Dodgers and Giants headed to the west coast. The Yankees had chased them out-of-town.

The Mayor's Trophy Game was revived June 20, 1963 at Yankee Stadium with a game between the Yankees and Mets. Casey Stengel, the Mets manager, used his best pitcher against his old team in a thinly veiled act of revenge. The Mets won 6 – 2. Over the next five years the games were split with the Mets winning three and the Yankees winning two.

Jack Moore arrived at Ryoya Akimoto's apartment carrying a bottle of Châteauneuf du Pape and four Sabrett hot dogs. He wore a New York Yankee baseball cap and carried a stuffed white cat. Ryoya went to her door regretting that she had agreed to watch the Mayor's Trophy Game on television with Jack. Frustration with the Claire Payton case weighed heavy on the New York City detective. She just didn't feel very enthusiastic or hospitable. Upon seeing Jack holding the wine, hot dogs, and cat she smiled. "With onions, peppers, and ketchup?"

"Yup, as sacrilegious as it is, just how you like them."

"And, what's the name of this creature?"

"What else—Babe."

"I must admit, you're good for my spirits. I think that's what I'll call you— Babe," Ryoya took the food and led Jack into the living room.

"You do realize it's the Yankees year?" Jack commented.

"Year to lose once more."

Jack placed the white cat on the table and said, "Not with Babe on the job."

"You are aware that the Mets have won nine in a row?"

"Against National League, 'I got it—no, you got it,' teams. Now, they have to play professionals."

"Professionals in fifth place."

"Yes, but they . . ." Jack broke into laughter as his argument fell flat.

By the end of the first inning the Mets led 4 – 0. With the meal finished, Jack and Ryoya sipped their wine and sat in silence. Ryoya's desultory mind leapt from enjoying the ball game to feeling guilty for not doing more on the Payton murder investigation. It felt good having Jack there but then at times she wanted to be alone. Finally, she had to speak, "Jack, I know I haven't been the best company, tonight."

Jack had a wise retort but the seriousness of Ryoya's tone caused him to remain silent. He rose from the couch, walked over, turned off the television, and returned to face Ryoya.

"The first thing a good detective learns is to not get personally involved with a case." Ryoya looked away at some distant vision found only in her head. "They tortured her." She looked down at the floor. "I let her down when I should have anticipated what would happen."

Jack wanted to respond, but decided upon discretion.

"I want them, bad," Ryoya's voice dripped with venom. "Only, I'm searching for a shadow in the darkness. We have no clues, no suspects, nothing to work with." Her gaze turned to Jack, "I'm also afraid. Afraid of what I might do when I do find the animals that did this crime."

Jack knew Ryoya Akimoto needed help—his help. He also knew that he couldn't solve her dilemma or fix it as is the first impulse of the male of the species. Indeed, she wasn't looking for a solution. He took a different track, "When I was a boy I had a fight with my friend. I mean a 'let's go outside and throw punches' fight. It didn't last long and we went our separate ways. My aunt was visiting at the time and witnessed the event. When I went inside she sat me down and said something I never forgot. 'If you're looking for a friend who is perfect you are going to be lonely.' Feel the regret and anger and fear and frustration and understand it's who you are. But, don't sit in judgement or expect perfection. You're not perfect, Ms. Akimoto, accept that fact and be a good friend to yourself."

"I want to turn back the clock and save Claire Payton."

Jack nodded.

"I know I can't," Ryoya admitted. "Something about her reached me. She committed a crime—murder to save a young girl. I did my job, arrested her, and let the judicial system take over. But, where did my job end? Once she was acquitted was that it? Why didn't she leave town—run away? Did the fact that she was arrested for Miguel Juarez' murder put a target on her back? Was I the one who shined that accusatory light on her? Did I mark her for execution? Am I complicit?"

This time Jack felt that he had to speak, "Detective Akimoto answer the lady's question. Was she to blame for the murder because she did her job?"

Ryoya had to think a moment as Jack's question asked her professional side to answer her emotional being. After a few moments of silence she responded. "Of course not."

"Then that's what you go with."

The two sat in silence. Ryoya stared at Jack and knew he was right. Her emotions were clouding her perception of reality. She would cry later for Claire Payton a poor soul caught up in a sordid world who saved a child from its horrid tentacles and paid the price for her good deed. Ryoya only hoped that the unnamed girl would make something good out of that new life bought for her at such a high price. Her attention returned to Jack, she rose, walked to the television, turned it on, and sat next to the dreaded Yankee fan.

The game was in the top of the third inning. The Yankees were at bat. With a man on first, Horace Clarke tripled, Gene Michael singled, and Roy White homered to tie the game. Given the situation and their conversation Jack sat in silence. Ryoya appreciated his reserve and smiled. She picked up the stuffed white cat and handed it to Jack and said, "Have at it. Let that cheer out before you rupture something."

Jack smiled, no grinned, then kissed Ryoya. As he leaned back he cheered.

Joe Pepitone got on base and a Frank Tepedino double drove him home. The Yankees led the game 5 – 4.

Ryoya left the room.

Jack hoped that he hadn't been insensitive.

When Ryoya returned she was carrying the stuffed black cat. In the bottom of the third a Shamsky two-run homer made it 6-5 Mets. The Mets scored again in the fifth inning. Then came the top of the ninth—the last chance for the Yankees. With one out three consecutive singles brought the Bronx Bombers to within one. Unfortunately for Jack and Babe the game ended with a Met's victory 7 – 6.

Ryoya tried to console Jack who pulled away and faux pouted. He looked like an oversized ten-year-old. Ryoya found laughter that escaped from deep inside. She leaned over and hugged the crestfallen fan. A black cat and white cat were left alone on the couch.

Lai Ngoc Linh, an eleven-year-old Vietnamese boy, walked along the river holding his six-year-old sister's hand.

70: Wednesday – October 1, 1969

Henry Kissinger wrote a memorandum to President Nixon outlining a conversation that he had with Soviet Ambassador Anatoly Dobrynin. In their attempt to get the Soviet Union more involved in bringing about a satisfactory solution to the Vietnam Conflict pressure was being applied at all levels. Kissinger told Dobrynin that there would be no special treatment for the Soviet Union until Vietnam was solved. He emphasized his point by saying, "The train had just left the station and was heading down the tracks."

In Vietnam, Lance Corporal Wellington Marsh was given his CAP area assignment—Quy Hoa. He was also introduced to his local liaison and interpreter Nghiem Duc Hung. For the next two days each CAP leader would become familiar with the village, terrain, history, known threats, and strategic value of their Tactical Area of Responsibility (TAOR).

Hung produced photographs of the three villages. The two on the west side of the river were craftsmen villages known for making furniture and tools. The larger village on the east side was agrarian. All combined the population was approximately 1,200 persons. Aside from areas cleared for farming, the terrain was mainly mountainous and heavily forested. They used small woven bamboo basket boats to cross back and forth across the river. Villagers lived in thatch roof huts with a few of the more established families in wood houses. A number of small lakes could be found in the surrounding mountains, as well as three large caves, one a water cave.

The location of the Quy Hoa villages were in the Central Highlands northwest of Pleiku and Kon Tum approximately six miles southeast of the Laos and Cambodia borders. Both Pleiku and Kon Tum were sites of major battles during the 1968 Tet Offensive. Hung explained that the Viet Cong bypassed his villages to attack the larger population centers. His fear was that they would eventually discover Quy Hoa and try to obtain control and force the villagers to make war materials.

Wellington's orders assigned him to 1st Combined Action Group (CAG) under Lieutenant Colonel David F. Seiler with a CAP designation of 1-6-2.

Mathew Ellis put down the *Bergen Record*. He had been reading the newspaper when on page seven he came across an article titled: Cause of Airliner Crash Inconclusive.

United Airlines Flight 266 left Los Angeles International Airport on January 18, 1969 at 6:17 PST en route to General Mitchell International Airport, Milwaukee, Wisconsin via Stapleton International Airport, Denver, Colorado. There were 32 passengers and 6 crew members onboard the Boeing 727. Four minutes after takeoff the aircraft crashed into Santa Monica Bay approximately 11.5 miles west of the airport. All onboard perished. Eight months later the preliminary NTSB report has been issued indicating the cause was most likely an electrical malfunction whose cause could not be determined.

The Boeing 727 aircraft, registration N7434U, had a nonfunctional #3 generator for several days prior to the accident. As is standard operating procedure, the crew placed masking tape over the switches and warning lights for that generator. A month earlier the aircraft had been fitted with a generator control panel that had been passed around several different UAL aircraft because of several malfunctions. After being installed in N7434U, generator #3 experienced operating problems and was swapped with a different unit. That generator was subsequently tested and found to have no mechanical issues. The control panel was identified as the problem after it caused further malfunctions with the replacement generator. Due to busy operating schedules and limited aircraft availability repair work on N7434U was put on hold, with the #3 generator disabled.

Approximately two minutes after takeoff, the crew reported a fire warning on engine #1 and shut it off subsequently taking the #1 generator offline. With only one functioning generator they radioed departure control stating that they needed to return to the airport. That was the last transmission from Flight 266.

The NTSB investigation found that shortly after the #1 engine shutdown the #2 generator ceased operating for an unknown reason. Investigators were also unable to explain the #1 engine fire warning in the absence of a fire. It was surmised that either an electrical failure or cracked duct allowing hot gasses to set off temperature sensors was the cause. Tests indicated that an overload condition could result from the abrupt shifting of operating load following the #1 generator shutdown.

A reconstruction of events led to the belief that with the loss of all electrical power to lights and flight instruments the pilots quickly became spatially disoriented in the darkness. They were flying at night under instrument flying rules (IFR) due to overcast conditions. The flight-control system would not have been affected by the loss of electrical power since it relied on hydraulic and mechanical lines. However, investigators concluded that the pilots couldn't use flight controls without instruments. They believe the backup electrical system had not been activated because the crew couldn't locate the switch in the dark. Consequently, the crew lost complete control of the aircraft and crashed into the ocean in a steep nose-down angle, killing everyone on board.

The Board determined that the probable cause of this accident was loss of attitude orientation during a night, instrument departure in which the attitude instruments were disabled by loss of electrical power. Further, the Board has been unable to determine (a) why all generator power was lost or (b) why the standby electrical power system either was not activated or failed to function.

When Matt finished reading the article he realized that he had been sweating profusely. In fact, his moist hands left marks on the newspaper. Another disaster involving electrical failure. Could that jet or control panel been wired with Orztech wire? His mind flashed back to the many contracts he helped finalize with aircraft manufacturers. Were they contracts or death warrants?

It took twelve innings but the New York Mets won their tenth game in a row and their 100th game of the season. It happened in Chicago at Wrigley Field when they beat the second place Chicago Cubs 6 - 5. Meanwhile, the New York Yankees won their sixth game in a row at Yankee Stadium beating the Cleveland Indians 4 – 3. The Bronx Bombers would finish the season in fifth place.

Jack Moore once again entered the dark recesses of the criminal underworld.
"What the hell am I—your private police force," Don Carmine Spacini bellowed.
"I just want to know if you heard anything," Jack insisted.
"This lady cop, she's pulling your strings?"
"She doesn't know I'm here."
"That's even worse. You've been thunder struck by her."
"She's really bothered by this murder."
"A street walker," Carmine said, "the one that got my boy Carl to disappear. That pissed me off." Don Spacini leaned back in his chair, "Maybe, I had something to do with it."
"I know better than that."
"You don't know better than to come around here."
"Yeah, well, sometimes I do dumb things."
"Like fall for a cop." Carmine Spacini lit his cigar, "Why don't you let me introduce you to a nice Italian girl?"
"Maybe, some other time."
Carmine said in a more friendly tone, "I'll ask around, but don't get your hopes up. Chasin' pimps is a little out of my line."
"Can I quote you on that?"
"Quote me on this asshole, 'two things I hate; reporters and cops' and you bring me both. Sei una rottura di palle."
"By the way," Jack added, "I hear Ray Esposito has a high stakes poker game somewhere downtown. You wouldn't know where?"
Jack found himself out on the street with his jacket a little rumpled.

Lai Ngoc Linh and his sister, Lai Thanh Tuyen, looked up at the sky to watch a military jet pass over the village.

71: Thursday – October 2, 1969

Richard Anderson was called into his boss's office. It was a regular occurrence so he wasn't concerned. With just nine days on the job at his father's publishing company there really wasn't a lot he could have done wrong. In fact, he had been pleasantly surprised to find that the editors of many of the magazines welcomed his involvement in the process. Even the Director of Graphic Services, Harlan Osterbrook, seemed pleased to have the young hippie on board. The fifty-year-old bald manager told Ritchie on his first day that what was needed was fresh thinking. He pointed out that with a small staff of artists that had limited design training they were hard-pressed to do any more than a standard photo on the cover of the magazines. With a sincere smile he told Ritchie to, "Show us what you got and take that stupid bow out of your hair."

"What possessed you to put fishermen on a merry-go-round?" Harlan Osterbrook asked with curiosity.

"Actually, it was inspired by the story titled *Endless Hunt* about fishermen's perpetual search for the perfect spot to cast their line. The writer addressed all of the theories, myths, and streams-of-logic used by anglers as they try to identify the exact place that offers the best catch potential. The story concludes by saying that ultimately they end up where they started." Ritchie shrugged, "a merry-go-round."

"You read the article?"

"I have to read the articles, man, to get a clear picture of what is being said or else I'm working in the dark. In which case, I can't graphically do an adequate job."

"A merry-go-round? I like it," the older man stated. He looked at the layout for a moment and concluded, "It's different. It will definitely get newsstand attention."

"Thanks."

"So, now we have to find a merry-go-round for a photo shoot."

"That's not my area," Ritchie offered as he leaned back in his chair.

"Ah, but it is," Harlan informed Ritchie. "You're the art director on this cover, which makes it your responsibility."

"Do I have to do the photography, as well?" Ritchie asked sarcastically.

"There ya go—you're catching on," Harlan said with a grin.

"Seriously?"

"This, my young friend, is a low-budget operation. You can check out a camera in supply. Also, send out a memo asking for volunteers to be fishermen on their day off. It pays the standard twenty bucks."

"Well, I believe there is a merry-go-round at Palisades Park. Maybe we can rent time on a Sunday morning."

"Rent time? Are you nuts? Tell them we'll give them a mention. Or else, find a merry-go-round someplace else that won't cost us."

"I'll start looking tomorrow."

"What's wrong with today?"

"I have a meeting with the editor of *My Bike* who wants to know why I want to put a bicycle in a tree."

Detective Akimoto stared at numerous photos of the crime scene hoping to see something that was previously missed. Something, anything, new had to turn up. Her logical mind was stuck in neutral having run out of ideas and it didn't make her happy. She examined photo after photo but nothing in the way of a clue presented itself. Detective Donovan had gone downstairs for coffee. He was as frustrated as her. By all indications this was going to be one of those unsolved murders that law enforcement professionals hate. Time was their enemy and it was quickly running out. They would soon be assigned a new case and the Claire Payton murder would languish as a cold case.

The telephone rang and Ryoya unconsciously picked up the receiver. A muffled voice that sounded like a male with a distinct Spanish accent stated, "The killers you seek are named Eduardo and Phillipe. They are from Lodi, New Jersey."

Caught by surprise Ryoya quickly wrote down what she heard and asked, "What are their last names and where in Lodi?"

The connection went dead.

Detective Akimoto looked at the note pad with her hurried scrawl. It was a lead—small as it was—a lead.

Michael Donovan returned carrying two Styrofoam cups of coffee.

Ryoya greeted him holding up her note pad, "We have a lead."

"A lead? Damn! What kind of lead?"

"An anonymous caller gave me two names and a location. Vague and not much, but a starting point."

"More than we had when we got here this morning."

It's interesting how when all seems lost the slightest positive event or ray of hope can re-energize the human mind. Ryoya Akimoto and Michael Donovan shared that feeling of excitement after more than a week of steadily running in place and getting nowhere.

After Ryoya relayed the information she had received to Michael, he asked, "Do you know how many Eduardos and Phillipes there are in the metropolitan area?"

"Fewer than total the number of Hispanic males," Ryoya replied. "We're closing in on the perpetrators."

"Uh, huh."

"We know that they have to have some kind of association with Miguel's happy little gang of cutthroats." A pang of remorse struck Ryoya as she remembered how Claire Payton died. A light comment said in haste had dramatic effect.

"Let's check arrest records for known associates of the late Miguel Juarez. If we turn up an Eduardo and Phillipe that would definitely be something worth following up on," Detective Donovan stated.

As they headed to records Detective Akimoto thought out loud, "I wonder who called and why."

On a chilly afternoon in Chicago with clouds threatening inclement weather the New York Mets played their last game of the season. They faced the Cubs at Wrigley Field. Only 9,981 diehard fans attended the game. The Mets jumped out to a 3 -0 lead but ultimately lost the game 5 − 3.

President Richard Nixon read the memo from Henry Kissinger that discussed Duck Hook. In it Dr. Kissinger cautioned, "Since we cannot confidently predict the exact point at which Hanoi could be likely to respond positively, we must be prepared to play out whatever string necessary." The wording was similar to that of the memo sent to Captain Rembrandt Robinson of the Joint Chiefs of Staff by Kissinger aides Roger Morris and Anthony Lake a few days earlier. In addition, the National Security Advisor wrote, "To achieve its full effect on Hanoi's thinking, the action must be brutal." "The action must be brutal" was underlined. Finally, Henry Kissinger asked the unavoidable question, "Should we be prepared to use nuclear weapons?"

The President placed the memo on top of a draft of an eighteen-page address he planned to deliver to the American people on the day Duck Hook would be initiated— if indeed it was. In the speech he would explain the reason for the dramatic steps he was about to take. It read, "This warning was privately confirmed to Hanoi's chief negotiator in Paris at the beginning of August. He was informed that if no major progress toward a settlement of the war had been made by the first of November, we would be compelled to take measures of the greatest consequence. But tonight— after months of the most thorough study and deliberation—I must report to you that Hanoi has indeed made a tragic miscalculation of our will and purpose. They have not heeded our clear warnings. They have refused to credit the word of the United States." The speech also made reference to the need to take extreme action. This might have been a pre-announcement to the American public of the planned use of tactical nuclear weapons in Vietnam. It ended with the words, "That decision had to be my responsibility. It is our common responsibility—yours and mine—to demonstrate our unflinching resolve to end this war."

Richard Nixon knew a tough decision had to be made. He prayed for the wisdom to make the right one.

Two Bell HU-1 Huey helicopters flew low above the trees. By Marine definition one was a Shark (gunship) and the other a Dolphin (transport). On the Dolphin were Wellington Marsh, his CAP squad, and interpreter Nghiem Duc Hung. The large side doors of the aircraft were open. For the first twenty minutes of the flight after they left Da Nang the landscape was relatively flat with rolling hills passing beneath them. Then, almost abruptly, mountainous peeks appeared. Updrafts caused the Huey to bounce and sway.

Little conversation took place due to the deafening noise of the rotors. Every once in a while, Hung would poke Wellington and point at a landmark below. Wellington liked the older Vietnamese man but in the back of his mind were the words of Sergeant . . . Wellington realized he didn't know the Sergeant's name . . . but his words rang clear, "Trust no one, not even your interpreter."

Midday they hovered over a clearing that was approximately two miles from the Village of Quy Hoa. The gunship remained at a higher altitude ready to strike if the dolphin received any enemy fire. All was quiet. The Huey touched down and the CAP squad rapidly exited the aircraft and spread out taking up defensive positions. Wellington signaled for two of the rifle team members to reconnoiter the woods to the west. Once they were all clear the Huey lifted off. It was at that moment Lance Corporal Wellington Marsh knew they were on their own and he would be tested in ways he couldn't even imagine. He felt like throwing up but instead signaled for the team to head in the direction of the two members on point.

Hung tapped Wellington on the arm and as he shook his head said, "No VC. If here we would know by now."

Wellington nodded but remained cautious.

Hung walked upright and unafraid into the woods.

"When you go into a village, everyone is the enemy until they prove otherwise," words of advice on a long flight from America echoed in Wellington's mind.

"We go," Hung said gesturing in the direction of the village.

Wellington signaled for the squad to follow at an interval. After half an hour they came to a cliff that overlooked a valley. Below they could see cultivated land, huts, wooden buildings, a dirt road, pastures, orchards, and a river beyond. Villagers scampered about doing their daily chores unaware that they were being observed.

"Quy Hoa," Hung pointed with a smile.

"Yes, Precious Flower," Wellington acknowledged. He pointed at an area that was free of trees and undergrowth, "We will spend the night here."

"Good. I go to my village. Tomorrow, we meet the old men."

After Hung left Wellington informed the team that they would move half a mile east to another relatively clear spot. He explained that they would leave two men to observe the area where they said they would be to see if any VC showed up. Observers would be relieved every two hours. The team understood his motives and gained confidence in their leader.

Lai Ngoc Linh sat on the ground watching a wood carver rapidly working on a piece of rosewood he clamped tightly with his feet.

72: Saturday – October 4, 1969

After two days there were no signs of Viet Cong. Wellington and his team had entered the village the day before to watchful eyes. Hung had arranged a meeting with the leaders of the three villages. The old men expressed their desire to live their lives as their ancestors had for hundreds of years. Generation after generation had lived in the valley, farmed, fished, hunted, and crafted fine furniture. Politics and war were of no interest to them. Wellington was able to use their desire to be left alone as a way of convincing the leaders that the CAP team was there to protect them from outside forces. Emotionless stares left him wondering if he had made his point.

On this morning they met with the few villagers who would help combat "outside forces." In all, there were seven old men and twelve young boys. Wellington quickly concluded that if the Viet Cong entered the village in force they wouldn't meet much resistance. Why they hadn't up to that point he didn't know. Maybe, the village didn't have any strategic value. Or, in the back of his mind, he wondered if they had struck a deal with the communists. If that was the case he and his team were in real jeopardy.

Wellington asked Hung how far the Cambodian and Laotian borders were from the village. Hung told him about six miles. From the border the Ho Chi Minh Trail was approximately twenty miles farther west. During the training session Wellington remembered being told that the two villages east of Quy Hoa, Kontum and Pleiku, ten and eighteen miles away respectively were where major battles were fought during the Tet Offensive. He asked Hung why Quy Hoa was spared.

"Xa mat, cách long," Hung said. He looked at Wellington and translated, "What cannot be seen cannot be touched."

"You hid the village?"

"We caused them to look the other way."

"How so?"

"I show."

Hung led them west through a thick forest on winding almost non-existent trails. The travel was mountainous, tough, and confusing. Often Wellington looked back at where they had come from to memorize the path but saw only trees and undergrowth. There was no trail. At times they climbed what seemed straight up. Other times they walked along narrow ledges on high cliffs. Wellington became anxious as he realized that it would be easy for Hung to deliver them into Viet Cong hands. After three hours, near exhaustion, they reached a peak that overlooked a canyon below.

Hung pointed north and said, "Laos." He pointed south and said, "Cambodia."

"Is this where the Viet Cong cross?" Wellington asked.

"Cross many places."

"Can we go down there?"

"No go." Hung waved his hand across the landscape and said, "Very dangerous." Hung then waved for them to follow him once more. They maneuvered through thick brush and heavily treed forests. At the edge of one forest Hung pointed at a clearing. There was a dirt road that led off to the northeast. It looked well-traveled. He smiled and said, "We build. Viet Cong take easy route." He pointed at the thick seemingly impenetrable forest, "Quy Hoa."

"You led them away from Quy Hoa. Very good."

Hung went on to explain that every route to the village had been camouflaged to keep outsiders away. Rough, but easy to find, routes insured that travelers found their way without going near the hidden villages. It was the American helicopters that ultimately found Quy Hoa. When that happened they knew they had to make a critical decision. Wellington and the CAP squad were the result of that decision.

They continued along the edge of the forest for a mile when Hung grabbed Wellington by the sleeve and motioned for the team to hide. Wellington leaned close to listen to what Hung had to say. The Vietnamese interpreter whispered, "American soldier over there." He pointed farther up the dirt path they had been paralleling.

"How do you know?" Wellington whispered.

Hung made a motion that mimicked smoking and sniffed the air.

Wellington sniffed but couldn't distinguish cigarette smoke. He listened but didn't hear any sound of a military force. "We should go meet them."

"No."

A bird flew up from a tree in the distance to the west. Hung pulled on Wellington's sleeve once more and pointed. Wellington saw the bird.

"Viet Minh," Hung whispered.

"Are you sure?"

"Ambush."

Wellington looked for any sign of the enemy but saw nothing. "We need to warn the Americans."

"No."

"Yes."

"Ambush there," Hung pointed at a high point above the dirt path with large rocks for cover. "We go there," he pointed to a spot above the protected ambush position.

Wellington examined the surroundings. When he was satisfied with the plan, he moved cautiously back into the woods. In a low whisper he explained the plan to the CAP squad. Slowly and as silently as possible they moved to the edge of the forest above the dirt road and ambush position. Once in position they waited.

Carl waited. A police car had arrived at Lark's Run. When Nick saw it coming up the private road he nonchalantly said to Carl, "You should take a walk in the woods." He nodded toward the distant vehicle.

Without saying a word Carl disappeared behind the barn and made his way up a little traveled path into the thicker part of the forest. He made his way through brambles and vines and fallen limbs. After a short climb up a steep slope he found a spot where he could remain invisible while also observing the farm below.

Nick walked up to the arriving police car and greeted the driver, "Good morning Fred, what brings you to Lark's Run?"

"Morning Nick, how's it going?"

"Looks like we'll have a good fall crop this year and I'm brewing an Octoberfest beer."

"I'll be sure to come by when I'm off duty."

"Do that, we'd love to have you," Nick nodded toward the police car, "However, you presently are on duty."

"We have an alert about an escaped convict being in the area," Patrolman Fred Leonardo produced a sheet of paper that contained a photograph of the fugitive.

From his vantage point Carl watched the police officer and Nick. Was that a wanted poster for a murderer from New York City? Would Nick turn him in? He wouldn't blame him. Nick had to protect Lark's Run. Carl considered disappearing into the mountainous wilderness of Western Pennsylvania. The problem was he was a city boy with little idea how to survive in the wild. His mind pictured Laurel and he felt loneliness. He missed her as deeply as he had ever missed anything in his life and he hadn't even left. When the police car left he knew Nick hadn't betrayed him. Slowly, he made his way back to the barnyard. Once there, he saw the paper Nick had been given. It wasn't him. Carl wanted to run to Laurel and hug her but knew at that hour she would be at the hives collecting honey.

Wellington heard a noise to his left. When he glanced in that direction he saw two soldiers in black peasant clothing moving stealthily along the side of the road. He concluded that they were the point men. What struck him was that they were without military gear of any kind. One carried an AK-47 while the other carried an old rifle the origin of which he had no idea. One looked up in their direction but didn't seem to notice anything unusual. The CAP team remained motionless and hidden.

Silently, the two Viet Cong moved up the path. They passed around a bend and out-of-sight. Suddenly, they came running back. Without any equipment they moved swiftly and relatively quietly. Wellington watched them pass beneath where he crouched and disappear behind a rock outcropping to the left. Then from the left came twelve Viet Cong. All but one wore black peasant clothes and carried a wide array of rifles. Wellington saw two M-16s which most likely came from dead Americans. When they got below the position of the CAP squad the single soldier in a real green fatigue uniform looked around and pointed at the exact spot Hung had said they would use for cover to ambush the American soldiers. Wellington wondered how he could possibly have known that these two forces would be here at this time and place. He looked over at the interpreter who was intently watching the action below.

The sound of boots on the path and clanking of equipment was heard to the east. The American force was approaching the ambush. The black-clad VC waited and watched the road. With a hand signal Wellington ordered his team to open fire. In what seemed a blink of an eye a vast number of rounds rained down on the unsuspecting ambushers. None were able to get off a shot. Wellington signaled for two Marines to go down and check the fallen VC, but Hung grabbed his arm and said, "No. We go."

"We need to check and meet with the Americans."

"No. We go."

Wellington felt anger well up inside. He was in charge of the CAP squad— not Hung. There was no reason to not meet with the Americans. Yet, a weathered Vietnamese face stared at him, not in anger, rather with a look of pleading or fear. Wellington looked down at the ambush site. He considered the options but couldn't find a logical answer as to the best action to take. He looked at Hung and said, "We go."

Hung smiled broadly and led the squad through a maze of vegetation until they had disappeared into the landscape. An American Marine reconnaissance platoon maneuvered their way to where they had heard gunfire until they came to the ambush site. Twelve Viet Cong lay dead. The Second Lieutenant in charge examined the carnage, looked up at the hillside above, and commented, "What the fuck?"

At 2:37 p.m. in the afternoon the New York Mets faced the Atlanta Braves at Atlanta Stadium in a best of three series for the National League championship. It was the first post-season game the Mets had ever played. Over fifty thousand baseball fans packed the stadium. The Mets had the better season record with 100 wins and 62 losses while the Braves won 93 and lost 69. Yet, the Atlanta Braves were favored by odds makers.

After six innings the score was tied 4 to 4. A Hank Aaron homerun in the bottom of the seventh inning gave the Atlanta Braves a 5 to 4 lead.

Then came the top of the eighth inning. Wayne Garrett led off with a double. Cleon Jones followed with a single driving in Garrett to tie the score. The third batter, Art Shamsky, singled and Al Weis was put in to run for him. Cleon Jones stole third base with Ken Boswell at bat who ultimately hit a ground ball which got Weis thrown out at second. Ed Kranepool then hit into a fielder's choice. The Atlanta Braves' first baseman, Orlando Cepeda, threw to home but Jones scored on an error. Boswell stopped at second and Kranepool was safe on first. The Mets led 6 to 5. Jerry Grote was the next batter who grounded out allowing the baserunners to advance. Atlanta then walked Bud Harrelson to load the bases with two out. That was when the wheels came off the trolley. J. C. Martin was put in as a pinch hitter for pitcher Tom Seaver. Martin hit a single to right field. Boswell and Kranepool scored and on a throwing error Harrelson also crossed home plate. J. C. Martin was thrown out trying to reach second base. The New York Mets led 9 to 5 which was the final score.

"Ah shit!" Wellington said in his mind. He saw the two Viet Cong that he shot at fall. Whether it was his bullet or someone else's that dropped them he couldn't know. What he did know was it left him with a sick feeling. He wanted to throw up. In the subdued light of the forest he looked at his team. They were all young, probably the same age as he. It was most likely their first action, as well. Shortstop had a funny look on his face. Wellington knew, as the team leader, he had to help them, and himself, over this hump. He signaled for them to gather round. In a low voice he said, "You all performed well. Thank you. Those enemy soldiers were prepared to ambush American soldiers and we eliminated that threat. For those of you who this is the first action that you've seen a seasoned Gunnery Sergeant told me you have to get past it and get past it quickly. Don't let it screw up your head. He told me, 'say ah shit,' and move on."

Hung came over to Wellington and said, "We go."

CAP Team 1-6-2 followed a circuitous route back to Quy Hoa. It was so complex that Wellington wasn't sure if they took the same route back as they had taken earlier in the day. He was sure of one thing it would be very easy to get lost in those mountains. At dusk they arrived back at Quy Hoa.

Detectives Donovan and Akimoto rode north on Third Avenue. They were headed to Spanish Harlem. When they crossed 102nd Street Michael Donovan said, "One block over on Lexington Avenue is Duffy's Hill. It runs between 102nd and 103rd and is the steepest hill in Manhattan. It was named after a Tammany Hall Alderman, Michael James Duffy. The guy was a big developer. He built a bunch of rowhouses in this area in the late 1800s."

"Have you been talking to Jack?" Ryoya asked sarcastically.

"I think New York history is fascinating. Take Duffy's Hill, they had so many accidents because street cars had trouble going up and down that they had to keep guards at the intersection of Lexington and 103rd 24/7" When the detectives reached 110th Street they stopped at a red light, "This all used to be farmland."

"In what century?" was Ryoya Akimoto's response.

"The 19th century, but after the Civil War houses were built over there," he pointed east of Third Avenue. "At first it was German, Irish, Scandinavian, and Jewish immigrants. Then in the 1870s Italian laborers were brought in as strikebreakers to lay trolley tracks on First Avenue. They settled in the area around 115th Street. As a matter-of-fact that area was the first in Manhattan to be referred to as Little Italy. It also was the birthplace of the Mafia with the Black Hand and where the founder of the Genovese crime family lived, as well as home of the murder-for-hire Purple Gang."

"You know quite a bit about this area."

After the First World War Puerto Rican and Latin American immigrants established a neighborhood in the western portion of East Harlem. I think around 110th Street. It became known as Spanish Harlem and spread wider and wider until it gobbled up all of East Harlem. The Italians moved to Bronx, Brooklyn, Upstate New York, and New Jersey. And that is your history lesson for today. There will be a test on Friday."

"I'm looking forward to it. Now, can you find La Serpiente Roja?"

"Two blocks up, one block over."

They turned east on a side street. Abandoned cars lined the rutted pavement. On one side of the street were deteriorating buildings that very well could be original to the area. Across the street was an empty lot filled with garbage and discarded appliances. Next to the lot was a laundromat and a bodega. Finally, on the corner was a three story red brick building. The ground floor was a bar whose doors were located at the corner. Next to the doors was a flight of stairs that led to a basement. The entire façade was painted bright red. Over the door a hand-painted sign read "La Serpiente Roja" under which was a red snake.

Ryoya reviewed the sheet of paper upon which were five names, three Eduardos and two Phillipes. All five had criminal records. Whether or not they knew Miguel Juarez or any members of his crew was unknown. La Serpiente Roja was a known hangout for that unsavory bunch so was a logical starting point. The two detectives entered the establishment. It being early evening there were a good number of patrons inside. Spanish music blared, conversations and laughter came from various parts of the bar, three young men played pool at the single table on one side of the room, and two bartenders were busy filling orders. When their presence became know a hush fell over the room. Only the Spanish music continued. Countless eyes followed the two detectives as they approached the bar. Michael Donovan showed his badge as he summoned one of the bartenders. He showed the man the list of names and asked, "Do you know any of these individuals?"

The bartender examined the list, looked at Detective Donovan, and shook his head negatively.

"Let me put that another way," Michael Donovan said, "if you don't help me find one or more of these people I will spend all my nights here checking green cards, looking for weapons, and making drug busts."

The man's eyes grew large as he considered the threat. He then nodded in the direction of the pool table and said softly Phillipe and Eduardo Pena.

"Thank you."

The uneasy silence continued as Michael Donovan made his way to the pool table. Detective Akimoto remained near the entrance. She watched for any sign of trouble. Her hand was in her purse holding her 38 Special.

"Phillipe, Eduardo," Detective Donovan said when he arrived at the table.

One of the pool players dashed for the door. Ryoya stepped in front of the fleeing man. He reached out to push her out of the way only to have an aikido wristlock drop him to his knees. Detective Donovan led the other two men toward the door. Curses in Spanish were heard from different parts of the room but no aggressive action was taken. The two police detectives walked outside with their three detainees.

"Who is Phillipe?" Donovan asked.

A skinny young man with greased back hair nodded with a sneer.

Donovan turned to the other man in his charge and asked, "So, you're Eduardo?"

The other young man with a mustache nodded.

"Who are you?" Donovan asked the third man who was still held by Ryoya.

"¡Bésame el trasero!"

"Wrong answer," Donovan said as he produced handcuffs and snapped them on the man's wrists. He turned back to the brothers, "Phillipe, Eduardo, where do you live?"

Phillipe answered, "123rd Street."

Detective Donovan nodded knowing they were not the two they were looking for who lived in Lodi, New Jersey. He reached in his pocket and pulled out a five dollar bill. As he handed it to Phillipe he said, "Enjoy your game." The two brothers went back into La Serpiente Roja.

"What about me?" The man in handcuffs asked.

Detective Donovan decided to take a shot as he asked, "Where is Eduardo Torres?"

"Never heard of him."

"Ah, see now I try to be nice and you lie to me. Now, we go downtown and I book you."

"Wait," the man said as he looked around to make sure there weren't any witnesses, "Torres lives in the Bronx. But, he's not there. He's in the Tombs—assault."

"That wasn't on his rap sheet," Ryoya stated.

The man in handcuffs turned toward her and explained, "He was picked up last night."

"We'll check," Detective Donovan warned, "If he's not cooling his heels in the Tombs you'll be there waiting trial on multiple charges, including assaulting a police officer."

"What assault?"

"I saw you try to shove Detective Akimoto."

"I . . ." he looked pleadingly back and forth at the two detectives.

Michael Donovan removed the handcuffs and said, "Get out of here."

"No five dollars?"

"I'll give you five knuckles."

The man disappeared into the bar.

"Well done," Ryoya said, "we now have two possibilities; Eduardo Fernandez and Phillipe Lopez."

"And it only cost you five bucks."

"Me?"

"I did all the work. And, remember the night we rousted those bikers? That cost me ten bucks—you're getting off easy."

Wellington Marsh lay on his poncho in the dark. Creatures crawled and landed upon him looking for their evening snack. On this occasion he was less aware of the assaults as he relived the action earlier in the day. Killing those soldiers left an indelible mark on his conscience. One part of his mind rationalized that they were preparing to kill American soldiers from ambush. He and his team saved those Americans. However, they did so from their own ambush shooting the unsuspecting combatants in the back. All the television westerns he had watched as a kid made it clear that only a coward shoots a man in the back. But, this was war, not a shootout on Main Street. Yet, he did kill those men. With the wave of his hand he snuffed out twelve lives. God said, "Let there be life," and Wellington Marsh said, "Let there be death." They probably had families who wait for their return. How did he come to this time and place to be a hired gun? It wasn't by choice—that was for sure. And, now he managed a killing machine.

Through the trees Wellington saw a single star. It hung silently in the sky. A lone speck of light floating in the universe made him lonely. Indeed, it made him homesick. Like some little boy he wanted to cry. He wanted someone to hold him and tell him everything was going to be alright. The darkness reflected his heart. Hope seemed a foreign concept. The star disappeared. A cloud drifted over their camp and Wellington jumped up to rouse the team. He quickly divided the fourteen team members into pairs of two. As each man carried half of a tent, one tent pole that can be split into three sections, and tent pegs seven pairs would share shelter. Wellington and the Navy Corpsman shared a tent. They crawled inside just as the rain began to fall.

Lai Ngoc Linh and his sister listened to the rain. By its intensity they knew the next few days would be wet.

73: Monday – October 6, 1969

President Richard M. Nixon decided against Duck Hook. He wasn't convinced that it would be effective and both Defense Secretary Melvin Laird and Secretary of State William P. Rogers warned against military escalation. Given past experience, they believed that hitting multiple targets once with conventional weapons would not convince North Vietnam to negotiate any more seriously. Only extreme measures, such as the use of tactical nuclear weapons, would get their attention. Nixon was not prepared to take such action.

As an alternative strategy the President decided to raise the level of interest on the part of the Soviet Union. He believed that by posturing the United States as raising its level of nuclear preparedness it would give the impression that the use of nuclear weapons in Vietnam was being considered. Nixon hoped the Soviet Union would then pressure North Vietnam to negotiate for peace.

After two days of rain the sky became clear. While a welcome relief everything remained wet or damp. All members of CAP 1-6-2 tried to find ways to dry their clothing, packs, weapons, and bodies. It was a futile effort.

Lance Corporal Wellington Marsh had met with Nghiem Duc Hung the day before to lay out plans for protecting the Village of Quy Hoa. It was not a typical situation like what was outlined during the training sessions. There they were taught tactics for defending a position, identifying ambushes, finding tunnels, and identifying collaborators. In Quy Hoa the entire population was apolitical. At least that was Wellington's initial impression. They definitely didn't want to live under the rule of ruthless communists, but conversely had no interest in the corrupt South Vietnamese government. Simply, they wanted to be left alone. Reluctantly, they agreed to the United States Marine CAP squad after lengthy negotiation during which it was promised that the soldiers would be there to defend the village and its way of life. Hung was a major supporter of the idea. He had seen the pain and suffering that came when other villages fell under communist control. If the day came when they would need to defend their homes he knew they would require assistance.

At the present time the goal was to keep Quy Hoa an unseen phantom hidden in the mountains. To do this, they had to make sure that no identifiable trails leading to the three villages could be discovered. Some of this was achieved through misdirection as Wellington had seen two days prior. Not a single path led directly to the village. All trails wound away from Quy Hoa. Only those who knew the secret were able to depart a trail in the correct place to head in the direction of the villages. Within the villages inventive ways were utilized to make sure no smoke rose above the trees, that fire and lights were shielded during the night, care was taken to make sure no artifacts of civilization were allowed to drift downstream, and travel in and out of the area was closely monitored. They even went so far as to create sounds of nature with wood flutes that hung in trees which in a breeze mimicked birds.

Wellington asked Hung about the chances of strangers coming downstream and discovering the village. He was told that it was impossible as less than a mile upstream was an unpassable fifty-foot waterfall. Hung smiled when he said that they have, on occasion, had a broken boat and bodies drift by floating downstream. "Those visitors did not stop," was Hung's comment. In the opposite direction, those wishing to sail upstream met equally unpassable rapids. Quy Hoa was well positioned.

Wellington and Hung developed a strategy to keep enemy soldiers away from Quy Hoa. The first tactic would be to carry two wooden wheels and an axle to one of the trails that had been cleared that led away from the villages. There they would assemble the wheels and push it along the path leaving a clear track. At one point, they would turn away from Quy Hoa into the forest. It would give the impression that something was going on in that direction. With luck the VC would be compelled to investigate and assume there was activity where indeed there was none. Their attention turned in one direction would cause them to ignore the other.

A second tactic would be to create a hot zone a good distance from the village. It would consist of booby traps, ambushes, and misleading materials. Among the materials would be parts of maps of areas far from the villages. The VC would have to expend time and personnel monitoring and policing the hot zone. And, as soon as they gained control a new hot zone would be created by CAP 1-6-2. Keep them busy and off balance and they don't have time to explore for a village that isn't there.

The final tactic had been to set up a surveillance network manned by members of the village militia. Old men and young boys hid where they could watch for any intruders who ventured in the direction of the village. Painstaking effort was made to find or create ideal observation posts. Eight locations were established. In addition, means for quick communication with the village were devised. For example, one location was north of the river and the waterfall. Hidden in the underbrush at the edge of the river was a brightly colored waterproof box that would both float and withstand the drop over the waterfall. If any villager saw that box floating past they would alert the elders. Another observation post was on a hilltop. Should an unwelcome guest be spotted the observer would travel half a mile to where a tree trunk lay tethered on the ground. He would release the line and the tree trunk would slide down a slope and over a cliff. When it did it would pull down a dead 100 foot tall deciduous duu baan tree that had been carefully placed to be seen on the distant hilltop miles from Quy Hoa. Villagers became accustomed to glancing in that direction whenever they were in a clearing where they could see the distant mountain. As long as that needle pointed skyward they knew they were safe.

Wellington was extremely impressed by the efforts of the people of Quy Hoa to remain hidden and live their lives as they wished. He thought of America. The only thing these folks wanted was to be free. Lance Corporal Marsh wasn't sure what was going on elsewhere in Vietnam, but at that moment in that place he knew why he was there.

Matthew Ellis walked aimlessly along New Milford Avenue until he came to Dumont High School. He graduated from that school in 1947. Slowly, he walked onto the campus. School was in session. He could see activity inside and gym classes on the track and football field. A part of him wished he could start over, but he knew in life that was impossible. The path he chose was the path he would have to follow and there was no turning back, retracing steps, or undoing what was done.

Memories continued to unfold and the crimes that he and Lida Petropoulos perpetrated became clearer. It was they who devised the scheme, they alone. What troubled him was the fact that the wire seemed to perform so poorly. He had been assured that the cheaper substitute wire was so close to the original specs that no difference would be noticed or experienced. Apparently, that was not the case. But, why? Was it the stranded metal wire or the sheathing or both? Matt wanted to know. He remembered that he had a roll of the wire. It was clear that he couldn't afford the fees of a testing laboratory and didn't have the facilities to experiment. He then wondered if Stephanie's ex-boyfriend, what was his name Ritchie, could help.

Ritchie stared at the photographs of fishermen on a merry-go-round. The day before, a Sunday morning, he and eight volunteers from the staff traveled to a small town in upstate New York where there was a vintage merry-go-round in the town square. It didn't run but stood proudly as a memory of good old days long gone. The plan was to arrive together, quickly set up, and take as many photos as possible before they were asked to leave town by the local police. That is not exactly what happened.

Before the first three volunteers could climb upon the merry-go-round a police car drove up. Officer Tank Garrison questioned the nine out-of-towners. Ritchie, hair blowing in the wind, tried to explain what they wished to do and that they would be careful not to do any damage.

"Well, you can't climb on our merry-go-round—that's trespassing," Officer Garrison stated with authority.

"We don't want to trespass," Ritchie said, "Is there any way we can get permission for just an hour?"

"It's Sunday, you'll have to come back tomorrow and talk with the mayor."

"Is there anyone we can talk with today?" Ritchie asked, "We've come a long way."

"It's Sunday, nobody's at town hall."

"Could we call someone at home?"

"It's Sunday, I don't want to bother people at home on Sunday."

Ritchie was running out of ideas. After a pause he asked, "What about your chief of police can we talk with him?"

"It's Sunday, he's at church."

"Are you the only police officer on duty?"

"It's Sunday, there are only two of us me and Sergeant Wilkins."

"Can we speak with Sergeant Wilkins?" Ritchie said then added quickly, "I know, it's Sunday, he's unavailable."

"No, it's Sunday, he's at police headquarters," Officer Garrison smiled.

"Where is police headquarters?"

"Right there," the patrolman pointed at a red two story wood clad building across the square.

"Thank you. We'll have a chat with Sergeant Wilkins."

"You can't do that."

"Why?"

"It's Sunday, the building is locked."

"Can you get in touch with him?"

"Of course."

"Can you ask him to let us in and meet with us?"

"It's Sunday, he doesn't like to be disturbed unless it's an emergency."

At that moment the radio in the patrolman's car crackled and then beeped. Officer Tank Garrison walked over and spoke for a few moments. He turned back to the nine strangers and said, "I have a call." He pointed and ordered, "Stay off the merry-go-round."

Left alone, one of the volunteer models asked, "Now what?"

Another suggested, "We could try to get a few quick shots and blow town."

Still another stated, "I don't feel like spending the night in jail."

"It's Sunday," Ritchie said, "Let's go disturb the Sergeant."

The faux anglers made their way across the town square to the red two story wood clad building. As expected the door was locked. There wasn't anything that looked like a doorbell so Ritchie knocked. Nothing. He tried once more. Nothing. Finally, he pounded on the door. This got a reaction.

With a resounding creak the door opened. Before them stood a rotund police sergeant with grey hair eating a piece of fried chicken. Between bites he stated officially, "It's Sunday, we're closed except for emergencies." As he focused on the group before him he smiled and said, "You lost—looking for a lake?"

Ritchie explained why they were there and requested permission to use the merry-go-round.

The police sergeant rubbed his chin and thought out loud, "Well, I don't know. I'm not sure that I have the authority to approve such a thing. That would be the mayor's call and it being Sunday."

Impulsively, Ritchie suggested, "Maybe, you would be willing to be in the photo. How'd you like to be on the cover of a national magazine?"

"Me?" the sergeant smiled and patted his huge girth, "I'd be a big fish in a small merry-go-round."

A wild idea struck Ritchie, "Sergeant Wilkins, it's your town's merry-go-round. Why not have local townspeople be the fisherman—you included? We'll give credit to the town and show a picture inside the magazine."

"The mayor would love that," Sergeant Wilkins admitted. He thought for a moment and then said, "It's Sunday, but let's give the mayor a call."

Things took off after that. The mayor showed up and quickly got onboard. Calls were made and before long the square was full of fishermen and women. Ritchie knew he would create unnecessary debate and disappointment if he simply picked eight candidates. He discussed the situation with the mayor and asked which four persons should definitely be in the shot. It turned out to be the mayor, Sergeant Wilkins, chairman of the town council, and the wife of a prominent businessman—don't ask. With those four placed, Ritchie picked groups of four additional townspeople and added them to the shot. In all, he photographed twelve different groupings. Everyone was satisfied with his explanation that the final decision as to which group would be on the cover was to be made by the managing editor of the magazine.

The excitement generated by the photo session created a festival atmosphere. People began bringing food and setting up tables. Children appearaed to be evrywhere, running this way and that. A local guitarist played in front of town hall. People picnicked in the square and local politicians made speeches. Ritchie was glad that he got all of the photos taken before the scene got completely cluttered with people.

When they left, the festivities were going strong. As they drove back toward

New York City, Ritchie commented, "It's Sunday, they should be home watching football."

Shea Stadium was packed with over 54,000 fans at two in the afternoon. The Amazing Mets were ahead in the three-game series 1–0. Unlike any other game at Shea Stadium this one had a flavor to it and it wasn't hotdogs. It was a flavor called the World Series. One more win and Met's fans would taste heaven.

However, the game didn't start the way Met's fans would have liked. The second batter up for the Atlanta Braves, Tony Gonzalez, singled to left field. This was followed by a Hank Aaron homerun. Before the Mets ever came to bat they were behind 2 – 0. It wasn't until the bottom of the third inning that the Mets scored on a Tommie Agee homerun. A two-run homer by Ken Boswell in the bottom of the fourth put the Mets ahead 3 – 2. In the top of the fifth the Braves came back with an Orlando Cepeda two-run homerun. However, the Braves 4 – 3 lead was short-lived as the Mets scored three runs in the bottom of the fifth inning and added another in the sixth. The final score of 7 – 4 opened a path to the bright lights of the World Series a goal that never seemed possible when the season began.

Detective Ryoya Akimoto was at her desk when the telephone rang. When she picked it up she heard Jack's voice singing, "Meet the Mets, Meet the Mets, Step right up and greet the Mets!" He then changed the lyrics, "You were right and I was wrong. That's why I'm singing this ridiculous song." Jack then announced, "In case you haven't heard the Mets won 7 – 4 sweeping the series."

"I hope you are prepared to sing that theme song in Grand Central Station when they win the World Series," Ryoya reminded Jack of his impulsive offer made a few weeks earlier.

Lai Ngoc Linh stared out over the landscape far below him. It was his turn to be on watch at this observation post. He was determined that if any outsiders came in the direction of Quy Hoa they would not pass without his sending the alarm.

74: Friday – October 10, 1969

Eduardo Fernandez and Phillipe Lopez were two possible suspects in the Claire Payton murder. They were known associates of the late Miguel Juarez and had criminal records. An anonymous informant indicated that the killers were named Eduardo and Phillipe and lived in Lodi, New Jersey. Information from the Bergen County Prosecutors' Office showed an Eduardo Fernandez and a Phillipe Lopez, residents of Lodi, New Jersey, both had extensive criminal records in the Garden State.

After a conversation with local law enforcement authorities, Detective Michael Donovan told his partner that there had been no sign of the two men in or about Lodi or the apartment where they lived. Local detectives suggested that there was a very good chance that the two men fled to Puerto Rico right after the incident.

General Earle Wheeler, chairman of the Joint Chiefs of Staff, issued a top secret message to military commanders around the world. It stated that orders had come down from higher up to raise their preparedness to respond to a possible confrontation with the Soviet Union.

During the summer of 1968, before Nixon was elected president, the candidate discussed an idea he had about the Vietnam War with close friend and political advisor H.R.Haldeman. "I call it the Madman Theory, Bob. I want the North Vietnamese to believe that I've reached the point that I might do anything to stop the war. We'll just slip the word to them that for God's sake, you know Nixon is obsessed about Communism. We can't restrain him when he is angry, and he has his hand on the nuclear button and Ho Chi Minh himself will be in Paris in two days begging for peace." As President, Nixon was ready to put that strategy into motion.

President Richard Nixon ordered the Air Force and Navy to raise their level of nuclear preparedness through a number of military exercises. The Strategic Air Command (SAC) was ordered to cease training missions and increase the number of nuclear armed B-52's ready for deployment. These actions became known as the Joint Chiefs of Staff Readiness Test.

The President hoped the Soviet Union, Communist China, and the North Vietnamese were listening.

CAP squad 1-6-2 moved silently through the underbrush to the east of Quy Hoa. After taking a circuitous route through mountainous terrain they came to a thick impassable portion of the jungle. During a five minute rest Hung explained that they were about to come to a point where they could overlook a paved road. It ran Southeast to Kontum and Pleiku. Pleiku Air Base was shared by the South Vietnamese Air Force (VNAF) and the United States Air Force. "Much traffic on road. Many soldiers. Americans," he said.

"That's good," Wellington responded. "We don't have to worry about this direction."

"We worry."

"Why."

"Many soldiers come, watch road, plan ambush."

"You mean Viet Cong?"

"Yes."

"So, we watch Viet Cong, who watch Americans?"

"Yes."

"Do you think they are a threat to Precious Flower?"

Hung smiled hearing the English translation of Quy Hoa. He picked up a stick and drew a map in the dirt. He indicated the locations of Quy Hoa, Kontum and Pleiku. Then showed the main trails that led from the Laos and Cambodian borders to the road they were going to observe. By all indications no path came close to Quy Hoa. "After ambush, they will not take known trails back. They will find or make a new route. If we know where their ambush might be we can help them choose correct path."

"Away from Quy Hoa," Wellington concluded.

Hung nodded, "Leave others here. You me go."

The patrol welcomed an extended rest. Some questioned the idea of Wellington going off alone with the Vietnamese interpreter. Wellington made the final decision to go hearing comments like, "It's your neck." Shortstop was the most vehemently opposed wanting to go along to protect his friend.

Wellington and Hung moved in a direction that appeared to go nowhere. After a short distance a tall mountain stood before them. They faced a flat rock wall that towered far above. One thing was clear there wasn't any chance of climbing it. At its base the jungle grew right up to the wall and in many areas up the wall. Hung pushed through some bushes and stepped behind the trunk of a large tree. He seemed to disappear. Wellington looked behind the tree. Low on the rock wall behind the tree was an opening. To proceed it was necessary for him to stoop. While one would expect to enter a dark cavern that was not the case. Light filtered down from above. Wellington looked up to what appeared to be the opening of an extinct volcano. Enough light filtered through the sparse trees around the opening to illuminate the cave. Once his eyes adjusted to the subdued light Wellington was surprised to see stairs carved out of stone.

Hung explained, "Many hours it took to build. Our ancestors discovered it and carved the stairs to the top. The secret has been kept for generations. If village knows I show this I would be executed."

"Then why did you show me?"

"Trust."

"I won't tell anybody."

"That I know."

Wellington looked at the older man who had a strange look on his face and was compelled to ask, "Why me?"

"Follow me—then you will know."

Laurel walked in the woods of Lark's Run. Along with her was a black basenji. It hadn't taken long for the two of them to bond. After all, they were unique free spirits that others found strange. Fetch, true to the basenji personality, would take off after a squirrel, bird, or other creature that came within the sight hound's range. When she did Laurel would watch and wait for her return. Laurel never scolded the canine as she knew it was natural. Fetch never caught anything even though she could. It was simply sport. In truth, she liked people food better. She also sensed that Laurel would not approve.

When they returned to the farmhouse Carl was waiting. He asked, "Where've you been?"

Laurel picked up on his tone, but ignored it. "We've been rabbit hunting."

"I bet. I don't see any rabbits."

"We didn't want to kill them, just visit with them."

"You know on a farm things get killed?"

"Not by my hands."

"But, you enjoy eating them."

"Yes, I do."

"Isn't that hypocritical?"

"No, it's cowardly. I am unable to kill." Laurel looked directly at Carl.

For a moment Carl felt ashamed, then defensive, and finally anger found its way into his mind. Was she throwing the fact that he was wanted for murder into his face? Was she looking down on him? Don't judge me bitch, he thought and immediately regretted the thought.

"There are those who have the strength to do what has to be done to survive. Us cowards live as a result of their kindness," Laurel continued.

"I'm sorry," Carl said more as an apology for his thoughts than what he said.

"Do you have a flashlight?" was Laurel's surprise answer.

"I can get one."

Laurel and Carl walked into the woods at Lark's Run. They arrived at a stone path that climbed upward and to the left. Laurel led and Carl followed. In a short period of time they came to a cave entrance. Carl then knew why he was asked to bring a flashlight.

At the top of the stone stairs was a chamber. It appeared to be large but only a small amount of light made its way in. Hung reached in and retrieved a candle which he lit. What Wellington saw took his breath away.

Carl handed Laurel the flashlight. She then led the way into the cave. The entrance was narrow but once inside it opened to a larger area. On one side was a flat rock wall. When Laurel shined the flashlight upon it Carl could see a carved mural. It was less than half complete. What had been carved was complex and filled with images.

Wellington looked at intricately carved images covering most of the walls. Many were of symbols and letters that he couldn't understand. Others were of designs and maps. There was something hauntingly beautiful by the entire display. In one area there appeared to be gems embedded into the wall. Wellington turned to look at Hung. In the subdued candlelight he beheld a man who reflected devoted reverence. Nghiem Duc Hung stood still as a statue staring at the great wall. It was better not to speak in this holy place. Behind Hung, Wellington observed another wall with what appeared to be a long list. Of course, it being in Vietnamese he could only surmise that it was a list of names.

Laurel said nothing. In silence, Carl gazed at the mural. Amidst flowers and creatures various objects were displayed. As would be expected musical instruments floated amid images of places and people. Some depictions were of a childhood of abundance. Others, of traveling or searching. Images of Lark's Run seemed the freshest. Then he saw it.

A strong hand touched Wellington's shoulder. Hung motioned for them to leave. Outside the chamber the Vietnamese interpreter said, "It is history of our village started long ago."

"It was amazing and beautiful," Wellington commented.

"You remember where to find."

"I'll try."

"You must."

"I will."

"Cam on nhieu. Thank you, Werrington March. You are part of village history, now."

Carl looked into his own eyes carved into the stone. It was actually a good likeness because it didn't make him look mean. He wondered how accurate that really was given his particular history. In his mind he saw a mural of his life filled with violence and evil deeds. After a few moments he realized that over his head was carved a tiara.

When they left the cave Carl said, "It's a remarkable mural."

"My life for all to see," she smiled, "Or, none to see."

"Why the tiara?"

"A tiara is empowering," Laurel smiled and headed back toward Lark's Run.

Lai Ngoc Linh and his sister, welcomed uncle Hung back when he returned late that evening.

75: Saturday – October 11, 1969

Jack Moore arrived at Ryoya Akimoto's apartment at 8:00 a.m. on the dot. They had decided to have breakfast together at a café along the East River. After that, Ryoya wanted to do some shopping which simply thrilled Jack. All they had to do was get back to her apartment in time for the first game of the World Series between the New York Mets and Baltimore Orioles.

At breakfast Ryoya shared an update on the Clair Payton case. It would go into the cold case files up until or when the Lodi, New Jersey police had any information on the whereabouts of Eduardo Fernandez or Phillipe Lopez. They may or may not return to their apartment. After offering that information she looked at Jack and said, "I still don't know why that anonymous informer called me." After taking a sip of coffee her burning stare returned and she added, "Or, how they knew who to call."

Jack knew any attempt at a logical explanation would show he was hiding something so he simply said, "Interesting."

"How is it interesting?"

"That you received a call and wonder why. As a reporter, that happens quite often to me."

"Did you get a call?"

"No."

"Did you tell anyone to call me?"

"No."

"Did you have any involvement with whatever actions led to me getting the call?"

"I don't even know what that means," he said. "Why all the questions, detective?"

"Because I seem to remember when I was investigating the Miguel Juarez murder and had a Carl Pythacyk dead to rights it was you who told me that you had a contact who, let me get this right, 'emphatically stated that Carl Pythacyk couldn't have done it.' With that, I pursued a different direction and ultimately got a confession from Claire Payton. Now, that same Claire Payton is murdered and I get this anonymous call heading me in a direction I probably wouldn't have uncovered on my own." She leaned forward, "The whole thing smells of Jack Moore."

"Me?" Jack asked innocently as he sniffed his armpits to see if he offended.

"Don't give me that. I realize that you have contacts in low places. Also, I know as a newspaperman you have to protect your sources. But, I want you to know, mister, I'm on to you." She smiled and added, "I'm watching you."

Jack spilled his coffee.

Mark Peterson pulled the generator from the tail section of a Boeing 727-100 that had failed. The aircraft had landed safely after which a maintenance report was filed. It had required some extraordinary flying skill and luck for the jet to come home in one piece.

The mechanic brought the suspect generator to the testing bench and went to work. Electrical power on the Boeing 727 is provided by three Alternating Current (AC) generators that produce 115 volts each. To achieve this they spin at a constant RPM through the use of a Constant Speed Drive (CSD). When everything is operating correctly the electrical load is shared equally by synchronized output. Key to coordinating both alternating current and direct current output is the generator control panel.

After extensive testing Mark found the offending generator was in perfect operating condition—nothing wrong. He reinstalled the generator in the 727. Unknown to him was the fact that a wire inside the control panel was the cause of the malfunction.

The aircraft tested fine, was put back into service, and would fly off to its ultimate destiny.

Ryoya and Jack wandered down First Avenue to Houston Street where various shops provided the ultimate shopping experience. The first stop was a designer shoe store. Jack didn't know a pump from a mule and listening to the conversation with the salesman couldn't help but think of a barnyard. His fertile mind drifted taking him back to Woodstock. A distant cow beckoned, flower girl smiled, Jerry the hippie in the tent who lost his brother in Vietnam reflected sadness, love beads from a young girl, Night Bird, mud, and that marihuana high.

Next, was a lingerie shop. Men love to see sexy undergarments on women but for some unexplainable reason get very nervous when seeing the silky items on hangers. Maybe, it's seeing how the sausage is made syndrome. Or, that latent crossdresser fear that might break free if exposed to too much temptation. Or, feeling lost in a strange world they just plain don't fully understand. Whatever the reason, Jack wanted to be somewhere else. This time his mind sat him at a table with Don Carmine Spacini. No doubt, he was a bad guy. In no way could Jack justify some of the acts of which Carmine was accused. Yet, Carmine also exhibited an admirable level of honor. Jack knew he could trust his boyhood friend. Given different circumstances the Don might have been a noble leader. Of course, there was no way that would ever be known. Carmine Spacini would continue to be a target for Jack's column and only the two of them would ever know there was an unbreakable bond between them.

"You like?" Ryoya's voice chased Carmine away. She held up a peach negligee.

Jack smiled and replied, "Jack, like."

Lance Corporal Wellington Marsh and Nghiem Duc Hung sat on the bank of the river that separated the three villages. The two men had come to a point where they trusted each other. In a war-torn world filled with subterfuge, misplaced loyalties, betrayal, and savagery it was a rare occurrence. And, in spite of the first encounter with the VC and prevented ambush it had been relatively peaceful. Quy Hoa was an oasis amid the madness.

"Your country," Hung asked, "how is it so peaceful?"

Wellington looked at his friend and saw a tired and worn soul. Hung had spent his entire life living amidst war. It was no wonder that he had difficulty conceiving of a peaceful existence. "We have laws and police who protect us and courts to put bad guys in jail and make sure everyone is treated fairly." Wellington knew that wasn't much of an answer but didn't know how to tell someone who didn't experience it firsthand how the American system of government worked.

"You don't fear your government?"

"No, we elect people to run the government. If we don't like what they do we don't re-elect them."

"It is a good place to live?"

"It is a great place to live."

"But, they send you here."

"Yeah, that's not really something I wanted, but it's part of being a good citizen."

"Life here is plenty tough."

"Yes, it is."

"Life would be good in America?"

Wellington wasn't sure where Hung was going with his questions. He knew that he didn't have the power to get Hung to America if that was what the interpreter was getting at. What Nghiem Duc Hung asked next surprised him.

The first game of the 1969 World Series began at 2:13 p.m. at Memorial Stadium in Baltimore. Jack and Ryoya returned from shopping in time to be in front of her Zenith color television set. Ryoya prepared popcorn and they drank Rheingold beer to support the sponsor.

Things did not start off well as the most the Mets could muster was a single in the top of the first inning. To make things worse, the leadoff batter for the Baltimore Orioles, Don Buford, hit a homerun to deep right field. Ryoya raised her arms and exclaimed, "What the hell!"

Neither team threatened to score in the second or third innings. Top of the fourth the Mets again failed to score. Bottom of the fourth with two out Elrod Hendricks singled. Then after a long hitter/pitcher duel Davey Johnson walked. Orioles' shortstop Mark Balenger came to bat and singled driving in Elrod Hendricks. It appeared that would be all the damage as the pitcher, Mike Cuellar, who was not a hitting threat came to bat. To the surprise of over fifty-thousand fans and one NYPD detective he hit a single driving in Davey Johnson. Ryoya jumped up and paced the room shaking her head. Then Don Buford hit a double allowing Mark Balenger to score. The inning finally ended with a ground out and the score Baltimore 4 and New York nothing.

By the end of the sixth inning the score remained the same with the Mets having only two hits so far in the game. Ryoya was not pleased. She reached a point of desperation and disappeared into the bedroom to return with the stuffed black cat. With a sheepish look she walked over to the couch and sat next to Jack rubbing the fur-covered magic lantern.

Donn Clendenon led off the Mets seventh inning with a single. This was followed with a Ron Swoboda walk. "Now, we're pulling it together," Ryoya exclaimed hugging the cat. After Ed Charles hit a fly out, Jerry Grote Singled. The Mets had loaded bases with one out. Ryoya stared intensely at the television. Second baseman Al Weis hit a flyball for the second out allowing Donn Clendenon to score. Rod Gasbar pinch hit for the pitcher but unfortunately grounded out. The score was 4 to 1 and Ryoya concluded, "We have two more innings to turn it around."

The eighth inning was uneventful bringing the game to the top of the ninth.

Ron Swoboda led off for the Mets with a single. Ryoya was on her feet. A fly out and strikeout later she was sitting on the couch clutching a black cat. Then Al Weis walked and Art Shamsky was put in as a pinch hitter. The tying run was at the plate. A long drive to left field had Ryoya once more on her feet. Hope was alive! It drifted foul. Finally, two pitches later, a ground ball and final out slammed the door on hope and game one was lost.

Jack trying to be supportive said, "I really like that peach colored thing you bought."

Ryoya spat, "You wear it," and stormed out of the room.

Nghiem Duc Hung looked around at the villages that surrounded the two men. This was his life. He would protect them from communists and government alike. To keep them safe and hidden would take his life and beyond he feared. That was his destiny. After searching for the right words he asked Wellington, "This America is good for children to grow in?"

"Yes, very good. We have schools and activities and doctors all to help children grow up well."

"I lose em re, my brother-in-law, to war. My sister to fever. They have two children cháu gái và cháu trai now my care." With strong hands he gripped Wellington's arm, "You take to America."

"What?" Wellington was completely surprised by the request and added, "I can't. I mean, it is not in my power to do it. The Marines wouldn't allow it."

"You try, Werrington March," the man pleaded.

"I wouldn't even know where to start."

"At the beginning," Hung smiled.

Lai Ngoc Linh and his sister, Lai Thanh Tuyen, walked on the other side of the river. They had no idea that they were the subjects of a conversation.

76: Sunday – October 12, 1969

"I was gonna rap with you about Paul McCartney being dead," was the statement made by a caller to the Russ Gibb's radio show on WKNR-FM in Detroit.

Surprised, the radio host asked, "What's this all about?"

The caller, a local student named Tom, explained, "When the song *Strawberry Fields Forever* is played backwards a voice says, 'Turn me on, dead man.'"

When the disc jockey played the record backwards more and more callers joined the discussion. Clue after clue was offered as proof that the Beatle had indeed died three years earlier and a lookalike was being used by the band.

One of the lyrics, "blew his mind out in a car," supposedly referred to an early morning car crash on an icy road November 9, 1966 where Paul McCartney was partially decapitated. It was based on a police report of an accident that involved McCartney's Aston Martin.

The cover of the *Abbey Road* album released in September 1969 provided numerous other clues for believers.

John Lennon wore a white suit which symbolized mourning in some Eastern religions. Ringo Starr wore more traditional black. And, George Harrison wore denim the color of mourning in Canada.

A major clue pointed out by almost everyone was the fact that Paul McCartney was barefoot. In some cultures the dead are buried without shoes.

A subtle clue was the fact that McCartney was out-of-step with the other band members while crossing Abbey Road.

Although left-handed, Paul held his cigarette in his right hand proving to believers that he was an imposter.

On the back cover of the *Abbey Road* album the Beatles sign has a crack running through it. This symbol might have actually had significance as the band had secretly already broken up. *Abbey Road* was to be their last studio album.

Also on the back cover is a girl in a blue dress. On the day of the supposed car accident McCartney had been driving with a fan named Rita. The theory is it is meant to symbolize her fleeing the crash scene.

Other theories truly stretched the bounds of credulity. The license plate of a Volkswagen Beetle in the background read 28IF. Those who chose to accept the fact that Paul was dead suggested that he would be 28 if he lived. Truth be known he would be 27. On the back of the album there are a series of dots that if connected formed the number three representing the remaining band members.

There were, however, some accurate facts about the iconic album cover. The original idea for a name of the album was Everest, named after the brand cigarettes that sound engineer Geoff Emerick smoked. The band had planned to take a private plane to the foothills of Mount Everest to shoot the cover photograph. As it became more and more involved Paul McCartney suggested they go outside the recording studio take the photo and name it *Abbey Road*.

For the photoshoot police held up traffic and gave photographer Iain Macmillan just ten minutes to get the shot. He stood on a ladder and various shots were taken.

McCartney wore sandals for the first two shots, but afterwards took them off and walked barefoot. Thus the clue to support the Paul is dead theory.

An interesting aside; the man standing on the right side of the street in the photo is Paul Cole an American tourist, who was totally unaware he had been photographed until he saw the album cover months later.

In an ironic macabre twist, the Abbey Road photograph was taken at 11:30 a.m. on the morning of August 8, 1969. Only hours later, the same day Sharon Tate and her guests would be brutally murdered by members of the Manson Family. This was not the only connection between the crime and the Beatles. Charlie Manson wanted to start a race war and adopted the song *Helter Skelter* from the Beatles *White Album* in 1968 as a name for it.

The Paul is dead hoax would be put to rest a month later when writers from *Life Magazine* interviewed McCartney at his country home in Scotland. He refuted the clues of his death and simply requested, "Let me live in peace."

Stephanie Ellis sat across the table from her father. It was a pleasant Sunday morning with temperatures warmer than usual for October. Her father had progressed steadily to where he was almost back to full health. He even commented about getting a job. Stephanie decided it was time to tell him of her plans. "Dad, as you know I've gone back to school." Matt nodded. "I'm going to get a degree in social work and non-profit management and help run an international adoption service."

"You are?"

"Yes, it's what I've chosen for my career."

"I think that's wonderful. How can I help?"

"Dr. Tallman said he would cover the cost of Community College."

"That's very generous of Dr. Tallman. He is a nice man."

"He is." Stephanie added, "After that, when I transfer to college, I will have to try for a scholarship and just work two jobs, if necessary."

"I guess it's good that I'm getting well enough to get a job of my own."

"There's more."

"OK."

"That reporter you've been talking to, Jack Moore . . ."

"What about him?"

"He introduced me to a man who is interested in founding an adoption agency. His family has money so it's more than a pipe dream."

"I see."

Stephanie hesitated, looked down at the table, then back at her father, "The adoption agency will be in Texas."

"Oh, Texas, that's a long way off."

Quickly, Stephanie stated, "Of course, I won't go until I know you will be alright."

Matt smiled, "Princess, I'll be fine. You have your whole life ahead of you. Don't worry about me. I only hope it turns out to be everything that you want and makes you happy."

"Daddy, I can't just leave you here alone."

"You've already done so much for me. I will be fine. I want you to follow your dream. That's what will make me happy."

Stephanie rose and went to her father. They hugged and she said, "I love you. I can't go and leave you." After a silent pause she said softly, "I wish mother was here."

Ritchie found himself on a Sunday morning at the World Trade Center construction site. A great deal of progress had been made during his short absence. Both buildings now stood well-above ground. In his hand he held a newspaper article. It was about the controversy surrounding the project.

It all began with protests and lawsuits concerning the relocation of hundreds of retail, commercial, and residential tenants from buildings on Radio Row on the lower west side. Then private real estate developers and members of the Real Estate Board of New York expressed concerns about all the subsidized office space that would go on the open market, competing with the private sector, when there was already a glut of vacancies. Lawrence A. Wien, owner of the Empire State Building, joined the chorus requesting that the scale of the project be reduced to keep it from replacing his building as the world's tallest. The World Trade Center design brought criticism, as well, from the American Institute of Architects and other groups. Lewis Mumford, author of *The City in History* described it as "just a glass-and-metal filing cabinet." Broadcast networks feared the buildings would interfere with television reception. Even the Linnaean Society of the American Museum of Natural History opposed the World Trade Center project, citing hazards the buildings would impose on migrating birds.

Ritchie took photographs of the buildings as they stood like skeletons of future twin knights of commerce and international understanding. While the design created by architect Minoru Yamasaki seemed simple, Ritchie was aware of distinct design elements. Yamasaki designed Saudi Arabia's Dhahran International Airport with the Saudi Bin Ladin Group. He was influenced by that experience as he incorporated Arabic architecture into the design of the World Trade Center. There were pointed arches, a minaret-like flight tower, and arabesque patterns in the design. In fact, the plaza was modelled after Mecca. It included features such as a vast delineated square, a fountain, and a radial circular pattern. Yamasaki stated he saw the plaza as, "a mecca, a great relief from the narrow streets and sidewalks of the Wall Street area."

A breeze off the river blew Ritchie's long hair. For some reason he thought of Manidoo-giizhikens, the Witch Tree in Minnesota. It seemed so long ago that he and Carl and Wellington stood before that weathered cedar tree offering gifts and contemplating their future. None could have guessed what lay ahead. Carl was safe in Lark's Run. Ritchie knew he was in a good place for the time being. Wellington, the reluctant Marine, was the one to be concerned about. He was somewhere in the middle of a war, probably suffering physical hardships, and living in a never-ending state of fear.

"What's the score?" Shortstop asked the radioman.
"Nothing, nothing, bottom of the third inning."
Shortstop walked back to where Wellington Marsh was standing and looking out over a valley. They had moved their camp three times in the past week to avoid being caught by surprise. It now seemed an unnecessary tactic as no bad guys had come anywhere near the villages.
"No score in the World Series game," Shortstop announced.

"What? Oh, yeah. Thanks."

"We goin' out again?"

"Not today," Wellington stated. "Tomorrow, I think we better check that road to Pleiku Air Base. It's been too quiet. Don't want any VC getting curious and exploring our little neck of the woods."

"We got lucky," Shortstop concluded.

"Yeah, we did."

"I mean, really lucky."

"Let's hope our luck holds."

"Donn Clendenon just hit a homerun for the Mets in the top of the fourth," Harry Van Ryker announced as he walked out of his back door. The bartender and owner of More-Or-Less carried two cans of beer.

Jack Moore looked over from where he was digging a post hole. He had arrived earlier in the day to help his friend repair a dilapidated fence in his back yard. As he accepted the beer he said, "Let's hope the Mets win. Ryoya can't take the pressure. If they lose we might find her out on a ledge."

Harry laughed. "She is a rabid fan. I think it's cute. I think she's cute,"

"Hey watch it."

"I think you're cute."

"I think you're nuts."

"I think you're goldbricking."

"It's called resting," after a pause, "or cardiac arrest."

"Yeah, you are getting old—too old for that vibrant young woman."

"Mets lead one nothing after five," Matt Ellis heard a driver tell his friend who stood on the corner. He had been walking and thinking. Stephanie's decision about school and excitement about an adoption agency warmed his heart. She was a caring and sweet person—much like her mother. He wished he could help her but was in no position to do so.

The weight of guilt seemed heavier than ever with each revelation and recalled memory. There was no longer any doubt as to his involvement in a fraud that shattered many lives and was destined to continue to unleash more and more pain.

"The Orioles scored in the bottom of the seventh to tie the game," Nick told Carl who was chopping wood.

"Damn! I hate Baltimore," Carl replied.

"I'm from Baltimore," Nick stated flatly.

"Oh, sorry about that."

"I'm screwing with you," Nick admitted, "I'm actually from Cincinnati. I'm also pulling for the lowly Mets. Hate the Orioles."

"I know a bunch of guys who probably have a lot of money riding on these games," Carl said as he recalled his days with Ray Esposito. "As a matter-of-fact I know a pretty cool cab driver from Baltimore, named Sid, who is probably cheering right now."

He looked around the farm and was grateful to have escaped a life that would have been less fulfilling if not short-lived.

"Still tied after eight innings," Colt McIntyre told a passerby in the park who had inquired upon seeing him with a portable radio. The native of Victoria, Texas relaxed on a bench wearing a fashionable black cowboy hat with an embroidered Mets NY. He was quietly taking in the sights of New York City. In four days he would be thirty years old and heading back to the Lone Star state. Indeed, he had seen the elephant, tugged its trunk, shoveled its manure, and tasted life.

While going home was a good thing he had an odd sense of loss. He had made a lot of friends along the way. There were people who accepted him as he was, liked his sense of humor, or downright couldn't stand him. Colt smiled.

Ryoya Akimoto sat in her apartment sipping a glass of white wine watching the game. It was the top of the ninth inning. Donn Clendenon came to bat and struck out. "Ah, Donn, couldn't you squeeze out one more homerun?" Ron Swoboda then grounded out. "You chased a bad pitch, Ron." Third baseman Ed Charles kept the inning alive with a single to left field. "OK! It's rally time," Ryoya picked up the stuffed black cat and hugged it. Jerry Grote fouled off numerous pitches but refused to be struck out. Finally, he hit a single to left field allowing Ed Charles to reach third base. "Yes! That's the way to hang in there Jerry." Al Weis came to bat. He was not a power hitter or, for that matter, a batter with a high batting average. Ryoya held her breath. On the third pitch she heard the crack of the bat. The ball sailed into left field in the same general area where the other two singles had gone. Ed Charles scored and the Mets led 2 to 1. Ryoya was glad it was white wine that had been spilled. The pitcher Jerry Koosman came to bat and grounded out.

In the bottom of the ninth inning the Orioles failed to score and the Mets won. The World Series was tied one game apiece. Ryoya Akimoto cheered. She sat back on the couch and smiled. Then she wished Jack had been there to share the moment with her.

Lai Ngoc Linh and his sister listened to Uncle Hung as he described a magic place where people lived free and in peace.

77: Tuesday – October 14, 1969

Wellington Marsh leaned against a tree with one foot up behind him resting on the trunk. He had been listening to Navy Corpsman Gordon Lassiter on the condition of the team. There were numerous scratches and abrasions from treks through thick jungle without trails. One team member had a nasty rash. Another enjoyed the pleasures of dysentery. Two had what appeared to be a significant number of insect bites. And, finally, there was Henry Atwater with a broken finger from taking a fall. All in all, they were in tip top shape.

"Atwater wants to know if he qualifies for a Purple Heart," Corpsman Lassiter said with a straight face.

"If he can prove there was an enemy soldier anywhere in the vicinity at the time, but that's not going to happen," Wellington replied with a smile. He looked around and added, "You know, Gordon, we are damned lucky to be where we are."

"Roger that," Lassiter replied.

Wellington thought for a moment and then asked, "How much do you know about regulations?"

"Regulations about medals, about going over the hill, regulations pertaining to what?"

Wellington told the corpsman of Nghiem Duc Hung's inquiry about his niece and nephew going to America.

"Yeah," Lassiter replied, "that's not going to happen either."

"I know, but I owe him at least a try."

"OK, marry a girl in the village, adopt the kids, and bring them home as dependents," Corpsman Lassiter joked.

Wellington laughed, as well, but then said seriously, "You know, something like that could work."

"There are regs to keep something like that from happening," Lassiter explained. "You can't get married without permission which means going through channels. Every step of the way is designed to make it impossible. You'd be a little old Lance Corporal before you got through the process. And, even then, they'd turn you down." The Navy Corpsman ran his fingers through his hair and continued, "Adoption? Sheez. That would be even harder to do. The kids would be full-grown by the time you get turned down."

"Have you seen anyone be successful?"

"One. A colonel's kid. Daddy pulled some pretty high strings to make that marriage happen. It still took months."

"I know it's a fool's errand, but the guy wants to give the kids a chance. I get that."

"Hey, I get it too. I also get that Uncle Sam doesn't care about Uncle Hung."

"He doesn't care about Uncle Wellington or Uncle Gordon, either," Wellington quipped.

Navy Corpsman Lassiter smiled, began to walk away, turned back to face Wellington, and said thoughtfully, "You know anyone back in the world with pull?"

"Not really." Wellington thought for a moment, then with a huge grin said, "I only know a hippie, a criminal, and an Indian Chief. I doubt they'd do me much good."

Now, that's a story I'd like to hear, someday," Corpsman Lassiter remarked as he walked away.

Carl leaned against a tree looking out over the valley. It sure was beautiful with the leaves turning bright red, orange, and yellow. He wondered what winter was like in the Western Pennsylvania mountains.

From behind, Nick's voice disturbed his reverie, "We're not going to have any firewood that way."

Carl turned to look at Nick, "Across the valley," he pointed, "Over there. Who owns that land?"

"Thinking of homesteading, are you?"

"Just curious."

"Curious, my ass. You're dreaming of the day you and Laurel have your own farm."

"Is that a bad thing?"

"Not from my perspective. However, it's what the lady wants that counts, isn't it?"

"I don't know what the lady wants," Carl admitted, "I'm just daydreaming."

Nick put his hand on Carl's shoulder, "It's a good dream. But, it's not the kind of dream one does alone. You and Laurel have something together. Whether or not it has staying power, only time will tell. Share your dream. It might be mutual or it might scare her off. That, my friend, is a chance you have to take."

"I like it here. There's something clean and fulfilling about honest work and seeing the fruits of your labor. People who never experience this don't know what they're missing."

The World Series came to Shea Stadium. The game was sold out so Ryoya and Jack were not among the 56,335 rabid fans that filled the stands. Besides, both had to work. As it turned out the game was relatively one-sided. In the bottom of the first inning Tommie Agee led off with a homerun to right field. In the bottom of the second inning, with two out, Jerry Grote walked and Bud Harrelson singled. Then the pitcher, Gary Gentry, surprised everyone with a double that drove in two runs. After two innings the Orioles were hitless and the Mets led 3 to 0. The Mets went on to score again in the sixth and eighth innings with the final score 5 to 0.

"What's this?" Jack asked.

"The words to the Mets theme song," Ryoya answered with a smile. "I can provide directions to Grand Central Station if you're not sure how to get there." Her grin was so mischievous and cute Jack had to join her.

They had agreed to meet for a late dinner at a small Chinese restaurant near Ryoya's apartment. Ryoya used chopsticks like a pro and Jack held his own with a slip here and there. While picking up a piece of errant chicken he said, "It would have been nice to be at that game."

"Don't rub it in," Ryoya said absently, "all three games in New York are sold out and the scalpers want the price of a Buick for the bleachers."

"I can't even wiggle my way into the press box," Jack admitted.

"There should be a loyalty test for tickets," Ryoya mused. "You know, we misguided optimists who have backed the team since the bad old days? We should have a shot at tickets." She shrugged and went back to eating. As she picked at her food a set of chopsticks holding World Series tickets crossed before her. "Are you kidding me?" she said with a mouthful of food and a combination of surprise and excitement.

Jack pulled back the tickets and explained, "It's the best I could do on short notice."

"Let me see," Ryoya demanded sounding like an excited sixteen year old.

"Now, I don't want you to be disappointed," Jack warned as he held the tickets out of view.

"Is it inside the park?"

"Of course."

"Then, that's good enough for me." She repeated, "Let me see."

"Now, wait, I have to explain."

Ryoya got a serious look on her face, "This better not be a joke, Jack."

"A joke?"

"I'm armed."

"I know."

"I'll shoot you, so help me."

"Right here, in a Chinese restaurant?"

"No, right there in your Yankee loving nose."

Jack laughed. "I have to explain," he began. Ryoya sat back with her arms folded in front of her giving him her full attention. "As you found, tickets are not to be had." Her stare was a cross between a child waiting to be allowed to open Christmas presents and an angry mother wanting an explanation. Jack continued, "I made a few inquiries but came up empty." The stare. "Even my usual 'don't ask any questions' sources had nothing." The stare. "I had one opportunity but would have to sell a kidney to afford it." The stare. "Quite frankly, as much as I wanted to surprise you, I gave up." The stare. "This morning when I was walking to the office a black limousine pulled up to the curb. I was, let us say, invited to get in. That's when I was given these tickets."

"So, you don't want to tell me how you got the tickets?"

"No, I don't want to tell you who gave me the tickets. I just told you how I got them."

"A stranger in a limousine picked you out of a crowd and gave you World Series tickets."

"No, an acquaintance, who I know, gave me the tickets. He wanted you and me to enjoy the game. How he got the tickets I have no idea. Why he thought of me I'm not sure. I know he's not much of a baseball fan so it's no surprise."

"I get the feeling that if I knew who gave you the tickets I wouldn't want to use them."

"That's a possibility."

"OK, don't tell me. Ignorance is bliss. Let me see them."

Jack handed the tickets to Ryoya. When she glanced at them she abruptly stood up from the table and exclaimed. "These are box seats! On the first base line! What the hell! No Jack, you don't get box seats for nothing. What have you done?"

"I turned a daughter against her father."

"What does that mean?"

"It means he was grateful."

"Why are you talking in riddles?"

"I'm not. In my mixed up crazy world it makes sense."

Ryoya returned to the tickets. "These are for Thursday, I'll have to get the day off. If they win tomorrow it could be the championship game." She looked up and said, "Wow, Jack."

Jack smiled as a piece of broccoli flew through the air when it escaped his chopsticks. He didn't tell Ryoya that he had, in fact, four tickets.

Lai Ngoc Linh hid in the underbrush as he watched the Americans. He was fascinated by these strange men and their odd actions.

78: Wednesday – October 15, 1969

On the Today Show coverage of the day's planned Vietnam Moratorium dominated. Hugh Downs read through a list of planned demonstrations across the nation. The organizers had focused on major cities and college campuses. In addition, he reported that sixteen U.S. senators–eight from each party–had endorsed the Moratorium, along with over 50 House members, and other elected officials. Locally, Mayor John Lindsay ordered all flags on city buildings to be flown at half-mast. This included Shea Stadium where game four of the World Series was to be played. Baseball commissioner Bowie Kuhn vetoed that plan and the flags remained at full staff.

It was a chilly day and to say the least the statistics were equally chilling; 45,000 Americans had been killed in the conflict and almost half a million remained deployed in Vietnam. Regardless of the efforts President Richard Nixon was making to move peace talks along many simply wanted out.

Earlier, activists in Europe congregated outside US embassies. Future President Bill Clinton organized and participated in a demonstration at Oxford where he was a student. In London approximately 300 demonstrated near the US embassy in Grosvenor Square.

There were also those on the other side of the issue who showed their support of the government by driving with their headlights on, waving American flags, and holding their own rallies. Many New York City police cars and fire trucks drove with their lights on that day.

Approximately, 250,000 demonstrators converged on the Capital in Washington, D.C. About 100,000 attended a speech by Senator George McGovern in Boston. Some estimates placed the total participants nationwide at nearly two million making it one of the largest demonstrations in American history.

While an afternoon rally took place at Bryant Park, behind the Fifth Avenue Public Library between 40th and 42nd Streets the fourth game of the World Series was being played on Long Island.

Donn Clendenon hit a leadoff homerun in the bottom of the second inning to give the Mets a 1 – 0 lead. The game then became a pitcher's battle between Tom Seaver for the Mets and Mike Cuellar for Baltimore. Inning after inning neither team could score. Finally, in the top of the ninth inning with one out Frank Robinson hit a single. He was followed by Boog Powell who also singled. Brooks Robinson hit a long fly ball for the second out, however it allowed Frank Robinson to score and tie the game. At the end of nine innings the score was tied.

In the top of the tenth inning the Orioles threatened but couldn't bring anyone home. The Mets brought up the bottom of the batting order in the bottom of the tenth inning. Jerry Grote hit a leadoff single and the crowd was on their feet. Rod Gaspar was put in as a pinch runner. Al Weis then walked. Gil Hodges then put J.C. Martin in to pinch hit for pitcher Tom Seaver. Martin attempted a sacrifice bunt up the third base line but a throwing error caused the ball to fly past first baseman Boog Powell. Speedy Rod Gaspar was able to score from second base and the Mets won 2 – 1 thus going up 3 games to 1 in the series.

When the afternoon Post came out columnist Pete Hamill wrote, "It's going to be the biggest, loudest 'NO' anyone's heard. The way to get out of Vietnam is to just get out." On the 7:00 o'clock CBS Evening News Walter Cronkite called it, "historic in its scope. Never before had so many demonstrated their hope for peace."

In a mountain jungle in Vietnam the members of CAP team 1-6-2 huddled under the branches of trees in an attempt to stay out of the rain. They had watched the clouds roll in as they patrolled west of Quy Hoa. A few miles from the Laos and Cambodian borders they prepared for a drenching. The storm promised to be a long wet event.

It was early afternoon when Wellington heard gunfire west of their position. He rallied the team and they headed in the direction of the gunfire. Hung led the way through thick jungle. The team proceeded to investigate what had occurred. No additional gunfire was heard through the driving rain. The Marines did the best they could to keep their M-16s dry under their ponchos. It was slower going than usual as rocks, fallen trees, and undergrowth were slick with moisture.

Out of habit Wellington glanced back in the direction of the signal tree. It stood tall and straight pointing at heaven. The rain caused visibility to be limited. No sounds of movement or voices could be heard. They proceeded west, although with Hung's twists and turns it was hard to tell. Ultimately, they came to the edge of a dense forest and peered into an open field. Shadowy figures moved across the field. Through relentless rain it was difficult to tell who they were. Their movement was away from Quy Hoa so they didn't represent an immediate threat.

Hung tapped Wellington on the shoulder and indicated that they could move parallel with the intruders while remaining unseen. Wellington agreed with the strategy. For ten minutes they observed the small group of combatants. Finally, both groups came upon a trail. The outsiders turned toward Wellington's team. As they drew near he could tell they were U.S. Army soldiers on patrol.

Wellington called out, "Hold you fire—U.S. Marines."

The Army squad dropped into defensive positions. A voice called out, "Advance and be recognized."

After signaling for his team to stay where they were Wellington stood and walked out onto the trail. "Lance Corporal Wellington Marsh."

One of the Army patrol members stood and came forward to meet Wellington. When he was convinced the Marine was authentic he led Wellington back to meet with their LT.

"Lieutenant Jorgensen, 23rd Infantry. What brings you out on this fine sunny day?" the young officer asked with rain dripping from his face.

"We heard gunfire and came to investigate."

"Yeah, my guys are a little jumpy," LT Jorgensen said. "I think there are some water buffalo that were scared to death back there."

"I don't blame them. This close to the Cambodian and Laotian borders there's a lot of enemy activity around here," Wellington said.

Lieutenant Jorgensen looked around and asked, "Where are your guys?"

"In the jungle, over there," Wellington nodded in the correct direction. "We followed you for a few hundred yards before we knew you were Army."

"Never knew you were there," LT wiped his face, "That makes me feel real safe and secure. Good thing you weren't gooks."

Wellington looked around and said, "This area is ripe with VC just itching to ambush an American patrol. Stay off the paths and keep the noise to a minimum. Also, avoid smoke breaks they can smell it a mile away."

The young lieutenant looked at Wellington appraisingly and asked, "How long have you been out here?"

Before Wellington could answer one of his team broke from the jungle and approached. "We have company," he said in a low voice as he nodded to the west. Using hand signals the Army patrol faded into the jungle and joined the Marines. Before following, Wellington and his fellow team member used branches to remove boot prints in the mud as best as they could. Once finished, they dissolved into the surroundings. In silence the combined force watched the muddy path. Rain continued to soak the landscape which helped wash away residual tracks.

Though masked by the showers, sounds of an approaching force was heard. Whatever it was, there were more than just a few and they had some type of mechanized equipment with them. The combined American team waited. The squeaking of wheels became distinct as did the sound of a large motor. Obscured by rain, the first image of the approaching force was no more than a shadow. In a few seconds it became clear.

A Soviet-built T-54 tank chewed up the trail as it muscled its way along in the rain. It being a light tank with a wide track negotiating mud was not a problem. Thirty-six tons of steel driven by a 500 horsepower diesel engine was a fearsome sight. The 100-mm D-10T gun projecting from the turret added to its lethal appearance. No one wanted to tangle with that armament. Smoke spewed from its exhaust as it passed within twenty yards of the American's position.

Behind the tank a force of thirty to forty North Vietnamese regular soldiers in full battle gear trudged along in the mud. They looked around as they passed, but with vision impaired by heavy rain saw nothing.

After what seemed a prolonged amount of time the column disappeared to the east. All the soldiers in the combined American force breathed a sigh of relief. Conditions and the odds were not in their favor even with an ambush.

Lieutenant Jorgensen tapped Wellington on the shoulder, "They're headed in the direction of Kontum or Pleiku Air Base." He looked up, got a face full of rain, and concluded, "No aircraft are going to be flying, today. We need to radio HQ and report troop movement."

"In these mountains you're not going to get anybody, except that tank," Wellington warned.

"You're right," LT agreed.

More sounds were heard coming from the west. The Army and Marine patrols remained hidden as they watched. In a few minutes a second T-54 tank came rumbling along the trail followed by NVA soldiers. They passed without incident.

Wellington pulled Hung aside and asked, "Is there any way we can make it through the hills, bypass Quy Hoa, and get these guys to Pleiku Air Base?"

"In rain, very dangerous," Hung cautioned, "We go."

Jack Moore sat in his apartment writing his column that would appear the next day. It had indeed been an eventful day. He felt the need to acknowledge the Moratorium but he believed so much had already been said. Words began to appear on the paper in his typewriter.

HOW WE GOT HERE
by Jack Moore

After Wednesday's protest activities, I have very little to add. A large number of people expressed their disagreement with the war in Vietnam. A possibly equal number expressed their support for the government in their own way, such as flying flags or driving with their headlights on. I won't take sides. What I will do is take a step back and look at how we got here.

In the 1950s President Eisenhower sent military advisors to aid the South Vietnamese government. It was to be a limited mission. After John F. Kennedy became President in 1961, he sharply increased military and economic aid to South Vietnam. He considered the growing insurgency a real threat to international peace as communist powers were spreading in the region. Unfortunately, chronic military and political shortcomings on the part of the South Vietnamese government created an unstable situation.

Originally, Army Special Forces (Green Berets) organized the highland tribes into Civilian Irregular Defense Groups (CIDG) to counter the insurgency. Within a few years, approximately 60,000 highlanders had enlisted in the CIDG program. Together, the forces defended villages, executed offensive guerilla activities, and initiated border surveillance and control measures.

In August, 1964 North Vietnamese patrol boats attacked the USS Maddox in the Gulf of Tonkin. This led to passage of the Southeast Asia Resolution by Congress giving President Johnson authority to defend allies in Asia. The resolution gave legal justification for deploying US conventional forces and the commencement of open warfare against North Vietnam. So, U.S. military strength in South Vietnam increased from under 700 at the start of 1960 to almost 24,000 by the end of 1964.

February, 1965, communist forces attacked an American compound in Pleiku in the Central Highlands. President Johnson responded by approving a campaign of direct air strikes against military and industrial targets in North Vietnam. Also, in 1965 the Army created the 1st Cavalry Division air mobile unit using helicopters. This dramatically changed tactics in the war. Unfortunately, political turmoil and a coup in the mid-60s along with poor defense of rural villages allowed the Viet Cong to gain greater control. As a result, by the end of 1965 U.S. military strength in South Vietnam reached

184,000, in 1966 it was 385,000 and 1967 nearly 490,000. The number of American forces in Vietnam reached its peak March of this year at 543,000.

Since taking office President Nixon opened Paris peace talks, made an offer for mutual pullout by America and North Vietnam that was rejected, announced the Vietnamization program, began withdrawing troops, reduced draft calls, established a draft lottery, and I'm certain is doing a great deal more behind the scenes. My point being, those who point fingers and claim he has done nothing are ill-informed. Remember, it took three previous Presidents to dig this massive hole.

Contrary to the idealists who state, "If you want to end the war—just leave." While that may sound good it is an over-simplification that is not a realistic solution. Logistically, it is impossible and would put countless lives at risk. I understand every day American soldiers are dying and each one is important. However, even more would die in the chaos that would follow a massive retreat.

Yesterday a lot of Americans made their opinions clear, for and against a war of which we all have grown weary. Many other Americans went about their business without expressing an opinion. Free speech is a beautiful thing. Bless a nation that not only allows it but defends it even when we don't agree.

On another subject; today I will be attending the fifth game of the World Series. The amazing Mets could very well win the championship, today. If they do, I invite you to join me at Grand Central Station on Saturday morning at 10 a.m. to exercise our right to free speech by singing the Mets theme song to celebrate.

Hung guided the combined American force south of Quy Hoa along treacherous mountain passes and ledges. Swollen streams added to the danger. Finally, after a rocky climb they arrived on a summit. Through the rain they could see in all directions. For the most part the landscape was covered by trees or obscured by other mountain ranges. Wellington had an idea in which direction precious flower lay but it remained hidden.

"Your radio might work from up here," Wellington told the young lieutenant.

At first reception was poor. However, after making a few adjustments they were able to make contact. Troop movements by regular North Vietnamese armored forces were reported and the lieutenant received praise from his superiors. Three hours later they came to an established road that went in the direction of Pleiku Air Base.

"Be careful, there may be more VC around," Wellington said as he parted with the Army patrol.

Lieutenant Jorgensen complimented the young Marine, "Thanks, it's been quite an experience working with a seasoned soldier who knows the ropes. I only hope when I'm out here as long as you I get my shit together as well."

Wellington nodded. He didn't have the heart to tell the LT he just arrived a few weeks ago.

Lai Ngoc Linh helped repair the roof that had begun to leak.

79: Thursday – October 16, 1969

A black cat roamed in the shadowy subterranean world it considered home. And a fine home it was with ample places to sleep, food to be scavenged, creatures to hunt for sport, and plenty of entertainment. A vast empire ruled by a single feline. Silently it padded across an empty area toward a beam of sunlight that streamed in through an opening. A sound caught its attention; it stopped, crouched, raised its ears, and peered in the direction of the noise. The opening through which sunlight spilled grew wider. A breeze explored the domain carrying the distinct aroma of a man. Unafraid the cat walked in the direction of the door. Unnoticed by the grounds crew the tomcat walked out into the warm morning sun. Ever observant, it noticed increased activity much like the day before. A meow welcomed the day as the black cat anticipated the crowds that would arrive later and leave a feast for the only permanent resident of Shea Stadium.

The creature didn't know it had magic powers or was held in high esteem by thousands of superstitious fans who couldn't help but believe. It neither had any plans to make an appearance nor to support either team. Through the years it watched many games with fascination—not understanding. Over time, however, the activities in the stands became of greater interest. Something strange was always happening when this many human beings got together in one place. From whatever vantage point the feline chose to observe it was never disappointing. What odd creatures are these human beings.

Jack walked along East Twenty Third Street toward Ryoya Akimoto's apartment. There was a chill in the air but the sky was blue promising a good day for going to a baseball game. Jack was looking forward to spending the day with his "treasure" and hoped that the Mets would win the World Series at home, on this day, with Ryoya sitting on the first base line. He was, however, also looking at the upcoming day with trepidation. He had no idea how events would unfold.

As it was the World Series, Jack was a little more formally dressed than was usual for a baseball game. He wore black slacks and blue front-button woven short sleeve shirt. When Ryoya opened the door she was wearing black slacks and a blue blouse. Upon seeing Jack she didn't greet him. Instead, she said, "I'm changing."

Ryoya and Jack had breakfast together at a local café. By that time she wore tan slacks and a green pullover top. Around her neck was the "treasure" necklace. She was bubbling with enthusiasm and anticipation of the upcoming game. "Kooz is on the mound."

"I know."

"He won game two in Baltimore."

"I know."

"Kept Baltimore hitless for six innings."

"I know."

"Held them to one run on two hits."

"I know."

Ryoya gave Jack a funny look as she said, "What you probably don't know is Jerry Koosman went 17-9 during the season with a 2.28 ERA and 180 strikeouts." She sipped some coffee and added, "He won eight of his last nine regular season games. He's hot. He's on his game." She picked up a piece of toast and pointed it at Jack stating, "We're going to win."

"There's a good chance of that."

"Nice move, by the way, inviting fans to join you at Grand Central Station to sing the Met's theme song. Now, instead of being embarrassing it's a publicity stunt."

"That was my thought."

Ryoya returned to the subject, "Last year, his rookie year, Koosman was 19-12 with an amazing 2.08 ERA and 178 strikeouts. His seven shutouts was a club record."

"Well, it was the Mets," Jack pointed out.

A piece of toast passed by Jack's ear. "He should have been Rookie of the Year." She wiped her mouth with her napkin and said, "Lost by a single vote to Johnny Bench."

"I see you've given this some thought."

"I wonder if Casey will show his face," Ryoya said with a smile referring to the Met's famous black cat.

"If he does, the game's in the bag."

Ryoya looked at Jack and Asked, "Are you superstitious?"

"I like to think I'm above all that. Yet, when you get something in your head it's hard to shake. How many people fear Friday the Thirteenth? Or, how many people feel if they make a prediction it could jinx the outcome?" Jack sat back and said to the ceiling, "I believe things happen for a reason, but it's up to us to recognize opportunities and make the best of them." He looked at Ryoya, "Today, is a perfect example."

Ryoya studied Jack Moore. She wasn't sure how to interpret his last remark. In the back of her mind she remembered him proclaiming that if the Mets won the World Series he would marry her. Maybe that would happen in another universe—not her world. First, such a dramatic decision is not to be the subject of a bet. Second, he made it sound like punishment. And the all-important third strike was Takashi and Mitsuki Akimoto, her father and mother. She was nisei and its hold on her was potent. It was undeniable that no force on earth was more powerful than the bonds of tradition.

Jack was a wonderful man who made her feel complete. What was it Harry Van Ryker, the bartender and owner of More-Or-Less, had said? Jack would make it easy for her to be herself. He made a lot of things easy. And, he would probably be easy to live with, but that would never be known.

Game time was 2:14 in the afternoon. This, of course, meant fans would start arriving at the ballpark at noon. One didn't want to miss any of the pregame activities. Jack and Ryoya arrived just before one o'clock. They had spent the morning wandering around Greenwich Village.

Jack and Ryoya walked down the steps toward Middle Field Box 111. As they did Ryoya looked around. What she saw was a sea of blue and orange. Shea Stadium was half full with throngs of fans slowly shuffling to their seats. Everywhere excited fans smiled and laughed and conversed with friends. To a person they believed this was the day the miracle would be realized.

Right behind the additional field-level seats was their box. Blue cushioned seats waited for the chosen few. Ryoya leaned over and said to Jack, "Don't ever tell me who gave you these tickets."

"A stranger in a black limo," was all he said.

In the box that seated eight were two other fans. One had on a black cowboy hat that Ryoya recognized. "That's Colt!" she stated with enthusiasm. She stopped on the steps and asked, "Just how many tickets did you get?"

"Four."

"Then besides Colt who else is coming?"

Jack continued walking down the stairs followed by Ryoya. She looked at the person seated beside Colt McIntyre but at that distance from behind didn't recognize him. A few more steps later they were at the box. Jack was between Ryoya and the seats. When he stepped aside to allow her to enter the box Ryoya recognized the fourth individual—it was her father.

"Papa? I didn't know you would be here."

Takashi Akimoto stood upon seeing his daughter. "Your friend wished it that way," he slightly bowed in Jack's direction.

Ryoya turned to look accusingly at Jack.

He shrugged, "I wanted it to be a surprise."

"Well, it was."

"A good one, I hope."

"You could have warned me. I would have dressed differently."

Jack turned to Ryoya's father, "Takashi-san, I know it's not the Giants, but it could be a big day for New York."

"Yes, and for Ryoya."

"She's quite a fan."

The old man smiled, "We share baseball."

Ryoya sat next to her father. Jack sat next to her with Colt McIntyre on his right.

Jerry Koosman paced in the bullpen before the game. The left-hander didn't want to throw too many pitches and overwork his arm. Still fresh in his memory was a game in April against the Expos in Montreal. It was an especially cold night. In the fifth inning his pitching arm went numb. He left the game and was sent back to New York. X-rays didn't reveal anything but when a doctor put pressure on his teres minor muscle, part of the rotator cup configuration, he winced in pain. It turned out to be a severe knot in the muscle that required long and painful massages to relieve. He was sidelined for almost a month.

Jerry Koosman had a deadly fastball and was one of the best at throwing a cutter fastball. A cutter is a type of fastball which breaks slightly toward the pitcher's glove side as it reaches home plate. Often when a batter hits a cutter fastball he only makes soft contact due to the movement of the ball. Koosman also had a big curveball he used effectively.

Ryoya and Takashi Akimoto discussed the strengths and weaknesses of both teams—offensively and defensively. As they did, Jack and Colt talked about the young man's plans to return home. His time was up, he had seen the elephant, it was his thirtieth birthday, and he was set to return to Victoria, Texas.

"It's been quite an experience," Colt said, "I'm glad that I did it. I'm also grateful to have met you and Ms. Akimoto."

"That, my friend, is mutual," Jack said, "We definitely won't forget you. Happy birthday. I wish your thirtieth was a year from now. Let's keep in touch. Who knows, maybe the Victoriaville Mudslinger will need an out-of-work reporter."

"I'll put in a bad word for you."

"I knew I could count on you. When do you leave?"

"I plan to fly out on Saturday."

The game started uneventfully with the Baltimore Orioles going three up and three down and the New York Mets enjoying two walks but no hits and no runs.

Jack heard Takashi Akimoto say to his daughter, "Koosman is favoring one leg."

Ryoya replied, "I noticed. That won't do his curve ball any good."

As it turned out they were right as in the top of the third inning Mark Belanger of the Orioles had a leadoff single. This brought up the pitcher, Dave McNally, who shouldn't have been a threat. Jerry Koosman wound up and threw a curveball that hung over the plate. McNally swung and hit a homerun deep to left field. After a ground out and a strikeout Koosman again had a curve ball fail to move as he wished and it was hit out of the park by Frank Robinson. After three innings the Orioles led 3 to 0.

In the Met's dugout Jerry Koosman told his teammates, "Let's score some runs, boys. They will not get another run off of me." He dropped the curveball from his arsenal of pitches.

Neither team scored in the fourth or fifth inning.

"We need Casey," Jack stated, referring to the black cat.

"We need some hitting," Ryoya replied.

"I got a good feeling about this next inning," Colt said with enthusiasm.

"I'm going with your feeling," Ryoya smiled. She turned to Jack and said softly, "My father is truly enjoying this game. Thank you."

"Thank the stranger in the black limo," Jack quipped. Then seriously he said, "You told me your father was a big baseball fan. Unfortunately, it's the San Francisco Giants, but, hey, they're not in the World Series."

"Right," after a pause Ryoya asked, "How do you know he is a Giants fan?"

"I'm a reporter. Besides he looks like a Giants fan." Jack then added, "He told me when I offered him the ticket."

Top of the sixth inning Baltimore had a single but failed to score. The leadoff batter for the Mets was Cleon Jones. The third pitch was low and inside and he had to jump in an attempt to not get hit. The ball appeared to bounce off the ground and into the Met's dugout. Jerry Koosman picked it up. The home-plate umpire, Lou DiMuro, ruled it a ball. Met's manager, Gil Hodges, told Koosman, "Slide it on your shoe and throw it here." He did. Hodges then took the ball out to DiMuro and showed him a streak of shoe polish on the ball. Cleon Jones was awarded first base for being hit by the pitch.

Ryoya laughed and said to her father, "That's some heads-up managing."

Donn Clendenon then came to bat and when Dave McNally threw an off-speed pitch it was hit for a homerun deep to left field. The stadium erupted. It was so loud that conversation became impossible. Everyone was on their feet. The next three batters failed to get on base and the inning ended with the Orioles leading 3 to 2.

In the seventh inning the Orioles went three up and three down. Then came the seventh inning stretch. This tradition purportedly began in 1882 at Manhattan College in New York City. On a hot and muggy day in June the college team was playing a semi-pro team coincidentally named the Metropolitans. In the middle of the seventh inning Brother Jasper, the baseball coach, noticed fans getting restless because of the heat. He called timeout and instructed everyone to get up, stretch, and move around. It worked so well they began doing it at every game. Shortly thereafter the New York Giants adopted a seventh inning stretch. By 1969 the seventh inning stretch was standard practice at all major league ballparks. It was a good time for fans to move around and make that last trip to the restroom or refreshment stand. Also, purchase a beer as the sale of alcohol is terminated at the end of the seventh inning. During the break, Jane Jarvis, the organist at Shea Stadium, played the Mexican Hat Dance as she had done since 1964.

"What do you think, Mr. Akimoto, can we win?" Jack asked.

"Except for the third inning, Koosman has held them to two hits. Absolutely, the Mets can win," Ryoya's father looked directly at Jack and added, "After all, this is the year of miracles."

In the bottom of the seventh inning the leadoff hitter for the Mets was Al Weis. After waiting for the right pitch, which finally came, he tied the game with a homerun to left field. It was the first homerun he had ever hit in Shea Stadium. After seven innings the score was tied.

Ryoya was ecstatic. She hugged her father, hugged Colt, and finally hugged Jack. When she did she whispered, "Thank you. This is so wonderful. I'm glad we can share it together."

"You can join me at Grand Central Station on Saturday, if we win," Jack deadpanned.

"We'll see," she teased as she turned coquettishly away.

Colt overheard the invitation and said, "I'll be there. My flight's in the evening."

Jerry Koosman continued to dominate as the Orioles went three up and three down in the top of the eighth inning. Cleon Jones led off with a double for the Mets. Ryoya was on her feet. Donn Clendenon grounded out. Ryoya sat down. Then Ron Swoboda hit a long drive up the first baseline for a double allowing Jones to score. Ryoya was on her feet. The entire stadium rose with her as did the noise level when the Mets took the lead. Ed Charles hit a fly ball for the second out. The Met's catcher Jerry Grote hit an infield ground ball for what appeared to be the final out but a throwing error allowed him to reach first base and Swoboda to score. Ryoya was on her feet. Al Weis struck out to end the inning. The Mets led 5 to 3 after eight innings.

When Jerry Koosman walked to the mound to begin the ninth inning the noise at Shea Stadium and his own nervousness made him acutely aware of the fact that he couldn't throw control pitches. They would be all over the place. He decided to rely on his awesome fastball and just try to get it over the plate. Unfortunately, he walked Frank Robinson to begin the inning. He then got Boog Powell to ground into a force play and Brooks Robinson to fly out to short center field. With two out and the tying run at bat and a count of two balls and one strike Jerry Koosman delivered his fast ball. With all the noise, he didn't hear the crack of the bat as Davey Johnson hit a fly ball to deep leftfield. Almost dreamlike the stadium fell silent as the ball carried toward the left field fence. Koosman turned to watch the ball and feared that the game had just been tied. He watched left fielder Cleon Jones running in the direction of the orb's flight and on the warning track caught the ball for the final out. The dream became reality.

Ryoya screamed and hugged her father. Fans poured onto the field from every corner of the ballpark. Jack looked at Ryoya hugging her father, ball players hugging each other, fans trying to hug ball players, and finally turned to Colt and hugged him. Colt shouted into his ear, "This doesn't mean I'm going to take you home to meet my parents."

While pandemonium raged at Shea Stadium a strange phenomenon took place throughout New York City. Office workers opened their windows and began throwing out papers, confetti, adding machine tape, computer printouts, clothing, and every other type of non-threatening material they could put their hands on. Almost every street had its own ticker tape parade. In some places it was knee deep.

In Middle Field Box 111 four fans sat and watched the celebration that unfolded all around them. Ryoya looked at Jack and winked. Then a smile dominated her face as she said, "How's the voice?"

Jack smiled but didn't answer. Ryoya returned his gaze, tilted her head, and took his hand. While holding it she said softly, "Thank you."

Takashi Akimoto watched the exchange. He said to no one in particular, "Me wa kuchi hodo ni mono o ii." A translation is, "The eyes speak as much as the mouth." He thought about a conversation he had with Jack Moore the day before. It was at the Akimoto home. The occidental newspaper reporter expressed his love for Ryoya, respect for her heritage and culture, wish for her parent's blessing, and pledge to abide by their decision. He went so far as to stumble through a Japanese phrase, "Sugitaru wa nao oyobazaru ga gotoshi," which meant, "Let what is past flow away downstream." He would neither complain nor continue to see their daughter if that was their wish. Both of her parents were polite, yet unrevealing of their opinion. Jack left not knowing what would be his fate.

Ryoya turned toward her father when he put his hand on her arm. Without saying a word her father reached into his pocket, retrieved a small blue box, and handed it to Ryoya. Somewhat confused, she took the box and examined it. Her gaze went from her father to Jack then back to Takashi. They stared at each other for a few seconds at which time he nodded and said, "Shikata ga nai."

Ryoya sat. She held the box knowing quite well what it contained. The noisy celebrations occurring at Shea Stadium disappeared as her mind turned inward. For some odd reason she saw the blue bicycle leaning against the wall of their cabin in Yuba City left there when they were taken to a relocation center. It was the bicycle her father gave her to ride to school. He accepted the inevitable then, no matter how unfair or distasteful, by simply saying, "Shikata ga nai." Was that what he was doing at that moment accepting the inevitable? She couldn't—no wouldn't—do that to him. After a long pause, she handed the box to her father and said, "Papa, you do not need to do this."

Takashi Akimoto did not take the box. He smiled and said, "A kite breeding a hawk. You are a splendid child born from common parents. We left our way of life many years ago to come to this country. There were those who shook their heads. Your mother's father turned his back on me and my mother wept. We traveled across an ocean to a strange new land. It was not our intent to reject our heritage but we knew Gou ni itte wa, gou ni shitagae—entering the village, obey the village. Our new life had to be a blend of old and new—an alloy that made the sword stronger. We are issei, Japanese-born immigrants, our road had many twists and turns but always we moved forward in the land of our adoption. You are nisei whose roots are here in America. If we didn't wish for you to be the stronger sword we never would have made the journey. Your children will be sansei and old traditions will be shadows on the wall. Shikata ga nai—it cannot be helped. But, it should not be feared."

Ryoya looked at her father and saw wisdom she had somehow long missed. Tears honored the man.

Takashi Akimoto continued, "This man Jack-san considers you his treasure. He respects our heritage and wishes to keep it alive with you. If your mother or I opposed such a thing he has agreed to abide by our wishes. A brave act that brings with it risks of invisible scars. My giving you that box is our answer. Now, it is up to you. Only you, my daughter of whom I am very proud, can decide the path you wish to take. Once you decide, Shikata ga nai."

Eleven-year-old Lai Ngoc Linh watched the foreign soldiers as they listened to the World Series game. He spoke some English but had no idea why they were acting so wild.

80: Saturday – October 18, 1969

Grand Central Station was rarely busy on a Saturday morning. However, on this Saturday the main concourse was rapidly filling with people. All sporting Mets hats, jerseys, and other paraphernalia, they came to join Jack Moore of the *Tribune* to sing the Mets theme song. It was 9:45 a.m. when the reporter appeared at the top of the main staircase wearing a Mets uniform. By then more than three hundred fans had congregated in the building. Upon seeing him a cheer erupted. He turned around to reveal the number 69 on his back below the name Miracle. The volume of the cheer increased. In his hand he held a bullhorn. With the crowd's attention he spoke through the device, "They said it couldn't be done." Cheers. "They said it would take a miracle." Cheers. "We knew better!" Cheers. "There's a new champion in town and they're called the Mets." Cheers. "And, they have the best fans in the world." Cheers. "And, the best black cat in town." Laughter and cheers. "Did you see the blizzard Thursday afternoon?" Cheers. "Even Yankee fans got caught up in the excitement." Boos followed by cheers. "Come'on; today every New Yorker is a Mets fan." Cheers. "But, we know who the real fans are." Cheers. "So, let them hear what real fans sound like." Ryoya Akimoto and Colt McIntyre joined Jack at the top of the stairs. To everyone's surprise they were also joined by a string quartet—two violins, a viola, and a cello. The lead-in was quite beautiful in an orchestrated way. They played *America The Beautiful, New York, New York,* and *Take Me Out To The Ballgame.* As they played, two volunteers unrolled a large banner displaying the lyrics of *Meet The Mets.* Abruptly, the music changed to an upbeat tune and the crowd joined in.

> Meet the Mets, Meet the Mets,
> Step right up and greet the Mets!
> Bring your kiddies, bring your wife;
> Guaranteed to have the time of your life
> because the Mets are really sockin' the ball;
> knocking those home runs over the wall!
> East side, West side, everybody's coming down
> to meet the M-E-T-S Mets of New York town!
>
> Oh, the butcher and the baker and the people on the streets,
> where did they go? To Meet the Mets!
> Oh, they're hollerin' and cheerin' and they're jumpin' in their seats,
> where did they go? To Meet the Mets!
> All the fans are true to the orange and blue,
> so hurry up and come on down -
> 'cause we've got ourselves a ball club,
> The Mets of New York town!
> Give 'em a yell! Give 'em a hand!
> And let 'em know your rootin' in the stand!

Come on and Meet the Mets, Meet the Mets,
Step right up and greet the Mets!
Bring your kiddies, bring your wife;
Guaranteed to have the time of your life
because the Mets are really sockin' the ball;
knocking those home runs over the wall!
East side, West side, everybody's coming down
to meet the M-E-T-S Mets of New York town!
Of New York town!

Then a roar came from the crowd as members of the New York Mets team wandered into the crowd and began shaking hands, handing out souvenirs, and signing autographs. A photographer from the *Tribune* recorded the event as did a cameraman from WOR-TV, the Mets local broadcast station. A few local politicians attempted to use the event to further their campaigns but went relatively ignored.

From their perch atop the stairs, Jack, Ryoya, and Colt watched the celebration. It became clear that this impromptu party was going to continue for some time.

Ryoya turned to Jack and said, "Well, no one can ever say you welch on a bet."

"A man is only as good as his word," Jack remarked. With a wry smile he said, "I'm glad you got your miracle. It was both an honor and a pleasure to have shared it with you." Jack kissed Ryoya on the forehead, turned, and walked away.

Colt MacIntyre watched the exchange and when Jack left asked, "What's going on?"

"I said no," Ryoya commented.

"She said no," Carl told Nick.

"That's what I would have expected," the Special Forces turned farmer said.

"I would have thought she would welcome the idea."

"She's not that kind of lady."

"She surprises me every day."

"Get used to it." Nick pulled the fencing wire taut and hammered a staple into the post.

"I don't know that I ever will," Carl admitted.

"That's a good thing, wouldn't you say?"

"It keeps me off balance—that's for sure." The two men walked to the next fencepost. Carl asked, "What do you think of my idea?"

"It's risky," Nick concluded. "I don't know what you are wanted for, but if it's more than petty theft you could be talking big time, if convicted."

"Murder," Carl stated flatly.

"That's heavy," Nick said as he stopped what he was doing and looked at Carl. He then asked, "Did he need killing?"

"He was trying to kill me."

"So, you claim self-defense?"

Carl walked over to the trailer that was attached to the tractor and got a cup of water, "I should have stayed and turned myself in when it happened. When I left him, after our fight, I didn't know he was dead. I just wanted to get the hell out of there. Then the next morning I find out he's dead and I know they're going to come looking for me. I panicked. He must have hit his head or something."

"Who started the fight?"

"He did," Carl answered immediately, "In fact, it was a set-up. I was going to meet some guy to help out a friend and this Miguel steps out of the shadows and points a gun at me." Carl looked at Nick and added, "He planned some crazy shit. I was lucky to get loose and take him down."

"And now you want to go back and face the music?"

"If I'm going to have any chance for a life with Laurel I have to get past this."

"And, she said no?" Nick reiterated.

"She doesn't want to take the chance that I get sent away for life. She said something I'm still trying to understand."

Ritchie Anderson examined the two strands of wire given to him by Matthew Ellis. They appeared to be identical. He looked up and said to Stephanie's father, "They appear to be the same. I don't know any metallurgists, but there is an electrician who is always experimenting and testing things who might see if there is any difference."

They had met at a small diner on Madison Avenue in Dumont, New Jersey. Stephanie arranged the meeting but declined to attend. In her mind the relationship had run its course. Besides, she had to remain focused on her goal.

"I really am interested in their relative capabilities. They might prove to be the same, but if they are different the question is how different?" Matt explained. He had taken samples from the beginning of the spool of wire and about fifty feet into the roll.

"I'll get them to Hank and ask him to test them," Ritchie agreed. He sipped his coffee and asked, "So, how is Stephanie doing?"

Matt wasn't sure how much of his daughter's plans he should reveal. He decided to play it close to the vest, "She's gone back to school."

"What is she studying?"

"I really don't know. I guess I should have shown more interest and asked her. I was just happy that she went back."

"She's a smart girl. Whatever she studies she'll do well." Ritchie hesitated, then asked, "Is she seeing anyone?"

Jack Moore sat on his regular stool at More-Or-Less. It was dinnertime and he hadn't eaten all day. His nerves were raw, mind racing in different directions, and emotions spent. He fully expected Takashi and Mitsuki Akimoto to put an end to any thoughts of marriage. For that he was prepared. When Ryoya's father presented her with the ring, in essence blessing the union, Jack's heart soared. Her postponing a decision was a surprise, after all the Mets won the World Series. It was her ultimate decision to decline the proposal that was an unexpected punch in the gut. He had all he could do to participate in the morning's activities after she informed him of her decision on their way to Grand Central Station. In truth, he wanted to run and hide somewhere to clear his head. However, that was not an option. He held it together long enough to do his part and payoff the bet then had to get away.

Harry came over to greet his friend, "Saw you on TV on the news. Jeez you're ugly and that Met's uniform, have you no shame?"

"I have plenty of shame," Jack said trying to be upbeat, "I have enough shame for both of us." He paused then asked, "By the way where were you this morning?"

"Polishing glasses."

"Couldn't prove it by this filthy glass," Jack held up the empty glass Harry had just placed in front of him.

"See if you get anything poured into that glass, ya son-of-a-bitch." Harry looked around and asked, "Where's your lady? You flying solo tonight?"

"Well," Jack said solemnly, "that's a long story."

"What did you do?"

"I forgot rule number one—don't leave your heart out where someone can step on it."

"It sounds serious," Harry said with sincere concern. "What are you drinking? Then tell me about it."

"Do you have any food back in your freezer?"

"I have some bar pies."

"I'd like one and a beer."

"You got it."

While the pie heated in the oven, Jack sipped his beer and told Harry the order of events. He explained that Ryoya didn't seem angry at anything that he did. She simply told him that she wouldn't marry him.

"Did she give any explanation?" Harry asked.

"Nope. She simply gave me the ring and said she was sorry but she couldn't accept it."

"Did you ask her why?"

"Harry, I'm in a cab, wearing a stupid baseball uniform, heading to Grand Central Station to make an ass of myself. I wasn't expecting an answer at that time—especially that answer. I mumbled something incoherently and then dropped the subject."

"I'm sorry, pal. It doesn't mean you're not going to see each other does it?"

"I think I smell my pie burning."

"We have insurance."

"I'm starving!"

As Jack tried to eat a steaming piece of pizza, Harry repeated his question, "Are you still going to see each other?"

"I really don't know. That's why I'm here, to pick up another chick."

"Just don't include Amanda on your list of targets."

"How are you two doing?"

"I hate to say."

"Look, don't feel bad because I'm a burned out hulk of a man. If you have a good thing going I'm happy for you."

"She's one-in-a-million and we have a lot in common."

"Get away from me, you bastard!"

Colt MacIntyre arrived at Kennedy Airport at 9:00 p.m. He had a late flight to Dallas and then a hedgehopper to Victoria. A black cowboy hat with Mets emblem was on his head.

He and Ryoya had visited for a while after Jack abruptly left Grand Central Station. While aware of all that had transpired at Shea Stadium, Colt was surprised to hear that Ryoya had turned Jack down.

"I thought you two had something really special," he remarked, "At least from what I observed."

"We do," Ryoya paused, "or did."

"Then why won't you jump the broom?"

"First, it can't be the prize in a bet."

"Ah, that was just an excuse. It's a yahoo's way of asking without asking. Fear of rejection and all that." He thought for a moment and then said, "I guess that went out the window."

"I want to be asked—one knee and all that."

"I see."

Ryoya looked at Colt and added very seriously, "I'm nisei and you don't just turn that off."

"Your father led us to believe that Jack was acceptable to your parents."

"Yes, he did, but is that how he really feels?" She shook her head with frustration, "I have to know for sure. If there is any chance that marrying Jack would hurt or disappoint either of my parents then I can't do it."

"How do you plan to find out how they really feel?" Colt asked.

"I'm a detective—I'll find out," she stopped speaking for a moment and then in an obviously sad voice said, "It may not matter in the end after the way he left."

"Shucks, when you gave mitten, his feelings got hurt and ego bruised. Once he has some alone time he'll come around."

"You're a good friend, Colt MacIntyre," Ryoya said as she hugged him.

He smiled and said, "I'm just a gadabout—heading home."

A Boeing 727-100 that had been out-of-service to repair a faulty generator waited to board at Gate 7A. The pilot and co-pilot went through the pre-flight check list. Initially, a red fault indicator had come on for a generator but after reset all was normal.

Passengers began boarding at 9:20 p.m. Colt MacIntyre sat in seat 14F. He was tired and planned to sleep during the flight. The plane pushed away from the gate at 9:42 p.m. and headed to the runway to begin its four hour flight. Once in the air Colt settled back and nodded off. Flight 367 turned and headed southwest. It would not land in Dallas, Texas.

Lai Ngoc Linh listened to his sister sing a Vietnamese children's folk song.

81: Sunday – October 19, 1969

Ryoya Akimoto was awakened by a knock on her door at 3:20 a.m. Whether it was the first or twentieth knock she had no way of knowing. Wrested from her sleep it took a moment to gather her thoughts and retrieve her off-duty revolver. She slipped into her robe and went to the door. The knocking continued. Through the peephole she saw Jack Moore's face. A combination of anger, confusion, and concern co-mingled in her mind. She quickly opened the door and asked, "Jack, what are you doing here? What time is it?"

Jack had a serious, emotionally drained, look upon his face, "I had to come to tell you in person."

"Tell me what? What is it Jack?"

"Colt MacIntyre's plane went down over Tennessee. I couldn't sleep so I turned on the television and caught a news story. There was very little information. The pilot radioed that they were having electrical problems and asked to be diverted to Memphis. That was the last transmission."

"Are you sure it was the plane Colt was on?"

"Non-stop to Dallas, it was the flight number he gave me."

"Are there any survivors?"

Jack shook his head and said, "They hadn't located the aircraft the last I saw."

Ryoya hurried over to her television set. As she did she said over her shoulder, "Please, come in, Jack." He followed.

One of the networks had continuing news coverage of the missing flight. "Residents in the Lakeland area of Tennessee reported hearing a loud boom. Authorities are searching in that area, but the mountainous terrain makes it difficult at night."

"Poor dear Colt," Ryoya mumbled as she settled onto the couch.

Jack sat next to her but remained silent.

The television news reporter continued, "The flight was a Boeing 727-100 nonstop from New York to Dallas with 82 onboard. At this time no sign of the aircraft has been found."

Ryoya changed the channel but there weren't any other news programs providing coverage. She turned to Jack, "I spoke with him this morning at Grand Central. He was so happy to be going home." Lost in thought she stared off at nothing in particular. To no one she commented, "No matter how much I've seen as a detective, I've never been able to grow a shell. It always gets to me. I see the human side. And, when it's someone I know—it hurts. That crazy, sweet, lovable cowboy touched me. Why couldn't he have been a jerk? Why did he have to be someone with so much to offer? Why did our paths have to cross? Why couldn't he have had a shot at life?" She turned back to Jack and with moist pleading eyes said, "Why?"

"Shikata ga nai," Jack said softly, adding, "When I first heard that phrase I really wasn't sure as to its meaning. To accept the inevitable seems over-simplified. When something happens accept it. Then on my way over here it struck me that there was far more to shikata ga nai. It's an understanding of the ebb and tide of life and the total unpredictability of even the simplest of events. It does not mean simply going where the wind takes you. You choose whether to stand against the wind or be carried by it. But, you do not deny the existence of the wind, shikata ga nai. I don't know why, but it helped me with the loss of a friend. Colt is most likely lost. I pray for a miracle, but if it turns out he is, I am grateful to have had what time I did with him. He made an impact on my life, one that will last my lifetime. He is an important part of what we had. After all, he did make our first date successful. It is now up to me to decide how I will react to the loss of my friend, Colt MacIntyre of Victoria, Texas. I will honor him for he was an honorable man. I will emulate him because he was a better human being than me. I will celebrate him because that's what he would have wanted. I will remember him because without question he was memorable. And, I will miss him."

"Do not deny the wind," Ryoya said thoughtfully, "You would make a good Japanese."

"At this moment, I just want to be a good friend," he pulled Ryoya to him. She didn't resist.

"Wreckage has been found in a remote area north of Lakeland, Tennessee. There are no apparent survivors."

Matthew Ellis watched the television news program with intense interest. After he arose in the morning he sat with his coffee and turned on the television. The ongoing story of an airline disaster slapped him in the face. He didn't want to watch but was compelled to. The words he feared most came loud and clear through the television speaker, "The pilot radioed that they were having electrical problems and asked to be diverted to Memphis. That was the last transmission." His heart sank. Was it due to faulty wiring? If it was, the endless suffering his former self unleashed on the world was more than he could bear. He wondered, why did he ever wake up?

Stephanie entered the room. After a few moments of watching the news coverage she said, "That's so sad. Those poor people."

Matt didn't answer—he couldn't. What could he say? That jet may well have gone down because of his cold, callus, greed. He also knew there were jets, automobiles, submarines, helicopters, space craft all at risk because of his and Lida Petropoulos evil actions. He wondered what kind of monster had he been? A memory flashed before him which answered that question.

It was the fall of 1963. Valerie was home sick. He had told her he would try to leave work early to come home to take care of her and help with their twelve-year-old daughter, Stephanie. Mid-afternoon his telephone rang. When he answered, Lida Petropoulos voice said provocatively, "I'm out of Champagne. Pick up a Moet Reserve on your way."

"What? I'm not planning . . ."

"I'm wearing the red silk georgette negligee you like so much."

"Ah, that's tempting, but . . . "

"I need some strong hands to massage my tired tanned and oiled body."

"That would be nice."

"And, I will be nice in showing my gratitude in that special way."

Matt's mind replayed the evening he spent with Lida Petropoulos. The two of them enjoyed each other with abandon.

When Matt arrived home after ten he found both Valarie and Stephanie asleep in their beds. His reminiscence dissolved with the ringing of a telephone. Stephanie answered. She listened, made a few comments, listened, and then said, "Thank you," and hung up the telephone. With a look of shock on her face she walked over and sat in front of the television. In a weak, faraway voice she said, "That was Jack Moore, the newspaper reporter. He said Colt MacIntyre was on the airplane that crashed." Stephanie looked at her father who had a confused countenance so she explained, "He was the man who wanted to start an international adoption service in Texas." Tears flowed from her eyes as she sat staring into space.

Matt wanted to comfort his daughter but overwhelming guilt made him feel that he had no right. He very well might be the cause of her pain.

"It's not fair," Stephanie said to no one, "He was so kind and caring and wanted to do so much good. It's just not fair."

Silence settled in the room as two individuals were both personally affected by the news report but in distinctly different ways.

Carl sat with Laurel in the gazebo. She had asked him to join her there which, of course, he agreed to do. When he arrived the first thing he noticed was that she was wearing her tiara. As a result, her peasant dress looked out-of-place. Yet, in Carl's eyes she always looked exquisite.

Laurel began, "Yesterday, when you told me your plan, I said 'a released tiger never returns.'"

Carl nodded.

"Once back in the jungle its instincts take over. If you go back to New York I might lose you two ways. They might put you in prison or you may discover your old ways suit you once again."

In almost a whisper Carl assured Laurel, "That will never happen."

"I'm sure the tiger feels the same way."

Carl explained, once more, "My reason for going back is to remove the threat of someday being arrested and taken back in handcuffs. In some strange wild illogical way my fear of being taken away from you is what is driving me to face that risk head-on now. Maybe, just maybe, I'll be found innocent because he attacked me. They don't know my side of the story. That punk, Moe Black, knows it was an ambush. If the police question him they'll know I was the victim."

"And, if they don't locate him you most likely will be found guilty."

Carl rose and walked to the edge of the gazebo and looked out at the landscape, "I love Lark's Run. I've found peace here. I've found meaning for my life. I don't want to leave." He turned to face Laurel, "I found love so pure and clean and true that all else seems insignificant. To me you are a precious flower outshining all around you. In my wildest dreams, before coming to Lark's Run, I could never have conjured up anyone like you. My mind was incapable of imagining a being so divine. The thought of leaving you and going back to New York makes me shudder. I want to marry you but can't entertain such a thought with a wanted poster over my head. You deserve better."

Laurel sat in silence.

Carl walked over and sat beside her. At that moment he wanted her more than ever. How could the tiger not return? When he's gone Carl knew the only thing he will think about is returning. The only thing that will give him strength would be the hope of returning. Hope—such a small word with such enormous meaning. Finally, he made a decision and said, "If you don't want me to go, I won't."

Laurel sat for an excruciatingly long time neither speaking nor moving. Carl waited. He expected her to tell him not to go. What she said he never expected. It was just not something he ever considered. Laurel turned to Carl and said, "I'm going with you."

Wellington Marsh sat on the bank of the river that dissected Quy Hoa with Navy Corpsman Gordon Lassiter. The sun was shining and the temperature was a comfortable 78 degrees. It had been a quiet few days which allowed them to train some of the local militia. Old men and young boys with a language barrier proved quite a challenge. As it turned out Hung's nephew, eleven-year-old Lai Ngoc Linh, understood enough English to be a significant help. It was then that Wellington decided to begin English lessons with Hung's niece and nephew.

"Tell me Gordon, what do you think are the odds of a Native American tribe adopting those two kids?"

"Are you still pining about those kids?"

"I've got to give it a shot," Wellington admitted. "I'll probably fail but I have to try."

"Well, that's a new one on me—an Indian tribe."

"What do you think?"

"They do have their own laws, but I don't know how you'd ever get the kids out of Vietnam."

"One step at a time."

"You know an Indian Reservation isn't the most desirable place to live?"

"As compared to this?"

"Toe-ma-toe, Toe-may-toe."

"I sent a letter to my hippie friend and only hope that by now he doesn't have short hair and is in basic training."

"Good luck. Let me know if anything comes of it."

Anna Six Trees sat on the steps of their cabin. She held the fox totem that hung around her neck and missed her brother with all her heart.

82: Monday – October 20, 1969

Crowds began to gather along the parade route called, "Canyon of Heroes." This was to be the first tickertape parade for a sports team in New York City history. The media gave a start time of 11:00 a.m.

Tickertape parades in New York City began by accident on October 28, 1886, as an impromptu parade occurred in honor of the dedication of the Statue of Liberty. As celebrating citizens marched up Broadway, employees in the financial district spontaneously threw ticker tape out of their office windows to join in the celebration. From that time on parades were held to celebrate special occasions. The first individual honored with a ticker tape parade, in 1899, was Admiral George Dewey who was a hero of the battle of Manila Bay.

A tickertape parade starts at the furthermost southern point in Manhattan at Battery Park. Participants march up Broadway from Bowling Green to Chambers Street, approximately 1.2 miles. Along the way they pass Trinity Church at Wall Street and end with a ceremony at City Hall Plaza at 1:00 p.m.

On this day the New York Mets were to be honored. Thousands of excited fans lined the route eight deep from the street. Celebrations were everywhere. Fans who endured the lean years and those who jumped on the bandwagon alike waited to see their heroes.

Another event occurred that went relatively unnoticed one block south of Chambers Street at Warren Street. A black cat crossed Broadway and entered City Hall Park. It was not clear whether or not his name was Casey.

On this day with fans crowding the parade route, three fans would neither attend the parade nor the ceremony; Jack Moore, Ryoya Akimoto, and Colt MacIntyre.

"This is what both of you wish to do?" Nick confirmed. Both Carl and Laurel nodded. "I can't tell you if you're right or wrong. I guess only time will provide an answer to that question." Nick looked across the kitchen table directly at Carl, "You know you will be booked. Then you'll be arraigned and charges specified. Given the severity of the crime and the fact that you fled you will most likely not get bail. You will be held until a trial date is set which could be months. Finally, at a trial you will not believe the way facts can be manipulated by both sides. In the end, it will come down to twelve people and what they accept as fact, as well as how they perceive you."

"Are you trying to scare me?" Carl asked. "Because you're doing a great job."

"I'm trying to put it in perspective," Nick explained. "They're not going to say thanks for coming by, have a nice day."

"My hope is that they will hear my side of the story and realize that I'm the victim."

"They have a murder on their hands that they have to solve. Someone is going to go on trial," Nick paused, "unless you accept a plea bargain."

"Like what?"

"Well, it was a mutual fight. Unfortunately, when you won your opponent lost his life. That sounds more like manslaughter—even involuntary manslaughter. You didn't mean to kill him."

"I didn't. All I wanted to do was get away."

"I don't know, maybe a good lawyer could convince a jury it was self-defense."

"I'll pay for a lawyer," Laurel said softly. When both men looked at her she stated, "Nick, you know I have money."

Nick stood up from the table and paced around the kitchen thinking. Carl took Laurel's hand. Fetch stuck her snout under Laurel's other hand. Sounds from the farm could be heard outside. Nick stopped. He slowly turned to face the couple and announced, "I'm going with you."

Dark clouds once more cast shadows over Stephanie Ellis' world. Where there was hope now there was despair. Where she had a well-defined goal she now had nothing. Where her life was beginning to have meaning it was now adrift. And, most importantly, after meeting Colt MacIntyre and sharing a dream with this kind, intelligent, funny, and remarkable man, she lost a friend.

As hard as she tried she couldn't find any consolation. She was lost in a swirling tumult of emotions. Grief from the loss of her angel. Anger aimed at a God who would allow such a pointless thing to happen. Sadness for all those children who would not be given a better life. Fear of an endless stream of disappointments that was her future. Jealousy of all those who seem to have charmed lives. Regret for having done nothing of note in her life. Sadness at the thought that there would end up being nothing of note in her life.

Energy, electric and tormenting, caused Stephanie to be unable to find comfort. She had to reach out to someone. Unfortunately, her father had retreated into his own mental world and shut down.

Stephanie found herself at Dr. Tallman's office just before lunch. The receptionist told her he was with a patient but it was the last one for the morning. She asked Stephanie to wait and that she would let the doctor know she was there.

As Stephanie waited she kept seeing Colt MacIntyre's face with his Texas grin. He seemed like such a genuine character that she knew she could trust and with whom she wanted to work. In her imagination, she had seen the two of them welcoming babies and children at the airport and introducing them to their new families. She even got a little excited about moving to Texas. Maybe, she would learn to ride a horse, or buy some cowboy boots, or a Stetson. Her whole future looked so bright. And then, another accident. It didn't matter if it was a head-on collision on Route 9W or a plane crash in Tennessee, fate once more stepped in to demolish her dreams. Slowly she lowered her head into her hands and began to sob.

A hand touched her shoulder and with red moist eyes she looked up. It was Colt MacIntyre. "Lass, you can't be caterwaulin' over me. Wipe your chin and listen. Nobody knows how long they got between being born and the bone orchard. Some get more days than others. Most don't do anything worth a hill of beans in their born days while those special few shake this old world. You may not know it but you are a world shaker. I knew you were a gal I should tie to because there are hundreds, maybe thousands, of lives that are going to be improved due to your efforts. And, I ain't putting on too much mustard. I saw it in you the first time we met. You're a mustang that can't be broken. So, raise your head high and make our dream yours. Little lady, you're going to cry in the future, again and again and again, tears of joy. And, that ain't stretchin' the blanket. I told my daddy about you and our plans. He was bang on in favor. You call him. He's hurtin' too. There are some fishin' poles that aren't going to be used and some yarns that won't get told. And, some good bourbon that won't get shared that's for dang sure. And, I won't be able to tell him how much I love him. The sadness of things not said. My old man's got sand and will get through it, but he also has a heart and talkin' to you will help. Don't bring up the adoption service, let it be his idea. He'll dance around it and try to get a handle on your thinking. Believe me, after all his yammerin' he'll post the pony. It will be his way of honoring me, not that I deserve it. Remember his name Clinton MacIntyre of Victoria, Texas. I'm counting on you, Stephanie Ellis. Oh, and about this conversation, keep it dry, uh, our little secret."

The opening of a door caused Stephanie to look to her left. When she looked back at Colt he wasn't there. Dr. Tallman walked in and sat next to Stephanie. Upon seeing her tears, he asked, "What's wrong Stephanie?"

Stephanie told Dr. Tallman the events of the past few days. She explained how she had come to see him because she couldn't break free from the despair. Quickly, she added that she somehow felt that Colt would want her to continue on with their plans. Something told her it was going to work out and she was compelled to follow that belief. When she finished she asked, "Am I crazy?"

Dr. Tallman took Stephanie's hand and said softly, "You are not crazy." He paused, then looked into her eyes and said, "I'm sorry to hear about your friend. It's always a tragedy when one dies so young. There is never anything that can be said to ease the pain."

"If I can, I'm going to build the Colt MacIntyre International Adoption Agency so that his spirit can live in the lives that are given a better chance. He deserves that much."

"You were touched by the girls at Woodstock and influenced by a young man. Inspiration can come from anywhere. If his loss is a driving force that keeps you going when it gets difficult then some good will come from a tragedy."

"I think in some strange way he might guide me."

"He very well may. In medicine there are far too many unexplained events for us to doubt the existence of a power beyond our understanding."

"I came here because I was lost. I didn't know what to do next. Just sitting here I found the answer."

"You go out there and make a difference," Dr. Tallman stood and smiled. "I'm counting on you, Stephanie Ellis."

"Life sucks!"

"Yeah, I can agree with you on that one."

"Just when things are looking good, someone throws a bag of shit in your face."

"Yeah, a bag of shit."

"It's getting harder and harder to make sense out of things."

"Why try?"

"Even a punching bag gets tired of being hit."

"Yeah, a punching bag."

"How many times can someone get knocked down and get back up?"

"Don't know."

"People have their limits."

"We all do."

"I lost a friend and it really hurts."

"Damn shame."

"Sometimes I just want to give up—stop trying."

"Understandable."

"But, then I have to look in the mirror."

"Ya gotta do that."

"What I see is not a quitter."

"I agree."

"I might get pissed off, but damn it, I won't get pissed on."

"Good for you."

"So, the truth is I just have to keep trying."

"That's the truth."

"Whatever the outcome, at least I faced it head on."

"Like a man."

"The heart is heavy, but the spirit won't quit."

"Not a quitter."

"All right, back into the fray."

"Good luck."

"Thanks."

"You're welcome."

"Sometimes you just need a different perspective."

"A different angle."

"You really were there for me."

"Glad to help."

Jack walked out of More-Or-Less.

Anna Six Trees found a picture drawn by her brother. It was a swan that she had asked him to draw back in the spring. She stared at it hoping to feel his spirit.

83: Wednesday – October 22, 1969

When her clock radio sprang to life, Peter, Paul and Mary were singing *Blowin' in the Wind.* Ryoya opened her eyes and lay in bed listening to the lyrics.

How many roads must a man walk down,
Before they call him a man?
How many seas must a white dove sail,
Before she sleeps in the sand?

How many times must the cannonballs fly,
Before they're forever banned?
The answer, my friend, is blowing in the wind,
The answer is blowing in the wind.

How many years must a mountain exist,
Before it is washed to the sea?
How many years can some people exist,
Before they're allowed to be free?

How many times can a man turn his head,
And pretend that he just doesn't see?
The answer, my friend, is blowing in the wind,
The answer is blowing in the wind.

How many times must a man look up,
Before he can see the sky?
How many ears must one man have,
Before he can hear people cry?

How many deaths will it take till he knows,
That too many people have died?
The answer, my friend, is blowing in the wind,
The answer is blowing in the wind.

At the song's conclusion, Ryoya thought about the reference to the answer blowing in the wind and Jack's statement about not denying the existence of the wind. It seemed an odd coincidence. They hadn't spoken since early Sunday morning when he came to her apartment to inform her of the plane crash. Since that time the wreckage had been found and a list of passengers and crew released. Colt MacIntyre was lost to the world that dark, dark, night.

At work a number of push-in robberies and assaults had kept her and Detective Michael Donovan busy. In a way she welcomed the heavy workload because it kept her from feeling the overwhelming grief that hid just beneath the surface. As she went through files her mind kept returning to the wind. For some reason it made her think of the phrase, "the winds of change." Change, for better or worse. Losing Colt was definitely for the worse. Losing Jack, as it appeared was possible, was also for the worse. Michael Donovan walked over to her desk and dropped another stack of files on top of the ones she was going through. He looked at her and said, "We're getting nowhere fast."

"By the time we go through all these files the perpetrators will have grown old and retired to Florida," Ryoya quipped.

"Not a fingerprint match from any of the crime scenes."

"I can't even see any pattern."

Detective Donovan picked up a folder and began to look through it. As he did, he asked, "Have you heard from Jack?"

"None of your business."

"Then, that's a no."

"It's a none of your business."

Michael Donovan leaned forward and said, "Listen, Rita, your miserable. It doesn't take a first-grade detective to see that. And, it is my business. We're partners which means we look out for each other on and off the job. Now, I've heard and seen you two together and there's a spark there that you share. You're good for each other. Whatever centuries old tradition, or 'stick with your own kind' attitude, or 'think about the kids' malarkey that's getting in the way is bullshit. You deserve to be happy. He deserves to be happy. Yin and yang, oil and vinegar, Popeye and Olive Oil whatever it is it works. You'll be a little old retired detective sitting with her cat if you cling to tradition. And, tradition won't warm your feet at night. Don't end up wondering what might have been. You know I'm right. I'm not just blowin' wind."

Ryoya looked at Michael. He was a good partner and a good friend. She couldn't get angry as he spoke the truth. He returned her stare and nodded as if to indicate that he had his say. Ryoya picked up the telephone and dialed. When Jack answered she said, "Lunch today. One o'clock. Patsy's on Third," and hung up.

Stephanie used directory assistance service to get the telephone number of Clinton MacIntyre of Victoria, Texas. She was nervous as she dialed the number. After three rings a man's voice answered. Stephanie asked, "May I speak with Clinton MacIntyre."

"This is he."

"Mr. MacIntyre, my name is Stephanie Ellis. You don't know me."

"Stephanie! Of course I know who you are. Colt told me all about you. He was very impressed."

"I was so impressed with Colt," tears began to well up in her eyes, "I'm so sorry about his loss."

"We will miss him very much." After a pause, "My boy was a breed unto himself. He saw things others missed. I watched him grow and develop into a man—a man you had to respect. There wasn't a day that I wasn't proud of him. There won't be a day that I won't miss him." Silence.

Stephanie felt compelled to speak, "Mr. MacIntyre, Colt was looking forward to coming home. He spoke of fishing, sharing tales, and enjoying a good bourbon with you."

"He told you that?"

Stephanie didn't know how to answer so she simply added, "He wanted you to know how much he loved you."

"How do you know that?" Clinton asked not as a cross examination, rather out of curiosity.

"Let's leave it as he shared that with me."

"I appreciate you telling me."

"I know nothing will make this less painful. When my mother died I walked around in a fog unable to find anything good anywhere. It was as though I was dragging a huge anchor behind me. Just going through the motions of carrying on day-to-day responsibilities was a major effort. It left me exhausted. The only thing that got me through it was what Dr. Tallman said. He told me, 'You honor her by the life you live.'"

"He sounds like a wise man."

"He is a special kind of man."

A long silence followed. Stephanie thought the connection may have been lost. Just when she was going to ask if he was still there, Clinton MacIntyre said, "We will honor Colt by how we live." Another pause, then Colt MacIntyre's father said, "There will be a memorial service for Colt after the authorities release the remains. I'd like you to attend."

"I, uh, well . . ."

"I'll pay your travel expenses."

"That's very generous but Colt and I only knew each other a short amount of time."

"Colt knew you long enough to want to build a business with you."

"The truth is all we did was share a dream of helping children."

"It was a dream he felt quite strongly about. He told me about the Holt organization and your experience at Woodstock and wanted me to provide the seed money." After a pause he continued, "I didn't give him an answer, but he knew me well enough to know that I would help."

"I think he knew."

"We need to build his dream, Stephanie. It can be a legacy from a too-short life. Can I count on you?"

"Mr. MacIntyre . . ."

"Call me Clint."

"Sir, I haven't even gotten my degree, yet."

"All I ask is a commitment. If you will help create Colt's dream we can work out the details. He put his trust in you, therefore, so will I."

"But, I don't know if I'm the right person. I could fail and then that doesn't honor Colt."

"When Colt was a small boy he wanted to learn how to rope and ride. Well, he was just a little nub but I taught him the basics. The first time he tried to throw a lasso while riding a horse he tumbled off and landed in a pile of manure. Then he lassoed his own horse. That boy was a danger to everyone and everything around with that rope. He got so frustrated that he threw his rope against the barn wall and cussed." As an aside Clint said, "He got tanned for that one." Colt's father then finished his story, "For the next two weeks he tried and tried failing dismally. I thought, this lad just doesn't have the eye hand coordination to rope and ride. He proved me wrong—in spades. Not only did he master it he won at the rodeo. His comment was, 'When I failed I learned what doesn't work. Eventually, I had to run out of failures.' I laughed." Clint MacIntyre fell silent.

Stephanie knew the senior MacIntyre was having trouble—a kind of trouble no words would help. She waited a reasonable amount of time and then said, "I wish I had known Colt longer. I would have learned so much."

"He taught me." Clinton MacIntyre cleared his throat and said, "All I have is his dream. Help me keep the dream alive for my boy."

"Mr., uh, Clint, I would love nothing more but I'm afraid I'll let you down."

"Stephanie Ellis, you won't let me or Colt down. Let's give er a try."

Ritchie Anderson and Matt Ellis met at the same diner where they had the past weekend. On the table were two strands of wire. One had black electrical tape around it to differentiate it from the other.

"By all appearances they are identical pieces of wire. That's what I thought and that's what my friend thought," Ritchie explained. "He ran alternating current and direct current through at different voltages. At first he said he didn't see any difference. But, then he noticed after a short period of time the wire with the black tape allowed less current to reach a lamp and upon examination had begun to heat up. He used all kinds of technical terms; impedance, capacitance, inductance, and ohms. Bottom line this wire," Ritchie picked up the wire with black tape, "begins to have a lot of resistance at certain voltages but only after a period of time. That would indicate a slow build of resistance. Turn off the power they both work the same once more. Then slowly the weaker wire loses conductivity and heats up." Ritchie sipped his coke as he looked at his notes. "He cut open a portion of the wires and looked at the metal strands. In the better wire they are all the same. The weaker wire, on the other hand was made up of strands from different metals. He has a theory that the different metals conduct electricity at varying rates thus creating counter flows that fight each other generating heat. It seemed more pronounced with direct current."

"So, this wire is noticeably inferior to the other wire?" Matt asked.

"There's more. The insulation on the taped wire is thinner and contains contaminants that conduct electricity. Even though only a small amount of energy escapes, at a higher current level the wire can arc burning away the insulation." Ritchie looked at Matthew Ellis and stated with conviction, "Someone's trying to pull one over on you. Run, don't walk, away from this wire it will burn your house down. Whoever is saying it is equal to the other wire should be thrown in jail."

Jack Moore walked into Patsy's and looked around. Nowhere in sight was a Japanese woman. As it was one o'clock, middle of the lunchtime rush, there were no open tables. He sat at the bar and ordered a beer. In his mind he had gone through every possible scenario; Ryoya had asked to meet so that she could accept his proposal, or admit she was confused and didn't know what to do, or tell him goodbye. He tried to prepare himself to handle whatever transpired. If it was the worst outcome he would accept it with dignity. The best outcome and he was buying beers for the house.

Time passed and Jack remained alone. Given that he was meeting a police detective there were a plethora of reasons why she would be late or not show at all. He tried to be mature about it, but sometimes it's more difficult than others. Anger was held at bay. A second beer allowed a small amount of frustration to slip through. The third beer was the key to the door that swung open and Jack was pissed. His time was as valuable as hers. He couldn't be sitting around doing nothing. A glance at his watch revealed that he had been waiting over a half hour.

Finally, Ryoya entered the pub. She spotted Jack at the bar and went directly to him. She apologized, "I'm sorry, Jack, we got tied up downtown and couldn't get back."

"Sure."

"I said I'm sorry."

"OK."

"We really did get tied up."

"Fine."

"Knowing you, you were on time," Ryoya smiled.

"That's right, old dependable Jack was on time."

"I said I was sorry."

"Yes, you did."

"I didn't do it on purpose."

"So you said."

"Maybe, this wasn't a good idea."

"It was your idea."

"Yes, it was. I thought we needed to clear the air."

Jack turned to face Ryoya, "There's nothing to discuss. You already made everything quite clear."

"I don't think so."

"Well, I got the message loud and clear."

"You're not being fair."

"How did I become the bad guy when all I did was try to do something good?"

"You're not the bad guy. But, you put me in a difficult position."

"I'm sorry," Jack stated sarcastically.

"You obviously don't want to talk about it at this time."

"I was ready to talk a half hour ago."

"I see. This was a mistake. Good bye, Jack." Ryoya turned and left Patsy's.

Jack sat at the bar wondering to where the mature adult had disappeared. He knew he had been unreasonable even as he was being unreasonable. Anger ruled the moment. The last thing he wanted to do was argue with Ryoya, yet it was the first thing to come to mind. It was obvious that he was losing her. That was not what he wanted. Unfortunately, due to his actions it was becoming a self-fulfilling prophecy. His fear of losing her was driving her away. While his heart ached, anger wouldn't let go. He did everything he could to make things right. Takashi Akimoto, Ryoya's father, had been polite and hospitable. He expressed the expected concern about a mixed marriage and cultural differences. It was clear that Jack was not his preferred choice. Jack appreciated the man's honesty and they ended the conversation with Jack literally leaving the decision in Takashi Akimoto's hands. If he withheld the ring Jack would accept the verdict. If he gave the ring to Ryoya, thus accepting Jack, it would be his unspoken decision. As it turned out her father approved. Jack got over the biggest hurdle. You would think she would have appreciated the effort. Instead, she became the problem. In Jack's mind it had become a one-way street. He was doing everything to build a relationship and she was doing nothing—except being late. When did he become a beggar? What the hell happened? Why should he feel guilty? Who else would jump through so many hoops? Jack looked at the door through which Ryoya had left. He turned and ordered another beer.

Wanda Six Trees and her daughter, Anna Marie, enjoyed a lunch in the lodge of Chief Michael.

84: Friday – October 24, 1969

There was a wrinkle before the trip even began. Nick had checked over the Lark's Run 1959 Chevrolet Nomad station wagon, filled the gas tank, and parked it in front of the farm house. At six in the morning they loaded their bags and were ready to start out. Nick hugged and kissed Penelope, his wife. As he did Fetch, the black basenji, invited herself along by jumping into the back seat and settling down next to Laurel.

"You're not going," Carl told the pooch.

"Come'on, out," Nick ordered.

Fetch didn't move.

"We can't take a dog," Nick stated, "The hotel doesn't allow dogs in the room."

Fetch stared him down.

Carl looked at the canine and said, "She's got a mind of her own and can be pretty stubborn."

"Are you talking about me?" Laurel asked in jest.

Confused, at first, Carl thought for a moment and then explained, "Uh, no, uh, I was talking about your buddy there." He pointed at Fetch.

"I think we have a fourth adventurer," Laurel said as she patted the pup's head. After a pause, she added, "She'll be company on the ride home if they throw Carl in jail."

"That's a comforting thought," Carl said.

"It's reality," Nick pointed out. "If you're having second thoughts—now's the time."

"I'm having second, third, and fourth thoughts, but it's something I have to do—like it or not."

Nick put the ten-year-old Chevy station wagon in gear and they headed toward the gate. When they passed through, Carl couldn't help looking back at his Shangri La and wondering if he would ever see it again. A cold chill ran through his body.

Matthew Ellis returned to 347 Madison Avenue where he found an office suite that once was home to LPAmerica. This time he sought the building manager. When he inquired as to whether or not LPAmerica left any forwarding address the answer he received was, "If they had we would know where to go after them for back rent."

He left the building and walked downtown on Madison Avenue. Alone, once more, with no idea where to find any answers Matthew Ellis walked in a daze. People all around him were invisible. The sounds of the city were muted. He had no destination. When he reached Forty-Second Street he turned right and headed west. In two blocks he reached Bryant Park behind the Library. There he found a park bench and sat. Fatigue mixed with guilt. Mathew Ellis felt he could search no more.

Wellington Marsh and his CAP team had become accepted by the Quy Hoa villagers. They smiled and greeted them when they passed through while others brought food to where the team camped. Except for when they went on patrol the team was essentially separated from the war.

Hung and Wellington looked at a map as they planned their next patrol. There seemed to be increased Viet Cong activity and Hung was concerned they might begin looking for alternative routes to Kontum and Pleiku through the mountains. He expressed his concern that it was a matter of time before the village is discovered. Given this concern he once more brought up the subject of his niece and nephew. Wellington explained that he wrote a letter to a friend in the United States but didn't hold too much hope it would get past the military censors. Even if it did, there weren't a lot of options that seemed plausible. Hung simply nodded and went back to the map.

Four travelers from Warren, Pennsylvania arrived in New York City at 1:53 p.m. From experience, Carl knew the Midtown North precinct was located at 306 West 54th Street. Miraculously, they found a parking space on the same block. They approached the four-story tan building with a large American flag hanging from a flagpole attached at the second floor. The cornerstone read 1938. Above two green doors they saw the number 306 and a sign stating 18th Precinct.

Upon entering, the group was greeted by the musty aroma of an old building. There seemed to be activity everywhere with uniformed and plain clothes officers sitting at desks behind glass walls, talking in small groups, or walking from one place to another. A large polished wood counter stood across the room. Behind it were three uniformed officers. No one in the building seemed to notice three adults and a dog enter.

Carl walked hesitantly up to the wood counter where a patrolman looked at him and said, "Can I help you?"

"Uh, yeah," Carl said, "I want to turn myself in."

"Turn yourself in, for what?"

"I'm wanted," Carl said. He didn't want to add for what crime.

"What are you wanted for?"

"Murder."

"Sergeant!" the officer called out immediately. "This guy says he's wanted for murder."

A middle-aged greying sergeant walked over and looked at Carl. After a few moments he stated, "I know you. You're Pitachuk."

"Pythacyk, Carl Pythacyk."

"Yeah. There was a flyer on you. Step over here." He waved Carl to the far end of the wood counter where there was a swinging gate. The sergeant walked through and took Carl by the arm. He led him to an open area where there were a number of chairs. Nick, Laurel, and Fetch followed. The sergeant looked at the trio and asked, "Who are you?"

"We're with him," Nick stated with authority.

"Well, you're going to have to wait out there. He's being taken into custody."

Reluctantly, they moved to the waiting area that was indicated.

"Put your hands behind your back," the sergeant ordered and Carl complied. After being handcuffed, he was led into a back room out-of-sight.

Laurel looked at Nick and said softly, "I hope we are doing the right thing."

"The decision has been made, we now have to see it through."

Inside the holding area Carl sat on a wooden bench. Three other detainees were present. A young punk with wild eyes stared at Carl as if challenging him. A businessman in a nice suit sat with his head down mumbling to himself. And, appearing to be asleep, an old derelict. Carl thought, well I'm back and nothing has changed. His mind wandered to Lark's Run and it seemed so far away. Almost like one of those dreams where you are running toward something but never can get any closer. Then he heard Laurel's voice singing her Celtic tune, so sad, so beautiful, so distant. The cold barren cobble stones of New York City had nothing to offer in comparison to the fields and streams and mountain trails and beehives of Lark's Run. Carl smiled. The young punk with wild eyes spat, "You think something's funny?"

Carl, ripped from his reverie, looked at the young man and saw himself. He simply shook his head.

"Pittinger," an officer announced.

When no one answered Carl said, "Pythacyk?"

"Yeah, come with me." The police officer motioned for Carl to follow. They walked up a flight of old creaky wooden stairs. Carl moved carefully as it was somewhat awkward with his hands cuffed behind his back. On the second floor they entered an interrogation room and Carl was ordered to sit in one of the wooden chairs.

"What kind of a dog is that?" an old man in the waiting area asked.

Laurel answered, "A basenji—African barkless dog. Only she's Americanized and barks."

"She's a pretty little thing," the old man smiled.

Carl sat alone and waited. He knew the drill. They make you wait so you know who's in charge. For whatever reason, Carl thought about Wellington Marsh. At that moment while he sat in a safe police station his Marine friend was probably in a jungle facing death. Their Minnesota adventure replayed in his mind.

"I had a dog, Skipper was his name, he was just a mutt," the old man explained. "We had a time together. Skipper and I went everywhere together. That is until those hoods killed him."

The door opened and a Japanese-American woman entered the room. "My name is Detective Akimoto."

Carl nodded.

"You are Carl Pythacyk. Wanted for the murder of Miguel Juarez," she stated looking at a paper in a manila folder.

Carl nodded, once more.

Detective Akimoto sat down opposite Carl and said, "Why don't you tell me what happened."

This was probably the only chance Carl had to convince anybody that it was self-defense and he knew it. He also knew all he could do was tell the truth. After explaining how he and Miguel had an ongoing feud, he described the events of the night Miguel was killed. Carl finished by saying, "I didn't know that he had died."

"What happened to the gun?"

"I took it and threw it in the river."

"And, the knife?"

"He dropped it when I hit him again. I picked it up and tossed it."

"Then what happened?"

He started to jump up, I knocked him down, he hit his head, and was unconscious so I left." Carl added with sincerity, "I didn't know he was dead."

"Did anyone witness the encounter?"

"Nobody that I know of."

"When you left the alley, did you see anyone?"

"No."

"Which way did you go when you left the alley?"

"Toward Ninth Avenue."

"Why did you run?"

"I heard the next morning that he had been found dead."

"Where have you been all this time?"

"I'd rather not say."

"Why not?"

"I don't want others to get into trouble. They had no idea I was on the run."

"I see." Ryoya made some notes and asked, "Why did you come back and turn yourself in?"

Carl hesitated. Detective Akimoto waited.

"It's tough having a dog in the city," the old man said adding sadly, "I miss Skipper."

Carl finally explained, "I found another way of life that is clean and pure and where I would like to be, but I can't with this hanging over my head."

"If you are convicted of murder you won't be able to return to that way of life."

"It's a chance I have to take. It was self-defense."

"You are willing to risk your life to have that other way of life?"

"Yes."

"That must be some way of life."

"It is."

Ryoya changed the subject, "You were associated with Don Carmine Spacini before you ran?"

"Yes, for a short time."

"Don't you miss the action?"

"No."

"Do you have anything you could tell us about his activities that could cause us to look more favorably on your case?" Ryoya went fishing.

"No."

"A little information, just between us."

"I have nothing."

"I wish I could get out of the city. But, with a rent controlled apartment and fixed income I'm trapped," the old man lamented.

"Mr. Pythacyk, why did you stab Miguel Juarez?"

Carl looked surprised, "I didn't stab him. Was he stabbed?"

"Your story doesn't fit the facts, Mr. Pythacyk."

"I told you exactly what happened."

"Up to where you stabbed him."

"I didn't." Carl slumped into the chair, "If I stabbed him I would never have come back."

"Your fingerprints are on the knife."

"I told you, I tossed it aside."

"What would you say if I told you we have a witness?"

"I'd say they will tell you that I'm telling the truth."

"Carl," Ryoya acted more friendly, "are you sure you didn't see anyone else when you left the alley?"

"I just wanted to get out of there. I didn't see anyone."

Ryoya went over her notes. She said as she read, "This Moe Black is the one who set you up."

"That's right."

"And, Miguel Juarez was waiting for you."

"He stepped out of the alley holding a gun."

"What happened to Moe Black?"

"I have no idea. I never saw him, again."

"Does the name Claire Payton mean anything to you?"

Carl thought for a few moments, "No, I don't recognize the name."

"I believe that's all I need," Detective Akimoto stood and went to the door, "Sit tight."

Once more Carl was alone with his thoughts. He knew he didn't stab Miguel. Why did she ask if he did? Could someone else have killed Miguel? What really happened in that alley?

The door opened and the uniformed police office that had led Carl up to the interrogation room entered. He removed the handcuffs and said, "Thanks for coming in. You're free to go."

"What?" Carl said in disbelief.

"You're free to go. There are no charges."

"But, what about the murder?"

"That case was closed weeks ago."

Carl walked into the waiting area. Laurel and Nick looked at him with wide eyes. Carl smiled.

"What happened?" Nick asked.

"They said thanks for coming in."

"You're free—that's it?"

"Yup. Someone else killed the guy."

Nick laughed and Fetch barked. Laurel wrapped her arms around Carl and said, "I knew you weren't a killer. I couldn't fall in love with a killer."

When they got to the car they found a parking ticket under the windshield wiper arm. Nick looked at the summons, looked around, and then asked, "Where does it say official police vehicles only?"

As they crossed the George Washington Bridge Carl asked Nick, "You think we can stop and see Ritchie? I have his parent's address."

"Why not? We can give him the good news."

Detective Akimoto said to her partner, Detective Donovan, "Can you believe that? The kid was willing to risk his life to be able to go back to where he was hiding out. It must be some little piece of heaven."

"Makes you wonder, doesn't it?"

The trio, plus dog, arrived in Haworth, New Jersey shortly before six o'clock. It took some searching but they eventually found the Anderson household. A large Victorian abode on a sprawling wooded lot stood before them.

Nick parked in front and said, "We now know from what well hippies spring."

"It's no apartment in the Bronx, that's for sure," Carl added.

"One is not responsible for the castle from which they originate," Laurel stated which indicated she may have lived in just such a mansion.

Fetch had no comment.

Ritchie's mother answered the door. She didn't know what to make of the group but was pleasant and hospitable. They were sitting in the den when Ritchie arrived. The group almost didn't recognize him in a suit and tie with his long hair pulled back. Fetch had no problem and ran to greet Ritchie. It was a touching, if also wet, reunion.

"Fetch, what are you doing here? How are you doing? It's good to see you. Have you been good? Did you miss me?" Ritchie went on and on.

"Who are you and what have you done with my hippie?" Carl asked from across the room.

Ritchie looked up while still petting Fetch and smiled, "I'm 4F, working for my father, living at home, a complete sellout."

"You look good," Nick declared, "Almost respectable."

Suddenly, Ritchie turned his attention to Carl, "Carl what are you doing here? Aren't you afraid of being caught?"

Nick answered, "Our boy turned himself in only they tossed him back. Someone else did the crime, he's free and clear. Can you believe it?"

"Oh, that's great news, man."

Carl said, "Now, all we need is for Wellington to get home safe. The three river rats would be back together."

"You know, I got a letter from him," Ritchie stated as he stood. "There were a lot of parts cut out but the gist of it was that he's doing OK." Ritchie walked over to the group followed by Fetch. "There was a part in the letter that was curious. He asked if I knew of any way to get two Vietnamese orphans adopted in the United States."

"He wants to adopt them?" Nick asked.

"That wasn't clear."

"There was a lot of that kind of thing being considered by GI's when I was there but it's made so difficult essentially all forgot it," Nick explained.

"I wouldn't even know where to begin," Ritchie said, "My ex-girlfriend's father told me she is interested in working in international adoption but she hasn't even finished school."

Nick added, "It would take an act of Congress to do something like that."

"Well, I owe it to Wellington to at least look into it."

The subject turned to Fetch. Laurel said to Ritchie, "We love having Fetch in our family but she is your dog. Now that you aren't going to be drafted she can stay with you—if you wish."

Ritchie looked at the little black dog and knew he missed her. Brown eyes stared at him. He faced reality. His new job, which he found very challenging and fulfilling, demanded long hours. At present, he lived in his parent's home. He hoped to have a social life, eventually. In truth, if she stayed with him, Fetch would not get the attention or freedom she enjoyed at Lark's Run. He loved her enough to let her go.

Wanda Six Trees sat in the dark. Her daughter Anna was asleep in her bed. For the thousandth time a grieving mother blamed herself.

85: Saturday – October 25, 1969

The ride back to Lark's Run had been light-hearted and filled with optimistic plans. Nick told Carl he would teach him how to brew beer. Carl expressed interest in reading more about a new type of no-plowing planting. Laurel played with Fetch and also played her flute. In addition, she wore her tiara. All in all, the ride was pleasant, sky clear blue, temperatures comfortable, and traffic inconsequential.

When they passed through the gate at Lark's Run Carl had an odd sensation of freedom. He was free of murder charges, free of his past life, and free to be something he never thought possible—happy. To the surprise of his traveling mates Carl began to laugh. It was a laugh that waited a lifetime to emerge. Laurel tried to ask what was funny but Carl's laugh was so contagious she soon joined him. It didn't take long for Nick to get pulled into the stew. As a result, when the car stopped in front of the farmhouse its occupants were seemingly out-of-control. Nick's wife, Penelope, walked over to the car and was surprised to see Carl. In no time she also fell victim to the hilarity and joined in. It took more than a few minutes for all to calm down.

As Fetch chased a squirrel, Lark's Run returned to normal.

Ritchie picked up Stephanie at her apartment. It had taken a little convincing before she finally agreed to have lunch with her ex-boyfriend. He took her to the Iron Horse in Westwood, New Jersey. She loved their hamburgers. As they rode to the restaurant, Stephanie told Ritchie about Colt MacIntrye, their plans, his loss, and her conversation with his father. Ritchie told the tale of his journey to Canada, the two friends he made, and the sad events on an Indian reservation. He also explained how he became 4F in the draft and ultimately went to work for his father.

"I'm glad to see that you've become more serious," Stephanie said as they ate lunch.

"I guess it had to happen. I got to a point where a decision had to be made—completely drop out or accept reality and join in," he munched on a french fry, "In truth, I'm enjoying being a graphic designer on the magazines. It's a creative challenge."

"I'm happy for you."

"I'm sorry about the loss of your friend," Ritchie said sincerely. "As a matter-of-fact I wanted to get your thoughts on the very subject of adoption."

"I'm not in a position to give advice. Maybe five years from now, but you know as much about adoption as me."

"When your father told me you were getting involved in adoption I assumed you knew people in that field."

"Unfortunately, no."

"Oh, well, I guess I'll have to seek answers elsewhere."

"What is your interest in adoption?" Stephanie asked out of curiosity.

Ritchie told Stephanie about his friend Wellington Marsh, the letter, and the two Vietnamese orphans. After what happened in Minnesota she understood his desire to help.

"I guess I'll write to him and explain that I don't have any idea where to begin." Ritchie thought for a moment, "Still I should at least try."

That evening, Stephanie received a telephone call from Clinton MacIntyre. He told her the memorial would be held on the upcoming Wednesday and that she should fly in on Tuesday. He reaffirmed his offer to pay her travel expenses and told her she could stay with him and his wife at their home. During the conversation he asked Stephanie to tell any other friends of Colt's that she knew the details about the service.

It being Saturday, Stephanie didn't know how to get in touch with Jack Moore. She hated to wait until Monday which wouldn't leave the reporter very much time if he wanted to attend.

Jack walked into More-Or-Less and over to his favorite barstool. It was a chilly evening. He removed his brown hat and brown coat and placed them on the stool next to his. The bar was not crowded and relatively quiet. Harry Van Ryker, the owner bartender, walked over to greet his friend, "Stag, tonight?"

With an expressionless face, Jack replied, "I think that relationship has run its course."

"Oh? Sorry to hear that."

"Let me have a bourbon and Adam's Ale," Jack said ordering what Colt MacIntyre had ordered when he visited the bar.

"In honor of a lost friend," Harry concluded as he placed the bourbon and water in front of Jack and said, "I liked that young man."

"I did too. More than I realized."

"He was a character."

"He had character." Jack sipped the bourbon, wrinkled his nose, and said, "Not very good taste, but character."

"I never can get used to losing the good ones."

"When I heard his plane went down I felt numb, not wanting to believe it. At first, I hoped he had missed his flight. Then I prayed that maybe there were survivors. In the end, it's a tragedy for all involved. So many families were thrown into the horror of unexpected loss. A vicious slap in the face telling us that nothing is guaranteed or permanent." Jack held his nose and sipped the bourbon.

"I wish there was something I could say that would make sense out of it," Harry said. "I guess I'm just not that smart."

"You're a bartender—you're supposed to have a line for all occasions."

"How about; we're better for having known him?"

"I'll drink to that," Jack raised the glass, looked at it, put it on the bar, and said, "but, not with that. Give me a scotch on the rocks. Sorry, Colt, I guess I'm just a mossback."

Harry placed a fresh drink in front of Jack, "Now, tell me what happened with Lotus Blossom."

"None of your damn business."

"It is my business, if you remember, I am the one who got that whole thing started."

"That's right. Thanks a lot." In a serious tone Jack continued, "I do mean thanks. We had a real good time together. She is an incredible woman. I guess things just moved too quickly. It created stresses and pressures that brought the ever present cultural divide front and center. More my fault than hers." Jack took a sip of the scotch and nodded his approval. "Isn't that the way it always is? The guy falls for the gal before she's ready to be fallen for and then something beautiful turns into something uncomfortable. Once the relationship gets into those rough waters, nine times out of ten, it's sunk."

"So, you're through?"

"I think we need a little breathing room. Let things cool off."

"Sounds like Jack the Ripper got loose."

"What? No. I like to think of myself as easy going."

"Do you even own a mirror?" Harry quipped getting an icy stare in return.

"I guess my ego is bruised by the rejection and I'm not being fair or reasonable. At least I can see that much. Rather than being a pain-in-the-ass to deal with, it's better that I keep my distance."

"That must be tough."

"You want to see me cry?"

"Not particularly."

"Then let's drop the subject."

"OK," Harry agreed. He looked around to see if any patron needed anything. When his attention returned to Jack he said, "I'm getting married."

"Jesus Christ! You think that helps? Your timing is incredible." Jack downed his drink and tapped the bar.

Harry refilled the glass. Jack looked at his friend, smiled, and said, "Congratulations, birdman."

"Yeah, you are a pain-in-the-ass, but thanks."

"I am happy for you—you deserve it," Jack offered his hand.

Harry gripped his friend's hand and held it, "Amanda and I would like you to be best man, because our twelve other choices are unavailable."

"I don't think you have twelve friends."

"Amanda does, which brings up a now sensitive subject. She has asked Detective Akimoto to be Maid-of-Honor."

"I see."

"That's not going to be a problem, is it?"

"Of course not. It will just rip my heart out and throw it on the floor to be stomped on by all in attendance."

"As long as it's not a problem."

"Harry, for you, what's a little heart stomping?"

The telephone rang and Harry left to answer it. Jack turned on the barstool to observe the room. More-Or-Less started getting busy. He decided not to hang around too long. A thud behind him caused Jack to turn around. Harry had placed the telephone on the bar, "It's for you."

Somewhat confused, as no one knew he was there, Jack took the receiver and spoke, "Jack Moore."

"Mr. Moore this is Stephanie Ellis."

"Stephanie, how are you? Better question, how did you know I was here?"

"I didn't, but I remembered that's where you and Colt hung out. So, I had to try. Mr. Moore, I spoke with Colt's father and the memorial service is being held at Saint Francis Episcopal Church in Victoria, Texas on Wednesday. I though you ought to know so you can decide whether or not to go."

"Thank you, Stephanie, I appreciate you finding me."

"It's no problem. I'm going to the service."

Jack thought for a second, "I really hadn't considered it, not knowing what was planned." Jack sipped his drink, "Maybe, I'll see you there."

Lai Ngoc Linh and his sister watched a body float down the river that must have gone over the waterfall.

86: Wednesday – October 29, 1969

Stephanie woke up in a strange bed in a strange house in a strange state—Texas. She had flown in the day before and was met at the airport by one of the foremen on the MacIntyre ranch.

"Howdy, little lady, my name is Chester Steele. You are Stephanie Ellis?"

The ride out to the ranch was quite a distance. They rode in a 1969 white Jeep Wagoneer. It was a big heavy vehicle which made the ride comfortable. Stephanie was just glad to be on the ground. The flight to Dallas was on a large commercial jet. This was followed by a flight on a small twin engine propeller plane to Victoria Airport. Even though she knew it was silly she found she was afraid of flying. As it was, this was her first experience and, given the accident that took Colt's life, she was very apprehensive.

On the ride Chester Steele reminisced about Colt and the many antics he pulled on the ranch. "He was a rip—always into something. One time he was driving his daddy's pick-em-up truck and decided to take a shortcut. Got stuck in mud up to the axles. He and his pal were out in the middle of nowhere. His friend tells him to leave the truck and start walking. Now, Colt, he doesn't ever give up. He finds two good size branches and ties them to the rear tires with some rope. They stick out from the tires like oars. Colt hops in and slowly spins the wheels. When the branches come around and hit the ground the truck lifts up out of the mud driving over the branches and moves forward. He bounced that truck again and again until they were completely out of the mud." Stephanie enjoyed hearing that and all the other tales about Colt that Chester Steele shared. Unfortunately, it also caused her to miss him all the more.

That evening she had dinner with Colt's parents, an uncle, and two cousins. His sister was supposed to arrive the next morning. Clinton MacIntyre was a tower of strength. What he was feeling inside remained hidden. He expressed pride in having such an admirable son and regret that their time together was far too short. What started as a subdued dinner quickly became more energized and lighthearted as memories of Colt's antics were shared. Stephanie found she was more of an observer than anything else. She was an observer who came to know what a fine human being was absent from that table.

At one point Clinton MacIntyre told the group that their guest, Stephanie Ellis, had planned on being partners with Colt in an international adoption enterprise. He went on to explain that Colt was far more interested and dedicated to following that path than even she realized. The level of enthusiasm he heard during a conversation with his son made it clear that this was his passion, his hope, and his dream. Clinton finished by stating, "I pressured Ms. Ellis to make a commitment to help build that dream. It was a father's zeal. My support remains, but I wish to give the young lady the courtesy of allowing her to decline the opportunity if she feels she was unduly coerced."

After getting over her initial surprise, Stephanie addressed the group. "When Colt and I were introduced it was because we shared a common interest—international adoption. Neither of us had any direct experience in that area, but we agreed to do whatever was needed to create and run a service that would help children. I only wish

I were already in a position to do some good. There are two Vietnamese orphans who need a safe home that I would help, right now. Unfortunately, it would take an act of Congress and me being appropriately trained for that to happen." She paused having gone off track. Then looked at Clinton MacIntyre and said, "I continue to be committed to making Colt's dream reality."

Later in the evening Stephanie sat on the back deck of the huge ranch house and looked out over a pond, small patch of trees, and wide open spaces. It was hard for her to believe that she was actually there. She only wished that Colt had been there with her. A part of her would even welcome another spectral visit. A cool breeze made her shiver and she looked around for Colt. Instead, it was Clinton MacIntyre who walked out of the house and toward her.

"Colt and I fished that pond when he was young," the older gentleman observed.

"He looked forward to fishing with you when he got home," Stephanie said sadly.

Clinton smiled a father's smile, "We made it a competition." He walked over to the rail and looked off into the distance, "Who caught the first fish, the largest fish, who cast his line farther, how many total fish, you name it. It was a game."

Stephanie couldn't help thinking how lucky Colt was to have a father while he was growing up.

Clinton MacIntyre turned and walked over to Stephanie and sat opposite her, "Tell me more about these Vietnamese orphans."

"There really isn't much I can tell you," she admitted, "My friend told me about them because of a letter he received from a Marine."

"Does the Marine want to adopt them?"

"I don't think so. I think he just wants to find them a home away from the war."

"I tell you what—when you get back home find out what you can about these young'uns. Call me with what you have."

"It might not be much."

"As Colt would say, 'it's more than we have now.'" He leaned forward and said, "Now, let's talk about you."

As Stephanie lay in bed the following morning she thought about that conversation. Colt's father offered her an opportunity to attend the University of Texas in Austin to get her degree. If possible, he would help her get part-time employment with social services in order to get practical experience. In her spare time the two of them would research and plan the Colt MacIntyre International Adoption Service. If she agreed they would make a trip to Austin to begin making arrangements. Stephanie remembered stating that it all sounded so attractive but she wasn't sure she could get into the University of Texas and definitely could not afford the tuition.

Clinton MacIntyre's only comment was, "You let me worry about that."

Stephanie got out of bed and dressed. When she entered the kitchen a half hour later she found Colt's mother sitting at the table. Maureen MacIntyre offered Stephanie coffee and offered to cook some breakfast. Stephanie accepted the coffee but wasn't hungry.

"Empathy is a mother's curse," Maureen said softly, "I keep seeing my boy in the final moments afraid and helpless. My instinct is to comfort him," her voice takes on a pitiful tone, "but I can't." She looked around as if seeking something, though she wasn't. It's no more than the actions of someone who is lost not knowing in which direction to go. She fumbled with her coffee cup and slowly rocked back and forth.

Stephanie could see the poor woman was in turmoil not knowing how to deal with her loss.

"My boy so loved life. Why his was so short, I just don't understand."

Stephanie went to the stove and got the coffee pot. After she filled both of their cups, she said, "It's sad, but the better the person the greater the pain. I believe if Colt were here in spirit he would take your hand and tell you that he is proud to be his mother's child. He would thank you for giving him faith, teaching him to work hard, to be honest, and to care. You taught him right from wrong, allowed his imagination to run free, and made his world beautiful."

Maureen MacIntyre looked up at Stephanie and said, "Thank you."

"Mrs. MacIntyre, I know you and Mr. MacIntyre are in pain and grieving. I came here to honor Colt, but I'm not sure that I can be his monument. He deserves to have his name on something that is special and successful in so many meaningful ways. I appreciate Mr. MacIntyre's offer to help me with education, employment, and the founding of Colt's dream, but there are so many other ways to do it more quickly and with less risk of failure. I can't take advantage of you two in a weak moment when you may not be thinking as clearly as you will six months from now. It is better that I return to New Jersey and continue my education there. Maybe when I graduate I can get a job at the Colt MacIntyre International Adoption Service."

"Miss Ellis," Maureen MacIntyre said with greater strength, "Clinton doesn't have a weak bone in his body. If he asked you to do this and offered to help, it is because he has a firm grip on the situation and believes this is the best way to go about it. My boy trusted you and my husband trusts you—that's enough."

"Who broke into the liquor store on Ninth Avenue? I think it was Carl Pythacyk," Detective Michael Donovan said from his desk at the Midtown North Precinct.

"So, now every crime we don't have a suspect for you're going to blame on this Carl Pythacyk fellow?"

"That sounds about right."

Detective Akimoto smiled. She noted, "The poor guy went all that time thinking he was wanted, then had the courage to turn himself in, and finds out he wasn't even being sought. I think that young lady with the dog was part of the motivation."

"Could be. It's amazing what a guy will do for a broad."

An entire town turned out for a memorial service to show their respect. Saint Francis Episcopal Church was filled to capacity. Without question, the MacIntyre family and Colt MacIntyre in particular were held in high esteem. Stephanie sat with the family. At one point when she glanced back at the growing crowd she saw a familiar face—Jack Moore.

After he learned of the memorial, Jack had called Ryoya Akimoto to give her the details. She appreciated his thoughtfulness and told him she would not be able to attend. At that time he hadn't made a decision. The next day Jack made arrangements to make a trip to Victoria, Texas. He arrived the morning of the service.

After the service, at the gravesite, Jack spoke with the MacIntyres and was invited out to the house. In the late afternoon, he found himself on the back deck with Colt's parents, sister, and Stephanie Ellis. It was then that it was revealed that Jack Moore introduced Stephanie Ellis to Colt MacIntrye.

Jack explained, "Colt met a lot of people in his quest to see the elephant. After meeting those people who adopted children from Korea he became driven. He said he didn't want to spend his life barkin' at a Knot."

Clinton MacIntyre smiled, "He pulled that cowboy jargon on you, I see."

"He had me all balled up. Made me feel like a ten-cent man. But, he had a spark that lit fires inside of you. I liked being around him and will always value a far too short a friendship."

Colt's sister, Amy, asked, "Did he mention me at any time?"

Jack looked at the young woman who was about five years younger than Colt. "He told me he was looking forward to getting home and seeing you," Jack lied.

"When he wanted to go off and see the world, I told him he was being foolish. We argued and I said some mean things. In truth, I didn't want him to go because I would miss him. I didn't answer his letters and now I can't tell him that I'm sorry." She neither cried nor showed any emotion. It was clear that she was holding it together but feeling powerful emotions inside.

Jack was compelled to add, "He never mentioned any disagreement, only that he wanted to see you. I think he understood."

"Mr. Moore," Clinton interjected, "You are a newspaper reporter, correct."

"Correct."

"I'd like to ask a favor."

Jack turned his attention to Clinton MacIntyre.

"This little lady," Clinton indicated Stephanie, "has very limited information about some orphans in Vietnam. Can you use your skills to gather more in-depth facts about them?"

"I'm not really sure."

"All I ask is that you give it a try."

"I can do that, but may not find out anything."

"Good."

The rest of the evening was spent chatting about Colt, Texas, politics, the weather, the Mets, and people. It was done over a few glasses of good bourbon.

At 10:30 the first message ever sent on ARPANET, which stood for Advanced Research Projects Agency Network, was logged. It was one of the world's first "packet switching networks" a progenitor of the internet. At the time, all communications worked through circuits comprised of intermediary lines that led from point A to Point B. The concept of packet switching sends data on a single communications link to a designated machine. Interface Message Processors (IMPs) act like modern routers. On this particular day, by comparison to modern technology, these communication interfaces were archaic.

The initial ARPANET consisted of four IMPs: the first at the University of California, Los Angeles; the second at Stanford Research Institute's Augmentation Research Center; the third at University of California, Santa Barbara; and the fourth at University of Utah's Computer Science Department. The first message on the ARPANET was sent by UCLA student programmer Charley Kline from Boelter Hall. He transmitted from the university's Sigma 7 Host computer to the Stanford Research Institute's 940 Host computer. The message was a text word "login." Unfortunately, after the "l" and "o" were transmitted the system crashed. Therefore, literally the first message transmitted over the ARPANET was "lo." An hour later the full message was delivered.

Wanda Six Trees listened to an old radio given to her by Chief Michael.

87: Friday – October 31, 1969

Matthew Ellis sat at the little table in their apartment and listened to Stephanie as she related her experience in Texas. If she wished, she could begin classes at the University of Texas in Austin during the spring semester, a part-time job opportunity was arranged with a religious-based children's services non-profit, and she together with Clinton MacIntyre would begin creating the Colt MacIntyre International Adoption Service. Her obvious enthusiasm was beyond anything Matt had seen in his daughter since waking up from a coma. It both warmed his heart and broke it.

With an air of sadness and resignation, Stephanie indicated that she couldn't go to Texas and leave her father alone under the present circumstances. Immediately, Matt reassured her that he was fully capable of taking care of himself. His health had progressed to a point where he could get a job and combined with his disability payments would have enough to allow him to keep the apartment. Matt smiled, held his daughter's hand, and said warmly, "Your future is in Texas and I couldn't be happier for you. We'll talk on the phone so you can keep me up-to-date on your progress. I love you and want you to be happy. Who knows, maybe someday, I'll move to Texas."

"I just don't know if I can leave you," Stephanie said softly.

After a telephone conversation with Stephanie, Ritchie wrote a letter to Wellington Marsh in Vietnam. He gave the young Marine an update on being 4F, as well as working for his father. "My long hair is safe," he joked. Next, he gave an account of the surprising turn-of-events with Carl. "Lady Laurel has her knight." Finally, he explained about the interest expressed by a wealthy Texas family in the two Vietnamese orphans. "Send me as much information about the children as you can. Can't promise anything, but it's a chance. Maybe this time we can save both." As he finished the letter Ritchie thought about the amazing adventure the three of them had shared. In a short period of time a bond developed among them that was stronger than any other he had experienced in his life. He finished by writing, "Don't take any risks and come home safe."

A firefight began on the trail that led from the Cambodian and Laos borders to the paved road than ran southeast to Kontum and Pleiku. CAP Squad 1-6-2 had placed themselves on the north side of the trail on a ridge. It provided ample cover and a good view of the trail. Tread marks from the North Vietnamese armor that passed through a little more than two weeks earlier were still visible. The plan was to harass any enemy troops that passed on the trail and then dissolve into the jungle. If they were pursued it would be in a direction away from Quy Hoa.

The team had spent the last few days creating trails leading into mountainous terrain far north of Quy Hoa. They wanted to leave the impression that somewhere in those hills was a village. To add to the deception they left artifacts of a village around. By all appearances, hidden somewhere in that rough terrain, there was an undiscovered village. The ruse would keep any curious interlopers busy for a long time searching.

Just when they settled down on their perch overlooking the trail a Viet Cong patrol arrived. They apparently had the idea of using the same high ground for an ambush as they left the trail and started to climb in the direction of CAP Squad 1-6-2. Initially outnumbered, surprise allowed the Marines to gain an edge. There was less than one-hundred yards between them on the hillside with the Americans holding the high ground when they opened fire. After a barrage of bullets flew in both directions fighting became more sporadic as combatants maneuvered for position and only fired when targets presented themselves. It turned into a standoff. Numbers were still on the side of the Viet Cong as they slowly made their way on the two flanks of the Marines. They planned to climb higher than the Americas so that they would be able to effect a cross fire.

Lance Corporal Marsh picked up on the movement. It was then he remembered his father talking about tactics on a rooftop in Detroit. "If you know what your opponent is going to do you can develop your own tactics." Wellington could see that the enemy was trying to flank his team and put them in a cross fire. This he could not allow. The terrain was relatively steep. It was also heavily wooded so there were ample places to hide and shoot from. Then it struck him, they had divided their force. Quickly, he pulled his team close in and told them they would attack the smaller force on their left. With hand signals he gave them their orders.

CAP team 1-6-2 moved rapidly to their left and still holding the high ground engaged the approaching VC who were climbing toward them. A brief firefight ensued. The few remaining Viet Cong retreated down the slope as CAP Team 1-6-2 faded into the jungle. The other half of the VC patrol didn't follow.

A company that would forever change the face of retail was incorporated on this day. Wal-Mart Stores Incorporated became reality seven years after being founded in 1962 by Sam Walton.

Samuel Moore Walton was born in Kingfisher, Oklahoma on March 29, 1918. He grew up during the Great Depression. To help with family finances he milked the family cow and sold the surplus, delivered *Columbia Daily Tribune* newspapers, and sold magazine subscriptions.

While in the eighth grade in Shelbina, Missouri he became the youngest Eagle Scout in the state's history. Sam then attended the University of Missouri as an ROTC cadet. While there he worked various odd jobs including waiting tables in exchange for meals. He also became a member of the national military honor society Scabbard and Blade and served as president of Burall Bible Class, a large class made up of students from the University of Missouri and Stephens College. Walton graduated in 1940 with a bachelor's degree in economics.

Upon graduation Sam Walton joined J. C. Penney as a management trainee in Des Moines, Iowa. The position paid $75 a month. With the onset of World War II, Walton resigned from J. C. Penney and went to work at a DuPont munitions plant near Tulsa, Oklahoma. Shortly, thereafter, he joined the U.S. Army Intelligence Corps, supervising security at aircraft plants and prisoner of war camps. When he left the Army he had reached the rank of Captain.

In 1945, at the age of 26, Walton purchased a Ben Franklin variety store franchise in Newport, Arkansas from the Butler Brothers chain. He did so with a

$20,000 loan from his father-in-law, plus $5,000 he had saved from his time in the Army. Right from the beginning he introduced many innovative concepts. Sales more than doubled at the first store which led to a second. After scouting numerous locations by automobile with his brother James they purchased a small second-hand airplane. James had been a pilot during the war and Sam eventually also became a pilot. By 1962, along with his brother, he owned 16 stores in Arkansas, Missouri, and Kansas.

The first Wal-Mart Discount City store opened on July 2, 1962, in Rogers, Arkansas. Walton's assistant, Bob Bogle, who was responsible for signage, came up with the name "Wal-Mart" for the new chain. Originally, Walton made a determined effort to market American-made products. By 1967, the company grew to 24 stores across the state of Arkansas. In 1968, Wal-Mart opened its first stores outside of Arkansas in Missouri and Oklahoma.

The future world's largest retailer was born.

Jack walked into More-Or-Less on this Halloween day to find Harry Van Ryker and his fiancée Amanda Shay trying to look like Sonny and Cher.

"Oh, I've got to find another place to get my booze," he stated as he walked to his favorite barstool. After studying the two behind the bar Jack spoke to Amanda, "With that long black wig every guy in the bar, and possibly some gals, are going to hit on you."

Amanda ran her hand down the long hair and replied, "I hope so."

"Hey!" was Harry's response.

Amanda turned to Harry and said, "I was thinking of tips, dear."

He looked at her and smiled, "You have fun, just remember who's taking you home."

"And in whose arms you're gonna be," Jack sang the next line of the song, "so, darling, save the last dance for me."

Harry looked at Jack and deadpanned, "Don't quit your day job."

Amanda wandered off and Harry leaned forward and rested his elbows on the bar, "She's glad you agreed to be best man. We set the date. It's December 20."

"I'll be there."

"You seem preoccupied—what's up?"

"Oh, is it obvious? I've been working on a story but can't seem to get any concrete information to go on. It could be something big, but I keep coming up empty. The linchpin is a woman."

"Isn't it always?"

"Yeah, her name is Lida Petropoulos, however, by all indications she doesn't exist and never did."

"What'd she do?"

"She and this guy in New Jersey apparently sold misrepresented poor quality wire to NASA. It may have been the cause of the Apollo I fire that killed Gus Grissom, Ed White, and Roger Chaffee."

"You're kidding."

"I seem to get a little information here and a little there but nothing conclusive. I can't locate anything on Lida Petropoulos and the guy in New Jersey had been in an automobile accident and in a coma for six years. He can't remember shit."

"So, what are you going to do?"

"At this point, I have to shelf it. Unless something turns up there are no more leads to follow." Jack nodded his head and concluded, "If she exists, she did an outstanding job of staying under the radar. Without question, this wasn't her first scam."

"Nor, will it be her last."

"I just can't put any more time into it even if it is a big story. It's a big story that eludes me."

"If they sold bad wire to NASA, who else did they sell wire to?" Harry asked.

"That, my friend, is a good question. Maybe there is one more lead to pursue." Jack finished his drink and headed for the door, "Thanks." He passed Amanda on the way and said, "Dump the bum run away with me, Cher baby."

"Thanks, that's the worst offer I've had all evening."

Lai Ngoc Linh used a rope with a slipknot to try to catch a goat that had escaped. He got irritated and cursed as he missed again and again.

88: Monday – November 3, 1969

Carl and Laurel stood on a hillside holding hands as they looked up at the sky. Snowflakes drifted down landing on their faces. It was only a flurry but was the first snow of the year. In the hills of northwestern Pennsylvania heavy snow is common due to lake effects from Lake Erie. Carl grew up in New York City where snow was an event that usually didn't last very long. His winter memories were of black snow after it had been on the ground longer than a day.

"Tá an gheimhridh ag teacht," Laurel said. She looked at Carl who was obviously confused and translated, "Winter is coming."

"And me without a coat or boots."

"We need to go shopping," she said excitedly pulling him in the direction of the farmhouse.

"At least now I don't have to fear being recognized," Carl said as he was dragged along.

They borrowed the farm's 1959 Chevrolet station wagon and headed to Warren. Laurel drove as Carl didn't have a license. As he sat in the passenger seat watching countryside go by he remembered Ray Esposito telling him to get a license. Even though he was glad to be away from that life he still liked Ray Esposito, Fat Tony, and East River Vito. He couldn't help but smile remembering the humor and ribbing that went on.

Outdoor gear was foreign to a city boy. Laurel took over. In the end he had a cache of outdoor gear which included a goose down parka with a fur lined hood, waterproof deep snow pac boots, hiking boots, leather fedora, insulated gloves, scarves, shirts, pants, and thermal underwear. When he commented on the underwear, Laurel said, "Coinnigh mé te san oíche. How else are you going to keep me warm at night?"

Livia Petralia strolled casually along Fifth Avenue. Dressed impeccably well and fashionable her passing was noted by men and women alike. Her long dark hair, finely chiseled features, and seductive walk were enhanced by a flocked Milano knit long-sleeve navy dress, Monili-Collar graphite dyed lamb shearling coat, curve-conforming suede black high-heel knee length boots, and hand-woven grey cashmere scarf. She was a standout even on crowded Fifth Avenue. By all appearances she was unaware of the effect she had on those around her, however, nothing could be further from the truth. Keen awareness of all that surrounded her was a well-developed skill. A slight glance at an admirer most often caused them look away in embarrassment, move awkwardly, or on-occasion trip or walk into an object or other person.

On this morning she was shopping. For Livia only the best would do. Many establishments on Fifth Avenue offered the level of quality, luxury, and uniqueness that she desired. After an hour she became bored with her quest for the perfect color or size and decided to have a bit of lunch. It had been a while since she dined at Eleanor's which became her destination.

As usual, Eleanor's was crowded at lunchtime. In fact, it was always crowded.

However, when Livia Petralia entered she miraculously found herself at the head of the line. A smile and nod and unspoken possibility of an afternoon of sensual pleasure was all it took.

When the maitre d' began to usher Livia to a table, a waiting diner spoke up, "Whoa, buddy, as much as I can understand your actions, I winked and smiled just as well, and I wager that I'm just as hungry." He looked at Livia and said almost apologetically, "for food and nourishment, that is." When she turned to face him and he saw her face he added, "Ah, hell, give her my table."

Livia smiled, acknowledged her benefactor's existence, and with a warm and inviting tone offered, "Would you join me?"

Jack Moore and Livia Petralia were led to a table situated along one of the walls. He was fascinated with his attractive and obviously sophisticated lunch partner. Part of him wondered how it happened. Usually, his big mouth and outspoken manner got him thrown out of places. This time he got thrown for a loop.

"I'm sorry I made such a scene," Jack apologized.

"Don't spoil it."

"OK," Jack said a little confused.

"You stood up for yourself," Livia leaned back and appraised the man opposite her, "I like that."

Jack found that he didn't have an answer so he felt it better to leave it alone. Instead, he offered his hand and introduced himself, "I'm Jack Moore."

"Livia Petralia."

"Livia; that's an interesting name."

"I've been told it means olive," she said. As she seductively leaned forward she added in a hushed voice, "Maybe, that's why I like martinis."

"Then by all means we should order some."

Livia sat back as she pondered, "Jack; that's an interesting name."

"It's short for Jack, which means able to lift an automobile."

"You must be powerful," she replied with a slight smile.

Jack returned her smile.

With martinis ordered the conversation continued, "Are you from New York?" Jack asked.

"No, I'm only visiting."

"Vacation, business, sightseeing, boyfriend?"

"Shopping."

"Well, you came to the right place."

"I'm aware of that. And you are a New Yorker," she stated rather than asked.

Jack looked down at his suit, "Does it show?"

"A great deal about you shows. More than you realize."

"Oh, what else about me do you see?"

"Let's not ruin the moment."

Silence blanketed the table. Jack wondered who this extraordinary woman was. She was obviously educated, sophisticated, cultured, and confident. Rather than a potential conquest he saw her as a unique personality in his never-ending search for answers as to who we are as human beings. Through the years he had met and interacted with so many diverse types it was sometimes hard to imagine that we are all of the same species. As he regarded her he experienced a flashback to Woodstock and the teens who gave him shelter during a rainstorm. Night Bird came to mind. By contrast she was innocent, not sophisticated, probably not highly educated, yet more connected to life than he or his dining partner. Night Bird rejected the artificial trappings of society. She didn't require expensive attire or practiced gestures to define her. She simply was Night Bird. It was pure and real and unadulterated and refreshing. On the other hand, Livia was a designer homo sapien. What he saw was the carefully forged image so perfectly fabricated that it provided a protective shield around an imperfect, scared, lost mortal. He wondered if she wore designer underwear. There was, indeed, something alluring about her that was enhanced by her faux image. Her appearance made his loins tingle and testosterone sent signals to his brain washing away logical impulses. While Night Bird was an acoustic guitar, Livia was an orchestra playing *Bolero*.

"You seem lost in thought," Livia observed, "Anything you wish to share?"

"Do you like music?" Jack asked.

"I do."

"*Bolero?*"

"Too pedestrian."

"Bach?"

"Tchaikovsky."

The *1812 Overture* began playing in Jack's head. He saw in his mind's eye the end of a children's television program where Quaker Puffed Rice was shot out of cannons toward the screen to the sound of the finale of the *1812 Overture*. He smiled.

"Ah, I see you know Tchaikovsky," Livia concluded. "And, what music do you enjoy?"

"Frank Sinatra, Sammy Davis, Jr., Kingston Trio, The Turtles, and Miles Davis."

"You like jazz?" Livia tilted her head and gazed at her dining partner, "Are you familiar with *In A Silent Way?*"

"Absolutely. What about Ella Fitzgerald *How High The Moon?*"

For the next half hour as they ate two strangers discussed jazz. In the end it was an enjoyable lunch and Jack picked up the tab. They parted when Jack put Livia Petralia in a taxi. He had given her his business card but didn't expect her to ever use it.

Livia Petralia arrived at her next destination for a two o'clock meeting with a young executive from an industrial construction company. They had arranged to meet away from his office at a coffee shop. This was his first face-to-face encounter and he was visibly impressed. They sat off in a corner.

"As we discussed, you have a desperate need for case hardened 18-8 Stainless Steel alloy custom keyway security bolts at a competitive price," Livia stated in a no-nonsense manner.

"Exactly," the young man looked around nervously then spoke in a low voice, "A bolt may not seem like much of an expense, but by the sheer number that will be incorporated into the project it represents a significant investment. It literally could change the nature of our bid."

"Don't you worry, Ira, we're going to help your company win that bid," a captivating smile punctuated the reassurance.

"I know I shouldn't have shared the costs provided by our regular supplier but, well," he blushed ever so slightly, "you convinced me on the phone."

"And, now I'm going to show you how not only will we win that bid, but you will enjoy the rewards of your extra effort," she moved her head to toss her long dark hair out of her face. A piece of paper that she retrieved from her purse slid across the table face down. Ira Hadstein reached for the paper. Livia's hand gently held his hand down, "There are three numbers on this document. The first is our regular price for the exact specified type of bolt in the sizes and quantities required. The second number is our special price for a comparable alternative product that your company will be charged. The third number is what LPAmerica will pay you as a commission for the business."

"I don't understand."

Livia removed her hand and said, "Look at the paper."

The young man did as instructed. His eyes grew large as he reviewed the document. He sat silent for a prolonged period of time. Finally, he looked up and stated, "The first price is higher than our regular supplier. However, the second price is significantly lower—unbelievably lower."

"In order to give you that extraordinary price our technicians made a few adjustments to the specs," Livia explained. "To begin, the raw material mixture was adjusted from 72% stainless steel, 18% chromium, 10% nickel to 66% stainless steel, 22% chromium, and 12% nickel. Our tests found it results in the same tensile and yield strength at a 7.5% material savings. Then by doing "through hardening" rather than "case hardening" we eliminate a time consuming and costly step."

"But, through hardened metal is usually more brittle than softer metal so that approach is not suitable for our application. Case hardening will provide a bolt that won't fracture because the soft core will absorb stresses without cracking while the harder outside will provide adequate wear resistance."

"True if you use the 72-18-10 mixture. With our adjustment to 66-22-12 it improves the strength and hardness of the metal. And, my friend, it is able to handle every kind of stress we tested without any failure or cracking."

"I . . . I can't . . . take the chance. This project and others like it that will follow is a nuclear power plant. There are specific tolerances that must be met."

"If your company doesn't win that bid the whole question will be moot, won't it?"

"We just don't have time to test your bolts and the project manager wouldn't even entertain the idea at this late hour."

"So, don't tell him."

"What?"

"I'm offering you a superior product to what was spec'ed at significant savings. By all appearances it is the same stainless steel alloy that was specified. No one is going to melt down the product and then calibrate the mixture to determine if there is an insignificant variation. If they want to test its strength they will find it outperforms the minimum requirements of 100,000–150,000 psi."

"But, over time, the enormous stresses experienced at a nuclear facility may eventually lead to premature failure of the fastener."

"May eventually? Can you guarantee that of the bolts manufactured to exact specifications none will ever fail?"

"Of course not."

"So, my technical experts come up with a better product by tweaking the raw material mix and offer it to you at incredible savings that almost guarantees your company wins the bid and you worry that one bolt sometime in the distant future may eventually fail. The facility will most likely reach its life expectancy and be shut down before that happens." Livia sat back and showed her disappointment.

Ira Hadstein sat silently, once more. He concluded that she did make sense in one aspect—if they don't win the bid the whole question about stainless steel alloy bolts didn't mean a thing. He also knew there were redundancies on redundancies on redundancies and an overabundant use of component parts at these plants. For instance, at a pipe joint with a gasket that could adequately be joined using eight bolts generally twelve were specified. A full third of the bolts could fail and the joint would still be sound. He re-examined the paper Livia had given him.

When Livia saw Ira look at the document once again she knew she had a sale. She waited.

"How do I explain this incredible price?" he asked.

"You don't."

"How do I do that?"

"Ira, your bid is a summary of all the materials, services, fees, and outside costs your firm anticipates to fulfill the contract. There are thousands of numbers. You are responsible for a large number of products and materials. Do you really think they are going to scrutinize the bid to such a degree that they will even know that the cost of bolts is substantially lower than industry standards? The only person who would know that fact is the one who deals with that product—you."

"I never thought of that."

"Ira, I want your firm to win this bid and others that follow. If we make this happen we all will prosper—me, your company, and you."

"About that, I'm not sure that a commission would be appropriate. It seems like a conflict of interest."

"It's my way of showing you that I'm being honest with you. I could have put that money in my pocket. You would never know. That is not how I work. By showing you there is some excess profit and sharing it with you we will have a better relationship going forward."

"I just don't know."

"OK, you have a choice. Take the money and know there will be more in the future or apply the money to the cost estimate and I'll thank you another way. How about a blow job?"

Ira tried not to show his surprise at Livia's offer. He nervously looked at the commission, which represented a good sum of money, and observed, "That would be an expensive blow job."

Livia laughed, "Take the money. If you play your cards right—who knows."

At 9:00 p.m. Eastern Standard Time President Richard Nixon addressed the nation. "Good evening, my fellow Americans: Tonight I want to talk to you on a subject of deep concern to all Americans and to many people in all parts of the world–the war in Vietnam."

He began by describing the situation he found when he was inaugurated on January 20, 1969. "The war had been going on for 4 years. 31,000 Americans had been killed in action. The training program for the South Vietnamese was behind schedule. 540,000 Americans were in Vietnam with no plans to reduce the number. No progress had been made at the negotiations in Paris and the United States had not put forth a comprehensive peace proposal. The war was causing deep division at home and criticism from many of our friends as well as our enemies abroad."

He then told how America became involved in Vietnam. "In response to the request of the Government of South Vietnam, President Eisenhower sent economic aid and military equipment to assist the people of South Vietnam in their efforts to prevent a Communist takeover. Seven years ago, President Kennedy sent 16,000 military personnel to Vietnam as combat advisers. Four years ago, President Johnson sent American combat forces to South Vietnam."

Nixon explained why simply leaving was not a realistic option. "For the South Vietnamese, our precipitate withdrawal would inevitably allow the Communists to repeat the massacres which followed their takeover in the North 15 years before. They then murdered more than 50,000 people and hundreds of thousands more died in slave labor camps."

In less than a year the President attempted to find an amicable solution using various approaches which he outlined. "Soon after my election, through an individual who is directly in contact on a personal basis with the leaders of North Vietnam, I made two private offers for a rapid, comprehensive settlement. Hanoi's replies called in effect for our surrender before negotiations. I, personally, have met on a number of occasions with representatives of the Soviet Government to enlist their assistance in getting meaningful negotiations started. I sent a letter to Ho Chi Minh. I received Ho Chi Minh's reply on August 30, 3 days before his death. It simply reiterated the public position North Vietnam had taken at Paris and flatly rejected my initiative. No progress whatever has been made except agreement on the shape of the bargaining table."

His strategy, given no interest to negotiate on the part of North Vietnam, was summarized, "In the previous administration, we Americanized the war in Vietnam. In this administration, we are Vietnamizing the search for peace." He added, "After 5 years of Americans going into Vietnam, we are finally bringing American men home. By December 15, over 60,000 men will have been withdrawn from South Vietnam— including 20 percent of all of our combat forces."

Richard Nixon was a man who inherited an unsolvable problem. He tried to initiate change while being condemned for a lack of progress. This left him with a choice that he made on the public stage. "I can order an immediate, precipitate withdrawal of all Americans from Vietnam without regard to the effects of that action. Or, we can persist in our search for a just peace through a negotiated settlement if possible, or through continued implementation of our plan for Vietnamization if necessary—a plan in which we will withdraw all of our forces from Vietnam on a schedule in accordance with our program, as the South Vietnamese become strong enough to defend their own freedom. I have chosen this second course. It is not the easy way. It is the right way."

The President finished his address, "Let historians not record that when America was the most powerful nation in the world we passed on the other side of the road and allowed the last hopes for peace and freedom of millions of people to be suffocated by the forces of totalitarianism. And so tonight—to you, the great silent majority of my fellow Americans—I ask for your support."

Anna Six Trees sat silently and watched Lauma White Feather do her jingle dress dance and wondered if she could ever be that graceful.

89: Sunday – November 9, 1969

Amanda Shay and Ryoya Akimoto sat opposite each other at a table in a small restaurant in midtown Manhattan. It was a pleasant cool Sunday morning. They had decided to meet to discuss plans for Amanda and Harry's wedding that was a mere six weeks away.

"We want simple but elegant," Amanda said.

"Have you selected a church?"

"Yes, we agreed on Holy Trinity Lutheran Church on Central Park West and 65th Street. It fits our religious needs, the pastor is a dynamic speaker, it's a beautiful building that was built in 1904, and they have an outstanding musical reputation. Last year they introduced their Bach Vespers program."

"I'm not familiar with that—what is it?"

"I'm not an expert. I can only tell you what I read. Johann Sebastian Bach, in the 1700s was an organist and composer. He wrote sacred cantatas for the liturgy and other occasions for the Lutheran church. A cantata is music meant to be sung with by a soloist or choir. Over a period of time, Bach wrote one a month for years. There are hundreds of them. Holy Trinity is the first church in the Western Hemisphere to perform the cantatas of Bach on the days designated by him corresponding to the liturgical calendar. Bach Vespers are played on Sunday evenings from October through April. This is the second year they are doing it."

"Is there a Bach cantata for a wedding?" Ryoya asked.

"Yes, they generally include soprano arias so we have to decide if we can afford the expense."

"I'm not familiar with Lutheran weddings," Ryoya admitted.

"A Lutheran wedding is primarily a worship service. They reserve socializing and celebration for the wedding reception, leaving the ceremony as a time for worshipping God and honoring the marriage. Harry and I like the idea."

"I look forward to experiencing the whole thing."

Amanda nibbled at a piece of toast lost in thought. She looked at Ryoya and tried to ascertain what her friend was feeling given the turn of events in their lives. Unfortunately, Ryoya's expression and actions revealed nothing. The only way she would know how her friend was feeling was to ask, "Ryoya, are you alright with all of this?"

"It's not up to me," Ryoya responded, "It's what you and Harry want that is important."

"No, I mean with us getting married so quickly, Jack as best man, and you and Jack . . ." her voice trailed off.

Ryoya smiled. It wasn't a happy smile as much as one for a friend. She said in a level unemotional tone, "You and Harry are adults. There's no rule as to how long people have to know each other before they fall in love. If you were teenagers I'd have reservations."

"And, Jack?"

"A good choice for best man. He and Harry go back a long way."

"What about you and Jack?"

"That shouldn't be your concern."

Amanda pressed on, "You are my concern—your happiness."

"My happiness is my responsibility—not yours."

"You know what I mean."

Ryoya sipped her coffee, put down the cup, looked directly at Amanda, and explained, "As a teenager, I lived in a relocation camp during the war. My parents lost everything. In a dirty dusty hell hole called Gila River 13,000 people formed a community. Traditions and culture gave us strength and an identity. I graduated from high school at Gila River. After the war we rebuilt our lives in New York. When soldiers who fought in the Pacific looked at us it was with hate in their eyes. Some spat on the sidewalk. I turned twenty-one in 1950, five years after the war, and I still looked down at the ground when I passed men with war wounds. Remarks, like arrows, left scars. I am nisei, second generation Japanese-American. My parents are issei, born in Japan immigrated to America. They made the decision to leave Japan and seek a new life. Maybe, that's why it is easier for them to abandon their culture than it is for me. At the World Series game when my father presented Jack's ring I saw a man who had been treated like an animal by the nation he loved. He endured and forgave and started once more with nothing but courage. I looked into his eyes but couldn't see his heart. Was he making one more sacrifice without complaint? Was this "shikata ga nai" another time when "it cannot be helped" and resignation that he is powerless? Maybe we nisei cling more tightly to culture and tradition because we witnessed our parents having it stripped away. No one should have to see their father kneel in the mud and bow. He used "gaman" which means perseverance to remain silent when I became a police officer. At that time, I didn't understand. Now, I do. I will not be the instrument that causes him to give up any more of his heritage."

Amanda sat in stunned silence. Her heart ached for her friend. At the same time she felt guilty for not having been more aware of the turmoil Ryoya faced alone.

Ryoya smiled and took Amanda's hand, "You didn't ask for my life history. I am so happy for you and Harry. Don't spend a moment being concerned about me. This is your time and we have to stay focused. We don't have a lot of time to get everything done."

"Ryoya, I . . ."

"Did you pick out rings, yet?"

"We're going shopping tomorrow."

"And, did that tightwad get you an engagement ring?"

"Tomorrow. Ryoya . . ."

"What about a dress?"

"I want your help with that."

"We should start this week. I'll let you know when I'm off," Ryoya said.

Amanda concluded, "You're not going to talk about it anymore, are you?"

"What about a reception? Do you plan to have one?"

Early in the morning a group of approximately 250 Indians from different tribes gathered at Fisherman's Wharf in San Francisco. They called themselves "Indians of All Tribes" and planned to boat over to Alcatraz, formerly a federal penitentiary that closed in 1963, and claim it for the Indian people. The boats they expected did not arrive so they abandoned their plans.

One chartered boat, the Monte Cristo, was boarded by Richard Oakes (Mohawk), Jim Vaughn (Cherokee), Joe Bill (Eskimo), Ross Harden (Ho-Chunk) and Jerry Hatch. It proceeded to a place near the island where they jumped overboard and swam ashore. In the name of Indians of All Tribes they claimed Alcatraz citing the 1868 Treaty of Fort Laramie which returned to Native American people all retired, abandoned, and out-of-use federal lands. As Alcatraz had been declared as surplus land by the government it fit that definition.

The Occupation of Alcatraz Island was about far more than land. They wanted to focus attention on broken treaties, broken promises, and treatment under the 16 year old Indian Termination Policy. In 1953 the United States government began terminating Indian reservations and relocating inhabitants, many to urban areas. To illustrate their position the Indians of All Tribes issued the Alcatraz Proclamation.

To the Great White Father and his People 1969

> We, the native Americans, re-claim the land known as Alcatraz Island in the name of all American Indians by right of discovery. We wish to be fair and honorable in our dealings with the Caucasian inhabitants of this land, and hereby offer the following treaty: We will purchase said Alcatraz Island for 24 dollars in glass beads and red cloth, a precedent set by the white man's purchase of a similar island about 300 years ago. We know that $24 in trade goods for these sixteen acres is more than was paid when Manhattan Island was sold, but we know that land values have risen over the years. Our offer of $1.24 per acre is greater than the 47 cents per acre the white men are now paying the California Indians for their land. We will give to the inhabitants of this land a portion of that land for their own, to be held in trust by the American Indian Government for as long as the sun shall rise and the rivers go down to the sea—to be administered by the Bureau of Caucasian Affairs (BCA). We will further guide the inhabitants in the proper way of living. We will offer them our religion, our education, our life-ways, in order to help them achieve our level of civilization and thus raise them and all their white brothers up from their savage and unhappy state. We offer this treaty in good faith and wish to be fair and honorable in our dealings with all white men. We feel that this so-called Alcatraz Island is more than suitable as an Indian Reservation, as determined by the white man's own standards.
>
> By this we mean that this place resembles most Indian reservations, in that:
> 1. It is isolated from modern facilities, and without adequate means of transportation.
> 2. It has no fresh running water.
> 3. The sanitation facilities are inadequate.
> 4. There are no oil or mineral rights.
> 5. There is no industry and so unemployment is very great.

6. There are no healthcare facilities.

7. The soil is rocky and non-productive and the land does not support game.

8. There are no educational facilities.

9. The population has always been held as prisoners and kept dependent upon others.

Further, it would be fitting and symbolic that ships from all over the world, entering the Golden Gate, would first see Indian land, and thus be reminded of the true history of this nation. This tiny island would be a symbol of the great lands once ruled by free and noble Indians.

The occupying members of Indians of All tribes were escorted off Alcatraz Island by the United States Coast Guard a few hours later.

Matthew Ellis sat watching the NFL St. Louis Cardinals destroying the New York Giants at Civic Center Busch Memorial Stadium. It was the end of the third quarter and St. Louis led 28 to 10. Fran Tarkenton had thrown a touchdown pass in the first quarter but they had been held to a single field goal since then. A loss would drop the Giants to a 3 and 5 record.

The telephone rang which rescued Matt from the agony of defeat. When he answered a familiar voice greeted him. "Mr. Ellis this is Jack Moore. We haven't spoken in a while and I thought we could catch up."

"I, uh, oh, the reporter."

"Right. Have you had any other memories surface which might help us locate Lida Petropoulos?"

"I haven't had any recollections and quite frankly have decided that I am not going to pursue the past any longer. I've got to look to the future."

"That's understandable. It's too bad we weren't able to locate her. She could probably have shed light on what really happened."

"It is frustrating."

"I wish I could have helped more."

"You could only do so much and I wasn't much help."

"You tried and I appreciate it," Jack paused, then asked, "Other than NASA what industries did you deal with? Do you remember?"

"I really don't," Matt saw a red flag and decided not to provide any more information.

"After all, wire is used in practically every industry. If we knew you dealt with another industry we might find a clue to Lida's location."

"I've tried to find other hints but nothing has surfaced," Matt lied.

Jack was a seasoned reporter and knew when he was being told a lie. Matthew Ellis knew more than he was admitting. To get him to reveal what he knew would require a delicate touch. "I don't know what it's like to have partial amnesia. It has to be discouraging to want to remember something but not be able to find it in your mind."

"It can be disheartening, especially when it's something you want to remember. I have no memory of my wedding or bringing my daughter home the first time. It's not like losing your keys, you've lost your life story."

"That really is sad. Does it always require something familiar to act as a memory jogger?"

"No. Sometimes memories reveal themselves in my dreams. Other times, memories cascade with one leading to another and another. It really isn't predictable and I rarely have any control over what will be revealed."

"You have some control. How did you remember working at Orztech?"

"That was something I just knew. It wasn't a revelation. Lida first came as a dream but I didn't know who she was. She haunted me. Then I remembered where we met. I was in the city and I stopped in a coffee shop one day. It was the very coffee shop where she and I first met. She had made the initial contact after reading about Orztech getting a large military contract for wire. I agreed to meet with her because we had exceeded our manufacturing capacity with all the various contracts. It seems that I did too good a job selling."

"Nobody could blame you for that," Jack said, "I guess NASA was the crown jewel in your sales."

"It was a long laborious process far more difficult than the aeronautics folks who simply provided specs and wanted the best price."

Jack wrote on a yellow pad, military and aeronautic industry. He continued, "Can you remember if all the contracts were fulfilled?"

"Not really. I assume they were, wait, some were which was why I trusted Lida with the NASA bid. Without any records there isn't any way to know for sure." Fran Tarkenton threw a five yard touchdown pass in the fourth quarter. Matt watched the television screen. "Mr. Moore, I am not going to drive myself crazy seeking lost memories any more. So, there's no reason to call. I don't wish to be rude. But, I have to get on with my life. It's important that I do so." Matt thought about his daughter, Stephanie, and how he had to make it easy for her to go to Texas where her future lay.

Late in the evening fourteen Native Americans made their way across San Francisco Bay and landed on Alcatraz Island. It was the second occupation that day. No one came to remove them.

Chief Michael read of the occupation of Alcatraz with pride and a sense of hope. In his mind he saw the spirit of Robert Six Trees join his brothers on a faraway island.

90: Monday – November 10, 1969

Stephanie Ellis dressed for work with the television in her living room on. It was tuned to channel 13, the public broadcast station. What she expected to hear was a news program. Instead, a musical tune emanated from the small black and white television.

> Sunny Day
> Sweepin' the clouds away
> On my way to where the air is sweet
>
> Can you tell me how to get,
> How to get to Sesame Street
>
> Come and play
> Everything's A-OK
> Friendly neighbors there
> That's where we meet
>
> Can you tell me how to get
> How to get to Sesame Street
>
> It's a magic carpet ride
>
> Every door will open wide
> To happy people like you--
> Happy people like
> What a beautiful
>
> Sunny Day
> Sweepin' the clouds away
> On my way to where the air is sweet
>
> Can you tell me how to get,
> How to get to Sesame Street...
>
> How to get to Sesame Street

It was the premiere of a new children's program called *Sesame Street* which was the brainchild of television producer Joan Ganz Cooney and Carnegie Foundation vice president Lloyd Morrisett. Years earlier, they had discussed a television program that would use the power of the medium to help prepare young children for school, especially children from low-income families.

The show's development began in 1967 when Cooney and her team combined research with television production. They enlisted the aid of Harvard professors Gerald S. Lesser and Edward L. Palmer to create educational objectives and develop research to determine how effective they were. Cooney stated, "From the beginning, we—the planners of the project—designed the show as an experimental research project with educational advisers, researchers, and television producers collaborating as equal partners."

A year later, in 1968, the Carnegie Institute awarded an $8 million grant to create the new program and establish the Children's Television Workshop. Additional multi-million dollar grants were procured from the U.S. federal government, the Arthur Vining Davis Foundations, Center for Public Broadcasting, and the Ford Foundation.

Joan Ganz Cooney was *Sesame Street's* first executive director, at the time it was called, "one of the most important television developments of the decade." Immediately, she assembled a team of producers, all of whom had previously worked on *Captain Kangaroo*. The show was comprised of Jim Henson's Muppets, animation, short films, humor, and cultural references. Based on recommendations by child psychologists the show's human actors did not initially interact with the Muppets. It was felt that it would confuse young children. However, after it was found children paid greater attention during segments with the Muppets, Big Bird and Oscar The Grouch were born.

Stephanie, along with 1.9 million households across America, watched the new unusual show with fascination. It was different and refreshing. She could understand children becoming enamored with it. After turning it off and heading out the door to go to work, she smiled and thought it was an omen that she had chosen the correct direction.

Ritchie Anderson sat in a conference room with a number of editors from various magazines published by his father's company. They had gathered to discuss the upcoming 1970 editorial calendars. Before the meeting began an informal discussion had taken place about the fresh new look on a number publication's covers and how well they had been received by readers. One editor commented, "After that issue most of the letters we received complimented our cover rather than pointing out every minute error in our editorial." Another stated, "My sales manager has noted an uptick in advertising sales." Finally, one editor said sarcastically, "First newsstand circulation increase in years. I wonder what has made this difference. Can't seem to put my finger on it." He looked sheepishly at Ritchie.

As the meeting progressed and an editorial calendar was created for the various magazines a degree on negotiating began to take place. It was impossible for Ritchie to design every cover on every magazine. So, the editors began to pencil him in on those issues they especially needed his talents. Deals were made and arguments ensued and the tenor in the room rose. Finally, one bald editor stated loudly, "I need the kid for this issue—that's final." He looked at Ritchie and said, "You do this issue and I'll grow my hair and wear a ponytail."

Ritchie found himself in a strange situation. There he was in a conference room surrounded by middle-aged businessmen, the enemy of all he stood for, and he found that he truly liked them. They were hard working serious individuals who sincerely cared. There was no resentment of him, or snide remarks, or any form of rejection what-so-ever. He found his whole perspective on the business world turned upside down. As a result, he wanted to help each and every one of them.

As they continued to work the door to the conference room opened and the company Owner/CEO, Ritchie's father entered. It was an unexpected visit. The old man didn't say anything upon entering, yet the editor who had been speaking fell silent. Nathan Anderson was a tough and demanding business leader. The editors of the various magazines knew it. Every one of them at one time or another had been called to his office and been dragged over the coals. You didn't argue with him. You listened, apologized, swore to do better, said a prayer, and went back to work. The CEO nodded toward the editor who had been speaking indicating that he should continue. The meeting resumed and Nathan Anderson observed.

What he saw was an energized group of professionals. They took pride in their publications and were optimistic about the future. He himself had been impressed by the new graphics and covers of some of the magazines. Could his son, in such a short period of time, have had that much of an impact? He glanced over at Ritchie who was smiling and conversing with an editor. Way back, Nathan had wanted his son to become a part of the business, but they never could get past the hippie thing. They locked horns and both dug in not wanting to give an inch or hear what the other was saying. Maybe, that's how it had to be. Whatever the reason they were together now and a father's pride welled up within him.

Nathan Anderson stood, smiled, and announced, "It looks like you have everything under control. Keep up the good work. I appreciate it." He left the room.

Lai Ngoc Linh rowed his small boat over to an island down river from Quy Hoa, he stepped off and claimed it in the name of his ancestors.

91: Tuesday – November 11, 1969

"That, my friend, is a dead maple tree. It's clean-burning and not too hard to split," Nick pointed at a bare tree that leaned precariously over the edge of a slight hill. Carl looked at the forty-foot tree they were preparing to cut down. Its size and the angle it was on made the task at hand seem quite difficult. "Are we going to use this to heat the farmhouse?" Carl asked.

"Eventually."

"Why eventually?"

Nick stopped and faced Carl. "Wood has to be seasoned before it is useful for heating," he explained. "You know the wood that we had stacked outside on pallets with the tarp over it? That's green wood we were drying. When you first cut a tree down half the weight of each piece is moisture. It's no good for burning. So, you leave it outside for a summer and let it dry. Then during the winter you store it in a woodshed."

"How can you tell when it's dry?" Carl asked.

"There are ways. You can check the end for cracks. Or, look at the color. Wood gets darker as it dries. Bang two pieces together. If it sounds hollow it's dry, solid it is still wet. Dry wood weighs less than wet wood. And finally, if it hisses when you try to burn it you have wood that's not ready."

"So, this tree won't be ready until next year?"

"Or longer. Dense hardwoods sometimes take longer to season. But, when it's ready it will produce a good strong heat and long lasting coal bed." Nick walked around the large tree. Bare branches stuck out on all sides twisting and bending in irregular and beautiful patterns. It must have been a magnificent tree in its day. Overall, it had about a thirty foot spread. Carl watched. Nick stopped and looked at the other trees around the dead maple. He then examined the ground and the hill. Finally, he backed up and said, "The only way that tree is coming down is over the hill," he pointed at the slope. "There are too many healthy trees on all sides, except down the hill. And, that lean makes it impossible to go in any other direction." Nick then waved his arm upward and said we have to top it and cut a lot of those branches before we fell this puppy."

"So, what's the plan?" Carl asked.

"I've got to climb up there and cut those longer branches off to keep the tree from getting lodged among the branches of other trees. That would be a pain in the ass."

"Let me climb up," Carl requested.

Nick considered Carl, "Carl, this is a dead tree. That means there could be rotting branches. You don't have any experience in this area. A branch could snap from under you and I'd have to be the one to tell Laurel you broke your neck."

"One could snap from under you."

"I have a little more knowledge of what to look for, listen for, and feel."

"Then teach me. How the hell else will I learn?" Carl turned away and looked down the hill. He said over his shoulder, "I'm part of the team, now. I want to pull my weight. I have a lot to learn, I know that, but I'm going to make it my business to do just that."

Nick had to respect the young man's desire. He looked up at the tree. With the proper safety gear it might be a good tree to learn on. Problem was they didn't have the proper safety gear. After a few moments of pondering the situation he said, "Tell you what. I'll climb up and top the tree and do the upper branches. Then you can do the lower ones. But, you watch and listen to me while I do my part. Deal?"

"Deal."

"Now, we're not lumberjacks—don't have the right equipment—have no business doing what we're doing. We're a couple a squirrels who shouldn't be climbing that tree."

"We're nuts."

"No, we're squirrels."

"OK."

Nick went to the trailer that was hooked to the tractor. He retrieved a leather harness, stepped through the two leg straps and tightened the waistband. Two large metal rings were on either side of the waistband. He took a length of rope and doubled it, slipped it through one of the rings and pulled both lengths of rope through the loop securing the double rope. He then slipped the two ends of the rope through a ring on a metal swivel eye double lock safety hook. Nick then showed Carl how to tie a double fisherman's knot to adjust the length of the rope. "When you're up there loop the rope around a strong limb, adjust the length so that you can work, and lock the hook on the waistband ring." He pointed a finger into Carl's face, "Don't do a thing until you've hooked up your safety harness."

Nick climbed the maple as high as he dared. He pulled the gas powered 18" chain saw up by rope and proceeded to cut limbs. One by one they felt to the ground and slid down the slope of the hill. Carl noted that everything that Nick did he did slowly and carefully. After Nick had cut two thirds of the larger limbs he lowered the chain saw to the ground and climbed down. "I hate heights," Nick confessed upon reaching the ground.

Once Carl had on the safety equipment and was given final instructions from Nick the city slicker began to climb the maple. From the ground it didn't appear that high. However, as Carl moved upward he got a sense of what Nick meant as a tingling of fear sprang from his groin. It almost made him a little weak in the knees. He continued his climb until he reached the highest and first limb he was going to cut. After securing the safety line around the trunk of the tree Carl pulled the chain saw up to his position. The cut went fine and the limb tumbled to the ground. Two more limbs surrendered to gravity. Carl then climbed down to the next victim. When he attached the safety hook to his waistband he heard what sounded like a firecracker and the limb he stood on was gone. There Carl hung swinging in the air. The harness caused him to flip over to where it appeared he was swimming in the air.

"Are you OK?" Nick asked from the ground.

"Are you kidding me? I'm hanging fifteen feet from the ground."

"I'd say it's more like twenty."

"That helps! How do I get down?"

"Stay calm. I'll help you get down." Nick went to the trailer for another length of rope. As he returned he began to laugh.

"What the hell's so funny?" Carl bellowed.

"Well, you look like a piñata hanging there. Just be glad there aren't fifty kids with baseball bats around."

"Very funny. This harness is cutting into my stomach."

Nick stood below Carl and tossed him an end of the rope. It took a few attempts before Carl could grab it. When he did Nick pulled him toward the trunk of the tree where Carl could grab another limb and get his footing. Admirably, he stayed in the tree and finished cutting the limbs that needed to be removed before they could fell the tree.

The next few hours were spent cutting and hauling wood.

Continental Flight 172 from Los Angeles to Phoenix began boarding at 5:10 p.m. Among the many passengers was Jim Morrison of the rock band The Doors. Along with him was his drinking buddy actor Tom Baker. Also in the party was photographer Frank Lisciandro and writer/producer Babe Hill. When they arrived at the airport both Jim Morrison and Tom Baker were already inebriated. They were loud and obnoxious as they were seated in the first class section of the aircraft. The four were not seated together. Jim Morrison was seated one row in front and across the aisle from Tom Baker who had an aisle seat.

They had decided to fly to Phoenix to attend a Rolling Stones concert at the Veterans Coliseum. Morrison came up with a practical joke idea of standing outside the stadium and handing out Stones tickets and saying, "This is courtesy of your old friend Jim Morrison. Enjoy the show." He was doing it in response to the Stones criticizing The Doors concert in 1968 at the Hollywood Bowl as not being exciting.

Due to an electrical problem with a generator the Boeing 727 departure was delayed. As they sat on the tarmac Tom Baker became rowdy. First, he tried to grab the stewardess as she passed his seat. Then he got up and stumbled around the first class section. Meanwhile, Jim Morrison lit a cigar ignoring the "no smoking" sign.

After the plane took off the two oafs continued their boorish behavior. Tom Baker was the main culprit. He kept grabbing at the stewardesses as they attempted to serve drinks. Then he and Morrison began loudly telling obscene jokes. Passengers in first class complained and the stewardess threatened to report their behavior to the captain. For a short period of time things calmed down.

The two alcohol soaked spoiled lushes slowly began to act up once more. Baker went to the lavatory and returned with bars of soap which he began throwing around the cabin. One landed in Morrison's drink which he mockingly complained about. The stewardess informed Captain Craig Chapman who came out of the flight deck to confront the two troublemakers. He found himself trying to reason with two drunks. Quickly, he concluded that Tom Baker was the cause of most of the trouble. They laughed and mocked his words. Frustrated he warned that if they didn't cease their antics he would either turn the plane around or land at the nearest airport and have them arrested.

When the captain returned to the cockpit the harassment began anew. Flight attendants refused to serve the two more than two drinks at which point they began passing back and forth a bottle of Cognac hidden in a comic book. Tom Baker headed to the lavatory, once more, and upon seeing the stewardess who reported them to the captain standing near the door threw it open purposely striking her. His assault continued as he later tried to trip her as she went up the aisle.

Captain Chapman radioed air traffic control in Phoenix requesting that police meet the aircraft upon arrival. The jet landed at Sky Harbor International Airport at 7:10 p.m. As it taxied to the terminal Jim Morrison and Tom Baker agreed that they needed to make a quick escape. They gathered their belongings and waited by the door. At the gate the two culprits were met by Phoenix police officers and FBI agents. Both were placed under arrest. Charges included: Drunk and Disorderly (misdemeanor), Crime Aboard Aircraft (felony), Assault (felony), and Interfering with A Flight Crew (felony). They were taken to the Phoenix jail.

Continental Flight 172 was scheduled to continue on to El Paso and Houston. However, it was delayed as passengers were interviewed regarding the incident. During this time mechanics found and replaced a faulty wire in the generator control panel.

Jack Moore sat in his apartment and read through his voluminous notes. He had spent two days searching for any mention of Orztech Incorporated in any military or aeronautic contract. It was the proverbial needle in a thousand haystacks endeavor and he had come up empty.

Lai Ngoc Linh sat with Uncle Hung as the older man described to the young man the various hidden trails that helped keep Quy Hoa a hidden treasure.

92: Wednesday – November 12, 1969

Independent investigative journalist Seymour Hersh released his findings on the My Lai incident to the Associated Press wire service. As would be expected the story spread quickly. The reporter obtained much of his information through extensive interviews of First Lieutenant William L. Calley, Jr.

The event took place on March 16, 1968 in My Lai 4, which was actually part of a cluster of hamlets that made up Son My village in the Son Tinh District of Quang Ngai Province in the coastal lowlands.

As the result of a spontaneous initiation of indiscriminate killing at least 175–200 Vietnamese men, women, and children were massacred. Of those, only 3 or 4 were found to be Viet Cong. The soldiers had believed that the villagers were Viet Cong sympathizers which ignited the fires of hatred. In their minds a sympathizer was the same as a combatant. What followed was a complete breakdown in discipline as unfettered frustration and anger touched off mindless depraved violence.

The incident was misrepresented by military command as a daylong firefight during which 128 communist fighters were killed. Due to rumors about the slaughter Brigadier General George H. Young ordered the 11th Light Infantry Brigade's commanding officer, Colonel Henderson to investigate. After interviewing several soldiers who were involved in the attack, in late April, Colonel Henderson issued a report stating that 20 civilians were inadvertently killed during the operation. This did not quell the rumors. In fact, other soldiers came forward to describe ongoing brutality against civilians.

Thirty-one-year-old Army Major Colin Powell was ordered to investigate the accusations. Powell concluded, "In direct refutation of this portrayal is the fact that relations between Americal Division soldiers and the Vietnamese people are excellent." Seymour Hersh's findings ultimately portrayed that conclusion as fiction. Sadly, soldiers who exercised restraint, did their jobs, showed compassion, and served with honor were caught up in the characterizations that followed the release of Hersh's report.

Ninety-three miles southwest of where the My Lai incident occurred, Wellington Marsh and CAP Team 1-6-2 were making their way through the jungle to the LZ that was two miles east of Quy Hoa. They were familiar with the terrain and the almost non-existent paths that led to the LZ, therefore, Hung was not with them. At 1100 hours they arrived, posted outlying guards, and waited.

"How long we been here? I lost track of time," Shortstop asked from his crouching position.

"It will be six weeks tomorrow," Wellington answered as he scanned the sky.

"Six weeks, huh? We done a lot in six weeks."

Wellington looked at his friend, "We should be grateful that we got assigned to Quy Hoa—Precious Flower. I bet other teams have had a far more difficult time."

"Yeah, I guess you're right."

The distinct flap, flap, flap, flap of helicopter rotors drew their attention. Because they were flying low the two aircraft were not visible. The radio crackled and a voice emerged, "CAP 1-6-2, this is Dragon Fire 1, what is your status, over?"

The radio operator handed Wellington the handset. "Dragon Fire 1, this is CAP 1-6-2, all quiet, clear to land, over."

"Roger that."

A Bell HU-1 Huey helicopter appeared over trees to the south. It hung above the LZ for a moment. Higher than the dolphin (transport) was the shark (gunship) that hovered and stood guard. The helicopter slowly drifted downward and landed in the open field. Wellington signaled for some of the team to unload the chopper. He walked over to the right side window and spoke to the pilot, Lieutenant Trick Underwood, "Do you have any dispatches for me?"

The pilot handed Wellington a sealed manila envelope. "Anything going back on the return?"

"No casualties."

"Good to hear." The pilot, a lieutenant not much older than Wellington, added, "This is my last trip. Got my orders."

"You going back to the world? A double-digit midget?"

"More like a single-digit midget," the pilot smiled, "In three days I'm on that airliner back to the arms of Angela De Larossa."

Wellington thought about Teresa Champion, the girl who waited for him— maybe. "My short time's so far off I can't even imagine it."

"Keep your head down and your eyes open—you'll get there."

"Roger that."

With the unloading finished, Wellington stepped away from the Huey helicopter. The aircraft lifted into the sky and the twins disappeared heading south. Before long even the sound of their rotors was gone. Wellington took inventory of the supplies that had been delivered. The team then picked up the boxes and headed into the jungle. They hadn't traveled more than five minutes when the radio squawked. Wellington was given the handset and he listened, "CAP 1-6-2. Dragon Fire 1 is down."

"CAP 1-6-2, Where?" Wellington responded.

"About two klicks south of the LZ."

"Survivors?"

"Unknown."

"Unfriendlies?"

"Unknown."

"We're on it."

"I'll guide you in."

"Roger."

CAP Team 1-6-2 grabbed additional ammunition from the supplies and crossed the landing zone heading south into the jungle. It was unfamiliar territory so they proceeded with caution. Wellington reminded them to watch out for booby traps. The only sounds they heard were those from the various indigenous birds and other wildlife. Private Washington was on point. The thirteen man team worked their way through the thick undergrowth.

Wellington knew time was an important factor. If there were injured pilots they would need treatment and evacuation. If VC saw the aircraft go down they would be on their way to capture or kill the flyers. Finally, the shark helicopter could only hang around until fuel became critical. Cap Team 1-6-2 had to get there quickly but not at the expense of caution. They came to a small clearing and Wellington looked up as he spoke into the radio handset, "Dragon Fire, we're in a small clearing, don't see you, what's your 20, over."

Static, then a voice, "CAP 1-6-2 there is a clearing approximately fifty yards from a river to the east. Don't see you. Get to the river, over."

"Roger."

The Marine squad made their way east. When they broke through the forest to the bank of a fast-moving river they stopped. Wellington looked skyward. "There!" one of the team members said as he pointed toward the sky to their right. The Bell HU-1 Huey gunship hovered in a clear blue sky.

"Dragon Fire, we have you just south of our position. What is the status, over?"

"Dragon Fire 1 down in the river. No sign of enemy activity, over."

"Roger." CAP Team 1-6-2 made their way along the bank of the river. It was slow going as the undergrowth and trees grew right out to the river in various places. As they got closer they could hear the flap, flap, flap of their guardian angel.

When they rounded a bend in the fast-moving river they saw the downed chopper precariously lying on its left side in the middle of the river. One of its twin rotor blades pointed straight up. At first there was no sign of life, but as they drew nearer they could see movement inside the cockpit.

"We've got to get them out of there," Wellington stated.

The radio crackled and a voice said, "CAP 1-6-2, med evac on its way, low fuel, have to leave, use blue smoke marker, over."

"Roger, Dragon Fire, thanks, over."

Wellington looked out at the fallen bird in the water and saw a red 1964 Ford Fairlaine sedan. He also saw haunting eyes of a brave Native American child who met death without so much as a whimper. The swiftly running water told Wellington they needed to make a chain as was done in the woods in Minnesota. He directed the team to take off their web belts and loop them around their wrists. The largest member of the team, Billy Garvin, was designated as the one to lash himself to a tree and hold the human chain. After they moved upstream from the helicopter, Wellington led the way into the rushing water. He carried a long somewhat straight branch to steady himself. The rapid flow of water made it difficult to keep one's footing. He tried to anticipate the angle on which he would have to proceed to get pushed to the chopper. It was a lesson learned a long way off at a very high price. They inched closer and closer. In water over their waists movement became almost impossible. One of the team members went under. The Marine on either side of him helped pull him up.

As Wellington drew near he could see the pilot, Lieutenant Trick Underwood, moving inside. He reached the Huey and its enormous size became apparent. On its side it stood 8' 6.6" high. With three and a half feet underwater the uppermost skid hung five feet above the water. The rotor, pointing straight up, soared twenty-four feet into a blue sky. Wellington felt helplessly small. Then he saw that the bracket for the skids curved inward before being attached to the fuselage. When he reached up he could grip near the point of attachment. As the aircraft was pointing downriver the current tried to pull Wellington away. He fought the powerful flow and pulled himself upward. As more and more of his body was raised above the waterline the effects of the current dropped. Finally, while feeling nearly exhausted, he climbed onto the upper skid, and pulled open the hinged door to the cockpit.

"I think my leg's broken," Lieutenant Underwood said.

"We'll get you out of here," Wellington replied.

"The engine just quit. Got some funny readings and alarms. Then no power and we dropped."

"There's not much I can do for your leg, it's gonna hurt."

"Let's go."

Wellington pulled the pilot toward the door. The man screamed out in pain. He tried to encourage the pilot by saying, "You think Angela wants to marry a wuz?"

"Fuck you!"

With another quick tug Wellington pulled Trick free and they both fell five feet into the river. The pilot screamed in pain. Carried by the rushing water they headed downstream. CAP Team 1-6-2's human chain swung them toward the bank. The two men got hung up on a tree root. Members of the team who were not part of the chain rushed to their aid and pulled them ashore. Navy Corpsman Gordon Lassiter attended to the pilot's injured leg.

"The other pilot, what's his condition?" Wellington asked.

"He banged his head. I think he's unconscious."

"We better get him out of there."

The team was exhausted so a new group lashed their arms together with web belts. They went upriver and repeated the approach. Wellington had retrieved a new walking stick for stability. His hands shook from exhaustion as he moved closer and closer to the helicopter. When he was about eight foot away the rotor shifted causing the aircraft to turn and nose down deeper into the water. It appeared very unstable. Wellington paused and looked at the precarious vehicle, then said, "Not this time!" He moved as quickly as he could and climbed onto the skid. Because of the shift of the Huey he reached the full length of the human chain and couldn't get into the cockpit. Without hesitation, he unlashed his arm and made his way into the helicopter. The other pilot remained unconscious. Practically falling he moved down to where the man lay. Once there, Wellington could see a large gash on the man's head. He felt for a pulse but none was found. He tried listening at his mouth for breathing with the same results. Finally, Wellington listened at the man's chest but neither heard breathing nor a heartbeat. He was dead.

From the bank, Shortstop watched as the rotor of the helicopter shifted once more and snapped. The Huey began to be carried downstream. Shortstop yelled, "Wellington!" The top-heavy aircraft flipped upside down and sank as it moved into deeper water. CAP Team 1-6-2 tried to follow but the river became wider and deeper and there was no sign of the Huey, the co-pilot, or Lance Corporal Wellington Marsh.

Jim Morrison and Tom Baker plead not guilty to a Drunk And Disorderly misdemeanor and were released on $66 bail. They were scheduled to appear in court on December 2, 1969. The two miscreants were turned over to U.S. Marshalls at 2:30 p.m. They pled not guilty to federal charges and Bill Siddons, the promoter of the Rolling Stones concert, paid their $2,500 bail. A November 24, 1969 court date was set. The pair faced up to $10,000 in fines each and possible sentence of up to 20 years.

Anna Six Trees stood with her mother before Manidoo-giizhikens, the Witch Tree, and offered gifts in honor of the three men who saved her life.

93: Friday – November 14, 1969

The Apollo 12 mission patch features a clipper ship arriving at the Moon which represents the Command Module named Yankee Clipper. It is symbolic of the fact that the entire crew was made up of U.S. Navy Commanders. The windjammer flies the American flag as it trails fire depicting the changing mode of explorers. In the background the area of the moon shown is the Ocean of Storms which was where Apollo 12 planned to land. The patch includes a wide gold border with small blue trim which are traditional U.S. Navy colors. Finally, four stars are in space behind the ship. Three stars represent the crew of Apollo 12. The fourth star is in memory of Clifton Williams, a U.S. naval aviator and astronaut who was killed on October 5, 1967. He trained as part of the backup crew for the Apollo 9 mission, and would have been assigned as Lunar Module Pilot for Apollo 12. An electrical failure caused the controls of his T-38 trainer to stop responding ending in a crash.

Apollo 12's crew consisted of Mission Commander Charles Conrad Jr., Lunar Module Pilot Alan L. Bean, and Command Module Pilot Richard F. Gordon Jr. The Lunar Module (LM-6) was named Intrepid. At 11:22 a.m. EDT a huge Saturn-V booster rocket lifted off Launch Pad 39A at Cape Kennedy into a cloudy, rain-swept sky. It was the first launch ever attended by an incumbent U.S. President—Richard M. Nixon.

Thirty-six-and-a-half seconds after lift-off, lightning discharged through the vehicle and down to Earth through the Saturn's ionized plume. In the Service Module protective circuits engaged and took all three fuel cells offline. Loss of the fuel cells switched the Command/Service Module entirely to batteries, which were unable to maintain the 75-ampere launch loads. One AC inverter dropped offline. Resulting power supply problems lit nearly every warning light on the control panel and caused most of the instrumentation to malfunction. A second lightning strike occurred at 52 seconds after launch. This strike knocked out the "8-Ball" attitude indicator.

At Mission Control information from the launch vehicle was garbled and unusable. Fortunately, the vehicle continued to fly correctly which meant the Saturn V had not been affected. The problem was that they needed to bring the fuel cells back online or the mission would be aborted. This could not be executed from Mission Control.

John Aaron, Electrical Environmental and Consumables Manager (EECOM), at Mission Control remembered a test that had been done when a power supply malfunction converted raw signals from instrumentation to standard voltages for the spacecraft instrument displays and telemetry encoders. He radioed the spacecraft and instructed them to, "Try SCE to aux." SCE, or Signal Conditioning Equipment would then be switched to backup power supply. This was not a common switch and Flight Director Gerald Griffin, CAPCOM Gerald Carr, and Mission Commander Pete Conrad did not immediately recognize it. However, Lunar Module Pilot Alan Bean did, located it, and brought the fuel cells back online restoring instrumentation and telemetry. The mission was able to continue. Once in Earth orbit, they carefully checked out the spacecraft for damage.

At Mission Control there was concern that the lightning strike could have caused the Command Module's parachute mechanism to prematurely fire, disabling the explosive bolts that open the parachute compartment. If that did happen the Command Module would drop unfettered into the Pacific Ocean killing all onboard. As there was no way to determine if this was the case or not, Mission Control decided not to share this concern with the astronauts.

Matthew Ellis had the television set on to watch the launch of Apollo 12, however, he wasn't paying attention. He was focused on a blank piece of paper. What he knew for sure was that Stephanie's future lay in Texas. Sacrificing what she wanted to do and giving up an incredible opportunity to remain in New Jersey and take care of him was out of the question. It was clear he had to convince her to leave.

After her conversation with Lodi, New Jersey police Detective Allen Ferrara, Detective Ryoya Akimoto decided they were going to New Jersey. The police had picked up Eduardo Fernandez, one of the suspects in the Claire Payton murder. They were holding him on a bench warrant for a misdemeanor and failure to appear. He would be held so that the New York City detectives could interview him.

Detective Michael Donovan drove across the George Washington Bridge as they discussed their strategy.

"You know he won't confess," Donovan said.

"Probably not—he has nothing to gain,"

"So, we need more than a scared anonymous informer's accusation to have him arrested and extradited."

"Kind of a challenge—isn't it?"

"Kind of a waste of time."

"We'll see," Ryoya looked out the window at the passing scenery. "People live out here among the trees, tangles of highways, and long commutes."

"Weekend escape."

"I guess," Ryoya thought for a moment then concluded, "We know there were two of them. One we have in custody."

"For the time being."

"Right. Maybe he will turn on his pal to save himself."

"It's a long shot."

"But, one worth taking."

"Consider the odds."

"The Mets won the World Series."

"Point taken."

Once in Earth parking orbit, all systems were checked and everything was functioning at nominal range. The Command Service Module separated from the vehicle, turned 180 degrees, and docked with the Lunar Module Intrepid. The maneuver was televised to Earth. Charles Conrad and Alan Bean entered the Intrepid and checked for damage from the lightning strikes. After they found nothing unusual they re-entered the Command Service Module. The newly configured space craft then re-ignited the S-IVB third stage for trans-lunar injection. After jettisoning the spent rocket the three astronauts settled in for 10 hours of sleep.

Matt fell asleep in the chair. Reading for a lengthy amount of time had that affect. He had given up on the blank piece of paper. Once his mind was released from consciousness it was free to wander in deep corners of the past. At first, simple images presented themselves. Then a brief undetermined scene played out. Finally, his id found that for which it was looking. Lida Petropoulos walked into a room. She wore a casual light green dress. Matt passed a mirror and saw his reflection. He wore a dark blue suit without a tie.

They sat on a couch and faced each other. Lida held a manila folder in her lap. She smiled and patted the item. "You and I have made a great deal of money from this little wire escapade. Once NASA signs on the dotted line we'll make even more." She got a serious look on her face and added, "There is one problem."

"What problem?" Matt asked.

"Contamination," she replied, "At one plant—the largest—there was a flood. A large portion of the raw metal was compromised. A combination of rust and dirt will cause premature deterioration of the core increasing the potential for failure."

"What does that mean?"

"If we replace the bad materials it will move the delivery date, as well as increase the cost to us."

"What if we use the damaged materials?"

"I'll be honest with you. The wire we are producing at present is pushing the envelope. The cheaper metals will work for the most part but a sudden surge could cause a short. If we introduce contaminants into the mix the possibility of sudden failure increases exponentially."

"So, does that mean failure in a month, a year, five years, twenty?"

"It's unknown, just more likely."

"What about cost?"

To keep the price to Orztech the same you and I would receive very little return if we have to purge the bad materials."

"Let me get this straight. Time and money are at stake."

"That sums it up," Lida crossed her legs.

Matt noticed. He sat in silence weighing the options. They were dealing with both a known and an unknown. The known was delivery on time and cash in his pocket. The unknown was whether or not the wire would fail—if ever. And, what if there was an occurrence? A light might not illuminate—bulbs fail all the time. A machine might malfunction—they do all the time for various reasons. Critical equipment has redundancies. What risk could the failure of one small wire pose? There just wasn't sufficient reason to give up profit. He looked at Lida's legs then up at her eyes, "Stick with the delivery schedule and make sure that I get my cut."

"I was hoping you were going to say that," Lida stated with a seductive smile.

"Problem solved," Matt replied. "Now, how are we going to use the rest of our time together?"

Lida took Matt's hand and led him into the bedroom.

The sound of a book hitting the floor woke Matt. At first, he was groggy and disoriented. The image of the dream remained. After a few moments he stood and walked toward the kitchen. On a shelf in the living room was a picture of Valerie. He gazed at her smile and sweet expression and innocent loving eyes. There she was, his

Odette, his love, his reason for shame. How he let things get so out-of-control he didn't know. He turned and went into the bathroom. In the mirror he saw a cold heartless monster.

Eduardo Fernandez sat in the interview room at the Lodi, New Jersey police station, an arrogant sneer upon his face. "What the hell is this all about? You have no reason to arrest me."

Ryoya stated flatly, "You're not under arrest. You're being held for questioning."

"Then I can go?"

"No."

"Then I'm under arrest."

"You are being detained. Based on your cooperation and answers to our questions a decision will be made as to whether or not you will be taken into custody."

"You're a New York cop—you have no authority here."

"Well, there you are wrong. I may not have jurisdiction but upon my recommendation Detective Ferrara can place you under arrest. The choice is yours— will you answer a few questions?"

"I don't have any choice."

"I'd say that's an accurate statement."

Detective Michael Donovan chimed in, "The only choice you have is whether you go to jail for murder or face a lighter charge."

Eduardo acted surprised, "Murder? I haven't killed anyone."

"That's not what we've been told," Donovan responded.

Detective Akimoto continued, "Does the name Miguel Juarez mean anything to you?"

"No."

"That's your first lie," Detective Donovan shouted abruptly as he stood over the young man.

Ryoya asked, "Were you in New York City in September?"

"No."

"Strike two!" Detective Donovan bellowed. "With strike three you won't believe what happens."

Eduardo looked at the detective, who towered over him, then at the Japanese woman across the table with a stern serious expression, "OK, I was in New York, but I didn't kill no-one."

"We have witnesses that say otherwise," Ryoya said in an unexpectedly soft voice. "How do you think we found you and are looking for Phillipe Lopez?"

Eduardo Fernandez didn't answer.

She continued, "We have enough to convict both of you for kidnapping, aggravated assault, and first degree murder. So, you might ask yourself, why would I even take the time to interview you?"

Eduardo Fernandez showed interest but didn't answer.

"It's quite simple, nothing is a sure thing. A sleazy lawyer might get you both off—or not. But, I like to play the game with the odds in my favor," Ryoya leaned back, "I'd rather get one sure conviction than risk getting none. What that means is the first one of you who makes a statement will get a real chance at a reduced charge."

"But, no bullshit," Donovan interjected, "remember strike three."

The young punk was no longer cocky. He looked back and forth between Akimoto and Donovan. It was obvious that they had gotten his attention. He was torn—on the fence—unsure what to do.

Ryoya recognized his indecision and acted appropriately, "Do you want something to drink?"

"Uh, yeah."

"How about a Coke?"

"Yeah, that will be good."

Michael got the cue and left the room.

Ryoya spoke in a kind friendly voice, "Eduardo, I'm a detective. My job is to identify and bring the guilty party to the District Attorney who ultimately decides charges. I use forensic evidence from the crime scene, witness information, and statements from those who were involved. We know you were there. What we don't know is what part you played. This is your opportunity to paint the best picture that you can about your involvement. If Phillipe was the perpetrator and you only played a minor role the District Attorney might cut you a deal for your testimony." Ryoya paused to let what she said sink in. She couldn't directly coach the suspect, but she could convince him to make a statement. After that it was out of her hands. "Of course, Phillipe Lopez has the same opportunity when we locate him. He could very well make a statement that implicates you. Fortunately, you are the first one we caught. You have the advantage," again she paused, "for the moment."

Detective Michael Donovan re-entered the interview room. He carried a can of Coca Cola. After sliding it over to Eduardo he asked, "Has our friend decided to lose the attitude and tell us what happened?"

"He hasn't decided," Ryoya replied, "He may let Phillipe Lopez set the tone and make a statement first when we catch up with him."

"And, we will catch up with him."

Ryoya smiled for effect, "We always do."

Silence hung in the room. The two detectives were seasoned enough to know to wait. Eduardo had to face the facts and work out his best next move for himself. If he bought the story about the existence of forensic evidence and witnesses he would believe that cooperation was the only answer. Rejection of those facts and he'd close up like a clam. Time would tell.

After two days of searching, the rescue and recover mission of the helicopter pilot and Lance Corporal Wellington Marsh was discontinued. Sergeant Curtis Willens called the team together to inform them of his decision. He had taken command of CAP Team 1-6-2 after the loss of Wellington Marsh.

His arrival on the day of the disaster was none too pleasant. Right from the start there was a dramatic difference from their prior team leader. Willens was an arrogant, rude, short little tyrant who only seemed to hear his own words. When he stepped off the chopper he asked for details of what had happened. After being told, his comment was, "Dumbass!" This didn't endear him to a team that had grown to respect and care about their lost leader.

When Hung arrived the next day, after hearing about Wellington, Sergeant Willens immediately tried to establish his authority. The Vietnamese interpreter and guide attempted to explain the relationship that Quy Hoa had with CAP Team 1-6-2 and the strategy to protect the villages. Sergeant Willens looked off at a distance as Hung spoke. He then stated, "We're going to have to open up some trails for easier access and quicker movement." Hung insisted that secrecy was their best defense. Willens peered at the older man and replied, "We're your best defense so get used to it. I'm calling the shots on this team. Either follow orders or go fishing."

"I'm surprised that you can read," Sergeant Willens said to Shortstop when they were back at camp. The young Marine was looking through his lost friends gear and personal possessions. "Bag his shit and ship it."

Detectives Akimoto and Donovan were headed back to Manhattan. In their possession was a statement from Eduardo Fernandez admitting to being at the scene of the crime and implicating Phillipe Lopez as the murderer. He also named Carlos Batista as the member of Miguel Juarez' crew that set up the kidnapping and murder. Eduardo held nothing back when he made the decision to throw everyone under the massive wheels of justice to save himself. He even indicated where the murder weapon was hidden in a vent in the apartment where they lived in Lodi. Subsequently, he was placed under arrest to be held for extradition and the Lodi police sought a search warrant to retrieve the knife.

"The Mets may have won the World Series, but we solved the unsolvable case," Detective Michael Donovan said as he drove east on Route 4. It was dark and they were on overtime.

"I still wonder what brought that informer forward," Ryoya said.

"Maybe, he had a grudge he wanted to settle."

"Or, maybe he got a nudge from someone."

"Why would anyone want to help us on such a low profile case?" Detective Donovan asked.

"That's exactly what makes it curious," Ryoya said as she pictured Jack Moore.

"Don't try to solve that riddle—it'll drive you nuts."

They drove onto the upper level of the George Washington Bridge. The Manhattan skyline at night was always an impressive sight. Ryoya looked downtown at the tall buildings of midtown. Suddenly, she yelled, "Michael pull over!"

"On the bridge I can't."

"Right there—look!"

A figure barely visible in the dark stood on the rail holding onto one of the vertical cables. Detective Donovan switched on his red and blue police flashers embedded in the headlights and brake lights and slowed to a stop. Ryoya Akimoto slipped out of the car, climbed the two foot cement curb, and slipped between the two-rail guardrail. She approached the figure cautiously. It was a man wearing a dark colored suit. He stood on top of the outer guardrail looking down.

Detective Akimoto spoke softly, "Sir, you don't want to do this."

"I have no choice," the man replied without turning around. "Don't try to stop me."

"I won't try to stop you, but I would like to have a conversation with you."

Matthew Ellis stood on the rail looking down at the Hudson River that appeared black at that time of night. In the black abyss he saw all the harm that he had caused and all the sorrow that waited to happen. There was no denying that he was an evil monster. Why did he ever wake up? It would have been easier if he simply drifted away into oblivion.

A cold breeze caused Ryoya to shiver. They were almost in the center of the span where the winds were strongest. "Please, at least tell me what brought you to this point. Maybe, I can help."

Matt's mind relived what he now knew was his past. The love of Valerie, a sweet innocent beautiful person, had deserved better. Stephanie, his daughter, who endured so much at such a young age needed to be set free. Lida, who was his Eve holding the apple had tempted him and he eagerly submitted. Yet, the evil that was done he did willingly. The betrayal of the woman he loved was intentional. The harm that was to come was unstoppable.

Ryoya continued to try, "Nothing can be so bad that it is worth giving up your life."

Matt spoke, "There is evil in this world that is a threat to innocent people."

"What kind of evil?"

"Unseen acts that cause endless misery."

"Please, come down. We can talk about it," Ryoya sensed that this was more than a broken heart, lost job, or other minor occurrence blown out of proportion. More than likely this was a psychotic episode which meant logic was out the window. "Can you help me understand the evil?"

Matthew Ellis turned and looked at the female standing below him on the walkway. "I don't know the man I was before I awoke. He is as a stranger. The things he did I would never consider doing. Yet, I am he. I am branded by the sins of my former self and nothing can wash that away."

"What did you do?"

"I found out the truth—a truth too reprehensible to bear. A truth no sentient being could live with. It was there hiding in my mind and my mind finally gave it up. I searched for it, sought it, and now have been condemned by it."

Ryoya found the entire conversation difficult to follow, yet she had to try. If she could make some type of connection with the poor suffering soul before her maybe there could be a positive outcome. She asked, "What truth did you find?"

Matt stood tall and stated, "I am evil!" He pivoted on his heel and stepped off thinking, one more step into hell. As he drifted into the blackness below he saw Valerie encased in a snow pile looking directly at him and he sobbed.

Stephanie began to wonder where her father had gone. He rarely stayed out that late. She decided to check his room to see if he left any indication of where he had gone. On his pillow was an envelope with her name on it. Inside, she found a handwritten note.

> Stephanie,
>
> I don't know how to tell you all the things that will make what I have to do easier for you to understand. As my memory has returned I've come to realize that before my accident I wasn't a very nice person. No, I was a very bad person. In my business dealings I cheated and am guilty of fraud. Inferior wire was substituted for specified wire and I received kickbacks from the manufacturer, although I don't

know where the money went. This may sound like just being an unethical businessman, but it is far more serious. As a result of my actions innocent people have died.

It is hard to explain, but I don't know the person I was. Somehow when I slept, I changed. Today, I could never do what I did. But, it doesn't change the facts. There are thousands of feet of bad wire out there that could fail at any time. I wouldn't even know how to find it all. More people are going to die because of me. I cannot live with that. It is the coward's way out but my only solution. I won't ask you to forgive me because what I have done is unforgiveable.

Go to Texas, help children, and live a good life. Forget me and don't cling to a false image.

In a panic, Stephanie looked around the room to find any clue as to what her father planned or where he might have gone. She found nothing. Neither the living room nor the kitchen provided any hint. With no other ideas, she picked up the telephone and called Ritchie. It was after ten at night. When Stephanie explained the situation, he told her he would come right over.

As Ritchie drove to Stephanie's apartment he listened to the news on the car radio. There was a report of a man committing suicide by jumping off the George Washington Bridge. Ritchie said in the dark cab of his van, "Oh my God, it can't be."

Nghiem Duc Hung sat with his eleven-year-old nephew, Lai Ngoc Linh, and six-year-old niece, Lai Thanh Tuyen and told them that they would not be going to the magic safe place of which he had once spoken.

94: Saturday – November 15, 1969

Two hundred feet below the surface of the Barents Sea the USS Gato glided silently through the water. The Barents Sea is part of the Arctic Ocean, located off the northern coasts of Norway and Russia. Due to its strategic position a significant number of missions were sailed by various nations in those waters.

The USS Gato was a Thresher-Class nuclear submarine nicknamed either "The Goalkeeper" or "Black Cat." She carried 12 officers and 115 crew. Captain James Greider Partlow was in command. On this morning, everything was going as planned until a short in a wire momentarily knocked out the boat's inertial navigation system leaving them unsure of their actual position.

Submarines navigated underwater using an inertial navigation system which kept track of relative motion from a known starting point. Because there were always small errors in calculation a submarine would have to rise to periscope depth periodically to update its position from Loran shore stations. Loran stood for long-range radio navigation. On this morning the need to check their position was hastened by the equipment failure. The captain prepared to go to periscope depth.

At 7:13 a.m. the crew of the Gato heard a scraping sound on the hull and experienced a shudder throughout the boat. They were unaware that a Soviet Hotel-Class submarine, the K-19, had collided with the Gato. It was a glancing blow where the bottom of the Soviet boat scraped along the sail of the American submarine. The Soviet boat was able to surface only after an emergency ballast tank blow. The impact completely destroyed the sonar pods and mangled the torpedo tube doors of the K-19. The USS Gato was relatively undamaged.

The K-19 had been hurriedly built when the Soviet Union tried to keep up with the United States in construction of nuclear submarines. Before it was even launched, eleven people died due to accidents. It then was plagued with a long list of breakdowns and accidents.

On July 4, 1961 during its initial voyage the K-19 was conducting exercises in the North Atlantic close to Southern Greenland when it suffered a complete loss of coolant to its aft nuclear reactor. As no backup system had been installed the temperature of the core kept rising despite control rods being inserted via a SCRAM mechanism. Captain First Rank Nikolai Vladimirovich Zateyev had to make the difficult decision to send eight engineering officers and twenty-two crew members into high-radiation areas to build a new coolant system by cutting off an air vent valve and welding a water-supplying pipe into it. Radioactive steam was subsequently released which spread to other sections of the boat. The new cooling system worked but the entire crew received substantial doses of radiation. Some of the repair crew died within a month with all the others dying in two years. After repairs, the K-19 returned to the fleet with the nickname "Hiroshima." The Soviet submarine would continue to suffer accidents and deaths through the years. Ultimately, it would be the subject of a 2002 movie titled, *The Widowmaker*.

It began on Thursday night, continued throughout Friday, and ended at 7:30 a.m. in the morning on this day. Called the "March Against Death" over 40,000 individuals silently walked single file carrying a placard with the name of a dead American soldier or destroyed Vietnamese village. When each participant arrived at the Capitol building they placed their paper in one of eleven wooden coffins.

Organized by the New Mobilization Committee to End the War in Vietnam, an estimated 250,000 demonstrators rallied in Washington, D.C. They came to demand a rapid withdrawal of United States troops from Vietnam. Most of the marchers were college age with a scattering of older adults in attendance. Interestingly, the percentage of blacks in the crowd was relatively small.

In preparation for the march, police had cleared a 24-block area around the White House allowing in only those who lived or had business there. The buffer zone was virtually deserted. More than 2,000 metropolitan police were on duty and in each of the federal buildings on or near the parade route Army and Marine Corps troops were held in reserve.

Ritchie had remained with Stephanie for the entire night. They watched the eleven o'clock news but the George Washington Bridge jumper had not been identified. The only information they had was from an interview with a New York City detective, who was on the scene, that indicated the victim said he was evil before he jumped.

"I know it was him," Stephanie sobbed.

Ritchie felt the same after reading her father's note. He wasn't sure what to say or do to help Stephanie face the tragedy or handle both the truth and the loss. Everything had come as such a surprise. A few weeks ago when her father asked him to have two wires tested Ritchie had no idea that it was he who had done such an unscrupulous thing. Somehow, he had to help Stephanie come to terms with the fact that her father was a criminal who was responsible for an unknown number of deaths. "Stephanie, there is a good chance that your father did commit suicide. He told you why in his note. The man you knew as a child apparently led two lives. He was a good and loving father and, on the other hand, he did many bad things in business. But, we don't have to judge him because he judged himself. He found himself guilty and decided the punishment. You should remember the man who awoke from a long sleep and was good and kind and remorseful."

Stephanie was tired, so very tired. It was difficult to make sense of anything that had happened. The father she loved and cherished confessed to being a despicable person, yet by some quirk of fate had metamorphized into a good kind person with a conscience. It didn't take away the bad things he had done but in a way, it did. She was all mixed up. She loved her father and wanted him to walk through the front door and tell her it was all a big mistake. However, she knew that was impossible. He was gone and she would never see him again. Stephanie began to wail as her emotions twisted and turned and sought relief from unendurable anguish.

Ritchie immediately went to Stephanie and held her close. When he first touched her she stiffened and tried to pull away. Then abruptly melted into his arms as if she had swooned. Gently, he lowered her to the couch and cradled her. Odd sounds emanated from her as she fought for control of her emotions. Time became meaningless.

It was a breezy morning with temperatures in the low 30's. The Vietnam Moratorium march began at 10:25 a.m. Three drummers led the way followed by demonstrators carrying the eleven coffins that contained the placards with the names of the dead. They were surrounded by other youth who joined hands.

Many of the marchers chanted, "One, two, three four. Tricky Dick, stop the war."

There were musical performances by the likes of Peter, Paul and Mary, Arlo Guthrie, and Pete Seeger. Seeger led the crowd in singing John Lennon's *Give Peace a Chance*.

In a storefront building with a curved facade at 257 E. Broad Street, Columbus, Ohio a new restaurant opened its doors. It offered funny square hamburgers, sea salt fries, and a form of soft serve ice cream mixed with frozen starches. On the sign was a red headed girl with pigtails and the name Wendy's Old Fashioned Hamburgers. It had been the dream of Dave Thomas who named his new enterprise after his fourth child Melinda Lou "Wendy" Thomas.

Born in 1932 in Atlantic City, New Jersey, Dave was adopted at birth by Rex and Auleva Thomas. When he was five-years-old his mother died and he lived with his grandmother while his father traveled looking for work. Always industrious, at the age of twelve, he worked at a restaurant in Knoxville, Tennessee and at Walgreens as a soda jerk. When he was fifteen his father landed a job in Fort Wayne, Indiana where Dave went to work at the Hobby House Restaurant. Years later, when his family moved, Dave remained in Fort Wayne, dropped out of school, and continued to work at the Hobby House Restaurant.

After serving in the Army, Dave Thomas returned to the Hobby House Restaurant where in 1956 he and owner Phil Clauss opened The Ranch House Restaurant. It was while working there that Thomas met Colonel Harland Sanders, founder of Kentucky Fried Chicken. Sanders' restaurants were struggling and he was impressed by the work of Dave Thomas. They entered into a partnership deal. Thomas turned around the failing stores and made enough profit to purchase more.

In 1968, at the age of 35, Dave Thomas sold his Kentucky Fried Chicken restaurants back to the company and followed his dream of opening his very own restaurant. Wendy's offered made-to-order hamburgers with fresh meat. The slogan was, "Quality Is Our Recipe."

No body had been recovered. New York City police searched the lower Hudson River but found nothing. Without any other clues the authorities had no idea who the Washington Bridge jumper was. All they could do was wait for someone to come forward and make a missing person's report or for a body to wash ashore.

No body was recovered so Sergeant Willens filed a "Missing In Action" report. Neither the other helicopter pilot nor Lance Corporal Wellington Marsh were found.

Mid-morning Willens called CAP Team 1-6-2 together. "We're going to pay these little villages a surprise visit and check them out," he announced. "Find any weapons or VC paraphernalia that you can."

"These villagers have been friendly and supportive," one Marine pointed out.

Sergeant Willens glared at the young Marine. "Gooks will smile and be friendly until they get a shot at your back. Now, you're gonna find me some sympathizers. Is that clear?"

At midday, a solid mass of humanity extended from the Capitol building ten blocks up Pennsylvania Avenue to the Treasury building and four blocks along Fifteenth Street across the mall to the Washington Monument. A counter demonstration was executed by Ambrose P. Salmini, a manufacturer of marine equipment from Yonkers, New York. He hired an airplane to fly over the capital trailing the message, "Will Vietnam satisfy the Reds?" By 2:00 p.m. the last stragglers joined the immense crowd.

Apollo 12 made a midcourse maneuver onto a wider path toward the moon. The spacecraft slowed so that it would arrive with the most desirable solar illumination on the selected landing site. A color television signal was beamed to Earth showing the interior of the Yankee Clipper.

CAP Team 1-6-2 entered Quy Hoa in a skirmish. At first the villagers were confused. They had become accustomed to the Americans and felt they offered no threat. The Marines were welcomed into the businesses and homes of the villagers until they began tearing apart the structures and overturning the contents. As that occurred the villagers began to protest.

Nghiem Duc Hung hurriedly caught up with Sergeant Curtis Willens and ordered him to stop the assault. The little martinet turned on Hung and snarled, "You've got VC here. Point them out!"

"There are no VC here," Hung insisted.

"Give them up or I'll tear this village to the ground. Where are the tunnels?"

"Quy Hoa is at peace—leave us that way."

"Don't lie to me asshole! VC leave you alone because you support them—you're VC."

"VC don't know we are here."

"Bullshit!"

"You go. Take your men and leave," Hung ordered.

"Not likely," Sergeant Willens snapped, "I'm going to clean out this nest of commies."

"You go," Hung insisted as he pointed east.

"Get out of my way," Willens shoved Hung aside and continued the assault on Precious Flower.

After an hour the search was complete with nothing suspicious having been found. Sergeant Willens was livid. "You bunch of clowns couldn't find your dick if a whore offered it for free." He paced back and forth in the bivouac area. "Pack your gear we're moving our operation."

The members of CAP Team 1-6-2 were not happy with the turn of events. They missed Lance Corporal Wellington Marsh. They knew no good was to come from the change in tactics. They feared for the inhabitants of Quy Hoa. They felt guilty for what they had done. Yet, they knew they had to follow orders.

CAP Team 1-6-2 moved west through the mountainous jungle toward the Laotian and Cambodian borders. Without a distinct trail to follow they chopped and trudged along creating a clearly identifiable path.

Hung watched from a distance and shook his head in disgust. He was struck with an overwhelming feeling of sadness.

In a few hours CAP Team 1-6-2 came to the trail that led from the Laotian and Cambodian borders to the paved road leading to Kontum and Pleiku Air Base. They stopped and observed.

By midafternoon only one arrest had been made. Dominic Angerame, a 20-year-old from Buffalo, New York was charged with disorderly conduct for painting a peace symbol on the Washington Monument. Temperatures only reached forty degrees which caused demonstrators to build small fires with their signs and placards.

President Richard Nixon made a statement about the march, "Now, I understand that there has been, and continues to be, opposition to the war in Vietnam on the campuses and also in the nation. As far as this kind of activity is concerned, we expect it; however, under no circumstances will I be affected whatever by it."

Detective Ryoya Akimoto read through her report. There were few details, yet a sizeable number of observations. The man had a New Jersey accent. He spoke of waking up and a former self indicating some type of medical or psychological event. The victim was distraught and felt guilty about something he had done. He referred to them as, "the sins of my former self." This was probably not a painful romantic breakup. It is highly likely that he was not trying to escape from anything. By all appearances, he was executing himself.

"There was something about John Doe that made him different from your run-of-the-mill jumper," Ryoya observed.

"Yeah, you said that," Detective Michael Donovan replied.

"No, I mean this guy was tortured by something."

"What kind of something? You think we have a murder/suicide?"

"Not exactly." She made a note, "once we make a positive identification we need to investigate the individual's background to determine if he is implicated in any criminal activity."

A sound was heard to the left of their position. Silently the members of CAP Team 1-6-2 waited and watched. Other sounds followed. After a short period of time they observed shadows moving slowly along the trail. Five, six, ten enemy soldiers moved cautiously along. As they did they looked left and right for any sign of an ambush. CAP Team 1-6-2 waited. The enemy patrol slowly moved closer. It would only take a few more minutes for them to step into the trap. Suddenly, they stopped and dissolved into the trees. No sign of their existence was left. The hidden Marines froze not wanting to reveal their presence. Only the sounds of the indigenous creatures could be heard. Time dragged on.

A bullet whizzed past one of CAP Team 1-6-2's members and struck a tree. Where it came from they didn't know. The report of rifles echoed from everywhere followed by another and another. Bullets hit the ground, rocks, trees and finally one of the Marines. "I'm hit! Corpsman, I'm hit!"

The Marines fired at where they thought the rounds were coming from. They had been discovered and were under attack by a well-hidden force. Another bullet found its mark and a team member fell holding his side. They tossed grenades in the direction of the attack. Sergeant Willens yelled in a panic, "Drop back, drop back." He moved in the direction of the path they had followed to get to the point where they were ambushed. More incoming rounds hit all around the retreating Marines. The wounded men were dragged along. A third Marine was struck.

As they moved back into the jungle the attack came from a different direction. The team was in a deadly crossfire. In desperation, they fired wildly as they retreated. Another Marine was hit and dropped instantly. It was obvious that he was dead. CAP Team 1-6-2 followed the trail they made earlier into the hills. The attack ended.

The Marines carried their dead and wounded as they made their way back to Quy Hoa. A safe distance behind the North Vietnamese regulars tracked their vanquished foe. It was unknown territory to them and quite a discovery when they saw the small villages on the river.

Late in the afternoon approximately 6,000 demonstrators broke from the crowd and advanced on the Justice Department at 950 Pennsylvania Avenue, NW. Led by members of the Youth International Party, known as Yippies, they threw rocks and bottles and burned American flags. In the end almost 100 perpetrators were arrested.

Most demonstrators began leaving the city at 8:00 p.m. and by 11:00 p.m. all was quiet.

Jack Moore sat on his favorite bar stool at More-Or-Less. It was late Saturday night and the crowd had thinned. The temperature outside had dropped to near freezing and Jack was in no hurry to see his breath puffing out before him.

"So, the GW jumper—who was he?" Harry asked from behind.

Jack turned to face his friend, "That's what everyone wants to know."

"I thought a big-time investigative reporter like you would know."

"Why don't you ask Detective Akimoto. Apparently, she was there."

"Did I detect a little animosity in that comment?"

"First denial—then bargaining—then anger whatever the steps are."

"Don't be too hard on her. She's carrying a lot of baggage," Harry advised.

"I'm not really angry and I don't blame her. It just wasn't meant to be. You can't put a Yankee fan and a Mets fan in the same cage and not expect fireworks."

"Yeah, I'd say that sums it up—if you're into oversimplification."

"She's a great gal and I miss her but it's better not to postpone the inevitable. It would only make it that much more painful—you son-of-a-bitch why did you have to bring her up?"

"I didn't—you did."

"Don't cloud the subject with facts."

"What about the demonstrations in Washington?" Harry changed the subject.

"When I was at Woodstock I met a lot of young people. They were idealists and peaceniks and nature lovers and free lovers and simple and authentic. There wasn't any pretention. If the kids that marched in Washington are like those at Woodstock they are sincere and care. They might be a little naïve about international affairs but aren't we all?"

"I don't know. Sometimes it pisses me off," Harry admitted.

"I can see that. We should be supporting our troops and our nation."

"When the North Vietnamese see all the unrest in America they have no reason to negotiate. They've won a psychological victory which will ultimately lead to a military victory. What these demonstrators don't get is that more American soldiers will die due to their actions."

Jack finished his drink and stood. As he put on his topcoat he asked, "How are the wedding preparations coming?"

"We're moving along. Amanda and Ry . . . Amanda bought her wedding gown. Of course, I'm not allowed to see it until the wedding."

"I'm looking forward to it. I know you two are going to be happy. You both deserve it." Jack turned and walked out into the cold dark night.

Anna Six Trees walked in the snow and remembered how much she and her brother enjoyed walking in the snow on a moonlit night.

95: Monday – November 17, 1969

Stephanie Ellis sat in her small living room with two New York City detectives. She had called the police department looking for the detective who had been on the George Washington Bridge Friday night when an unknown man jumped to his death. It was clear to Stephanie that the man was her father. He had not returned home.

After being put on hold and bounced around she finally was connected to Detective Ryoya Akimoto. The detective was genuinely sympathetic and, after hearing the words in the note, agreed there was a distinct possibility that the jumper was her father, Matthew Ellis. While she only saw him in the dark for a brief period of time a photograph provided by Stephanie helped confirm the identification.

"Your father was obviously distraught and riddled with guilt over this wire fraud. Do you know what he meant that innocent people died?" Ryoya Akimoto asked.

"He never talked about his business activities that took place before the accident," Stephanie told the detective. "I guess I was just glad that his health was improving. He would go off for long periods of time and return without telling me where he had been." She paused then thought of something and said, "Wait, there was this newspaper reporter who met with my father. They discussed something but I think neither one was sure of the facts."

"Do you know the reporter's name?"

"Of course, it is Jack Moore. He's with the *Tribune*."

Ryoya was shocked to hear Jack's name but didn't show it. She wrote the name in her notebook. "Is there anything in your father's things that might help us solve this puzzle?"

"You're welcome to look," Stephanie indicated the bedroom.

Among the few possessions that Matthew Ellis had the detectives found a spool of wire. It was the spool with dark gray wire and the Orztech logo Matt had found in the empty LPAmerica offices. They also leafed through numerous papers that were in a suitcase and number of boxes. Nothing else concrete was found.

"Do you mind if we take this wire with us?" Detective Akimoto asked.

Stephanie looked at the spool of wire. As she did, she recalled her father's note. Before her was the poison that took her father's life. That gray obscenity must be the bad wire of which he wrote. It drew her attention in a hypnotic manner. The wire that coiled around a metal spool was a powerless specimen. Elsewhere in the world, there were endless lengths in nameless locations carrying current waiting for the moment when they would cease to function. What would be the result—a minor annoyance or more lives put at risk? How many times in how many places was an interruption destined to happen? And in the end, what would be the financial cost or what would be the toll in human lives? It was almost too frightful to conceive. Like some hideous virus unleashed on an unsuspecting population there was no way to know where it would turn up next. Stephanie felt lightheaded and reeled. As a fog descended upon her she understood why her father chose the course of action that he did.

Apollo 12 beamed a television transmission back to Earth prior to lunar orbit insertion. They showed the Earth, moon, and interior of the spacecraft. All was AOK.

Jack Moore was surprised to hear Ryoya's voice when he answered his telephone. She was pleasant and friendly, however, got right down to business by asking him if he knew a Matthew Ellis.

"Yes, I do," he replied, "I was investigating allegations of fraud on the part of the company that he had once worked for."

"Orztech Corporation?"

"That's it. What is your interest in Ellis?"

"He was the individual who jumped from the George Washington Bridge last Friday."

"Are you sure of that?"

"We met with his daughter this morning and confirmed the identification through a photograph."

"Suicide, I didn't see that coming."

"Apparently, neither did his daughter."

"What drove him to take his life?"

"I thought you would know."

"It may have something to do with the fraud investigation."

"He left a note. Guilt over what he had done drove him to jump."

Jack shared what information he had concerning the wire fraud. He was surprised that the police had a spool of the wire in question. It would obviously be the subject of examination and testing. Among the pieces of information Jack shared were the names Parker Adolphson, former president of Orztech Corporation, and Lida Petropoulos. Finally, he pointed out that from his conversations with Matthew Ellis the wire was possibly used in military applications, the aeronautic industry, automotive idustry, and NASA.

"NASA?" Ryoya asked in disbelief.

"An anonymous source at NASA confirmed the wire was used in the space program. In fact, it might have been the cause of the Apollo 1 fire that killed three astronauts. And, has been used in various parts utilized by the Apollo program."

"There is a spacecraft headed for the moon right now," Ryoya stated the obvious.

"And on that spacecraft might be strands of that wire that could fail at any time."

Apollo 12 went behind the moon approximately 97 miles above the surface. A six-minute lunar insertion burn was executed placing the spacecraft in an elliptical orbit ranging from 69 to 195 miles.

Marvin Press, known as Shortstop, rested in a hospital bed aboard the hospital ship USS Sanctuary. When he got wounded he didn't know he had been shot. It felt like someone had punched him in the stomach. Other than that—no pain. When it happened he kept moving through the jungle with CAP Team 1-6-2 as they retreated. Next thing he knew he was lying on the ground looking up at the trees with his head spinning. He wasn't sure how he got in that position but didn't have the strength to get up. Navy Corpsman Gordon Lassiter leaned over him and said, "Lay still Marvin, I've got to slow the bleeding." Shortstop drifted in and out of consciousness. In a daze, he felt himself being lifted and carried. There were distant sounds of a firefight. Handling was rough as they carried and dragged him to safety. Suddenly, it became quiet. The only sound he heard was the rustling of the canvass that held him. Then someone screamed. It was a hauntingly plaintive sound. Animal-like and desperate the sound was one of a dying creature. Corpsman Gordon Lassiter appeared once more above him, "Hang in there Marvin, we're getting you on a dust-off helicopter. You'll be in good hands really soon. I know it hurts." Shortstop passed out. After a quick stop in Da Nang he was transported to the USS Sanctuary. He'd lost a kidney and a lot of blood but the prognosis was good.

Lai Ngoc Linh and his six-year-old sister, Lai Thanh Tuyen stood and watched as soldiers in black uniforms shoved and hit the villagers and held them at gunpoint.

96: Wednesday – November 19, 1969

On the prior day, Charles "Pete" Conrad Jr., and Alan L. Bean had entered the Lunar Module, separated from the Command Module, and settled into an orbit around the moon. This day in the fourteenth orbit the descent maneuver began. While behind the moon a 29 second burn of the descent engine lowered Intrepid's orbit to 9 by 69 miles from the surface. A new navigation computer program promised a precision touchdown at the intended site. Charles "Pete" Conrad controlled the descent semi-manually for the last 500 feet. Without incident, Intrepid landed in the Ocean of Storms about 535 feet northwest of where the unmanned probe Surveyor III had landed on April 20, 1967. The landing site would thereafter be listed as Statio Cognitum on lunar maps. Conrad nicknamed the intended touchdown area "Pete's Parking Lot."

A knock on the door gained Stephanie Ellis' attention. She rose from the small kitchen table, walked over, and opened the door. Before her stood Clinton MacIntyre. Tall and fit, wearing a dark brown business suit and his black Stetson, he said in a fatherly voice, "I came as soon as I heard."

"How did . . . I don't understand."

"Your friend, the newspaperman, called me and told me the sad news and I didn't want you to feel all alone."

Stephanie stood in disbelief. Her tortured mind wasn't able to process quickly. After an uneasy pause, she said, "Please, come in."

"Thank you." Clinton MacIntyre entered the apartment, turned to face Stephanie, and said, "It's so difficult to know what to say to bring someone comfort at times like this. I can't take away your pain, but I can be here and help you face it. Maureen and I would like you to come to Texas. You can stay with us until the college semester begins."

"Mr. MacIntyre."

"Clinton."

"Mr. MacIntyre, I really appreciate your kindness." Stephanie shook her head, "But, Colt and I just met and I don't feel right taking so much . . ."

"Wait," Clinton MacIntyre interrupted, "you are not taking anything. In fact, you are giving. If you wish to pursue the dream of building an international adoption agency it will require time and effort and dedication on your part. The money is insignificant. If Colt were alive, he and I would have come to this point together." Clinton smiled, "I would have made him sweat. However, the outcome would be the same." He took Stephanie's hand and led her to the couch. She sat and he continued, "The only decision you have to make at this time is whether or not this is something you want to do. I don't want you to feel pressured. If you decide you are not interested in building an adoption agency, that will be the end of it. On the other hand, if it is your goal, focus on getting there." The big man paused, looked down at his hands, and said with a note of first-hand experience, "Sometimes it's best to look forward and not dwell on the past."

"The world seems so surreal. Everything is upside down," Stephanie said softly sounding like a lost child—which she was.

Clinton MacIntyre looked up. He raised a daughter so was not in unfamiliar territory. Yet, Colt's younger sister, Amy, enjoyed a rosy and comfortable childhood unlike the young lady with whom he sat. He searched for the right words. Then as if from a source beyond him he thought of words once spoken by Colt. "When you're confused and hurt and down it's the perfect time to take a chance cause you've got nothing to lose."

Stephanie thought about those words. There really was very little to keep her in New Jersey. She hadn't lost her interest in adoption. Yet, she still had trouble accepting so much from relative strangers.

"You know it's the right thing to do," Clinton MacIntyre said giving her a nudge.

"I still don't feel comfortable with it."

"I'll tell you what I'd tell my daughter Amy," Clinton offered, "I expect you to take college seriously and work hard. You're going there for a reason and it's not partying or acting out. You goof off and you'll hear from me," he smiled and added, "And stay off Sixth Street."

"Sixth Street?"

"It's where all the bars and hangouts are located in Austin."

Stephanie laughed. It felt strange to do so. She looked at Clinton MacIntyre and felt a kind of bond with him as both of them experienced a painful loss so recently. "I'll stay away from Sixth Street," she said.

The decision made they discussed how she was to make the move to Texas. She would have some things shipped and pack a few things to take with her. It was a big step but she had to take it.

Pete Conrad and Allan Bean slipped into their space suits. After doing so, they reviewed the lunar checklist attached to the wrist of each suit. Conrad examined the checklist flip-book. To his surprise, he came face to heavenly body of Angela Dorian, *Playboy* Miss September 1967 with the caption "SEEN ANY INTERESTING HILLS & VALLEYS?" Following that was a picture of Reagan Wilson, Miss October 1967 and the caption "PREFERRED TETHER PARTNER," which referred to the emergency sharing of life-support systems. In Allan Bean's wrist flip-book were photos of Cynthia Myers, Miss December 1968 "DON'T FORGET–DESCRIBE THE PROTUBERANCES" and Leslie Bianchini, Miss January 1969 "SURVEY–HER ACTIVITY." The backup crew being all Air Force had slipped in the reduced size photocopies as a prank on their all Navy counterparts. The third member of Apollo 12 was not overlooked as Dick Gordon, on board the Yankee Clipper in lunar orbit, found a November, 1969 calendar featuring DeDe Lind, Miss August 1967, in a locker.

Astronaut Pete Conrad opened the hatch to Intrepid and after a prolonged effort to get through climbed down the ladder. As he stepped onto the Lunar Module pad at the bottom he said, "Whoopie! Man, that may have been a small one for Neil, but that's a long one for me." Conrad at 5'6" was referring to the fact that Neil Armstrong was much taller. A pet peeve of Pete Conrad was the public belief that NASA told the astronauts what to say on their missions. He knew Neil Armstrong's words were his own. One afternoon during the summer an Italian journalist, Oriana Fallaci, visited the Conrad home in Houston where she stated that she was convinced NASA told Neil

Armstrong what to say. It was then that Pete Conrad decided what he was going to say and bet her $500 that he would do so. She accepted the bet. Although he won he never collected the money.

"I'm going to step off the pad," Conrad told Mission Control. He placed a foot on the moon's surface and remarked, "Off the . . . Oooh, is that soft and queasy." As he clung to the ladder he said, "Hey, that's neat. I don't sink in too far." He let go of the ladder, "I'll try a little . . . Boy, that Sun is bright. That's just like somebody shining a spotlight in your hand." After a pause, "Well, I can walk pretty well, Al, but I've got to take it easy and watch what I'm doing." Pete Conrad walked around, back to the LM, and looked east. "Boy, you'll never believe it. Guess what I see sitting on the side of the crater!"

From inside the LM Alan Bean replied, "The old Surveyor, right?"

Conrad laughed, "The old Surveyor. Yes, sir. Does that look neat! It can't be any further than 600 feet from here. How about that?"

A color television camera had been carried to the moon on Apollo 12. Unfortunately, Al Bean unintentionally pointed it directly into the Sun which destroyed the Secondary Electron Conduction tube. Thus, television coverage of the mission was impossible.

The two astronauts spent three hours and thirty-nine minutes on the lunar surface. Conrad collected surface samples and deployed the S-band communication antenna and equipment that took measurements of the Moon's seismicity, solar wind flux, and magnetic field. These were part of the first nuclear-powered Apollo Lunar Surface Experiments Package (ALSEP) station on the Moon to relay long-term data back to Earth.

The crew of Apollo 12 were good friends. So good that they convinced a car dealer in Cocoa Beach with contacts at General Motors to get them three matching gold Corvettes with license plates signifying their Apollo 12 assignment; CDR for Conrad, CMP for Gordon, and LMP for Bean.

Pete Conrad was a jokester. Because he was a collector of baseball caps he tried to get a huge blue and white one made that he could fit over his helmet. He wanted to walk in front of the television camera on the Moon wearing it. Unfortunately, he was unable to sneak it aboard the spacecraft.

Eduardo Fernandez waived extradition and was transported to New York custody. Phillipe Lopez was still at large, probably hiding in Puerto Rico. The case was now in the hands of the district attorney. Of course, Eduardo painted a picture of innocence and being in the wrong place at the wrong time in his statement.

Detective Ryoya Akimoto finished typing her report on the George Washington Bridge jumper. In her report, she referred to his suicide note and the spool of suspect wire. Due to the potential widespread tragedies that could occur she recommended that further investigation of the wire fraud be implemented as quickly as possible.

Sergeant Curtis Willens pulled CAP team 1-6-2 away from Quy Hoa. When they arrived at a safe LZ he requested that they be removed from the area as the villages had been overrun by North Vietnamese regulars. In half an hour two Huey helicopters arrived and removed the remaining team members. They were flown to Pleiku Air Base where he was debriefed by an Army Major.

"It was touch and go," Willens stated. "They were definitely commie sympathizers. After we did a search of the village that so-called interpreter Nghiem Duc Hung called in the North Vietnamese regulars. We were severely outnumbered. I don't know why the lance corporal I replaced didn't check the place out. Maybe he was over his head, or incompetent, or scared, but he never investigated the villages."

"Are there NVA there now?"

"Last reconnoiter we did they were hanging around like old buddies."

"Do you think this is a stopping off place for insurgents crossing the border?"

"Affirmative."

"And the locals are complicit?"

"Affirmative."

"I'll forward this to command. You and your men will be redeployed. That is all."

Anna Six Trees had a dream of a far-off place. It was an island and native Americans were dancing and chanting.

97: Thursday – November 20, 1969

Seventy-Nine American Indians eluded a Coast Guard blockade in San Francisco Bay to once again land on Alcatraz Island. Among them were students, married couples, and six children. It had been weeks since their first occupation of the island and they felt no progress had been made with the government.

Over the years, the San Francisco Bay area had become a location with a large urban Native American population. As is normal with any culture, they found comfort with their own people. Community centers and college campuses became regular meeting venues. Frustration grew as did their need to take action. On this day, a large group landed on the island with the intent of staying.

One of the leaders, Richard Oakes, sent a message to the San Francisco Department of the Interior. "We invite the United States to acknowledge the justice of our claim. The choice now lies with the leaders of the American government—to use violence upon us as before to remove us from our Great Spirit's land, or to institute a real change in its dealing with the American Indian. We do not fear your threat to charge us with crimes on our land. We and all other oppressed peoples would welcome spectacle of proof before the world of your title by genocide. Nevertheless, we seek peace."

Ritchie Anderson helped Stephanie with some final packing. She didn't have a lot of boxes which Clinton MacIntrye made arrangements to have picked up and shipped to Victoria, Texas. Among the items she was taking were a number of paintings that Ritchie had given her. He picked up one and examined it. It was a portrait of a small black dog. Fetch had that mischievous look on her face that dared you to turn your back. The time when he created that painting seemed so long ago. He smiled at that funny little face and missed his friend. She was better off where she was but that didn't take the sting out of seeing those brown eyes.

"Did you hear from your soldier friend?" Stephanie brought Ritchie back to reality.

"What? Uh, no," he replied. "It's only been a couple weeks. Things move really slowly in the military. I doubt he even got my letter, yet."

"When you do, you know where to reach me. I believe Mr. MacIntyre was serious about wanting to help those children."

"As soon as I hear anything, I'll let you know," he reassured her.

"I appreciate everything you've done to help me," Stephanie said sincerely.

"I'm sorry things turned out as they did," Ritchie said softly. He walked over and put his hands on Stephanie's shoulders and followed with a more enthusiastic statement, "You're going to do great things in Texas. Think of this as a new beginning to the happy part of your life. Spread your wings and fly."

Thirty B-52s were preparing for takeoff from Kadena Air Base on the island of

Okinawa. Strategic Air Command (SAC) established the 4252d Strategic Wing (SW) on 12 January 1965 and assigned it to the 3d Air Division. Missions were then flown over Vietnam on a daily basis.

The B-52 was designed to carry nuclear weapons as a deterrent. When the decision was made to use these aircraft in Vietnam they were modified to carry conventional high explosive bombs. Each B-52 could carry eighty-four 500-pound bombs internally and twenty-four 750-pound bombs on underwing racks. As a result, the destructive power of a single B-52 was enormous and lethal.

In the briefing before the mission the pilots were given their primary and secondary targets. This mission was aimed at the influx of men and material along the Ho Chi Minh Trail from Laos and Cambodia.

The pilot and navigator of the aircraft designated as Green 4 discussed their primary. "From what I can tell there's nothing there," the navigator stated while looking at the map.

"The Laos and Cambodian borders are approximately 100 miles west of Kontum and Pleiku. Right here where the two borders intersect is where the suspected infiltration trail enters Vietnam. Somewhere in the mountains to the south of that trail is a village named Quy Hoa that is harboring Charlie. It's on this river," the pilot explained.

"We have the coordinates, we'll just have to flatten everything in that area."

"If there is a village there, it won't be when we drop our load."

The thirty-jet mission named Roadblock 1 took off on time and began its three-and-a-half-hour flight to Vietnam.

"We don't have time to chase shadows," Lieutenant Klein stated when Detective Akimoto inquired about follow-up to the Orztech wire fraud.

"If there is bad wire out there that could fail and cause accidents shouldn't we investigate and alert those at risk?" she inquired.

"According to your report, this Orztech Corporation went out of business a couple years ago."

"Correct."

"Do you have any specific information on where this wire is in use?"

"Not specific."

"Then there's no one to alert."

"Maybe, we should at least inform manufacturers in the industries indicated not to use Orztech wire if they have any on the shelf."

"What percentage of the Orztech wire is inferior?"

"Unknown."

"What proof do you have that the wire ever failed?"

"An anonymous statement from a NASA employee."

"Not much to work with, is it?"

"Not much."

"Be realistic, we have no way of knowing what companies to inform. Besides, it's not our job. We have enough to do, while shorthanded, solving crimes. Is that clear, detective?"

"Yes, it's clear."

An hour and a half earlier than planned, Pete Conrad and Alan Bean began their second EVA. While on the lunar surface they collected about 85 pounds of rock and dirt samples. In addition, they retrieved samples from as deep as 32 inches below the surface. Finally, they made their way over to the 650-foot-wide crater where Surveyor III landed. Numerous photos were taken of the unmanned vehicle. The seventeen-pound camera was removed to be returned to Earth. The EVA lasted three hours and forty-eight minutes. In the end, the two astronauts climbed aboard the LM, slipped out of the pressurized suits, and jettisoned them onto the Moon.

Approximately six hours later the LM ascent engine was fired for about seven minutes to lift off of the lunar surface and achieve orbit. Three and a half hours later in an orbit between 10 and 54 miles, Intrepid rendezvoused with Yankee Clipper. The maneuver was televised to Earth. Once Conrad and Bean were safely aboard the Command Service Module, Intrepid was released and its engine fired to have it leave orbit and impact on the lunar surface. Plans were then made for the return trip home.

In a small dingy office on Parris Island a large black man with a serious look on his face sat reading a sheet of paper. It was a casualty report. On it Sergeant Kincaid stared at the name Lance Corporal Wellington Marsh M.I.A. He knew the names of all his recruits that he tried desperately to turn into Marines in an ever-shorter period of time. It bothered him every time he saw one of their names followed by K.I.A or M.I.A. Yet, there was something about this particular young man that stood out. He had many skills, a good attitude, leadership capabilities, intelligence, and an undaunted spirit. He was an impressive individual and would have had a good future in the Corps. Sergeant Kincaid hated this war. He hated all war. However, he knew if brave young men and women didn't stand up to aggression and evil freedom would be on the casualty list followed by K.I.A. Peace on earth was an unachievable myth. The best you could do was keep tyrants and evildoers at bay. Minimize their impact. The fight would go on and on and on. And, like it or not, good young people with promising futures would sacrifice those futures to protect the inalienable rights of others. Good versus evil has no end.

The drill instructor picked up a pen and began to write a note to the parents of Lance Corporal Wellington Marsh. It was not his policy to write parents and he wasn't sure why he was compelled to do so in this case. He wanted Marsh's parents to know they had raised an exceptional son. Whether this would bring them a modicum of comfort or increase their sense of loss he didn't know. What he did know was he shared a feeling of loss.

"Hey, yo-yo," a young woman with long straight black hair that hung past her shoulders said while standing in Jack Moore's office door.

Jack immediately recognized "Cleavage" from Woodstock. She didn't look the same, as instead of a vest over bare breasts she wore a white cotton blouse over a pleated dark blue skirt. "Hi, what a surprise, come in. I'm sorry I can't offer you a dovetail."

The young woman laughed and replied, "You're not wearing the beads I gave you."

"They clash with my suit."

"I can see that."

Jack motioned to a chair, "Sit, what brings a girl from Danbury to the Big Apple?"

"I thought about what you said at Woodstock," she began.

"I said a lot of things."

"Actually, it was what you wrote," she reached into her purse and pulled out a newspaper clipping. It was Jack Moore's column—the one where he confessed to smoking, albeit secondhand, marijuana. "At the end of your column you wrote, 'Woodstock is destined to become a defining moment for the counter-culture in America. It's easy to point out things that are unfair or unreasonable. It's not as easy to make a difference. And, I know one thing for sure; you don't change things that you believe are wrong by running away. It's the coward's way out.' It was like you were talking directly to me."

"In a way, I was," Jack said.

"I decided to heed your advice and instead of dropping out pitching in. I'm back in school studying journalism. I want to be a reporter—not just any reporter—one like you."

"I'm flattered, but it would be better if you were a reporter just like you. One thing that is universally true is that the world keeps changing, evolving, and redefining itself. I'm old school—soon to be a dinosaur. My values and mores come from the world I started my career in. Your perspective will be different. I hope for the better but sometimes wonder."

"In our tent, in the rain, you treated us with respect and were honest. That really struck me. All the other accounts of Woodstock painted such warped pictures. I was there and know the truth. It wasn't all rosy and beautiful, but it also wasn't a complete breakdown in society and gathering of uncivilized savages."

"No, it wasn't. There was an air of cooperation, kindness, and compassion that I haven't seen since. Although, there was also a lot of drug use."

"In your column, you told the truth," Cleavage said. "However, there is a good side to coming face to face with such truth. It allows you to change what can be changed and to accept that which you have no control over," she quoted one of Jack's lines from another column. She got a serious look on her face, leaned forward, and said with determination, "I want to speak the truth. It's the only way to affect change."

"You mean effect," Jack corrected.

"Effect?"

"Yes, to bring about. Affect means to act on. At Woodstock, you affected me many ways."

"It was the grass."

"Yeah, let's leave it at that."

His guest began to laugh. "That could be interpreted many ways."

"I guess it could." Jack paused and then confessed, "I have to admit something, here. I don't know your name. Did you ever tell it to me?"

"I did, you wrote it down along with my telephone number, and promised to call. You never did."

"I don't remember that."

Once again, she laughed, "I'm goofing on you. I never told you my name. It's Denise Chamberlain."

"For someone who wants to tell the truth, you lie well."

"It's a knack."

"I see. How can I help you, Denise Chamberlain?"

"How does one get a job as a reporter?" She quickly added, "I know, I have to finish school and get a degree. But, I don't want to waste any time. If I start now, I might have a better grasp on the whole thing by the time I graduate."

They spent the next two hours discussing types of reporters, different media, some cold hard facts about the business, and her goals. Denise was a smart girl with a quick wit. It appeared that she had the tools, all she needed was a plan of action. Jack gave her some pointers about doing freelance work, executing primary research studies and writing about the findings, targeting smaller media outlets to begin, and creating a personal image. Denise enthusiastically took notes and was grateful for the guidance.

When they finished, Denise changed the subject and asked, "How did things work out with your police honey?"

"I'm afraid that I played that one wrong. You called it." Jack shook his head, "Too much pressure. She bolted."

"Sorry to hear that," Denise said. She then advised Jack, "Give it time and give her space. Sometimes things work out. If not, it's better to know now."

"Maybe you could start an advice to the lovelorn column," Jack quipped.

"I don't think so. You see how well I did with you."

"So, you're back in school and becoming a part of the establishment. How do your Danbury pals feel about it?"

"They understand. Sometimes you just gotta be a yo-yo."

Twelve-year-old Nghiem Duc Hung heard the sounds of many large planes and looked skyward.

98: Monday – November 24, 1969

A snowball—soft, white, fluffy, cold, and wet found its mark. With an almost imperceptible thump it exploded on the back of Carl's head.

"What the . . . hey!" Carl exclaimed.

Laurel didn't say a word as she disappeared into the woods. Carl followed. Snow was eight inches deep, therefore running was out of the question. As they plodded their way Carl knew where they were headed. In about ten minutes they reached the cave.

Inside the cave, it was dark but, without the stiff breeze, somewhat warmer. Laurel began lighting candles and placing them around the stone retreat. Candlelight created a milieu of dancing shadows. In an odd sort of way flickering flames made the cave seem even warmer.

"Who are you—Carl Pythacyk?" Laurel asked as she sat upon a rock.

Surprised and confused by her question he responded, "What do you want to know?"

"I know what you have done since coming here, that you saved a child's life, and that you're not a murderer. You come from New York, are afraid of bees, and love me."

"Not true."

Laurel pouted, "You don't love me?"

"I'm not afraid of bees."

"Yes, you are."

"OK, I am. I'm terrified of bees."

"And you love me."

"You are making it very difficult." Carl wiped the back of his head which was still wet.

"I'm making it interesting."

"To say the least."

"So, answer my question," Laurel smiled.

"What was the question?"

"Who are you? What are your values, goals, desires? What makes you happy. Besides bees and me what are you afraid of?"

"You? I'm not . . . never mind."

"If I were even to consider marrying you, I'd have to know a lot more about you. Don't you agree?"

"Marrying me? I haven't asked you."

"Not yet, but you're planning to—aren't you?"

"No."

"No?"

"You deserve better than some common street thug."

"I do. That's why I want to know who you are. Is that all you are—a common street thug?"

"That's what I was."

"That's what you were. I want to know who you are."

Carl thought for a moment. "For a long time, all I was trying to do was survive—

make my way on the mean streets of the city. You either were a victim, scared rabbit, sellout, or top dog. I preferred to be on top."

Laurel stared directly into Carl's eyes which made him uncomfortable. He felt that he had to choose his words carefully because she was hanging on every one. Something made him feel like he had to explain more, "Look you have to have been there to understand the world I come from. In some ways, the city is more of a wilderness than these mountains. If you didn't watch your back, someone would put a knife in it. Here, life is so much more pleasant and meaningful. We grow things, build things, share things, see things, and enjoy things. I never knew such a place existed." Carl walked over to one of the candles and gazed into the flame. It brought him back to when Laurel sat in front of the fireplace. "The first night that I was here and you sang I forgot about everything that I left behind. I only wanted to be in that room hearing your voice, watching you play the guitar, seeing your hair sway with the music. I didn't want to leave and head to Canada but I was on the run. When I left here I felt as though my life had ended." He turned back to face Laurel, "You asked what makes me happy? Being right here with you. I could do without the snowball, but if that's part of the package."

"It is," Laurel pointed out. "Being unpredictable is part of my nature. You'd have to get used to that."

"I can adjust."

"Do you want children?"

"Never thought about it."

"What about your parents. Are they in New York?"

"I don't want to talk about it."

"Then leave."

"What?"

"If you don't wish to talk anymore you are free to leave."

"You're throwing me out?"

"Not at all. I wish to talk and you do not. Therefore, you may leave."

"Your way or the highway," Carl remarked.

Laurel looked toward the mouth of the cave, tilted her head, and replied, "It's more of a snow-covered path."

"Some things are painful, "Carl admitted.

"Less so, when shared."

Carl told Laurel the story about the destroyed book from the old country and he and his father's falling out. He also told of how he replaced the damn book. While his voice sounded angry, Laurel was acutely aware of deep unrelenting pain.

"We have to go to New York," Laurel said.

"Why?"

"You and your parents have to reconcile."

"Never happen," Carl snapped.

"It must and it will."

"You don't know my old man."

"I fear you don't know him." Laurel took Carl's hand, looked directly at him, and explained, "If you harbor anger and pain you cannot fully open your heart. Until you face your demons your love for me is a shallow stream lacking the depth to support life."

"You're wrong. I love you with all my heart."

"If that were true there would be no question about going to New York."

"I guess we're going to New York."

Laurel smiled and kissed Carl. They blew out the candles and left the cave. Carl led the way as they followed the path back to the farmhouse. A snowball hit him in the back of the head.

Before leaving the Moon, Alan Bean tossed his silver astronaut pin into a lunar crater. A silver pin is given to an astronaut who completed training but had not yet flown in space. Bean had worn his pin for six years. It was a common tradition for military pilots to ceremoniously toss their original flight wings when awarded others. Bean would receive a gold pin after completing the mission.

The return flight to Earth was uneventful. On Saturday, a mid-course correction maneuver was executed about 208,000 miles from Earth. On Sunday, they held a press conference from space 108,000 miles from Earth. As Apollo 12 prepared to re-enter the atmosphere a number of technicians discussed their concern that the lightning strikes during launch might have disabled the parachute explosive bolts. If the system failed the astronauts would plummet to their deaths. It was decided that there was no value in alerting the crew.

At 3:58 p.m. EDT Yankee Clipper returned safely to Earth. Splashdown occurred approximately three miles from the target area. It landed in the Pacific Ocean about 500 nautical miles southeast of American Samoa. The entire mission took 244 hours, 36 minutes, 25 seconds—a mere 62 seconds longer than planned. During splashdown, a 16mm film camera was dislodged from its storage rack and hit Alan Bean on the forehead. He was knocked briefly unconscious, suffered a mild concussion, and required six stitches. The vehicle was recovered by the aircraft carrier USS Hornet. The three astronauts were flown to Pago Pago International Airport for a reception and then on to Honolulu.

Wanda Six Trees told her daughter Anna about the brave Indians of all tribes claiming an island far to the west.

99: Wednesday – November 26, 1969

After lengthy debate and less than unanimous agreement from his staff President Richard Nixon issued Executive Order 11497—Amending the Selective Service Regulations to Prescribe Random Selection. A draft lottery was to be created that prioritized selection based on date-of-birth and first letter of individuals' surname. A drawing would take place on December 1, 1969 and be implemented on the first day of 1970. The lottery would include all male registrants between the ages of 18 and 26.

Ritchie found himself with an old friend—actually two old friends. The twins hadn't gone anywhere while he was away. All they did was go upward and were now significantly above ground level growing toward the sky. It was a cold morning intensified by a stiff breeze off the Hudson River. The plan was to use a photo of the construction of the World Trade Center on a cover of one of the financial magazines his father published. Of course, this also allowed Ritchie to add to his own portfolio of the project.

The artist in Ritchie drove him to take shots from many different angles. At one point, he took a shot through the upright steel external frame that had the appearance of a forest. The view brought him back to an Indian reservation in Minnesota. His mind reflected on the Witch Tree, Chief Michael, and a young boy. As he drifted back to that place and time an inspiration hit him.

For their outdoor magazine, he would use Chief Michael and some other members of the tribe in a wilderness setting. Winter snow would make a beautiful backdrop. He decided to run the idea past the editor.

In a small room at the Corona State Prison for Women in California, Sergeant Michael Nielsen, badge number 7945, of the Robbery-Homicide Division interviewed inmate Virginia Kathleen Graham. It was 3:15 in the afternoon. She had briefly spent time as a cellmate of Susan Atkins at the Sybil Brand Institution for Women in Chino and had come forward after that member of the Manson family confessed to murder. Atkins was known within the Manson family as Sadie Mae Glutz.

". . . at first I had no idea what she was there for and she's very young and looks real sweet and I thought, oh, you poor little kid, you know. She just looks that way—to me anyway," Graham told Nielsen.

"And I started talking to her one day. We were sitting on two little stools and we just started chatting and I asked her, 'What are you here for?' you know, I started like I was going to scold her and she said, 'First degree murder.' So, I just looked at her and I said, 'Oh, you are, huh?' And then she told me she had a case and she had a co-defendant over in the county jail and she dropped it."

"So anyway, then she came up one evening. She started talking to me very serious about it, you know, just as serious as she could, and I was very frank with her. I said, 'If you did what you are here for, if you did—now I don't care, you sure talk about it an awful lot. If you want to take a piece of advice from somebody that's a little older than you. I wouldn't talk as much as you do, because you never know.' She said, 'Oh, I know. I haven't talked about it to anybody else.' She started saying, 'Oh, well, there's so much that they don't know,' and I said, 'Well, what do you mean?' She said, 'Well, you know, there's a case right now, they are so far off the track they don't even know what's happening.' I said, 'What are you talking about?' and she said, 'That one on Benedict Canyon.' I said, 'You don't mean Sharon Tate?' and she said, 'Yeah.' And with this she got real kind of like excited, you know, and everything came out real fast. I mean you could see the girl was really excited."

Sergeant Nielsen asked, "She didn't need much prompting to tell you the story?"

"Not at all, not at all. In fact, just before she said that, she said, 'You know, I can look at you and there's something about you. I know I can tell things to you.' And, I laughed, so she told me about a fellow named Charles Manson and two other girls, there was four of them all together."

"Did she name the girls?"

"She did not. She just named the fellow, and she said that they were given instructions by him. And, he must have had a tremendous influence on all these girls and obviously, there was quite a few girls from the way she spoke to me about it. And also, her co-defendant had been in their sect too, but he had nothing—from what I could gather—to do with this murder on Benedict Canyon, you know. And, anyway, she said that they had decided they wanted to do a crime that would shock the world, that the world would have to stand up and take notice. And, of course, I know the little girl had been on LSD and speed."

"What did she tell you about Benedict Canyon?"

"She said that they went to this house because it was isolated and they picked these people from random. In other words, they didn't know these people at all, but she knew this house because she told me that Terry Melcher, who is Doris Day's son, had owned it and she knew Terry from a year or so back. So, she said that they went up; they cut the wires. She said the service wires or something. I said, 'Well, wouldn't that have taken off all the electricity?' and she said something, about, 'No, just for the phone.' And then she said that they killed the boy first, Parent. She said that they shot him four times. They felt that he saw them. So, I think she told me—I'm not positive. I think she said that this Charles shot him."

"Did she say how they got in?"

"No. No. She didn't?"

"Okay. Go ahead."

"She said that they went on into the house and that the girl, Ann Folger, was sitting in the living room reading, and when they came in she didn't look up. She didn't hear them or something. It seems, from the way she told me, that two people stayed in the living room and two went to the bedroom. She said that Jay was sitting on the edge of the bed talking to Sharon. She said, 'She had on a bikini bra and panties,' and I said, 'You're kidding. And she was pregnant?' you know. And she said, 'Yeah. And they looked up and they were surprised.'" Virginia Graham paused, then continued her tale, "She just went on and said that Sharon was the last to die and that they had strung Jay and Sharon up with the noose around their neck, but she told me they did not put a hood over his head."

Sergeant Nielsen didn't say anything. He didn't want to break her stream of thought.

Virginia continued, "She held Sharon's arms back behind her and Sharon looked at her and said, 'Please don't kill me. Please don't kill me. I don't want to die.' She said she was crying and she said, 'Please, I'm going to have a baby.' And Sadie said to her, 'Look, bitch, I don't care if you're going to have a baby, you better be ready. You're going to die and that's all there is to it. Then we killed her a few minutes later.' I asked, 'Hey, why did you kill them?' And she said that they wanted to release them from this earth you know, so they could go on and that they loved them so much that they had to kill them and that this man, this Charlie Manson, obviously had schooled all these girls and boys, whatever, that there is a hole in the middle of Death Valley and that there are people living down underground and that they are going to start a new society and that they are the chosen few, they are elected, this group of people, to pick people at random and execute them."

Sergeant Nielsen asked, "Was she coherent?"

"Oh, completely. As coherent as I am speaking to you. Excited, but it was like a child that runs to its mother, 'Oh, mommy,' and I have to tell you something real fast type of thing."

"She appeared perfectly sane?"

"Completely. In fact, she told me that she's very good at playing crazy. Well, I said, 'You better be careful with something like this. If there are other people involved, somebody's going to spill the beans.' She said, 'No way, they wouldn't dare. They are so afraid, they know better, because that there's a lot of us.' She called this group of people something like they named it helter-skelter."

Virginia Graham went on to describe more gruesome facts and the events that she was told took place after the murders. Susan Atkins spoke of Charles Manson in admiring terms and indicated that there were three other murders in the desert.

Sergeant Nielsen asked, "Would you be willing to stand up and tell what she told you in court?"

Virginia replied, "Uh huh. Yeah. Yeah. I would, yes. I thought about that, too, because I am scared to death, because if there is a group of people like this, it's not a fantasy in her head, I don't know where they are and I'm sure I wouldn't want them to come and get me, but, yeah, I would. I mean if you felt that you had a case, then you got me."

This tip-off was the L.A. Police Department's first major break in the Sharon Tate/La Bianca case.

100: Thursday – November 27, 1969

Jack and Harry had breakfast in a small coffee shop on Third Avenue. It was seven in the morning and cold. As they ate the conversation turned to the upcoming wedding.

"So, is everything ready for the big day?" Jack inquired.

"How the hell do I know," Harry commented over his cup of coffee. "I just go where I'm told, do what I'm told, and agree with everything. It's easier that way."

"You learned quickly," Jack observed.

"Running a bar you get to see what works and what doesn't."

"I guess this will be our last year doing this."

"Maybe—maybe not," Harry concluded, "Who knows, maybe Amanda will join us."

"She might just do that—she's the caring sort."

"Yeah, and she isn't much of a cook, so this could be a better alternative."

"Are we ready?"

"Let's do it."

The entire house had the welcoming aroma of turkey in the oven, stuffing, potatoes and gravy, casseroles, biscuits, and more. Ritchie's mother hummed as she made final preparations. In her mind this was a special Thanksgiving as there was not only peace in the family but also hope. Richard and his father seemed to be working well together, magazine sales were up and there was talk about adding new titles, the military draft had been postponed and a new draft lottery offered even more hope, and her son was home even if only for the moment.

As had been their tradition for ten years, Jack Moore and Harry Van Ryker proceeded to the Sixth Street Mission where they helped prepare a feast for those who needed a Thanksgiving. From early morning until the end of the day the two of them, along with other volunteers, served hundreds of meals.

It was a mixed bag of experience. Some visitors arrived in a jovial mood, others somewhat sour, and still others quiet and withdrawn. It was the quiet ones that always drew Jack's attention. They were enigma. In some cases, they had simply seen too much of life's vicissitudes and folded inside themselves as a form of defense. Some just didn't want to be bothered with other human beings. Then there were those who were rookies—new to the destitute scene. They seemed to be confused or embarrassed or lost. It was a new and difficult episode in their life. Rookies were easy to spot.

On this day one rookie stood out. He was a young man, clean-cut, relatively neatly dressed—not your typical down-and-outer. By all appearances, he should have been on the serving side of the long table. Yet, here he was standing in line.

When the rookie got to Jack, who was serving mashed potatoes, he neither smiled nor frowned simply held out his plate.

"Lumpy or non-lumpy?" Jack asked in jest.

To Jack's surprise the young man said in a sad voice, "I already had my lumps—non-lumpy." He offered a sad smile. After his plate was filled the rookie found a quiet place off to the side alone and sat to eat.

Lark's Run always had a bountiful table. It's one of the nice things about a successful farm. After venturing out in the snow the day before to deliver food to various organizations around Warren, they settled in to have a relaxing day. Everyone pitched in to make the day festive.

Nick made a toast and acknowledged their two new members Night Bird and Carl Pith-something. He also pointed out that he had a new and improved beer for all to try. Fetch barked, at which time Nick commented, "None for you." He then went on to say, "Life on a farm can be challenging. It is definitely a great deal of work. Even in winter we have cows to milk, animals to tend to, eggs to gather, canning, repairs, and planning for the planting season. The chores seem endless. Not simply on this day, but every day, I couldn't think of a better group of people to be with, to share the burden with, and to enjoy the rewards of our labors. Eat hearty and let your spirits fly free."

As Jack served additional guests he kept his eye on "Lumpy." The young man didn't seem aware of his surroundings. He stared directly at his plate as he ate slowly giving the appearance that he didn't want it to end too quickly. When there was a lull in activity, Jack grabbed a piece of pumpkin pie and walked over to where the young man sat. He placed the pie before the rookie and asked, "Mind if I sit?"

"I'd rather be alone—if you don't mind."

"That's what I would say, if I were you. Even though I would welcome having someone to tell what pile of shit just fell on me."

Lumpy smiled ever so slightly and said, "Sit."

Jack sat and said, "I'm not looking to meddle in your life. It's just, not so long ago, I got the proverbial punch in the gut and was lucky to have a friend I could talk with. He didn't judge me or offer stupid advice or make some worthless prediction about good days ahead." Jack paused, looked over at Harry and stated, "As a matter-of-fact he was no help at all." Once again, Jack paused before adding, "But, I was glad he was there. It kept me from talking to myself and giving myself bad advice."

Lumpy looked over at Harry and asked, "Is he the friend?"

"Loosely speaking, yes."

"Maybe, I should talk with him," the young man smiled.

"He didn't bring you a piece of pie."

"Oh, yeah, that's right, there's no such thing as a free piece of pie."

Jack smiled, "How were the potatoes?"

"Lumpy."

"Sorry, I must have taken them from the wrong side of the bowl."

"Don't apologize—it's a sign of weakness."

In unison, they both said, "John Wayne in *She Wore a Yellow Ribbon*."

This time Lumpy laughed. He looked at Jack and said, "That's the first time I've laughed in two weeks."

"It feels good even when nothing seems to be going right," Jack offered.

"I got fired two weeks ago, no severance. My girlfriend blamed me and threw me out, no place to live. The few dollars I had in my wallet ran out, no food. I've looked for another job, no luck." Lumpy shrugged. "So, here I am mooching a meal."

"Why did you get fired?" Jack asked.

"I wouldn't lie to a client to cover up a mistake."

"Did you like the job?"

"Not particularly."

"So, as I see it, you kept your honor, found out your girlfriend was shallow, didn't particularly like what you were doing, and now have the opportunity to get a fresh start," Jack said.

"Do you really believe that?"

"Not in the least. What happened sucks—there's no getting around that. Do you need a ride to the Verrazano Narrows Bridge so you can do a Matthew Ellis and show those people who did you wrong?"

"Matthew Ellis?"

"He's the guy who did a yard dart off the George Washington two weeks ago."

"I'm not suicidal, just cold, dirty, and hungry," Lumpy pushed the pie back toward Jack. "Thanks, but no thanks."

Jack smiled, "Eat your damn pie, then wash your hands, and join us on the serving line. We can use the help."

Detective Ryoya Akimoto walked into the small bedroom of the apartment on East Sixty Third Street. Police had been called because of a disturbance heard by neighbors. When patrol officers arrived, they banged on the door but received no response. A neighbor told them that there had been a loud violent fight heard from that apartment. This was enough probable cause to force entry. When the patrolmen did enter they found a male and female dead in the bedroom from apparent knife wounds. Once they confirmed that both victims were, in fact, deceased they secured the scene and called for detectives.

Detectives Akimoto and Donovan were on duty on this holiday. They arrived eleven minutes after the patrol officers. What they found was a neat and clean apartment with a table set in the small kitchen that included an uneaten turkey dinner. The bedroom, on the other hand, was a shambles that reflected a fierce fight of some kind. The male, wearing blue jeans and a white tee shirt lay slumped against a wall near the door. He had multiple stab wounds to the chest and abdomen. The female subject, wearing a gold pullover blouse and black slacks, lay face down on the bed. Her wounds were not as apparent. Blood spray and stains were found around the room. On the floor was a kitchen carving knife covered with blood.

Ryoya left the bedroom and joined Michael Donovan who was interviewing the patrol officers. He looked at his partner asking the unspoken question. "Looks like they had a knockdown drag out fight that they both lost," she stated without emotion. "Who stabbed who first we may never know. We'll wait for the photographer and crime scene folks."

Michael Donovan looked at the inviting table with all the prepared food and said, "Happy Thanksgiving."

Lumpy joined the volunteers behind the tables and helped serve food to the continuing line of hungry men, women, and children. As he did he looked into their eyes and saw suffering that eclipsed his. Until two weeks prior he had been relatively comfortable with plenty to eat, warm clothes, and an optimistic outlook. Some of the souls he served had all the appearance of having been barely surviving for an extended period of time. Even under those circumstances most smiled and said thank you when given their helpings of food.

A tap on his shoulder caused Lumpy to turn and face Jack. Jack pointed at a man near the end of the line handing out cups of coffee and tea. He was heavyset with gray hair wearing a blue dress shirt and grey pants. "He knows people. People who are looking for an honest man who will do an honest day's work," Jack said. "He wants to talk with you later." Lumpy looked at the man once more who seemed to have a kind word for everyone he served. There was something friendly about the man that was felt more than seen. This caused the young rookie to look at the other volunteers on the line. It struck him that they were not doing charity work handing out free food to the downtrodden out of pity or sense of duty. They were enjoying the camaraderie with each other and their guests. A mother with two small children stopped at his station. As he put green beans on their plates he said to the children with a smile, "Make sure you get some pumpkin pie it's really good." A young girl's grin made him forget his troubles.

"I know we have a lot to be remorseful about," Clinton MacIntyre began as he stood at the head of the table. "However, the true measure of a person's character is the ability to go on under the worst of circumstances. We've all suffered loss. That cannot be changed. Tears have been shed and memories shared. Going on does not mean leaving those we loved behind as long as we keep them in our hearts. So, I'd like to have one minute of silence to honor those who cannot be with us. Then we go on, enjoy each other's company, celebrate our good fortune, and make optimistic plans for the future. We all know those who we miss would want it that way. Now, a moment of silence."

After the period of silence, Clinton offered a prayer, "Lord, take into your arms those who you have called home. Give all at this table the strength to live good, decent, constructive lives, the wisdom to make sound decisions, desire to treat all others with respect, and compassion to help those in need. We ask this in Jesus name, Amen."

Stephanie Ellis looked around the table and indeed was thankful to have been rescued by this incredible family.

Four hundred Native Americans joined together on the island of Alcatraz. Since it was reoccupied a week earlier, there had been a steady stream of supporters visiting the island. Press coverage was both significant and positive which led to public support. Joseph Morris, a Blackfoot longshoreman, rented space on Pier 40 to transport supplies and people to the island. Rock band Creedence Clearwater Revival donated $15,000 for a boat that would provide reliable transportation. Many others made donations for the cause. On this Thanksgiving Day, the largest number of occupiers was present, to date. Some called the occupation "The cradle of the modern Native American civil rights movement."

A husband and wife sat in deep silence eating their Thanksgiving dinner. Because neither wanted the traditional turkey feast they picked at baked chicken and macaroni and cheese. Each drifted silently among their own thoughts. They relived past experiences and sought to give their lives some semblance of meaning. In the past, Thanksgiving had been a much-anticipated day that was filled with food, family, and joy. Not so—this year. There was nothing to be thankful for and nothing for which to look forward. Even if they wanted to console each other they didn't know how. A dark malevolent shadow hung over the table. Food seemed tasteless and any sounds produced by silverware echoed in the emptiness.

The husband rose and left the room. He dragged himself into the bedroom. There he retrieved the telegram from his dresser and reread it for the thousandth time.

> 727A EST NOV 13 69 CTA 175 CT CT WA186 XV GOVT PD
> WASHINGTON, DC 14 559A EST
> MR AND MRS PETER W MARSH,
> DON'T PHONE DON'T DELIVER BETWEEN 10 PM AND
> 6AM REPORT DELIVERY
> 321 BRANDYWINE AVE SOUTHFIELD MI
> THE COMMANDANT OF THE MARINE CORPS HAS ASKED
> ME TO EXPRESS HIS DEEP REGRET THAT YOUR SON,
> LANCE CORPORAL WELLINGTON MARSH IS MISSING IN
> ACTION IN VIETNAM AS OF 12 NOVEMBER 1969.
> HE WAS LOST WHILE ATTEMPTING TO SAVE THE LIFE
> OF A DOWNED HELICOPTER PILOT. SEARCH AND
> RESCUE OPERATIONS TURNED UP NO SIGN OF LIFE.
> PLEASE ACCEPT MY DEEPEST SYMPATHY. THIS
> CONFIRMS PERSONAL NOTIFICATION MADE BY A
> REPRESENTATIVE OF THE U.S. MARINE CORPS
> L W WALT GEN USMC ACTING COMMANDANT OF THE
> U.S. MARINE CORPS
> (17).

The Rolling Stones were at Madison Square Garden for a concert. Opening for them was Tina Turner, who had turned thirty years old the day before. Also, there was Janis Joplin who had long been an admirer of Turner. When Janis Joplin first entered the music world in the mid 1960's, Tina Turner had been performing and recording for more than five years. Although Turner was relatively unknown in the United States Joplin knew about her and was highly influenced by her singing style.

On July 18, 1969, Janis Joplin appeared on the Dick Cavett Show. During the interview, she was asked who she goes to see when she wants to see a good concert. She answered, "Tina Turner—she's the best chick ever! Fantastic singer, fantastic dancer, fantastic show."

The first-time Tina and Janis met, Turner observed, "Honey, you can't continue to sing like that or you'll have no voice."

On this evening, Janis was watching from the wings as Ike & Tina performed. It was during *Land of 1,000 Dances* that Joplin couldn't contain her enthusiasm and she jumped on the stage. The two ladies ended up singing an unplanned duet.

Wanda and Anna Six Trees were guests of Chief Michael along with other members of the tribe to celebrate Thanksgiving.

101: Monday – December 1, 1969

"Jack Moore," he said into the telephone receiver in his office.

"Jack, Ryoya."

Jack sat straight up hearing her voice, "Ryoya, what a surprise—nice surprise. How was your Thanksgiving?"

"Double murder. A couple decided to carve each other rather than the turkey."

"I'd have to say, mine was better."

"Probably goes without saying. I hope you had a good day."

"In many ways, a very good day."

Ryoya changed the tone of her voice to one of concern, "Jack, remember Matthew Ellis, the GW bridge jumper?"

"I do," for some reason saying those two words made Jack think about the elusive wedding that would never be. He also thought about Cleavage, Denise Chamberlain, who had given him great advice that he wished he had followed—tic toc."

Ryoya continued, "He confessed to perpetrating a serious fraud. There are countless numbers of feet of defective wire out there that could fail at any time putting numerous lives at risk."

"Have you shared this information with your superiors?" Jack asked.

"Of course, however, they aren't interested in pursuing it any further."

"Don't they realize what's at stake?"

"They don't seem to think it's NYPD business. Fact is, any investigation is not going to be initiated from here. That's the reason for my call," Ryoya explained.

"The power of the press, I presume," Jack responded in a businesslike voice.

Ryoya picked up on the switch in tone but didn't overtly react, "This isn't something that should be ignored. There are untold numbers of innocent lives at risk. I can't get anything going here, but that doesn't mean the whole thing should be dropped."

"You have to remember that I can only deal with facts—not conjecture," Jack countered.

"The suicide note/confession is fact," Ryoya stated firmly.

"Can I read it?"

"Absolutely."

"What about lunch, today?"

At lunch, Ira Hadstein was animated and exorbitantly upbeat. He wore his best two-button, dark grey, wool, pin-stripe Brooks Brothers suit. His hair had been recently barbered and shoes highly shined. A starched white shirt and deep blue tie completed the look. By all indications, he had taken care preparing for this encounter. Across the table sat Livia Petralia, known to Matthew Ellis as Lida Petropoulos, wearing a three-piece ensemble consisting of a slim skirt and double-breasted coat in matching medium and deep teal blue star-check fabric along with a blue long-sleeved turtleneck sweater. As usual, she looked enchanting.

"This is big—really big," Ira said enthusiastically. "We won the bid and the contract. What I didn't know at the time is it was one of many." He leaned forward and attempted to speak in a low voice but it came out at a raised level, "Over the next ten years we are going to build over 15 nuclear power plants. That's almost two a year."

"One point five," Livia corrected.

"Yeah. We're going to need one hell-of-a-lot of custom steel alloy bolts at the price you quoted." He stopped, looked directly at Livia, and with a slight sound of panic asked, "You can deliver them, can't you?"

"Watch me."

"And they'll perform as requested?"

"I assure you the bolts we deliver will provide the strength and longevity required."

"What about delivery? Work is beginning immediately. It will take time for site preparation, containment building and reactor vessel construction, and turbine installation. After that the coolant loop and steam pipe plumbing and core will be fabricated using thousands of these bolts. They have to be available at that time."

"Has the timing you requested changed?"

"No."

"Then you have nothing to worry about."

"What about the huge number of additional bolts for all the other projects?"

"Give me the quantities and timing and I'll make it happen."

"I knew you would," Ira leaned back, with a broad smile he added, "That is a load off my mind."

Livia returned his smile and added, "You do realize that this involves a significantly larger budget than originally discussed?"

"That won't be a problem. This is a huge company. We pay our bills on time."

"What I am trying to say is that you and I will enjoy far more compensation than originally anticipated."

"Yeah," Ira nodded, "I guess so."

In a seductive tone, Livia Petralia cooed, "What are you going to buy me?"

"What do you want?"

"I'm sure I will think of something," she ran her perfectly manicured nails across the back of his hand.

Eight years after that lunch, on September 24, 1977, the relief valve for the reactor pressurizer at the Davis–Besse Nuclear Power Station approximately 25 miles east of Toledo, Ohio failed to close. Inadequate stainless steel bolts, weakened due to enormous stresses and heat, caused the valve to shift and thereby remain locked in an open position. As the reactor was running at only 9% power, shut down due to disruption in the feedwater system occurred without further incident. The valve was replaced and new stainless steel bolts installed. They came from the excess supply inventoried from original construction of the plant.

Eighteen months after that incident, on March 28, 1979, a stuck-open pilot-operated relief valve in the primary cooling system of reactor number 2 at Three Mile Island Nuclear Generating Station (TMI-2) in Dauphin County, Pennsylvania allowed large amounts of nuclear reactor coolant to escape. This time the reactor was operating at 97%. The crisis began at 4:37 a.m. EST. Steam generators no longer received feedwater, therefore, heat and pressure in the reactor coolant system increased and the reactor executed an emergency shutdown (SCRAM). Within eight seconds, control rods got inserted into the core to halt the nuclear chain reaction. Because the reactor continued to generate decay heat and steam that was no longer being used by the turbine, heat no longer was removed from the reactor's primary water loop. Adding to the problem, operators, due to a mistaken conclusion that the system was being overfilled, decided to turn off the emergency core cooling pumps, which had automatically started after the pilot-operated relief valve stuck and core coolant loss began. At 4:15 a.m., the relief diaphragm of the pressurizer relief tank ruptured and fission products were released into the reactor coolant. Since the relief valve remained stuck open primary coolant with fission products and fuel were released into the auxiliary building located outside the containment boundary.

Seven hours into the emergency, new water was pumped into the primary loop and a backup relief valve opened to reduce pressure so that the loop could be filled with water. After 16 hours, the primary loop pumps were turned back on and the core temperature brought down. Unfortunately, a large part of the core melted and the system had become dangerously radioactive.

Over the next week, steam and hydrogen was removed from the reactor using a catalytic recombiner and then controversially vented straight into the atmosphere. The worst nuclear power accident in United States history caused by faulty bolts changed public opinion of nuclear power. Unfortunately, the cause of the accident would never be officially determined.

March 20, 1982 in Scriba, New York, Nine Mile Point Unit 1 experienced a recirculation system piping failure at a junction due to fastener failure. The unit was shut down for two years for repairs.

June 18, 1982 in Seneca, South Carolina, feedwater heat extraction line failure at Oconee 2 Pressurized Water Reactor caused the system to execute an emergency shut down.

February 12, 1983 in Forked River, New Jersey, the Oyster Creek Nuclear Generating Station failed a safety inspection due to numerous loose fittings and was forced to shut down for repairs.

Ira Hadstein would sit in his office wondering when the defective bolts would be determined to be the common thread. His numerous attempts to contact Livia Petralia went to no avail.

Detective Ryoya Akimoto walked into McCann's Bar and Grill. This time she was on time. Immediately, she spotted Jack Moore sitting at a corner table. It was near the end of the lunch hour so the restaurant had thinned out. Jack saw Ryoya enter the establishment and his emotions stirred. He watched as she approached. She wore a black unbuttoned pea coat under which was a dark blue blouse and grey skirt. Memory of his over-emotional actions when she was late to their previous meeting reminded Jack to keep his head on straight. He rose when Ryoya reached the table.

"I'm one time, this time," Ryoya offered with a smile.

Jack felt it was better not to broach that subject, therefore he said, "It's good to see you. Here sit, I'll get our food. What would you like?"

After discussing the menu, making a trip to the counter, and returning Jack sat and asked, "How have the wedding plans been going?"

"Very smoothly. Amanda has a clear vision of what she wants and is very decisive."

"She has Harry in line, that's for sure."

"Is he complaining?"

"Not at all."

"That's good." Ryoya reached into her purse and retrieved a sheet of paper in a plastic sleeve. She handed it to Jack and explained, "It's still evidence so I can't leave it with you. You can read it and take notes."

Jack examined the document and wrote down the exact words. When he was finished, he handed it back to Detective Akimoto and commented, "Matthew Ellis was an interesting individual. From my dealing with him he was quite polite and cooperative and forthcoming. I believe he was telling me the truth," Jack paused. He absently nodded and added, "At least, until the end. He was desperately trying to reconstruct his memory that was lost in the accident. I believe he recently found what he was looking for. From this note, it appears he was convinced that he was guilty of fraud and, as a result, responsible for people dying." Jack looked directly at Ryoya and lamented, "I wish he had hung around long enough to help identify and alert those who were misled and now unknowingly operating with ticking time bombs."

"Does that give you enough for a story?"

"It gives me an ending to a vague story that I was pursuing. Only, if no one picks up on it—that's all she wrote."

"It's all we have," Ryoya concluded.

"Unless we can locate Lida Petropoulos, his partner in this crime."

"I'll run her name through the police wires but unless she's been arrested there won't be any trace of her."

"Matthew Ellis' daughter moved to Texas," Jack changed the subject unexpectedly.

"She did?"

"After the suicide, I called Colt's father and he flew up here to console her and take her back to Texas. The MacIntyres are going to put her through college and after she graduates establish an adoption agency with her. It was a dream of Colt's." Jack reflected, "She's been through a lot. Without them, she would be facing her father's confession and suicide alone. They are a Godsend."

"I only see the seedy side of life," Ryoya admitted. "It's nice to hear about good people doing good things from time to time." She took a bite of her sandwich and looked directly into Jack's eyes. "I enjoy your columns when you highlight the good things people do."

He felt the warmth of her non-physical touch and wanted to beseech her to reconsider his marriage proposal. They could work out any perceived problems and make a life for themselves. His first impulse was to take her in his arms and show her that his love had not diminished one tiny bit. Damn, he'd give up his Yankees, if that's what it would take. He sat so near the object of his desire and felt compelled to not let the opportunity pass. Tic toc. "How's the sandwich?" Jack asked nonchalantly as he mentally cursed Cleavage.

"We have an excellent financing program," the salesman said as he presented a stack of papers.

"We'll pay cash," Carl stated.

"Uh, cash?" the surprised man gushed. He reviewed the papers and stated, "The total price is $3,972, which includes registration."

Carl reached into his pocket and pulled out an envelope. Before he could count out the cash, the caught-off-guard salesman led them to the business office of the dealership. A nice middle-aged lady with horn-rimmed glasses started, "And, how would you like to finance . . ."

"They are paying cash," the salesman interrupted.

"Oh, uh, well, uh, please, sit down." She reviewed the purchase. "Let's see; 1969 Jeep Wagoneer, Four Door, Fawn Beige and black fabric interior, with the new Buick Dauntless V8, 4 Wheel Drive and 3 Speed manual transmission, Air-conditioning, and the towing package."

"It's Unit 275 on the lot," the salesman interjected.

"And, it is to be registered in Pennsylvania," she added. "We can give you temporary dealer plates until the actual ones are mailed to you. However, you have to get insurance within thirty days when our coverage runs out."

Nick had driven Carl and Laurel twenty miles north on Route 62 to Jamestown, New York where the closest Jeep dealer was located. They walked the lot and found the perfect vehicle for them and Lark's Run. Carl brought the money that he had taken with him when he fled New York City to avoid being arrested. He handed the lady forty 100 dollar bills. The Jeep was put in Laurel's name as she had a driver's license. She also would drive the new car/truck back to Lark's Run as she had experience with a standard transmission. Nick had jokingly stated that Lark's Run could use a pickup truck. Yet, because he knew of their long-term plans agreed the Jeep was a good choice.

On the drive back to Lark's Run in the new Jeep Wagoneer, Laurel reminded Carl, "Remember what you agreed."

"I know, I know."

"And, what was it you agreed to do?"

"Don't push it."

"I only want to be sure that we both remember correctly," she turned toward Carl and smiled.

"I've got it straight."

"Tell me," she coaxed.

"We both know."

"Carl, my love, we are embarking on a great adventure. Together we are going to light the heavens. Wondrous things lie ahead. We will sing a new song that is all ours and find true happiness. But, first there is much to be done." Laurel paused and in a firm but non-threatening voice ordered, "Now, tell me."

Carl relented, "I will learn to drive a stick and get a driver's license."

"And?"

"And, we will go to New York to see the Christmas lights."

"And?"

"And, I'll show you all the sights."

"No, that's not it. And?"

"We'll stay in a nice hotel and I'll make love to you."

"Not if you don't finish what you agreed to do."

"OK," reluctantly, Carl stated the final point, "I will introduce you to my parents."

In Los Angeles, California LAPD Police Chief Edward Davis announced that warrants had been issued for Charles Manson, Charles "Tex" Watson, Patricia Krenwinkel, Susan Atkins, and Linda Kasabian, seven counts of murder and one count of conspiracy to commit murder; and Leslie van Houten, two counts of murder and one count of conspiracy to commit murder.

It only took the grand jury twenty minutes to hand down the indictments. Krenwinkel's and Watson's fingerprints had been collected by LAPD at Cielo Drive. In addition, another piece of critical evidence had been re-found. On September 1, 1969, Bernard Weiss' ten-year-old son found a gun on their lawn in Sherman Oaks. It was a dirty and rusty .22 caliber Hi Standard Longhorn revolver with a broken gun grip. He gave it to his father who immediately called LAPD. Weiss, after reading about the indictments in the newspaper, called LAPD Homicide to see if the revolver he had turned in was the murder weapon. He got passed from person to person until one officer told him, "We don't keep guns that long. We throw them in the ocean after a while."

"I can't believe that you'd throw away what could be the single most important piece of evidence in the Tate case," Weiss replied.

"Listen, mister, we can't check out every citizen report on every gun we find," he was told.

Frustrated, Bernard Weiss called a television station, who in turn, called the LAPD. After a hurried search, the gun was found where it had been left in the Van Nuys police station. Subsequent tests indicated that it was the murder weapon.

Watson and Krenwinkel were already under arrest in McKinney, Texas and Mobile, Alabama respectively having been picked up by local authorities. Linda Kasabian, hearing of a warrant for her arrest, surrendered to authorities in Concord, New Hampshire.

Thirty-five-year-old Deputy District Attorney Vincent T. Bugliosi was assigned the Tate-LaBianca murder cases.

At the Selective Service National Headquarters in Washington, D.C. U.S. Representative Alexander Pirnie of New York, the senior Republican on the House Armed Service Committee's special subcommittee on the draft, drew a blue capsule from a large glass container. This began the first selective service draft lottery since 1942. Inside the capsule was the date Sept. 14.

The drawing determined the order of induction for men born between January 1, 1944 and December 31, 1950. In the glass container were 366 blue capsules with each date of the year including Feb. 29. The lottery system replaced the "draft the oldest man first" method that had been used to determine order of call. With the old method, a man would go through seven years of uncertainty about being drafted.

After the initial capsule was drawn, young men and women from the Selective Service Youth Advisory Committees from each state drew additional capsules. One young man, David L. Fowler representing the District of Columbia, said he had been "notified" not to draw and walked out. When he did the Selective Service Director, Lt. General Lewis B. Hershey, who had a reputation of being tough, rose from his seat and shook the young man's hand.

The top ten dates were: Sept. 14, April 24, Dec. 30, Feb. 14, Oct. 18, Sept. 6, Oct. 26, Sept. 7, Nov. 22 and Dec. 6. Following the selection of dates, a second lottery was executed establishing the order of induction of the first letter of the last name of each registrant. The nation's 4,000 draft boards would be notified and begin selecting eligible young men in the prescribed order on January 1, 1970. Once a board fills its draft quota for the year, those men whose birthdays have not been reached will be free of all draft liability except in time of extreme national emergency.

It was expected that those born on the dates in the upper third of the list would definitely be drafted. Those in the middle third were in question and the last third had avoided the draft.

102: Tuesday – December 2, 1969

As would be expected, Ritchie read the morning newspaper with great interest. The evening news, the night before, only gave the top ten draft lottery dates. His was not one of them. He found the full list on page nine and looked for his birth date. Richard Anderson was born on March 14 which came up a glorious 354. His mother jumped when he let out a yell of relief.

"Good news, Richard?" she asked.

"Great news. I'm number 354. I won't be drafted."

"That's wonderful! Oh, however, I feel sorry for those young men who are seeing their number and know they will be drafted."

"If they would just end the damn war and bring everybody home no one would have to be drafted."

Nathan Anderson, Ritchie's father, entered the kitchen. As he poured a cup of coffee he asked, "You are traveling today, correct?"

"Yes," Ritchie answered, "I'm going to be away a few days getting photographs for a few covers."

His father sat and said, "I keep getting good reports on your work. You bring a new fresh perspective to our magazines. I'm glad you joined the team."

"Thank you. It's been a challenge but also a lot of fun."

As he played with his gold watch, Nathan Anderson said, "Maybe, when you get back we can toss the baseball."

"I'd like that."

On an overcast morning with a brisk breeze from the west one of the first Pan Am Boeing 747s rolled up to gate 11 at the South Concourse of The Port Airport in Seattle, Washington. It was a special Press Flight planned after the 747 received its FAA airworthiness certificate which occurred the day before.

Onboard 191 people, most of whom were reporters and photographers. Excitement and anticipation was everywhere as passengers prepared for the five-hour flight to New York City. Until this day none of the passengers had ever been on an aircraft this large. Some wondered, with trepidation, how it would get off the ground.

In 1963 Boeing competed with other aircraft manufacturers for a contract to build a large-capacity military transport that could carry 115,000 pounds payload, fly 500 miles-per-hour, and travel an unrefueled range of 5,000 nautical miles. The cargo area had to be 17 feet wide by 13.5 feet high and 100 feet long with access through doors at the front and rear of the jet. To accommodate loading in the front Boeing moved the cockpit above the fuselage with a pod that ran from just behind the nose to just behind the wing. In the end, Boeing didn't win the contract.

At the same time as the military concept was being developed, Juan Trippe, president of Pan American World Airways, approached Boeing with a request for a larger passenger aircraft. Airports had become congested with smaller jets and he believed large capacity aircraft would be a solution. While management at Boeing agreed, they were concerned that supersonic passenger aircraft would become the standard. With this in mind they designed the Boeing 747 to also be a cargo aircraft which meant keeping the hump to allow for front loading. The passenger version of the 747 had two-and-a-half times greater capacity than a Boeing 707. Juan Trippe predicted that the 747 would be "a great weapon for peace, competing with intercontinental missiles for mankind's destiny."

Development of the 747 put the very existence of Boeing at risk. The company borrowed heavily to cover costs. This included the cost of building a facility large enough to assemble the aircraft. Boeing bought a 780-acre site near a military base at Paine Field outside of Everett, Washington in June of 1966. At the time, the plant was the largest building, by volume, ever built. As the development and production of the new "Jumbo Jet" neared completion Boeing was in debt for more than $2 billion. "It was really too large a project for us," Boeing president William M. Allen later admitted. However, the gamble paid off as Boeing was the dominant player in the production of very large passenger aircraft for many years.

The Boeing 747 taxied to the end of runway 34 and prepared for takeoff. People onboard and people on the ground watched as the four Pratt & Whitney high-bypass turbofan engines went to full power. The huge aircraft rose gracefully into the sky changing air travel forever.

At approximately the same time as the Press Boeing 747 was landing at Kennedy Airport, Ritchie Anderson arrived at Lark's Run. He stopped his 1966 blue Ford Econoline van in front of the farm house behind a sparkling brand new Jeep Wagoneer.

The first one to see Ritchie was Night Bird. She had just fed hay to the goats in their barn. Immediately, she recognized Ritchie, walked over to him, smiled, and said, "I know you, you're one of the three wise men."

"Hey, Songbird! I don't know how wise I am driving out here in the snow."

"It's Night Bird."

"Oh, sorry, not that wise, huh?" Ritchie smiled.

"They're inside, come on in."

When they entered the farmhouse the first person Ritchie encountered was Nick. He was coming from the kitchen carrying two cups of coffee. As he handed one to Ritchie he said, "Saw you drive up. Milk and sugar correct?"

Ritchie took the cup and said, "Thanks." He quickly added, "354."

"Then I guess you're not headed to Canada—congratulations."

"Well, I am headed to Minnesota."

They entered the great room where the fireplace blazed and warmth welcomed them. In the room were Nick's wife Penelope, Carl, Laurel, and Night Bird. Upon seeing Ritchie, Carl stood and hurried over to his friend offering his hand, "Hey, hippie, what brings you to Lark's Run?"

"As I told Nick, I'm heading to Minnesota. I plan to do a photoshoot."

Nick pointed out, "An empty van on snowy roads—yeah—that's a formula for success."

"I really don't have much choice," Ritchie responded. "Besides, I want the snow in the photos."

"Well, at least, let's puts some logs in the back over the tires to improve traction," Nick recommended.

"Where in Minnesota are you going?" Carl inquired.

"I'm going to go see Chief Michael, then visit the Witch Tree."

"That's what I thought," Carl said. "I'd like to go along."

Laurel looked at Carl but didn't speak. She immediately understood his desire to revisit the place where he had a life-changing experience. It was like a soldier going back to the scene of a battle many years later. Something draws you there. Could it be a need to confirm that it really exists, therefore, it really happened? Whatever the reason she wouldn't stand in his way. However, she was concerned about the treacherous roads. That van wasn't the best vehicle for such a trip. Finally, she spoke, "I have an idea. Why don't we take the Jeep? I'd like to meet Chief Michael and see the Witch Tree."

All eyes turned to Laurel.

"We?" Carl asked.

"Yes, we. Are you going to drive?"

"I, uh, well . . ."

"We," Laurel confirmed.

"I'd like to go," Night Bird surprised everyone with her announcement. She looked at their faces and added, "I can drive a standard transmission."

Nick chimed in addressing Ritchie, "What are trying to do—put us out of business? You're talking about taking half the staff of Lark's Run." He leaned back and said sarcastically, "Why don't you hire a bus?"

"I was just passing through. I didn't know I'd be picking up stowaways," Ritchie pointed out innocently.

Carl said, "Too bad Wellington isn't here." He looked at Ritchie, "Have you heard from him?"

"Not recently. I got a letter from him weeks ago and wrote to him but haven't received a response."

"How was he doing?"

"Seemed to be doing OK. He wanted to know about adoption. Apparently, there are some Vietnamese orphans he wants to help."

"Yup, that's our little Marine."

"So, when do we leave?" Laurel asked.

Late in the afternoon, in the Phuoc Long province, Republic of Vietnam the men of the 2nd squad of the 2nd Platoon of Bravo Company, 1st Battalion, 8th Cavalry, 1st Cavalry Division were on a reconnaissance mission when they discovered a bunker complex that was still under construction. As they proceeded north into the complex they engaged an enemy force of unknown size to their northwest. Automatic small arms fire was exchanged and two members of the squad were killed. They called for assistance.

Second Lieutenant Robert Ronald Leisy led the 2nd Platoon and the remainder of Bravo Company into the area to reinforce the 2nd squad in the firefight. As they approached the area they came under intense enemy fire to their front and both flanks. The twenty-four-year-old Second Lieutenant moved from position to position directing his men as they countered the attack.

Lieutenant Leisy then moved to the front with his radio operator to gain a better perspective of the situation. At the last moment, he spotted an enemy sniper in a tree fire a Rocket Propelled Grenade (RPG) at their position. The University of Washington graduate shielded the radio operator and radio with his body. Other soldiers who were nearby were also kept from serious injury. Although mortally wounded, Lieutenant Leisy continued to direct the actions of his platoon.

Bravo Company attempted to come to the aid of the 2nd Platoon but came under heavy machine gun fire and RPG attack. After two air-strikes and artillery fire against the enemy positions it was decided they would have to withdraw. The soldiers from 2nd Platoon fought their way back and were finally able to rejoin Bravo Company by 5:58 P.M. A firefight continued until about 6:15 P.M. when darkness caused a breakoff of hostilities.

Medevac helicopters arrived and Lieutenant Leisy refused medical treatment until the most seriously wounded soldiers around him were treated. He died of his wounds before reaching the hospital. Second Lieutenant Robert Ronald Leisy would receive the Congressional Medal of Honor posthumously.

> Ordinary individuals
> facing extraordinary circumstances
> with courage and selflessness
> answer the call
> and change the course of destiny.
> Medal of Honor

103: Wednesday – December 3, 1969

"We can't publish this," the Editor-In-Chief stated as he handed the papers to Jack Moore.

"I thought that might be the case," Jack replied. He added, "Everything in it is true and factual."

"I have no doubt the suicide note is real and that a crime took place. The problem is we will be inciting panic without any proof that the wire was used in more than just a few occasions, or that it hasn't already been replaced, or that it will ever fail."

"Matthew Ellis believed it was a real danger."

"Yes, but he's dead and he didn't leave any information we can use."

"I know." Jack stood and walked toward the office door. He stopped and turned, then said, "What bothers me is that there is a distinct possibility that, somewhere out there, lives are at risk and we have no way of alerting the manufacturers or operators of whatever equipment is involved of the danger."

"It's not our responsibility."

Jack walked down the hall to the elevator bank. He understood why the paper couldn't tell its readers the sky is falling and spread panic. NASA had discovered the defective wire and stopped using it. The anonymous source from the space agency also indicated that it was impossible to replace all the wire that had already been installed. That would probably be the case with all the other users. He thought about a commercial airplane and the thousands of feet of wiring hidden in walls, snaked through conduit, behind instrument panels, and elsewhere. Without question, they can't take an aircraft out of service and entirely rewire it. He wondered if he was the president of an airline what he would do—keep the fleet flying or ground all aircraft and go out of business. It was a logical, business, and moral dilemma. It's a kind of electrical Russian Roulette. If nothing bad happens the correct decision was made. If even one plane crashes due to defective wiring who shares the blame? Jack's mind switched to the military. Where was Orztech wire used? Was it military aircraft, tanks, ships, or ground installations? He pictured a submarine under the Polar icecap losing navigation capability. It was then that Jack decided his only course would be to call and write letters to the CEO's of major airlines, automobile manufacturers, and the Secretary of Defense. What course of action they chose to take would be up to them.

The elevator door opened and a voice greeted Jack, "Hey, Yo yo, I was on my way to see you."

Over the snickers from other occupants of the elevator, Jack said as he boarded the car, "Denise, what are you doing here?"

"Coming to see you, silly."

Jack glared at the others who snickered, once more. "Do we have an appointment?"

"I don't need an appointment. You're my cosmic guide, you wear my love beads."

Snickers, "Denise . . ."

"Don't get so uptight, we're where it's at."

Snickers. "I don't . . ."

"You're a freak—wear it with pride."

Laughter, "This isn't . . ."

"Don't flip out. After Woodstock, it's our karma."

The doors to the elevator opened on the floor where Jack had his office. He and Denise Chamberlain exited the car. As the doors closed Jack heard laughter.

In a firm voice, Jack asked, "What was that all about?"

"They wanted a show, so I gave them one."

"And ruined my reputation in the process."

Denise tilted her head and shifted he weight so that one hip jutted out, "Or, enhanced it."

Jack looked at the young woman and felt a pang of desire that he knew was inappropriate. Her eyes stared directly at him—challenging him. He laughed, "OK, you win, I won't hassle you. Why are you here?"

"I have an idea for a column that I can write while in school. I thought of calling it 'Far Out' and writing about the counter-culture generation."

"I see."

"Then, I thought most establishment types wouldn't read a column with that title." Denise leaned forward reminding Jack of her nickname, Cleavage, and said, "And, let's face it most of the problems are the fault of the establishment. So, I changed the name to 'Akimbo' which is standing with your hands on your hips—like your mother used to do when she said, 'Why did you do that?' I think it fits."

"Have you written anything yet?"

"Yes," she reached into her purse and pulled out a typewritten sheet of paper. "It might not be any good, but I'd like your opinion." Denise handed the paper to Jack.

THE LOTTERY OF LIFE
by: Denise Chamberlain

We just had a draft lottery that determined who would be called for military service and who would not. In truth, those with high numbers that will not face the draft won the lottery of life. You have been given a second chance at life. Take this as an omen. It is not simply a quirk of fate. You have been given freedom from the fate some of your brothers now face. To ignore this wonderful opportunity is an insult to those who are being called in your place.

Open your eyes and open your mind. Make that gift of guaranteed time worthwhile. Don't squander it. Get involved. You might pursue a career that helps mankind, such as; medicine, science, teaching, or social work. Or, volunteer at a charity. Or, enter law-enforcement. Or, run for office. Just don't drop out and leave the future to others.

In life, we are actors in a play with the power to change the script. Let's pursue that better day and show the world the power of the human spirit. Together, we can shine a light so bright that it cannot be ignored. A light that offers hope, brings warmth, and shows the way. We have that power. We only need to choose to use it.

Jack finished reading Denise Chamberlain's column. He thought for a while, then spoke, "It's good, I like the perspective of telling those who lucked out to appreciate their good fortune and not waste it." He looked up at Denise and told her, "One thing, don't lecture—point out. People don't like to be told how to act. 'Open your eyes and open your mind' might sound better as, 'This is your opportunity to open your eyes and open your mind.' It's more of an observation than an order."

Denise Chamberlain stared directly at Jack with hungry eyes.

"'The power to change the script' is good, I like it," Jack continued. "You change the reader from a victim to a player with power. And I like the analogy of life being a play."

Denise continued to stare and hang on Jack's every word.

He returned her scrutiny and said, "You have talent. Most important, you are a thinker. Too many journalism students are mechanics. They know how to construct sentences and how to cover all the points but never with a different or fresh point-of-view."

Denise smiled but didn't take her eyes off Jack.

"Think of your writing as the sharing of thoughts or pulling back of a curtain to reveal what the reader may have missed. But, most of all develop your own style. Your professors will condemn you for it, but in the real world you have to make waves to get recognized and valued."

Denise reached out and took Jack's hand.

He tried to ignore the gesture, "Don't expect everything you write to be Pulitzer material. Just make sure it's honest."

Denise spoke softly and seductively, "Would you like to make love?"

Jack fought a battle between his intellect and libido. Initially, it was one-sided but slowly cold hard cognitive power gained control. He replied, "More than ever, however, it would be the last time that I would be able to help you as everything between us would have changed. As difficult as it is to say, I believe we should keep this on a professional basis so that I can continue to work with you." He looked at Denise for a reaction.

"OK," she said breezily, "So, you think I can be a writer?"

Carl brushed snow off of the Jeep Wagoneer.

"I guess we should have parked it in the barn," Nick said as he helped.

"Who knew?"

"When we build your cabin, we should include a garage."

"We haven't even gotten the land, yet."

"That land, contiguous with Lark's Run, you and Laurel are interested in isn't on the market," Nick stated. "However, they are distant owners so I believe they could be convinced to sell."

"It's still a lot for me to get my head around."

"You know Laurel comes from a wealthy family and has money?"

"We talked about it. That doesn't mean I feel it is right. It just makes me feel uncomfortable."

"I wouldn't think much of you if it didn't," Nick stopped brushing off snow. "You don't feel right taking a woman's money. You're supposed to be the breadwinner, not a gigolo. Right?"

"That about sums it up," Carl admitted.

"When Penelope and I bought this place, we pooled our resources. Quite honestly, I can't remember who had more funds at the time. We committed to build our dream together."

"In our case," Carl lamented, "I do know. Laurel is putting in all of the money."

"If it bothers you that much keep the property in her name." Nick smiled, "That way she can kick your ass off of it anytime she wants."

"Oh, that's comforting."

"You are getting married—correct?"

"Yes."

"You love her—right?"

"Yes."

"Just because she has money and you don't, do you think it's right that she lives in poverty?"

"No."

"So, get your head out of your ass and be grateful for your good fortune."

"I guess you're right. We love Lark's Run and want to be a part of the expanded Lark's Run when our property becomes a part of the operation."

"It's going to keep us busy, that's for sure."

A snowball appeared from nowhere and hit Carl in the back of the head with a splat. He didn't turn around for he knew who threw it. Instead, he looked at Nick and said, "You could have warned me."

"Yeah, I could have."

Jack hung up the telephone receiver. He had spent over an hour talking with stranger after stranger trying to get to the appropriate person at the Department of Defense. He explained the reason for his call to one person who transferred him to another and then another. After each conversation, he was told they had nothing to do with procurement. Finally, he reached a logistics officer who assured him the military checks and double checks all materials used in equipment. "Last thing you want is a breakdown in a hot zone." When Jack pressed him about military equipment built by outside companies he was told everything was built to mil spec so there was nothing to worry about.

Laurel, Carl, Ritchie, and Night Bird left Lark's Run in the 1969 Jeep Wagoneer. Laurel drove with Carl at her side. Behind Laurel sat Ritchie with Night Bird on his right. Between them was an unexpected traveler—Fetch the black basenji. She had insisted on going by jumping in the vehicle and refusing to leave.

They drove north on Route 62 to Jamestown, NY. North of Jamestown, they picked up Highway 86 west. The trip to Duluth would normally take fifteen hours on a good day. Snow on the roads portended a much longer timeframe.

From the backseat, Ritchie said, "We can make Chicago in eight hours. There's a guy who owns an apartment building that lets travelers crash for the night in an empty apartment. Then tomorrow we can get to Duluth in a little over seven hours."

"Works for me," Carl offered.

"I'm just taking in the glorious snow-covered scenery and the outrageous snowflake ballet," Night Bird stated as she stared through the side window.

"Snowflake ballet," Laurel repeated, "I like it. Let's just hope the performance doesn't go on too long."

Carl sat in silence for a while trying to find the right words. He thought about his conversation with Nick and was indeed uncomfortable with living on her money. It just wasn't done. Yet, if they depended on him they would remain in the farmhouse at Lark's Run and not have a home of their own. He could handle that, but would it be fair to Laurel. He looked over at his love with her hair in a ponytail driving the car. There too, the man should be driving the car—if he knew how to drive the car. Everything he learned growing up was being turned upside down. After all, he grew up on the tough streets of New York, took no shit from anyone, and took care of his own business. He was not beholden to anyone. He called the shots. He was on his way up in the Spacini family. He was a man. Now, he wasn't sure what he was. However, with all those desultory thoughts bouncing around in his head—he was one thing—happy. He thought of Laurel hitting him with snowballs and laughed.

"What's so funny," Laurel asked.

"You're driving," Carl quipped.

In a faux hurt voice, she asked, "What's wrong with my driving?"

"Nothing. I just said that," Carl admitted. "I've been thinking about our plans."

"Stopping in Chicago?"

"No, our plans—you and me."

"I know. I'm just making you work for it."

"Thanks. There is a part of me that has a problem with using your money to buy the property next to Lark's Run."

"Well, when we are married it will be our money," Laurel pointed out.

"It still is yours. I feel like somehow I'm taking advantage of you."

"Do you plan to continue to work on our combined farms?"

"Of course."

"Are you going to treat me right?"

"Yes," Carl said, then added, "However, I do owe you a few snowball strikes."

"That might hurt. So, you plan on hurting me?"

"No, absolutely not! I will never hurt you."

"Carl, you make it too easy. I know you will never hurt me, I'm teasing you."

"Well, stop."

"Is that an order? Do you plan on ordering me around?"

"Of course not, but, will you let me finish? I'm trying to be serious."

"OK, I was fortunate to be born into a wealthy family. My parents are both successful and I have a generous trust. They don't fully understand why I have taken the path in life that I have but want me to be happy. Earlier this year they visited Lark's Run and witnessed me with the bees. My father cried. I'd never seen him cry before. He explained that they were tears of joy. Every father wants his daughter to be safe and happy. What he saw was that I had found my magic place and he was overwhelmed with joy. While he could never have imagined me in such a scenario he was pleased to know that his little girl was going to be alright."

Laurel reached over and took Carl's hand. "You come from a different place. You had to fight to survive. You faced hardships I can't even imagine. Life gave you a tough skin. Yet, you liked my voice, my music, my smile, my tiara and let me sneak in under that tough skin. You even risked going to jail for life for me. You never realized that you are a kind and caring person. I have no doubt that you will protect me and work hard to make our lives wonderful and love me and eventually be a grand father." She removed her hand to shift the car. "My parents gave me money. The money we used to buy this Jeep you earned on mean streets. Now I ask you, given our backgrounds, which one of us paid the higher price to get where we are today?"

Carl thought for a few moments then said sincerely, "I don't think we should try to figure out who did what."

"Then shut up."

"Are you giving me orders?" Carl said sarcastically.

"Yup."

In the offices of their theater company, the Really Useful Group, Andrew Lloyd Webber and Tim Rice chatted with John Lennon of the Beatles. Their third musical, *Jesus Christ Superstar,* was to debut in 1970 and they offered the lead role of Jesus to Lennon. Lennon declined the position but said his wife would be interested in the role of Mary Magdalene.

As darkness began to fall the Lark's Run travelers entered Chicago on Route 90, went west on Route 290, and took exit 27C.

"We go four blocks up and make a right on West Monroe," Ritchie directed. "It is in the middle of the block, 2319."

Carl commented, "This is kind of a seedy neighborhood. Reminds me of New York."

"You think the car will be there in the morning?" Laurel asked.

"He said we can park in the back," Ritchie answered. "It should be safe."

Wanda Six Trees carried more wood into the cabin. It promised to be a cold night and the fireplace, though in ill-repair, was their only source of heat.

104: Thursday – December 4, 1969

At 4:45 a.m. a tactical unit of fourteen Chicago police officers silently arrived at 2337 West Monroe Street. They were assigned to the Cook County State's Attorney's Office and were there to execute a search warrant. The objective was to find and seize illegal weapons. They divided into two teams, eight in the front and six to the rear of the apartment. In a coordinated effort, the two teams entered.

Mark Clark, twenty-two-year-old member of the Black Panther Party, was in the front room with a shotgun in his lap. He was on security duty. When the police stormed the apartment, Clark fired a single round and was killed instantly by police automatic weapons fire. This began a series of events that left Black Panther Party Chairman, Fred Hampton, dead and four of the other seven occupants of the apartment wounded. Two Chicago police officers suffered minor injuries. The surviving suspects were arrested and held on a variety of charges, including attempted murder.

Carl, Laurel, Ritchie, and Night Bird were awakened by the sound of gunfire. Fetch barked. Instinctively, Carl was the first on his feet. He headed to the front door of the apartment they were in and checked to make sure it was locked. After that, he peered out the front window. To his left, he could see a number of police vehicles blocking the street. The other three members of their party joined him.

"What's going on?" Ritchie asked.

"Some kind of police action," Carl concluded.

"What time is it?" Night Bird asked.

"Four-thirty-two," Ritchie answered. He then asked Carl, "What do you think?"

"I think we stay the hell inside until they finish what they are doing. No reason for us to go anywhere near there."

Laurel walked up behind Carl and put her arms around him. Carl placed his hands on her arms and said to Ritchie, "Nice place you brought us to."

"The brochure showed a much more inviting resort," Ritchie quipped.

An ambulance passed the window on its way to the crime scene.

A few hours after the incident Cook County State's Attorney Edward V. Hanrahan held a press conference. He accused the Black Panthers of instigating the gun battle and praised the police for their restraint. Photographic evidence was presented of bullet holes allegedly made by shots fired by the Panthers. It was further pointed out that many of the individuals under arrest had numerous run-ins with the law, including weapons violations and assault.

A flurry of accusations soon followed. Public outcry and media involvement resulted in the Federal Bureau of Investigation looking into the case to inquire whether there were possible violations of federal law.

On December 16 the Internal Inspections Division (IID) of the Chicago Police Department concluded an investigation of the incident. It found that the police were innocent of any wrongdoing and that their actions were justified.

The American Civil Liberties Union issued a press release dated December 24, 1969 stating that they did not find a directed national campaign to get the Panthers, but government official's statements and actions helped to create a climate of oppression and encouraged local police to initiate crackdowns.

As a result of continued pressure the city created a special Blue-Ribbon Coroner's Inquest composed of prominent citizens, black and white. It was headed by deputy coroner Martin S. Gerber and convened on January 6, 1970. Twelve days later the verdict was justifiable homicide.

On January 30, 1970, a Cook County grand jury indicted the seven surviving occupants of the apartment on charges ranging from attempted murder to illegal possession of firearms. No indictment was brought against the police.

On May 8, 1970, the state dropped all charges against the seven survivors.

Due to the unique wake-up call the Lark's Run travelers got an early start. At 1:00 p.m. they arrived in Duluth, Minnesota. The snow had stopped and roads were clear.

"Now what, Great Pathfinder?" Laurel asked Ritchie.

"We go north on 61."

When I-35 became Route 61 the road narrowed with mounds on snow along the edge. Travel became slower. They passed many small, almost imperceptible, towns; Clifton, Palmers, Knife River, Two Harbors, and finally after a long stretch of wilderness came to Beaver Bay.

"There's the Lemon Wolf Café," Ritchie stated as he pointed to the place where they had a confrontation with Ojibwa lumberjacks. "Turn left on Lax Lake Road."

Laurel looked for a road but only saw a snow-covered forest. Finally, what appeared to be a driveway was in fact the road she sought. Travel became treacherous as they inched along. In the distance, she saw a figure on the road. It was an old man in a shearling coat with a tattered hat and walking stick trudging along headed toward them. Ever so slowly he approached.

Suddenly, Carl leaned forward and shouted, "It's Chief Michael!"

"I'll be damned," Ritchie said.

The two men jumped out of the Jeep and walked briskly toward Chief Michael. The old man saw the two young men and stopped. When they got to him, he asked, "You couldn't get here earlier and save me this long walk?" His eyes smiled.

"Why are you out on a day like this?" Ritchie asked.

Before the old man could answer, Carl remembered, "Your Thursday ritual."

They let Chief Michael sit in the front seat while Carl and Ritchie squeezed into the back. After introducing Laurel and Night Bird, Carl said, "We have to turn around."

"That's easier said than done," Laurel remarked.

"We have to go back to the Lemon Wolf Café."

"Aye, aye, Captain," Laurel said as she looked for a place wide enough to turn around.

Chief Michael sat in silence as they made their way back to the small restaurant. Inside they sat at a round table and the waitress took their orders. When she didn't take Chief Michael's order Laurel pointed out the error.

"She knows what I wish to have," Chief Michael stated. He then turned his attention to Carl and Ritchie and stated, "I waited for you these past three weeks."

"How did you know we were coming? We didn't know until last week," Ritchie asked.

"When the young soldier reunited with the boy you could not save the spirits were strong. I felt them in a dream and knew Manidoo-giizhikens would beckon you."

"Reunited with the boy? What does that mean?" Carl asked.

"Do you mean Wellington is dead?" Ritchie asked in amazement as a cold rush of fear passed through him.

"It was bawaajigewin, a dream. You will visit Manidoo-giizhikens, yes?"

"I would like to see the Witch Tree," Laurel said.

Chief Michael turned and looked at Laurel. His gaze was neither threatening nor judgmental. It was more of an inquisitive and welcoming study. She returned his peer. After a moment, Chief Michael turned to Carl and said, "Ininigaazo, she is held a certain way by you."

"Yes, how do you know?"

"Her eyes told me. You—my brave, sought your destiny in the wrong direction. When you returned from the north and went back your heart was full. Now, your destiny sits among us. Her spirit is strong." The Chief turned to Laurel, "Why do you wish to visit Manidoo-giizhikens?"

"She sent Carl back to me," Laurel responded. "I wish to thank her."

Once more Chief Michael stared at Laurel while contemplating. After a moment, he said, "I will go with you."

On her day off Ryoya Akimoto walked with her father in the garden behind his house. It was a cold and grey morning. Ryoya walked among the evergreen trees and stared at the raked sand and stones.

Takashi Akimoto, her father, who was behind her said, "I very much value the doragon. It will be revered in our household."

With her back to him she smiled.

"You have mastered your skill in origami, daughter."

Ryoya turned to face her father. She looked into his tired eyes and said, "You were born the year of the dragon. The zodiac sign tatsu, the most peculiar of all the 12 signs."

"Yes, it is said we are short-tempered and stubborn."

"And, honest, courageous, and disciplined."

"I am but a small dragon."

"You have the spirit of Ryu Jin, the dragon king known for his nobility and wisdom."

"You are too kind."

"He also had beautiful daughters," Ryoya quipped.

"Then Ryu jin it is."

Father and daughter went back into the house. They sat in the living room and Ryoya poured tea that her mother had left into her father's cup. In Japan, it is considered rude to pour into your own cup. He reciprocated and sat back knowing his daughter had something on her mind.

"I fear," she began hesitantly, "I fear that I am losing my identity—my heritage."

Takashi Akimoto nodded but let his daughter continue.

"I am Japanese, yet I am not. I look Japanese, but in the dark you wouldn't know. I don't act Japanese. I act gaijin. I am American by birth, but the culture has stolen my seishin. My Japanese identity has slipped away."

"Your mother and I are issei, we brought Nihon no dentō, our Japanese customs, with us. Those customs were from Meiji Japan of the early twentieth century. Since that time, Japan changed dramatically. Even we would not understand it today if we returned." He sipped his tea. "You as nisei are caught between old Japan and modern America. But, you have never known Meiji Japan so American customs dominate."

Ryoya listened to her father attentively. She felt out-of-place both in Japan and America. Yet, she was more American than Japanese. This created a gap or a thirst. Her family practiced many Japanese customs, but for an unexplainable reason she wanted more. She wanted to be more Japanese and proud of her heritage. She looked at her father and said softly, "I don't want to lose, no I want to better understand Nihon no dentō."

Takashi Akimoto smiled and said, "Ryoya means 'moonlit night.' Let that light shine and vanquish the darkness. Your desire to better understand your heritage is a good thing. But, never forget your life is a fine blend of old Japan and new America."

In an almost pleading voice Ryoya said, "I just want to feel Japanese."

Five riders and a dog arrived at Chief Michael's lodge. They had agreed to spend the night and in the morning visit Manidoo-giizhikens. As they sat in the great room in front of a fireplace Ritchie told the Chief of his desire to take outdoor photos for a magazine. He asked the Chief to pose and to recommend other members of the tribe that might be willing to participate. It was explained that a small stipend would be given and that if their photo was used they would receive a larger payment.

Chief Michael thought for a moment then said, "I know three lumberjacks who might agree." He didn't smile but the look he gave Ritchie told him he already knew these individuals. "There is another," he said in a serious voice, "the mother and child you saved. She is a woman covered all over."

Ritchie gave him a quizzical look.

"A woman who is alone and takes on the role of a man in addition to that of a mother is called a woman covered all over. No matter how small the stipend she can use the money."

"A mother and child in the snow," Ritchie contemplated. "That's good. It would more than likely be used. In the meantime, I will increase her stipend out of my pocket to help."

"Count me in," Carl added.

"It has been a difficult time for her."

Wanda Six Trees placed another blanket on her sleeping daughter, Anna. The cabin was chilly, filled with breezes from many gaps in windows and doors. She went to her bed and lay down, pulled up her cover, and thought of her lost son.

105: Friday – December 5, 1969

A light snow drifted down outside Chief Michael's lodge. Inside the four visitors, Chief Michael, and his daughter crowded into a benchlike table. Breakfast consisted of a casserole made of wildlife that had been captured, vegetables, and rice. Flat breads with Maple syrup and herb tea completed the fare.

"We will meet the lumberjacks, then visit Manidoo-giizhikens, Little Cedar Spirit Tree," Chief Michael proclaimed.

"I'd like to get some good shots in the snow, if they're willing," Ritchie said.

Chief Michael looked directly at Ritchie and said confidently, "They will agree."

Unexpectedly, Chief Michael's daughter spoke up, "I wish to go." She was a captivating woman in her thirties. After her husband died on Lake Superior in a boating accident she moved in with her father.

"It's going to be crowded in that Jeep," Laurel warned.

"I'll ride in the back behind the seats with Fetch," Ritchie offered.

The loaded Jeep made its way up Highway 61 to a place where Chief Michael instructed them to turn onto a barely visible road. After winding through the forest, they came to a clearing with a row of cabins and a larger building. The Chief left the vehicle and entered one of the cabins. They waited.

When Chief Michael returned, he was followed by four large Ojibwa lumberjacks. After a short discussion, they all walked up a path into the woods and posed for numerous photographs in a variety of locations. Ritchie was overjoyed with the photos and said a silent prayer that the film would develop without any problems. After an hour, they were through. Ritchie paid a small stipend to the braves and they walked back to their cabin without any mention of the altercation earlier in the year.

The Grand Jury Foreman read an opening statement. "Between the late evening hours of August 8, 1969, and early morning hours of August 9, 1969, the following five persons were murdered by either gunshot and/or multiple stab wounds at the Roman Polanski residence located at 10050 Cielo Drive, Los Angeles, California: One, Abigail Anne Folger. Two, Wojiciech Frykowski. Three, Steven Earl Parent. Four, Sharon Marie Polanski. Five, Thomas John Sebring."

"The prosecution intends to prove by direct and circumstantial evidence that suspects Charles Manson, Charles Watson, Susan Atkins, Linda Kasabian and Patricia Krenwinkel entered into a conspiracy to murder any and all persons at the residence and pursuant to the conspiracy did, in fact, murder said victims."

"Sometime between 2:00 a.m. and 10:30 p.m. on August 10, 1969, Leno LaBianca and his wife, Rosemary LaBianca, were murdered by multiple stab wounds inside their residence located at 3301 Waverly Drive, Los Angeles."

"The prosecution intends to prove by direct and circumstantial evidence that the aforementioned five suspects and Leslie Sankston and Steve Grogan entered into a conspiracy to murder any and all persons inside a residence they had not yet selected. That pursuant to the conspiracy they selected the LaBianca residence and proceeded to murder Mr. and Mrs. LaBianca. Any member of the Grand Jury who has a state of mind in reference to the case, or to any of the parties involved, which will prevent him from acting impartially and without prejudice to the substantial rights of any of the said parties, will now retire."

All Grand Jurors present remained.

Susan Denice Atkins was called as a witness and sworn in. She was then questioned by Vincent T. Bugliosi, Deputy District Attorney. What followed was a long and often upsetting session. Among her statements or answers to questions were the following.

"Charlie is the only man that I have ever met—I'm not taking away from any other man—on the face of this earth, the only man that I ever met that is a complete man. He will not take any back talk from a woman. He will not let a woman talk him into doing anything. He is a man."

"I never recall getting any actual instructions from Charlie other than getting a change of clothing and a knife and was told to do exactly what Tex told me to do."

"Did Tex tell you why he and you three girls were going to Terry Melcher's former residence?"

"To get all of their money and to kill whoever was there."

"I walked back to the room and went into Abigail Folger's bedroom, put a knife in front of her, and said, 'Get up and go into the living room. Don't ask me any questions. Just do what I say.' She then proceeded to get up out of bed and walk down the hall and was met by Katie."

"Tex ordered them all to lie down on their stomachs in front of the fireplace. Jay Sebring didn't follow Tex's orders and Tex shot him."

"I forgot who said it, but one of the victims said, 'What are you going to do with us?' Tex said, 'You are all going to die.' And at that time, they began to plead for their lives."

The gruesome murders were revealed in detail as the session continued.

Stephanie Ellis sat looking out the window of her room. The MacIntyres had been extraordinarily kind. They made her feel at home and tried to help her come to terms with her father's suicide. In a mere three weeks, everything in her life had changed. She felt so out-of-place and yet welcome among this unique family.

Her mind drifted and she thought about her mother, Valerie. Together they did the best they could and, in spite of the hardships, there were good times. She thought of the night they went "rabbit hunting" for the record album with *White Rabbit* on it. The great chocolate pudding war also came to mind. She saw her mother's face which seemed so gentle and kind and yet tired. How she missed her mother.

Maureen MacIntyre, Colt's mother, gently knocked on the open bedroom door. Stephanie turned. "I'm going into town to do some shopping. Would you like to come along?"

"I, uh . . ."

"You need to get out and start to live, once more, as do I. Maybe we can help each other."

Stephanie looked at the older woman and saw the same tired appearance she remembered on her mother's face. Maureen MacIntyre had lost her son and was struggling to cope. In a small way, it made Stephanie feel less self-pity. There was so much pain weighing everybody down. It was there and couldn't be denied, but maybe ever so slowly they could find meaning in life once more. Her mother's awkward attempts to cheer her up when she was younger were now cherished memories.

Stephanie stood and walked over to the door and said as brightly as she could muster, "Let's go rabbit hunting."

At exactly twelve noon the earth shook. One minute later, dust suspended in the air by the shock wave. A 20-kiloton nuclear device had been detonated deep beneath the surface of the ground at the Nevada Test Site approximately 65 miles northwest of Las Vegas.

Code named; Diesel Train this was the twenty-seventh detonation in the planned 52 tests of the Mandrel Nuclear Test Series. The energy of the nuclear explosion was released in one microsecond. A few microseconds later, the test hardware and surrounding rock were vaporized by temperatures of several million degrees and pressures of several million atmospheres. A bubble of high-pressure gas and steam formed within the melt-cavity. Twenty-Three minutes later, as the gas and steam cooled the roof of the blast cavity collapsed into the void. Subsequent levels of rock and dirt continued to drop into the pit forming a chimney and finally a depression in the surface called a subsidence crater. It joined many other craters in the countryside.

Chief Michael stood majestically in front of Manidoo-giizhikens. Both he and the cedar had lived through many winters. Yet, together they embodied life. There was an energy one could feel. At that moment, it appeared that no force of nature could move that little tree or dampen the spirit of a weathered Ojibwa Chief. Ritchie took photograph after photograph not wanting to miss a thing. His artist's eye found every angle appealing. The juxtaposition of the cedar tree and the Ojibwa Chief was striking. Ritchie knew he had his magazine cover.

On a whim, Ritchie told Laurel to stand by Manidoo-giizhikens.

"I wish I had brought my tiara," she mentioned.

"Here," Carl handed her the tiara.

"How? Why?"

"Ritchie told me to bring it."

Laurel walked over to the tree and posed. She was slightly uncomfortable not knowing what posture to take or where to put her hands. Ritchie helped by giving her direction. "Look to your left. Now, down at the ground. Place your hands behind your back. Turn sideways. Now, look up at the branches of the tree."

That was when it happened.

A red Northern Cardinal drifted down from the grey sky and landed on a branch of the Witch Tree right above Laurel. Its distinctive red crest and black mask stood out given the dramatic contrast with Laurel's grey coat.

"Don't move," Ritchie said softly as he took shot after shot.

The little nine-inch-tall bird stared at Laurel tilting its head one way then another. A soft trill escaped its throat. Laurel smiled and the red bird jumped down to a lower branch nearer to her. Ritchie continued taking photographs. Laurel raised her hand to shoulder height and the little red bird jumped onto her finger. The two did a short duet of sounds and then the Cardinal was gone.

"That was amazing," Ritchie exclaimed.

"Bees, birds, what's next—bears?" Carl said.

Chief Michael walked over to Laurel and said, "Birds and other animals are messengers from gichi-manidoo, the Great Spirit. Misko-binens, the red bird, came to you because you are manidoo-waabiwin, seeing in a spirit way. I have seen mashkawide`ewin in you." He took her hand and explained, "great strength of heart. You are Manidoo-Binesiikwe, Spirit Bird Woman."

In that sacred place under the watchful spirit of Manidoo-giizhikens no one spoke. Small waves lapped the shoreline but no other noise was heard. Blankets of snow had deadened all sounds. Chief Michael took a piece of parchment from his jacket and placed it among the branches of the little cedar. His daughter followed by putting a beaded necklace on the tree. Night Bird walked over and hugged the tree then placed a button she pulled from her dress. She had nothing else to offer. Ritchie knew he was coming to this spot and came with something he considered of great value. He placed a photograph of Wellington Marsh in a branch. Carl walked over to Laurel and placed his arm around her. The two of them faced the tree and said a silent prayer. From his pocket, Carl retrieved an Italian silk tie. He looked at it and thought how long ago he had worn it. From then on Manidoo-giizhikens would sport that tie.

Finally, Laurel, who felt all eyes upon her, looked skyward for any sign of the Cardinal. In an odd way when he did not appear she felt a sense of loss. Slowly, she reached up and removed the tiara from her head and placed it at the base of the tree.

"You are truly Manidoo-Binesiikwe—Spirit Bird Woman," Chief Michael said. Once more he took Laurel's hand. This time he used a small sharp tipped knife to prick her finger. Laurel watched as if watching someone else. She felt no pain. The Chief then pricked his finger and rubbed the two wounds together.

"Now, we are sisters," Chief Michael's daughter said warmly.

As they rode back to Route 61 Chief Michael told the legend of the Cardinal. "Ensiban, a racoon, passed ma`iingan, a wolf in the woods. True to his nature the racoon insults the wolf. Upon hearing the insults the wolf takes chase. The faster raccoon runs to a large tree where he hides on a limb that hangs over a creek. When the wolf arrives, he is thirsty and exhausted. As he laps up the fresh water, he sees the raccoon's reflection and dives in to get him. It is then he realizes it was only a reflection. The wolf nearly drowns before making it back to shore. Tired from the ordeal the wolf falls asleep. It is then the raccoon comes down from the safety of the tree limb and plasters the wolf's eyes shut with clay from the bottom of the creek. Soon after, the wolf awakens but he cannot see. He struggles to wipe the hard clay from his eyes but is unable to do so. In desperation, he howls. Upon hearing the poor wolf's cries, an unattractive little brown bird comes to see if he can help. The kind bird begins pecking at the clay around the wolf's eyes until the last chunk of clay is gone. The grateful wolf asks how he can possibly reward the little bird. When the brown bird declines the wolf's offer, the wolf has an idea. 'Jump up onto my shoulder,' the wolf says and away they run through the woods to the rock that oozes red paint. The wolf plucks a twig from a tree and chews the end until it is soft and pliable like a paint brush. He then paints the feathers of the little bird bright red. Then in a booming voice the wolf declares from this day forward you are a beautiful red bird, misko-binens, and all of your children will be born with beautiful crimson feathers. So began the tradition that all boy children wear red feathers."

Chief Michael patted Laurel's hand and stated, "Misko-binens, the red bird, is bawaagan, your guardian spirit animal."

"His song will remain in my heart," Laurel replied.

"Cardinal medicine symbolizes relationships, courtship, and monogamy," Chief Michael explained, "During courtship, the male feeds seed to the female beak-to-beak. Cardinals are monogamous birds whose relationships with their spouses are harmonious, romantic, and musical. The male and female sing duets, calling similar songs to each other. You, Spirit Bird Woman, and my brave have been blessed by gichi-manidoo. This is a good thing."

"Like, wow," Night Bird said in the back seat.

Stephanie Ellis and Maureen MacIntyre returned to the ranch. Two women from completely different worlds put aside their pain and sadness and shared an afternoon together. What they faced were ideas, values, and perspective distinct from one another. And yet, they also found common ground upon which to build a relationship. For a few hours, they shared moments of peace, solace, and hope.

Maureen bought Stephanie her first pair of cowboy boots. When Stephanie balked the older woman simply said, "My dear, this is Texas."

Stephanie learned more about the MacIntyre family and found that she felt very fortunate to have fallen in with them. Everywhere they went people knew Maureen and spoke highly of her and Clinton and their children. The MacIntyre's were an important part of the community. When individuals met Stephanie, who was with Maureen MacIntyre, they treated her with obvious kindness and respect.

Before returning to the ranch they stopped in a small café and had a snack. The conversation was pleasant. Stephanie once more expressed her gratitude and accompanying discomfort with accepting so much from the MacIntyres.

Maureen looked at the young woman and said, "From this moment on I don't want to hear any complaints or concerns about money or other things we might give you. We are a wealthy family with the means to make a difference in your life. That is what we have chosen to do and you, by golly, will accept it without reservation or guilt or other unnecessary objections. I can be a stubborn old broad so don't refuse."

Deep in the woods was a small cabin nestled among evergreen trees. Small wisps of smoke rose from the chimney. No sign of life was apparent. Not even footprints in the snow. Laurel drove to a clear flat area and stopped the Jeep.

Chief Michael climbed out of the vehicle and with his walking stick carved the number twelve in the fresh snow. "Cardinals are seen twelve months out of the year. They often have twelve eggs in their nest. Twelve is the number of good fortune. It is for you on this day."

They were welcomed into Wanda Six Trees home. Chief Michael explained why they were there and she agreed to pose with her daughter for the magazine pictures. Before going in, Carl and Laurel had handed Ritchie additional money for the stipend. The photoshoot went just as well as the previous efforts. Ritchie found he had so much material that he started considering putting together a book showing an Ojibwa Winter. In fact, he began feeling so close to these people that in a small odd way he was jealous of Laurel who was now an adopted member of the tribe.

Anna Six Trees was a perfect subject. An uninhibited six-year-old mind allowed her to find ways to hide and stand and pose that Ritchie could never have imagined. At one point Ritchie took a close-up of the fox totem that the young girl wore around her neck. He remembered that it was the very one that Robert Six Trees wore that fateful day. Back in the cabin Ritchie looked around at the meager possessions of the Six Tree family and felt shame about living in a big comfortable house wanting for nothing.

Wanda Six Trees was very interested in Spirit Bird Woman and her encounter with the Cardinal. She hung on every word. Finally, she rose and went to a small cupboard. When she returned, she held three red feathers, "These belonged to Robert. They now are for you."

As they continued to talk Wanda Six Trees braided Laurel's long dark red hair. When she was finished, a long braid hung from either side of Laurel's head. The Native American hostess then tied a beaded cloth with yarn around Laurel's head and placed the three red feathers, one up and two down at the back. "There, you are Ojibwa, Spirit Bird Woman."

Ritchie immediately took out his camera and started taking photographs.

Laurel quickly held up her hand and said, "Please, not now. This is too personal and too special." She turned to Chief Michael, who sat watching, and asked, "How do I say thank you?"

"Miigwech."

Laurel looked at Wanda Six Trees and said with the greatest sincerity, "Miigwech."

Wanda Six Trees nodded her head in approval.

106: Saturday – December 6, 1969

First rays of morning sun reached out to Chief Michael's lodge. The sky was blue and clear promising a good day for travel. Carl was the first of the travelers to rise. He and Chief Michael sat in the kitchen.

"I love Spirit Bird Woman," Carl told the old Ojibwa Chief.

"You are fortunate. The spirit is strong in her."

"I've known that from the very first time I saw her."

"Yet, you left."

"I did."

"But, you could not truly leave for she was in you."

"I had to return."

"Nothing in the world had color while you were apart," the Chief pointed out.

"Nothing in the world had meaning."

"A brave believes he is ojimaa, leader of his lodge. He acts as the leader. He speaks as the leader. He stands tall as the leader. What he doesn't realize is that he sees the world through her eyes."

Carl looked out the window and pondered the Chief's words. Ever since Laurel entered his life his perspective had changed. Indeed, he had changed for the better. Yet, it never seemed like she forced her opinion or point-of-view upon him. It was more like a veil had been removed allowing him to see more clearly.

Chief Michael continued, "Spirit Bird Woman shares her world with the many spirit animals. A rare gift. Watch her and protect her for she will open the skies to you and let you have a glimpse of gichi-manidoo."

"I will protect her."

Chief Michael leaned forward and told Carl, "If I were a younger man, I would steal her from you." A fleeting smile crossed his face.

Night Bird, Ritchie, and Fetch entered the kitchen.

"Are we ready for a long ride?" Ritchie announced. He then turned his attention to Chief Michael, "I want to thank you for your help. These photographs are more than I anticipated. I'll make sure that the magazine pays everyone for their use."

"They are all in need of zhooniyaa, money."

A sound drew their attention. Into the kitchen walked Chief Michael's daughter and Laurel. Laurel's hair was no longer braided, but hung on either side as long pigtails tied with leather strands. She wore a beaded headband, although the three red feathers were not present. Spirit Bird Woman sat next to Carl and said, "We've been trading."

"Oh, and what have we been trading?"

"Lots of things."

At 9:00 a.m. Pacific Time the gates opened at the Altamont Speedway on the border of Alameda and San Joaquin Counties, about 30 miles east of San Francisco, California. In answer to criticism that ticket prices had been too high during the Rolling Stones' American tour promoters decided to end with a free concert.

A regular area venue, Golden Gate Park, was unavailable as the Chicago Bears were meeting the San Francisco 49ers at Kezat Stadium. So, Grateful Dead manager Rock Scully and concert organizer Michael Lang made arrangements to hold the event at Sears Point Raceway, an auto-racing track well-known in Northern California. The site had a natural amphitheater and good fencing. Two days before the concert, Chip Monck, who had put together the Woodstock Festival, had a stage built and towers for lights erected. Unfortunately, Sears Point was owned by Filmways which operated Concert Associates in Los Angeles. Concert Associates had booked the Rolling Stones in Los Angeles and had expected a second concert there that never materialized. As a result, the relationship had become strained. Representatives from Filmways met with Ron Schneider, the Rolling Stones business agent, and made unreasonable financial demands which ended the possibility of a concert at Sears Point.

Thursday night Chip Monck visited Altamont Speedway and reluctantly said it would do. Altamont Speedway was a barren, lifeless, forbidding location without a tree or grass or anything green. A problem with the concert site became immediately apparent. The stage area was a mere four feet high with the audience section slanted toward it. This vastly increased the possibility of concert attendees pushing forward and climbing onto the stage.

Approximately 300,000 concertgoers ultimately packed Altamont Speedway. And, as with Woodstock there were insufficient portable facilities, food vendors, or medical services.

Altamont Speedway owner Dick Carter had hired professional security guards to protect his property but they were ineffective in crowd control or safety. Due to concerns about the low stage, members of the Hells Angels motorcycle club, led by Oakland chapter head Ralph "Sonny" Barger, were asked to surround the stage to provide security. They were recommended by the Grateful Dead and Jefferson Airplane who had both used the Hells Angels at previous concerts for security. The deal was made at a meeting among Sam Cutler, road manager of the Rolling Stones, Grateful Dead manager Rock Scully, and Pete Knell, a member of the Hells Angels' San Francisco chapter. The price was $500 in beer.

Grace Slick of Jefferson Airplane observed, "The vibes were bad. Something was very peculiar, not particularly bad, just real peculiar. It was that kind of hazy, abrasive and unsure day. I had expected the loving vibes of Woodstock but that wasn't coming at me. This was a whole different thing."

"That was an ugly crowd," Rock Scully concluded, "When you'd get up to go to the john, you'd get karate chopped on the legs as you stepped through the crowd."

The concert lineup included: Santana; Jefferson Airplane; Flying Burrito Brothers; Crosby, Stills, Nash and Young; Grateful Dead; with the Rolling Stones closing the concert.

By nine in the morning drunken Hell's Angels were throwing beer cans, acting out, and even fighting among themselves. The concert was scheduled to begin at noon. Things didn't start well. When Mick Jagger of the Rolling Stones got off of the helicopter a long-haired youth ran at him screaming, "I'm gonna kill you! I hate you!" He punched the singer in the face. While Jagger was only bruised, it set the tone for the day.

Santana was the first act to take the stage. Most of their performance went smoothly with a few interruptions but all seemed well. However, as the day progressed the large crowd became more and more unruly. Fights broke out in various sections of the audience. The Hells Angels sat on the edge of the stage and drank beer after beer.

At one point, one of the Hells Angels' bikes caught fire. The audience was packed right up to the stage where the bike was parked. Hells Angels jumped from the stage and moved the crowd back. In the process, numerous concertgoers were beaten.

Grace Slick and Jefferson Airplane were the next band to perform. Jack Casady, bassist with the band, later said, "It happened pretty fast. We were all busy doing the set, playing our music. At the same time, you're looking around and notice that everything's way out of hand. Usually we try to continue playing, no matter what." As they sang *The Other Side of This Life* their lead singer, Marty Balin, jumped offstage in an attempt to stop Hells Angels from beating a young black man. One of the Angels punched Balin knocking him out.

On stage, Grace Slick went over to drummer Spencer Dryden and asked, "What the hell is going on?"

"The Angels are kinda beating up Marty."

At one point during the altercation Marty Balin had exchanged words with a Hells Angel and ended up saying, "Fuck you."

The thug knocked him down and said, "You never say fuck you to an Angel."

Marty said it again and was knocked unconscious.

Paul Kantner, Jefferson Airplane guitarist, who was still onstage walked over to the microphone and stated, "I'd like to mention that the Hells Angels just smashed Marty Balin in the face and knocked him out for a bit."

After their set, Jefferson Airplane wanted to leave quickly but had no helicopter or ride. They made their way to the parking lot and found a young man passed out on the hood of a Mustang. "We told him if he let us drive him to San Francisco, we would buy him a Mexican dinner. He said okay and that's how we got out of Altamont."

Things seemed to calm down during the Flying Burrito Brothers set. However, trouble recurred when Crosby, Stills, Nash & Young sang *It's Been a Long Time Coming.* By three in the afternoon frustrated audience members began to leave. Given the continued violence Grateful Dead refused to play and also left the area.

Late in the afternoon, when the sun went behind a range of hills it became cold. The remaining crowd waited for the Rolling Stones and became more and more agitated. Finally, the Rolling Stones came on in a burst of energy, surrounded by Hells Angels and their own New York guards. The crowd roared. Four to five thousand fans pressed against the edge of the stage. It was then when the Hells Angels began to take their job seriously when individuals attempted to climb onto the stage.

As things became more violent, Rolling Stones lead singer, Mick Jagger urged everyone, "Just be cool down in the front there, don't push around."

During the third song, *Sympathy for the Devil,* a fight broke out at the front of the stage. The Stones stopped playing. Keith Richard put down his guitar and yelled, "If you don't cool it, we're not going to play."

At the start of *Under My Thumb* the Hells Angels grabbed a fan who was trying to get on stage. He was eighteen-year-old Meredith Hunter wearing a bright lime-green suit. One of the Hells Angels grabbed his head, punched him, and chased him back into the crowd. Patty Bredehoft, the young man's girlfriend, tried to calm him down and convince him to move away from the stage.

Rock Scully, witnessed what was taking place and later said, "I saw what he was looking at, that he was crazy, he was on drugs, and that he had murderous intent. There was no doubt in my mind that he intended to do terrible harm to Mick or somebody in the Rolling Stones, or somebody on that stage."

Meredith Hunter was enraged and high on drugs. He returned to the stage and pulled a long-barreled .22 caliber revolver from inside his jacket. Hells Angel Alan Passaro saw what was happening and charged Hunter from the side. In the melee he stabbed the man two to five times in the upper back. Several other Hells Angels joined in and stomped the fallen man on the ground.

Mick Jagger was singing when the encounter occurred. He stopped and yelled, "Brothers and sisters, come on now...everybody just cool out, everybody! Come on now." He leaned over the edge of the stage and asked, "Are you all right?" Then announced, "We need a doctor and an ambulance."

Alan Passaro was free on bail at the time of the Altamont killing. He had been arrested in San Jose in July, 1969 for selling marijuana and theft. He pled guilty to the marijuana charge but was waiting for trial on the theft count.

A medic from the San Francisco Public Health Hospital, Robert Hiatt, carried Meredith Hunter backstage. "He had serious wounds, it was obvious he wasn't going to make it."

Dr. Richard Baldwin, a volunteer in charge of the medical facilities, said, "There's nothing they could have done to save him."

Around eleven that night, Meredith Hunter's body was delivered to the coroner's office. An autopsy the following day showed he was high on methamphetamine and had been stabbed and beaten to death.

A young female attendee at Altamont said sadly, "There was no love, no joy. In twenty-four hours, we created all the problems of our society in one place: congestion, violence, dehumanization. Is this what we want?"

Mick Jagger was upset by the events of the evening. When questioned later in the evening at the Huntington Hotel he said, "I know San Francisco by reputation. It was supposed to be lovely here—not uptight. What happened? What's gone wrong? If Jesus had been there, He would have been crucified."

Waiting at the hotel was Phil Kaufman who worked as the Rolling Stones' road manager. He had spent time in prison and was a friend of Charles Manson. After release, he lived for a period of time with the Manson Family. On this night while Charlie sat in a prison cell Phil sat in a hotel room with the Rolling Stones.

Small world.

Wanda and Anna Six Trees played a game of toss. They knew good fortune was coming having been visited by Spirit Bird Woman.

107: Monday – December 8, 1969

Detective Michael Donovan walked into the squad room carrying a folder. He walked over to Ryoya's desk and plopped it in front of her. Detective Akimoto picked up the folder read the title and said, "Ray Esposito."

"Yup. Word is his game is still going on."

"We know that. What we don't know is exactly when or where."

"We may have a lead."

"Oh? Do tell."

"A guy was picked up Saturday night D and D. No one thought anything about it. However, he opens his yap in holding to some of the other guests about having been at a high stakes poker game. They ignore him until he says it's the Esposito game."

"Is this guy a high roller?"

"No, he's a wannabe."

"So, what makes you think there's anything to his story?"

"He's a United States Senator's aid in town for some conference with the Senator."

"Then maybe the high roller is the Senator."

"Now, you're with me."

"But, that still doesn't get us anywhere," Ryoya concluded. "By now, they are back in Washington."

"Except for the fact that his aid had an address in his pocket."

"Oh?"

"44 West Grove Street. It's at the corner of Grove and Bleecker."

"So, all we have to do is guess when the next game will be and stake it out."

"Something like that."

Laurel stood on the edge of a ravine and looked out over the hillside. Snow covered the ground and trees. The sky was blue and clear. A frigid breeze pushed her long hair forward around her face. They had arrived back at Lark's Run the evening before. Stories were shared and thanks given for their good fortune. Laurel had been touched by her experience in Minnesota and the Ojibwa title Spirit Bird Woman, Manidoo-Binesiikwe. In a trancelike state she sang an Irish tune *My Singing Bird.*

> I have seen the lark soar high at morn
> Heard his song up in the blue
> I have heard the blackbird pipe his note
> The thrush and the linnet too
> But there's none of them can sing so sweet
> My singing bird as you.
> If I could lure my singing bird
> From his own cozy nest
> If I could catch my singing bird
> I would warm him on my breast

For there's none of them can sing so sweet
My singing bird as you.

Standing alone looking out over the property that she and Carl proposed to purchase Laurel was lost in thought. The breeze was cold but also refreshing. It made her feel alive. It brought her back to Manidoo-giizhikens, Little Cedar Spirit Tree. She couldn't explain, even to herself, how deeply spiritual the experience had been. The valley before her was quiet. By all appearances, she was standing in Minnesota.

A voice reached out from behind, "If you put a porch on the west side of the house you will be able to enjoy many beautiful sunsets." It was Nick.

Laurel turned to face the Vietnam veteran and owner of Lark's Run. "We'll have to remember that."

"The owners indicted that they would be open to selling that land."

"I'm glad to hear it. Did they provide a price?"

"I believe they are leaving it to us to make an offer." Nick picked up a stick and threw it into the valley, "I've got the realtor putting together an appraisal and offer recommendation."

"Thank you. You've been so much help. We don't know how to show our appreciation."

"Don't mention it. I will admit it's going to be real interesting."

"We'll still be one big family. The farm will just be somewhat larger."

"I know and wouldn't want it any other way."

"That makes me feel better."

"Have you thought of a name for your acreage?" Nick asked.

"I have, although I have to get Carl's agreement," Laurel said, "It's Cardinal's Gate."

"Sticking with the red bird theme, huh?" Nick looked across the valley at the property in question, "I like it." He turned back to face Laurel, "Lark's Run and Cardinal's Gate, sorta a tale of two birds." Nick smiled.

Laurel returned his smile. "Carl and I are going to New York," she announced.

"So I heard."

"I won't marry him until he reconciles with his parents."

"I understand." Nick paused then added, "Carl is a good guy."

"Carl is a gentle tiger who can be fierce when necessary."

"A good kind of tiger to have."

Laurel nodded when something caught her eye. As she turned to see what had gotten her attention a Northern Red Cardinal drifted down and landed on a tree branch. "I knew you would come," she said to the little bird that gazed at her.

Nick turned and walked away mumbling, "Nobody's gonna believe it."

The Los Angeles County Grand Jury indicted Charles Manson, 35; Charles D. Watson, 23; Patricia Krenwinkel, 21; Linda Kasabian, 20; and Susan Atkins, 21 on seven counts of murder and one of conspiracy in the deaths of actress Sharon Tate and six others. In addition, Leslie Sankston, 19; and another girl, were named on two counts of murder and one of conspiracy in relation to the LaBianca murders.

Jack Moore sat on his favorite bar stool. His campaign to inform manufacturers and users of Orztech wire had come to an end. Nobody cared. Short of pulling wires out of equipment, he could do no more. In a funny way making the decision to stop tilting at unseen windmills gave him a sense of relief.

"Did you get fitted for your tux?" Harry Van Ryker asked from behind.

Jack turned on the bar stool to face his friend, "Tomorrow, I have to lose ten pounds first."

"You mean twenty-five."

"Yeah, probably. What about you?" Jack asked.

"Me? I'm squared away. Nothing to do until the big day." He took Jack's glass and filled it. "You do remember how to pull a beer, don't you?"

Jack had agreed to run More-Or-Less for the short honeymoon that Harry and Amanda planned. He took vacation time and would watch the bar for the four days they planned to spend in the Poconos. The bar would then be closed on Christmas and the happy couple would be back at work on Friday the twenty-sixth. "Don't you worry about a thing. I'm thinking of having a "buy one get two free" drink nights."

"I'll take it out of your salary."

"Salary?"

Harry leaned on the bar and said seriously, "You still OK with the bridesmaid/best man situation?"

"Tic tock, Tic tock," Jack responded, although Harry had no idea what it meant.

"I'll take that as a yes."

"You can." Jack sipped his drink, looked at the golden liquid, and said, "I miss her. Sometimes more than I care to admit. However, I respect her enough to not wish to cause her any more anxiety or pain. What we had was a fleeting thing. It was good—damn good—for both of us. But, due to unseen forces that I missed, it was doomed from the very beginning. I have to accept that fact. Doesn't mean I have to like it. I'll always have a place in my heart for My Treasure."

Ryoya Akimoto stood in front of her dresser. As she did she peered into the mirror. Her long black hair and almond shaped eyes reflected Japanese heritage. However, her countenance was one of a strong woman which was incongruous with a traditional Japanese female. For a long time, she stared at the woman in the mirror and wondered who she was. Where did she fit in? Why was she so confused?

Her eyes focused on the necklace she wore, a gold chain with two Japanese letters that meant "Treasure." Slowly, she reached up and undid the clasp. With care, she placed it in her jewelry box and closed the lid.

108: Wednesday – December 10, 1969

The envelope contained numerous contact sheets of the innumerable number of photographs Ritchie had taken while in Minnesota. He could hardly contain his excitement. They better have turned out, he thought. One-by-one he placed the sheets on the drawing-board in front of him. How he took so many pictures he couldn't imagine.

With a printer's magnifying glass, he studied the photographs. Each one brought him back to that wonderful return to the Witch Tree. At one point, he congratulated himself for having such a good eye and steady hand. It was then he came upon a photograph of Chief Michael in front of the little cedar tree. There was something powerful in that shot. The tree had the appearance of having its arm around the Chief holding him, protecting him, connecting with him. Ritchie could almost feel energy emanating from the small photographic proof. His mind returned to the shoreline of Lake Superior. The red bird had come from nowhere. Why at that time in that place?

Ritchie sat upright. He always believed that there was more to life than just trudging along seeking pleasure and avoiding pain. There was a spiritual element to existence. Had he witnessed first-hand proof? He wondered what Laurel Fitzgerald was feeling at that time.

Suddenly, a random thought imposed itself upon him—Chief Michael's dream. What meaning did it have? Was Wellington dead? Did the young boy, what's his name Robert Six Trees, take Wellington to the spiritual world? Why hadn't he heard from his Marine friend? He thought of the Witch Tree and silently asked for her to watch over Wellington Marsh.

The door of Ritchie's work area opened and the publisher of the outdoor magazine for which the photoshoot had been done walked in. "Are you trying to single-handedly break the bank?" the man said with feigned anger.

"What?"

"How many photos did you take?"

"A lot."

"You bet your ass, a lot." The older man with a stern face and large mustache walked over to the table, "Let me see what was so impressive that it took thousands of shots."

Ritchie handed the publisher the magnifying glass.

As he reviewed the contact sheets, the man was visibly impressed, "These are outstanding. Jeez, that's good. Oh, this one says everything. I can see why you took this shot. My god, that Chief is perfect. Good. Good. Good. Who's the lady? How'd you get that bird to do that?" He looked up, "Damn, Ritch, this is a gold mine. I don't know how we will be able to select just a few."

"I've been thinking about that," Ritchie said from the side, "We have enough to do a special issue. We could call it Cherokee Winter and do a whole feature on the Minnesota tribe."

"A special issue?" the publisher thought out loud. "That's a major undertaking. We could only do it if we had sponsors. I'll have to talk with the advertising department.

There are probably a number of advertisers who would jump at the idea."

"We can interview Chief Michael," Ritchie offered with a tone of excitement.

"It might just work."

"In fact, it could lead to four seasonal special editions," Ritchie pointed out. "Like, Amish Spring, Cajun Summer, and Mormon Fall."

The publisher nodded, "As long as it doesn't require that you take a thousand photographs each time." He then pointed at the photograph of Laurel with the Cardinal on her finger, "So, who's the lady?"

Ritchie told the tale of their visit to Minnesota and all that had transpired. As he did, he thought of Wanda and Anna Six Trees in that drafty cabin and hoped the special issue would become a reality so that they would get paid more for the use of their photos.

Superior Court Judge William Keene of Los Angeles County ordered a cessation of all public discussion by attorneys, police, and other officials concerning the case against the three young women charged with the murder of actress Sharon Tate and six other persons. He indicated that there was a conflict between the need for a free press and a fair trial, but believed both could be preserved if certain pretrial restrictions were imposed. The ban prevented lawyers and prosecutors from even discussing the importance of evidence that they have presented. Judge Keene said that any infraction of the ban would be treated as contempt of court.

Jack Moore's telephone rang. When he answered, a voice he found strangely familiar said, "Jack Moore, this is Lida Petropoulos."

"Lida Petropoulos? I've been trying to find you," Jack stated when he gained his composure.

"Well, I found you."

"I'm glad you did. Can we meet? I have a lot of questions that you might be able to answer."

"I'm afraid I'm leaving New York shortly so this will have to be your opportunity."

Jack pulled a yellow writing tablet out of his desk drawer and wrote across the top Lida Petropoulos; telephone interview, 12/10/69. "To begin, why did you call me?"

"We have, or had, a mutual friend, Matthew Ellis. After his suicide, you wrote in your column that there was a great deal of mystery surrounding his decision to take his own life."

"I'm flattered that you read my column."

"I didn't until we met."

"We met? When, where?"

"That's not important."

"It is to me."

"Oh Jack, let's leave it that we had martinis and discussed jazz."

Jack tried to remember such an encounter but nothing came to mind.

Lida continued, "In your column you mentioned a dragon lady, an evil vixen who led him astray and ultimately brought him to the point of no return."

"I did."

"Nice turn of phrase. However, I'm not the evil vixen of whom you wrote."

"I might have been harsh. Without question, there are two sides to every story. Sans your side, I could only guess," Jack explained.

"Yes, you were harsh and judgmental and mistaken."

"I, uh . . ."

"Don't be concerned, I was not offended. How could I be when your characterization was flawed?"

"Well, Ms. Petropoulos, now is your opportunity to set the record straight."

"How formal. Have I made you uncomfortable?"

"Not at all," Jack lied as he was well-aware that he was losing control of the interview. He needed to regain the lead. "Why don't you tell me about the relationship you had with Matthew Ellis."

"Very well, Matthew was a driven man who insisted on having everything his way. We met a number of years ago, before his accident, when he worked for Orztech Corporation. They had landed a number of large contracts and sought to outsource some of the production of their wire product. He provided the specs and we manufactured the product. After his accident, we continued to work with Orztech until the contract was completed. It was a straightforward business relationship. A far cry from the 'evil vixen' narrative."

"Did you know the wire was not up to the standards required for the proposed uses?"

"As I stated, Matthew Ellis wanted everything his way. He provided the specs. We had no knowledge of whom the end user would be. What we delivered was exactly what he ordered."

"You know there was a suicide note?"

"You alluded to it in your column. Did it say an evil vixen drove him to it?"

Jack did not react and stayed on his course of questioning, "Did you provide any financial rewards to Matthew Ellis for the business?"

"Jack, Matthew Ellis was a tough negotiator. There wasn't enough margin to give any gratuity. We were barely able to make a profit."

"Is that why you started producing inferior wire?"

"I should hang up on you. If your accusation was correct, I would. However, I understand with you being a newspaper reporter it is your awkward technique to infer facts that are not supportable. How do you say, throw it out there and see if it sticks?"

"Lida, when did we meet?"

With a slight laugh, Lida Petropoulos answered, "This dance is becoming interesting. If I'm not careful you will cause me to make a statement that incriminates me."

"Where did we meet?"

"It was a Monday."

"What were you wearing?"

"Now, you sound like a school boy. I thought better of you."

Jack knew he had to get back to the subject before she ended the conversation. He asked, "At any time, did Ellis change the specs of the wire?"

"No."

"What would you say if I told you I have a spool of the wire in question?"

"It wouldn't be a surprise there are thousands of them that were manufactured."

"What if I told you the wire doesn't meet the specs of the wire ordered by Orztech Corporation?"

"I would suggest you ask Mr. Ellis about that, but of course, you can't."

Jack made notes on the writing pad and found he had doodled a musical note. It must have been her reference to jazz that caused him to do that. He pictured a woman with whom he had a conversation about jazz but couldn't place when or where. She had long dark hair, piercing eyes, and was dressed impeccably.

"Jack, Matthew Ellis may have perpetrated a fraud with his company. We have no way of knowing about that. Obviously, he felt remorse which led to his taking his own life. It is sad and unfortunate. However, we had nothing to do with his questionable activities."

"Did you meet with Matthew Ellis after his accident?"

"No."

"Did you inquire about his condition?"

"No."

"Weren't you curious?"

"As I indicated it was a strictly business relationship. After his accident, I dealt with some middle manager that was overseeing the contract. When someone leaves a company, or gets fired, you continue to work with the company—that's business."

"Why did you close LPAmerica?"

"We had interests elsewhere in the world."

"Yet, you left no trace of ever having been in the United States," Jack observed.

"That was purely unintentional."

"Why did you call me?"

"Shortly after I met you, Matthew Ellis took his life. You wrote a column in which you placed blame on an evil vixen. I knew that wasn't true and considered calling you on a number of occasions, but always put it off. When we met you seemed a fair-minded individual. Then, last week you wrote a column in which you wrote about the intrinsic value of truth. Call it pride or vanity, I simply want to correct the story and present the truth. This is my last opportunity as I am leaving the States today."

"Did you have any dealings with Parker Adolphson, president of Orztech Corporation?" Jack pressed on.

"Never met the man."

Jack reviewed his notes. Lida Petropoulos story was hard to believe, to say the least. It painted her as the innocent business professional who simply provided what was ordered and had nothing to do with the fraud. This call could be laying the foundation for a defense should the need arise.

"Will you provide a contact where I can interview someone at the manufacturing facility."

"That will be impossible."

"Why?"

"Jack, I called as a courtesy to clear up your misunderstanding of the events that led up to the suicide of Matthew Ellis, not to open some pointless investigative reporting that will misrepresent the facts."

"Talk about harsh," Jack said.

"Sometimes that truth you value so much hurts."

"Eleanor's! A navy-blue dress, dark grey coat, black boots, and grey scarf," Jack recalled.

"I'm impressed, as well as flattered."

"I believe you gave me a different name."

"I did."

"Why?"

"When I meet a stranger I often do so incognito. It's a simple defense mechanism we involved in international trade prefer to use."

"I have to ask," Jack said, "Was our meeting a chance meeting?"

"Of course." Lida laughed ever so slightly and seductively, "Call it fate, kismet, chance, whatever you will. It was, however, a delightful lunch."

"Thank you," Jack replied, then asked, "Is there any way I can contact you after you leave America? Where are you going—by the way?"

"A good traveler has no fixed plans and is not intent on arriving—Lao Tzu."

"The person attempting to travel two roads at once will get nowhere—Xun Kuang."

"Ah, now we are philosophers. Jack Moore, we might have been good friends under different circumstances. You have much to offer that I find rare in other men. Some lady will do well to be held in your arms."

"Now, it's my turn to be flattered," Jack said. "Can we not stay in touch?"

"I'm afraid not. But, we'll always have Eleanor's."

"In the background, I hear, *As Time Goes By*."

"And, you remember how *Casablanca* ended? He put her on the plane. I must leave, Jack. You'll be with me for the beginning of my journey. Au revoir mon amour." The telephone connection was broken.

Jack sat in silence staring at the yellow writing pad. He had sketched the little he remembered about Lida Petropoulos' features. An ethereal beauty stared at him. It was at that moment that he understood Matthew Ellis better than he had ever before. The lady was seductive in many, many ways. Her charm drew you in and intellect snuck up on you. Before you were aware it was happening, she was manipulating reality to fit her needs. It wasn't weakness that made one fall prey to her wiles. She had the power to turn one's own strength upon themselves, whereby they decide what she wishes them to decide.

Jack realized that he could easily accept Lida Petropoulos' version of the story and lay all the blame on the late Matthew Ellis. He stood and walked around his office to clear his head. A part of him was thankful that he didn't have to deal with the evil vixen any longer. For surely as she had done to one man, and an unknown number of others, she would reach inside and pull the malevolent, unprincipled elements of his soul to the surface. At that moment, he had the subject of his next column; My Conversation With The Devil.

Anna Six Trees tried in vain to draw Spirit Bird Woman but was not nearly as capable as her brother had been.

109: Thursday – December 11, 1969

Laurel and Carl headed east on Route 80. Fetch, with her paws on the center console and rear on the back seat, stared out the front window. Apparently, she was making sure that they didn't get lost.

"The last time we made this trip I didn't think I was coming back," Carl observed.

"Neither did I," Laurel admitted.

"It's funny how things work out."

"I'm glad that they did and I'm proud of you for being so brave."

Carl looked over at Laurel and remarked, "Who'da thought I'd be sitting here with Silly Bird Woman."

"That's Spirit Bird Woman," Laurel corrected, then added, "There's a difference between being brave and being foolhardy, my friend."

In a more serious tone Carl said, "Speaking of being proud, I was very proud of you in Minnesota. From the first day I saw you, I could see you were really something exceptional and rare. Then at the Witch Tree you went beyond my expectations on a spiritual level I think most people never imagine. Yes, you are Spirit Bird Woman and, even more importantly, you are my Spirit Bird Woman."

"Thank you," Laurel took Carl's hand.

He added, "I like your red feathers."

Fetch stuck a cold wet nose into the couple's hands.

Time passed quickly as they talked about their plans for building a cabin in the Pennsylvania hills and developing Cardinal's Gate. It was during this conversation that Carl learned of the magnitude of Laurel's trust fund. By any standard, she was wealthy. Once again, his male ego reared its ugly head. He sat silently trying to rationalize the situation. Their last conversation on the subject took some of the sting out of the fact that they would be living on her money, however, the amount was overwhelming. As hard as he tried Carl still could not escape from feeling that he had very little power in the relationship. He would be the damn wife.

After a while Laurel could tell something was bothering Carl. She asked, "What's wrong?"

At first, Carl simply didn't want to talk about it, so he responded, "Nothing."

Laurel knew that was not the case. "Something is bothering you."

"It's not important."

"If it bothers you, then it's important to me."

"I don't want to talk about it."

"Is it something that I said?"

"I really don't want to talk about it."

"I just want to help."

"If you want to help—drop it!"

With that Laurel turned her attention to the road. They rode for another twenty minutes in silence. Fetch grew bored, curled up in the back seat, and slept.

As they crossed into New Jersey, Carl finally spoke, "I'm still having trouble with this whole money thing."

"Why? I thought we talked about it."

"Once I heard how much you have—you're rich for crying out loud. That makes me a . . . a . . . gold digger."

"Is that why you love me, for my money?"

"No, I fell for you before I knew you had money."

"Then it shouldn't be a problem."

"You don't get it. By the very fact that you have all the money you have all the power in the relationship. That's not easy to swallow."

"So, you want more power?" Laurel asked, "You want to be Lord of the Manor?"

"It's not like that," Carl insisted.

They rode for a short distance in silence. Fetch jumped up and looked out the back window and barked at the car behind them.

"I want us to be partners—a team," Carl stated.

"But, with me having all the money I will always be in a position to be the one who makes all the final decisions," Laurel concluded.

"In a way—yes."

Laurel surprised Carl when she said, "How can you think so little of me?"

"What? I didn't . . ."

"You clearly stated that I would take advantage of my financial standing and force my will upon you. Why would you even consider marrying such a small, petty, spoiled, opportunistic, self-centered shrew?"

"That's not what I meant."

"There's no other way to interpret it," she paused, then added, "You don't trust me."

"I do trust you. In fact, I trust you more than any other person on earth."

"But, you don't like the fact that I control the purse strings." They rode in silence for a moment. Laurel then said, "You realize, I didn't earn that money. It was given to me by my parents. They want me to have the freedom to follow my heart and do what makes me happy." Another period of silence. "Should I refuse to accept the money?" Laurel asked. Before Carl could answer she offered, "If you are so concerned about the money and not having a say in the relationship, I'm going to give you power—the power to choose our future direction. You decide, do I refuse the money or do we accept it as our money?"

"Laurel . . ."

"You make the decision. We can stay at Lark's Run and be part of the group or build Cardinal's Gate which can only happen if you decide that we accept the money. I will abide by your decision."

"Laurel, whether at Lark's Run or Cardinal's Gate I want to be with you."

"Decide."

"That's not what I meant by power."

"Decide."

"You're putting our whole future in my hands."

"Decide."

"It should be our decision."

"Decide."

"I want you to be happy and have a bright and wonderful future. I can't decide to make you, uh us, paupers who struggle just to get by. I have my pride, but I also have my senses. You keep the money."

Laurel said pointedly, "OK, so from now on it's our money, our lives, and our future. Neither of us earned the money. What we do with it, what positive things we achieve is now our responsibility."

"Agreed," Carl looked out the side window at the passing countryside. After a few minutes of reflection, he asked, "What would you have done if I had said not to take the money?"

"That's easy—I would have driven us into a tree," Laurel answered.

"No doubt about it—I have to get a license."

American Airlines flight 511 boarded at Weir Cook Municipal Airport in Indianapolis for a fifty-five-minute flight to Chicago O'Hare Airport. The Boeing 727 left the terminal area and headed to the runway. As it did, a truck drove into its path with the driver waving a flashlight. The aircraft stopped and shortly after Captain S.R. Heath made an announcement, "Ladies and gentlemen, we are going to pull out here a little bit further into the field and stop. We are going to deplane as a precautionary. In other words, we had another one of those telephone calls and we are going to deplane through the aft stairs. As I say there is no emergency. However, as a precautionary move we are going to deplane and I would like you to follow the instructions of the stewardess."

The jet was parked away from other airport buildings and the engines shut down. Everything was executed in an orderly fashion. Passengers were taken to area hotels as the baggage was removed and examined and the entire jet checked by technicians. No bomb was found.

The three travelers crossed the George Washington Bridge. It was dusk and had been a long day.

"Stay in the right lane," Carl ordered. "We want to go north on the Henry Hudson Parkway."

"What's the speed limit?" Laurel asked.

"Doesn't matter," Carl replied, "the cops are too busy chasing criminals to worry about traffic."

"I hope this isn't anything like your Chicago lodging," Laurel said.

"To begin, Ritchie set that one up. Second this is a guy who rents rooms to students from the College of Mount Saint Vincent—a good Catholic school. And third, he's doesn't mind us having a dog."

"I feel much better."

"This is also a nice part of the Bronx."

Laurel looked out to the side and saw a boarded-up tenement building, "I'll have to take your word for it."

"Take the next exit."

They got off the highway at 241st Street and then made a right onto Riverdale Avenue. Eventually, they made a right onto West 261st Street followed by a left onto Tyndall Avenue after three blocks. A large house half way down the block on the left was their destination. Luckily, there was a single parking space on the block.

Stephanie finished washing the dishes. Even though wealthy, the MacIntyres did not have household staff. After a long discussion with Maureen MacIntyre where Stephanie insisted on pulling her weight in the household, a number of chores were agreed upon. It both made Stephanie feel less like a freeloader and gave her a sense of purpose.

All the paperwork had been done and arrangements made for Stephanie to begin at the University of Texas at Austin in the Spring semester. She looked forward to getting started, as well as dreaded what lay ahead. It had been a long time since she was in school, with the exception of a short period of time in a community college.

The thought of school brought a memory back to Stephanie. Valerie, her mother, had volunteered to be a chaperone on a school trip to the Museum of Natural History. Stephanie was in eighth grade and twenty-six students climbed aboard a yellow school bus for the trip to New York City. A teacher and two volunteer chaperones were with them.

During the day they visited the dinosaur exhibits, North American mammals, birds of the world, reptiles and amphibians, meteorite exhibits, and more. It was when they entered the Butterfly Conservatory that something unexpected happened. Stephanie's mother, Valerie, began telling the students all about butterflies. She explained how butterfly wings are actually transparent. Thousands of tiny scales cover the wings and reflect various colors. Butterflies taste with their feet, by drumming on the leaves of a plant. Because of the unique structure of their mouth they only feed on liquids, usually nectar. And, they can't fly if they are cold. When the temperature drops below 55 degrees they are immobile. Also, butterflies can see a range of ultraviolet colors invisible to the human eye and actually see these colors on some flowers. She finished by telling about how the Monarch butterfly migrates annually over 4,000 miles to winter in Mexico and usually in the same tree.

Stephanie was amazed by her mother's knowledge of butterflies, especially the Monarch. She asked her mother about it when they got home and her mother said, "When I see a butterfly I feel like I'm looking at a tiny angel. I find their quiet beauty fascinating, especially the Monarch."

Stephanie shared her memory with Maureen MacIntrye.

110: Friday – December 12, 1969

Laurel walked up behind Carl and wrapped her arms around him. As she held him tightly she said soothingly, "It's going to be alright. Wait and see."

"Yeah, that doesn't mean it's gonna be easy."

"It will be easier than you imagine."

"Anything is easier than what I'm envisioning."

Laurel snickered, "Don't worry, I'll be there."

After getting dressed Laurel, Carl, and Fetch climbed in the Jeep Wagoneer and headed south on Broadway which took them past Van Cortland Park. At 225th Street they turned left and headed east. After a short distance it became Kingsbridge Road. Carl instructed Laurel to turn right on University Avenue which was a wide four-lane street. They began looking for a parking place and found one halfway down the block.

"Your parents haven't seen or heard from you since late August, correct?" Laurel asked.

"That's right."

"I'm sure they are going to be pleased to see you."

"My mother, maybe."

Laurel sighed and then said to Carl, "What happened between you and your father took place a long time ago. If you ask me, it's a case of two stubborn, bull-headed males unwilling to give an inch. The result, a lot of lost time where you both could have enjoyed each other's company. Well, that stops today."

They walked up the twenty odd wide cement steps that led to a courtyard with bushes and flowers and small evergreen trees. Directly in front of them proudly stood a three-story high Christmas tree.

"This is really lovely," Laurel observed.

"The super and his wife do a great job keeping up the garden and maintaining the building."

There were four entrances to the building each leading to three groups of apartments identified by letters; A,B,C; D,E,F; G,H,J; K,L,M. They went through the G,H,J entrance door, climbed four flights of stairs, and stood outside apartment 4G.

"Here goes," Carl said as he knocked on the door.

He had a key to the apartment but felt it better to not just walk in. They heard movement inside. A lock turned and the door opened slowly. An old woman peered out. At first, she seemed confused. Then her eyes widened and she threw open the door, "Carl, my son, it's you!"

"It's me, momma," Carl said as he held open his arms to accept her hug.

"Where have you been?" his mother said, "I've been so worried." She then stopped, looked at Laurel, and asked, "And, who is this pretty lady?"

"This is Laurel Fitzpatrick. She is my friend, uh fiancé," he looked at Laurel as if asking if that was correct.

"You haven't asked me, yet," Laurel deadpanned. She offered her hand to Carl's mother and said, "It's so nice to meet you, Mrs. Pythacyk."

"Please, to come in," Carl's mother stepped back to allow them to pass. "And, you have another friend, Carl."

"This is Fetch."

"I see."

After Carl's mother put down a bowl of water in the kitchen for Fetch, they all sat in the living room. She looked at her son and said, "Back in the summer, Carl, some detectives came looking for you."

"I know, momma. That has all been cleared up."

"So, you are not in trouble?"

"Not at all."

"That is good. Your father will like to know that."

Carl looked around and asked, "Where is he?"

"Your papa is on the roof. He is putting up a new clothesline. The old one broke and all the clothes fell."

"Why don't you go up and see if your father needs any help?" Laurel suggested.

"Well, I uh . . ." he looked into Laurel's eyes, "guess I'll go up on the roof."

After climbing two flights of stairs, Carl opened the door onto the large flat tar-covered roof of the apartment building. Around the perimeter of the roof was a low two-foot high wall. Television antennas, clotheslines, mechanical equipment, and exhaust stacks cluttered the roof. Carl looked around. There were a few people on the roof, but he didn't see his father. As he walked around on the roof he remembered the many times as a boy he played on that roof and fire escapes of the building. He saw a man who had his back to him working with a rope. At first, he didn't recognize his father. The old man had aged. Carl walked up to the man and said, "Papa, can I give you a hand?"

Josef Pythacyk turned to face his son. He looked at the young man with an expressionless face. Without saying a word, he handed an end of the rope to Carl. They pulled the rope taut and tied it off. With the job completed, Josef picked up his tools and headed for the door to the stairway. Carl followed.

When they got back to the apartment Carl's father walked past the living room to the back bedroom. Carl joined Laurel and his mother in the living room.

"What did he say?" Laurel asked with a smile.

"Absolutely nothing."

"He must have said something," she said in disbelief, "hell-o, hi, something."

"Not a word," Carl confirmed, "Let's go, we're leaving."

Laurel took Carl's hand and pulled him down onto the sofa next to her. "We're not leaving until I hear your father's voice. I don't care what he says, but he is going to say something."

"Don't bet on it."

Laurel turned her attention to Carl's mother, "Would you ask your husband to join us, please?"

The old woman smiled and left the room.

"I like Florentyna," Laurel said referring to Carl's mother. "She was very worried about you."

"I've given her a lot to worry about through the years."

"I assume you did, but that's behind you, now. We're here to start a new chapter."

Mr. and Mrs. Pythacyk entered the room. Florentyna sat in a chair and her husband, Josef, stood by the window that overlooked the courtyard. Silence hung heavy in the room. A clock ticked on a shelf. Fetch looked at the silent humans and tilted her head trying to figure out what was going on, or who was going to speak first.

Laurel answered that question when she said to Josef Pythacyk, "Your son has come home to see you."

"I have no son," the old man replied defiantly.

"You have a son and he is here."

"No hooligan is a son of mine."

"You're right. The man in this room is no hooligan, he is a decent, caring, brave man who is a farmer. He risked his life to save that of a child. And, he is well-respected by those who know him."

"I only see a criminal."

"You see what you created when you turned your back on him," Laurel countered. She rose and walked over to Carl's father and in a softer tone said, "I see who he really is. He's gentle and kind, a tireless worker, a strong leader, and an honorable man in spite of being thrust out on the mean streets of this city when just a boy."

Josef Pythacyk looked over at his son as if noticing that he was in the room for the first time.

"He is not the boy you remember," Laurel said gently. She took his hand, "Come, meet the man who would make you proud. Meet Carl Pythacyk—farmer, a good brave man. Meet my future husband." She looked over her shoulder at Carl and added, "even though he hasn't asked, as yet."

Josef walked over to where Carl sat, "Is this true—you are farmer?"

"Yes, papa. I drive a tractor, chop wood, plant seeds, gather vegetables, herd cattle, and even milked a cow."

"You do all these things?" the old man said in disbelief.

"I am happy doing all those things."

"What about the police?"

"I turned myself in and was cleared of all charges."

"That is good."

Carl stood, "I couldn't fix the book that was destroyed, but I replaced it. That's all I could do."

Josef walked back to the window and peered out. "How such a little thing like a book could have such a big effect, I don't understand," Carl's father lamented.

"It's behind us," Carl said. He walked over, put his hand on his father's shoulder, and turned him toward Laurel as he said, "Let me introduce you to my fiancé. A special lady who won my heart the moment I met her. She is the essence of innocence and embodiment of all that is good about the human race. Her name is Laurel, the Ojibwa Indians call her Spirit Bird Woman, and I call her my gift from God."

Father and son spent the afternoon getting to know one another. Laurel and Carl's mother participated but also seemed to get unmeasured pleasure simply watching. At four o'clock Carl told his parents that they had to leave. He had planned to take Laurel downtown to see the Christmas lights and have dinner. Before that they had to drop Fetch off at the room where they were staying in Riverdale.

"She's a good dog," Carl's mother observed, "She can stay here. This way she won't be lonely."

"Listen, she can be a handful," Carl pointed out.

"Nonsense," Carl's father chimed in, "I can walk her—she'll be no problem."

With arrangements made Carl and Laurel left the apartment and headed to the Jerome Avenue subway. A cold December breeze was intensified on the elevated subway platform. Laurel pulled the collar of her bluish green textured wool coat tighter. Carl noticing, put his arm around her to help keep her warm. The number 4 train arrived and they walked into a relatively empty car. At that hour, most of the riders were outbound. Carl looked around and was struck by something. The subway car was filthy. He never noticed it in the past but there was dirt, grime, and debris everywhere. He brushed off a seat and motioned for Laurel to sit. At least the train had heat. They changed trains at 161st Street and caught a downtown D train. After twenty minutes, they arrived at the 47-50 Street Station, Rockefeller Center.

"Are you ready?" Carl asked.

"I can't wait," Laurel replied with enthusiasm.

They walked around the corner and entered Rockefeller Plaza. There before them stood majestically an 84 foot Norway Spruce decorated with over 50,000 lights. Atop the tree, eleven stories above, was an illuminated white star.

"Oh, I've always wanted to see the tree in real life," Laurel said as she gazed upward at the glowing evergreen. "Isn't it just beautiful?" She turned to Carl and said, "You must've come here every year."

"Actually, this is my first time," Carl admitted.

"You never came to see the tree?"

"It's common for people who live in a city to not visit the places of interest to tourists," Carl noted. He added with a slight tone of resignation, "Besides, Christmas hasn't really meant that much to me."

Laurel stood in the multi-colored glow of the towering Christmas tree and looked at Carl. How much he must have endured as a street kid. He grew up without knowing how good life could be. It must have been quite the opposite where he fully knew how bad life could be. In the multi-colored glow of the tree Carl appeared strong, yet vulnerable. She knew he could be tough, yet tender. She both admired him and felt sorry for him at the same time. They were, indeed, opposites but the spirits brought them together. There was a reason for that and a great adventure lay ahead. Laurel took Carl's hand and said with joyous affection, "From now on Christmas is going to mean a lot to you and is going to supply many fond memories."

"As long as you're a part of it—I'm in."

On Christmas Eve in 1931 when the nation was deep into the Great Depression, workers at the Rockefeller Center building site put their money together to buy a Christmas tree. It was a 20-foot balsam fir. They decorated it with handmade garland and ornaments. It was a little bright spot in a city filled with despair and desperation. It made quite an impact.

Two years later the owners of Rockefeller Center decided to make the tree an annual tradition. That was the year they held the first official tree-lighting ceremony. Three years later, in 1936, they opened the ice-skating rink and put up two trees to mark the date. An ice-skating competition was also held that year.

During World War II the lights on the tree were red, white, and blue. While in 1944 the tree went unlit due to wartime blackout regulations.

Then in 1951 the lighting ceremony was televised for the first time. The Kate Smith Show on NBC did a special broadcast.

Carl and Laurel had the pleasure of seeing the work of sculptor Valerie Clarebout that was on display for the first time in the Channel Gardens in Rockefeller Plaza. Twelve eight-foot-tall metal wire herald angels, each holding a six-foot-long brass trumpet angled toward the brightly lit tree.

Below street level was the skating rink. Carl and Laurel stood at the rail watching skaters down below on the ice. Some were highly talented figure skaters, some possible hockey players, other general skaters, and the always entertaining beginners.

"Do you know how to skate?" Laurel asked Carl.

"Never learned."

"Me either," she looked down at the laughing smiling people and concluded, "It looks like fun. When our pond freezes, we should get some skates and learn."

"Does the word concussion mean anything to you?"

"Oh, stop."

The couple walked out onto Fifth Avenue. A blistering breeze welcomed them. Carl wrapped his arm around Laurel. They walked downtown looking at the creative, heart-warming Christmas displays in the windows of the department stores. "I wonder how many couples walked down this street having their hearts filled with the Christmas spirit."

"I wonder how many had their pockets picked," Carl retorted.

Laurel stopped and turned toward Carl. She looked directly into his eyes and said, "Are you going to have a negative remark for everything I say?"

Carl looked at the love of his life, who brought beauty, and music, and hope into it. He realized his attempts at humor were not being taken as humor. "I guess it's this city. I'm like a wild animal back in the jungle. Old ways sneak back. In your eyes, everything is pure and sweet and kind. My eyes watch for danger. But, when my eyes look at you I see all that is good. I'll try to do better." Laurel smiled and Carl added, "So when the pond freezes, I'll fall on my ass and laugh."

They resumed going from window to window and found themselves transported back to another time. The warm refreshing spirit of Christmas reached out to them. Then they came to a window in front of a book store. The scene was one of a colonial family in a log cabin. A simulated fire blazed in the fireplace. Wooden furniture was scattered about the room and a large Christmas tree stood in a corner. A father, mother, son, and daughter completed the scene. The young girl was standing and pointing at the tree. When they looked in the direction she indicated there on the branch of the tree was a red Cardinal.

Laurel caught her breath and squeezed Carl's hand.

When he saw the bird on the branch he said, "I don't believe it."

"It's an omen. Cardinal's Gate must become reality."

"It will," Carl promised.

When they reached Forty-Fifth Street Carl hailed a taxi. A Checker Cab pulled to the curb and two cold tourists climbed into the expansive back seat. "Eleventh Avenue and Twenty Third—Santino's," Carl directed.

"You got it, Mac," the cabbie responded with a distinct Brooklyn accent. After a few minutes of silence, the cabbie asked, "I've never been there. The food any good?"

"Very good—molto bene," Carl replied. In the dark recesses of the taxi he couldn't help smiling as he thought about his only meeting with Don Carmine Spacini. In the shadow of the West Side Highway, Santino's resided in a two-story building where it had been for over forty years. The outside of the restaurant had a simple sign lit by two spotlights. Dark green pain on the wall and window frames made the restaurant blend into the background. No other business was visible in the area. They entered.

The moment they were inside a short Italian man wearing a white shirt and green vest hurried to greet them and said fawningly, "Mr. Carl, it'sa so good to see you."

He looked at Laurel and said, "Mia signora, benvenuto a Santino's." The man grabbed two menus and led Carl and Laurel to one of the choice tables on a raised portion of the restaurant surrounded by a brass rail. "It'sa been a long time, Mr. Carl. Let me tell Gino you are-a here." He hurried off.

"I see you've been here before," Laurel observed.

Almost immediately, Gino arrived. "Mr. Carl, how good to see you. And, bella signora, welcome to Santino's." He returned to Carl, "Don't you worry about a thing, Gino will make sure everything is molto bene."

"Gino, this is my fiancé, Laurel," Carl said.

"Auguri, bella signora. Felicità maggio di seguire tutte le giornate."

"Grazie, Don Gino. Sono onorato di essere nel vostro ristorante e sono ansioso di una deliziosa esperienza," Laurel answered, to Carl's obvious surprise.

"Ah, siamo amici, mia signora. Farò qualcosa di molto speciale per lei e il signor Carl." Gino hurried off.

"You speak Italian," Carl said.

"Doesn't everybody?" she replied, then added, "Si, parlo italiano."

Carl made hand motions as he asked, "So, what was that all about?"

"Well, he offered his best wishes and said, 'May happiness follow you all your days.' I thanked him and said I was honored to be in his restaurant and looked forward to a delicious experience. He said we were now friends and he would make something very special for us."

"Here I was trying to impress you and once again you impressed me," Carl admitted.

Carl and Laurel enjoyed a meal fit for the Pope. Gino brought out a bottle of Zenato Amarone della Valpolicella, a classic red wine and once tasted by Carl poured generously into their glasses. The appetizer was Chickpea Bruschetta, followed by a Tuscan panzanella savory salad made with tomatoes, stale bread and plenty of fresh herbs and topped with kale, peaches and white balsalmic vinegar. The meal consisted of Stuffed Peppers using Italian sausage, Arborio rice and Gorgonzola and mozzarella cheeses. On the side was Broccolini with Anchovies and Garlic, as well as Caponata a Sicilian eggplant stew.

When the main courses were being served, Gino brought a bottle of Giacomo Conterno Barolo Monfortino. He explained with pride that this wine was from old vines and probably the most long aging Italian red wine which is kept in casks for years. Made from native Italian nebbiolo grapes it offers a deep mineral flavor enhanced with wild berry and spices. They finished with Homemade Cannoli and Espresso.

Barely able to move, Laurel and Carl talked about their wonderful evening and future plans. Gino walked up to the table and inquired as to everything being satisfactory.

Laurel said, "I miei complimenti allo chef."

Carl followed with, "Gino, every time I come here I leave knowing I won't be happy with other restaurants for a long time."

"That is good. I'm glad you enjoyed your visit."

"Now, if you would bring us the check I will gladly pay it."

"No!"

"Please, it would be my honor to pay for such a fine meal."

"No! You and your lady are my guest."

"I can't let you do that." Carl remembered that Gino associated him with Ray

Esposito. "Gino, I no longer . . ."

"This is my restaurant. I decide who is my guest. Don't insult me."

"I won't insult you, my friend. The meal was molto bene. Grazie."

Gino smiled and said, "Please, come again."

Carl asked the maître d to call a taxi for them and they headed downtown.

"Where are we going, now?" Laurel inquired.

"It's Friday night. I want to show you where I spent some of my Friday nights."

They rode down Ninth Avenue, onto Hudson Street, which became Bleecker Street. Just before they got to Grove Street Carl had the cab pull over to the curb. He pointed across Grove Street at a red brick building. "Right there, in that building, I worked a high stakes card game. I got quite an education along with some generous tips. It really wasn't . . ." Carl glanced down the street on the opposite side of Bleecker Street. A man and a woman sat in a nondescript black car. Because Bleecker Street was "one way" their backs were to him.

"Really wasn't what?" Laurel inquired.

"Uh, wait a minute." He told the cabbie to drive on down the street slowly. As he did Carl glanced to the left at the couple in the black car. When he recognized Detective Ryoya Akimoto he quickly slipped down in the seat. She didn't pay any attention to the passing taxi. Carl had the driver go to Washington Square Park which was a few blocks away. When he spotted a telephone booth he had the driver stop and they got out.

"What's going on?" Laurel asked.

When they were away from the taxi Carl explained, "Like I told you there is a high stakes poker game in that building back there. I used to work it. The guy who runs it was good to me. As a matter-of-fact two of his guys saved my life the first time Miguel tried to kill me. That black car parked across the street is a police car. They're staking out the game."

"Carl, you're not part of that life, anymore."

"I know. The problem is I feel I owe them. In my world where you could trust no one they were good to me."

"What are you planning to do?"

"I thought the least I could do is alert Ray about what I saw. That's all."

"You'd still be helping a criminal."

"I know. But, if I do nothing, I'm turning my back on a friend."

"A friend who is breaking the law."

Carl paced a few steps in each direction. He stood staring into Washington Square Park. Then slapped the telephone booth with his hand. Finally, he looked at Laurel and said, "Laurel, you are all that matters to me. My life is with you. My loyalty is to you. I love you and trust you. I'm stuck trying to figure out what is right and what is wrong. I know what is legal and illegal, but a part of me doesn't know how to turn my back on a friend. Everything is spinning round and round. Right here, right now, I need your help—your judgment. You decide. Do I call Ray and warn him or do we head back to the Bronx? There will be no second-guessing you or blame of any kind. I'm smart enough to know that I can't make a reasonable decision at this time. Whatever you recommend is what we do. I trust you Spirit Bird Woman."

Laurel looked at Carl and could see what turmoil he was going through. In truth, she could see both sides. She also could see the risk. There might not be great legal risk, but a psychological risk was evident. Carl could find himself drawn back into that life. The allure of power can be compelling. They just had a fine dinner—on the house. And, criminals are expert at persuasion. Carl, for all his street smarts, was vulnerable and a bit naive. But, what about the lingering effect of turning his back on a perceived friend? Spirit Bird Woman, indeed, she needed her own guidance.

A New York City police officer approached the couple. "Good evening, is there anything wrong?"

"Good evening officer," Laurel said with a smile.

"We're sightseeing," Carl offered.

"It's a cold night to be out," the patrolman observed.

"Tell me about it," was Carl's response.

Laurel explained, "We saw the Rockefeller Center Christmas tree and all the window displays on Fifth Avenue and had a fabulous dinner in an Italian restaurant."

"What brings you down here?" the police officer inquired.

"I was showing her where I used to hang out," Carl said, "I'm originally from New York."

"Where are you folks from?"

"Warren, Pennsylvania," Carl answered.

"Don't know that I'm familiar with Warren."

"It's in the northwest corner of the state," Carl pointed out, "Usually, buried in snow."

The policeman smiled, "So, I guess you're accustomed to cold weather." He paused then asked, "Do you have some form of ID?"

Laurel answered, "I have a driver's license." She rummaged through her purse, found her license, and handed it to the police officer.

He examined the document and handed it back to Laurel. "What about you?" he asked Carl.

"I don't have a license. Coming from New York, I never had need for one. She does all the driving," he shrugged, "I really need to get one—if you know what I mean. She scares me to death."

"Pennsylvania drivers," was all the patrolman said.

"Officer," Laurel interjected, "maybe you can help us." Carl looked nervously at Laurel.

"If I can."

"If you had a friend who you thought was doing something wrong. Something that might get them fired, for instance. Would you warn them to stop or mind your own business and let things happen as they happen?"

"I'm not sure I can answer such an abstract question. However, I will say this, a good friend looks out for you and tells you the truth even at the risk of losing you as a friend. I wouldn't turn my back on a friend."

"That helps," Laurel said, "Thank you."

The police officer smiled, nodded, and said, "You have a good evening."

When they were once again alone, Laurel said to Carl, "Make the call."

Carl entered the telephone booth and dialed Ray Esposito's number that he still remembered. When it was answered, he said, "Mr. Esposito, I just passed the location of the game and there are police staking it out."

"Who is this?" Ray inquired.

"Carl Pythacyk."

"Carl, I thought you blew the country, kid. Where are you?"

"I'm in a phone booth at Washington Square. Mr. Esposito, there's a black car across the street from the location with two detectives in it. I recognized one."

"Hold on," there were muffled sounds and then Ray Esposito returned. "OK, we're going to use an alternate site. You want to work the game?"

"No. I'm just visiting New York. When I saw the stakeout, I had to tell you. You were always good to me."

"Where've you been?"

"I'm working on a farm and getting married."

"The hell you say. That's great, kid. I hate to lose you. The boys will be glad to hear you're alive."

"Thank you. And, thanks for everything—I mean that."

"Carl, you're a sharp kid. You take care." The phone call ended.

Anna Six Trees lay in her bed and hoped to dream about Spirit Bird Woman. She was held in high esteem by her school friends for having actually met Manidoo-Binesiikwe.

111: Saturday – December 13, 1969

Detective Ryoya Akimoto sipped her coffee. It was early and they had spent a late night sitting in an uncomfortable car waiting for participants in an illegal card game to show. None did. A little after midnight they shut down the stakeout.

"What do you say—try again tonight?" Detective Michael Donovan asked as he leaned on her desk.

"Not my decision," she replied, "and not my problem."

"It is our case, therefore our decision, and we are shorthanded."

"Meaning?"

"I was just told if we want that location staked out tonight, we have to do it."

"Great."

"Also, we don't get overtime. So, if we are going to sit in a stinking car for hours tonight we have to leave early to turn up those hours."

"I would have bet that last night was the night," Ryoya stated. "From what I've been able to determine the Senator arrived in town Friday afternoon. We don't know his whereabouts on Friday night, but he was at an official dinner on Saturday night." She leaned back in her chair and concluded, "I don't think the game will be held tonight. In fact, I think they made us last night and either cancelled or moved the damn thing."

"You could be right," Michael Donovan said, "So, now what?"

"If they made us, that location is history. And, we don't have anything else to go on."

"So, a hot lead turns into a cold slice of pizza," Detective Donovan surmised. After a moment of thought he added, "You know what? I bet it was that Carl Pith Helmet. He warned them."

Ryoya looked at her partner and smiled, "I see, Carl Pit . . . Pissa . . . Pita Bread drove all the way to New York from somewhere in Pennsylvania, saw us, and warned Ray Esposito."

"Sounds logical to me."

"Right." Detective Akimoto concluded, "Ray Esposito has a guardian angel, that's for sure."

When Carl and Laurel picked up Fetch the night before they agree to join his parents for lunch. As they sat around the small kitchen table Laurel filled in the gap between when they last saw Carl and the present. Both his mother and father were captivated by the tale. Neither one ever imagined their son on a farm. Josef, Carl's father, laughed when he heard that Carl was afraid of bees.

"That's not so strange," Carl protested.

"No, my son," Josef said, "I laugh because I too have a fear of them."

Carl smiled. It was not because they shared a phobia as much as it was the first time he could remember his father calling him "my son."

Florentyna, Carl's mother, then said, "And, now you are getting married?"

"I still haven't been asked," Laurel said teasingly.

Carl ignored the dig and said, "We have an offer in on some land on which we are going to build a farmhouse."

"Not with criminal money," Josef warned.

"No. My parents are very successful and gave us money," Laurel explained.

"Oh? That is better," the old man said.

"We do not have money to give," Florentyna apologized.

Laurel looked at Carl's mother and said sincerely, "This meal is as valuable as the money was from my parents. Your love is precious to us. We will leave here far richer and happier. There is no price that can be put on happiness."

Carl's mother took Laurel's hand and said, "Thank you. My Carl, did indeed find an angel."

"Spirit Bird Woman," Carl corrected with his mouth half full.

"Don't talk with your mouth full," his mother chastised.

Carl nodded.

"If things go well, we plan a spring wedding," Laurel explained. "My family lives in St. Louis which is where we will get married. We'd like you to be there. Of course, we will pay the travel expenses."

Florentyna looked at Josef.

"We can afford it," Carl stated.

Boeing 747-21 with designation N732PA was manufactured in July, 1969. It had been used for flight testing, certification, and demonstration purposes. It was scheduled to be ferried from Boeing Field in Seattle to Renton, Washington for final refurbishing and configuration before delivery to a customer.

The original pilot was unavailable for flying on that day. His replacement, Ralph Clyde Cokeley, was a former military pilot with 121 flying hours in the 747. Co-pilot John Worthington Harder had only simulator time on the 747.

Because Renton Airport had a short runway, 5,300 feet, the pilot decided to do a practice landing at Boeing Field. He was familiar with N732PA as he had flown the aircraft for over five hours the day before on its last scheduled test flight. They took off at 10:45 a.m. Pacific Standard Time, circled the field, fell in line with air traffic, and landed on Runway 13. The jet touched down 700 feet past the threshold and came to a complete stop 2,500 feet down the runway using heavy braking and reverse thrust.

Later that day eleven persons were onboard the aircraft for the short ten-minute flight to Renton. The Boeing 747 took off at 11:04 a.m. Pacific Standard Time. The landing gear was left deployed due to the short flight and to cool the brakes from the practice landing. The jet flew at 2,500 feet along the Lake Washington eastern shoreline. It began raining which meant the stopping distance on the runway would be greater. The pilot executed a descending left turn over the East Channel Bridge. It was then that Ralph Cokeley noticed that they were slightly high so he made a glide slope adjustment. They were given clearance to land on Runway 15 and informed that there was a slight crosswind.

Co-pilot Harder called out the aircraft's altitude in 100 foot increments. Two miles out they were flying at 128 knots at 600 feet. Once they reached 100 feet he began calling out ten foot increments. When he called out 30 feet the shoreline passed under the cockpit at which time the aircraft abruptly sank. No one onboard was aware of the fact that a short in a wire caused the number four engine to slow.

At 11:11 a.m. the right landing gear wheels hit the lip of the lake bank 30 inches below the level of the runway and 25 feet short of the pavement. The impact tore off part of the landing gear and caused the right wing to dip dragging the number three and four engines on the pavement. Small fires erupted in those engines that were quickly extinguished unfortunately wiping out any evidence of the wire failure.

The pilot did an amazing job keeping the huge aircraft on the centerline and bringing it to a stop in just 3,500 feet. There was structural damage to the right wing landing gear, right flap assemblies, and number three and four engines. A cause for the sinking of the jet was never determined.

Harry Van Ryker leaned on the bar and asked, "You watch Johnny Carson?"

"Sometimes, when I'm not out walking," Jack responded.

"Oh, you doing that again?"

"It relaxes me."

"Still creating scenarios of women in apartments where lights are on?"

"I imagine who might be in an apartment, what they are doing, how their life is going, what problems they face, whether or not they're watching Johnny Carson. It's a form of creativity that keeps me mentally in shape."

"I think you're a peeping tom."

"You're probably right."

"Back to Johnny Carson," Harry said, "Do you know next week that weird falsetto singing flake Tiny Tim is marrying this Miss Vickie on the Carson show?" He looked up in the air, "The same week I'm getting married."

"Yeah, but you're not getting married on the Tonight Show."

"That's not the point. They're making a mockery of marriage the same week I am taking sacred vows!"

"And, you believe they're doing this just to screw up your wedding?"

"No, of course not. It's just the timing sucks."

"You know what I think?"

"No, and I don't want to know."

"I think you're getting nervous. You realize what a life-changing thing this is and it's only seven days away. In seven teeny days, your socks will no longer be welcome on the bedroom floor, or dirty dishes allowed to age, or Playboy Magazines left on the coffee table, or the toilet seat . . ."

"OK, OK, you made your point," Harry conceded. "Maybe, that's part of it."

"That's all of it." Jack held up his empty glass, "You have to look past the little adjustments that need to be made and see the wonderful possibilities. Shopping will become a regular form of entertainment. Your closet—well you can find other places for your stuff. Also, you'll become more efficient once you start sharing a bathroom. There's no end to the possibilities."

"You're a son-of-a-bitch, you know that?"

"You're right," Jack admitted. "I will say one thing, though. When the two of you start sharing your lives together you'll wonder how you survived so long with so much emptiness in your life. Everything will become more exciting, beautiful, and meaningful when you can turn to that special someone and share an experience. You're going to step into infinite happiness."

"I'm sorry," Harry said sincerely.

"Don't be—I am a son-of-a-bitch."

"Not for that." Harry put a new drink in front of Jack. He then put his hand on his friend's arm and said, "I'm sorry you didn't get your infinite happiness."

112: Sunday – December 14, 1969

Three tourists from Warren, Pennsylvania headed west on Route 80. Their visit to New York had been a complete success. Josef and Florentyne Pythacyk agreed to attend the wedding and even wanted to visit Cardinal's Gate sometime in the future. Carl closed the book on Ray Esposito. And, Laurel got to see the Christmas lights.

They took his parents out to dinner and spent the evening with them. At one point Florentyna and Carl disappeared for a few minutes. When they did, Josef walked over a sat next to Laurel, stared at her, nodded, and said, "You saved my boy. I am so ashamed to have failed him. He was dead to me and you gave him life. Thank you."

Laurel sat in silence, nodded, and smiled. No words were necessary.

When Carl and his mother returned to the room, he walked over to where Laurel sat, got down on one knee, and asked, "Laurel Fitzpatrick, will you marry me?" In his hand he held an antique ring.

Laurel looked at Carl and recited the lines of a Celtic song, "If you could be music, the song you would sing, and all of the beauty, and joy you would bring. The world would stop turning, to hear the refrain, and the peace and the harmony, you bring, when we are together." She then smiled and added her own words, "I will marry you for without you my heart would live in unbearable silence."

Now, on their way back to Lark's Run they had only the future before them. Carl found that he was at ease, maybe for the first time in many years. In his mind he envisioned a farmhouse.

"You realize, of course, the most difficult part lies ahead," Laurel broke the silence.

"Oh, what might that be?"

"You have to meet my parents."

"And, you see that as a problem?"

"Let's say a challenge. One you might not be up to. Or, one that will leave a lasting mark on your psyche."

"Great, now I have something new to deal with as if my ego isn't bruised enough."

"When they're through, shattered might be a better term."

"Can I take back my proposal and grandmother's ring?"

"Nope."

"Any advice on how to approach them?"

"Very carefully."

"You make them sound dangerous."

"I'm just trying to be fair and give you adequate warning."

"Give me some pointers. What do I do. And, what do I not do?"

"That's really hard to say." After a pause, Laurel added, "They do like square dancing. Maybe you and I can brush up on your square dancing."

"Brush up? I wouldn't know a square dance from a can can."

"Well, we have some work to do."

"And, that will make your parent's like me?" Carl inquired hoping it would.

"No, it may make them tolerate you." Another pause, "My father is an amateur sculptor—mainly nudes. He might ask you to pose."

"Hell, no!"

"If you love me you won't refuse."

"Look I gotta draw the line somewhere."

"Not there," Laurel stated. "You can draw the line by not participating in the pagan ritual to honor Cernunnos the Celtic God of the Wild Hunt, fertility, and masculine energy. It gets pretty bizarre at times."

"What? Who the hell are these people? Where did you come from?"

"I'm a witch."

"That does it."

Laurel began laughing at which point Carl knew he had been had. She had taken him into the forest and down a rabbit hole and he went blindly along. "You are a witch—you know that?"

"Yes, but I'm your witch."

A grin dominated Carl's face, "I wouldn't have it any other way."

"Good answer. You don't want me to put a curse on you."

"You already have."

Ritchie Anderson stood in front of the World Trade Center site and looked up at the buildings that had sprout out the ground and were growing toward the sky. As he did, his thoughts drifted to the great escape trip that never reached Canada. Three strangers found themselves in a life and death struggle that both defined them and colored their futures. He knew Carl's future would be positive, but what about Wellington Marsh? There was no letter in response to his. And, Chief Michael's dream couldn't be ignored. Was Wellington dead?

Ritchie wondered what is it that causes things to happen? Is it simply chance? Or, are there unseen forces manipulating their lives? If he hadn't made the decision to flee to Canada, then picked up a young Marine, met an Indian Chief, gone to visit a tree, and come across a family in distress would he even know who Wellington Marsh is—or care? Since it all began with his decision to head to Canada he wondered was there some force that prompted that decision. Receipt of his reclassification to 1A certainly started the ball rolling. Or, was it snow ball rolling?

A bird drifted down and landed on the fence that surrounded the World Trade Center site. Ritchie's mind switched to another course of events. Would Carl have met Laurel if he hadn't picked up the on-the-run hitchhiker? If he hadn't brought Carl to Lark's Run the guy would never have known the place existed. Chance or Divine Design? Ritchie wondered.

His mind pictured Stephanie Ellis. All that happened to her pushed her in so many directions. Her father's accident, mother's death, boyfriend leaving, loss of Colt MacIntyre, and subsequent father's suicide all had dramatic impact on her life. Yet, she had nothing to do with those events. A black cloud seemed to hover over her. If there was such a thing as Divine Design, Ritchie prayed that Stephanie's move to Texas would dissipate the clouds and let her step out into the warm, life-enriching sunshine.

A cold breeze slapped Ritchie across the face. It brought him back to the job at hand. He resumed taking photographs of the skyline-changing project. Not strictly due to the immense size of the buildings that were the center of his attention, at that moment Ritchie felt very small. He was a grain of sand on an enormous beach waiting to be dragged out to sea and eventually deposited he knew not where.

Amanda Shay brought out two glasses of white wine. She handed one to Ryoya Akimoto and sat in a chair next to the couch. A slew of papers were spread on the coffee table. They had spent the day going over all of the final preparations for the upcoming wedding. Everything appeared to be in order.

"That's it," Ryoya remarked, "now you can sit back and relax. All you have to do is show up at Holy Trinity Lutheran Church on Saturday."

"And, hope that Harry shows up," Amanda replied.

"Is he getting cold feet?"

"No, but knowing him he'll get involved with someone who needs a helping hand and forget what day it is."

"I'll call him in the morning to remind him," Ryoya offered.

"You joke, but that could be a good idea."

"So, noted." Ryoya sipped her wine, "And, what is the temperature of your feet?"

Amanda smiled and answered, "I'm good, not nervous, and no reservations." Suddenly, she got a stricken look on her face. "Reservations! I bet Harry hasn't made reservations at the Skytop Lodge. It's a quaint old hotel near Scranton, hidden in the mountains, a perfect getaway for a few days. He was supposed to take care of that."

"I'll check with him tomorrow," Ryoya said.

"You've been so helpful. I don't know how to thank you," Amanda stated.

"No need. Two wonderful people found each other, fell in love, and are going to make a life together. Just to witness the happiness is all that I need."

"And, what about your happiness?" Amanda asked impulsively.

"Right now, I'm trying to find Ryoya Akimoto. When I do I might just determine where lies my happiness."

At eight o'clock on CBS the Ed Sullivan Show came on. This evening the audience was introduced to Michael Jackson and the Jackson Five from Gary, Indiana. Michael Jackson was ten-years-old, yet had an air of confidence about him and impressive vocal range. They began by singing Sly and the Family Stone's *Stand.* They followed with a blues rendition of Smokey Robinson's *Who's Loving You.* The last song they sang was their first single hit *I Want You Back.* Ed Sullivan was visibly impressed with the group and said, "The little fella in front is incredible."

Wanda Six Trees sipped herbal tea, looked at her daughter asleep in her bed, and wished for her a bright future.

113: Saturday – December 20, 1969

Jack Moore woke up with a headache. His mouth was dry and stomach wasn't sure which way to push its contents. Some call it a hangover. Jack called it the exclamation point on a stupid statement made the night before. He and Harry Van Ryker had been up late into the night reminiscing. They'd known each other for a long time, shared many experiences, given each other support when needed, and formed a lasting friendship.

It was Harry's wedding day and Jack knew he had to pull himself together for his friend. He also knew he had to check on the barkeep to make sure that he makes it to the church on time. When he tried to sit up the weight of his head kept it glued to the pillow. Then he realized it wasn't his pillow. It was his balled-up overcoat and he wasn't in his bed. He was laying on the living room floor still fully dressed. This posed a new problem. He couldn't roll out of bed, he had to climb up from the depths of depravity.

A noise caught his attention. Was it an atomic detonation? Or, earthquake? Or, refinery explosion? Harry entered the room carrying two cups of coffee.

"What the hell are you doing in my apartment?" Jack asked from his dignified position on the floor.

"I could ask you that same question," was Harry's bright, fresh, unaffected response. "You're in my apartment."

"No."

"Yes, here have some black coffee," Harry stooped down and put the cup in front of Jack's face.

"How did I get here?"

"Hard to tell."

"You must know."

"Oh, I know, the story is hard to tell."

"Oh crap! What did I do?"

"You remember us having a few drinks between friends?"

"Yeah."

"We closed the bar, sat at a table, and opened a good bottle of Johnny Walker Black."

"I'm with you."

"We shared a lot of experiences over the years—good and bad."

"Is this particular one good or bad?"

"Depends on how it turns out."

Jack fought his way to a prone position leaning on his elbows. Shaking hands brought the coffee cup up to his lips. The aroma punched him in the face. A sip of the hot black liquid laser-beamed into his stomach. He fought the impulse to return it to its original location.

Harry continued, "We finished Mr. Walker and went our separate ways. I was home for about a half hour, about to get into bed, when there was a pounding on my door. At two in the morning people frown on door pounding."

"Me?"

"You. Apparently, you found an all-night club and got Mr. Walker a friend."

"Sounds like me."

Harry sat on the couch, "Jack, you were shit-faced. More importantly, you were distraught. It's clear you're not over Detective Akimoto and from the sound of it will never be able to fully let go. She got under your skin. You opened the vault that surrounds your heart, risked everything, and it bit you in the ass. In a way, I'm sorry I made that happen."

"Don't be. It was a bright spot in an otherwise dull life. A supernova that burned out too quickly. Yet, I wouldn't have missed it for the world. I touched heaven, Harry."

"Yeah, and then fell all the way down to hell."

Jack tried another sip of coffee, "So, what else did I do?"

"You were concerned about how you would react when you saw her today. As you put it, 'I don't want to fuck up your wedding.' You told me you loved her. As matter-of-fact you told me you loved me, loved Amanda, the guy who sold you the booze, and the cab driver who brought you here."

"He was a good cabbie."

"Then you decided to leave. That's when you took up residence on my floor. I thought it was best to leave you there. At least this way I could get you up and moving in the morning."

"I'm sorry, Harry. This is your big day and you don't need to play nursemaid to a sot."

"Jack, if you're going to make a jackass of yourself, I'd rather it be with me."

Jack fought his way to a sitting position. "Is my head as big as it feels?"

"It's about right, but your eyes look like two red traffic lights."

"I better go and pull myself together. Don't worry, I'll be there on time and I'll be a good boy."

"I know you will," Harry helped Jack up. After a Three Stooges routine, they were successful in getting a wrinkled overcoat onto a not-too-steady best man. Jack made his way out the door.

Ryoya Akimoto brought breakfast to Amanda's apartment. As Maid-of-Honor it was her job to make sure Amanda got her hair done, make-up, dress and accessories, and arrived at the church on time. She also needed to make sure the bride got something to eat and that all the little surprises that seem to appear on one's wedding day got handled.

"Did you get a good night's sleep?" Ryoya asked.

"Slept like a baby."

"Good. We have some running around to do, but everything seems to be progressing as planned. I even spoke with Harry and he knows what day it is and that he has to be at the church at 5:30."

"This is a lot easier than my first wedding," Amanda observed. "That wedding was a major production. Of course, my parents were still alive and we had practically the entire NYPD force in attendance."

"I must say this wedding, although planned hastily, has come together quite well."

"At our age, Harry and I don't need a big wedding."

"I'd say it's big enough with your and Harry's friends."

Amanda then became serious and asked Ryoya, "Did Harry say anything about Jack?"

"No. However, I'm not worried. Jack is a mature adult and will not do anything to detract from this special day."

"I love you both and don't want the wedding to stress either of you."

"The only thing you have to worry about is answering the pastor's questions correctly."

Amanda snickered. She then contemplated, "It's so funny how things turn out. When you brought Harry and me together I would never have imagined I'd be sitting here preparing to get married. Life is so totally unpredictable. The unexpected comes to happen while what seemed obvious turns out to not be," Amanda caught herself and said, "Oh, I'm sorry."

"No need to apologize. As you said, life is unpredictable. In a way, it might have been better if the Mets had lost," Ryoya lamented. Then with a forced smile she said, "What am I saying?"

Jack Moore made it to his apartment on East Sixty Third Street. His head throbbed from the unrelenting sounds of the city. Not one of his smarter moves, he thought. Get plowed after the wedding—not before. Now, he had to contend with a hangover on top of the emotional strain of walking down the aisle with Ryoya only to go their separate ways after the wedding. That's the time to get stinko—idiot!

After a shower and change of clothes, Jack felt . . . like crap. He knew he had to get something to eat in an attempt to settle his stomach. However, eating was the last thing he wanting to do.

Jack Moore walked out of his apartment building onto East Sixty Third Street. Cold air squeezed what little bit of life he was feeling from his body. His intent was to pick up a tame turkey sandwich at Goldstein's Deli. That was not going to happen. Before Jack could take four steps, a black Cadillac stopped in the street adjacent to where he walked. The newspaper reporter quickly became aware of his stalkers. Immediately, a large mean-looking character emerged from the car and sauntered onto the sidewalk, blocked Jack's path, and said, "Jack Moore, someone wants to see you."

Jack surmised who the culprit was and said, "Tell whomever it is they can call my office and make an appointment."

"He wants to see you—now!" the man replied not showing any sense of humor. Jack was directed into the waiting black Cadillac. It was clear that he couldn't refuse such a polite invitation. He had made his defiant statement but now had to comply or run the risk of going to Harry's wedding in a cast. Jack entered the automobile.

Carl entered the automobile. He and Laurel were on a mission. On their return trip from New York they discussed their many plans. One part of their goal was for Carl to get a driver's license as quickly as possible. He passed both the eye test and written test earlier in the week and now had a learner's permit. With Laurel beside him he made an effort to develop the skills needed to take the driver's test.

"You know, it's going to feel good to sit back and let you drive," Laurel stated.

"I don't mind. I rather enjoy driving," Carl replied.

The black Cadillac pulled up to a building with which Jack was very familiar. He was invited to enter with a friendly shove. Once inside, Jack found himself seated at a table upon which was a bottle of wine and two glasses. Just the thought of alcohol made his stomach threaten to rebel. He was pleased that the bottle wasn't open as he knew he couldn't handle the aroma of alcohol.

After a short wait, Don Carmine Spacini entered the room, sat in a chair opposite Jack, and said, "You look like shit—fachabroot."

"You always were an observant son-of-a-bitch," Jack retorted.

"It keeps me alive—which is more than I can say about you based on appearances and your wiseass mouth."

"Thanks, you're more right than you realize."

Carmine took out a corkscrew and began twisting it into the cork that sealed the bottle of wine.

"Please, none for me," Jack gestured.

"Don't insult me," was the don's reply as he pulled the cork from the bottle with a pop. "Good friends drink together and share the pleasure of a fine vintage."

"Really, I'm in no condition."

"Nonsense," Carmine said as he poured the red liquid into each glass. "A man can control his physical response, while a boy falls prey to over-indulgence."

"You really are an evil man," Jack concluded.

"Yes, I am," Carmine raised his glass, "Saluto!"

Reluctantly, Jack picked up his glass and held it up in a shaking hand, "Saluto, il mio amico." He sipped the wine. In spite of his condition he found the flavor to be full, fruity, and robust. It was not too sweet nor too dry. Carmine had, indeed, made a fine selection. The hair of the dog actually eased some of Jack's stomach discomfort, but the teeth of the dog gnawed at his aching head.

"This is Dolcetto d'Alba," Carmine pointed out. "Dolcetto is a hearty little grape that is easy-growing and early-ripening. In Italy, Dolcetto is found in the Piedmont region of northwest Italy particularly in cooler higher elevations. Dolcetto means 'little sweet one' but that's a misnomer. These grapes produce a dry wine."

Jack examined the bottle which was unlike most tall narrow wine bottles. This one was shorter and rounder, much like a bottle of cognac. In his glass the deep red color of the wine was attractive and inviting.

Carmine continued his lesson, "A document from 1633 shows the presence of Dolcetto in the cellars of the Arboreo family of Valenza. In 1700, Barnabà Centurione sent the wine as a gift to Queen Anne of Great Britain. The Spacini family in the hilly region of Monchiero have vines dating back to 1763. Dolcetto wines are known for black cherry, licorice, and prune flavors, with a characteristically bitter finish tasting of almonds." He took another sip and indicated for Jack to do the same.

Jack complied and waited. He knew his friend well enough to realize he wasn't invited to get a degree in winemaking.

Don Carmine Spacini put his glass down. He took out two cigars and offered one to Jack. When both men had enjoyed the first two or three puffs, Carmine looked across the table and said, "I require of you a favor."

Richard Anderson walked along in the Bergen Mall doing his Christmas shopping. He didn't have a long list but wanted to get something special for each individual for whom he was buying. Unfortunately, it being the Saturday before Christmas, the mall was so crowded it was like Grand Central Station at rush hour.

In spite of all the people a soldier in uniform caught Ritchie's eye. The young man was walking slowly with his girlfriend looking in store windows. Ritchie's mind soared across continents and oceans to a jungle in Vietnam. Where was Wellington Marsh? Was he alive? Why hadn't he answered the letter? Was Chief Michael's dream an omen? Could he be making too much of the lack of information?

Jack didn't have to remind his friend that he would do nothing illegal or compromising. They both understood that. For this reason, Jack didn't respond when Carmine requested a favor.

"Do you recognize the name Carl Pythacyk?" Carmine Spacini asked.

"Of course, I came to you for information on him. He was accused of murder but cleared."

"Correct."

Jack waited. His stomach felt better but his head refused to forgive him for the night before.

"Last week this Carl Pythacyk did Ray Esposito a favor. He didn't have to, but he saved Ray from, uh, let us say, embarrassment." Carmine leaned forward and stated, "The kid didn't do anything illegal. In fact, I hear he's working on a farm and getting married."

"And, you want me to find him," Jack concluded. "Can't do it."

"Stoonod! You're an asshole."

"You know I can't do it," Jack insisted.

"Listen, sciocco, I don't want you to find him."

"Oh? Then what do you want?"

"I want you to find him . . ."

"What the hell?"

"Stata Zeet! I want you to find him, not tell me where he is."

"Then what?"

Don Carmine Spacini rose from the table and walked over to a sideboard. There he retrieved a package. It was shoebox size wrapped in brown paper. When he returned he placed it on the table. "I want you to get this to the young man. He made a gesture as a friend and showed respect. Now, he has a chance to go straight. I want to show my appreciation for what he did, but not draw him back into the life."

Jack heard sincerity in Carmine's voice. It was the same sincerity he heard when Carmine asked Jack to keep his daughter on the right side of the law. Don Carmine Spacini could be tough, ruthless, and downright dangerous. To a certain few, he could also be compassionate and thoughtful. He looked at the box and asked, "What's in it?"

"It's a cutting from the original Dolcetta grape vine cultivated by the Spacini family in the hilly region of Monchiero. It was brought to America and has been grown on my estate for many years." Carmine patted the box, "I want Carl to have a cutting so he can grow the Spacini Dolcetta grape and make fine wine." The don leaned back and added, "Who knows, maybe someday he'll send me a case."

"You know as much about his whereabouts as me."

"Yes, but you have a girlfriend, that detective, who most likely has his address."

Jack took another sip of wine. "We are no longer seeing each other," he offered.

"Oh, I'm sorry to hear that," Carmine said sincerely. He waved his arm across the table and inquired, "And, is this a reason for your present situation?"

"Part of it. I'm best man at Harry Van Ryker's wedding today and she is Maid-of-Honor."

"The bar owner," Carmine reflected, "Today? And, I am keeping you."

"It's an evening wedding."

"La femmina è difficile da capire, the female is hard to understand."

"Tell me about it."

"If I could, I would rule the world."

Jack laughed and raised his glass, "You are a wise man, Don Spacini."

Carmine Spacini nodded. He leaned back and said, "So, now, will you grant me this favor?"

"I'll do whatever I can to get the gift to the young man."

"Grazie," Carmine poured the last of the wine into their glasses. As he examined the deep red color he said in a friendly tone, "Now, how about I introduce you to a nice Italian lady?"

"Too soon, my friend."

More people than anticipated filed into Holy Trinity Lutheran Church on Central Park West. It seemed that both Amanda Shay and Harry Van Ryker had more friends than they realized.

As a Lutheran wedding is primarily a worship service, there is little pomp and ceremony. The organist played a number of hymns as a prelude. Shortly after, the pastor and groom entered the sanctuary and stood in the front.

Due to short notice the couple had decided to only have a Maid-of-Honor and Best Man. Amanda would come down the aisle alone. When planning the wedding, the pastor explained that much of traditional wedding music was inappropriate in the Lutheran worship service. He explained one reason a church may give for considering certain pieces unacceptable is the music's original setting. For instance, the traditional *Wedding March* was from the opera *Lohengrin,* which was a very tragic tale. Further, it did not have a religious origin. In addition, the popular Pachelbel's *Canon in D* did not originate in a Christian worship context. In the end, the pastor made a recommendation which the couple accepted.

When the music changed Ryoya Akimoto walked out of the side room into the vestibule. From the opposite direction, Jack Moore entered. He wore a dark tuxedo. Across the room stood his treasure wearing a dark grey, sleeveless, floor-length, A-line, empire waist, chiffon evening gown. A crisscross bodice created V-necks front and back. Detailed ruching pleats extended from the waist to the floor giving the light chiffon skirt volume and movement. The rippling flow as she walked was mesmerizing. Jack was unprepared for how stunning and seductive she appeared. He ached to be near her, but knew it would not be.

Ryoya glided across the room and turned at the doors leading to the center aisle. Jack joined her. Neither spoke. The music changed and the doors opened. Jack and Ryoya walked together down the long aisle. Jack Moore tried to squeeze a lifetime into that interlude. In a dreamlike state, he relived previous shared moments of unfettered joy and infinite promise. When they reached the front, the music stopped.

After a pause the organist played *Jesu, Joy of Man's Desiring* by Johann Sabastian Bach. All eyes turned to the vestibule doors. Amanda Shay appeared. She wore a champagne lace cap sleeve dress with a lace sheer illusion overlay with matching silk sash. The length was long and loose with an embellished waistline. It was a perfect dress for the occasion.

Jack looked at his friend. Harry Van Ryker was lost in the magic of the moment. His eyes were fixed on his bride, lips parted, and head ever so slightly tilted. It was the essence of amazement and joy. Jack both envied Harry, as well as was pleased to see his longtime pal find his treasure. It was then that Jack realized that Ryoya was not wearing the necklace he had given her.

Stephanie Ellis spent most of her Saturday volunteering to do various jobs around the ranch. She just felt better if she was busy doing something constructive. In addition, it was all new to her. She grew up in a suburb of New York City and had very little exposure to a rural lifestyle. There was something refreshing about it. Yet, Stephanie also came to realize it was very hard work. Late in the afternoon Clinton MacIntyre walked over to where Stephanie was moving some small pieces of wood.

"Always look carefully before lifting anything," he warned. "Snakes like to hide under rocks and wood and other debris."

Stephanie looked up and replied, "I've been warned and have been careful. If I see a snake I'm heading back to Jersey."

Clinton laughed. "We're going out to dinner, tonight. Why don't you call it a day and get cleaned up?"

Clan MacIntyre went to 302 S. Main Street in Victoria, Texas. Their destination was Fossati's Delicatessen. The misleading name was actually the oldest deli in Texas, as well as one of the oldest restaurants in the United States. Fraschio Napoleon Fossati opened his restaurant in 1882. Three years later he had a building constructed in the square in downtown Victoria. It sported red and white checkered tablecloths, a bar, and in the backroom a huge bookcase filled with hundreds of cookbooks. Fossati's Delicatessen was a regular gathering place for Victoria's citizens. Political functions were also common in this welcoming establishment.

On this night, the restaurant was relatively crowded. Of course, everyone knew the MacIntyres. A steady stream of visitors stopped at their table to chat and were introduced to Stephanie. By the end of the evening she was well known in Victoria. She also was asked by a number of young men if they could call her.

After the wedding service a reception was held at the Empire Hotel three blocks from the church. The lounge was reserved with a buffet and cash bar available. Once more, the bride and groom did not expect much turnout. However, the crowd grew and grew until it filled the room.

Jack did not seek to find Ryoya. He didn't want to take the chance of doing something stupid.

At the appropriate time, Jack Moore stood and raised his glass. The crowd took a few moments to quiet. When he had their attention, he made his toast, "I tried to find a quote about marriage that I could use. Unfortunately, they all seemed to address the challenges of marriage and adjustments needed to live together and warnings of what not to do. It was enough to scare anyone away." A few snickers were heard in the crowd. "So, I thought about what marriage really is. In my mind, when something good happens to you the first person you want to share it with is your partner. On those occasions when you need support they bring you strength. Nostalgia is defined by those times you create memories together. When you wish to be alone you have the freedom to do so without cutting all ties. You have available twice the judgement, enhanced strength, eyes in the back of your head, moral support, and a view of the world through a magnificent prism only the two of you understand. I'll call it marriage perspective where two people blend individual experiences and values to form a new and unique life view that defines them, while allowing each to be completely comfortable being themselves. Amanda and Harry, go hand in hand with confidence and anticipation of infinite happiness in your new world."

On the other side of the world a frustrated Henry Cabot Lodge quit his post as chief U.S. negotiator at the Paris peace talks. He found that President Nixon was right the North Vietnamese had no interest in a negotiated peace.

114: Monday – December 22, 1969

Jack picked up the telephone and dialed a familiar number.

"Detective Akimoto."

"Ryoya, Jack."

"Yes, Jack, how are you?"

"I'm fine."

"It was a lovely wedding."

"Yes, it was." Jack's tone became businesslike, "I need some information."

"What kind of information?"

"Do you remember that kid, Carl Pythacyk, that was wanted for murder?"

"I do. He was cleared of all charges."

"I know. Do you have his address?"

"I don't believe he ever gave us an actual address. What is this all about?"

Jack knew that question would be asked so he was prepared with an answer, "An acquaintance of his wants to send him a Christmas card."

"I smell a rat," Ryoya commented.

"Why not a reindeer?"

"Because Santa doesn't send Christmas cards." After a pause, Ryoya said, "Listen Jack, the kid is out of the mob—let him be."

"You've got it wrong. No one wants him back. I simply want to get in touch with him."

"As I said he didn't provide an actual address. In fact, all we have is his parent's address in the Bronx."

"That's a start."

"Give me a second." Ryoya leafed through some files and returned to the phone, "2515 University Avenue, Apartment 4G. I'm not sure they know where Carl is living."

"I'll start there."

"Jack, as I said, the kid got away from the criminal life. I'd hate to see that change."

"It's called trust, detective," Jack ended the conversation before he said something he would regret.

The special Cherokee Winter issue of the outdoor magazine had been approved as a sufficient number of sponsors signed up to make it profitable. Ritchie Anderson was excited as he knew that he was going back to Minnesota along with a team to do interviews and additional photographs after the first of the year. It also meant that Chief Michael and Wanda Six Trees would be rewarded. A young Ojibwa boy's eyes haunted Ritchie's optimistic images.

Jack Moore took the subway to the Bronx and found himself at the door of Apartment 4G. A woman answered. After he explained who he was and why he was there she invited him in. Jack learned a great deal about Carl Pythacyk and that he was living on a farm called Lark's Run in Warren, Pennsylvania.

Two Navy F8 Crusader jet fighter aircraft were practicing Air-Combat Maneuvering (ACM) west of San Diego on a cool clear morning. Suddenly the jet fighter flown by Lieutenant Cyrus M. Riddell experienced a complete loss of power—a flame out. He attempted to return to Miramar Naval Air Station, fifteen miles northwest of San Diego. At 10:20 in the morning as he approached the runway while rapidly losing altitude he was ordered to eject. Lieutenant Riddell, aimed the jet at the runway and ejected at 400 feet altitude approximately one mile from the end of the runway.

His wingman Lieutenant Commander J.E. Graham watched in horror as the 45,000-pound pilotless jet veered to the right and nosedived at 250 miles per hour into the north doors of hanger K-277 and skid into two F-4 Phantom jets. A huge fireball erupted with flames and fuel spewing in all directions.

Approximately 60 persons were inside the acre-size hangar at the time. Navy personnel and civilians ran from the building yelling as ejection seats of six other jet planes exploded. One tore through the roof of the structure. Flames shot 150 feet into the air and the entire area was blanketed in black smoke.

Emergency crews reacted immediately. A yellow crash truck drove right into the hanger to fight the fire. Some Navy personnel who had rushed to the scene pushed two F-4 Phantom jets out of the hanger. Other fire trucks and ambulances arrived quickly and Navy helicopters flew injured and burned men to San Diego after emergency treatment at the base. In the end eleven men died, including two brothers, and fourteen were injured. The pilot of the crippled jet was not physically hurt, but carried unrelenting guilt about the accident for the rest of his life.

"Today is the winter solstice," Nick announced as the crew of Lark's Run sat down for dinner. "This means we will enjoy the longest night of the year."

"Does that mean we get to sleep late," Audra inquired.

"Bad Temper Barney doesn't care where the sun is when he starts to crow," Nick replied referring to the resident rooster.

"Look, it's snowing," Night Bird said as she pointed at the window.

Large white snowflakes drifted lazily downward. A slight breeze caused them to swirl and dance in the light from the farmhouse.

"That looks like more than a flurry," Carl concluded.

Snow continued falling all evening. By the time most went to bed there was at least five inches on the ground. Nick added some wood to the two Franklin stoves that heated the house. He then poked at the fire in the fireplace in the great room. Afterward, he settled into a comfortable chair with the intention of reading. Laurel entered the room.

"I like snow," she stated, adding, "even though it makes our work more difficult."

"Even as a kid I always got excited when it began to snow," Nick said.

"I don't think Carl likes snow."

"He might if you would stop hitting him in the back of the head with snowballs."

Laurel grinned, "But it's such a big head—easy to hit."

Nick put down his book and asked, "What's on your mind?"

"Carl and I love Lark's Run. We've found our little bit of paradise here. If we buy the property across the stream, we don't want it to have a detrimental effect on Lark's Run."

"Why should it do that?"

"Well, to begin, it will double the area that is involved. And, when we build a house there will be maintenance and upkeep that will take us away from Lark's Run. That will leave fewer people to operate Lark's Run."

"I see," Nick replied. "Before Night Bird and Carl arrived we kept things going pretty well, didn't we?"

"Yes."

"When they did join us it allowed us to do more. Now, when you and Carl establish, what was it, Crow's Cavern?"

Laurel Laughed, "Cardinal's Gate."

"That's it. When you set up Cardinal's Gate we will have just that much more to work with. We could add some beef cows in a pasture, or expand our selection of vegetables, or add a greenhouse for year around growing. If anything, it will improve Lark's Run."

"We just don't have enough people."

"Maybe, we'll get lucky and have some new visitors who choose to stay. Or, maybe, we can recruit some new members. I'm optimistic. Our two farms, Lark's Run and Pigeon's Pouch will be a haven to those who want to work the land and escape the industrial revolution. It will be a stopping off point for travelers and a new beginning for those who fell on hard times."

That last statement gave Laurel pause. She thought of her red feathers. A gift from a mother struggling to raise her daughter in the harshest of conditions while also bearing the pain of a lost son came to mind. Would such a woman want to join their merry band or would it be an insult to ask her to leave the reservation and her way of life. Laurel shared her thoughts with Nick.

"That, I believe, is a question you should pose to the chief, Spirit Bird Woman."

"If I have been adopted by the Ojibwa Tribe why can't Cardinal's Gate be a branch of the reservation, much like an embassy in a foreign country?"

"It would be interesting."

"I'll have to discuss it with Carl."

Nick looked around, "Where is the lad?"

"He's outside hiding with a snowball. I told him I was going to check on the cows before going to bed." Laurel stood and said cheerily, "Well, I'm going up to bed. Good night."

For a brief moment, Nick considered saving Carl. He laughed and opened his book.

Wanda Six Trees dreamed of a faraway place where green fields and dense forests nestled among hills.

115: Wednesday – December 24, 1969

All the homes on Brandywine Avenue were decorated using multi-colored Christmas lights—with the exception of one. A small brick ranch house at 321 Brandywine Avenue had only a small yellow porch light. It created a shadowy foreboding appearance in a sea of festive light. A dark maw of ominous meaning.

In the past on Christmas Eve that home would have been brightly lit with multi-colored lights along the roofline, a large star on the roof, and large plastic candles on either side of the porch. This year, however, all the decorations remained in boxes in the attic. There was no reason for celebration.

Inside 321, Peter and Judith Marsh sat in their living room. The black and white console television was on but neither of them payed it much attention. Each was engulfed in their cherished memories as they attempted to read a book or magazine. Time had passed since they received the telegram from the Acting Commandant of the U.S. Marine Corps informing them their son, Lance Corporal Wellington Marsh, was missing in action. Time did not heal their wounds. Time did not bring them good news for which they prayed. Time did not make day-to-day living any easier. Time only made them feel old. Time was also not on their side. Each passing day lowered the odds of Wellington being found alive and returning to them. There would be no Christmas for the Marsh family in 1969.

It was snowing outside and the street grew quiet. Neither Peter nor Judith spoke. They had shared their feelings over and over and were drained of emotion. Now, they turned inward and simply existed. A single car was heard on the street. Snowy conditions muffled its sound. After it passed an eerie quiet returned to Brandywine Avenue. Suddenly, the doorbell rang. It startled Judith. Peter rose slowly and glanced out the front window. He saw the shadow of a police officer or a soldier. Immediately, he knew if it was a soldier it could be the bad news they feared most that Wellington had been confirmed dead. A part of him wanted to run into the bedroom and pull the covers over his head to avoid the inevitable. His missing boy was gone forever. The doorbell rang once more. Hesitantly, Peter Marsh walked to the portal to face the un-faceable. He rotated the lock on the door, turned and looked at his wife who sat staring blankly at him, returned his attention to the door, and opened it.

"I don't have my key," Wellington said apologetically.

Peter Marsh stared at his son in disbelief. It was like a dream from which he feared he would wake. There before him stood Wellington in his Marine uniform with a duffle bag beside him on the porch under a single yellow light. The son he feared would never return was standing before him. Shock kept words from the older man.

"It's good to be home, dad," Wellington said to his father.

"My holy, dear lord, you're real. It's really you," Peter Marsh said excitedly, "Come in, it's cold." Peter Marsh hugged his son, grabbed the duffle bag, and yelled, "Judy, your son is home."

He was surprised to hear her voice from right behind him, "My baby is home!" Nearly hysterical, she bellowed, "Lord have mercy, my prayers have been answered! My baby is home!" She forced her way between her husband and son to grab ahold of

Wellington. "Come inside, you'll catch your death," she ordered. Tears flowed down her cheeks and she wiped her eyes.

As Wellington entered his parents noticed he was limping.

"You're hurt!" Judith exclaimed.

"It's nothing," Wellington said brushing the subject aside.

"Why didn't you call us?" his mother chastised as she clung to her son's arm.

"Every time I thought I had an opportunity something made it impossible," he explained.

"We were told you were missing," Wellington's father stated.

"I was."

"Let me get you something to eat. Are you hungry?" Wellington's mother asked.

"I'm starved. I haven't eaten since yesterday." Wellington walked over to the couch and sat. "Where's the Christmas tree? All the way home I looked forward to seeing the Christmas tree."

Peter Marsh said, "For obvious reasons we weren't in a holiday mood."

"I know, I'm just being funny," Wellington admitted.

Peter Marsh pulled a coat out of the closet and put it on, "Com'on we're going out to get a tree."

"It's snowing out there," Wellington pointed out.

"Let's go. We have more reason than ever to celebrate Christmas this year."

"Wait!" Judith Marsh ran behind the two men and handed Wellington a sandwich and bottle of soda.

As they walked out the door she heard Peter say, "We're getting a tree and when we get back we're putting up the lights."

Jack looked out the window of More-Or-Less and saw light snow falling. His plan was to lock up the bar at the end of the evening, get in the car he had rented, and drive through the night to Warren Pennsylvania. He had nothing else to do for Christmas so why not play Santa and deliver Don Carmine Spacini's gift to one Carl Pythacyk. With the snow, he figured it would take seven or eight hours to go the estimated 350 miles. Once there, he had no idea what he was going to do.

Peter and Wellington Marsh dragged a snow-covered Christmas tree into the living room.

"Where on earth did you find a tree at this hour in the snow?" Judith Marsh asked in amazement.

"The lot up on Park Road," Peter replied. "It was closed, but a note on a pole said help yourself—remaining trees are free. So, we picked the best one."

In the corner of the room they saw boxes of ornaments. "I see you've been busy," Peter commented.

"Those are for the tree. I don't want you out in the snow putting lights on the house. You'll either slip and fall or get electrocuted."

With the tree decorated and another sandwich consumed, Wellington and his parents settled down in the living room. His parents sat on the couch and Wellington sat in a comfortable chair. Peter Marsh and his son each had a beer while his mother sipped tea.

"Tell us what happened," his mother said.

Quickly, his father added, "That is if you are up to talking about it."

"I don't mind, but it's a long story."

"We have all night," his father pointed out.

"My CAP Team was assigned to a village whose name translates to 'Precious Flower.' We were really lucky because the village is hidden in the mountains and didn't have any enemy contact. Most of the time we just did what we could to keep the village secret. Our interpreter, Hung, was a seasoned veteran and good guy. I got to trust him and learned from him. It really was a good assignment."

"Then 12 November we got supplies delivered by helicopter. Everything went smoothly. It was actually a nice day and we all felt like we could take it easy. Then we got a call that one of the choppers went down. Engine trouble of some kind. We went downstream guided by the other Huey and found the one that crashed. It was on its side in the middle of a river. The water was moving really fast so we formed a human chain and got the pilot out to safety. He had a broken leg. I went back for the co-pilot. To reach him I had to let go of the other guys and climb inside the aircraft. He was dead."

"Oh, I'm sorry," Judith Marsh said softly.

"Then the helicopter broke loose and everything turned upside down—literally. I was tossed around inside the cockpit and couldn't tell what was up or what was down. Water rushed in and I became lost in the silt and debris. I panicked. It was clear to me that I was going to drown, but something made me want to fight until my last breath."

"The helicopter continued to tumble as it was dragged downstream. Inside, I became tangled in wires and seatbelts and whatever else was loose. They say your whole life flashes before your eyes when you face death. I was too busy trying to avoid death. Then my air ran out. Darkness engulfed me. My heartbeat in my ears begged for oxygen. I had to fight to keep my lungs from forcing out the bad air and inhaling water. I wanted to scream—but couldn't. The sunken helicopter bumped into something. I was thrown against some part of the fuselage. At that point, my strength gave out and I accepted my fate."

"Gradually, an image seemed to form before me. At first, I couldn't tell what it was. As if in slow motion it took shape. I forgot about breathing. It was almost like a runner's high that I experienced in basic training. I became fascinated with what I was seeing. Finally, I found I was staring into a child's eyes. They were strangely familiar. I moved toward the aberration but it remained the same distance from me. How long I followed, or was led, or in what direction I went I couldn't tell. Then the image dissolved into light and I broke the surface of the water. I gasped for air as the rapidly moving current carried me downstream. I didn't have the strength to fight it."

"At one point the river turned to the right and I was deposited on the shore. There I lay trying to catch my breath and regain my senses. How long I remained there I don't really know. Slowly, the sound of rushing water returned and I became aware of birds in the trees. I was alive. It was clear that a child saved me. The very child that I was unable to save on the Indian Reservation. Did I live his nightmare? I couldn't say. But, I know in my heart, he saved me from my red Ford."

"The Lord sent you back to us," Judith said softly.

"After a period of time, I heard another sound. It was the click of metal on metal. I looked up and peered into the muzzle of an AK-47. It struck me as funny that I could have survived drowning only to be shot. Three men stood over me all with weapons trained on me. At first, I didn't know if they were friend or foe. Then one kicked me in the ribs, so I knew they weren't friends. I couldn't understand what they were saying but they indicated for me to move in a certain direction. I tried to get up but my strength hadn't returned. Again, I got kicked."

"Bastards!" Peter Marsh spat.

After brushing snow off his rental car, Jack climbed in and started the engine. He let the car warm up as he reviewed the map. It appeared to be a pretty straightforward route to Warren, Pennsylvania. Next to him on the seat was a thermos of coffee. In the back seat was the box with the grapevine cutting he was to deliver. The snow had stopped and the streets seemed relatively clear. With a sense of adventure Jack put the car in gear and thought, let the journey begin.

Wellington Marsh continued his story, "They dragged me to my feet, pulled my arms behind me, and tied me with some kind of leather strap. I looked around but had no idea where I had landed. If my team was looking for me they wouldn't know how far downstream to look."

"My head spun as we walked through the high grass. Every once in a while, I would be poked in the back with the muzzle of an AK. I decided to cooperate until I regained my strength. We walked for quite a long time. It became slightly hilly which made walking difficult with my arms tied behind me." Wellington looked at his father and confessed, "Dad, I was really scared. I didn't know if they were going to kill me or put me in some horrible prison."

Peter Marsh nodded.

"At dusk, they stopped in a small clearing. I was tied to a tree. Unfortunately, where I sat was near an ant hill and the little bastards started biting me. I couldn't move away and struggled to keep them off. My captors started laughing as they watched me twist and turn. They spoke to each other but I didn't understand what they were saying. I called out, 'I'm being bitten. I need to move.' Finally, one of the men walked over and untied me, led me over to a different tree, and retied me. He gave me some nasty water that tasted good after being dry for so long. They didn't give me anything to eat."

"I looked at the three Vietnamese and concluded that they weren't North Vietnamese regulars. Probably, local insurgents. I was only able to sleep due to exhaustion. In the morning, we began walking once more. By late morning we got to a small village. My captors were very rough on the inhabitants. They pushed the old men around, slapped the young boys, and helped themselves to whatever they wanted.

While they were eating and drinking, a local woman came over to me and fed me some rice and fish and gave me water. She showed me a weak smile and quickly hurried away. Then we were walking once more."

"Late in the day we came to a larger village filled with armed men. They cheered and congratulated their comrades on the capture. As I was led through the village I was struck with sticks, gun barrels, fists, and even rocks. They led me to a wooden building and I was shoved inside. It stunk in there like a latrine. There were no windows. In the dim light I saw three wooden doors. My captors opened one, untied my arms, and shoved me in. It was small maybe four by six, I really couldn't tell when they first pushed me in. Then the door closed and it was black as pitch. My arms hurt and it was difficult to move them around to the front of my body. I had to do it slowly, gasping when I did. Both my shoulders ached. I just stood in the dark trying to regain the motion of my arms and get a sense of where I was. My ears picked up on a sound to my right. It was the buzzing of flies. I slid my right foot along the dirt floor until it struck something. After tapping it with my boot I realized it was a pail. I knew what that was for. Time passed. How much, I don't know. At first, I paced slowly gaining a feel for the dimensions of my cell. It was four and a half feet by almost six feet. It had a hard-packed dirt floor, solid wood walls and, as far as I could tell, wooden roof. It was stuffy and hot. When my eyes adjusted to the darkness I became aware of a small source of light. It was the space beneath and around the door. The door swung on old wooden hinges and was secured with a wood bar on the outside. My mind began to imagine how to escape, but even if I could get through that door there were many armed men outside. When fatigue set in I sat on the floor leaning against a wall facing the door.

Fatigue began to weigh heavy on Jack as he drove in the darkness. The snow had subsided and the highway was clear. However, it being Christmas Eve there was more traffic than usual. Everyone trying to get to grandma's house, Jack concluded. He listened to a steady stream of Christmas Carols on the radio. It brought him back to other Christmases. For some reason not having a family or someone to share the holidays with bothered him more than usual. What he concluded was that he had gone from being an interested observer who wrote about others to an individual who wished to be a part of the experience. How could he have existed so long not realizing what he was missing? He knew why but didn't want to acknowledge the fact.

Wellington Marsh sipped his beer and noted the intense look on his parent's faces. They didn't want to hear about their son's captivity, but had to hear it none-the-less. "As I sat in my cell I thought of home. How I wanted to be here. In a way, my desire to get back here and see you gave me the strength to endure what was happening. Even thousands of miles away family can give you strength. I fell asleep. How long I slept I don't know. One of my captors had taken my watch. I was awakened when the wood door creaked open and light blinded me. A guard started yelling something in Vietnamese, but I couldn't understand any of it. I raised my arm to shade the light and saw him motioning with his AK-47. It was difficult getting up but I made my way to the door. I was shoved outside the building. Suddenly, I was hit from behind and knocked to the ground. A group of soldiers pulled at my clothes and hit me. I was being attacked from every direction. When it was over they had taken my boots, and clothes, and I was left in my underwear."

"I lay on the ground knowing that I couldn't escape into the jungle with no protection and no sense of direction. My survival instinct kicked in so I raised my hand above the ground to see which way the shadow went. Because it was morning I could determine which direction was east. I then tried to look around to see the layout of the village. It was then that I was grabbed by the arms and dragged over to a small wooden fence and my arms tied to a rail. When the first blow from a bamboo stick struck my back, I let out a scream of both surprise and pain. Then a second and third. As much as it hurt I didn't make another sound. I wasn't going to give them the satisfaction. Things began spinning in my head and I blacked out. I woke up in complete darkness. I was back in my cell. My back was raw and the flies were nipping at the wounds. It became clear that I had to escape or I would die."

Up ahead Jack saw flashing red lights. Traffic slowed. He wondered if it was an accident. A sea of solid red lights joined the distant flashing lights as taillights announced the complete stoppage of the highway. Jack looked around to see if there was an exit he could take to go around the stoppage but none was apparent. "It's going to be a long night," he said to no one in the car.

Traffic inched along. Jack wasn't in a hurry, but every minute that passed meant he would be on the road that much longer. Taillights stretched down the highway as far as he could see. Time passed.

"How much time passed I didn't know. At one point the door was opened and a tin cup and a tin pan were placed inside the door. It was closed quickly and I was once more in the dark. Thirst and hunger drove me to the tin ware. The water was warm and nasty but it was water. In the tin pan was some rice and something I'd rather never know what it was."

Peter Marsh smiled and nodded, "I'm with you on that."

"The next day—I guess the next day—they dragged me out and gave me some bamboo sandals and a smelly tunic-like thing to wear. I was led to a field and put to work pulling roots up and putting them in a basket. Two guards watched me but I think they knew I wasn't going to run. There was no place to run to. My escape would have to be in the dark of night." Wellington looked at his mother and said, "In a way doing physical work took my mind off of the pain of my wounds."

"My poor baby," Judith Marsh whispered.

"On a brighter note, that night I got more water and a larger portion of nasty rice. I guess they wanted me to have enough strength to work." After another sip of beer Wellington continued, "That went on for probably two weeks. It became a kind of routine. I developed a pretty good sense of what direction I would travel when I escaped. Also, in my cell I found a loose board between my cell and the one next to mine. To the best of my knowledge it was empty and the door wasn't barred. When the time was right, I planned to pull the loose board free and use it as a lever to remove other boards. Once inside the other cell I could exit the cell and building. That was when I would face the greatest risk as I had no idea if any guards watched the building. At night, I tried to listen for conversation or footsteps, or any other sign of movement. Unfortunately, before I could execute my plan things changed."

"One morning the wooden door opened and I was ordered out. I had become accustomed to a routine so thought nothing of it. Unfortunately, on that day things were not routine. A number of North Vietnamese soldiers waited outside. Just like on the first day I was knocked to the ground. My arms were tied behind my back and a leather strap tied around my neck. It became obvious that I was being turned over to those soldiers."

Five Christmas Carols later Jack inched up to an exit ramp and decided to leave the petrified highway. Along with a dozen other cars he freight-trained up the exit ramp into darkness. He assumed the drivers of the other vehicles in front of him knew the area, therefore, the best way to parallel the highway and get back on after the accident or whatever was the problem. All-in-all, he felt better because at least they were moving. At the end of the ramp half of the cars went left and the other half turned right. Jack chose to go left. More vehicles went in different directions at a stop sign. Jack found himself behind two cars heading in what he believed to be the correct direction. Instinctively, he checked his gas gauge and found he had plenty of fuel. The few houses they past were brightly lit with Christmas cheer. One of the two lead cars turned off onto a side street. Jack remained behind the last remaining guide car. It was his only choice as he had no idea how to get back to the highway.

"By the end of the day I had no idea where I was. One fact I did know was that we were traveling west, not north. We were heading toward Cambodia or Laos. It appeared we were on the trail that my team often watched—but I wasn't sure. They made camp for the night and I was tied to a tree. It had rained and the mosquitoes were vicious. With my hands tied I couldn't do anything but let them feast upon me. Needless to say, it was a long night."

"The next day I was sure we were on the trail that led from the Laos/Cambodian borders to the road to Kontum and Pleiku. On my left hidden in the mountains was Quy Hoa, the village my team protected. It was out there so close, yet unaware of my passing. I assumed my team had a new leader, prayed that they were scouting the area, would see me captive, and initiate a rescue. That prayer went unanswered. We entered Laos."

The lead car turned left and Jack instinctively followed. When it stopped he realized he was in a driveway. The driver of the car got out carrying a shotgun. Jack froze. As the man approached, Jack rolled down the window and said, "Merry Christmas. Can you tell me how to get back on U.S. 80 west?"

The homeowner smiled. He was a tall man in his late fifties wearing a brown leather bomber jacket and fedora. "I guess you followed the wrong car," he said with the shotgun pointing straight up.

"I was following a guy in a sleigh with reindeer but I couldn't keep up."

"That would be my brother. He was always a speed demon," Shotgun said with a grin.

"So, can you give me directions or rent me a room?"

"Once we entered Laos I knew there wouldn't be any rescue. It was up to me to escape. But, I had no idea how. I was hungry and thirsty, chewed on by mosquitoes, tired, and bruised. The good news was the weather was warm and dry. After three days, we came to a makeshift prison. There were other POWs in large bamboo cages. It looked like some of them had been there a long time. They mainly lay around on bamboo mats or the bare floor."

"There was a post in the middle of an open area with a crosspiece forming a tee. It didn't take much imagination to know what that was for. As we entered the prison compound one of my captors tripped me causing me to fall onto the ground.

They laughed and another kicked me prodding me to one of the large bamboo cages. I was angry but also smart enough not to fight back. Inside the cell that I was put in there were four other Americans. None of them spoke. I opened my mouth and one of them held up his hand to stop me. It was clear talking was not allowed."

"Among my cell mates were two Army soldiers and two Marines. The highest ranked was a Marine sergeant. I guess due to rank he was in charge as others looked to him for direction. Me being the new guy I simply watched what everyone else was doing and followed suit."

"After I was there a few days there was an incident where a POW in one of the other bamboo cells complained loudly about something. Almost immediately the guards were upon him. They dragged him out, tied him to the post, and whipped him with bamboo switches. While they were busy enjoying their game the Marine sergeant sat next to me and whispered, 'Any excuse.' I nodded while trying not to be bothered by the man's screams."

"He told me his name was Teague and his call sign was three taps. I quickly learned that there was a communications system that had been established consisting of tapping. It was almost like Morse Code. To address someone, you tapped two taps three times then their call sign. My call sign became five taps." Wellington demonstrated on the coffee table, tap tap, tap tap, tap tap, tap tap tap tap tap.

"No conversation of any kind was allowed in khuk kongnoa 23, that means Kong River Prison number 23. You got to where the taps were like words. We even had alerts. For instance, if you saw a venomous snake near someone you couldn't yell out a warning. Instead, a steady fast tapping caused anyone who heard it to stop what they were doing and look around. The person tapping the alert would point at the threat. On rare occasions, there were late night whispered conversations, but only when absolutely necessary. The guards were always looking for 'any excuse.' I had a whispered conversation with Sergeant Teague. He explained that we were 'jungle POWs' and of no value. In fact, they wanted to cause us as much pain as possible to scare us off or for us to die. Which really didn't matter. The valuable POWs were officers and pilots. They could be pumped for information or used for propaganda. I asked him the question that I really didn't want to know the answer to, 'Why don't they just kill us?' He explained that from time to time they could sell us as slave labor. They also had some warped point-of-view that if we died in captivity it was more honorable than just outright killing us. One thing was clear—they hated us."

"Food was scarce, while dirty water was plentiful. Hunger became my main focus. If a snake or rodent wandered into our cell it became part of our dinner."

Wellington looked at his father, once more, and said, "I'm not sure how long I could have endured khuk kongnoa 23."

Peter Marsh stood, walked over to his son, patted him fatherly on the shoulder, and said, "There is more courage and strength in you than you realize. I can't tell you how proud I am of my son." He then asked if Wellington wanted another beer.

Jack Moore drove through the dark Pennsylvania countryside following Shotgun's directions. There was little evidence of civilization outside his vehicle. At first, the directions seemed spot on. Turn here, follow the road, left at the stop sign, go two miles, and the highway will be on your left. After approximately twelve minutes, Jack found Route 80. There it was his path to his destination. However, it was, to say the least, poorly marked. He made a quick decision and rocketed onto the highway. As it was growing later, traffic had thinned to just a few other vehicles. "Ah, now we're moving," he thought.

After a mile, Jack saw flashing lights in the far distance. "Not again," he mumbled, "I hope it's on the other side." He got his wish. A tractor trailer had jack-knifed on the highway going in the opposite direction. Behind the accident, traffic was at a standstill and backed up as far as the eye could see. Jack's side of the road continued to move smoothly. It was just after passing the blockage Jack saw a small sign indicating that he was on Route 80 east—he was driving in the wrong direction.

"There's a funny thing about hopelessness," Wellington said.

Both his father and mother looked at their son as only parents do when they feel the ultimate pain of seeing their child suffer.

"When there seems to be no solution, no relief, no hope your mind responds by creating images of possibilities no matter how far-fetched. I saw myself breaking the bamboo bars and slipping off into the jungle. Dreams showed me a thousand ways to escape. And yet reality was I was looking at a long torturous stay and most likely was going to die in that foul nasty place."

"After six, seven, eight days—I'm not sure—we were outside our cell clearing an area for another bamboo cell to be built. It was a sunny day and getting hot. Then there was a sound in the jungle. Tanks were coming down Ho Chi Minh Trail which was less than a mile away. They got louder and louder. How many there were I couldn't determine. Then the sound seemed to change. It was different in an odd sort of way.

"Son-of-a-bitch!" Jack cursed as he headed in the direction of New York. In a few miles he took the next exit off the highway and found himself back where he had left the road earlier. "Now, if I can only remember the route I took before," he said to himself. He retraced his steps to the tune of *Little Drummer Boy.*

"In addition to the mechanical sounds of the tanks there was a drumming sound. It was high as if above us. I looked up and that's when I saw the B-52s. A dozen or more floated high in the sky. The guards also saw the aircraft and began shooting at them. I knew they couldn't do any damage at that distance, but they continued to try. A hand touched my back. When I turned I found Sergeant Teague pulling me toward the jungle."

"Suddenly, a new sound joined all the others. It was a whistling. Moments later the world exploded. Huge detonations shook the ground, dirt flew up into the air, men were yelling, the guards dove into spider holes, trees fell, and Sergeant Teague dragged me into the jungle. It was horrifying. Consider what a hundred freight trains all crashing into each other with you in the middle is like. All I could think of was to follow Sergeant Teague. He led and I followed as we ran through thick underbrush. Some of the plants had thorns but we didn't care. It was our ticket out of that hell-hole and we were taking it."

"The bombing ceased so we stopped, crouched down, and listened. I think one or two of those bombs hit the prison. That meant they would be busy for a while. I wondered if other prisoners had made a run for it. Some I knew physically couldn't. When we didn't hear any movement in our direction we decided to cautiously continue. Unfortunately, we had gone west which took us deeper into Laos."

Jack finally found himself back on Highway 80 going west. His little detour had added over an hour to his trip. With the accident behind him holding traffic up he was the only car on the road. His first thought was to speed up to make up for lost time, however, he decided he didn't want the hassle of sitting on the side of the road while a State Trooper asked, "Where's the fire?"

Surrounded by darkness and staring at two yellow beams of light Jack's mind wandered. He was sitting in the stands at Shae Stadium. Beside him was Ryoya Akimoto. He heard her voice yelling at the pitcher to keep it high and tight. In the darkness of the automobile Jack smiled. She was the epitome of the rabid Mets fan. She was not afraid to "get in the game" and support the team. She was a fringe lunatic. She was fun to be around. The radio played *Silver Bells* as Jack admitted to himself, alone on a dark highway in Pennsylvania, how much he missed her. He blinked to hold back tears.

"We were free but in a very precarious situation. The enemy knew the terrain and the trails that led back to Vietnam. Without question, they would be patrolling and looking for any escapees. There was no way to know if the locals were friendly or not. We had no food or water. And, we were a long way from any American installations. The odds definitely were not in our favor. What we had going for us was that there were two of us and we were Marines," there was a hint of pride in that last statement.

"Darkness fell and we had to hole up in a small bamboo forest. Sarge found two strong bamboo stalks that we sharpened on one end on a rock to create a spear. We took turns sleeping with the man who was awake brushing mosquitoes off the other while listening for intruders. At sunrise, we discussed our strategy and decided to go south for some distance before turning east. Job one was to find water. You can live a long time without food but without water you won't last very long."

"At one point as we moved south we heard voices. We hid and waited. A VC patrol passed by east of us. They didn't seem too interested in looking for escapees as they sauntered along chatting among themselves. We decided to shadow them." Wellington stopped talking for a moment, looked at his mother, and said, "Mother, what I did next I had to do to survive."

In a dark car in the middle of the night a man can do some very strange things to entertain himself. Jack Moore was no different. He became bored with the endless Christmas Carols. Finally, he shut off the radio and began writing a fictional story in his head while reciting all the parts. It was a murder mystery. A financier had been bumped off and his wife hired a private detective, Luke Foritt, to help find the killer. "When did you last see your husband?" Jack asked in the confines of the car. He changed his voice to simulate a female, "He left for his office early in the morning. He was supposed to come home early so we could go to the Euwarr party." Male voice,

"Not the Dwight Euwarr party?" Female voice, "My husband never came home."

"We moved as quietly as possible as we trailed the patrol. I really appreciated my Marine training at that time. One of the VC broke from the patrol to relieve himself in the bushes. The others continued on. Sarge and I waited for him to be, uh, distracted. Then we jumped him, covered his mouth, and broke his neck. He never made a sound."

Wellington looked at his mother who did not show any outward reaction.

"In an instant, we removed his clothes, sandals, and equipment. After covering the body with brush, we disappeared into the jungle. There was no telling if his friends would miss him and come looking. Once we got a safe distance we looked at what we had gotten. I left it up to Sergeant Teague to decide who got what. The VC had a full canteen which we really appreciated. These were Chinese copies of WW II Japanese canteens. Sarge tossed me the goonie hat and he kept the Ho Chi Minh Freedom Sandals. They are made from old truck tires with straps cut from inner tubes. The man's uniform was too small for either of us but we kept it for the cloth. I was given a machete and Sarge kept the AK-47 and three magazines. The soldier also had a rucksack with various items in it. We found some paper-wrapped food and devoured it immediately."

"Once again, we headed south. There was no sign of the patrol and we avoided any trails. By the end of the day we came across a small stream and filled the canteen. We settled down in a small cave. Sergeant Teague told me, 'tomorrow we turn east.' He also told me he had been part of a special operations team that was spotting the Ho Chi Minh Trail for the bombers. Some locals, who they had given food to, turned them in. He was the only survivor."

"For two days, we made our way through the jungle. We saw a few patrols but they never saw us. I don't think I would have gotten that far without Sergeant Teague. Finally, we entered Vietnam and began looking for American patrols or installations. After another two days, we made contact with an Army patrol."

"Mrs. Stopshear, did you hear from your husband Buck at any time during the day?" Jack asked in his detective voice. "He never called," his female persona answered. "So, what makes you think Buck Stopshear was murdered?" "He had been getting threatening phone calls."

Jack continued his play as the miles drifted by. Then some white specks on the windshield told him he had more to be concerned with than where old Buck had gone. At first, the snow was light and rather pretty. It blew around and danced upon the hood of the car. Then more and more of their sparkling white friends joined the party.

"We got medevacked to Pleiku. After doctors checked us out, gave us numerous shots, and treated our wounds, we were flown to Cam Ranh Bay to be debriefed. That's when I found out that CAP Team 1-6-2 had been in a firefight. I was shocked to hear that Quy Hoa was on a primary target list for the B-52s. This Blue Falcon Sergeant Willens had his head up his ass when he listed my village as hostile. All I could think about were those peaceful villagers going about their day-to-day business and having

500 pound bombs rain down upon them. From my prison experience, I know first-hand what that is like." Wellington showed visible anger. He took a moment before continuing, "I have no idea about the status of Precious Flower or the people or Hung or the two children. The actions of Sergeant, FUBAR, Willens led to some of my team being killed and others wounded. I did get Quy Hoa taken off the target list. Also, I have to write letters to the parents of the Marines on CAP Team 1-6-2 who were KIA."

"Because of my experience, I was given a thirty-day convalescent leave which is non-chargeable. I tried to call home but all the lines to the States were tied up—Christmas. Then I had a chance to get on a transport that was leaving right then so I grabbed it. When I got back to the world a pilot who deadheaded on the transport told me he had a connection for a flight to Chicago and I could tag along. I did. In Chicago O'Hare Airport, I couldn't believe it when people called me names, cursed at me, and gave me the finger. I just escaped hell and that's the reception I get! I guess I shouldn't have been surprised. There were anti-war demonstrations before I went to Nam. But, complain to the government, I didn't declare war or choose to go there."

The highway became snow covered as Jack proceeded. He took Exit 111 onto State Highway 153. It was a two-lane road that was covered in snow. In the dark, he had trouble telling where the road actually was. "It's clear this road isn't getting plowed any time soon," Jack told his invisible passenger. High beams reflected the snow and made it more difficult to see. He went back to standard beams. Without question, his only option was to proceed with caution.

"Would you believe every phone at O'Hare Airport was being used? I tried to get a cab to the bus station but due to the snow there was a long line of travelers waiting ahead of me. What drove me crazy was that I was so close to home but couldn't find a way to get here. I stopped a police officer and asked him how far away the bus terminal was. He asked where I was trying to go. When I told him Southfield, Michigan he started to laugh. I got ticked off and told him I just crawled through Laotian and Cambodian jungle after being a POW to get back to civilization and I didn't appreciate his thinking my trying to get home was funny. He held up his hand and said, 'Don't be offended, I'm laughing because I was just talking with a stewardess who told me she was hopping a private flight to Detroit to connect with a commercial flight to Miami. Maybe she can get you on the Detroit leg. Come'on I know where she's sitting.'"

Jack's arms ached from his tight grip on the steering wheel. He was navigating through snow-covered hills in the dark. There were no street lights, houses, guard rails, or reindeer. At times, it appeared the road dropped off on the sides to depths unknown. Other times he literally had to stop to determine where the road twisted and turned. He felt completely alone and vulnerable. If he went off the road they wouldn't find the body until spring.

Finally, he came to a T and turned right onto Highway 219. It was more of the same. A two-lane road, maybe, who could tell when it was covered with snow? There was one good sign, tire tracks. Some poor soul was in front of him leading the way. As long as those tracks didn't drive off the side of a mountain he had an ersatz guide.

"The stewardess was very nice, but she explained to me that she was flying to Detroit in a friend's Cessna 310 twin engine prop that seated four and all the seats were taken. She nodded toward three other stewardesses in the waiting area. I thanked her and said I understood. As I turned to leave one of the stewardesses said she wasn't feeling well and decided not to go. I could have her seat. It didn't take a genius to see through her lie. I thanked her and turned down the offer. At that moment, the pilot showed up and said he was ready to board the airplane and get in line for takeoff. One of the other stewardesses tried to give me her seat and I again said no. The pilot was ex-military and asked each of the stewardesses what they weighed. Afterward, he looked at me and said, 'OK you can ride in the co-pilot seat.' So, we trudged out to the rather small airplane waiting in the snow."

Jack entered Ridgeway, Pennsylvania. He was never so happy to see a traffic light in his life. When it turned red he actually cheered. There was no sign of life as it was the middle of the night, but there was something reassuring about buildings, street lights, and traffic signs. He pulled over to take a break and to review his map. He felt like he had been driving all night and, in fact, he had. Jack looked in the back seat at the package from Don Spacini and said sarcastically, "Fa, la, la, la, la, la, la!"

A police car, probably the only one in Ridgeway, pulled up behind Jack's car. The red flashers came on. When a patrolman walked up and tapped on the window Jack rolled it down and said, "Merry Christmas."

"Merry Christmas. How are you doing?"

"I've been driving all night on my way to Warren, Pennsylvania," Jack explained.

The patrolman looked upward and said, "You picked a good night for it."

"Tell me about it. There were times when I had no idea where the road was," Jack got hit in the face with a large snowflake and suggested, "Why don't you get in out of the snow?"

"Thanks, but I better not."

"By my map, somewhere up there I turn right onto 948 North."

"Three blocks up, at the bank, turn right. Highway 948 becomes 666 then 6 but it still is 948. It might not be too good an idea to drive that road at night in the snow if you're not familiar with it."

"It's a rental car."

"Well, if you insist, drive carefully, take it slow, there are some treacherous curves, and some steep hills."

"You make it sound so inviting."

The police officer snickered and offered, "If you decide to wait until daylight the police station is on the left four blocks up. You can get a cup of coffee and a place to rest."

"I'm going to go on. By morning, the snow will only be deeper."

"I understand. Merry Christmas."

Jack drove three blocks, turned right, and embarked on the final leg of his journey. It was not without a little trepidation.

"I have to admit, I was a little more than worried as our twin-engine propeller plane moved slowly in line behind huge jets. Our pilot joked, 'There is a huge plane behind us. I know he can't see us. I only hope he remembers we are here.' Tiny wipers brushed the snow from the windshield as we creeped along. Behind me, the stewardesses were partying and having a great time."

"Then it became our turn. We sat at the end of the runway waiting for clearance. The pilot said, 'We have to turn right after takeoff to avoid the jet wash from the previous aircraft. It can be a bitch.' At that point I was looking for the door handle."

Peter Marsh laughed.

"We got into the air, turned, and were bounced back and forth. The pilot said, 'See what I mean?' After that we climbed above the clouds and things got real peaceful. I actually was able to relax."

There's something very peaceful about driving in the woods on pristine snow at night. Unconsciously, Jack began whistling *White Christmas*. As he did, he followed the snow-covered road by keeping the guardrail a set distance to his right. Whether or not he was in the middle of the road or in his lane really didn't matter. He figured that he had a little over an hour left on his Odyssey.

Then the guardrail disappeared. Jack's mind announced, "I've reached the end of civilization. I'm now on my own." He slowed his pace and stared intensely out the window. Trees and an occasional street sign helped him determine where Route 948 was and where it was going. Thankfully, the snow was soft and fluffy, not wet and heavy which would be far more slippery. He drove on. At one point, a combination of wide treeless terrain and increased snowfall caused Jack to be lost in total whiteness.

"All I saw through the airplane's windshield was whiteness. The pilot told me he was making an instrument approach. This is where he is using radio signals to know where the airport and runway are. There's something eerie about traveling over a hundred miles-per-hour in white soup. If anything was out there it couldn't be seen. We would blast into it without ever knowing what it was."

"I watched the pilot as he read his instruments, referred to a map on his knee, and made adjustments. He didn't seem at all concerned. I gotta tell you I was—very concerned. Even the stewardesses became quiet."

"When he got clearance to land the pilot switched a few switches and made some more adjustments. Still we flew in a white cocoon. After what seemed two hours the airplane came out of the clouds and we could just barely see the ground through falling snow. Nowhere could I see the airport. Slowly, we dropped lower and lower. Buildings began to look larger and larger. I almost jumped when the plane banked right. The pilot pulled back on the throttles and the engine slowed. I sat there sweating. He lowered the landing gear. Then finally, through the snow I could make out the runway lights. We lined up on them and came in for a soft landing. The pilot looked over at me and said, 'With the extra weight I may not be able to stop this thing.' Flyguy humor."

As he proceeded down a steep incline Jack noticed yellow markers at the bottom indicating that the road curved. Which direction he couldn't tell. He wondered if he was going to be able to stop. His stomach muscles ached from being tense for so long. Closer and closer he came to those yellow markers. The car slid slightly sideways and finally ground to a stop. Jack perused the dark landscape and determined the road went left so he proceeded. About a mile farther down the road he cheered as he passed a sign that read, Warren County.

"I came halfway around the world—got damn lucky—and the hardest part of my trip was getting from Detroit Airport home. I decided not to call because I was almost home and wanted to surprise you. I tried but couldn't get a taxi so I set out hitch-hiking. There wasn't much traffic and the cars that did pass just kept going. After a half hour, I was ready to give up when of all people a priest stopped. When I told him where I was headed he said with God's help he could get me home and make it back for midnight mass. I kid you not, the snow stopped. The guy was a maniac on the road. It was almost as scary as that small plane flight. He got me here, blessed me and my family, and shot away. I expected to hear hi yo Silver."

In Warren, Pennsylvania Jack found the police station and got directions to Lark's Run. Twenty minutes later, he stood before the gate. A tired, but relieved, smile crossed his face as he read the sign, "Deposit your anger in the barrel and open your heart as you open this gate."

"Your wounded leg," Wellington's mother asked, "How did that happen?"
Wellington looked at his mother, smiled, and replied, "I slipped on the snow on our front path and twisted my knee. It was dark."

116: Thursday – December 25, 1969

The gate swung open as the eastern sky began to brighten. Jack Moore drove through, closed the gate, and proceeded up the gravel path to the farmhouse at Lark's Run. A tall, slender man with long brown hair tied back into a ponytail walked out onto the porch. He paused, walked down the stairs, and greeted Jack, "Welcome to Lark's Run. Merry Christmas. I'm Nick."

"Not Saint Nick, I hope, that would mean I drove too far north," Jack quipped.

"Yeah, the sleigh's in the barn," Nick replied, "Wow, what a long night."

"Tell me about it, I've been on the road all night."

"You must have really wanted to get here," Nick concluded, then asked, "Who are you?"

"My name is Jack Moore. I'm a newspaper reported with the *New York Tribune*."

"You came all the way out here in the snow for a story?"

"No, I came all the way out here to play Santa."

"Well, come inside and get some coffee, Santa," Nick said welcomingly.

When they entered the great room, Jack heard a familiar voice call out, "Yo, yo, you came!" Night Bird ran across the room and threw herself into his arms.

Jack caught the young girl and said, "Night Bird. So, this is where you went."

"This is my little bit of heaven. Are you going to join us?"

"No, I'm just here to make a delivery."

"We're just sitting down for breakfast. Please join us," Nick's wife Penelope said.

Ritchie sat in the kitchen drinking coffee. He had gotten up early and shoveled snow from the walk. Everything seemed so pleasant to him, even throwing shovelfuls of snow. He was no longer threatened with the draft, was overjoyed with his job at his father's publishing company, was going to be able to help Chief Michael and the young Ojibwa woman, happy that Stephanie had been kind of adopted and found a direction, and Carl was no longer on the run. Strange how things work out. In the quiet of the kitchen Ritchie's mind once more turned to Wellington Marsh. He hated not knowing if his friend was alive or dead, in a prison camp, or wounded.

Ritchie's mother entered the kitchen, "Richard, you're up. Merry Christmas, sweetheart. Why do you have on your coat and hat?"

"I shoveled the walk and driveway."

"Oh, that was good of you. But, too much for one person."

"I didn't mind, I need the exercise."

Nathan Anderson entered the room and bellowed, "Merry Christmas." It had been a long time since Ritchie had seen his father so jovial. His father looked at him and said, "Take off your coat and hat and stay awhile."

Ritchie snickered at his father's humor. As his mother poured coffee into two cups, Ritchie said, "I have presents for each of you under the tree. But, I also have one additional present for you."

Ryoya Akimoto rose early, showered, and dressed. She was on duty the night before and had gotten in rather late. On her way out the door she picked up the presents that she had purchased for her parents. They were typical gifts given by someone with a busy schedule and little time to shop. For her mother she chose a gold pin and scarf. Her father was to receive a shirt and Mets baseball cap with World Champions emblem.

Clinton and Maureen MacIntyre were up early, as usual. Both felt the pain and anguish of their first Christmas without their son, Colt. In the subdued light of the kitchen, they sat in silence. Each wanted to comfort the other. Only there weren't any words of comfort that could be offered. Just being together gave them needed strength as it had throughout their marriage.

Finally, Clint said, "The young lady, Stephanie Ellis, is also suffering from loss. We should do all we can to help her through this difficult time."

"I know, dear," Maureen replied, "I did my crying in the shower."

Clint smiled and said, "Colt would have pointed out that you probably saved water."

"He would have," she smiled and agreed.

"I believe he's here with us and would not want us to ruin a perfectly good Christmas."

"Another Coltism?"

"Probably. When I look across the table I see him. Sitting by the tree, he will be there. If at any time I lose the joy and spirit of the season he will look at me with those disapproving eyes."

"A hundred children," Maureen whispered.

"Excuse me?"

"A hundred children. When his vision for an adoption agency places a hundred children in safe and loving homes then his soul will rest."

"A thousand—my boy thinks big."

After sitting up half the night, the Marsh family slept late. A Christmas tree glowed in the living room. No presents were to be found under the tree as the greatest present of all lay asleep in his bed.

Jack was amazed by the abundance of food at the Lark's Run breakfast table. He was indeed hungry after his all-night ordeal. The food tasted so good he couldn't remember experiencing such wonderful flavors. Fresh from the farm would be a subject of a future column. In addition, there was an energy and excitement and camaraderie demonstrated by the members of Lark's Run. Jack couldn't help but feel refreshed by the very environment.

After breakfast, in the great room, different individuals exchanged gifts. Jack observed. He was particularly interested in Carl and Laurel. He watched as Carl handed Laurel a small package. It had that "male-wrapped" disheveled look. She carefully opened the package to reveal a blue box. Inside was a tiara. Carl said, "You gave your tiara to the Witch Tree and she made you Manidoo-Binesiikwe—Spirit Bird

Woman. If anyone on the Earth deserves to wear a tiara it is you." Laurel placed the tiara upon her head, leaned forward, and kissed Carl. She then handed him his gift.

Carl removed the wrapping paper to reveal a shoebox. When he opened it he sat and stared at the contents. Jack wondered what could be so impressive. Laurel said, "With our money we can pretty much have most of the things we desire. I wanted to give you a meaningful gift. What I give you money can't buy."

Carl looked up at Laurel and said, "I wish I were a poet. I'd write of tiaras and trees and songs and bees and of the one I love."

"You just did," Laurel said.

Carl put down the box and they embraced. Jack sneaked a glance into the box and saw three red feathers.

Ryoya entered her parent's house and smelled Cedarwood incense. While they celebrated Christmas, it was subdued with a small tree in the window and some colorful lanterns outside. Japanese generally celebrate New Year's more so than Christmas. They send New Year's cards called nengajyo and decorate the house with kadomatsu decorations which are made from bamboo, pine branches, and strips of white folded paper. When she was a child, on New Year's Day Ryoya looked forward to her otoshidama which was a small decorated envelope with money inside. It was like a second Christmas.

Because they lived through lean times in the camps and had to start over after the war, gifts exchanged were generally simple and in small numbers. Ryoya placed her packages beside the tree.

"Daughter, Merry Christmas," Takashi Akimoto said.

"Merry Christmas." Ryoya said as she became aware of Beethoven's *Ninth Symphony* playing on the record player. Ludwig van Beethoven's final complete symphony was published in 1824 and known as *The Choral* because it used four vocal soloists and a chorus during the final movement. Words from Friedrich Schiller's poem *Ode to Joy* were sung making it a choral symphony. This piece became the traditional music played by many Japanese households during Christmas.

In the kitchen, her mother was finishing the traditional Christmas Cake—a sponge cake, covered with whipped cream, strawberries and small Santa Claus figures. Ryoya remembered an old saying she heard an aunt say, "Spoiled like a Christmas Cake." It came from the 1950s and referred to an unrefrigerated cake after the 25th which was compared to an unmarried woman over the age of 25. She thought to herself, having turned forty-years-old that year, that cake is long gone.

Stephanie Ellis joined the MacIntyres in the kitchen. At first, she didn't know what to say given the situation.

Clinton MacIntyre set the tone with a joyous, "Merry Christmas, Stephanie. Ho, ho, ho."

She couldn't help but smile. The MacIntyres explained to Stephanie that while they missed their son and would carry that pain for the rest of their lives they also knew that he would want them to live those lives to the fullest. To honor his memory Christmas would live in their home and the joy of the season would reign.

After breakfast, they went into the den and sat by the Christmas tree. Stephanie stood while Clinton and Maureen sat. She looked at the presents under the tree and said, "I don't have any money and I'm not very creative with my hands, but I want to give you something for Christmas."

Clinton thought of saying it wasn't necessary but judged by the serious look on her face that she had more to say. He decided to wait.

"I am so grateful for everything that you have done. A short time ago you had no idea that I existed. We met under the worst of circumstances, yet you opened your home and hearts to me. It's hard for me to imagine that people like you are real and yet from the short time I knew Colt I can see why he was such a wonderful person. Maybe, over time some of your essence will have a positive effect on me." Stephanie smiled. "I thought about the Christmas Carol *Little Drummer Boy* where he had no gift to offer the baby Jesus, only his talent. The only thing that I have is standing before you. This is my gift to you and Colt." Stephanie picked up an envelope from under the tree and handed it to Clinton, "It's for both of you."

Clinton opened the envelope and took out a handwritten piece of paper.

Mr. and Mrs. MacIntyre

On this Christmas day in 1969 I make this pledge.

I will dedicate all my efforts and talents to achieve my, and Colt's, and now your dream of building an international adoption organization that will help children from around the world enjoy better, safer, more fruitful lives.

I will work to complete my education as quickly as possible in order to have the necessary credentials to operate such an organization.

I will gain as much practical experience in the field of adoption while completing my education so that we can establish the Colt MacIntyre International Adoption Services in the shortest possible length of time.

I will treat people with the same respect and kindness that I received in this home.

I will never forget who made all of this possible.

Signed: Stephanie Elizabeth Ellis

Clinton MacIntyre read the pledge then handed it to Maureen. She smiled and said in a motherly tone, "I know you will dear. It is a fine gift."

"There needs to be one addendum added, "Clinton said. He picked up a pen and wrote on the document an addition pledge: I will enjoy life as it is a gift from God. He handed it back to Stephanie.

Stephanie read the addition and tears filled her eyes. She sputtered, "I'll try."

"You will," Clinton ordered.

"Our gift is not as special or valuable as yours, but we hope you like it," Maureen said as she handed Stephanie a small box.

Stephanie opened her present and found a hand-painted gold Monarch Butterfly pin. "It's beautiful," she said sincerely.

"When you told me the story about how your mother liked butterflies, I knew what I had to get for you," Maureen explained. "Your mother said when she saw a butterfly it felt like she was looking at a tiny angel. You deserve your own tiny angel. It may let you keep a little of your mother with you."

Ritchie and his parents went into the den. As they entered his mother said, "Richard, you must take off your coat and hat."

"I plan to, mother," he replied. Then he said, "This is my special gift to you." He removed his coat and then his hat. Before Nathan and Helen Anderson stood a clean-cut young man. His long hair was gone. They both stood with their mouths open. "I've grown-up a lot this year. My experience in Minnesota, meeting two friends from different worlds, taking responsibility with the draft, and going to work with you, dad. It all had an effect on me. I see things from a new perspective. Life is unpredictable and precious. But, it's what you do with your life that really counts. Instead of judging and condemning everyone else I need to focus my attention on me. I need to be the best that I can. Maybe, someday I'll have a family and I have to be a role model." Ritchie looked at his father, "I really like working at your firm and I'm grateful for you giving me the opportunity. Lord knows, I didn't give you much reason to take a chance. I only hope that I bring real value to the company and make a positive difference."

"You already have, son," Nathan Alexander said as he walked over and hugged his son.

Nathan reached under the tree, picked up a present, and gave it to Ritchie. When he opened it, Ritchie was stunned. It was his father's gold watch. "I tried to think of something to tell you that I was proud of what you have done with the magazines and proud that you are my son."

It was late when Peter, Judith, and Wellington Marsh stumbled into the kitchen. Merry Christmases were flung this way and that. It was indeed merry—the Christmas that wasn't now was. Smiles were abundant as they ate breakfast and small talk ruled the day. The horrors of Vietnam had all been shared through a long night.

When the conversation experienced a lull, Wellington said, "I'm going back."

"You are?" his surprised mother asked.

"I have to."

"They're sending you back?" his father asked.

"I volunteered," Wellington said nonchalantly. The silence that filled the room compelled him to explain, "If Quy Hoa still exists the people need CAP Team 1-6-2. Without us they are vulnerable to attack. Another Sergeant Willens might come along. There are old men, women, and children just trying to live their lives in peace in the middle of the madness that is going on. Hung and his niece and nephew may not be alive. If they are, they deserve a shot at life. They might not get a chance to come to America, although God knows I'm going to try. I got command to agree to reassign me and my team there when I get back." More silence. "And, finally, I'm a United States Marine," he said with pride. "I'm good at being a Marine. I've been put in for a bronze star and they offered me OCS after my tour."

"OCS?" his mother asked.

"Officer's Candidate School. They believe I have the leadership skills, intelligence, now experience, and earned my shot by escaping a VC prison." Wellington looked at his father and said, "I'm going to stay a Marine. I've found my calling."

Peter Marsh stood walked over to his son and offered his hand, "As difficult as these past months have been, I understand. I'm proud of you. You'll make an outstanding Marine." He smiled and added, "Just, cut back on the heroics."

With all the gifts given Jack excused himself and went out to his car. He came back and handed the box to Carl. "A friend of yours asked me to give you this. He does not want you to change your mind or contact him. This is an honorable gift from an honorable man."

Carl took the box and removed the plain brown paper. He found a shoebox, "This must be the year for shoeboxes." When he opened the box he found a grape vine cutting in a plastic bag. At first, he had no idea what it was, but a note included in the box explained everything. "It's from Don Spacini. This is a cutting of a Dolcetto grapevine from the region of Monchiero in Italy. The Spacini family brought it to America. It is a gift from Don Carmine Spacini. He says I showed respect and he wishes to show his gratitude. It also says that I've chosen the correct path and he never wishes to hear from me, unless it is to deliver a case of wine from this gift." Carl smiled, "I know he is a bad man, but I liked him." He turned to Jack and asked, "Will you relay my thanks for this precious gift? Tell Don Spacini that I will do all I can to cultivate this vine and will remember his kindness as I fumble at trying to learn how to make wine."

"I'll tell him," Jack stated.

"There is one more gift to be unwrapped," Laurel said as she handed a small box to Nick. "Carl insisted that we get rid of the last of the money he brought with him from New York."

Nick opened the box and said, "This better not be what I think it is." He removed a set of keys from the box. On them was emblazoned a Chevrolet emblem.

Carl said, "It's a 1969 four-wheel-drive Chevy pickup." He scratched his head as he added, "There is one problem, though. I didn't get my license in time so your truck is parked at the dealer. You'll have to go get it."

As he fiddled with the keys Nick said, "I really can't let you do this."

"It's done," Carl stated.

"You and Laurel are very generous, but there is a limit to what I feel comfortable accepting."

"Accept it," Nick's wife Penelope said.

"Wait, we are relatively self-sufficient at Lark's Run. We own the land, the house, the stock, and our Chevrolet station wagon. This is way beyond a gift."

"It is as much a gift for us as it is for you," Laurel said.

"I don't understand."

"Women are made to be loved, not understood; Oscar Wilde," Laurel replied.

Nick sat in silence staring.

"What she means is that when we build our house and start our farm we will most likely borrow your truck from time to time," Carl explained.

"What makes you think I'll lend it to you?" Nick quipped. "You don't even have a license, for God's sake."

"That hurt," Carl jested.

Jack watched the conversation and enjoyed all the light-hearted banter. It was a refreshing interlude in his not-so-perfect life.

The Akimoto family enjoyed a fine dinner and then sat in the living room. They exchanged their gifts and enjoyed each other's company. It was then, Takashi handed his daughter an envelope. "Your mother and I have one more gift for you, daughter."

Ryoya opened the envelope and found a folder from a travel agency. It was a trip to Japan with open dates. She looked at the outline of air transportation to Tokyo, hotel, rental car, travelers checks, and more. Finally, she looked up and said, "I can't accept this—it is too much."

Her father said in a calm encouraging voice, "You should go. Not so much for the modern culture—walk the land, breathe the air, taste the food, and experience the history. Nihon no basho is where our ancestors lived and died. Feel what they felt, touch what they touched, go where they went, see what they saw—be Japanese. Just remember, modern Japan is not the Japan we left so long ago. For that you seek a ghost."

"Maybe, if I touch my heritage I will be more comfortable with my identity. Where did you and mother come from in Japan?"

"A small village named Yomikaki in Shinano Province. At the base of Mt. Ontake. It may not exist anymore."

"I will look for it."

"Take many photographs."

"This is too much, but I am grateful." Ryoya sat in silence. Her mind raced as she tried to determine when she could get vacation time to make such a trip. Yet, it had to be expensive and a great sacrifice for her parents. They most likely did it to help her work through her doubts and confusion. She tried to think of a way to refuse the gift without insulting them. That would be impossible. Then she had an idea and said, "Why don't you come with me?"

"Thank you, but this is for you," her father replied.

"But, it would mean so much more if shared." She quickly added, "Let me give a travel gift to you."

"It is expensive," Takashi insisted.

"It is a wise investment," Ryoya responded.

Takashi Akimoto looked at his wife who smiled and nodded. He turned to Ryoya and said "Shikata Ga Nai."

"Take a look at the pin," Maureen MacIntyre told Stephanie.

Stephanie tried to lift the pin out of the box but it was stuck. Carefully, she tugged on it not wanting to do damage. The cardboard it was pinned to lifted and came out of the box. Dangling before her were a set of keys. "What is this?"

"Those are the keys to an Aztec Aqua 1969 Mustang," Clinton stated loudly. "It's a little 'girly' with an automatic transmission, but Maureen insisted. You need something to get back and forth to Austin and around campus. Just one thing, young lady, no drinking and driving."

Stephanie, once more had tears in her eyes as she said, "I promise."

Clinton turned toward Maureen and asked, "Do you believe her?"

"I do."

"It's out in the barn," Clinton said, "Let's go take a look. Of course, you'll have to get a Texas driver's license."

Maureen watched her husband and their ersatz adopted daughter head outside. She thought how her heart ached for Colt, but could see all the good that had come from Stephanie joining their family. They might spoil her some, as doing so helped relieve the pain, but the girl had character and sensitivity. Just maybe they could help her with the sorrow she endured. In the end, they all might face a brighter future.

A weak surface low-pressure system formed over northern Texas. The resulting storm system moved slowly to the east. As it did a low-level jet stream delivered warm air to areas east of the storm center. Jet stream winds reached velocities of 120 miles-per-hour and fostered heavy precipitation. The developing extratropical cyclone spawned sixteen tornadoes and waterspouts in Louisiana, Georgia, and Florida. This became the largest Christmas Day tornado outbreak on record. Further north, the storm system dropped heavy snow over the Appalachian Mountains.

Ahead of the cyclone a high-pressure area pushed extremely cold air into the northeast. Albany, New York experienced its coldest Christmas on record with temperatures as low as minus 22 degrees Fahrenheit.

Jack sat in the den in the farmhouse at Lark's Run as the evening news weatherman described the extreme weather. Outside, heavy snow had already left ten inches on the ground. He had planned to spend the night and get on the road in the morning. It appeared that may be impossible. He said to Nick, "I planned to leave tomorrow but may have to take advantage of your hospitality a bit longer."

"You're welcome to stay," Nick replied, "We can use the extra hands. It looks like this is going to be a big one."

That evening Laurel played her guitar and sang, Carl watched in adoration, everyone enjoyed a glass of wine in front of a roaring fire, and Jack fell asleep on the couch.

When Night Bird noticed, she went to the desk and retrieved a magic marker. She drew an owl and wrote "Night Bird" on Jack's forearm. "There, now he's mine," she stated proudly.

117: Wednesday – December 31, 1969

The 1969 nor'easter that raged between December 25 and December 28 included a tornado outbreak, record snow accumulations, damaging ice, and flooding rains. Roads were blocked by thirty foot drifts, airports closed, power outages were widespread, fatal traffic accidents occurred, and the Northeast came to a standstill for four days. It was indeed an atypical year with many weather records set.

Lark's Run received eighteen inches of snow. Jack Moore enjoyed his unplanned vacation and finally got on the road on December 29. He almost hated to leave a group of individuals who had carved out their Utopia in a mountain in Pennsylvania. His Night Bird tattoo had almost faded so he had her reapply it. Why? He wasn't sure. He just wanted to bring a little of Lark's Run back with him. Now, on New Year's Eve Lark's Run was a fond memory.

The night was clear, but temperatures were freezing. Detectives Ryoya Akimoto and Michael Donovan had drawn duty that night. They spent time between their unmarked car and walking along streets that fed into Times Square. Piles of black snow lined the curb. In spite of the cold, thousands of people flocked into Times Square to ring in the new year—new decade.

On one trip to their vehicle they drank hot coffee from a thermos.

"New Year's is a big holiday for Japanese," Ryoya said. "We thoroughly clean our houses and go around driving out evil spirits and inviting in good luck. In Japan, a huge gong is struck 108 times to wipe away the 108 sins of the previous year."

"So, do you have a gong in your apartment?" Michael Donovan asked in jest.

"No, but I do have a Daruma doll."

"A Daruma doll?"

"It's like those Russian dolls without arms and legs. Daruma dolls have a face with a mustache and beard. Only their eyes are white. You color in one eye when you make a resolution. If you keep the resolution or achieve a goal that you set you color in the other eye."

"I see."

"I have a lot of one-eyed dolls in my closet."

"What about this year?"

"This year, I have a lot of work to do. After my parents and I return from Japan, I have to come to terms with where my happiness lies."

"That sounds deep. Do you know where that is?"

"I have an idea."

Jack watched the ball drop in the comfort of his apartment on East Sixty Third Street. After his sojourn at Lark's Run he needed the rest. Strangely, he found himself restless. He donned a heavy coat and he decided to take a walk and breath some 1970 air. As he left his apartment, as a whim he put his Mets cap on his head.

His trek took him west on Sixty Third Street, north on Madison Avenue, and back east on Sixty Fifth Street. At one point he stopped, lit a cigar, and looked up at an apartment building's windows. It being New Year's Eve, many were still brightly lit. One caught his eye. She was in there. Probably, a dancer stretching and working out to remain limber. Hers was a highly competitive profession and short-lived if you didn't stay physically strong. She might not even know it was New Year's Eve as she focused on dance steps that filled her head. Jack flicked ashes off his cigar and thought, I have to stop these fantasies.

Jack Moore began walking, stopped, and looked back. It was as though he was looking back in time. "What a year," he said to himself. It was plain to see that the world was rapidly changing. He wondered if it would be for better or worse. The war would eventually end with broken bodies and broken hearts spread across the nation. The youthful subculture would have an impact, but what kind? Drugs raised a black flag of death destined to cut down lives in their prime. A jet flew over and Jack looked up. He thought of Matthew Ellis and his wire time-bombs. How many more lives would be put in jeopardy? How many, at that moment, were thousands of feet in the air dangling on a thin strand of wire? The devil did her work, that was for sure. Harry and Amanda were all cuddly and sappy when they returned. "I have to find a new watering hole," he decided. Jack wondered if the next decade would be an age of Aquarius or a Rude Awakening. He puffed his cigar and said softly, "Shikata Ga Nai."

When he reached the corner of Second Avenue and Sixty Fifth Street he saw three young men running toward him.

Detective Michael Donovan took the radio call while Detective Akimoto talked with some tourists. He beeped the horn. When she got in he said, "We have our first homicide of the year. Second Avenue and Sixty Fifth Street."

About The Author

Kenneth J Munkens

Kenneth J Munkens is a storyteller with a remarkably creative mind that never seems to rest. There is nothing common about his work. Known for his complex stories populated with multi-dimensional characters he takes readers on an emotional and intellectual journey whose destination is unpredictable.

Enter the world that Munkens creates at your own risk. His stories will make you laugh, cry, smile, wonder, and care. Empathy serves him well as he understands the wide range of emotions involved in human relationships. His humor will sneak up on you while your heart will be stung by a depth of emotion so rare these days.

Character development is an art perfected by this author. He creates real human beings that stay with you long after you finish reading. Readers often state that they feel as though they know the characters as well as they know their friends and relatives. Many long for a sequel to continue to follow the lives of characters with whom they have become attached.

Born in the Bronx, congenital eye problems and loss of his mother at a young age shaped Munkens' character giving him the strength to face the real world head on with a non-yielding spirit. Married over forty years with two grown daughters, he values family, his enthusiasm is contagious, sense of humor notorious, and fascination with those strange creatures called human beings limitless.

Other Works by Kenneth J Munkens
Downtown Dreams
Black Ice
2076AD

Downtown Dreams
438 pages

Downtown Dreams takes you on a remarkable journey into the world of advertising. Meet the creative minds and emotional souls of those who practice the fine art of persuasion—adpeople, contradictions wrapped up in a world of creativity, feeding on challenge, ignoring stress, reaching for the stars, and ultimately finding each other.

Black Ice
212 pages

A patch of black ice sets in motion life-changing events as a father and daughter search for meaning in a world turned upside down. Music, the universal language, relates the haunting story of a young girl with a violin and a secret. Sometimes as complex as a symphony or simple as a child's tune, her story is one of hope disappointment, passion, courage, and the power of the human spirit. Just as black ice can sneak up on you, words in this tale will unexpectedly touch your heart and long be remembered.